GILBERT MORRIS

Appomattox Saga

(Part 3)
1863–1864

FOUR BOOKS IN ONE
1) WALL OF FIRE
2) STARS IN THEIR COURSES
3) CHARIOTS IN THE SMOKE
4) WITNESS IN HEAVEN

BARBOUR
PUBLISHING

Wall of Fire © 1995 by Gilbert Morris
Stars in Their Courses © 1995 by Gilbert Morris
Chariots in the Smoke © 1997 by Gilbert Morris
Witness in Heaven © 1998 by Gilbert Morris

ISBN 978-1-60260-180-2

All rights reserved. No part of this publication may be reproduced or transmitted for commercial purposes, except for brief quotations in printed reviews, without written permission of the publisher.

Scripture quotations are taken from the King James Version of the Bible.

This book is a work of fiction. Names, characters, places, and incidents are either products of the author's imagination or used fictitiously. Any similarity to actual people, organizations, and/or events is purely coincidental.

Cover images: (field) Michael Melford/The Image Bank/Getty Images; (couple) © Philip Gould/CORBIS

Published by Barbour Publishing, Inc., P.O. Box 719, Uhrichsville, Ohio 44683, www.barbourbooks.com

Our mission is to publish and distribute inspirational products offering exceptional value and biblical encouragement to the masses.

Printed in the United States of America.

Genealogy of the Rocklin Family

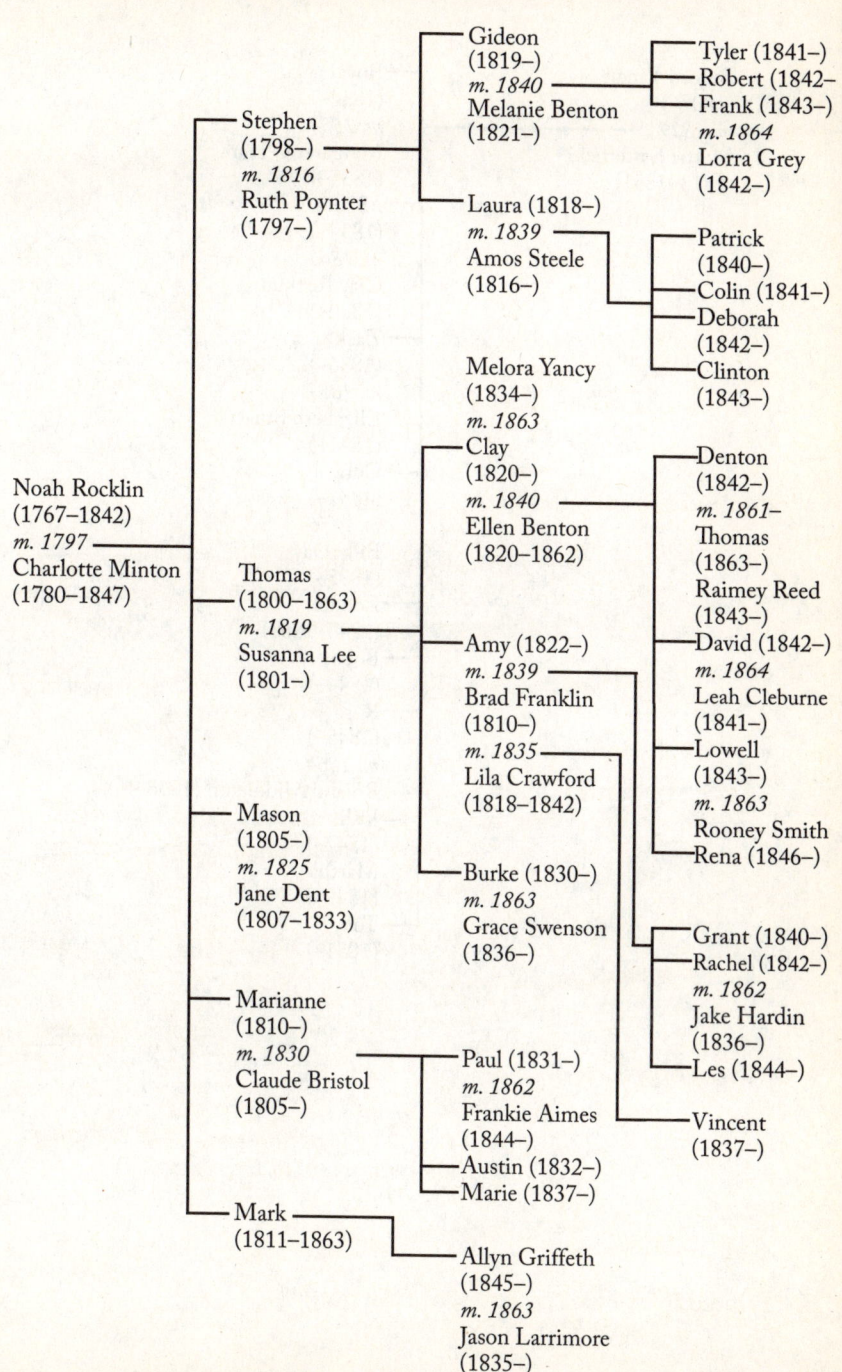

Genealogy of the Yancy Family

Buford Yancy
(1807–)
m. 1829
Mattie Satterfield
(1813–1851)

- Royal
(1832–)
m. 1854
Margaret O'Hara
(1835–)
- Melora
(1834–)
m. 1863
Clay Rocklin
(1820–)
- Zack
(1836–)
m. 1859
Elizabeth Stuart
(1841–)
- Cora
(1837–)
m. 1855
Billy Day
(1835–)
- Lonnie
(1843–1863)
- Bobby
(1844–)
- Rose
(1845–)
m. 1864
Roland Middleton (1836–)
- Josh
(1847–)
- Martha
(1849–)
- Toby
(1851–)

WALL OF FIRE

PART ONE
Clash at Gettysburg

CHAPTER 1
A DIFFICULT CHOICE

Allyn Griffeth knew the French Quarter of New Orleans very well, but as she made her way down a narrow street late one Tuesday evening, she felt a chill of fear. *Shouldn't have come this way!* she thought, and the faint sound of movement coming from an alleyway ahead gave her a warning as plain as the cocking of a gun. She whirled around and dashed back down the dimly lit street. The flickering yellow streetlights threw her shadow on the walls that lined the narrow corridor. Her feet made a quick patter on the cobblestones, and the shadow became a leaping gargoyle.

No good to scream, Allyn thought. The sound of pounding feet behind her caused her to turn her head. Two men were almost on her. She knew she could not outrun them—and she knew what terrible things lay ahead if they had their way. Young women disappeared from the streets of the Quarter—most of them sold into white slavery, chattel for one of the many brothels in New Orleans.

Stopping abruptly, Allyn rammed her hand into her coat pocket and whipped out the small revolver. She had never fired it—she wasn't even certain that it *would* fire, but as the two men converged on her, she lifted the weapon and pulled the trigger.

The explosion echoed through the streets, and both men stopped as abruptly as if they'd run into a brick wall.

"Nom de Dieu!" one of them gasped.

In a thick French accent the other cried out, "Do not shoot!"

Allyn leveled the pistol at his head and pulled the hammer back as she had learned to do. "Get out of here, you scum, before I put a bullet in your brain!" She held the weapon high until the two scurried frantically away. When they vanished in the fog, she lowered it and began to tremble.

A window opened over her head, and a voice demanded, "Who's doing the shooting?" Allyn hastily pocketed the pistol and hurried away. The police of New Orleans paid little attention to anything that happened in the Quarter, but she didn't want to take the chance that they might investigate. Her breathing was shallow, and the narrow escape brought a weakness to her legs, but there was no time to linger.

Avoiding the side streets, she hurried to Bourbon Street. Though she knew she would be accosted by men, at least she was in no danger of being dragged away. Keeping her eyes straight ahead, she ignored the crude invitations from the men she passed. They all assumed, Allyn well knew, that a lone woman walking through the Quarter was available.

This is an evil place, Allyn thought, not for the first time. New Orleans seemed to be covered with some sort of dark presence, and all her life she had sensed the evil miasma that lay over parts of it—especially the French Quarter. She had learned to avoid the dangers of the narrow streets as a Cajun girl would learn to avoid cottonmouths and other deadly wildlife that lurked in the swamps.

As she turned into a saloon with the words GAY PAREE painted in elaborate letters over the wide front door, she felt safer at once. The large room was filled with the odor of whiskey and cigarette smoke in addition to the smell of many unwashed bodies. A hand caught at her arm, and a short, round-faced man grinned as he said, "Hey, Allyn, you come and give me three or two dances, no?"

Allyn smiled briefly and said, "Some other time, Frenchie. I've got to talk to Sam." The man shrugged elaborately, and she made her way to the table along the back wall, where a very fat man with a gleaming bald head and a tawny mustache looked up from a game of solitaire. Allyn asked without preamble, "No word from Lucas, Sam?"

Sam Barker, owner of the Gay Paree, was a native of Virginia, and the soft accent of his boyhood still threaded his voice. "No, Allyn, I ain't heard a word." Barker laid his thick forearms on the table and studied the girl out of a pair of hazel eyes.

What he saw was a young woman of eighteen, taller than average, dressed in a worn, cheap, brown dress. The shapeless garment, however, failed to conceal the rich curves of her figure. Her face was squarish, dominated by a pair of aquamarine eyes that were large and well shaped. The structure of her face made a definite, strong, and pleasant contour often seen in Welshwomen. Her hair was dark red and was bound up in braids that formed a corona that gleamed as the lamplight brought out tints of gold. She had a long, composed mouth and a temper that could at once charm a man or chill him to the bones. This was a competence a girl acquired in the French Quarter of New Orleans, the manner of a girl raised in rough circumstances.

Barker said, "Maybe he'll write."

Allyn met his gaze and shook her head, saying briefly, "I

don't think so, Sam." There was a fatalism in her attitude, the reflection of hard lessons and many disappointments.

"Aw, Allyn, you know how Lucas is. . . ."

Her answer was short, and bitterness lay cold on her voice. "Yes, I know how he is. He's run from every responsibility that ever came at him. He won't be back this time."

Barker tossed his cards down and stood up. *She's right about him*, he thought. *Lucas Rawlings never had any backbone and never will.* Aloud he said, "How's your ma?"

"She's dying."

The bluntness of the girl's reply caused Barker to blink, and he shook his massive head. "Naw, maybe not, Allyn."

"Maybe not today, but she'll never get better, Sam. She knows she won't live long."

Reaching into his vest pocket, the saloon keeper pulled out some bills. Peeling off a few of them, he shoved them toward the girl. "Get the doctor, Allyn. Buy some medicine."

Reluctantly Allyn took the bills. "I—I hate to take this, Sam. I'll pay you back."

Barker waved his thick hand, protesting. "No problem!" He wanted to say something to comfort the girl but knew that there was little hope. Beth Griffeth had been sick for some time—consumption, the doctor had said. Barker had seen her "husband" getting more and more nervous, for Lucas Rawlings was not a man one could lean on in a pinch. Barker laid his hand on the girl's shoulder and said in a kindly fashion, "Look, now, Allyn." She was a proud girl, and as her eyes fastened on him, he chose his words carefully. "None of us likes to take charity. But you've got to think of your mama. She's going to have a tough time, and I want to help a little. You stay with her and let me worry about the bills for a little while. All right?"

Allyn Griffeth was not a crying young woman, but the unexpected kindness on the part of the saloon keeper brought tears to her eyes. She dashed them away and nodded, saying huskily, "Thanks, Sam!"

"Now you go to your mama," Barker said quickly. "Wait—I better go with you. It ain't safe on the streets this late."

A touch of grim humor came to the girl's eyes as she said, "I'll be safe, Sam. I had to use the gun Lucas gave me." When she related the incident with the two men, he frowned angrily then smiled.

"Next time, don't miss. Shoot one of them varmints and it'll get the rest of them to understand you're serious."

After the girl left, Barker sat down, his thoughts moody. When a tall man in the garb of a gambler came up and asked, "What's wrong with Allyn?" Barker clamped his bulldog jaws together then said, "Lucas—he's run out."

"Well, he's the runnin' kind, Sam."

"Never was no good!" Barker began to lay out a new game then stopped and gave the gambler a sharp look. "Keep your eye out for the girl, Tom. She'll need all the help she can get. Her ma won't make it, and you know what a good-looking girl can expect at a place like this."

Allyn made her way through the Quarter without further incident, coming to a small frame house set back between two large warehouses. The door was unlocked, and she pushed inside, thinking, *I have to get a lock—anybody could come in while I'm gone.* The house consisted of three rooms—one that served as a kitchen, dining room, and living area plus two tiny bedrooms. She lit a lamp that threw an amber glow over the shabby, makeshift furniture then moved at once to one of the bedrooms.

"Mama? Are you awake?"

11

The woman who stirred and tried to sit up was thin, and her face was gray with strain. Only a trace remained of the beauty that had been Beth Griffeth's, for poverty and sickness had drained that away. "Yes, I'm awake." Her lips were pale, but she managed to smile, saying, "I've been thinking of making a pie."

Allyn came over and helped her mother into a sitting position. The birdlike bones of her mother and the shrunken frame frightened her, but she said cheerfully, "Now that's a good idea. We've got some apples—how would an apple pie go down?"

The women chatted as Allyn helped her mother get out of bed and supported her as they made their way to the kitchen. Allyn sat her mother down in the battered horsehide chair and said, "Now you can direct this pie making. Nobody can make pies like you, so you just give me the orders, and I'll do the work."

For thirty minutes Beth Griffeth sat in the chair giving instructions and listening as Allyn talked of small matters. From time to time a smile touched her wan lips, but there was a sadness in her eyes that she could not conceal. When the pie was in the oven, she said, "Come and sit down. You must be tired."

"Oh no, I'm fine, Mama."

But sickness had not dulled the mind of Allyn's mother. She studied the lines around the girl's eyes and the drawn appearance of the wide mouth. "That factory is too hard on you. I wish..."

Allyn saw her mother hesitate and said quickly, "It's all right Mama. I don't mind it. Lots of jobs would be harder." Actually, she despised the bottle factory, where her job consisted of putting tops on small glass bottles. It was monotonous work for long hours and a pittance of pay, but she'd taken it to help out with expenses. Now she knew that somehow she had to be with her mother until...

"I expect we'll hear from Lucas," Beth said. "When he gets work he'll send for us."

"Why, yes, Mama. Maybe we'll hear this week."

Beth gave her daughter a glance and then shook her head in denial. She had lived with Rawlings for two years—the last of a succession of men she'd taken up with—and knew what he was. "No. He won't write."

"Oh, Mama!"

"He's been good to us. At least he never bothered you, like some of the others."

"No, he never did." Allyn leaned down and took her mother's hand. "We'll make out, Mama. I don't want you to worry."

Beth seized Allyn's hand with surprising strength. "What will happen to you when I'm gone? You won't have anybody!"

It was the first time her mother had stated the possibility of death, and Allyn saw that she was terrified. Holding to the thin hand, she leaned forward and pushed a lock of hair from her mother's fevered brow. "I'm strong, Mama," she said quietly. "You mustn't worry about me."

"How can I help it?" Tears ran down the pale cheeks, and anguish came to the eyes of the sick woman. "You haven't had any life at all—nothing!"

"Oh, Mama!"

"It's true. I've given you nothing."

"We've made out. It hasn't been so bad."

"If I could have found a good man, things could have been different."

Grief seized the older woman, and when she began to weep, the action brought on a paroxysm of coughing. Her frail body was torn with gagging coughs that went on without end. There was nothing that helped the sick woman, and Allyn could only watch helplessly. Great hacking coughs continued until finally the woman was exhausted.

"Come on, Mama," Allyn said gently. "Maybe you'd better lie down. You don't cough so much that way."

"It doesn't matter," Beth whispered. When she was back in bed, her face pale as paste, she looked up out of tragic eyes and murmured, "I haven't given you anything, baby, and I wanted you to have a good life."

"She's given up, I'm afraid." Dr. Kinsman shook his shaggy head then added, "There's only one end to that, you understand?"

"I know," Allyn said, nodding. For two weeks she'd seen her mother go down steadily, and she knew what that meant. The two of them had stepped out of the sick woman's room, and the doctor had hesitated before speaking. Allyn looked tired, for she had been up all night trying to make her mother more comfortable. Now she brushed a wisp of auburn hair back with a weary motion and said bitterly, "She gave up a long time ago, Doctor."

Kinsman was a thin, bespectacled man in his forties. He stared at the young woman then said bluntly, "She could go at any time. Can't you get someone to be with you?"

"One of the neighbors will come in later, but Mama gets restless if I'm not there."

Kinsman nodded then reached into his black bag to extract a large brown bottle. "Give her all she needs of this to make her comfortable."

"Thank you, Dr. Kinsman."

After the doctor left, Allyn slumped down in the ragged horsehide chair and put her head back. Weariness washed over her, and she went to sleep almost at once. She awoke sometime later, aware of the familiar sound of her mother's coughing. Quickly she rose and went to the basin to dash her face with cold water. Then she took the bottle of medicine and entered the bedroom.

Carefully she helped her mother sit up then poured a large spoonful of the dark liquid. "Take this, Mama. It will make you feel better."

Beth took the medicine, struggled to control the cough, then lay back and closed her eyes. "You need to get some rest, baby," she whispered. "You were up all night again."

"I'll take a nap later, Mama."

"You're not eating right, either." Stirring slightly, Beth looked over at her daughter, who had seated herself beside the bed. For a long time she said nothing, and when she did speak, her speech was already beginning to slur from the powerful narcotic. She was nothing but skin, bones, and nerves, and as she lay there she was aware that the end was not far.

"I could—go easy, baby—if I wasn't worried about you."

Allyn said quietly, "I'll be all right, Mama. You mustn't worry about me." She went on speaking, hoping that her mother would drop off into a deep sleep. She gave such assurances as she could, but they had been over this many times.

"I wish you could have had a good home," Beth whispered faintly. "A nice house—a father to love you. You never had that."

"Lucas wasn't bad," Allyn said quickly. "He was never mean to either of us."

"No, meanness wasn't in him, but he wasn't a strong man."

"He taught me how to play cards," Allyn murmured. "I got good enough to beat him most of the time."

Beth shook her head faintly. "Gambling was his curse. He could have been a better man, but he wouldn't leave cards alone."

A silence fell over the room, the sounds from the street outside muffled. The sick woman lay so still that she seemed almost to have given up the struggle. Allyn studied her mother's worn face, remembering how pretty she had been years ago. Now little was left of that charm except the bone structure.

A thought came to her, and she let it lie in her mind for some time without speaking. Finally, she said, "Mama? Can I ask you something?"

"Yes, baby." The voice was weak, but Beth opened her eyes and smiled slightly. "What is it?"

"Who was my father?"

The question was one that Allyn had asked ten years earlier, but her mother had put her off, saying only that the past was better left alone. Now, however, the shadow of death was on Beth Griffeth, and she knew there would be little time. Her lips were dry, and she said, "Give me some water." When she had swallowed some of the tepid water, she lay back and studied her daughter. "That's strong—the medicine," she whispered. Then she began to pluck at the coverlet with thin hands, her eyes dim.

"He was a gentleman, baby," she said finally. "A fine gentleman. We met right here in New Orleans. It was in April, and I remember the magnolias were filled with lovely white blossoms. And he used to bring me flowers—all kinds."

"Where was he from, Mama? What did he look like?"

"He was from Virginia, and he was a handsome man, tall and dark—" She broke off and put her hand out to touch Allyn's cheek. "You look a little like him, baby."

"Did—did you love him, Mama?"

"Yes! And he loved me, too."

"Why didn't he marry you?"

Beth's eyes were cloudy from the drug, and she was fighting against the drowsiness. "He. . .came from a fine. . .family," she whispered. "I was nobody. . .and he was quality."

Allyn had to bite her lips to keep from saying, "He wasn't quality—not to abandon a girl who loved him and had a baby!" But it was too late for that. She spoke softly, getting as many details as she could. For years she had longed for a father, though she had managed to bury some of that desire. Now she knew that once her mother died she would have no one to ask.

But the medicine was powerful, and soon her mother was deep in a comalike sleep. Regretfully Allyn sat there, her eyes on the worn face. *I'll have to find out more about him,* she thought just before she dozed off in the chair.

But she had little chance to find out more about her father. Her mother was in such pain that it was necessary to keep her drugged, and her speech was incoherent most of the time. When she was conscious, she seemed reluctant to talk about Allyn's father—saying once, "If it would help, I'd tell you, baby, but it was all so long ago!"

The next day the end came. Allyn had been cooking some eggs over the small stove when she heard her mother call. Putting the pan off the stove, she hurried into the bedroom. Her mother was lying flat on her back with her eyes wide open. "What is it, Mama?" Allyn asked, going to stand beside her.

Beth Griffeth's eyes were staring at the ceiling, almost

blindly it seemed. "Mama? Are you all right?"

"I...have always...loved you...." The words were so faint that Allyn had to bend down to hear them.

Fear came to her then, for she saw that the breathing was very shallow. "I'll go get Dr. Kinsman."

"Too late." The words were a gasp, and then the dying woman seemed to recognize that the time had come. With the last of her strength she reached up, and her words were almost inaudible. "His...name was...Mark!"

"My father?"

But the effort was the last. The pale lips formed the word *baby*, and then Allyn's mother relaxed in that terrible finality into the great silence.

"You want to do *what*?" Sam Barker had been lifting a beer to his lips when Allyn had made her request. Staring at her, he put the stein down and shook his head. "Why, not in a million years would I let you do a thing like that!" His bald head gleamed, and he brushed his mustache fiercely as he did when something displeased him.

"What's wrong with it?" Allyn asked quietly. She came into the saloon three days after her mother's funeral, and when Sam had seated her at his table, she said, "Sam, I want to deal blackjack for you in the Gay Paree." She had known he would say no, so she had sat there patiently, her eyes determined.

"What's wrong with it?" Barker shot back. "Everything! This ain't no place for a young girl." He reddened as Allyn looked at the women who were serving at the bar. He snapped, "I won't have no part in making you into one of *them*, Allyn!"

"Look, Sam, all I want is a way to make money. I can't go on at that factory. It's just another kind of death." She gestured toward the saloon girls, saying, "I know what they do, and that's not for me. But I can't get any other kind of work." Her eyes were enormous, and there was a fierce determination in her. "Won't you at least let me try it, Sam?"

Barker was a hard man, but he had a soft spot for this girl. He'd had a daughter himself once. She had died, but he had never forgotten her. He was honest enough with himself to admit that he'd spent considerable time worrying about the fate of Allyn Griffeth. Now he sat still, his agile brain working. Finally, he grunted, "What makes you think you're good enough to deal for me?"

"Lucas taught me."

"He wasn't much good himself."

Allyn smiled. "Try me!"

Sam had always liked the girl's spunk. He grinned, picked up a deck of cards, and tossed them in front of her. Allyn picked them up, shuffled expertly, then dealt the cards. Ten minutes later, Barker laughed, "Well, you're good enough to beat me, I reckon."

"Can I do it, Sam?"

"We'll try it." He dug into his pocket and handed her some bills. "That's an advance. Go get some fancy clothes. You'll start tonight."

That night Sam was shocked when Allyn walked into the saloon. He'd never seen her wear anything but worn, drab clothing. The sight of her wearing an emerald green dress that was modest by the standards of the Gay Paree but still revealed her stunning figure hit him hard.

"You look nice," he said. "Never seen your hair like that."

Allyn's rich auburn hair was done up in the latest fashion, but two tendrils hung down in front of each ear. "I borrowed these jade earrings from Marsha," she said, touching one of them. Then she said, "Sam, I'm—I'm a little nervous, to tell the truth."

"Why, these high rollers will be standing in line to lose their money to you!"

"What if I lose?"

"You won't lose." Sam grinned as he added, "You're so good looking they'll be watching you instead of their cards. Go on, girl, you'll be all right!"

Allyn said softly, "Thanks, Sam!" Then she moved to the blackjack table and soon had a lively group gathered around. The tall gambler came over after an hour to say, "Sam, I didn't know you were so smart." He nodded at the group of men gathered around Allyn, adding with a grin, "She's going to do all right."

After the saloon closed, Allyn said, "I didn't make your fortune, Sam, but I didn't lose nothin', either."

Barker was pleased but felt a warning was in order. "You did fine, Allyn, but this isn't much of a life for a woman. I know you think you can make out, but this sort of thing hardens a man—much less a woman."

Allyn put her hand on Sam Barker's thick forearm. "I've got you to look out for me. That's why I'm not worried."

Barker flushed then nodded seriously. "I had a daughter once, Allyn. I—I wish you could think of me as sort of a father."

Allyn felt intensely the loneliness that had been with her for years. "I'd be happy to think of you like that. I don't trust men very much. I've had...some bad experiences."

"You never knew your father, did you?"

# WALL OF FIRE

The words, he saw, seemed to harden her, and she said, "No—nor do I ever want to, Sam. He abandoned my mother and me!"

"Well…that happens, I guess." He had touched a nerve and wanted to change the subject. "You go get some rest. Then you and me will go out to Antoine's and eat a big steak—all right?"

"I'd like that a lot, Sam." She turned and left the saloon, and Sam sat down and began to deal solitaire. His thoughts were not on the cards, however, but on Allyn.

Chapter 2

Kings Go Forth

Melora awakened instantly as the mockingbird greeted the dawn. He and his mate nested in the wild hedge outside the cabin, and the pair carried on eternal warfare against a yellow tomcat who stayed in the small barn. He had a scarred hammerlike head and never seemed to learn that the mockingbirds would peck him bloody when he approached the hedge.

Cautiously Melora climbed out of bed and tiptoed toward the door. Looking back, she cast a loving glance at Clay, who was still asleep. Five days constituted her marital life, and she was amused that she experienced a shock at finding a man in the bed beside her each morning. *Just an eternal old maid—that's all you are!* she jeered at herself.

She let her eyes rest on her new husband's calm, strong features, admiring his hair, dark as her own, and tentatively put out a finger to touch the slight cleft in his chin. Then she stopped, not wanting to awaken him. They had stayed on the river running a trotline until nearly three in the morning, and Melora thought of the times he had taken her fishing when she was a child. *I fell in love with him when I was no more than ten years old.* And then the memories came rushing back to her—how Clay had come to fill her life when he was a grown man and she was still a little girl. She'd been the daughter of a poor farmer while he'd been a member of the wealthy planter class—a monumental wall between two people. Memories flickered as she thought of Clay's hapless marriage to Ellen Benton. She had tricked him into marriage, and despite the four children who came to the pair, Ellen had led an immoral life and made a hell on earth for Clay.

You were faithful to her, Melora thought, looking lovingly at Clay. *Most men would have sought another woman, but you never did.* She had loved him for that, loved him through all the years that had transformed her from a leggy adolescent to a tall, stately woman.

Now Ellen was gone, and Clay was hers. In a normal world they would have waited a year to marry, but the war had changed all sense of time. Clay would be marching off with the Richmond Grays under the command of Robert E. Lee and his Army of Northern Virginia. They knew he might never return, and Melora had said, "Let me have what time there is, Clay!"

"But what if I don't come back—and there's a child?"

"Then I'll have part of you to keep and treasure!"

Melora smiled at Clay. *Even if I never have more than these few days, I'll have had more than most women!*

The mockingbird screamed, and Melora crept into the kitchen and peered out the window. The scruffy tom was retreating, head down and bloody from the lethal bills of the mockingbirds, who were swooping down in great dives and peppering the hapless cat mercilessly.

Melora was on the side of the birds. *Go get that worthless tom!* she urged. *Peck his old head off!*

And then she uttered a short cry of alarm—for a pair of

strong arms suddenly wrapped around her from behind.

"Got you!"

"Clay! You let me go!"

Melora turned and put her hands against Clay's broad chest and shoved, but he held her easily, laughing at her struggles. She flushed, as she did every morning when he first looked at her and took her in his arms. A rich color rose to her cheeks, and she had no idea how attractive she was to him at that moment. "If you don't stop, I'll—I'll—"

"You'll go off into the woods and eat woolly worms?" he teased. Ignoring her protests, he pulled her close, and her eyes widened as he looked at her then kissed her.

Clay was very tall and, even at the age of forty-three, was almost as lean and strong as he had been at twenty. She ran her hand down his muscular back, delighting in his strength.

Clay held her in his arms, marveling at the silken sheen of her skin. She was twenty-nine now, a mature woman, with all the love she'd harbored for years overflowing as he held her in his arms. He said, "We've missed a lot of years, Melora."

Melora knew he still grieved over the past, and at once she pulled his head down and kissed him. When she pulled back, she whispered, "We have each other, so never look back, Clay. We mustn't do that!"

She was, he had long known, a woman who possessed a rare wisdom. Now he realized she was speaking the truth. "No—never that." He held her close, murmuring quietly, "I've got the whole world—right here in my arms!"

*

Clay soaked up the last of the sorghum molasses with a flaky biscuit half, placed it in his mouth, and chewed slowly. "Got to make the taste of this last," he said, shaking his head. "The Army of Northern Virginia doesn't serve breakfast like this." Melora had fixed all Clay's favorite things for their last breakfast—eggs, bacon, grits, hash brown potatoes, biscuits and sorghum, and a pot of scalding coffee. It was the last of the real coffee, for the Confederacy was cut off from that item. Melora had hoarded the precious grounds, knowing how Clay disliked baked acorns and other substitutes.

"Maybe you could take me along as your aide," Melora teased.

Clay examined her critically. She was wearing a thin robe over a silk nightdress—and even with her hair slightly tousled from sleep, she looked beautiful. "Nope, I don't think that would work." He shook his head regretfully. "You don't look like any aide I ever saw in the army." He sipped his coffee, eyes running over her curves, then added, "General Lee wouldn't like it." He reached over and took her hand, a knowing smile on his lips. "Now *I'd* like it mighty well, myself—"

Melora slapped at his hand then rose to clean the table. He helped her as he always did, and afterward they left the cabin and walked toward the small stream that led to the river. The hammer-headed cat slunk toward the hedge and was promptly bombarded by the dapper mockingbirds. Both of them laughed as he crept away with his head down in abject humiliation.

"He never learns, does he?" Clay remarked.

"I don't care if they peck his old yellow head off!" Melora snapped. She loved birds, and the thought of anything preying on them angered her. But it was only a passing anger, and she was soon holding Clay's hand and laughing as they made their way along the river. When they reached the bank, they sat down on a grassy knoll, and after a while Melora said wistfully, "It's almost over, isn't it?"

Clay was thinking the same thought. "For a while, Melora." Regret came to his dark eyes, and he shook his head. "I wish we could stay here forever."

"Wouldn't that be fine?" She reached over and took his hand, stroked it gently, then said, "We've had only a few days, but I've learned something about being a wife."

Clay's eyes gleamed, and he closed his hand on hers. "Yes, I'll say amen to that!" he said with a sly grin.

"Oh, you!" Melora colored slightly then grew still. He had grown accustomed to this from her. There was more life in this woman than in any he'd ever seen, but at times she would seem to withdraw, her mind and spirit moving in some realm that he could only imagine. Finally, she began to speak, and there was a wonder in her still face. "I can't find words to say it, Clay, but it's like I'm lost without you—no, not lost—but somehow *not complete*. I guess that's what the pastor meant when he said we'd be one flesh. When you're not right with me, I get a queer, strange feeling inside—"

A large fish came to the surface, a black bass, and she broke off, eyeing the silvery flash as he rolled over and took a bug that had fallen into the water from an overhanging branch. He sank back into the green depths, and Melora turned again to Clay. "Sometimes when you're just sitting by the fire or eating breakfast—or when I look at you when you're asleep—I feel like my heart's going to bust wide open! Just crack and run down inside of me. I'm so proud that you're my man, my bones just—just sort of turn to jelly and a shiver runs over me." She turned her face away from him and whispered, "And that's what love makes me feel like, Clay."

He was deeply moved, for she had never voiced her feelings so strongly. He put his arms around her and drew her close, savoring the clean smell of her hair, the firm curves of her body, and the sweetness that was part of her. "I wish I'd said that, sweetheart," he said quietly. "I feel like that, too, but a man—well, he can't seem to say those things so easy." Then he turned her around and kissed her. Drawing back, he smiled, adding, "But I'm going to learn how to say what I feel. I don't know much, but I know women like to be told they're loved."

Melora's eyes suddenly grew mischievous. "You can practice on me, Clay Rocklin. I'll let you know when you do it right or when I've heard enough!"

They both laughed and sat there making foolish talk, and finally Melora grew serious. "How long do you think the army will be gone?"

Clay picked up a flat rock and skipped it expertly across the water. As he watched it sink, he grew thoughtful. "Hard to say, Melora. But things can't go on like they are. The South grows weaker every day, and the North grows stronger."

"Do you think we'll lose?"

"If something remarkable doesn't happen, I think we will. It comes to this: Either we draw our army around Richmond and stand a siege—which will end sooner or later in surrender—or we invade the North."

"Isn't that what we did when the army went to Maryland?"

"Yes, and we have to do it again." Clay's eyes grew sober, and he shook his head in a moody gesture. "We'll be taking every man that can be spared, and somewhere we'll have to meet the Union army. But I don't know how long we'll be gone—nobody knows that."

Melora felt a sudden stab of fear but knew that she must

never show it to Clay. She changed the subject, and later that day they packed their things and left the cabin. As they left the clearing, Melora clung to his arm. "It was the finest honeymoon any woman ever had, Clay!"

He saw the sadness in her eyes and said huskily, holding her with one arm, "We'll come back here as soon as I get home, Melora."

They turned and walked slowly toward the river, clinging to each other with a desperation that each of them had to fight down. The bass rose to take a shining minnow, breaking the water with a loud splash, but neither of them noticed the sound.

Rooney Smith scooped off a spoonful of the steaming broth that simmered in the large black pot and carefully tasted it. "This chicken soup needs more of something, Dorrie, but I can't tell what."

"Gimme dat spoon!" The black woman who spoke had been kneading biscuit dough, turning it relentlessly. She was tall and straight despite her sixty years, her face was barely lined, and there was a nobility in her features. She took the spoon, tasted the broth, then frowned as she said, "Needs mo' thyme—and mebbe a little mo' rosemary."

Rooney shook her head in disgust. "I'll *never* learn to cook like you, Dorrie," she groaned. She was an attractive girl of seventeen with curly auburn hair and large blue eyes shaded by thick black lashes. "I guess Lowell will have to hire a cook when we get married."

Dorrie glanced at the young woman, and a smile curled the edges of her lips upward. "You doin' fine, Miss Rooney," she said.

WALL OF FIRE

"Never seed a girl learn to cook as quick as you. Mr. Lowell, he's gonna git fat as a possum when you gits a chance to feed him." She went back to pounding her dough, asking, "When you and Marse Lowell gettin' married?"

Rooney gave her head a toss, saying as she added the ingredients to the broth, "As soon as the army comes back." An impatience stirred in her, for she was a quick-spirited girl. "Lowell was afraid something would happen to him in the army. But Clay and Melora got married, so I don't see why we can't."

"Humph!" The short explosion that issued from the lips of Dorrie expressed her disgust. "Miz Melora been a-waitin' for Marse Clay 'mos' as long as you been *alive*! So you jis' settle back—learn how to cook and how to treat a man!"

Rooney smiled at the older woman, mischief in her eyes. "How *do* you treat a man, Dorrie? You and Zander have been married a long time. Did he ever take after another woman?"

Again the explosion: "Humph!" Then Dorrie said, "I doan reckon you needs to know *everything* 'bout it—but he did git to looking at a little ol' yellow gal onst. I cotched him at it!"

"What'd you do, Dorrie? Take a broom to him?"

"No! I made him a pie every day and tole him whut a handsome man he wuz!" Dorrie tried to frown, but instead a smile came to her. "And I wuz nice in other ways, too. You gonna have to learn, honey, dat when a man git steak *at home*—why, he ain't gonna be looking around to find chicken backs somewheres else!"

Rooney giggled abruptly and would have questioned Dorrie more closely, but Susanna Rocklin entered at that moment. "What are you two plotting?" she asked, noting the merriment on the girl's face.

"Dorrie's teaching me how to hold on to a man," Rooney

answered. "She says you make everything so nice he won't *dare* run away. Is that right?"

Susanna laughed aloud, saying, "It worked for me, Rooney. And Lowell is so spoiled already—mostly by me and Dorrie—that you'll have to treat him better than most new bridegrooms." The mistress of Gracefield was sixty-two years old and still had the steady blue-green eyes and trim shape she'd had when she'd come to be the bride of Thomas Rocklin years earlier. A faint shadow lay over her, for the death of her husband had left her lonely. *Now I've got two new daughters to care for,* she thought. *Melora and Rooney will need me more than they know.*

The three women talked for a time, and then Rooney said, "I've made some chicken soup for Mark. He's not been eating well."

Susanna shook her head, for she had been concerned for her brother-in-law. "He's lost so much weight—I'm worried about him. Maybe I ought to get Dr. Maxwell out to see him."

Dorrie gave her mistress a quick glance and shook her head. "He ain't done no good, Miz Susanna, not since he got shot in dat battle. I'm plumb worried 'bout Marse Mark."

"He was always your favorite, wasn't he, Dorrie?" Susanna asked gently.

"I doan know 'bout dat!" Dorrie spoke sharply, turned, and left the kitchen abruptly.

"She always loved Mark," Susanna said to Rooney. "Maybe it was because he was such a lost man."

"Lost? How?"

"Oh, Mark was always a rebel. Dorrie practically raised him, was a mother to him almost. Finally, he left and became a Mississippi riverboat gambler—and worse, I suspect. He would come home from time to time, but he always stayed on the outside of our family." Susanna began to spoon the soup into a bowl, her brow drawn up. "He's not been one to share himself," she murmured. "He never married, and we've always known there was some kind of a tragedy, though he's never spoken of it."

Rooney glanced at Susanna sharply, hoping that she wouldn't be asked if she knew anything about Mark. But Rooney said only, "I'll take him his soup. I can get him to eat usually."

Susanna nodded, studying the young woman. "He thinks a lot of you, Rooney. What do the two of you talk about so much?"

"Oh, different things," Rooney said evasively. She quickly prepared a tray then moved out of the kitchen into the broad hall. When she got to the room at the end, she knocked once then entered. "Now then, Mark Rocklin," she said cheerfully as she set the tray down on a small table, "You've got to eat every bite of this!"

Mark was sitting in a chair beside the large window that let in the bright sunlight. He was a tall man, but illness had drained him of vitality. His dark eyes were sunk into their sockets, and his hair was lank, having lost its dark luster. He smiled, however, saying, "Sit down, Rooney. I've been lonesome."

"I'll sit as long as you eat," Rooney pronounced and proceeded to practically force him to eat all of the soup. She was a clever young woman and had learned how to cheer the tall man. For an hour she sat with him, entertaining him with tales of her attempts to learn how to function on a large plantation. She had been a city girl, and her romance with Lowell had been stormy. Even now her mother, Clara, was just out of prison leading an immoral life, and this was a constant grief to Rooney and her younger brother, Buck.

Mark sat quietly, smiling at her sprightly accounts, careful not to let the pain that came to him show on his face. At least he tried to do this, but Rooney was very quick. "You're in a lot of pain, aren't you, Mark?"

"I can't complain," he said quickly then added, "You've learned a lot about wounded men, working at the hospital. But I'm all right." He had little hope left that he would recover from his wound but wanted to go with as little trouble as possible. "Tell me about Lowell. Is he champing at the bit to get married?"

Rooney answered Mark's questions, but she was thinking of the time she'd cared for him when he'd been in a delirium. He'd spoken of a woman who died, a woman he was in love with named Beth. Rooney had never mentioned what Mark had said but had cautiously probed Dorrie—who knew every detail of the Rocklin family—and had discovered that even she knew nothing about this part of Mark's history.

Now as she finished feeding Mark the soup, she watched his drawn face and the pain behind his eyes. She thought, *He loved a woman once—and it ruined his whole life!* But she couldn't bring herself to ask about the woman or her daughter. So she said nothing, and when she left, there was a weight on her. As much as she'd come to like and respect Mark Rocklin, she could see no glimmer of hope for him.

On the morning of June 8, 1863, Major General Jeb Stuart greeted his commander, Robert E. Lee. Stuart cut quite a figure, wearing a brand-new uniform and a slouch hat with a long black ostrich plume fastened with a golden clasp. Stuart sat astride a horse decked with garlands of flowers, and one of Lee's staff quipped, "It's Stuart in all his glory."

WALL OF FIRE

Stuart was proud—and had reason to be. His command—now five brigades comprising nearly ten thousand cavalrymen—had demonstrated time and again its ability to ride rings around the Federal cavalry. Now as he and Lee took position on a hilltop at Brandy Station, a whistle-stop on the Orange & Alexander Railroad just north of Culpepper, Virginia, Stuart gave a signal.

Bugles blared as twenty-two cavalry regiments wheeled into a column four across. While three bands played, horses pranced as the troopers moved out beneath their flags, which waved with the blowing of the breeze. A large dust cloud billowed up from the grand parade.

As the parade moved by, Lee thought of the meeting he'd just had with President Jefferson Davis and his cabinet in Richmond. He had laid his plan for the invasion of the North before them and had seen that some of them disapproved. Quietly Lee had said, "Mr. President—and gentlemen—we have just won a victory at Chancellorsville. But we lost General Stonewall Jackson—who cannot be replaced. Now we *must* force the action."

"Why, sir?" Davis had demanded. He was an impossible man. "We cannot leave Richmond unprotected."

Carefully Lee had given his three reasons for the proposed invasion. "First, there is the matter of supplies. We must have adequate food and clothing for the army and forage for the horses. An invasion of Pennsylvania would give access to that rich storehouse and would allow the people of Virginia to stockpile supplies. Also, sir, the Peace Democrats in the North will press harder to end the war under favorable terms to the Confederacy."

Now as the last of the troopers filed by, Lee felt the

weariness that had come from that struggle to convince the president and cabinet of the necessity of the blow against Pennsylvania. He complimented Jeb Stuart then turned the iron gray horse away from the field.

"Sir, we will whip the Yankees again!"

Lee gave the flamboyant Stuart a hooded glance but said only, "It will be as God wills, General."

The bugles began to blow again, brazen and harsh to Lee's ears. He had heard many bugles blow in his time, but Lee heard an ominous note to the sound this time. . . .

The leader of the Union cavalry was General Alfred Pleasanton—a small man who was addicted to straw hats and kid gloves. He was sick of getting whipped by Jeb Stuart and had determined to hand the flamboyant Confederate a sound thrashing. "If you do," he had been told by Hooker, "it will be the first time our cavalry ever did anything but run from Stuart! But go see what you can do with him."

Pleasanton had at his command some fine officers, but perhaps the largest asset to him, in this case, was the review of the Confederate cavalry, for Jeb Stuart was so elated over the affair that for once he let down his guard. Thus, for the first time in the war, the Federal cavalry caught its enemy off guard. Pleasanton got his men down to the upper fords of the Rappahannock at dawn on June 9 and sent them splashing across the stream yelling like madmen. They struck the Confederate outpost line, pushed it aside, and drove from the riverside to Brandy Station—not far from where General Stuart lay asleep, as though the enemy was still in Washington.

WALL OF FIRE

Lowell Rocklin had risen before dawn, groomed his horse, then shared a breakfast of bacon and biscuits with Lieutenant Lafe Hebert, a dark Cajun from Baton Rouge. "Gimme three or two of them biscuits, Rocklin. I'm hungry as a bear, me!"

Lowell grinned and leaned forward to pick up the biscuits, but he stopped and turned his head to one side. "Hey—what's that?"

"I don't hear nothin'," Hebert said.

Lowell tossed his plate down and stood up, alarm on his face as he turned toward the east. For one moment the two men stood still, and then Lowell yelled, "That's a charge, Lieutenant! Hear that trumpet?"

"Wake the men! The Yanks are comin'!" Hebert cried. He rousted the drummer boy, and a sharp staccato brought the troopers out of their blankets. They were none too soon, for by the time the officers had gotten their men into the saddles, a terrific roar of guns shook the woods to their left. "They're all along the river," Hebert shouted. "Rocklin—go tell General Jones we got trouble!"

Lowell shot away from the camp and found General Jones—called Grumble Jones by friend and foe—without difficulty. The general appeared barefoot, hatless, and coatless as Lowell tore into the command post. "What's going on?" the general demanded.

"Yankees are attacking, sir," Lowell said. "A big force. Sounds like they're spread out along the river—and coming hard!"

Jones and Stuart did not get along, but the general was too good a soldier to waste time blaming his superior. "Come along, trooper," he commanded Lowell. "I'll need you to take a message to General Stuart when I get this sorted out."

Lowell followed General Jones, who sized up the situation

very quickly after arriving at the line of battle. The field was covered with a mingled mass, fighting with pistol and saber, and Jones immediately saw a weakness. "Go down there and tell Captain Chew there's a big gap in those woods. They'll be setting up their artillery right there!"

"Yes, General!" Lowell spurred his horse and without a moment's hesitation drove into the center of the fight. He drew his pistol, and when a maddened Yankee drove for him with saber raised high, Lowell lifted it and shot the man out of the saddle. The battle was a wild, confused affair, not a simple charge where two lines of cavalry are clearly defined. Before he had crossed the field, Lowell had ridden past several Federals and had emptied his revolver, but he did reach Captain Chew and gave him Jones's orders. At once Chew ordered his guns brought up, cutting down scores of Federals. But the Union charge powered on, and the Confederates were driven back.

Lowell carried messages for General Jones several times, and when Grumble Jones saw the enemy flanking Fleetwood Hill, he sent Lowell to find General Stuart. "Tell him we've got more Yankee cavalry than I've ever seen, and we're about to get flanked."

Lowell rode away, managing to avoid the center of the melee. Stuart was not far away, and when Lowell rode up and gave him Jones's warning, Stuart said with irritation, "Tell General Jones to attend to the Yankees in his front, and I'll watch the flanks."

Lowell wheeled his mount, and when he gave Stuart's reply to Jones, the crusty warrior glared toward where Stuart was located. "So he thinks they ain't coming, does he? Well, let him alone—he'll darned soon see for himself."

And Stuart did, for the flanking force appeared across from

Fleetwood Hill and began shelling the hill.

Jeb Stuart had never been flanked—and even now found it difficult to believe that the Federals were at him in force. When he heard the shelling, he commanded James Hart of his artillery, "Ride over and see what this foolishness is all about." But before Hart could leave, a courier confirmed the news. It was then that Stuart decided to throw his entire force against the enemy. "Order every regimental officer to get to Fleetwood at the gallop!"

Lowell was with General Jones when the order came, and he ignored the fact that he was a courier. He was one of those who made the charge. Later he wrote his father, saying, "It was a thrilling sight to see these dashing horsemen draw their sabers and start for the hill a mile and a half away. The lines met on the hill, and it was like what we read of in the days of chivalry—acres and acres of horsemen sparkling with sabers. The flags above the two lines were hurled against each other at full speed, and when we met the earth seemed to tremble!"

Stuart's chief scout, young Captain Farley, was right in front of Lowell, and he went down, knocked from his horse by a shell. Lowell had gotten close to the man and pulled his horse up at once and dismounted. Kneeling down, he saw that Farley was hard hit. The captain's leg had been blown off above the knee, and Lowell at once put a tourniquet around the stump. Farley was pale but asked, "Are we winning? Did the charge drive them back, Rocklin?"

"Yes, sir. They're leaving the field," Lowell said as he looked across the field. "Take it easy, sir. I'll get you a couple of stretcher bearers."

Farley looked down at the wreck of his leg and managed a grin. "I guess we'll be a matched set, won't we? Reckon you can get your man to make me a leg like yours?"

"You bet, sir."

Lowell found the ambulance wagon, and when he directed it to where the captain lay, he found Farley much worse. He had lost a great deal of blood, and when the soldiers picked him up to put him inside, he pointed to his leg, which lay ten yards away where it had been flung by the shell.

"Bring it to me, please," he whispered. Lowell was shocked but did what the captain asked. "It's an old friend, and I don't want to part with it," Farley said. Then he looked at Lowell and whispered, "I know my condition. Good-bye, Lowell—thank you for your great kindness...."

Lowell mounted and rode toward the front, deeply saddened. *He's in love with a girl named Alice. He's going to marry her—if he makes it.* He was hoping that Farley would survive the wound but was not optimistic. After the battle ended and the Yankees were driven off, he went to the field hospital. When he asked about Farley's condition, the doctor shook his head. "I'm sorry. Captain Farley died an hour ago."

Stuart had lost over five hundred men, and Rooney Lee, the son of General Robert E. Lee, had been badly injured. Later in the month, while he was recovering, Federals captured him. Stuart ordered his camp set up at the site where the battle had been, but when he got there he discovered bluebottle flies swarming over the bloody ground thickly and bodies of men and horses covering the field. He chose another spot.

The battle of Brandy Station proved one thing: Federal cavalry *could* stand up to Rebel cavalry in open combat. As one Confederate critic put it, "It *made* the Federal cavalry!"

Jeb Stuart was criticized for his conduct. Charles Blackford, a member of Longstreet's staff, said, "The fight at Brandy

Station can hardly be called a victory. Stuart was certainly surprised, and but for the gallantry of his subordinate officers and men, it would have been a day of disaster and disgrace. Stuart is blamed very much."

But the invasion of the North was under way, so Stuart led his men on a mission to screen the movement of General Lee. As Lafe Hebert said to Lowell, "If we wasn't 'bout to get in a big fight, I reckon General Lee would spank Stuart—but we gonna need every man we got!"

Robert E. Lee was a man of daring. One of his opponents had said of him, "Good Lord—Lee makes a Mississippi riverboat gambler look like an old maid! I've never seen a man with such nerve!"

And now it was time to gamble again, not for money but for a nation. And the table stakes would be not currency, but the rich red blood of men. Men and boys. The Confederacy had reached the end of its resources. The bravest had gone first, throwing themselves into the Cause with reckless abandon. When they were gone, there were no others like them to fill the gaps. The draft now drew men of fifty and boys of sixteen. Men with white beards and boys with no beards at all.

It will be for everything—we will lose or win on this invasion. Lee reached down and patted the shoulder of the great horse, then said quietly, "Come, Traveler—it's the time when kings go forth to war."

CHAPTER 3

OUT OF THE PAST

Robert E. Lee was poised to strike. The Army of Northern Virginia would be the weapon with which he hoped to demolish the Army of the Potomac. However, the death of Stonewall Jackson meant that the army must be reorganized.

The Army of Northern Virginia had been organized into two corps, one under Jackson and one commanded by Lieutenant General James Longstreet. Each corps comprised about thirty thousand men—too many, Lee felt, for one officer to handle. He decided to divide his army into three corps.

The Confederate I Corps would remain under the command of Longstreet, the solid Georgian whom Lee fondly called "my old warhorse." In fact, Longstreet was opposed to the invasion of the North but agreed provided that it should be offensive in strategy but defensive in tactics, forcing the Federal army to give battle only when the Confederates were in strong position.

Lee selected Lieutenant General Richard S. Ewell to take Jackson's place as head of II Corps. This was a gamble, for Ewell was not the same Ewell who had fought well under Jackson. He had lost a leg, and big wounds change men. All through the campaign officers and men noted that Ewell did not have the drive he once had—but Lee could not know this before the fact. Ewell had made two acquisitions prior to the invasion. One was religion, which tempered his whole outlook. Formerly profane, he was now mild in manner. The second acquisition was a wife—a wealthy widow who in her youth had rejected him to marry a man with the undistinguished name of Brown. Ewell could scarcely believe his luck and sometimes forgot himself so far as to introduce her as "my wife, Mrs. Brown."

The commander of the new III Corps was Lieutenant General Ambrose Powell Hill, a fierce fighter indeed, but also highstrung and impatient.

Thus Lee launched his greatest campaign without the incomparable Stonewall Jackson. And of his three commanders, one was skeptical about the mission, while the other two were totally inexperienced as corps commanders.

Across the Potomac, the matter of leadership was even more confusing. "Fighting" Joe Hooker had fallen into general disfavor following his defeat at Chancellorsville. Although President Lincoln liked him personally, Secretary of War Stanton and General in Chief Halleck were determined to oust him. Their response was perhaps natural. After the defeat Lee and Jackson administered to the Army of the Potomac at Chancellorsville, Washington fell into deep dejection. Horace Greeley cringed in print that the finest army on the planet had been defeated by "an army of ragamuffins." When Lincoln received the bad news, his sallow face turned ashen gray, and he muttered as if dazed, "My God! What will the country say?"

It was a turning point in the war—this terrible defeat of Hooker's army. Nobody consciously made any decision about anything, yet people began taking something for granted that they had not known before: that the war would have to be fought out, no matter how many ups and downs it might have, that there would never be any turning back, that out of the horror of this lost battle in a forest fire there would come a renewed determination and an unutterable grimness. The high watermark of the rebellion had been left behind, though many would have to die before it was over.

Somehow in the North, except for the new graves and the thousands of maimed men in the hospitals, it was nearly as though Chancellorsville had not been fought. The battle had been almost totally devoid of results. The army had been defeated again, but that did not seem to matter.

Why this attitude in the North? Some said that the Army of the Potomac had come of age. It was a professional army now, built around the volunteers of 1862 who had come in singing songs and dreaming dreams. But the songs had come to be doggerel, and the dreams had been knocked out of the men.

And so the two armies moved toward each other—and they were not the same.

The spirits of the men in the Army of Northern Virginia had never been higher. They set out with a dream of defeating the enemy so soundly that the war would end. The men in the Army of the Potomac had no such exuberance, but they had a grim determination to fight until the South was back in the Union.

The Army of Northern Virginia moved north through the Shenandoah and into Maryland and then Pennsylvania—and the Army of the Potomac tarried. To the east, Hooker paralleled Lee's course but remained at least two days behind. There were a few skirmishes along the way, but it was at a spot far ahead that the two mighty armies would clash.

"Buck—you leave those chickens alone!"

WALL OF FIRE

Rena Rocklin aimed a warning kick at the big dog, who had been engaged in chasing a banty rooster. "You don't mind a thing I say," she complained, but then when the huge animal came to paw at her leg, she knelt and put her arms around him, whispering, "Buck, I wish the men didn't have to go to the stupid old war!"

Buck whined and tried to lick the girl's face, but she stood up and shoved him away. "Come on, let's get the worms dug before Josh gets here." She moved quickly away from the house, and when she reached the barn, she picked up a tin bucket and half filled it with dead leaves. She turned to go inside the barn, but someone called her. She turned back to see Josh Yancy come around the house.

"Josh, hurry up," the girl called impatiently. "Where've you been?"

"Had to go to the mill for your grandmother." Josh Yancy at the age of sixteen was fully six feet tall. He had greenish eyes—as had all the Yancys—tow-colored hair that fell over his forehead, and a few freckles across his tanned face. "You get the bait?"

"No, I just got here. Come on, I want to get a mess of fish before it gets too hot."

"Here, give me the bucket." Josh took the bucket and shot a covert admiring glance at Rena. She was wearing a pair of old overalls that had once belonged to one of her brothers. The legs were cut off so she wouldn't trip over the ends, and her youthful girlish figure was evident even though they were men's pants. She wore a light blue cotton shirt, and a tan straw hat covered her dark brown hair. Her eyes were so dark they appeared black, not sharp as were her father's and brothers', but gentle and kind.

The pair moved to the barn and began kicking a pile of dried manure and rotten leaves. "Gosh, they're thick today!" Josh exclaimed. Reaching down he made a stab and captured a long worm that wiggled frantically in its efforts to escape. "Never seen so many!"

Rena bent over and came up with a long worm in each hand. When she put them into the bait can, Josh grinned at her. "Remember the first time I brought you to get night crawlers? You screamed like a panther!"

Rena sniffed and kicked up the leaves, then when she'd come up with another wiggling night crawler, said, "Dorrie says digging worms isn't ladylike. She says I ought to be sewing and doing needlework."

"Not near as much fun as catching f–fish," Josh teased her.

Rena noted that he stumbled over the word and glanced quickly at the tall young man. When she had first met Josh, he had stuttered so badly that he refused to speak. But as time had passed, he had lost most of the stutter, so that now only in moments of crisis was his handicap noticeable. Rena almost commented on this but caught herself in time, knowing that Josh didn't like anyone to mention it. Instead, she said, "Let's go over to the big pool today. Maybe we'll catch that big ol' bass that got away last week."

"All right."

Thirty minutes later, the two were watching their corks in a large pool made in the bend of the river. The air was still and it was cool, though the rising sun would soon lay a baking heat on the ground. Soon the bluegills began to bite, and Josh spent most of his time baiting Rena's hook. She disliked the job, and he contented himself with sliding the hook into the frantically wiggling worms and stringing the plump redear sunfish that Rena brought in.

"You get as excited over a one-pound bluegill as I would over a five pound b–bass," he said with a grin, extracting her hook from the mouth of a fish. Slipping the fish on the stringer, he replaced it in the water, rummaged in the bait can, and began threading a new worm on her hook. "I'm going to put this big one on. I'm t–tired of these little fellows." When the hook was baited, he nodded at a strand of willows that formed the boundary of the water. "Put this sucker right in them willows."

"I'll get hung up," Rena protested.

Josh grinned at her and leaned back on the grass. "Best way to catch a big bass is to get your bait in where you c–couldn't get it out no way."

Rena stared at him then followed his instructions. The red cork bobbed on the small waves, and she watched it carefully. The sun turned the stream red, and they could hear the sound of a cow in the distance. The water gurgled over the stones at their feet, and Josh idly said, "Shore wish I could make a living fishing. Beats work all hollow."

"I guess so."

There was a note in the girl's voice that caught Josh's attention, and he swiveled his head toward her. She'd removed her hat, and he admired her hair—dark brown like walnut. He had learned her ways very well over the past weeks and now saw that her natural gaiety was subdued. "What's the matter, Rena?" he asked.

Rena bit her lower lip then took her eyes off the bobbing cork long enough to face him. She had creamy skin, and her eyes were wide, shaded by thick black eyelashes that Josh admired. "I'm worried about Father—and about Dent and Lowell."

"Why, they'll be all right, Rena!"

"How do you know? Every day it seems like we hear about

somebody getting killed. Yesterday the Baineses got word that their oldest boy was killed in Tennessee."

Josh picked up a stick and began to probe the sandy bottom of the stream. A silvery cloud of minnows fled as he raked the stick through the silt, their scales flashing in the early morning sun. He was troubled by her statement and finally nodded. "I know. Guess I worry about my brothers, too, especially since Lonnie got killed. But it don't do no good worryin', does it? If somethin's gonna happen, why, I guess it will."

"You don't believe that, Josh," Rena said sharply. "You wouldn't go to sleep on a railroad track, would you? God gave us sense enough to keep from doing foolish things!"

Something seemed wrong about this to Josh. He shoved his hair back from his forehead, thought hard, then shook his head. "It ain't the same thing. I don't *have* to sleep on no railroad track, but we *do* have to fight the Yankees!" He was pleased with this and added, "Anyways, it would be downright uncomfortable sleeping on a railroad track."

Rena laughed aloud, amused by his thinking. She reached over and grabbed a handful of his hair. Giving it a sharp yank, she said, "You can't think—that's your trouble!"

"Hey—that hurts!" Josh grabbed her wrist, but she clung to his hair stubbornly. He was strong enough to have freed himself but feared hurting her. He grabbed her other wrist and rolled her over on the grass, but she fought back, squealing shrilly. Josh ordered, "Turn me loose, you crazy female!"

"No! What's going to happen is going to happen!" Rena said, panting. "So what's happening is I'm pulling your hair!"

Josh began to laugh and with an easy strength shoved her back on the grass. He clasped her dainty wrists with one of his big hands then reached over and took a night crawler from

WALL OF FIRE

the bait can. Holding it over her face, he grinned down at her. "All right, it's *supposed* to be that I put this ol' worm in your mouth!"

Rena struggled frantically, her eyes enormous as Josh lowered the wriggling worm. "No! Don't you dare, Josh Yancy!" she cried.

Josh held her easily and let the worm drop another two inches. "Why, I'm just trying to prove a point. My grandpa was a preacher, and he allus said, 'What is to be will be.' Now it's just *got* to be that this worm—"

But Rena suddenly stopped struggling and looked up at him piteously. "You're so mean to me," she whispered, and to Josh's horror, tears welled up in Rena's eyes.

"Oh, g–gosh!" At once Josh released his grip. He was horrified at what he had done and threw the worm away and pulled the girl to a sitting position. "I never m–meant—," he stuttered vainly, but Rena's shoulders were shaking, and her face was buried in her hands. "Oh, R–Rena—for gosh sakes, don't c–cry!"

But she was quivering now, and Josh felt terrible. Awkwardly he put his arm around the girl's shoulders and tried to apologize. "Aw, Rena!" he muttered and was thinking, *Now you done it, you big ox! That's all you needed, wasn't it—scare her to death!*

But as he was muttering his abject apologies and begging her not to cry, she drew back—and she was laughing! Her eyes were clear, and her white teeth gleamed as she said, "There! Now I guess you'll keep your old worms to yourself!" Her dark brown eyes glowed with a merry light, and she held herself, giggling at the look on Josh's face.

Josh was thunderstruck. He stared at the girl in disbelief; then his face reddened. "Why—why, you little—"

"What are you so mad about?" Rena jibed. "Maybe you'll

keep your ol' night crawlers to yourself from now on!" But then she saw that she'd gone too far. Josh, she knew, was as sensitive as a human being could be, and he stared at her with a mixture of humiliation and shame in his eyes. At once Rena put her hand on his arm, saying contritely, "Oh, Josh—I was just teasing you—don't be mad!"

But her words seemed to make things worse, for Josh got to his feet and turned his back, saying, "I d–didn't think y–you'd fool me like th–that."

Rena came to her feet, grasped his arm, and pulled him around. "Oh, Josh, I'm sorry!" She put her arms around him impulsively and buried her face against his chest. Her voice was muffled as she whispered, "I shouldn't have teased you like that. I'm truly sorry."

Josh had been angry, but now as Rena clung to him he felt the anger leave. She was pressing against him, and he was conscious of the pressure of her young form. Then she lifted her face and whispered, "I'm sorry, Josh."

He had kissed her once, and now he did so again. It was a natural thing, and her lips were firm and sweet under his. Then there was a splashing sound, and Josh looked down to see that Rena's fishing pole had been jerked into the water and was headed downstream.

"Hey!" Josh released Rena so abruptly that she almost fell. He took a wild leap into the river and missed his stab at the pole. Sputtering, he began to swim after it, calling back, "It's a big 'un!"

Rena stared at Josh as he thrashed the water and caught the pole with one hand. As the boy fought to get his footing, she saw that his face was alive with excitement, and she angrily kicked at the bait can. It sailed through the air, fell, and rolled on its side. When it came to a halt, she saw the night crawlers come boiling out and snapped, "Go on—all of you!" Then she looked back at Josh, who was fighting to land the bass, and slowly the anger left her. Her lips curved upward into an amused smile, and she said, "Josh Yancy, only you would leave off kissing a girl to catch an ol' fish!"

⁂

"Look at that, Rooney—Josh and Rena." Mark Rocklin had spotted the pair as he sat in the scuppernong arbor, watching the slaves as they worked the fields. He had not felt much like coming outside, but Rooney had bullied him into it. The warm sun had felt good, and except for the gnawing pain in his stomach that never completely ceased, he felt good.

Rooney glanced up from the fabric she was stitching to see a pair of figures emerge from the tree line. "Those two have gotten close," she said. Biting her lip, she shook her head. "It might not be a good thing."

"Why not?"

Rooney shrugged without speaking for a moment. Then she said slowly, "He's a poor boy, and she's a rich girl."

Mark put his eyes on her, understanding at once what she was thinking. "I'd have thought you'd know better than to think that, Rooney," he said quietly. "You and Lowell went through all that, didn't you?"

"Yes, but it's different, Mark. You know it is." Her thoughts troubled her, and she picked nervously at the cloth she was working on. Finally, she looked up and said, "A rich man can marry a poor girl, but it doesn't work the other way around. The Rocklins are wealthy planters, and the Yancys are poor farmers.

You'd never have them in to have dinner with you."

"I'm not so sure about that," Mark mused. "Before the war, all the time I was growing up, maybe it was like that. It was one of the things I didn't like about the South—maybe why I ran away from it. But now it's different. And after the war, no matter which side wins, it'll never be the same."

"I guess it will, Mark," Rooney disagreed. "Money makes a difference—and the raising you get. How could a girl raised like Rena ever be happy in a shack with nothing?"

Mark lifted his heavy eyebrows but said nothing. Something about the conversation, Rooney saw, unsettled him. He sat in his chair, his hands clasping and unclasping nervously. *He's gone downhill so much,* Rooney thought. *And it's not all the wound, either. Something's bothering him.*

The two sat there letting the silence run on. It was one of the things that Mark had always liked about Rooney, her manner of falling into the quietness of a mood. Not many people could do that, he'd often thought. Now he seemed to forget her and, lost in his thoughts, let his eyes fall on the June landscape.

Rooney thought that he'd forgotten the subject, but to her surprise, he said abruptly, "You're right—about rich and poor."

"Oh, I'm not sure I was," Rooney answered quickly. "I'll learn your ways, and if Rena and Josh ever got serious, Clay would take Josh in." She smiled at him fondly, adding, "When two people love each other, there's always a way."

"No!" The word almost exploded from Mark's lips, and he gave her a look that was filled with anguish. "That's the way it *should* be," he said grimly, "but sometimes a man—or a woman—doesn't understand that."

Rooney strongly sensed the emptiness in Mark Rocklin. *Why, he's so lonely!* she thought. *Something in him is crying out for help*. She was a compassionate young woman, and as she sat there she remembered how he'd spoken of a woman he'd once loved. *I can't mention it,* she thought, but looking at the pain in his eyes, she felt this was one time when Mark might need to speak of whatever it was.

"Mark, when you were in a coma—I took care of you." Rooney hesitated, on the brink of turning back, but then forged ahead. "We talked once about how you once considered marriage. Was her name Beth?"

"Beth? Where did you hear that name?" Mark anxiously asked.

"From you, when you were delirious. You said you loved a girl named Beth, and that she was beautiful. Was she the one you wanted to marry?" For one moment Rooney feared she'd gone too far, because Mark Rocklin's dark eyes were fixed on her in what seemed to be anger. Gently she said, "I don't mean to pry, but I've wondered why you never married."

Now Rooney thought the silence louder than any battlefield could ever be. Mark, she saw, had dropped his head, and the muscles in his jaw were working tensely. But then he lifted his eyes to her, and she saw that they were filled with pure misery.

"It was. . .a long time ago," he whispered. A deep breath stirred his thin chest, and he shook his head, his voice frail in the stillness of the morning. "Her name was Beth Griffeth," he said.

When he said no more, Rooney asked gently, "Was she from around here?"

"No, I met her in New Orleans. She was. . .the most beautiful thing I'd ever seen!" Mark shook his head as memories came flooding back. "She was Welsh, and she had dark red hair and green eyes. And how she could laugh!" He stirred in his chair, adding, "We'd dance all night then go have johnnycake and fried oysters at Antoine's for breakfast...."

The singing of the men in the field floated to the arbor, slow songs in rich male voices. Honeybees made a lazy humming as they sought the sweetness of the clover, and from high in the sky came the plaintive cry of a distant bird. These sounds melded together to form a faint background for Mark's voice, and for a long time Rooney sat very quietly. She understood without being told that it was the sort of thing that Mark could not have easily shared with any of his family.

"She was not 'quality,'" Mark finally said, almost spitting out that last word, bitterness twisting his lips. "How I hate that word! She was from a poor family and had no education. As if that mattered! But it did matter—at least I thought it did. I should have married her, but I was a fool!"

Rooney asked gently, "What happened?"

Mark shook his head, and there was a bitter note in his voice as he answered, "I left her, Rooney. She cried when I left. I've never been able to get away from the sound of her weeping as I left the room for the last time!"

"What happened to her? Did you ever see her again?"

"No, never. Once I got a letter from a friend of mine who lives in New Orleans. He knew about us—Beth and me—and was against our marriage. He told me she'd never be accepted in the family. Well, he wrote awhile later and said...that she'd gotten sick and died."

"How awful!"

Mark lifted his eyes and saw the compassion on the girl's face. "She was like you, Rooney," he said finally. "If I'd married her, we'd have been happy. Maybe I wouldn't have wasted my life...."

WALL OF FIRE

Rooney wanted to say something to comfort him, but she could think of nothing. Mark Rocklin was a strong man, but he'd let his life be ruined by a tragic mistake. Finally, she said, "I'm sorry, Mark."

"Yes—so am I, Rooney."

The two of them sat there, and neither of them spoke for a long time. Finally, Mark said wearily, "I've never told my family about this, Rooney. Please don't say anything to them. Nothing they can do, and it would give them more pain."

"I won't say anything," Rooney agreed.

Mark turned to look at her, and his thin face was etched with grief as he whispered, "She was a lot like you, Rooney."

Chapter 4

Colonel Rocklin Meets the President

The calamity of the defeat at Chancellorsville had appalled the North. But two bitter years of war had made many callous. Business was good, factory wheels were turning, and there was wild speculation on the stock market. The humblest man could pocket a large bounty by donning the uniform of his country.

But the price was high. The wounded cumbered the Washington wharves. To Gideon Rocklin, who was now making his way past a large group of wounded who had been almost dumped off a stern-wheeler, the prostrate young bodies symbolized the very figure of the Union itself, and his spirit grew heavy at the familiar scene.

The compact caravans of ambulances had become a monotonous part of the pageant in the streets, but Gideon never got used to it. The procession of the maimed with their empty sleeves and trouser legs moved him no matter how many times he saw such scenes. Even death had become commonplace. Once, the death of one man, Elmer Ellsworth, had thrown the entire capital into mourning. Now from the silver-mounted rosewood of the higher officers to the cheap pine slats of the ordinary soldiers, the business of death was plied like that of any other prosperous trade.

Gideon Rocklin left the wharf, swung into the saddle of a mottled gray stallion, and headed toward the center of the city. The sun was hot on Washington, and he sweated through his wool uniform as he passed through a section of the city where the *rat-tat* of the coffin makers' hammers sounded from the open doors of the cabinet shops. Outside he noted stacks of long, upended boxes—coffins that were a grim fever chart of battle.

He arrived at the War Department thinking that the city had a surfeit of misery. But if the horror of blood beat like a wound in the back of every mind, the faces on the streets were smiling. The soft summer air carried the plaintive mechanical melodies of the organ grinders, and on the avenue, under a huge transparency that advertised embalming, the promenaders sauntered in the sunshine. Gideon threaded his way through the hacks, the wagons, and the caracoling horses of the officers. Fashionable ladies drove in barouches with black coachmen and footmen. On the sidewalks, salesmen cried the merits of patent soaps, and the proprietors of telescopes and lung-testing machines clamored for customers. Pineapples, oranges, and tomatoes were piled in colored pyramids, ice cream dealers were stationed in the shade of the trees, and Italians roasted chestnuts in little portable stoves.

It's like a carnival! Gideon Rocklin thought with disgust. *They don't even know the names of the battlefields, some of them! Men are dying, and they're parading like it was a holiday!*

He made his way down Pennsylvania Avenue, arriving at the President's Park. The White House was here, flanked by four massive buildings that housed the State Department, the Treasury, the War Department, and the Navy Department. He dismounted, tossed the reins to a private, then entered the War Department.

When he walked into the large office occupied by General Halleck, the adjutant, Lieutenant Sellers, said at once, "General Halleck wants you to come in, Colonel."

"Very well, Lieutenant."

"Sir, the president is with the general."

Gideon's hand was on the door, but he hesitated, giving the adjutant a questioning look. "What's going on, Sellers?"

"I don't know, sir—but the president is worried."

Gideon thought for a moment of the state of the country then grunted, "Well, he's got plenty to be worried about, I guess." He knocked on the door, and when the general's voice said, "Come in!" he pushed it open and entered.

"Ah, Rocklin—come in, come in!" The general in chief of the nation's armies was a small man with the air of a snapping turtle. He nodded toward the president, saying, "Colonel Rocklin, Mr. President."

"Yes, the colonel and I have met." Lincoln had a smile on his homely face as he came over to offer his hand. "How's that niece of yours, and the young private she was so fond of?"

"Miss Steele is fine, sir, and you may have read some of the reports Noel Kojak has written for the *New Review*."

Lincoln thought, then nodded. "I did read some of them. Sensible writing, very powerful."

"I thought they stressed the misery of our men too much," Halleck grumbled. He had been displeased, along with some other high-ranking officers, when the stories written by young Kojak had been published. Most of the reports up until then had been patriotic and filled with flag-waving. Kojak had told the story of the misery and terrible trials experienced by the common soldier. "We don't need the people reading that sort of thing!"

"The truth is always hard," Lincoln remarked, "but is usually best, I reckon."

"I'd argue that, Mr. President," Halleck shot back. "We're having a hard enough time filling the gaps in the army. When men read how terrible it is, why, it'll be that much harder."

Lincoln only gave a faint smile to Halleck. Gideon saw him often enough, but almost always at a distance. Now he saw that the president had aged. His face was lined with strain, and his eyes were sunk into craggy hollows. *This war's killing him*, Gideon thought, but then Halleck began to speak.

"Colonel Rocklin, the president wanted to hear firsthand about the battle of Chancellorsville. You were right in the center of the action. Give us your report and leave nothing out—" Halleck paused then added carefully, "Even about the behavior of the commanders."

An alarm went off inside Gideon. *They want to know about Hooker*, he thought instantly. He was trapped, for he knew he could not give his commanding officer a bad report. But Lincoln said at once, "General Halleck has told me of your loyalty to the army and to your fellow officers, Colonel Rocklin. I appreciate that and honor you for it." The gaunt man looked straight at Gideon and said evenly, "But I must know the truth—how else can I make decisions?"

"It's—an awkward position for me, Mr. President," Gideon said. "I don't want to be thought of as one of those officers who is never satisfied with the men above him."

"Just give us your critical judgment of the tactics of the battle, Colonel," Lincoln said, nodding. "That's all we expect."

"Very well, sir." Rocklin knew as did every other officer in the army that Major General Darius N. Couch had been so outraged at Hooker's vacillating conduct during the battle that he refused to serve under "Fighting" Joe any longer—and at least two other corps commanders were maneuvering to have Hooker replaced. As he began to give his report, Gideon knew that General Halleck had never liked Hooker and was anxious to replace him.

With the two men listening to him carefully, Gideon traced the battle. He was unable to tell the story without placing blame on Hooker, but he said finally, "General Hooker is a fine officer. He's done a good job of pulling the army together since the battle, but he found difficulty in dealing with General Lee and General Jackson."

"Name me one general who hasn't!" Lincoln exclaimed. "We send out enough men to overwhelm the Rebels, and they come back whipped! Why can't we beat them?"

Gideon hesitated then said, "Without any disrespect to former commanders of the Army of the Potomac, Mr. President, I believe you must find a man who is not. . .reluctant to close with the Confederates."

Lincoln stared at the officer then nodded. "A man with a killer instinct—just what I've said. But who among our choices has such a quality?"

"It's not my place to say, sir—but I've always felt that you saw this sort of determination in General Grant."

"Yes, Grant's a bulldog." Lincoln nodded. "But he's at Vicksburg. He'll win, but we've got to face up to this invasion, and—" The president knew that he could not ask a mere colonel for more than this one had given. He smiled, saying, "You'll be leaving with your regiment, General Halleck has told me." He put out his big hand and, when Rocklin took it, said warmly,

"God be with you and all your brave men, Colonel Rocklin!"

"Thank you, Mr. President—and my prayers will be with you as you carry this impossible burden." Gideon left the office, and when the adjutant probed to find out what the president and the general had wanted with a mere colonel, he said, "Oh, nothing much, George. He just wanted to know who to appoint as commander of the Army of the Potomac."

The lieutenant laughed at what he felt was a rebuff, but Gideon thought for the rest of the day of how difficult it would be to make such a choice. *McClellan, Pope, Burnside, and Hooker—they all were too timid to go after Lee. This time if the president chooses the wrong man, he knows that thousands of our men will die—and for nothing!*

Gideon arrived home after a long day and found that Deborah Steele and her fiancé, Noel Kojak, were there. "You're late, Uncle Gideon," Deborah scolded him. She came to kiss his cheek. "Come! Sit down to dinner. We've all been starving."

Gideon grinned at the young woman, admiring her fresh beauty as always. He'd longed for a daughter, but this niece was as close as he'd come. She had blond hair and large violet eyes, and most men turned around to watch her when she passed. "You see what you're letting yourself in for, Noel? This woman will run your life worse than any sergeant in the army!"

Noel Kojak was no more than average height and was not handsome. He had the short nose and high cheekbones of his European forebears, and a pair of steady gray eyes. "I guess it's worth it, sir," Noel said.

Deborah pinched his arm, smiled, and said, "You have your

moments, I guess. But why don't you say flowery things to me? You know, 'Your eyes are like sparkling pools; your lips are like rose petals'? What's the good of having a writer for a sweetheart if I don't get any of that sort of thing?"

Noel gave her a wry look, saying, "I'm a journalist, not a poet. Maybe I'll get a book of poetry and steal some of the best things for you."

"Why, that wouldn't be the same! I want something just for *me*!"

"You two stop arguing and come to the table." Melanie Rocklin appeared suddenly, came over to take Gideon's kiss, then started to scold them about letting the food get cold. But even as she spoke, a knock sounded, and when Gideon opened the door, they heard him say, "Why, Uncle Mason!"

"I'm late, Gid, as usual." A stooped man wearing the uniform of a major entered and, seeing the others, stopped and apologized. "Sorry I'm late, Melanie. I got tied up at headquarters."

"You're just in time," Melanie said and came forward to give Gideon's uncle a quick hug. Mason was a rare guest but a welcome one. "All of you come and sit down. Everything's ready."

Ten minutes later they were all seated at the round oak dining table heaped high with roast beef, new potatoes, green beans, and fresh bread. Mason tasted the meat, shook his head, and said, "Gid, you've got the best cook in Washington!"

"Or anywhere else for that matter," Gideon said with a wide grin. "I'm getting fat! When will your unit leave, Mason?"

"In the morning." Mason had been a Union officer for years, spending a great deal of time in the Far West. He'd served in Mexico with General Scott and was a trusted member of General Winfield Scott Hancock's corps. "What about you?"

"The regiment's ready. We'll pull out and join General Hooker day after tomorrow."

Noel studied the two older men and said abruptly, "I wish I were going with you—in the ranks, I mean." Noel had served in the army, but a wound he'd taken had never healed completely. Now he stared down at his plate with a disgruntled expression on his face. "I feel like I'm pretty worthless."

"Don't be silly, Noel!" Deborah reached over and squeezed his arm. "You're doing your part with your writing!"

"Can't stop a Reb charge with a turkey quill pen." Noel shrugged. "And from what I can pick up, they're coming at us with everything they got this time."

"I think so." Gideon nodded. He chewed thoughtfully on a morsel of beef then added, "Lee will have to win big this time, and he'll hit us with all he's got."

"And that's a lot," Mason put in. He was fifty-eight years old, and years of hard service had stooped his shoulders and lined his face. "We've got to stop them this time—or it could all be over!"

Noel looked up quickly. "How is that, sir?"

"The Peace party's looking for one more big defeat of the Federal army. If we don't stop Lee this time, I think the country could give it up—let the South go its own way."

"Why, that can't happen!" Deborah was the daughter of Amos Steele, a strict abolitionist, and was herself a fiery opponent of slavery. "We can't let slavery go on!"

"I hope not, Deborah," Gideon said slowly. "But people are tired of losing. They're sick of their husbands and sons and brothers dying—and nothing happening. I think Mason is right. We've got to whip the Rebels soundly this time!"

Mason nodded, and as the talk flowed around the table, he listened but said little. He was a widower and owned half of his brother Stephen's munitions factory. His wife had died in 1833, and he'd never remarried. His life was the army, and he was grieved over the war that had turned brother against brother. Having no children of his own, he was very fond of his nephews and their children.

"How are the boys?" he asked. "Are they all seeing action?"

Gideon shot a quick look at Melanie then nodded. "Tyler and Robert are under Grant at Vicksburg. Frank will be with me, of course—my aide."

"What about your brothers, Deborah?"

"Pat is home on sick leave, but Colin and Clinton are with General Hooker now."

Mason shook his head sadly. "All the fine young men—they ought to be going to college or making careers!"

"They will, sir, when the war is over," Noel said quickly. The strain in the dining room was palpable, and no more was said.

The next afternoon when he and Deborah were on the way to his family's house, Noel mentioned his feelings again. He shook his head gloomily, saying, "I can't help it, Deborah," he muttered. "Your brothers and Tyler and Frank—all fighting for the Union. And all I do is write stories!"

Deborah didn't argue, for they had gone over this many times. She was secretly relieved that Noel was not in the army and felt some guilt over this feeling. She thought of how she'd gone to Richmond and found him sick and dying in a Confederate hospital, and it had taken a miracle to get him out and back home. His recovery had been slow, and she knew that he was anxious to serve. But she said now, "Every man has to do what's best for the country, Noel. Right now, until you get well enough to go back into the army, that's writing. People at home need to hear about what's happening, and God's given you the gift of putting things down so that they seem real."

"It seems so—so *little* to do, Deborah!"

She took his arm and said, "Noel, let's get married."

"You mean now?"

"I mean right away. You were too sick when you first came back from the hospital, but you're fine now." Her violet eyes filled with humor as she added, "Maybe you can't march twenty miles with a full pack, but I expect you can take care of your husbandly duties!"

Her boldness shocked Noel, for he was a reserved young man. "Why, Deborah—I don't think—"

"Don't you love me, Noel?"

"Sure, of course I do! Great Scott, Deborah, I never thought to have a girl like you!"

"Well, you've got me." Deborah moved closer to him and whispered, "Now what are you going to do with me?"

No red-blooded young man could have resisted a pair of lips so inviting! Noel held her fast, and there was such a sweetness in her that when he lifted his head, he gasped, "Deborah—I do love you!"

Deborah stroked his cheek, whispering, "I want to be a wife, Noel!"

As the carriage made its way to the section where Noel's family lived, they talked about getting married. Deborah steadfastly maintained that they loved each other—and that settled it.

Noel had led a difficult life, and as he drove into the

Swampoodle district, the stench seemed to depress him. The section consisted of ramshackle houses with privies behind them. The visual impact of the area offended the eyes almost as much as the smell offended the nose. There was no beauty in Swampoodle, only line after line of shacks unpainted and scoured to a leprous gray-brown by wind and weather. There was almost no attempt at decoration—no flowers or fresh curtains, and all was crude and plain and depressing.

Noel pulled the buggy up in front of a frame house, got down, and helped Deborah to the ground. The door was open, and when he called out, a woman appeared. "Noel!" she cried out and moved to embrace him.

"Ma, how are you?" Noel asked gently.

"Fine, son, and here's Deborah!" Anna Kojak was in her early forties but looked ten years older. Her brown hair was streaked with gray, and only faint traces of an earlier beauty remained. "Come in. Can you stay for supper?"

"No, we're going to a meeting," Deborah said. "Noel's going to speak to a group of writers, Anna."

"Well, ain't that fine!" Anna led the way inside, and when the pair were seated she said, "This place you helped us buy is so nice, son!" She looked around the simple room with pride, and Deborah thought of the wretched shack the Kojaks had lived in when she'd first met Noel.

"Where is everyone?" Noel asked curiously.

"Bing won a fight last night," Anna said. "Nothing would do but he'd take the kids to a circus."

"I hate for him to fight, Ma," Noel said with a frown. "I wish he'd get a job."

"So do I, but he makes more money fighting. He won't hear to quitting."

The three of them sat there talking for half an hour; then

they heard the sound of excited voices approaching. "That sounds like them," Noel said. He got up and looked out the door then turned with a smile on his face. "Looks like they had a good time," he remarked; then the small room was filled with Kojaks.

Bing Kojak led the way, his eyes gleaming. He was twenty-one, a year younger than Noel, but much larger. He was tall and muscular, with a shock of wavy black hair and a bruise under his left eye. "Well, look who's here—the bride and groom!"

Noel took the hard handshake from Bing, and Deborah smiled as the big man gave her a rough kiss on the cheek. "Did you see the elephant?" she asked, and as the younger Kojaks began noisily describing the beast she mentioned, she studied the family.

Bing she knew best, for it was Bing who had helped her when she had gone to Richmond to get Noel out of prison. He was a rough young man who wanted much out of life and had found a way to get it with his fists.

Grace Kojak, age seventeen, was not pretty but had a pair of sharp brown eyes. She wore a dress that could have used washing, and her hair was in the same condition. She was, Deborah had discovered, the smartest of the children—except for Noel.

Holmes, at the age of thirteen, and Joel, five years younger, both had fine brown hair and thin faces. They were loud and boisterous, and for the next ten minutes vied with each other in describing the circus.

Finally, Noel asked, "Where's Pa? Did he go to the circus, too?"

Bing looked a little awkward then said, "Oh, he stopped off on the way back."

This, Deborah had come to understand, was the usual way

of describing Will Kojak's trips to the bars. He would come back dead drunk, or Bing would go find him and haul him back bodily. She had learned something of the class to which Will Kojak belonged, and it stirred her compassion for Anna and the children and even for the father himself. *He drinks to forget his poverty,* she thought.

The two stayed for an hour, and when they got into the carriage, Noel said, "Bing, come and ride with us."

Bing, never one to refuse an invitation, climbed into the buggy. Noel slipped his mother and his brothers and sisters a little money. "Use it on something foolish," he jokingly said. They understood that to mean they were to use it for themselves, not give it to their father for drink.

As they moved along the street, Noel said, "Ma loves the house, Bing. It was a fine thing you did, buying it for her."

Bing shrugged off the comment, saying, "Ah, you know me, both of you. I'd have blown it on foolishness. Anyway, I couldn't have done it if you two hadn't chipped in."

"Bing, I hate to see you get involved in fighting," Deborah said. "My uncle will give you a good job in the factory."

"Ah, Deborah, I can't stand that kind of work!" Bing protested. "I can make more from one fight than I can working for a month in that place."

"But you don't get your brains beat out at the factory," Noel argued.

"I don't get bored to death fighting." Bing listened tolerantly but shook his head, saying, "Nope, I'll just keep on as I am."

"Ever think about joining the army again?"

Bing shook his head emphatically. "Nope, that's not for me." He shot a quick look at Noel then nodded. "You'd like to go back, wouldn't you?"

"Yes, I would." Noel's eyes were thoughtful as he added, "I guess I'd like to do anything that would bring this country back together again."

"Lots of men in shallow graves in Virginia and other places," Bing muttered. "They had the same idea as you, but they're dead. And from what I hear, we ain't much closer to gettin' this thing settled than when we started."

"But don't you see, Bing," Noel said quickly, "if we let it all drop—all those men really *did* die in vain. But if we win, why, their deaths *mean* something!"

Deborah held to Noel's arm, and when she heard this, she knew that she was hearing the real reason for fighting the war through to the end. "Noel's right, Bing. We've got to go on. As Mr. Lincoln said, this nation can't endure half slave and half free."

Bing Kojak was a healthy young man with an appetite for life. He was not a coward, but he strenuously objected to risking his life—unless he was pretty sure that it was for something worthwhile. The steel-shod hooves of the horses clattered along the cobblestones as he sat loosely beside the pair.

"Well, you can let me out at the Palace Saloon. I'll hang around until Pa's too drunk to care; then I'll take him home."

Noel and Deborah knew Bing too well to argue, so they said no more to him. When Noel pulled the team up in front of the Palace, Bing leaped lightly to the ground. He looked up at them with a challenge in his bright brown eyes.

"If you find anything for me to do to end this war, let me know. But I've only got one life, and I'm not about to throw it away unless I know it really counts!"

Noel and Deborah watched as Bing passed through the

swinging doors. Then as Noel spoke to the team, she said, "He could be something great, Noel. He really could!"

"Yes, he could," Noel said soberly. Then as the buggy clattered on down the street, he said quietly, "But he'll never be much until he learns what's worthwhile in this world and what isn't! And that's the hardest lesson for anyone to learn, isn't it, Deborah?"

"I guess it is, Noel."

Chapter 5

Mark Calls on a Friend

"Mr. Larrimore?"

Jason Larrimore looked up from the poker table and narrowed his eyes against the smoky atmosphere of the room. He saw a young man—a boy, really—who had entered the Golden Nugget and had come to stand beside him. Larrimore took in the plain dress of the young man and could not remember ever having seen him before. "Yes, what is it, son?"

"My name is Josh Yancy. Could I talk to you a minute, sir?"

One of the cardplayers seated across from Larrimore, a tall, sallow-faced individual with a bristly mustache, grinned suddenly. "What'd you do, Larrimore? Have it fixed up with this kid to come in and get you out of the game when you're ahead?"

Jason Larrimore smiled at the man and shook his head. "No, it wasn't that way, Simon, but I'm tired of taking your money anyhow. How about we break up and start in again tomorrow?"

The man named Simon and the other two were all weary, for the game had gone on for hours. "All right," he said. "You can't win all the time. Meet you here tomorrow. Same time?"

"You got it. Twelve noon on the nose." Larrimore raked in the pile of bills and coins in front of him and stuffed them into the pocket of the frock coat that hung on the back of his chair. Then, standing up and slinging the coat over his shoulder, he said to the young man, "Come along, Josh. Let's get a little fresh air."

"Yes, sir."

Larrimore led the way out of the saloon. He was very tall, almost two inches over six feet, but lean and very quick. His blond hair was worn long, and he had exceptionally light blue eyes, wide spaced and penetrating. He had a wide mouth and high cheekbones reminding his acquaintances of the Vikings who had stormed across the sea to conquer the world in earlier days. His hands were very strong looking, yet he had long fingers that had made him into an expert cardplayer. There was something in his face that revealed a little of the cynical nature that was a part of him. It was a rugged face with sharp, angular planes, and the set of the mouth was firm. As Josh glanced at the man, he thought, *He looks like a pretty tough fellow. I'd hate to have trouble with him.*

Larrimore walked to a restaurant, where he was greeted by a waiter who said, "Ah, Mr. Larrimore, your usual table?"

"That'll be fine, Robert." He turned and followed the waiter down a line of tables and seated himself in a chair at one of them. Waving his hand, he said, "Sit down, Josh. How about a bite to eat?"

Josh hesitated. He had traveled far and had had nothing to eat since early morning at breakfast. "Well, I guess I could eat a little bit," he said.

"Fine—bring us some bacon and eggs and some of those biscuits of Millie's, if there are any. Bring us a pitcher of milk and some coffee. That do you all right, young fellow?"

"Yes, sir. It sounds fine."

The waiter nodded his assent, said, "It won't be long, Mr. Larrimore," and then turned and made his way across the room.

Larrimore looked at the young man and said, "I don't know you, do I?"

"No, sir, you don't," Josh replied. "I was sent by Mr. Mark Rocklin."

The name caught Larrimore's attention. "Is that so? I haven't seen Mark in quite awhile. How is he?" He leaned back in his chair, pulled a thin black cigar out of his pocket, and clipped the end of it off. Inserting it between his teeth, he lit it with a match he drew from another pocket. Then, sending a puff of purple smoke into the air, he smiled. "We've had some times together, that man and me. I'd like to see him."

"Well, sir, did you hear about his trouble?"

"Trouble? No, I didn't hear anything about that." Larrimore removed the cigar and leaned forward slightly, his eyes narrowing. "What sort of trouble is Mark in?"

"He got shot," Josh said softly, "in the war."

Larrimore leaned back and said, "I never heard anything about Mark being in the army. I thought he was still up north somewhere. How bad was it?"

"Well, sir, it was pretty bad. They didn't think he would live for a while, but they brought him back home to Gracefield, and Miss Susanna and the other ladies, they been taking care of him." Josh gave the details of the wound and finally shook his head, saying, "I sure was plumb sorry to see how bad he's doing. He just gets weaker all the time."

Jason lost interest in his cigar and put it down. He probed at the boy in a way that was his manner, extracting every bit of information that he could from the young man. When the waiter came with their food, he continued to inquire about Mark and the situation while they ate. Josh ate quickly, for he was hungry, and he answered the questions the best he could.

"I hate to hear that," Larrimore said slowly, his mouth twisted. "Looks like there's enough scoundrels in the world to get shot without a good man like Mark taking a bullet." He shoved the plate back then reached over and picked up the coffee cup. Sipping it, he shook his head. "That's the way it is with this blasted war. It takes the best of them and leaves the scoundrels like me."

Josh hardly knew what to make of a man who would call himself a scoundrel, but he said, "Yes, sir, that's the way it is, all right, but I'm going in just as soon as I'm old enough."

Jason Larrimore gave the young boy a quick glance. *He's just like all the rest of them,* he thought bitterly. *Can't wait to get into a war that's going to get him killed. And for what? The South can't win, slavery's doomed, and this boy never owned a slave in his life. Well, I can't tell him that because he wouldn't listen.* Aloud he said, "What message did Mr. Rocklin give you for me, Josh?"

"He wants you to come and see him, if you can," Josh said quickly.

"And he's at Gracefield? That's the old family place, isn't it? How far is it?"

"Oh, not too far," Josh said quickly, "and I've got a carriage with me. Mr. Rocklin, he said I was to wait as long as I needed to and to bring you if you could come."

Jason thought quickly about his schedule and then nodded. "My ship won't be ready for a while. Let me take a bath, change clothes, and get a few things together."

Josh was surprised at the quickness with which the man made up his mind. "You mean—right now—today?"

"Sure," Jason said with a grin. "We don't know about

tomorrow, do we, Josh? Whatever we do, we'd better do it right now. I think that's scriptural, isn't it?"

"I guess so. I'll wait outside for you."

"Come on up to my room, and you can wait there, Josh. Won't take too long."

Jason rose to his feet, put some money on the table, then turned and led the way out of the restaurant. As he went, his brow was broken by a slight wrinkle. He was thinking, *Sure hate to hear that about Mark. From what the boy says, it doesn't sound like he's going to make it.* He was a man who was used to hard knocks and always expected the worst. He had pleasant memories of Mark Rocklin, and Rocklin was one of few men he respected wholeheartedly. As he was soaking in his bath, he said aloud, "Got to help Mark if I can. I've owed him a debt for a long time, but what in the world can I do for a man like him?"

※

The woman who met Larrimore at the door was very attractive, and Larrimore pulled off his hat at once. "I'm Jason Larrimore," he said. "Mark Rocklin asked me to come and see him."

"Oh yes, come in, Captain Larrimore. I'm Susanna Rocklin. Mark is my brother-in-law."

She put out her hand, and as he took it he was impressed by the firmness of her grasp. "Josh must have found you very quickly," she said as she led him inside the large foyer. "We weren't expecting you so soon. Josh only left this morning."

"It's a lucky thing he caught me when he did," Jason answered. "My ship is being refitted, so I have more time on my hands now than usual. I'm glad he caught me."

Susanna led him out of the foyer into a hallway then turned

to him. "Did Josh tell you about Mark?"

"Yes, and I'm sorry to hear it. He's been a good friend to me." Jason bit his lip then shook his head. "This war is taking the best of them, isn't it?"

"Yes, it is."

"How badly is he wounded?"

"Very badly, I'm afraid." Susanna's eyes were cloudy with worry. She said quietly, "I don't think he can live, Mr. Larrimore."

Her words shocked Jason. Even though he was a pessimist, he hoped that the wound wasn't as bad as it had sounded. "That's tough, Mrs. Rocklin. Does he know it—that he's going to die?"

"Oh yes. Mark's very perceptive, and he's quite alert. Doctors say he might live for some time, but he's not hopeful."

Larrimore clenched his fist and struck his palm. "Blast this war," he exclaimed. "I hate it!" Then he blinked and shook his head. "I'm sorry, I get carried away sometimes, but it makes me angry to see this waste. I hate to see anything wasted—especially men like Mark."

A smile touched Susanna's lips. She said gently, "I feel exactly the same way. I always have." Then she said, "I have a room all made up for you, just in case you did come. I hope you can stay for a few days."

"I'll stay as long as I can. I've got a couple of weeks or so before I have to ship out. Do you think Mark will be awake?"

"He was thirty minutes ago. Come along—he's so anxious to see you."

Larrimore followed the woman down the hall. She turned to a door, knocked, then opened it when a voice replied. She stepped inside and said, "Mark, Captain Larrimore is here to see you."

Larrimore entered and was shocked at the sight of his old

friend. He was, however, an accomplished poker player and let none of this show on his face. "Hello, Mark," he said with a wide grin. He crossed the room with swift strides, put out his hand, took the thin hand of the sick man, and added, "I see you've found a way to get out of work and to get people to wait on you. You always were a lazy scoundrel."

Mark had been sitting in his chair reading the Bible. He had dozed off but now was awake, his drawn face showing excitement. "You're a fine one to talk about laziness," he said. "I never knew you to do an honest day's work in your life." He looked over at Susanna and grinned. "I guess you've got the two laziest men in creation right under your roof, Susanna."

Susanna smiled, glad to see Mark showing such life. "You two visit. I'll bring you something to drink. We have some things left over from supper. I'll heat a plate for you, Captain, and I'll bring you something, too, Mark."

When the woman left the room, Mark said, "Sit down, Jason." He waited until the tall man had seated himself and said, "Josh didn't have any trouble finding you, I take it?"

"No," Jason said. "I was at the Golden Nugget taking some money away from some sorry cardplayers." He looked over and paused. "Sorry to hear about your bad luck, Mark."

Mark shrugged. "It happens," he said briefly. Mark had never been a complainer, Larrimore knew, and in that he had not changed. Larrimore was shocked, however, at Mark's appearance. He had been prepared for some changes, but the strong, healthy man he knew was hardly to be seen in the thin, pale man who sat quietly in the chair. Mark Rocklin had always been a man filled with life, had met it with a shout, throwing himself into whatever was at hand with all his strength. Now, Larrimore saw, that was over. Mark's eyes were sunk back into his head, and his cheeks were sunk in. Pain had given his mouth a pinched look, and there was a fragility about him that frightened Larrimore.

Mark caught his glance and said, "Well, as you can see, I don't have much time."

"Oh, you never know about those things," Jason protested.

Mark shook his head. "I know about myself. I've been around awhile, Jason. I've had some close scrapes, but this time my time's about up." He held up a thin hand, as if in protest. "I'm not complaining, you understand. No man likes to die, but I suppose I've had a better life than most."

Larrimore sat there unable to answer. He felt a pang of grief for his friend, but he recognized the truth of what Rocklin had said. Death was in his face, and now Larrimore could only say simply, "Whatever I can do, Mark, you've got it."

"That's like you, Jason."

"Well, I don't think it is, really." Larrimore pulled a cigar out of his inner pocket then hesitated. "I guess I shouldn't smoke in here."

"It won't hurt my health much."

Larrimore grinned at the slight joke. He lit the cigar, leaned back, and shook his head. "Mark, you know me better than most. I'm not much of a one for charities, but I owe you one for that time you saved my bacon when nobody else would, or could. I haven't forgotten it, you know."

"It wasn't that much," Mark said quietly. "I was glad to help you. I don't want to presume on that, but—I don't have a lot of choice, Jason." He clasped his hands and sat there and thought for one moment, then said, "I don't have much to show for my life, Jason. I've got some money, sure, but that doesn't seem to account for much at this stage of the game. Looking back on it,

I see some turns I made that were wrong."

"I guess everybody feels like that."

"Maybe, but there's one thing I want to see before I die, and I can't do it for myself. That's why I sent for you." Mark looked up quickly and said, "I loved a girl once, years ago. I was too blasted proud to do anything about it. Had some stupid idea about aristocracy and the gentry, nonsense like that. If I'd married her, I'd have been a better man, but I was a fool, so I let it slip."

Outside, the sun had finally set, the golden dusk replaced by the darkening night sky. The room itself grew dark as well, with only a single lamp lit in the corner. Mark said, "Light that other lamp, will you, Jason? My eyes don't see as well as they used to." He watched as Jason drew a match from his pocket, struck it, lifted the chimney of the lamp, and turned it up to a steady yellow flame. Then when Jason sat back, he continued speaking softly.

"Her name was Beth—Beth Griffeth. We met in New Orleans, and I fell in love with her. She was young and beautiful, sweet, all that a woman ought to be. She loved me, too, more than I deserved." He broke off suddenly and looked out the window. A bat fluttered by, shuddering in quick, ecstatic motion, and something in the movement of the flying mammal attracted Mark's attention. He was having difficulty speaking of his past life, for he was not a man to speak of himself. He had no choice now, he well knew, so he turned back from the window and said, "There was a child, Jason, a girl. But I didn't know this until a few days ago." A pained smile briefly crossed Mark's face. "I didn't even know Beth was still alive. Years ago a friend of mine wrote and said she died. But four days ago I got a letter from Beth. She said she was dying and she thought a man ought to know when he had a child. She also said she'd always loved me."

Jason sat there taking a puff from the thin cigar from time to time, studying the face of the man before him. Finally, he said, "What is it you want, Mark?"

"I want you to go to New Orleans and find my daughter and bring her here."

It took a great deal to startle Jason Larrimore, but Mark had succeeded this time. "Are you sure that's what you want, Mark? I mean, how old is the girl now?"

"She's eighteen."

"Does she know about you, that you're her father, I mean?"

"No, I don't think so. Beth said she never told her who her father was."

Larrimore was troubled. He stood up, walked to the open window, and looked outside. Holding out the cigar, he knocked the ashes on the ground below then turned around and said abruptly, "What if she won't come?"

Mark shrugged. "If she won't come, she won't. That's not your problem, Jason. But I've got to try. I did her mother an injustice too many years ago. Now my time's running out. I've got to do something to right the wrong. Will you go?"

Jason shrugged. "Of course I'll go. I have two weeks before my ship's refitted. Of course I'll go." Something, however, troubled him about this whole thing. He wanted to say no, but not because he didn't want to take the trouble. He was afraid it might be a disappointment for this dying man whom he respected so much.

"Things don't always turn out like we want, Mark," he said slowly, "except in storybooks. I'll go to New Orleans and find the girl. I'll do my best to bring her here, but there's always the chance that it won't work out."

Mark nodded. "I know that, Jason. I've thought about little else for the past few days. She may hate me. She may not like the life here. She may be married. But, whatever I can do, I want to do it." He looked up and said, "It's asking a lot. I know you're a busy man."

"Don't speak of that," Jason protested. "I'm glad to do it, Mark, and I'll give it my best effort—but I guess I'm not very hopeful about most things."

Mark looked at him and said, "You and I have always been a lot alike, Jason. Both of us have been pretty cynical about things, but when you come to the end of the road, as I have, you get a little different perspective." He reached down and touched the Bible that was on his lap. "Don't worry," he said, seeing the look in Jason's eyes, "I'm not about to start preaching at you, but I've found something in this that's been good for me. You met Susanna. She's one of those arguments for Christianity that I could never answer. I could laugh at the Bible and see the hypocrites in the church, but there was always Susanna and some others that I couldn't explain away."

"And you've found God, have you, Mark?"

"Yes, I have. Not much else to do here but read, and Susanna keeps a Bible in every room, it seems. Well, I got reading the Gospels and talking to Susanna about what I read. I realized the loneliness I felt could only be filled by Jesus. I'd spent my life wandering around trying to find happiness, and I wound up finding it lying in my room." Mark paused and grinned slightly. "I guess I was going to preach after all." There was a quiet assurance in the sick man's voice as he said, "I found God very late, but I'm glad that it's not too late."

"I'm happy for you, Mark," Jason said. "I'll go to New

Orleans and find the girl. I'll leave first thing in the morning."

The two men sat there and talked, long into the night, Jason listening as Mark told him what little he knew about Beth Griffeth. Susanna brought a plate in, and he ate a little. Then, seeing that Mark was growing tired, he said, "I'll say good-bye now, Mark. I'll leave early before you get up."

Mark put his hand out and when Jason took it, he said, "God be with you and help you to find my daughter."

Chapter 6

The Sound and the Fury

The protection of Richmond was the major concern of the Army of Northern Virginia, but General Robert E. Lee reasoned that to hold on to the Southern capital, he needed more than a defensive position. After his victory at Chancellorsville, Lee decided not to wait. He chose to carry the war into the North, into Pennsylvania, hoping to draw the Federal Army of the Potomac after him and away from Richmond.

The high-spirited Army of Northern Virginia contained seventy-seven thousand men under three corps commanders. On June 3, the Confederates marched west, turning northward up the Shenandoah Valley. They crossed the Potomac River and headed toward Pennsylvania.

It took Major General Joseph Hooker nine days to discover that his enemy had badly deceived him. Lincoln sent word to Hooker that his first responsibility was the protection of Washington and the pursuit and destruction of the Confederate army. Hooker's problem was that he did not know where Lee was. Nevertheless, he struck north, hunting the Army of Northern Virginia. Lee was as badly informed as his opponent, for he did not know where Hooker was. Jeb Stuart's cavalry had gone off on a raid, leaving the Southern commander without any notion of his enemy's presence. On June 28, a spy named Harrison came to Confederate headquarters with the alarming news that the Union army was very close. He also revealed that Hooker had been replaced by Major General George E. Meade.

Lee immediately recast his plans. He issued orders for his three widely dispersed corps to concentrate at Cashtown, close to Harrisburg, the Pennsylvania state capital. At the same time, General Meade began to pull his troops together, and the gap between the two armies started to close.

Just outside of Gettysburg on the afternoon of July 1, Brigadier General John Buford, commander of the First Cavalry Division, encountered Confederate infantry who were on their way to commandeer some shoes that were reported to be in Gettysburg. His two brigades were understrength; nevertheless, they managed to delay the Confederates until reinforcements arrived. Neither commander wanted to fight at Gettysburg, but the two armies had accidentally collided, and both commanders quickly poured troops into the area.

Confederate General Richard Ewell failed to take the high ground south of the town of Gettysburg, so it was Major General Winfield Hancock who formed a defensive line shaped like an inverted fishhook two and a half miles long in this prime position. The Federal right lay on Culp's Hill, and the line curved through Cemetery Hill, extended down Cemetery Ridge, then rested its left on two hills known as Little Round Top and Big Round Top.

The battle of Gettysburg was actually a play in three acts. On July 1, the first day of the battle, Confederate strength on the battlefield was greater than that of the Union troops. General Jubal Early's division made a slashing attack that crumbled the Union right flank. This threw the entire line of the Eleventh Corps into confusion, and the Union army beat a path back to the town. Early pursued the beaten divisions to the clogged streets of Gettysburg, capturing many. He then stopped to reorganize and sent part of his troops out on the York Road to protect his flank.

The heavy fighting that day left many dead and wounded on the grass and in the town. The day's casualties amounted to ten thousand for the Union and seven thousand for the Confederates.

All day long and far into the night, the numerous divisions in blue and in gray, with their supporting artillery, had been snaking along the roads that converged at Gettysburg. The men of both armies were driven at a rapid pace by their officers to get there first—but without knowing just where they were going or what they would meet when they got there.

The men of the Richmond Grays saw no action this day, but when Clay pulled his horse up and spoke to one of the staff officers, he returned to say to Dent, "We're too late for action today, but no doubt we'll be in it tomorrow."

Dent looked at his father, his eyes alive with excitement. "We'll get them this time, won't we, Major?" He always used the correct military title when in situations like this. He looked around and said, "The boys are ready for a scrap."

Clay looked over toward the low-lying hills almost hidden in the darkness. He stood there quietly, listening to the booming of cannons still sounding and the far-off rattle of musket fire, and then looked to Dent. "I think we're in for the biggest fight we've ever seen, Dent. Pass the word to the men. Have 'em carry all the ammunition they can, and see that they get a drink from the well. They'll be going dry almost at once."

At dawn the next day, Colonel Gideon Rocklin led his Federal troops onto the field of battle. His men were well trained, he knew, but that day nothing seemed to work as planned. Gideon turned to his aide midway through the morning's fighting, saying soberly, "We can draw our plans on the maps—but once the first shot is fired, you can throw them all away!"

The biggest problem turned out to be a weakness on the left side of the Union line, Little Round Top, the Union anchor on the south. General Dan Sickles moved his men to what he thought was a better position and sent out Berdan's sharpshooters to probe the Confederate position. Without securing Meade's permission, he moved his entire corps forward about 1:00 p.m. and took position in the Peach Orchard. Part of his troops were in the vicinity of the Devil's Den, an area of enormous boulders. As a result of Sickles's movement, Little Round Top was left unoccupied, and Meade's scheme of defense was sadly upset.

The Southern troops were about as confused as the Federals. They were slow to take advantage of the Union weakness. If they had captured Little Round Top, it would have been possible to attack the Union line from behind, which would almost have assured a Confederate victory.

Longstreet, always slow to move, consumed more than three and a half hours marching and countermarching west of Seminary Ridge. It was four thirty when he finally started his infantry attack, which was badly conceived. He found one of Sickles's divisions directly in his front. Furthermore, Hood was not permitted to work around the south of the Round Tops as he wished to do. This disposed of Lee's idea that the attack would be a flanking operation.

For four long hours the battle raged. Sickles's corps was so badly chopped up it practically disappeared. The bloody fighting spread over the landscape until it engulfed the Wheat Field, Devil's Den, and the slopes of Little Round Top.

"We're gettin' beat!" Major Summit gasped, coming back to report to Gideon. "They're driving us back."

"We can't fall back!" Gideon shouted. "Throw every reserve we have into the line!" He stood there tall, walking along the lines, listening not at all to the bullets that whipped by close to his head. Cannon exploded all around—from both the Federal artillery and the Confederate guns. Everywhere men lay shot to pieces, some of them lying in that eloquent stillness that death brings, others crawling along the ground, leaving their scarlet blood on the rocks, in the dirt, and on the grass.

By the end of the second day, both armies were bled dry. Every man, no matter what side he fought on, knew that the third day of Gettysburg would decide the fate of this battle—perhaps the fate of the entire war.

When the Battle of Gettysburg broke out, twenty-year-old Jenny Wade was at the home of her sister, who lived on Baltimore Street at the foot of Cemetery Hill. There was a new baby in the McClellan home, and Jenny was helping her sister with its care.

There was no heavy fighting in the immediate area, but a Federal picket line did run behind the little brick house. There was intermediate skirmishing between it and Confederate outposts in the town proper. On the third morning of the Battle of Gettysburg, while Jenny stood in the kitchen kneading dough, a bullet pierced two wooden doors and struck her in the back, killing her instantly. The cries of her sister and mother attracted Federal soldiers, who carried Jenny's body to the cellar. Later, she was buried in a coffin some Confederate soldiers had fashioned for an officer. Jenny was engaged to a Corporal Johnson Skelly, who, unknown to her, had been wounded two weeks earlier in the Battle of Winchester. News that he had died in Confederate hands came several days after the Southern army had withdrawn from the Gettysburg area. The death of the young woman was one of many that day of July 3, 1863.

Basically, the battle that day consisted of a charge led by Confederate General Pickett with his Virginia troops. Longstreet had argued strenuously with Lee that no troops in the world could cross the long, level plain and survive the fire thrown down by the entire Army of the Potomac as it kept its position on top of the high ground.

Lee had been suffering from the heart problem that would one day kill him. He had also had a ferocious two-week attack of diarrhea. Added to this was the fact that he had lost Stonewall Jackson at Chancellorsville and had gone into battle without this favorite commander. For whatever reason, Lee insisted on the charge. As Pickett rode back and forth in front of his troops, he called out, "Up, men, and to your posts! Don't forget today that you are from old Virginia."

Clay was one of the officers who lay in the woods with the commands. His company was finely trained, but as he looked up and down the line, then across that long field, he said to Bushrod Aimes, who was standing beside him, "A lot of us are not going to get back off that hill."

WALL OF FIRE

Aimes shook his head. "General Lee knows we'll do our best. We've never failed him."

Suppose you placed infantry behind a stone wall and had one rank fire and then fall back to reload while a second rank instantly took their place. Then you had these men fire and repeat this action so a constant hail of bone-smashing minié balls ripped the air in front of that wall. Now suppose you gathered the finest soldiers to be found and marched them a quarter of a mile across a flat field then up a slope into the muzzles of those guns behind that wall. The result of this sort of fighting was proven conclusively at Gettysburg on July 3, 1863—it was a slaughter!

Not that the men of the South failed for want of trying. They marched in behind their officers, lined up as if on a parade ground. For almost two hours the Confederate artillery had pounded the Federals on top of the ridge. When Pickett led his men out, the long gray lines moved out from the protection of the trees and corrected their alignment as though on dress parade. A sudden dramatic hush fell on the battlefield. In three lines, the Confederates marched forward across the open field, their fluttering battle flags adding a brilliant touch of color to the impressive scene.

Watching the pageant from Cemetery Ridge and holding their fire until the enemy was in effective range, Gideon's troops paid silent, grim tribute to the magnificent courage of the Confederates as they marched steadily forward, the lines closing doggedly as the shells knocked out huge segments of the attacking force. Only a few of the twelve thousand who started the charge reached the Union position through the hail of cannon fire and musketry. Over the stone wall went that intrepid handful, but after initial success, they were either killed or driven back.

Sick at heart, Clay had watched his men drop and was fearful of the lives of the rest of them. They were driven back, and finally he gave the command to retreat. He picked his way back through the lines of the wounded, giving commands that as many of them as possible be carried back, when he looked up to see a small force of Union soldiers practically upon them. "Major! Pin those Yankee troops down! Form a line!" he yelled. He joined the line, and his men began to pick off the Union troops as they charged down the hill to capture them.

"We'll be cut off! Watch on the right flank!" Clay screamed over the rattle of musket fire.

And then it was that he saw something he could not believe. Clay had always had good eyesight, and when he looked up and saw the officer who had come out with the attacking force, he saw that it was his cousin Gideon Rocklin.

Gideon had been given the order by one of the generals to lead a force to take as many Confederates captive as he could. At once he had gathered a sizable force and led the charge down the hill. Now he was on foot and waving his sword, urging his men onward.

Clay stared at him. "Go back, Gid!" Clay whispered. "Go back!" But the officer had no intention of going back. As Clay watched, Gideon leaned over, picked up a musket, then ran straight down the hill. But he had not gone five steps before a bullet struck him, turning him around. He slumped to the ground, but by his movements Clay saw that he was not dead. "He'll be a target for every man in this line," Clay yelled to Dent, who had come to stand beside him.

Something came to Clay then—a thought that seemed to explode in his mind: *That's why I'm here!*

The thought blazed through him, and he immediately ran

forward. Without a backward look, he charged the enemy. He heard Dent shout, "Father, come back!" but he did not even slow down. Every soldier along the line saw the Confederate officer rush right into the guns of the Union foes, and it was then that Dent cried, "Charge!" and led the Richmond Grays back toward the Union troops.

All the world was covered by a red haze to Gideon. The pain, however, did not block everything out. And he looked up to see an officer in gray, almost upon him. He tried to pick up the musket, but his fingers lost their strength. Then he heard a voice saying, "Gid!"

Gideon thought, *I must be dreaming!* when he looked up and saw the face of Clay Rocklin. "Clay—," he muttered.

The two men clung to each other as the battle raged around them. Dent dashed up to say, "We've driven them back. Let's get the prisoners out of here!"

Clay wanted to leave Gid, knowing the hard fate of prisoners, but the fire from his lines was strong. "You men, take this officer back to our lines," he commanded. As four privates picked up Gideon and carried him off the field, the battle raged on.

When they were behind the Confederate lines, Gideon awoke long enough to see tears running down the brown face of the man who held him. Memories came to him of the days when he and Clay had roamed the fields of Virginia as young boys, and later as young men. "Clay?" he whispered, and as the darkness came up to envelop him, he whispered, "I've missed you, Clay." The warm darkness moved over him and Gideon Rocklin knew nothing more.

Part Two
The Bargain

Chapter 7

"A Woman Should Be Gentle"

The *Natchez Belle* rammed into the pilings so abruptly that Jason Larrimore grabbed at the railing to keep his balance. A tall man with a full beard standing beside him jostled against him with a shock. He looked at Jason, saying, "Not much of a captain, is he? Next time he'll knock the whole blasted wharf down!"

Jason smiled and shrugged. "At least we made it. I was afraid a couple of times we would ram another boat." With a look toward the bridge, Jason agreed, "No, he's not much of a captain."

The whistle gave a piercing shriek, and at the signal the deckhands lowered the gangplank. Picking up his small suitcase, Jason joined the crowd that jostled one another to get ashore. He was sleepy, for he had stayed awake most of the night engaged in a ferocious poker game. He had come out a winner by a slight margin, but his eyes were scratchy as the bright New Orleans sunlight hit them.

Reaching the crowded dock, he shouldered his way through the crowd, trying to decide how to approach the problem that had been dumped in his lap by Mark Rocklin. He was not a man given to introspection, preferring to plunge into action at once. He had made his way to the top of his profession by following this method and now, as he strolled along the streets, decided that he had no time for fine intellectual thought.

"Must be over 150,000 people in this city," he murmured, dodging as a group of Union officers headed down the sidewalk toward him. "I can't go from door to door looking for the girl. I have to find a better way than that."

He knew New Orleans well, having spent much time there. It was the port where his own ship most often docked. However, since the Federals had taken the city, he had not been back. Still, he had some fond memories of the place, and as he strolled along he enjoyed the polyglot of accents that he heard around him—the twangy nasal dialect of the officers from New Hampshire, Massachusetts, and other New England states; the soft murmur of the Southern peoples; the almost unintelligible sound of the slaves chanting along the roadside, selling the wares of their masters. Above all, as he moved along, he heard the soft murmur of French, for New Orleans was French in nature, the only truly international city in the United States.

He was hungry as he made his way to the Majestic Hotel, where he had often stayed before. He was greeted by the room clerk, a small, round-faced Frenchman whose eyes lit up when he saw him. "Ah, Monsieur Larrimore! You are back!"

"Yes, François, I'll be here for just a short time. Do you have a room?"

"Ah, it is crowded, monsieur, but for you I will find something. How about the room over the courtyard that you always liked so much?" The Frenchman smiled. "You see? I still remember you."

"That will be fine," Larrimore said with satisfaction. "Please have someone take my bag up, and I'll go have breakfast."

"But *certainement.*" The clerk raised his eyebrow and a small Cajun lad appeared magically. "Take Monsieur Larrimore's bag to room 216," he commanded. Then, turning to Jason, he said, "You're here on business, monsieur?"

Larrimore extracted a long cigar from his inner coat pocket, stuck it between his teeth, and lit it. Sending a haze of purple smoke upward, he eyed the clerk and said, "I don't suppose you've ever heard of a woman named Beth Griffeth?"

"Griffeth, is it?" François pondered the name, tasting it on his tongue, so it seemed, then shook his head regretfully. "But no, Monsieur Larrimore. I do not know the name, but I will ask around."

"Thank you, François." Larrimore nodded, turned, and walked at once into the café. He was remembered there by the maître d', who greeted him warmly and seated him at a table by the window. The warm yellow sunlight filtered in, and Larrimore sat back in his chair, allowing the waiter to fuss over him. He ate a fine breakfast of eggs, pancakes, and toast with a rasher of bacon, washed down with café au lait, a drink of equal parts coffee and hot milk.

As Jason sat there, he thought about Mark Rocklin. He liked the man and owed him a debt—and Larrimore was a man who paid his debts. He believed in very little, but he did believe in honoring his debts. To him, a welsher was the lowest form of animal life. It was this ideal that had brought him back to New Orleans. His mind darted back and forth. The strains of Mark's talk came to him. *He said she probably would be in the poor section of town,* he thought. Sipping his coffee, he shook his head almost in despair. *I guess that would describe most of New Orleans. I won't have to filter through the rich planters, but that's not much help.*

Finishing his breakfast, he went into the barbershop, took a bath, got a shave, then went up to his room, where he put on his clean clothes. He was rather a fancy dresser when not on duty and slipped into a pair of fawn-colored trousers, a white shirt with a string tie, and a brown, brocaded waistcoat. He wore over it a light brown wool frock coat. He paused long enough to look into the mirror and brush his blond hair back carelessly, then left the hotel room. Before leaving the building, he stopped at the desk. "I'm not expecting any visitors, François," he said, "but if anyone does come by, make sure you take a message."

His only idea was to start at the city hall. As he made his way along the streets filled with Union soldiers, he noted that the citizens of New Orleans had lost their gaiety. *They don't like being captives of the Yankees,* he thought grimly. He remembered General Ben Butler, probably one of the worst of the Union's generals, but so strong politically that Lincoln couldn't fire him. When Butler had come to New Orleans, he had been accused of stealing silverware from one of the fine homes and was called "Spoons" Butler for a time. Later he got a worse name. The women of New Orleans were fiery Southern patriots and took occasion to vent their hatred of the Yankees by insulting the officers. Butler had retaliated by issuing a special order that stated bluntly that any woman who insulted a Union officer would be treated as a prostitute. This order had caused Butler to be hated worse than any Yankee, and he was henceforth known as "Beast" Butler.

Arriving at the city hall, Jason found the usual bureaucratic snarl. After impatiently going through two clerks, he found himself talking to an older man with a pair of tired gray eyes. "My name is Jason Larrimore," he said. "I'm looking for a woman who lives in New Orleans." He had decided not to give the full story and said, "A distant relative is seeking to find her. Her name is Beth Griffeth."

"You have an address?"

"No, nothing except her name. Do you think you can help me?"

The man, whose name was Jenkins, shrugged. "I doubt it. If some of her male relatives are registered to vote, we may have an address. I'll check for you."

He disappeared and did not come back for fifteen minutes. Finally, when he returned, he said, "We have no Beth Griffeth listed. We have seven Griffeths on the tax rolls. It is a rather unusual name, or there would be more."

"I suppose I'm lucky her name wasn't Bourdeaux," Jason said with a grin. He took the list the man handed him, studied it, and said, "Thanks a lot, Mr. Jenkins. I appreciate it."

Leaving the city hall, he hailed a carriage, stared at the first name on the list, and asked the cabdriver, "Do you know where Alexandria Street is?"

The cabdriver was a small, dark Cajun with black eyes. "Why, yes, I know that."

"Take me there."

The cabdriver took what seemed to be a circuitous route to the address, and Jason felt he was padding his pocketbook by making the trip last longer. However, he said nothing. When he arrived at the plain frame house that sat close to the street, he got down and said, "Wait here. I probably won't be long." He went to the door and knocked.

When a woman opened it, Jason removed his hat and gave his best smile. "I'm looking for a lady named Beth Griffeth. Would you know of her by any chance?"

"Beth Griffeth? No, I've never heard of her."

"I suppose you know most of the Griffeths here in New Orleans? It's not a common name for this part of the world."

"Yes, I think I know most of them, but I've never heard of a Beth. Why are you looking for her?"

"Just a business affair," Jason said. "Thank you very much for your time."

Going back to the cab, he picked the second name on the list, and again the cabdriver seemed to take a great deal of time. He was a small, well-built man who announced that his name was Louis Prejean. "I been driving a cab ten years, me," he said cheerfully. "Better than getting shot at in the army, no?"

"Much better." Jason grinned, and as the two crossed through the small twisted streets of New Orleans, he listened as Prejean gave him a rundown of his family life, which was in poor shape, it seemed. He listened as Prejean told about how his wife was never satisfied with anything he did and now, if he had it to do over again, he would never marry. Finally, the cab drew up in a much more affluent section of town, in front of a brick building of French design.

"I will wait for you, yes?"

"Yes, Louis. It won't take long, I shouldn't think."

It didn't take long, for the large man who came to the door had never heard of a Beth Griffeth and doubted that there was any such in New Orleans. "I know all of our people here," he said, "but I know of no Beth Griffeth. A rather unusual name," he announced proudly.

"If you think of anyone, I'll be at the Majestic Hotel. My name is Jason Larrimore. I would appreciate it if you would contact me."

Jason went back to the cab and for the rest of the morning and part of the afternoon sought out the names on his brief list.

Finally, after the last futile call, he came back and sat down in the cab, feeling defeated.

Prejean turned and said, "We go now, monsieur?"

"Take me to the Majestic, Louis," he said. "I've run out of names."

"*Oui.*" The small cabdriver spoke to the horses in French and for a while chatted as he had all day. When they drew up in front of the Majestic, Jason asked the fee and, when it was given, paid it cheerfully, though it seemed a little large. He added a ten-dollar gold piece to the sum, saying, "You've done a good job, Louis. I appreciate it."

"If I can be of further service, you tell me, no?"

"Well, there's one thing you might do. I'm looking for a woman named Beth Griffeth. You might ask around among your people down in the Quarter. I'll be looking myself. If you hear of anything, there'll be a couple more of those gold pieces for you."

The liquid eyes of the small, muscular driver grew wide. "Twenty-dolla' gold, you betcha! I ask plenty, me." He leaped into the cab and whipped the horses up, dodging through the crowded street expertly.

Jason turned and went into the hotel. He asked at the desk, but there were no messages. He had expected none, so he went upstairs, undressed, and took a nap. He rested fitfully for a time, trying to think of some way to narrow the search, but thought of nothing. Again he thought, *I can't go from door to door looking for the woman.*

Finally, he awoke, dressed, went down to lunch, and spent the rest of the afternoon and evening wandering through the French Quarter. He was approached by many ladies of the evening taken by his tall form and fine clothes but shook them off.

He went into businesses, shops, asked the police officers, but got no help from any of them.

Dejectedly he went back to the hotel, ate supper, and went to bed. "I'll give it three days," he said. "If I don't find her by then, I'll have to give up."

The next morning he was brought out of a sound sleep by a knock on the door. Startled, he slipped his hand under the pillow—where he always kept his pistol at night—and rose up on one elbow. "Who is it?" he asked groggily.

"It's me, Louis Prejean."

"Prejean? Wait a minute." Jason rolled out of bed, pulled on his pants, and went over to the door. When he opened it, he saw that Prejean was grinning broadly.

"Beth Griffeth, you look for her, no?"

A shock ran through Larrimore, and he awakened fully. "Yes, did you find her?"

"I find where she usta was," Prejean said. "I think they don't like Cajuns much there, but if a gentleman such as yourself go, they might tell you something."

"Where is it, Louis?"

"A boardinghouse over by Lake Pontchartrain. Not a very nice place." He shrugged. "I ask around, and one of my friends, he know. He met a woman named that once. I think his wife did. Anyway, I chase him like a bird dog all night long, and there she is—116 Chartres Street. You find out something there, maybe."

"You're a fine fellow, Louis." Jason smiled, stuck his hand in his pocket, and pulled out two gold coins. He looked at them a moment then added a third. "Here you are. Now you wait until I get dressed and get something to eat, and you can take me out there."

"Oui. I do that, you bet."

Larrimore threw his clothes on, went downstairs and ate a quick breakfast, then went outside. Louis was waiting with the cab, and he quickly got in, saying, "Now we go."

Soon they were in a poor district on the north side of town, and Louis pulled up before a dilapidated two-story building. "This is where the woman lived," he announced.

"Wait here, Louis." Larrimore stepped down, went to the door, and knocked. It seemed like a long wait, but finally the door opened a crack. An older woman with her gray hair in disarray grumbled, "What do you want?"

"I am looking for a woman named Beth Griffeth."

"What do you want with her?"

"I'm looking on behalf of a distant relative. I think there's some kind of estate involved. Do you know her?"

"I did know her. She's dead now. Didn't you know that?"

"I did hear that," Larrimore said evenly, "but I understand she has a daughter."

"That she has."

When the woman stopped abruptly, Larrimore sensed greed almost palpable in the air. "It would be worth twenty dollars gold to me to find the young woman."

At once the door opened, and the woman mustered a smile. "Well, that's business. You'll find her in the Gay Paree dealing blackjack."

Larrimore was shocked, for he had expected almost anything but this. "Are you sure it's the same young woman?"

"Didn't I know her all my life?" she said. "Allyn Griffeth, that's her name. You'll find her there tonight."

"Allyn?"

"Well, she spells it *A-l-l-y-n*," the woman said and sniffed.

"But it sounds like *Ay*-leen."

"Do you know where she lives?"

"No, I don't. She'll be dealing cards in that saloon. How about that twenty dollars?"

Jason handed her the money, which she looked at carefully and stuck into her pocket with satisfaction. "Tell her Millie sent you."

"Thank you very much." Larrimore nodded. He turned and went back to the cab with a sense of accomplishment and at the same time a sense of foreboding. When he got into the cab and had Louis drive back to the hotel, he thought, *Dealing blackjack in the Gay Paree? Doesn't sound like the kind of daughter Mark needs—but at least I found her.*

❦

As soon as Jason stepped into the Gay Paree, he spotted the object of his quest. Moving to the bar, he ordered a drink and turned to look at the woman who was dealing blackjack across the room. He had rarely seen a woman so attractive—and he had seen many. He asked the bartender as he paid for his drink, "I take it that's Allyn Griffeth?"

The bartender, a husky individual, gave him a careful look. "Yeah," he said briefly, "that's Allyn."

Jason turned and studied the young woman carefully. She was wearing a rose-colored silk dress overlaid with some sort of pink lace flounces. It was fairly modest for a saloon, but he saw at once that the girl had a fine figure. She had dark red hair, and her green eyes caught the reflection of the chandeliers overhead. She had, he noted, a strong, squarish face and a creamy complexion.

Jason finished his drink, walked over, and stood watching as the man in front played cards. As soon as he got up, Jason slipped into the seat, saying, "Good evening."

"How are you?" the young woman said. There was a watchfulness in her eyes that told him she would not be easy to fool, and he sat there for a while playing. He soon discovered she was a good player; she had a quick mind and handled the cards well. He lost a few dollars then said, "Miss Allyn Griffeth, isn't it?"

"That's right." The answer was spare, but the watchfulness in the green eyes was even more pronounced.

"I'd like to talk with you for a few moments," Larrimore said.

"Go ahead and talk."

As they were talking, two men had come over to watch them play. Looking at them, Jason said, "A little more privately than this."

"If you want to play cards, go ahead. Otherwise, I'll ask you to let one of these gentlemen have your seat."

Jason flushed at the hard tone, and his temper flared. "Look, all I want to do is talk—"

Jason felt his arm grasped as if by a vise. He was pulled to his feet and turned quickly so that he faced the giant of a man with a red face and blunt features who was holding him. A smaller man had come to stand on his other side and said, "I'll have to ask you to leave, sir."

Jason pulled against the grip, but the large hand on his arm simply tightened, almost cutting off the circulation.

"I only wanted—"

"I know what you wanted," the man said. "This is my place, and I'm asking you to leave. Take him out, Toby."

Jason glanced down at the girl and saw a small smile on her

lips. However, he had no time to do more, for he found himself simply turned around and walked across the floor. He had an idea of making a fight of it but was fairly sure that there were others at hand as rough as the one who held him. He found himself outside, and the big man said, "I don't think I would come back if I was you. Good night, sir."

Inside, Sam Barker said, "Come on; let's take a break, Allyn."

Allyn smiled up at him and shook her head. "No, it's all right. Just another fancy man. Thank you, Sam," she said. "I'll be all right."

Barker examined her carefully then nodded. "All right, I'll keep an eye out in case he comes back."

"I don't think he'll do that, Sam."

Allyn played the rest of the night, took a break occasionally, and put all thoughts of the tall, blond-haired man out of her mind. Finally, at eleven, she said good night to Sam and started for the door.

"Toby, see Miss Allyn gets home all right," Barker called to the large bouncer.

"Sure, boss."

Allyn was accustomed to this, although she had often protested she would be all right alone. Tonight, however, she walked the two blocks toward her room speaking occasionally to the huge man beside her. He left her at the gate, and she said with a fond smile, "Thank you, Toby."

"Yeah, sure, Miss Allyn. Good night."

Allyn entered the courtyard, went to the stairs that led upward, then stopped on the balcony to fumble for her key. She had just inserted the key when a voice said, "Miss Allyn?"

She turned and saw by the streetlight the tall, blond-haired man who had been put out of the saloon. She was not a fearful girl, but he loomed large in the feeble light. She had not heard him approach at all.

"What do you want?" she asked coldly. "Go away and leave me alone."

Jason took off his hat and nodded. "I know this looks bad, but I have to talk to you. I mean no harm."

"Come back in the morning."

"I'll do that if you insist," he said quietly. He knew he had to calm her somehow and finally said, "You don't have to be afraid of me."

"I'm not afraid of you. I just don't want to talk to you."

"It's about your father. He sent me to find you."

Allyn had reached into her bag, where she carried a small pistol called a pepperbox. It would fire four bullets at the same time, and Sam had given her careful instructions on how to use it. She had been prepared to draw it, hoping that it would frighten him, but his words shocked her. She blinked her eyes and stared, trying to see his face more clearly. "My father? What are you talking about?"

"My name is Jason Larrimore. Your father asked me to find you." He looked around the balcony and said, "I know it's late, and I'll come back tomorrow if you'd rather, but I think you'll want to hear what I have to say."

Allyn hesitated then made a decision. "Come inside," she said. She turned, unlocked the door, and entered. She lit the lamp and turned the wick up. Allyn wheeled to him, her eyes large in the amber light, and said, "What are you talking about? My father? I don't have any father."

Larrimore was aware that the caution she exercised was habitual. He knew that his words had come as a shock and that her calmness had been broken. Carefully he said, "Your father's name is Mark Rocklin. Did you know that?"

"I don't—" Allyn stopped and then remembered her mother's words: *"Your father's name is Mark."* Inexplicably she began to tremble, and her knees felt weak. Quickly she moved to a chair and waved to another, saying, "Sit down." When he was seated, she said, "Your name is Larrimore?"

"Yes."

She stared at Jason. "I never—my mother never told me about who my father was."

Jason nodded. "It's not up to me to go into the past, Miss Griffeth. All I can do is pass the message along." He hesitated then added, "I *will* tell you two things. First, your father was not even aware that you existed. He got a letter from your mother saying she was dying. In the letter, for the first time, she mentioned you. Mark had no idea that he had a daughter."

Allyn stared at him with disbelief in her eyes. "What's the second thing?" she asked rather coldly.

"The second thing is that your father's a sick man. He was wounded in the war and—well, I don't think he has long to live."

Allyn had gotten better control of herself now. She studied the face of the man in front of her. She had been forced to learn men rather well during her brief life. She had learned that fine clothes and fine manners did not necessarily mean quality. The face of the man in front of her was strong and bold. There was a fearless quality about him that she had seen in a few men. His features were carved and strong, his wide-set eyes fixed on her. He had a broad mouth and a long English nose. Something about his bearing told her he might be hard, but there was not a viciousness in him that she had seen in other men. "Why should I believe you?" she said.

"I have a letter here from your father." He shrugged. "But since you don't know him, that doesn't mean much." He hesitated again. It was harder talking to this girl than he had thought. He tried to put the words together in his mind before he spoke them. "I know that this comes as a shock, but after you've thought it over, I think you should go see your father. I'll be glad to escort you there, if that's what you want."

"Why should I go see him? He left my mother. She told me that much."

"I can't go into that," Jason said. "It's not my affair."

"I won't go," Allyn said almost harshly. "He's had eighteen years to find me. If he was really interested, he would have done something before this."

Jason shook his head. "As I said, he didn't know you existed. In fact, he heard your mother had died long ago. But if that's the way you feel, then I suppose nothing I do will change it. But let me tell you a little about your father. . . ." He began to talk, relating the time that he himself had been destitute and had hit bottom. He told her how it had been her father, Mark Rocklin, who had reached out and single-handedly saved him from ruin. "He gave me a new hope," Larrimore added thoughtfully. "If it hadn't been for him, I think I would have killed myself. Can't tell you how low I'd fallen, but it was low as a man could get. Mark didn't have any reason for helping me. We were no kin, but we were friends. I know he hasn't been everything a man should be, but I haven't been, either. I can tell you this: He is a man of honor, and if he tells you that he didn't know you were alive, you can believe that that was the way it was."

Allyn had listened to this recital carefully, watching the face of the man who sat across from her. Her heart was beating faster as she remembered all the years she had thought about her father, as a child how she had longed for a father and there had been none. Now she recognized the bitterness of those lost years and shook her head abruptly. "I don't need him now. He wasn't there when I did need him, so why should I go to him?"

Larrimore wanted to argue, but he saw that against this girl arguments would be useless. He leaned back in his chair and studied her carefully. She grew nervous under his inspection, and finally he said, "A woman should be gentle."

A flush touched her smooth cheeks, and she dropped her eyes for a moment. His words angered her, yet at the same time, there was some justice in what he said. Only the ticking of a small clock on her dressing table broke the silence. Finally, she lifted her eyes and met his. "I haven't had a chance to learn how to be gentle. A young girl doesn't learn gentleness on the streets of New Orleans."

"I know," he said, "and I ask your pardon. I spoke too soon." He abruptly got to his feet and said, "I've done all that I can do. I'll be leaving New Orleans tomorrow." She rose at once as he added, "I wish you would think about this. I know it's a big decision—you'd be leaving your life here and joining a brand-new one. The Rocklins are a big family."

"I'm sure they'd be glad to see a saloon girl coming to join them," Allyn said bitterly.

"You'd have to know this family to understand. They're fine people, planters just outside of Richmond, most of them. Mark's one of the older members. The younger ones are fighting for the Cause. There are some Rocklins in the North serving the Union army, but let me tell you this, it's no shame to anyone to be a Rocklin." He saw the doubt in her eyes and added, "I think there's a good life for you there, Miss Griffeth. Without being judgmental, I'd say the one you have now probably isn't the best for a young woman. I'm no judge of that—but I can tell you you'd be doing yourself a favor if at least you'd go for a visit to Gracefield."

"Gracefield? What's that?"

"That's the Rocklin plantation."

Allyn struggled with herself for a moment, and as she stood there, a desire to see the man who called himself her father grew in her. Abruptly she made a decision, which was not unusual for her. She had been forced to make decisions all her life, and now she said briskly, "All right, Mr. Larrimore. I'll go with you for a visit—that's all, just a visit."

Larrimore took a deep breath and nodded. "I think that's wise. There'll be a ship out in the morning. We'll have to do some dodging to get through the patrols, but if you'll come with me, I'll be glad to see you to your father."

Allyn studied him and said, "I don't like to put myself in the power of a man, and I don't even know you."

Jason shrugged. "That's your decision. I can't change what I am, but I can give you my word that you'll be safe with me. Mark's my friend, and I wouldn't let harm come to his daughter for anything."

Something in his words assured Allyn, and she said reluctantly, "All right, I'll be ready to leave tomorrow."

He bowed and said, "I'll see about the passage. Shall I come back here?"

"Yes, I'll tell Sam tomorrow that I'll be taking a vacation. I'll wait here until you come."

"Good night, Miss Griffeth."

He turned and left quickly, and for a long time she stood staring at the door. Then she walked over to the bed and sat

WALL OF FIRE

down, discovering that her hands were trembling. She could not think clearly, and for a long time that night she lay awake thinking of the man called Mark Rocklin.

Chapter 8

"I Didn't Know What Love Was!"

The large four-story building that had been converted to Libby Prison loomed over the sluggish James River as Clay and Melora walked down the dock. Glancing with distaste at the structure, Melora said, "It's an awful-looking place, isn't it, Clay?"

"Yes, but then, I guess all prisons are. I don't suppose there's a pretty one anywhere." They approached the two guards who stood outside the main door, and Clay pulled a paper from his pocket. "Major Rocklin," he introduced himself. "I'm here to visit with one of the prisoners, Colonel Rocklin."

The guard, a man in his late fifties or early sixties, studied the paper carefully then nodded. "Yes, sir. I'll take you to him myself." He turned to a fat young man who stood watching and said, "Corporal, you stand watch while I take the major inside."

As Clay and Melora entered the ancient building, they both gagged as they were struck by the rank smells of the bodies of unwashed men and human waste, all mixed in a nauseating way with the odor of boiled cabbage. The corridor led through the building to a stairway, and the sergeant led them up to the third floor. There he addressed a private who stood guard outside one of the two doors in the corridor and said, "Visitor for Colonel Rocklin."

The guard, a very young man, no more than sixteen, saluted Clay and said hastily, "Yes, sir." He pulled a large iron key from his belt and inserted it in the lock. There was a clanking rattle as the door swung open. Clay stepped inside, saying, "Where'll I find the colonel?"

"Well, sir, we've got just one private room here. I guess you can use that." He pointed over across the wide-open crowded room that was filled with men sitting on the floor or milling about aimlessly.

Clay said at once, "Yes, we'll take the room, Private."

He led Melora along the wall, and some of the officers stepped aside to let them pass. When he opened the door, the two stepped into a ten-by-ten room. It was occupied with a desk, a chair, and several shelves filled with supplies.

"It's worse than I thought," Melora said, "and if the officers' prison is like this, think what it must be like for the privates!"

"Well, it's pretty bad." Clay nodded. "But maybe we can help Gid. We are allowed to bring in food, I suppose."

They stood there quietly, waiting, thinking of how strange the war was, that one cousin would be captured, another free. Finally, the door opened and Gideon came in. "Hello, Clay." He smiled. "You must be Melora! I'm glad to finally meet you, though I wish the circumstances were better."

Both Clay and Melora were speechless. Gideon was in terrible condition! His uniform, which was torn in several places, was unwashed and stiff with food and dirt. Noticing their glances, he shrugged. "Not much of a chance to keep very neat around here. You'll have to excuse the way I look."

"We'll do something about that, Gid." Clay stepped forward,

put his arm around Gideon's shoulder. "By the good Lord, I hate to see you here like this!" he exclaimed. He was shocked at the frail shoulders beneath his grasp. Gideon had always been a strong-bodied man, heavily muscled, but already during his short time here, he had lost so much weight his uniform hung on him.

Melora moved forward, put her hands out, took one of Gideon's in hers, and said, "I'm sorry to see you here, too, Gideon. How have you been?"

"Well, I'm alive." Gid smiled slightly. His face was drawn and his cheeks sunken from lack of good diet. His eyes were sunk back in his head and were bright with fever.

Clay could tell that his body was hot, and he said urgently, "You're sick, Gid. You need to be in a hospital."

Gideon shrugged and answered in a rather hopeless tone, "Hospital's full, Clay. To get in there you have to be almost dead. I'll make out all right here."

Clay felt helpless, and a burst of anger ran through him as he looked at the emaciated form of his cousin. He and Gid had been suitors for Melanie Benton when they were younger, and there had been a time when Clay had hated Gideon with all his heart. But that was all gone. Now he felt pity and love for the feeble figure who stood before him. "Here, sit down, Gid," he said.

Gideon sat down and said with a wan smile, "That feels good. We don't have any furniture, you know."

"No furniture!" Melora exclaimed. "Not any at all?"

"No, I guess the Confederacy hasn't gotten around to making beds and chairs for prisoners."

"That's terrible," Melora exclaimed. "Would they let us bring some in?"

"I don't know what they'd do," Gid said, shrugging. "You can try, I suppose. Sure would be nice to lie down on a good pad again. If you can't get a bed in, some kind of a mattress—even shucks—that would be better than that hard floor." He looked up quickly and said, "I don't mean to complain. I know it's not your fault."

Clay's mind was working rapidly, and he said, "This place is terrible, Gid! There must be some way to get you exchanged."

Gideon shook his head. "I had hoped for that, but exchanges move awfully slow. It has to go through both commands, you know—Confederate and Federal. So somebody somewhere is sitting around figuring who to trade for who. But there's always hope."

"I'll write to Melanie at once," Clay said. "And in the meantime I'll pull all the strings I can to get you a better place. Now what would you like us to bring you?"

Gid sat before them in the chair, his hands grasping the arms. He licked his lips, which were cracked, and shook his head. "I guess we need about anything you can think of—medicine, bedding, food." He looked up suddenly and said, "You know, Clay, I thought a lot about getting killed in battle, and I thought about getting wounded, but it never once occurred to me that I would be captured. That's funny, isn't it?"

Melora put her hand on his shoulder and said, "You just wait, Gideon. We'll be going pretty soon, but when I come back, you'll see what I have for you!"

"Thank you, Melora. I appreciate that." He looked up at Clay and said, "I've written to Melanie. Don't tell her how bad it is here. No point in worrying her. I'm sure I'll be all right."

"Of course you will! The good Lord's going to take good care of you," Clay said heartily. For twenty minutes the three talked. Then Clay, seeing that Gideon was getting tired, said quickly, "We'll be going now, but we'll be back this afternoon with some blankets—maybe a bed. I'll see what I can do in the way of getting you out of this place."

"Thanks, Clay," Gideon said. He got to his feet slowly, like an old man, and looked at them fondly. "We've come a long way since the old days, haven't we? We Rocklins go back a long way. I remember hunting for bear with you out in the Black River bottoms. You remember that?"

"Sure I do," Clay said. "We'll do it again one day, too, when this is all over."

Gideon looked at him but made no answer. He turned toward the door, and Clay stepped to open it. They watched as he went back through the crowded room toward a dark corner. Then Clay said, "Come on, Melora, let's get out of here. We've got things to do."

When they were outside, Clay took a deep breath and shook his head. "Awful! Just terrible! Look, you go start getting some things together—food, clothes, whatever kind of medicine you think might be good. I'll go talk to the commandant."

"Do you know him, Clay?"

"I know who he is. His name is Major Thomas P. Turner. He's commandant of both Libby Prison and Belle Isle. I hear he's a hard man, but I don't see how he could object if we feed prisoners. Come along—I'll get you out of here, and we'll do something about this!"

The coal-burning engine loosed a piercing blast as it pulled into the station at Richmond. As soon as the train ground to a halt, Jason rose to his feet and led Allyn down the narrow passageway. Stepping down, he reached back for her hand and took it, and as she stepped to the cobblestone pavement, he said, "We'll have to rent a carriage, Miss Griffeth. I think we'll find one down this way."

Allyn was tired after the journey that had brought them into Richmond. The coach had been hot, and cinders had flown in through the open windows so that she felt coated with soot. "Please," she murmured, "isn't there somewhere I could go clean up before we leave?"

"Why, certainly. As a matter of fact, I think I could use a little washing down myself. Come along."

He led her to a line of carriages and helped her into one, and they drove to the Patterson Hotel, where Jason had a permanent room when he was ashore. Going to the desk, he spoke to the clerk. "I'll have a room for this lady, James. We'll be leaving early in the morning, so one night will be sufficient."

"Yes, Mr. Larrimore. Number 200 is vacant. Will that be all right?"

"Yes, and have a bath drawn up for her, if you please."

He turned to Allyn and said, "Why don't you go up to room 200 and have a bath? We'll leave in the morning."

"That would be fine," she said gratefully.

He nodded and said, "I'll have your bag sent up."

She made her way to the room and soon was soaking in a tub of steaming hot water brought by two tired-looking maids. She scrubbed and scrubbed—grateful for the luxurious soaking. As she got out and dried off, she discovered the journey had exhausted her. Slipping into a simple gown, she lay down on the bed. The journey had been hard on her in more ways than one. Physically it had been demanding, as all travel was, but even harder had been her emotional tension. She had felt ill at ease with Larrimore. After he had made several attempts at conversation, to which she had responded almost in monosyllables, he had taken a newspaper and spent most of his time reading or dozing.

Now as she lay down, sleep came to her quickly, but she thought as she dozed off, *I almost wish I had never come here. I can't see what good it will do to see him. Still, I've always wanted to see my father. Now's the chance.*

The next morning she awoke refreshed. She dressed, putting on a light gray dress with white lace at her throat and wrists. It was a simple dress with plain, clean lines that fit her well. She put on a small, fashionable hat then went downstairs, where she found Larrimore waiting in the lobby.

"A hot bath and a good night's sleep do wonders, don't they?" he said. "Are you ready for a meal?"

"Yes."

After breakfast he led her outside, where he had brought their carriage. He helped her inside then drove the carriage through the town. She examined the streets of Richmond curiously, thinking how different the city was from New Orleans. It was the busiest place she had ever seen. The streets were packed with Confederate soldiers of all ranks, all hurrying as if they had very urgent business. Intermingled with them were tradesmen, clerks, businessmen, and poor people of all sorts, all shoving and jostling each other. They passed by factories as they moved out of the city, one of them with huge smokestacks belching out large clouds of black smoke. "That's the Tredegar Ironworks," Jason informed her. "Makes most of the armament for the Confederate army."

"Richmond's a busy place, isn't it?" she murmured.

"Busiest place in the South, I suppose," he said.

He had discovered she was not a talkative woman. *She's either sullen or perhaps a little frightened of what lies ahead of her.*

Choosing to believe the latter, as soon as they were out of the city, he tried again to carry on a conversation. As they passed through the open fields and she commented on the lack of crops, he explained, "The men are all gone to the army—most of them, anyway. Besides, about all people know how to grow around here is cotton, and there's already cotton enough to supply the world, I guess."

"Can't the slaves grow the cotton?" she inquired.

"They can do the work, but what will the planters do with it? It's stacked up on the wharves now high as a mountain. They could sell it if they could get it to England, but the blockade has stopped that." He thought about it for a while then turned to her. He looked alert, and his light blue eyes were almost electric. "One of your relatives, Major Clay Rocklin, has the right idea. He says all the farms ought to grow food to feed the army, not cotton to sit on some wharf somewhere. But as usual, a prophet has no honor in his own country. They laughed at Clay, but another year of this starving and they'll listen to him, I think."

"What do you think of the war?" she inquired suddenly. He had not said anything about his own feelings. Yet it was apparent that he was a man who could become a soldier. Allyn was accustomed to seeing healthy men in uniform. Even in New Orleans, during the early part of the war, men were jeered at and ridiculed who did not serve, and she was curious about this big, strong man who obviously was fit in every respect.

"I'm just an innocent bystander." Larrimore grinned at her. He seemed cheerful enough about the matter, but as the carriage rolled on through the fields, occupied by slaves who were working in cornfields, he added, "I didn't grow up in the South, so my loyalties aren't here."

"Then you're for the North."

"No, I don't suppose so, at least not enough to put on a uniform and fight."

"But what do you think about the war?"

"I think it's going to ruin the South before it's over. Already the best and finest of the young men have died. That's always the way in a war, I suppose. The best go first and get killed; then the second-rate men have to go. They've been conscripting men for a while. It's not very popular, but that's what it's come to."

The carriage rolled on, and Allyn enjoyed the beauty of the countryside. She was accustomed to the flat land of the delta—New Orleans itself being below sea level. She could see the rising hills to her right and far ahead a blue ridge of mountains. *It's beautiful here,* she thought, *but I wish I knew what I'd find at the end of this trip.*

Jason sat silently in the seat beside her. He was impressed by her beauty. And though he had known many beautiful young women in his life, never had he seen one quite as beautiful as this. She lacked the tenderness or gentleness he liked to see in a woman, but he could understand something about that. *Growing up on the streets of New Orleans must have been a hard thing for a young woman,* he thought. *Men must have been after her. For a young girl, it's either give in or build a wall, and I guess it's best that she's built the wall. I wonder how she and Mark will even talk to each other. I'm afraid he's going to be disappointed if he's expecting her to fall on his neck. I can see she won't do that.*

As they approached Gracefield, he nodded and said, "There's Gracefield over there, one of the finest plantations in the county."

Allyn looked up, startled at the large white house that sat back off the road. As Larrimore drove the carriage around the large circular driveway, she was impressed with the size and the gracefulness of the house. Large white pillars rose on three sides of the house, and the sunlight struck the many glassed windows as they approached.

Jason stopped the carriage, and a slave came out at once to hold the horses' heads. Leaping down, Jason said, "I guess you can water them and give them a little grain, if you've got any." The slave nodded, and after Allyn stepped to the ground, he led the team off.

Allyn felt more nervous than she ever had in her life. "Will you—will you be staying for a while, Mr. Larrimore?"

Glancing at her quickly, and understanding her nervousness, Jason nodded. "Why, sure! I'm going to be around for a little while. Come along now. You'll like your father's sister-in-law. She's one of the finest women I've ever known. She lost her husband, Thomas, a short while ago. She'll be glad to see you."

Allyn took his arm as he held it out, and they climbed the steps that led to the large double doors. Before they got there, the door opened and a woman came out. Allyn was taken aback when she came over and held out her hands, saying at once, "You must be Mark's daughter. I'm so glad to see you, my dear! Come in! You must be tired after your long journey."

"Thank you," Allyn murmured. She was impressed with the attractiveness of Susanna Rocklin, who at sixty-two had lost little of her youthful beauty. There was a little gray in her auburn hair, but her blue-green eyes were as bright as ever and her skin still fresh and smooth.

When they were inside, Susanna said, "Why don't you come in the drawing room? We can have something to drink and talk." She gave Allyn another smile and said, "I'm so glad to see you. Come now." She led the way to an opulent drawing room and sat them down, and a black woman came in when she rang a silver bell. "Bring us some lemonade, if you have any of those lemons left, Dorrie."

"Yes'm, we got some."

Susanna turned to the man, saying, "I'm glad to see you again, Captain Larrimore. Mark has talked about you so much since you've been gone that I feel like we're old friends."

"I hope he didn't tell you everything." Larrimore smiled. "Some of my escapades aren't fit for the ears of ladies, I'm afraid." He felt slightly uncomfortable and said, "If you don't mind, I think I'll walk around the plantation. Might even take a ride on that black horse Mark's told me about."

"Why, certainly, you go right ahead, Captain." Susanna recognized the tactfulness of the tall man, and as soon as he bowed and left the room, she said, "He certainly is a fine-looking man, isn't he?"

"I suppose so."

The reply was spoken rather shortly, and at once Susanna put aside her light manner. "This must be very difficult for you, my dear," she said quietly. "Mark has told me a little of the story about your mother. It must have been very hard for you."

Suddenly Allyn wanted to pour out the whole story to this woman who seemed so gentle, so receptive. But years of habit kept her lips shut, and she said merely, "We made out, Mother and I."

Susanna read the face of the young woman, saw the tightness of her lips, and knew at once that there was bitterness in the young woman's heart. She also knew it was too soon for her to start giving advice, so she asked quietly, "Would you like to go up to your father's room now? He was awake a little while ago."

"Y–yes," Allyn said, "I suppose so." She looked at Susanna and asked, "How sick is he?"

"Very ill, I'm afraid. The wound he took has never healed, and the doctors are afraid it's not going to get any better. We're praying for him, and I believe God has done a work just keeping him alive this long." She hesitated then said, "He's had a strange life, your father. I've never really understood him. He's been different from the rest of the family. He's been grieving all his life over what happened between him and your mother. He said so to me, so I know you'll be kind."

Allyn nodded but lifted her head in an impetuous gesture. "If you'll take me to him—"

"Of course. His room is right down the hall."

Allyn followed Susanna out of the room and down the hall, where she paused before a large oak door. She knocked twice, and when a man's voice said, "Come in," she opened the door and entered. When Susanna was inside, she stopped and nodded to Allyn. "Come in, my dear."

Allyn felt light-headed, and her knees were not quite steady as she entered the room. She was breathing rather shallowly as she stopped and faced a tall man who had been sitting in a chair beside a window. He got up rather painfully, and when he turned to Allyn, a shock ran over her. He was not well, she saw at once, but even though he was ill and drawn, she recognized what a fine-looking man he was. Even as this thought came to her, a bitterness touched her, and she thought, *He must have been very handsome when he left my mother.* She had come partly out of curiosity, but now the sight of the man who had deserted her mother brought a hardness to her. She stood there unsmiling as she waited.

"Allyn, this is your father," Susanna said. She hesitated and said, "I'll leave you two alone to get acquainted." She turned and left the room, and when she was outside, she shook her head. "She's bitter against him," she murmured. "I could see it in her eyes and in the very straightness of her back."

The weakness that swept over Mark Rocklin was hard for him to bear, for he was used to keeping himself under control. But now at the sight of the young woman, he felt utterly inadequate. Nevertheless, he forced himself to step forward and said, "My dear, I know this must be very hard for you."

When she did not answer but stood there staring at him with large green eyes, his heart sank, for he recognized the hardness that lay in the young woman. Desperately he said, "Sit down. You must be tired after your long trip."

"Thank you." Allyn sat down and waited for him to speak. She saw how carefully he moved, and as he seated himself in the chair, a spasm of pain touched his face. *He's very sick,* she thought, and then she said nervously in an artificial tone, "I was very surprised when Captain Larrimore found me in New Orleans."

"How much did he tell you of—of your mother and myself?"

"Very little," Allyn said. She hesitated then said, "I asked my mother several times who my father was, but she would never tell me anything."

Mark Rocklin sat back in the chair, tried to organize his thoughts. They ran through him riotously, and nothing that came sounded right. Finally, he said in a weary tone, "It's too late to change the past. Nobody can ever do that, can they? But let me explain that I never knew you existed. If I had, things would have been different."

"Why did you leave my mother?" Allyn demanded suddenly.

"Didn't you love her?"

Mark stared at her; then a smile pulled the corners of his lips up. "You're very like her, you know. You look like her, same eyes, same red hair. Have you ever seen this?" He reached inside his pocket and pulled out a locket of mother-of-pearl and gold. Unsnapping it, he opened it and handed it over.

It was a miniature of her mother. She had never seen it. Taking it in her hand, she held it and studied the young face, the wide, innocent eyes, and the gentle lips. "I've never seen this," she said. "She was very pretty."

"You are very like her, Allyn," Mark said quietly. "And her ways, too. She was a strong woman. Much stronger than I," he added with a trace of disgust in his voice.

He took the locket when she handed it back and said, "You'd like to have this one day, and you will." He put the locket back in his pocket and then said, "Well, no time for defense—and I have none to make." He looked out the window, his eyes growing dreamy. "I was a much younger man than I am now and had little sense. I went to New Orleans to have a fling. I was looking for a good time. Instead, I found. . .your mother. . . ."

Allyn sat there listening to him, feeling as if she were an onlooker at the scene rather than a participant. As he spoke of those days with her mother in New Orleans, she tried to go back and picture them. Her memories of her mother were of hard times when life had been difficult, and she could not imagine the young woman whom Mark Rocklin spoke of.

Finally, Mark said, "You ask if I loved your mother. I can only say I was a fool. I didn't know what love was. Maybe I still don't. I don't know if anybody does. But I can tell you this one thing—I never got away from her." He turned his eyes back on her, and she saw the pain that was in them. "I've lived to be an old man now, and I don't think a day has passed that I didn't think of her in one way or another. I never married because I never found a woman that could stand beside her in my mind." Suddenly he dropped his eyes, and his fingers tightened as he grasped them, and she had to lean forward to catch his words. "I didn't know," he repeated, "what love was."

A silence ran across the room, and for a time Allyn did not know what to say. She had come with a hardness in her, angry at this man who had deserted her mother. Now, seeing him sick and alone, some of that melted. Yet it was too much for her, and she finally said, "I don't suppose I'll be staying long, but I–I'm glad that I got to see you at last."

At once Mark looked up and said quickly, "Allyn, I didn't send Captain Larrimore to get you just so I could meet you." He hesitated then added, "I didn't do anything for your mother —except bring her heartache. Let me do something for you."

"Something for me?"

"Why, yes." There was surprise in his voice; then he laughed shortly. "Well, I've thought about it so much, somehow I guess I thought you knew what I had in mind." He leaned forward then, and excitement came to his tired eyes. "I don't know about your life in New Orleans. You may be very happy there. Is that so?"

"You don't know where Captain Larrimore found me," she said evenly. Watching him carefully, she said, "I was dealing blackjack in the Gay Paree saloon."

Mark blinked in surprise then shook his head. "I'm not your judge, Allyn. I know it's been hard for you, and you have to do what you can to make it. It would be hard for any young woman."

"After Mother died," she said, "Sam Barker was really the only friend I had. He owns the Gay Paree. My stepfather taught me how to play cards, so I went to Sam and asked him to let me deal blackjack." She drew herself up, and there was pride in her eyes as she said, "And that's *all* I do—deal cards—as perhaps Captain Larrimore will tell you."

"What happened?"

"He showed a little bit too much interest in me and got thrown out of the place. Devil fly off!" she exclaimed. "Probably the first time a rich important man like him ever got thrown out of a saloon."

"I'd like to have seen that." Mark chuckled. "Imagine, Jason Larrimore getting bounced out of a saloon." He looked at her and smiled fondly. "'Devil fly off,' you said. That's what your mother used to say."

"I guess I got some of my Welsh expressions from her," Allyn said. Then she straightened up. "Anyway, I can take care of myself. It's not a very good life, but at least I can have independence."

"Independence is a fine thing," Mark said, "but it's a lonely thing, too." He ran his hand over his graying hair and said, "I ought to know about that. I've been independent all my life, so I know how lonely that can be." He suddenly gripped his hands together and said, "Allyn, stay for a while. There could be a good life for you here. I have some money that I've been putting back. Never knew what I wanted to do with it. But we could buy a place, a plantation. They are cheap enough now that the war has come. You could be independent there, too."

"Me, stay in Virginia?" Allyn had thought about this, but now it seemed impossible. "What would I do here? I don't know anyone. My whole life is in New Orleans."

Mark had gained considerable wisdom over his years, and he knew that this proud young woman could not be coerced, so he did not try. "You may want to go back to New Orleans, and if you do, I'll help you so that you don't have to work at all, if you don't want to. I don't want to run your life, Allyn. All I want to do is help you." He looked out the window and swept his hands in a gesture at the gracious lawn outside. "But Gracefield is your heritage. Your grandfather was here. Your roots and your people are here." He looked back at her and said, "If you'd just give them a chance, they'll accept you."

"A blackjack dealer from a New Orleans saloon?" she jibed. "I don't think so. That's not the idea I have of Southern gentry."

Mark knew it was useless to argue, but he said, "Will you stay for a week? Just meet the family; then if you want to go back, we'll work out something for you there."

Allyn struggled for a moment then finally nodded and said, "All right, I'll stay for a week. We'll see how it goes."

"Fine, fine," Mark exclaimed. He reached out, and before she thought, Allyn took his hand. He held it gently, put his other over it, and studied her face. A silence ran through the room, and finally he said, "You're very like your mother, my dear. Very like her."

CHAPTER 9

A BALL AT GRACEFIELD

Melora sat at the kitchen table peeling potatoes. When Rena came in, she looked up and smiled. "Sit down and help me peel these potatoes. I don't think I'll ever get through with them."

Rena was wearing her usual garb—a pair of old pants that were faded with many washings and a brown-and-white-checkered shirt. "Oh, I *hate* peeling potatoes!" she complained, but nonetheless flopped down beside the other woman. Picking up a knife, she began spiraling off potato peelings. After the two women had talked for a while, Rena said, "I don't know what's wrong with Mark's daughter. She just doesn't seem to fit in here, does she?"

"Well, she's had a different kind of life than you, Rena," Melora answered. "A harder life in a lot of ways. It will just take her a little time to settle down."

"She's not very friendly," Rena complained. "She stays by herself most of the time. I've offered to take her riding, but she says she doesn't care anything about horses."

"I wish you'd keep on making yourself available, Rena. Allyn needs a friend. She's at a critical time in her life right now, and she needs all the prayer and help and friendship that she can get. You can imagine, can't you, how it would be if you were plucked up out of Gracefield and plumped down in New Orleans in the midst of that kind of life, without any family? Think how hard it would be for you." She looked across at the girl with a smile and said, "It's been hard for me coming to Gracefield."

Rena looked up with surprise, her wide eyes taking in her stepmother. "Hard for you? Why, you've been around Gracefield most of your life, and we've known you forever, it seems."

"It's not the same thing." Melora shook her head and placed the potato she had just peeled on top of the stack of those already completed. Putting down the knife, she wiped her hands on her apron then leaned back in the chair, her eyes thoughtful. "I grew up in a world almost as different from the one you have here as Allyn's. I was the daughter of a poor farmer. Why, Rena, you can't imagine how I thought about the life here at Gracefield! To me it was like a fairyland where everybody wore pretty clothes all the time and nobody ever worked and life was just one constant stream of dances and fancy affairs. And all the time I was out feeding hogs and chopping cotton."

"Well, it's not always like that," Rena said rather indignantly. "We *do* work around here—as you've found out by now!"

Melora laughed. "Yes, I know now. I'm just saying it was hard for me to come here, and it's even more difficult for Allyn." She smiled gently, adding, "That's why we must be very kind and very open to her."

Rena picked up another potato. She thought for several minutes about what Melora had said then murmured, "She's so beautiful, Melora, isn't she?"

"Yes, she is."

"But Uncle Mark doesn't seem happy at all. I thought he would be after he got her back again."

"Well, he doesn't actually have her *back*. She's just here for a visit. But I know he'd like for her to stay." She rose and picked up the potatoes, saying thoughtfully, "I suppose that's enough for now." Going to the sink, she put them down, poured some water from a bucket over them, then turned back to Rena. "I've tried and tried to think of some way we could make her feel more at home—perhaps persuade her to stay here. But she's built a wall around her a mile high."

Rena rose and shrugged. "Well, I don't—" She halted abruptly, a light coming into her eyes as she said excitedly, "I know what we could do, Melora!"

"Do? Do about what?"

"Do about Allyn, of course!" Rena's eyes shone, and she spoke rapidly as she always did when she was excited. "Melora, she's all alone out here—never meets anybody. Why don't we have a party—or even a ball here at the house? She would meet people, and I think that would bring her out of herself. She's so pretty, and the soldiers would swarm her like flies to honey! Now *that* would make her feel at home!"

Melora's first impulse was to reject the idea, but as she stood there, she realized that Mark's desire was not likely to come to pass. "We do need to do *something*," she murmured thoughtfully.

"Oh, let's do it!" Rena said. "It'd be *fun*, Melora! We haven't had anything around here for so long, and after Gettysburg, it's been so miserable! Everybody's so depressed and downhearted. We *need* something like that!"

Rena was correct in her evaluation, for after the carnage of Gettysburg, the city of Richmond had become one huge hospital. The wagons had struggled home bringing thousands of wounded men. Almost every house contained at least one of them, and Chimborazo, the largest Confederate hospital, was packed to capacity. The defeat at Gettysburg had sapped the spirit of the Confederacy. When Lee had led his army forth, it had been with high hopes that one battle would convince England to come in and recognize the Confederacy as an independent nation. If that had been done, loans could have been negotiated, the blockade could have been broken, and the future of the South would have been bright indeed.

Now, however, after the debacle in Pennsylvania, as Lee brought the broken army of Virginia back home, the entire Confederacy seemed to be broken—almost as badly as the army. Life went on, as it had to, but the grief of thousands of families who had lost husbands and fathers and brothers hung like a pall over the land. Enlistments in the army practically came to a halt so that another conscription obviously would follow soon. The factories at Richmond continued to pour out the tools of war, but something had gone out of the Confederacy.

The high tide of the Cause for which the South had gone to war had been reached when George Pickett led his Virginians in the last futile charge at Gettysburg. A few had reached the summit of the hill, and for one brief moment it seemed as though the South would win—that Lee's forces would be victorious. But then, overwhelmed by the superiority of numbers, Pickett's men were driven back down the hill, leaving a carpet of blood shed by dying and wounded men. From that moment on, it seemed the South had lost that fervor that had led them into secession. Now, though Jefferson Davis tried to whip up excitement and patriotism, it was not the same as it had been during the early days of the strife. Most people knew the inevitable outcome of the war—defeat—but no one would speak the thought aloud.

Melora thought of this and nodded. "I think you're right,

Rena. There's been so much grief, so much sorrow. Maybe what we need is a little gaiety in life. I don't know what Clay will say, though."

"Oh, Daddy will do whatever we tell him to," Rena said airily. She smiled suddenly, adding, "Ever since he came back again, I know how to handle him. He's easy, Melora! All you have to do is just hang on him a little bit and pat his cheek and tell him how nice he looks. Things like that, you know. Even if he says no, if you keep on, he'll always give in."

Melora laughed with delight. "You are a caution, Rena Rocklin!" She stared out the window at the tall oaks then nodded firmly. "All right, we'll have a ball. Come now, let's sit down and figure out how we can afford it and when it will be."

"Well, I know one thing," Rena said excitedly as she sat down with the older woman. "I'm going to make Josh buy a fancy suit. And I'm going to have the first dance with him and the last one, too, maybe."

"That young man"—Melora shook her head solemnly—"will never know what hit him. Come now, let's make some plans...."

As balls go among the gentry of the South, the affair held at Gracefield was not much. The large ballroom that occupied part of the lower floor of the mansion was comfortably filled, but not to overflowing as it had been during happier times. This was primarily because so many of the young men were away in the army, many of them in Tennessee—and even those in the Army of Northern Virginia were scattered out in a thin line to defend the city.

Nevertheless, when Josh Yancy rode up on his bay gelding, his heart almost failed him, for it looked like a fairyland to him. He arrived at dusk, when the lanterns had been lit and were casting their amber gleam over the outside of the house. He could see through the large windows the women in their colored dresses and the officers in their gray uniforms. It startled him, and he muttered, "Gosh, I won't fit in this place at all! I don't know why I let Rena talk me into this!"

He halted, pulled up the bay, and swung to the ground. Box, one of the slaves, came to him with a flash of gleaming white teeth. "Yes, suh, Mistuh Josh, let me take that fine-looking hoss."

Feeling very awkward, Josh grinned. "I almost turned around and rode away, Box, when I saw all the fancy dresses and uniforms in there. I'm as nervous as a long-tailed cat in a roomful of rocking chairs!"

"Naw, suh, you go right on in and find Miss Rena. She been looking fo' you. You look mighty fine, Mistuh Josh! You go right on in and have yo'self a fine time!"

Josh took some courage from the friendly words. He walked to the steps and joined those who were filing in. When he entered, he heard the sound of music and turned at once to the ballroom. He looked around with shock, for he had never seen the ballroom decorated for a party, and he now studied it carefully.

Lighted prisms dangled below glass shades on the lofty ceiling. They cast miniature rainbows on the dancers who already whirled and glided across the glistening parquet floor of the ballroom. All around the walls, green velvet draperies framed the scene. Intricately wrought Spanish ironwork decorated a broad staircase that led to a second floor with a balcony that accommodated the musicians. It was really late in the year for flowers, but somehow some had been found, mostly wildflowers, and these filled vases, adding splashes of color to the room. Overhead on the small balcony nine musicians worked at sending out the music that floated over the room. There were two violins, a dulcimer, several guitars, and even an accordion and a couple of banjos.

Shifting his gaze to the dance floor, Josh saw that the dominant color was the gray of the officers' uniforms, set off by the black sheen of boots and the golden flash of brass buttons. But it was the dresses of the women that caught his eye, as they flashed to the strain of a waltz. Some of them were startlingly décolleté, glowing in brilliant colors of sapphire, yellow, pink, green, and white.

"Josh—I've been waiting for you!"

Rena appeared before him and took his arm possessively. She was wearing a yellow dress with puffed sleeves and tiny blue stripes on the skirt. Her hair was done up in a way he had not seen before, and for a moment Josh felt that she was a total stranger. "Gosh, you look...you look..."

"Well, how do I look? Tell me," Rena teased him.

Josh was not a young man with a free flow of words. He had struggled with a stutter most of his life, and now in this strange environment, he knew he had to be very careful. "You look pretty as a wildflower," he said slowly.

Rena's eyes widened, and she said, "Why, Josh, you're getting to be a poet. That's the nicest compliment!" She stood back and looked him over. She had insisted he take the money he was going to spend on a new rifle and buy himself a new suit for the ball. She had not seen the suit yet, and now she examined him closely. "Why, Josh, you look so *handsome*! That's a beautiful suit!" She eyed the suit, which consisted of a pair of light brown trousers, a fingertip-length dark linen coat, a wine-colored waistcoat, and a ruffled white shirt with a black string tie. He was a tall, lean young man, and in his new suit he looked very masculine and handsome.

Rena smiled and grabbed his arm. "Josh, you stay away from that Mary Wadsworth," she whispered. "She's already told me how handsome she thinks you are—but if she makes a move at you, I'll scratch her eyes out! Come on, now—let's dance."

Josh blinked his eyes and shook his head. "Well—I don't know, Rena, I'm not much of a dancer."

"I've taught you, and I'm a good teacher," she said. "Come on now!" Soon he was moving awkwardly through the steps of the dance, and the two were chatting away.

"My brother and Rena make a nice-looking couple, don't they, Clay?" Melora and Clay were standing beside the refreshment table. He lifted his eyes to see the couple. "Yes, they do," he said. He looked at Melora and grinned. "Not as nice looking as us, though."

"Well, of course not!" she mocked him, and then she giggled. "We're so vain, aren't we? But we are nice looking for an old couple."

Clay looked down at Melora, who wore a green dress that brought out the color of her eyes, and said, "You'll never be old. When you're ninety, you'll be as beautiful as you are right now."

Melora squeezed his arm. "I'm glad you think so, but you're going to have to put up with me no matter what I look like."

Now they stood there chatting for a while. Finally, Clay said, "Look, there's Larrimore. I thought he had left on one of his blockade-running expeditions."

Melora glanced in the direction of his nod. "Why, I thought so, too. I'm glad he came, though. He seems to do Mark so much good. He always cheers him up."

"He's a strange companion for Mark, isn't he?"

"I don't think so. As a matter of fact, they are alike in a lot of ways."

"Alike? How?" Clay asked.

"They're both alone. I imagine Jason Larrimore is a lot like Mark when he was that age." She looked across at Larrimore, who was dancing with a young woman who was staring up at him with fascination in her eyes. Melora shook her head. "He's a handsome thing, isn't he?"

"Oh, I don't know about that, but he's a good captain—or so I hear. He runs through that blockade like he's going for a stroll in the park. He's probably the best blockade-runner the Confederacy has, and he's getting rich at it, too."

Melora glanced at the stairs and said, "Allyn hasn't come down yet. Let me go up. It would be better if I came down with her and introduced her."

"Well, you'll have to fight some of these officers off, I think. I don't believe their manners are as excellent as their shooting."

Melora left the ballroom and climbed the stairs to where Allyn had been given a room on the second floor. She paused at the door and asked, "Allyn, can I come in?"

"Yes, come in."

When Melora entered, she stopped abruptly and stared at the girl. "Why, Allyn, how nice you look!"

Allyn was wearing a ball gown made of fine silk. It was a delicate dove gray with rose stripes. Clusters of pink rosebuds gathered the fullness of her billowing skirt into festoons above a silken laced petticoat that rustled with the slightest motion.

Her shoulders were exposed and looked creamy and smooth. Her auburn hair was done up in a graceful swirl, and her eyes looked enormous, though somewhat troubled.

"That's a beautiful dress. You got it in New Orleans, I suppose?" Melora asked, coming over to touch the material. "My, I've never seen a dress so pretty."

"Well, I don't know what made me buy it. I never thought I'd have anywhere to wear it," Allyn said. She seemed subdued and looked at Melora. "I feel so—so *strange*," she said. "I wish I didn't have to go to the ball!"

"Why, of course you're going—and you'll have a fine time, too. There are some of your family you'll have to meet—Clay's son Dent and some of the Bristols and the Franklins, too. Come along now."

"Well, I suppose I must." Allyn stood there diffidently and finally said, "I don't belong in this place. I feel like a total stranger. I—I just don't belong here."

"Well, neither do I," Melora said quickly. "You know, I've told you the kind of family I had, where I came from, but God's put me here."

Allyn's eyes narrowed, and her lips grew thin. "I don't believe in God," she said rebelliously.

If she had expected to shock Melora, she did not. Melora had already discovered that Allyn Griffeth was a girl who had been so hurt and bruised by life that she had closed her heart to all thoughts of God. Now Melora only smiled and said gently, "You may not believe in Him, but He believes in you."

Her statement caught Allyn off guard. Her lips parted with surprise, but she could think of nothing to say and stood there examining Melora. Finally, she shrugged. "I've been talking to my father. He wants to adopt me legally, but I don't know what to do."

Melora felt a great urge to put her arm around the girl, but she knew that there was still a wall there. "Why, I think that would be wonderful, if you would agree to it, Allyn. Not that we would love you any less if you kept your mother's name. But it would make your father so happy—and all of us, as a matter of fact."

The gentleness of the woman took some of the rebellious light out of Allyn's eyes. She had not expected Mark's proposal of adoption, which he had made only the night before. It had disturbed her, and she could not understand why such turbulent thoughts came to her over this. For long hours she had lain awake wondering what to do, but when she had awakened early in the morning, she still was confused. All day she had kept to her room, except for one long walk through the woods that surrounded the mansion. Now as she stood before Melora, the decision was clear. "I think I will," she said. She twisted her hands nervously and added, "There's really nothing for me to go back to in New Orleans. I don't know how it will be here, but I'd like to stay for a while, anyway."

Melora then did move forward and kissed the girl on the cheek. "I think you're making a very wise choice," she said gently. "Your father loves you, and you'll have a family. Come along now, and I can introduce you as Allyn Rocklin, the daughter of Mark Rocklin."

Allyn moved along the hall, something like fear coming to her. She had made a decision that she knew would impact her whole life. She had no idea what the days to come would bring, but she had grown weary of life in New Orleans, of fighting off unwelcome advances, of the tawdriness of the life that she led dealing cards in a saloon. Some of the gracefulness of the life at Gracefield still remained, though scarred and battered by the hammering of the war effort. And she had seen in Melora, Rena, Rooney, and Susanna—the women of the plantation—a quality that she admired. She knew herself to be much harder than any of these and regretted it, but now, as she moved down one of the curving stairways, she thought, *No matter what happens here, it couldn't be any worse than dealing cards in the Gay Paree!*

When she reached the foot of the stairs, at once she was met by Clay, who took her hand, saying, "You look beautiful, Miss Allyn. Come, let me introduce you to some of my officers."

They were surrounded instantly by a group of young officers. One of them, a tall, dark-haired man in a captain's uniform, seemed to edge himself forward, past the others, and Melora smiled. "Gentlemen, I want you to meet the newest member of the Rocklin family, Miss Allyn Rocklin, from New Orleans. Some of you have served with her father, Mark Rocklin."

The tall captain bowed at once and said, "Miss Allyn, let me be the first to welcome you to your new home. May I claim the first dance?"

Clay laughed. "This is Captain Will Farley, Allyn, one of our most dashing young officers. He is headed for promotion. You can see how he's outmaneuvered the rest of his fellow officers."

A groan went up from the other officers, but Farley simply stepped forward and held out his arm. "Come, Miss Allyn. As we dance I'll tell you about what terrible fellows these are so that you will be forewarned."

Allyn liked the look of the tall young man and said, "Why, of course, Captain, but then I'll have to ask Major Rocklin to tell me all about *your* shortcomings."

A laugh went up as the two moved off to a waltz, and Clay

said, "You fellows will just have to wait your turn. Looks like you'd better form a line."

"Clay," Melora said, "why don't you go and see if Mark would feel like coming to the ballroom. I'm sure he would enjoy seeing Allyn dance."

"That's a good idea. I was just about to do that."

Clay moved out of the ballroom, walked quickly to Mark's room, and knocked on the door. When he entered, he found Mark dressed and seated in his usual place beside the table. "You feel like a little trip, Mark?" he asked. "Allyn's already got half the company ready to shoot each other. She's a beautiful young woman."

Mark looked thin, but there was a light of anticipation in his eyes. "I believe I can make it if you'll stick close beside me. I don't want to go in a blasted wheelchair."

"You'll do fine—just hang on to me if you need to," Clay encouraged him.

They made their way down the hall and entered the ballroom. Clay maneuvered Mark over to the line of chairs along one side of the wall and said, "Here, let's sit down and watch for a while."

Clay was concerned about Mark, for his face was pale, and pain drew his mouth into a thin line. They talked for a few moments, and several of the officers came by to express their concern and to see how Mark was faring. Mark only half paid attention, for he had eyes only for Allyn. He watched her as she danced with first one and then another young officer and said, "Clay, she's the prettiest thing I've ever seen!"

"Well, I haven't seen an ugly Rocklin woman yet," Clay said. "She is a beautiful young woman." He shifted his weight, wanting to ask a question but not knowing how. "How are you two doing?" he asked finally.

Mark rubbed his hands across his chin thoughtfully. "Better than I have any right to expect," he admitted. "But she's an unhappy young woman, and it's mostly my fault." Pain struck him along the side; he took a deep breath and tried not to show it. The pains were becoming more frequent now, more severe, and he knew that he could not conceal them from the sharp eyes of those who knew him. Taking a deep breath, he said, "I've got to do something for her, Clay. I've failed her all my life, and now I can't let it go on like this."

"What do you want to do, Mark?"

"Why, I'd like to buy a place and have her be the mistress of it. Not as large as Gracefield, of course," he added quickly, "but I've been saving some money most of my life." He smiled at Clay, saying, "You didn't think that, did you? You thought I was the prodigal, throwing money away right and left. I guess I was for a few years. But then I got tired of that. I've been making a few investments."

"Not in Southern stocks, I hope."

"No, mostly in Northern railroads, and they're doing very well. I can cash in now and have enough to buy a nice place."

Clay said excitedly, "You know, Twelve Trees is for sale. Jennings is giving up."

Twelve Trees was a medium-sized plantation five miles away from Gracefield. It had a fine home, not elaborate, but well built and solid. The mention of it at once caught Mark's attention. "Twelve Trees—I've always liked that place. Not too big, just a nice size. How much do you think Jennings would have to have?"

"Well, it's a buyer's market," Clay said with a shrug. "You know how much plantations are worth as much as I do." He looked over and asked, "Would you like Jennings to come over and talk to you about it?"

"Yes. Will you go see him tomorrow?"

"Sure. That'd be a fine place for you and Allyn."

"I don't know about me, but I would like to leave her a legacy. If she doesn't want that, I'm going to leave her the money anyway. Somehow I think she needs roots, and her only family in New Orleans is gone. She needs a family, but I've robbed her of that."

"Mark, you've got to stop beating yourself up about this," Clay interrupted. "You did a wrong thing. All right, so have we all. Think about what I did; I forsook my family and left them to come up alone—and I knew about my children. You didn't. So I've done worse than you, but God has given it all back to me."

The remark struck Mark, and he said, "You know, that's right, isn't it? Since I've started reading the scripture and asked God to come into my life, I've found out that God can do anything He wants to."

"That's right. Now we'll just have to pray that Allyn will find her way, that she'll accept us as a family, just like we accept her. And it'll happen, too—you wait and see!"

As the two men talked, Allyn swept around the floor. She was dancing with a rather overweight young lieutenant when she saw her father and said, "Oh, look. I really ought to go speak to my father."

"Why, certainly, Miss Allyn. Let me do the honors." Lieutenant Grigsby led her across the floor, disappointed at being robbed of some of his time with her, but hopeful that he would make it up on another dance.

"Don't get up," Allyn said to Mark. "I just wanted to come and say what a nice ball it is. Father, this is Lieutenant Grigsby.

Lieutenant, my father, Mr. Mark Rocklin."

The two men shook hands, and Mark's face glowed with pleasure at her reference to him as "my father." He said, "You look absolutely beautiful, Allyn. Are you having a good time?"

"Oh yes. Lieutenant Grigsby and his fellow officers are all quite gallant."

"Well, you'll have to watch out for this one," Clay said. "He has a fiancée, you know."

"Why, sir, didn't I tell you?" Grigsby said. "My fiancée and I—well, we decided to call it off."

Allyn was amused at the young lieutenant's agony and said, "Well, perhaps you'll make it up with her, Lieutenant." This did not seem to assuage Lieutenant Grigsby, but finally when Allyn allowed him to take her back on the floor, Clay smiled. "She has a real sense of humor. A fine girl."

"Yes, she has. But she's also hard, Clay, but what could you expect after what she's been through?" Suddenly Mark said, "Look—there's Larrimore. He's cutting in on that poor lieutenant of yours."

Lieutenant Grigsby felt a hand on his shoulder, and when he turned, he found himself maneuvered out of position. The tall man asked, "Do you mind too much, Lieutenant?" Then, without waiting for an answer, he simply waltzed off with the young woman.

Allyn was startled by the sudden appearance of Jason Larrimore. She looked up at him and said, "I thought you were going off on a voyage."

"No, the ship wasn't quite ready, but I'll be leaving soon." He looked down at her and said, "You look lovely. Have you enjoyed your time here?"

Allyn nodded. "Yes," she said diffidently, "it's been very nice."

A thought came to her, and she said, "I suppose now that I'm going to be a Rocklin, you've come to court me."

Jason grinned down at her. He was wearing a fine gray suit, and a large diamond stickpin glittered on the cravat at his throat. "Well, I'm not the marrying kind, Miss Allyn. Now if you're interested in other arrangements—"

His words suddenly angered her, and she drew back. "No, Captain Larrimore, I am *not* interested in your 'other' arrangements!" She turned and left him standing alone on the floor. He watched her go and shook his head, saying to himself, *You're a fool, Larrimore. Why'd you have to say a thing like that?*

Josh and Rena had been watching the pair, and as Allyn left the tall man standing alone, Rena said, "They've had a quarrel of some kind."

"Yep." Josh nodded. "She looks mad as a wet hen, doesn't she? Wonder what he said to her?"

"I don't know. Josh, you go dance with that girl over there, and I'll see what I can find out."

"You mean that ugly one?"

"She's not ugly. She's just plain."

"Oh." He sounded rebuked but said, "Well, I really would rather dance with that girl over there, the one in the green dress."

"No," Rena said firmly, "you wouldn't want to dance with her. Just do what I tell you. That girl is Mary Higgins, and she's a very nice young lady. Now you go dance with her, and I'll go talk to Allyn."

She turned and walked away, and Josh shrugged. Melora came to stand beside him. "What was Rena telling you?"

"She was telling me to go dance with that ugly—I mean *plain*—girl over there in the red dress."

"Well, are you going to mind her?" Melora teased him.

Josh grinned at her and nodded. "Reckon I will. You always mind Mr. Clay, don't you?"

"He likes to think so," Melora said smoothly. She reached up and patted his cheek, saying, "Go along now and do what Rena told you."

As soon as he was gone, she made her way to Jason Larrimore, who had moved off the dance floor and was headed for the door.

"Are you leaving, Captain Larrimore?"

Larrimore turned and nodded. "Why, yes, Mrs. Rocklin, I suppose I am."

She said, "Please don't go yet. Go and sit with Mark awhile. He enjoys your company so much."

"I'd be glad to. I'll be leaving soon and won't get to see him for a while. But"—he shrugged as he spoke—"Miss Allyn is not too pleased with my company." He frowned and said, "I guess I'm just a rough sailor. I've hurt her feelings, I'm afraid."

"You've done her a great service," Melora said. "She'll recognize that. Don't mind if she gets upset."

He smiled at her and said, "All right, I'll go visit with Mark for a while."

He went over, and Melora watched as the three men sat there talking. Mark, as always, was glad to see Jason Larrimore, and Melora nodded with satisfaction. "I wonder how he hurt her feelings," she murmured then turned and went back to her duties as hostess.

Chapter 10

"I'll Have What I Want!"

The day after the ball, Allyn slept until ten then went down for a late breakfast. She found Susanna looking worried as Dorrie set the food on the table.

"That was a wonderful ball last night," Allyn said as she ate the eggs the black woman put before her. "I suppose you've seen bigger ones before the war."

"Oh yes," Susanna affirmed.

Susanna seemed unusually quiet, unlike herself, and Allyn said, "What's the matter—is something wrong?"

Susanna sipped the cup of sassafras tea that she usually drank in the morning. The pressures of running the plantation were great, and she looked tired. "Your father's not well this morning. I suppose going to the ball was too much for him last night." She sipped the tea, made a face, and put it down. "How I'd love to have some good China tea again! They don't have room on the blockade-runners for luxuries like that. It's all bullets and gunpowder now." She paused, put on a happier face, and said, "I'm glad you've decided to become a Rocklin."

The simple sentence seemed to trouble Allyn. She flushed slightly and pushed the eggs around her plate with the silver fork. "I thought about it and decided that would be best, but I still feel strange here."

"Why, the family all accepted you. Surely you could see that after last night?"

"Oh yes, they were all very nice, but that's not like being a member of the family."

"Time will change things. You'll grow more accustomed to things here. Now I think you should go see your father this morning. He wants to talk to you."

"All right, I will."

Allyn got to her feet and left the small dining room. When she reached Mark's room, she knocked on the door. After a brief silence, a voice said, "Come in." She entered the room and saw that Mark was still in bed. Pausing, she said, "Oh, I didn't know you weren't up." Turning, she said, "I'll come back later."

"No, come in, Allyn." Mark struggled to a sitting position and tried to arrange the pillows behind his back. Seeing that he was in pain, Allyn walked over and helped him adjust the pillows. "Thanks a lot," he said. "Sorry to be such a confounded baby."

"I took care of Mother a lot when she was sick," Allyn said. She sat down beside him and said, "I'm sorry to see you're feeling so bad today."

Mark shrugged his thin shoulders and said, "I can't complain. I get better care here than I would anywhere else." He looked at her and said thoughtfully, "It's good to have you here, Allyn. I watched you at the ball last night. I was very proud of you."

"I'd never been to a ball like that before. One of the things I missed, I suppose."

"Didn't you go to any dances, parties, or anything like that?"

Allyn leaned forward, her eyes thoughtful. "I can remember when I was twelve years old—Mother bought me a new dress. There was a party at our school. I know she worked hard to save the money for it. It was pink and had blue bows on it, I remember. We didn't have the money to get my hair fixed, so Mother did it herself. I remember how excited I was when I went to the party."

Mark, seeing that an unhappiness had come into her voice, asked, "What happened?"

"Oh, it wasn't any good. I was an outsider, and you know how children are. Two of them get along very well, but you put three of them together, they'll shut one out."

Mark blinked his eyes in surprise. "Why, I never noticed."

"You never watched that with children?"

"I guess I haven't been around too many children. Is that really the way they are?"

Allyn pushed a strand of hair back over her ear and nodded. "Yes, most of them, and it doesn't stop with the children, either. Most people are like that, I guess. They like to form little clubs where they can be at the top and close everybody else out."

Mark thought about it and nodded abruptly. "You know, that's right. When I think back on it, that's the way most of life is, everybody wanting to be at the top." He gave her a quick glance, adding, "I guess if everybody were at the top, there wouldn't be any way to be exclusive. You are a very bright young woman."

"Oh, not very," she said. She was uncomfortable in his presence. Somehow the very knowledge that he had sent for her disturbed her. She had been angry with him subconsciously all of her life and now found it impossible to simply say that all was well. As she sat there, the two of them talking, she noticed that even during her brief stay, he seemed to have gotten worse. His skin was a sallow grayish hue, with very little color in it, and she could tell his eyes were filled with the same sort of pain her mother had had. *I wish I could like him better,* she thought. *But how can I after what he did to Mother and to me!* "Would you like for me to read to you, or play cards maybe?" She managed to smile, saying, "I don't think you could beat me, though."

"You don't? Well, we'll find out. I think there's a deck over in that bureau drawer."

Allyn got the cards, and for the next hour they played various games. They were pretty evenly matched, and Mark was surprised. "You're a good cardplayer," he said. "Better than any woman I ever saw, at least at poker and blackjack."

"I had a good teacher"—Allyn shrugged—"my stepfather. He wasn't much good for anything else, but he was a good cardplayer—but not good enough to stop losing all his money. If it weren't for him, though, I wouldn't have been able to get that job in the Gay Paree dealing blackjack. I don't know what I'd have done if it weren't for that. Nothing very good, though."

Mark's face grew more sober as she made this remark. He said, "I'm sorry I wasn't around, Allyn."

"Look, you don't have to apologize every time we talk. You've said all that before." Her voice was a little sharp. She said, "Let's not mention it again, if you don't mind."

"All right, then, I won't." He sat there for a moment silently and then said, "I was talking to Clay last night. Something came up that I wanted to talk to you about."

"What is it?"

"It's about your future. He told me about a plantation called Twelve Trees. It's not too far from here, about five miles. It's a nice place, not big like this one, but it has a nice house on it. I've been there several times; our two families visited quite a bit. The owner's selling out now—going north, I suppose." He hesitated, not knowing how to say what was on his heart. He wanted more than anything else in the world to please this girl, to bring happiness and joy into her life. But somehow that had become a spiritual matter as well. Part of his repentance, he assumed. He needed to make things right, and now he said quietly, "Allyn, would you live there, if I would buy the place?"

"Live there?" She was taken off guard. "You mean permanently—from now on?"

"Yes." He grew eager and said, "We could find someone to help with the work there. There's a good overseer, an older man. He takes care of the place mostly. Too old for the army, and there are enough hands to keep things going. Oh, it'll never be a great plantation, but we could buy it, and it would be in the clear. No matter what happens with the war or whatever, you'd always have it."

He hesitated and dropped his head. He fingered the gaily colored quilt that lay across his lap, tracing the orange and red and green designs that had been made by his mother; he'd always loved it. He asked for it every time he came to Gracefield—a touch of the past that always moved him. Now he said, "It would give you some options. It would be yours, of course, after I'm gone, to do with as you please. If it didn't work, you could always sell it for what it was worth and do something else." He lifted his eyes, and there was a pleading in them as he asked, "Would that please you, do you think?"

Allyn stared at him for one moment, disconcerted by his offer. She had felt that he would make this sort of an offer, and yet it caught her off guard. "You mean you want to spend all your money and buy that place—just for me?"

"I want to make up for the pain I've caused you, Allyn," he said simply.

For one brief moment she wanted to break down her defenses, reach out, and take him in her arms. There was a gentleness in this girl, but she had buried it so deeply it could find no way of expression. Now she sat there in the silence of the room, watching this man who had suddenly appeared out of nowhere, emerging from a past that was so dim she had no inkling of what lay there—and she didn't know what to say. The long years of bitterness were too strong, and finally she heard herself saying, "I'll do it, but I want you to know it's just because I'm selfish. I'll have what I want. You and I can never be very close. Now do you still want to do it?"

Mark studied the girl and said quietly, "That's what I did. I took what I wanted, and it's not wise. It doesn't bring any happiness, Allyn."

She lifted her chin defiantly. "If you want to buy it, I'll live there. I'll do my best to take care of you, too, but I can't forget all the years that you abandoned me. I'm sorry to talk to you like this when you're sick—but at least you'll know where I stand."

"You're an honest girl," Mark said evenly. "Your mother was the same. Nobody ever had to wonder what she thought." He sat there quietly then nodded. "All right, we'll buy the place. I think we'll get a bargain." He hesitated then said, "I hope as time goes by, we'll get closer."

She shook her head, saying quietly, "Don't hope too much for that. It's hard to forget the past."

The sale of Twelve Trees proceeded. Clay talked to the owner, and a lawyer came the next day to talk to Mark. They sat together talking for a long time, and later that day Mark said to Allyn, "I think it's going to go all right. He wanted more than it was worth, and I wanted to pay less, but it looks as though we'll own Twelve Trees before too long."

Allyn studied him carefully then managed to smile. "If you're sure that's what you want, then I'm glad for you. Would it be soon?"

"I think within a week we could take possession. I made an offer on all the furnishings, so all we have to do is move in." He hesitated then said, "I think we'll have to have one of the slaves come as a body servant, or hire someone. I take a lot of care, I know."

"Oh, I think I can manage," she said calmly. "There'll be some maids there, won't there?"

"Yes, I'm sure there will be. It's just a small place, as I said, but there's an older slave couple that has been there a long time. They have a daughter. They take care of the house, mostly, with some help from one of the younger girls. But I don't want to be a burden on you."

It disturbed her that he seemed to be giving up so much, but Allyn simply said, "All right. We'll manage."

The word soon spread among the family, and the slaves, of course, knew everything that went on in the Rocklin family. All the others seemed pleased that Allyn and Mark would be living close, but Dorrie had no pleasure in the thought. She was one of the oldest slaves, and she had shared the responsibility with Susanna of managing the huge plantation for so long that she knew the family better than anyone else. It was this familiarity that brought her into conflict with Allyn.

Allyn had come in from the fields where she had been

walking, her face flushed. She had picked a bunch of wildflowers and saw Dorrie standing there as she came in the back door. "Dorrie, I need a vase for these flowers. Aren't they pretty?"

Without a word, Dorrie walked over to a cabinet, pulled out a large vase, and handed it to Allyn.

Allyn took the vase and stared at the round face of the older woman. Allyn turned, filled the vase with water from a bucket, and began to arrange the flowers. She said quietly, "Well, Dorrie, it appears you don't like me."

Dorrie had turned to leave, but she stopped now and turned squarely to face the young woman. Her face was lined now, and her step was slower, but her loyalty to the Rocklin family was a fierce thing—after her church and her God, the strongest thing in her life.

"Dat's right," she said evenly.

Allyn looked up and met the eyes of the slave. "Why not?" she asked.

" 'Cause you doan treat Mistuh Mark right," Dorrie said firmly.

"Why do you say that?"

"He's sick. He ain't got long to live, and he need somebody roun' him with love—and you ain't got none of dat in you."

Startled at the black woman's declaration, a quick anger ran through Allyn. "How do you know that? You don't know anything about me."

Dorrie knew that most slaves would never be honest in a face-to-face encounter with a white owner, but to her the Rocklin family was almost sacred. Now she faced the young woman fiercely, her lips turned down in a frown. "I knows love when I sees it, and I knows it when I *doan* see it. Mistuh Mark, I knowed him all my life. He's a good man. He ain't always done right. He caused lots of heartache for his family—fo' me, too—but he's good, and now he's done foun' the Lord."

When the older woman stopped, Allyn said, "I didn't ask to come here, Dorrie." She knew that most white women would have lashed out at the slave, yet the direct stare from the brown eyes of Dorrie intimidated her. "I didn't even know who he was. You can't expect me to just walk in and start loving somebody without even knowing them!"

Dorrie hesitated, not wanting to go too far, and yet it infuriated her when anyone mistreated one of the family. "Dat ain't all dere is to it. You're a pretty woman, but dey's a *coldness* in you. You is hard! Mr. Mark don't need dat! He needs someone dat will be good to him, dat will love him. I wish you hadn't never come to dis place!"

Again anger flashed in Allyn's eyes. "You don't know how hard it was for me to grow up without a father."

"Don't I?" Dorrie snapped. "You think I had a father? I didn't have *nothin'*, but I learned to love people, and you ain't never learned dat and I doan think you never will."

Allyn could not meet the woman's gaze. She slammed the vase down on the floor so that it broke with a tinkling crash. "You don't know anything about it!" she cried angrily. "I don't have to listen to talk from an old nigger!" she shouted then whirled and ran from the room and out the front door.

The sun was hot on her face as she left. She heard someone call to her, but she did not turn around. She walked quickly until she found herself back in the trees that bordered the east side of the plantation. A small road led to the summerhouse where Clay had lived when he came back. Rooney and her brother used it now. She had learned that much of the family history. Blindly she walked down the road, shocked to find tears rolling down her face. She had not cried for years, and now she found herself trembling. "She doesn't know anything about it!" she muttered furiously. "It's none of her business, anyway!"

The August heat was cut off by the trees that arched overhead, forming a cathedral-like atmosphere. The ground was soft from a rain that had come the night before so that she made little sound as she walked along the road. Slowly she began to regain her composure and was startled when a large dog came bounding from around the turn, saw her, and came toward her with his head up, barking.

Allyn had never been around large animals, and the dog frightened her. "Get away," she cried, and the dog circled her, barking loudly.

"Buck! Buck! You stop that!"

Rena had appeared, and she came running forward, saying, "Don't pay any attention to Buck. He's all bark and wouldn't hurt a flea."

"I'm afraid of dogs," she said. "I never grew up around animals."

Rena said, "Pet him on the head."

Cautiously Allyn reached forward and touched the animal's head. He licked her hand and barked a booming "Woof!"

"He looks so fierce!" Allyn said, feeling slightly better about Buck.

"Well, I guess he'd bite anybody that tried to hurt me," Rena said. She thought and said, "You know, when Daddy first came home, I didn't like him at all because he deserted me and my brothers and my mother. At one time, when he first got here, Buck thought he was going to hurt me and he bit him, laid his arm open." She straightened up, her fine young eyes moody with the thought. "I think that's when I first began realizing that he really cared for me. He let me wash the wound out, and after that he showed me the books that he had brought with him. From that time on, it was all right."

"Must have been hard for you, being brought up with your father gone like that. It was for me."

"Oh yes." Rena nodded. Then she said quickly, "But it was worse for you, I expect, because I had brothers around to help me."

Allyn had liked Rena from the time she met her. She admired her trim young beauty, her enthusiasm. The two were close enough in age so that they could be friends, but when she looked at Rena and saw the innocence in her eyes and thought of her life, she felt almost like a mother to her. "Well," she said, "I guess I'll be going."

"I'll walk back to the house with you. Come on, Buck." The two young women walked back, and Rena chattered on about the ball. "Wasn't Josh fine looking in his new suit?"

Allyn smiled. "You're very fond of that young man, aren't you?"

"Oh, I guess so. You know, when I first met him, he had the most awful stutter. It was because he was afraid to be around people."

"Really? Why, he doesn't stutter at all now."

"No, and you know, I think I was able to help him with that. He was so bashful that he couldn't even look at me, but when we became friends and we fished together, he stopped stuttering so much. Now it's only when he gets excited or angry."

"Are you in love with him?" Allyn asked.

Rena flushed. "Oh, I don't know. Maybe someday it'll come to that. He's the best friend I have in the world—except for Daddy, of course. Do you like him, Allyn?"

"Yes. I don't know him very well, but he seems like a fine young man."

"It's going to be so good when you and Uncle Mark get moved. Will you have me over to visit with you?"

"Why, I guess I will," Allyn said. She laughed shortly. "I'm not used to being mistress of a house. I don't know a thing. You know a lot more than I do. Maybe you could come over and teach me how to keep house, things like that."

"I couldn't cook an egg, I don't think."

Allyn laughed. "I can't either, but we can learn." Allyn hesitated then said, "Dorrie doesn't think I'm good for my father, says I don't love him."

Rena halted, and the other girl halted as well. "You don't love him? Why would she think that?"

"I don't know. She says I'm hard—that I don't love anybody."

"Oh, Dorrie's just an old grouch." As she said this, Rena felt a streak of disloyalty, for she loved the old black woman. Now she saw the loneliness in the young woman and said, "She's just hard to get to know. You'll like her when you get to know her better." The two girls walked on toward the house, and Rena later told Susanna, "I'd better go and stay with Allyn when she and Uncle Mark move. I think she needs me."

Two days later Mark was pleased when he looked up and saw Jason Larrimore riding up to the house. "Look, there's Jason," he said to Allyn, who was sitting with him. The two were playing cards out on the veranda—a habit they had formed lately—and he said, "Hope he can stay for a while."

Allyn rose and said, "I'll let you two visit."

When she had left and Jason had come up on the porch, Mark said, "Sit down, Jason. Got some things to tell you."

Larrimore shook the thin hand that Mark extended, noting how it seemed to grow more skeletal each time he came. He had a deep concern and a premonition about this man whom he was so fond of, but he let none of this show in his face. He sat down, and soon Susanna came out, bringing them some lemonade to drink.

As the two men sat there, Mark faced Jason with excitement as he explained the adventure of buying Twelve Trees. "I think it's going to work out fine, Jason," he said, nodding his head. "It's not a big place, but it's going to be just what Allyn will like, I think. Of course," he said, "I don't know much about her. We'll be together all the time there. I think she'll learn to care for me."

"How have you two been getting on, Mark?" Jason inquired.

"Oh, you know me, Jason." Mark smiled, but there was strain in his face. "I always like to work and get things done. But you can't do that in a situation like this. I can't expect Allyn to just pick up and start being a daughter as if I've had her all my life. I've put her through a hard time, and now I've got to pay my dues—show her that I love her and want to take care of her."

"Well, you're already doing that," Jason said. "Twelve Trees is a nice place, I hear. When do you think you'll be going?"

"Oh, we should take possession within a week or so, but it will probably be a couple weeks before we move in. You'll come and see us there, won't you?"

"Why, sure I will. I've got to make a run now, but by the time I get back, you two ought to be all settled in."

The two men sat there talking, and finally Allyn came back. "Hello, Jason," she said as she put her hand out. He arose and took it. "It's good to see you again."

He did not remark on their last meeting; he had been somewhat ashamed of himself. "Good to see you, too, Allyn. Your father has just been telling me about your new home. I know you'll be happy there."

"Thank you." The words were spare and rather short, but Jason paid no heed to that. He looked down at the cards on the table and smiled. "You two are a pretty good match, I would guess. How about a three-handed poker game?"

"Fine," Mark cried, "sit down. I need to take some of that cash away that you've been stacking up."

As they sat down and began to play, they talked amiably, mostly Mark and Jason. Allyn, from time to time, made a comment. When Susanna came out and saw them, she said, "Well, looks like I've got a gambling parlor started on my front porch. You suppose I could play, too?"

"Why, you don't know how to play cards, Susanna. You never could," Mark said with a grin. "If you ever got in a game, I'd win this place from you."

"You probably would," Susanna agreed, smiling, "so I'd better not play. Jason, you'll stay for supper and stay the night, won't you?"

"Well, I have to sail in the morning, have to be back to the ship—"

"Why, a young fellow like you doesn't mind an early morning ride!" Mark said quickly. "I wish you'd stay."

Jason glanced at Mark and saw the desire there in the older man's eyes. "If you can put up with me, I will."

"Good, I'll go tell Dorrie to kill another chicken," Susanna said.

The three began to play again. It was a pleasant morning,

but Mark grew tired quickly and went to bed. Jason spent most of the day riding over the fields. He had never had a home like this, having grown up roughly, but the sight of the rolling hills and the scents of summer, the odors of earth, the clouds rolling overhead—all of it pleased him. He paused on a ridge and looked down on the valley where the fields were ripening and said, "A man has this, he has everything. Makes a ship look pretty lonesome."

He was not a man to think of himself much. He was a man, basically, who demanded action. For that reason the sea satisfied him, for it was a hard, demanding type of life. He had learned his trade well. Now, however, as he rode the sleek black horse he had taken from the stable at a swift gallop down toward Gracefield, he thought, *Maybe someday, when I get too old to captain a ship, I can have a place like this.*

He dismounted, and when the slave stripped the saddle off, he gave him a coin, saying, "Rub him down, will you? He's a good horse." Then he turned and went across the yard, entered the house, and went at once to his room, where he lay down for a while—an unusual thing for him. Later he arose and found Mark awake and feeling well enough to come down to the supper table.

Jason had a good supper that night—fresh sweet potatoes, thin slices of Virginia ham, new potatoes, and carrots. "The best meal I've had in a long time," he said to Dorrie, who had come outside. "Why don't you leave this place and come and cook for me on board the *Eagle*?" he said. "I'll treat you better than these folks do."

Dorrie, who had learned his ways already, smiled at him. "You hush now, Mistuh Jason! You know I ain't gonna get on no old boat!"

"Well, I'll bring you a present next time I come, Dorrie. Pick you out the best silk petticoat I can find."

Dorrie glared at him then sniffed, saying, "I ain't studying no petticoats!" and turned around and walked off, her chin in the air.

"Don't make the cook mad!" Mark laughed.

"Don't worry. I think I know women well enough to know she'll take that red petticoat, if I can find one."

"I didn't think you hauled petticoats much through the blockade," Susanna remarked. "I thought it was all medicine and ammunitions."

"Mostly it is, but I always bring back a few small things. Anything you'd like? French perfume? Something like that, Susanna?"

"Oh, what would I do with French perfume?" she scoffed. "You might bring some for Allyn and Rena, though."

"Oh yes, Captain Larrimore," Rena said eagerly. "Bring me some of that!"

"Don't be a beggar!" Susanna said sharply. "You know better, Rena Rocklin."

"Well, you suggested it, didn't you?" Rena said innocently. "And I bet Allyn would like some, too, wouldn't you, Allyn?"

"I'm sure the captain has lots of demands more pressing than French perfume."

"Why, not at all." Larrimore smiled at Allyn. "After all, a bottle doesn't take much room. Of course, you never know what we'll find, but I'll see what I can do."

Later in the evening, after a short game of cards that Rena joined in with much merriment, Mark went to bed early. It was Larrimore who said, "I think I'll take a stroll around." He glanced at Rena and Allyn and inquired, "Why don't you two young ladies come with me?"

"All right, we will. Come on, Allyn," Rena urged. "I'll show you the new foal down at the barn."

It was still early enough for light to cover the scene as the three of them walked along. Rena chattered on about the virtues of the new foal. She brought the animal out, and it was duly admired by Allyn and Larrimore. Finally, Rena said, "I've got to go down to the summerhouse. Why don't you come with me?"

"Not for me," Allyn said quickly. "Captain Larrimore may want to go."

"No, I guess I'd better turn in early. I've got to leave before dawn. I'll walk you back to the house, Allyn."

The two of them turned and made their way back to the Big House. Allyn again felt the strange discomfort this man always brought to her. Perhaps it was because he had seen her in the saloon. *I wonder if he thinks of me as a cheap saloon girl*, was the thought that came to her. It was difficult to tell what Larrimore thought, for he masked his feelings carefully.

They talked idly about the foal; then as they approached the house, Larrimore said, "I want to talk to you a minute."

Allyn turned in surprise. "Yes, what is it?"

Jason Larrimore was better at commanding a ship than he was at talking to young ladies about serious matters. He had thought much about what he wanted to say, but now as she looked up at him, he found it difficult to put into words. Her face seemed carved out of old ivory in the fading light. Her eyes were large and luminous. Once again he was acutely conscious of how attractive she was, and this disturbed him. "I don't know how to say this. . . ." He hesitated. "Don't take it wrong."

Allyn looked at him, wondering at his meaning. "Take it wrong? What is it?"

"Well, I've thought a lot about you and your father. I guess I think as much of Mark Rocklin as I've ever thought of any man. I'd hate to see him get hurt."

"And you think I'll hurt him, is that it?"

Jason hesitated. "I don't think you'd do so intentionally, but have you thought about what's going to happen if you let him buy Twelve Trees, then you decide to leave?"

Allyn had indeed thought of this, and it had troubled her. She had persuaded herself that it was the best thing to do. But now his words stirred the earlier anxieties in her. She grew faintly irritated, for he had touched on the very thing that had troubled her, and she was aggravated to find that he was wise enough to see what was in her. "I don't think that that's any of your business, Captain."

Jason grew angry suddenly. "Yes, it's my business, all right. Anytime a bad thing happens to a friend of mine, it's my business." Jason saw that he had shaken and angered her. "I'm sorry to talk to you like this, but right now it wouldn't be much trouble for you to pull out. If you don't mean to stay with him, I think you ought to."

"It's easy for you to make that decision, isn't it? You've never had to do without anything," she snapped. The anger, which she recognized as irrational, rose in her, and she said, "I don't need any help from you to make decisions, Captain Larrimore!" She turned to go, but he grabbed her by the arm.

Now he was angry and said, "Why don't you go back to New Orleans and deal blackjack?" As soon as he had said it, he let go of her arm, and he could have bitten his tongue off. But now he could only say, "Wait—I didn't mean to say that."

"Yes, I think you did," she said. "Let me tell you this. He owes me something."

Larrimore stared down at her. She looked rather small and fragile in the gathering darkness. He wanted to reach out and shake her, but she looked up at him with an indomitable look in her large eyes. "And you're going to collect. Is that it?"

"Yes, I'm going to collect! There's no reason why I shouldn't."

Larrimore knew that he had failed and cursed himself for approaching the matter at all, certainly as awkwardly as he had. But he was still angry with her and snapped, "Well, I've got to go run the blockade and get rich." He stared down at her again. He reached out, took her by the arms, and said, "I'm as selfish as you are."

Allyn opened her mouth to argue with him, but before she could, he pulled her close against him. He was very strong, and though she struggled, it was hopeless. She found herself pressed against his body, and then his lips covered hers. She could not move away for one moment. He was so strong that she was like a child in his grasp.

And then, despite herself, despite the anger and rage that rose in her at his touch, something in his embrace touched some well deep down in her that she had not known existed. His lips were firm on hers—hard and demanding, and she found herself surrendering to his embrace. She had spent so much time fighting men off, and now this man, with all of his exuberance and love of life, held her tightly. She felt his strength and power, and perhaps it was all of the years she had spent fighting her own fights that suddenly caused her to crumble. She surrendered to his embrace and added a pressure of her lips to his. The moment flowed on, and then she realized that he had stepped back.

"Well," he said slowly, "I guess that was a good-bye kiss."

Jason Larrimore had known many women and had kissed many,

but somehow this young woman had stirred him as no other ever had. He had kissed her in anger to show her his contempt, but somehow as their lips had met and he had felt her stiff defenses surrender, something had changed in him. But he could not speak the words, could not say what he felt. He saw her looking at him with something he could not define in her eyes and said, "I guess we're just two selfish people. Good night, Allyn." He turned and walked into the house.

Allyn went slowly after him. She went to her room, donned a nightgown, and found that her hands were trembling as she prepared for bed. Finally, she stood at the window and looked out at the darkness. The swifts were darting—black aerial acrobats, making arabesque patterns on the night sky. Slowly she reached up with one hand and touched her lips, remembering his kiss. The moment came back to her and she whispered, "What was I thinking of? What was in me to let me give in to him like that?"

But no answer came. As she lay awake that night, her thoughts centered on Captain Jason Larrimore.

Chapter 11

A Visitor for Colonel Rocklin

Robert Simms was a cabdriver who made most of his money by being able to spot good fares. He had decided long ago that the best possibilities were Yankees, and even though he himself was a rabid secessionist and had lived in Richmond all his life, still he had a living to make. "This Confederate money," he had complained to his wife, "ain't worth nothing. Takes a wagonload of the blasted stuff to buy a sackful of groceries!"

He spotted at once the well-dressed woman who stepped down off the car pulled by the ancient wood-burning engine and beat out two other cabbies by stepping forward and saying, "Yes, ma'am! Give you a hand with your baggage, ma'am?"

Melanie Rocklin was weary from her long journey from Washington. It had been a difficult task persuading her children that she had to go do what she could for Gideon. They had all protested that she had no business going to Richmond, but in the end she had simply ignored them and gotten on the train, leaving them notes saying she would be back when Gideon was exchanged or the war was over. "Yes," she said, "I have a small trunk also—that one right over there, the black one. Would you please get that for me?"

"Yes, ma'am." Robert grabbed the bags with alacrity and led her away with the small trunk over one shoulder and her valise in his other hand. All the way to the carriage he chattered, talking about the weather, the war, and what was wrong with the way things were going in the world. When he reached the carriage, he plumped the trunk down soundly with a thud that made Melanie blink her eyes, tossed the bag in beside it, and then turned to her. "Let me help you in this carriage, ma'am."

"Thank you, Robert." She had gotten his name as they walked to the carriage and now accepted his aid. As she settled into the seat, her body was racked with fatigue. *I'm not as young as I used to be,* she thought wryly. Then when he settled into the seat beside her and cocked his eyebrows, she said, "Take me to the Majestic Hotel."

"Yes, ma'am. Majestic it is!" He spoke to the horse, whose ribs were rather prominent, and the carriage moved out with a jerk. "Hot weather we've been having, but it's good for the crops. I don't reckon you're from around here, ma'am?" he inquired.

Melanie concealed a smile behind her fan, amused by his curiosity. "I used to be," she said. "I grew up here as a girl. My family's name was Benton."

"Benton! Would that be James Benton, ma'am—Major Benton?"

"Yes, that's right. You know him?"

"Oh, well, we ain't personal acquainted, ma'am, you understand, but everybody knowed Major Benton. You been off on a visit, I'd say."

She saw him eyeing her fashionably designed clothes and decided that she may as well tell him the truth. *Be like putting it in the papers,* she thought. "I'm married to one of the Rocklins," she said. "Colonel Gideon Rocklin of the Union army."

A change traced its way across Robert's face, but he concealed it quickly. "Oh yes, ma'am. That's been quite a spell ago that you married Mr. Rocklin. I still see Mr. Clay pretty often."

Melanie listened as he outlined the family history and realized he was a walking newspaper, knowing everything apparently about everybody. When they got to the Majestic, she said, "Let me go in and see if there's a room available. If there is, I'd like for you to unload my baggage for me."

"Yes, Miz Rocklin."

Robert hopped down and helped her from the carriage. Going inside, she inquired at the desk for a room. The clerk looked doubtfully at her and said, "Well, we've got one little room, ma'am, up on the third floor. It's pretty small and nothing fancy."

"That will do very nicely," she said. "I imagine you're pretty crowded."

"Oh yes, ma'am, full to busting out. Would you sign the register?"

Melanie signed the register and saw him read it, and he looked up to say, "Why, Mrs. Rocklin, I remember you. I heard that your husband has been taken prisoner. You come to see about him, did you?"

Melanie saw there was no secrecy or privacy in this world. "Yes, I'll be staying for a while. I'll be wanting to visit him. May I have the key, please?"

Thirty minutes later Melanie was back in the carriage with Robert. She had had him wait while she washed her face, refreshed herself, and changed clothes. Now she had settled herself back, saying, "Take me to Libby Prison, Robert."

"Yes, ma'am, shore will. Is that where they got the colonel, ma'am?"

"Yes, it is."

Robert kept up his customary rapid-fire conversation all the way to Libby, and when they arrived in front of the large, three-story brick building, he leaped out to help her down. "Shall I wait for you, ma'am?" he asked.

"If you don't mind, Robert. I don't think I'll be too long this first visit."

"Sure, I'll be right here, ma'am. You just bet on it."

Melanie made her way to the entrance, where she was stopped by the two guards. "I'd like to see Colonel Rocklin," she said.

The guards examined her papers, and she wondered, *Maybe they think I'm a Union spy*. They did indeed give her strange looks but were accustomed to this sort of thing. One of them, who opened the door and let her inside, said, "We often get Yankee visitors coming to see their people, Mrs. Rocklin. Come this way, if you will."

Melanie followed him to the third floor and was appalled at the odor that struck her when he opened the door. It was fetid and nauseated her. There was no privacy whatsoever, she saw, just one large, open room with men sitting on the floor or lying down on old blankets. None of the prisoners were near the windows, which Melanie learned later was to avoid the risk of being shot at by the guards.

"Right this way, Mrs. Rocklin."

Melanie followed the guard to a corner of the room and at once saw that the man lying on the cot was her husband. Stepping forward, she said, "Gideon. . . ?"

Gideon's eyes flew open, and he batted them blindly for a few moments. Carefully he swung his feet over, rubbed at his eyes, then looked at the woman who had knelt beside him.

"Melanie!" he whispered incredulously. He put his arms out, and she came to him, holding him fiercely.

"Oh, Gid! My dear!" she whispered. He was so thin, and she held him to her breast as a mother would hold a child. For a long time she could do nothing but fight back the tears that sprang to her eyes. Finally, she drew back and said, "I'm so glad to see you!"

Gid could scarcely believe it and said so. "I thought maybe," he said with a warm smile, "that I'd died and woke up in heaven. You look like an angel to me." He looked down and said, "I guess I look pretty bad."

She reached out and pushed a lock of his hair back from his face. It was lank and greasy. She knew how he liked to be clean and neat and always kept his hair washed better than any man she ever knew. An immense pity welled up in her, but she put a cheerful note in her voice and said, "I've come down to take care of you! I'll get to boss you like I've always wanted to."

Gideon smiled one of the few smiles since his imprisonment. "Well, I've got lots of bosses," he said. He looked at her, took in the smooth cast of her features, the wide eyes, and shook his head. "Mercy, you look good to me! How I've missed you, sweetheart!"

She reached out and held his hand, noticing how thin it was. "How are you?" she asked quietly.

"Oh, pretty well." He tried to appear jaunty. "Clay and Melora have been coming down and babying me pretty often. Rena and Rooney Smith, too. They bring groceries in here by the wagonload, it seems." He waved his hand around, saying, "Of course, I can't eat before all these fellows, poor devils. So I share it with them. They've made this ward kind of their mission field, I guess."

"Well, I'll just have to join their ranks," Melanie said. "Now how do you feel, Gid? How's the wound?"

"Oh, pretty well. Still a little infection, but I don't get the fever so much now as I did. That was what was so bad. I wouldn't be surprised if it wasn't a slight case of the smallpox, as it pops up here from time to time, I'm told. Left me weak as a kitten." He shook his head, saying, "I don't want to talk about that. Tell me everything. How are the boys? Where are they?"

For the next forty-five minutes she sat there, straining to remember everything as he drank in her words hungrily. Finally, she said, "I have to go now, Gid. I need to write to the children—they're worried to death about you. I'll come back first thing in the morning and bring you something you'll really like."

"Just bring yourself. You're what I want most of all."

His broad face seemed very thin, and his eyes were sunk back in his head farther than she would have liked. She leaned forward, held him again, kissed him firmly on the lips, and whispered, "I'll be back first thing in the morning."

She stood up, left the prison, and discovered, when she got outside, that she was shaking. Robert at once saw her troubled face and said, "Well now, Miz Rocklin, let me help you back." He helped her in the carriage, got in, and sat beside her and spoke to the horses. Despite his garrulous manner, he was a kindhearted man. He knew a little something of the awful conditions that prevailed in the prison and, like most decent men, was unhappy about it. Finally, he said, "Not a very nice place, ma'am. It's all we can do in the Confederacy here to feed ourselves. We have to stretch it mighty thin to feed all these prisoners that we've took. Wish it was better."

"Thank you, Robert," Melanie said. "Nice of you to say that.

I suppose we have prisons in the North just as bad. Just another horror of war, isn't it?"

"Yes, ma'am." He drove along silently for a few moments then said, "Would you like to go back to the hotel now?"

"If you don't mind, Robert, could you go shopping with me? I want to find some nice things for the colonel, some food and maybe some fresh underwear and socks and clothes. I don't know Richmond anymore. Perhaps you could help me."

"Why, I'd be plumb glad to, Miz Rocklin," Robert agreed at once. "Just come right along with me now, and we'll get that man of yours fixed up like a Boston lawyer!"

Melanie moved among the stores and shops of Richmond, noticing how eagerly they snatched at the gold pieces she had brought from the North. She was forced to take Confederate money in exchange, knowing that it would be worth very little. Still, she had to have things for Gideon. Finally, she got in the carriage, and Robert drove her back to the hotel. He helped her out, and when she asked the price, he hesitated then named a figure.

"Oh, it was worth much more than that!" She smiled and gave him an even larger amount. "I'll be wanting to take these things to the colonel in the morning early, if you'd care to come by. As a matter of fact, I'll be going every morning. Maybe we could work out a regular thing. You could go and leave me, then pick me up later."

"That'd be fine, Miz Rocklin," Robert said quickly. "I'll be glad to do it." He bowed to her and, when he went back outside, said to one of his fellow cabdrivers, "Wal, Ed, I hate Yankees, but that Miz Gideon Rocklin, now she's a real lady!" Then as if ashamed of showing such tender sentiments, he added quickly, "'Course—she's a good Southern girl to begin with, which accounts for it."

Melanie went to her room, which was indeed small. There was only one battered table inside, but it did for a nightstand and for a place to write. Sitting down, she quickly began to write to the children, telling them her news. When the letters were finished, she took them out and mailed them. Then as she walked back to her hotel, she thought, *I've got to get word to Susanna and Clay. They'll be able to tell me more about Gideon than anybody else.* She went back to the hotel room and for a long time sat on the single chair beside her bed reading her Bible. Finally, she closed it and said, "Oh God, You will have to help us with this. It's too much for me!"

"Why, this is terrible!" Noel looked across at Deborah, who had opened the letter. He had come straight to the house and found Deborah, and when she had come down, he'd given her the envelope. She had seen it was from Melanie and had torn it open and read it rapidly.

After her exclamation, she got up and began to pace the floor. She was a forthright girl, active and ever ready for any task at hand.

"What does it say? Is the colonel all right?" Noel asked anxiously.

"No, he's not all right! Here—read for yourself." Deborah thrust the single sheet of paper at Noel and, as he scanned it, continued to pace the floor. She twisted her hands, and when he'd finished she said, "There, you see? He's sick and wounded and likely to die in that place!"

"Well, maybe it's not that bad."

"You know it is! We hear all the time about our men dying

in Confederate prisons. Noel, we've got to *do* something."

"Do what?" Noel asked in surprise. "Mrs. Rocklin's down there to take care of him. We couldn't do anything anyway."

Deborah looked at him, her eyes flashing. "Well, we've got to do *something*!"

Noel watched her carefully. He was accustomed to her ways and well knew there was no way in the world to stop her in her headlong rush. Once an idea possessed her, everything had to give way before her. He thought for a while then finally said, "Why don't we go down to the War Department and find out who it is that takes care of prisoner exchanges? Maybe we can put pressure on him somehow or other."

At once Deborah halted. She turned to him, her eyes sparkling, and came over to give him a hug. "Oh, Noel, that's a wonderful idea! And I'll tell you what," she continued. "If he won't do it, you can tell him you're going to write a series of articles exposing what a worthless thing he is!"

"Why, I can't do that!" Noel said in alarm. "We don't know the first thing about this man."

"I know it, but you know how bureaucrats are. We just have to do something to get them moving. Come on, Noel—let's go right now!"

"All right," Noel said with resignation. He led the way out of the house. All the way to the War Department as they rode along in the carriage, Deborah talked excitedly about how they could get some action.

When they got to the War Department, as Noel expected, they found it difficult to see anyone with any authority. They spent quite some time talking to a pompous captain who leaned back and assured them that nothing could be done that wasn't being done. "Why, my dear young friends," he said expansively, "you can't appreciate the magnitude of this task of working out exchanges." He had a full set of whiskers that wiggled when he talked and a set of small eyes that were almost hidden in the fat of his face. "It's a terrible task, I assure you, to work these things out. Those of us here in the exchange department work late into the night when you folks are all asleep. Why, it's worse than combat!"

"You've been in combat, have you?" Noel demanded, angered by the man's manner.

"Ah, well—no. That is to say—"

"Then how do you know this is worse?" Deborah demanded.

Angered by their attitudes, the officer said haughtily, "I'm sorry, but I have no time for you. You'll have to wait and go through the regular channels."

Deborah stared at him. "Well, that's it. We'll just have to go see the president."

The fat officer laughed at them. "Yes, you just go see the president," he said. Obviously he'd had this sort of threat before and said, "I'm sure he's just *waiting* for you to come up and tell him how to run the War Department. Good day!"

Noel had to pull Deborah aside. She wanted to continue the argument, but he simply dragged her outside. When they were out of his office, Noel said, "You can't argue with a man like that. He's not in charge, anyway."

"Well, why don't we go see the president?"

Noel was aghast. "Why, Deborah, we can't do that. That poor man is burdened down with a thousand...a million details. He wouldn't have time for us."

"I'll bet he would," Deborah said defiantly. She lifted her chin and said, "Come on, we're going to his office."

Noel suddenly laughed. "You are *something*, Deborah Steele!

Going to see the president!"

"Well, are you coming or not?"

"I'll come," Noel said, "but it'll be a waste of time."

So it proved to be. The president was out of town and would not be back for over a week. The secretary was kind when Noel explained their mission and said, "I'm sure the president would like to do something for you. He's a good friend, of course, of Mr. Stephen Rocklin. Perhaps I could put this in a note, and he could look at it and get in touch with you when he gets back or have one of us do it. Would that be all right?"

"We'd appreciate that so much," Deborah said. They turned and left the office, and her shoulders sagged. "Well, if he were here, I bet he'd do something about it."

"I don't know. He does the best he can," Noel said.

They moved on back to the carriage and drove away. As they drove along, Deborah said, "I can't stand the thought of it—Uncle Gid being in prison."

Noel shook his head. "Me, too, Deborah, but I'm glad he's alive. He could have been killed—but those prisons are awful places. I guess all we can do is pray."

Deborah was silent for a long time. Finally, she looked at him and said, "We're going to have to do more than pray. Noel, you're smart, and I'm smart, too. When two smart people like us get together and we ask God to help us, we can't fail, can we?"

"Fail at what?" He stared at her with a puzzled light in his eyes.

"Can't fail to get Uncle Gid out of that old jail," she said. Then, reaching over, she grasped his arm and squeezed it hard. "We've got to do it somehow. So start praying!"

Noel Kojak knew better than to argue with this girl. He loved her with all of his heart and realized if they ever married, she would run him half crazy—but that didn't seem to matter. Looking at her, he said, "You know, it's quite an education being around you, Deborah Steele. A fellow learns all sorts of things."

"Things like what?" she asked suddenly.

"Why, things like how to mind when you crack the whip." He grinned. Then, seeing anger come into her eyes, he said, "Now wait a minute. I *like* it. So if you command me to pray, so help me, I'll pray." Then he got serious and said, "And I will think on it. There's got to be something we can do."

"Will you, Noel?" She leaned forward and kissed him, oblivious to the people who had caught sight of her, and laughed. "That's like you. Come on now. Let's go home, and we'll sit down and write down every possibility!"

Part Three
The Bridegroom

Chapter 12
Death of a Ship

At the very beginning of hostilities, General Winfield Scott, commander of the Northern armed forces, had proposed what he called the "Anaconda Plan." Basically, this plan as implemented had two parts. The first was to gain control of the Mississippi River, thus cutting the Confederacy in two. The second was to blockade all the Southern coasts, cutting off all supplies from Europe. McClellan and others scoffed at this plan, saying it was too slow; however, after Little Mac had a taste of Robert E. Lee and the Army of Northern Virginia, the military had quickly learned that there was no quick and easy solution to the rebellion. Scott's plan, therefore, slowly became *the* plan by which the Union attempted to win the war. In July 1863, Vicksburg fell, which opened the Mississippi River to Federal control, splitting the Confederacy in half and barring shipments of goods from west of the river eastward.

The attempts at blockade went more slowly. At the beginning of the war, the North had a very small navy. Soon, however, shipyards were turning out ironclads and ships of all descriptions to throw a ring of iron around the Southern coast. Such a thing was not easy, for there were hundreds of harbors stretching all the way from New Orleans, at the mouth of the Mississippi, around Florida and along the eastern coast of the country.

One of these, Fort Sumter, at Charleston, where the war had begun, was the scene of a furious assault in August of 1863. Major General Quincy A. Gillmore was assigned the task of subduing the major seaport of the Confederacy. This involved seizing Battery Wagner near the northern tip of Morris Island, which was defended by twelve hundred Confederate troops and several heavy guns. Gillmore was overconfident and, hoping to gain a quick strike with only two and a half regiments, advanced on the battery. He suffered a terrible defeat, the Seventh Connecticut Infantry losing 108 out of 196 men, while the Confederacy suffered only twelve casualties. Sobered by this defeat, the North began to throw added weight into the struggle, bringing the total to six thousand infantry. Though they tried hard, it was only after a long struggle that Battery Wagner was taken. Charleston, South Carolina, was all but lost as a Southern port. The Union dead, many hideously mutilated, littered the beach in front of Wagner. One Charleston journalist wrote that "probably no battlefield in the country has ever presented such an array of mangled bodies in a small compass."

Charleston had been the home port of Jason Larrimore, but with the attention the Federals were paying to the batteries at the mouth of the harbor, he avoided that city and chose a small, hidden harbor north of Charleston. He had run the blockade twice and had come back to unload his small ship into wagons, which he sent into both Charleston and Richmond. He arrived at the small town that marked the harbor and went at once to where the *Eagle* was anchored in a natural lagoon. He had been fortunate to find it, for the fingers that formed the lagoon were covered with palmetto trees that shielded the harbor from the eyes of lookouts on Federal gunboats. Dismounting from his carriage and walking out to the small wharf, he saw his first officer, Malcolm Davis, on deck. He quickly crossed the gangplank, stepped on board, and shook hands, saying, "Hello, Malcolm. Things going well?"

Davis, a short, muscular man with reddish hair, had been an officer in the United States Navy but had resigned his commission, enjoying the freelance fighting for his home state of South Carolina and the Confederacy. He was the best sailor Jason had ever seen and kept the *Eagle* as clean as a woman's kitchen. "Aye, sir, ready to go whenever you give the word." He gave a cautious look to the sky and said, "Going to have cloudy weather for the next night or two, I think. If you're ready, I think we ought to go tonight."

"I've got some supplies coming that we can sell on our trip over," Jason said. "As soon as they come, we'll load them and get under way."

He was glad to get back to the ship and spent the next two days anxiously awaiting the supplies. When they finally came and were loaded, he said, "I believe we'll go out at midnight, Malcolm. What do you think?"

The red-haired seaman chewed his lower lip nervously. "Our cloud cover was gone last night and probably won't be back tonight. The moon's a little bit full for my liking."

"Well, we'll chance it. I think we can outrun anything we're likely to meet." Jason smiled and clapped the shorter man on the shoulder. "The *Eagle*'s never been caught yet, has she?"

"No, that's right, but God's been with us so far."

"You always put everything at God's front door, don't you, Malcolm?" Jason smiled as he said this. He himself was not a believer, but he had come to respect Davis's religion. On shore or on board the *Eagle*, the first officer was always the same, a hardworking, hard-driving man, but with a total commitment to the scripture and to God.

"We're not alone, Jason," Davis said. "You'll find that out someday."

Davis had never attempted to force his belief on Larrimore, but there was something in his straight, direct gaze that caused the captain to fidget. "I hope you're right," he said. "I've seen a lot of hypocrites in my time, but I've seen enough of the real thing to know that there's something there that I'm missing." Quickly he said, "Well, get everything ready. We want to make a quick run. We ought to make a bundle this time. The Confederacy's starving to death. We could bring back a load of nothing but coffee and get rich off it." And then he smiled and said, "But I know you. You want to bring back shot and shell, something to win the war with."

"That's what I'd like," Davis said, "but we'll have to take what we can get." Davis was an ardent patriot, firmly believing in the rightness of his cause, and there was no hesitation as he said, "God will be with us."

At midnight, Jason stood at the wheel of the *Eagle*. The weather was clear, but there was a brisk breeze for which he was thankful. As the crew maneuvered the sails, he held the wheel firm in his hands, guiding the ship expertly through the narrow channel. As he kept his eye on the shoals, he thought of all the tricks and ploys that had been used by the North to stop the blockade-runners. In England, a reward of thirty pounds was offered to anyone who could supply reliable information concerning vessels leaving for blockaded ports. When the North learned that blockade-running ships used anthracite coal because it burned without smoke, all shipments of this fuel to foreign ports were banned. When the runners discovered that Federal ships were waiting to seize them, they learned to go to intermediary ports, such as Nassau and Bermuda, sometimes transferring their cargo to smaller crafts that could be sneaked into ports along the Southern coast.

As the sails caught the full breeze and the *Eagle* passed out into the open sea, Jason felt the ship tremble beneath his feet. There was always something miraculous about this to him, how the dead tons of wood lying in the water, almost like a log, suddenly came alive as the sails filled and the power of the wind lifted the ship out of the water and sent it flying along the surface. The wind blew through his hair, and he took a deep breath, inhaling the salt fragrance of the sea. The only sounds as they skimmed along were the hissing of the water along the sides of the ship and the harsh guttural cries of the seagulls that followed, as always, hoping for a free meal.

"Going to be a good trip," he said aloud, his eyes already scanning the horizon, searching for those tiny dots or wisps of smoke that could mean disaster or even death. He was happy to be back at sea, as he always was. The land to him seemed to be a prison at times, and only when he stood on the deck of a ship and looked around at the limitless sea that surrounded him did he feel free.

He stood at the wheel for four hours; then Davis came and relieved him. "Not a sign of an ironclad," Jason murmured as he stepped back, giving the wheel to the first officer. "Maybe this will be one of those good ones that will be like a cruise on a ferryboat. I hope so."

"I've prayed to that intent," Davis said, nodding.

His simple words caught at Larrimore. He stood there moving instinctively to the roll of the ship and thought about what the shorter man had said. "How do you make it all line up, Malcolm?" he asked.

"Make it all line up? What do you mean by that, sir?"

"I mean, when you pray for something and don't get it. Doesn't that discourage you?"

"Why, not a bit." The ship gave suddenly under their feet, pitched down into a trough, then rose again like a bird. Davis planted his feet, held the wheel firmly, and commented, "We may run into a bit of weather—getting into some swells already." He had not forgotten the question, however, for he turned and gave his companion a steady look. "When you were growing up and you asked your parents for something, they said no sometimes, didn't they?"

"I guess they did."

"Why do you suppose they did that?"

Jason thought for a moment and said, "Sometimes they said no because they couldn't provide what I wanted, what I'd asked for."

"Aye, but that's never true with God, is it? He owns everything there is. His hand is not shortened. There's not a thing a man's mind could think of that God couldn't provide—if He wanted to."

"I suppose that's so. But still, you don't get everything you pray for, do you?"

Davis shook his head. "I'm afraid not, but if you'll stop and think, there were other reasons why your parents didn't give you everything. If you were like most boys—like I was, for instance—you wanted some things that wouldn't have been good for you. I always loved firearms, and I asked my father for a gun when I was ten years old. Do you think he gave it to me? Not likely! I'd have probably blown my head off with it. So you see, sometimes we ask for things, and God says no because He knows we're not ready for them."

Jason nodded. "I can see that, but I heard a preacher once in Montgomery—I don't know the verse or where the verse is found—but he preached for two hours on the subject 'Ask for whatever you want, and if you believe, you'll get it.'"

"Oh yes, that's in the twenty-first chapter of Matthew, verses 21 and 22." He narrowed his eyes, thought for a moment, then quoted the scripture, "'Jesus answered and said unto them, Verily I say unto you, If ye have faith, and doubt not, ye shall not only do this which is done to the fig tree, but also if ye shall say unto this mountain, Be thou removed, and be thou cast into the sea; it shall be done. And all things, whatsoever ye shall ask in prayer, believing, ye shall receive.'"

Jason stared at him with unconcealed admiration. "You must have the whole Bible memorized, Malcolm. You're just a walking concordance."

"Oh no, I wish that were true, but it's not."

Jason looked across the waters and thought he saw the first pale breaking of dawn. But he was not through yet with his questioning. "But what about when you ask and don't get what you ask for? That verse just says you'll get it. Doesn't that prove the Bible is wrong?"

Malcolm said quickly, "No, the Bible is God's Word. Sometimes it *seems* to be wrong, but it never is. What's wrong is our understanding of it. For example, many of us have struggled with the thing you have just mentioned. God seems to promise we'll get what we ask for. Sometimes we ask, but we don't get it—what does that mean?" He gave a quick glance at his friend and said, "Why, it means we have misunderstood the scripture."

"How have I misunderstood this one? It seems clear enough

to me. 'Whatsoever ye shall ask, ye shall receive.'"

"Well, here is the truth of this doctrine, as I see it. When Jesus was about to be crucified, the last time He met with His disciples, He spoke of this very thing again. This is in the sixteenth chapter of John, verses 23 and 24, I believe. He said, 'Verily, verily, I say unto you, Whatsoever ye shall ask the Father in my name, he will give it you. Hitherto have ye asked nothing in my name: ask, and ye shall receive, that your joy may be full.'"

"Why, that sounds like about the same thing to me as the other verse."

"Only one thing is different. Jesus said we have to ask in His name."

"Well, people do that, don't they? Usually people end their prayer by saying, 'I ask this in the name of Jesus.'"

"Oh, that's what we do, all right. But I think the Lord Jesus meant much more than putting a little tag on prayer asking for whatever we wanted. I think when He said, 'Ask in my name,' He was really saying, 'Ask for the sort of thing that I Myself would ask for.' Do you see the difference?"

"I suppose so, but it's a pretty fine distinction."

"Perhaps, but not when you think of it, Jason. Look, there are two reasons for men to ask things of God. One of them is selfish, and one of them is unselfish. If, for instance, I want to get a lot of money so that I can spend it on myself, that's selfish. Was that the sort of thing Jesus would do? Of course not. He said, 'I do always those things that please him,' meaning the Father. I think there is a point in a person's life when prayers become unselfish and we pray for things that would bring the kingdom of God to this earth in our own hearts. So that's the way I try to pray now."

Jason frowned and said, "I'm afraid I don't get it, Malcolm.

Aren't we supposed to ask for what we need?"

Malcolm nodded at once. "Yes, what we *need*. But our needs are very simple. It's our *wants* that get us into trouble. That's why I don't pray for things until I've decided they're in the will of God. If I want a house, I wait until God tells me it's His will for me to have that house. Then I pray for it, and I always get it. Don't be too quick with your praying." He grinned suddenly. "You might get what you ask for, and that might be the worst thing in the world for you."

Jason studied the face of the small, short, blocky man and wondered, not for the first time, how such a tough, hard-driving character could be such a devoted Christian. Finally, he shook his head and said, "I guess my head is too thick for such things, Malcolm. I'll never get it."

Malcolm reached out and put his hand on his captain's shoulder. "It's not your head that's the problem. Not with you, Jason. It's the heart. One day, the Lord Jesus will come knocking at the door of your heart. You'll know it's Him, and you'll have to decide who's going to be boss, Jason Larrimore or Jesus Christ." He took his hand away quickly and shook his head. "Didn't mean to preach, but I would dearly love to see you find God, Jason."

Jason turned and left, somewhat embarrassed by the encounter. He had had many talks like this with his first officer, and always, when they were over, the subject seemed to get stuck in his head and he could not escape it.

Dawn was approaching rapidly, and he began to walk around the deck, cautioning the hands from time to time, "Keep a sharp eye out. We may be encountering gunboats pretty soon." As the ship glided over the water, he went to the rail, put his elbows on it, and scanned the sky. Small areas of pale blotches appeared in the east, and he kept his eyes constantly in motion. At the same time, he remembered Allyn Rocklin. The memory came to him of their last meeting. He was disturbed and shook his shoulders restlessly as he thought of how her kiss had affected him. He did not like to be thrown off balance, being a self-sufficient man, and the thought of how the touch of her body against him and the firmness of her soft lips under his had shaken and bothered him. He pulled his cap down over his forehead with a half-angry gesture. "I'm not a boy to be set on my heels by a woman's kiss!" he muttered angrily.

He quickly shifted position, moving to the other side of the ship. Still, the memory would not leave his mind. He thought over the entire history of his encounters with the girl and thought, *She's not a woman a man could get involved with. She's selfish to the core and will take poor Mark for everything she can get!* The more he thought, the more dissatisfied he became with his part in bringing Allyn to her father. "When I get back," he announced defiantly to the breaking waves that he stared at, "I'm going to talk Mark out of giving her everything. That would be a bad mistake!"

"Captain! Off the port! Federal warships!"

Jason, hearing the lookout's cry, whirled and threw himself around the superstructure. Gazing over the side, he narrowed his eyes. Sure enough, a tiny dot broke the clean edge of the horizon formed by the sea. At once he whirled and called Malcolm. "First Officer, hang every inch of canvas!"

"Aye, sir." Davis had seen the sail as well and gave the orders that sent the hands scurrying up the mast to unfurl every sail available. He came to stand beside Jason and said, "It may be another blockade-runner."

"I don't think so—too big for that, and she's got the wind on us. Look." They stood watching for a time until half an hour later, Jason said, "She's Federal, all right." He put the spyglass down and said, "And a fast one, too."

Davis grinned. "Don't worry, sir. Those Yankees don't have a ship that can catch the *Eagle*."

A premonition swept over Jason Larrimore. He did not believe in such things, yet a feeling such as he had never had came to him. "Wet the canvas down," he said. "It may get us just the speed we need to outrun that ship." Davis gave him an odd glance but at once gave the orders. By wetting the canvas down, the sails held the wind a little better. For the next hour they maintained this tactic, constantly dousing the sails.

Finally, Davis came to stand beside the captain and said apprehensively, "You're right—she's a fast one, Captain, and she's got a bead on us."

"I think once we get clear of Pirates' Reef we'll be all right." He spoke of a range of the coast that had become a graveyard of many ships. It was a treacherous spot of water luring unwary captains into what seemed to be deep water, only to rip the bottoms out of ships.

Jason and Malcolm stood tensely behind the wheel, watching the enemy ship. Malcolm commented once, "That's only a cutter. Maybe we can put her out with the three-pounder."

"Give it a try, Malcolm," Jason said. "If you manage to dismast her, we could walk away and leave her."

At once Davis was yelling orders at the crew, who gathered around the small three-pound rifled cannon that was the single armament of the *Eagle*. Davis and the captain had had long discussions about how much armament to carry, and finally Jason had said, "We can never carry enough to fight off an ironclad. We'll rely on speed, which means getting rid of all the extra weight." Davis had argued and gotten his way in having the three-pounder mounted. It was only a small gun but was capable of piercing the side of a small vessel, such as the one pursuing them.

Soon the small cannon was booming regularly, and small dots of water showed that the shots were falling closer.

"That's it, Lieutenant!" Jason said with excitement. "You've got the range now."

During the next half hour, several hits were observed, but nothing stopped the other ship, which had now begun to answer with her own heavier armament.

A shot whizzed overhead, making a neat hole in the canvas. Larrimore looked up at it with alarm. "They've got our range, too," he said. He looked at the ship and shook his head. "We'll be at the cove in a moment, and she'll have to turn. We can outrun her on a straightaway. So just keep firing that pop gun, Lieutenant."

The enemy ship, a schooner, evidently constructed for chasing just such blockade-runners as the *Eagle*, had to turn, and as soon as she fell into the same parallel as the *Eagle*, it became apparent at once that she was no match in speed for the Southern ship. A cheer went up from the crew, and Davis turned and said, "There, you see. I told you no ship could keep up with the *Eagle*."

Jason grunted. "Keep every sail full. I want to put her out of sight as quick as we can."

For the next hour they watched carefully as the Federal vessel fell behind. Jason finally drew a deep breath and was about

WALL OF FIRE

WALL OF FIRE

to congratulate Davis on his gunnery, but a cry came up from a lookout—"Two sails off starboard!"

Whirling, both Jason and the first officer saw what they most dreaded—two sails in front of them spread out exactly the right distance so they could not hope to dodge them. "Those aren't schooners," Davis said. "They're ironclads."

Jason thought rapidly. "They'll blow us out of the water if we try to dodge between them. We can't fall away because of that fellow behind us." He said sharply, "We'll have to hug the shore. They can't come in close or they'll tear their bottoms out. They draw so much more than the *Eagle*. Hug that shoreline!" he commanded.

Davis rubbed his chin, shook his head. "You know what Pirates' Reef is like," he said. "Seems like there's a devil down there that reaches up and tears the bottoms out of ships."

"I can't help that. It's the only chance we've got." He looked at the two ironclads that were coming steadily onward and said, "They'll take us into port. You and I'll probably land up in prison for the rest of the war. No, we'll make a try at it. Hard aport," he called, and the two men watched nervously as the *Eagle* wheeled over and headed for the shore.

The water hissed along the sides of the ship, and the mast creaked as the sails caught a full wind. "Could tear the sticks out of her," Davis said.

"We don't have any choice, Malcolm. Look, those ironclads are penning us in. They can't come after us, but their guns will be able to reach us if we don't get by in the next few minutes."

Like pieces on a chessboard, the ships maneuvered along the narrow stretch of land. The two ironclads moved steadily to pen the smaller vessel in, while the Federal warship behind them plugged that area of escape. The *Eagle* headed straight for shore, heeling over only at the last minute when Larrimore gave the command. "I'm going forward," he said. "Maybe I can spot the reefs. You stay here and follow the commands."

"Aye, sir."

Larrimore went forward and stood at the very prow of the ship. His practiced eye searched the waters ahead of him, and once he saw a finger of coral reef reaching upward, he turned and yelled, "Hard aport—!" He watched, holding his breath as the *Eagle* heeled over and seemed to brush by the coral. "Straighten her up," he yelled when they were by.

All the time he was keeping his eye on the warships. Then suddenly he heard the booming of cannon. He waited, watching the ocean, and saw the shot send a small geyser of water into the air a hundred yards from the *Eagle*'s starboard. There was nothing he could do. They would just have to stand the fire. Looking ahead, he was hopeful. *If we can just get past that reef, we'll have it made. They can't outrun us, and they can't reach us with their guns. Come on,* Eagle—*let's see you fly!*

The *Eagle* did seem to fly over the water, skimming lightly, and although the shells were falling closer to the ship, there was open water ahead. *I'll be able to turn soon,* he thought and quickly turned and raced back toward the deckhouse. He had reached the deckhouse when the shell struck. It was a single iron ball, but it tore through the wooden frame of the *Eagle*, sending splinters flying, and then struck the mainmast. Already strained with the full sails, the mast broke in two and fell with a creaking, groaning noise, striking the deck with a crash and maiming one man who could not escape.

Jason was not aware of that. The same shot that had parted the mainmast had sent a splinter flying across the tiny wheelhouse, and it struck him high in the back. It drove him to the deck, and a searing pain raked along his side. When he tried to move, he cried out involuntarily. At once Malcolm shouted, "Are you all right, Captain?"

Jason could hardly speak for the pain but said, "Keep going—try to make it! We've got to get away!"

But it was hopeless. With the mainmast down, the two warships were catching up easily.

Malcolm Davis made a decision. "Get the lifeboats out! We've got to get off this ship!" he yelled. He stayed at the wheel while the men swung the two small lifeboats out, then said, "Get the captain into one. He's been hit."

Davis himself stayed at his station until the two lifeboats were well under way. Then he slapped the wheel with a hard fist. "Good-bye, my lady," he said regretfully. "You've been a good ship!" He turned the wheel toward Pirates' Reef, tied it there, and quickly ran and dove off the side. Swimming rapidly, he caught up with the boat that contained the captain and was heaved on board by the crew. He came up just in time to see the *Eagle* strike the reef. It reared upward like a deer that had been shot, then settled back.

"She's gone, sir," he said to Jason, who was being held carefully by one of the seaman. "Now let me have a look at that splinter you took."

As Davis pulled off his shirt, pain raged through Jason Larrimore, but the pain of losing the *Eagle* was far greater than anything that could touch his body.

"There'll never be another one like her," he gasped, and then—as Davis opened his knife and began to cut the splinter out—he passed into a merciful oblivion.

Chapter 13

"Every Woman Needs a Man"

Clay rode into the fields toward Gracefield after having been away for more than a month. The orange pumpkins dotting the fields brought good memories of the pumpkin pies that he had enjoyed in happier days. He was tired to the bone, and the horse he had finally scrounged was even wearier. Men and animals had been worn thin by the Gettysburg campaign, so that when they had reached the relative safety of Richmond, the army seemed to have simply given up. The rest of the summer had been spent regaining the army's strength and planning its next move.

As he rode slowly down the circular driveway that wound in front of the Big House, he saw Melora coming from around the house, and his gloomy mood lifted. Standing up in the stirrups, he lifted his hat and called, "Melora!" then spurred the tired animal into a gallop.

Melora glanced up and, seeing him, raised a hand to her lips. She ran forward to meet him, and when he came off his horse and took her in his arms, she clung to him fiercely. "Clay—Clay!" she whispered huskily. "I'm so glad you're back!"

He held her tightly, savoring the firmness of her body as he kissed her soft lips, then grinned down at her. "Nice to be welcomed home by such a beautiful lady," he said. Then with a glint of humor he added, "You sure look better than anything I've seen lately—of course, all I've seen is hairy-legged, dirty soldiers."

"Oh, *you!*" she laughed. "Come on in the house and tell me everything." Drawing him into the kitchen, she sat him down at the table, saying, "Now I've got a surprise for you." Turning to the pie safe, she opened the door and brought out a pie and set it before him. "Pumpkin pie—your favorite. Now you eat that; then you can tell me everything."

The two sat there, Clay wolfing down the succulent pie in huge bites. He related the details of camp life and assured her that his sons and her brother were getting along fine. When he halted, she told him about Melanie, who had come to do what she could to take care of Gid. He nodded at once. "I'm glad of that. I'd hoped he'd be exchanged, but until then he needs her. What about Mark?"

Melora shook her head. "He's worse, I'm afraid—weaker than ever. He stays in his wheelchair most of the time and is in a great deal of pain."

"What about Allyn? Are they doing better together?"

Melora leaned forward, put her chin in her hands, a thoughtful look in her eyes. "I can't tell, Clay. She's a strange girl. She's built a wall around herself."

"She's had a hard life, I suppose, and this is all strange to her. She hasn't been here all that long, you know, only a couple months."

"That's true. She spends a lot of time with Mark and seems to cheer him up. But the two of them have never really gotten close. Allyn's hard to get close to. I've tried, and so have Rena and Rooney. Lots of the young men in the neighborhood drop by—those that aren't off in the army. She doesn't seem too interested in them, either."

"Well," Clay said, shoving the plate back and taking a long swallow of coffee from a thick mug, "it'll probably be all right. It'll just take some more time."

She leaned over, took his hand in hers, and caressed it, noticing that he had a fresh scar on the back of it. "It'll take time," she said softly. Then she added, "But that's the one thing that Mark doesn't have."

The day after Clay returned, Lowell rode in. Stepping off Midnight, his horse, he made his way up the steps, limping slightly. The artificial leg that he wore was better than he ever thought such a thing could be. As soon as he stepped in the door, he shouted, "Hello! Where is everyone?"

His call brought Susanna and Rooney out of the kitchen. They both ran to him and smothered him so that he cried out, "Hey—wait a minute! You don't want to choke a fellow, do you?" He kissed Susanna lightly on the cheek, saying, "You're still the—" He paused, looked over at Rooney, and winked. "The *second*-best-looking woman I know."

Susanna slapped him playfully on the chest. "Well, you've learned a *little* about women, I'm glad to say. Now you two go for a walk while I finish cooking."

"Oh, I'll help you, Miz Rocklin," Rooney said at once.

"Lowell didn't ride in to watch you work. Now you two go on."

Lowell took Rooney's hand and nodded. "You always listen to your elders, young lady—and since I'm older than you, that means me. Come on now." He led her outside, and the two strolled along the brick walk that led around the house. When they came to the east side of the house, Lowell grinned suddenly. "Come on, I know where we can go." He led her to the scuppernong arbor. The vines completely covered the latticework so that it effectively hid those who stepped inside. An ancient wooden bench was there, and Lowell pulled Rooney down so they were both sitting on it. "Here," he whispered with a grin. "Now I've got you where I want you!"

Rooney started to speak, but he threw his arms around her, drawing her close. She responded by putting her own arms around his neck, pulling his head toward her. She was an emotional girl and held him closely, savoring the touch of his lips on hers. Finally, he pulled his head back and said with a grin, "Well now, that was worth waiting for!"

"Yes, it was," she said demurely.

Lowell grinned at her. "Well, I guess it's time for me to get back to the war!"

He had started to get up, but Rooney pulled him back down vigorously. Rooney's eyes had an elfish light of humor. "Oh no, you don't. Jeb Stuart's seen enough of you. Now it's my turn." With that, she kissed him again.

When their lips parted, Lowell stared at her. He was enjoying the fresh smell of her hair, the light that gladdened her eyes, the smoothness of her skin. He had missed her more than he knew, and as he sat there with his arm around her, he leaned over and whispered, "I feel it's time for us to get married, sweetheart."

Rooney lifted her eyes to his. She reached up, brushed his hair back off his forehead, then said, "Oh, Lowell, that's wonderful!" She paused. "Are you sure that's what you want, Lowell?"

"Of course that's what I *want*. But it may not be best for you." He took her hand, held it, stroked it gently, and said, "I may not come back, you know. You may be a widow—maybe even with a child."

"That's what your father told Melora, but they got married. I guess we can do what they did, can't we?"

"Yes, we can." He kissed her again, holding her longer this time.

She clung to him, enjoying his touch, then finally pulled her head back and said, "I think that's almost enough, don't you?"

"*Never* enough—I'll never get enough of you, Rooney."

Pulling away from him, she stood up, and he saw there was a troubled light in her eyes. Standing quickly, he said, "What is it? Something's wrong."

Rooney shook her head. "Not between us. I love you so much, Lowell, and you're the only man I've ever loved. But—I worry about my mother."

Lowell had thought about Rooney's mother. She was a common woman, and even now was only shortly out of jail and living a dissolute life in Richmond. Lowell disliked her but at the same time felt pity for her. But he knew he had to somehow convince Rooney that he was willing to accept that responsibility. "We'll help her, Rooney," he said quietly. "Perhaps she'd want to come and stay with you for a while."

The kindness of his offer touched Rooney. She knew that her mother would not fit at all in a setting like this. *Ma would never come here—she's too tied to the life she lives,* was her thought. "That's sweet of you," she said. "She'd never come here, but I can go see her and spend more time with her."

"It's settled, then. Let's seal the bargain with a kiss." He did so promptly and cocked one eyebrow. "You know what? This kissing could get to be a habit."

"Yes, I'll have to limit you. I'd say about three a day," she said mischievously.

"Three a day! That's no good for a man in my condition—in love so bad I can hardly walk!" Then he said, "I think the wedding should be late in October. Will that be too soon?"

"No, not too soon." She leaned forward and whispered, "You've already had your three kisses, but I'll give you an advance if you want one."

"I may be gone a long time," he said. "We'd better work our way forward a couple of weeks." Then he took her in his arms again.

❧

Clay and Lowell's presence had brought a new sense of life to Gracefield. The first two days they were there seemed almost like an extended party. Underneath the gaiety, however, lurked the knowledge that they had to rejoin their units. Fear would come like a cold hand to the women, an eerie whispering that these young men—so alive and vital—might lie in shallow graves very soon. They hid these fears, going out of their way to make the time as happy and meaningful as they could. Clay did not speak much of the war, nor did Lowell. It was as if they wished to close that part of their lives and take the few precious hours that they had, storing them up, as it were, against the lean, hard days they knew lay ahead of them.

Clay spoke of this once to Melora as they were walking through the leaves that had already begun to fall. "You know, all over the South—and the North, too, I suppose—men and women are doing just as we are."

"What's that, Clay?" Melora asked quietly.

He didn't answer for a moment. Finally, he took her hand, and they ambled along under the shade of the huge walnut trees that lined the path leading to the small creek. "Oh, trying to forget about the war." A fox squirrel popped up over his head, chattering angrily. Clay picked up a stick and threw it. It missed, but the squirrel disappeared almost magically. They both laughed, and Clay said, "I'd like to have him in a pot with some dumplings!" Then he went back to his original thought. "After a battle, everyone's stunned, I think—especially after Gettysburg. It was as if we couldn't think or move or act. If it hadn't been for the timidity of George Meade, the war would be over. All he had to do was send a big force at us and the Army of Northern Virginia would have been wiped out. It's a good thing that General Grant's commanding in the west! He'd have sent every man he had after us, and we'd have been helpless."

"It was very bad, wasn't it?"

"Very bad. The worst I've ever seen. Pickett's charge up that hill—" Clay shook his head. "I never saw anything like it! It makes you wonder what's in our men. They lined up like soldiers on parade and marched up that hill. When a man in front was shot, another one simply stepped in his place. It was the most devastating musket fire I've ever seen in my life!"

"Was it a mistake, Clay?" Melora asked gently.

"I think it was. It seems like our leaders just can't learn not to march mass troops against troops that are dug in. It happens over and over again. The Yankees took about as bad as we got at Gettysburg when they tried it at Fredericksburg. Our losses at Malvern Hill were about as bad." He shook his head firmly. "We're still fighting European style, and it seems these new weapons have made that style obsolete."

They walked along, the leaves crisp under their feet, losing their brilliant yellow and orange and red. The woods seemed to be full of game, and finally he said, "I'll have to get Josh, and we'll take a gun and clean some of these deer and squirrels out—"

Even as he spoke, Allyn appeared, stepping around the pathway. Clay called, "Allyn!"

Melora looked up and called out, "Hello, Allyn." The two strolled forward to greet her. Melora said, "Come and walk with us."

Allyn was wearing a light green dress that reflected the color of her eyes. Her rich dark red hair caught the gleams of the September sun. She gave them a slight smile and shook her head. "No, I promised Father I'd play chess with him." Then she made a face. "I hate that game!"

"So do I," Melora said. "Clay makes me play with him, and I can never remember how those little men move."

Clay smiled at the young woman. "Try checkers, Allyn. You'll have a better chance at that."

"All right, I will. You two go on now, and I'll go see if I can do any better with checkers." She turned and walked away, but as soon as the two were out of sight, she thought of how awkward she had felt with them. *I should have joined them, but they need all the time they have together. When he's gone, I know she'll save all these times in her memory.*

She made her way down the road, enjoying the brisk wind that stirred the leaves and bent the dead grasses over. They seemed to bow in obeisance to the power of the breeze. She had come to love Gracefield and the country that surrounded it. All of her life she had been confined to the narrow streets of New Orleans, and now the freshness of the open countryside, the smell, the sights, the touch of raw earth under her feet had all come to be precious to her.

When the house came in sight, she admired as always the fine lines of the classic mansion. She knew nothing about architecture, but there was something about the mansion at Gracefield that was pleasing to the eye: the stately white pillars on three sides, the tall windows that caught the gleam of the late afternoon sun, the carpeted lawn that now was turning brown but was still evenly clipped and level. She thought of the mean, ugly streets of the section of New Orleans where she had lived—and dreaded the thought of going back to such a place again.

As she entered the yard, she spoke to several of the slaves, who grinned at her, saying, "How are you, Miss Allyn?" She wondered again about her feelings about slavery. She had grown up with it, and it had been a part of her world, so deeply entrenched she could not have imagined any other world. The war itself had not been as meaningful to her as to some, for she had not had a father, brother, or lover who was risking his life. Now, however, that she had come to know some of the Rocklin men, it gave her a chill as she thought that Clay, Lowell, or Dent in a few days might lie dead in some bloody field.

She entered the house through a side door, went at once to Mark's room, and knocked on the door.

"Come in."

She opened the door and entered, smiling at him. "I've got an idea," she said.

Mark sat in his wheelchair, as usual. He'd been waiting for her, as he always did. He'd noticed that he counted the hours until she came, and now he said, "Good. What is it?"

"I'll never learn to play chess. Let's play checkers instead."

Mark grinned at her. When he smiled, some of the pain

seemed to leave his face, and she thought, *What a handsome man he must have been when he was young—before he got hurt.* Moving to the cabinet, she picked up the board and a box containing some checkers. Placing them on a table she pulled over in front of Mark, she drew up a chair, set up the board, then asked, "How do you feel, Father?"

"Oh, very well today," Mark said. "Tell me what you've been doing."

Allyn knew he didn't like to talk about his illness. He never complained, and he always wanted to know all that she did. She began tracing her day for him, putting in the little things, and as she spoke, she was unaware of how his eyes were fixed to her face. Her own eyes were fastened on the board as she studied the pieces.

Mark let her win the game and was pleased to see the delight that such a simple thing brought to her. Thoughtfully he said, "You look very like your mother, Allyn, when she was your age."

Allyn shook her head. "I don't think I'd ever be as pretty as that picture of her."

"You are, though."

His words pleased her, but she had been thinking of her position at Gracefield, and now she leaned back and stared at her father. "I can't go on forever like this," she said suddenly.

"What do you mean, Allyn?"

"Why, all I do is walk around and play games with you. I don't do any work." She moved restlessly. Some of the energy that was in her seemed to spill over. She got up and walked to the window and looked out briefly, then turned to him. "Everybody has work to do but me. I'm just a guest."

"Why, that's what you are, Allyn," Mark said. He was

surprised at the girl and added, "You wouldn't want to do housework or anything like that, would you? You'll have enough to do when we are able to move into Twelve Trees."

"I don't know. I just feel—oh, sort of useless, I guess you'd say."

"You're never that." He hesitated then held out his hand. She came over and took it. He looked up at her and smiled again. "You've been a godsend to me, daughter."

His simple words embarrassed her. She was not accustomed to being told things like that. His hand felt thin and fragile under hers, and she knew that if she squeezed it, he would not be able to withstand the pressure, he was that weak. He looked at her then said quietly, "Sit down, Allyn. I want to talk to you."

She gave him a curious glance and then sat down. Folding her hands in her lap, she asked carefully, "What is it?"

Something, she saw, was troubling the sick man. Running his hand over his graying hair, he dropped his eyes for a few moments, seeming to study the intricate patterns in the carpet. In the quietness they could hear the slaves calling to one another outside the window out in the yard. Their voices made a happy sound, and he sat there quietly trying to organize his thoughts. He finally lifted his eyes and said seriously, "Allyn, I'd like for you to marry."

"Marry!"

"Now wait—" He raised his hand to interrupt. "I know that sounds bossy, and maybe even crazy to you, but hear me out, will you?"

Mark's proposal had caught Allyn off guard. She had expected practically anything but this. Now she stared at him, her eyes wide with surprise, but she nodded and said, "Go ahead. I'd like to hear it." There was a wry tone in her voice that he did not miss. She leaned forward a little bit, her interest caught.

"Allyn, every woman needs a man. Don't you think so?"

Allyn seemed to get defensive. Her lips drew together, and she shook her head. "I don't need *anybody*—especially a husband!" she replied curtly.

"It's a pretty bad thing to be alone, Allyn." A bitterness came to his eyes, and he looked down again at his hands. "I guess I ought to know that better than anybody. I've been alone all my life. I've already told you how I made a fool out of myself about your mother. We could have had such a *good* life, but I didn't have sense enough to know it. I'd hate for you to make the same mistake I made."

Allyn shook her head stubbornly. "Why, it's not the same at all! You were in love with my mother, but I'm not in love with anyone."

"I don't know much about love," Mark said slowly. "I loved your mother. I see people like Clay and Melora that just seem to be meant for each other—and now Lowell and Rooney. But this is a hard world, Allyn. I don't have to tell you that. A woman, I think, has a harder time alone than a man."

"I don't think that's so, not necessarily," Allyn said. "I can take care of myself. I don't want a man."

Her own words sounded harsh to her ears, but she was not ready to consider marriage. She had not thought that far ahead. She sat there as he began to talk, but there was a resistance in her that would not surrender.

Mark began to explain how he felt. "You know what it's like for a woman," he said gently, "but if a woman has a good husband, he can take that load off her. A woman has a difficult way to go in this society. She can either get married or teach school. There aren't many other options, are there?" He continued to speak, hoping to persuade her. But seeing that her back was straight, finally he said gently, "Allyn, you know I'd like you to have everything when I'm gone, but I want you to have a strong man to share it with."

Allyn shot him a glance that was almost harsh. "What do you want me to do? Advertise in the Richmond paper for a husband?"

"Why, you wouldn't have to do that," Mark protested. "I've noticed how many young men have stopped by. They have all kinds of excuses, but they come just to see you. Yet you won't have anything to do with them."

"I don't really want to talk about it," Allyn said shortly.

Mark leaned back in his chair and studied her. He put his fingertips together and formed a peak and let the silence run on. Finally, he asked, "Did some man hurt you somewhere, Allyn?"

She gave him a strange, half-frightened look. "I've seen the way that men have treated my mother over the years. Let's just say that I would rather do without what a husband can provide."

Mark saw that she was tremendously upset. He himself was shaken, for he had planned this carefully in his mind. It had been his concept that she would agree to marry and would begin to look around among the young men. He had been sure that, as beautiful as she was—and with some property—finding an acceptable husband would not be a problem. Now, however, he saw that she was both angry and frightened of the idea.

A weariness came to him, and the pain that lurked always just below the surface of his nerves suddenly attacked him. He sat there enduring it, until finally it grew to a dull throbbing. Finally, he said quietly, "Allyn, I can't be around to help you, not for long. All I can do is be sure that you'll have someone who will take care of you."

"I can take care of myself!"

"You have a lot of determination. But a woman can be victimized—and I'd hate to see that happen to you. If I just handed you everything with no restrictions, I'd be afraid of what might happen."

"I don't want anything from you, Father," she said firmly. "I just came to meet you. Now I've done that. . .and I can. . .go back." This was not what she wanted, and she had to force the words out.

He saw that she did not mean what she said, and he reached out and put his hand on hers. "Allyn, until I can be sure, I can't sign the property over to you. Everything I have will be yours someday, but until you get married, we'll have to do something a little different."

Allyn felt a sudden burst of pity go through her. She had learned to respect this man. The antagonism she had brought with her when she came to meet him was now gone. She knew that he was telling her the exact truth, that he really wanted to help her. Nevertheless, she lifted her eyes and said, "Father, I'll never marry a man just to get a piece of land or money." A bitterness touched her lips, and she shook her head and said vehemently, "I've already seen too much of that."

Mark knew she meant exactly what she said. "Well," he said as weariness marked his face with deep lines, "at least you're here and you have time—a little, anyway. I'll just pray that God will come into the situation." He looked at her and forced a smile. "I'm not much of a hand at praying," he admitted. "I came to it late in life, but somehow I know that God's got a man for you out there, and all we've got to do is find him."

Allyn didn't argue. Not wanting to give him more pain, she leaned forward, saying quietly, "It'll be all right. Now let's play another game of checkers."

Chapter 14

A Bold Plan

The South was wearing down as the war ground on, and the North was also having serious problems. On March 3, 1863, the first Federal conscription act was passed. It stated that all able-bodied males between twenty and forty-five were liable for service. Prior to that the North had obtained its troops from volunteers and state militia called into Federal service. But when the conscription act was enacted in July, draft riots broke out at once.

Opposition to the act was widespread. Many were already lukewarm to the war effort. Secret societies for resisting the draft were formed, and in some areas draft officers were assaulted by mobs or run out of town. In almost every state there were protests, outbreaks of violence, and other forms of resistance.

By far the worst explosion took place in New York City in July 1863. New York had strong Southern sympathies, and its Democratic political machine despised Abraham Lincoln. The drawing of the first draftees' names touched off three days of rioting in which mobs roamed the streets and fought pitched battles with police. Several blacks were lynched, and the

Colored Orphan Asylum was burned to the ground. Army units were rushed from Gettysburg to join the police and militia in quelling the riots, and the draft resumed in New York. It was, however, a sign of the weariness of the North with the terrible conflict that drained it of young men and consumed all of its effort.

In Washington, with its still-unfinished Capitol, the streets were filled with the crumbs of war, soldiers, clerks, all the baggage of war, veterans back on leave, recruits, spies, spies on spies, politicians, slackers, harlots, Negro boys who organized butting matches to please the recruits, tattooers, and fortune-tellers. All seemed to converge on Washington.

Perhaps the loneliest man in the entire city was Abraham Lincoln, who had lost a son but had no time to grieve him.

It was still hot in Washington that September. It was hot in the city, hot in the White House rooms, and sweltering hot in the office where Deborah sat waiting to see the president. The sentinel on his post clicked back and forth, and in the crowded bureaus the pens moved slowly as she sat there. The damp clerks, wet with sweat, watched the clock. Deborah mopped her brow with a handkerchief already soaked but stubbornly refused to leave. This was the second day she had sat in the office. The lieutenant in charge had done his best to persuade her to leave both days, but she had said quietly, "I'll wait, Lieutenant."

A short brigadier general exited from the door, and the lieutenant nodded to him then stepped inside the office. He found the president standing at the window, staring out, and he said, "Sir, General McCauley has been waiting all morning."

Lincoln turned and asked, "Who else?"

Lieutenant Smith shrugged. "The office is full, Mr. President, as it always is."

A smile touched the lips of the president. He stood there making a tall shape against the window, his coarse black hair awry, his body lank but muscular. He was weary and had to draw upon a tremendous energy, and now even that was growing weak. He was tired of the war, tired of the cabinet, tired of excuses, and weary to the bone of bearing the burden of this government. "Well," he said quietly, "I don't suppose it matters much. I guess I'll see the general—unless you have a better candidate."

Lieutenant Smith thought quickly. "Well, sir, there's a young lady out here. She's been waiting for two days."

"What does the girl want? Does she have a sweetheart she wants to get out of the draft?"

"I don't know, sir. She won't tell me, but I'll tell you one thing, she's better looking than anything else out there in the office."

Lincoln, always quick to appreciate a good joke, leaned forward and said, "Let's have her, then, but don't tell my wife I'm seeing attractive young ladies."

"No, sir, of course not."

Deborah looked up with little hope when the lieutenant came out, but then he came over and smiled at her. "All right, Miss Steele, the president will see you now, but only for a few minutes. I put in a good word for you."

Deborah rose at once and gave the lieutenant a dazzling smile. She put out her hand and said quietly, "Thank you, Lieutenant. I appreciate it."

She moved inside at once, and the president came forward and put out his hand. "It is good to see you again, Miss Steele. How are you?"

"I'm fine, Mr. President. Thank you. I'm surprised you remembered," Deborah said.

"Yes. You're Colonel Gideon Rocklin's niece."

"Yes, sir." She knew her time was short and said at once, "I'll try to be as brief as I can. Actually, Uncle Gideon is the reason I'm here."

He grew serious then and said, "I am sorry to hear of his being captured. That can't be very pleasant in those Confederate war prisons." His lips grew tighter, and he said, "Our own aren't much better, I'm afraid."

"I've come to see you, Mr. President," Deborah said almost breathlessly. "I've tried everything I can to get my uncle exchanged, but it doesn't seem to have done much good. I've come to ask you if you could do anything to get him back."

Lincoln listened to her carefully then nodded. "I'll write a letter, of course, but this thing has become very difficult, exchanging prisoners."

"How is that, Mr. President? We give them a man; they give us a man."

Lincoln shrugged. "Nothing seems to be simple in this war. In a bureaucracy, I suppose, nothing ever is. But I can tell you one thing," he added dryly. "If the Confederates knew for certain that the president of the United States wanted a certain man released, that would make it ten times as hard to get him. They'd hold out for the world with a fence around it in order to let him go."

"Oh," Deborah said in disappointment. Then she nodded, saying, "Yes, I can see that. But we're so worried about him, I just thought that—"

"Of course, Miss Steele, we're all worried about our men in prisons. They're dying there at an awful rate. I will write the letter, as I said, and authorize the officer in charge of exchanges to exert every effort to get Colonel Rocklin back, but we can't know how much good that will do. As I say, it is a confusing matter."

Deborah knew that she could go no further. "Thank you, Mr. President. I do appreciate it." She hesitated then added, "I'll pray for you, not only for this but that you'll be able to bear this tremendous load that's on your shoulders. God bless you for what you're doing."

Lincoln's homely face lit up. He put out his large hand, which swallowed hers as he squeezed it gently. "Thank you, my dear," he said quietly. "Unless the Almighty sustained me, I could not go on for one day."

At the exact time that Deborah was speaking with the president of the United States, her fiancé, Noel Kojak, was in a much cruder setting. He had agreed—against his better judgment—to accompany his brother Bing to one of his bare-knuckle prize-fights. It was not Noel's first fight. He had seen several others but never without a sense of disgust. Nothing could be much more depraved, he had thought, than watching two men beating each other into a state of insensibility.

The fight was held on a barge anchored offshore in the Potomac River. Noel had crossed over in a small boat along with Bing and his manager, a short, muscular man named Sam Phillips. Phillips himself had been a pugilist in his youth and now had found his glory in steering younger men down that same pathway.

"Cheer up, Noel. You look like you're going to a funeral."

Bing Kojak grinned at his older brother, adding, "This is supposed to be entertainment."

Noel glanced at the referee, who was standing in the center as he gave the instructions. "I wish you'd quit this foolishness, Bing," he said. But he knew that it was useless. He had talked to Bing so many times that now it had become automatic. He glanced at his brother, over six feet tall, strong and powerful with black wavy hair and dark brown eyes. He was very quick, which had saved his face from being marked in his fights. Even now there was a look of anticipation on his face, and Noel thought with amazement, *He likes it! I can't understand it.*

Phillips came over and massaged the thick muscles in Bing's neck. He was smoking a foul-smelling black cigar that seemed to be permanently attached to his face. Noel had never seen him without one and wondered at times if he smoked when he took a bath—if he ever took baths, that is. "You gotta watch this pug, Bing," he said, raising his voice above the noise of the crowd that lined the shore. "He's slow but strong as a bull. Just dance around him awhile. Let him wear himself out."

"Sure, Sam." Bing nodded carelessly.

The referee motioned to the two fighters, who went to the center of the ring. As he spoke to the two men, Noel looked over the crowd that lined the bank of the river. It was a male crowd, of course, composed almost equally of soldiers in the lower ranks and workingmen. Prizefighting was not a respectable form of entertainment, but no matter how many laws were passed against it, it appeared that people would always be willing to see two men come together to try to destroy each other. *I wonder why that is?* Noel asked himself.

Bing and Sam Phillips came back. Phillips jerked the robe from Bing's shoulders and growled, "Remember, don't let him catch you with that right of his."

"Sure, I'll watch it," Bing said with a grin. Then he moved forward, his left hand extended, his right cocked. He was wearing a pair of black tights and was naked from the waist up. He moved like a great cat, crossing the floor of the barge to meet the huge man who came roaring out like a mad bull.

"That fighter, he's pretty tough," Phillips informed Noel. "But Bing'll take him—if he don't get ideas of his own."

"What kind of ideas?" Noel inquired. He watched Bing simply move to one side as Fred Cartwright sailed by. He was amazed to see Bing reach out and strike the big man on the neck negligibly. The blow did not seem hard, but the force of Bing's 190 pounds was behind it, so it sent Cartwright to the floor, mostly as a result of his own momentum.

"End of round one," the referee announced. Every knockdown constituted a round, and there had been fights with as many as one hundred rounds. The fighters had thirty seconds between rounds.

Bing came back, took a swig of the water that Sam gave him, and said, "Pretty good crowd, eh, Noel? We'll go out and celebrate after I've polished this bohunk off." Then he turned and saw that Cartwright had come back to scratch, standing in the middle waiting for him. The big man weighed well over two hundred pounds, and his face looked as if it had been battered by an ax handle.

"Stay away from him," Phillips warned. "That brother of yours, he don't think he'll ever get hurt. He could be champion of the world if he'd pay attention to me." He shifted the cigar around to another position then shook his head. "Never saw anybody more stubborn in my whole life. Does it run in your family?"

"I don't think so, Sam," Noel answered. "That's just Bing."

Noel watched as Bing moved almost contemptuously around the bigger man. Cartwright bellowed and shoved and bulled his way toward the smaller man, but trying to hit Bing was like trying to hit a sunbeam. He simply was not there. Despite himself, Noel felt a twinge of admiration for his younger brother. *Well*, he thought, *I think it's a despicable way to make a living, but he's good at it, all right.*

Time after time, Cartwright went to the deck but seemed to be indestructible. He had won most of his fights by the thick sheathing of muscle and bone that made him almost impervious to pain. He simply outlasted his opponents, soaking up whatever they had to give until they grew arm weary, then finally stepping in and battering them down.

After what seemed a long time, Bing came back after a knockdown and asked, "How many rounds is that, Noel?"

"I don't know; I've lost count. Aren't you getting tired?"

Bing shrugged. "A little, but he's slowing down, too. He's got a lot more beef to move around than I have."

This was true. Cartwright was moving slower. Now he simply plodded across the ring. Bing backed away most of the time, ignoring Cartwright's curses and jeers at his cowardice, biding his time. "He's doing fine," Phillips said, "if he just keeps on backing up—but look out, there he goes!"

Cartwright had propelled himself forward, desperately throwing a vicious roundhouse right that would have torn Bing's head off had it landed. Ordinarily, up until now, this was the sort of thing that Bing had dodged, but now that he was getting tired himself, he decided on a new tactic. As Cartwright's fist whizzed by him, he blocked it with one forearm and threw himself forward. The force of his blow began with his right foot, traveled up his leg, then his torso. As his arm flashed out, his fist caught the bigger man coming in. It was like being hit with a battering ram! The force of the blow drove Cartwright back, and his mouth was bloody as he hit the deck. He lay there, slowly moving his arms and legs as if he were swimming. Bing came back breathing hard.

"I told you to stay away from him," Phillips complained.

"Oh, that stopped his clock," Bing said. He watched the other fighter carefully and said, "I can tell. He won't be able to come back to scratch."

Noel watched as Cartwright's manager tried to get him upright. He poured water from a bottle over his face, hauled at him, but the bigger man's legs seemed to be made of rubber. After counting the thirty seconds between rounds, the referee said, "Eight seconds to come back to scratch."

Noel counted off the seconds, as did the crowd. Then a cheer went up as the referee came over and lifted Bing's hand, shouting, "The winner: Bing Kojak!"

Bing laughed as Phillips reached up and pulled him down with a hard hug. Then Bing reached over and ruffled Noel's hair. "How about that, older brother?" he said. "Not bad, was it?"

Noel managed to grin. "Well, it's a good thing he didn't catch you. I believe he would have put you in a grave if one of those blows had struck."

"He didn't, though." Bing laughed, and his white teeth flashed in the light of the setting sun. "Let me get cleaned up, and we'll go out and eat."

Bing had brought extra clothes, and after he took a quick wash at a rooming house where he stayed sometimes, he put on a new suit and came out looking fresh as a daisy. "I'm starved," he said. "Let's go eat."

"I told Deborah I'd pick her up."

"Good, we'll take her out. She'll give us a touch of class, eh, Noel?"

Deborah glanced across the table at the two brothers, thinking, not for the first time, how dissimilar they were: Noel, with his light brown hair and gray eyes, was not over five ten or 160 pounds, while Bing was over six feet and exuded raw strength. He was much better looking than Noel with his black wavy hair and dark brown eyes. Noel was not handsome. His features were regular, with a short nose and a wide mouth. It was something on the inside that drew her to the smaller man.

"Tell me about the fight," she said after they had ordered their meal.

Bing said, "Oh, it was easy, Deborah—like taking candy from a baby."

"It wasn't all that easy," Noel said. "If that big brute had hit you, you'd have been in the hospital."

"Don't ever worry about what might have happened," Bing said airily. "That's my philosophy. There's something like that in the Bible, isn't there?"

Deborah smiled at him. Bing was a good-natured young man, wild and undisciplined yet devoted to his friends. She had learned to trust him when they had worked together to get Noel out of a Confederate hospital. Now she smiled at him, reached over, and patted his large hand. "I wish I could have seen it," she said. "Next time I'll go along with you."

"You can't do that, Deborah," Noel gasped. "There are no women at prizefights."

"Then it'll be a first," she said. She enjoyed teasing Noel, who was far more straitlaced than she. Catching the look on his face, she laughed delightedly and said, "Would I be an embarrassment to you, Noel?"

"You certainly would!" he said. "I wouldn't permit you to go to a thing like that!"

"Why, there are worse things than prizefights," Bing protested.

"I'd like to know what!" Noel growled. "Two men beating each other into unconsciousness is barbaric."

"Unconscious?" Bing frowned. "Why, I'm about as conscious as a human being can be. Anyway, it'd be educational for you, Deborah." He winked at her and grinned. "You and I'll sneak off and go next time. We won't tell the preacher here."

"It's a date," Deborah said. She had no intention of doing such a thing, but she liked to tease Noel, who sat there looking disgusted with the conversation. "After all, Queen Elizabeth loved bearbaitings," she said.

Bing asked, "What's bearbaiting?"

"Oh, back in the days of Queen Elizabeth, it was considered great fun to chain a bear to a tree and then turn dogs loose to kill it."

Bing's jaw hardened and his eyes narrowed. "Now that's what I call barbaric," he said. He looked at Noel, saying, "I'd be against a thing like that—but fighting, why, it's a test of skill."

Noel sat there, really enjoying himself. He knew the two were making fun of him, but his nature was such that he didn't mind it. Somehow Noel Kojak had risen amid some of the worst circumstances in the world to become a scholar of sorts. He had never attended school, having been taught by his mother to read. He wrote poetry—which he was ashamed of and would let no one see—and had become a respected writer for several

Northern newspapers. He had a gift, a flair for describing a scene so vividly that the readers could sense the sights, smells, and colors of the event.

Now as he looked across at Deborah, he thought about their history—how she had befriended him and his family when he had never thought a young society girl would do such a thing. To him, she was the most beautiful woman in the world, and he never ceased wondering why she had chosen him out of all the men she knew. *She could have anybody,* he thought and was fiercely proud that she had agreed to marry him.

They talked cheerfully until their steaks came, then ate the food with the appetite of youth. Afterward they ordered ice cream, cake, and coffee. After the meal, Bing patted his stomach and said, "I couldn't eat another bite! Now I'll have to do a lot of roadwork to get rid of this paunch I've put on tonight."

"It was good, wasn't it?" Deborah said.

Then as the two men talked, she fell into a silence that did not go unnoticed by Noel. He turned from Bing, asking, "What's wrong, Deborah?"

"I can't hide anything from you, can I? After we get married, how will I manage that? Women are supposed to have some secrets."

"Are you worried about something?" he asked, ignoring her joking.

Deborah bit her lip and said, "I finally got in to see the president this afternoon."

The two men stared at her, and it was Bing who exclaimed, "You mean—President Lincoln?"

"Yes, I've been sitting in his office for two days."

"I can't believe it!" Noel exclaimed. "I thought you were joking about going to see him."

"No, I wasn't joking. I haven't been able to think about anything except Uncle Gid and that awful Libby Prison."

"What did he say—the president?" Noel asked eagerly. "Did he say he'd help?"

"He said he'd write a letter, but he said if the Confederates found out that the president wanted Uncle Gid out, they'd ask for the moon and the stars for him."

"I expect that's right," Bing said. "Didn't he give you any hope at all?"

"Not much. He said he'd write the letter, as I said, but I could tell he didn't expect it to do much good." She leaned forward and put her chin on her fist and said, "President Lincoln is so tired. I don't see how he stands it. The office was full of people, every one of them demanding to see him, and that goes on every day." She shook her head almost angrily. "I felt bad taking up just that much of his time. But he was so kind."

The three sat there quietly. The two men respected Colonel Gideon Rocklin deeply, and of course, he had been Deborah's hero since her childhood, spoiling her completely.

"I wish I could help," Noel said heavily, "but I don't see any way."

Bing said suddenly, "You remember once I said I wouldn't risk my life for nothing, but if you ever found anything I could do that had some meaning to it, why, I'd go for it?"

Both Noel and Deborah looked at the large young man. "I remember," Noel said. He looked at his younger brother curiously. "What are you thinking, Bing?"

Bing leaned back in his chair. As they had talked of Deborah's uncle, an idea had come to him. Now he said casually, "Well, I think I'll go down there and bust Colonel Rocklin out of that jail."

Deborah's eyes flew open with surprise. "Bing!"

"What are you talking about, Bing?" Noel exclaimed. "You can't do a thing like that."

"Tell me why I can't." Bing had spoken half in jest, but now he saw the expressions of the others and grew excited. He had hated his short stint in the army—the discipline, the lack of freedom—but he had looked back often and thought of the excitement that had been in him when he and Deborah had worked to get Noel out of the prison hospital. Now his face grew flushed as he leaned forward, saying, "Aw, it's just one prison, ain't it? And they got all the tough guys fightin' the war. Bound to be a bunch of old men and young kids serving as guards. Why, that's the way it was when you was in the hospital. Don't you remember, Noel?"

"I remember how we could have all gotten killed getting out of that place," Noel said in rebuke. "But he's not in a hospital—he's in a prison. And from what I hear, in those prisons they shoot people who even *look* like they want to escape."

"Ah, you're just a worrywart," Bing said, dismissing Noel's concerns. He was enjoying the sensation his announcement had made. Leaning forward, he said, "I don't have another fight for a few weeks. I think I'll just go down and bust him out. Be some excitement in that, I reckon."

Deborah said clearly, "That's fine, Bing, and I'll go along with you."

Now it was Bing's turn to blink in surprise. "Why, you can't do that, Deborah!"

"Tell me why I can't," she said, echoing his words. A rash grin touched her lips as she said, "You've got to get him out and get him back into the North, and it's going to take more than you to do that."

Noel felt this was getting out of hand. "This is crazy! Both of you are crazy," he said. "Don't you know that that's about the same thing as being a spy? They hang spies down there pretty often, you know."

"They have to catch us first," Bing said. He was now totally enamored with his proposition. He knew that Deborah was smart enough to do the thinking and said so. "You do the planning, and I'll do the busting, Deborah." Then he looked over at Noel and slapped him on the shoulder, saying, "I'll just have to borrow your fiancée for just a little while. You don't mind, do you, big brother?"

Noel understood that these two could not be stopped. Both of them had an excitement in their eyes, and their whole faces were lit with thoughts of what was to come. Heavily he drew a breath then shook his head. "No, I won't lend her to you—but I'll go along with you." He grinned as the other two suddenly grabbed at him and pounded at his shoulders. "Hey!" he said. "Don't beat me to death! Somebody with some brains has got to go along to be sure you two don't go to jail."

"We'll do it! We'll all three go," Deborah exclaimed in delight, "and we won't tell anybody. We'll just go get Uncle Gid out, and then you can write a story or a book about it that will make us rich and famous."

The three talked excitedly until the restaurant closed for the night. None of them had the vaguest glimmer of an idea about *how* to get Gideon Rocklin out of the prison, but they were all totally committed to the task and pledged themselves to do whatever was necessary to get the job done.

It was Bing who said, "Why, it'll be a piece of cake!"

Chapter 15

Store-bought Husband

"You wait right here, Sonny," Allyn said to the tall young slave who had driven her into Richmond for supplies.

Sonny looked around apprehensively and said, "I'd better comes wif you, missy—you don't know dis heah place. Dey's lots of bad folks here!"

Allyn laughed. "Don't be silly. I'll go make my purchases; then you can come bring the wagon around and pick them up." She stepped down, ignoring his protests, then made her way along the street that seemed to be more than unusually crowded.

For thousands of Southerners, Richmond had become a city of refuge. Runaway slaves, destitute soldiers' wives, and army deserters all flocked to the capital, along with loyalists ejected from Federal-occupied zones. Largely as a result of this migration, the city's population had trebled to 128,000. As the diarist Mary Chestnut put it, "Richmond was filled to suffocation, hardly standing room left."

For an hour Allyn moved among the stores, but most of them had bare shelves and demanded exorbitant prices. When she got home, she sat down and talked to Mark about it.

"Well, it's bad, and it's going to get worse," he said. "In

April there was a bread riot in Richmond. A group of angry women led by a woman named Mary Jackson cornered Governor Letcher."

"What did he say?"

"Nothing much he *could* say—and not much he could do, either, when the women went on a rampage."

Allyn stared at him wide-eyed. "But—what did they do?"

"They raided the stores," Mark answered. "Just swarmed in brandishing knives and hatchets. Wrecked the stores and came out with food and whatever else they could lay their hands on."

"How awful!"

"Well, it was. But it didn't go on long." A thin smile came to Mark's lips, and he added, "President Davis stopped it. It was something to see, according to what I heard. The president reached into his pockets and gave them all his money. But when that didn't satisfy them, he took out his watch and said, 'I don't want to see any of you harmed—but this must stop. If you don't disperse in five minutes, you'll be fired upon!'"

"Did they leave?"

"Oh yes. I think they believed the president."

"Do you think he would have ordered the soldiers to fire on civilians?"

Mark gave her a thoughtful look and then nodded. "I think he might have done it, Allyn. He's a compassionate man at heart, but he sees everything in terms of war. Of course, things are getting worse every day."

"Well, I don't know about everything," Allyn said, "but I know grocery prices are terrible! Soap was only ten cents a pound, Susanna said, but now it's a dollar ten a pound. That's one-tenth of a soldier's monthly pay. Half a pound of green tea costs sixteen dollars."

WALL OF FIRE

"I know. I feel so sorry for the families of the soldiers who are fighting. I know they're suffering at home, and I fear it's only going to get worse."

Allyn had sat down across from Mark. She had taken him in his wheelchair to the porch, where they were watching a grouping of low-lying clouds skim along. The moon was yellow as old cheese as they sat drinking in the beautiful, dark scene. Far away they could hear the sound of singing from the slaves' quarters, and now the cry of a lonesome, mournful dog somewhere floated to them on the cool September breeze.

Mark looked up and said, "Look, those clouds are going to hit the moon." As they watched, the clouds blotted the moon momentarily then slowly unveiled it so that the pale silver rays fell on the earth again, casting their gleam on the dead fields that surrounded the mansion.

"Have you heard about Jason Larrimore?" Mark inquired.

"Why, no, I haven't heard anything. What happened to him?"

"Bad news, I'm afraid. Something I've been afraid of all the time, I suppose. The Federals penned his ship along the coast. Too bad!"

"Did they capture him?" Allyn asked quickly.

"No, he was wounded, but he and all the crew got away. They had to scuttle the ship, though, and everything he had was in it."

"Why, I thought he was rich. I thought all blockade-runners were rich—the successful ones, that is."

"He put all his money in that ship. It cost a fortune. He told me he had put all he could get his hands on into it, but he thought he would make a profit with this run through the blockade and back. He could have, too," Mark said regretfully.

The silence ran on, and Allyn asked finally, "What will he do now?"

"I don't know. He's in Richmond trying to raise money for another ship, but he won't have any luck. Money's hard to come by these days."

"Why don't you help him, Father?" Allyn asked.

"It's too risky," Mark said quickly. "It would cost all I have to get a ship like he needs, and the same thing could happen to it that happened to the last one. It's a dangerous business. No, I can't do that."

"I feel sorry for him," she said. "He's a little arrogant, but I suppose most captains are that way. I guess they have to be."

"Jason has had a tough life, Allyn. His parents died when he was fourteen. He went to sea as a cabin boy," Mark said quietly. "He rose all the way to captain on the strength of his fists and his quick wits. He bought a piece of a ship that had been condemned and kept it afloat somehow. He told me that he ran slaves once, but it sickened him."

"He's very cynical, isn't he?"

"Well, he doesn't believe in much. I guess he's had enough hard knocks to convince him there's very little honesty and kindness in this world." He stared across through the moonlight at her and said, "You didn't like him, I could tell. Did he mistreat you in any way in New Orleans or on the way here?"

"Oh no," she said quickly. "It's not that. He's just—oh, I don't know."

Mark let the silence linger and then said, "The papers are ready for signing. Twelve Trees is a wonderful place," he urged gently. "You and I could go there, and we could have some peace for however long I've got left. It's a little isolated, but I wouldn't mind that."

Allyn shook her head. "I'll go with you, but I won't marry." She saw that her answer disappointed him and wished that it were different. She found herself growing fonder of him and knew that except for that hard streak that had built up in her during her childhood and adolescence, she would have felt this affection even more strongly. She could not free herself from the resentment. She knew it was wrong, but that was the way she was.

"I'll have the papers anytime you are ready," Mark said quietly. "I'll go ahead and buy the place, but it'll stay in my name. Then if I die, I'll leave Clay as the executor. He'll be that until you marry, then he'll sign it all over to you."

A lump came up in Allyn's throat and she said, "I—I don't want you to think I'm ungrateful. It's not that, but I've not been able to get very close to a man. Maybe I don't have any love in me. Sure, I loved Mother, but as for men. . ."

At once Mark said, "I won't rush you, Allyn. Maybe it's best this way. And who knows? I'm a tough old bird! I might live a long time."

"Yes," she said quickly and reached over and patted his hand. "You probably will. Let's do it. You buy the place, and I'll go there with you and you can teach me how to play chess. That ought to take a lifetime, at least." Neither of them referred to the subject again, and for several days she seemed unusually quiet. Early one morning she came to him and said, "I'm going into Richmond. I want some time to think. I may stay for several days. Is that all right?"

"Why, of course. Here, take this money. Rooms will be high in the hotels there, if there are even any vacancies. Have a good time." Secretly he hoped she would meet some young man and fall in love with him. "Go on now—bring me something back, maybe Dickens's latest novel if you can find it."

He watched as she left the room, then later spoke with

Susanna about it. "I wish she'd meet somebody, but I don't think she will. She's afraid of men, I think."

Susanna said quietly, "A lot of women are—and some of them for good reason." Warmly she smiled at him and said, "But there's a man for her somewhere. You and I, we'll just beat on the gates of heaven until the Lord hears our prayer and gives her just the one she needs."

"Why, I'm sorry, Captain Larrimore, but you must understand that the money in this bank doesn't belong to me. It belongs to the depositors, and I can't take risks with it. I have to put it into sound ventures—and buying a ship to run the blockade, why, that's about as risky a venture as I can think of!"

Jason had expected little from Giles Goodman, the president of Planters' Bank. He rose to his feet and said quietly, "Well, I didn't really expect you could, Giles, not after I just lost one ship."

Goodman rose at once and protested. "Now wait, Jason—" He was a tall, portly man with muttonchop whiskers and a head of bushy white hair. "I think something might be done in time, some private subscriptions maybe. Let me talk to a few of my friends. But as for a bank loan"—he shrugged his big shoulders expressively—"I'm afraid that's just out of the question."

"Sure, I'll be around," Jason said. He shook the big hand and, turning a little too quickly, felt a twinge in the wound in his back that had not completely healed. He left the bank, stepped outside, and blinked in the bright sunlight. The streets, as usual, were crowded, and he walked carefully to avoid being jostled by the many soldiers who hurried busily along. For over an hour he walked the main streets of the busy city and finally went back to his hotel and started to go to his room.

"Ah, Captain Larrimore?"

Jason turned to see the clerk, a small man named Robbins, looking at him. Moving to the desk, he said, "Yes, what is it?"

"Well, I hate to mention it, Captain, but..." Robbins seemed embarrassed. He tugged at his collar and let his eyes drop to the register. He fiddled with it with his hands then finally lifted his eyes and shrugged his thin shoulders. "The fact of the matter is, Captain, if you could pay just a *small* portion of your bill?"

Jason had already spent a small fortune at the hotel. He stared hard at the clerk then shrugged. "How much is the bill?"

"It comes to a little over $170, Captain."

Jason reached into his pocket and pulled out a thin roll of bills, peeled off half of them. "There's a hundred—I'll pay the rest tomorrow."

Robbins took the money and said regretfully, "You know, I hate to ask. You've been such a good guest, Captain Larrimore, but the owner—"

"I know, Robbins," Jason interrupted. "It's not your fault. Don't worry about it."

He turned and walked back outside. As always, when there was trouble, he liked to be near the water. He walked down to the James River and watched the deckhands on the small boats. Finally, he talked with one of the captains and found himself almost asking for a job. But then he knew he would never be content on a small riverboat. He bid the man good-bye and turned back toward his hotel.

"I'll have to go to sea," he muttered. "Ought to be able to find some shipping company that needs a good captain."

But he was not happy with the decision. Having been a ship

owner had spoiled him for anything else, and he knew it. But when he ran over the possibilities in his mind, he found there were none. He had no way of raising the money to buy another ship except by a stroke of luck. He might take his remaining small roll of bills and win big in a poker game, but in his experience the very time a man needed to win was the time he usually lost. Quick and impulsive, however, he decided, "I might as well try it." He moved to a saloon nearby and soon was sitting in a game. He ran his stakes up to over three hundred dollars then lost it all on one hand.

When he left the saloon, he was as broke as he'd ever been in his life. He rammed his hands down in his pocket and came out with a coin. "Ten cents," he muttered. "That's my bankroll." His lips drew into a thin smile, and he shook his head. "It looks like I'm going to have to go to work. I hate to work for anybody! I guess I'm just too independent for that."

He did not even have enough money for supper, so he went to his room, lay down on his bed, and stared at the ceiling. He was essentially a man of action. If there was a job to be done, a risk to be taken, there was no hesitancy. But waiting was a different story. Now there stretched out before him a time of inactivity or of boring work. The truth was that he was enamored with running the blockade. There was enough risk in it to whet his appetite for adventure and enough profit to bring in the money to follow the kind of life he wanted to lead.

Now that was all gone, and he could think of nothing but leaving the next day and going to the coast. *Probably go back north—more chance of getting a ship there than in the South with this blockade.*

He dozed off and started when a knock at the door awakened him. "Who is it?" he called out, sitting up at once.

"Captain Larrimore?" Jason advanced to the door, opened it, and saw Robbins there. "Captain," he said, "there's a young lady downstairs that wants to see you."

"Young lady? What's her name?"

"She didn't give it, Captain." Robbins smiled. "She's a fine-looking young woman, though. Dressed real nice. I offered to let her come up to your room, but she wouldn't do it. Shall I tell her you'll be down?"

A few possibilities ran through Jason's mind. He did know several attractive women in Richmond, but none would be coming to seek him out at his hotel. Or if they were such, he was not anxious to have them come up. "All right, Robbins, I'll be right down," he said.

Quickly he washed his face, combed his thick blond hair back, and put on his coat. Leaving the hotel room, he started to lock the hotel door then smiled grimly. *I don't know what they could get except my clothes.* He went down the stairs and looked around the lobby. Quickly his sharp eyes caught the woman who was standing beside a large potted plant over to his left. Her back was to him. He walked over and said, "Hello, I'm Jason Larrimore."

And then the woman turned, and he saw, with a slight shock, that it was Allyn Rocklin. "Hello, Captain," she said unsmilingly. "I'm sorry to disturb you like this."

Jason shrugged his shoulders. "I wasn't doing anything." He stared at her and asked quickly, "You wanted to talk to me?"

She glanced around at the busy hotel lobby. "Can we go somewhere and sit down?"

Jason looked over at the door to his left and said, "We can go into the restaurant. It's too early for most people to eat. I expect that'll be quiet enough."

When they entered, Jason saw that only a few tables were occupied. A waiter came at once and showed them to a table off in the corner of the room. Jason asked, "Are you hungry?"

"I suppose I could eat a little something." She listened as the waiter rattled off the entrees and then gave her choice. Jason shrugged, saying, "I'll have the same."

The waiter wheeled and left the table. Jason leaned back in his chair and waited for her to speak. She seemed nervous and was pale. *It must be about Mark,* he thought. *I wonder if he died? No, she would have told me that right off.* Aloud he said, "How's your experiment turning out?"

"Experiment?"

"Why, yes, I thought that was the idea, your coming to Richmond, to Gracefield, to see if you could become a part of the Rocklin family. Wasn't that the idea?"

Allyn nodded but said nothing. She seemed to have trouble concentrating, and for a while she stumbled over her words, giving him some of the details of Mark's illness. She talked about the family there and seemed very interested in the coming marriage of Rooney and Lowell Rocklin.

"Women always like weddings," Jason remarked. "Tell me, why do they always cry?"

"I don't know. I've never been to a wedding," Allyn said simply. "Not a fancy one, anyway. A girlfriend of mine got married once, but it wasn't very impressive, and I didn't cry."

"I don't suppose you cry about much. You're not a crying woman, are you?"

"Is that a way of telling me I'm hard and unfeeling?"

"Why, not at all. I don't cry myself, but I'm not hard and unfeeling. Matter of fact, I think we're alike, you and I."

"No, we're not alike," Allyn said abruptly.

"I think you're wrong, but we won't argue about it." He knew that she had not come to see him to talk about anything as trite as women crying at weddings—but whatever it was, he would have to let it come out. When the meal came, he ate slowly and watched her closely, thinking all the time what a fine-looking woman she was.

Finally, she pushed her plate back and said, "I have to say what I came to say." She'd eaten almost nothing, and he noticed that her hands were fidgeting nervously with the napkin.

A thought came to him. "Are you in some kind of trouble, Allyn? If that's it—"

"I am in trouble, but not like you think." She raised her eyes to his and waited for a moment then said, "My father wants me to get married."

"Married? Married to whom?"

"He hasn't said," Allyn said wryly. She shook her head. "I don't think he's thought about it. He has this idea that a woman's not able to take care of herself, that she needs a husband."

"Well, that's true, isn't it?"

"Not always, but that's what he thinks. Anyway, he's been having trouble getting his money out of the Northern banks, so the sale of Twelve Trees has been delayed. While he's been waiting, he decided that he'd keep the plantation in his name until I got married; then it would be placed in my name."

The waiter came back to refill the coffee cups, and they waited until he was gone to resume their conversation. There was a desperation in her that Jason had not seen before, a vulnerability that he had not suspected. She seemed younger, more susceptible. Larrimore asked carefully, "Surely he must have some candidate. He wouldn't want you to marry just *anybody*."

"I think he'd take any man who was decent and respectable.

He's got this fear of a woman being preyed upon if she doesn't have a husband. He's afraid that'll happen to me."

"Well, I've seen it happen to others." He studied her carefully then shook his head. "I don't think any man would take advantage of you. I don't think he'd have the chance."

She lifted her head impetuously and demanded, "What do you mean by that?"

"I mean you're pretty and look soft and gentle—but inside there's a hard streak in you, Allyn. That's what I meant when I said we are alike. I've got the same thing in me." He drank the coffee slowly and looked at her. "Both of us came up the hard way. That does something to a person—being poor, having to learn to fight to survive. Most of the Rocklins don't know anything about that. They're good people, but they always had money, family, someone to lean on." He leaned back, half shut his eyes, stirred the coffee gently, then said, "Sometimes at night I go by houses that are lit up and know there are families inside. Those people have everything."

"Why, I've thought that myself," Allyn said in astonishment. She had not considered this side of the tall man, for he had never revealed the softness or gentleness that she saw now.

And then he looked up and said, "Well, are you going back to New Orleans, or are you gonna get a husband and stay here? It's that simple, isn't it?"

"I could stay here with Father. When he dies, Clay will be the executor. But that's not what I want." She hesitated then said, "You've been independent, Jason. You had a hard time, as you said, when you were a boy, and you've had to fight your way. But you had the one thing that most women can't have—you had freedom and independence."

"I had that, all right." Jason shrugged, a slight smile pulling the corners of his lips up. "Sometimes I wish I had somebody to run to, but there's never been anybody like that."

"That's what I want—independence," Allyn said firmly. She hesitated for one moment, gathering her courage, then said, "And I can think of only one way to get it."

Jason Larrimore looked at her curiously. "How are you going to accomplish that? Mark insists on you getting married. Are you just going to wait until a husband comes along?"

"That's—that's what I came here for, Jason." She took a deep breath and said, "I've heard about your misfortune with your ship." She saw his lips tighten, and she nodded slightly. "I'm sorry for it."

"I've been broke before." He looked around, and a whimsical thought came to him. "I hope you've got the money to pay for this meal," he said, "because I don't."

What he said seemed strangely to encourage her. Allyn leaned forward, her green eyes glowing. "Jason, you'll probably think I'm crazy, but here's why I came: You need a ship, and I—I need a husband." She smiled at his sudden reaction, for his mouth parted, and his eyes blinked. "Yes, we both need something, and I know I'm willing to do my part to see that you get your ship if you're willing to help me get what I want, which is freedom and independence."

Jason Larrimore had known many women and heard some strange proposals. Carefully he asked, in order to clarify things, "Let me get this straight—we get married, you buy me a ship, and you get Twelve Trees. Is that it?"

"Yes, that's it."

Larrimore smiled broadly, leaned forward, and shook his head. "I think you're crazy," he said amiably. "I never heard such a wild scheme in all my life."

Allyn's face flushed a rich red. She felt the heat rising to her cheeks, and she said harshly, "If that's the way you feel about it, then that's all there is to it."

She started to rise, but Larrimore reached across the table and pulled her down. "Wait a minute," he said. "I didn't mean to hurt your feelings, but you've been thinking about this for some time, haven't you? Now you just tossed it at me. Give me a minute to think."

Allyn said, "What I'm proposing is not a real marriage. You can buy your ship, and I think you could make your fortune with it. But Twelve Trees will be *mine*." She hesitated and said in a lower tone, "And my life will be mine." A sudden color suffused her cheeks, and she gave him a direct stare as she said, "I don't want you in my bed."

Larrimore stared at her bluntness. "That's plain enough," he said. "Speaking right out, aren't you?"

"I don't think I'll ever love a man," she said quietly. "But I would love to have a place, and I would love to have the freedom to do what I please. Those are the things I want. You probably don't want to even think about this. I know men want a wife in—in every sense of the word, and there's no reason why you should be any different." Allyn shook her head in resignation. "Oh, why did I come? It's just a crazy idea!"

Once again she attempted to rise, but he said, "Wait, Allyn—" When she paused, he said, "I don't think you know what you're asking. Marriage is for a long time. If we got married, I could never have anybody else; neither could you. Divorces are hard to come by, especially in the South."

"I don't know how much time I have, but I want to do something more than just be a slave to some man," she said coldly. His refusal or semi-refusal had angered her. She was embarrassed and humiliated that after steeling herself to make such an offer, he was turning her down. She said abruptly, "Forget that I even mentioned it!"

Larrimore leaned back and looked at her. He thought about the long days ahead, about his penniless condition, and as the silence ran on, his choice became clear. "I think it would be a mistake," he said finally, "but I want a ship more than I want to live. I'll tell you what—give me a day, and you take a day, and we'll think about it. I'll meet you here tomorrow at two o'clock. If that's what you want and that's what I want, we'll do it."

"All right, I'll see you tomorrow at two o'clock. Come to my room at the Patterson."

She arose and started to leave. He called after her, "Didn't you forget something?"

"Forget what?"

"You didn't pay for the supper."

Allyn flushed, reached into her purse, and put some money on the table.

"You'll have to give me enough to pay my hotel bill," he said, "and I need a shave and a few other things. A hundred dollars ought to tide me over." He smiled and said, "Until we get married, that is. Then you can tell me what my allowance will be. I'm not up on the rules of being a kept man."

Allyn saw that he was not serious. She handed him a few bills then turned, saying, "I'll see you tomorrow, but I can tell you right now, I won't change my mind. I'll keep my part of the bargain." She gazed at him and said in a steady tone, "And if we do this, you'll keep your part of the bargain—*all* of it."

"Or what?" Larrimore demanded in an innocent tone. "Will you shoot me if I try to break into your bedroom?"

Allyn Rocklin stared at him thoughtfully then nodded and

said, "Yes, I will shoot you." Then she turned and walked away.

Watching her go, Jason Larrimore found that her answer had delighted him. "By George, I think she'd do it!" he muttered. He got up and left the room, wondering what his decision would be. When he was back in his room, he thought, *I want a ship, but do I want it this bad?*

At two o'clock the next afternoon, a knock came at the door of Allyn's room. She had dark shadows under her eyes, for she had not slept at all well. She had risen at daylight, dressed, and gone for a long walk, but had eaten nothing.

She stared at the door almost in fear for a moment, raising her hands to her breast, her eyes wide with anticipation. Then she straightened her back, walked over, and opened the door. "Come in, Jason," she said calmly.

Larrimore entered, pulled off his hat, and turned to Allyn. For a moment he said nothing and then murmured, "I didn't sleep much last night."

"Neither did I."

Larrimore considered her carefully and then said, "You know, I said yesterday that we were alike. You were angry about that."

"I remember. I still don't agree."

"Well, we're alike in one way. We both mean to have what we want no matter what it costs to get it."

Allyn raised her hand to her throat and for one moment could not think of what to say. Finally, she said, "Does that mean that you'll go through with it?"

"Yes." A calculating look came into his eyes. "You remember I kissed you."

"Against my will," she reminded him quickly. She had been ashamed ever since that kiss at her response to his touch. And now she stared at him and said, "Don't start this way. I've told you my terms. If you're not willing to meet them—"

"You don't have to worry about my keeping the bargain," Jason said at once. "Let's be agreed. You buy me a ship, and I satisfy the requirements for your getting the money and the property. We live together, but as you put it, we don't share the same bedroom. But what about other women I might see?"

A flush came to her cheeks, and she held her head high. "I'll never ask you about them. I don't want to hear."

A smile touched his lips, and he asked almost idly, "Well, what about your men friends? Am I supposed to ignore them?"

"You don't seem to understand, Jason," Allyn said. "This is a business partnership, nothing else. What you do with your life is your own business—what I do with mine is none of your business." She halted then said, "I think both of us are crazy for even thinking about it."

"You're probably right." He hesitated then put out his hand. She took it, and he held it tightly for a moment. "These are insane times we're living in. It's infected everybody, I think." Her hand felt fragile in his, soft and defenseless. He'd thought about this long and hard, and now he said, "Make sure this is what you want, Allyn."

"I'm sure," she whispered then pulled her hand back. "Like you say, you'll get what you want, and I'll get what I want."

"We're probably both fools, but I've been a fool about other things," he said. He stood staring at her then said, "We'll have to put on some sort of a masquerade, I suppose, for Mark and your family."

"I suppose. I'll go home today. You come tomorrow, stay a couple of days—then we'll tell my father."

"A whirlwind courtship! Sorry I don't play a guitar and can't sing love songs."

"That won't be required," Allyn said. Now that the thing was settled, she had to fight down the feelings that seemed to close her throat. "We'll just each remember our part of the bargain."

"All right—it's settled, then." He turned to the door, opened it, then stood looking back at her. He started to speak, and she waited. But whatever it was he intended to say, he changed his mind. "I'll see you tomorrow," he said quietly and turned and shut the door.

Allyn walked over and sat down on the bed. She found she was trembling so much that her knees were unable to hold her up. Finally, without explanation, she turned over and buried her face in the pillow and began to weep.

Chapter 16

All Brides Are Beautiful

"I'm surprised that Jason has stayed so long, even though it's only a couple of days." Mark Rocklin was sitting in his wheelchair looking out the window of his room as Susanna made his bed. Below him he watched as Allyn and Jason Larrimore strolled past. "Jason's not a man to waste time. He's always been active, on the go."

Susanna patted the pillow in place then turned to come over and stand beside him. She, too, watched the pair, silently for a moment, then expressed her thoughts. "I don't know him as well as you do. He's restless, though; anyone can see that."

Mark looked up at her and said, "You know, everything that Allyn could wish lies ahead of her. All the good things."

Susanna reached out and touched his hair, saying, "I've got to cut your hair; you're getting shaggy." She considered his words and finally said, "Everything that lies ahead of her probably won't be good. It never is, is it? We have to learn to take the good with the bad." They both remained silent, and she finally added, "I've prayed that the good things would come to her, and I know they will. God will hear us." She looked at him fondly and said, "You've come a long way in a short time, Mark. Not many men, or women, learn to know God as quickly as you have."

He shook his head. "I'm a child," he said. "If I'd found God years ago. . ." He stirred his shoulders restlessly then smiled at her. "You can't go back, can you? None of us. All you can do is accept where you are, live in the time that God's given, and maybe try to make up for lost time."

The two sat there talking for a little while until Susanna rose and left the room, giving him a cheerful word. Again he turned and saw that his daughter and Larrimore had moved over to the line of trees. As he watched, they sat down on an old log, appearing to be engaged in some sort of earnest conversation. Mark thought about the things that can come into a person's life, the sounds of a family through a house, the deep midnight silence of that house when people slept in peace, the first stirrings of spring, the smell of hay rising from a sickled meadow, the voice of one you love calling to you fresh and clear. These were the little experiences that when put together made a life. If a man took them as they came and stopped for them and lived each good moment of them, he was a rich man. He realized, with a deep grief, that his own failure had been the failure to stop. Somehow he had lived for the future and had been impatient for today. So he had hastened through the day and lost the wonder of these full moments. Now he realized that over the years he had starved himself. He stirred, put his hands out on the windowsill, and said aloud, "On this earth there's only one moment in which to live—that little bit of time we call *now*!"

Later in the day Allyn came to him. She said at once, "Jason went out for a ride. He loves horses, doesn't he?"

"Yes, I think if he hadn't been a seaman, he might have turned out to be a jockey, although he's too big for that, of course." The light filtered through the window and fell on her, sending golden glints dancing in her hair. "You look very nice today," he said. "Is that a new dress?"

She was wearing a blue dress with a white collar and cuffs that fit her snugly. "Yes, I bought it when I was in Richmond. I felt like a fool paying as much as I did, but everything's so high there." She sat down beside him and talked for a few moments. Finally, she said, "What can I fix you to eat tonight? Anything special?"

"Just whatever the rest of you eat." He had no appetite and ate primarily to satisfy the pleadings of the women, who somehow felt that food would solve all problems. "I'm surprised at Jason," he said. "He doesn't usually stay this long in one place—not unless there's a card table or horse race or some excitement going on. Pretty dull life for him." He fingered the coverlet over his knees then asked, "Has he said anything about losing his ship?"

Allyn hesitated then said, "It really tore the heart out of him, Father. He said once that he didn't care much about anything after he lost that ship. It was almost like a wife to him, he said." The thought amused her for a moment, and the corners of her full lips turned up. She made a fine picture as she sat there in the amber rays of the sun. There was a fullness and a spirit of life about her that pleased Mark as he looked at her. She caught his glance and smiled. "He said ships made better wives than women because you could control them better. Just a matter, he said, of putting the sails up and down and hauling the rudder around one way or the other. Not a very complimentary thing to women."

"Well, that's Jason's way. I'm not sure he means all he says. Sometimes I wonder if I've ever known him. He's pretty outgoing, but deep under all that talk, I think there's a pretty sensitive fellow." He saw that she was restless and finally asked quietly, "Is something wrong?"

Allyn licked her lips and then said, "I've got something to tell you. I'm—I'm not sure how you'll take it."

Apprehension ran along Mark's nerves. He had suffered such terrible misfortunes that despite himself and his newborn faith, he could not help feeling some dire portent in her words and in her demeanor. "What is it, Allyn?" he asked quietly, preparing himself for the news that she was going back to New Orleans. He hated to see her throw her life away in a place like that, and although he had already determined to help her all that he could, he longed for her to be with him for whatever time he had left.

"I–I've been thinking about what you said, about getting married, about a woman needing a husband." She hesitated for a moment, and he saw the uncertainty that lay over her. It was unusual, for despite her youth she had an assurance and a determination that flashed forth out of her spirit. It showed in the set of her back, the way she lifted her chin when she made statements. But now she was fragile and more vulnerable than he'd ever seen her. He could not imagine what she wanted to say. Finally, she said it. "I think you were right, so I'm going to be married."

An alarm went off in Mark's mind, and he said abruptly, "Married? Why, Allyn!"

"I know you'll think it's rash, but it's what you wanted, isn't it? And I suppose you can guess who the man is."

At once all the pieces fell into place in Mark's mind. Surprise washed over him, and he exclaimed, "You can't mean Jason?"

"Yes, I do."

Mark suddenly realized he had done the girl a grave

disservice. "I pushed you into this, Allyn," he said, regret and remorse marring his face. "I can see that now."

"No, you were right. A woman is alone in the world. She does need someone. That's the way the world is, so Jason and I have decided to get married." She lifted her chin in a gesture of defiance, but her eyes pleaded with him for understanding. "I know it's sudden, but we have big plans that you'll like. One of them is that we're going to take part of the inheritance that you're making available to me and buy Jason a ship. I think it's only fair for you to know, before we marry, that that's what we'll do. He's a seagoing man, and he needs a ship."

Mark was shaken by this disclosure. As she spoke on, he tried to think of some way to prevent this girl from plunging ahead. "But you don't love him," he said finally.

"I—don't think I shall ever love any man the way the books tell about it, Father. But we have an understanding. He is a good man, and I'll try to be a good matron of Twelve Trees."

"That's not much to build a marriage on."

"It's more than some have," Allyn said quietly. "Anyway, he'll be coming to talk to you. I wanted to tell you first, and I want to ask you not to worry. You and Jason and me, we'll go to Twelve Trees, and it'll be good." She got up suddenly and did something very unusual. She leaned over, put her arms around him, and held him tightly for a moment.

Mark felt the warmness of her body against him, then the soft touch of her lips on his cheek. Without a word, she turned and whirled away, and he could see the distress written on her face. The door closed, and he sat there unable to think clearly.

Five minutes later, when Jason entered the room, Mark said at once, "Jason, this is wrong. You don't love that girl."

Jason came over, moving softly for a big man, and sat down

in the chair. He leaned back, his blue eyes fixed on Mark, and said, "I came to make you a promise, Mark."

"A promise?"

"I know this seems rash to you. It does to me, too." He looked down at his hands, spread them open, then closed them and looked up again. "You're a smart man, Mark. I've never known anyone that I admired more, so I just want to promise you that no harm will ever come to your daughter through me. I'll do the best I can to take care of her."

"There's one thing you can't do," Mark said, his voice grating. "You can't love her. That means you can't give her the thing that a husband ought to bring to a woman."

"In that, you are right," Jason admitted reluctantly. "I don't think she loves me, either. What we have here, Mark, is a situation of two people who need each other. You know me, I've been one of the roughs. But I want you to know that I'll take care of Allyn. Twelve Trees is hers, and I know I can make it this time with a ship, so she'll be provided for." He leaned forward, intensity drawing his face fine. He was a powerful man, and strength seemed to flow out of him. "This country is going to the devil, Mark, and we both know it. The South's not going to win this war, and when it's over, who knows what will come? Even if you gave Allyn a place, there's no guarantee she could keep it. She needs somebody to help her fight for it, and that's what I propose to do."

Mark sat there quietly as the big man spoke. Jason finally leaned back and shrugged, saying, "I hope you'll understand. It's something we want to do. When I made up my mind, I was thinking partly of you. I owe you a lot, Mark. This is one thing I can do for you—take care of your daughter. And you never know—maybe we can come to love each other the way you feel we should."

Mark studied the face of the blond man, the sturdy shoulders, strong hands, the face like a Viking. He knew this man, his strengths and weaknesses, better than most, and finally did what he felt he must do. "All right, Jason," he said. "God give you the strength, you and Allyn both, to do this thing."

Rooney looked across to where Allyn was sitting in a chair sewing and said, "I declare, Allyn, I'm jealous of you."

Allyn looked up at the girl who was observing her and said, "Jealous? What do you mean, Rooney?"

Rooney put her own sewing down, flexed her fingers, and stood up, arching her back. Then she smiled at Allyn and said, "Why, here I'm the one that's had the wedding date set, but you and Jason are getting married before Lowell and me. It's not fair!"

Allyn put her sewing down and leaned back in the chair. She and Jason had set their wedding date only a week away, which had brought shock waves throughout the entire Rocklin world. Susanna had been disturbed when Mark had given her the news, more disturbed than Mark had ever seen her. The two had talked long into the night, and finally Susanna had said, "It's not right, Mark. No man and woman should try to live together as man and wife unless they love each other."

Mark had agreed with her, but finally after talking with Allyn, Susanna had seen the adamant quality of her spirit and had reluctantly agreed to do all she could. The wedding would be at Gracefield so that Mark would be able to attend, for he was too weak to make a trip even to the church.

The rest of the family had received the news with the same

sort of sheltered amazement. They had done their best to welcome Jason, to make him feel at home, but still there was an air of unreality.

Now Allyn looked across and saw the petulance on Rooney's lips and smiled. "I know it's hard on you. A bride wants to be the center of attention, I suppose. But Jason's got to find a ship. Perhaps even have one built. We want to get started in a hurry on that project; then we've got to settle down at Twelve Trees and make a place for my father."

"Oh, I know, Allyn," Rooney said, and a smile softened her features. She said, "I guess I'm just nervous. I don't know the first thing about being a wife."

"I don't suppose I do, either," Allyn said. "But don't worry. Why, you and Lowell are perfect for each other. Anyone can see that. He lights up like a candle every time you walk into the room."

"He's so—so sweet," Rooney said. She looked around cautiously and said, "Allyn, I hate to ask you this, but I don't know anything about—about…" She flushed richly and blurted, "Well, I don't know how to be a *wife*—do you know what I mean?"

Allyn knew exactly what she meant, and her own face became suffused with color. Then she said, "Well, I don't know anything, either." The humor of it took her, and she said, "Here we are, two brides-to-be that don't have the vaguest idea of what to expect. It's like shoving off to sea in a sieve, isn't it?"

Rooney giggled and hugged Allyn. "We'll make out all right. I think I love Lowell so much that I'll be whatever I have to be to make him happy."

Her words struck against Allyn and brought a sudden halt to the light conversation. She got up at once and said hurriedly, "I—I think I'll go see how my father's feeling. We'll finish this sewing later."

WALL OF FIRE

When she left the room, Rooney stared after her. "That was odd," she murmured. She ran over in her mind what she had said, thinking she might have offended Allyn, and realized it was when she talked about loving Lowell that a door had seemed to close down and the light had died in Allyn's eyes. She hurried at once to Susanna, repeated the conversation, and asked, "What's wrong? Is Allyn just afraid of getting married, do you think?"

Susanna hesitated, not knowing how to answer. "I suppose most brides are that way—apprehensive. And after all, Allyn and Jason haven't had the opportunity of getting to know each other. But they'll be all right, I am sure."

Rooney left the room shortly after that. Dorrie, who had been standing at the other end of the kitchen mixing biscuit dough, turned and came over to say, "Humph! Dat ain't so, what you just said."

Susanna, accustomed to Dorrie's dire proclamations of gloom, looked up at her. "What's wrong, Dorrie?"

"Ain't nuffin' wrong wit me. It dat woman—dat's whut's wrong."

"Allyn? She'll be all right," Susanna said quickly. "We'll have to help her all we can."

"Humph!" Dorrie snorted again, disgust filling her face. She shook her head and put her hands on her hips, saying, "Ain't no good gonna come outta it. You mark my words! Dat's a triflin' man, dat sailor! I guess I ought to know one when I sees one. I seed 'nough of 'em in my days. He ain't gonna make dat girl happy." She snorted emphatically then turned, walked back, and began pounding the biscuit dough with short vicious jabs of her fist.

Susanna thought, *Dorrie knows more about people than most*

anyone I know, and she feels about this even more strongly than I do. She thought about the fragile situation—Mark's illness, the newly born relationship between the father and the daughter, and now this tall stranger who had come in and would be a part of that.

A pang of apprehension flooded Susanna. She sat there feeling helpless as a swimmer caught in a strong current, and all she could do was say, "Oh God, help us all through this! Don't let them make some terrible mistake!"

"It's a good thing this train is so crowded," Bing said as he helped Deborah to the ground. He leaned closer and whispered, "Nobody'll pick us out as spies out of this mob, will they?" His brown eyes sparkled with excitement as he turned to Noel, who was struggling with two heavy suitcases. Reaching forward, he took them and said, "You get the rest of them, Noel. I'll find us a carriage."

He moved through the crowd that had disembarked from the train, using his bulk to force a way. He held the two heavy suitcases as lightly as if they were filled with air, and Deborah followed in his wake. Finding a carriage drawn by a lop-eared ancient mule, Bing tossed the suitcases into the back and said, "You two go on. I want to look the town over a little bit. I'll meet you at the Spotswood Restaurant for supper tonight."

"That might not be the best," Deborah said quickly. "I don't want us to be seen together any more than necessary. We'll meet you out on the docks about six o'clock."

"All right," Bing said cheerfully. He picked his suitcase out of the back of the wagon bed and moved away.

"It'd be all right for us, I suppose, to be seen together," Noel said, "since we're engaged and I'm here on official business." He helped her into the carriage and then climbed up to sit beside her. "Take us to the Spotswood, driver."

"Yes, sir!" The driver urged the weary-looking mule into a stumbling walk.

"I hope the mule doesn't die before we get there," Noel whispered into Deborah's ear. "That would call attention to us." He was sitting close to her and impulsively put his arms around her and kissed her cheek. She turned to him and opened her lips to protest, but he closed them firmly with another kiss. "That's the way to stop a woman from talking," he said with satisfaction as he sat back.

"Noel! You shouldn't do that—not in public!" She was actually pleased, for Noel had not been brought up in a demonstrative family. She had had to educate him. Now she was pleased with the gesture, for it was the first time he had ever kissed her in public.

"Shouldn't do it in public? Well, let's get somewhere in private, then," he joked. Noel was feeling better. He had been apprehensive about the project at first, but as they had made plans, he had grown more and more excited. Now that he was actually in Richmond, his dark eyes glowed with excitement. As they moved along the street toward the Spotswood, he thought over the plan. He remembered what he had said when he had sprung it on Bing and Deborah.

"What we'll do," he had said, "is march right into the lions' den. We've got to have some excuse for being in Richmond, and there's bound to be someone that'll remember you, Deborah. I don't think we can go around wearing disguises, but these whiskers of mine will be my disguise. Besides, I was almost a scarecrow when you and Bing got me out of that prison. What we'll say is that I'm your fiancé and you've come to visit your family. A lot of that goes on—people from the North coming South to visit those they've left behind here."

"Well, what excuse will you have for being here?" Deborah had demanded. "You've got to have some reason for coming along with me."

"Ah! That's the heart of my plan," Noel had said. "We'll let it be known that I'm a writer and that I've come to write a series of stories giving the North a more sympathetic view of what people in the South are like. The power of the press, you know. They'll put on their best faces for us—I hope!"

But as they trundled along, watching the crowds that thronged the streets of Richmond, Noel was growing apprehensive again. "I hope this scheme works," he murmured. "It's the only game in town. I'm going to stop by the newspaper office as soon as I get you settled and meet the editor. That way it will establish my credentials, and hopefully I'll get on the inside of things a little bit."

Deborah shook her head. "No Yankee's going to get on the inside of many things," she said. "Not here in Richmond. You know how they hate us down here."

"I know, but at least it's a way of explaining our presence. It'll be all right, you'll see."

They arrived at the Spotswood and rented two rooms. After depositing Deborah and her luggage in her room, Noel threw his bag in his room and went at once to the newspaper office.

The editor of the *Richmond Examiner*, a tall, stooped man named Tim Franklin, greeted him with a great deal of suspicion. He leaned back from where he sat behind his desk and smiled frostily. "So you've come to get a story on what wonderful folks we Rebels are, if I understand you, Mr. Kojak?"

Kojak saw the skepticism in Franklin's eyes and grinned brashly. "Well, I hardly think I could put it that strongly," he answered. "I intend to report what I see honestly—and if you think the South can bear the light of honest reporting, I'm your man."

Franklin shrugged his wiry shoulders. "I don't think you'd ever get anything printed in the North that smells of truth," he said. He was a rabid secessionist and despised Abraham Lincoln with all of his heart, but he seemed to see something in the young man that he found acceptable. "All right, make this your headquarters while you're in town, Mr. Kojak. As a matter of fact, I'm going out now to do a little investigative reporting, I guess you'd call it. Come along. I'll introduce you to some prominent Rebels."

It was a stroke of fortune, Noel found, going to the newspaperman. All afternoon he trudged along with the tall editor, and by the time he got back to the Spotswood, he was glowing with excitement. "It's going to be all right, Deborah," he bubbled over. "Franklin's introduced me to the mayor, to one of the generals, and they've all made me kind of a guest. I guess Franklin convinced them I was part honest"—he grinned—"as honest as a Yankee could be, so we're going to be all right."

"Oh, that's wonderful," Deborah said. They were in her room, and she went over and gave him a quick squeeze. "Tomorrow I'll go see Uncle Gid. I'll have to find Aunt Melanie, but she's here in town and shouldn't be too hard to find."

They went that night to meet with Bing, who announced he had found a place in a rooming house. They set up a meeting place and a system of messages and then parted. The next morning Deborah found Melanie by going from hotel to hotel asking for Mrs. Melanie Rocklin. At her third attempt, the clerk said,

"Why, yes, Mrs. Rocklin's here." He gave her the room number, and she went up at once and knocked on the door.

When Melanie opened it, she stared at Deborah in astonishment. "Deborah! What in the world—!"

"Aunt Melanie!" Deborah flew into the room and grabbed her aunt, whom she'd always loved dearly. She squeezed her so hard the older woman gasped, then gave her a delighted grin. "I'm so glad to see you."

"What are you doing here, Deborah?" Melanie gasped. "How did you get here?"

"Got here on the train," Deborah said with a smile. Her eyes sparkled, and she suddenly realized the door was open. Turning, she closed it then turned back and said, "Aunt Melanie, Bing and Noel are with me."

Melanie stared at her without comprehension. "Why, that's dangerous for Northerners to come into Richmond at a time like this."

"Listen, here's the way it is. We're going to get Uncle Gid out of prison." Seeing the shock touch her aunt's eyes, she said, "Wait a minute! Come and sit down; let me tell you all about it. I know you think I'm crazy, but Noel and I have a plan. Sit down, and we'll talk about it...."

*

The wedding of Jason Larrimore and Allyn Rocklin took place on October 10. Dorrie and Susanna had struggled to make the house a substitute for the church where Rocklins usually married. The family—as many as could come—were crowded into the rooms. Since the army was ensconced, for the main part, within Richmond, the house swarmed with Rocklins. Denton

Rocklin was there with his wife, Raimey. Raimey was glowing with health, as was her baby, Thomas.

Lowell, of course, was there, never getting more than two steps away from Rooney. Rooney's brother, Buck, was in and out of the festivities. He was only thirteen and had been brought up under a hard school, along with his sister, Rooney, but life at Gracefield had brought out the best in him.

As the morning of the wedding dawned, the family began to arrive. Clay was granted leave, and he and Melora were there to greet them. They greeted Amy Rocklin Franklin and her husband, Brad, who came from Lindwood. Two of their children were there, Rachel and Les, while the other two, Vince and Grant, and Rachel's husband, Jake, were gone on duty. Marianne Bristol and her husband, Claude, from the Hartsworth plantation were there along with two of their children, Austin and Marie.

It was a time of happiness for Susanna to see the children filling the house, and she said to Dorrie, "Isn't this wonderful to see so many of the family together again?"

Dorrie nodded grumpily. "If you has to cooks for dis army, it ain't so much fun!"

Susanna hugged her quickly and said, "You don't fool me, Dorrie. You love this as much as I do."

The day went by quickly, and at two o'clock in the afternoon, the ceremony took place. Clay stood beside Jason as they waited nervously in an outer room for the music to call them into the large hall, the only place large enough for such a wedding. It was a ballroom, actually, but chairs had been moved in, and it was now packed. Jason tugged at his collar and said, "Major Rocklin, how does a man endure all this?" He glanced nervously at the door that led out to the hall, then at the outer door. "What I'd like to do is run right through that door, get on a horse, and ride away as fast as I can!"

Clay had learned to like the tall sailor, so he came over and clapped his hand on his shoulder. "A typical reaction. All bridegrooms are the same."

Jason gave Clay a look and shook his head. "I'll bet you didn't do that. Not from what you've told me."

Clay, realizing he had overstated the case, shrugged. "Well, I confess I didn't have any temptation to run away, but it's common enough to be nervous, I suppose. Like before battle"—he grinned widely—"once you get into it, you'll be all right." He grew serious and said, "Listen! That's the music; come on."

Jason Larrimore pulled himself up straight. He was wearing a gray silk waistcoat with satin stripes over his pleated shirt with a turned-down collar and a starched bow-tied cravat. He wore a frock-coated wool suit and looked very handsome, but his face twitched nervously as he passed through the door. Once he stepped into the large ballroom, the nervousness increased. It was filled with strangers, and he had had no real peace about this plan since its conception.

This is all a mistake! he thought wildly. *If I had any sense, I'd run away right now!* He knew he would not, so he stood beside Clay and the minister, his eyes fixed on the door through which his bride would enter.

Allyn had been assisted into her wedding dress by Rooney and Rena. They had fussed over her, and Rena had said mischievously, "I don't think you could even button your shoes, could you, Allyn?"

"I don't think I could," Allyn said faintly. She stood there getting into her dress, which was a white silk satin overlaid with pale peach lace flounces. She wore a stole and a pair of white kid gloves, and carried a small bouquet. Some small silk flowers were pinned to her bosom. She glanced at herself in a mirror and saw that her face was almost dead white. Then the music sounded.

"Here comes the bride," Rooney said. "Come along, your father's waiting for you."

Feeling like someone in a vague dream, Allyn allowed herself to be escorted to the door. When she passed through it, she found Mark, wearing a brown suit, in his wheelchair. He reached up one hand and she took it, and he felt it tremble. "Don't be afraid," he said, noting that her lips were tremulous and her face pale. "God will be with us."

He nodded, and Rooney stepped behind the wheelchair. They moved down the hall and then passed through the door that led to the ballroom. The room was packed with visitors, all of whom turned to look at her, and Allyn felt totally weak and inadequate. Mark squeezed her hand and said, "Come now, I'm proud of you. You look so beautiful!" He looked up at her, saying, "All brides are beautiful, but I've never seen one like you."

Allyn began to move forward as Rooney propelled the wheelchair, and then she looked up. The visitors, the surroundings, the flowers—all faded when she looked into the face of Jason Larrimore.

She seemed to float down the aisle, unconscious of her feet—even of the steps she made—but she found herself standing in front of the minister, who began to speak. She was so frightened and overwhelmed by what she was doing that she could barely understand the words. Finally, he asked, "Who gives this woman?" and she heard Mark say firmly, "I give her," and then he released her hand and she found herself standing by Jason. She could not look up at him as the ceremony moved on. She heard the words "to love, honor, and obey. . .with this ring I thee wed. . .cling to each other as long as you both shall live," but she was mostly conscious of his large hand as it held hers. As he slipped the ring on her finger, however, she looked up.

He was staring down at her with a strange expression on his bronzed face. His lips were tight, and his eyelids were half closed over his blue eyes. Studying her carefully, he seemed to be a stranger. *I'm giving myself to him—a stranger!* she thought wildly.

And then she heard the words "I now pronounce you man and wife." Jason's hands closed on hers, and the minister said, more lightly, "You may kiss your bride, Mr. Larrimore."

Allyn felt his hand on her back, and she was turned to face him. She lifted her head, and her lips were half parted, her eyes filled with fear as he bent over her. She felt the firm pressure of his lips, his arms drew her closer against him, and she thought for one flashing moment of the other time that she had felt his kiss.

And then it was over. The pianoforte played the "Wedding March" as they exited in spirited fashion, and when they stepped out and were headed down the hall toward where the reception was to be, he suddenly stopped her and said, "Are you afraid?"

Allyn looked up at him and said quietly, "Yes. I am afraid."

Surprisingly, he nodded. "Me, too. I guess it's like jumping off a cliff in the dark. You leap off and don't know how far you're going to fall or how bad it will be when you hit." Then he studied her face carefully and said, "Come along; we'll be all right."

It was not much consolation, but she followed him toward the reception room, where they were surrounded almost at once by what seemed like hundreds of people coming by to shake her hand, to hug her, to claim the traditional kiss.

But all Allyn could think was, *I've done a foolish thing!*

Chapter 17

The Wedding Night

After the noise and laughter and the happy talk of the reception, Allyn was glad to escape to the carriage. Her hand was warm from the many times it had been grasped, and she had felt strange about the Rocklin family who had come to her one at a time, the women kissing her cheek, sometimes the men also. *Nearly all of them,* she thought, *said something nice about my being a member of the family now.*

Soon she shifted her eyes to catch a glimpse of Jason, who had gotten into the seat and spoken to the horses. They started with a jolt, and the cries of those who'd come to say their farewells rose in the late afternoon air.

"Turn around, smile, and wave at them," Jason whispered. "Like this." He turned around, lifted one hand, and gave them a broad smile, adding to Allyn, "A bride should be happy."

Allyn did as he urged. Her eyes ran over the crowd, picking out Susanna, whose eyes even now held some sort of reluctance. Behind her, on the porch, Dorrie glared at her in absolute disfavor, almost hatred. *She thinks I'm mistreating Mark,* Allyn thought but quickly pulled her mind away from the black woman. Her glance picked up Rooney and Lowell waving, then Josh and Rena, the Bristols, the Franklins. As the carriage reached the outer road and turned right, she leaned back in the leather padded seat and gave a gusty sigh of relief.

Jason looked at her quickly. "I guess we're both glad that's over," he mused. "It never ceases to amaze me how much trouble people will go to to get married. If it had been my choice, we would have just gone to a preacher."

"No, Father needed this," Allyn said. "It was for his benefit, not yours, not mine. I guess it was partly for the whole family. They needed some kind of assurance, I suppose."

He gave her a cautious look. She had clean-running physical lines, and her face was a mirror that changed with her feelings. She took up the material of her dress now and let it slide through her fingers. Even in that small act, he noted, she was graceful. Then she turned to look at him, and he saw pride. Yet something smothered this like a cloud. The horses clipped along at a fast gait, but neither Jason nor Allyn spoke. As they rode on, the sun grew large and red on the horizon. Except for a few murmured remarks, both of them kept their silence, their own thoughts pressing in on their minds. Finally, after what seemed like hours but was only a short time, they pulled up to the driveway that led to Twelve Trees.

"Glad to be getting here before dark," Jason said as he guided the horses toward the house that sat back off the road half sheltered by a line of beech trees. They had been at Twelve Trees twice during their brief engagement, meeting the servants and slaves and moving a few things into their quarters. "It's a nice-looking place," Jason continued. "I never cared for the big, fancy houses, even like Gracefield. Something always seems too showy about it to me, but this place," he said, waving his large hand toward it, "it's got something about it that's more homey."

Allyn looked and saw what he meant. It was a small house, compared to Gracefield, at least, built in the manner of early Southern plantations, with a porch that spanned the entire front. The windows were evenly spaced, and on the second story lantern lights were already casting their glow out in the gathering darkness. It had a steep-pitched roof broken by brick chimneys, and white smoke lifted gently out of them, curling in lazy spirals into the darkness of the upper air.

Jason pulled the horses up, and at once a muscular black man was there, saying, "Yes, suh, Captain. Let me take dis team."

"Hello, Caesar," Jason greeted cheerfully. "How's everything?"

"Oh, fine, suh," Caesar replied. "Everthin's ready in de house. You and Miz Allyn go right on in. Dey's waitin' supper fo' you."

Allyn took the hand that Jason extended, stepped to the ground, and moved toward the house. "I'll bring yo' bags in, Marse Jason," Caesar called out, and he murmured their thanks.

They climbed the white steps, where they were met by the servants. Flossie and Ned, both in their sixties, greeted them at once. Flossie said, "You come on in, now. We wuz afraid you wouldn't get here 'fore dark. We got a nice supper all fixed for you."

Ned bobbed up and down, his white hair catching the last rays of the lanterns on the porch. "Yes, suh, it's gonna be the best weddin' supper you ever had, I bet!" He grinned broadly, his teeth very white against his ebony skin.

Jason smiled at them, reached into his pocket, and passed some coins to Ned. "You take Flossie to town tomorrow and buy her something pretty. Get yourself something, too, Ned. Sort of a wedding present in reverse."

"Yas, suh! I'll just do dat," Ned said.

However, Flossie promptly reached over and put her hands out. "You give me dat money. You ain't got sense enough to spend it right."

She took the money that Ned surrendered reluctantly, and they stepped aside. Allyn walked into the house and, as nervous as she was, admired again the polished heart pine floors, the ten-foot ceilings, the walls covered with delicate paper, and the fine furniture—mostly of gleaming oak and walnut.

"You go to your room, missy," Flossie said, "and fresh up. Den you comes back and we'll have supper."

"All right, Flossie," Allyn agreed. She moved up the curving staircase, running her hand along the smooth oak stair rail. Everything was handmade in the house, created by craftsmen who took pride in their work. She moved down the hall to the room that they had chosen and entered. She stopped momentarily and stared around. Two lamps shed their pale amber light over the room. The large walnut bed was made with fresh linen and turned down carefully. She stared at the bed for a moment—then pulled her eyes away from it. As soon as Caesar brought the trunk in, she gave him his wedding present, saying, "Buy yourself something nice, Caesar. Thank you for your trouble."

"Yas, ma'am," Caesar said. "Anything you wants, you jest let me know."

Allyn changed at once out of her traveling dress, donning a simple blue dress of linen. After washing her face and brushing her hair, she went downstairs. When she entered the dining room, she found Jason already seated. He arose, motioned toward the place across from him. "A little lonesome in here," he said, "just the two of us. The Jennings must have had lots of company, didn't they, Flossie?"

"Oh yas, suh. Dey was entertaining folk—neighbors come from all around to eat wif de Jennings." She had a broad face and deep-set, almost black eyes that caught the glint of the lantern. She smiled, revealing a gold tooth in front, saying, "Dey gonna come see you, too, Captain—you and yo' lady. It's gonna be happy times here at Twelve Trees."

"We'll be bringing my father here shortly. We'll have to make up the downstairs room for him. He's an invalid, you know."

"Yas, ma'am, I knows. We'll take good care of him—you don't worry 'bout dat."

The meal was excellent—chicken, potatoes, mushrooms, and a cut of meat that Allyn didn't recognize. "What is this, Ellie?" she asked the small servant girl who was filling the water glasses and doing the work of a waitress.

"Oh, that's coon, Miz Larrimore. Ain't it good?"

Allyn had always loved the sight of coons, thinking them clever animals. The idea of eating one was rather like eating a cat to her. She abruptly put her fork down and took a sip of water.

Jason grinned across the table at her, took a bite of his portion of the rich meat, and said, "Nothing better than coon—unless it's a nice, fat, greasy possum."

"You like possum?" Ned had come up to bring fresh bread. "Oh, dat's good, Captain, 'cause I know how to cotch 'em! And Flossie here, she know how to cook 'em. You take a nice juicy possum with a sweet tater in his mouth—ain't nothin' no finer!"

"We'll look forward to it, won't we, dear?" Jason said, his lips turned up in a grin.

Allyn stared at him and then said reluctantly, "I think I prefer the chicken."

They finished the meal, except for Allyn's portion of raccoon, and afterward went into the drawing room, where Ellie brought them coffee in fine china.

Jason sat down, stretched out his long legs, and looked utterly at peace with the world. Sipping the coffee, saying nothing, Allyn, who was sitting at his right, had a chance to examine him. She noticed that he had a scar on his neck that ran into the thick blond hair, and she wondered where he'd gotten it. She discovered another scar on his chin; this one was less noticeable. He was staring at the books, which lined the wall, with a remote and angular smile. She saw behind the toughness the years had somehow beaten into him. He sat with a looseness, and she could not help but admire his strength. He was over six feet and didn't show the bulkiness of his two hundred pounds. It was a distributed weight lying in the muscles of his chest and upper arms, on the broad flats of his shoulders and in the girth of his legs. He had big bones, she saw. His fingers were long and blunt at the ends and looked very strong.

"I'll be leaving fairly soon." He broke the silence suddenly. "We'll make the arrangements for me to write a check for the ship."

"That's fine," Allyn said quickly. "I—I hope you get a good one. Tell me about your last ship."

Looking at her, he raised one eyebrow curiously and shrugged his shoulders. "Didn't know you were interested in ships," he murmured then began to tell her about the *Eagle*. As he spoke, his voice made a pleasant baritone rumbling in the quiet room. He spoke almost lovingly of the ship he'd lost and finally gave Allyn a quick glance. "I guess I'll never find one I like as much as that one."

"Maybe so," Allyn said. "She'll be what you make her, won't she? I mean, don't the men who sail the ship pretty much determine what kind of a ship it is?"

He was impressed by her quickness. "I'm surprised that you'd know that, but that's the way it is. I've seen a few good hands and a good captain take an old tub and make a real clipper out of her." He spoke for a long time of ships he had sailed, some of the storms he had passed through, and some other difficulties. A large grandfather clock ticked the minutes away in the hall, and Allyn was acutely conscious of the passage of time.

Several times Ellie or Flossie came in to see if they would care for more dessert or more coffee. Finally, Jason yawned and said, "Well, I suppose I'm getting old." Flossie was picking up the coffee cups and deliberately not looking at them. Jason found this amusing, and he said, "Well, bride, I suppose it's time for us to go to bed. Come along."

Allyn got to her feet, and Jason came over and took her arm. "Good night, Flossie. We'll probably sleep late in the morning and won't require an early breakfast."

"Yas, suh."

Allyn walked out of the room, aware of the touch of Jason's hand on her arm. When they got to the hall, she pulled away deliberately, a gesture that amused him. Neither of them said anything until they had reached the landing and turned to go to the large bedroom at the end of the hall. When they got there, they noticed that the door was open. Stepping inside, Jason saw Ellie busy carrying fresh linens inside. "I brought you some fresh towels," she said. "If you wants any, I'll bring you some fresh hot water whenever you calls for it."

"Don't guess we'll require anything tonight. Good night,

Ellie," Jason said. He waited until the small maid had left the room, then shut the door.

Jason looked very large and formidable to Allyn as he stood there. She had assumed he would simply find another room to sleep in. But now she didn't know what to do. Her mind moved quickly as she walked over to the wardrobe and opened it up, saying nervously, "I suppose I'll have enough clothes. I don't guess there's much social life out here in the country."

"Oh, we'll be going to Richmond since it's not too far. Got to show off my new bride, don't I?" Jason moved over to the window. He sat down on the sill, turning his back to the outer air, and pulled one of the thin cheroots from his pocket and lit it up. He tossed the match outside and crossed his arms casually. "You know how it is," he remarked, a glint in his eye. "People expect newlyweds to stay sequestered for a while, but after that they need to get out and be seen."

Allyn moved over to the mirror, sat down, and began to brush her hair. She could not think of a thing to say, and the silence began to be oppressive. Jason suddenly got to his feet and said, "I'll go down for a time. I need to talk to Caesar about a horse for traveling back and forth to Richmond."

He left the room, and Allyn put down the hairbrush with almost a violent gesture. As soon as she heard his footsteps go down the hall, she walked at once to the door and slipped the lock. Then, turning her back, she leaned her head back and closed her eyes. She was incredibly weary; she couldn't remember ever being so tired and exhausted in all her life. It was not, she understood, the physical exertion, but the emotional reaction to the whole thing had enervated her, drained her until there seemed to be no strength left.

For a long time she stood there, her head back against the

door, her eyes closed. Then, finally, she took a deep breath, shook her shoulders slightly, and moved over toward the trunk. She stripped off the dress she'd worn for dinner, then the plain petticoat she'd worn under it. She glanced nervously at the door then quickly sponged off with the tepid water in the large basin on the washstand, drying herself with a thick, fluffy towel. Moving to the trunk, Allyn dug through her possessions and produced a long white cotton nightgown with green lace on the cuffs and collar. *This probably isn't what normal brides wear on their wedding night,* Allyn thought with dark humor, *but this isn't any normal marriage.* Then she sat down and began to brush her hair again.

The act of brushing her hair always seemed to calm her nerves. Her long cascade of auburn hair reached down to her waist, and there was a pleasure in running the brush and comb through it, feeling the shimmering mass beneath the ivory teeth of the comb.

Finally, her arm grew tired, so she put the brush and the comb back on the dressing table then walked over to the window. Outside, the air was cold and biting, but she enjoyed the brisk wind as it came inside and touched her face. It made her flesh stand up in goose bumps. She rubbed her arms quickly but remained there, looking out across the yard. A pale moon threw its beams on the trees and the open spaces, and Allyn wondered, *How will it be here? What kind of life will I have?*

Allyn started to go to bed, but she found that as tired as she was, she was too nervous to sleep. So instead she went to the trunk, pulled out a thick cotton robe, and put it on. Then she went back down to the kitchen to get another taste of Flossie's desserts.

"Why, Miz Larrimore! What you doin' down here? You'z

s'pose to be wit yo' husband."

"Oh, Flossie," Allyn said, surprised that Flossie was still up and about. "I guess it's just wedding night jitters." She moved over to the cabinets and took down a plate. "I thought I'd come down for another piece of peach pie. I've never tasted any so good!"

"Well, just doan take too long eatin' dat. You husband might get lonesome," Flossie said with a smile. "I see you folks in da mornin'." And she went off to her quarters.

Allyn did take her time eating the pie, savoring each bite. Eventually she cleaned the plate and couldn't think of another excuse not to go back to her room. Putting down her fork, Allyn stood up and walked out of the kitchen and toward the stairs.

As she approached the bottom of the stairs, Jason walked in the front door and headed for the stairs. "I thought I put you to bed," he said lightheartedly.

She was startled at his voice, surprised that so many people were about this late at night. "Oh, I just wanted a little more pie," she said, explaining. "And what are you doing up and about?" she asked with suspicion in her voice.

"I was just coming up to your room to—"

"My room!" Allyn had assumed that Jason had gone for the night. She stood there awkwardly and without thinking said, "Don't even think about going to my room. I don't want you in there."

Jason had come back to tell her that he would stay in the room until the house had gone to sleep, then would find another place. He tried to explain, but she wouldn't let him.

"Just because it says we're married on a piece of paper doesn't mean you can invade my privacy anytime you want! You remember, we had a bargain. I thought you'd abide by it."

Jason had tried to be understanding, but her accusations enraged him. Without thinking, he stepped toward her and firmly placed a hand on her shoulder. She tried to wrench free, but his grip held the robe tightly.

"Don't touch me!" Allyn ordered.

Jason looked at her. Her hair hung down her back, and her eyes, as she looked up at him, were large with rage. Jason thought of her as a mouse angrily glaring at the cat that held him in his paws. "It seems we need to get a few things clear, *Mrs. Larrimore!*" Jason said.

Her eyes narrowed. "I hate you!" she whispered. "You'll never know how much I hate you!"

Jason laughed at her. "No, you don't hate me. Or if you do, it's only with your mind. I think your heart's saying something else." She tried to pull away, but he held her, saying, "Look, Allyn, I promised your father I'd take care of you. I promised you that this marriage would be just a counterfeit thing."

"Yes, you did," she cried. "Now get out of here and leave me alone. Don't ever come back."

He put his other hand on her other shoulder and held her as if she were a child. "What a shame! There's a real woman hidden somewhere inside. All that beauty on the outside, and inside nothing but ice! You don't trust me at all. I'd thought that you might wake up, but it's like I said at the beginning—we're both of us two pretty hard people. We're alike, you and I."

"We're not! We're not!" Allyn denied vehemently. She wrenched away and stepped back from him. She held her hands tightly together and said, "Will you please leave?"

"All right, I'm going, but I hope I'm around when you decide to open up and trust someone, Allyn."

He spun and walked out the front door. Allyn ran up the

stairs, into her bedroom, and quickly locked the door.

Turning, she looked in a mirror and saw herself. Her face was flushed, and her eyes were red and watery. She quickly removed the robe and crawled into the bed, hoping to take refuge there. She found she was trembling, and for a long time she bit her thumb to keep back the sobs that seemed to rise within her.

What's wrong with me? Why am I acting like this? she thought.

Finally, she went to sleep, but the night was interrupted by dreams. Once she awoke shaking, and when she remembered where she was and the scene that had taken place, she got out of bed and walked for a long time. Eventually she went back to bed but was racked by bad dreams.

She rose at dawn, dressed, and went downstairs. She met Flossie, who looked at her with astonishment. "Why, Miz Allyn, what you doin' up dis early? The captain, he say you sleep late."

"No," Allyn said, a flush on her cheeks, "I thought I'd get up early and take a walk. Is my...husband here?"

"Why, no, ma'am, he gone."

Allyn stared at her blankly. "Gone? Where did he go, Flossie?"

"I reckon he say in dis paper." Flossie reached into her pocket and handed a single sheet of paper to her mistress.

She looked at it and discovered the bare words: "Going to find a ship. Your loving husband, Jason."

Shock ran along her nerves, and she could not understand why. She managed to keep a straight face and then nodded. "It's all right. The captain will be gone for a few days."

Allyn turned and walked out the front door. She sat on the porch looking out over Twelve Trees, but the beauty of the autumn woods did not please her. She ran over the scene of the previous night, finding it was so vivid that she seemed to feel his hands on her. Gripping the top rail of the banister that lined the porch, she whispered in an agonized voice, "It can never be right. Never!"

Chapter 18

Another Wedding

This was the third autumn of the war, and the South was still besieged but breathed a bit easier than during the disastrous midsummer. The Confederates had been successful at halting the drives on Charleston and Texas and had won at Chickamauga. On the other hand, the North was in Chattanooga, and troops were rallying to their relief. The most significant event went almost unnoticed. General U. S. Grant was ordered to Washington, where he was given the command of the military division of the Mississippi. Lincoln had had practically no success in appointing generals. Hooker, Burnside, McClellan—all had failed him in the east. Lincoln now turned to the stubby, unobtrusive man who had failed at everything in civilian life, and placed in his hands the fate of the western theater. Meanwhile, in Washington, President Lincoln issued a proclamation calling for three hundred thousand more volunteers for Federal armies.

Allyn lived through the days more quietly than she had dreamed possible. Twelve Trees was off the beaten track, and days went by when she would see no one except an occasional rider who would stop at the house asking for information. She formed the habit of rising early and walking in the woods, then coming back to have a late breakfast. Much of her time she spent learning the affairs of a plantation. She had seen some of this, of course, at Gracefield, but now, as the first week came to an end, she began to realize a truth. *This is mine,* she thought. *I've never had a place before, but now I can call it mine.* A love of the land was born in her, and she got Caesar to choose a horse for her. The tall black slave rode with her day after day, showing her around the place.

"She sho' do love this place already," Caesar said to Ellie, the small black waitress with whom he was passionately and blindly in love. "She want to see ev'ry stalk of corn and ev'ry tree, I think. Gonna wear me out ridin' aroun'!"

Ellie came over and pushed herself against him. "Never mind that," she said. "You pay attention to me." She was a born flirt, and this kept Caesar constantly on his toes to be sure that her eyes were for him only.

"Come here, woman. I'll teach you what a real man's like!"

Allyn had been watching the pair from where she stood. She smiled as the two romanced, then walked into the house through the back entrance. "Flossie," she said, "I want to learn how to make pancakes like you do. They're the best things I've ever eaten."

"Why, sho', Miz Allyn," she said. "You jes' watch me, and I'll make you de best pancake maker in Virginia." She began to throw the elements together expertly, explaining the process. When the first pancake was placed into the pan, she said, "You jes' wait until a little bubble comes up on the top; then you turn 'er over, you see?"

Allyn picked up the turner and stared down at the pancake. "You make it look so easy," she said. "I don't think I'll ever be able to cook like that."

Flossie grinned at her. "You don't have to, Miz Allyn, not as long as old Flossie's here to do de cooking for you!" She watched the young woman, who intently kept her eye on the frying pan, and asked, "When Captain Larrimore coming back? He been gone, seem like a long time now."

Allyn looked up at her and saw the wisdom in the old woman's eyes. *She knows something's wrong with us,* she thought. *No man would run off and leave a bride unless there was something terribly wrong.* Aloud she said, "He didn't say, but he has to have a ship. That's—that's why he went off so suddenly, Flossie."

"I don't know about going off on no ship," Flossie declared. "I wants my foots on de *ground*!"

"I'll be leaving this afternoon, Flossie," Allyn said. "I don't know how long I'll be gone, but I've got to go to a wedding back over at Gracefield. When I come back, I'll bring my father with me, so I guess Caesar better go with me."

"You watch out for dat worthless man! Any of them young gals wink at him over there, he go down like a tree! He thinks ever' gal he sees is plumb in love with him." She looked over at her young mistress, who was now turning the pancake over. "We got de big room on de first floor all fixed for yo' pappy. We'll take care of him real good, Miz Allyn; don't you worry. The good Lawd's gonna take care of you."

Allyn had turned the pancake, and now she glanced up. "I don't know much about the Lord," she murmured. "I've missed out on that somehow."

At once Flossie shook her head. She had developed an interest in and a concern for the young woman. Her years had brought her a great deal of wisdom, and she had sensed at once the difficulties between the couple who now owned Twelve

Trees. Her tone grew soft and gentle, and she wanted to reach out and put her arms around the young woman—but it was too soon for that. "Ain't none of us can do widdout the good Lawd," she said. "I been through some hard times, and if it wasn't for the Lawd Jesus, I don't know what I'd done!"

Allyn could not answer. She had felt an emptiness and a loneliness; although it had been a time of rest for her spirit, she realized it was only a stasis of peace. Soon Jason would return, and the very thought of that made her tense. She straightened up and asked quickly, "Is this pancake done? How can you tell when the bottom part's done?"

"You just has to know. Pick up the corner and peek at it, if you wants to." Flossie saw that Allyn was reluctant to talk about God. Later on she said to her husband, Ned, "That girl's running from God. Ain't no two ways about it. You and me, we'll have to pray that He'll catch her pretty soon." Then she added, "She got lots of misery, dat girl. Until she lets God get inside her, she ain't gonna do no good."

Allyn found Caesar at the barn later that day and said, "Caesar, I've got to go over to Gracefield. Mr. Lowell Rocklin's going to get married, and I have to be there for the wedding."

"Yes'm, I'll get the carriage ready."

"I don't think so," Allyn responded. "I'll be bringing my father back, and he won't be able to sit up for the journey, I don't think. We'll take a wagon and perhaps set up some padding so he can lie down in the bed of the wagon."

"Yes'm, I'll get a pallet, plenty of quilts from de house. We'll make him a fine bed, and I'll drive real keerful so yo' pappy won't be bumped."

"That's fine, Caesar. We'll be there overnight and will come back tomorrow." Her eyes sparkled suddenly. "You better be sure and give Ellie enough kisses to do her until then." She laughed at his startled expression then shook her head. "When are you two getting married?" she asked.

"I don't know." He scratched his woolly head. "Dat's up to her, but I reckon pretty soon now. I be ready when you are, Miz Allyn."

Allyn went upstairs and chose and packed the dress she would wear to the wedding. She then put on a traveling dress of gray cotton and pulled out a cloak made of fine black wool. It had a hood, and she weighed it in her hands, thinking, *It'll be cold coming back. I'll have to remember to get plenty of blankets for Father.* She went over to the window and stared out at the trees that were stripped bare. They raised their naked arms to heaven, it seemed to her, in prayer. A leaden sky overhead proclaimed the danger of bad weather. *I hope it doesn't snow,* she thought. *But I suppose it's too early for that. We'd better take an oilcloth cover in case it does get bad.* A dull spirit had come to her, and she realized she didn't want to leave Twelve Trees. It had been a haven for her, and now she was about to leave it. Finally, she sighed and said, "I wish I could just stay here. When I get Father here, we'll pull up the drawbridge and not even know what goes on outside." She knew this was not possible, but it comforted her a little to think that once she got her father here, they would be cut off from the world.

Later that afternoon when she left, sitting beside Caesar, she waved to Flossie and said, "I'll be back. Take care of things, Flossie. And watch out for her, Ned." She pulled the cloak around her and settled down for the long ride. Caesar chirped to the horses, who stepped out with a rapid pace. As they left the yard, the wind began to blow. It made a keening noise that blew her hair wildly for a moment; then she pulled up the hood, patted it into place, and tried to get comfortable.

By the time they got to Gracefield, it was late in the afternoon. "Go right over there to the barn, Caesar," she said. "Get Box to show you where to put the horses." She stepped out of the wagon, saying, "Then come to the house, and I'll see that you get something to eat. I know you're hungry."

"Yes'm, I'll be there. I'll bring yo' suitcase up, too."

Allyn went directly to the house, where she was greeted by Susanna. The house was swarming with people. Susanna said with a harried look, "Allyn, I'm so glad you got here." She looked around and laughed ruefully. "Looks like everybody in the country's here for the wedding. Every bed's taken, and there are pallets all over the floor. Do you suppose you could make a pallet in your father's room?"

"Of course. Don't worry about it." Allyn smiled then said at once, "I'll go to him now; then I'll come back and help."

She left Susanna and made her way through the milling guests, and several of them spoke to her. She stopped long enough to greet Lowell and asked, "How's the bridegroom?"

Lowell's face was flushed, and his eyes danced with excitement. "I've always heard bridegrooms are supposed to be scared, but I'm feeling pretty good right now." He looked over her shoulder and said, "Jason didn't come with you?"

"Oh no," Allyn said quickly. "He's gone to buy a ship. I don't know when to expect him back. Not until he gets one, I suppose." She answered that same question in one form or another many times in the hours that followed. Now, however, she hurried to Mark's room, where she knocked on the door and entered when he answered.

Stepping inside, she closed the door and threw off her cloak. Dropping it on the chair, she went to him and sat down beside his wheelchair. He reached out his hands, and she took them and impulsively leaned over and kissed him on the cheek, saying, "I've missed you. I should have come earlier."

"No, you had to get settled," Mark said. His voice was thin and reedy, and she saw that his cheeks were even more sunken and his thin body more emaciated than when she had left. Her heart smote her when she saw how he had gone down, and she set about making amends. "You're going to have to put up with me tonight," she said. "Susanna says every nook and cranny of the house is full and that I'll have to make a pallet in here."

"You can sleep on the couch," Mark said. He sat there listening as she chattered, and he could tell that something was wrong. Finally, he asked, "Jason came with you?"

Allyn hesitated then shook her head. "No, he left to go buy a ship." Defensively she added, "He said it might be hard to find just the right one." Again there was a break that revealed to the sick man that all was not well. "He—he said it might look odd for a bridegroom to leave so quickly, but these are not normal times, are they?"

"No, they're not. Now tell me about Twelve Trees."

Glad to get off the subject of her husband, Allyn spoke rapidly, stopping once to fix tea. As the two of them sipped the fragrant brew, she spoke with some excitement about her new home. "You'll love it, Father! We had a big room downstairs made up just for you."

"You like it, do you, Allyn?" he asked softly.

"Oh yes! It's so beautiful, and it's so private! I guess I've been with people in big crowds all my life one way or the other. When I'm there," she said, leaning back to sip her tea, her voice thoughtful, "it's like the world is somewhere far off, and I can just sit and let it go by." Then she smiled and said, "I can't wait to get you there. I'll have you all to myself then."

Mark looked down at his hands then glanced up and smiled at her. "That will be good," he said, "but I'll be a trouble."

"How could you be that?" she asked, rebuke in her voice. Then she said, "It must be close to suppertime. Let me go get a bite to eat and see that Caesar is fed. I'll bring you back a tray."

She rose and left the room, and Mark sat there looking after her. He was tired and had no appetite, but when she returned shortly with food, he did his best to pick at it, to make some sort of a showing. She was aware of what he was doing and did not urge him to eat more, not wanting to become a nag. Finally, when he had eaten a little, he put the tray aside, and she took it away.

Then she came and sat down beside him, breathing a deep sigh. "I talked to Rooney for a little while. She's so excited." Her voice was thoughtful, and weariness had come to her. From different parts of the house they could hear voices speaking, and somewhere far away the sound of a fiddle came to them, making a happy, cheerful sound. "That's 'Dixie' they're playing. Wonder if they're going to have a military review?"

"I wouldn't be surprised." Mark smiled. "About half of Lowell's company managed to get leave. I think they're camping out somewhere in the barn. When they leave, they're going to have to pass under one of those sword things—you know, where they form a canopy of swords."

"Won't that be nice!" Allyn exclaimed. "Something she and Lowell can remember for a long time." She grew quiet, and he could see that her mind was occupied. Finally, she said, "They're going to be very happy, aren't they, Father?"

"I think so. They're young and strong, and if Lowell's spared in the war, they'll be a fine family." Then he asked hesitantly, "I don't want to probe, but what about you, daughter?"

She flushed, knowing at once that he was asking, as tactfully as he knew how, about her relationship with Jason. She dropped her eyes and traced the pattern of her skirt. The silence ran on for a time, and the fiddle ended the song and began a plaintive ballad. "Oh, we're fine," she said finally. She looked up at him, and his eyes were on her. *He doesn't believe that,* she thought. *I never was a very good liar, but how do I tell him what it's like when I don't even know myself?* Quickly she said, "I'm tired. Would it be all right if I made up a bed and turned in a little early?"

"Sure. I'm ready myself."

She brought him his medicine to dull the pain and leaned over him. His hair had once been as black as a crow's wing, but now it was streaked with gray and lay lank about his head. She reached out and smoothed it, whispering, "When we get to Twelve Trees, things will be quiet. You and I can spend whole days talking and playing chess and just being together."

"That will be good," he murmured. He reached up and took her hand, then surprisingly kissed it. "You are very like your mother," he murmured, "very like." Then he closed his eyes and fell asleep so quickly that it alarmed her.

She placed his hand on his chest and moved over to fix a bed on the couch. She turned down the lamps until there was only a small light in the darkness. Then she lay down on the couch and pulled a blanket over her. It was rough and scratched her cheeks, but she was tired and for a short time lay there listening to the fiddle. The unknown player was a fine musician, and then she heard the sound of a clear tenor voice raised in song. She had heard the song before—everyone in the North *and* South had heard it, for that matter. It had a plaintive quality to it. As the words came to her, they seemed to sink into her spirit:

WALL OF FIRE

Into the ward of the clean whitewash'd walls
Where the dead and the dying lay,
Wounded by bayonets, sabers, and balls,
Somebody's darling was born one day.
Somebody's darling, so young and so brave,
Wearing still on his sweet yet pale face,
Soon to be hid in the dust of the grave,
The lingering light of his boyhood's grace.

A weight pressed on Allyn as the chorus followed:

Somebody's darling, somebody's pride,
Who'll tell his mother where her boy died?

The thought came to Allyn, *Why—that could be about Lowell!* She had grown fond of the young man, and the thought of his lying cold and dead frightened her. *What must Rooney think when she hears this?* she wondered. She hoped that the singer would break off—or choose a happier song—but it did not happen.

Matted and damp are his tresses of gold,
Kissing the snow of that fair young brow;
Pale are the lips of most delicate mold,
Somebody's darling is dying now.
Back from his beautiful purple vein'd brow
Brush off the wand'ring waves of gold;
Cross his white hands on his broad bosom now,
Somebody's darling is still and cold.
Somebody's watching and waiting for him,
Yearning to hold him again to her breast;

> *Yet there he lies with his blue eyes so dim,*
> *And purple, childlike lips half apart.*
> *Tenderly bury the fair, unknown dead,*
> *Pausing to drop on his grave a tear;*
> *Carve on the wooden slab over his head,*
> *Somebody's darling is slumbering here.*
> *Somebody's darling, somebody's pride,*
> *Who'll tell his mother where her boy died?*

As the last words faded and seemed to drop off, the house grew quiet and Allyn lay still, thinking of the harvest of death that had fallen on the land. Then she thought of how Jason had stared down at her and accused her of being unwilling to be the woman she was meant to be. What if something happened to him after he found a ship and things were never fixed between them? *What if he died hating me?* She couldn't figure out why she cared about his feelings about her. Finally, she dropped off into a sleep, Jason's strong, tanned face framed by his long blond hair recurring in her dreams.

Gideon lifted his head and stared fuzzily around. He had been half asleep and was startled when a voice said, "Uncle Gid?" He tried to sit up and found that he had trouble. *Weak as a blasted baby!* he thought. Then he felt a strong hand helping him into a sitting position. The light from the tall window struck his eyes, and he blinked owlishly and licked his dry lips. He coughed, cleared his throat, and then the face of the woman who had helped him swam into view. "Why, Deborah," he gasped. He could say no more, for he was shocked to see her here of all places. He attempted to stand up, but she put her hands on his shoulders and held him down.

"Don't try to get up, Uncle," she said. "Here, let me get the chair." She reached over and pulled the folding chair close beside his cot and sat down. "It's cold in here," she said. "Do you need me to bring you more blankets?"

"No, Melanie got enough. I shared some of them." He waved his hand at some of the men in the vicinity.

He put his eyes on her, and she saw that they were sunk deep in their sockets. He'd gone down so much that she had to mask her true feelings, which raked against her nerves. Her uncle had always been so strong, and now he was as weak as a kitten. "I brought you something good," she said. She reached down to a large basket and opened it up to let him peer inside. "Some fresh beef and some pies that I had specially made."

Gid looked down into the basket then looked up and smiled at her. "That sounds good," he said. "This is probably the best-fed ward in the whole prison, thanks to Melanie and the others."

"Can you eat something now?" she asked.

"Maybe a little later." He stared at her in the gloomy light of the room and asked, "What are you doing here, Deborah? Is something wrong?"

"No, not really," she said. She hesitated for one moment then decided to tell the real reason for her coming. Leaning forward, she whispered, "Bing and Noel are here with me, Uncle Gid."

The news surprised him, and he said quickly, "That's dangerous, Deborah. Neither one of them are in the army now, but they both were at one time. They could be arrested for spies. You don't know how bad the feeling is around here." He shook his head sadly. "Just last week a man who was just suspected of being a Union agent was pulled out of his hotel room and whipped, then tarred and feathered." He bit his lip and added, "The South is losing, and they're lashing out at anything that moves." He stared at her and said, "Why are you doing this?"

Deborah hesitated. It had all seemed so logical and so possible back at home, but now that she was here in this solid building with guards standing at every door, it did not seem quite so possible as it had then. Nevertheless, she reached out, took his hand, which she noted was very thin, and whispered, "We've come to get you out of here, Uncle Gid."

He blinked at her, shock running across his nerves. "Why, that's impossible!"

"That's not what the Bible says—the Bible says that with God all things are possible!"

Gideon grinned despite himself. "That's what comes from trying to argue with a preacher's daughter. You've always got some sort of a text to throw at a man, haven't you?" He sobered and waved at the room. "There are escapes made from most prisons, but this is a tough one. Once someone gets outside, there is always a chance to break away. But I'm in such poor shape, I couldn't 'break' for anything. You've got to call it off, Deborah." He squeezed her hand and said, "You know what I would feel like if anything happened to you. That would be worse than being a prisoner."

Deborah had prepared all her arguments, and for the next fifteen minutes she sat there stubbornly refusing to be moved. Finally, Gideon said, "You're just like your mother—stubborn as a mule! Like all Rocklins, I guess."

"That's right, and you're as bad as any," Deborah said with a smile. She was glad to see that he had lowered his guard to some degree, although she knew the battle still lay ahead. "This was Bing's idea," she said. "I've never seen him so set on anything, except the time we were here to get Noel out."

"He's a rough young fellow, isn't he? But he's got a good heart." Gideon frowned and shook his head. "This'll be tougher than getting Noel out. This place is better guarded than Chimborazo was. There are guards around the clock, and they've got orders to shoot anybody that tries to make a break. So far nobody's tried it, for they know it would be the same as asking for a bullet." He leaned over and opened the basket, pulling out one of the pies. "Why don't you cut this up, and we'll divide it among ourselves here. I'm not hog enough to eat the whole thing."

"All right." She cut the pies into small segments, and soon they had been distributed. She saw how the men did not gobble it down, but took small mouthfuls and savored the taste of the fresh apple pie. They were all officers in here, most of them fairly well cleaned up and presentable, though their uniforms were torn and patched. Some of them had been here a long time, she had discovered.

As she watched them eat, Gideon asked, "What's your plan?"

Deborah hesitated then confessed, "Well, we don't have one right now, but we'll think of something." Then she smiled and said, "It's crazy, isn't it? Come down here without a plan. But really, Uncle Gid, we think the Lord's in it. Even Bing thinks so, and he's not even a Christian. But this is good for Noel. He feels useless not being in the army."

"He's doing his part, writing stories that help the war effort."

"I know, but he doesn't think it's a help. He always respected and loved and admired you, so all three of us feel like we are doing something if we can get you home again. Now eat your pie. I'll bring some more tomorrow. At least I can do that. I brought all the money I could get ahold of with me, and we'll do what we can for the men in here till we get you out."

Gideon sat back, nibbling at the pie, staring at the girl. She had a determined light in her eye, and he said quietly, "Well, I'm willing to be got out. I'll have to admit this isn't my idea of living, but don't take any chances. I'd rather stay here till the war is over than see any one of the three of you hurt." Then he began to eat the pie, and they spoke of other things.

"I don't think we can put this off much longer," Bing said morosely. He was slumped in a chair in the room that Noel had rented for himself and looked over to where Noel and Deborah were seated together on a couch. "I can't see that we're doing any good."

"You have to be patient, Bing," Deborah said. She herself was tired of the waiting. Two weeks had gone by, and every day she had gone to visit Gid. She had spent a lot of time with Melanie. She'd even gone out to Gracefield once for a quick visit with Susanna, whom she dearly loved. The time had passed, but almost daily the three of them had met. Most of the time they asked each other, "What do you think we ought to do next?"

Bing was worse off, for he was basically geared to action. He got up now and paced the floor back and forth, stopping once to look suspiciously toward the door. "Sooner or later," he said, turning to face them, spreading out his large hands in a gesture of impatience, "somebody's gonna catch on to the fact that we don't really *belong* here. We've gotta do something!"

WALL OF FIRE

"Do what?" Deborah protested. Her own temper was short, and she said, "If you weren't ready to wait, you shouldn't have come here."

"Maybe I shouldn't," Bing snapped. He stared at her angrily and would have said more, but Noel interrupted.

"Wait a minute! We can't afford to fight among ourselves." His calm voice seemed to bring a relief into the room, and he smiled. "I feel just like you two, but we can't just pick up guns and go charging into the prison, can we? That wouldn't do any good."

Bing cast an apologetic look at Deborah, saying, "Sorry, Deb. I'm just nervous."

Noel sat there, his chair tilted back. There was a quietness in him that the others did not possess. He was by nature reflective, and he had walked the streets of the city hours each day, circling the prison, considering every possibility. Like Bing, he wanted to take some action, but caution held him back. Now, however, he put his chair down and stood to his feet. "I've got an idea, but it might get us all killed."

Bing at once flashed a grin. "Well, they can't kill us but once, can they? What is it?"

Noel hesitated. The idea had come to him, not all at once, but in bits and pieces. He had toyed with it as a man would play with a puzzle, trying to fit different pieces, rejecting those that wouldn't fit, searching for other parts. It was, he understood, a tricky and dangerous business. He had hoped for something better to come. Now he said carefully, "I'm not sure about this at all, but this is what I've put together...."

Deborah and Bing leaned forward and listened as Noel spoke slowly. Both of them had come to appreciate this young man who had a calmer spirit than either of them. He had often served as a brake for their rather unbridled emotions, and now, as he spoke logically, taking point upon point, Deborah and Bing paid careful heed.

"That's it," Noel said. "It's not much, but it's all I've been able to come up with."

Bing leaped forward and pounded Noel on the shoulder. "That's it! Brother, you're a genius!"

Deborah came over and threw her arms around him. "We'll do it!"

Noel protested, "It won't be easy, and like I say, it'll be dangerous."

"Crossing the street's dangerous," Bing stated. "You can get run over by a wild horse. When can we start?"

Noel looked at the two and took a deep breath. "All right, we'll do it. Here's what we'll do first...."

Part Four
The Last Chance

Chapter 19

"What Is a Marriage?"

Jason's homecoming caught Allyn completely off guard. She had not even realized he had arrived, but when she came back from a ride and entered the house, she found him standing in the foyer. He stood still, not coming to meet her, and she felt awkward. When she said inanely, "Why—hello!" she felt even more foolish.

Then he did come forward, pausing before her. "I just came in thirty minutes ago," he said easily. "You been out riding?"

"Yes. I'm not very good at it, but with some advice from Caesar I'm doing better."

At that moment Flossie came in and said, "You come and set down, Captain. I know you ain't had no fit cooking since you been gone, but I got some ham, and I battered you some eggs. Dey'll do till supper tonight."

Larrimore turned to smile at the heavyset black woman. "Thank you, Flossie, and you're right about not very good cooking. Those Yankees can build ships, but they can't cook a meal fit to eat."

"You come, too, Miss Allyn," Flossie insisted. "I'll fix you a plate."

"Oh, I'm not really very hungry," Allyn protested. Nevertheless, she entered the kitchen and sat down at the table. Flossie kept up a constant stream of questions, for she was fiercely curious about the world of the Yankees. To her, they all had forked tails and carried pitchforks. She was rather disappointed at Jason's assurance that they were just men, no better or worse than the ones she knew.

"I can't believe dat!" she said emphatically, slamming a plate of biscuits down that she had taken out of the oven. "Why they coming down here with all their shootin' and killin' if they so good? You tell me dat!"

Jason grinned at her then secretly winked at Allyn. "Well, maybe you're right, but I'm too hungry to argue the point."

He began to eat, and when Flossie had left the room, Allyn asked, "Did you get the ship?"

"Yes." He chewed thoughtfully on the eggs, sliced a biscuit open, and dipped a knife into the bowl of butter. Spreading it evenly, he took a bite of that, chewed on it for a moment, then nodded. "She's right about cooking, you know. Yankees can't cook." He took a swallow of coffee then piled a heap of yellow eggs on his fork. Before he put it into his mouth, he said, "I got a good one. Didn't have enough money to pay for it, but the owner took a note."

"Tell me about it. How big a ship is it?"

"Different kind than I've seen, for the most part," he said. "She's built low and long, a rakish sort of craft, has short masts and convex forecastle decks."

"Why is that?"

"Well, a ship like that will go through the rough seas instead of bouncing along on the top. At least, that's the theory," he admitted with a grin. He put the eggs in his mouth, chewed on them, then swallowed. "The idea is that while the Yankee gunboats are bouncing around on top of the water, this ship will plow right through and outrun them."

"What color is it? White?"

Jason laughed at her. "Bless you, no! A dull lead color." Seeing her disappointment, he said, "If you want a pleasure ship, we'll try to get one and paint it red, white, and blue. For this business, the less visible a ship is, the better."

"Oh, I see. I suppose that's so." Allyn knew nothing about ships and leaned forward as he described the vessel carefully. Finally, she asked, "Have you named it yet?"

He grinned at her sardonically, a grin touching the corners of his eyes. "The *Last Chance*," he said.

Allyn looked at him with surprise. "The *Last Chance*? That's the name of the ship?"

"Yes."

"But that's an awful name," she said. "Why don't you call her the *White Lily* or something like that? Anything but the *Last Chance*." She shook her head, sending her mass of curls bouncing. "Where did you get such an awful name?"

Jason put his fork down, picked up the coffee cup, and sipped from it. He was tired, and lines of strain showed around the corners of his mouth and the edges of his eyes. "Because that's about what it is, I suppose," he said quietly. "Can't afford to lose this one." He put the cup down and stared at her and said, "I've had second thoughts about all of this. It's not fair to you, Allyn."

"What do you mean, not fair to me? It's what we agreed on."

"I know it, but it doesn't seem right."

"The plantation's in my name. Even if you lose the ship, I'll have that."

"Yes, but it takes money to run a plantation. I don't know

much about it, but every planter I know is head over heels in debt. He makes and spends all his money, uses all the credit he can, and then when the crops come in, if they do, he pays it off. The trouble with that is," he said glumly, "crops aren't bringing anything. You can't sell cotton—no place to take it." He picked up the fork and pushed the eggs around on his plate; then he looked up at her, his blue eyes startling to her as always against his tanned skin. "I guess I should have thought of all this before I plunged in and bought the ship."

She was pleased by his concern. "It'll be all right, Jason," she said. "I've heard of fortunes being made. Why, you made a lot of money yourself."

"If I don't get caught, we'll be all right," he said. "But there's always that chance. It's riskier than a poker game, Allyn."

They sat there talking, and finally he stretched and said, "I think I'll go lie down awhile. I don't think I've slept a whole night since I've been gone."

She rose, asking, "When will you leave?"

"As soon as I can. I've got Davis getting the ship fitted out. As soon as it's ready, we'll make our run. I've got to earn my keep around here." He glanced at her curiously and said, "What have you been doing with yourself?" A glint touched his eyes. "Explaining to people why your new husband ran off and left his new bride?"

Her cheeks flushed, but she managed to smile. "I just told them you'd gone to buy a ship. They seemed to think that was very patriotic of you. It's amazing how much everybody's depending on you and the blockade-runners."

He shrugged, saying, "No other way to get things, but we're not heroes, Allyn. We're in it for the money."

"I suppose so. After you rest awhile, maybe you'd like to take a ride around the place. You haven't seen it all."

"No, I left a little abruptly, didn't I?" He laughed at her then nodded. "Yes, we'll do that." He turned and left without another word.

Later that afternoon when he awoke, they did ride through the fields. The early November wind was rough, but it brought a rouge to her cheeks that he found admirable and said so. "This country air is good for you," he said. "You're looking well."

"Why—thank you," she said, "but I've been busy taking care of Father. He can't get out much in this kind of weather."

"How is he? When I talked to him, he didn't seem any better."

"No, he's not." She bit her lip. As the horses moved along, she swayed easily with the movement of her animal. "I worry about him. He doesn't worry, though."

"No, he doesn't." A puzzled look spread across Jason's face, and he shook his head. "Mark's got lots of nerve. I never knew anyone with more. We've been in some pretty tough spots together, and he acted like there wasn't any such thing as fear. But this is a little different."

Allyn glanced at him. He was wearing a light brown jacket over a white shirt, tight-fitting, fawn-colored breeches, and polished boots that came up to his knees. She thought he looked very masculine and strong. "What do you mean, different?" she asked.

"Well, when you go into a battle, you've got a chance of getting out of it, and that's what you always think about." He shrugged and added, "The fellow on the left of you or on your right, *they* may go down, but you don't think you'll ever be the one. But in a thing like this, Mark knows he's going down, and he's not afraid."

Allyn thought about what he had said. She, too, had been

impressed by the quiet and solid dignity that her father had shown. He bore without complaint the pain and the indignities that accompanied sickness, and he spoke of his death indifferently, expressing only the regret that he would not be around to help her. But as for himself, she knew he was absolutely resigned and had, as Jason had said, no fear.

"It has something to do with his belief in God," she said. "He told me that."

"He told me that, too," Jason said. He shook his head. "I'm a pretty sorry subject for a sermon. I guess Mark knows it, but I admire the real thing. I've seen it in a few—in Susanna and Clay, and now in Mark. That whole Rocklin family seems to have a hand on God somehow, don't they?"

"Yes, they do," she said quietly. They rode along a narrow trail with the leaves crisp beneath the hooves of the horses. The winds caught bundles of them and sent them in small whirlwinds over the ground, where they settled to fall back onto the earth. The clouds were white against the light blue sky. They skittered along, and Jason said, "They look like the sails of huge ships, don't they? I always did like clouds."

"So did I," she said in surprise. "Sometimes I get a crick in my neck from just walking along, looking up. Ran into a post once, and everybody laughed at me."

He looked at her, admiring the color in her cheeks. He'd never seen anything like the satin silkiness of her skin, and there was a piquant quality in her expression. She looked, almost, like a very young girl. He almost told her so but felt it might not be wise.

When they approached the house, he said, "Well, I solved one problem for you."

"Problem? What problem is that?"

"I told Flossie that I wanted my own room." As he expected, she reddened, and he laughed at her. "Don't worry, I took all the blame for it. Told her that I talked in my sleep terribly. I don't think she believed it, but she didn't say anything."

"Thank you—that was thoughtful of you."

"Don't mention it. We husbands always want to be gentlemen and do the right thing by our brides."

She found no answer for that but sat in her saddle straightly, her body trim, outlined by the gray riding outfit she wore. She had left her hair loose, tied simply in the back with a single ribbon, and it cascaded down her back, catching the afternoon sun.

"Aren't you going to ask if I had any female companionship on my travels?" he said, a sparkle in his eye.

"No," she said shortly. "I'll never ask you anything like that."

"And I needn't ask you if you had any gentlemen callers, I suppose?"

She did not answer him but spurred her horse. His laugh followed her, and he came up alongside her. When they dismounted, he reached over and caught her hair for a moment. She gasped and turned to look at him, not knowing what he was up to. But he simply held it and said nothing. Then he dropped the strand and went into the house. "I'll spend some time with Mark before supper."

For two days Allyn and Jason kept an uneasy truce. Neither of them felt comfortable, and Mark was well aware of it. He knew, of course, that they were not sharing the same room, although he never spoke of it to either of them. It had been Flossie who had informed him of the fact. She had also said, "That ain't right, and you know it ain't right, Mistuh Mark."

"We'll have to let them work out their own problems, Flossie," Mark had said. Now as Jason entered his room, he studied the big man and said, "Did you have a good ride? I saw you and Allyn through the window."

"Yes." Jason fell into a chair and tossed his leg over the arm. "She's a good rider."

"Tell me, what do you think of Twelve Trees?" Mark asked.

"Fine place. I've never seen better. Small, but I like that. I never did see any sense in having twenty thousand acres of land that you couldn't even walk around. Always felt the same way about ships, too," he said thoughtfully. "Take a man-of-war, ship of the line, with a thousand men on them. Why, they're like towns, but small ships, small crews—you know, Mark, they're like family."

They talked on for a while, Mark listening mostly as Jason talked about the sea and about the blockade and how he intended to beat the Federals at their own game. Finally, when Jason got up to leave, he said, "Jason, I don't know how to say this."

Jason halted, cocked an eyebrow. "Why, just let me have it straight, Mark. We've always been that way with each other."

"All right, here it is: What is a marriage?"

Jason knew what his friend was getting at. He had not spoken of any of the intimate details, such as they were, but he suddenly was aware that Mark knew. He wanted to tell him more, to explain that this was Allyn's idea of a business relationship, but he felt that it was her place to say those things. Now he said, "Why, it's a man and a woman living together. I'm no expert."

"It's more than that," Mark said. "I missed it myself, but you've seen it, haven't you? A man and a woman really one, both just one creature, almost, made out of two parts, the man and the woman. It always made me sad when I saw it because I knew that I had missed probably the greatest thing on earth, aside from God Himself."

"You don't see it much," Jason muttered.

"It's there, though," Mark said. He leaned forward and said, "I can't interfere with you and Allyn. What's done is done, but—be gentle with her, Jason. That's all I ask."

Jason blinked his eyes then nodded shortly. "You can believe that I'll do that, Mark. I'll not be the best husband in the world, but she'll never know meanness from me."

When Jason had left the room, Mark leaned back, fatigue overcoming him. The pain was worse now, and he bit his lip to choke the cry that would have escaped. Finally, he whispered, "Marriage is more than not showing meanness to someone!"

*

Rooney and Lowell rode over the following day, arriving at noon. They were glowing with happiness and could not be separated from each other by more than a distance of two feet.

"They make me feel a hundred years old," Jason remarked as the two laughed and joked with each other. He was standing with Allyn, looking out the window where the new bride and groom were walking along hand in hand, Rooney laughing at something Lowell had said.

Allyn came over and looked out at the young couple. She watched as Lowell reached down and pulled Rooney to him, kissing her thoroughly. She seemed embarrassed for a moment but then surrendered and put her arms around his neck.

"That's very sweet," Allyn whispered. "They're so in love."

"I suppose."

"You *suppose*!" Allyn looked up at him. "Can't you see it?"

"I see a lot of men kissing a lot of women, but that's not love." He gave her a straightforward look. "I guess I'm just not romantic. But then, you'd hate it if I were, wouldn't you?"

Allyn turned and left at once. He had a way of hurting her—whether or not intentionally, she could not tell. She could not understand her feelings about him. Somehow she wanted to strike out, for at times he seemed arrogant or hard. Mark had told her that this was part of his rough upbringing, and she wanted to believe it. At times he was different. He seemed almost gentle. Certainly when he talked to the slaves, there was an openness he never showed to her. *He's always got his guard up around me,* she said to herself as she went to Mark's room. Then she put her lips together firmly, thinking, *But then, so do I.*

She entered Mark's room and saw that he was awake.

"I came to ask you what you want for supper," she said with a smile.

"Some of that squirrel and dumplings I think I could keep down," he said. "Jason went out and shot a bunch this morning, he told me."

"Yes, he took me with him. He's such a good shot." She laughed suddenly, a delightful sound. "He let me shoot, but only once. He was afraid I'd blow his leg off," she said.

"Tell me about Rooney and Lowell," Mark said. He lay there while she spoke of the young couple, and finally, when she'd finished, he nodded. "They'll be all right."

"Yes," Allyn said, adding more soberly, "if he gets home from the war. I don't know how Rooney would handle it if anything happened to Lowell. She's caught up in him so much. Why, she needs him just like she needs air."

"That's a poetic way of putting it," Mark observed. He

thought for a moment then made a decision. "Sit down, Allyn. I want to talk to you."

Surprised, she looked at his face and saw that he was serious, so she slipped into a chair. "What is it?" she asked.

"I'm worried about you," he said. "I pushed you into this marriage, and now, looking at it, I think I was wrong."

"I made up my own mind," Allyn replied at once. "You can't blame yourself for anything. Besides, it's going to work out all right."

"You think so? You really think so?"

Allyn said with much more confidence than she felt, "Yes, it will."

Mark had prayed much about the marriage of his daughter. He felt that it had been a mistake. It had never been part of his plan for her to marry a man like Jason. Now for the last few days he had tried to find some way to make a contribution, but how do you pull a marriage together? How do you push a man and woman toward each other and make them care for one another? He had agonized over this and prayed about it. Only two nights earlier he had been searching the scripture, praying, and an idea had come to him. The idea seemed so strange to him that he could not think it was from God.

But he carried it in his heart and meditated on it. More than once he whispered, "I wish Susanna were here to help me pray about this." But Susanna was not there, and now as he lay in the bed looking over at Allyn, he knew he had to at least try to make her understand.

He lay there gathering his thoughts, trying to muster up some strength, and felt the weakness creeping up on him. *Oh God*, he prayed, *help me to help her make the right decision.* Then he said aloud, "Allyn, I want to ask you to do something. You may think this is very strange, but I've prayed about it, and I think I'm giving you what God has given to me."

She stared at him blankly then leaned forward. "Why, I'll do anything I can. You know that. What is it you think God has told you?"

"I think you should go with your husband on this trip."

Allyn stared at him, shock raking across her nerves. "Why—why would you ask me to do a thing like that?"

"I'm not blind, Allyn," Mark said quietly. "It's obvious that you two are not man and wife." He saw her eyes drop, her long lashes falling on her cheeks. She could not meet his gaze, and he said softly, "Don't be ashamed. I haven't given up hope."

Allyn then lifted her eyes and licked her dry lips. "It's—it's not a normal marriage we have, Jason and I. It's more of a business matter. He needed a ship, and I needed a husband to get the house."

Mark shook his head. "As I told Jason, marriage is more than most people think. If it doesn't have love, it's nothing."

The silence ran on, and he waited for her to speak. He was afraid for a moment that he had said too much. He saw that she was vulnerable; her lips were soft and trembling. She whispered, "You can't make people love, can you, Father?"

"I think," he said carefully, "you can put yourself in the way of love. I don't know what's gone on between you and Jason, but I do know you can't go on forty or fifty years the way you're going now."

"But—but how would going with him solve this?"

"I don't know. I do know it won't solve anything if he goes off and leaves you here. You've got to be with him—be together. Maybe on a ship. A ship's a lonely place. If you seek the Lord and if you want to find love, Allyn, that might be the place for it." He hesitated then said, "Will you go?"

"I—I don't know if he'd let me."

"Will you try?" Mark urged. He lifted his hand, reached over, and squeezed her arm with surprising strength. "It's your life I'm talking about, Allyn. Go with him; open yourself up to him. He's a good man—a little hard perhaps, but a woman can do a lot to soften a man. Will you try?"

Allyn reached up, put her hand on his, and held it. "I'll ask him," she said, "and if he'll have me, I'll go with him."

Chapter 20

Maiden Voyage

As soon as the *Last Chance* slipped outside the small bay where it lay hidden from cruising gunboats into the moonlit waters, Allyn gasped. The bow rose then fell, and she held on to the rail with all of her strength. She had never been in anything larger than a rowboat, and that on a still pond just outside New Orleans. Now the swells of the sea began to catch the long, low-lying craft as she steamed forward, the land rapidly falling behind. She had eaten a fish supper earlier—against the advice of Jason, who had warned her it was a rather heavy meal.

Now as the ship dipped forward and rose again, her stomach seemed to do the same. A queasiness came to her, and for five minutes she stood there clinging to the rail, getting sicker by the moment. She decided to go below and lie down, but when she was halfway to the hatch that led below, she knew she would never make it. Staggering against the rollings and the dippings of the ship, she came to the rail, barely making it before she threw up.

Jason was standing in the wheelhouse and happened to glance down. He saw Allyn clinging to the rail and shook his head. *That'll get worse before it gets better,* he thought to himself.

He could not leave the wheel at the moment, for the critical time of a blockade-runner was getting away from the shores. The gunboats lay offshore, cruising back and forth, and at any moment one or more might suddenly appear.

Malcolm Davis came to stand beside him, saying, "The engine's running smoothly, Captain." Then he stood there silently, the two of them sweeping the horizon carefully. There were lookouts posted on the tops of the masts to catch the first glimpse of smoke or an enemy vessel.

For over an hour, Jason held the wheel. Finally, he took a deep breath and said with relief, "I think we made it, First. I think we've passed through the net."

"God was with us," Malcolm said quietly. "He'll be there all the way to the pickup, too." They had an appointment to rendezvous at a port in the Bermudas to pick up the cargo that had been shipped from England. It would be a quick run.

Jason looked down and saw that Allyn was gone. "Take the wheel, Malcolm," he said. "I think my wife isn't going to be a very good sailor."

He descended from the pilothouse, went below, and made his way to the door of the small cabin that would have been his. Tapping on the door, he waited for a moment, heard a small moan, and stepped inside. Allyn, he saw, was lying on the bunk, her face pale and her eyes shut. "Sorry it took you like this," he said. "I'm hoping we'll get out of some of these swells when the weather lets up."

"I think I'm going to die," she whispered feebly.

He moved to her side and looked down on her. "Everybody thinks that, but I never saw anyone yet die of seasickness. Sometimes I've wanted to," he added. "Stay in your bunk. After a while, I'll bring you some hot tea."

"No—don't even *mention* it!" she moaned.

He grinned at her, shook his head, then said, "You'll be all right, Allyn. I'll be back soon."

For the next two days, Allyn kept to her cabin. The first day she took practically nothing at all except tea in small doses, which she threw up half the time. Once she had looked up at him as he held a towel in front of her and said, "I'm so much trouble. I should have stayed at home."

He had looked at her and said, "Well, you wanted a life at sea, and this is part of it."

He left the room, and she wiped her face with the wet towel that he left in the basin. As long as she lay still, it was not so bad. The weather had calmed, and the *Last Chance* was a smooth ride, all things considered. It was the sudden dips that brought the wrenches to her stomach, and she lay there praying they wouldn't happen again.

But on the third day she awoke in the morning to find herself hungry and without a trace of nausea. Getting up, she sat on the bed carefully and waited to see if it would return. When it did not, she took a deep breath and began to wash her face. She stripped off her nightgown, took a complete sponge bath, dried, and then put on a warm, blue wool dress. Her black cloak was hanging beside it. She fastened that about her shoulders and stepped outside into the passageway. Before she got to the ladder, she learned that she would be able to live with the slight motion of the ship and felt rather proud of herself.

She climbed the ladder and met the first officer, Malcolm Davis, whose name she remembered after a moment's struggle.

"Well, good morning, Mrs. Larrimore," Davis said with a smile. He touched his hat. "How do you feel?"

"Oh, much better, thank you." She gave him a wry smile

and shook her head. "That's the sickest I've ever been in my life! Does it happen at the first of every voyage?"

"Well now, for some it does, but we'll pray that the good Lord will give you a better stomach and make a good sailor out of you." He smiled, his square face friendly and warm. "Being married to a sailor, a lady like you needs to have sea legs and be able to take a blow now and then. Why don't you go up and see the captain? He'll be glad to see you're feeling better. I know he's been worried."

"Thank you, Mr. Davis. I believe I will."

She made her way along the deck and climbed the ladder leading to the wheelhouse. Jason turned to greet her with a surprised look on his face. "Well, you're better," he said.

"Yes, it went away as quick as it came."

"You're probably hungry," he said. "Clinton, take the wheel; hold this course."

"Aye, sir."

Jason took her arm and moved her through a door that led into what seemed to be a small galley. "Sit down. I'll have the cook make you some eggs. They're usually the safest thing. Some toast and a little milk, perhaps?"

"That sounds good."

She sat there and he left, then came back after a moment to sit down across the table from her. "Ollie's making you something nice. Be sure you brag on him." He grinned, saying, "You don't want to alienate the cook on board ship."

She looked around and said, "It's not very ornamental, is it? I was on a riverboat for a few minutes once in New Orleans. It was all gold gilt and carpets and big chandeliers."

"No, you won't find any of that on the *Last Chance* or on any blockade-runner." He looked at the bare walls, the stark furnishings, all rough and slightly greasy. "This isn't a pleasure boat. We'll get that when we get our cargo back and sell it. Then we can take a trip on one of those fancy riverboats. Be nice to go all the way to New Orleans—but the Yankees are controlling the river now, so we can't do that."

"I'd like to do it sometime," she said. "I always wanted to ride on one of those big riverboats. They have music and dancing and things like that."

"Oh yes, they're floating palaces. I'll take you on one when there's time."

Jason studied her carefully, without appearing to do so, while they were waiting for the food. She was a little pale, but the sickness was gone from her eyes. She had shoved the hood back and now sat at the table, her hands in front of her. He was considering her offer to come. She had come to him saying, "I'd like to make the first trip with you." He'd argued against it, naming the discomforts on board a ship like the *Last Chance*, but when she had insisted, he reluctantly agreed. It had come as a surprise to him, for he had not thought she would want such a thing. Even more surprising was the fact that he had agreed to let her come. Now as he sat watching her, he wondered why he had given in.

A short, fat man with hairy arms came in bearing a tray and set it down before the couple. "I made you an omelet, missus," he said with a grin, exposing a line of gold teeth that glittered brightly. "If you've been seasick, you wouldn't want some of the greasy food that we'll have at our regular meals. You can come to me, and I'll see that you get something good until you get your strength back. Me name's Ollie."

"Thank you, Ollie," Allyn said. She dug into the omelet and tasted it then gave him an appreciative look. "Oh, this is *good*!"

"I'll make you another if that ain't enough. Captain, what can I bring you?"

"Just coffee, Ollie."

"Aye, sir, I'll be right back with it."

Allyn ate hungrily, and Jason watched her languidly. When she was finished, he said, "Like to take a turn on deck? Feel up to that?"

"Yes. I'm tired of that cabin." She rose, pulling the hood up over her head; then the two went out on deck. She walked the deck with him for some time, delighted with the passage of the ship over the gray-green waves. Finally, they came to stand at the very prow of the ship, and she stood there looking down at the froth that the sharp-cutting edge of the ship threw high in the air. "It smells good," she said, "crisp—different from the land."

"I miss the smell of the sea when I'm on the shore," Jason said. They talked for a while, and finally he asked, "Why did you want to come on this trip, Allyn? Were you just bored?"

The impulse came to Allyn to tell him what her father had said, but she knew she couldn't do that. Looking at him now, she studied the smooth line of his jaw, the strength that lay in his shoulders, and the light in his blue eyes. *He's hard and strong,* she thought. *I don't know how to get close to such a man.* Aloud she said, "I just thought it would be nice to see what it is you do, Jason." She looked out over the sea and said, "I can understand a man wanting to be a sailor."

"It isn't always like this," he said. "Sometimes the storms come and throw us around like a ball. The food gets bad on long journeys, and the water's not fit to drink."

"I suppose so," she said. "But it's exciting anyway for someone out the first time."

After a while one of the sailors came and said, "The first officer asked me to tell you he wants you to come to the engine room, Captain."

"I'll be right there." Jason turned and said, "I'm afraid you'll have to entertain yourself, Allyn. I'll be busy most of the time, but we'll plan a good supper tonight. I'll have Ollie make something special."

"All right, I'd like that."

The rest of the day Allyn spent walking the deck. She never got tired of the endless stretch of the ocean. She was aware that the lookouts constantly swept the horizon looking for enemy ships, and she hoped fervently that they did not see any. Finally, she went to her room and rested. She woke up an hour before supper, washed her face, and sat down to pick up the Bible that she had brought with her—one that Mark had given her. She had grown interested in the scripture, which was mostly Susanna's doing. For a long time she sat there reading. Then she closed the Bible and went to the galley, where she found Jason and Malcolm Davis waiting for her.

"No white tablecloth at this captain's table," Jason said, "but Ollie's got something you'll like, I think."

It was a fine meal, and Ollie outdid himself with grilled chicken, well-roasted beef, and fresh bread from the oven. There was fresh juice that tasted delicious. After the meal, the three of them sat around drinking coffee. The two men talked about other voyages they had made while Allyn listened. Finally, she said, "It must be nice to have been with someone a long time. You two go back a long way, don't you?"

"Yes, we do, Mrs. Larrimore," Davis affirmed. "And you're right. It is a good thing to have friends. The scripture says that two are better than one."

A mischievous light suddenly glinted in Jason's eyes. He leaned back and said, "I know that one. I've heard you quote it enough. 'Two are better than one; because they have a good reward for their labour. For if they fall, the one will lift up his fellow: but woe to him that is alone when he falleth; for he hath not another to help him up.'" He looked over at Allyn and said softly, "'Again, if two lie together, then they have heat: but how can one be warm alone?'" A smile tugged at the corners of his lips, and he said no more.

Allyn felt her face grow warm, for she knew the way he had of using a barbed wit sometimes that hurt, and he was making fun of her.

Malcolm Davis missed that byplay, but he nodded seriously. "'Woe to him that is alone when he falleth.' I've thought about that verse a lot," he said quietly. "Nothing much worse than being alone in this world."

"Most of us are, though," Jason commented. He had moved a finger along his nose, scratching it, then dropped his hand. There was a thin veneer of cynicism that came to him often, and it seemed to be on him now. "Most of us live alone, even in the midst of crowds," he said.

At once Allyn lifted her eyes and stared at him. "Why, I've always felt that way!" she said.

"Have you? I wouldn't have thought it."

"Yes, I have. I've often wondered at people who have a lot of friends. I wish that I could have many, but I just haven't been able to make them."

"It costs to have a friend," Malcolm said. "The Bible says that if you would have a friend, you must show yourself friendly."

"You've always got a scripture to fit everything, Malcolm." Jason grinned at his friend and said, "You should have been a preacher, not a sailor."

"I didn't have the call," Davis said. "They have a hard life, the ministers of God. I do all I can to help them. It's a glorious calling to have, to proclaim the glorious gospel of the Lord Jesus. I can't think of a higher one. Greater than an emperor, I think."

"That's nice," Allyn said thoughtfully. "Not many people speak that well of preachers."

They talked until Allyn got to her feet and said, "Well, it was a lovely meal. I really enjoyed it." She left and went to her cabin. For a time she sat reading, and then a knock came at her door. "Yes?" she said.

"It's me, Jason. Can I come in?"

Allyn put the Bible down and moved to the door. "Yes," she said carefully, "come inside."

He entered, having to duck his head. "These things were made for smaller-sized men, weren't they? Not for tall cranes like me." He studied her for a moment then held up a bottle in his hand. "I found this wine when I was on shore. I'd forgotten about it. We haven't had our drink celebrating our first cruise together." He had two glasses in his pocket, and he took them out and handed one to her then filled them. "A toast, then. Shall you make it or I?"

"I don't know how to make a toast."

"All right. Here's to a successful voyage and a safe return."

Allyn smiled and said, "Yes." She drank the wine, which she had never tasted before, and said, "I don't know whether I like this or not."

"The second one's always better. Can we sit down?"

"Yes. There's not much room, though." He took the chair and she sat on the bunk as he poured the glasses full again. "I don't drink, you know," she said.

"This is only wine. I didn't come to get you drunk."

She flushed, saying, "I didn't think you did. It's just that—"

"I know," he said, "you're afraid of me."

Allyn looked at him and lifted her chin and eyes. "No, I'm not afraid of you, not anymore."

"Then let's drink our wine."

They sat there quietly listening to the sibilant sound of the waves as the ship cut through them. She said, "I don't know much about you. Tell me about yourself, about your boyhood, things like that."

He shrugged and for a few moments spoke of his early life. He ended by saying, "Not a very interesting story."

Impulsively she asked, "Were you ever in love?"

He looked at her, the smile leaving his face. "Once," he said.

"Who was she?"

"Just a girl."

Noting his reluctance, Allyn said quietly, "If you don't want to talk about her, if it hurts that bad, then she's still inside you. I can hear the echoes inside."

Jason looked at her and said, "You're a very clever young woman, but you're not right this time. It's all over." He shook his head, took another sip of the wine, then said, "I was very young, and she was from a fine family—at least a rich family." A grimace moved across his face, and he said, "She married a son of one of the richest men in the state." He took a swallow of the wine and said, "I remember she came to me and told me how it was, that she didn't want to do it, that we'd never be suited."

"Do you think of her often?" Allyn asked, almost timidly.

"Sometimes." Then he looked at her and said, "What about you?"

"No, there's been nothing like that in my life."

"Can't understand it, a fine-looking girl like you."

"Oh, there've been men enough chasing me, but I've never loved anyone."

Jason was interested. He leaned back, gazed at her, and said finally, "You know, it cut me pretty deep when she walked out on me, but something was even worse—at least it seems so now."

Allyn leaned forward. He was utterly serious, she saw. His lips were tight, and his shoulders moved with some sort of agitation stirred by an inner feeling. Something in him went very deep, and she asked, "What was that, Jason?"

"Well, it may sound funny coming from me, but I wanted to get married because..." He hesitated and seemed almost embarrassed. "I never had a family, so I wanted one. Most of all," he said, "I wanted a son."

From outside the cry of a lookout came. He straightened, listening carefully, then said, "No danger. But there's always a chance of a warship." Then he put the cork in the bottle and set it down along with the glass. Looking across at her, he said, "I still want a son."

Allyn grew still. She searched his face and saw that he had somehow changed. At once she said angrily, "That's why you came here tonight, isn't it?"

The mood of the cabin suddenly became charged, and Jason stared at her. "Do you always have to have your guard up? You might as well get a suit of armor and put it on! You always think I'm after you."

Allyn rose and said, "I don't want to hear any more. We made a bargain, and I'm not ready to change. I've kept my part of it."

He got to his feet and stood staring down at her. For a moment she thought he meant to put his hands on her, but he simply stood there, his eyes filled with regret. He did not seem to be angry, which surprised her. Finally, he said in a clipped tone, "You know that verse of scripture tonight, the one that Davis was quoting. I think you should have listened to it. 'Two are better than one.'" He waited a moment then shook his head. "You'll never be 'two,' Allyn. You're too frightened of what you are and all the rest of it. You'll always be alone—and you'll always sleep cold."

He whirled, left the room, and slammed the door shut. The sound seemed to hit her like a blow. She opened her mouth to cry, "No, that's not true!" but the words were muted. He had the power to shake her, and seeing that her hands were trembling, she clasped them together. She paced quickly back and forth in the confines of the small cabin then sat down and buried her face in her hands. She thought of the words of her father, who had asked her to open herself to love.

"I can't do it," she said between clenched teeth. "What's *wrong* with me? I *wanted* him to stay. Why did I act like I did?" And then she began to weep.

Chapter 21

Noel and the Secretary

A chill hung over the large room that Gideon shared with the other prisoners. Almost all the men wore blankets over their shoulders to keep out the jaw-breaking cold. There was no stove or fire of any kind, and those men who had to sleep on the floor had trouble rising the next morning, so stiff and sore they were. They slept spoon-fashion, a line of them clutching each other for warmth, so that if one of them wanted to turn over, he called out, "Turn," and the whole serpentine row was forced to roll over.

"These blankets you've brought have been a lifesaver for us, Melanie," Gideon said. He was sitting on his bunk sipping a cup of lukewarm coffee that she had brought to him in a covered pot. "I don't think some of the men would have made it without your help."

Melanie looked over the men, whose faces were gray with illness, and shook her head. "I wish I could do more. It breaks my heart to think about the men that are in even worse shape."

"Yes, I hear they are dying like flies at Belle Isle and Andersonville. I'm thankful I'm here instead of one of those places."

"You're looking better," she said. She was seated across from him in a chair. Reaching forward, she put her hand on his as it rested on his knee. A smile lit her face, and she said cheerfully, "All you needed was a good nurse."

Gideon turned his hand over and clasped hers. "I'm not sure I would have made it if you hadn't come. I can face battle, but this—" He looked around the gloomy prison and shook his head. "It's the worst thing I've ever encountered. But you came. It's like you, Melanie."

"Oh, I haven't done anything," she said. She looked at him steadily and asked, "Don't they ever let you out for any kind of exercise?"

"No, I don't guess they have the manpower for that. I've been walking back and forth, getting all the exercise I can now that I'm up on my feet again."

"How's your wound?" she asked. "Let me take a look at it."

He put the coffee down, and she examined the wound then said with satisfaction, "It's all knitted together. You heal quickly."

Again he said, "That's because of you and the good care you've given me."

The two sat there talking quietly, mostly about their boys. They got few letters, for communication between North and South was difficult. Finally, Melanie said with a puzzled look, "I can't figure out why Deborah came. Of course she wanted to help, but it seems strange she would just pull up, leave home, and come here with things as hard as they are. Also, why did she bring Noel and Bing along with her?" She stared at him and asked, "What's she up to, Gid?"

Gideon and Deborah had already agreed he would reveal nothing to Melanie about the plan, thinking it would be best if she knew nothing. "Well, for one thing, I guess Noel came to get a story. From what I hear, he's quite a celebrity—a Yankee in

Rebel land. That editor from the *Richmond Examiner* has introduced Noel to every big shot in the Confederacy, I think."

"Yes, Noel said that he'd met the president the other day, just for a minute. I'm surprised that they let him run loose."

"I asked him about that. He said that most of the stories he wrote about the North were pretty blunt and took a pretty charitable view of the South—for a Yankee, that is. I guess they figure they need all the help they can get along those lines." He leaned back, picked up the coffee, and sipped it. "He told me he was going to see the secretary of war today. I wish he'd talk him into exchanging me. I'd like to get home again. Get back to living."

Melanie smiled gently. "We'll get there, Gid—you just watch. God's going to do something for us."

Later that same day Noel was ushered into the office of the secretary of war by a lieutenant. He had been waiting in the outer office for over an hour, along with a crowd of people, and was surprised to be ushered in ahead of several high-ranking officers. When he entered, he said at once to the man behind the desk, "Secretary Seddon, I appreciate your seeing me. I know you're a busy man."

Secretary of War James Alexander Seddon rose and came over to offer his hand. A smile touched his lips, and he said, "I've been anxious to meet our visiting Yankee journalist, Mr. Kojak. Please have a seat."

"Thank you." Noel sat down and studied the face of the secretary carefully. "Sir," he said, taking out a pencil and pad, "I know how unusual it is for cabinet members to grant interviews to the Federal press, but I'd appreciate your views on the conduct of the war."

Seddon suddenly laughed. He seemed to be a pleasant man but one who was shrewd enough not to give away any vital information. "I don't think I'm much inclined to give you our strategy for winning the war, Mr. Kojak. However, if you'll ask specific questions, I'll be glad to answer them."

"Fine, sir. Now are you comfortable with the conscription act, and is it working?"

"Yes to both. Of course, Mr. Lincoln has passed the same sort of act in the North." Seddon leaned back, picked up a short paper knife, and toyed with it as he said thoughtfully, "The volunteers came early and without pressure, but this war has gone on so long that those men were quickly used up. We went to conscription—as did the North—as the only way of filling the vacancies in the ranks."

Kojak kept the secretary's attention by his shrewd, often humorous remarks, and the two got along well. Finally, after nearly half an hour, Kojak said, "General, I know I can't take up any more of your time, but I do have a favor to ask."

A wary look crossed Seddon's face, and he asked, "What is it, Mr. Kojak?"

"I'd like to visit the troops in the west—in Chattanooga."

"I don't see any harm in it. Of course, we allow the British journalists to go right along with the troops. I'll have to ask you to submit the story you file with our authorities there, perhaps even General Bragg or someone he designates."

"That will be fine, sir. I'd be happy to do that."

"I'll make you out a pass." Seddon picked up a paper and a pen. He dipped the pen in an inkwell then stared at the paper. "I hate this grade of paper we're being forced to use."

"Well, the war has brought everything down some, I suppose," Kojak said. "I notice the newspaper's printed on wallpaper. I suppose all paper is in short supply."

"Yes, that is true." Seddon wrote a few lines on the paper, signed it with a flourish, then handed it to Kojak. "There you are, Mr. Kojak. Be sure you don't lose this. We are very careful about people traveling back and forth to the site of the action."

"I'll need passes for two men, General. I have a colleague who is traveling with me, another journalist."

When the passes were made out, Noel hesitated, snapped his fingers, and fumbled through the small case he'd brought with him. "Dash it all! I've come to the end of my paper!" He showed the general that he'd used the last page. He laughed with some embarrassment, saying, "I was going to get a few more interviews with some of your staff, but I'm out of paper. Could you spare a couple of sheets, sir?"

"Why, certainly. Help yourself."

Seddon picked up a small sheaf of papers and extended them toward Kojak. "Why, this'll be fine, sir," Noel said, taking a couple of them. He put them in the small case, along with his pencil, and put out his hand and said, "Thank you for your time. I appreciate it very much."

"I hope you will write honest stories, which I understand is your habit." The secretary of war rose, put his hand out, and said, "We in the South need the truth to get to the Northern people."

"I always try to be as honest as I can," Noel said. "Good afternoon, sir."

Noel was outside and walking through the corridor leading to the outer door. He passed outside into the cold air, muttering, "Well, that's a lie. Nothing very honest about what I'm doing right now. I hate to do a thing like this to the secretary, but that's the way things are."

※

"Getting colder out there!" Noel exclaimed. He moved over, putting his hands close to the small wood-burning stove that radiated heat. "Well, I think we're on our way."

Bing was eating a piece of beef, gnawing it hungrily, but he looked up at once and said, "What do you mean? Are we ready to bust Colonel Rocklin out of that joint?"

"I think we've got a chance. Come along." He looked over at Deborah, who had poured a cup of coffee into a mug and handed it to him. "Thanks." He sipped it gratefully and said, "I'd hate to be one of those poor fellows in that jail with no fire at all."

Deborah asked quickly, "Did you get to see the secretary?"

"Oh yes." Noel sipped the coffee and grinned. "It was easier to get to see him than it was some of the underlings in our own War Department. He seemed like a nice enough fellow. I liked him."

"Why did you want to see him?" Bing demanded. "Is he part of the plan?"

"Yes." Noel set the coffee down on the table, held his hands out, and warmed them, putting things together in his mind. When his hands were warm, he picked up the cup, sipped the coffee again, and said, "All right, I've got it all now." A wry look touched his lips, and he shrugged, saying, "It'll probably get us all hanged, but it's the best I can come up with."

"Tell us about it, Noel. What are we going to do?"

Noel began to speak, slowly and distinctly. That was his way, to impose a solid methodology on anything that he had to do. He alone of the three was a careful planner, and he well knew that the burden rested upon him. Bing would be handy for the execution of the plan, but he knew his brother was no thinker, and Deborah was far too impulsive.

"We can't bust into that prison by force; we know that. We've got to use our heads. We've got to somehow get the colonel *outside* the building."

"I don't know how we'll do that," Bing complained. "They never take any prisoners out, that I can tell. They go in, but the only time they leave is when they take some out to be exchanged, and then there's a big guard—too many for us."

"That's right, Bing." Noel nodded. "Of course, if he were going to be exchanged, we wouldn't be here. What we've got to do is create a situation where they bring Colonel Rocklin out all by himself."

"And this has something to do with your visit to the secretary?" Deborah asked. Her eyes were bright, and she leaned forward eagerly as she waited impatiently for his reply.

Noel reached over, picked up the small case, and opened it. "Look at this."

The two looked, and Deborah exclaimed, "Why, it's passes for two men to travel by train to Tennessee."

"Yes, and the most important thing is that we have a sample of the secretary's handwriting, and we have paper that came off of his desk." He held up the paper, which was a peculiar shade of brown and had the secretary's name printed across the top. "That look official enough?"

"What are you going to do with it?" Bing asked curiously.

Noel hesitated and said, "I'm going to forge an order. It's going to go to Major Thomas B. Turner."

"Who's he?" Deborah demanded.

"He's the commandant in charge of Belle Isle and Libby prisons."

She was very quick, this girl with the bright eyes and eager face. "I know—you are going to say something in that order that will get Uncle Gid out."

"That's right. I've been thinking about it a lot, and the order will say that the secretary commands that Colonel Rocklin be brought at once to the War Department."

Bing exclaimed, "And while the guard's taking him, we hit them!"

"Well, that's pretty much the idea, but now that I think of it, it's got some holes in it."

"It can't be in daylight," Deborah said at once. "The streets are so crowded. You can't just stop a squad of armed men in broad-open daylight, Noel. You'd be seen."

"We'll have to do it at dusk, but even that will be dangerous. There're only two of us to do the kidnapping."

"Three!" Deborah snapped.

"Well, three, then," Noel surrendered. "But I've been thinking about this ever since I came back. Here is the final part of the plan—and the most dangerous." Bing was curious, as was Deborah, and the two stood there waiting until Noel had gotten the thing firmly in his mind. Finally, Noel said, "We'll procure a couple of uniforms—an officer's uniform for me and a private's for you. We'll deliver this order in person. Hopefully they'll turn the prisoner over to us, and we'll just walk out of there and that's it."

"But what if they don't?" Deborah demanded. "What if they send a whole squad with you?"

"I don't think they have the kind of manpower for that,"

Noel said. "If they do, we'll just have to do the best we can."

They talked for a long time, picking the plan apart, finding every fault they could.

Finally, Deborah went over and gave Noel a hug. "It's a good plan," she said. "I'm proud of you."

Bing said, "I ain't gonna hug you, but I think it'll work. You've given us the brains, and I'll do the rough stuff. We're gonna make it."

Noel shook his head doubtfully. "Well, lots of things can go wrong, but it's the only chance we have." He hesitated and said, "If we get caught, it could be rather—unpleasant. I want you to stay out of it, Deborah."

She smiled softly, saying, "You're going to learn pretty soon, after we get married, that we Steele women are used to getting pretty much what we want."

"I've noticed that," Noel said. He could not contain the smile that came to him as he said, "I guess I'll just have to get used to it."

"Good! You're learning!" Deborah smiled at him. "Now let's go over it again."

Chapter 22

Action at Sea

The light-blue skies began to change to a duller color and finally were transmuted into a dull leaden hue. The slight breeze that had barely filled the sails of the *Last Chance* swelled into heavy, forceful gusts that sent the ship scudding rapidly through the water. In her cabin Allyn felt the entire ship shudder as it plunged into a trough. She grabbed hold of the edge of her bunk, and after what seemed a long time, the ship slowly recovered. Nervously she waited for a return of the nausea, but it did not come. "I guess I'm over that, for this trip anyway," she said.

The sailors had told her that once her stomach had become adjusted to a voyage, she was fairly safe. One of them had said, "Been at sea twenty-nine years, ma'am, and every time I go out I'm sick as a dog. After that, I'm all right."

There was no porthole in the small cabin, and when the ship began to plunge more sharply, Allyn put on her cloak and left the cabin. She made her way down the corridor, holding on to the walls. When she reached the deck, she was greeted by a fine drizzle that was sending slanted lines across the horizon, making dimples on the roiling billows. The waves seemed to rise like mountains, lifting the *Last Chance* high then letting it slide down into the trough—only to rise again for the next wave.

Allyn was frightened by the power of the sea. She realized how fragile a thing the ship was; only a fraction of an inch, the thickness of the hull, kept her and the crew alive. She flattened her back against the bulkhead and watched as the rain swept across the deck. Seeking shelter to keep from getting drenched, she dodged into the hatchway that led to the galley. When she entered, Ollie saw her and called out, "Heavy weather, missus, ain't it now?"

"It seems very bad to me," Allyn said as she grabbed at the table that was bolted to the deck and asked, "Does it get worse than this?"

"Worse than this?" Ollie grinned. "Why, yes indeed, missus. But you just don't go wandering around on that deck by yourself. Many a man's been washed overboard by a wave, taken off in a moment to meet his Maker."

"I'll be careful," she said quickly. The ship took a nosedive, and she lurched backward. She made a grab at the table but missed, so she pitched back, falling full length on the floor.

At once Ollie sprang forward, crying, "Watch out, missus—"

At that exact moment the door opened and Jason stepped in. He saw Allyn struggling on the floor and came forward to help her. He seized her arms and lifted her upright as he would have a child. "Here. Sit down," he said gruffly.

Allyn slid into the seat and held on to the table, whispering, "Thank you."

Jason paid her no further heed but turned to Ollie, saying, "Ollie, don't try to cook anything in this weather. Just serve the crew a cold lunch today. Maybe it'll calm down and you can heat the galley up tonight."

"Aye, sir."

Ollie dismissed himself, and Jason turned to put his eyes on Allyn. "Are you feeling all right?" he asked shortly.

"Yes," she said. "I thought I might be sick with the way this ship is pitching, but I think I'm all right."

"Good."

He turned and would have left, but she said quickly, "We're not going to sink, are we?"

Jason stopped abruptly, turned, and placed one hand against the wall to gain his balance. "No, not unless it gets a lot worse than this."

It was the longest remark he had made to her since they had had the confrontation in her cabin. For two days she had kept to her cabin, leaving only to go for walks on the deck or to take her meals in the dining room. She had talked to Malcolm Davis considerably and knew that the first officer understood that she and Jason were at outs—although he had said nothing. She had found that Ollie was an entertaining sort of fellow and had spent some time in the dining room and the galley listening to his exaggerated stories of sea life, but Jason himself had kept his silence.

It was the first moment she had had alone with him, and she forced herself to say, "Jason, I'm—I'm sorry for what happened in my cabin."

Surprised, he looked at her and studied her carefully. Ever since that incident he had been forced to keep his anger throttled down. He could not understand why he was being so sensitive and irrational. He had not revealed himself to many people, and he never told anyone about the girl who had touched his life in the past, who had been such an influence in making him reserved. When Allyn had taken his statement about wanting a son as an advance on his part, nothing had been further from his mind. After he had stormed out of the cabin and tried to cool down, he had muttered to himself, *Why do I let her get to me like that? I knew what she was when I married her. I can't go the rest of my life with a short fuse, blowing up. I'll just let her go her way and I'll go mine.*

This had been the reason for his aloof behavior. He had deliberately cut her out, speaking only when necessary. But he had not been able to obliterate the thoughts that came to him, especially as he lay on his bunk at night or stood the long watches behind the wheel. In the quietness of the wheelhouse, he found himself thinking of her. Over and over again he went over his first meeting with her in New Orleans. He realized now that there was a strange attractiveness about her. He was accustomed to the favors of women, but there was an innocence about this girl that both drew him and baffled him. It was not her attractiveness, although her trim figure and beautiful features were enough to stir any man's blood. Nor was it the fact that she was virginal—although this piqued his curiosity and caused him to behave rather stiffly toward her. He was convinced she had never had an affair with a man, that she was, indeed, totally innocent in this respect. He'd come to respect this in her, and now as he looked at her as she sat at the table, he suddenly felt like he had been a boor. He sat down at the table cautiously and folded his hands in front of him. "I guess I forget," he said apologetically, "how this must look to anyone who's not used to the sea." He waved his hand toward the sea, saying, "This isn't really bad. There's no danger at all. I think it'll blow over tomorrow or the next day. Don't look for it to get any worse than this." He was ignoring her remark, but then he knew that would not do. "I guess I did look pretty scary to you, and what I said could have meant something else."

Allyn knew at once that this was his apology. She accepted it for what it was. She said quietly, "It seems, Jason, you and I have the ability to say the wrong things to each other and—to do the wrong things. I'm sorry, too. I—I know I'm too sensitive."

She looked small and fragile as she sat there, which made Larrimore even more aware of the fact that he had behaved badly. "Well," he said, "I suppose that's right, but we're in a strange situation." He thought about it for a moment and said, "If we were lovers, it would be different."

Startled by his words, she looked at him, trying to see what lay beneath the remark. She thought about it for a moment then asked, "What does that mean, Jason?"

"Why, when lovers have a quarrel, they know they've got to make up. No matter how bad the quarrel was, they don't have an option. Strangers can shrug and say good-bye, but not lovers."

It was an aspect Allyn had never considered, and she gave him a sudden surprised glance. *Not many men would think of a thing like that to say.* She thought about what he said then added to it, "Then you mean that married people don't have the freedom to leave each other—so they have to learn to get along?"

"Exactly. Divorce isn't very popular. When a man or woman goes through that, they say good-bye to a lot of things."

Allyn was intrigued by his thinking. "I've never thought of it like that, but I didn't know anybody that was divorced in New Orleans. We heard about it, but it was mostly high-society people who had money and influence."

"Money always makes a difference, but it shouldn't. I always thought," he said slowly, forming his thoughts and stating them rather flatly, "that some problems you have with people are somewhat like the flu—it hurts pretty bad at the time, but you get over it and later it's almost as if it never happened. But a divorce wouldn't be like that." He clasped his big hands together and studied them, thoughts running through him. Finally, he looked up at her and said, "I'd think when a man and woman are married and love each other, if they ever did separate and get a divorce, it would be more like a—well—like losing a leg. That's not like the flu! You never forget losing a leg. You might get an artificial leg and learn to use it, but you'd limp around the rest of your life with it."

Allyn's features grew soft, and she stared at him, fascinated by what he'd just said. She had not suspected such insights to rest within this big rough man. "I never expected to hear you say anything like that," she murmured. "If you think marriage is that strong, why did you marry me?"

"I was a fool, and so were you," he said bluntly. "I knew it beforehand, but like most fools, all I could think of was what I wanted at the moment. I guess that's the way most troubles come to us. We jump into things, give everything to get something we want—then repent at leisure."

Allyn said quietly, "We could get a divorce, Jason, if that's what you want. I won't hold you."

"On what grounds?" he shot back. "Adultery is the only grounds most courts will listen to. One of us would have to give the other an excuse."

"I can't do that," she said at once.

The wind whistled through the cracks of the door as if it were a wild beast seeking to get in. The ship rolled sideways, falling into the trough, then recovered, and the engines beat more steadily. "It may come to that," he said. "I've been lying awake at night thinking about us. We made a bad mistake, Allyn." He wanted to say more but could not think of any way to frame the thoughts within him. They were a mixture of disappointment, anger at his own foolishness, and bewilderment concerning this beautiful woman who sat across from him. He was restless and unhappy and did not know how to fight it, and he could not say these things to her. Suddenly he rose and said, "I've got to get back to the wheel."

After he left, Allyn thought, *He's as unhappy as I am—and that's saying a lot.* She, too, was feeling depressed, and all of the happiness she had hoped for when she had left New Orleans had vanished. "When I get back, I'll take care of my father, as long as he lives. That's something," she said. But as she rose and went back to her cabin, the grayness of the sky reflected what was in her spirit.

"Look, Captain!" the first lieutenant called out, lifting his voice above the keening of the wind. "There she is! I knew I saw a ship!"

Captain Ernest Webb of the United States Navy held on to the rail, narrowing his eyes. Darkness was falling fast, and the sharper eyes of young Lieutenant James Troy had picked up something that he had not been able to see. But now, just a glimmer of movement came to him that was not of the waves. "Full speed ahead, Lieutenant," he said, "and we'll see what it is."

The USS *Cormorant*'s engines stepped up their speed, and the gunboat plunged forward through the rolling waves. As they drew nearer, Lieutenant Troy shouted, "It's a blockade-runner, Captain! See the lines of her?"

"I believe you're right, Lieutenant. Have the crew man the guns."

"We won't be able to hit much with the ship tossing around like this," Lieutenant Troy said, his face falling. Then he lifted his eyes and said with determination, "We'll do the best she can."

"You won't get much of a chance. But I don't think she spotted us yet," the captain said. "I expect she can outrun us from the looks of her, so the best we can hope for is to get in a broadside that would knock her sticks down or dismantle her engine."

"Aye, sir, I'll have every gun ready."

"I'll pull up as close as I can; then when she starts running away from us, we'll turn the ship to port. That'll give your starboard guns one good shot at her."

"Aye, sir, I'll have the guns loaded and run out."

The young lieutenant raced through the ship, screaming orders, and the crew, startled, at once caught his fervor. Falling out of their bunks, they scrambled toward the guns, where the bosun and gunnery captains began screaming their orders, which were almost drowned out by the sound of the whistling wind. Soon the guns were loaded, and Lieutenant Troy stood along the line of cannon calling out, "You're only going to get one shot. It's dark and we're pitching like a chip in Niagara, so make it count, men!" He stood there waiting, feeling the roll of the ship, and soon he felt the ship begin to turn to port.

"Ready to fire," he called out, his brain racing. He could not fire her broadside, letting all the cannons go off on one side all at the same time, but knew that he had to trust the individual gunners to place their shots on the small target as it presented itself. *Not much chance at a hit*, he thought grimly, *but there's such a thing as luck!*

He was caught off guard when one of the cannons suddenly roared out, filling the small confined space with the tremendous explosion. Then another down the line. One by one the cannons went off, not in order, but spasmodically.

Up on the bridge, Captain Webb had his glass out. Even with it, he had only intermittent views of the small ship. It was low in the water and obviously had spotted them. "He's getting away, blast it!" Webb muttered. He saw one of the cannonballs strike a hundred yards behind the ship and shook his head in despair. "No platform for shooting," he muttered. But he watched hopefully, for it only took one shot to knock down a mast, which might give them just the edge they needed to catch up with the blockade-runner.

He heard a clatter and glanced around to see Lieutenant Troy, his eyes alive with excitement, come barreling into the pilothouse. "Did we hit her?" he cried.

"No," Webb said shortly, "she keeps pulling away from us."

Lieutenant Troy let out a blasphemous curse, for which the captain rebuked him. "Well, sir, it just ain't right," he muttered. "Here we had him right in our hands, and now we've lost him."

"We'll follow, and perhaps we'll see him again." But the captain knew that was not likely. The captains of these blockade-runners were as wily as foxes and as hard to catch. In his mind he said good-bye to a lost chance and said, "Back engines, Lieutenant. We'll continue our patrol."

But Captain Webb had been wrong. All of the shot had missed the *Last Chance* except one—and that one had been an explosive shell that had pierced the thin hull of the blockade-runner. By chance it had passed through the cabin next to the one Allyn occupied. It had exploded, demolishing that cabin and sending fragments of wood and iron through the thin walls that made up the other three sides. One small fragment had struck Allyn as she sat on her bunk. She had been trying to read by the light of the flickering oil lamp, having no idea that they were under fire, for the sound of the crashing waves and the screaming wind blotted out the cries of the seamen. She felt something strike her back and at first thought something had fallen off the wall. But then, falling forward, she was struck by a terrible pain that ran through her nerves and exploded in a blinding flash of white. She thought as she fell, *I've been struck by lightning!* Then she knew no more.

"Captain! Captain Larrimore!"

Jason whirled to see the master-at-arms, who had come crashing through the door of the pilothouse. "What's wrong, Simms?" he demanded.

"Sir, it's your wife." Simms, a short, rotund individual, shook his head. "You'd better come to her cabin."

Jason stared at him only for a moment then said, "Take the wheel, Malcolm," and dashed out of the hatchway with Simms following close behind. "What's wrong, Simms?"

"I was passing by her door, and I heard her moaning, Captain." Simms gasped as he scurried along the soaking deck. "I knocked on the door but didn't get no answer. Finally, I opened it up, and there she was, sir."

"What do you mean?"

"A shell, sir—it must have come from that ironclad. It went off in that cabin next to hers and—well, sir, she got hit."

Jason's jaw clenched, and he scrambled over the deck and plunged down into the hatchway. When he reached the cabin door, he leaped inside and saw Allyn lying facedown, her back wet with crimson blood.

"Help me get her on the bunk." The two men placed her

facedown on the bunk, and Jason put his hand on her wrist, feeling for a pulse. He felt it beating and gave a sigh of relief. "She's alive," he said. "Go get the first officer, Simms."

"Aye, sir."

Taking his knife from his pocket, Jason carefully slit the material of the dress, peeling it back, and his heart sank when he saw the jagged wound that was pulsing with a flow of blood. He whipped out his handkerchief and held it on the wound. *She could bleed to death like that,* he thought, his mind racing wildly, *and no doctor on board.*

Almost at once it seemed, Malcolm came to the door, his eyes troubled. He looked down at Allyn, asking, "How bad is it?"

"I don't know. I wanted you to take a look." Jason lifted the blood-soaked handkerchief, and Malcolm drew a sharp breath. "I hope it missed the lung," he said. The wound was high on Allyn's back, in the vicinity of the shoulder blade. "If it went straight in," he said slowly, "I'm afraid it's trouble. Could be close to the heart—but maybe it hit at an angle. You can't tell with a wound like this."

"What will we do?" Jason demanded. He himself had no skill with such things, but Malcolm had served some time working on a hospital ship and knew considerably more.

The first officer's eyes were grave as he said, "That's got to come out, Jason. I wish we had a doctor here."

"Can you take it out, Malcolm?"

Davis hesitated. He knew it was no job for an amateur, but there was no other choice. "I'll do my best, Jason. No promises. God will have to help."

Usually Jason smiled at such statements. He knew that the thickset officer believed that God was in control of all things.

He felt no such assurance. But now, as the ship tossed and he looked down at the gaping, ragged wound that marred the smoothness of his wife's skin, he said, "Tell me what to do."

Malcolm was standing over Allyn, looking down at her face. His own face was pale and his hands were not quite steady. They had been steady enough as he had extracted the fragment of shell that had penetrated Allyn's flesh. "It's a good thing it went in at an angle, or we'd have lost her, I think."

Jason looked down at Allyn's pale face. He had stood by while Davis had probed for the metal, and at one point he had thought he would vomit. It was one thing to suffer a wound himself, but another to see the big hands of the first officer probing with the pliers that would pull the metal fragment out. It had been a bloody affair, and now as he stood there, he was surprised to find himself unsteady, his knees suddenly weak.

Davis looked around at him. "Here, sit down, Jason." He pushed the big man into a chair and smiled at him faintly. "It takes you that way sometimes, but she's going to be all right, I think. The Lord was with us."

"What—what do we do now?" Jason asked, taking out a handkerchief and mopping his brow.

"She'll be out for a while. I had to overdose her because I didn't want her jarring around while I was trying to get at that piece of shell. I think one of us ought to sit with her."

"I'll do that," Jason said quickly.

"All right, I'll go see to the ship."

"Davis." Jason reached out and caught the smaller man's arm as he moved toward the door, and when the officer turned to look down at him, he said, "Thanks, Malcolm. If it hadn't been for you, I—I don't know what I'd have done!"

Malcolm Davis had never seen the big man so shaken. *He must think more of her than I thought.* He put his hand on Jason's shoulder and squeezed it. "She'll be all right. Just give God the glory."

"I do," Jason said shortly and pressed his lips together. He sat there with a preoccupied manner, hearing the door slam, and looked down at Allyn. She was still lying on her stomach, the left side of her face visible. Carefully he wrung out a rag and dabbed at her forehead, not knowing anything else to do. He was shocked at the ragged torrent of emotions that had shaken him down to the very core of his being. He had been through hard things before, but the sight of her still face and the thoughts of the gaping wound had taken something out of him. Drawing a deep breath, he expelled it—then he looked down at his hands and saw that they were trembling. "I didn't think anything in the world could do that to me!" he muttered. He clasped them together and leaned forward, his eyes fixed on her face. She was breathing lightly, her back rising regularly, and he pulled the sheet higher around her neck, tucked it in around her shoulders. For a long time he sat there, looking down on her and noticing the incredible length of the lashes that lay on her cheek, the perfect bow of her lips, and the smoothness of her complexion.

The ship plunged on, and still he sat there. Malcolm came back an hour later to change the dressing on the wound. "I'll spell you, Jason."

"No," he said quickly. "I want to be here. Do you think she looks all right?"

Malcolm looked at her, put his hand on her forehead, and nodded. "Aye, she looks good. The danger, of course, is infection from the wound. That's what kills most people."

"What can we do?"

"Pray," Malcolm said simply. "I know you haven't been much of one for that," he said, "but it's different now, isn't it?" He had seen the agitation in the movements of Jason Larrimore and felt that this was the time God was going to speak to the big man. "Things like this make us realize how helpless we are, Jason," he said gently. "That's when we have to learn that a man needs strength that comes from outside himself. That can only be from God." He could have said more but felt that that was enough. "I'll be back after a while and spell you."

Jason remained beside Allyn for four hours. Malcolm came back several times, but each time Jason had simply shaken his head. He felt that he was on duty and could not leave. As the hours went by, more and more he felt the strangeness of his feeling for this girl. She was his wife, and yet, not his wife. Finally, he put his hand on her hair, smoothing it with a gentle motion, and as he did her eye moved and opened. At once he knelt by the bed so she would see him and whispered, "Allyn—Allyn, can you hear me?"

The long eyelashes fluttered; then her eyes opened all the way. She looked at him with confusion, licked her lips, and asked, "What happened to me?" Her speech was thick, and she spoke slowly. She tried to prop herself up on her elbows, but the pain was too great.

Jason kept his hand on her hair and reached out and pressed her hand, which had fallen back to her side. "You had an accident, Allyn," he said, "but you're all right now. Just lie still."

She looked up at him, and he saw her eyes clear. She studied his face carefully and looked down and saw that he was holding her hand. "How long have you been here?" she whispered.

"It doesn't matter," he said. "Can I get you anything? Is the pain bad?"

"Some water—"

Quickly he put her hand down and moved to fill a glass, then turned back to her. "Try just to lift your head." He put the glass to her lips, and she managed a small sip at first.

Allyn was still lost in half-consciousness. It was like a dream to her. The pain gnawed at her, but she was more conscious of Jason's face in front of hers as she sipped at the water thirstily.

When she finished drinking, she whispered, "What happened?"

"A shell went off in the cabin next door. You took a bit of fragment," he said. "It was Malcolm who took it out. But you're going to be all right now."

She felt sleep coming back and with it fear that she might never wake. Instinctively she held up her hand, and instantly it was grasped by his. "Jason?" she whispered, her voice frail.

"Yes, what is it, Allyn?"

"Stay with me. . . . !"

She drifted off to sleep, her hand nestled in his, and he whispered tenderly, "I'll stay with you, Allyn."

The *Last Chance* had touched a tiny spot in the Bahamas called Nassau. The ship's crew had worked hard jury-rigging the hull for the return trip, loading the supplies that had been waiting and replenishing the food and the water. Then, without pause, once all the tasks were accomplished, the engines started, and the ship moved out of the harbor, heading back for the mainland.

All day they sailed, and Jason had said, "Malcolm, the

Federals know we come to Nassau to pick up supplies. I wouldn't be surprised to see a fleet of gunboats around here."

Well might he think it, for the United States Navy was aware of the part that Nassau played in the economy of the South. Salt, which was worth $6.50 a ton in Nassau, brought $1,700 in the South, and coffee selling for $249 a ton in Nassau commanded $5,500 Confederate on the Southern market. A successful ship captain might make as much as $5,000 on a single run. But profit was not on the mind of the captain of the *Last Chance*. As the ship plowed along, he stayed on the deck for two hours looking for enemy gunboats, then finally drew a sigh of relief. "Take the wheel, Malcolm. I'm going to see to my wife."

"She's doing fine," Davis said. He waited for one moment then said, "Hope you know it was God's doing."

"You had a part in it, Malcolm."

"Oh, God uses men, no doubt. But still, it's God. As the scripture says, 'The lot is cast into the lap but the whole disposing thereof is of the Lord.' "

"What does *that* mean?" Jason demanded.

"Why, it just means that a man does what he can, but in the last event, it's God that's in control."

"Well, I've been thankful to God that He had you on this ship. I don't think Allyn would have made it if I'd have had to take care of her. I could never have gotten that fragment out."

"I'm glad I was here. You're a fortunate man, Jason Larrimore. I hope you know that."

Jason gave him an odd glance and nodded shortly. "I'm beginning to learn it, Malcolm." He turned then and left the wheelhouse.

He went at once to the galley and obtained a pitcher of fresh juice, then went down to Allyn's cabin. He knocked on the door, and she said, "Come in."

WALL OF FIRE

He entered and saw that she was sitting up. "You're looking very fine indeed, Mrs. Larrimore," he said. He sat down on the bunk, poured a glass of fresh juice, and said, "Here. Doctor's orders."

She drank it thirstily and said, "That's good!"

She was wearing a thin blue robe of silk that he had bought at Nassau, and he asked, "How does the robe feel?"

"Oh, wonderful." Her eyes were bright and clear, and she ran her free hand over the material. "It's so light. The only one I have is so hot."

"I'm glad you like it," he said. "If they'd had one big enough, I'd have got one for myself."

She drank some more of the juice and inquired, "Where are we, Jason?"

"On the way home. The hard part lies ahead, getting through the enemy fleet. But we'll make it. We'll stay out and go in after dark. They don't have anything that can catch us. We'll be all right."

They sat there, and he explained the maneuvers necessary to get through the enemy fleet. When she had finished the juice, he said, "Let's have a look at that wound."

"It's all right," she said.

"Don't argue with the doctor." He stood up and pulled her to her feet. "Is there much pain?" he asked as she turned around.

"It hurts a little, but I don't want to take any more of that medicine. It makes me feel like my mind's wrapped in a blanket." She hesitated then loosened the robe, turned her back, and let it drop to midback while she held the front of the robe closely to her chest.

He lifted the bandage and studied the wound carefully. "I want to change this bandage." He had learned to do this from

Malcolm, who had told him the best thing that could be done was to keep the wound clean. "You're going to have a little scar," he said.

She felt strange standing there half naked before him and whispered, "That's—that's all right. It won't show."

Carefully he reached over, got a cloth, cleansed the wound carefully, then retied the bandage. Pulling her robe up, he said, "You can fasten that now." She pulled the robe together and tied it, and when she turned around, she was blushing but did not comment.

"Feel like talking a little bit?" he asked.

"Yes," she said quickly. "I get lonesome down here, although I know you're busy." She added quickly, "I'm not complaining."

"You never do," he said. This was true. Most women, he had decided, would have complained considerably, but she had never uttered one word of complaint. As they talked, he thought about when she was first wounded. "Do you remember much about the first night after you were wounded?"

"I remember you and Malcolm and a lot of pain," she said.

"You had us pretty worried," Jason said. He leaned back and shoved his hand through his crisp blond hair. "I don't want to go through that again."

"What was it like? How did he get that piece out? I didn't know he had that kind of skill."

"I think Malcolm's just about the best man I know for things like that. He can do anything on a ship. Thank God he was here." He sat there quietly thinking about what he had said. "You know, that's true. I've been going along most of my life without even thinking about God, but that night, I did. I thought you were going to die and—"

He broke off suddenly and bit his lip. She looked at him

curiously. "I wouldn't think you'd be afraid of anything."

"Well, I thought I had my share of nerve, but you were so—so *helpless*," he said. "There was nothing I could do. I found myself calling on God and asking Him to do something." He smiled suddenly and said, "And He did."

His smile broke something loose inside Allyn, and she put her hand out, saying, "Thank you, Jason. I know this hasn't been easy for you."

He held her hand for a moment then asked, "Do you remember talking that night after the operation, after Malcolm dug that steel out?"

"No," she said in surprise. "I don't remember anything."

He turned her hand, noticing the fine shape of the fingers, the nails, then released it. Leaning back, he hesitated and said, "You had some bad dreams, I guess. You talked about when you were a little girl. I guess those were bad times for you."

Allyn dropped her eyes. "They weren't very good. I hope I didn't say anything—"

"Oh, just mumbling, mostly." He hesitated, not knowing whether to say anything more or not. Finally, he said, "You did say one thing. I don't know if you want to hear it or not."

Her curiosity rose at once, and she said, "I hope it was nothing that I'd be ashamed of."

"You might think so," he said. When he saw her eyes widen, he shook his head. "I don't know—just one sentence, and I may have heard you wrong, but you said, 'Jason, don't leave me.'"

Allyn bit her lip and looked down. Then she looked up at him and said gently, "I've always been afraid of being left alone. I guess you were all I had, Jason. And you didn't leave me, did you?"

"No—and I won't," he said. "This is no time to speak of it,

I suppose, but I want you to know, Allyn, that our arrangement may have been just a bargain, a business matter, but I don't look on it like that anymore. I'd like us to be more. It's not possible for a man and a woman to be just items on a ledger. Mark wanted more than that for you."

"Yes, he did." Now it was Allyn's turn to hesitate. After a moment she said, "That's why he wanted me to come on this trip with you." She saw his surprise and smiled. "He thought we could get to know each other better on a cruise."

"He didn't know much about blockade-running," Jason said. He looked at her and admired the clean sweep of her jaw, the fine set of her eyes, and said gently, "Anyway, what I wanted to say was, I don't want you to worry. I'm not much, but I've never broken my word. I promised Mark I'd take care of you, and I will, Allyn." Suddenly he arose, as if he had said too much. "I don't want to come on too strong," he said. "I've already done that, haven't I?"

"Yes," she said. But when she looked at him, there was a smile in her eyes, and she said, "It's good to hear, though."

*

At midnight, Jason handed the wheel over to Davis and said, "So far, so good. We'll be in day after tomorrow, I think. We'll wait till dusk or maybe even midnight, and we can thread our way in."

"There won't be much moon," Davis warned. "We don't want to pile 'er up."

Jason clapped him on the shoulder. "Why, I've got the best night runner in the business. You won't do that. Good night." He left and went down below, as was his habit, stopping at Allyn's cabin. He didn't want to awaken her, so he opened the door softly and stopped, for he saw that she was tossing and throwing her arms around.

Quickly he stepped inside and moved over to her. He knelt beside her, ignoring the chair, whispering, "Allyn, are you all right?"

Then he was shocked to see that she was crying. He saw, also, that she had a slight fever, which alarmed him. She had had it before, and Davis told him it went with the shell wound, but now alarm ran through him. He knew wounds could go bad. He whispered, "Allyn, are you all right?"

She opened her eyes, and he saw fear in them.

"I had bad dreams," she said.

"You're all right," he said. He was kneeling awkwardly beside her, holding her hands, and said, "Let me bathe your face."

Quickly he dipped a cloth in the basin beside the bed and began to bathe her face and neck. "Is that better?" he asked.

"Yes," she whispered.

But he saw that she was still disturbed. Putting down the cloth, he said to Allyn, "What's troubling you? Is it the old days?"

"No, I had a dream about—I don't know what it was, but I was somewhere, and I was all alone."

He knew her fear of being alone, for she had mentioned it more than once. He said quickly, "You won't be alone. I'm right here. I'll stay here. You can go back to sleep. I won't leave you."

"Won't you, Jason?"

"No, I promise."

She lay there quietly, and he reached out and put his hand on her hair. "You have such beautiful hair," he whispered, "the most beautiful I've ever seen."

The pressure of his hand on her head seemed to give her peace, and she lay there looking up at him. Then the memory of the dream came, and she stirred uneasily. "I dreamed I was in some kind of a big room, and I looked down and I saw that my hands were wrinkled. And there was a mirror. I looked in it and, Jason, I saw I was old. I tried to get out of the room and couldn't."

"It was just a bad dream," he insisted. "Don't think about it."

But she could not leave it alone. "The worst thing was not being old, but being alone. It frightens me, Jason!"

She looked very fragile and vulnerable, and he wanted to comfort her. Carefully he reached over, put his left arm under her, lifted her slightly, and held her in the crook of his arm. "Don't worry," he said quietly, "you'll never be in a room like that alone. I'll be with you." He looked down at her and saw that her eyes were enormous. They caught the light of the yellow flame of the candle, and he saw that her lips were trembling. Suddenly all the things that he had thought, the doubts and the fears, agonizing over the situation with this woman, seemed to rise up in him. He groaned suddenly. "Allyn, I've been a fool."

She reached up tentatively and touched his cheek. "No, you've been wonderful," she said. Then she pulled his head down and kissed him on the lips. A shock ran through him, for her lips were even softer than he remembered. There was a gentleness and a vulnerability in her as he put his other arm around her, being careful of her wound. He held her gently and held the kiss. Her lips moved slightly beneath his, and there was a sweetness and a gentleness such as he'd never dreamed. This was not like the other times when he was demanding. He was giving this time, and as he held her, savoring the wild sweetness, he thought, *Why, this is what I always wanted!*

Allyn rested in his arms, and a sense of well-being and safety came to her. His arms were strong and hard beneath her, and she thought, *He would never let anything harm me.* She held him tightly, pulling him ever closer. There was a strength and a cleanness in his lips that she needed, and she held him, clinging to him with all the strength in her arms.

Finally, she moved her head back, and the kiss ended. He whispered, "Allyn, I love you."

Those simple words seemed to set off some kind of signal in her, and she felt the tears run down her cheeks. All her life she'd wanted someone to say that simply and plainly.

"I love you, too, Jason," she whispered and then pulled his head down again.

He held her for a long time and said finally, "Allyn, don't ever think you'll be alone. We've come a long hard way, but I love you as I never loved anyone."

She lay there and knew that she had found what she had been searching for all of her life.

CHAPTER 23

A DESPERATE VENTURE

The two men who had approached the hulk of Libby Prison stopped, the smaller one putting out his hand. He was dressed in the uniform of a Confederate captain and spoke to the other, who was wearing the uniform of a private.

"Have you got it straight now, Bing?" Noel demanded. He looked up at the sky and said, "I think we've got it timed about right. It'll be pretty dark by the time we get on the streets—if this thing works."

Bing glanced up and nodded. "It'll be dark enough, all right." He held a musket in his right hand, and underneath his uniform overcoat, he had a heavy navy .44 revolver fully loaded. A worried look crossed his face. "I been hearing about this Major Turner, the commandant here. He's a pretty tough hombre, so they say. What if you can't talk him into letting Colonel Rocklin go?"

Noel smiled. "I forgot to tell you. That's part of the plan, Bing. Turner won't be here."

"Won't be here? Where will he be?"

"I found out that he goes to inspect Belle Isle every Thursday. That's the other prison he's in charge of. He leaves a lieutenant in charge of Libby. I figured we could handle a lieutenant easier than we could a tough major in the regulars." He looked at Bing thoughtfully. "Don't say any more than you have to. Just one word could give either one of us away."

"Don't worry. I've got it all down. Let's do it."

"All right." Noel marched ahead, and they approached the guard, who at once said, "You have a pass?"

Noel snapped, "I have to see Major Turner. I've got an order here from the War Department."

The guard looked at his fellow guard, who shrugged and said, "Major Turner ain't here. He's gone to Belle Isle like he always does every Thursday."

"Who's in charge?" Noel demanded.

"That'd be Lieutenant Bates."

"Well, I'll see him, then."

"Yes, sir." The first guard opened the door and called out, "Corporal Helleman—officer here to see Lieutenant Bates."

An older man, wearing a rather worn uniform, came and peered at Noel and then at Bing. "Have to see your pass, sir."

Noel held up the sealed envelope and said, "This is straight from the War Department. I need to see Lieutenant Bates at once."

The guard gave it a careless look and said, "Yes, sir. Right this way." He moved along the corridors to a door at the end of the hall, then opened it. "Lieutenant Bates, there's a captain here to see you."

"Have him come in." Lieutenant Bates was sitting at a desk, and he glanced up curiously at the two men who entered. "What can I do for you, Captain?" he asked. He was young and stood to his feet rather nervously.

"I have an order here from the secretary of war," Noel said

rather loudly. "It's rather urgent. I had expected to speak to Major Turner."

"He won't be back until the morning, Captain. Can it wait until then?"

"The secretary says no. I expect you'd better take care of it, Lieutenant."

Lieutenant Bates took the envelope, opened it, and read it quickly. "Why, I can't release a prisoner, Captain! You'll have to wait until tomorrow for Major Turner."

Noel had anticipated this. "You want me to return that answer to the secretary of war? That Lieutenant Bates refuses to obey a direct order?"

"Oh no, you can't do that, Captain!" Bates raked his hand through his thin blond hair frantically. He looked at the order again and said, "Very well, I'll get the prisoner. I'll send a squad along with you."

"I brought a guard with me," Noel said diligently. "That won't be necessary."

"Oh, it's regulations, Captain. You understand, three guards have to go with every prisoner that's transferred. I couldn't release him otherwise."

"Very well," Noel said in a bored tone. "Hurry it along, will you? The secretary is an impatient man, as you probably know."

Lieutenant Bates did not know firsthand, although he had heard. He at once dashed out the door. Noel waited tensely for a few moments, listening to the commands being called; then the lieutenant entered. "I'm having the colonel brought in." He looked at the order again and said, "I don't quite understand. How long will the prisoner be there?"

"Well, the secretary hasn't let me in on all his plans, you understand, Lieutenant. I think he wants to interrogate several of the officers. Colonel Rocklin will be the first. He'll probably keep him overnight."

"You'll have to send the guards back and then send for them when he is to be transferred again. I'm short of men," he complained.

"Yes, I'll take care of that."

Noel stood there chatting with the lieutenant, putting on an air of impersonal boredom. Inside he was tense as a steel wire. All that had to happen was for one officer to challenge his identity. He had no papers, no proof, nothing except the uniform he wore. He was relieved when a knock at the door sounded, and the corporal said, "Prisoner's ready, sir."

"Very well, Captain. I'll turn the colonel over to you."

"Thank you, Lieutenant. I'll mention to the secretary that you are doing a good job here."

The remark pleased the harried young lieutenant, and he said, "Thank you, sir."

There was a tense moment when Noel stepped outside, for Gideon Rocklin was waiting, dressed in his tattered uniform. Noel's eyes met his, and for one minute he was afraid that Gideon would give them away. But he saw at once he need have no fear. "Colonel Rocklin, I'm Captain Hagan. You're going to have a short interview with the secretary of war."

Gideon had been aroused from a nap and simply told he was making a short trip. He had quickly become alert, suspecting that Noel and Bing were at the bottom of it. Now he nodded and said, "I'm glad to know you, Captain."

"Come this way." Noel led the way outside, where he found three guards already there waiting, with Bing standing to one side.

The corporal said, "Have to put the prisoner in that

ambulance. That's the way we always transfer them."

"Very well, Corporal." Noel nodded and watched as Gideon climbed inside. "Suppose it'll be all right for me to ride with the driver?"

"Why, yes, sir, that'll be fine. Here, Clyde, you drive this ambulance over. Bring it back in one piece, you hear me!" Then the corporal turned to the other two and said, "You two mind your manners." He gave Bing a sharp glance and said, "You go along, too, I guess."

Noel climbed up on the seat and sat down by the private named Clyde and said, "Let's go, Private."

"Yes, sir." The soldier slapped the horse with the line, and the ambulance moved off down the street. Out of the corner of his eye, Noel saw that the two guards were ambling along behind the ambulance and that Bing had joined them.

"Going to be dark pretty soon," he observed. "Do you know your way to the War Department, Private?"

"Oh yes, sir, I know how to get there."

The skies grew darker, but not dark enough to suit Noel and Bing. Both of them were wishing that it was pitch black, but the timing had been hard to figure. What Noel had wanted was to pass through the streets in that interval between the time darkness fell and the streetlamps were lighted. He thought to himself, *I believe we've got it about right. Maybe a little early, but no help for that.*

The ambulance moved slowly through the streets, and Noel carefully watched, seeing that the streets at this hour were fairly empty. He knew it would have been impossible to carry out the plan during the busy hours, but he had studied it carefully. This was the one time when there was almost no one stirring. He knew that he couldn't count on that, so he waited until they got to a street in one of the seedier elements of town and said, "I know a shortcut. Go down this street, Private."

"Sir? I don't think—"

"Do what I tell you, Private!" Noel snapped. "I don't have time to argue with you. We're in a hurry."

"Well, all right. If you say so, sir."

The driver turned the horse's head down the narrow street, which was really an alley more than anything else. It led between two factories, both of them built of red brick and neither in operation at the moment. It was a long block, and the two buildings cut off most of the light. Uneasily the ambulance driver asked, "Are you sure this is the way, sir?"

"Yes." This was the critical part of the plan. Noel glanced back, seeing the forms of the men plodding along behind. Suddenly he gasped and bent over. "Oh!" he said, crying out as if in pain.

The driver stared at him. "What is it, Captain?"

"I took a wound at Seven Pines," he gasped. "It gives me problems." He leaned forward and said, "Stop! Stop the ambulance, Private!"

At once the private pulled up the horse and sat there, not knowing what to do. "Can I help you, Captain?"

Noel was not an actor, but so much depended on it that he threw himself into it. He began to cough and cry out, saying, "Oh, it's terrible! I can't stand it! Help me!"

"What can I do, sir?"

"Help me down to the ground—I've got to lie down for a moment!"

Instantly the private fastened the lines and leaped to the ground. He ran around the wagon, saying, "Here, you guards! Help me get him down."

The two men came forward, and one of them said, "What's wrong?"

"Officer's sick! Help me! Put him on the ground there."

The two guards leaned their muskets up against the wagon—which was exactly what Noel had hoped for—and he resisted as much as he could, saying, "Oh, be careful, it hurts!" Soon all three of them were struggling to get him on the ground. He glanced over the shoulder of one and saw that Bing had put his musket down, too, and had drawn the .44. As the three eased him to the ground, Noel reached under his overcoat and pulled out the heavy pistol he had stuck in his belt. He pulled the hammer back, and it made a resounding click in the darkness. He shoved it under the chin of the private who had been driving the ambulance and said, "Just stand still, soldier—don't move!"

At once the other two guards reared back. One of them turned to make a grab at his musket and found himself staring into the muzzle of a heavy revolver. The big soldier who had said not a word now spoke. "You two scratch for it. Put your hands up, or I'll let a hole in you!"

"What is this?" the driver gasped. "What are you doing?"

"We're taking a little detour," Noel said. "Stand aside." He shoved the driver aside and reached up and unlocked the padlock on the outside of the door. Opening it, he said, "You can come out now, Colonel."

Gideon looked out, saw the situation, and at once climbed to the ground. He didn't say a word, but his eyes glowed in the growing darkness. Noel flashed him a quick smile then became sober.

"Into that ambulance—you three."

"What are you going to do with us?" one of the guards protested.

"Just gonna take you for a little ride. You won't get hurt if you do what we say. Now get in there."

As they climbed in, Bing grabbed one of them, pulled his head back, and laid the muzzle against his temple. "I hope you have a full life, sonny," he said. "But if you make one peep in there, I'll have to see that you don't." He shoved the man inside and slammed the door, fastening the lock. "Let's go," he said quickly.

Noel climbed up on the seat, followed by Gideon. He spoke to the horse and said, "Giddup," then turned to see that Bing had taken position slightly to the rear, but close enough to get to the door if any of the prisoners acted up.

Gideon clapped him on the shoulder, saying, "I never was so glad to see anyone in my life! How'd you arrange this?"

"I'll tell you all about it, but we're not out of the woods yet. Are you all right?"

"I'm feeling better every second." Gideon took a deep breath and said, "That fresh air's the best thing I ever smelled in my life!"

Noel nodded then drove the team down to the end of the alley. He took a sharp right and went two blocks, and Gideon saw they had come to a large open space. A pasture had been left, a small one, with a barn to one side. "I think they keep the horses here for some of the members of the cabinet who live in town," Noel said. "Anyway, that's where we're headed." Gideon looked up and saw, as they approached, there were no houses anywhere near, only the barn. Noel pulled up, and as he did, a door opened and a voice called, "Noel?"

"Yes, it's us, Deborah. Open the doors."

Gideon got down and watched as the doors opened. When Noel drove the ambulance inside, he moved forward and put out his hand, saying, "Deborah?"

She came to him at once and gave him a hug. "Uncle Gid!"

She hugged him tightly, and then Bing came up to say, "You can save that for later. We still ain't safe."

Stepping inside the barn, Noel stopped beside the door and said, "You fellows in there keep quiet. I don't want to hear a peep out of you."

He came over hurriedly and said, "Colonel Rocklin, you've got to change clothes. Where are they, Deborah?"

"Right here." Deborah swiftly moved over to pick up a package and said, "You wouldn't get far in that uniform, Uncle Gid. Change quick as you can."

Gid ducked into a stall, shucked off the worn uniform, and slipped into the black suit with matching boots. There was even a hat to go with it, and he pulled it down. It was a little too large, but that caused it to fall over his face, hiding it a little more effectively. Stepping outside, he said, "Well, good-bye to the uniform. What now?"

"We've got to get out of Richmond," Noel said. "I've got passes for two men on the train that leaves in an hour. You and I'll be on it."

"What about Bing and Deborah?"

"Bing will stay here and keep these fellows company until we've had plenty of time for the train to get out of town. Then he can fade away. They won't be looking for him once he gets out of that uniform. And Deborah will just go back north as soon as possible, since she was just here visiting relatives."

"I wish we could all go together," Gid said. He looked over at Bing, who was watching with a broad grin on his face; he stepped closer and put out his hand. "I understand this is all your idea, Bing," he said. "Can't tell you how much it means to me."

"Well," Bing said, embarrassed, "I ain't much of a soldier, Colonel. You know that, but I'm glad I could do this for you. Feels like I'm really doing something." He laughed aloud. "Maybe I could make a habit of busting prisoners out of Confederate jails."

"I don't think you could work this twice." Gideon smiled back at him. He held on to the man's thick hand and squeezed it, saying, "God bless you, my boy. My family and I will be eternally in your debt."

"We'd better go, Colonel," Noel said. "I want to be at the train station just kind of out of sight. We'll get on the train just before it pulls out. They won't have time to look at the pass very carefully."

"All right," Gid said. He reached out and hugged Deborah and whispered against her ear. "You paid for your raising this time, young'un," he said. He held her tightly and said huskily, "Hang on to that young man. He's worth keeping." Then he released her and said, "All right, I'm ready, Noel."

Noel moved forward, kissed Deborah, and said, "Go as quick as you can."

She kissed him back and said, "I will."

Then Noel turned to Bing and hit him lightly on the chest. "You big sucker, I owe you one for this! When you get back, we'll go out and have the finest steak in the city."

"Yeah, you bet we'll do that," Bing agreed heartily. Then the two faded away into the darkness. Bing watched them go; then he turned to Deborah. He put the pistol in his belt and smiled at her. "Well, we done good, didn't we, Deborah?"

"Yes," Deborah said proudly, "we done real good, Bing."

Chapter 24

Homecoming

As Allyn looked down at the dock to stare at the crowd that had gathered to greet the *Last Chance*, it seemed that every available foot was taken. She whispered to Jason, who stood closely beside her, "I never saw anything like this, even in New Orleans at the docks."

"The people in New Orleans were never hurting for supplies as bad as the people of Richmond," Jason answered. He stood close to her and looked down at her, asking, "How do you feel? Are you sure you're able to make this kind of a move? I can have an ambulance, if you like."

"Oh, don't be foolish," she said, smiling up at him.

They had been forced to lie outside the sea-lanes for almost a week. The weather was beautiful: the sun shining and the winds still, which was not to their advantage. She had been surprised when Jason had said, "I'd rather have a typhoon. Easier to dodge the patrol boats that way." Then she remembered he had smiled and said, "We'll just have a little pleasure cruise while you heal up."

They had cruised twenty miles off shore, keeping a careful look for the ships that maintained the blockade, and they had seen several. During those days, Allyn and Jason had spent much time together. His duties were light, amounting only to giving a few orders. The two of them had sat for long hours in the galley, which he had fixed up with a comfortable chair, padding it with mattress pads. He had discovered her desire to learn how to play chess, and she had developed, under his tutelage, into a surprisingly good player. During the milder periods of the day, he had walked her around the deck, his arm around her much of the time, although she protested she didn't need it. "Still a little swelled here," he had said. "Mind your doctor's orders."

Now as they stood at the rail, she thought of those times and turned to him. "These last few days, they've been—" She started to say *wonderful* then changed her mind. That sounded too exotic. "They've been very good for me, Jason."

"Have they? I'm glad to hear that."

"Yes, I needed some sort of assurance, I guess. That night that you held me and told me you'd never leave me—ever since then I felt—well, secure." She hesitated again, and a slight flush touched her cheeks, which was not brought on by the sharpness of the wind. "I guess being sick makes you want to know you're wanted." A thought struck her. "I guess that's the way my father feels."

"I think maybe it is." He looked down on her and smiled. "We'll make him feel wanted when we get to Twelve Trees. Come along."

He called out to Davis, "First, you're in charge of the ship. Get all you can out of these folks. We need to make money to pay for this ship."

"Right you are! Where will ye be headed, Captain?"

"I'll be taking Mrs. Larrimore to Twelve Trees. I'll stay there for a while. When everything's done, you come out. We've got a room for you. We'll talk about the next run."

"Yes, sir. I'll be there."

Jason led Allyn down the gangplank and waved to a carriage. He helped her in and then said to the driver, "You've got a long fare this time, but I'll make it worth your while. Go out the North Road."

"Yes, sir." The carriage driver beamed. "Yes, sir, Captain. It'll be a good trip."

It was a good trip, the wind brisk, but the November sun shone down, shedding pale beams over the seared landscape. Jason had the carriage stop twice to let Allyn get down and walk a little so she wouldn't stiffen up. She had laughed at him. "Why, I'm fine, Jason," she had said, but that he was worried about her had pleased her. When they had pulled up in front of Twelve Trees, she said, "Come along; I'm anxious to see how Father is."

They moved across the yard. As they went up the steps, he said, "Don't move so fast. You might get that wound to bleeding."

"No, I'm fine," she said. "Come along." She reached out and took his hand and started up the steps. When they reached the landing, both of them stopped. Allyn said, "Why, Susanna!" and then she asked quickly, "Is it Father? Is he worse?"

Susanna Rocklin held the door open and said, "Come in. He's not been doing too well. I thought I would come over and help until you got back."

The two of them entered, and Susanna had not missed the fact that Jason had been holding Allyn's hand. That pleased her, and she said, "Did you have a good trip, Jason?"

Jason removed his hat and bowed his head. "Why, yes,

Susanna, we did—except for her."

Susanna shot a quick look at Allyn and said, "What's wrong?"

"Oh, she got hit with a cannon shell." Jason's eyes were gleaming as he saw her startled expression. "She's all right. Just has to take it easy. She'll tell you all about it, I'm sure."

"Oh, it's nothing. I'm fine. What about Father?"

"Dr. Maxwell was by yesterday," Susanna said. "He wasn't very optimistic, but then, he never is. Come along; I know Mark'll be anxious to see you."

The pair followed Susanna down the hall, and when she opened the door, they all entered. Mark was lying in bed, his eyes open. As soon as he saw them, he said quickly, "Allyn! Jason! How was the trip?" He struggled to sit up, and Allyn ran over and helped him into a sitting position.

She saw at once that he was much weaker, that the wound had drained him, but she said nothing of this. "We had good fortune," she said. "Come along, Jason. Sit down on the other side."

Jason moved over and took the chair, reached out his hand, took the thin one Mark held up to him. "Well, I brought her back, almost whole," he said. When Mark lifted his eyebrow, he said, "Tell them about your adventure, wife."

At the use of the word *wife*, Mark shot a quick glance at Allyn, and she looked flustered, but she immediately plunged into her story. When she finished, she said, "Ever since I got hurt, Jason's been treating me like a piece of fragile china."

"You should have gotten shot earlier," Mark said with a smile on his lips. "That's a good way to get sympathy."

"Oh, don't be foolish!" Susanna said. "Now I'll leave you here, but don't tell all the story. I just want to go get your rooms ready."

She left the room, and at once Mark asked, "Now how was it?"

"Well, I guess I can retell it later to Susanna," Allyn said, and she began telling of her adventure. Mark sat there quietly, watching the excitement in her eyes. He sensed there was a difference in her. He studied her face and the animation that was there, the liveliness in her eyes, and the fact that more than once she looked over at Jason for some detail. There was a freedom between the two that had not been there when they left.

Maybe, he thought, *I've done the right thing for once. They look at peace, as if they have fought their battles out.*

Finally, Allyn said, "It was so exciting. I'm going to go again the next time Jason goes." She glanced at Mark and said, "As soon as you get better, that is."

"You don't have my permission for that," Jason said. "The next trip might not go as easy as this one did—and that was no picnic at times. You never know when you're going to run into these gunboats." He leaned back and nodded. "We made plenty of money this time, Mark. Enough to pay the boat off, I think—so at least we start even the next time we make a trip."

"What did you bring back?" Mark asked.

For a while the three sat there talking about the voyage, and finally the visitors saw that Mark was getting tired. Allyn said, "I'm tired. Let me go lie down a little, Father, and I'll come back after I've had a little rest."

Mark said at once, "Yes, I want to hear more about all of this."

Allyn left the room, and Mark looked at Jason. "She seems happy, Jason," he observed.

"Well, we had a few misunderstandings, but things are better now."

WALL OF FIRE

"I'm glad to hear that." Mark said no more and felt weakness creeping up. He put out his hand, and when Jason took it, he said, "Thank you. I know it's going to be all right." Then he dropped off to sleep.

Quietly Jason got up and left the room. He found Susanna and Allyn talking about the patient, and he said, "He doesn't look good at all."

"No, he's not," Susanna said. She bit her lip and shook her head. "He could go at any time. Dr. Maxwell thinks his heart's been affected by all of this, and it's very erratic."

"Can't something be done?" Allyn whispered. "I mean, I've just found him. I can't lose him now!"

"We'll pray, but somehow in my spirit I feel that he'll be taken soon." She saw the hurt look in Allyn's eyes and said, "But just think what he's done, Allyn! He's found you and made a home for you here." She looked at Jason and smiled. "He's seen you married. That was what worried him most." She saw that Jason looked uncomfortable at this, so she passed on over it to add, "And he's found God. That's the most important thing of all."

"It's so hard," Allyn said.

"Why, yes, it's hard not to get to see the ones we love, but it's something we all come to. And if we're right with God, we know that those separations are only for a little while."

Susanna stood there quietly watching their faces. She sensed that both of them had reached some sort of crossroads or a fork in the road. She knew that God was working on them, and she prayed, *Oh God, bring them in! Bring them in!*

❦

Mark Rocklin lingered for three days after the return of Allyn and Jason. Most of the time he slept peaceably. During the times when he was awake, he was very content, they could all see. The pair stayed very close beside him, and when he was awake, he seemed happy just to have them there. They did not talk much, though more than once he would look at them and say, "God has been good to me." He did not speak much, for the effort seemed to tire him.

There was only one end to this, of course, and it was Susanna who came to awaken Allyn in the middle of the night. Upon seeing her aunt standing in the doorway, she said, "Is he going?"

"Yes, put on a robe and come quickly, Allyn."

Allyn pulled on the wool robe that lay beside her bed, stepped her feet into the house shoes, and without even giving her hair a touch followed the older woman. They moved down the hall, and she saw that Jason was there. Pain was in his face, but he said nothing.

When they entered, Flossie was standing over to one side. "He done been callin' for you, Miz Allyn," she said, tears running down her face. She was an emotional woman, and although she had not known Mark Rocklin long, she had grown to respect him greatly. She moved back into the shadows and stood there silently watching, her ebony face full of grief.

Allyn moved quickly to the bed, and Jason went to the other side. Leaning over, Allyn whispered, "Father, are you awake?"

His eyes opened, and Mark studied her carefully. There was a peacefulness about him, a calmness that she had never associated with death. She did not know whether this happened often or not, but when he lifted his hand, she took it and held it. She could not hold the tears back, and as the hot drops fell on his hand, he said with some surprise, "Why, daughter, you mustn't cry!"

"I can't bear to lose you," she said and fell against him, holding him tightly.

His free arm came over her and he held her shaking shoulders. A smile came to his thin lips, and he said nothing for a while. Finally, he whispered, "The pain, it's all gone now. The first time since I was wounded—all gone."

Allyn pulled back, lifted her head, and could not speak, her throat was so tight. Mark seemed to be falling asleep again, but he opened his eyes and saw Jason sitting silently beside him. He reached out his free hand, and Jason took it at once. "Jason—my friend," he whispered, "faithful are the wounds of a friend. You've been good to me, Jason."

Tears stung Jason's eyes. He was not a crying man, nor could he remember the last time he had wept—but he knew he was losing something very precious. He held the fragile hand in his, thinking back to the time when that hand was as strong as his own. Now his throat grew full as he said, "I'll miss you, Mark."

Mark's eyes fastened on him, and his frail hand tightened its grip. "You must not miss the greatest thing there is," he whispered. "Jesus is the only answer. I want you to trust in Him, Jason."

Jason had heard about Jesus from Mark, Malcolm, and others, but no one had really asked him directly if he would trust God and accept Jesus as Lord. He thought about what the others had told him about Jesus, and how he'd called out to God when Allyn was wounded. Now that he was asked to decide one way or the other, he found he couldn't refuse. Jason swallowed hard then nodded his head shortly.

Susanna came and placed her hand on his shoulder, tears running down her cheeks, and she could not speak, except to say, "Praise God!"

"It doesn't take a lot—just ask Him. Would you do that, Jason? It would make me feel good if you would."

Thus it was that Jason Larrimore, who had never asked anything of any man, bowed his head and simply called on the name of Jesus as he held the fragile hand in his. Finally, he lifted his eyes and whispered, "It's done. I'll serve God all my life, Mark—all my life."

A great happiness came over Mark, and he turned his head. His voice was weaker, and he said, "Now, daughter, can you do that? Jesus loves you so much."

Allyn was weeping fully now, tears rolling down her cheeks. She looked up at her father with diamonds in her eyes and said, "I've already done it. I prayed while Jason did. I'll serve God as long as I live!"

Mark looked over at Susanna and said, "Susanna—" She came over and bent over beside him, touching his cheek. She kissed him, and he whispered, "You've been faithful—I couldn't have made it without you. Now the circle's unbroken. They're all in God's house."

"Yes, Mark, they're all home now." Her face was transfused with a joy that went beyond anything this world had to offer as she said, "I'm so *proud* of you, Mark."

Mark Rocklin held on to them for a few moments, but they could see that life was leaving him. Five minutes later, he straightened out on the bed, looked around the room, and smiled. He did not speak again except to say, "Lord Jesus"; then he took a deep breath, held it for a moment, and relaxed. His eyes were closed as he lay there, and they all knew that Mark Rocklin had gone to be with God.

The funeral had been difficult for Jason. There were many

branches of the Rocklin family, and all of these Southern branches came, but it had taken two days for them all to gather. Jason had kept to himself most of that time. It was hard; he had never been in a house where there was a loss. People came and went, and he ate when Flossie or Susanna or Allyn urged it upon him, but there was something in his spirit such as he had never sensed in all of his life. It was more than the loss of Mark Rocklin, he knew. As the body of his friend was lowered into the grave, he had felt a tremendous sense of loss—but then a sudden sense of certainty came upon him, and it was almost as if a voice said, "You will see him again."

Since that moment he had kept more or less to himself. Allyn, he knew, was worried about him, but his new commitment to God occupied his mind. He went for long walks, and on this day he had gone to the woods and stayed out all day and into the night.

He was sitting by a pond, thinking of what had happened and marveling at the peace that had come into his heart. He was startled when a slight noise attracted his attention. He was a man who had spent his life in dangerous situations, and when he heard twigs snap behind him, he spun around and jumped to his feet. "Stop! Hold it right there! Who is it?"

The form moved into a shaft of moonlight that poked through the trees, and he could see that it was Allyn. "What's wrong? Are you all right?"

"Yes, I'm fine," she said. "I just thought a walk would be nice." He came to her, and she put her hands out. He grasped them and held them. He felt strange in the darkness, wondering all sorts of things, but they said nothing for a time.

"Allyn, your hands are freezing," he said finally, not thinking of anything better to say.

"Really? I hadn't noticed." Her voice was low, so low he had to lean forward to hear it—and when he did, he smelled the scent of lilacs very faintly. He had smelled it before. It was the scent that had come to remind him of her no matter where he smelled it. The moon passed behind the cloud then emerged and bathed them again in silver, as if a spotlight in the wilderness.

"Jason," she said quietly. "Jason—!" She suddenly put her hands around his neck as she had done once before and pulled his head down. He put his arms around her and drew her close. She let her lips linger on his and then she moved her head back, the moonlight dancing in her eyes.

"Jason—I'm your wife," she whispered.

His nerves tingled as he realized what she was saying. He held her in his arms and for one moment could not believe what was happening. "And, Allyn," he said deliberately, "I'm your husband."

"I love you, Jason," she said at once. Her voice was not quite steady, and he could feel that she was trembling.

"Mark would be so happy to see us out here, saying what we're saying. But," Jason mused, "maybe he is watching us, smiling down from heaven." He gazed into her eyes. "Shall we return to our home, wife?"

She took his hand, and they began walking back toward Twelve Trees. As the house came into view, Allyn stopped, kissed Jason on the cheek, and whispered faintly, "I feel like I've come home at last."

"We both have," agreed Jason. Without a word, they walked hand in hand to start their lives together truly as man and wife.

Stars in Their Courses

PART ONE
The Actor
March–June 1863

CHAPTER 1

EARLY MORNING ENCOUNTER

"Anybody who would eat goose liver deserves a bellyache!"

As Frank Rocklin strolled down Fourteenth Street, he glanced at Willards Hotel and smiled faintly. The structure, outlined in the darkness by the flickering amber of oil-burning streetlamps, brought a quick memory of the very late supper he'd eaten there a few hours ago. The meal had included fried oysters, steak and onions, blancmange, and pâté de foie gras. He rubbed his stomach as he walked along in the predawn darkness.

Rocklin spoke the words aloud then quickly moved down the deserted streets of Washington. He was on his way home after a long night at the poker table, and his eyes were gritty from lack of sleep. Overhead a sullen moon hid behind skeins of dark clouds, and the silence of the streets lent an eerie tone to the capital. By day the area Rocklin passed through was in essence a Southern town, without the picturesque quality but with all the indolence, disorder, and want of sanitation. When Frank had walked down the same street early the previous morning, lounging Negroes had been a reminder of the war—for many of them were in Washington as contraband. He'd passed through flocks of geese while moving past the Capitol, and hogs of every size and color roamed in the grassy area that surrounded the War Department.

A wagon rumbled by, the driver stopping now and then to pick up night soil, and the thousands of privies sending forth their rank odors brought a frown to Rocklin's face. "I liked you well enough before the war," he murmured, addressing the city as if it were a troublesome child, "but you're spoiled forever."

He quickened his pace and passed along a row of roughly built structures, anxious to get home. "Should have hired a cab," he muttered. As he spoke, the sound of muffled voices came to him. Glancing up alertly, he strained his eyes trying to pierce the stygian darkness. Slowing his pace, he drew himself up, well aware that the dark streets were the hunting ground for predators—two-legged ones.

As Rocklin advanced along the wooden sidewalk, he realized that the muted voices were coming from a gaping cavity between a hardware store and a gun shop. Placing himself close to the gun shop front, he eased himself along until he stood framed in the opening. The flickering yellow light of the streetlamp threw four figures into relief, two of them bulking large in the murky dimness.

A rough male voice rasped, "All right, let's have that ring, dearie. And I'll have that stickpin from you, fellow!"

A woman's voice answered, quick with fear. "This was my mother's ring. Please, let me keep it, and I'll give you money."

"We'll have the money *and* the ring, dearie." A high-pitched giggle followed, and the shadows melded as one of the roughly dressed men suddenly moved forward. "Don't scream, or I'll have to slit that pretty throat of yours!"

Rocklin moved forward, noting that the woman's companion was backed against the wall of the hardware store, held there by a knife pressed against his chest. The woman was struggling with the smaller of the two hold-up men, pleading with him to leave her ring.

Rocklin stepped closer then said loudly, "All right, you two—let those folks alone!"

At once both men whirled, both holding knives in fighting position. One of them was very tall, over six feet two or three, and his features were blunt. His smallish eyes searched the opening, and seeing only one man, he grinned, exposing broken teeth. "Well now, looks like we got us another contributor, Ollie."

The smaller man had a foxlike face, sharp and keen. His lips were thin and now curved into a smile. "Right, mate. Now suppose you take the gentleman's money."

A glimmer of light traced the blade of the knife, and a hungry grin appeared on the thick lips of the big man. "Let's have it, now—no funny stuff."

Rocklin's hand dipped into his coat pocket, and he came out with a revolver. "Would you say this is funny stuff?" Neither attacker said a word, so Rocklin said casually, "I like this gun. It's a LeMat—the same kind that Jeb Stuart carries." Lifting it to aim at the head of the smaller man, he observed mildly, "It shoots six .42-caliber slugs, enough to tear a pretty nice hole in fellows like you. But if you survive all that, there's a 20-bore shotgun barrel underneath—see?" He lifted the LeMat slightly then added, "Pretty messy thing, getting hit in the belly with shotgun shells."

"Now—just a minute—"

"Drop those knives and get out of here!"

The two men at once threw down their knives and scurried away, disappearing into the darkness like nocturnal animals. Rocklin slipped the revolver into his pocket then asked, "Are you two all right?"

"I think so," the man said and turned to the woman. "All right, Carmen?"

"Y–yes." The voice was low and trembled only slightly. She came forward and peered upward into the face of Rocklin. "If you hadn't come, it would have been terrible."

"Let's get out of here," her companion spoke up. "They might come back." He moved quickly onto the sidewalk, drew a deep breath, and shook his head. The light falling from the streetlight revealed the lean face of a man in his late twenties, aristocratic and handsome. His voice was a rich baritone as he said with a grateful smile, "And your name, sir?"

"Frank Rocklin."

"Ah, Mr. Rocklin, my name is Roland Middleton—and this is Miss Carmen Montaigne." He hesitated slightly, as though expecting Rocklin to recognize the names, then said, "Come along; we'll have a drink to celebrate our timely rescue."

"Thanks, but it's late—or early, I should say." Frank smiled, adding, "I'd either take to carrying a gun or keep off the streets during these hours."

"Please, Mr. Rocklin, I'd feel much safer if you'd walk with us to our hotel," Miss Montaigne said. She was an attractive woman in her late twenties, Rocklin guessed, possibly older, with black hair and a striking face that had a foreign flavor. Her voice was strong and clear as she urged, "We're staying at Willards." There was a magnetism in her voice, and her eyes were compelling as she turned them fully on him.

"Why, of course," Rocklin answered.

The trio made their way down the street, Middleton speaking of the dangers of the city, the woman saying nothing. She let her arm brush against Rocklin's as though for security, and when they reached Willards, she put out her hand. "I'll never forget your help," she said, smiling up at him. "I insist that you give Roland and me a chance to show our gratitude."

"Why, certainly!" Middleton reached into his waistcoat pocket and came out with several small slips of paper. "I don't know if you're a man who likes the theater, but you must come for our performance—tonight, if possible."

Carmen examined Rocklin closely, taking in the tall, strong figure in a glance, then noting the deep-set dark brown eyes under heavy black brows. He had olive skin, a straight nose, and high cheekbones. His mouth was wide, and his slightly waving hair was black as her own. He was a handsome man, somewhere in his early twenties, she estimated. His hands were square and rather thick. He wore a dark brown coat, a pair of tan trousers, low-heeled black boots, and a black hat with a medium brim shoved back on his head in a careless fashion.

Rocklin peered at the tickets then looked up to ask quickly, "You're with Mr. Booth's company?" He had been aware that John Wilkes Booth, the brother of the most famous actor in America, Edwin Booth, was appearing in a production of *Romeo and Juliet*. He loved the theater and said so. "I'll be glad to come. Which roles do you play?"

"Juliet," Carmen answered. "And Roland here is Mercutio."

Frank nodded. "My favorite in the play, Mr. Middleton."

"Really? Well, I'd rather play Romeo, but John insisted on that role." There was a droll look on Middleton's face, and he grinned suddenly, adding, "But you have good taste."

"I played the role two years ago—a very bad, amateurish production," Rocklin confessed with a half-embarrassed laugh. "I was terrible! But I liked the sword fight."

Carmen Montaigne laughed aloud, amusement in her dark eyes as she cast a mischievous glance at Middleton. "Do you now? Roland *despises* the fencing!"

"Fool sort of thing." Middleton flushed. "Somebody's going to get hurt—and it'll probably be me!" He managed a smile, saying, "Bring a couple of your friends, and we'll have dinner at Willards after the performance."

"Maybe John will join us," the woman suggested.

Middleton turned his nose up in an imperial gesture. "I shall not ask him. He's a pompous bore!" He shook his head, adding, "He's a fire-eating Rebel, Mr. Rocklin. I wish he'd go join the Confederate army—then *I* could play Romeo!" He had an engaging wit and now put his hand out, giving Frank a surprisingly strong grip. "We'll tell the ticket taker to put you in front-row seats. And as for your help, I can no other answer make, but thanks and thanks—and ever thanks."

"*Hamlet*," Frank said with a nod, recognizing the quotation.

"You *do* know your theater!" Middleton stared at him with pleasure. "We'll look forward to the dinner."

"I hope you enjoy the play," Carmen said, putting out her hand. Her hand was smooth and strong, and there was a promise in her dark eyes. When Rocklin turned and left, she waited until he was out of hearing then murmured, "Most men wouldn't have risked helping us."

"A knight in shining armor, Carmen?" Middleton asked, his gray eyes on her.

Carmen Montaigne knew men well. She had found most of them to be less than they should be—but as she watched the tall figure of Rocklin moving away, she said sharply, "Don't be so cynical, Roland." She turned and moved into the hotel. "There are a *few* good men in this world."

<hr />

Stephen Rocklin looked with satisfaction around the dining room. He had designed and furnished it himself, saying to his wife, Ruth, "We'll be spending plenty of time in here, so I want to feel comfortable." Fortunately, as owner of a prosperous ironworks, he had not been limited, and there was a richness in the room and the furnishings that gave him satisfaction each time he sat down for a meal.

Along one wall rested a large sideboard made by Thomas Sheraton, supporting on its gleaming mahogany top a golden pitcher and sparkling crystal goblets. The serpentine front allowed one to reach easily across and serve with agility. Two large oil paintings directly over the sideboard added color, and the features of Noah and Charlotte Rocklin, Stephen's parents, were finely executed. In the opposite wall was a large fireplace with a walnut mantel that supported patent lamps on gilded tripods. Behind Stephen two ten-foot-high windows were covered with scarlet draperies, a gilt-edged mirror between, and light was regulated by blinds that blocked out a distracting glare. The Wilton carpet was protected by a baize floorcloth, and overhead an adjustable ceiling lamp was suspended to shed a brilliant light over the handsome dining table and chairs.

The room pleased Stephen, but tonight it was the company that gave him the most satisfaction. He ran his eyes around the table, taking in each face, then said to the woman on his left, "I wish Gideon was here, Melanie," thinking of his son, who was on active duty with Hooker.

"So do I, sir." Melanie Rocklin reached over and put her hand on her father-in-law's arm. She was an attractive woman of forty-two, wife of Stephen's only son, Gideon. "But at least we have all three of the boys."

"That's a minor miracle with this war going on," Stephen said. He glanced fondly at the three young men sitting to his left. At the age of twenty, Frank was the youngest—and the most trouble. His brothers had joined the army almost as soon as the war began. Tyler was the oldest at twenty-two, and Bob was only a year younger, and both of the older boys wore blue uniforms. Stephen asked, "Well, Frank, when are you joining the army?"

The question brought a pause in the hum of conversation, and Frank gave his grandfather a rash grin. "I don't have to worry now, Grandfather," he said. "Looks like I'll get conscripted. Lincoln signed the act yesterday."

At once his cousin Deborah Steele, who sat across from him, said sharply, "I don't agree with the president. The North has plenty of young men who'll fight!" She was an attractive young woman with decided opinions. "I read the act, Grandfather. It says that any drafted man can hire another as a substitute for three hundred dollars. This isn't a rich man's war!"

Frank winked slyly at Noel Kojak, Deborah's fiancé, saying, "I didn't know that, Deborah! Only three hundred dollars? Why, that solves my problem. Noel, keep your eye out for a good, strong young man for me, will you?"

Deborah opened her mouth to reply angrily, but Noel squeezed her arm. He was a small young man with light brown hair and gray eyes. He had been wounded at Bull Run and was not fit for active duty, but his writings on the army and the war were becoming more and more popular. President Lincoln had been heard to remark, "Why, that young Kojak can just make a man *see* what's going on—and he's got good sense, too!"

Ruth Rocklin, Stephen's wife, said sharply, "I think it's a good idea. There are plenty of men who have other things to do. You find a decent young man, Frank. I'm sure your father will understand."

"I doubt that, Grandmother." Frank shook his head wryly. "No colonel in the Union army wants his son to sit out this war." He glanced around and saw that only his grandmother favored such a cowardly act as buying a substitute, and he quickly changed the subject. "Ty, what's going to happen next? Will Lee whip us again like he always does?"

Tyler Rocklin wore the uniform of a second lieutenant of artillery. He forced a grin and shook his head almost sadly. "Well, I hope not, Frank. But unless we get a real fighting general at the head of the Army of the Potomac, he just might do it. But the best man would be Grant."

"Old 'Unconditional Surrender'?" Stephen mused. Ulysses S. Grant had scored the most significant Union victories for the North by capturing Fort Donelson and Fort Henry. By a curious coincidence, his initials fit the terms he'd demanded from the Confederates—unconditional surrender—and the name had stuck.

"Grant won't lead the army against Lee," Bob Rocklin said slowly. He was a quiet young man, the deepest thinker of the three boys and the gentlest. He looked more like his mother than the other two, and now he shook his head. "Somebody's got to take Vicksburg. Until we take the whole Mississippi and split the Confederacy, we can't put the rebellion down."

"Bob's right," Tyler agreed. "I expect both of us will be

pulling out soon to do that. And it'll be a big job. No port on the river is as well fortified as that place."

The talk went on for thirty minutes, and then Frank snapped his fingers. He fumbled in his waistcoat pocket, pulled out the tickets Middleton had given him, and grinned at his grandparents. "Got a treat for you—I'm taking you to see a play. I've got three tickets down front for *Romeo and Juliet*. And after the play, we'll have supper with a couple of the actors."

Stephen stared at his grandson and snorted. "Me? Go to a thing like that? And eat with *actors*?" He hated drama and despised actors. "I like real people," he said stiffly, "and real life, too. Take my advice, Frank, and throw those things away!"

But Deborah at once said, "Take Noel and me, Frank! I'd love to see the play!"

"All right, unless you fellows want to go," Frank offered, glancing at his brothers. "Or better yet, let's all go. I'll pay for the extra seats."

Tyler said roughly, "That's the play John Booth is in, isn't it? He's a copperhead, Frank! A real Southern sympathizer. I'd pay to send him to the South, but I won't go to see him act."

In the end it was Deborah and Noel who got into the cab. As the cabby spoke to the horses and sent them off at a brisk pace, Deborah said, "I'm not going to listen to John Wilkes Booth make a speech. I want some romance!"

"Well, nothing's more romantic than *Romeo and Juliet*, Deborah," Noel said. He put his arm around her and drew her close. "Maybe I'll get some pointers from this thing. You're always saying I'm not romantic enough." He winked at Frank, who was grinning at him. "Pretty hot stuff, is it, Frank?"

"Never mind all that, Noel!" Deborah sniffed and drew back. "You just stay away from those painted actresses!"

The trio enjoyed the play tremendously. Frank jabbed Noel in the ribs when Juliet came onstage, saying, "There she is, Noel. If you like, I'll take Deborah off someplace, and you and Carmen can have a private little supper. That all right with you, Deborah?"

Deborah gave Frank a frosty stare. "She's old enough to be his mother! Juliet's supposed to be fourteen years old!"

"Well, art has its limits, I guess." Frank shrugged. He, too, was of the opinion that Carmen Montaigne was too old for her role, but he had to admit that she *looked* better than any Juliet he'd ever seen. She wore a stunning white gown, and there was a sophistication in her eyes that no fourteen-year-old girl had. She added to the role a most sensuous quality.

Noel said at once, "Well, she's *romantic* enough, Deborah. I'm keeping my eyes on her; that's for sure!" He kept Deborah fuming by his under-the-breath remarks on the "art" of the actress.

Frank was interested in John Wilkes Booth, who played the role of Romeo with too much spirit, he thought. He had little of his older brother Edwin's skill, but moved with overdone gymnastic abandon all through the play. *Why, I could do better than that!* Frank thought. He'd seen Edwin Booth perform *Hamlet* in New York and had been amazed at the ability of the actor.

Roland Middleton was a good actor, but he had obviously been drinking. This surprised Frank a little, for though he was no prude, he believed in giving his best—and liquor never helped a man do that. Middleton did so well under the influence, Frank wondered how good he'd be if he was sober.

Finally, the third act began, and Frank leaned forward, for this was Mercutio's death scene. He thought of how the actor had scowled at the thought of fencing, and he wondered at it. He himself was an expert fencer and loved the sport. He watched as the quarrel between Tybalt and Romeo developed; then Mercutio entered. The actor playing Tybalt demanded of Middleton, "What wouldst thou have with me?"

Middleton looked pale, and his hands were not steady as he drew his sword, saying, "Good King of Cats, nothing but one of your nine lives!"

The duel began, and Frank noted how ineffectual Middleton was. The actor playing Tybalt was obviously an expert swordsman, his blade flashing as he circled Middleton. Booth as Romeo played his part well, coming in to thrust up the blades of the two men. In the play, he is attempting to make peace, but the treacherous Tybalt stabs Mercutio under Romeo's arm.

It was a tricky piece of stage work, and Frank remembered how hard he'd practiced with the actors when he'd played the part. It had to be done carefully or someone could get hurt.

And suddenly he saw it—Tybalt's blade shot under Romeo's arm—but Middleton was too slow to turn aside. The blade took him in the thigh and he dropped his sword, crying aloud. He recovered instantly, so that most of the audience didn't know that an accident had occurred. Turning to one side, Middleton concealed the blood that streamed down his leg as he said his final lines.

He's got plenty of nerve—even if he drinks too much, Frank thought. Middleton's face was pale as he cried, "Go, villain, fetch a surgeon."

A shaken Booth managed to speak his line: "Courage, man, the hurt cannot be much."

And then Middleton turned and happened to look directly into the face of Frank Rocklin. He smiled cynically, saying, "'Tis not so deep as a well nor so wide as a church door, but 'tis enough, 'twill serve." And then he laughed suddenly, giving the most famous pun of Mercutio, "Ask for me tomorrow and you shall find me a grave man!"

The actors helped the dying Mercutio off the stage, and Deborah said, "That looked so *real*!"

"It was real," Frank said grimly. "I'm going backstage."

"We'll go with you," Noel said at once.

The three rose and ignored the glares from the irate spectators. They made their way out a side door. Frank strolled purposefully down a hall leading to the back of the building and entered the backstage area. At once he saw a crowd of actors huddled around Middleton. He moved closer and bent down to see the wound. He found himself standing next to Carmen Montaigne, who looked at him with distressed eyes.

"Is he badly hurt?" Frank asked.

"I don't know. We've sent for a doctor." She would have said more, but a heavyset man chewing on the stub of a cigar came to say, "All right, get ready, Carmen—the rest of you, break it up. We'll take care of Roland."

Middleton had been sitting on a stool but now rose. Seeing Frank, he said, "Come along, Rocklin. I may need a little help."

Noel and Deborah went back to their seats, and Frank accompanied the actor to his dressing room, where Middleton collapsed on a chair. "Cut this blasted costume off, will you? Can't see how bad it is with the bloody thing on!"

Frank managed to cut the right leg of the tights off, and he said at once, "Not too bad, Middleton. If the blade had hit an artery, we'd see lots of bright red blood."

Middleton looked down, his lips puckered. "Looks like enough blood to me. Are you a doctor?"

"No, but when I was fencing regularly, this sort of thing sometimes happened. You'll be all right."

Soon a doctor came in, a small man with a thin face and intense gray eyes. "I'm Dr. Parnell. Let's have a look."

Frank stood back as Parnell examined his patient. He punched and probed, making Middleton squirm. "By heaven, that's painful!" he gasped. "Is it bad?"

Dr. Parnell stared at him. "You're not going to die—but you're going to have to stay off this leg for a week. A big muscle is torn."

Middleton didn't argue. After the doctor left, he gave Frank a pale-faced look. "Stick around, will you, Frank? Booth is going to hit the ceiling!"

Frank sat down, and the two talked until the play ended. The door opened, and Booth came rushing in. Glaring at Middleton, he cursed vividly, throwing himself around the room. While he was engaged in this, the door opened again and Carmen entered, followed by Noel and Deborah. "Is it bad, Roland?" she asked.

"Bad enough that he can't do his part for a week!" Booth snarled. "What am I supposed to do for a replacement? Blast a drunk anyway!"

Deborah watched the actors as they argued, fascinated by the behind-the-scenes action. She was intrigued by Booth, who was as handsome as he was famous. And she felt sorry for Middleton, who looked pale and sick. She was an impulsive girl and spoke up to interrupt Booth. "Frank, you always wanted to be an actor. Here's your chance."

John Wilkes Booth at once fixed his large, expressive eyes

on Frank. "Are you an actor, sir?"

"Why, just in an amateur sort of way—"

"John, he knows the lines, and he's an expert swordsman," Roland Middleton spoke up, anxious to turn Booth's wrath away. "He can be my replacement."

"Do you know the part?" Booth demanded. Then he said, "What follows this cue: 'And so bound, I cannot bound a pitch above dull woe. Under love's heavy burden do I sink'?"

Frank spoke the next line, lifting his voice, "And to sink in it, should you burden love, too great oppression for a tender thing."

"*Very* good!" Booth said, a surprised look on his face. "A fine voice. Now what follows this cue: 'In bed asleep, while they do dream on things true'?"

Frank had always loved Mercutio's speech on the fairy, Queen Mab. He spoke it quietly, but his love for the lines shone through his eyes and his voice. "Oh then, I see Queen Mab hath been with you. She is the fairies' midwife, and she comes in shape no bigger than an agate stone on the forefinger of an alderman, drawn with a team of little atomies. . . ."

The room grew still as he recited the long speech, and when it ended, Booth exclaimed, "Why, sir, you *are* an actor, no matter what you say! I've heard no better Queen Mab from any man." He was a handsome man, with black curly hair and magnetic eyes. He had forgotten his anger and said, "Come now, you must help our friend Roland."

"Why, Mr. Booth—!"

"I'd be in your debt—again," Middleton spoke up. He had fine gray eyes, and there was a pleading in them as he spoke.

"Grandfather will disown you, Frank," Deborah said, her eyes gleaming. "But I'd love to see you do it!"

"It would be a favor for all of us, sir," Carmen said, coming to stand by Frank. "Won't you do it?"

Frank Rocklin was a reckless young man. He had done more dangerous things than this, and the idea had a certain appeal. "Why, I'll do my best, but I may smell up your play with my amateur acting."

John Wilkes Booth laughed with delight. He, too, was a daring young man and clapped the newest member of his cast on the shoulder. "Rehearsal tomorrow at ten o'clock. You'll do a fine job!"

Frank Rocklin said wryly to Roland Middleton, "Don't worry about your job, Roland. A week of this, and I'll be glad to hand your job back to you."

But Carmen Montaigne put her hand on his arm in a possessive manner. "Don't be too sure about that, Frank. You may like it better than you think!"

Chapter 2

Dinner at Willards

Frank endured the morning rehearsal and, after satisfying Booth that he could get through the play, left the theater. He'd been more nervous than he'd expected, unable to do more than nibble at the excellent lunch he ordered. The curtain went up at eight, but Booth had warned the cast to be on hand and in costume by seven. Frank paced the streets nervously, dreading the time he'd have to step out on the stage. Finally, at six o'clock he made his way to Grover's Theater and found it surrounded by a noisy, milling crowd.

"What's the trouble?" he asked a tall, lanky man wearing a stovepipe hat. "Has there been an accident?"

The tall man wheeled and fixed a pair of steely blue eyes on Frank. "Accident? No, sir, not an accident—but an outrage!" He lifted his chin and pointed upward to the top of the theater. "Some Rebel has torn down the new flag that Mr. Grover installed on top of the theater—and some of us are ready to tar and feather the traitor!"

Lifting his gaze, Frank saw that two men were raising a mammoth flag. The stiff breeze caught it, and as it rippled freely, he said mildly, "Well, there's another new one."

"And it will stay unfurled, sir! Anyone who dares touch yon banner dies like a dog!"

A grin rose to Rocklin's lips as he thought, *He talks like one of the actors.* He suppressed it, saying only, "I hardly think a Rebel would dare touch the flag in broad daylight."

"There is nothing so low but that the traitors who have rent our Union asunder will stoop to it!"

"I suppose that is so." Frank had no inclination to argue with the man, for Southern sympathizers were legion in Washington and he did not want to be labeled as such. Lincoln's secretary of war, Edwin M. Stanton, had imposed an iron rule on the capital but had not succeeded in obliterating the movement. The city was rife with the rumors of Confederate spies, and Belle Boyd, the colorful Southern spy, had not been troubled with the high cost of living in the capital. She had been given one of the best rooms in Old Capitol Prison, which held more than two thousand Confederate captives.

A cheer went up as the huge flag fluttered in the breeze, and as Frank made his way through the crowd, he wondered if John Wilkes Booth was troubled by the anti-Confederate feeling that brought out such crowds over a single flag. He found the door to the theater locked, but when he knocked, he was admitted at once by Jed Hoskins. "Good evenin', Mr. Rocklin. You's early, sah."

Frank grinned at the tall black man who had been born a slave in Alabama but had fled to the North on the Underground Railroad. "I may leave early, Jed." He shrugged. "I feel as out of place as a frog on the middle of Pennsylvania Avenue."

Hoskins was a serious man, but he smiled with sympathy. "No, sah, you is gonna do real fine! Mr. Middleton, he say you a natural-born actor."

"Is he here?"

"Yes, sah. He backstage." Hoskins shook his head, a sad expression sweeping over his face. "I wish you could keep Mr. Middleton from likker, sah. He a good man, but dat whiskey is de ruination of him."

"Guess we all have our weaknesses, Jed," Frank murmured. He stood there uncertainly then shrugged and attempted a smile that didn't quite come off. "If they start throwing rotten tomatoes at me, Jed, I hope you'll stand by with a towel."

Hoskins shook his head vigorously. "No, *sah*! I watched you real good in de rehearsal. You do jest fine! And I say a special prayer dat Gawd will be with you. Dat'll answer!"

"Thanks, Jed. I need all the help I can get."

Making his way through the empty theater, Frank found Roland slumped in a chair, a pair of crutches leaning against the wall. He looked up to say, "Hello, Frank. You're early—which is a mistake."

"Coming early is a mistake?"

"Oh yes." Roland pulled a silver flask from his inside pocket, unscrewed it, and offered it to Frank, who shook his head. He lifted it, took two swallows, then shuddered as the liquor bit at his throat. "What awful stuff!" he muttered. "Tastes like varnish remover!"

"Maybe you need to buy better whiskey."

"No, it all tastes the same after a few swallows." Middleton looked tired, and his eyes were red-rimmed. He shifted in the chair, grimaced, and swore. "Leg is killing me!"

"You ought to be in bed, Roland." Frank sat down, gave a nervous glance around, then rose and paced the floor. "Why is it better not to come early?" he asked. He was not really interested in the answer but was not able to keep still.

"Because you pace the floor like you're doing now and worry about how it will go. But if you come late, other people have to worry." Middleton smiled and lifted his hand to smooth his dark brown hair. "If I were you, I'd leave now. Go to a saloon, have a few drinks, and get back just in time to get dressed."

Frank grinned, his white teeth flashing. "I'd get roaring drunk, and Booth would put that sword right through my middle." Then he realized that his words were an insult to Middleton—who had done just what he had mentioned. "I didn't mean—"

"Oh, you can't insult a drunk, Frank," Roland said with a trace of bitterness. "There was a time when I'd have called you out for saying that, but I'm past having my pride hurt." He pulled out the flask, unscrewed the top, and then hesitated, lifting his gaze to look at Rocklin. "Want to know why I became a drunk, Frank?"

"Yes."

"Nothing very original, I'm afraid." Middleton stared down at his feet as if he found them particularly interesting. He spoke in a low voice. "I was engaged to a young woman. Very much in love, of course—so much so that I would not beteem the winds of heaven visit her face too roughly." His lips twisted bitterly, adding, "As Lord Hamlet once said of another faithless woman. Well then, I had a friend—or thought I did. Can you guess the rest?"

"Your friend took your fiancée away from you?"

"Yes, so it was, and since that time I have tried to ruin my life by strong drink. You find that despicable, I suppose?"

"I find it tragic, Roland." Frank studied the lean face of Middleton, shook his head, and added, "There are other women—and not all men are like your friend. Take another try." Frank shrugged his shoulders and grinned. "I hate it when people tell me to do the obvious and right thing. When we decide to go to the devil, why, something in us gets some sort of perverse pleasure out of watching ourselves fall apart."

Middleton stared at Rocklin with a startled expression. "Where did you get that from, Frank? You've never been a failure, have you?"

"Some would argue that I'm one right now—my grandfather, for one. And maybe even my father—" He broke off as a knock sounded, and without a pause the door opened and Carmen walked in. Frank rose at once, saying, "Hello, Carmen."

"Frank, you're here early." Carmen was wearing a rose-colored dress that set off her figure well. Her cheeks were flushed, and there was a pleased expression in her large eyes. "I'm excited about your premier performance."

Frank laughed self-consciously. "I feel like I'm the guest of honor at an execution. Matter of fact, I'd like to back out of the whole thing."

Carmen came to stand before him. She was not tall and had to lift her head to look up into his face. She was a woman of much experience, but there was a youthful air about her as she said, "No, I won't let you do that. Now you get into your costume. We'll have time to go over your lines one more time."

"He knows them better than I do," Roland said. He smiled at Frank, saying, "My costume ought to fit you. Step outside, Carmen, and we'll see what he looks like in tights."

Fifteen minutes later Frank was wearing tights for the first time in his life—and feeling like an utter and complete fool. He stared at himself in the mirror on the wall and growled, "Roland—I can't go out in front of people wearing this! Why, it's indecent!"

Roland laughed but assured him, "You look good, Frank. All of us feel the same way when we first put on garb like that. Don't be nervous—it'll be fine."

Voices were beginning to filter through to the dressing room, and soon Booth breezed into the room, followed by Carmen, and smiled with satisfaction. "I was afraid you might run away, Rocklin. First-night nerves do funny things to a man." Booth was wearing a greatcoat with a flowing cape collared in fur. There was a velvet collar on his braid-bound jacket. He wore a seal ring on his little finger, and a stickpin was thrust in the center of his fine cravat. He was, in short, the picture of nonchalant dandyism. He walked around Frank, examining his costume carefully. "Good! You'll make a fine Mercutio!"

"What if I freeze up or forget my lines?"

"Roland will be sitting in the wings. If you forget a line, he'll prompt you. If you freeze up"—Booth smiled and struck Rocklin lightly on the chest—"I'll stomp on your toe." He laughed, saying, "You'll do fine. The rehearsal was good. See you onstage."

As soon as Booth left the room, Carmen said, "Come along, Frank. We'll go over your lines." The two of them went to her dressing room, where Frank stood stiffly, reciting his lines as she gave him the cues. Time dragged by slowly, but finally Jed Hoskins stuck his head inside, saying, "Curtain goin' up! Better git yoahselves in place, please."

"All right, Jed." Carmen had been sitting down but rose and came to take Frank's arm. "It'll be all right," she said then turned, and he followed her to the wings. He could hear the muttering voices of the audience, and the actors and actresses were strolling around in a casual way. The older man who played Capulet was reading a copy of *Uncle Tom's Cabin*, deeply engrossed in it.

He's probably been onstage so long, it's no more than taking a drink of water, Frank thought with a tinge of envy.

As the curtain rose, Frank's knees were unsteady and his palms were sweaty. He wanted to wipe his face but was afraid he'd smear the makeup that Roland had layered on. Mercutio did not appear in the first three scenes, and the tension grew worse. Finally, Booth came to stand by him, his dark eyes excited. "All right, Rocklin?" he asked.

Frank croaked, "All right," his throat dry as dust. When Booth walked out onto the stage accompanied by several other actors, he tried to follow—but seemed to be glued in place. And then Carmen gave him a kick, saying, "Break a leg, Frank!" When he stared at her uncomprehendingly, she smiled and explained, "It's the way we wish each other well in the theater. Now go do it!"

Frank was half shoved onto the stage by a thrust from Carmen, and the lights blinded him for a moment. The act began with Romeo and Benvolio speaking, and frantically he tried to remember his line but could not have told anyone his name. He stumbled forward, staring at the audience as if he were hypnotized, his mind reeling.

Booth caught a glimpse of Frank and saw at once that he was having a terminal case of stage fright. He'd seen it happen before and now moved close to Frank. He said very loudly the line that introduced Mercutio's first speech: "Give me a torch: I am not for this ambling." He took the torch handed him by one of the actors, then moved so close to Frank that he was touching him. "Being but heavy," he said even more loudly, "I will bear the light." As he said the last of the line, he lifted his foot and brought it down hard on Frank's toes!

Frank grunted involuntarily and spat out his line, running

it together so rapidly that most could not understand a word of it: "Nay, gentle Romeo, we must have you dance." As he gasped out the line, he glared at Booth, who laughed at him and whispered, "Now you're on your own!"

The grins of the actors inspired Frank Rocklin. He saw that they were amused, and for some strange reason this delivered him from the fear that had paralyzed him. He looked over the audience and saw Deborah, Noel, Robert, and Tyler sitting up front. Taking a deep breath, he lifted his voice and spoke his line clearly, "You are a lover. Borrow Cupid's wings, and soar with them above a common bound."

Booth was instantly relieved, and he winked at Frank slyly. He dominated the scene, of course, but Frank was able to throw himself into the play. This had happened to him before, in amateur productions—losing himself. He forgot the audience, or at least was able to concentrate on the action that took place on the stage. And as he did this, he seemed to enter into another realm. The world faded, and all he knew was the tiny cosmos that existed on the small stage.

Why, this is fun! he thought once, and when it came time for him to speak the Queen Mab speech, he was shocked when, at the end, the audience applauded. He blinked with astonishment, and Booth nudged him, whispering, "Blast it all, don't be *too* good, Rocklin! I hate to be upstaged by a bit player!" But he was smiling with approval, and as Frank made his exit, Carmen was waiting, her eyes like stars. She threw her arms around him, whispering, "You were *wonderful*, Frank!" And then she was gone, her voice floating to Frank as he stood in the darkness of the wings.

As he stood there, a sense of fulfillment came to Frank Rocklin. He listened to the voices of the actors, and to his total astonishment he found himself *anxious* to get back in front of the footlights. When Jed came by and patted him on the shoulder, whispering, "You done real *fine*, sah! Real fine actin' indeed!" Frank felt a wave of pride and thought, *A man could get used to this!*

Finally, the play ended, and Frank was pulled out for a curtain call. He stood there staring down at the audience, noting that his family was beaming at him with pride. Then he was startled, for Booth lifted his hand for silence and, when it came, said forcefully, "I want to give special thanks to Mr. Frank Rocklin, who played the role of Mercutio. He is one of your own, the son of Colonel Gideon Rocklin, and his two brothers right in front are, as you see, wearing the uniform of the United States. This was Mr. Rocklin's first professional appearance on the stage, but I know acting, and I insist that if he chooses to make this his profession, why, my family will have to look to its laurels!" He smiled at Frank, and the applause that followed seemed like thunder, sending thrills along that young man's spine such as he'd never felt before.

The dining room at Willards would hold fifteen hundred people—or so Mr. Willard boasted—but as the party of John Wilkes Booth was finally seated, it seemed to Frank that the enormous room could not hold one more person.

Booth had charmed the headwaiter into placing them at a good table, and as Frank held Carmen's chair, he said, "Not exactly a private little celebration, is it?"

Carmen turned to face him as he sat down, her lips curved in a smile. "The English hate this place," she said. "They like snug inns with private parties, and one of them told me that all they got here was heat, noise, dust, smoke—and spitting!" She was wearing a pale green dress with a low-cut bodice, and from her ears dangled two jade earrings. Leaning toward him, she said, "We'll have a private celebration for your triumph later, Frank, but Booth has to have this sort of thing. He thrives on attention—like all of us in the theater, I suppose."

And she spoke only the truth, for Booth was in his element. He was greeted by many, some wanting his autograph, and more than one stagestruck young woman practically threw herself at the handsome young star. Frank took in the actor, noting the ivory skin, the silky black hair and mustache, the white teeth and lustrous, heavy-lidded eyes. "He's fine looking—a little of a dandy."

"Women practically throw themselves at him. But he's not just a dandy, Frank. He's a fencer and an expert pistol shot. Look at his hands—see how strong they are?"

Frank nodded then turned to Deborah, who was seated on his left, saying, "Get Noel to dance with you."

Deborah smiled but shook her head. "That's not dancing, Frank. That's a can of sardines out there." She motioned to the dance floor, which was indeed packed. The floor was filled with officers wearing white gloves and snowy collars above their wool tunics. The West Point generals were splendid in gold-embroidered shoulder straps and gauntlets, and some of them even kept on their plumed hats. The colors were almost glaring, for the ladies wore dresses of pink and green silk and white tarlatan, and they tossed their curls in the mazes of the dance. Old and young, plump and lean, pretty and plain, the ladies all seemed to find partners. Grave statesmen and stout generals capered as friskily as boyish lieutenants on leave, and the sound of laughter and music and the soft plopping of champagne corks filled the air.

Robert said quietly to Tyler, "You'd never think that our men are dying out there in the field, would you, Ty?"

Tyler shook his head but didn't answer directly. Instead, he looked at Frank with a curious expression. "He was good, wasn't he, Bob?"

"I suppose so." He sipped his water carefully, a worried expression on his face. "It's a pretty frothy sort of existence, this acting business. I'll be glad when Frank signs up and we can get away from here. Washington's like some sort of circus these days."

Booth waited until their meal had been ordered then turned to speak to Noel. "Well, Mr. Kojak, I've read your stories—very fine writing. Honest and clear—a rare thing for a political writer."

"I must say the same for your acting, Mr. Booth," Noel answered quickly, and his reply pleased the actor. Noel added, "I must warn you that I've been asked to write a critical review of your play."

Booth laughed aloud, saying at once, "Well then, I must flatter you a good deal more than I have, sir! But since one of my company is your good friend, I'll hope you'll spare us the worst."

Carmen said firmly, "I never saw such poise in anyone with so little experience, did you, Mr. Booth?"

"No, indeed I have not." Booth turned to face Frank, his face serious. "Some men cannot be taught to act. Oh, they can memorize the lines and go through the role well enough. But there's a sort of—well, *magic* in drama. Some men and some women can make the audience forget it's in a theater. And those who do are the sort who themselves forget they're in a play. I saw some of that in your performance tonight, Frank. You belong on the stage. I hope you won't neglect the talent God's put in you."

Deborah saw that both of Frank's brothers were uneasy with this statement, and she herself was uncertain that Booth was right. But this was Frank's night of triumph, and so she waited until later to whisper to him, "I hope you don't go on the stage, Frank, as a career." When he looked at her with surprise, she smiled, saying, "You're far too attractive. You'd be besieged by impressionable young women."

"Oh, don't be silly, Deborah!" Frank protested.

"It's true, you know. When you were on the stage, I forgot that you were just Frank Rocklin, the young man I've known forever. There's some sort of magnetism in some men—Booth is one of them—and I was drawn to you."

"Don't tell Noel. He'd challenge me to a duel."

But Deborah was serious. "Haven't you seen how the women swarm around Booth?"

"Well, I'm no Booth—and not likely to be."

"That's good. Most men couldn't stand such adulation. I'd hate to see you get caught up in that kind of temptation."

Chapter 3

Frank Makes a Choice

As Frank took his final bow at the curtain call along with the rest of the company, he felt a sense of loss. For seven nights he had performed, but now Middleton was fit. Looking out at the audience, he thought, *I'm going to miss all this.* He turned and left the stage, and when he got to the dressing room, he found Roland waiting for him.

"You did well tonight, Frank. Even better than usual."

Frank shrugged and sat down to remove his makeup. "Thanks, Roland," he murmured. He listened as Roland rambled on, speaking of various aspects of the performance, then rose and stripped off the costume. "I'll have these washed for you, Roland," he said.

"Don't bother. I'll take care of it. It'll be good to get back on the boards." He tested his leg then grinned ruefully. "I hope Booth is more careful with that blasted sword!"

Frank slipped on his trousers, saying, "Roland, don't ever drink before a performance. It's too dangerous trying to handle a sword when you're drunk."

"Amen!" Roland's aristocratic features drew up into a frown. "I've learned that lesson," he said tersely. "I've heard enough about it from Booth." He sat down and grinned faintly. "I'll try to use more discretion in my progress to ruin. I'll only drink before performances that have no dueling scenes."

Frank buttoned his white shirt then reached for his coat. He slipped it on and turned to study the actor. He had grown fond of Middleton during the past few days, discovering that beneath the cynical facade that the man wore was a sensitive man—and a tortured one. Middleton made a joke of his painful experience with his sweetheart and best friend, but Frank was astute enough to realize that the betrayal of the two had scarred the man emotionally. Now as he sat down and pulled on his soft black boots, he tried one more time to help Middleton.

"You're tired of my preaching, Roland," he said quietly, "but I think we've gotten to be good friends. I hate to see you ruin yourself. You're a fine actor—and if you'd give up drinking, why, you could go to the top." He'd discovered from Carmen that Roland's reputation for drinking kept him from rising in his profession, and now added as he rose to his feet, "You're better than Booth."

"Wouldn't have to be too good to outact him." Roland came to his feet, testing his right leg carefully, then turned to face Frank squarely. "I'm not much at liking other men, Frank, but I like you. But I might as well tell you what you already know—don't waste your time trying to reform me. I'm a hopeless case."

"Don't believe that, Roland," Frank protested. "A man can do what he wants to do." Then he grinned and slapped Roland on the shoulder in a rough gesture of affection. "End of sermon. We'll now have the offering and the benediction."

"What will you do, Frank?"

"Don't know. Go into the army, I expect."

"You feel strongly about the war? You haven't said much."

Frank shrugged his shoulders, saying, "I'm against slavery, but not enough to get myself killed doing something about it. My father and my brothers have all the noble instincts in our family. I'm just a mutt, I guess."

Roland laughed at the expression on Frank's face. "Makes two of us," he said. Putting his hand out impulsively, he gripped Frank's hand with a surprisingly strong pressure. "Let's see each other, Frank. We'll be going to New York next week, but we can have a good time before then."

"Sure. I'll come tomorrow night just to be sure you do a good job." Grinning rashly, Frank added, "Why don't you pink Booth in the arm? Might give him a little humility!"

He turned and left the dressing room, going at once to knock on Carmen's door. When she called out for him to enter, he opened the door and stepped inside. She was sitting at her dressing table but rose at once and came to him. "I guess my brief career on the stage is over," Frank said, grinning ruefully.

"It doesn't have to be." She put her hands out and squeezed his as she looked up at him. "Booth likes you, Frank. He'll find you a place in the company."

"I don't think so," Frank said. They had spoken of this before, but he knew that he had little or no choice. "The only way I could become an actor would be to hire a substitute—and I won't do that."

"No, you wouldn't do that."

Carmen had become very fond of this broad-shouldered young man. Usually it was the men who became infatuated with *her*, but most of them were not men she'd think of seriously. She'd been interested in a few, but they had been married—or had no intention of marrying an actress. For the past week, she and Frank had been together every day, going out after the play to eat. They'd enjoyed each other's company tremendously—something Carmen thought wonderful. Most men would have pressured her into an affair, but though Frank had kissed her more than once, he had not asked anything more of her.

Now that he was leaving the company, Carmen felt a desire to keep him. "You promised to take me riding," she said, holding on to his arm.

"How about tomorrow afternoon?" Frank asked. "I'll pick you up at one. We can have a nice ride in the park." When she nodded, he turned and left the room.

He was on his way toward the exit when Booth stepped out of his dressing room and hailed him. "Frank, hold on there!" The actor came and held out an envelope. "You weren't leaving without saying good-bye—and without your salary?" His handsome face broke into a smile, and he shook his head. "If you're going to be an actor, never forget to take the money."

Feeling extremely awkward, Frank took the envelope but said, "I didn't do this for money, Mr. Booth."

"I know that—and it's refreshing to see someone who loves the stage for what it is." Booth sobered, his large eyes fixed on Frank thoughtfully. "I've been meaning to talk to you about joining the company."

"Why, you don't need me!" Frank was astonished at the offer. He knew that any young actor would snap up the chance to join the company of John Wilkes Booth. He was not the figure of renown his father was—or his brother, Edwin—still, he was a rising star on the stage.

Booth brushed his dark mustache and said briefly, "Roland's a good actor, but totally unreliable. You know that. He's been released before and will be again. I don't trust him. Why don't you come with me?"

Frank did not even have to think about it. "I appreciate your offer, but I can't accept." He hesitated, not wanting to sound sanctimonious, then faced Booth squarely. "We've not known each other long, but Roland and I are friends."

Booth was very much surprised. He had had no thought but that his offer would be accepted. Now he stared at Frank for a long moment. "Loyalty is a fine thing, sir," he finally said slowly. "I honor you for it. But it might be better placed, I think."

"I've talked to Roland. I think he'll do better in the future."

"Oh, he's always going to do better." Booth shrugged with contempt. "He's promised me a dozen times to lay off the bottle, but he just can't do it. He's hopeless, I'm afraid."

"I don't give up on people," Frank insisted. "But I do appreciate your offer, Mr. Booth." He found a smile, adding, "My family would probably cast me into the street if I did become an actor. They have little respect for the theater."

"Well, if you change your mind, I'll be glad to recommend you, Rocklin. You've got a real gift, and you're young enough to learn to craft it into something wonderful. I'll be keeping up with you." He smiled at a thought then added, "Carmen will keep me posted. She's quite taken with you, isn't she?"

Frank shifted uncomfortably, disliking the cynical expression that had come to Booth's face. "I expect we won't be seeing each other much—not if I go into the army."

"You're enlisting?"

"Have to, I guess. It's that or get conscripted."

"You don't think of hiring a substitute?"

"No. I won't do that. I must uphold my family's fine military tradition," Frank said, none too convincingly.

Booth stared at him, started to speak—then changed his

mind. "Good luck to you," he said cordially, shook hands, and turned back into his dressing room.

He was going to say something to me about the war, Frank thought as he left the theater. He knew that before the war John Wilkes Booth had been very popular in the South. He had, in fact, put on a militia uniform and gone to stand guard when John Brown had been hanged. Middleton had told him, "Booth is a Marylander—one of those who hate the Republican administration and who sentimentalize over the Confederacy. But he'll never join himself to its fortunes."

A light rain glazed the sidewalk as Frank emerged, and he thought of his future. He had no desire to go into the army, and the idea of becoming an actor tantalized him. But as he made his way home, he put those thoughts aside—and thought instead of his riding date with Carmen.

"I'm glad that acting foolishness is out of Frank's system." Stephen Rocklin leaned back in his chair and grunted with satisfaction at Tyler. The two had always been close, and there was a fond light in the older man's eyes as he examined his grandson. Tyler sat loosely in a leather-covered chair, his muscles lax. He was a muscular young man, his chest swelling the fabric of his blue uniform. He had a certain inner strength that matched the power of his sturdy frame, and there was a steadiness in his dark eyes.

"I'm not so sure it's over, Grandfather. You know Frank—when he gets an idea in his head, it takes an earthquake to blast it loose." A sudden grin pulled the corners of his lips upward, and humor glinted in his eyes. "Like you, I suppose."

Stephen glared at his grandson. "I'm *firm*," he snorted. "Frank is *stubborn*!" Then he slapped the desk in front of him and laughed at his own words. "You're right, Ty. I guess it runs in the blood. All Rocklins are pretty stubborn. Well, there are worse things for a man to be."

"Frank is good at things. He just never found anything he liked well enough to stick to. He'll find himself someday."

The two men were sitting in Stephen's office. Tyler had dropped by to spend a little time with his grandfather. It was understood that once the war was over, it would be Tyler who would be a driving force in Rocklin Ironworks. Gideon would never leave the army, and Robert cared little for the business—Frank even less. At the age of sixty-five, Stephen Rocklin was strong and vigorous, but now as he looked at his grandson, he felt a touch of mortality.

"You'll be sitting behind the desk soon, Ty," he said abruptly. "I wish you weren't in the army. I need you here. The business is too much for an old man. We're three months behind with orders now—and they keep piling up." He waved his thick, square hand at a stack of papers on his desk, adding, "The army can't get enough of anything."

"You know how I love to work with you, Grandfather," Ty said gently, "but I have to wear the uniform." He changed the subject at once, saying, "Frank needs to get into the company with Bob and me. That way we could watch out for him."

"Will he do it, Ty?"

"I talked to him yesterday, and he said he'd let me know."

"He told Bob he'd sign up for ninety days—but no more."

Ty frowned, saying, "Ninety-day wonders, we call those fellows. They're almost worthless. Not enough time to be trained, and as soon as they are, they're looking forward to getting out of the army. If a man's due to get out in a few weeks, he'll hold back when it's time to charge the enemy. We don't need that kind!"

The two men sat there speaking quietly, and finally Stephen asked, "What about this woman Frank's been seeing? What's her name?"

"Carmen Montaigne."

Stephen snorted and gave his grandson a cynical look. "I'll bet she was born Mary Smith!"

Ty laughed and rose to his feet. "I wouldn't be surprised, sir. If Frank went on the stage as a professional, he might change his name to Launcelot Fourtenier!" He picked up his hat but said before he turned to go, "That's another good reason for getting Frank away from here. She's a pretty sultry package. Enough to turn any man's head."

"Well, get him out of here, Ty," Stephen said, coming to put his hand on the thick shoulder of the younger man. "And watch out for him and Bob as best you can." His gray eyes grew troubled, and he said quietly, "I couldn't bear to lose any of you!"

* * *

The presidential residence was dismissed by most travelers from overseas as an ordinary country house without taste or splendor. As Frank and Carmen rode past the structure, Frank nodded toward it, saying, "Looks pretty much like a Southern plantation home. Sort of out of place here in Washington."

Carmen was hanging on to the reins of her mare tightly. She disliked horses and had agreed to ride with Frank only to spend time with him away from the city. Now she looked at the iron fence with large gateways that enclosed the grounds, and she shook her head. "It's not very pretty."

Frank laughed, turning to face her. "Smells bad, too."

"What *is* that awful smell, Frank?"

"All this area used to be a marsh. It was used as an outlet for sewage. And right over there is the old city canal. It used to be an inland waterway between the Potomac and the Eastern Branch, but now it's mostly a sewage canal. Come along. We can get away from all this."

Thirty minutes later they were walking their horses slowly down a lane shaded by huge oaks. "This is where most of the officers come for their rides," Frank said. "Pretty nice, isn't it? Wonder how long it will take the engineers to find it and mess it up."

They reached an opening where green grass carpeted the ground, and Carmen exclaimed, "Oh, look at the flowers!"

Frank glanced at the carpet of wildflowers and nodded. "Want to gather a bouquet?"

"Yes!" Carmen allowed him to help her to the ground and made a face. "I'm going to be sore tomorrow!" She laughed up at him, adding, "I'm no rider, as you've found out."

Frank tied the horses to a sapling then walked with her across the open ground. Carmen was delighted with the flowers that grew profusely and, as she picked them, asked, "I wonder what these are. They're so pretty."

"That's bloodroot," Frank answered, looking at the blossom, which was white with a golden center. "Be careful you don't get any of that juice on your dress." He pointed at a drop of red bloodlike liquid that oozed from the wounded stem. "The Indians use this to decorate their faces and their weapons."

Carmen stared at him with amazement. "How in the world do you know that?"

"My mother likes wildflowers. She used to take all three of us to the woods and fields." He stooped to pick a delicate flower with a purplish tint and held it out to her. "This is a wood anemone," he said. "William Cullen Bryant wrote a poem about it." Frank quoted a few words, touching the blossom with a forefinger:

"Within the woods,
Whose young and half transparent leaves scarce cast
A shade, gay circles of anemones
Danced on their stalks."

Carmen took the flower and held it gently, saying, "I've never known a man who knew wildflowers."

"No money in it," he said with a shrug. He was embarrassed and laughed ruefully. "None in poetry, either. What I need to do is get into selling life insurance or something profitable."

"You'd never like business," Carmen answered. The two wandered along the fringe of trees that outlined the open field and came finally to a large tree that had fallen. "I suppose you know what sort of tree this is?" she asked, sitting down on it.

"Elm," he remarked then sat down beside her. The air was still, and he could smell the scent of violets in her hair. She was wearing a hunter green riding outfit, and a small gray hat with a yellow plume sat on her head. As with all her clothing, the garment clung to the rich curves of her body. "This is nice, Carmen," he said quietly.

"Yes, it is." Carmen held a pink blossom to her cheek as she studied him, then asked, "What are you going to do, Frank?"

"I signed up for a ninety-day enlistment this morning."

Disappointment came to her face, but she was too

experienced to protest. "I'll miss you," she said. "We've had fun, haven't we?"

"We'll have more when I get out. Three months isn't long."

Carmen dropped the flower, which fell to the grass. Turning to face him, she whispered, "Yes, it is—a very long time."

Reaching out, Frank put his arms around Carmen and drew her close. She came to him willingly, taking his kiss fully, even eagerly. When he released her, she said, "You've had experience with women."

"Not too much," he protested.

"You're the sort of man who has his way with women."

Frank was stung by her remark and said almost roughly, "And you're the sort of woman who can make a man do anything."

"No, that's not right." Carmen placed her hand on his cheek, a smile coming to her lips. "If I were that, I'd have kept you with me. I tried hard enough."

He was a little shocked at her blunt response. "I've got to go, Carmen. There's no way out of it."

"I see that now." She was afraid that her aggressiveness had shocked him. Drawing back, she put her hand up and smoothed her hair. "What will you do when you get out, Frank?"

He stood up and gazed around at the field, noting that a flight of blackbirds was rising out of the lank grass across the field. She stood with him, and he shook his head. "I don't know, Carmen. Maybe go to work for my grandfather at the factory."

"I suppose that would be good for most men. It's a good business, isn't it?"

"Yes, very good." The thought of going to work behind a desk depressed him, and he said abruptly, "No sense thinking about that now. I've got three months to think about it." He was restless and said, "Let's ride over and see the Potomac. Maybe we'll see one of the new gunboats."

They spent the rest of the afternoon making their way in a leisurely fashion along the banks of the Potomac, and when Frank left her, she offered her hand. "Come back safely, Frank."

The next morning Frank accompanied Bob to the camp, where he was issued a uniform and the tools of his new trade. When he'd put his uniform on, Bob said with satisfaction, "Well, you *look* like a soldier, Frank. Now let's see if we can make you into a first-class fighting man."

The training period for the new recruits was almost over, and a week later Frank climbed aboard a railway car stuffed with yelling soldiers. He and Bob squeezed their way into a seat, and when they cleared the station and the men quieted down, they listened to the reckless talk of the recruits. One of them, a lanky young man with flaming red hair, said, "Why, we'll take Vicksburg in a week!"

A yell of agreement rose from the young soldier's friends, but Bob said quietly, "I think it'll take a little more time than that."

As the train crawled around the curves outside of Washington, squeezing between the banks of stone, protesting as the grade grew steep, a strange thing happened to Frank. He was looking around at the fresh, youthful faces of the members of his company—and the thought leaped into his mind, *Some of us who are so alive this morning will be dead before Vicksburg is taken.*

He tried to ignore the thought, but it came back, as

persistent as a tune that goes on inside one's head. Finally, he began to consider his own death. *What if I get killed?* It was an unsettling feeling, and as the train whistle uttered a shrill protest, it seemed to him that many things he'd always put a high premium on were not as important as he'd assumed. Finally, he joined a noisy poker game and managed to shake off the feeling.

The train turned southward, bearing the men who were to be thrown into the struggle for control of the mighty Mississippi. All day long it clattered over the joints of the rails, and as night fell and the men slept, there was a doleful sound as the engineer tugged at the cord over his head, sending what seemed to be a hoarse warning to the countryside. Into the ebony darkness the iron wheels propelled the men of Company H, and Frank Rocklin was not the only one aboard who could not shake the thoughts of battles that loomed ahead.

Chapter 4

Advance to Vicksburg

"He looks like a man who's lowered his head and seems determined to ram it through a two-inch-thick oak door!"

Thus one of the aides of General Ulysses S. Grant described his commanding officer. And it would take a man like this—stubborn as any officer who wore the Union uniform—to accomplish what *had* to be done before the Confederacy could be severed. Lincoln had said as early as 1861, not long after Manassas: "The war can never be brought to a close until Vicksburg is in our pocket. We may take all the northern ports of the Confederacy and they can still defy us from that stronghold!"

For nine months the Union struggled to take Vicksburg but experienced nothing but humiliating defeat in five separate attempts. Why were the powerful Union army and equally powerful navy unable to storm this bastion of Southern power?

General William T. Sherman, who was as scrappy a soldier as a man can be, lost heart in the struggle. "No place on earth," he stated flatly, "is favored by nature with natural defenses as Vicksburg, and I do believe the whole thing will fail." He pointed out that the city stood on a series of frowning bluffs above the Mississippi River. Fortifications along these precipices reached as high as three hundred feet, so that any gunboats had to face the fire of heavy land-based guns while unable to return the fire. As for attacking the city from the landward side, this was even more difficult. To come from the north meant that an army with heavy guns and wagons would bog down in the soft, low ground turned into a mire by the Yazoo River. To approach from the other side meant a terrible journey through bayous—with no supply lines. In this territory, the Union soldiers were hindered by chilly, rainy weather in low, swampy country. Everything—clothing, tents, bedding—was wet and stayed wet. Malarial fever and smallpox broke out, and under these terrible conditions any man except Ulysses S. Grant would have given up.

Finally, the winter passed, and Grant was ready to attack. But he was like a prizefighter who had been floored too many times. The gunboats of the navy would not take the city, nor could the engineers find a way to get at the stubborn Confederates. Something else would have to be tried, and the soldiers of both armies waited to see what Grant would do.

Ty Rocklin sat down on a log beside Frank, saying, "Well, Private, you've been yelling for action ever since we left Washington. Now it looks like you're going to get your wish."

Frank glanced up quickly, noting the excitement on his brother's face. "We're going into action?" he demanded. "When?"

"Well, General Grant hasn't given me all the details of his plan," Ty said, a gleam of humor in his eyes. "But I think the waiting is over." He reached and took a piece of hardtack from the skillet, juggling it to keep from getting burned. A few drops of the grease Frank had been frying it in fell on his boot, but he ignored it, since the caked mud hid the leather completely. "You know, this hardtack isn't too bad," he commented, nibbling at it cautiously.

"Not if you like shoe leather soaked in wallpaper paste," Frank answered. He glanced up as Bob came out of the tent, and said, "The general here says we're going to whip the Rebs, Bob. Here, you'd better eat some of this. It'll make you fight better."

"What's the plan, Lieutenant?" Bob asked, squatting down in front of the small fire. The April breeze blew the gray coals into a swirling funnel, and he turned away to avoid the smoke. He was thinner than he had been, for sickness had laid him low for the past week.

"Don't know much, except that General McPherson just called a staff meeting."

"I didn't know a lowly second lieutenant gets in on those things," Frank jibed. He picked up the blackened coffeepot, filled his tin cup with the tarlike substance, then asked, "What'd you and the general decide?"

Ignoring Frank's remarks, Ty looked down at the muddy waters of the Mississippi, where it purled around a stand of cypress trees. He studied it thoughtfully then shook his head. "We'll never take that place from the river. That hairpin curve just below it forces the gunboats to slow down to a crawl. Makes them sitting ducks for those big guns up there." He was a slow-talking man, like his father, and he now paused and nibbled at the hardtack. "We're going to head south along the west bank of the river. When we get out of range of the guns, we'll cross over."

"And what will that get us?" Frank inquired. He sipped cautiously at the scalding coffee, grimaced, and blew into the cup.

"They'll be ready for us when we get around them, won't they?"

"I suppose so—but at least they can't turn those big guns up on that bluff at us." He sat on the log, a big man seeming entirely indolent. He spoke for a time of the tactics of the campaign, then rose and grinned. "Be sure you take some dry socks on this march. I've got a feeling we're all going to get our feet wet on this one."

"Word is that Grant is sending a big cavalry force out to draw the Rebs away," Bob said.

"That's right, he is. Colonel Grierson's taking his troops out to stir up trouble. If he can draw Pemberton's force after him, it'll give us a chance to cross the river without the Rebs finding out about it. And Grant's leaving Sherman here to demonstrate against Vicksburg."

"But the boats are all north of Vicksburg," Bob argued. "We'll need them to get across the river."

"Admiral Porter will take them downriver," Ty said. "While the enemy is busy with him—and with Sherman and Grierson—we'll sneak down the river, cross over—and then we'll have them!"

Later in the day marching orders came, and Frank was exultant. "I'm sick of sitting on this old riverbank like a bullfrog in a mud hole," he said as he lined up beside Bob in marching order. "Anything would be better than more of this!"

But as with most battle plans, the execution of Grant's scheme proved to be more difficult than it seemed on paper. Some of his officers doubted that the plan would work, and truthfully it was hazardous. All communications and supply lines would be cut off once the army crossed the river. If they were defeated, all would be lost. But Grant was stubbornly determined to hit the Confederates, and he gave the orders for the operation to begin.

On the night of April 16, 1863, Admiral Porter led the Union fleet past the Vicksburg batteries. "I want absolute silence," Porter ordered. "Leave your pets behind—and the chickens, too!"

General Pemberton and his senior officers were enjoying a ball that night, but when Confederate pickets spotted the spectral shadows of the approaching ships, the ball ended abruptly. The batteries opened up, and several buildings were set ablaze. Barrels of pitch on the east bank were ignited, and suddenly, as Fred Grant, General Grant's twelve-year-old son, would recall later, "the river was lit up as if by sunlight."

The passage of the fleet was agonizingly slow. For five hours the bombardment lasted, but only one transport was sunk. Thus the first part of Grant's plan was successful. The second part was launched at once, as Grant sent Colonel Grierson on a raid that drew off many of General Pemberton's men. Grierson's cavalry made a great deal of mischief, as ordered.

All of this was academic to Frank Rocklin, for he was one of those who spent most of April struggling through the muddy bayous and swamps of Louisiana. They fought the heat, mosquitoes, snakes, sickness, and when they finally arrived at their destination, Frank exclaimed in disgust to Bob, "If fighting is any worse than this, I don't think I can take it, Bob!"

Bob Rocklin, struggling with the beginnings of a malarial fever, was pale, and his face was covered with a sheen of sweat. He glanced across the river silently then said abruptly, "Frank, this has been bad—but if we get into a fight tomorrow, I'd feel a lot easier knowing that you were all right."

"Why, I'll be fine, Bob," Frank answered at once. He understood instantly that his brother was not speaking of the physical danger. "I guess you're worried because I've never joined the church."

"It's more than that, Frank," Bob said. "None of us know when we'll die. A man can get thrown by a horse on his way to a party. But in battle, the odds are shorter." He wiped his face with a damp handkerchief then turned to say, "Why haven't you ever given your heart to God, Frank? It's been a grief to all of us—especially to Father and Mother."

"Can't say why, Bob." Frank was a man who could always find something to say—but now he discovered that he had no answer for his brother's quiet question. "I know God exists. I believe the Bible, too. But somehow it's just not come to me as it did to you and Ty. Guess some folks are just naturally drawn to such things—and I'm one of those who just isn't."

"That's wrong, Frank," Bob said instantly. He pulled out his worn New Testament, opened it, and read, "'For the grace of God that bringeth salvation hath appeared to all men.'" Looking up, he asked quietly, "Do you believe that Jesus is the Son of God?"

"Why, of course! I've always believed that."

Bob began to read the scripture. He was a quiet young man, not flamboyant or outgoing. But there was a steadiness in him that Frank had always admired, perhaps because he himself lacked the quality. It had been Bob he'd gone to all his life when he needed help or advice. Their father had been gone on duty for long periods, but Bob had always been there. More than once it had been this brother who'd steered Frank out of trouble or who'd been there to help when he'd gone wrong.

Finally, when Bob fell silent, having done his best to present his beliefs, Frank said, "Bob, I guess men don't have words to say some things—not like women do. But just in case something does happen—" Frank paused and looked down at his muddy shoes, then lifted his face, his eyes fixed on Bob. "Just in case,

I want you to know that I—well, I love you, brother. You've been the best friend I've ever had." Embarrassed by the voicing of his deepest feelings, he looked off across the river, studying the Federal gunboats as they steamed back and forth like huge beasts.

"Why, I appreciate that, Frank," Bob said. He was weak, and his hands were not steady, but he smiled, adding, "I believe that God will get all three of us through this thing, but we ought to say such things to each other." He hesitated then nodded slowly. "I'm not going to pester you with sermons, Frank. I know that won't do. You've heard the gospel just like Ty and I have. But I want you to know that I'm praying for you all the time."

Frank took a deep breath then expelled it slowly. "Thanks, Bob. I reckon I knew that." He clapped his brother on the shoulder, noting that it seemed thin and frail. "Well, let me do one thing. That fever's got you down. You still won't go to the surgeon?"

"No. I didn't come to be sick."

"Then I'll carry your pack on the march. No arguments. You had to carry *me* once, remember? That time we were coon hunting and I fell into a hole and twisted my ankle?"

Robert smiled, his face lighting up. "That was a good time, wasn't it? What were we, about thirteen?"

"You were, and I was mad because *I* wanted to be in my teens." His face changed, and the thought of that dim past had its way with him. His eyelids fell and his lips seemed to soften as he answered, "Funny how we're never satisfied to be what we are." Leaning back and clasping his leg, he continued, "When we're little, we want to be in our teens. But when that comes, we want to be grown men. I guess we're always looking for something better...."

Bob listened quietly as Frank spoke. The scent of cooking

meat was in the air, along with the lush, rank smell of the bayou. Overhead the sky was blue and looked hard enough to strike a match on. The air was filled with the sound of an army preparing to move—the clatter of equipment, men cursing mules who struggled to pull heavy guns through the soupy mud, a babble of voices, most with hard Northern accents. Excitement filled the air, and Bob thought, *Some of these men who are laughing right now will be dead or shot to pieces before this thing is over. Why can't they see what's coming?*

"Well, you stretch out and take it easy, Bob," Frank said. "I'll scout around and see what I can scrounge. Lots of grub here, but when we cross that river there, we won't be able to run to the store and buy a few groceries." He stood up on his feet, looked across the chocolate brown river that looked as strong as time itself, then shook his head. "I expect we'll do some fighting when we get on that other side."

He left Bob and spent a few hours scrounging food. He had the instincts of an old soldier and, by the time Ty found him, had collected quite a store. "You look like the quartermaster, Private Rocklin," Ty joked as he looked over the stock. "Going on a picnic?"

"No, sir, Lieutenant. Just tired of hardtack. Made a little dicker with a farmer and his wife." He waved at the stock of food with pride. "They were just about to start eating dinner, and I bought it from them. Look, got some ham, pork chops, baked potatoes, two loaves of fresh-baked bread—and the biggest part of a chocolate cake. Here, have a taste."

Tyler took a slice of the cake, ate it with pleasure, then wiped his hands on his handkerchief. "You're just a chocolate soldier, Private," he teased. Then he looked over toward where Bob was lying flat on the ground and sobered. "He ought to go to the hospital. He's in no shape to go into action."

"Won't hear of it." Frank shook his head. "Never saw him act so stubborn, Ty."

"Well, if he gets worse, I'll order him to go. Meanwhile, you look out for him."

"I don't think he can make a march. He's weak as a kitten, Ty."

Tyler thought for a moment. "I'll assign him to one of the supply wagons as a helper. That way he can ride. When we go into action, we'll have to see."

"That'll be better."

"Frank—"

Something in his older brother's voice caught at Frank. He glanced up quickly and saw that Ty's eyes were filled with concern. At once he said, "You're worried about us, aren't you?"

"Yes. It's going to be pretty hard, Frank. Some of us aren't going to make it."

"Bob's talked to me." Although Frank was not as close to Tyler as he was to Bob, he respected and admired him. Now he wanted to say so, but found it difficult. "I know all of you are disappointed that I've not been a church member," he said slowly, searching for the right words. "Maybe it will come to me, but a man can't force a thing like that. I'll just have to wait, Ty. I can't become a Christian just to please other people."

"No, but I'm hoping you'll find Christ for your own happiness, Frank." Tyler Rocklin was basically a private person and found it hard to speak of his faith. "I'm no preacher, Frank, but without Jesus, I'd be the most miserable man in the world!" He shook his shoulders together and his lips grew firm. "End of sermon."

"I told Bob how much I admire and respect him," Frank said awkwardly. Again he was embarrassed, and his face grew slightly red. "Well, you've been a fine older brother to me, Ty—and I want you to know I—I count myself lucky." He grinned suddenly, adding, "I can spout poetry by the yard! Why can't I say what I feel about my own family? Blast it all, Ty, I love you—and you'll just have to put up with my blathering! Must be the ham in me!"

But his words had pleased Ty, and he put his heavy hand on Frank's shoulder. He said only, "I feel the same about you, Frank." Then he was gone, and as he disappeared, Frank felt good. *Should have said those things a long time ago. It's a shame it takes a war before people can say what they feel!*

On April 30, the Union army crossed from the west bank of the Mississippi River to Bruinsburg on the east shore, a village thirty-five miles below Vicksburg. Grant wrote about his arrival in Bruinsburg, "I felt a degree of relief scarcely ever equaled since.... I was on dry ground on the same side of the river with the enemy. All the campaigns, labors, hardships and exposures that had been made and endured were for the accomplishment of this one object."

General Pemberton, Grant's opponent, telegraphed President Jefferson Davis for help, but Pemberton moved too slowly. Instead of striking at once for Vicksburg, Grant moved toward Jackson. He knew that once Jackson was taken, the Confederate supply line to Vicksburg would be cut.

Few Union military campaigns were as successful as that of Grant in the days that followed. He defeated a Confederate force at Port Royal on May 1, then was joined by Sherman to begin what would be called almost eighty years later a "blitz."

The Union army defeated the Confederates at Raymond on May 12 in drenching rain, and it was in this battle that the Rocklins were fiercely engaged. Company H was part of the First Brigade, the Third Division of the Seventeenth Army Corps. They were led by Major General James B. McPherson, a handsome young man from Baltimore.

As the army moved forward, Lieutenant Tyler Rocklin was disturbed about the condition of his men. He wrote in a letter to his mother, "The men need time to rest, but there is no time. The marches have been severe, and nearly one-third of our men have no shoes, having worn them out on the marches. Supplies are short, and the men are so tired, I've seen the whole company asleep as they trudge along the muddy roads. I'm especially concerned for Bob. He's weak after his bout with malaria. Pray for him, Mother, and for Frank, that he will find God. Much hard fighting ahead, but we must trust in the mercies of the Lord."

Jackson fell to Grant's army on May 14, and the army then turned to Vicksburg. Grant whipped Pemberton at Champion Hill, then again at Big Black River Bridge. Pemberton sensed defeat and ordered his troops to retreat to Vicksburg.

It was a great victory for Grant. In eighteen days his army had marched two hundred miles, fought five victorious battles, and captured more than six thousand prisoners and sixty-seven pieces of artillery. The relatively low Union cost was forty-five hundred casualties. Lincoln's faith in the squat and tough Ulysses Grant was amply justified!

"Now I guess we can get a little rest." Frank spoke as he looked down at his shoe, the sole of which was held in place by a piece of rawhide string. He was tired to the bone, and looking around at the squad, he knew that they were all played out. Bob was slumped in his blankets, and Kyle Morton—at the age of seventeen, the youngest man in the squad—had gone to sleep holding his bowl of stew. "Wake up, Kyle," Frank called out. "Eat that stew; then go to bed."

Kyle gave a start, looked around wildly, then grinned wearily at Frank. "Who made you a general, Private Rocklin?" he demanded. He lifted the spoon, ate the rest of the food, then looked around with bleary eyes. "I been a hero long enough. I want my medals now, Frank." He was an engaging young man, thin as a rail, but strong and active.

Frank had gotten close to the boy, feeling protective of the youngster, and now teased him. "If Martha Ann could see you now, she'd find another sweetheart."

"No, I'm too good looking," Kyle said with a wink. He had only faint wisps of a beard on his smooth cheeks, despite all his desire to grow a fierce beard. "She's too much in love with me to look at any other feller."

At that moment, a voice called out, "Form up! Form up!" The members of the squad groaned, and Kyle said, "Aw, Lieutenant, give us a break."

Lieutenant Rocklin's face was lined with fatigue. "We're moving in—we'll be skirmishers. Load your muskets and follow me!" He turned to Bob, who was acting sergeant. "Get them moving, Sergeant," he said then whirled and left to go down the line.

"Bob, we're in no shape to attack!" Frank whispered, pulling his belt on. "We're in poor condition."

"We'll make it, Frank. Watch out for yourself!"

But the attack was a failure. Grant, overconfident after

his success, was determined to take Vicksburg by storm. The Confederates had been able to fortify the approach, and the Union troops had great difficulty getting through the felled trees and steep ravines.

Frank's squad was in the thick of the fight. They advanced through the thickets, bullets screaming overhead. "Keep down!" Bob called out. "Crawl on the ground!"

Frank was beside Kyle as Bob called out. He turned to relay the order to the young man, but a bullet caught Morton in the stomach at that instant, driving him backward.

"Kyle!" Frank cried out. Dropping his musket, he leaped to kneel beside the wounded man. Kyle stared up at him, his face filled with astonishment and pain.

"Why—they shot me, Frank!"

"Take it easy, Kyle. You'll be all right."

But young Morton looked down to see his stomach drenched with crimson. He knew as well as any that the chances of a man recovering from a stomach wound were almost nonexistent. He lay there quietly and finally said, "It don't hardly hurt at all, Frank." But the blood was pouring from the wound, and he looked up to stare at his friend. "I'm going to die, Frank. Write my people for me."

"I'll get you to the hospital."

"Won't make no difference. Promise me you'll write to my ma. Tell her I died trusting in Jesus. And write to Martha, too."

The air was filled with the explosion of shells, and the musket fire was like thousands of sticks breaking. The cries of the wounded grated on Frank's nerves, but he nodded. "I'll...do it, Kyle."

Morton reached out, and Frank took the bloodstained hand. Kyle's face was pale, and he looked no more than fourteen years old as he lay dying. "Glad you stopped," he whispered, squeezing Frank's hand. "Wouldn't like...to die...alone."

Frank's throat was thick, and his eyes blurred. He sat there holding the young man in his arms and finally heard him whisper, "Martha." Then he seemed to relax, his hand going limp.

Frank Rocklin sat on the battlefield holding his dead friend. Soon the squad returned, beaten back by the Confederates. He looked up to see Bob standing over him. "He's gone, Bob," Frank said tonelessly. Getting to his feet, he gave one angry look at Vicksburg. "He died taking that place. I don't think Martha will think it's worth it."

Bob said only, "He was a Christian, Frank. He's with his Lord now."

But Frank shook his head, a bitterness in his expression. "I'm going to bury him, Bob. It's the last thing I can do for him." Lifting his eyes to stare at the city, he said nothing more.

Bob knew him well. *He's going to be bitter over this,* he thought. Then he said gently, "I'll get some shovels, Frank. We'll have a little service. It'll be something to tell his people." He saw that his words meant little to Frank, but there was nothing else he could say.

Chapter 5

Special Mission

A pale white sun poured heat over the ditch where the six sweat-soaked soldiers crouched. From time to time one of the Federal cannon would fire, and the men would blink and look upward. Sometimes it was possible to actually *see* the missile, or at least a faint black line, as it scored the summer sky. When it struck with a muffled *whump*, they would all relax.

That was when one of their own cannon fired; but when a shell rose from one of the Confederate batteries, that was a different story! They had all learned to identify the muffled cough of the Rebel artillery, and when it came, every man would draw his head in like a snapping turtle. Frank knew it was silly, for if a shell hit in his section of the trench, such a thing would not save him—but it was an involuntary action.

Now as he crouched in the dust with his legs drawn up, Frank heard the familiar sound and hunched himself into a fetal position. As the enemy shell rose, it screamed like a banshee, and for one moment Frank thought of the shell as a living thing—a sharklike demon with white teeth gleaming as it sought to find its prey of living flesh. Then the explosion came, some fifty feet behind him and to his right. He turned his head to watch the geyser of dust rise and then muttered, "Rotten shot, Reb!" He rolled over and pulled his canteen from underneath his side with a grunt, uncapped it, and took three small sips of the rank, tepid water. It tasted of metal, but he would have willingly drained it all. But water was short, and all along the twelve-mile length of the Union line, men were as thirsty as he.

Flies swarmed around his head, and he ignored them for the most part. But when one of them crawled over his lips, he couldn't stand that and shook his head, blowing out with a mild curse. He was tired to the bone and from time to time would doze off, only to be awakened by a howling shell and the shattering explosion that followed. Sleep came at night, and he longed for the searing heat of day to pass into the relative coolness. Mississippi was a hot place, and only during the darkness did he get any respite from the humid air that kept him bathed in sweat.

The siege had begun on May 18, and now it was growing toward the middle of June. Not a long time, relatively speaking, but digging holes in the ground under the sultry, burning Southern sun all day while dodging shells and the fire of lynx-eyed sharpshooters made it seem like an eternity. As he lay there, Frank heard the sound of singing and was forced to smile despite his misery. Both sides sang at night, but this was a new one—obviously composed by some witty Confederate. They'd sung it every night for a week and now had decided to serenade themselves under the sun. It was sung to the tune of "A Life on the Ocean Wave," and Frank hummed along with his Rebel foes:

GILBERT MORRIS

A life on the Vicksburg bluff,
A home in the trenches deep,
Where we dodge Yank shells enough,
And our old peabread won't keep.
On old Logan's beef I pine,
For there's fat on his bones no more;
Oh! give me some pork and brine,
And truck from a sutler's store.

"Sounds like the Rebs are getting hungry, don't it, Frank?"

Frank lifted his head cautiously to meet the eyes of Lafe Sutter, a lanky young man from Maine. He was something of a musician himself and cocked his head critically. "That ain't their regular tenor," he remarked. "Hope they ain't nothing happened to him. That there feller taking his place is pretty bad."

Frank grinned at the young man, saying, "They'd be sorry to hear their performance doesn't please you, Lafe. Maybe we ought to let them know that we've got a particular judge of music over here on our side." As the song started again, he thought of how strange it was that Lafe was concerned about the well-being of a man who was trying his best to kill him. But then, much of war was ridiculous, he had learned, and he listened to the rest of the song.

Old Grant is starving us out,
Our grub is fast wasting away,
Pemb' don't know what he's about,
And he hasn't for many a day,
So we'll bury old Logan tonight,
From tough beef we'll be set free;
We'll put him far out of sight,
No more of his meat for me!

Texas steers are no longer in view,
Mule steaks are now "done up brown,"
While peabread, mule roast, and mule stew
Are our fare here in Vicksburg town;
And the song of our hearts shall be,
When the Yanks and their gunboats rave;
A life in a bomb-proof for me,
And a tear on old Logan's grave.

As the ragged chorus of voices faded, Frank squirmed around to ask, "Bob, you ever stop to think that one of those fellows in those trenches might be named Rocklin?"

"Sure, I have." Bob was sitting with his back braced against the trench. His face was sunburned, and he was still weak from the fever that had plagued him from the beginning of the campaign. He traced a complicated geometric figure in the dust as he thought back, then glanced at Frank. "I think a lot of those cousins of ours," he murmured. "Can't forget that summer we spent there, all three of us—you and me and Ty. It was the best vacation we ever had."

"Sure was," Frank agreed, thinking of the summer of '57. He'd been fourteen and had run wild in the hills of Virginia. The three of them had stayed at Gracefield, where they'd learned to know their Southern cousins for the first time. He thought of the long, slow nights with the scent of magnolias and how he'd fallen madly in love with one of his cousins. "Remember how I fell for Rachel Franklin, Bob?" he asked. "Never did understand just how close kin we were, but I was sure crazy about her."

"She's married now," Bob said then smiled. "You were pretty gone on her." He paused then said more slowly, "I got real close to Dent. He was pretty wild, but I liked him." He glanced involuntarily toward the Rebel line of fortifications, saying softly, "Sure would hate to meet up with Dent. Don't see how I could pull a trigger on him."

"You think any of our kin might be in those lines?"

"Most of them are with Lee." He fell into a silence then shook his head. "This isn't like fighting some army from Spain or Germany. That would be easy. But to fight your own kin—it's hard!"

Frank said nothing, for he had thought of this. It was a brothers' war, with many families split right in two. *There's no way to sort this mess out,* he thought wearily. He hated the war, and he hated the trench warfare worse than battle. As he sat under the blazing sun, he thought, *When my ninety days are up, I'll get out of this!* He knew Bob and Ty were expecting him to reenlist, but he could not endure more of this sort of misery!

The day wore on, and finally he grew angrier. Yanking off his cap, he put it on the end of a stick and lifted it above the trench. Almost instantly he heard a sharp crack, and the cap jerked as a minié ball struck it then continued to plow a track in the dirt behind the trench.

"Rocklin, stop that blamed foolishness!" First Sergeant Jake Mulhullen, a square box of a man from Vermont, had been crawling down the line and had seen Frank's action. His face was the color of a ripe tomato, and he barked angrily, "If you want to play games, come along with me. I've got one you'll love!"

"Aw, Sarge, I was just seeing if the Rebs were awake!" Frank protested.

Mulhullen only glared at him. "Diggin' latrines—that's a good game, Rocklin. Just about your speed!"

Frank gave a despairing glance at Lafe, who shrugged,

saying, "Have a good time, Frank."

For the rest of the long afternoon, Frank joined the miserable crew who had displeased their superiors as they dug long, shallow trenches. One of his fellow sufferers paused long enough to say, "Well, at least we won't get picked off by one of them sharpshooters!" His sentiments might have been astute, but Frank was furious. For a while he took his anger out by making the dirt fly, but the short private to his right hissed, "Cut it out, will you? You're making the rest of us look bad. What you tryin' to do, set us a good example?"

Frank simmered down and settled into a slow, methodical motion that he refused to increase even when prodded by the sergeant in charge of the detail. Finally, the sun began to set, and the air cooled. Sergeant Mulhullen came to say, "All right, Rocklin, if you had enough fun, you can get chow. But if I catch you playin' around again, you'll dig a trench ten miles long!"

Frank stomped to where his squad had been pulled back far enough to have their evening meal. Several of the men laughed as he came to get his plate of beans and pork. "Gonna win the war by digging them ditches?" one of them jibed, and when Frank glared at him, he threw up his hands in mock fear. "Hold him, you fellers! It's that trench-diggin' terror, Frank Rocklin!"

Frank started for the soldier, but Bob was there to hold him back. "Here, better get some of this grub before these gluttons eat it up," he joked. He pulled Frank aside, saying, "Got a letter from Mother. It's to all of us, I guess. Ty's already read it." Bob watched as Frank read the letter then folded it and handed it back. "She's worried about us, of course, and about Pa, too."

Frank was still angry and, when Ty came by, said, "I didn't join the army to dig sanitary trenches!"

"They've got to be dug. We've lost more men to sickness

and disease than we have to Reb bullets." Tyler considered the stubborn expression on the face of his younger brother and then glanced at Bob. Something passed between the two men, and Tyler said, "Got some chores of my own. Got to detail a private to the job of taking care of the staff's horses. Be a change for you, Frank."

Frank gave the lieutenant a grateful look but said, "I don't want any special treatment."

"You won't get any," Tyler said with a smile. "Far as I see, Private, there's no such thing as a soft job in this kind of fight. Report to me first thing in the morning."

Afterward, Bob had a chance to speak with Tyler alone. "He's pretty touchy. Good for you to have him where you can keep an eye on him."

Tyler nodded thoughtfully. "He's not like us, Bob. We're pretty steady fellows—like Father, I suppose." Taking off his hat, he wiped his brow then replaced the hat, settling it firmly on his head. "Frank's more impulsive. He's the kind you can count on when things are hot and the action is heavy, but he's not built to take boredom too well. I'll be glad when this thing is over," he concluded. Staring through the darkness, he shook his head. "Wonder what the Rebs are thinking. No way for them to get out. Gunboats on the river, and seventy thousand of us to stop a breakthrough. They must be worse off than we are!"

Tyler Rocklin had been entirely correct in his analysis of the character of his youngest brother. That Frank was impulsive with a highly volatile streak, all the family well understood. But two days after Frank had been assigned to take care of the chores for the staff of the corps commander, General McPherson, Lieutenant Tyler Rocklin got the shock of his military career.

"Lieutenant, General McPherson wants to speak with you. Report to his headquarters at once." The order came in the form of terse, clipped speech from a slight young major named Benning. He snapped caustically, "The general doesn't like to be kept waiting, Lieutenant Rocklin."

"Of course, Major!" Tyler fell into step beside the officer, asking, "Do you have any idea what the general wants with me?"

"General McPherson will do his own talking, Lieutenant."

Tyler's mind raced as he accompanied Benning along the line of tents toward the headquarters of the commander. *I must have done something pretty bad,* he thought, but though he searched his memory frantically, nothing came to him. He was a tough-minded young man and knew that he'd done his duty, so when he arrived outside the tent of the commander, he was curious but not at all rattled.

Major Benning leaned to put his head inside the tent. "Sir, Lieutenant Rocklin is here."

"Come in—and you remain as well, Major."

Tyler stepped inside and found the general seated at his portable desk. He rose at once and returned Rocklin's salute. He was a trim young man in his thirties, with a pair of intense gray eyes and a firm mouth. "Good to see you again, Lieutenant. I hear good things of your company from Colonel Wesley."

"Why, thank you, General!"

"I served with your father once—fine officer! I know you're proud of him."

"I am indeed, sir!"

General McPherson studied the tall young officer for an extended moment then said, "You have two brothers serving with your company? Tell me about your youngest brother—Private Frank Rocklin, isn't it?"

Tyler's heart grew cold, for he was now certain that Frank had committed some frightful blunder! But he lifted his head and said firmly, "My brother Robert is enlisted for three years, General, and will rise in the ranks. Frank is—well, different from Robert and me. He's very impulsive, sir, and he's had hardly any training. No time for it before we left Washington." Tyler spoke slowly, giving an honest judgment, and finally asked, "Is Private Rocklin in some sort of trouble, General?"

At once McPherson shook his head. "Why, no, Lieutenant, not at all." He smiled then, adding, "I can see how you might think so—getting called up before the corps commander to explain your brother. But it's not what he's done. It's what he *wants* to do."

"Sir?"

"General Grant is going to have to make an attempt to take the city. We all know that, don't we? The country's eyes are on this place. It's become a symbol for the whole war. If Vicksburg falls, the end of the war is in sight. It's important that we have this victory."

As McPherson went over what every officer in the army knew, Tyler was wondering what under the sun all of this had to do with Frank. Finally, the general said, "Well, your brother's been listening to the camp gossip. Everyone wants to know if the enemy is ripe for an attack. How strong are they?" A smile touched McPherson's lips, and he shook his head with a sort of wonder. "These ninety-day men don't have the awe of generals that regulars do, Lieutenant. So this brother of yours came to my aide with a request to see me. Major Benning here was quite shocked, but when he heard the plan, he thought I should hear it."

"I still think it won't work, sir," Benning snapped. "He'll never pull it off."

"Pull *what* off, sir?" Tyler burst out. "What in the world does Frank want to do?"

"Why, he says he can get through the Confederate lines, scout out the situation, and get the information back to us."

Tyler stared at the two officers in dismay but asked cautiously, "And how does he propose to do all this, sir?"

"Says he's an actor," Benning snorted. "He's going to put on a disguise of some sort and just walk right into the city! Nonsense!"

"But if it worked, Major," General McPherson urged quickly, "it would be an invaluable piece of information." He put his steady gaze on Tyler and asked, "Is he capable of doing this, in your judgment?"

Tyler thought rapidly then nodded firmly. "It's the kind of thing *he* would do, sir. I couldn't do it, but I think Frank might be able to accomplish a mission like that."

McPherson laughed loudly. "He says it'll be better than digging latrines! I like his spirit. Now, Lieutenant, I want you to see to it that he gets what he needs. Anything! But it must be fast!" He hesitated then added, "You must see that he understands that he'll be shot at once if he's caught. He'll be out of uniform—a spy. We'd do the same if we caught one of theirs."

"I think he knows that, sir. He's no coward."

"Well, he'll be doing us more good in this way than taking care of my horse. Have him come and see me before he leaves. I'll have a few instructions for him, and you tell him what sort of military items he needs to look for—guns emplacements and so on."

"Yes, General." Tyler saluted, and as he left he thought, *Only Frank would think up a scheme like this!*

※

"Contraband Negro to see you, General."

General McPherson turned to find Major Benning, who had approached the rise that was covered with tall oaks. He'd come here to study the twisting line of battle—and to think. It was a quiet spot, and one of the few places where he could find some solitude. He frowned as he said shortly, "You can take care of these things, Major."

Benning was a stubborn young man, and he held his head high. "Sir, he says he's been in Vicksburg, that he knows something that might help us. He won't speak with anyone but you, sir."

"Very well!" McPherson stood still as the black man advanced. *He might know something—but he looks almost senile.* "Yes, Uncle, what is it?"

The man was very old. His kinky hair was white as snow, as was the beard that adorned his dark cheeks. His eyes were dark brown but almost hidden under droopy lids, and there was a slowness in his thick speech that made him almost impossible to understand. He walked painfully, leaning on a cane made from a sapling, and his snuff-colored hands trembled violently. "Is Marse Linkum heah?" he quavered in a rusty voice.

"President Lincoln? Why, no, he's not here. What do you have, Uncle? Tell me about Vicksburg!"

"Yas, suh, I done seed it." The features of the old man twisted, and his hand fluttered as he fumbled with the cane. He licked his thick lips then seemed to forget that he was in the presence of a general. He mumbled about someone named Carter then cackled in a high-pitched laugh, saying, "No, suh, us ain't been kotched—them pattyrollers ain't get us!"

McPherson gave the major a disgusted look. "See he gets something to eat, Major Benning—he's no help." He turned but then stopped when a strong voice said, "Private Rocklin reporting, General." Wheeling to face the man, McPherson stared with incredulous eyes as the bent figure straightened up and the eyes opened wide—and a broad smile split the darkened face. "Ready for duty, sir!" he said, a light of humor in his dark eyes.

McPherson burst into laughter. "Well, Private Rocklin," he said, "if you can fool the Rebs as well as you fooled us, you'll be all right. Did you know him, Major?"

"No, sir." Benning was as taken by surprise as the general and gave one of his rare smiles. "Maybe there is *some* use for actors in the world, Private Rocklin. You'll have a chance to prove it to me and the general."

The three men spoke for over thirty minutes as darkness fell over the land. Frank saluted then faded away without a backward glance.

"Do you think he can do it, sir?"

"I think he's got brass enough for it, Major." McPherson added, "I think we might take time to wish that young man luck—and a prayer if you've got one!"

Frank had found that a single man getting into Vicksburg after dark was not the problem he had feared. The lines were thin in spots, and he had moved stealthily through the darkness, grateful that there was only a sliver of a moon. Keeping to the line of trees that flanked some sort of rough cattle trail, he passed out of the Union lines. Once he heard a sentinel call out on his left, "Hey, Charlie, you got a chaw of terbaccy?" He froze at once, but when the guard left to get his chaw, he at once moved forward.

"Well, I'm in Vicksburg," he murmured as he made his way up the incline. He had no map nor any sort of paper to identify himself, but Major Benning had shown him on the regimental map where the city lay behind the lines. Soon he encountered a series of houses that he recognized as the outer limits of the city. The silence was broken occasionally by one of the Union batteries firing on the town. Frank made his way carefully toward the bulk of buildings and then decided to wait until morning to proceed.

He took shelter in a clump of trees but dared not light a fire. He had no canteen, but he had brought a piece of beef he'd scrounged from the general's mess, which he gnawed as he lay on the dew-soaked ground. It was tough and stringy, but better than hardtack, and it was something to do. The beef was salty and he grew thirsty, but he decided not to try to find water until daybreak.

It was a long night to him, and he could not sleep. As the shells exploded, making red dots in the blackness of the night, Rocklin thought with a gust of amusement of what he was doing. "Of all the fool stunts I've ever pulled, this takes the prize," he murmured, shifting to avoid a sharp stone that dug into his back. There was a strange mixture of humor and fatalism in him; he knew that if he were caught, there would be no long-drawn-out trial. The thought that he might be lying dead in a shallow grave in a few hours came to him, and he discovered that he was somewhat frightened by the concept. It wasn't death that troubled him, but the notion that life would be cut short. *Lots of things I want to do. If I get caught, it's all over.* He tried to think of what it would be like to be dead, but all he could make of it was that he would be out of the only place he knew. *When you're dead, it's the end of the world. Your family will still be living, and the war will be going on—but not for you.* He thought of the sermons he'd heard about hell and judgment, and he grew sober. He was no doubter and was convinced that he would face God one day. It had always seemed like something that was far away, a distant threat like thunder heard far off—only a low rumble. Now it was very close, and as the hours crawled by, he was silent, thinking about God and what it would be like to stand before Him.

When the first few gleams of gray appeared in the east, he was up and moving. Finding a small creek, he drank thirstily then ate the rest of the beef. When he emerged from the trees, he put himself on the road, careful to assume his role. Hobbling painfully, he leaned on his stick and kept his head down. The first person he saw was a woman who came out of her house and stared at him for a moment. She didn't speak, and Frank pretended not to see her. The brief encounter sharpened his thoughts, for he realized that just one false step with just one person would be a disaster.

As the sun rose, he encountered more people. He passed a gaggle of small children playing some sort of game that involved a ball, but none of them paid him the slightest attention. A man driving a scrawny cow appeared out of a side trail. He was a short, muscular man wearing a pair of faded overalls. "Better watch yourself," he called out as he passed close to Frank. "One of them shells wouldn't do you any good."

"No, suh," Frank mumbled. "Is it dem Yankees?"

"Shore. They won't git in heah, you can bet. Gen'ral Joe Johnston, he's on his way with 'bout a million of our boys." The stocky man nodded emphatically, adding, "He'll run them Bluebellies all the way back to ol' Abe!" The cow had stopped to pull a few mouthfuls of grass, and Frank stood there quietly, listening and saying a word now and then. He risked looking the man fully in the face and, to his relief, got no reaction. When the farmer asked him if he was looking to be free, he shook his head and mumbled, "I belong ter Mistah Edward Sullins. Ain't studyin' no freedom, no, suh!"

The man grinned then said, "Watch fer them shells, Uncle. You'll get to glory quicker than you think if one of them derned things lands on you." He tapped the cow with the long slender sapling he held and moved away.

Frank expelled his breath, feeling a little drained. He'd conceived this role of an older slave but hadn't been certain he could pull it off. He'd been around blacks when visiting in Virginia, but that had been several years earlier. Fortunately, he had a good ear for dialect, and the thick speech of Box, an elderly slave who was the blacksmith at Gracefield, had stayed with him.

People emerged from their houses as he passed through the residential areas. All of them scurried quickly along, ducking their heads when a cannon shell exploded. There was a determined look on most of their faces, but there was fear as well. Once when a shell exploded beside a small white frame house not fifty feet from where he walked, Frank almost darted away. The shell blew the side of the house apart, sending splintered fragments sailing into the air. A woman who was working in a garden in the back threw the hoe down and screamed, "Betsy! Betsy!" Frank watched as she ran in the back door, then felt a gust of relief as she emerged carrying a small, naked child.

Neighbors came running to the pair, and as the dust settled, Frank heard the woman say, "Take Betsy with you, Helen. I'll go see to the house."

All morning Frank roamed the town, moving slowly toward the river. He noted the artillery mounted in parapets made of timber and earth. He was studying the batteries and had decided that they were rifled thirty-two pounders, but he wrote nothing down. As he passed along the front, he stopped to watch as one gun crew carefully took aim and fired at a Federal gunboat that was edging along the far side of the river. When the missile bounced off the armored side of the vessel, the gun captain swore roundly then shook his head. "We only got twelve charges left. We can't waste no more on them iron gunboats."

He grew hungry after midafternoon and bought three potatoes, ten pears, and a loaf of fresh-baked bread from an old man selling vegetables. He ate one of the pears as he sat watching the soldiers who guarded the inner lines. Once, he gained some information that he knew would be worth the risk he was taking. He'd hobbled toward the Confederate lines that faced the Union invaders and had been greeted by a sergeant. "Come to jine up with the army, have you?"

"No, suh!" Frank said. "Jes' bin to see could I fin' some fresh vegetables for Mist' Sullins. My ol' legs, dey 'bout give out."

The sergeant nodded at an empty box, saying cheerfully, "Set fer a while." He turned away but later came to stand beside Frank, who offered him one of the pears. He took it, bit into it, then chewed it slowly, savoring the juicy fruit.

A lieutenant soon joined him, and Frank was more alert. He kept his head down and listened as the two spoke.

"Hope the Yanks try another bust in here, Lieutenant," the sergeant said. "They nailed us last time. Them Mississippi rifles warn't no good. Half of 'em blowed up—and a sharpshooter couldn't hit a bull elephant ten feet away."

The lieutenant nodded grimly but then grinned. "It'll be different next time they try it. These new Enfields will stop them!" The English-made Enfield rifle fired an elongated ball and was highly accurate. "We were lucky to get these rifles," the lieutenant grunted. "They were almost taken but got here still in the crates."

"I got the men all set with muskets loaded like shotguns, too, sir," the sergeant replied. "We'll let the Bluebellies get close then rise up and give 'em what they come fer!"

Frank sat on the crate for some time, soaking up information, then rose and hobbled off. The sun was going down, and he made his way to a hill on the northeastern part of Vicksburg, intending to spend the night in the woods.

As he moved down a worn path, he heard a voice say, "Stop!" and a sudden warning ran along his nerves. But when he turned, he saw only a young girl and an old man dressed in a suit. "Yas, suh?" Frank said, bobbing his head. "Kin I hep you, suh?"

"What's the word from town?" The man was in his late sixties, but his eyes were sharp and his voice strong. "Any word come about General Johnston?"

"He comin', dey says." Frank spoke slowly, thickening his accent. "But dey doan know when."

The elderly man nodded then said, "I don't know you. Who do you belong to?"

"Mist' Sullins, sah. His place ovah close to Simmsville. He sent me heah to find out 'bout his girl, Ellen. She live in Vicksburg. He say fo' me to take care of her."

At that moment a shell exploded not far away, and the man said, "Come on—they've got our range!" He grabbed the girl's hand and pulled her around. Frank saw no house, but when the man shouted, "Come on—get out of this, Uncle!" he followed him.

Frank saw an opening in the steep bank and realized that it was a cave. When he stepped inside, he saw that it was furnished like a house. A woman was cooking on a woodstove that was set back, and to the left a carpet covered the raw earth. A couch, several chairs, and a table were illuminated by two lamps, and the elderly man waved his hand, saying, "We've moved here until the siege is over. Too dangerous in our house. Sit down, Uncle."

Frank eased himself into a chair and for the next two hours learned about what war was like for helpless civilians. The family was named Taylor and were fine people, he decided. He said little, but the girl chattered to him like a parrot. She was a pretty thing with bright red hair and sparkling blue eyes. She was a singer of songs and a teller of stories, Frank discovered, and Mrs. Taylor warned him, "Patty will talk the hands off the clock!"

Finally, when the meal was ready, Mrs. Taylor handed Frank a plate of beans with a morsel of salt pork. His portion, Frank noted, was the same size as theirs. Mr. Taylor asked a simple blessing, and then they ate their supper. After they were finished, Frank pulled out his sack, saying, "I thanks you, and I is got something sweet." He passed out the remainder of his pears, and the family ate them at once. Afterward, Frank left, and as he hobbled away he thought, *Why does war have to be so hard on old people and children?*

He stayed in the city for three days and then made his way back through the lines under cover of darkness. He was cautious, for the Union pickets were trigger-happy at times. The next morning he appeared at the tent of General McPherson,

GILBERT MORRIS

who was delighted to see him. "Well, what have you got for us, Private?" he asked at once. He listened carefully, along with Major Benning. Frank ended with the words, "They're tough people, General. It's not going to be easy."

"I think you're right, Private," the general said. "You don't see any signs of their weakening?"

Frank pulled a piece of paper out of his pocket. "They've taken a lot, but they've still got a sense of humor, General. I took this from the wall of a hotel."

BILL OF FARE

Soup
Mule Tail

Boiled
Mule Bacon with Poke Greens
Mule Ham Canvassed

Roasts
Mule Sirloin
Mule Rump Stuffed with Rice

Entrées
Mule Head Stuffed à la Mode
Mule Beef Jerked à la Mexicana
Mule Hide Stewed New Style Laid On
Mule Spare Ribs Plain
Mule Liver Hashed

Side Dishes
Mule Salad
Mule Hoof Soused
Mule Kidney Stuffed with Peas

Jellies
Mule Foot

Pastries
Cotton Seed Pies
China Berry Tarts

Liquors
Mississippi Water Vintage 1492 Superior $3.00
Spring Water Vicksburg Brand $1.50

Meals at all hours. Any inattention on the part of servants will be promptly reported at the office.
Jeff Davis & Co.
Proprietors

General McPherson lowered the fragment of paper, his face grim. "No, they're not whipped," he murmured. "You've done a fine job, Private. I'll see that your father hears of it."

Frank saluted then left the tent. He found himself greeted warmly by his squad, and when he had time to talk with Ty and Bob privately, he said, "Those people won't give up."

"We've got to take it, Frank," Bob insisted.

Frank stared at the two. He was thinking of the bright eyes of Patty, the small red-haired girl in the cave. For him she had become the symbol of the futility of war. He had made a decision on his way back to the camp, and now he said flatly, "I'm out of it. When my ninety days are up, I'm going home." When his brothers started to argue, he cut them off shortly. "You do what you have to do. But I'm through with this war—and that's that!"

Chapter 6

A New Start

As Frank stepped off the crowded train, he found himself strangely despondent. Grabbing his gear, he fought his way through a noisy crowd, found a cab, and quickly tossed his knapsack into it. The driver, a lantern-jawed individual, stared at his private's uniform with a jaundiced eye. When Frank gave his parents' address, he muttered, "Cost you two dollars, solger."

"I think I can rake it up." Throwing himself into the cab, Frank tried to ignore the depression that had begun when he'd said good-bye to his brothers. They had not rebuked him for leaving the army—at least not with words. Both of them had wished him well, but there had been an uncomfortable feeling about the parting. Now as he rode through the crowded streets of Washington, he felt sullen and discontented. *What's the matter with me? I wanted out of the army—so I've got what I asked for.*

Moving his feet restlessly, he stared out the window and saw a huge crowd gathered in one of the park areas. He heard raucous shouts that sounded like threats; over to one side of the park a line of infantry stood with muskets at half rest. "What's going on?" Frank demanded of the driver.

"Why, it's them nigger solgers," the hulking driver said.

Turning to give his fare a hard glance, he shrugged, adding, "Been tryin' to get a nigger regiment ever since we got chopped up so bad at Chancellorsville. Ain't goin' to work, though!" He sent a stream of amber tobacco juice onto the street, disgust in every move.

"Why not?"

"Because they ain't enough of 'em, fer one thing. All the free niggers got good jobs as teamsters or laborers. And them that *do* sign up fer the army is likely to get shot at from *both* sides." Noting Frank's confusion, the driver added caustically, "Lots of whites in the North are from the South. They hate niggers being raised up and would just as lief take a shot at one of them for spite. And if the Rebels capture a nigger in a blue uniform, why, he's gonna put a ball in his head, don't you reckon? And one of the police right here said he'd shoot down a nigger wearing a uniform jest like he would a yeller dog!"

Frank stared at the thin line of black soldiers who were wearing army uniforms, wondering what would come of this. He said mildly, "Some of them are good fighters. I've just come from Grant's army in Mississippi. The Negro troops fought at Fort Hudson and Miliken's Bend as well as any men could." He got a cold stare from the driver and made no further attempts to speak of the matter.

Getting out at his parents' home, he paid his fare—to the penny—then walked toward the house, ignoring the furious stare of the driver. "You'll see about them niggers!" he called out spitefully. "They ain't got no souls like us white people."

Frank dismissed the driver with a thought of disgust and opened the front door. He found his mother alone, and she greeted him joyfully. "Why, Frank, come in! Are you hungry?"

Frank grinned as he held her tightly. "You'd offer a meal if the world was coming to an end, Mother." However, he allowed her to fix him a plate of gravy and biscuits, which he devoured with relish. As he ate, he gave her the news of Ty and Bob then asked about his father.

"Why, he's with General Meade, going to stop Lee."

"Meade? I thought Hooker was in charge."

"He was, but President Lincoln replaced him. I guess he was unhappy with the way he failed at Chancellorsville." Melanie's face suddenly turned heavy, and she gave Frank a troubled look. "I'm afraid for your father. He'll be right in the thick of the battle—like he always is."

Frank felt the same sense of discomfort he'd felt with his brothers and said abruptly, "I've left the army, Mother."

"I know, son." Melanie put her hand over his and shook her head. "It's a thing no person can decide for another."

"Do you think Pa will despise me?"

"Of course not! You know your father better than that, Frank!"

"Well, he's army to the heart, and I thought—"

Melanie shook her head, noting the uneasy expression on the tanned face. This son had always been more trouble to her and her husband than the other two. She studied his brooding expression, noting how much he resembled his father. *He looks like Gid, but Ty and Bob are the ones who act like him.* She smoothed his raven-dark hair back from his forehead, wondering what lay ahead for this youngest of her sons, but said only, "Well, what will you do with yourself?"

Frank looked up, his eyes suddenly bright. His broad lips turned upward in a grin, and he said, "Going to disgrace the family, Ma—I always knew I would."

"Why, Frank!"

Frank rose and took her in his arms, squeezing her. "You're still the best-looking woman in Washington," he said, grinning down at her. Then he held her at arm's length and shrugged. "I'm going to try my luck on the stage, Mother. I know you and Father will hate it, but I feel I've got to do it." When he saw the alarmed look on her face, he laughed, adding, "Don't worry—I'll probably be terrible. It'll be the shortest career in the history of the theater!"

"You'll do well at whatever you set your mind to, Frank Rocklin!" Melanie insisted. "Let me go—some letters came for you." He followed her into the drawing room, where she took several letters off the mantel. Handing them to Frank, she could not help observing, "They're from a woman. I can tell by the handwriting."

"Yes, from Miss Montaigne," Frank said. "I told her to write me at this address." He looked up from the first envelope and, seeing the curious look on his mother's face, asked innocently, "Do you want me to read them aloud, Ma?" He laughed when she flushed and left the room in a huff.

"You didn't get any of your insolence taken out of you in the army!" she observed acidly. "I don't care a pin about your old letters!"

Frank sat down and read all three of the letters at once. The first two were witty and full of descriptions of New York, where Carmen had been with Booth's troop. The play had been a success, and in the second letter, she spoke of how it was likely that Booth would bring the company back to Washington for a play—she wasn't certain what it would be.

The third letter caught at Frank instantly. It was dated only a week earlier, June 21, and was very brief. She wrote:

We are back in Washington to do Hamlet. I will be Ophelia, of course. Booth will play Hamlet, and Roland will play Laertes. I fully expect Booth to kill Roland! The sword fights are so intense! Mr. Ford is building a new theater. The old one he had, the Athenaeum, was actually a church! Remodeled, of course—but still I expect several deacons and pastors must have rolled over in their graves at some of the lines that were spoken in that place! We will rehearse at the old theater, but the play will open in Mr. Ford's new theater sometime around the first of July.

I have no idea when you will return, but long to see you! Write if you get this! I still remember our times together with pleasure!

Carmen Montaigne

Frank did some mental calculation, rose, and called, "Mother, I'm going downtown. Don't wait supper for me!" He went to his room, washed, and shaved carefully. Placing the uniform in a drawer—and feeling some sort of regret he couldn't understand—he put on his best clothing. The outfit consisted of a pair of white trousers tapered at the ankle, a white silk shirt, a square-cut waistcoat, and a double-breasted maroon frock coat. He stared at his reflection in the mirror, smiled wryly, and muttered, "Well, Mr. Rocklin, if looking like a fop will get you into the theater, you're well qualified!" Then he picked up a gleaming black top hat, stuck it on his head at a rakish angle, and left the house.

The rehearsal had not gone well, and John Wilkes Booth was in a rage. He had laid aside his fine clothes and wore a pair of gray trousers and a white cotton shirt—both now drenched with perspiration. His handsome face was drawn into a scowl, and as he glared at the actors across the stage, fury burned in his dark eyes. "Have any of you *read* the play?" he shouted. Slapping his hands together in a rash gesture, he moved like a cat around the stage, his voice ripping them like a rapier. "Before heaven, I've never seen such an insipid, mewing bunch of amateurs in all my experience!" A table barred his way, and he kicked it viciously, sending it flying over the edge of the stage to crash into the seats below. The gesture, Carmen realized, was typical of Booth. She paid little heed to his ranting, for long ago she had discovered that under the fine looks of the actor lurked a rashness, an anger that would flare out at times. The rehearsal had not been good, but Booth himself had performed poorly. However, none of the cast dared to say so. Therefore they stood there enduring the harsh words with as much patience as they could muster.

Finally, Booth seemed to exhaust the fit of anger and slumped down on a couch, moaning, "We'll *never* be ready for opening night."

Roland Middleton, looking tired and leaner than usual, said, "Well, Mr. Booth, we've done harder things. I'm sure we'll be all right."

But his words brought no comfort to Booth. He muttered, "If you'd learn to handle a blade, Middleton, that would help a great deal." He got to his feet, looked at them, then shook his head. "Well, let's do it again—and this time, let your voices fill this place. You're all mewing like sick kittens!"

Frank Rocklin had entered the theater just a few moments before Booth had exploded into rage. He stood back under the balcony in the darkness, dismayed at what he had witnessed. The theater was dark, only the stage lit by footlights, so he could not be seen. Now as he watched the company struggle on through the act, he thought, *This is not the best time to ask for a part.* He watched Carmen for the most part, admiring her as she played her role very well. She was wearing a simple light green dress and her hair was done up in a new fashion—but he admired her beauty. He'd forgotten how attractive she was, and now the thoughts of their times together floated back into his memory.

Finally, Booth said wearily, "That's all for tonight. Be here at ten in the morning."

Frank moved forward, and as he came into the range of the lights, Booth turned abruptly, catching the movement. He blinked and put up a hand to shade his eyes—then called out, "Bless us! Is this Rocklin that I see before me?" He ran to the edge of the stage and jumped over it, which caused the older woman playing the role of Gertrude to cry out a warning. But Booth was half acrobat, and he landed on the floor of the theater with perfect balance. He smiled and came with his hand out. "I thought you were in the army," he said then took in Frank's fine clothing and added, "but I don't recognize that as a uniform of the Union."

Booth's hand was hard and firm, and Frank was astonished that the actor showed such pleasure. "I'm an ex-soldier now, Mr. Booth. I did my ninety days and am now ready to bore you all with lying tales of how I saved my regiment from death and destruction."

Booth opened his eyes widely and smiled, exposing perfect teeth. "Let me get dressed," he said in an animated tone. "We're going out to dinner. I want to hear what you've been doing." As he wheeled and practically ran across to the side door, Roland came down the short flight of stairs, his usually glum face alive with pleasure. "Welcome home, the conquering hero!" he exclaimed, grasping Frank's hand. "When did you get home?"

"He can tell us all about it at dinner." Carmen had come to stand before Frank, and putting out her hands, she smiled warmly. "I'm glad to see you," she said huskily. "I'll go change. Don't go away."

As she left, Middleton said eagerly, "Are you home for good, Frank?"

"Yes. I've done my soldiering, Roland." He smiled, saying, "You looked good up there."

"I was as bad as everyone else. The play's sour before it even starts."

"Why is that?"

Roland shrugged. "No one can say why it happens, Frank. Sometimes everything is wrong, but the actors catch fire. Sometimes everything looks good, but nothing happens." He hesitated then said, "I think Booth's upset over the way the war's going. He's pretty pro-Southern, you know. He doesn't talk about it much—that wouldn't be smart. But his emotions go up and down according to the way the Confederacy prospers. When the South wins, he's high as the moon—but when they suffer a setback, he's impossible, like you saw him tonight."

"He'll be more upset, then—because Vicksburg is going to fall."

"Really? Well, that's good news for the country. But watch Booth when it happens."

Middleton left, and an hour later Frank was sitting at a table at Willards with Booth and Carmen. The other members of the cast had not come, and Booth at one point confided, "The cast is not doing well, Frank."

"It'll get better, I hope."

Booth shrugged then asked eagerly, "Tell me about Vicksburg. How does it look?"

Frank hesitated then said honestly, "It's hopeless for Pemberton, Mr. Booth." He saw the disappointment wash across Booth's face as he went on to describe the situation. He ended by saying, "The only hope the South had was to unite the armies of Pemberton and Johnston. Once Grant cut in between them and penned Pemberton up in the city, there was no real hope."

"Perhaps Johnston will come to relieve the city."

"Perhaps. But if he doesn't, it's just a matter of time. The people of Vicksburg are living in caves, and the food can't last."

Booth pondered this, and as Frank talked with Carmen, he noticed that the actor was in some sort of deep thought. Finally, Booth shook off his mood and asked, "What's for you now, Rocklin?"

Frank laughed shortly, his face flushed. "I want to learn the art of the theater," he said. "I might be no good, but I'd like to try."

Booth brightened up instantly. "Why, I think you'd do well, Frank!"

"Why don't you let him play Laertes?" Carmen suggested. "Roland hates the role, and after seeing Frank play Mercutio, I think he'd be a fine Laertes."

"Why, that's true! Both of those fellows were hotheads, too quick with their swords!"

"I won't take the role," Frank said instantly. "Roland's a friend."

"Don't let that hinder you," Booth said. "Middleton loathes the role, especially the swordplay. You've seen how inept he is, and the duels in this play are more demanding. You could handle that part of it perfectly. Middleton can take the role of

Rosencrantz. Do you know the play?"

"I've seen it three times and read it quite often," Frank said, then admitted, "but I'd have to memorize the lines and the actions."

Booth sat staring across the table at Rocklin, and it was one of those times for Frank when he felt that he'd come to a crossroads in his life. If Booth turned him down, he had no other contacts. But then Booth nodded and slapped the table hard. "All right—you're on! If you can't do it, I'll have to let you go, of course." He turned to Carmen and smiled with slight mockery. "I don't suppose you'd have time to teach Frank the part, Carmen?"

But Carmen gave him a steady smile and reached across the table to put her hand over Frank's. "I'm always glad to help a fellow performer, Mr. Booth."

After the meal, Booth left them alone, and it was Frank who said, "I don't know if I can do this, Carmen. It's one thing to play a role for a week that you know pretty well, but it's something else to make it your life."

Carmen leaned toward him, the lights bringing out the coral of her skin. There was a strain of imagination in her and a wild depth of feeling that leaped out from time to time. Despite the hard life that all actresses led, she had retained a warmth and even a gentleness that she revealed to only a few. Now as she sat before him, her lips were in repose and there was a longing in her brown eyes that she didn't try to hide.

"You'll be successful, Frank," she whispered. "You have a great talent. And I'll help you."

There was a promise in her words, and Frank felt again the reckless spirit that he'd seen in her, but now was conscious of a deep, mysterious glow that he had not seen before. Slowly he

STARS IN THEIR COURSES

reached out and, when he held her hand, said slowly, "You know how to draw a man, Carmen." He saw that his words pleased her, and he laughed aloud, the memories of the bloody violence at Vicksburg gone from his mind.

PART TWO

The Actress

January-August 1863

CHAPTER 7

LORNA

Lorna Grey started violently as a heavy hand slid around her waist and a sly voice whispered, "Now that's wot I calls a fine piece of work!"

Without hesitation Lorna lifted the hot pressing iron in her right hand and slapped it against the meaty hand of her employer, Mr. Norval Bates. The results were spectacular, for the hand was jerked away abruptly and Mr. Bates yelped with pain as he hopped around trying to jam the wounded member into his mouth.

"Ow! You burned me!" Bates stopped long enough to glare balefully at the young woman who had turned to watch him—holding up the iron in a defensive position. "I'll teach you—"

"What's happening here?" Mrs. Phoebe Bates materialized as if by magic, her agate hazel eyes fixed on the pair. She was a thin, sallow-faced woman, who for some unfathomable reason felt that every woman in London was a danger to her marriage. Her insane jealousy was beyond the comprehension of Lorna, who abhorred the man. He had put his hands on her at the first opportunity after she began working in the shop, and since that day she had found that boredom and weariness were the least of her problems. She had searched for another job, but work was scarce, and now she lowered the iron, saying quietly, "I'm afraid I burned Mr. Bates with the iron. I was too careless."

Mrs. Bates glared at her but, having no direct evidence of wrongdoing, turned to her husband. "Come along, dear. I'll put some ointment on that burn." She made comforting sounds as she led the hulking man out, but turned to say harshly, "I've warned you before, but now you'll have to decide. You can't do two jobs. Either you give your notice to that music hall, or I can't use you."

Lorna yearned to throw the iron at the woman, but the thought of hunting for employment came to her. "Yes, Mrs. Bates," she said wearily. "I'll give my notice tonight."

Her answer dissatisfied the woman, but she only grunted and left the room. As Lorna turned and began mechanically ironing a delicate white blouse, a young woman with a pale face and a sour mouth grinned from where she stood ironing a similar garment. "I wisht you'd stuck that iron in 'is ear! Why, 'e ain't nothin' but a beast! Can't never keep 'is blasted 'ands to 'imself." Whipping the blouse off the board, she placed it on a stack of finished ones then said, "Yer ain't gonna quit your actin', are you, Lorna?"

"I'll have to, Annie. It doesn't pay much, and I've got to live."

"Wot a shame—and you so good at it, too!"

Lorna put in the rest of the day, and as she was leaving, Mrs. Bates stopped her, saying, "Remember, you give your notice to those people. No self-respecting young woman would allow herself to be seen with them! And be here early in the morning!"

"Yes, Mrs. Bates."

Lorna left the building, noting that the bricks were so stained with smoke from thousands of London fireplaces that the original color was completely obscured. Her legs were trembling with weariness, for the day had been long—and Mrs. Bates did not believe in breaks. Twelve hours of standing over a hot iron was enough to drain the energy from anyone—and now as she moved across the dirty snow that covered the walk, she felt the weight of depression. Her room was located in a rough part of town, and several times men spoke to her, but she had learned to ignore them. Finally, she arrived at her room, where she looked longingly at her iron bed. The mattress was lumpy, and the covers long since had lost any grace or beauty—still she longed to fall into it and lose herself in sleep.

"Tomorrow I can come home and sleep," she said aloud then forced herself to clean up as well as she could. There was no bath, of course, and the room was icy cold. But she endured the cold water, washing herself even as her teeth chattered. Moving slowly, she put on her only clean dress and then sat down and fixed her hair. She had beautiful hair, long and the color of honey. Her eyes were gray, and there was a delicate beauty in her oval-shaped face. She studied herself dispassionately then applied a little rice powder to her cheeks. Finally, she rose and pulled on her thin black coat and settled a rust-colored hat over her head.

Leaving the room, she made her way along the streets, moving toward the theater. The smell of roasting meat came to her, and she considered treating herself to a kidney pie, but settled for tea and crumpets in the cause of economy. She was still hungry but had learned to live with that.

The Gem Theatre was not the place for royalty, and as she

reached the rather grimy two-story brick building almost hidden on a side street of Soho, she felt a quick pang of despair. Memories of the green countryside of her home came to her, and she stopped dead still in front of the side entrance used by the cast. The dancing heads of sprightly flowers and the carpet of emerald green grass on the rolling hills were strong in her mind. Regret sliced through her, but then she tightened her lips and scolded herself silently. *You hated your life there—buried like a potato in the mud! Couldn't wait to get away from the boring existence and get to the glittering world of London! Well, you're in London—and on the stage—so stop moping and do your job!*

She forced the memories of Yorkshire from her mind, entered the theater, and moved quickly to the shabby dressing room she shared with six other girls. The odor of strong, cheap perfume and sweat struck her at once, but that was part of the world of the Gem. Quickly she removed her street clothes and slipped into her costume, a gauzy pink dress exactly like the ones the other six girls wore. As she sat and arranged her hair, a voice from the past seemed to speak: *"You'll lose your virtue if you go on the stage—it happens to all them actresses!"* Lorna had heard her mother say that often enough and now wondered if there had not been wisdom in the warning.

Glancing around at the five young women who chattered like squirrels, she knew that all of them were free with their favors. They went out with the rather seedy men who came seeking female companionship, and they were contemptuous of Lorna for keeping herself aloof from men. She had made no friends among them, and now as she put on her makeup, the thought came to her, *How long will it be before I become as cheap and tawdry as they are?* The depression that had troubled her for days grew heavier, and as she rose when the stage manager bellowed, "All right—get with it, girls!" she thought with some relief, *Well, this is my last night—good-bye to the stage for me.*

The production was something called *Springtime in Dover*. It was a rather dreadful and unsuccessful attempt to join a light drama with some sort of musical score. But the producer had not wasted money on talented musicians or on singers. Most of the girls who made up the chorus had flat voices and either sang in a strident off-key manner or made no more music than a cricket. The story was so banal that Lorna was sick of it the second time she was exposed and could not explain why anyone would come to such a pitiful excuse for entertainment.

The Gem was, of course, a music hall, and it made no pretense of grandeur. The seats were filled with working-class people, desperate for any break in their monotonous lives. And as Lorna joined in the chorus, she felt a sense of defeat, for her dreams of being an actress had come to this. And now even this pitiful excuse for a stage career had come to an end.

When the time came for her one solo number, Lorna put herself into it. She had a fine contralto, untrained but clear and sweet and strong. As always the audience grew still as she sang, and it was the one moment of time in her bleak life that was vivid and alive. The song was not deep or profound—merely a ballad about a girl whose sweetheart had gone to war—but she always managed to get across the poignant grief of a girl who had lost her love. Her clear voice rose and fell, swelling with power then falling to almost a whisper as she finished.

And as always, when the song ended the audience broke into loud applause, and there were calls of "That's the way to sing it, girlie!" Lorna blinked back the tears, knowing it was the last time she would feel such—such *magic*—for such it was to her. She craved the stage as a drunk craves liquor, and she had to turn aside to dash the tears from her eyes. *Well, that's that!* she thought grimly, and as the performance ground to an end, she paid little heed, thinking of the grubby room she would go back to—and fighting off Mr. Bates the next day.

In the dressing room she mechanically removed her makeup and was about to put on her dress when the manager stuck his head in the door and said in an excited fashion, "Hey, Lorna, get yourself dressed! There's a real swell askin' for you!"

"Tell him I can't go with him, Barney."

Barney gave her an outraged stare. "Hey, this ain't no joke! I know this guy, Lorna." He paused and said impressively, "This is *Michael Dennis*!"

Every one of the other five young women swiveled their heads to stare at the manager. "Aw, you're puttin' us on, Barney!" a sharp-faced girl named Sally jibed. Then she shot a calculating stare at Lorna, adding, "If you don't want 'im, Lorna, I'll take 'im off your hands!"

Lorna had seen Dennis once, spending too much to see him perform. He was the most popular leading man in England, and curiosity rose in her. "Tell him I'll be right out, Barney." Conscious of the envious stares of the other girls, she quickly changed and left the dressing room. Barney was standing close to the door, nodding his head toward a tall man who was lounging farther toward the exit.

As Lorna approached, she felt a quickening interest. "Mr. Dennis?" she said, coming to stand before him. He turned to face her, a smile coming to his lips. He was six feet tall, very erect and athletic. His hair was a dark chestnut with a slight wave, and he wore a small mustache of the same texture. His light brown eyes, large and direct, were his best feature, and he fixed them on her, saying, "Miss Grey, I apologize for coming unannounced."

"Frankly, Mr. Dennis, I'm surprised that you're in a place like this at all."

Instantly Dennis grinned broadly, two creases springing up at the edges of his lips. Casting a look around the dilapidated interior of the Gem, he shook his head. "Frankly, I don't come to places like this often. But a friend of mine told me about you."

"About *me*? Why, I can't imagine why, Mr. Dennis." Lorna was perplexed, and then a thought came to her. "If you're looking for—female companionship," she said firmly, her eyes meeting his glance, "I can introduce you to several of the actresses who'd be charmed to join you."

Michael Dennis was accustomed to adulation. It was part of his life as an actor. Perhaps he was sated with female companionship, for he found himself intrigued by the firm rejection of what many young women would fight to obtain. He cocked his handsome head to one side, studied her, then said, "I appreciate the warning, Miss Grey. Actually, I want to speak with you about another matter. Would you join me for a late supper where we can discuss a professional matter?"

Lorna was mystified, but humor came along with a stab of curiosity. "I'll be glad to join you, but I must warn you: I'm starved. It will be an expensive meal."

Dennis's white teeth gleamed as he smiled and offered her his arm. "I've never heard a woman admit that," he remarked as they left the Gem. He handed her into a cab, told the driver the name of a restaurant, then got in beside her. He was cheerful as they drove along the dark streets, commenting on the weather but saying nothing of his purpose. When they reached the restaurant, Lorna felt badly out of place with her inexpensive dress, but she kept her head up as they were seated.

The next hour went quickly and very pleasantly. Dennis

tactfully helped her to order, then while they waited, asked her a few questions. He listened as she spoke, and when she finished, he told her amusing stories of the theater. The meal arrived, and Lorna ate hungrily. Afterward, when the waiter brought fresh tea, Dennis announced, "I want you to read for a part in my new play."

Lorna stared at him. If he'd told her she was going to the wilds of Africa, she would not have been more shocked. Her eyes grew large, and finally she asked, "Is it your custom to recruit for your company in third-rate music halls like the Gem, Mr. Dennis?"

Dennis had expected the young woman to leap at his offer and was taken somewhat aback when she questioned him so. He lit a cigar, taking his time; then when the purple smoke was rising languidly, he leaned back and observed, "You don't trust people too much, do you, Miss Grey—or may I call you Lorna?"

"If you like—and I suppose I do have some caution." She smiled slightly, her full lips curving in a most attractive manner. Her long blond hair caught the gleams of the chandeliers, and there was a piquant expression in her gray eyes. "I've not had many famous men beating a path to my door asking me to go on the stage." She sipped the tea and studied Dennis carefully. "Why me, Mr. Dennis?"

"You'll work cheap!" Dennis laughed aloud then leaned forward. "You're an honest young woman," he said abruptly. "Let me be equally honest. I'm getting a cast together to do a new play. I'm tired of paying managers and investors. This one will be all mine. Let me tell you about the play...."

Lorna listened as Dennis spoke with excitement about his project. In essence, he was putting up all the money, so he needed a cast who would work for modest salaries. He ended by saying, "You would be perfect for the character of Jenny in the play."

"You've never seen me act."

"No, but I've seen your face and I've heard you sing. This character, Jenny, isn't a major character, but she's vital to the play. She's a sweet girl with a beautiful voice, and she dies in the second act. Her death is the center of the action, and I can teach you what you don't know about acting." Dennis leaned forward and said quietly, "A friend of mine saw your performance and asked me to come to see you. Now that I have, I think there's a good chance you could do very well. As I've told you, I can't hire well-known talent. As a matter of fact, only the leading lady and I are established. I'm picking up the rest of the cast as best I can. Would you like to read for the part?"

Lorna agreed. "I love the stage, Mr. Dennis. If you think there's a chance for me, I'll work very hard."

Dennis was watching the girl's face carefully. *She's got whatever it is that makes people watch her. Never saw a good actress who didn't have it.* He smiled. "I think we're going to be working together. Let's have a toast." He lifted his cup of tea and, holding it toward her, said, "To a long and successful career for Miss Lorna Grey!"

Lorna felt a sudden rising of hope. She had given up, but now out of nowhere this man had come to offer her what she wanted most in the world. Gratitude filled her voice, and her lips trembled slightly as she lifted her cup, whispering, "Thank you, Mr. Dennis!"

She could say no more, and he saw that her eyes were brimming with tears. He reached over and took her hand, squeezed it gently, then said, "I'm glad I found you, Lorna Grey!"

STARS IN THEIR COURSES

※

Lorna felt Michael squeeze her hand hard, and she turned to smile at him. The footlights caught his face, and he whispered over the cheers of the audience, "You have them, Lorna! They love you!" He bowed again and led her off the stage, then turned at once and kissed her full on the lips, saying warmly, "You were wonderful, darling!"

Lorna had grown accustomed to Michael's caresses, and now she flushed with pleasure, ignoring the grins of the stagehands. "Let me get dressed; then we'll go out for dinner."

"All right, but it'll be a special dinner tonight." He released her, and she moved quickly to her dressing room. As she entered and began undressing, she thought of how opulent this room had been four months earlier. It had been the dressing room of Alice Fortiner, the actress starring with Dennis. But after the success of that play, she had been given the starring role in his second venture and had inherited the star's dressing room. The play was a costume drama, and she carefully removed the ornate silk dress then the farthingale and the numerous petticoats. Quickly she hung the costume in a wardrobe then put on her new dress. It had the fashionable pyramid shape, with bell-shaped sleeves and a tight-fitting bodice that closed around the neck in a V shape. Carefully she arranged her small straw hat so that it tilted over her brow, plucked up a matching silk parasol, and left the dressing room.

Michael met her, dressed as usual in the latest fashion. He looked dashing in a royal blue double-breasted frock coat, and around the gleaming of his white shirt blossomed a cravat with fringed ends. He hurried her outside, spoke to the driver, then got in. He was in a fine humor and soon had her laughing over some of the amusing things that had occurred during the performance.

Lorna sat close beside him, enjoying his witty conversation. He had been careful not to press her into private meetings for the first month of the play's successful run. He had spent long hours going over her part, rehearsing her until she was perfect—but it had been purely professional. After the first play closed, he had been excited about a new play—one that would allow her a starring role. Not as fat as his, of course, but second place to the brilliant Michael Dennis had been thrilling enough for Lorna.

The carriage stopped, and when Lorna stepped down, she looked up to say with surprise, "Why, this is your hotel, Michael. I thought we were going to the fanciest restaurant in London."

Dennis smiled and squeezed her arm. "Something better than that, Lorna. Come along now and don't ask questions. I've spent a lot of time planning this evening."

Lorna allowed herself to be led into the hotel, noting that Michael was greeted with deference by all the help. The manager came to say, "All is ready, Mr. Dennis. I think even *you* will be pleased with what I've managed to come up with."

"Thank you, Louis. I'm looking forward to it."

Lorna had been to Dennis's hotel suite twice, both times accompanied by other members of the cast. But now as she entered and looked around, she saw only two waiters, who were standing beside a table covered with a snowy white cloth. One of them said, "Whenever you're ready, Mr. Dennis."

"We're ready now, Andrew." He waited while one of the servants took their coats; then he led Lorna to a chair at one end of the table. When she was seated, he nodded at the waiter, saying,

"Let's have some wine—and some music, Andrew."

Lorna turned as a door opened and three men came in, all carrying stringed instruments. She turned to Dennis, her eyes shining. "You *have* planned all this, haven't you, Michael? How lovely!"

It was an evening such as Lorna had never imagined. The string trio played all her favorite tunes, and the meal was the best she'd ever eaten. Michael was charming, and his words of approval over her performance in the play excited and pleased her.

Finally, the table was cleared, and the musicians played one final medley then left after receiving warm approval from both Dennis and Lorna.

But the night that had been so wonderful for Lorna soon turned unpleasant. While talking on the couch, they had moved rather close to one another. Michael gently kissed her, but soon his kisses had become forceful. As his hands began to roam, she struggled against him and fought clear of his embrace. "I think it's time for me to go home, Michael," she said, disappointed in his behavior.

Dennis rose and came to stand before her. He caught her hands and asked, "Lorna, don't you care for me at all?" When she said rather awkwardly that she *did* care, at once he began telling her how much he loved her. Lorna was drawn to Michael as she had not been attracted to any other man. For many weeks she had felt herself in love with him, yet what he was suggesting was impossible for her.

"Michael, I—I don't know how to say this," she said quietly. "I know actresses are—well—lax in their relationships with men. But I can't be like that. When I marry, I want to be able to come to my husband as a pure woman."

A silence fell on the room, so that the loudest sound was the ticking of a large rosewood pendulum clock. It seemed to Lorna that the slow beat of the instrument was an echo to the beating of her own heart. She stood quietly before Dennis, offering no arguments, but there was a steely pride in her erect posture that he admired. Despite her rigid posture, there was something soft and gentle and appealing in her, and he said quietly, "I do love you, Lorna. I've never known a woman who was beautiful—and firm." He came closer to her and put out his hands, and when she surrendered hers, he held them gently. "I can't think of a woman I'd rather marry. Most actresses have egos as big as this hotel. You're not like that."

Lorna listened to him speak, and she was relieved to hear him finally say, "I'll take you home now." All the way back to her hotel, he was quiet, and when they stood outside the door of her room, he made no attempt to kiss her. He did stand before her quietly, his eyes taking in her face as though seeking the answer to some mystery. Finally, he said, "We'll talk about us later, Lorna. Good night."

Lorna entered her room and slowly began preparing for bed. She was shaken by the experience and knew there was little safety for her in repeating such things. When she had put on her nightgown, she sat down at the small desk beside her bed, took out a small book, and opened it. She had begun a journal six months earlier, when she'd first joined Michael's cast. Now as she read the pages, she saw clearly that she'd been falling in love with him. Finally, she picked up her pen, opened the small bottle of ink, and began to write. She recorded the scene as clearly as if she were an objective reporter. Then she paused and lifted her eyes, remembering how his caresses had brought an excitement to her. Then she wrote in her neat script, "I am in

love with Michael. That is very dangerous, for even if he loves me, he has loved many women." She hesitated, wrote slowly for a moment, then paused to look at the words she'd put on paper. "I am not certain if I am strong enough to keep myself from him. God help me to do so!"

Then she closed the diary, replaced it in the drawer, and blew out the light. Getting into bed, she thought of what it would be like to have a husband—and the memory of Michael's hands as he'd caressed her was disturbing. *What kind of a wife would I be? Can I please a man?* She had no answers and finally let herself drop off into a disturbed sleep.

Chapter 8

End of a Dream

"Ah, this is a most beautiful gown—the finest I have ever seen." The diminutive woman with the slight French accent who had shown the best of her goods to Lorna stroked the pale blue silk nightgown with a sensuous gesture. Madame Dubois was curious about the beautiful young woman who seemed rather nervous when shown the finest of undergarments. *She must be getting married. But she's behaving strangely about her underclothes—and about this nightgown.* She was good at her job and suggested with a smile, "Are you getting married, mademoiselle?"

Lorna had developed into a fine actress, but the question brought a rich flush to her smooth cheeks. Aware that the woman was smiling at her in a knowing fashion, she grew flustered, saying hurriedly, "Why—I will be—that is, I'm going on a short vacation—" She broke off, aware that she was only arousing the sharp-eyed woman's curiosity. "I'll take it—and that will be all."

"*Certainement!* I will have them wrapped carefully myself, mademoiselle." She took the garments into a back room and, as she wrapped them, gave a wicked smile to an older woman who sat at a table sewing a blouse. "That one, she is up to mischief, *ma tante*."

"Why do you say that? She looks respectable enough."

"So I thought." Wrapping the garments expertly, the small woman shook her head with a definite motion. "Only two kinds of women buy the sort of lingerie this one has chosen: the one who is going to be a bride"—she paused long enough to give the string a final knot then looked at the older woman with a gleam in her dark eyes—"and the woman who wants to please a man who is *not* her husband." Holding the package, she hesitated, her eyes moody. "I thought I knew both kinds, ma tante, but this one deceived me. She has the innocence of a bride—but she is not. *Voilà*, she is a woman out to snare a man!"

When Madame Dubois handed the packages to the young woman then took the cash for them, she smiled slightly, saying, "I hope you enjoy your vacation."

Lorna caught the emphasis on the word *vacation* and could not meet the woman's eyes. She turned and left the shop quickly, conscious that the sharp-eyed woman had seen something in her that she thought she had concealed.

The sky was a leaden color as she walked along the busy street, the brilliant blues of spring fading. Soon summer would come, then fall, then the dreary winter. London was not a pleasant place during the winter, at least not to Lorna. She loved the summer and spring, but the dreary months when the city was shrouded with fog, smoke, and dirty snow depressed her.

Turning into her hotel, Lorna was greeted by a stubby man in a rather flamboyant suit. She recognized him, saying, "Mr. Cooper, how are you?"

Thomas Cooper ducked his head, smiling at her hopefully. He had a reddish face, a shock of orange-red hair, and an abundant crop of freckles. "I'd be better if you'd consider my offer in a more agreeable light, Miss Grey." He added eagerly, "Now that your run is over, you'd be free to take another engagement. Now I'm willing to offer you the best terms I can, and it would be an *international* tour! All the way to America!"

Cooper had been insistent with his offers, and Dennis had laughed at them. "He's a poor show for a manager," he'd told Lorna. "Never had much success in this country, so now he's going to try it overseas. Don't give it a second thought, Lorna!"

Being kindhearted, Lorna had tried to let the man down as easily as possible and now said, "I'm very sorry, Mr. Cooper, but I have no desire to leave England. I wish you well, but you really must accept this as my final answer."

Cooper was not at all dismayed; he grinned cheerfully, saying, "Well, I don't want to be a pest, Miss Grey—but if you change your mind before the sixteenth, let me know. I'll always make a place for *you*!"

Cooper left, and as Lorna moved across the lobby, she returned the greeting of the desk clerk absently then turned to say, "Harold, I'll be gone for the next week. Will you hold any mail that comes for me?"

"Certainly, Miss Grey." The clerk was a fervent admirer of the young actress and said, "I was at the final performance of your play last night. You were *wonderful!*" He beamed at her then asked, "Will you be doing another play with Mr. Dennis?"

"I'm not sure, Harold."

"Oh, I *do* hope so! You two seem so—well, you act together so very well." Like most other fans of Dennis and Lorna, Harold Grimsely had spent much time wondering if the love scene that the pair acted out on the stage was a reflection of what went on offstage. Harold had been besieged by endless questioning concerning the pair and was disappointed that he could not give a report to his questioners. He compensated with innuendos and self-righteous proclamations: "Why, it would be unethical for me to say anything about Michael and Lorna!"

As Lorna turned away, the clerk could not conceal his avid curiosity. "Are you going on a trip with—" He halted abruptly as Lorna whirled, her eyes filled with anger. "I mean, will you be coming back soon? I believe I can hold your room for you, Miss Grey."

Lorna bit back the scalding words that leaped to her lips, saying only, "I can't say now, Harold."

When she was safely inside her room, she tossed the packages on her bed then took two or three turns around the room, clasping her hands tightly. Her face was stiff and her lips drawn into a tight line. Restlessness stirred her, and she moved to the window and stared out at the pale sun that seemed reluctant to touch the dusky streets with light. Finally, she turned slowly and moved to the mahogany chest and, opening the bottom drawer, pulled her diary from underneath the underclothes.

I'm ashamed to have anyone read what I've written in here for the last few weeks! she thought, an unusual bitterness rising in her. She flipped through the pages of the thin volume, noting that her relationship with Michael had grown more physical. She had managed to keep herself from making the final surrender, but the flesh had been stronger since he'd begun telling her he loved her. She was a young woman who longed for love, and his caresses drew her toward a consummation that he insisted would prove they were truly *one*.

Sitting down, she read the last entry, her brow drawn together in a worried expression. Her writing, she noted, was erratic and scarcely readable—quite unlike her usual neat script.

> *I don't know what to do! Michael has said that he loves me—and that we will be married! When he said that tonight, I wanted to give myself to him. But somehow I could not! He urged me to show my love and said that we would never be complete until we knew the limits of love. But when I asked him when we would be married, he said that we had our careers to think of. He said that the public wants a romance off the stage as well as on. When I told him I didn't understand this, he laughed and kissed me, saying, "Why, sweetheart, the people see that we're in love. And they'll come to see us play on the stage what they know is true in real life. We'll give them another play—a highly romantic one—and we'll announce our engagement. Then we'll be married and give them a dozen romantic dramas!"*

The sounds of traffic floated in, and Lorna paused for a moment. She looked at the wallpaper as if it might have some sort of message, then shook her head and began writing again:

> *I've agreed to go away with him for a week. He was delirious with happiness, telling me that we'll be truly one, that I'll know what love really is. But I'm afraid. It isn't right, and I know it. He says what matters is that we love each other and that one day soon we'll be married. He says that the marriage is only a formality.*
>
> *Perhaps he's right. I'll go with him, for we can't go on like this. I love him so much—and the thought of losing him is more than I can stand. God help me—but I must have him!*

Slowly she blotted the ink then stood and moved to the packages on the bed. Unwrapping them, she held up the silk nightgown. As she gazed at her reflection in the mirror, she found something in the sight that disturbed her. Slowly she began to pack and, when she came to her diary, had an impulse to throw it away. She held it over the basket for a long moment then put it into her suitcase and closed the lid.

Brighton was like nothing Lorna had ever seen before. When she walked along the boardwalk for the first time, her eyes grew large with wonder and she gasped, "Michael! It's like a fairyland!"

"The prince of Wales created it to look like that," Dennis said. "Nothing like it in all England."

The centerpiece of the city was something like an Indian mogul's palace with a great onion-shaped dome. Radiating out from this magnificent structure rose domes and minarets and cupolas. And the interiors of the buildings equaled the outer appearance. Within the Royal Pavilion, huge gilded rooms were filled with treasures, ornate and oriental. Lorna gasped as Michael took her into the famous banqueting room, stunned by a table set with priceless silver. She marveled as she saw, hanging from the ceiling, a giant palm tree out of which hissed a dragon!

Finally, as the afternoon drew on, Michael said, "It's been a long trip, sweetheart. Let's go to the hotel and have dinner." He took her to the dining room, where he ate with obvious enjoyment. The meal included a delicate turtle soup, lamb cutlets with asparagus, roast saddle of venison, plovers' eggs in aspic jelly, and finally ices and pineapple cream along with chocolate cream.

Lorna ate a little of each but had little appetite. She was dreading the moment when they would be alone together, but she did not allow her fears to show. Finally, when Michael finished the last of the tea and rose, saying, "Well, shall we go, my dear?" she followed him out of the dining room.

Their room was on the second floor, and a servant brought them hot water in covered vessels then left. Lorna sat down as Michael spoke with animation about the new play that he was planning, but she was not able to keep her mind on what he was saying. Finally, Michael gave her an odd look then said, "Why don't you get ready for bed, sweetheart? I'll just take care of a little book work."

"Of course." Lorna rose at once and left the sitting room. The bed was turned back, her trunk open at the foot. Slowly she took the silk gown from where it lay on the top, held it for a moment, then changed. She felt uncomfortable in the thin garment, and she turned abruptly and slipped into the bed. Pulling up the cover, she tried to relax but discovered that her muscles refused to obey her will.

For what seemed like a long time, she lay there, forcing herself to unclench her fists. Her mind was filled with fears and confusing thoughts, and she wished that she had chosen another way.

Finally, she heard the sound of voices from the sitting room and grew curious. At first she thought it was Michael talking to a bellboy, but there was a strident sound to at least one of the voices. She sat up in bed, for she recognized that one of the voices—the loudest one—belonged to a woman. She listened hard and then, as the voices grew louder, crawled out of bed. Slipping into a blue silken robe that matched her gown, she moved to the door and placed her ear against it. She listened for a time, and what she heard made her cheeks turn pale. Opening the door quickly, she stepped inside and saw a woman with an angry expression standing opposite Michael.

"Who is this woman, Michael?" Lorna demanded, turning to face him. His face, she saw, was pale, and he dropped his eyes, as though unable to face her. When he said nothing, she turned to the woman, demanding, "What are you doing here?"

The woman was in her thirties and was rather attractive in a hard sort of fashion. She was tall and well formed, with a round face and pretty features. She was dressed in expensive clothing, and there was an aggressiveness in her voice as she said, "What are *you* doing here would be a more fitting question." She had a pair of smallish blue eyes that studied Lorna with obvious disgust. Turning to Michael, she demanded, "Is this your latest trollop, Michael? I must say, she's prettier than some of the others."

"Michael! Who is this woman?"

"I'm his wife, that's who I am!" Anger and triumph flashed from the woman's eyes, and she cried out, "Well, tell her! I suppose you didn't bother to tell her you had a wife, did you?"

The room seemed to swim before Lorna for just one moment. *It can't be true!* was the thought that screamed through her mind—but when she steeled herself and looked at the face of Michael, she knew that it *was* true. Dennis's expression was filled with guilt. He stroked his mustache in a nervous gesture, saying, "Now don't be upset, Lorna. I can explain—"

"Can you explain that I'm your legal wife and you're here with another woman?"

Dennis stepped forward, making an angry gesture toward the woman. "Get out of here, Lillian! We've said all we have to say to one another!"

The woman saw something in Michael's expression that

caused her to shut her lips into a thin line. She blinked at him then muttered, "All right—but I want the money, Michael. If I don't get it, you know what will happen!" She turned and left the room, slamming the door.

Dennis stood still for a moment, his chest heaving, then gave a look of black despair to Lorna. "Well, there it is," he said heavily. "I wanted to tell you, but I was afraid I'd lose you."

"She's really your wife?"

"Yes, unfortunately." Dennis turned to her, saying, "Sit down, Lorna. It's a long story."

Lorna sat down numbly and listened as Dennis spoke bitterly of his past. In essence, he told her how he'd made a rash marriage when he was seventeen. He'd separated from his wife after a short time and had lost contact with her. After he'd become a star, she'd come demanding to take her place as his wife. He ended by saying, "I don't love her—I *never* loved her! I pay her to stay away from me, and she keeps promising to give me a divorce. That's what she came for tonight—to up the price."

"You should have told me, Michael."

"You'd have left me, wouldn't you?"

Lorna nodded and got stiffly to her feet. "I have to leave here."

Dennis protested but saw that it was useless. He said finally, "I'm sorry, Lorna. Stay here tonight. I'll get another room, and I'll see you back to London tomorrow." He hesitated then said, "I hope we can work together—even after this."

"No, Michael," Lorna said quietly. "I never want to see you again."

Thomas Cooper opened the door of his hotel room and was

shocked to see Lorna Grey standing there. "Why, Miss Grey!" he exclaimed. "I didn't expect to see *you*! Come in!"

"I'm afraid that would not be appropriate, Mr. Cooper."

"No, of course not. Let me get my coat. We'll go down to the restaurant."

A few minutes later the two were seated at a table, and when Cooper had poured two cups of tea, Lorna asked without preamble, "Would you still like for me to join your company?"

The question was so unexpected that Cooper almost dropped his cup! He recovered it then stared at the young woman. "Why, of course! It would be exactly what I need."

"Very well, give me your terms."

Cooper began to talk rapidly, and after he had set forth his terms and the time he planned to be in America, Lorna nodded. "I'll accept. When will we leave, Mr. Cooper?"

"Why now, I'd say we're ready for the day after tomorrow. Would that be too soon for you, Miss Grey?"

"No, not at all. I'll be at the Sterling Hotel. Let me know when the ship leaves." She rose and left with the briefest of good-byes, and Thomas Cooper sat down and sipped the last of his tea thoughtfully. When he rose and paid for the tea, he went back to his room, thinking, *I'd like to know what changed her mind.*

For the next two days Cooper drove himself frantically, but finally late one afternoon he stood braced against the rail of the *Priscilla* watching the shores of England fade into the dusk. Noting the latest addition to his company standing alone, he moved to take his place beside her. "Well now, we won't be seeing England again for a time, eh?"

Lorna turned to him, and he was shocked at the emptiness in her eyes as she said, "I don't care if I ever see it again." She turned and walked away from Cooper, the wind blowing her hair. Her back was stiff as she moved to the bow and stood watching the white froth as it flew by. She lifted her gaze and seemed to be trying to look over the thousands of miles of open sea to where America lay waiting for her. But there was a cynical twist on her lips as she whispered, "I hope it's better in America than here, but I think it's all the same no matter where you go!"

The gulls circled, their voices raucous. Their white breasts formed a glaring contrast to the iron gray sky and the sea beneath, and Lorna watched them until they rose, circled, then turned back toward the shores of England.

Chapter 9

The Winds of War

The war hovered over the North like a huge dark shadow during the early summer of 1863. The winter had passed with a sullen discontent, but by mid-June new defenders poured into Washington. But there was no relief in the city, for, louder and more perilous than the distant roar of guns at Vicksburg, an ominous rumble had sounded beyond the Blue Ridge. Daily hundreds of rumors flew along the streets of the capital. Frank Rocklin listened to these avidly, anxious for his father. The details were varied and contradictory, but one thing was clear: General Lee and the Army of Northern Virginia were marching north.

Frank Rocklin, caught up in trying to master a new profession, was troubled by all of this. He spent as much time with his mother as possible, and the two of them waited impatiently for word from Tyler and Bob. Vicksburg was invested and the siege was on, and though Frank said nothing to his mother, he felt the worst was yet to come for his brothers.

On June 16, the report of Rebels crossing into Maryland spread. A week and a half later, as Frank made his way from his home to Ford's Theater for the evening performance, he was aware that crowds were gathering in front of the newspaper offices. When he stopped to listen, he heard one of the editors repeating to the nervous listeners how Rebel troops were in Chambersburg in Pennsylvania. A sense of panic seized the city, and that night the audience was scant.

Booth was excited, the cast saw, and after the performance, he disappeared without a word. Frank knew the actor was sympathetic to the Confederate cause, and this troubled him.

On June 27, Washington listened to heavy artillery fire from the direction of the Bull Run Mountains. General Hooker was abruptly relieved of command of the army and replaced by General George G. Meade the next day. Meade was a little-known commander with a bleak scholar's face, and he at once moved to meet Lee's army.

The two armies groped blindly and finally found each other at Gettysburg. For three days Washington held its breath. All during the evening of July 3 and for most of the night, the burning of firecrackers, squibs, and rockets ushered in the celebration of Independence Day.

Late in the afternoon of the Fourth, Frank was with his mother at home. He looked up startled when a neighbor came running down the street waving a paper. "Lee's been beaten!" he yelled, and Frank and his mother went out on the front porch at once. Harold Dement's face glowed as he yelled, "We whupped the Rebels! The Army of the Potomac's whupped Lee!"

"Thank God!" Melanie whispered, leaning against Frank. "Now if we can just hear that your father's safe!"

Frank hugged her, saying, "He'll be fine, Mother! I know he will! And Tyler and Bob—we'll have them all home again soon." He held her tightly, speaking cheerfully, but he knew the odds of battle too well. *Three of them—and that's three chances for us to lose at least one of them!* He tried to brush the thought away, but as the two of them moved back into the house, he had a strange feeling that the men of the Rocklin tribe would not escape the fires of this battle unscathed.

The next day the news came that Vicksburg had fallen to the forces of General Grant. The double victory sent the nation into a heady celebration. Across the North boomed the salutes of guns. Bells rang and buildings were adorned with garish banners. People cheered the names of Grant and Sherman, the heroes of the hour.

But Meade did not destroy Lee's army. He could have done so, for the Confederates were broken, but he did not move. The Army of Northern Virginia crept back to Virginia bleeding but not destroyed.

"Meade let them get away!" Frank exclaimed with disgust. "He had Lee in his hand but didn't have the nerve to push at him!"

Lincoln felt the same way, and he wrote a scathing letter to Meade—then refused to mail it. "I wasn't there," he said sadly. "I can't judge General Meade from the safety of Washington."

And so the Union was not saved, and a longer war loomed ahead despite victories at Gettysburg and Vicksburg. The golden opportunity slipped away from the North, and grimly both North and South prepared for the bloodbath that all knew would come.

The city of Washington was not at all what Lorna Grey had expected. She had come to believe that the capital of the country would be somewhat grand, and when she got her first glimpse of the city, she was shocked at its crude appearance.

As Thomas Cooper took the company from the station to their hotel, she noted that there was a random sort of feeling connected with Washington. Outside the area where the population was concentrated were lonely tracts of woodlands and commons, broken at intervals by large estates, planted and bowered in trees. But adjoined to the rather attractive sections she saw shantytowns, their dusty streets lined with dingy buildings. Rain had turned the roadbeds into channels of mud, and the open sewer of the canal sent a malignant stink over the area.

Cooper kept up a running conversation as the carriage took the company down the city's main thoroughfare, Pennsylvania Avenue. "Now then, ain't this fine!" he exclaimed, apparently excited by the view of the restaurants and shops that were all located on the north side of the avenue. Lorna thought the hotels, which were a recent development, ugly to a fault, but said nothing.

Unfortunately, the company arrived in the capital when Congress was in session. At such times the hotels and all their halls, dining rooms, and bars were packed. The din as they entered their hotel, a smallish one called the Morgan House, was frightful. Cooper's face dropped when he negotiated the price for the room, for rates were high and the clerks haughty and short-tempered.

Finally, Lorna found herself in a very small room with a bed, a table, one chair, and a washstand. Eileen Fenton, her roommate, took one look at the lumpy mattress and complained, "I think I'll try the *floor*. It looks *far* more comfortable than that *bed*!" Eileen was a short, rather overweight actress who, at the age of twenty-nine, had passed the point of playing youthful heroines. She had been rather successful in such roles when she was eighteen and still persisted in trying to recapture her early triumphs. Cooper, desperate for actors and actresses to join him in the rash venture, had agreed to give her better roles than she'd been able to find in England. She was a nervous, high-strung woman who complained constantly, and now as Lorna unpacked her trunk, Eileen moved about the room finding fault with every element from the wallpaper to the water pitcher, which had a minuscule crack on the handle.

"We'll just have to make the best of it, I suppose," Lorna offered mildly. She was actually sick to death of Eileen's constant complaining and longed for nothing more than peace and quietness.

"I'm going to *demand* that Thomas get me a *private* room!" Eileen could not speak without emphasizing far too many of the words she uttered—which in effect meant that people soon stopped paying any heed at all to what she said. Now she turned and left the room, her shrill voice raised as she said, "How does he *expect* an actress to *perform* when she has no *privacy*!"

Lorna sighed with relief as the door slammed. She was exhausted, for the voyage had been stormy and the accommodations poor. For weeks the ship, a converted merchant ship with the unlikely name of *Pride of Albion*, had wallowed in the troughs of the roaring waves for what seemed like months. Eileen had been seasick and so frightened that she'd kept Lorna by her side constantly.

"I should have stayed in England," Lorna murmured then shook her head in a firm manner, knowing she could not look back. She had little money, and her only hope was to make the best of the situation. Removing her dress, she stared down at her petticoat, which was a new style, the forerunner of a hooped crinoline. It had been fresh and stiff once, but life at sea had offered no opportunity for keeping clothing in that condition. Stripping it off, she examined the parallel rows of stitching around the bottom that stiffened it, noting that the threads were pulling loose. She took advantage of the moment of privacy to strip off the Greek-style *zora*, which consisted of a silk garment wrapped around her upper body, then the lace-trimmed pantalets. She had not had a thorough bath for days, and now she used all the fresh water, luxuriating in the smell of soap and the sensation of cleanliness. Quickly she dried herself with the rather skimpy towel and put on a cotton nightgown. Fatigue struck her, and she stripped the covers back, fell into the bed, and was asleep instantly.

She awoke to the sound of Eileen's voice, complaining as usual. "And I told *him* that if I didn't get my *own* room—why, he could get *another* artist!" Eileen looked over and saw that Lorna was awake and said, "We're all going to the *theater*, Lorna. I *told* Thomas it wasn't likely we'd see any *acting*, but he says we *must* scout out the competition."

Lorna, refreshed by her bath and rest, rose and dressed. She had brought a small trunk filled with clothing and now slipped into ankle-length pantalets, a plain petticoat, and a crinoline "pouf" with hoops and ribbon ties to hold the front closure in place. Her dress was striped satin, blue and white, and after checking herself one last time, Lorna said, "I'm ready, Eileen."

The two found the rest of the company waiting, and after a rather poorly cooked meal, they left the hotel and, with some difficulty, packed themselves into a carriage. Since there were eight members of the company, Lorna found herself squeezed between Jonathan Bratton, the leading man, and Lyle Defore, who played either villains or heroes as was needed. Both of them had made advances to Lorna, which she had fended off so adamantly that each had made a truce with her. Across from Lorna three rather seedy actors shared the seat with Eileen. They all were tired and uncertain and therefore said little. Eileen's complaints, however, made up for that.

Lorna was relieved when they arrived, and when they were seated in Ford's Theater, she was pleased to find herself seated between Cooper and David Talbot, a young man of seventeen who was very shy—for an actor.

"What's the play, Mr. Cooper?" Talbot asked.

"Why, it's Mr. Booth's *Hamlet*." Cooper turned to add, "It's John Wilkes Booth—not his famous brother."

"Have you seen him act?"

"No, but if he's anything like his father or brother, he's excellent."

As it developed, Lorna was not at all impressed by the star of the play. He was, she thought, more of a gymnast than an actor. She watched as Booth cavorted about the stage, sawing the air with his hands constantly. Finally, she whispered to Cooper, "I don't care for him. He's like some sort of puppet that one winds up—and he goes until he runs down."

"I must say he's a bit *much*," Cooper agreed. "Some of the rest of the cast aren't bad. That young fellow playing Laertes is rather good. What's his name?"

Lorna peered at the program she held then whispered, "Frank Rocklin." She watched as the sword fight was enacted then commented, "I must say, Booth is better with a sword than he is with a line." When the play was over, they went backstage and met the star and his cast. Booth welcomed them and wished them well in their new venture. He frowned, adding, "There's need in our country for English excellency on the boards. I'll expect to hear great things from your company, Mr. Cooper."

Lorna shook hands with Booth then turned to find the young actor who'd played Laertes standing beside her. She hesitated then said, "I enjoyed your performance, Mr. Rocklin."

"Why—thank you, Miss...?"

"Lorna Grey."

"Miss Grey, I'm so new to this profession that I gather up any crumbs of appreciation that fall in my path." Rocklin was impressed with the poise of the young woman, as well as with her serene beauty. "Have you been acting long?" He listened as Lorna gave him a brief answer, then smiled at her. "Welcome to America. I wish you a prosperous tour." He was very handsome, his raven-dark hair and dark eyes set off by olive skin and even features. "I'll come to see you if I can. Where will you be playing?"

"We open in a week," Lorna answered. "At the Belleview Theater." She saw something in Rocklin's face change as she named the theater, and she asked, "Is something wrong, sir?"

"Well, not really." Frank Rocklin hesitated then said honestly, "The Belleview isn't quite as ornate as—well, as Ford's. But it's the performance that counts, not the place," he added quickly. He bowed and moved to speak to others who were waiting, but his reaction stayed with Lorna.

On their way back to the hotel, she thought, *The Belleview must be a pretty dreary place. I could see Mr. Rocklin was a little shocked that we'd be playing there.* She thought of this then shrugged, for there was nothing to be done. She did remember more of Rocklin than she did of Booth in the days to come. There was an intensity in him that impressed her. *He's going to do well*, she thought. *He has talent, looks, and he knows what he wants.*

"You're going to do *what*?"

Frank stared at his mother blankly, certain that he had misunderstood her. Since the news had arrived that Gideon had been captured at Gettysburg and taken to Richmond as a prisoner of war, Melanie had been quiet. Frank had been bitter, for he had heard of the terrible conditions of the camps and prisons where captured men suffered. He'd come down for breakfast and had been shocked as his mother faced him and spoke of her intentions to go to Richmond.

"I'm going to Richmond to take care of your father, Frank." There was an iron quality in Melanie's voice, and Frank knew that when his mother had that certain glint in her eyes, argument was useless. He listened as she told him that Clay had sent her a letter telling her of Gideon's location and condition. "You can read the letter," Melanie said, holding it out to him.

Frank scanned the short letter then frowned. "I was hoping he was doing better. But going to Richmond can be dangerous," he protested.

Melanie answered emphatically, "I don't care. Your father is sick, and he needs me."

"But you don't know that you can get to him!"

"God will be with me."

Frank protested the rest of the evening and thought he had convinced his mother to wait for official channels to help his father. But the next morning Frank found a note from his mother saying that she had left for Richmond and not to worry. "God will take care of me" was the last line of the note.

Upset that his mother had left on such a dangerous journey,

Frank couldn't sit around the house. He dressed and went out for a long walk. His square shoulders were slumped and his mouth was a bitter line as he wandered D.C. He went to the newspaper office and read the list of dead, wounded, and captured that was posted on the outside, his eyes bleak.

He straightened when he found no mention of his brothers, and a gust of relief passed his lips. "Well, there's hope," he muttered. Still, he knew that after a battle, many soldiers killed in the action were buried in mass graves and it was as if they had disappeared.

That would be the worst, he thought, turning to make his way to the theater. *Not to know—just to think about their bodies thrown into an unmarked grave!* He shook his shoulders, forced the thought out of his mind, and walked rapidly away. *They'll be all right—God won't let them die!*

※

A faint but persistent banging noise brought Frank out of a sound sleep. He had been dreaming of some ridiculous escapade in which he was vaguely aware that it *was* a dream. It involved a party in which he was involved with several animals that were making strange noises. Somehow the cries of the animals were transformed into a persistent knocking sound, and he came out of sleep abruptly, sitting up in bed with a start. Staring around wildly, he realized someone was knocking at the door.

Scrambling out of bed, he grabbed his pants and struggled into them; then when he dashed across the room, he kicked a low stool he'd forgotten was there.

"Blast!" he groaned, grabbing his shin and hopping on his other foot. The steady rapping continued, and he hobbled out of his bedroom. He groped his way to a table in the hall, found a jar of matches, and managed to light a lamp. Replacing the chimney, he made his way to the front door. Slipping the bolt, he pulled the door half open and peered at the dark, shadowy figure of a man outlined in the opening.

"What the blazes do you want?" he rasped, holding the light up so that the amber light fell on the face of the visitor.

"Hello, Frank."

Frank blinked with astonishment as he recognized the drawn features of his oldest brother. "Tyler!" he exclaimed and at once reached out and pulled him inside and closed the door.

"I thought nobody was home," Tyler said, taking off his coat.

"Did you get our letter about Dad getting captured at Gettysburg?" Frank asked.

"Yes."

Tyler looked exhausted, and he had a guarded expression on his face. At once alarm shot through Frank, and he grabbed Tyler's arm, his voice going tense. "Where's Bob?"

"Well—"

"He's dead, isn't he?"

"No! Nothing like that!" Tyler shot back. "He was wounded, but I got him out of Vicksburg."

Frank saw that Tyler was groggy with fatigue and worn thin with the rigors of battle. "Come on," he said, "I'll fix you something to eat while you tell me about it." He led the way to the kitchen, and shoving Tyler into a chair, he fired up the stove.

By the time the eggs and bacon were cooked, Frank had told Tyler all that he knew about their father's capture. Tyler began to eat hungrily, washing the food down with greedy gulps of strong black coffee. When he was finished, he shoved the plate back and began to speak of the last days of Vicksburg. He sketched the battle quickly then said with a bitter note in his voice, "Bob got hit just four days before the surrender."

"How bad is he, Ty?"

"A shell went off just over the trench we were in. Killed two men. Bob got some of the blast from the powder in the face. One piece of shrapnel got him in the chest. I got him to the surgeon, and he patched him up. He got a fever after the operation, and I thought he'd die." Tyler leaned his head down on his hands in a gesture of utter fatigue. He remained there for a few moments then lifted his head to stare at his brother. His voice was hoarse as he said, "He's blind, Frank."

Frank bit his lips, and he lowered his head to stare at the table. "Any chance he'll ever see again?"

"The doctors gave us no hope."

"That's bad," Frank said quietly. "What about the wound in his chest?"

"Making a good recovery. I left him in the hospital—used to be the old Union Hotel, but they've made a hospital of it."

"I'll go right down," Frank said, rising to his feet. "You go to bed, Ty."

"Think I will." Tyler rose, his eyes bleary with want of sleep, then pulled his shoulders back as he looked at Frank. "I'm grateful all three of us are alive," he said quietly. "But it's hard to take, Bob losing his eyes."

Frank could not speak of that but said bitterly, "He didn't have that kind of thing coming to him, Ty—not Bob!"

"A lot of good men got a rough deal, Frank, and some of them wore Confederate gray." He turned and made his way out of the kitchen, his back bent with fatigue. At once Frank cleaned up the kitchen and went to dress. There was a dullness in him as he saddled a horse and mounted. As he made his way along the darkened streets, headed for the hospital, bitterness rose in him.

"Why'd it have to be Bob?" he said aloud then clamped his lips together. He'd never been good with people who'd suffered tragedy. Going to a home where death had come had been a terrible thing for him. He could never think of a single thing to say that made any sense at all. Now he had to go to his brother, who'd lost the great gift of sight.

What can I say to him? If it were me, I'd kill myself, I reckon. He went over the situation in his mind and found guilt rising in him. *Maybe if I'd stayed with him, it wouldn't have happened,* he thought, and though the rational part of him told him there was no certainty of this, he could not shake it off.

When he dismounted and tied his horse in front of the Union Hospital, he had tried himself and returned a guilty verdict. As he mounted the steps and passed inside, bitterness seared his spirit like a hot iron.

Pausing before a large woman who sat at a table, he said, "I'm looking for Robert Rocklin."

The woman was rolling bandages, and there was a light of pity in her face as she looked up. "I'm Miss Alcott," she answered. "Your brother Tyler said you'd be coming."

"Can I see him?"

"I expect he's asleep. You can sit beside him if you like."

"I want to."

Miss Alcott rose and led Frank down a hall then into a long room filled with cots. Lamps burned faintly at each end, giving nurses enough light to see by. She stopped by a cot and whispered, "Are you awake, Robert?"

"Yes."

"Your brother Frank is here." She busied herself getting a chair and placing it beside the bed then whispered to Frank, "You have a fine family, Mr. Rocklin."

When the nurse left, Frank sat down and cleared his throat. "How do you feel, Bob?"

"Not bad. My chest hurts a little sometimes, but Miss Alcott gives me something for it. I'm pretty fuzzy right now."

Frank hesitated then said, "I came as soon as Tyler got home." He struggled to find words, and anger ran through him at seeing his brother stretched out blind and helpless. He fought it down then slowly reached over and took Bob's hand. At once he felt the pressure and returned it.

"I'm glad you're back safe, Bob," he whispered finally. The pressure on his hand grew, and the two sat there in the darkened room holding to each other. After a time, Frank whispered, "I'm sorry about—" He could not finish what he'd planned to say, and then he saw that Bob was asleep. He clung to the still hand, and slowly the tears ran down his cheeks unheeded.

Chapter 10

"God Let It Happen!"

The staff of Union Hospital had grown accustomed to the visitor, for he came often. Louisa May Alcott had asked one of the male nurses about the stout, gray-haired man and had been told, "Why, his name's Whitman—Walt, I think his first name is. Some kind of a writer."

It took Miss Alcott some time to discover that Walt Whitman had written a slender book of poems entitled *Leaves of Grass*. It was reputed to be vulgar, so she didn't read it, of course. She herself had begun to be known as a writer of tales and poems and made it her business to get to know Whitman.

"My brother was wounded at Fredericksburg," Whitman told her when she engaged him in a brief conversation. "I came to see him and got caught up in our brave wounded fellows." The poet was slow-moving and had opaque, heavy-lidded eyes and wore no tie. His spotless white shirt was Byronic, and there was an unusual daintiness about the big man. He was only forty-four years old but seemed older.

"The men are grateful for your faithful visits, Mr. Whitman," Miss Alcott said. "It's good of you to come so regularly. Do you have your own business?"

"Oh no, Miss Alcott! I do a little clerking, a little hacking for newspapers." Whitman shrugged. "I do some copying in the paymaster general's office for two hours or so each day." His bluff, reddish face grew sad, and he added, "I see some of our wounded men climbing to the top floor, and sometimes they find a hitch in their papers and can't get paid. It's a sad thing to watch."

"How terrible! But you always bring little presents—and the men are so grateful."

"I wish I could do more. I've asked some friends and my family to help, and they do." He lifted the haversack in his hand, his soulful eyes grown warm. "Look, I brought pens and pencils, writing paper and envelopes. And I brought some pickles and horehound candy—and some jelly, you see?" He smiled as she exclaimed over his small store, then added, "I give them plugs of tobacco, and sometimes I can spare a little cash to buy the fresh milk that's for sale in the wards."

"Are you a minister, Mr. Whitman?"

The woman's question seemed to amuse Whitman. "I believe we're all ministers, Miss Louisa," he said quietly. He left her then and passed into the ward. For three hours he moved from bed to bed, writing letters, reading to some, sometimes playing Twenty Questions. Walt Whitman believed in the curative properties of affection, and he often stroked the hands or feverish brows of the sick men, whispering encouragement.

"Well now, how are you today, Robert?" he asked, coming to sit down beside the soldier whose eyes were bound with a linen bandage.

"Fine, Mr. Whitman." Bob Rocklin turned his head to face the man who sat down beside him and smiled. "Did you bring your poems today as you promised?"

"Oh yes. But I brought something sweeter." Rummaging in his knapsack, he came up with a small orange and placed it in Bob's hands. "Nothing sweeter than a good orange!"

"Why, I've always been partial to oranges, sir. I'll eat it later."

"I've got the latest edition of the newspaper. Let me read the gist of it...."

Whitman read in a clear tenor voice, stopping to comment from time to time on the news. Finally, he noted a young man in rather dandified dress approach, and he stopped reading. "You have a visitor, Robert," Whitman said. He got up, but the young man shook his head. "I'll get this stool, sir," he said and moved a three-legged stool to the opposite side of the bed. "How are you, Bob?"

"Fine, fine. This is my brother Frank—and this is Mr. Walt Whitman."

Frank leaned over and shook the man's hand, saying, "Nice of you to visit with our men, sir. Miss Alcott tells me you rarely fail."

Whitman shook off the praise and said quickly, "I'll leave you two to visit—"

"Not before you read some of your poetry, Mr. Whitman," Bob broke in. "Frank's the real authority on poetry in our family. He'll probably have to explain to me what it means after you leave."

Whitman smiled gently then took a small book out of his knapsack. Opening it, he found a page and began to read:

"A child said What is the grass? fetching it to me with full hands;

How could I answer the child? I do not know what it is any more than he.

I guess it must be the flag of my disposition, out of hopeful green stuff woven.
Or I guess it is the handkerchief of the Lord,
A scented gift and remembrancer designedly dropt,
Bearing the owner's name someway in the corners, that we may see and remark, and say Whose?"

"Why, even I can understand that!" Bob exclaimed. Turning to Frank he demanded, "Why didn't you tell me poetry could be so easy?"

Frank was puzzled by the poem and shook his head. "Your poetry's not like any I've read, sir. I'd like to read more of it."

Whitman reached into his knapsack, pulled out another volume, and handed it to Frank. A humorous grin touched his full lips. "I have a library of two thousand books, sir, and I wrote every one of them."

Frank laughed, liking the man. He opened the book and began reading aloud where Whitman had left off:

"Or I guess the grass is itself a child, the produced babe of the vegetation.
Or I guess it is a uniform hieroglyphic,
And it means, Sprouting alike in broad zones and narrow zones,
Growing among black folks as among white,
Kanuck, Tuckahoe, Congressman, Cuff, I give them the same, I receive them the same.
And now it seems to me the beautiful uncut hair of graves.
Tenderly will I use you curling grass,
It may be you transpire from the breasts of young men,

It may be if I had known them I would have loved them,
It may be you are from old people, or from offspring taken soon out of their mothers' laps,
And here you are the mothers' laps."

Frank's voice was deep and rich, and when he paused, Whitman said, "You read very well, Mr. Rocklin."

"I've never seen poetry like this," Frank repeated. "Which poets did you model your work on?"

Whitman shook his head. "We must speak with our own voice. It may be the world will not hear a new voice, being content with old ones, but every man is different. In that book I say, 'I celebrate myself.' Some have said that is egotistical, but we are all specially made, all of us different."

"That's so, Mr. Whitman," Bob said, his voice quiet and certain. "And all made by God to serve Him."

"Do you believe in God, sir?" Frank inquired.

Whitman was not offended. He looked at the book in Frank's hands, saying, "Read on ahead, sir."

Frank scanned the page then read slowly:

"I wish I could translate the hints about the dead young men and women,
And the hints about old men and mothers, and the offspring taken soon out of their laps.
What do you think has become of the young and old men?
And what do you think has become of the women and children?
They are alive and well somewhere,
The smallest sprout shows there is really no death."

Frank looked up quickly, a frown on his brow. "It's hard for those who've buried their dead to believe this, Mr. Whitman."

"Death is not the end, Frank." It was Bob who spoke up, and there was a firm smile on his lips as he turned to face his brother. "Jesus came out of the tomb—and all of those who believe and trust in Him will do the same."

The eyes of the poet and the actor met across the body of the stricken man, and it was Whitman who said gently, "I honor your faith, Robert." He rose, saying, "I trust you will find something in my verses to your liking, Mr. Rocklin."

Frank watched the sturdy figure move away then shook his head. "What do you make of him, Bob?"

"He loves people. You can feel it, can't you?"

"I guess so. But he's sure a different kind of poet from any I've read." He sat beside Bob, giving him the details of his day. Finally, he said, "You look better. More color in your cheeks."

"I feel better. The doctor says I'm keeping a real sick man from a bed." Bob shifted and said, "I'd like to come home, Frank."

"I'll talk to the doctor." He remained for another hour, mostly reading from Whitman's book of poetry, then rose, saying, "I'll see you tomorrow. Ty will be in as soon as he gets back with the company—probably next week."

Frank left the ward and stopped by the table where Miss Alcott was working on her bandages. "Do you have a minute to spare?" he asked.

"Why, certainly, Mr. Rocklin." Miss Alcott rose and nodded to her left. "Come along, and I'll see if we can't have some tea."

Ten minutes later the two were sitting at a table in the mess hall, and as she talked, Frank studied her. Louisa May Alcott was thirty-one years old, he had discovered, and was plain and quite strong. She was a large, bashful woman with dark eyes and long hair bundled up in braids at the back of her head. Frank had watched her in action, and like other inexperienced nurses, she shed tears often, smoothed brows, and sometimes sang lullabies and placed nosegays on pillows. She joked and gossiped, played games with the patients, and armed herself with a bottle of lavender water to drown out the bad smells.

"How did you happen to get into nursing?" Frank asked. He liked this woman a great deal and knew that she had done much for his brother.

"Oh, I've always been a romantic," Miss Alcott confessed shyly. "I suppose I want to be like Clara Barton—rush to the battlefield as she's done—but I'll never do that!" She leaned forward, placed her chin on her hands, and smiled at herself. "I remember when I came here my first time. Forty wagons filled with wounded men were lined up right out there, Frank. They were brought in, and I nearly fainted! A more pitiful-looking sight you never saw! Ragged, gaunt, and pale, muddy, and with bloody bandages untouched since they'd been put on."

"And what did you do?"

"A nurse put a block of brown soap in my hands and told me to start cleaning the men up. I was flabbergasted—but there was no way out of it. There I was, a spinster lady, and I was to wash those men!" Laughter ran over the nurse's face, and she giggled. "My first man was old and Irish, and I scrubbed him down and stuffed him with soup. After that, it was all right."

Frank enjoyed listening to Miss Alcott but finally got to the subject of Robert. "How is my brother, Miss Alcott?"

"The wound in his chest is healing well. Dr. Anderson said he didn't anticipate any difficulty there."

"But his eyes?"

"Poor boy! Dr. Anderson said he'd never see again! So sad!"

"He wants to go home. Do you think he could?"

Miss Alcott thought hard then nodded slowly. "You'd have to check with one of the doctors. But with good nursing, he could go, I think. But unless you've got somebody to stay with him, he might be better off here until his wound is completely healed."

"My mother would do it, but she's out of town." Frank got to his feet, saying, "Thanks for the tea—and for all you've done for Bob."

"He's a dear fellow!" Tears welled in the dark eyes, and Miss Alcott shook her head. "He'll need love to get over the loss of his sight. I wish his mother were home. There's nobody like a mother in a case like this."

"Perhaps she'll be home soon. I'll ask Dr. Anderson if he'll release him."

Dr. Anderson said much the same as Nurse Alcott. "He'll need some care, but he'll be fine with that."

Frank then faced the doctor squarely. "Is there *no* chance he'll ever see, Doctor?"

Anderson was a burly man of sixty, with much experience in battlefield wounds. He was accustomed to giving bad news, but he never had learned to like it. Now he said bluntly, "I hate to raise false hopes, Mr. Rocklin. Better to face the facts, I think." He thought for a moment then said evenly, "The eyes are intact, but there's a great deal of damage apparently to the optic nerve. We don't know too much about that part of the body—and practically nothing about how to treat such injuries."

When Anderson paused, Frank stared at him hard. "So there *is* a chance, even if it's small? Is that what you're saying?"

"Don't allow yourself to hope—and don't offer any to your

brother. Miracles happen—at least things that we can't explain," Dr. Anderson shot back. "In Robert's case, that's what it would take. It's almost—" He sought for a way to put the concept into words then shrugged his thick shoulders. "It's almost the same as saying that a man who's lost an arm would have to grow another arm. I never heard of such a thing. It would be unwise for Robert to spend his life counting on it."

Frank nodded slowly then said, "I'll find someone to take care of him, Doctor. And as for the rest—"

"He'll have to fill his life with other things, Mr. Rocklin. It's not the end of the world. He has all his other senses; he can walk and learn to do some kinds of work. I'm sorry I don't have better news for you."

Frank thanked the physician then left the hospital. He moved through the performance that night, his mind on the problem of finding someone to stay with Bob. After the play he was surprised to see his aunt Laura Steele enter the backstage area. She was accompanied by her husband, Amos, a minister. Laura came to him with a bright smile, saying, "You were wonderful, Frank!"

Frank took her kiss on his cheek then turned with a smile to her husband. "I'm surprised to see you here, Uncle. I thought you were opposed to the theater."

Amos Steele was a tall man with piercing hazel eyes. He was not a man of great humor, but he smiled now, saying, "Your aunt is educating me, Frank. I suppose I'll be going to bet on horse races before she's through with me." He put his hand out, saying, "I'm impressed with your play. Always loved *Hamlet*."

"Come now, we've come to kidnap you," Laura teased. "We're going to feed you, and you're going to tell us all about the wicked ways of the theater!"

Frank truly enjoyed the meal with Amos and Laura. He'd always been fond of them and was aware that they had come to the play to show their loyalty to his choice. He listened as they talked about their children, especially about the coming marriage of Deborah and Noel. Clinton, their youngest son, was in college, while Colin and Pat were both in the army.

Finally, it was Laura who asked about Robert. The pair listened as Frank told them of the tragedy. His voice was unsteady, and he said bitterly, "God let it happen! It didn't have to be like this!"

Amos Steele resisted the impulse to launch into a theological debate, but with the aid of one warning look from his wife, he said merely, "I'm sorry, Frank. We're very fond of Robert."

"When can he come home?" Laura asked.

"Oh, he can leave the hospital now," Frank said. "But I'm gone every night, and with Mother in Richmond, there's nobody to take care of him."

A swift glance passed between Amos and his wife. "He'll come with us," Laura said firmly. When Frank started with surprise, she added tartly, "Don't look so shocked. We're family, I suppose you know? And you're coming to live with us, too. You'll be company for him."

When Frank tried to protest, Amos said sharply, "Don't argue, nephew. Laura and I rattle around in that big house with all the children gone. It'll be nice having young people there again. Besides," he added, "you know how well Robert and I always got on. He was planning to study with me. Well, we'll do it now!"

Frank felt a lump in his throat at the kindness and nodded. With some difficulty, he said, "I'll bring him tomorrow."

"It'll be a blessing having both of you," Amos said.

"Uncle Amos—I didn't mean to speak so—about God."

"I know, Frank," Steele said gently. "But He's probably used to our foolish speeches. Come now, let's look to Him in all things!"

※

The next day Frank came to stand beside Bob, who was sitting up on his bed. Something about the helpless attitude of his brother struck a sad chord in Frank, and he covered it by saying brusquely, "Well, you've soldiered on me long enough. Come on, time to move on."

"Move on?" Bob's lips tightened slightly. "I can stay here, you know."

"No, you can't." Frank had brought fresh clothing, including a flannel gown and robe. "Here, get into this. We're going to live with Aunt Laura and Uncle Amos—at least until Mother gets home."

Bob made no protest and slipped into the garments. Frank had paid two of the attendants to carry Bob on a stretcher, and they made the trip with no trouble. When they arrived, his uncle and aunt came down the steps. "We've made up Patrick's room for you, Bob—and you can have Colin's room, Frank. You'll be close together that way."

Amos came over to stand beside the still form of Bob lying on the stretcher. "Well now, Robert," he said loudly, "now we'll be able to get this matter of sanctification straight, won't we?" Leaning down he took the young man's hand and squeezed it warmly. "I trust that I'll be able to—ah—*enlighten* you on that doctrine." Then he straightened up and dismissed the attendants with a nod.

As Amos got Bob settled, Frank spoke with his aunt. "It's

wonderful for you to take us in, Aunt Laura," he said. "I was about out of ideas."

Laura smiled then kissed him on the cheek. "We're going to see God do great things, Frank. Now you go up and stay with Bob. I'll make one of those peach pies you both love so well." She went to the kitchen and stood there for one moment silently. Then, looking up, she lifted her hands and pleaded, "Lord, do a mighty work in Bob, and in Frank, and in all of us!"

Thomas Cooper had gathered the company into the stage area early in the afternoon. Most of the cast assumed they were going to be asked to rehearse and were sullen. But something about the pale cast of Cooper's face caught Lorna's attention. *He's afraid of something,* she thought, and she listened closely as the stubby manager called for their attention.

"Well now, I wish I had good news for you," Cooper said in a strangely flat voice. He took out a limp handkerchief and mopped his brow.

"Well, what *is* it, Thomas?" Eileen demanded. "What's wrong *this* time?"

Others of the company began complaining, and Cooper suddenly lifted his head. "Might as well give it to you straight." He hesitated one moment, shrugged, and said, "The tour is off."

Every member of the cast stared at him, and it was Lorna who spoke. "What's happened, Mr. Cooper?"

"It's a bust, that's all. You've seen how the house has been off. And two of the theaters I thought were booked have canceled." He gave them a defensive look, adding, "I'm sorry, but that's the way it is. I've got tickets to get us back home—and that's what we've got to do."

What followed was a tide of angry recriminations and threats of lawsuits. Most of the actors, however, were hardened to the facts of touring and made the best of it. When Cooper said the ship would sail the next day, there was a bustle to get to the hotel and pack.

Lorna stopped Cooper as he turned to leave. "Mr. Cooper, could I have my ticket, please?" she asked.

"Why, it might be better if I kept all of the tickets, Miss Lorna."

"I'm going to cash it in." Seeing the surprise on Cooper's homely face, Lorna said quickly, "I'm not going back to England—not yet, at least."

"But what will you do?" Worry etched itself on the plain features, for he felt responsible for the young woman.

"Don't worry about me, Mr. Cooper. I'll be all right." It took some persuasion on her part, but finally the manager saw that she was adamant. He gave her the ticket reluctantly; then she gave him her hand. "You'll be very busy, so let me say good-bye—and thank you. You've been very kind."

"Aw, now, I wish it hadn't come to this," Cooper muttered. "You take care of yourself, now! You've got talent, and looks, too. When you get back to England, you look me up. We'll do better another time!"

The next day Lorna waved good-bye as the ship bearing the company sailed down the river; then she turned and made her way back to the hotel. She had no idea what she would do, and fear came to her as she sat down in her room. She had very little money, no friends, and no marketable skills. Closing her eyes, she prayed for the first time since she was a small child.

"Oh God, I'm frightened! Take care of me, please, will You?

Don't let me go wrong!" She sat there quietly and was somewhat surprised when, after her rather desperate prayer, a sense of peace came to her. It wasn't much, but as the fear left, her courage rose, and she stood to her feet and left to face the world that lay before her.

CHAPTER 11

MR. PINKERTON MAKES A CALL

"Nothing smells better than a mimosa blossom, does it, Aunt Laura?"

Bob Rocklin stood shaded from the blistering August sun, holding a delicate bloom to his nose. The fine hairlike tendrils tickled his nose, and he smiled broadly. "I wonder why young women haven't come up with a way to make perfume out of this. I'd fall in love with anyone who smelled this good!"

Laura Steele had come to sit in the backyard, hopeful of catching some faint breeze. She looked up from the purple-hulled peas she was shelling and smiled at her nephew. "We called those silk flowers when I was growing up," she remarked. "The trees are always small enough for a child to climb, and I made many a bouquet of silk-tree blossoms."

Bob walked from under the tree, holding out his hands as he approached the house. He wore a pair of dark smoked glasses instead of the bandages he'd worn when he first came. Carefully he reached out until he touched the side of the house, then turned and leaned against it. He wore a pair of faded blue cotton trousers and a thin white shirt of the same material. His face had some color, and he showed little trace of the wound he'd taken.

"Did you change your bandage this morning, Bob?" Laura asked. She had been his nurse for a week after his arrival, but he soon rebelled, insisting that he could take care of his own needs.

"Don't really need one, Aunt Laura." Touching his chest, he nodded, saying, "The scar is all formed; no need to keep a bandage. I think the air is good for it."

"That's good. You need to gain a little weight, though."

"If you keep on stuffing me, I'll be as big as Mrs. Skeffington." He referred to a brood sow that he had raised as a young boy. He smiled at the memory, adding, "Just like an ornery boy, wasn't it, to name a sow after the pastor's wife."

"Well, Sister Mae *was* overweight," Laura admitted then smiled. "I wonder if she ever heard about that sow."

"I hope not. Boys are pretty heartless." Squatting down on his heels, Bob ran the palm of his hand across the stiff tongues of grass then dug his fingers into the ground, loosening the soil and letting it run through his fingers. Laura caught this and thought suddenly, *He has to be touching something all the time—to make up for his lack of sight, I think.* "I brought the newspaper out." She put the pan of peas down and, picking up the paper, began to read.

After the crisis of July, August had been fairly quiet. Robert E. Lee had led the Army of Northern Virginia home to rebuild, and there had been little major military action. On July 13, New York City had been rocked by a draft riot. The draft headquarters had been stormed, residences raided, and businesses looted. Only the troops returning from Gettysburg had stemmed the riot, but it had broken out again in other parts of the city for the next two days.

"It says here that General Lee has offered to resign from the army," Laura commented.

"Davis will never let him do that," Bob spoke up. "Lee's the one indispensable man in the South. They could do without Jefferson Davis, but it's the South's veneration for Lee that keeps them going."

"The navy is attacking Fort Sumter." Laura read the account of the attempts to retake Charleston Harbor then lowered the paper. Her eyes were thoughtful as she said quietly, "It seems like a lifetime ago that the war started—right there at Fort Sumter."

Bob was listening carefully to his aunt and caught the sadness in her tone. He had always been good at reading people, and since the loss of his sight, his hearing seemed to be more acute. "You're worried about Pat and Colin, aren't you, Aunt Laura?"

"I grieve over all of our men. It's like a fog over the land." Her face grew sad, and there was a faint trembling of her lips as she added, "No matter where you go, it's the same. Everybody's got someone in the army or the navy—and they're all in harm's way. We live under the shadow of death. And in the South, I know it's the same."

"One day it'll be over. Until then, we have to trust God, don't we?"

Laura found his faith encouraging. He'd never once complained about his injury but had manifested a cheerful spirit. "I wish Frank wasn't so bitter," she remarked. "He's turning into a sour man, and that's going to destroy him."

"I've tried to talk to him, but he's full of hatred. I think he takes my blindness worse than I do."

"He's worried about Gideon, too."

"Yes, he is. So am I, Aunt Laura, but the scripture says that with God all things are possible. God can keep Dad alive and get him home safely." Bob stood up and lifted his face upward as though seeking some sort of answer to the problems that faced them all. Then he turned his face toward her. "It's good for him to be here—with you and Uncle Amos. It would be good for anyone."

Laura rose and came to take his hand. "You have a sweet spirit, Bob. But don't you ever get depressed? Most people would."

"Sometimes I do," Bob admitted. "But then I know that God has something for me to do. If He didn't have, I'd have been taken home in the battle. I don't know what it is yet, but God will tell me when I'm ready for it. But one thing I can do now—while I'm waiting to find out God's will."

"What's that, Bob?"

"I can go to the hospital. I can visit with the men, take them little gifts, like Mr. Whitman does." This was something that had come to Bob as his strength had returned. He had planned it out, and now his face glowed with excitement as he spoke of his plans. "If you'll bake some cookies or a cake, I could take it to the hospital. And even though I can't read to the men, I can talk to them." He laughed and seemed almost boyish. "And I can practice preaching to them. If God calls me into the ministry, I'll have some experience."

Laura smiled at that and at once joined in helping with a plan. "I'll do the baking, and you do the preaching! When do you think you'll feel up to going?"

Bob was so enthused he was ready to begin that day, but Laura and Amos saw to it that he waited for a week. Frank listened as Bob spoke with enthusiasm of his venture, and he said at once, "I'll go with you as often as I can, Bob." He was glad that Bob had come up with something to throw himself into, and on the first visit to Union Hospital, he'd been glad to see the reception Bob got.

Miss Alcott's eyes had grown large, and she'd come at once to hug Bob, exclaiming, "Why, Robert Rocklin—look at you! You're brown as a berry!" She had taken him at once to the ward, where Bob was greeted by calls from his friends.

Frank stood to one side, leaning against the wall, watching with a faint smile as Bob moved from bed to bed. He wished he could join in, but a strange mood had come upon him— one he couldn't shake off and couldn't explain. Ever since he'd learned of the maiming of his brother, he'd been oppressed by some sort of dull-spirited moodiness. He was able to conceal this from people and had carried on with his work, but it was always there. He was worried about his father, and at times he thought that was his trouble.

At night he would toss on his bed, assailed by a bitterness at the tragedy of his brother. It did him no good to realize that Bob himself had accepted his blindness. Somehow he still had the nagging doubt that if he had stayed at Vicksburg, this might not have happened. He was aware that most of the men in his family wore the uniform—and this troubled him as well.

They're fighting and risking their lives for the Union—and I'm playacting! Even now as he watched Bob speak to a young man with two stubs for legs, Frank felt self-disgust rise inside him. He'd been a man of strong self-esteem, but now that seemed to have been replaced by loathing for what he was. He was in this sort of mood when a voice beside him said, "Good afternoon, Mr. Rocklin."

Frank snapped out of his gloomy reverie and turned to find that Walt Whitman had come to stand beside him. "Oh, hello, Mr. Whitman."

"Your brother is doing well," Whitman said. "I'm glad to see it."

"He's still blind."

Whitman's eyes narrowed at the flat tone of Frank Rocklin's voice. He was a perceptive man and at once understood the bitterness that marked the voice and eyes of the young man next to him. "It's a cruel war—but then, there's no such thing as a 'kind war,' is there?"

"He's taking it better than I am," Frank said in a spare tone. "I'd like to line up the men who got us into this war and shoot them all! The South started all this!"

Whitman listened as Frank Rocklin spoke with fervent bitterness of the war and what it was doing to the country. He made no attempt to speak, for he realized that the young man was using him as some sort of confessor. He was a good listener, this gray poet. He'd heard many voices speak to him what they were ashamed to speak to family or friends.

Finally, Frank halted abruptly and shook his head, a half-shamed and bitter smile on his lips. "Didn't mean to dump all my hard feelings on you, sir. Don't usually do things like that."

"I think we all need to speak what's in our heart, Mr. Rocklin. We think we're alone, that nobody else is as bad off as we are. But we're all alike, really. The whole land is filled with men and women who've suffered loss. Don't think you're alone, my boy!"

"I feel alone, sir!"

Whitman's eyes were large and luminous as he put his hand on Frank's shoulder. "You must not feel so. We are all tied by blood—all of us!"

Frank listened as Whitman spoke, and when the poet left, he thought, *He's a strange one! Wish I could feel like he does—but I can't!* He watched as Bob spoke to the wounded men and could not fathom how a man who'd been stripped of his sight could be so happy. Finally, they left the hospital, and on the way home, Bob said, "Poor fellows! I wish I could do more for them!"

Somehow this love Bob had for the men in the ward came as a rebuke to Frank. He had to force himself to be cheerful, and when he left the house to go to the theater, he muttered almost angrily, "I can't go on like this! I'm getting to be like a mean dog. Next thing I know I'll be snapping at people or biting myself!"

August was hot and sultry, but as it came to an end, the cooling breezes touched Washington with a soothing hand. The discontent that had shaken the city during the summer was less rampant, but everyone knew that the war was simply smoldering. In the West, Rosecrans and his Federal Army of the Cumberland were edging toward Chattanooga—where Bragg and his Army of Tennessee waited. The Army of Northern Virginia was being reformed, and any force that moved toward Richmond would have to contend with it.

As for Frank Rocklin, he struggled with moodiness, performing at night at Ford's, but less and less content with his life. He spent much time with Bob, but Amos Steele had taken his nephew in hand, and the two of them spent long hours in the study of the scriptures. Frank roamed the city aimlessly for hours, trying to find some sort of escape from the discontent that had destroyed his peace of mind.

One night after the performance, he was greeted by Tyler, who had regained his lost weight and looked tanned and fit. "Come along, little brother," Ty said after they'd greeted one another. "I'm starved. You can buy me a steak." The two went out to dinner, and as they ate, Ty recounted his activities. "No fighting—just marching around from one place to another." He drank from his coffee cup then said, "The play's still going well?"

"This is the last week. Booth told us last night we'd be closing."

Ty gave his brother a curious glance. "What happens then? Will you go into another play?"

"Don't know, Ty." Frank stirred restlessly in his chair. "Bob needed me for a while, but he's busy with Uncle Amos."

"I expect he'll make a preacher," Ty commented. "He was always bent that way."

"Can a blind man be a preacher?"

Ty caught the bitterness in Frank's voice. "What's the matter with you, Frank? You're down in the mouth. It's not like you."

Frank hesitated then began to speak of his moodiness. Finally, he ended by saying, "I can't get it out of my mind that if I'd stayed with you two, Bob might not have gotten blinded."

"Or he might have gotten killed—or *you* might have been maimed." Shaking his head, Ty said strongly, "No sense in thinking like that, Frank. You can't go back. And even if you could, you might make things worse." He spoke for a time then leaned forward with a speculative look in his eyes. "You've got something on your mind, haven't you?"

"Well, I guess I have." Frank moved his legs restlessly then blurted out, "I'm thinking of going back into the army, Ty. Never should have left it in the first place. What good have I done? Nothing but prance around on a stage spouting poetry!"

Ty stared at Frank, saying nothing for a time. He knew this younger brother of his fairly well, and finally he said, "It's more than that. I think you'll make a great actor."

"Can't win the war playing Hamlet!"

The two finished their meal, and when they parted, Ty said, "Don't be too quick to jump into a uniform, Frank. Think it over."

"I've got another week of the play. When that's over, I'm going to reenlist."

For the next two days, Frank grew more and more certain that he would enlist in the Washington Blues as soon as he was free. He said nothing to his family, not really wanting to hear their advice. But then he was met again by Tyler after the performance on Wednesday. "Got to talk to you, Frank," he said abruptly.

"All right." They left the theater and Frank asked, "Want to get something to eat at Willards?"

"No. There's a little place over on Elm Street. We'll go there." He led Frank to a small, dingy restaurant wedged between a hardware shop and a laundry. As they entered, he said to the waiter, "We'll eat with that gentleman back there."

Frank followed Ty to the table, where a man wearing a plain brown suit looked up at them. "Sit down," he said quietly. He was a smallish man with a clipped brown beard and a pair of small, steady eyes. "I take it this is your brother, Lieutenant?"

"Yes. Frank Rocklin."

"I've seen you in the play, Mr. Rocklin. Fine performance."

Frank said, "I didn't get your name, sir." He was aware that Ty had not given the man's name and was certain that the omission was deliberate.

"My name is Pinkerton—Allan Pinkerton."

Frank stared at Pinkerton, for he was aware that this was the famous head of the Secret Service. "Glad to know you," he murmured. He glanced at Ty, who shrugged but said nothing.

"Will you order now?" The waiter had appeared, and after

he had taken their order, Pinkerton said, "I suppose you're wondering what this is all about."

"I don't meet with Secret Service men often."

Pinkerton found this amusing. "I suppose not." He had a tight mouth, opening it to speak, it seemed, with some reluctance. "Tyler, perhaps you'd better explain why I'm here."

"Yes, of course." He turned to face Frank, asking, "You remember how I was wounded at Bull Run?"

"Yes. You were laid up for quite a while."

"Do you remember the young woman who nursed me? Frankie Aimes?"

"Why, certainly. She married our uncle Paul, didn't she?"

"Yes, but what you don't know is that she was an agent for Mr. Pinkerton—and so was I."

Frank stared at Ty with surprise, saying, "I didn't know that!"

"Neither does anyone else, and I'd appreciate it if you'd keep it to yourself," Ty said at once. He hesitated then said, "Ever since you told me you were going to reenlist, I've been thinking about something. Finally, I went to Mr. Pinkerton and laid it out. He was very interested, and I think you should hear what he's got to say."

Frank turned to look at Pinkerton, who said at once, "It's commendable of you to want to reenlist, Mr. Rocklin, but I think I've got a better plan." He smiled briefly, asking, "Perhaps you can guess what it is?"

But Frank was mystified. "What kind of a plan, sir?"

"I want you to join my force," Pinkerton said, smiling slightly at the shock that came to the face of the young man. Turning to Tyler he said, "He's as surprised as you were when I asked you to join us."

"Me? Become a spy?"

"An *agent*, Mr. Rocklin!"

"I don't see that calling it something different makes it better." Frank shook his head. "I'd be no good at that sort of thing—decoding messages and so on. I can shoot, and that's what I'm going to do."

Pinkerton grew stern, his voice firm. "You're determined to serve your country, but don't you owe it to your country to serve in the best way you can?"

"Yes, but—"

"We have one hundred thousand men to fire muskets, Mr. Rocklin, but almost no one can do the job I need *you* for." When Frank stared at him with an unbelieving expression, Pinkerton spoke rapidly. "We've lost battles because our generals had almost no reliable information. This war is going to be bloody to the end, so we must do all we can to end it quickly! And one way to do that is to provide accurate information to those who have to go in and do the fighting."

Frank listened as Pinkerton spoke with a simple eloquence about the job of the Secret Service. Finally, he shook his head, saying, "I don't disagree with what you say, Mr. Pinkerton. But I'm not fitted to do such work."

"Most of our men started as amateurs. There's no West Point to train agents. Your brother performed well, and I'm convinced that you can do a fine job."

"But why *me*?"

"Ah, you're in a position to move at once into place—because of your profession."

"You mean acting?"

"Exactly! What I propose has never been done—and that's why it will work!"

"Just what is it you have in mind, Mr. Pinkerton?"

"I want you to assemble a company of actors and take it to the South, to New Orleans and especially to Richmond." Pinkerton's smallish eyes gleamed as he spoke rapidly, outlining his plan. "Actors move often, and they meet everyone. You'd be invited to social events where people speak freely."

"But I'm not a star! It's not like I was Edwin or John Booth! I'd never be accepted."

"But Booth doesn't have a family named Rocklin—some of the men in the Confederate army," Pinkerton shot back. "All you have to do is indicate that you're sympathetic to the Southern cause and say that's why you've chosen to bring your company to the South."

Frank was stunned by the idea, but even as he thought of it, he saw the adventure and the difficulties. "But it would take money—"

"That's no problem. The government will foot the bills," Pinkerton said quickly. He was a quick-witted man, and for the next twenty minutes he spoke rapidly, covering most of the difficulties. Finally, he demanded, "Will you do this job, Mr. Rocklin?"

Frank was an impulsive young man. Despite his guilt over Bob, he had dreaded the idea of going into the regular army, but this was different. The romantic side of his nature drew him to such a venture, and he said at once, "I'll do it, sir!"

Relief washed across the face of Pinkerton. "Fine! Now your play is over this week. Can you begin as soon as you're free?"

"Yes, sir, I can do that."

"Good! Now you'll have trouble getting a company. No successful actor or actress will leave here to go into enemy territory. Get whomever you can—but secrecy is vital!"

"Yes, sir. But how do I get information back to you?"

"You'll be given very specific instructions, and you'll be contacted by a very good agent." Pinkerton rose, saying, "Be in front of the Capitol tomorrow morning at ten. You'll be contacted, and we'll give you what training we can. I'm grateful you'll be with us, Frank."

When Pinkerton was gone, Frank stared at the table, wordless for once. Tyler clapped a hand on his shoulder. "Well, it beats digging trenches, little brother. But if you get caught, you'll be executed—so be careful!"

Frank looked up and smiled. "It's a little more in my line, isn't it? I was never a good soldier—like you and Bob, and Dad, of course."

"It's like Pinkerton says, Frank. You might be able to help shorten the war."

Later as Frank made his way to the Steeles' home, he was surprised to discover that the gloomy despair that had oppressed him for days had lifted. He smiled briefly then murmured, "Well, it looks like I'm going to have to be a pretty good actor. I can't afford to put on a bad performance for the Rebels, or they'll stretch my neck!" He laughed aloud and with a zestful air found himself looking for the adventure that lay ahead of him.

CHAPTER 12

A NEW SORT OF COMPANY

Frank felt constrained to mention his plan to form a repertory company to John Wilkes Booth. The actor stared at him with a gleam of interest then demanded, "Why to the South? Do your sympathies lie in that direction?"

"Well, Mr. Booth, I have family there, you know, so I am not exactly anti-Southern," Frank said. "But the truth is, I'm not able to compete with you and the other established stars here in the North."

"But can you make a go of it financially? Things are pretty bad there, I understand."

"I'll have to pay short wages, but it'll be good experience. I think I can get some young people who haven't caught on here and maybe a few who are, well, past their best days."

Booth smiled and offered his hand. "I wish you luck. By the way, I have some friends in the profession there. I'll write you a letter of introduction. It'll open a few doors."

"Why, that's generous of you, sir!" Frank shook Booth's hand and went at once to rent a room at Willards Hotel. He placed an advertisement in the paper then made his way to the Steeles. Finding Bob in the parlor with his uncle, he said, "Well, I'll be out of your way by the end of the week."

"Are you *sure* you want to do this, Frank?" Bob asked. He'd been surprised when Frank had spoken of his new venture, but then, so had the Steeles. "Seems to be a pretty risky sort of thing."

Amos nodded, anxiety on his plain face. "I agree with Bob. As I understand it, acting is a pretty precarious sort of life at best, but to go to the South—!"

"Now we've been through all that," Frank said with a polite smile. He'd been reluctant to leave Bob, but he'd seen that Amos and Laura were what he needed. With that settled, he was happy in a way that none of his family could understand—except for his grandfather, Stephen. The old man had grunted, "He's not got all the foolishness knocked out of him yet. Got to let some of that life in him get spent. He'll probably go broke, but he'll have good memories to keep."

Frank said as he studied Bob carefully, "I'll try to get to see Dad. Mother could probably use some help taking care of him."

"Well, that's true," Bob agreed. "I'm hoping he'll be exchanged soon. When do you leave?"

"As soon as I get a company hired." Frank grinned as he added, "I don't have a lot of experience to get in the way. Talk about shoving off to sea in a sieve!" He laughed at his own foolishness then said, "I'll be staying at Willards until I'm ready to leave. But I'll be by to say good-bye before we shove off."

After Frank left, Amos said in a puzzled tone, "He's changed, Bob. He was pretty low for a while."

Bob said only, "Frank's not like Ty and me. He's got a reckless streak. But I'm glad he's got something to challenge him." He shook his head, adding, "He's never gotten to know God, Uncle Amos. I think he's put that out of his mind."

"Well, God knows all about Frank, as He knows about every man. When He wills it, Frank will get his call."

※

The job of recruiting a company proved to be less difficult than Frank had anticipated. He was somewhat shocked when applicants came thick and fast on the first day. Most of them lost interest when they discovered that the tour would take place in the South, but by the end of the second day, he had five solid volunteers.

One of these was Carmen Montaigne, which both pleased and disturbed him. She had smiled at his protests that the whole thing would probably fold up, saying, "It'll be fun, Frank. We'll smell the magnolias together." He'd warned her about low pay and poor conditions, but she'd leaned against him and put her hand on his cheek. "I'm tired of what I've got here," she murmured. There was a light in her black eyes as she whispered, "We'll go dancing in New Orleans. It's a romantic place, I hear."

The very first volunteer was a young man of seventeen named Albert Deckerman. He had apparently slept outside Frank's room, for when Frank opened the door to go to breakfast, he'd practically stumbled over the boy. Albert had only amateur experience, but he had enough theatrical ambitions for *ten* actors. Albert was thin and had long blond hair, of which he was inordinately proud. He also had a booming voice and was willing to serve as a props man and all-around handyman.

The prize of the company, Frank felt, was the Hardcastles—J. Harold and Elizabeth. They were both in their late fifties but strong and hale, and they had a wealth of experience. J. Harold was a short, overweight man with thinning gray hair and bright blue eyes. He had a bombastic manner of acting, a fashion out of date for thirty years, but he could play any role in the older age category.

Elizabeth Hardcastle was a dignified woman of some fifty-five years. She was thin and alert and had great presence. She had been an actress all her life and said in a regal tone, "We in the theater have a special calling, Mr. Rocklin. We must lift our audience *up*."

Frank was not exactly certain of what that meant, but he was grateful for the Hardcastles.

It was a word from Carmen that gave him another member of the company. "Roland's in jail," she had said grimly. "He publicly insulted the secretary of war. Go pay his fine, Frank. He'll be glad to come with us."

At once Frank had gone to Pinkerton and explained the situation, and on that same day Roland had been released with the condition that he get out of Washington.

Frank had offered him a job, warning him, "It's not going to be easy, Roland. We may be tarred and feathered by those Rebels in Richmond."

But Roland was happy to be out of jail—and glad to have work of any kind. He promised to remain reasonably sober and, as he looked over the script with Frank, beamed as he exclaimed, "We'll have a triumph in the land of cotton, my dear fellow!"

***

Lorna had risen early, determined to find some sort of work. She had her breakfast at the Northern Pride Restaurant, which included one egg, a small portion of fried ham, and biscuits.

Ora Jenkins, the owner, cook, and manager of the Northern Pride, passed by, paused to study the tired expression on the features of the young woman, and said, "I been asking around about some work for you, Miss Lorna. You could get on at the iron factory, but that's too rough for you."

"I'll have to take it, Ora."

Jenkins smiled ruefully, saying, "Well, I'll keep looking around. Something will turn up. Like the fellow in the Bible says, 'I have not seen the righteous forsaken, nor his seed begging bread.'" The thin owner had a scripture for all occasions. He left Lorna's table but was back in five minutes holding a paper in his hand. "I'll bet you didn't see this, Miss Lorna," he said, beaming and handing it to her. "Read that right there!"

Lorna took the paper and read the small advertisement under Jenkins's bony forefinger: "Wanted—actors and actresses willing to travel. Company being formed to leave immediately. Contact Mr. Frank Rocklin, Room 222, Willards Hotel."

"Now if that ain't the good Lord providing for you, I never seen it!" Jenkins was smiling broadly and added, "Was I you, Miss Lorna, I'd hie myself over without no preliminaries."

"I will, Ora. Thank you!"

Lorna's spirits rose as she walked the five blocks to Willards. *I wonder if Mr. Rocklin will remember me* was the thought that came to her. *I doubt it—he's met a great many actresses.* As she entered the hotel, she was conscious of both hope and nervousness. *I've just got to get on with this company! It's that or go back to England.*

She knocked on the door firmly, and when it opened, she smiled, saying, "Am I too early, Mr. Rocklin?"

"Why, no, of course not!" Frank stepped back, and when she had stepped inside, he asked, "I suppose you've come about the new company?"

"Yes. I'm very much in need of work."

Frank liked her straightforward admission, and he admired her appearance. She was wearing a stylish dress, light blue with white cuffs and collar. She had, he saw at once, the mobile features that were so necessary for anyone in the theater. He started to speak then hesitated. "Have we met before? You look familiar."

"You have a good memory for faces," Lorna commented. "I came backstage after one of your performances. I was with Mr. Cooper's company."

"Why, yes, of course. You were with the troupe from England as I recall."

"Yes. My name is Lorna Grey."

"Sit down, Miss Grey." Frank waited until she was seated in one of the two chairs in the room, then sat down across from her. He spoke briefly, setting forth his intentions to take a troupe south, and ended by saying, "It's really a rather risky venture, I'm afraid."

"Because of the war?"

"Well, there's always some danger of being caught in some of that, but I was referring to the professional risks."

"Aren't all plays risky? Most of the companies I've been with haven't made anyone rich. I think it's the nature of the theater."

Frank nodded, pleased by her sharp analysis. "That's true, Miss Grey. And you must understand that I've had almost no experience in this sort of thing. But I think this will be excellent experience." He smiled, his teeth white against his tan, and added with a wry tone, "I think I'm afraid of the competition here in the North. Where we'll be going, the critical response won't be so severe."

"I admire your ingenuity, Mr. Rocklin." Lorna was impressed by Rocklin's dark good looks and wondered how long it would be before he used them on her—if she got the part. "As I said, I must have work. Could I read for you?"

Rocklin knew that he would offer the young woman a place with the company but decided to make the thing look professional. He rose and picked up a book from the desk, found a page, and handed it to her. "You know this speech from *Romeo and Juliet*?"

Lorna glanced at the page and smiled. Putting the book down, she rose and walked to the window, looking down at the street for a moment. Then she turned and began the familiar speech:

> "O Romeo, Romeo, wherefore art thou, Romeo?
> Deny thy father and refuse thy name,
> Or if thou wilt not, be but sworn my love
> And I'll no longer be Capulet."

Frank was highly impressed by the young woman. Her beauty was set off by the pale yellow sunshine that filtered through the window; the bars of light caressed her long honey blond hair, giving off faint reddish gleams, and her large gray eyes were lustrous. Her lips were full and well shaped, and there was a regal quality in her bearing that he had rarely seen in a woman.

She ended her speech, saying, "Romeo, doff thy name, and for thy name, which is no part of thee, take all of myself."

Frank at once came to her, smiling and giving Romeo's response. "I take thee at thy word. Call me but love, and I'll be new baptized."

Lorna answered, and the two played out the scene. They

made a fine team, which both of them realized, and finally when they reached the end of the scene, Frank cried out, "By heaven, we'll have to do this play together."

Lorna was excited by how well she had done. "Am I accepted, then?"

"Accepted?" Frank's eyes glowed with admiration, and he took her hands and held them tightly, "Why, my dear Lorna, you will be a brilliant light in our little company." He was aware of her firm hands in his and released them at once. Smiling ruefully, he said, "I wish the salary were commensurate with your talent, but I'm afraid I can't pay much."

They talked for a time of the terms of her employment; then Frank slapped his hands together, saying with pleasure, "Now that's settled. I can't tell you how pleased I am to have you with us."

Lorna was feeling light-headed with relief. Her future had been dim and murky, but now she had a place and something to do. "I'm the one to be grateful, Mr. Rocklin—"

"Frank, if you will."

"Yes, Frank, then." Lorna smiled at him, confessing, "I was in a pretty grim situation. Getting a place with your company is like a gift from heaven." She smiled and her eyes glinted with humor. "You're not an angel in disguise by any chance?"

"After you see me in a few rehearsals, you won't accuse me of anything so nice as that! Many would say I'm rather spoiled." He looked very virile and masculine as he lolled in the chair across from her. "I hope *you're* not spoiled. Two prima donnas is one too many!" The two sat there, each of them feeling very good over finding the other.

"What play will we do first?" Lorna asked finally.

"When we get to New Orleans, we'll do *Romeo and Juliet*,"

Frank said. "Some of the company were in Mr. Booth's version, and we can cut back—do an abbreviated version. Plenty of Union troops there with Union cash. We can use that!" He rose and picked up a sheaf of papers then handed it to her. "Here's what we'll do when we're in Confederate territory. It's called *The Return of the Prodigal*."

"What's it about?"

"It's about the evil Yankees who've come to destroy the South. I play a noble young man who goes wrong but is brought back to the ways of righteousness—and to a place in the Confederate army—by a beautiful Southern girl—and that's you. There's a villainous Yankee officer, some fond parents, and so on."

"I don't think I know the play."

Frank grinned ruefully. "Not too surprising since I'm writing it myself!"

Lorna looked up, startled. "You're a playwright?"

"No, I'm a desperate amateur manager of a company who needs a surefire success in his first venture." There was a light of humor in Rocklin's eyes, and he suddenly laughed aloud. "I'll probably have us all come out waving Confederate flags and singing 'Dixie'! Anything you can think of to pander to the folks of the Confederacy, don't hold it back, Lorna." He shook his head, saying, "I'm afraid it's not very artistic."

"It'll be fun," Lorna maintained stoutly. She rose, saying, "I'll leave you now." Putting out her hand, she gave him a firm grip, saying seriously, "I'm not a very religious person, but the owner of the Northern Pride Restaurant told me that God worked in getting me this job. I'm very grateful to God and to you, Mr. Rocklin."

"We'll be good for each other, and hopefully it'll be some

fun, as you say." He reluctantly released her hand, saying, "Can you leave on short notice?"

"I can go *today*."

"Well, not *that* short! But possibly tomorrow." A thought came to him, and he asked, "Are you married—or anything?"

Lorna's lips curled upward in an amused smile. "I don't know what *anything* means to you, but I'm not married."

When Lorna left the room, Frank moved to the window and watched until she emerged from the hotel. He followed her with his eyes until she moved out of his sight, then clapped his hands together with a sharp gesture, exclaiming, "Well now, *that's* a stroke of luck." He was excited by the addition of a capable actress and walked around the floor making plans. "We can do *Romeo and Juliet*," he muttered under his breath. "She's a lovely woman, and she's not married—or *anything*!"

He thought of what she'd said about God being in her coming to him, and he grew sober. *If she knew what this thing was all about, she wouldn't be so quick to bring God into it!*

The thought depressed him, and he sat down and wrote for some time, making the arrangements for the tour. Finally, he stopped and looked at the wall blankly. He was a little astonished to find that much of the bitterness that had driven him into this venture had left him. *I'm still going through with it, but I don't feel all the anger that I did for a while after Bob got hurt. I wonder why that is.*

He had no answers, and finally went back to his papers. A thought came to him even as he wrote: *She's a beautiful Juliet! I'd like to do that play with her.*

PART THREE

The Company

August–October 1863

CHAPTER 13

UNDER SOUTHERN SKIES

Dark, rolling clouds obscured the skies as the *Saratoga* plowed through the choppy waters. Lorna drew her coat more closely about her and peered to her right, seeking a sight of land, but found none. The iron gray August heavens were bleak and cheerless. Far off in the distance, she knew, lay the sunny climes of Florida and the Gulf of Mexico. But now the sharp tang of the Atlantic breeze bit at her face, causing her to shiver slightly. Shoving her hands in her pockets, she thought almost longingly of England but quickly drove those thoughts out of her mind.

"I've made up my mind," she murmured, a look of defiance in her eyes. "There's no turning back. I should have found that out by this time." She was interrupted when someone called her name, and she turned quickly to find Frank Rocklin approaching her. He was wearing a pair of light gray trousers and a loosely cut blue frock coat. The wind ruffled his dark hair, and as he approached he tried to smooth it with his hand. "Cold out here. Hard to believe it's still summer. It'll be warmer if the sun comes out, though." Leaning on the rail, he peered out into the foggy outlines of the sea then shook his head. "I don't like ships much. It's too far to swim home." He turned to face her, and his broad lips broke into a smile. "If a horse goes lame or the wagon wheel rolls off, you can always walk home. Not out here, though."

"How far are we from New Orleans?"

Rocklin considered her question then shook his head. "I don't really know," he admitted. "It's somewhere around five days to a week, the captain says." He shook his shoulders together and said, "We've been invited to eat at Captain Woods's table. Are you hungry?"

"Yes, I am." Lorna turned from the rail and matched her steps to his as they walked down the deck. "Does Elizabeth feel any better?"

"I don't think so. Seasickness is a pretty bad thing."

Elizabeth Hardcastle had gotten sick almost the moment the company had come on board the *Saratoga*. Even when the ship was as steady as a house, the aging actress had begun to turn pale. And when the ship had drawn anchor then plunged out into the stream with a sharp dipping motion, she had gone abruptly to her cabin. Thinking about her, Rocklin shook his head. "I had a friend once that made the crossing to England. He was sick all the way over and all the way back. Said it was the worst thing that ever happened to him." A thought struck him as the ship bucked slightly, catching a broadside wave. He took her arm and held her until it settled down, then released her. "He said for a while he was afraid he was going to die." His eyelids came together with a hint of humor as he added, "And then he said after a while he was afraid he *wasn't* going to die."

Lorna smiled faintly. "I had just a touch of it on my way over from London," she said. "It didn't last long, but it's very bad." She stepped through the door, and the two of them walked down the corridor to the dining room.

The *Saratoga* was a combination cargo ship and passenger vessel, a little less of the latter. Some of the space had been carved up into cabins, and the dining room was fairly large for the twenty-five or so passengers who had gathered there. She might have been a fancy ship at one time, but age and smoke and hard wear had worn off whatever elegance she had once possessed. "The captain's waiting for us," Rocklin said, and the two of them approached the table. Frank pulled out Lorna's chair, and after she was seated he sat down between her and Roland Middleton. Albert Deckerman was flanked by Middleton and Carmen. There was a certain sickish look about Middleton's face, and Lorna suspected it was because he had been drinking.

"Well, it's good to have acting folks on board," Captain Leonard Woods said. He was a tall, broad man of fifty-five with pearly white hair that was always exceptionally clean. His blue eyes were almost hidden by the wrinkles after a lifetime of staring into the sun reflecting off the ocean. He looked around the table and smiled. "I don't suppose any of you ever crossed the equator?" When no one responded, he shook his head. "That's a pity. Now there's a voyage for you. No piddling around on these little creeks or rivers or in the blasted Gulf Stream!" He waved his fork around with violent gestures as the steward began to serve them. "Pitch in," he commanded brusquely. "We don't have fancy cabins, but we do have good grub."

Frank had been somewhat surprised to find out that the food on board the *Saratoga* was good. He had discovered that Captain Woods demanded the best on his table and had imported his own Chinese cook, whose wages he supplemented out of his own pocket for a special fare.

"How is your wife doing, Mr. Hardcastle?" Lorna inquired.

Hardcastle shook his head mournfully. "Not at all well, I'm afraid. She's no sailor." He plunged into his food, eating heartily. He was a man with a big appetite, Lorna had already discovered. As he put the food away, she was aware that he was one of those men who can never say no to any kind of food.

The talk ran around the table for some time, and finally Carmen asked, "Do you think we'll have a good run in New Orleans, Frank?"

"Not sure." Frank shrugged. He looked at the captain and asked, "What's it like in New Orleans, now that the Union army's taken over?"

"Lots of tension," Captain Woods said. He turned to the first mate, Charles Hardin, a tall dark man of twenty-eight. "What was that that you found out about Butler last time we hit port there?"

Hardin had been lifting a glass to his lips. He put it down and said with a grin, "Well, the ladies of New Orleans have been rather arrogant, I'm afraid. They treated some of the Union officers with disrespect." He glanced over at Carmen and smiled. "Some of them even spit on him, so I understand. Not very ladylike, but feeling is strong in New Orleans. Anyway, it got General Butler a new nickname." He picked up the water again, sipped it, and, when he put it down, added, "They call him 'Beast' Butler now. He gave an order that any woman who insulted a Union officer would be arrested and jailed as a prostitute."

Frank stared at him. "That's pretty strong medicine!" he exclaimed. "I wouldn't think he could get by with that."

"Butler can get by with about anything, sir," Captain Woods

said. "He's a pretty sorry general from a military standpoint, but he knows how to bring the votes in. Lincoln knows he's going to have to run for reelection, so I guess the Union army will have Butler on its hands as long as this war lasts."

The talk ran around the table, and Lorna found herself enjoying the conversation. Both Woods and Hardin had traveled widely, and the two entertained them with stories of their voyages over the past several years. When the meal was over, Lorna excused herself and went to her room. The ship began pitching slightly as the weather grew worse, but after a while it seemed to go calm again. For a time she sat down and studied the script of the play that they were to do in Richmond, *The Return of the Prodigal*, and agreed that it would appeal to the emotions of the Southern people. It was a thriller about a young man who had joined the Confederate army, a romantic sort of play that was not to her liking. Then she turned to the abbreviated version of *Romeo and Juliet* that they would perform in New Orleans. Lorna was cast as Juliet, and Carmen was assigned the part of the nurse. Soon she put it aside and lay down. Ordinarily the rocking of the ship would have put her to sleep, but sleep eluded her. She heard bells ring from time to time and slept a little, but finally was glad when she awoke and saw the beginning of a gray dawn out the window. Quickly she rolled out of bed, washed her face and hands, dressed, then sat down and did her hair. When she left the cabin and made her way along the rail, she saw a solitary figure and identified Roland Middleton. Stopping beside him, she said, "Good morning! You're up early."

Middleton turned at once to face her. He was wearing a rather disreputable brown jacket and a soft felt hat pulled down low over his brow. "Couldn't sleep," he muttered. "Never did like ships."

"Shall we go down and get some breakfast?"

"After a while, I suppose." He turned to her and studied her carefully. He was somewhat of a connoisseur of women, and he admired the well-made structure of her oval-shaped face. There was a liveliness in her gray eyes, although now they seemed a little clouded with some sort of troubled thought. "How do you like it here in the States?" he asked finally.

Lorna shrugged slightly. "All places are about alike, aren't they?"

Middleton was caught by her answer. He traced the iron rail with one long forefinger, thought about what she had said, and finally stated, "That's for an old cynic like me to say, not a good-looking young woman like you."

Lorna's lips curled up into a smile at his distinction between them. "Men and women are about alike, aren't they, in some ways?"

At once Roland shook his head. "Now that's where you're wrong. All places may be alike, at least to some of us, but men and women are no more alike than. . ." He hesitated, searching for a simile. "They're no more alike than birds are like turtles." He laughed at his own inept phrasing. "Not very well said, but you know what I mean."

He stood there awhile, and the two of them spoke of the trip. Middleton had found that she was a sensible young woman, but he sensed there was something unpleasant in her past. It had brought the serious look that so often came to her face and was reflected in her wide-spaced eyes. Finally, he murmured, "It's odd what you said about one place being like another." He looked out over the iron gray ocean that seemed to crawl under the dim light of the feeble sun, moving in an undulant fashion as far as the eye could follow it. "A little bit like this ocean—no trees, no mountains, no rivers." He waved his arms, saying, "It's all just alike, isn't it? If we stopped right here, it'd be just like stopping where we'll be two hours from now. And that's the way life is. Doesn't matter whether I'm in Washington, Chicago, or New Orleans. Scenes change a little, but they're all pretty much alike."

Lorna was interested in Middleton. Despite his dissipation and the thin strain of cynicism that lurked beneath his manners, she had found him to be a sensitive man and able to laugh at his own weaknesses. "I'm not sure it's really that way," she finally admitted. "I think we carry our own places about inside of us." She glanced up at the sky, where the last flickering stars were still barely visible through the broken cloud cover over to her left, before saying, "They say those stars are a million miles apart." For a moment she hesitated then reached up and tucked a strand of her hair under the hat that she had pinned on. "It scares some people to think about all that empty space, but it doesn't frighten me. I think we have it in ourselves—empty places, I mean—far more frightening than anything up there."

Once again Middleton was intrigued. "You're not old enough to think thoughts like that," he protested. "Have you had an unhappy life?" he inquired.

"No worse than some." The answer was clipped short, and Roland almost felt she had hung a DO NOT DISTURB sign over her past. He said nothing for a while; then finally she asked him about his own life. Roland began to speak slowly. They were alone, and he was lonely. He began to speak of places he had been and things he had done. He spoke about his childhood briefly, which had not been unhappy. Finally, he shrugged. "I'm afraid I have no excuse for being the miserable company that I am. My family was good. I can't blame them for what I've become—a drunk."

Lorna was shocked at the depth of self-loathing that had suddenly leaped into Middleton's tone. Looking at him quickly, she saw it was reflected in his face. His lips were drawn into a bitter line, and there was a dim hopelessness etched over his features. Without thinking she put her hand on his arm, saying, "I'm sorry. I didn't mean to pry."

"You didn't. I don't often talk like this, though," he said. "Might as well tell it all." He turned once again to stare out bleakly over the sea and let the moment run on. Finally, he said, "I had great hopes once. I have some talent. Not very easy to see it since I'm drunk most of the time. But I could've been more than I am on the stage."

"Why didn't you?" Lorna asked quietly.

"I knew a woman once. I thought the sun rose in her. I had heard before of those loves when someone became more than food or drink or even air. Didn't think it existed, though, until I met her."

When he said no more, Lorna asked quietly, "You lost her, did you, Roland?"

"Someone took her away—I lost her—in any case she's gone now." He turned and said, "Now, Lorna, *please* don't tell me there are other women in the world! I've said all that to myself a million times. I'm just a weak character."

The waves made a chafing sound as they slapped against the side of the iron hull of the *Saratoga*. The breaking whitecaps made startling flashes ahead as the prow of the ship dipped into the ocean, breaking the gray waters into flashing bits of froth. Lorna said slowly, "I know something about that." Her voice was quiet, but there was a tone in it that drew his gaze. "I've been disappointed, too, in love."

When she said no more, Middleton felt a sense of kinship

with her. He did not ask any questions as the two of them stood there alone. Tentatively he put his hand on her shoulder and squeezed it. "We're two of a kind, Lorna. But you're young. You'll find somebody."

His words brought her eyes up, and she shook her head suddenly. "I guess I'm like you, Roland. I'm just not looking for anybody. Not anymore."

*

"This sun feels so good, doesn't it, Frank?"

Carmen and Rocklin had been walking around the deck after the noon meal. The days had grown steadily warmer and the bad weather had blown itself out. As they rounded the Florida peninsula, the sun shone brightly. The blue-green waters of the gulf seemed to flicker with millions of tiny lights. The *Saratoga* had picked up speed and was now headed across the gulf in the direction of New Orleans.

"It beats what we've had, doesn't it?" Frank observed. He took a deep breath and enjoyed the salty tang of the air. Though the breeze was sharp, it was not like the northern breeze they had left. "Let's go back to the stern. Some of the sailors have put out lines. Maybe they'll catch something."

"All right." Carmen was happy as they walked along. She had shed her heavy clothes for a lightweight cotton dress that was an odd shade of bluish green. The wind flattened it against her figure, and her black hair was disturbed by the stiff wind. When they arrived at the fantail, they sat down and watched as one of the sailors, an older hand who smoked a pipe, watched over several lines tossed over the rail. He gave them a curious glance but said nothing. Finally, one of the lines made a thunking sound, and he leaped to his feet.

"What is it?" Carmen asked with excitement.

"Don't know, miss." The sailor shook his head. He picked up the line and gave it a tentative pull. The muscles in his arm kinked, and the line hardly gave at all. "It's a big 'un," he said with satisfaction. "Maybe a marlin. Most likely a shark, though."

Frank and Carmen watched with excitement as the sailor worked the fish in. The *Saratoga* was making at least twelve or fourteen knots, and whatever the sailor had hooked had that much going for him. Hand over hand, the sailor would haul for a while, then lean down, bracing the rope against the rail to rest his arms.

"Can I give you a hand?" Frank asked with excitement.

"Why, it's hard work, sir."

"Always liked to fish. Never caught anything that big, whatever it is," Frank said. Moving over, he reached out and grasped the line with both hands and hauled back. A look of surprise spread across his features. He considered himself a fairly strong man but discovered that he could not do with both hands what the sailor could do with one!

Carmen caught his expression and laughed. "Come on, Frank! Let's see you haul him in. You've seen how it's done."

A look of chagrin crossed his features. Frank gritted his teeth and began to pull at the line. He did succeed in making some progress, but the sailor said, "Here, sir. You ain't got the hard hands for this. You'd better let me do it."

Frank surrendered the line and looked down at his palms, which indeed were rubbed raw. He stood there glaring at them then forced a smile. "Every man to his trade, I suppose."

The two watched, and finally they could see a long, slim body trailing twenty feet behind the ship. "What is it?" Frank demanded.

"Shark," the sailor said quickly. He lifted his voice and cried with a stentorian voice, "Hey, Charlie! Come—get a couple of hands. Let's haul this fellow on board."

Twenty minutes later, after a tremendous struggle, Frank and Carmen stood looking at the monstrous beast that was flopping on the deck. One of the sailors took an ax and hit him on top of the head, but it made no difference. "That's a tiger shark," the older sailor observed. He looked at the great length, torpedo-shaped, and then at the row of enormous white teeth spread into a grin. "Could take your leg right off, that fellow could."

"Is he dead?" Carmen asked.

"Dead! Well, bless you. No, miss. Why, you could cut his head off, and twenty-four hours later I would vow he could still bite you."

"Just like a snapping turtle," Frank said. "What will you do with him?"

"Nothing much. Not fit to eat. They get hunted for their livers, though."

Carmen and Frank watched as the sailors got the enormous hook out of the jaws of the shark and flipped him overboard. "Will he live?" Carmen asked.

"Them fellows are mighty tough," the sailor said. He baited the hook, threw it back over, and shook his head. "Ain't good for nothing, them things aren't. Now if it was a big king mackerel, marlin, or a sailfish, then we'd have something to eat. Don't know why God made things like that."

As Frank walked away, he observed, "I've wondered the same thing about mosquitoes and bugs like that. Why does God make them?"

Carmen looked at him curiously. She said nothing about

that but looked around and said, "This is fun, isn't it, Frank? I wish we didn't ever have to get to New Orleans."

He laughed at her. "It'd be a long trip. I think we'd get bored with it. No, I like to get places."

Frank kept a sharp eye on the troupe now that they were approaching New Orleans. They had had plenty of time for rehearsal, and that night he persuaded Captain Woods to let them have the dining room to run through it. They all worked hard moving the tables and chairs out of the way, then running through the play, stopping to work on the more difficult scenes. Albert Deckerman, as usual, overplayed his part. He could not speak, it seemed, without waving his arms around, and once Frank said in disgust, "Albert, you don't talk with your arms. You talk with your mouth."

"Why, I've seen Mr. Booth. He waved his arms around something fierce," he protested.

Frank would not criticize another actor, but he said, "Never mind Mr. Booth. I'm going to fix you, Albert."

"What are you going to do?" Albert asked, his eyes growing large. He quickly found out, for Frank procured a length of line from a sailor and tied Albert's hands to his sides. The effect was ludicrous. As they ran through the play, Albert would open his mouth, but nothing would come out. This was hilarious to all the members of the company, and finally Lorna begged, "Don't be mean, Frank. Let him move his arms around if he wants to."

"Well, all right. I guess one of these days he'll just fly off, but looks like that's the way it'll have to be."

After the rehearsal they all had a cup of tea while they talked about what was to come. Elizabeth Hardcastle was much better, although still pale from her ordeal with seasickness. "I'll be glad when we get off this boat," she said. "I'll never get on another one."

"Now, my dear, don't say that," her husband said. J. Harold leaned over and patted her fondly on the shoulder. There was a loving relationship between the two that everyone noted. Neither of them had ever achieved any fame, but you would never know it to listen to them talk.

Later, when everyone had broken up to go to their cabins, Carmen and Frank stayed to clean up. "That's sweet, the way the Hardcastles love each other," Carmen said.

"Yes, it is. Something you don't see too often."

They worked together, speaking from time to time; then he said, "I'll take you to your cabin."

When they were outside, Carmen walked slowly with him till they reached her door. But instead of going in, she turned and went to the rail. He joined her, and the two stared out at the waters. The engines of the *Saratoga* were throbbing, and the boat moved swiftly through the waters. The moon was up and made a long, inverted V shape. "The Vikings called that path of light the Whales' Way," Frank observed.

Carmen turned to him. "How'd you know that?" she asked in surprise.

"Part of my useless education," Frank laughed. He thought about it for a moment and said, "I had a friend who loved to read about the old Vikings. He told me, I think."

"Tell me about the Vikings."

For a while Frank stood there speaking quietly, feeling the ship quiver beneath his feet. She seemed interested, and Frank finally said, "They had a pretty hard life, those Vikings, as I recall. Very short lives, most of them. Either killed in battle or by disease."

"I guess all of us have short lives compared to those up

there." Carmen waved her hand at the stars. "I wonder how long they've been there." She seemed preoccupied and said, "Tell me some more about the Vikings."

"One thing I always will remember about them—it's kind of sad," Frank said. He stroked his jaw thoughtfully, letting the memory come back. "My friend said their idea of what this life is like is strange. He said one of their poets said that life is like a bird coming out of a raging storm, beat and about dead. This bird flies into a nice warm building where there's heat, light, and peace. He gets his feathers all dry, and no sooner is he all over the storm, he flies out into the storm again." Frank leaned on the rail, stared down, and said thoughtfully, "He said that's what the Vikings thought life was—coming out of nothingness into a warm place where there's a little joy, a little fun, and a little light, and then flying out again into cold nothingness."

"Is that what you believe?" Carmen asked soberly.

Frank turned to her, his face serious. There was a steadiness in him that she admired, a rocklike quality that she had not found in many men. "No, I don't believe that," he said.

"What do you believe?"

"I believe the Bible," he said, then added quickly, "Believe it, but don't do it. At least not much."

"I don't know much about God," Carmen said, a sad note in her voice.

Frank looked at her. In the light of the moon, her face seemed to glow. He was curious about her and asked abruptly, "Were you ever married?"

"No."

"Ever engaged?"

She turned to him and lifted her face. "I never found a good man." She was studying him carefully; then her hands went up.

They came to rest on his chest and she repeated, "I never found a good man, Frank."

He reached out and pulled her toward him. Her arms went around his neck, and when he lowered his head and kissed her, she met him fully. There was an urgency in her that shocked him. He realized that this was a lonely woman, despite the fact that she had known men. He knew from her statement that she had been disappointed. Her lips were soft under his and returned his pressure. As her body leaned against him, there was both a tenseness and a surrender. She was a woman who had led an adventurous life but had never found what she was looking for. All of this came through to him as they clung to one another. Then she pulled her head back and put her hands on his chest. Her lips trembled and she whispered, "Good night, Frank. Don't think bad of me."

"No, I won't," he murmured. But she had turned and stepped inside her cabin. When she was inside, she shut the door and leaned back against it. She bowed her head, and for some inexplicable reason, tears came to her eyes. She had tasted life and its pleasures and found it to be bitter. Now there was a hope in her. It was like a light that someone sees far, far down a dark, dangerous road. Only a faint light, but it was more than she had had in a long time. Slowly she moved across the tiny cabin, got undressed, and finally lay down on her bunk. She thought of the kiss and knew that it would not leave her mind. Then she whispered, "He's different from most men." The thought seemed to comfort her, and she let her mind run over the times they'd had together, until finally she dropped off to sleep.

New Orleans was a beehive of activity. As Frank made his way down the gangplank, his ears were assailed by the polyglot of sound. There were cries of the sailors who were engaged in docking ships, captains screaming at mates, and mates shouting harshly at the hands.

When all the members were on solid ground, they heard the soft sound of French coming like a layer over them. Most of the deckhands seemed to be dark-skinned men with very white teeth. Not black slaves, but Cajuns, as they found out later. Frank and Middleton worked together to get the luggage separated, and finally, along with Albert's help, they managed to get it into two carriages.

"You know a good, cheap hotel?" Frank asked the carriage driver.

"Sure, I know a good one, me." The driver was a swarthy man with a patch over one eye. He looked suspiciously like a pirate, but he turned out to be fairly reliable. He located a reasonable hotel not far from the French Quarter. When he had gotten all their bags inside, he said, "You going to like it here, I'm telling you. This hotel, my uncle, he owns half of it. I get you a special rate."

Frank tipped him liberally, and then the members of the cast went to their rooms, tired from their voyage. By the time the day had ended, Frank had found a local building that had been used as a theater but now was vacant. When he got back he said, "Well, we're ready for tomorrow. I've had posters put up all over town, so we'll see what kind of actors we are."

The next night they did *Romeo and Juliet* and, surprisingly, received a standing ovation. The audience was a mixture of Union soldiers and native-born citizens of New Orleans, with a dash of foreign sailors from other ports.

After the theater was cleared, Frank said, "Well, they're easy to please." There was a roguish grin on his face and he shook his head. "I thought we pretty much made a hash out of it."

J. Harold Hardcastle cried out, "Not at all, sir! Not at all! First nights always seem like that." He fondly put his hand on his wife's shoulder and said, "Your performance was beyond anything I've ever seen, my dear."

"Thank you, Harold. As for you, the crowned heads of Europe would be privileged to see such a performance as you gave tonight."

Carmen was standing close to Lorna. "You did very well, Lorna," she said. "I wish I had an English accent."

Lorna smiled. "I just hope I can remember to change to a Southern accent when we go to Richmond."

Albert Deckerman had played the role of Mercutio and was highly satisfied with himself. "Did you hear the applause when I gave my best speech?" he asked. His thin, lank blond hair fell from beneath his cap. He had a wonderful voice, and Frank thought that it was a shame the young man's acting wasn't as good. "Wait till tomorrow. We'll show them what acting is!"

"Well, we've got a couple weeks here; then we'll be moving to Richmond," Frank said. He looked around the circle. "I don't see much point in rehearsing. I think they'd applaud if we stood on our heads."

"The best kind of audience imaginable," Roland said. He had played the role of Tybalt and done the sword duel with a minimum of complaint. "But I'll be happy to survive these blasted sword fights. Don't you think we might use pistols instead, Frank? A bit out of time, but more comfortable!"

They played New Orleans for two weeks, leaving the Crescent City on the tenth of September. As they boarded the train for Richmond, Middleton had a worried look. "Somehow I feel a little bit strange, a Yankee like me roaming the South. Does it bother you, Frank?"

Frank thought of his real purpose in going to Richmond. He thought, *If you only knew why we're really going, you would be upset!* But he only said briefly, "Nobody takes actors seriously. They don't think we have any politics."

As the train rattled over the rails headed north, Frank couldn't help thinking, *One false slip and I could be hanged. I wouldn't mind being shot in a battle, but I can't think of anything worse than dying like that!*

Chapter 14

An Officer but No Gentleman

The travel from New Orleans to Richmond was difficult. It meant moving from Union-held territory into the heart of the Confederacy. The acting troupe, however, had less trouble than most. Several times they were eyed sharply by what appeared to be those in charge of the train, sometimes military officers and sometimes the crewmen, but no one questioned them. They were forced to change trains several times. The North had a fine system of railroads—a network that covered practically the entire area. The South, however, had only bits and pieces of small roads. Some of them didn't even use the same gauge of tracks. In addition to this, the Union army nibbled away at the rail system so that in one month the Confederacy might have a particular line but, after being forced back, would have to reroute all traffic on a completely different system.

"I really don't see how these people keep up the battle," Frank murmured. He was sitting by Middleton, and the two men were staring out the window. They passed through part of the war-torn countryside where the battles had raged in previous months. The train clanked and rattled and had already stopped four times for what seemed to be major repairs.

Middleton looked out at the beautiful countryside. The hardwoods were beginning to turn scarlet, brown, and gold. "Reminds me of home," he said.

"Where's that, originally?" Frank inquired.

"New Hampshire."

"Ever get back there?"

"No, there's nothing to go back to. Family's pretty well given up on me," Middleton observed. He seemingly cared little for discussion of his past. As the train clicked over the joints of the rails, he began to speak of the company. "Do you really think this run will be successful, Frank?" he asked.

"I don't know. I wanted to try it, though."

"Why the South?" Middleton inquired. He raised one eyebrow and shrugged his shoulders. "From what I hear, the country's broke—Confederate money's not worth the paper it's printed on even now. If I wanted to take a troupe somewhere, it wouldn't be here."

It was the kind of question that Rocklin tried to avoid. "I don't know, Roland," he said uncomfortably. "My roots are here, in a way. My great-grandfather built a plantation in the middle of Virginia. Some of our people are still there. There're some Rocklins fighting right now against the Union." He stared out the window and thought about the situation, then shrugged, saying, "There's no use thinking about this. Anyway, I just thought this would be a good time to break in a company. If the South is as broke as everybody says and they're as sick of war, any play will be a hit. Time to sharpen up our skills; then we can go back to the North and put it on the road."

The train finally limped into Richmond after what seemed to be an interminable journey. When the passengers disembarked, once again there was a scuffle for baggage. Middleton found a man with a wagon who agreed to take their luggage to the Spotswood Hotel. "They say it's the best," he advised Frank. "It might be expensive, but Union money will buy anything, I suppose."

Middleton proved to be correct. The clerk's eyes widened when Frank paid for the rooms for a week with gold coins. He picked up one of the coins almost reverently, weighed it in his hand, and then shook his head. "Don't see too many of these, Mr. Rocklin. We're glad to have you staying with us."

"Glad to be here. I have some people in this part of the world. I don't suppose you know any of them? Clay Rocklin, perhaps?"

The clerk's eyes opened wide. "Why, certainly, sir. Mr. Clay stays in this hotel often when he's in town. Of course, I think he's out with his command now."

The accommodations were rather crowded. Richmond was a seething mass of people, as they soon discovered. It was the center of the Confederacy in more ways than one. For one thing, it housed many factories, most of them small, but the Tredegar Ironworks employed a host of people. It was practically the only foundry in the whole Confederacy capable of producing cannons and rifles.

The streets themselves were filled with soldiers, tradesmen, and workers on their way to the various factories. Frank, on his first foray into the city, found some difficulty in obtaining a place to stage the play, despite the contacts he'd gotten from Booth. He tried first to find an empty building and, seeing none that would answer, in desperation asked for the office of the mayor.

"Mayor Johnson, that'll be," answered a tall man with a stovepipe hat. "Right over there, sir. You'll find him on the second floor."

The building housed the mayor's office over the courtroom. Frank, as he passed through, noticed that the courtroom was filled to overflowing. "What's the trial?" he asked one of the clerks who was hurrying along.

"Big murder case. Clifford Haynes shot his wife's lover. He won't be convicted, though," he said confidently. "It'd be hard to convict a million dollars, and that's about what he's got, I guess."

Rocklin managed a grin at this bit of worldly sophistication, then inquired about the mayor's office. Following the clerk's instructions, he climbed a steep stairway, but he found Mayor Johnson a hard man to see. The office was full of applicants, but Frank managed to cut through them by leaning over and whispering confidentially to the clerk, "I have a proposition that might be financially enticing to the mayor."

The clerk peered up at him from under bushy eyebrows. "Financially enticing, is it? Well, I'll see what I can do."

Five minutes later, Frank was in the mayor's office, having found that in Richmond money talked, as it did elsewhere. "I'm looking for a place to put on an extended theatrical production," he said. He had worn his most expensive suit, a fawn-colored pair of trousers, a brown frock coat with a white ruffled shirt, and a pair of shiny black boots. "My company and I have just returned from a triumphant tour in Europe," he lied blatantly. "We decided that the South deserves the best in art, Mr. Johnson. But I'm a stranger here, so could you perhaps advise me about a theater?"

Cletus Johnson could indeed. "As it so happens," he said, "I'm part owner of a building that could easily be converted to a theater. I would be happy to work out any details with you—Mr. Rocklin, is it? Any relation to the Rocklins at Gracefield?"

"Yes, indeed. Clay Rocklin is my uncle," he said at once. He understood instantly that identifying himself with the Rocklins at Gracefield or any of the relatives in Richmond removed all suspicion and most questions about why he was in the South. "I understand that Uncle Clay is on duty right now, but I hope to see him during our stay."

Johnson called his clerk, gave him some rapid instructions, and then shook hands firmly with Frank. "We'll work out an arrangement, I'm sure, and you can expect to see me on opening night. What play will you be doing?"

"*The Return of the Prodigal* is the name of it," Frank said. "It's about a young Southern boy who flees his responsibility to the Confederacy and later comes to his senses and becomes a hero to the cause."

"Fine! Fine!" Johnson said. "I'm certain you'll have a good audience."

Frank spent the rest of the afternoon with business matters. He discovered that having posters printed was somewhat difficult. Paper was becoming scarcer and scarcer in the Confederacy all the time. The printer finally said, "I have some wallpaper here. I could use the backside of it. Will that do?"

"Excellent! Just so the print's big enough and it gets posted. When can I come back for them, sir?" He made the arrangements with the printer and spent the rest of the afternoon scraping together enough chairs for the theater, which was in effect a barn that had been converted into more or less of a meetinghouse. He found it necessary to hire a carpenter to put up a stage. By the time he had rounded up enough material for a curtain and engaged a seamstress to put it together, darkness was beginning to fall.

When he got back to the hotel, he found the others

waiting. "Let's go have dinner," he said, "and I'll tell you what I've done."

Dinner in the Spotswood Restaurant was a pleasant enough experience. The room was crowded, mostly with officers and their ladies, and also with black-coated businessmen. The main dish was chicken—as well as the secondary dish. "This war's hard on chickens," Middleton remarked, holding up a crusty fried leg. "I must say, they do know how to fry chicken here in the South."

"That's right," Albert Deckerman replied in his booming voice. "I always said you can't fry chicken north of St. Louis. Something happens to it. It's in the air, I reckon."

Lorna laughed and bit into the chicken carefully. "We don't have anything like this in England," she said. "We always bake it or broil it there."

Carmen studied the fare and said, "I should tell you about some of the meals I've had and some of the out-of-the-way places I've been. This is heaven compared to that."

As they were eating, Frank described what he had done and finally shook his head. "We're set to go on day after tomorrow night. I think the stage, the seats, and the curtain will all be finished." He shook his head dolefully. "It's not Ford's Theater," he said. "It's frontier style."

"I've played in a few of those," Roland said. "A small place, I suppose?"

"Yes, not too large."

"I thought so," Roland said. "The thing about that is the audience is right up in your face. If they don't like you, you don't have to wonder about it." He grimaced, his face twisting into a wry smile. "I hope they don't bring rotten tomatoes. They know we're Yankees."

"Not possible, sir!" J. Harold Hardcastle pounded on the table. "Audiences understand that the actor is not to be confused with the role he plays. I'm not a supporter of the Confederacy, but an artist must subdue his natural tendencies." He began to speak rapidly, saying, "After all, when an actor plays Hamlet, he doesn't have to be a prince; he just has to pretend to be a prince. When he plays Macbeth, he doesn't have to be a murderer filled up with ambition. That would be most retrograde!"

"You don't think it would help to be a murderer to play a murderer?" Lorna asked, amused at the older man's insistence.

"Why, indeed not! That is the essence of our art, to seem to be that which we are not."

"Then I reckon that most of the world could be actors and actresses," Middleton said, "because most people pretend to be what they're not. What's the difference between us, then, Mr. Hardcastle?"

"We get paid for it," Albert Deckerman boomed out and laughed at his own joke.

Frank was amused by Hardcastle's definitions, yet grew serious. "I've wondered a lot about acting," he said. "Why is it that people like to see plays? It's not real."

Middleton said at once, "Neither is a painting real. You know it's on a flat surface—that those mountains don't have any curves or bumps—but we like to see a painting, especially of places we've been to, that we know. We're just made so that we enjoy that sort of thing."

"I think drama does that when it's good," Lorna observed. "Was it Dr. Johnson that said, 'Shakespeare holds the mirror up to life'? When we see someone in a play, if they do it well, we're reminded of what we are. That's what drama is, I think. To show us what life is really like."

Carmen was listening to all this very carefully. "I never thought of it like that," she said. "I just thought it was for amusement."

"Well, it has to be that," Frank said. "Nobody's going to come see a play unless they're amused. But I think Lorna's right. There's something about a play that catches us. Why, there's something in the Bible about drama."

Middleton was interested, as well as the others. "What do you mean by that, Frank?" he asked. "I wasn't aware that there was drama in the Bible."

"Well, not drama actually. But do you remember in the Old Testament when David committed his great sin? Somehow he didn't seem to know it. He fell in love with Bathsheba, and after she was with child, he had her husband killed so he could marry her." Frank was caught up in his explanation, his dark eyes intent as they swept the table. "Then the prophet Nathan came to him. Do you remember what he did?"

"What was it?" Middleton inquired when no one spoke up.

"Why, he told a story, which is a form of drama," Frank explained. "He told about a man that had one little lamb that was like a member of his family. He'd carry it around because it was very special to him, and he'd feed him from his own table. Then there was a rich man who had thousands of lambs. He saw that one little lamb that the poor man had and took it from him."

"How awful!" Carmen said, her eyes flashing.

"That's what David said," Frank continued. "He said, 'Who has done this deed will die for it.' I can't quote it exactly," he said. "But he intended on having that fellow's hide, and that's when the prophet looked right at him and said, 'Thou art the man!' It hit David like a ton of bricks," Frank observed. "As soon as he heard those words, he saw himself for what he was. So the prophet used drama, in effect, to show David what he'd actually done. That little story—a drama if you like—made his crime come alive for him."

"Well, I didn't know I was quite as noble as all that," Carmen laughed. "I'll be asking for a raise now that I know what my profession really is."

Frank laughed at her. "I'm not interested in nobility right now, Carmen. If we can just keep these Rebs amused and entertained and make a little money, that's enough for me."

Frank rose early the next morning and set out to find his mother. When he walked into her hotel room, she was as surprised as he'd ever seen her. "Why, Frank! What are you doing here?" she demanded.

"Right now, I've come to take you to breakfast," he said with a grin, squeezing her tightly. "After that, I want to go visit Dad. Come along." He took her to a restaurant, and she listened intently as he told her of his new profession. She was surprised, of course, but said only, "I hope you succeed, Frank." After breakfast, they went to Libby Prison, where Frank was finally admitted after some difficulty. When they entered the huge open room, his mother led him to the section beside a high window. Gideon stood up at once, shock in his eyes. "Why, Frank!" he exclaimed.

Frank embraced his father, shocked at how pale and wan he seemed. The wound he'd taken at Gettysburg had sapped his strength, and there was little of the vigor of the man he'd last seen. After a quick explanation of why Frank was in the South, Gideon said, "Tell me about Bob."

It was a difficult time for Frank, but he concealed his bitterness and gave them the best report possible. Finally, he said, "He's handling it better than I would. Uncle Amos and Aunt

Laura have helped a lot. It wouldn't surprise me if Bob became a preacher."

"Any chance at all of his getting his sight back?" Gideon asked quietly.

"The doctor says it would take a miracle."

Gideon considered that; then a smile touched his lips. "I guess there are precedents, aren't there?"

The three of them talked for an hour, and as the visitors were leaving, Gideon hugged Frank again. "I'm glad to see you, son. I've missed you!"

Frank only nodded and muttered something. When they got outside, he said, "I wish I could get him out of that place. That'll take a miracle, too, won't it?"

Melanie hugged him at the door. "Miracles can happen, Frank. Don't forget that."

⁂

Two nights later, the play opened. Frank had hired a man to sell tickets on the mayor's recommendation that he was tolerably honest. In their jammed-up dressing rooms, which had once been several feed stalls, they heard the crowd filing in.

"Noisy bunch, aren't they?" Middleton said with a grin as he came out, dressed in his uniform. He loosened the sword, sighed, and said, "I hope I don't have to use this to protect myself."

Lorna came out, along with Carmen, wearing their costumes. Carmen looked very calm, but Lorna was somewhat pale. Listening to the crowd's noise, she asked, "Is that sort of thing usual? It sounds more like a circus than a drama."

"Oh, they'll be all right, Miss Lorna," Albert spoke up.

"They're just folks like anybody else. They'll appreciate good drama when they see it."

"All right, everybody get ready!" Frank commanded. He felt a fine sheen of perspiration on his forehead, and he tried to avoid any appearance of nervousness by speaking loudly. "We'll knock 'em dead. Let's go!"

When the curtain opened, the crowd burst into loud applause even though they had seen none of the acting. As the drama proceeded, Frank realized at once that this was a different kind of audience from anything he had ever seen. Primarily, he saw that the uniforms of the Confederate army made up most of the audience. Here and there were a few ladies, but it was a rough bunch of soldiers who had come to see the opening night performance. As the drama proceeded, the group made several blunders. But the audience readily went along with it. "You're all right there, boy!" one of them yelled when Albert forgot his lines. "Just sing a song if you forget what you're supposed to say."

Lorna was well received by the soldiers. Several of them called out endearments to her, such as "I'll meet you after the play, sweetheart. You're a real Confederate flower!"

Unaccustomed to this, Lorna faltered. But the crowd was good-natured and soon settled down to enter into the production.

The play itself was not much. The story was simple enough: A young man, played by Frank, ran away from home, went bad in his youth, and became a prodigal, breaking the hearts of his parents, played by the Hardcastles. Later on, he redeemed himself by joining the Confederate army, where he became a hero.

Middleton, who played the villain, was constantly hissed and booed by the audience. Once when they were behind the stage waiting for their entrances, Middleton grinned at Lorna. "I like being the villain," he said. "You don't have to please anyone. The worse you are, the better they like it. I just hope they don't try to charge. Some of those soldiers look pretty raunchy."

Finally, the play came to an end. The curtain was drawn, and Frank said quickly, "Let's take a curtain call, if they know what that is."

The audience did indeed know what it was. They whistled and applauded, all standing, and before they were satisfied, the cast had made five curtain calls, and finally Frank said, "That's enough. They'll have us going out all night."

They soon discovered that Southern theater, at least this one, was a little different. Part of the audience felt no compunction about simply strolling back behind the curtain, and the actors were soon besieged by admirers. Frank was amused by all of this, but he soon got a shock when a young Confederate lieutenant walked up with an attractive young woman by his side. "Mr. Rocklin?" the lieutenant asked with a grin on his face.

"Yes, Lieutenant. I hope you enjoyed the play."

The lieutenant put out his hand, and when Frank took it, he said, "Well, I guess I had to like it, seeing as we're kinfolk. My name's Lowell Rocklin."

"Clay's son, of course!" Frank remembered his genealogy. "Well, I'm glad to have you here, Lieutenant. It's always good to have kin in the audience."

"This is my fiancée, Rooney. Rooney, you've heard me speak of my uncle Gideon. Well, Mr. Frank Rocklin here is his youngest son."

"I'm pleased to know you, sir." Rooney said. She was an attractive, vivacious girl, nicely dressed in what seemed to be a new sky blue outfit.

"When will be the big day?" Frank asked.

"About a month away—October twenty-fourth, to be exact." Then she changed the subject by saying, "I thought the play was so good." She hesitated then said, "Of course, I haven't seen many plays."

"Why, Rooney, that's no way to talk to an actor," Lowell said. Then he turned to Frank. "I've seen quite a few plays, and I tell you, this was one of the finest ones. Father will be glad to see you when he gets back. How's your family in the North?" He spoke of the Northern Rocklins quite easily as the three of them stood there talking. Finally, Frank introduced them to the rest of the cast. Then he turned to the young couple. "I think I'm going to offer my relatives an early bridal supper."

"A bridal supper?" Lorna asked at once, coming to stand beside Rooney. "You will have a beautiful bride, Lieutenant," she said to Lowell.

Frank took the pair out for a meal, and on the way over, he noticed Lowell favoring one foot. Lowell was very quick, and he said, "I do limp a little. I lost a leg fighting you Yanks, but I'm with the cavalry now. Man in a saddle doesn't need two good legs like an infantryman."

"You're much to be commended, Lowell," Frank said earnestly. He was fascinated by Lowell. He had always been interested in his Southern relatives, and his first introduction to them was most pleasing. Finally, the supper was over, and Lowell said, "Mr. Rocklin—"

"Oh, call me Frank."

"Well, Frank, then. I'd like to invite you to a tea tomorrow afternoon at Mrs. Chesnut's home."

"Mrs. Chesnut?"

"Yes!" Rooney said eagerly. "Mrs. Mary Chesnut. Her

husband is a colonel, one of the advisers to President Davis. Everybody comes to their house, don't they, Lowell?"

"They surely do. I've seen General Lee, General Jackson, General Stuart, all three there—and I don't know who else—in the same room. I'd be pleased to have you as my guest. Let the flower of Richmond's society see that we Northern Rocklins have *one* artist, at least, in our family."

Frank's mind was working quickly. He was thinking about being able to pick up some information, and it sounded like an excellent place to do it. "I'd be happy to come," he said.

"Oh, and bring as many of your cast as you would like. There's always plenty of room at the Chesnuts'," Rooney said.

"Rooney! You can't invite a host of people to the Chesnuts' house," Lowell protested.

"Oh, it's all right," Rooney said. "I'll go by and mention it beforehand. She's so interested in books and art and things like that. She'll be glad to meet a real company of actors."

Lowell was not so sure, but he had learned that Rooney had a way of taking things into her own hands. "All right, then. But you'll have to make it right." He nodded and said, "Good night, Frank. I'll tell the rest of the family to be sure and come to the play."

"Will your father be back soon?" Frank asked.

"I think so. He's been out with the company on a scouting mission looking for the Union troops to make a drive from the northeast. That's where we've got all our forces scattered." Lowell spoke assuredly, and Frank filed that fact in his head. *It might be something Pinkerton needs to know,* he thought. But he smiled and said, "Fine. What time tomorrow?"

"Two o'clock. Ask anyone—everyone knows where the Chesnuts live."

"Miss Grey, I believe?"

Lorna looked up to find a tall Confederate officer wearing the uniform of a major. He had come to stand slightly behind her, and when she turned, he said, "I haven't had the pleasure of seeing you perform, but I propose to take care of that immediately." He was in his late twenties, she judged, with light blond hair and very light blue eyes. His face was thin in an aristocratic fashion, and his hair was cut fashionably long. He looked rather like a dandy to Lorna, but his eyes were intelligent and his manners were better than average.

"My name is Major Miles Taliferro. May I take you for some refreshments?"

"That would be very nice, Major." Lorna had arrived with the rest of the group at the home of the Chesnuts. She had been impressed by the graciousness of the house, with its heart pine floors, the stately windows, and the polished, gleaming furniture. The house, as Lowell Rocklin had warned her, was very crowded. There were no privates in this room, however. As a matter of fact, few lowly lieutenants. It was the cream of Richmond's society. Lorna had been very impressed by Mary Chesnut, who had charmed her at once by identifying her accent. "From England, I see. We're glad to welcome you to the South, Miss Grey. You must tell me more about how you got here."

Lorna allowed Taliferro to take her to the table. He placed a slice of cake on a fine china saucer, handed it to her, then proceeded to procure some for himself. Armed with this and a cup of delicious punch, the two sat down. "You're from England, I understand," Taliferro said. "How is it that you find yourself in this country?"

Lorna explained her coming very simply and was aware that Taliferro was very attentive. There was something about him that warned her that he knew women—perhaps better than a man should. Some men, she had long ago discovered, were primarily hunters. They perceived any attractive woman as their quarry, just as a hunter in the woods looks at a deer as his legitimate property. They felt that every woman was to be pursued. Not that he was rude or in any way forward in his manners. On the contrary, he was very smooth. The two sat talking, and finally Frank came over and introduced himself to the major. Taliferro greeted him and asked, "I take it you've been traveling quite a bit. Has your troupe been in the South long?"

At once an alarm went off in Frank's head. There was something about the question that seemed so innocent, yet perhaps was not. There was a sharpness in the major's light blue eyes, and instantly Frank decided to tell as much of the truth as possible. "Why, no. As a matter of fact, we came from New Orleans, where we played for a couple of weeks. Before that we were in the North. In Washington, to be exact."

"Ah." Interest lighted Taliferro's eyes, and he said, "Have you ever played before the president?"

"As a matter of fact, he did come to a play. I was a minor actor, of course. I've never met him. He does like the theater, although he likes comedy rather than serious drama."

"So I understand," Taliferro agreed. He sipped his punch and said, "I'm surprised you decided to bring your troupe to the Confederacy." A smile turned up the corners of his lips. "At the moment, we're engaged in business quite different from drama."

"I suppose it's natural that you would wonder," Frank said at once. He frowned slightly and looked down at his own refreshments. "As a matter of fact, Major, I probably made a mistake coming here."

"Oh, and how is that?"

"Well, it's obvious enough that the South is hungry for drama. I suppose any nation wants its entertainment, but"—he shrugged his shoulders eloquently—"it's not easy to make it a paying proposition."

"I suppose not, but then, you knew that before you came."

"Yes, I did." Frank decided to be a little daring. He was certain that the major knew of the Northern branch of Rocklins, so there would be no danger in admitting it. "My father is in the Union army, and so is my uncle Mason. But our families have been very close—that is, with those here in Virginia. The war, of course, has come and broken most of our communications." Frank looked up directly into the major's eyes and said as simply as he could, "I've only visited briefly in the South. I don't understand it. I think a lot of us from the North have that difficulty, so I thought I would come and see for myself."

Taliferro seemed interested in the explanation. "Well, I'm glad you've come, Mr. Rocklin. You have a fine family here, and I'm sure your own family back in the North are the same. It is a tragedy that we couldn't settle our differences without a war, and hopefully the day will come when we can sit down in peace once again."

It was a straightforward speech, and Lorna listened to it carefully, feeling gratitude for the major's temperance. He turned to her suddenly and said, "We are depending, of course, here in the Confederacy on *your* country for support, Miss Grey. When you were last in England, did you hear any talk about England recognizing the Confederacy?"

Lorna hesitated. "There's always talk, and there are people

who feel strongly on both sides of the question." She stopped then said, "I'm not much of a politician, I'm afraid. But I love your country, what little I've seen of it."

Taliferro said, "I'm sure. I'll be glad to show you more." He smiled engagingly. "After all, you only perform at night. That leaves all your days free."

"But not yours, surely, Major." Lorna gave him back his smile. "Soldiers have plenty to do, don't they?"

"Well, there are different kinds of soldiers." Taliferro hesitated then said, "The combat soldiers, of course, are on the front lines. But there is much to be done before they reach that stage. An army and a nation, especially a new army and a newly born nation such as ours, require a great deal of attention. I'm one of those who attempts to make it possible for my country to survive."

Soon Frank wandered off and encountered Mrs. Chesnut. She was a charming woman, no longer in her youth, nor was she beautiful. But there was some quality in her that drew men. Frank had seen it before in women who were almost plain. He spoke with her for some time then nodded to where Taliferro was speaking with Lorna. "The major seems quite taken with our leading lady," he said.

"Oh yes. Major Taliferro is not averse to pretty young ladies."

"Does he lead a battalion or some other unit in the Army of Northern Virginia?" Frank asked carelessly.

"Oh no. He is on the staff of the secretary of war." She hesitated then said, "It's fairly well known that he's one of the leaders of what you might call the Secret Service. I suppose every company has that sort of thing."

Frank's heart lurched, but he kept a straight, even face. "Yes, of course, they're necessary, I suppose." He continued speaking to Mrs. Chesnut until it was time to go. And finally, as they were on their way back to the hotel, Lorna asked him, "What did you think of them, Frank? Southerners, that is?"

"They're very gracious. But then, I knew that." He looked at her, paused, and then said, "The major was quite taken with you."

"Oh yes. He was very attentive, very gallant." She seemed almost uninterested, and when Frank prodded her, she shrugged her shoulders lightly. "Men are interested in actresses. They see them as easy game, I think."

Frank was a little shocked at her way of putting it. "Well, that's speaking right out. How long have you felt like that?"

"Why, I've always known that. I don't know as much of the history of theater as I should—not as much as you do—but I think in the early days, actresses were almost always women of low morals." She hesitated then bit her lip. "Many of them, I suppose, still are."

"Not all, though," Frank said quickly. "I've met some fine ladies in my short experience. And then there's you."

She looked up to see him smiling at her and returned the smile. "You do pay a nice compliment once in a while. But as for the major, I don't suppose I'll be seeing much of him. He'll be gone off to fight, I'd imagine."

Frank shook his head. "No, he's not that kind of a soldier."

"Not a fighting soldier? Don't tell me he's some sort of a clerk."

"A little bit more than that," Frank admitted. "Did you enjoy yourself tonight?"

"Very much. They're not like I thought they would be—Southerners, I mean. Back in England, we hear the awful stories of slavery, and I'm sure it's as bad as they say. But you'd never know that these people are cruel taskmasters."

"Not all slave owners are cruel," Frank said at once. "I know that much. My uncle's family owns slaves, and I've heard my father talk about how much care he takes with them."

"I'm sure you're right," she said.

When they got back to the hotel, Middleton spoke for a moment to Carmen. "Well, we were in fancy society tonight. The cream of the Confederacy. I fully expected General Lee to walk in."

"That major was taken with Lorna, wasn't he? I hope she's careful with him. I've seen his kind before."

Middleton gave her a quick glance. "Yes, I saw that. Well, I'm sure Lorna's able to take care of herself."

"I don't know that she is."

Middleton, surprised, gave her a direct look. "What does that mean?"

"Oh, I think you know, Roland. Lorna's not like most actresses. She has a—I don't know—she's vulnerable. A man could hurt her easily."

"But not you, eh, Carmen?"

Carmen dropped her eyes for a moment then lifted them and smiled. "I thought I was past being hurt, but maybe I'm not. Good night, Roland."

Roland went slowly along the hall to his room. When he got there, he sat down on the bed thinking about the evening. Slowly he pulled out the whiskey bottle that he kept in his suitcase. He uncapped it and lifted it to his lips, then suddenly shook his head and put the cap back on. Putting it away, he undressed and went to bed. Before he went to sleep, he muttered, "Lorna's vulnerable, all right. But then, so am I—so are all of us!"

CHAPTER 15

ROSE ATTENDS A PLAY

Josh Yancy counted the worn bills carefully, laying down each one on the table. When he had finished, he gathered them and shoved them into his pocket. Slowly he got up and walked around the room, staring aimlessly at the furnishings. The Yancys' house was a typical Southern cabin with few luxuries. It was comfortable enough, most of the furniture having been made by Buford Yancy and his sons. The walls were covered with pictures clipped out of magazines and newspapers by the girls, except for a few drawings of Stonewall Jackson and Robert E. Lee, which had been collected by Josh.

Josh sniffed at the smell of meat roasting then walked over to the fireplace, pulled his bowie knife from his belt, and pushed it into the carcass of the turkey that was slowly turning on a spit over glowing coals. The juice dripped to the coals, sending a heady aroma into the room. "You're going to be durned good," he muttered with satisfaction. "You'll do us a lot more good for supper than you did running around out there l–loose." The slight stutter irritated him, but he shrugged, thinking of how the habit was practically gone. He had shot the turkey only the day before and now had lingered around the house most of the morning watching it slowly broil.

The door to a bedroom opened, and his sister Rose emerged. She walked over to the turkey, stared down at it, then commented, "Looks good. Be sure you don't let it burn, Josh." Rose was a tall, willowy young woman of eighteen. She had the same black hair and light green eyes as her sister Melora and the same almost unearthly beauty one sees in a mountain girl from time to time.

"You watch it awhile," Josh said. He looked up and asked, "Where've you been, Rose? I didn't hear you go out this morning."

"Oh, I went over to see Sarah Green." Rose came and poked at the turkey with a kitchen knife then tossed it to the table and sat down. There was a restless dissatisfaction in her face.

"What's the matter with you?" Josh demanded. "You've been moping around like a sick possum for weeks now."

"Nothing's the matter with me."

"Well, I hope I don't have to look at that sour face you got on for the rest of your life," Josh snapped. He shoved his knife back in his belt and started out the door. "You watch that turkey. Pa ought to be back by dark, and I promised him we'd have it for supper tonight."

"Where're you going?"

"I'm going out to check the pigs."

"I'll go with you." Rose called for Martha to come and watch the cooking bird. When the younger girl arrived, Rose grabbed a man's coat from a peg in the wall and slipped her arms into it. The two left the house, and Josh looked carefully at the sky, searching for the flight of wild ducks. He was a woodsman and a hunter, as were all the Yancys, and his pale green eyes missed nothing as the couple made their way down a path that led through the woods. He knew every inch of this ground—every hill, every valley, and where the bees hummed around their trees. He had shot deer, wild pigs, rabbits, coons, possum—all the wildlife that made up the diet of a typical backwoods Southerner.

"I reckon you must be pretty bored if you want to go look at the pigs," Josh said finally. "What's wrong, Rose? You can tell me."

Rose kicked at a root that rose out of the ground and seemingly tried to snatch her foot. She was wearing a pair of heavy shoes and a rather ugly brown dress. "Oh, I don't know, Josh. Nothing really," she said. The quick gestures of her hands and the twitching of her shoulders told Josh differently. She gave him a quick glance and summoned up a smile. "You and I don't talk as much as you and Melora used to. I wonder why that is."

"No telling about those things," Josh said. "But it's not too late to start, sis. Something bothering you?" he asked for the third time.

Rose tried to match the long steps of the boy. At sixteen, he was slightly taller than she was, with the same lean build. She wore no ornaments, and the worn, rough coat concealed the curves of her young body. "I sometimes think I'll go crazy on this place, Josh!" she exclaimed finally. Biting her lip, she shook her head. The motion sent the black hair cascading across her shoulders. She was a lively girl who liked fun and hated to see the parties and dances that took place from time to time end. "I guess you're right. Any girl that'll go watch pigs is pretty bored."

Josh said nothing for a while. He seemed to be slow thinking, but actually he was very thorough in his mind. "I guess so. You don't hunt and you don't like to read like Melora does.

It must get boring for you out here." The two walked on for a while before he said, "I'm taking Rena to the play in town."

"A play?" Rose's eyes brightened at once. "Tell me about it! What kind of play is it? Who's in it?" she asked rapidly.

She listened avidly as Josh described the play and ended by saying, "The actor in it, why, he's kinfolk of the Rocklins. Mr. Frank Rocklin's his name. I think he's a nephew of Mr. Clay. Anyway, I've been saving up money from the hides that I sold, and I'm going to take Rena to see the thing."

Instantly Rose grabbed his arm and turned him around with surprising strength. "Oh, take me, Josh! Please?"

Josh was surprised at the intensity of her gaze. He really cared deeply for this older sister of his, as he did for Melora, but the two women were very different. He had known for a long time that Rose didn't like the farm, but he thought that was just part of growing up. Now when he saw her lips trembling with anxiety, he said quickly, "Why, sure, Rose. We'll all three go. We'll have a good time, too. I've got enough for us to have supper, I think."

"Oh, Josh!" Rose threw her arms around him and squeezed him so hard he grunted. When she stepped back, her eyes were dancing and she said, "I'll wear my green dress, and maybe Melora will let me wear her locket. What time will we leave?"

Josh grinned at her, pulled off his hat, and scratched his head. "Well, I guess about ten o'clock in the morning. Think you can be ready?"

"Yes!" Rose exclaimed. As she smiled, the dimple that adorned her right cheek suddenly popped into view. "You two need a chaperone. You're too old to be going out with a young woman without someone to watch you." She was merry the rest of the time, even at such a mundane chore as feeding the pigs.

That night when she told her father that Josh was taking her to the play, the younger children set up a howl to go.

"No, you let Rose and Josh go this time," Buford Yancy said. He was one of those tall, lean mountain men who never seem to grow older until they simply stop living one day. He said to the younger members of his family, "There's going to be a circus in two weeks. If you'll stop your yowling, we'll all go. I hear they got a critter there that you won't even believe when you see it. That be all right?" He smiled as the younger ones agreed and said to Josh, "You and Rose go on and have a good time. If there's anything in that play a young man orten to hear"—he winked at Rose—"you just reach out and clap your hands over his ears."

*

Rose Yancy had never had such a good time! She said so more than once as the three young people were sitting in the theater. Josh was wearing a new black suit that he had bought from his earnings when he worked for the Rocklins at Gracefield. Rena looked prettier than ever in a charcoal-colored dress with a saucy new hat pinned into her hair. "That was the best supper I ever had, Josh!" Rose exclaimed. "I wish we could eat out every meal."

"Aw, Rose, you'd get tired of that fancy café cooking pretty soon, I think. Why, they didn't even have any fritters and no grits a'tall!" He winked at Rena, who smiled back at him. "An ol' country girl like you, why, you'd go crazy if you didn't get some pig's feet every now and then."

"Oh, you hush!" Rose said. Her cheeks were glowing, and many of the younger soldiers were casting admiring glances at her.

Rena said, "You'd better be careful, Rose. These soldiers haven't seen anything as pretty as you in a long time." Rena was fond of Rose but had spent little time with her. She had always been very close to Melora, but this younger sister she knew hardly at all. "I've got to spend more time with Rose," she whispered to Josh. "I never knew she was so much fun to be around." Then she halted when Josh said, "Look! The curtain's going up."

Rose had never seen a professional drama before. She had been to entertainment of various kinds and one circus. But as she sat there watching the drama unfold, she was caught up in the action. She had nothing to compare it to; for her the acting was real. And when the hero was thought to be dying, tears rose to her eyes. When he revived, she found herself clapping her hands, saying, "Good! Good!" The dresses of the women seemed very beautiful, as did the women themselves. Once she leaned over and said to Josh, "Isn't it wonderful, Josh? I'd give anything if I could see a play every night!"

Josh nudged her with his elbow, saying, "No, it would get old every night, but it's a treat once in a while."

When the play ended, the audience rose to give a standing ovation, none applauding more than Rose. Finally, Josh said, "Come on."

"Why? Where're we going?" Rose asked in bewilderment.

"Going back to meet the actors. After all, they're Rena's kinfolk. Lowell and Rooney went back to meet them. I guess we can, too."

Josh led the way and Rose followed timidly. Josh immediately spotted Frank Rocklin and said, "Come on, that's your kinfolk, Rena."

Walking purposefully, he stopped in front of Frank and said, "Mr. Rocklin?"

"Yes?"

"This here's your kinfolk. This is Miss Rena Rocklin, Mr. Clay's girl. And I'm Josh Yancy, and this here's my sister Rose."

Frank looked instantly at Rena and smiled. When she put out her hand, he took it and bent over and kissed it in an eloquent fashion. "I didn't know I had such lovely relatives in Dixie. I'm glad to meet you."

Then he turned, and Rose blushed to the roots of her hair. Frank smiled, reached out and took her hand, and kissed it also. "I'm glad to meet you, Miss Yancy. Did you enjoy the play?"

"Oh yes. It was—it was wonderful!"

Frank laughed, his white teeth flashing as he said, "I wish the critics thought so."

"Why, it's a great play, Mr. Rocklin," Josh protested. "Makes them Yankees look like low-down dogs and makes us Confederates look pretty good."

"Well, that's what we wanted to do," Frank said. He liked the fresh appearance of the trio and added, "Let me introduce you to the rest of the cast."

Then followed the most memorable evening of Rose Yancy's life. She found herself caught up in a movement to go out and eat, as was the custom of the cast. And when they were in the restaurant, she was seated between the beautiful young actress Lorna Grey and the actor who had played the villain. She was a little standoffish with him, and Middleton at once understood the reason. He turned to her, saying, "You don't see many plays, do you, Miss Yancy?"

"No, this is my first one."

Winking at Carmen across the table, Roland assumed a ferocious look, "Well, how'd you think I played my part? Was I nasty enough to suit you?"

Rose blushed and dropped her head. Then she raised her eyes to his and said, "You're real mean. Once I almost got out of my seat and came up to—to—"

Everyone laughed, and J. Harold Hardcastle, who was listening, said, "Now *that's* the mark of a fine actor—one who can inspire that kind of emotion!"

Carmen leaned across and said, "You mustn't confuse the role with the man. Roland here is as harmless as any man could be. He wouldn't hurt a fly. He's not a Yankee officer."

"Oh, I'm so sorry!" Rose gasped. She turned to face Middleton, and he was captivated by the sight of her lips, which seemed very red and very vulnerable, and by her wide-spaced, enormous green eyes. He said to himself, *She is a rose out here in this desert of ignorance. Never saw a prettier one.* But he reached out, patted her shoulder, and said, "Don't apologize, Miss Yancy. I understand."

As the meal progressed, Rose began to gain courage. She listened avidly to all the talk that went on about acting. Eventually she began to speak with more freedom to Roland Middleton. He answered her questions easily. And finally she said, "It must be heavenly to be an actor or an actress."

Middleton caught Carmen's eyes and the cynical twist of her lips. Shaking his head, he said, "Well, it's a job. Not a very good one at times. A very few rise to the top and make a lot of money or get a lot of admiration from the public. Most of us are just poor drudges doing our job."

"But you get to move around and go from place to place. And you get to do new plays, don't you? You don't always do this one."

"Well, that's true, of course."

"Tell me about the plays you've done," Rose demanded.

Even after the meal was over, she was still listening, and Middleton felt flattered by her interest. Afterward they sat around drinking tea, and several officers came up to speak to Middleton, glancing at Rose, but he fended them off successfully. He sat looking at the young woman and said, "You remind me a great deal of my sister."

Rose lifted her eyes to his with surprise on her features. "Do I look like her?" she asked.

"A little, but she's excited easily, and her whole face lights up when she's pleased—just like yours. When I left home, she was about your age and about as crazy about the theater as you are."

"Did she go on the stage?"

"No, she married a barber, and they have four children now."

Rose wrinkled up her nose. "That sounds almost as dull as taking care of the pigs like I do."

Middleton was amused. "Some things about acting are about as bad as taking care of pigs," he said.

"I don't believe it!" Rose insisted. She made a fetching picture as she sat there, the dark green of her dress setting off the light green of her almond-shaped eyes. Her hair was as black as hair can be and hung down her back in a thick cascade. She had a heart-shaped face, and her features were delicate and at the same time strangely sensuous in an innocent way.

"Maybe you ought to leave the pigs and become an actress," Middleton teased her.

Rose stopped smiling at once. Her eyes grew smaller as she looked at him, and she whispered, "I'd do anything if I could do what you do, Mr. Middleton. Anything!"

Middleton was aware that she was totally serious and shook his head. "It's not as glamorous as it seems, Miss Yancy." He had no time to say more, for Josh and Rena had come to stand beside them, Josh saying, "It's time to go, Rose."

Middleton stood at once and smiled down at Rose. He looked rather handsome in his ash gray suit and said, "I hope you'll come back to see another performance. It's refreshing to have someone youthful like you admiring what we do."

Rose shook her head and said bitterly, "No, I'm afraid I can't come back, Mr. Middleton. So this is good-bye."

As the three left, Carmen came over and said, "Pretty little thing, isn't she, Roland? I suppose she's stagestruck."

Roland said nothing for a moment. He was watching the trio as they left, his eyes fastened on the form of the tall young woman. "Yes, she is. She's bored out of her head at that farm she lives on."

Carmen shook her head. "She's probably better off there—she'll marry a farmer and have a dozen kids." She turned to leave, but Roland stood for a long time thinking about the aching desire in the eyes of Rose Yancy.

Josh and Rena talked excitedly about the play on the long ride back to Gracefield. When they let Rena out, she gave Rose a swift look then reached up and pulled Josh's head down and gave him a resounding kiss on the cheek. "That's a thank-you for a wonderful evening, Josh," she said. Then she turned and ran into the house.

Josh climbed back into the wagon, spoke to the team, and slapped them with the line. "Giddyap!" The team started out with a sprightly pace and Josh said, "It's gonna be late by the time we get home. Do you want to lie down in the back and go to sleep, Rose?"

"No, I couldn't sleep."

Josh turned to look at her. A full moon was high in the sky, and the silver light bathed her face. "You really liked it, didn't you?" he asked.

"Better than anything."

Josh hesitated then said, "You talked a long time to that actor fellow, didn't you?"

"Yes. He was so interesting. He told me all about the stage."

"Well, you have to be careful with fellows like that," Josh observed. "Not that you're likely to see him again. But if you were, I'd have to tell you actors aren't all that nice in their behavior to women."

Rose sniffed. "How would you know? You don't know any actors."

"Everybody knows about actors."

Rose glared at him and pulled her coat more firmly around her shoulders. "You don't know anything, Josh, except that farm, just like me. We're not much better than those pigs out there rooting around!"

Josh stared at her. "That ain't so," he said. "What's the matter with you, anyhow? Here I bring you all the way to Richmond and take you to the theater, and you gripe all the way home."

Rose said nothing but settled back, her arms crossed over her chest. The wagon rattled over the road, and the harness tinkled from time to time. The horses snorted, the sound of their hoofbeats making a cadence that made Josh sleepy. When they finally got to the house, it was long past three o'clock. Josh hopped down, saying, "Not much sense in going to bed." When Rose didn't answer, he came over to her and put his arm around her. "I didn't mean to be sharp with you," he said. "But I hope you'll learn to like it on the farm."

Rose looked up at him, and he saw that there were tears in

her eyes. "I'll always hate it here," she whispered. She turned and disappeared into the house, leaving Josh looking after her. Finally, he turned slowly and led the team to the barn, where he unharnessed them and turned them loose in the corral after feeding them. Then he stood for a moment, leaning against the fence, thinking of Rose. "Women sure do know how to complicate things," he said aloud. Then he struck the top rail of the fence so that it gave a humming sound, turned, and walked into the house.

After the performance, Frank had excused himself and wandered down the streets of Richmond. He stopped idly in front of Planter's Bank, standing under the light of an oil lamp. Soon a man appeared out of the darkness to say, "Do you have a light?"

Frank reached into his pocket, obtained a match, and struck it. As the man leaned forward to hold his cigar to the burning match, he said, "The Union...now and forever."

Frank looked around nervously then replied, "Liberty at all costs."

The man nodded, saying, "Come along. This place is too public."

Frank followed the man, a short, barrel-shaped individual wearing a rather worn suit and a cap pulled down over his eyes. When they found a place in the shadows in a vacant lot across from a blacksmith shop, Frank said, "What's your name?"

"Right now it's Dave Perkins. Folks around here think I'm a jobber, a yard goods salesman. I even carry a few samples around. Nobody has any money to buy, of course, and I can't stay long.

What've you got?"

Frank rattled off the things he had discovered during his short stay and watched as the dark eyes of Perkins seemed to register it all. He had a catfish mouth that was pierced in the middle by the cigar. Finally, when Frank had finished, he pulled it out and sent a puff skyward. "Not bad. You'll get more as time goes on. What did you find out at the Chesnuts'?"

"There was a man there named Taliferro. He's Secret Service, I hear."

"Sure. Pretty sharp, too. Watch out for him." He continued to feed Frank information and finally said, "That's all for now. Meet me here again Tuesday night. I'll have some orders by then. Maybe you'll know something about military movements. Watch out for Taliferro." Without a good-bye he faded away into the darkness. Frank turned and walked back toward his hotel slowly. The wind was blowing, making a keening sound that sent a chill over him, and he turned his coat collar up and trudged heavily toward the hotel.

CHAPTER 16

AN ADDITION TO THE COMPANY

The skies were clear, but a stiff October breeze ruffled the blond hair of Miles Taliferro as he approached the long, low red brick building that housed the Signal Corps of the Confederate army. A smile tugged at his lips as he thought with a stab of amusement, *If Pinkerton knew that the Secret Service Bureau was in here, he'd love it.*

He entered the building, turned to his right, then walked across a large room where at least twenty men labored at battered desks. The Secret Service had come to include ten captains, twenty lieutenants, thirty sergeants, and scores of enlisted men from the ranks of army regiments. Many of those were out of the office the majority of the time, however, leaving only enough men to keep up with the book work. "Is Major Norris busy?" he asked a dapper-looking sergeant working on a cipher.

"He said for you to come right in, Major."

Taliferro nodded and stepped inside the office of the chief of the Confederate Secret Service Bureau. Major William Norris, a tidy, bearded man, looked up from a paper that he was signing. "Come in, Major," he said. Shoving the paper aside, he waved at a chair, saying, "Sit down." When Taliferro was seated, Norris questioned him for some twenty minutes about his activities on the mission he had just completed, and finally he nodded with approval. "You did a fine job," he said.

"Thank you, sir. I hope it will be of some help."

Norris rose to his feet, moved over to the window, and stared out of it moodily. "It would help if some of our leaders had more confidence in the work that we do."

"You mean General Lee?"

"He's one of them." Norris's tone was clipped, resentment obvious in his features. Robert E. Lee was a general who believed in the old, honorable ways of warfare. He wanted to be free and clear of spies, or scouts as he called them.

"He's a great general," Norris said, "but he's behind the times." Turning from the window, he marched up and down the floor in a jerky fashion, stroking his beard. "Of course, some of our agents are excellent," he argued. A frown crossed his face as he reached over and picked up a newspaper with SOUTHERN ILLUSTRATED NEWS across the top. It was the most important newspaper of the Confederacy. Major Norris said, "Look at that, Miles."

Miles took the paper and saw rather crude woodcuts of a woman on the front page. He grimaced and read aloud, "Miss Belle Boyd, the Rebel Spy." Shaking his head angrily, he said, "How does Belle expect to be a spy if she's got her picture on the front of every newspaper, North and South?"

"She's practically worthless," Norris answered. "It's not her lack of brains, but the woman loves publicity. That story there is fabricated out of half-truths and rumors. She ought to start writing novels!" he grunted.

"They're calling her the 'Siren of the Shenandoah,'" Taliferro said. "Or sometimes the 'Secesh Cleopatra.'"

The two men stared moodily at the paper that Taliferro had tossed on the table; then Norris said, "I've got something for you to look into. I hear from one of our agents in Washington that Pinkerton's stepping up his activities. Word we got was that he's going to be flooding us with new agents." Walking over to his chair, he sat down heavily and shook his head. "Sometimes I think we have more of their agents in Richmond than we do of our own."

"Any information about what they look like—names, descriptions?"

"Some information is on the way. I think we're going to have to take on more men. But I want you to go to all of our agents now and privately tip them off to be looking for new suspects."

"Yes, sir. And as soon as you hear anything from our man in Washington, you'll pass it along?"

"Of course." Major Norris waved his hand and said, "We've got plenty of rope. As soon as we catch them, there won't be any long, drawn-out trials, Major Taliferro!" With only a careless nod, he went back to the papers he was signing, and his visitor left the room, closing the door quietly.

"You are a very persistent officer, Major." Lorna smiled slightly at Taliferro as the two of them walked along the promenade outside the hotel. Lorna was wearing an oyster white dress over which she had put a lightweight woolen jacket made of a beautiful sky blue material. The hat that was perched on her head was the latest fashion, and she looked fetching as they moved along.

Miles Taliferro was a man who appreciated beauty in a woman, and he found it in Lorna Grey in abundance. He had learned, however, that she was wary of overt compliments, having heard too many of them, he suspected. "I'm considered to be rather firm," he admitted as they stepped aside to allow a woman pushing a large baby carriage to pass. When they resumed their walk, he said, "That's supposed to be an admirable trait in an officer. I hope you're not offended by my persistence, as you call it."

"Not at all." Lorna had rejected three invitations by the major, and each time he'd merely smiled and asked her in another form at a later date. "I suppose officers get accustomed to giving orders."

"I hope you don't think I've tried to do that with you," he said quickly. "I've desired your company—as have half the men in Richmond, it seems. But I'm sure you understand that we officers get lonely at times."

"So do women, Major."

Taliferro half missed a step and turned his head to look at her. "That's the most revealing thing you've ever said. Why should you be lonely, Lorna? You could have as many men as you want."

"How many men does a woman need?" she countered. Her lips turned up in a slight smile, and she added, "I think one's enough—if it's the right one."

"A wise reply. And you're right. One man, one woman. Is that it?"

"I think that's the biblical formula. Although it doesn't always work out in our society, does it, Major?"

"Would you please call me Miles? I keep expecting you to salute," he said with some asperity. "Yes, you're right."

"I think you look on women as a challenge to your ability," Lorna said.

Her words caught Miles off guard, and he flushed slightly. "Women have played games with me and I've responded. I think some of them expect such things." Quickly he added, "Not you, of course."

Lorna's gray eyes studied him for a moment; then she shrugged. "It's the only game women have, Miles. Men can have a career, but for most women their only option is to find a husband."

"Unless they're actresses, or perhaps schoolteachers."

"Never the twain shall meet!" Lorna exclaimed.

They had come to a side street, and he took her arm as she stepped down. "It will do me no good to tell you this," he said abruptly, "but you're very close to being the most beautiful woman I've ever seen."

"Thank you," she said easily. "I never know what to say when someone pays me a compliment." She laughed suddenly. "What would you think if I said, 'Yes, I am beautiful, aren't I?'"

Her wit amused Taliferro. "Well, we'd be agreed in that case." The two walked on down the street and afterward stopped in a shop, where he bought her a cup of sassafras tea. As they sat there, she said, "I've never tasted this before. What's it made of?"

"Some sort of root, I believe." He sipped the liquid, frowned, and shook his head. "Like everything else in the Confederacy, we're having to use substitutes. One day it'll be different."

"Will you be leaving Richmond for your duties, or are you stationed here all the time?"

"I sometimes get called to other parts of the Confederacy," he said guardedly. He studied her for a moment, and as he moved the glass around, leaving a trail of water on the table, he asked, "What's it like in the North now? Does everyone there hate us?"

"Not everyone. There's a strong Peace party that would like to end the war, and many there, best I could tell, have strong Southern sympathies. But since I'm a foreigner, you'll have to ask others." She gave him a covert look then said, "I understand that you're in some sort of antispy organization."

Miles shook his head sadly. "It's supposed to be the *Secret Service*, but of course, it isn't. Everyone knows what's going on." He laughed suddenly, saying, "Would you like to know where we get most of our information about the movement of Federal troops?"

"Yes."

"From the Northern newspapers." Taliferro laughed aloud and leaned back in his chair, his thin aristocratic face showing amusement. "Fortunately, there are many more newspapers in the North than we have in the South."

Lorna was fascinated. "Are there many spies in Richmond?"

"I'm afraid so." He leaned forward suddenly and put his hand over hers. "Perhaps you're one of them. After all, it would be a natural thing. You're English, and that wouldn't put you under suspicion. Actors travel everywhere, pick up all kinds of information. No one worries about their being spies. Are you a spy?" he asked with a smile.

Lorna was conscious of his hand over her own. She let it remain there, pressing hers lightly, and smiled at him. "I will see if you're a good enough Secret Service man to find out. If I am, I will certainly report to Mr. Pinkerton that one Southern officer is very alert."

The two of them had a pleasant walk together. When they

finally returned to her room, the corridor was vacant. She turned to say good night, but Taliferro pulled her forward, holding her tightly and kissing her. It was something he did very well, and Lorna did not struggle. When he released her, she smiled and said, "There. I surrendered that kiss to you. Now you'll tell me more of your secrets when we go for a walk. Good afternoon, Major Taliferro."

Taliferro was amused and tantalized. *She's a beautiful one*, he thought when she had closed her door. *I've never met anyone like her.* As he left the hotel, he was already planning new ways to entice her into spending more time with him.

※

As soon as Josh entered the house, he took one look at his father and asked abruptly, "What's wrong, Pa?"

Buford Yancy gave his son a troubled glance. "It's Rose," he said. "We had a fight."

Josh tossed the package he'd brought onto the table and turned to ask, "What was it about?"

"The same thing it always is," Buford said. "She's tired of the farm. She wants to go live in Richmond."

"Why, she can't do that!"

Buford Yancy reached up and rubbed the back of his neck. His pale green eyes were as sharp as when he'd been a younger man. He had only a few lines around his eyes, and it was the sinking in of his cheeks that showed his true age. "Well," he grunted, giving his head a disconcerted shake, "she may have done more than talk this time."

"Where is she, Pa?"

"Gone to visit that friend of hers—Millie—the one that

lives just outside Richmond."

"You shouldn't have let her go there."

"She's eighteen years old. What am I going to do? Tie her up to the hitching post?" Buford was disturbed. With the help of Melora, he had raised a large family without a wife. Most of the children had been easy to raise, but there had been a rebellious streak in Rose almost from the time she could walk. He remembered when the girl was first learning to walk. He had tried to get her to hold his hand, but she'd pulled back, arguing, "No, I do it." No matter how many times she fell, she never asked for help. Buford walked over and sat down heavily in the chair. He had not shaved in several days, and the bristles of his beard formed a white shadow on his cheeks. "I dunno whut to do with that girl, Josh," he said finally. "If I hadn't let her go, she'd have run off."

"I'm afraid for Rose." Josh suddenly slapped the wall of the cabin with his hand then turned to his father. "I'll go bring her back, Pa."

"No, I said she could stay for a week."

"What good does that do? This place isn't gonna change. She'll hate it just as bad."

A harried look came to Yancy's eyes. "I'm gonna talk to Melora. She's the nearest thing to a ma that Rose ever had."

Josh shook his head. "She loves Melora, but she won't listen to her. She won't listen to anybody." Josh was not accustomed to this sort of problem, and he said in a way that made Yancy look up, "What are we going to do, Pa? We gotta do something!"

Josh had not asked questions in such a plaintive way in a long time. He was a sturdy boy, able to take care of himself—almost a man. But something about the look in his eye reminded Buford Yancy of when he'd been a small boy. He wished he had an answer, but he had none. Deep in his heart, he was afraid there was none. Sighing deeply, he shook his head. "Young'uns grow up, Josh. They leave their home and make their own way. Some go right; some go wrong. Me, you, and Melora will just have to pray that Rose turns out to be one who went right."

✦

"Come in." Roland Middleton half turned, his hands raised to put on his makeup. He was surprised to see Rose Yancy enter the small dressing room. "Why, Miss Yancy!" he exclaimed, getting to his feet at once. He had not seen her except for the one time but was once again impressed by her fresh beauty. Now, however, he saw that her eyes were wide and her lips were drawn tight. "Is something wrong?" he asked immediately.

"Mr. Middleton, you've got to help me!" Rose was wearing a simple brown dress and over it a worn wool coat. Her hair had been blown by the stiff breezes, and she put her hand up, smoothing it down unconsciously. She seemed to be out of breath, which indeed she was, for she had come at almost a run to arrive at the theater before the performance.

"I—I don't know how to tell you this," she said breathlessly. There was a poignancy in the girl's green eyes, and she had a charm that was not polished but natural and free. "Can I talk to you for a minute, Mr. Middleton?"

"Well, we have about—oh, ten minutes before the curtain goes up. Can it wait till afterward?"

Rose hesitated then nodded. "Yes, sir, I can wait that long."

"Fine! Why don't you sit there and let me get this blasted makeup on; then after that we'll talk." As he applied the makeup, he spoke quietly to the young woman, wondering what had brought her to his dressing room in such a state. When someone called, "Places! Places, everybody!" he said, "Why don't you watch the play from backstage? It'll give you a different view of the theater."

"Oh, could I do that?"

"Certainly. Come on. I'll find you a place where you won't get run over by the thundering herd."

Rose spent the next two hours standing at one side of the stage. She was not visible to the audience, but all of the cast members were aware of her and spoke to her as they made their entrances and exits.

For Rose it was a fascinating two hours. She was disturbed over her argument with her father but soon lost herself in the action of the play. Surprisingly enough, it was the intricacy of the thing that interested her. When she had seen the play from the side of the audience, she'd lost herself in it. Now, however, her interest sharpened as she saw how the play really worked. Several of the players acted multiple roles, so they were constantly charging to a dressing room and whisking out in a new costume, talking to themselves as they made the adjustment. She was especially amused at Albert Deckerman, who played not only the role of a young man, but the role of a much older man. He stopped once beside her, muttering to himself, then turned and asked, "Are my whiskers on straight?"

Rose saw that he had glued a set of false whiskers on with some sort of substance. They were crooked, and she reached out and straightened them. "Now they look fine. You're doing so well, Mr. Deckerman. I don't see how you remember all those lines."

Albert Deckerman was not accustomed to being complimented by beautiful young women. He was highly pleased, for he got few compliments on his acting ability. "Not hard once you get the hang of it," he said airily. "Well, there's my cue." He shot off onto the stage, his booming voice dominating the theater as it always did.

"He's loud, isn't he?"

Rose turned to find Carmen Montaigne standing beside her. The actress was dressed in a beautiful gown of some wine-colored material. Her hair was wound around her head in a fashion that Rose had never seen before, and her eyes were curious. "Oh yes," Rose said. "He sure is. You look so pretty," she burst out.

Sophisticated as she was, Carmen appreciated the obviously earnest compliment. "Thank you—Miss Yancy, isn't it?" She hesitated then said, "You came to see the play?"

Rose hesitated and dropped her head, showing confusion. When she lifted her eyes, she saw that the older woman was looking at her with compassion. "Yes, well, I did want to see the play—" But at that moment, Carmen's cue came and she moved out on the stage.

Rose was almost sorry when the play was over, but it had given her time to think. Middleton came by and said, "Let me get out of this costume, and we'll go someplace where we can talk. Maybe have a cup of tea or coffee." He left at once and was soon back. He led her out of the theater to a café two doors down. It was only half full, and he chose a table near the rear of the room. As soon as the waiter had taken their order, he said, "Now I can see you have some sort of problem. You want to tell me about it?"

Rose began to speak nervously. She twisted her hands together, and her youthful face was almost painful to watch. The actor, accustomed as he was to hard times and his own troubles, found himself feeling an unexpected burst of pity for the girl. It was an old story to him, of course: a young girl wanting to go on the stage. He was rehearsing his speech, one that he'd given several times. It always began with "I know you want to be on the stage, but there's more to it than you see...."

Finally, Rose said, "So you see, I *can't* go back to that old farm, Mr. Middleton. I hate it there."

Roland shook his head and traced a pattern on the top of the table with his forefinger. "There're worse places than a farm, Miss Yancy. I've been in some of them myself."

"Oh, I know that, but I've just *got* to do something else. I can't go on taking care of pigs the rest of my life."

"A pretty young thing like you wouldn't have to worry about that."

Rose flushed at the compliment. She made a charming picture in Middleton's eyes as she sat there. Her skin was almost translucent, as beautiful as anything he'd seen. Her long eyelashes curled upward, and her widely spaced eyes looked at him with an innocence and yet a pain that he found hard to meet. "I could get married," she said simply. "But it would be just moving to another farm. I don't want to spend my life doing that. I want to do something with a little color in it. Something different!"

"Well, the theater's different, all right. May I call you Rose?" he asked suddenly. "I've gone through this with many young people, young ladies and men. The theater seems glamorous enough when you're sitting out there—bright lights, fancy costumes, moving from place to place." He leaned back, his eyes moody, and he shook his head. "It isn't like that really. It's just another job after you've done it awhile. And not a very good job at that—except for a few." He sat there and waited for her objections, which came as he'd expected. He listened for a long time and wished that he had the wisdom to counsel this girl. He knew, however, that it was not wisdom that she needed. Her mind was made up to leave, and there was no mistaking that.

Rose dropped her head finally and bit her lip. "I—I shouldn't have told you all this, I suppose." She looked up, and her lips were soft and warm and vulnerable as she added, "But I had to talk to somebody. And you were so nice to me before, just like you are now."

Roland Middleton had known many women, but never had he known one with the charm, innocence, and unspoiled beauty of Rose Yancy. A thought came to him: *Someone's going to sell her a bill of goods. She's fair game for some adventurer who doesn't have any compunction about things like that. She'll wake up one day and find herself totally lost.*

His mind worked quickly and he said finally, "Well, Rose, it's not my company. Mr. Rocklin would have to say. I'm not hopeful, but at least we could ask him." At the use of the word "we," Rose smiled tremulously. "Would you go with me to talk to him?" she asked quickly. "I'd feel so much better if you would."

"Yes, I'll do that. But you mustn't get your hopes up."

Twenty minutes later they were standing in Frank Rocklin's hotel room, where Rose was making her plea.

Frank listened carefully, and once his glance met that of Roland Middleton, as if to say, *Why did you bring this to me?* Finally, when Rose was finished, he shook his head. "I'm sorry, Rose. This is a small company. We just don't need another actress."

"But I'll do anything," she said. "You need someone to keep up with the costumes and the guns and the things you use in the play...." Rose's voice almost fell over itself. Her eyes were pleading as she stood before the two men. "Just let me go with you. You wouldn't have to pay me. Just a place to sleep and something to eat—that's all I want."

Frank was troubled by the girl. "Does your father know you're here, Rose?"

"He—he knows I'm in Richmond," Rose said. "He thinks I'm at a girlfriend's house. But he wouldn't mind. Not if you asked him, Mr. Rocklin."

"I couldn't be responsible for you," Frank said. Disappointment leaped into the young girl's eyes. "You can see how it is: a young woman going all over the country with a bunch of actors and actresses. I don't think your father would agree to it for a moment."

"I'm eighteen years old, Mr. Rocklin," Rose said, straightening up. She had removed the coat, and she made an attractive picture. She lifted her chin and said, "I'm not afraid to work. You won't have any trouble with me. I just want to leave the farm."

Middleton had been thinking and said suddenly, "Frank, we could use some help with the costumes. Especially when we go on tour. Nobody's really responsible, and we've got some walk-on parts with just short dialogue. It'd save Lorna and Carmen from having to make all those changes."

Frank gave Roland a disgusted look. He'd hoped that the actor would realize the difficulties. "Are you volunteering to be responsible for Miss Yancy, Mr. Middleton?" he asked sarcastically.

A sense of surprise ran through Middleton. He was not accustomed to putting himself out for anyone else. For so long a time his only concern had been drowning himself in drink and satisfying his own needs. Now he found himself saying, "She'll be all right. I'll do all I can—so will you. Lorna and Carmen will be her chaperones. It's respectable enough. After all, we're respectable people, aren't we?"

He caught a caustic look in Frank Rocklin's expression and was forced to grin. "Well, *you* are respectable, and it might do me good to have some responsibility." He hesitated then said, "Give her a try, Frank. At least while we're here in Richmond. See how it goes."

Frank Rocklin felt he was making a mistake. He argued for five minutes then threw up his hands. "All right, you can stay. I can't pay very much, and I'll have to talk to your father. He'll have to agree. You understand that, Rose?"

"I'll talk to him," she said breathlessly. There was a joy in her face that was obvious to both men. Her lips trembled as she turned and said, "Thank you, Mr. Middleton. I won't give you any trouble, I promise."

"I'm sure you won't, Rose," Middleton said. He was somewhat shaken now that he realized what he had promised. And when Frank told him to see about getting the girl a place to stay, they left, and Middleton turned to her and said, "Well, I guess I'm elected to take care of you." He grinned uncertainly. "I never had a daughter before, so I don't know how to start."

Instantly Rose looked at him. "You're not near old enough to be my father!" she said in a sprightly fashion. "An older brother, maybe."

Of course the whole plan had to be worked out. The next day, Rose sent word to her father. Yancy came, accompanied by Josh, and the pair talked with Frank Rocklin and Roland Middleton for a long time. Finally, they called Rose in and Buford Yancy said, "Rose, these two gentlemen have promised me to do their best to see you do right. They can't *make* you do right any more than I can. They'll be here for two more weeks. I've said you can stay that long; then we'll talk again."

"Oh, Pa!" Rose ran to her father and threw her arms around him, squeezing him hard. When she looked up, there were diamonds in her eyes, and she whispered, "I'll be good, Pa. Don't you worry."

Later on, Frank said dryly to Roland, " 'Don't you worry'—that's what she told her father. And I'm not going to. She's *your* responsibility. You take care of her."

Then a hard expression formed around Frank Rocklin's lips. "Roland, I like you, but you're not much good. I'm telling you this—I don't want that girl abused! You understand me?"

Roland Middleton was not offended. "Don't worry, Frank. I haven't done many good things with my life. Maybe if I can help Rose find herself, it'll be one mark in my favor." He turned and walked away, his head already filled with thoughts of what to do with this young girl, so alive, so vulnerable, so ready for life—so unaware of how life *really* was!

Chapter 17

A Matter of Loyalty

For the first few days of Rose Yancy's apprenticeship with the Rocklin Theatrical Company, things went well. Rose herself was ecstatic over the excitement and color of her new life, and finding work for her was no problem. She threw herself into keeping the costumes clean and in perfect condition and was always available for any errand or piece of work. Albert Deckerman had previously strewn his various costumes recklessly, so that from time to time he appeared on the stage wearing the wrong costume. His booming voice was often heard saying, "Rose, I don't know how we got along without you backstage."

The other aspect of Rose's new job included prompting the actors, although this was scarcely ever needed. On her fourth night, however, she was permitted to make a brief appearance on the stage. The play had called for a neighbor of the heroine to appear, say a half dozen lines, and then disappear. Either Carmen or Lorna had been forced to change costumes, make a quick appearance, and then rush backstage and change again. It had been Middleton who had said, "Rose, I think you ought to do a little acting." His eyes had sparkled with fun. And when she had taken a deep breath and nodded vigorously, he had gone to Frank and suggested that the girl be given a chance. Frank Rocklin had been happy enough, and both Carmen and Lorna had been very helpful. Neither of them relished the quick change, and together they had helped Rose find a dress that would do and coached her on the scene.

Just before Rose was to go out, Middleton was standing beside her, soothing her nerves. "You'll do fine, Rose," he said. "Just forget about the audience and look right at Frank as you say your lines. Did you ever play any make-believe games when you were little?"

Rose was nervous, but his remark caught at her. "Yes, I always did. We playacted all the time. I made my brothers and sisters be in plays whether they wanted to or not."

"Well, it's just like that now. We're all playing a big game up here. Sometimes when I was first beginning, I'd pretend there was a big brick wall at the footlights, that no audience was actually sitting out there. It worked pretty well for me. I got to the point where I could just ignore the audience." His face grew a little glum and he said, "I still do that sometimes, when I do a bad job."

"You never do a bad job, Mr. Middleton!" Rose argued quickly. Her eyes were shining, and she added, "I sure appreciate what you've done for me. I know Mr. Rocklin would never have let me come to work unless you had agreed to look out for me."

Roland Middleton shrugged off the compliment, but actually it pleased him. "I'm glad I could help, Rose. But you mustn't get too caught up with this kind of life. It's a very fragile way to live. Look, there's your cue. Out you go now!" He reached and patted her on the shoulder as she moved onto the stage.

Rose saw that Frank Rocklin was standing in the middle

of the stage waiting for her. She did not do as Middleton suggested, however. She took a quick glance at the audience and saw the faces packed in the long rows, all looking at her. But for some strange reason, it did not frighten her. She turned calmly to Frank and spoke her lines clearly. Frank smiled at her and winked, his back being to the audience, as he returned his own lines. And when she went offstage, J. Harold Hardcastle and his wife, Elizabeth, were waiting for her. They both hugged her and said, "You did fine, child, just fine."

"It was such fun!" Rose beamed. She turned to Middleton, saying, "Oh, Roland, you didn't tell me it was such *fun!*"

Middleton noticed that it was the first time she had used his first name, and he was pleased. "I'm glad you enjoyed it. Maybe I'll write in a few more touching scenes or add a new motif to the play."

"What's a *motif*?" Rose demanded instantly. But he had no time to answer, for he heard his cue.

After the curtain had fallen and they had taken their curtain call, Roland stopped long enough to say, "Still excited over your opening night, Rose?" He smiled at her, the smile making his face look much younger.

Rose started to answer, "Oh yes, Roland, I've—"

"Hey there, pretty gal! I've come to take you out on the town."

Middleton and Rose both turned to see a burly, red-faced soldier wearing a sergeant's uniform. He had come backstage uninvited, as was the custom, but they both saw at once that he had been drinking. His face was blotchy, and his speech was slurred. He suddenly took Rose by the arm. "Hey! I've been looking for a purty little thing like you. Come on, now—let's you and me go out and celebrate."

Middleton at once scowled, saying, "You're welcome to congratulate the lady, Sergeant, but that's all."

The burly soldier stopped smiling. He was one of those, Middleton saw at once, who turned ugly when he drank. And now his small, piggish eyes were squeezed almost shut as he said loudly, "Well, you're almost as pretty as she is." He laughed vacantly and added, "But I ain't taking *you* out. On your way, purty boy!"

Middleton stepped forward at once and struck the forearm of the soldier so that he dropped Rose's arm. "Let's not have any trouble about this. Life's too short for things like that," Middleton said. He turned half away and only caught a flash of the hamlike fist of the soldier as it came. He managed to pull himself partly out of the way, but the fist struck him on the shoulder and drove him backward. He almost lost his balance but caught himself and then turned. The sergeant laughed raucously, saying, "I guess you need a lesson in manners, purty boy. Get outta here 'fore I give it to you." He turned to make another grab at Rose, and as he did Roland stepped forward and hit him squarely in the nose. It drove the soldier backward, and instantly his nose started bleeding. He looked down in bewilderment at the crimson stain spreading across his shirt. The blow had sobered him up, and when he realized what had happened, he uttered a wild roar and threw himself at Middleton.

Roland Middleton was not an expert in the art of brawling. He had had a few fights as a youth, practically none since he had become fully grown. The sergeant, on the other hand, obviously was a brawler of some experience. He came in, catching Roland high on the temple with a tremendous left hand. Roland tried to block the blow, but the sergeant was simply too strong for him. Flashing lights seemed to dance before his eyes as he was knocked backward. Before he could recover, another blow caught him square in the mouth. He fell at once to the floor.

The sergeant laughed and drew back his foot, yelling, "You won't be a purty boy when I git through with you!" But before he could deliver the kick, someone grabbed his foot and wrenched it high in the air. "Hey, what the—!" The soldier fell facedown, trying to break his fall, but his forehead banged against the floor. Before he could move, a steely arm went around his throat and he was jerked to his feet. He struggled wildly, but the arm tightened mercilessly, and all he could do was gag. His arms thrashed and he tried to pull away, but as the oxygen grew thin, he became frantic. His voice gurgled in his throat, and he felt himself helpless against his unseen assailant.

Rose had been shocked at the scene. As little as she knew about fights, she realized that if the kick had been delivered, it would have broken Middleton's ribs. She had not seen Frank Rocklin, but he had come from nowhere, yanking the soldier's foot upward. And when he hit the floor, Rocklin had grabbed him around the throat and hauled him to his feet. Rose grew frightened as she saw the sergeant's face grow a brilliant red as he tried to suck air into his lungs. Frank's face was tense with anger, and for one moment she was afraid he would kill the soldier.

But Rocklin loosened his grip and instantly applied a hammerlock to the sergeant and pulled him across the room. As everyone stared, he walked to the door, opened it with his free hand, and said, "Sergeant, I'm going to allow you to leave this time. If you come back, it'll be unhealthy for you." With that he shoved him through the door. The sergeant hurtled out, and as Frank shut the door, they heard the sergeant gasping as he fell. Frank turned and walked over to Middleton. "You all right, Roland?"

Middleton's mouth was bleeding, and there was a raw scrape over his right temple. He tried to struggle to his feet, and Frank leaned down and pulled him up. "That was one of the roughs," he said. "Come along. We'll get you patched up. That's a bad cut on your lip there."

"Oh, I can do that," Rose said quickly. The fight had taken place so quickly that she had had little time to think, but now she led Middleton away to his dressing room. She shut the door and said, "You sit down right there."

Middleton's head was swimming, his head and mouth giving him considerable pain. Rose disappeared and came back soon with a pan of water and clean cloths, and he sat quietly while she dabbed at his wounds. "I don't think I'm going to go into boxing as an occupation," he muttered.

"He was *mean*!" Rose said with indignation. She was standing very close to him—so close he could smell a faint scent of lavender. Even though he was hurting badly, he was aware of the smoothness of Rose's skin and the clearness of her large green eyes. "I wish Mr. Rocklin had broken his dumb old neck!"

Middleton grinned, which hurt him, then inquired, "Have you had a lot of experience nursing beat-up actors?"

Rose was carefully dabbing at his mouth. She lowered the cloth and touched it with her hands, her touch gentle as possible. "That's going to hurt. I wish I had my medicine from the farm," she said. "It'd take some of the pain away."

"I'll be all right," Middleton said. He stood up and ran his tongue along the cut.

She watched him and whispered, "I sure thank you, Roland. You—you didn't have to do that."

"Why, sure I did. I'm your big brother, aren't I?"

Rose stared at him, an unspoken thought in her eyes. Finally, she said, "No, you're not my big brother. You're my friend, though. The best friend I have in the world."

※

Early the next morning, Lorna sat beside Middleton at the breakfast table. "How do you feel?" she asked quietly.

"Why, pretty well," he said. "My mouth's going to be a little sore, but it could've been worse." Roland shook his head. "Wonder where Frank learned to roughhouse like that. If he hadn't pulled that brute off me, I wouldn't have a whole rib in my body."

"He must have learned it in the army. He's very quick—and strong, too."

"Good thing for me he is." He looked down the table to where Rose was sitting, talking to Elizabeth Hardcastle in an animated fashion. "I wonder what it would feel like to be fresh, unspoiled, and excited about life like Rose."

Lorna's gaze switched to the young woman, and she said, "I wonder that myself."

It was not the first time Lorna had aroused Roland's curiosity. He had made such a tragic affair out of his own life. He hated to see anyone as young and beautiful as this English girl headed down that same road. "I hate to see you so low, Lorna," he said finally. "You've got everything. Oh, you've had a bad bump, but don't feel sorry for yourself. That's worse than getting kicked in the ribs by a drunken sergeant," he said bitterly. "The ribs heal up easier than the heart, I think." He laughed aloud rather harshly, saying, "I sound like a real bad romance novel, don't I? *Ribs heal easier than the heart!*"

Lorna gave him a quick glance. "Why, I think you're right, Roland. Any doctor can tie ribs up. Getting at the heart—that which is inside of us—who knows how to do that?"

"The preachers say it can be done," Roland observed.

"Do you believe that?" Lorna asked instantly. "I hadn't thought of you as a religious man."

Middleton hesitated then said, "I can't forget my mother. Every time I hear people talk about how Christians are hypocrites who don't mean what they say and there's nothing to religion, I think about her. My father and I didn't get along. He was hard. Still is, I guess. But my mother never gave up on me." He leaned back in the chair, toyed with his coffee cup, then finally lifted it and drank. He flinched as the hot liquid hit the cut in his mouth, and then he said, "Every time I think of her, I know there's something to it. God was in her. No question about it."

"I've known two or three people like that," Lorna admitted. Then she looked over and smiled bitterly. "But not us. We're too smart for that, aren't we, Roland?" He didn't answer, and finally she shook her head. "I'm sorry. I don't mean to be so caustic. I don't know what's the matter with me." She tried to smile then reached over and put her hand on his arm. "We'll be all right, eventually. We just haven't found our way."

Frank had been watching the two talk together and wondered what they were talking about. As always, he was impressed by the fresh attractiveness of Lorna, and the thought came to him, *What if those two fell in love? It wouldn't be good for her. I think a lot of Roland, but he can't even take care of himself.* Finally, he spoke up, saying, "I've got an announcement to make. We have an invitation."

"An invitation to what?" Albert Deckerman questioned loudly.

"An invitation to a fancy ball." Frank pulled a note out of his pocket and held it up. "My relatives, Uncle Brad and Aunt Amy Franklin, have invited the whole company out to Lindwood, their plantation. We're all invited to come. Would you all like to go?" At once the voices of the company assured him that they would. He stuck the paper back into his pocket with a grin and said, "All right. You'll have to behave yourselves, though. I don't want my Southern relatives to find out what a disreputable company I've really got!"

Rose came to Frank afterward, a little distressed. "You didn't mean me, did you, Mr. Rocklin?"

"About what, Rose?"

"About the party at Lindwood."

"Well, of course you're going. The note's from my aunt. She especially asked me to bring you."

Rose's face colored as she smiled and said, "Well, I just wasn't sure about it. We Yancys aren't great folks, you know. Not like the Rocklins or the Franklins."

Frank smiled, for he found this touching. "Well, *I* think you're great folks," he said. "It'll be an honor for them to have you. I'm sure your sister and all of them will feel that way, so put your best bonnet on, because we're going to a ball."

The sun was setting as Clay and Melora rode into view of Lindwood. The cool October air brought a flush to Melora's cheeks as they rode in the open carriage. They both looked impeccable, dressed for the autumn ball given every year by Clay's sister, Amy, and her husband, Brad Franklin. Clay sat ramrod straight in his ash gray uniform complete with a crimson sash around his lean middle. He had come home only two days before, and the two of them had been as loving as if they had just gotten married. Clay looked at Melora and nodded at the dress, a plum-colored fare of silk that he'd paid far too much for in Richmond. "You look beautiful," he said simply.

"Why, thank you, sir," she answered demurely. "And you'll be the handsomest man at that ball."

"Don't tell Rooney that. She thinks Lowell is."

"He is fine looking. So are Dent and David. All you Rocklin men are handsome devils." Then she asked suddenly, "What do you think about Rose? Going to be on the stage, I mean."

Clay shook his head. "Took me off guard. What do you think?"

"I don't know," Melora said, shrugging her shoulders. "She never was like the rest of us. Always unhappy on the farm—you know that, Clay."

"Maybe she needs a good spanking. But I guess at eighteen, it's too late for that. I'll have a good talk with my Yankee nephew. I hope he's got some of Gid's good sense. Never thought of having an actor in the family. Almost as bad as having a jockey or a lawyer, isn't it?"

"Now you hush," she said quickly.

Clay grew serious and shook his head. "She's a sweet girl, but not like you at all. She always craves excitement, and the farm just doesn't give it to her."

They had reached the front steps of Lindwood, and Clay pulled the horses to a stop. Bruno, one of the Franklins' stable hands, took hold of the horses, and Clay stepped down from the carriage and walked around to Melora's side. "Come along, now."

He helped her down, and the couple made their way inside

and met Brad and Amy, who were greeting guests as they arrived. Then they turned and entered the ballroom. "There's Rose," Melora whispered. "I know who that is with her. He's got the Rocklin look."

The two approached, and as soon as they were there, Melora gave Rose a hug. "How pretty you look!" she said.

Rose had worn one of Lorna's dresses and said at once, "This is Mr. Frank Rocklin."

"You don't have to introduce us," Clay said. "I remember you well, Frank—you, Ty, and Bob."

"That was a long time ago, sir," Frank said. "We had a good time, even though it didn't last long enough for us. I hope that soon we will all be able to gather here again." He turned and said, "I'm happy to meet you, Mrs. Rocklin." He took Melora's hand and bent to kiss it. "My grandmother's letters did not do your beauty justice." Frank gestured toward a small group and said, "Here's the rest of my troupe. Let me introduce them to you."

Frank introduced his company, and when he was finished, Clay said, "I'm halfway tempted to ask you to put on your play tonight since the whole group's here. But I'll let you off this time. Come and sit down with me. I want to hear what's happening with your brothers—and your whole family, for that matter."

Frank followed Clay Rocklin to an alcove, where they sat down. For the next thirty minutes, they chatted, with Frank doing most of the talking, about his family. Finally, Clay said, "I'm glad to hear the family's doing well. I wish your father were out of Libby. I'm trying hard to get him exchanged." The two spoke of Gideon for a time; then Clay hesitated and said, "Frank, I've got to talk with you seriously. I hope you won't take it wrong."

"Why, of course not. What is it, Uncle Clay?"

"It's about Rose. Melora's worried about her. She's not sure—about the life of an actress."

Frank at once said, "I understand your concern." He went on to explain how Rose had come to him and how he had offered her a place for as long as the company was in Richmond. "Her father came by," he said. "I explained it to him. Did he tell you?"

"I haven't seen Buford. But if he told you it was all right, then of course it is."

Frank said, "I can't guarantee anything. All I can say is Mr. Middleton and I will do our best to watch out for the girl. But you know she's a handful. Actually, I hesitated to take her, but she begged so hard that I just couldn't say no."

Clay grinned rashly, his white teeth gleaming against his golden brown skin. "Those Yancy girls have a way of doing that," he said. "Well, you watch out for her the best you can, Frank. That's all I ask."

The two returned to the party, and the evening was a pleasant one for all of them. Frank danced with his relatives and spent a most enjoyable thirty minutes with Susanna Rocklin, his great-aunt. She was a beautiful woman at the age of sixty-two, with a sharp wit. Finally, he found himself dancing with Carmen, who had been besieged by some of the young officers gathered for the ball.

"You're a hit," he said as they went around the polished floor.

"Any woman who wasn't actually hideous would be a hit here," she said. "Officers are all the same, North or South, aren't they?"

"If you mean that they appreciate a beautiful woman, you're right," he said. Then he asked, "What do you think of this place?"

Carmen looked around the floor at the colorful dresses of the women, the gray uniforms of the men, the flashing of brass buttons reflecting the chandeliers, and shook her head. "It's beautiful," she said. "But it isn't really the South, is it?"

"No, not really. There are few plantations and lots of poor folks, but the North has far more poor than rich as well," he countered.

"Do you think they will let Rose stay with the company?"

"It looks that way. We'll have to be very careful about her, though. These Southerners are very protective of their young women."

"Roland seems to be doing a good job at that," she announced and nodded toward the two who sailed by, gliding in a waltz in and out among the dancers. "Have you noticed that Roland's doing better? He's not drinking. Do you suppose Rose has a good influence on him?"

"I think so. He doesn't like to look bad in front of her, which could be a good thing—or a bad thing."

"What could be bad about it?"

"If he fell in love with her. That would be bad."

"Why? Roland's a good man."

"Sure, but you know Roland. He can't even take care of himself, much less a wife and a family."

Dissatisfaction and something almost like pain swept across Carmen's face. "He can change, can't he, Frank? Anyone can change, given the chance."

Surprised at the intensity in Carmen's voice, Frank looked carefully at her. She was beautiful in her crimson dress, a daring one that not many women could wear. "Of course they can, but they have to want to. I'm not sure Roland wants to."

Carmen wanted to talk more with Frank, but the dance

stopped. She was at once claimed by a tall colonel who swept her off for the next dance.

Frank wandered around the floor awhile and finally saw Lorna slip out one of the side doors. Quickly he followed her. The sound of the music faded as he stepped outside and closed the door. Lorna turned to face him, and he said, "It's cool out here. Should I get your wrap?"

"No, I'm not staying long, Frank." She studied him then said, "I like your family very much."

"My father thinks the world of Clay," he said. He came to stand by her and smelled the jasmine that was in the scent she wore. Overhead the stars twinkled brightly against the velvet sky, and he said, "The story is that my father and Clay Rocklin were both in love with my mother—and Clay lost."

"It must've been a hard choice for her. Your father must be quite a man to have beat Mr. Clay Rocklin out. He's so fine looking! Such a fine man, too, from what I understand."

"Yes, he is. But he wasn't always that way." He hesitated then said, "He had a bad experience in marriage, and it's taken him a long time to come back. The family talks about it sometimes. His first wife was not amiable, but Clay was always faithful to her, even though he loved Melora for years."

"I think that's very sweet. Melora's very beautiful." She let the silence run on then said, "It's not very often the story turns out like that, is it, Frank?"

"You mean happily? Well, I suppose some of the time it does; some of the time it doesn't."

"But mostly it doesn't," she said.

Frank was interested in this. "Why do you say that, Lorna? I've wondered about you." He turned her around and stood facing her. "You're a puzzle to me."

"I think I'm a very simple woman," Lorna said quietly. She looked up, facing him, and said, "I think men put complexities in women that aren't really there."

"And sometimes," Frank countered with a slight smile, "women have complexities that they try to cover over with simplicities." He reached out, took her hand, and held it for a moment. "I didn't mean to sound like a half-baked philosopher. But I've been waiting for a chance to tell you how much I appreciate your coming with the group. You've been a great help."

Lorna was very conscious of his warm hand holding hers. She was troubled by it at the same time—or troubled by something that went on inside her. "I was glad to get away from England," she said quietly. Then the memories from the past rose in her and her face grew sad. "I wouldn't want to go back again."

Frank Rocklin was suddenly conscious of the vulnerability of this young woman whose hand he held. Her flesh was soft, warm, and vibrant, but there was a fragility in her that he could not identify. He wanted somehow to see her put it aside and manifest the joy that a beautiful woman should let the world see. "What's to be so sad for?" he whispered. "I hate to see that in you."

They were very close, and Lorna looked up intending to speak, but she found she could not. The sadness that lay not too far beneath the surface suddenly caught up with her, and Frank Rocklin saw it. "Don't be sad," he said. "Life is good." He reached out and drew her close. She lowered her cheek against his chest, and he held her there quietly. There was a strength in him that she yearned for. His arms closed warm and strong around her, and in that moment she felt safe and secure. There was a sudden desire in her for whatever it is that a man brings to a woman. She had missed it, and in missing it she had feared she would never have anything like love again. And now for this one moment as he held her tightly, she felt something of what a woman ought to feel when a man protects her.

Frank was moved by her surrender. She was, he knew, a strong woman, not one to give herself easily. There was nothing in her but an intense femininity—that mystery that is woman, female—that the male must have. And now as she leaned against him, almost like a tiny bird nestling in a set of strong hands, he felt protective of her. Reaching up, he touched the back of her hair, caressing it, and when she looked at him, he said, "Don't be sad. You have so much, Lorna." He wanted to kiss her but felt that would be wrong. Instead, he touched her cheek with one hand and said quietly, "I want you to have what every woman should have. And you'll have it one day, I promise you."

Lorna was moved by his words. She had expected him to try to kiss her, and when he did not, paradoxically she was both disappointed and relieved. Taking a deep breath, she nodded and stepped back. "I'm sorry, I don't often let these moods throw me," she said. "I suppose we'd better go back in."

"Are you all right?" he asked quietly.

She smiled, her face becoming quite serene. The moment had done something for her, and she knew she would think of it often. "Yes, Frank. I'm all right now. Let's go inside."

Chapter 18

The Secret Discovered

Major Miles Taliferro was dissatisfied. His profession lent itself to disappointment, for being a spy in both the North and the South was of necessity a matter of amateurism. There had been no professional spies, as such, when the war began. But now both sides realized the need for information about the movements of the enemy.

Since his superior had warned him that an influx of agents from the North was to be expected, Taliferro had worked hard at instilling in his subordinates the necessity of rooting them out. This, of course, was most difficult. Some of the agents they had apprehended had *seemed* more Southern than those born in the South. Some of them had, indeed, been born in the South but had given their loyalty to the North. Now as Taliferro looked over the paperwork scattered on his desk, he grew irritable. Finally, he shuffled the papers around and shoved them into a folder. Moving across the room, he leaned down and twirled the dial of a huge safe. It had been in a bank once, but Taliferro had managed to obtain it for storing his own files. The doors swung open. He put the folder carefully on top of a stack, shut the safe, and spun the dial again.

Moving swiftly, he left the office, saying, "I'll be gone for the rest of the day, Sergeant."

"Can I reach you at any particular place, Major?"

"I'll be moving around quite a bit. If you have to find me, I'll eventually be at that makeshift theater where Rocklin's company is playing."

The sergeant grinned. "I saw that play myself. It ain't bad, is it, sir?"

"It's all right, I suppose."

For the rest of the afternoon, Taliferro moved from point to point. He had a phenomenal memory for names and faces, and when he saw someone who looked slightly out of place, a stranger he didn't recognize, he managed to discover something about the party. Sometimes he did this by striking up a conversation directly, and other times he would move around, following the suspect and asking others for information. By five o'clock he gave up and moved to the Spotswood Hotel, where he entered the dining room. It was only half filled this early, and he was able to obtain a good table. He was in the process of ordering when he looked up and saw Lorna Grey enter. At once he said to the waiter, "Hold on. I hope to have company." Moving across the floor, he came to stand in front of Lorna, saying, "Have pity on a poor, lonesome soldier—have dinner with me."

"I'll be glad to, Major." Lorna allowed him to escort her to the table. He seated her then negotiated the meal, warning the waiter he'd have the place closed if the food wasn't prepared just right.

As the waiter left, Lorna smiled at him, amused by his threats. "Would you really have the restaurant closed?" she asked idly.

"I'd be shot if I did." Taliferro grinned. "This is the best place to eat in Richmond." He studied her for a moment then asked, "How's the play going?"

"Very well, I suppose. At least all the seats are filled every night."

"I suppose that's due to many factors."

At once Lorna understood his meaning. "Not very complimentary, Major. But true enough. Any kind of entertainment would play to a full house around here. It's not a very good play, I'm afraid."

"Not a good one for you, at least. You should be doing something quite different. Tell me about your career."

But Lorna, after touching on the subject, chose to lead him away from it. She spoke of the company, and when she mentioned Rose, Taliferro glanced at her sharply. "Rose Yancy? Who is she?"

"A girl from the country. Her sister's married to Clay Rocklin."

"That's unusual. I didn't know the Rocklins went in for the theater."

"The girl comes from a very poor family, I think. I understand she's not going to be with the company for long. When we leave Richmond, I'm not sure her father will let her accompany us."

"Mr. Rocklin—has he said when you'll be leaving?"

"No, he hasn't mentioned it. But he did say when we left Washington that we'd be touring the South, so I presume we'll be performing in some other cities down here."

They talked idly until the food came, and then as they ate, Taliferro picked up the threads of the conversation again. "As I told Mr. Rocklin, it seems a strange thing to bring a theatrical company here." A sour look came to his face, and he said, "I'm sure you've discovered that Confederate money is worth very little." He took a bite of the steak before him, chewed it thoughtfully, and said, "Mr. Rocklin said he wanted to see the South again, but it doesn't seem to be a wise or professional move."

"I suppose that's so. But I know nothing about Mr. Rocklin's plans."

"He visits his father every day, I'm told."

"Yes, he does. I think he's very concerned about his condition."

For some time they sat there talking. And finally Lorna became aware that there was some sort of pattern to the conversation. Taliferro would speak idly of certain things, but his questions always came back to the company, especially to Frank Rocklin. She said nothing to him about this but filed it in her mind. Later on, after they had parted, she thought, *I wonder why he's so interested in Frank.* The thought would not leave her, and from that moment on she began to pay more attention to Frank's movements.

The skies had grown completely dark, and as they left the theater after the performance and moved back to their hotel, the company had little to say. Middleton was walking with Rose, and once he looked up and said, "We'll have rain before morning."

Rose followed his glance and agreed. "Yes, it smells like that, doesn't it?"

They arrived at the hotel, and the company said good night

and went to bed. But Lorna suddenly remembered that she had left her purse at the theater. It contained all the money that she had, and she was not certain it would be safe. She went to Frank's room to get the key, but to her surprise he was not inside. Puzzled, she thought, *But he just came here. Where could he be?*

Albert Deckerman took care of the props, and she knew that he had a spare key. She went to Albert's room, borrowed his key, and told him she'd return it the next morning.

"You'd better let me go with you if you're going back to the theater," he proposed.

"No, I'll be all right. I'll take a cab. You go to sleep, Albert."

"All right, but I'd be glad to go."

Lorna did not take a cab, for the theater was only a few blocks away. She walked along the sidewalks, the oil lamps casting enough light for her to see clearly. When she arrived at the theater, she went inside and found her purse in the dressing room. Then she left the theater, locking the simple hasp back in place. Turning to go, she saw a man across the street and was surprised to identify him as Frank Rocklin. He was walking with his head down, for a few drops of rain had started to fall. Lorna remembered her conversation with Taliferro and on impulse crossed the street. She kept far enough behind Rocklin so that she could not be identified. Frank walked for two blocks then stopped suddenly as a man came out of an alley. The two spoke to each other then moved back into the darkness of the alley.

Alarm ran along Lorna's nerves, and she moved closer to the building and waited. *What could he be doing here? And why's he so secretive about it?* she asked herself. She knew little of Frank Rocklin's business. There could be any number of reasons or explanations of why he was meeting someone at this time of night, but she couldn't think of one. Finally, Rocklin came out and turned back toward her, and she saw the other man emerge and turn in the other direction. Rocklin was headed straight for her, and fearful of being seen, Lorna turned and walked as rapidly as she could along the boardwalk. When she got to the street where the hotel was, she crossed and went at once to her room. She unlocked the door, stepped inside, and, after she shut it, moved across to the window. She watched as Frank came down the street, turned, and entered the hotel. Curiosity came to her even stronger, and she moved to the door and cracked it. She saw Frank reach the landing and turn to his own room. He opened the door and shut it very quietly, as one who didn't want to be heard.

"How very strange!" Lorna murmured. She undressed, washed her face, took a sponge bath carefully, then put on her nightgown. For a time, she sat on the side of her bed wondering what it all could mean. Finally, she shrugged. *He probably has a good explanation for it,* she thought then lay down and went to sleep.

The next morning at breakfast, however, something more disturbing happened. In the middle of the conversation, Middleton said he hadn't slept well. "How about you, Frank?" he asked. Lorna was sitting directly across from Frank, and she saw a break in his features. "I went right to bed and slept like a log," he said and continued eating. *That's a lie!* Lorna thought. *He did no such thing.*

Frank looked up and saw her watching him. "What do you plan to do today, Lorna?" he asked. "Like to take a ride around town? You and Roland and Carmen and I could maybe see a little of the town."

"That would be nice," Lorna agreed.

They went on their ride later that afternoon. Carmen and Middleton were jaded with strange places, but Lorna found Richmond fascinating. Once, they passed by a slave market, and she said, "Could we see that?"

Frank looked at her strangely. "I suppose so." He drove the wagon to a hitching post, got out, and came to help her down. The four of them made their way into a huge barnlike affair, where the sale was already going on. Lorna found herself disgusted by the entire thing. The auctioneer had just brought a woman in her middle thirties and a small boy to the front. "What am I bid for this fine pair?" he demanded. "Come over, gentlemen. They're worth the money. This buck will make a fine field hand. This woman's capable of bringing lots more like him into the world."

Lorna watched as the prospective buyers went to the front. Some of them prodded the woman's body as if she were an animal. More than one rude remark ran around the room. But the ending was more shocking. One of the bidders made a high bid for the woman but said, "I can't use the boy."

The auctioneer at once said, "We'll sell them separately."

The woman reached out, grabbed the small boy, and held to him, her eyes defiant and filled with fear. The auctioneer nodded. Two strong-looking men came and held the woman, who screamed while the boy was ripped from her arms.

"Let's get out of here," Frank said grimly. "I've had all of this I want to see." The others were ready, and they hurried to the wagon. The afternoon was spoiled for all of them, and when they got back to the hotel, Frank said, "That's the other part of the South—the ugly part. People get fooled by the magnolias and the nice weather, but any system that'll tear a child from his mother has got to go!"

Lorna agreed at once. "Inhuman slavery was outlawed in Great Britain years ago. I think it's indecent that this country permits it."

"Well, I don't think they'll permit it long," Middleton said. "That's what this war is all about."

The play stretched out to a three-week run. And it was in the middle of the third week that Lorna had opportunity to observe Frank Rocklin's strange behavior again. She had noticed that he went out at odd times, and one night while sitting at her window after a play, she saw him exit the hotel. At once she knew that he was off on another one of his missions—whatever it was. Instantly she grabbed her coat and left her room, and as she left the hotel, she saw him turn a corner. Without knowing why, she felt she had to know what he was doing. Something in her revolted against the idea that he was not what he seemed. The idea had been growing in her that he was perhaps involved in the Southern Secret Service. She had thought of Major Taliferro's questions and had finally decided that perhaps he was Frank's superior. It didn't make much sense to her, but she could not come to any other conclusion.

She had been very clever, she thought, about following Frank. He made his way down the street past the place the last meeting had been, and two blocks later he turned to cross into what appeared to be two vacant lots between two wooden structures. There were no streetlights on this side street, and Lorna felt her way along.

Once, she stopped, listening for the sound of voices, but

hearing none, she kept moving forward. *They've got to be here somewhere,* she thought. Far away the distant tinny sound of a piano came to her from one of the saloons that was still open, but ahead there was no sound at all. Then, abruptly, before she could even move, a pair of strong arms went around her from behind. When she opened her mouth to scream, a hard hand was clapped over her lips, cutting off her cry. She struggled and fear raced through her. Fiercely she kicked with her sharp heel and had the satisfaction of raising a grunt from her assailant, but his hands remained firmly in place. She heard someone else coming, moving from her side, and then she heard Frank's voice demanding, "Who is it, Perkins?"

"I've been watching her. She followed you all the way down the street and turned in here after you did. She's got to be a spy."

Lorna did not recognize the second voice, but she did recognize Frank's. And now she heard him ask, "What'll we do?"

"We can't let her go loose," the first voice said.

Frank said quickly, "Let her talk. I can't believe anyone followed me."

Dave Perkins was a hard man and had done hard things. "We'll have to get her out of here—kidnap her till we find out what she's up to. I think she's one of Taliferro's agents."

Lorna found herself being held tightly, but the hand moved away from her lips. Perkins said, "Who are you? What are you doing following us?"

Lorna said at once, "Frank, it's me, Lorna!"

"Lorna!" Frank was aghast. Then he said abruptly, "It's all right, Perkins. She's one of the actresses in our company."

"It's not all right," Perkins said. "Why is she following you?" A thought came to him and he said, "Is she your woman?

Maybe she was just jealous."

Lorna struggled with his grip, and he released her but kept one hand on her arm. "No, I'm not his woman," she said angrily. She looked at Frank and said, "Who is this man, Frank?"

Frank hesitated then knew he would have to tell the truth, but not here. "It's all right, Perkins. I'll take care of it."

Perkins said angrily, "You can't take care of it. We'll have to get her out of here. She knows too much."

"You don't know what she knows," Frank snapped. "I said I'd handle it." He reached over and took Lorna's arm. "Come on, Lorna."

Lorna was relieved to feel the man called Perkins release her. She stumbled along as Frank pulled her out of the darkened lot. He said nothing until they were half a block away. Then when she said, "Frank—," he muttered, "Don't talk—not here."

He led her back to her room, and when she unlocked it, he stepped inside, following her, then shut the door. She was trembling and asked at once, "What are you doing, Frank? I have to know."

Frank nodded slowly. "Yes, you do have to know." He hesitated then said, "Sit down. It's a long story." He waited until she was seated then began by saying, "I have a brother. The best man that ever lived. . ."

Lorna sat listening to the story, and when he was through, she stared at him. "So you're a spy for the North. That's it?"

"That's it," Frank said wearily. He drew his hand across his forehead then lowered it. "I'm sorry you found out about it. It has nothing to do with you. You're not involved in this war."

Somehow Lorna was feeling a pain she hadn't expected. She could not understand it. Her mind went back to the time when she had stood with Frank and he had held her. She remembered the comfort that had come to her, the strength that had flowed out of him and that she had trusted. That grew bitter now, and anger rose in her. "No, it's not my war, but I hate to be used."

Frank stared at her. "What do you mean *used*?"

"You're using us all," Lorna said, her voice cold. "All of us. None of the rest of them know anything about this, do they? They think you're doing it because it's your profession. But you'll drop the whole company if you want to. Anything to get even for your brother, is that right?"

Frank stared at her. "Don't put it like that, Lorna," he said quietly. "I want this war to be over. This is the way that I've chosen to help." He, too, was remembering how he had held her in his arms and how she'd responded. "Please don't be upset," he said finally. "I couldn't tell you. You wouldn't have come—nobody would've come!"

"That's right," Lorna said flatly. "I wouldn't have come, and I'm not staying."

Frank stared at her. A sense of disloyalty came to him. He had felt the same way when he had been at Lindwood, using his family to get information for their enemies. He felt it now as he stood before Lorna, her eyes angry, her lips drawn tightly together. He felt that he'd like to throw the whole thing over, but he'd gone too far for that, and he hadn't completed his job. "I can't stop you if that's what you want to do," he said at last. "Are you going to tell the others?"

Lorna found herself trembling. "No," she said. "And I'll stay. It wouldn't be fair to them for me to leave. I care about them, even if you don't."

It was a hard moment for Frank Rocklin. He had learned to admire this young woman, and he'd lost her trust. That moment of harmony and gentleness they had shared together was now gone, he saw. He said wearily, "Well, I thank you for that. I'll keep you clear of it. Hopefully it won't be for too long. Then we can go back." He stood then moved to the door. When he got there, he turned back to her again and said simply, "Lorna, I'm sorry." Then he turned and left the room.

Lorna closed and locked the door behind him; then she went to the bed, fell across it, and began to weep.

PART FOUR
The Last Act
November–December 1863

CHAPTER 19

JOSH GIVES A CHALLENGE

"I'm glad to be back in Richmond." Carmen was sitting in the dressing room applying her makeup. She looked up at Lorna, who was doing the same at the other makeshift dressing table. "I've seen about all of the South that I want to see," she added.

Lorna carefully put the final touches on her face, murmuring, "It was interesting to me. I was surprised at how small most of the so-called big cities are here in the South." They had gone on a short tour, playing in Montgomery for two weeks. After the first two days, the troupe had found little to draw their attention.

Rose, who had come in with dresses freshly pressed for the two women, listened as the actresses talked. "I thought it was fun. I wish we could travel some more." She helped Carmen put on her dress, and when the actress left the room at her call, she said to Lorna, "You think I'll ever get to be a real actress, Miss Lorna?"

"I'm sure you will." Lorna smiled with encouragement. "Though I'm not sure it's what you really ought to do. It's a hard life—as you've found out on this tour."

"Not as hard as living on a farm," Rose insisted. She fastened up Lorna's dress and stood back in admiration. "Now you look right pretty," she said. Then she held out her skirt and asked, "How do I look? All right?"

"You look fine, Rose, just fine."

The two women left the dressing room and went to stand in the wings. The timing on the play had become so perfect that Lorna had learned how to leave the dressing room with only seconds to spare. As she arrived in the wings, she heard her cue and walked out on the stage speaking her opening line: "Why, Davis! What are you doing here?"

Frank turned as she entered, showing his profile to the audience, and spoke his line: "I had to get away. I had to see you, Alice." He crossed the stage to her and took her hand. The two stood there speaking their lines until the culmination of the love scene. Lorna's face was half turned toward the audience, and she kept a loving expression on him. "I love you, Davis," she whispered, reaching up to pull his head down. When his lips came down on hers, she could not help but remember how close they had been for a time. And even now, in view of a full house, she was moved more than she liked to admit by his kiss. He clung to her, pressing her closer, and seemed to savor the kiss more than was necessary. She broke away and continued the scene.

After the two had left the stage and the Hardcastles were heard doing their part of the play, Frank said, "That was well done, Lorna."

Lorna stopped and looked at him. She'd been distant since discovering what his actual purpose was in raising the company, and now she said sharply, "I don't think you have to hold me quite so tightly in that scene, Frank."

Turning to look at her, Frank lifted his eyebrow. He knew that she was distrustful of him. He was disturbed that they had lost the warmth that once existed. "As an actress you ought to know we've got to live our roles, at least out on that stage."

"I think I know the difference between acting and what you've been doing."

Frank stared at her but could say nothing, for he knew that she was partly right. He ducked his head, bit his lip, then lifted his eyes to her, saying, "I'm sorry." He tried to think how to explain himself, and finally shrugged. "If I feel something for you, I guess it comes out when I'm close, especially in a kiss. I don't know how to kiss a woman without some sort of response." The other actors moved about, getting into their places, and although there was no time, he said, "I'd hoped that we'd get back to what we were once, Lorna. I think about you all the time."

Lorna hesitated. There was a faint longing in her that stirred to life as she thought about their past. She had been drawn to Frank Rocklin as she never had been to any man. Yet the memory of her tragic experience with Michael Dennis was still with her. She had raised a wall since discovering Frank's activities with the Secret Service and could not seem to put it behind her. Wearily she said, "I'm sorry I said anything. Forget it, will you, Frank?" Turning, she walked away and entered the dressing room.

After the play was over, the company went out to eat. But Frank noticed at once that Lorna did not accompany them. As he was sitting down with Carmen to drink his coffee, he mentioned the fact.

"I expect she's just tired from the tour," Carmen answered carelessly. "She's not tough enough for things like that, I suppose." Finally, she reached over and put her hand over his. "These English ladies are meant for drawing rooms and tea and things like that."

Frank reached over, picked up her hand, and held it for a moment. He smiled, saying, "You've been great for the company, Carmen."

Disappointment rose in the woman, for she had been hoping for something more intimate. She, too, had noticed the cooling off between Frank and Lorna and had hoped that it meant that Frank would be devoting more time to her. When he released her hand, she felt a vague sense of dissatisfaction. "I wish we could stay here for a long time," she said finally.

"There's not much money in it," Frank replied. "You certainly don't need the experience."

Something about the remark displeased Carmen. She had thought much about herself during the days of the tour and about Frank Rocklin. Carmen was perhaps oversensitive about her age. At thirty-two, she was past her youth, and Frank was so much younger. She had known men to marry older women and was aware that she did not look her age. Nevertheless, his remark about her "experience" somehow hurt her. Finally, when the two rose and left, she said, "It's not too cold to go for a walk, is it?"

"No, of course not. Just a little snappy is all. Nothing like our Northern falls, is it, Carmen?"

The two walked along the streets, the brisk wind snatching at their clothing, making it flutter. "There might be some snow in that," Frank observed, walking along. "The sky looks like it wants to, but I think it's too warm for that. I wouldn't mind seeing a little snow. I always liked it." She stumbled slightly, and he took her arm and held lightly on to it. "I like to make snowmen, have snowball fights, and go sledding."

They took two turns around the block then entered the hotel. He accompanied her up to her room, and, opening the door, she turned to him. "Thank you for the walk. It was nice," she said. She waited for him to say something, and it was on her mind to invite him in. She sensed that would be a mistake. She had been free, too much, with her favors in the past, and it had to be different with Frank. Still, she knew how to look up and entice a man, and so when she did, he leaned forward and kissed her on the lips. She pulled away at once and whispered huskily, "That was sweet. Good night, Frank."

As the door closed, Frank turned and walked to his own room. He was thinking about so many things. He had been concerned about Perkins, who had been hinting at some great action that would have to take place, although he would not say what. He was also buried in thought about keeping the company going. He had discovered one thing—that acting was the life for him. Entering his room, he shut the door and locked it, then undressed and went to bed. For some time he lay thinking about problems that existed, especially about his brother. He still felt a bitterness at what the war had done to his family and could not shake it off.

"Got to stop thinking like that," he said. His mother had talked with him, as had others. He remembered how Bob had smiled and said, "You can't let bad things turn you sour. God's too good to let that happen. He's going to do something in you, Frank."

Frank Rocklin thought of these words and finally drifted off to sleep. His last thought, however, was of the softness of the lips of Lorna Grey. "Stage kiss," he murmured, "but I wonder if it will always be like that."

"I'm going to do something about it, Rena." Josh Yancy had been walking with Rena along the stream that bordered Gracefield. It was a favorite place for the two of them. They had caught pumpkinseed perch, fat and thumping, in the summer. And they had seen deer drink from its waters then bound away in that airless fashion of the breeze. It was here that they had come to talk when they had had problems. And now as they walked along, a thought came to Josh. "You know," he said, "I hardly ever stutter anymore. You broke me of that habit."

"I think you did it yourself, Josh," Rena said. She was very pretty that day, wearing a dark green dress and, on her head, a felt cap that she and Melora had picked out. It had been expensive, but Josh had liked it, and that had been enough. Now they came to a narrow place in the creek. "Let's cross to the other side," she said.

"All right." Josh followed behind her, saying, "Don't fall in. It's too cold for that."

They moved along the north side of the creek. The grasses were brown and dead now, and the trees were orange, red, and a brilliant yellow. "What is it that you're going to do, Josh?" Rena asked.

"I'm going to do something about Rose. She can't go on like she's been doing."

"But what can you do?" Rena asked. "She's grown up. She's eighteen. If she wants to be an actress, you can't stop her."

"Maybe not, but I'm going to try," Josh said. He was filling out now, his lanky frame showing the beginnings of strong muscles, his shoulders broadening. There was a maturity in his face that had not been there a year ago. "I'm going to Richmond tomorrow for Pa, and while I'm there I'm going to have a talk with Rose. Maybe even with Mr. Frank Rocklin. I sort of like him, even if he is a Yankee."

"Well, he's a Rocklin—part of my family," Rena said quickly. "He is nice, and good looking, too."

Josh glanced at her, and a mischievous light came to his eyes. He lost his troubled expression for a moment and reached out and took her arm. She squealed as he held her toward the creek, leaning over. "I think I'll just dunk you in the water," he teased. "That'll stop you from looking at these good-looking actors."

"You let me go, Josh Yancy!" She struggled in his grasp but was powerless in his strong hands. "Please, Josh!" she said. "Don't let me fall."

At the piteous tone, Josh hesitated then pulled her back. "I wouldn't do that," he said. "But don't be looking at any of these handsome fellas around here. Mr. Rocklin's your cousin, but I saw you looking at Sam Goodwin the other day in church. He's plumb loony over you." He hesitated and said, "Some would even say he's good looking, even better looking than me."

"Those with eyes," Rena said pertly. Then at the look on his face, she laughed and hit him then took his arm. "Come on, let's walk. I'm not interested in Sam Goodwin."

The two finished their walk. He took her back to the house, and before he left, he had a word with Susanna. He had great confidence in Rena's grandmother and talked with her for some time about his concerns for his sister. Melora came in while they were talking and listened quietly. Finally, he turned to her and said, "Melora, why don't you go talk to Mr. Rocklin? He'd listen to you."

"It's not Mr. Rocklin that you need to think about. It's Rose. She's headstrong, and there's nothing Mr. Rocklin can do about that. I don't think you ought to go, either."

Josh was usually an agreeable young man, but it had hurt him that his sister had gone on the stage. For some reason, he had strong feelings about people in the theater. He had heard enough stories about the immoral lives of actors and actresses, and he wanted none of that for Rose. He shook his head stubbornly and said, "I'm going to talk to her and Mr. Rocklin, too."

When he had left, Melora turned to Susanna, saying, "It won't do Josh any good. Might even make Rose more stubborn. I wish he wouldn't go."

"Well," Susanna said, "he's going, and that's all there is to it. You Yancys have a pretty stubborn streak." She reached over and patted her daughter-in-law on the shoulder. "But I'm proud of all of you. Clay couldn't have had anything better happen than to get you, Melora."

As soon as Josh had finished the business for his father in Richmond, he went to the theater. He found Frank Rocklin without any trouble and said quickly, "Can I talk to you alone, Mr. Rocklin?"

"Why, sure, Josh. Come on to my dressing room. We'll have a little privacy."

Josh sat down then began nervously, "I'm worried about Rose, Mr. Rocklin." He went on to explain his difficulties, and Frank felt a great sympathy for the young man.

When Josh had finished with a plea for Frank to do something, Frank spread his hands out and said, "Josh, I appreciate your concern for Rose. I wish I could do something, but the only thing I could do is fire her. If I did that, what would happen?"

Josh thought hard and said, "She'd be madder than hops."

"That's right, and disappointed, too. Your father allowed her to travel to Montgomery with us, so he must have some confidence in our ability to take care of Rose. And after working with us for a while, maybe she'll learn that the theater isn't too good a life. Why don't you just let her stay? Mr. Middleton and I are looking out for her, and so are Miss Montaigne and Miss Grey."

At the name of Middleton, Josh seemed to bridle. He said nothing, but a rebellious streak rose in him. He wanted to argue but saw that it was useless. "Well, thank you, Mr. Rocklin. I appreciate your looking out for my sister."

At the same time that this pair was talking, Rose and Roland were riding in a buggy. She had teased him into taking her for a ride, and the two had driven out of the city. She had shown him around the parts that she knew of the countryside, and now they were on their way back.

"Oh, it's been such fun, Roland!" she said. "Can't we stay a little longer?"

"Not if we're going to make the curtain tonight," Roland said. He glanced at her, admiring the rosy complexion stirred by the wind. She had the clearest eyes he had ever seen; they were the most peculiar shade of green. He had noticed the same shade of green in the eyes of Melora Rocklin and also her brother Josh. "You look very pretty," he said, paying her a rare compliment. "Those Confederate officers that line up to meet you, I'll have to fight them off with a stick tonight."

Rose flushed and shook her head. "You won't have to do

that."

"Does it make you feel good to have men flocking around you like bees after honey?"

"I don't care about that," she said sharply. Then she glanced at him quickly. "I didn't mean to be short with you, but I'm happy as I am. I don't need to be thinking about any officers. All I want to do is be an actress."

They had had this conversation many times, and Roland had given up trying to argue against this desire to act that burned in her. They drove along at a leisurely fashion, Rose speaking freely and gesturing with her hands, as was her way. Roland sat listening, enjoying her company. Finally, they came into town and returned the buggy to the livery stable.

As they made their way back to the hotel, he began telling her, at her request, of some of the famous people he had met. "I have some pictures somewhere of Mr. Booth—not John, but his father—whom I met when I was a child. And some other famous stars of the theater."

"Oh, could I see them? Do you have them with you?"

"I think so," he said. "I think they're in the bottom of the trunk, if I remember."

When they got to his room, she said, "Please, Roland! Let me see the pictures. It won't take long. We have time."

"Well, all right. Come in." Prudently he left the door ajar and said, "Sit down, and I'll see if I can dig them out."

Five minutes later Roland had found the pictures and then carried in the chair from Rose's room—since his room only had the one chair—and sat down next to her at the small table in his room. Spread out on an oak table were various tintypes and daguerreotypes. Rose was exclaiming with delight as he pointed out the famous actors he had known.

"This is the whole cast of *Macbeth*." He grinned and asked, "Can you guess which one is me?"

"Why, of course!" Rose said indignantly, putting her finger on the photograph. "That's you right there." She looked up at him and smiled. "I don't like you with whiskers."

"Well, I don't either, to tell the truth." He rubbed his smooth cheek with his hand and smiled. "All for art's sake. You sometimes have to suffer to be an actor."

For a few minutes they sat there; finally, she gathered up the pictures and put them neatly in a stack. "You need to put these in a scrapbook," she scolded. "They're going to get scarred if you don't."

"Don't have time."

"Well, I do," she said. "Do you have anything I could put them in? We can buy a scrapbook, and we'll start right away. You can help me, but I'll paste them in after you show me the order."

"I don't think it's going to be a very valuable scrapbook. Not like Frank Rocklin's. I think he'll be a great star one of these days."

"You could be a star." She held the pictures carefully and looked down at one of them. "You could do it if you wanted to."

"I guess I've just lost my ambition. A man gets tired of trying to keep up a front."

"Why are you so sad sometimes, Roland?" Rose asked.

He hesitated then said, "I've never told you this, but I got hurt pretty bad once."

Rose Yancy was an intuitive girl and at once asked, "Was it a woman?"

"Yes, it was. I guess I've forgotten most of it."

"No, you haven't." She looked into his eyes, and her face had grief in it. "There's something in your voice when you talk about it. It's like echoes from your past. I'm sorry," she said simply.

"Things like that happen, but it seems like it's hard to get over."

Rose impulsively took one of his hands in hers. Looking up to his face, she whispered, "I wish I could do something to help you. You've done so much for me!"

Knowing that it was not right, Roland reached over and pulled her closer. He gave her plenty of time to reject him—to shove him away—but she did neither of these. Her eyes grew large, but she said nothing. Her hand was trembling in his, but he saw that there was no real fear of him in her eyes. "You're a sweet girl, Rose. I wish I'd met you a long time ago." Then he bent and gave her what he meant to be a quick kiss, but somehow it was not. The touch of her lips stirred him, and he put his arm around her and drew her close. There was a youthful innocence in the girl, and her lips were soft and pliant under his. It was different, he knew, from other women's kisses, and he knew that he would not forget it.

Rose had been kissed a few times, but she had grown very fond of this tall, thin man who had been so kind to her. And now as he held her, she felt drawn to him and put her hand on his neck. He was gentle, and she knew that he was feeling something of the same emotion that had risen in her.

Suddenly a voice broke out, startling both of them. "Rose!"

Rose broke away from Middleton and leaped to her feet to face Josh, who had entered through the half-opened door. Rose flushed, for she knew the situation looked bad. Middleton turned pale, and he said at once, "Now, Josh, this isn't what it seems—"

"I reckon I can see what it is!" Josh stated flatly, his face drained of color, his mouth drawn into a thin, straight line. "I knew you were no good," he said in a shrill voice. "I knew it all the time! I knew what you were like."

"It's not what it looks like," Rose said. "We were just—"

Josh ignored her. "I don't know what you Yankees do when you catch a fellow messing with your sister, but I know what I'm going to do. A friend of mine will call on you. I don't care whether it's guns, knives, or what, but I'll have satisfaction."

"Don't be ridiculous," Roland started. "I'm not going to fight a duel with you."

"That's up to you," Josh said. "Either you'll fight me on those terms, or I'll shoot you out of the saddle when you go out for a ride."

"Josh, don't be foolish." Rose ran to him and shook his arm, but he jerked away from her, his eyes cold.

"Are you going home with me and forget all about this, Rose?"

Rose hesitated. "No, I can't."

"Then it'll have to be a fight." He turned and left the room, slamming the door.

"He'll do it, Roland," Rose said. "You've got to leave town."

Roland said, "I can't do that." Then he knew the despondency that could only come with despair. "You'll have to go now, Rose," he said.

She gave him a strange look then turned and left the room. Roland Middleton stood there feeling bleak despair. Finally, he looked up at the mirror on his wall and said aloud in the bitterest of all tones, "Well, Roland, you've done it again, haven't you? Not content with messing up your own life—now you have to ruin the life of an innocent young girl."

GILBERT MORRIS

He slammed his fist against the raw pine-board wall and then leaned against it, pressing his face against his arm—and wishing he could go back and be the man he once was.

Chapter 20

"Why Hast Thou Forsaken Me?"

"Well, we've got another invitation from my family."

The company had been having breakfast together, and all of them looked up as Frank spoke. "Not to a ball this time." He held up a letter that he had just opened. "It's from my grandmother. She wants us all to come to church. It's a Thanksgiving service."

The response to his announcement was mixed. The Hardcastles eagerly agreed to go. But Albert Deckerman and Carmen shook their heads stubbornly. "I had enough of being made to go to church when I was growing up," Albert boomed. It seemed as if he couldn't speak in a normal voice, and some of the people at other tables looked over at him with distaste.

Carmen said quickly, "I think I'll stay in and rest today."

"I'd like to go," Rose said, casting a quick glance at Middleton.

"I suppose I'd better go, too," Middleton said. "I need it." He had been depressed since Josh had made his threat. He had told Frank about it, and Frank had tried to comfort him. "Too bad it had to happen, Roland. But he's just a hotheaded boy. I'm sure we can calm him down." He had ridden out to Gracefield and spoken to Melora, explaining the matter to her. And Melora had talked with Josh and her father. The matter seemed to have calmed down, but Middleton was still depressed about it. He knew he had been in error, and his low self-esteem had dropped even lower.

"I'll rent a carriage," Frank said. "We'll leave about eleven o'clock. It's a special afternoon service."

Frank finished breakfast and an hour later was in his room reading when a knock came at his door. Thinking it was one of the cast, he said, "Come in."

The door opened, and Frank was shocked to see Dave Perkins slip inside. He came off the bed at once, saying, "Perkins, you shouldn't be here! We don't need to be seen together."

"I was careful." Perkins had a strange catlike walk, and he was very quick despite his short barrel shape. He moved over to the window, looked out, then turned back to Frank. "I was careful, but I had to see you."

"What is it? Something happened?"

"I've got this thing penned down." The quick black eyes of the agent gleamed as he looked at Frank. "Our people have been having fits trying to interpret the ciphers of the Confederates."

"I thought they had it all figured out," Frank answered.

"They did for a while. Do you know much about ciphers?"

"No, not a lot."

"Well, here's one here." Perkins pulled out a small slip of paper and handed it to Frank. It was a square with letters in random fashion, in different rows. "Here's the way it works. First, you have to have a key. The key to this one is the words *complete victory*. You have to have that to make the cipher work, but once we got that, we were able to interpret all the messages pretty well. Lucky for us, the Confederates don't have their own lines.

STARS IN THEIR COURSES

They have to use the public lines, so we can pick them up."

"What's the trouble, then, if you've got the message?"

"They've gotten onto us. They know we can read this code." He took the paper back and stuck it in his pocket. "What they've done is gone to another method." He reached into his inside pocket, pulled out an object, and handed it to Frank. "Ever see anything like this?"

Frank took the object, which was a large brass disk. It had letters from *A* to *Z* around it on the outer edge. There was an inner ring that moved also with the letters from *A* to *Z*. In the middle was printed "U.S.A." "How does it work?" Frank asked. He listened as Perkins explained.

"To encode each letter, you have a *key letter*. Let's say it's the letter *B*. Then you put this letter under the letter *A* on the outer wheel. Then all you have to do is take the letters of the message on the outer wheel, and right beneath each of these letters, you substitute the letters on the inner wheel. We've got to have it, Frank! If we can get it, every time they send a message, it'll be just like sending it to General Grant."

"Where is it?" Frank asked. "They keep it pretty safe, I imagine."

"Yes, that's the trouble." Perkins frowned and shook his head. "We're pretty sure it's in Taliferro's office. He's got a safe there that's pretty well foolproof, right in the middle of the Secret Service Department." He bit his lip and shook his head again with despair. "But we've *got* to get it out of there. One of our agents," he explained, "got the information somehow that it's in there."

Frank examined the cipher and handed it back to him. "How do we get it? We can't bust in with guns, can we, and hold up the Secret Service?"

"No, we're going to have to turn burglars."

Frank stared at him. "How are we going to get into the building?"

"There's a back way—an alley. There are guards, of course, but nobody's looking for anybody to break into the Secret Service offices." He grinned, saying, "It'd be a first if we pull it off."

"All right, I'm in," Frank said. "I'd like to see a little action instead of all this sneaking around. What do we do—take the disk?"

"No, that wouldn't do any good. We've got to see the cipher, make a copy of it, and put it back. They can't know that we've seen it. That's the secret of the whole thing."

Frank stared at Perkins and shook his head. "Well, I can't open a safe. I'm no safecracker," he said. "Can you get into it?"

"No, but we've got a man that made a living along that line for a while. He claims he can open any safe in the world if he has enough time. That's where you and I come in." Perkins took out a cigar, bit off the end and spat it out the window, then lit it with a kitchen match. When he had it drawing, he said, "We'll get him in and get him out. Hopefully we won't be spotted. But if we do get caught, we may have to fight our way out. Do you have a gun?"

Frank nodded. "Yes, but I don't want to use it. If we get caught, we get caught."

"If we get caught, we get hanged, so use it if you have to. I'll give you word when it's on. Be ready! I'll be outside the Secret Service building about a block down, checking the outside."

"All right." Frank watched as the agent disappeared. He sat down on the bed and thought of what was about to take place and tried to feel comfortable about it. "Well," he said finally, "that's what I came here to do, so now I've just got to do it."

He changed clothes, went out, and met the others. They had a pleasant carriage ride to the church in the country. The sun was shining, and the wind was much warmer than it had been. When they arrived at the white frame church with columns in front, he saw Susanna Rocklin standing and waiting. "I hope we're not late," he said. He tied the team and helped the women down, and then the group hurried to the church.

"I'm so glad you could come," Susanna said.

"Are we late?"

"No, just right. Come inside."

As they entered the church, Lorna looked around curiously. She was accustomed to large, ornate Anglican churches in England, though she had not attended in years. This was far more to her liking. The pews were made out of white pine and heavily coated with varnish. The ceiling was high, and the tall windows along each side let in sunlight. Up in the front on a raised platform two men were sitting, talking quietly, and there was a cheerful aspect to the entire congregation, she thought.

"Here we go. We'll have the whole pew," Susanna whispered. Lorna found herself sitting between Susanna and Frank and felt strange about it all. She glanced at Frank and saw that he was tense, and she wondered why that should be. The singing began, and although she did not know most of the songs, she quickly picked up some of the tunes by the second verse. When Susanna whispered, "You have a beautiful voice, my dear," she turned to her and smiled, whispering back, "My two talents: I have a little singing voice, and I can see for a mile. I like your church," she said.

Susanna smiled at her; then the two began singing again.

The service was very simple. Frank had been in many services like it, for his family attended an evangelical church in

Washington. He joined in the songs, but he knew the words so well he could sing them without thinking of them. His mind actually was on the robbery. It was not that he was afraid. He had seen battle and was not troubled about that aspect of it. But somehow he felt disloyal to his relatives. He glanced over to the two women and saw the placid calm on the face of Susanna Rocklin, and guilt washed over him. *I shouldn't be using them like this. Lorna's right—it's wrong to use people, no matter what the excuse.*

Finally, the song service was over and the minister got up. He was a tall, well-built man with a pleasant baritone voice. He began by reading a group of scriptures and spoke for a time about being thankful. "That's what we're here for," he said, "to remember that we owe everything to God. But I'm going to do something a little bit different this afternoon." He looked down over the congregation and said, "Open your Bibles, if you will, to the fifteenth chapter of Mark's Gospel."

The leaves of the Bibles rustled all around him, and Frank was startled when a man behind him handed a Bible over his shoulder. He took it, mumbled his thanks, and found the place.

The minister said, "This, of course, is the chapter that deals with the death of the Lord Jesus Christ. And I would like to read you a portion of it." He began reading at the first, when Jesus was brought before Pilate, and then later, when the soldiers led him away and put a crown of thorns on his head. His voice slowed to a solemn cadence when he read, "'And they smote him on the head with a reed, and did spit upon him, and bowing their knees worshipped him. And when they had mocked him, they took off the purple from him, and put his own clothes on him, and led him out to crucify him. And they compel one Simon a Cyrenian, who passed by, coming out of the country, the father of Alexander and Rufus, to bear his cross.'"

He looked out over the congregation and paused briefly. Then he continued, "'And when they had crucified him, they parted his garments, casting lots upon them, what every man should take. And it was the third hour, and they crucified him.'" The minister began to speak about the death of Jesus. Frank, even though he had heard the sermon or one like it many times, found himself putting aside his own problems and listening. The minister made it so graphic that he found himself entering into it. A strange feeling seized him as he heard how Jesus suffered on the cross. And finally the preacher said, "Let me read you what Jesus said: 'My God, my God, why hast thou forsaken me?'"

Frank felt strong emotions stir within him. He had heard and read the words many times, but somehow this was different. He looked down at his hands and found that they were clenched tightly together. Deliberately he unclenched them, but the tension in his spirit did not lessen. He sat listening while the minister said solemnly, "Why did God forsake Jesus? So that He would not have to forsake you. We're here for Thanksgiving, and I'm going to preach you the gospel this morning—for that is the good news. That is what every man, every woman, and every young person on the planet needs to hear—that Jesus died for their sins. That is Thanksgiving."

For the next forty-five minutes, the preacher roamed through the Bible, pulling scriptures out from the Old and New Testaments and tying them together. The longer he preached, the more miserable Frank got. He could not keep his hands from trembling, and there was a thickness in his throat.

He was not unobserved. More than once Lorna glanced at him, and Susanna was very much aware of her young relative's problem. She, unlike Lorna, knew what was happening. *He's under conviction. God's dealing with him,* she thought and, bowing her head, began to pray.

When the minister reached the end of his message, he said, "We're going to pray now, a prayer of thanksgiving for what Jesus has done for all of us. If you have not let Him into your life, if He is not your Savior, one simple cry will make all of that different. As the thief on the cross cried out, 'Remember me,' will you not cry that today? For He will remember you. If you will turn from your sins and believe on Him and call, you will be a new creature in Christ."

As they stood, Frank was aware that his eyes were filling with tears. He blinked but could not keep the tears back. Quickly he pulled out his handkerchief and wiped his eyes, and when he turned his head, he saw that both Lorna and Susanna were watching him. With some embarrassment, he turned his head from them and endured the prayer. But as the preacher prayed, he began to feel a misery and a hope. He knew that Christianity was true and he prayed simply, "Lord, I've been far away. Don't give up on me! Help me!" He cried out within his spirit, and he *knew* that something remarkable was happening to him.

And then it was over. Frank did not remember much about leaving the church. But when he did, he found Susanna waiting for him. She took his hand and said quietly, so only he could hear, "God is going to do a work in your heart, my dear boy."

Frank did not say a word. He made his way back to the carriage, helped Lorna inside, and, when the others were settled, began to drive back to town. The Hardcastles talked freely behind him, and Lorna joined in. But finally they reached the hotel. When he got down and he and Lorna were moving toward the hotel, she asked, "Something happened to you in church, didn't it?"

"Yes," he said briefly. "I'm not sure what it was. But I know one thing—I know that God is real, for He came and rescued me."

Lorna marveled at him. He had seemed so far away and thoughtless. And now there was a brokenness in him that she did not understand.

*

Carmen had been upset, and Frank could not understand why. If he had known women better, he would have read her emotions a little more easily. In fact, she was disturbed that Frank had not insisted on her going to church. She had known that she would *not* go under any conditions. But when they returned from church, she had been watching as Frank and Lorna had paused to speak outside the hotel. She had noticed later that they had had several long conversations, and a rash jealousy arose in her. *Maybe things are not as distant between them as I assumed,* she thought.

Lorna was aware of this, but Frank was not. She did not mention it to him, for she felt that it was not her place. The day after the service, she was greeted during a noon meal by Major Taliferro. He appeared suddenly and she invited him to eat with her. He was charming, as usual. But now that Lorna understood the deadly duel going on between him and Frank, she was more apprehensive. However, when he asked, "Would you like to see where I work and what goes on in those mysterious offices in the War Department?" she agreed at once. "Why, yes, Miles. I'd like to see it very much."

He was delighted at her response, and after lunch he engaged a carriage to take them to the department. When they were inside the building, he took great pleasure in showing her the operation. When they went into one room, he said, "Have you seen anything like this?" He handed her a doll consisting of a rag-stuffed body but a hard, plaster-of-paris head. "Why, it's just a doll, isn't it?"

"Not quite." Miles grinned at her and, taking the doll, deftly removed the head. "Look at this," he said. "See, the head is hollow. We use it for getting things through the lines. Medicine and other drugs for one thing. You'd be surprised how easy it is to get a doll like this past even watchful guards." He picked up a ring and showed her how it came apart. "Inside, you see, you can put a very tiny message on onionskin." She was holding the ring, and he looked down at her and said, "Here I am giving away secrets. You're not an agent of the Union, are you, Lorna? I'd have to arrest you, you know."

She looked up at him and smiled. "Would you really do that?"

"I'd arrest my own mother," Miles said with a curt smile. "That's what they pay me for. Come along, now, and you can go into the inner sanctum." He led her to his office and seated her at the desk across from him. He showed her several papers and spoke, if not a little boastfully, of his triumphs in tracking down Union agents.

The door opened and a sergeant came in. "Sorry to interrupt, sir, but General Williams says he has to have the papers on the. . ." He looked over at Lorna and hesitated. "The papers you're doing for him."

Lorna said at once, "Shall I leave the room?"

"No, that won't be necessary. I'll get them, Sergeant."

Rising from his desk, he walked over to the safe, stooped down, and began to work the combination. Soon it opened with a click. Reaching inside, he removed an envelope. Closing the safe, he moved across the room. "There you are, Sergeant. Tell the general they're all intact."

"Yes, sir."

After the sergeant had left, Lorna said, "I really must be going now."

"So soon? Well, you must allow me to take you out for a drive tomorrow. I know some of the better places."

"That would be nice," she said. She allowed him to drive her back to the hotel, and when he left, she went to her room to lie down before the performance. She woke up half an hour later refreshed. She dressed and was brushing her hair when a knock came at her door. "Come in," she said. She turned, and when she saw who it was, she said, "Why, Frank."

"Can I talk to you for a moment? It's important."

"Of course. Come in. Here, take this chair."

Frank shook his head. "It won't take long. There's something I have to tell you—two things really." He took two or three steps back and forth; then he paced across the room, apparently trying to put his thoughts together. Then he came over and sat down in the chair across from her. "I have to tell you this, Lorna. You were right to be upset with me when you found out what I was doing. I should never have done it."

"Being an agent, you mean?"

"Not that so much as using my family. I could hardly stand to look at Susanna in church. I feel like a—a snake! I just can't do it anymore."

Lorna felt a great pleasure from his speech. "I'm glad you feel that way, Frank. I know there are spies and agents and that they're honorable men—some of them—but I just hated for you to be one of them."

"I was doing it for the wrong reasons. I was angry because of my father being captured and my brother being blinded. I just wanted to strike out. I guess soldiers get angry at the enemy sometimes." He paused and said, "Slavery's wrong. But if I want to stop it, I'll have to do it another way."

"You're giving up the tour?"

He paused and nodded. "I have one more thing to do; then I'll call it off. We haven't made enough money to claim any success. I don't think anyone will be too surprised if we pack up and head back to the North."

She looked at him curiously. "What's the one thing you have to do?"

Frank hesitated. "One job that I have to help Perkins with will be over this week. If we can pull it off, I'll have done enough to pay for the training they gave me."

She hesitated then asked, "What's the other thing you came to tell me?"

Frank Rocklin was not a man who had trouble with words, ordinarily. This time he did. For a while she thought he wouldn't say anything. He looked out the window silently. She could tell something was troubling him greatly. "What is it, Frank? You can tell me," she said softly.

He looked at her and said, "I think I can. It's—what happened in church. I don't understand it, but I know one thing—I've got to serve God. I've got to call on Him and find out what He wants with me. I'm going to do it, too!"

Lorna was accustomed to church being a thing of habit. She said, "I don't understand this intimacy. People talk of knowing Jesus, and all I know is that He's in the Bible."

"There's more to it than that," Frank insisted. "I've seen it in my parents and in my brother Bob. Jesus Christ is in him, with him, and all around him. And I guess now He's in me. That's how I know Jesus still wants to be with people. That's the only way I know to put it." He rose to his feet, and she rose with him. Putting out his hands, he took hers and said, "I'm sorry I got you into all of this, Lorna. I'll do my best for you, though." He hesitated then said, "I've never known a sweeter, more generous woman."

A flush rose to Lorna's cheeks. She was very conscious of his hands holding hers. Then without meaning to, she whispered, "I feel—I feel very strongly about you, Frank."

He stared at her, incredulous, then reached down and touched her cheek. "It's something we'll have to talk about, isn't it?"

"Yes, it is. I want to."

He said no more but turned and left the room. Lorna went to the window and looked out, but she did not notice the view. She reached up and touched her cheek where he had put his hand. It seemed to burn under his slight caress, and she felt pleasure when she recalled his words. "Nothing can come of it," she whispered, but she did not believe it in her heart.

Chapter 21

A Time to Embrace

Roland Middleton had known little of contentment. His life had been fragmented by a disastrous love affair, and he had taken a downhill turn ever since. Somehow, though, as he finished shaving and put his razor carefully away, he had a sense of well-being that was unusual for the actor.

"Must be going into my second childhood." He smiled into the mirror at his lean, aristocratic face then picked up a set of brushes and began to brush his hair. When he finished, he put on his coat and left the room. Still, he was thinking of his future, and although he realized he had wasted his talent, he was still young enough at twenty-seven to turn around. *I just never had the desire to do it before,* he thought as he moved down the street toward the theater. *But a man can't go drifting along like I've been all of my life.* Inevitably his thoughts went to Rose, for he understood himself well enough to know that her coming into his life had made a change. She had the same youthful exuberance that he himself had once had, and being around her had restored this quality to him. As he passed by a store window, he saw a bottle of perfume and on impulse went inside and bought it. "Put it in a nice wrapping, will you?" he instructed the clerk.

"Is it a birthday present, sir?"

"No, just a present." He waited until the clerk wrapped the package, tucked it into his pocket, then went out of the shop and began whistling. He was a little shocked at himself to feel the excitement that ran through him as he approached the theater. But once again he knew that it was Rose Yancy who had brought this new quality into his life. He entered and was met at once by Albert Deckerman, who had a strange, serious look on his face. Albert usually had a rather foolish grin, but now his lips were drawn down, and he said soberly, "Mr. Rocklin says for you to come to his dressing room right away."

Surprised, Middleton gave the young man a look. "What's the trouble, Albert?"

"You'll have to go ask him."

Middleton's eyebrows went up, for Albert was always willing to talk on any subject. *It must be bad,* he thought, *if Albert's not going to talk about it.* At once he made his way to the rear of the theater and went to Rocklin's dressing room. When he knocked on the door, Frank's voice said, "Come in," and he entered. As soon as he got inside, he saw Josh Yancy standing with his back against the wall, his face set in a determined look. Quickly he glanced over and saw Rose, who stood across the room from him, and at once knew what had happened.

"Come in and shut the door, Roland," Frank said quietly. He was sitting at his dressing table but was not putting on makeup. He gave Middleton a direct look and said, "Got some news that you're not going to like." He glanced at Josh and said, "Rose's father sent a letter."

"He wants me to come home, Roland," Rose said. She lifted her face, and he saw that her lips were trembling. She was a highly charged girl emotionally, and he knew her well enough to recognize that she was on the verge of tears.

"I see." He looked at Josh and was silent for a moment. "Is this because of what you saw—Rose and me, together?"

"Yes," Josh said defiantly. "I won't have my sister playing loose with an actor, or anybody else for that matter."

Rose cried out angrily, "It's none of your business, Josh! It's my life, and I'll do with it what I please."

Josh shook his head stubbornly. "Pa says for you to come home, and you'll have to do it, Rose." He looked at Middleton, his face set with grim determination. "I don't know you, Mr. Middleton. I do know that Rose wouldn't be happy with a man like you. You're just not steady."

"Been asking questions about me, Josh?" Middleton inquired mildly. All the lightness had left him. At first he wanted to lash out at the boy, but then he thought, *I've got to try to see it from his point of view. To him, I'm just a seedy, run-down actor that's had maybe a lot of women. That's the way it looks to him and his father, too.*

Josh flushed but did not flinch. "Yes, sir, I have been asking about you, and what I've heard hasn't been very good."

"He is good!" Rose cried out. "He's just had a hard time."

Josh cast his gaze on her and then said, "Maybe that's so, but you're my sister, Rose. Pa's worried about you, and he says to come home and talk about it. It'll have to be between the two of you."

Frank said, "No more of this crazy duel business, Josh, is that right?"

Josh dropped his eyes. He had been ashamed at his rash threats to shoot the actor. And now as he raised his head and began to speak, some of his stutter returned, as it did occasionally. "I c–can't—I was wrong about th–that," he said. "But I'm not wrong to ask you to go see Pa. That's the least you can d–do, Rose."

Rose saw that there was nothing else to do. "I'll have to go," she murmured, dropping her head.

"I think that's probably best, Rose," Frank said quickly. "You and your father talk about it; then we'll see." He rose to his feet and came to her, putting out his hand. "You've done a fine job, but you have to listen to your father." Rose took his hand, shook it, and then turned to leave.

"I'll get my things, Josh." Her voice was dead, and all the liveliness had gone out of her face. When she left the room, Josh looked worried. "I didn't want to hurt her, but I just don't think she's going down the right road." He turned to Middleton and said, "I may be all wrong about you. Rose says I am, and she's always b–been an honest girl. But I don't want to take a chance when it comes to one of my sisters. I'm sorry it turned out like this."

Middleton smiled and said, "I'm glad you see it that way, Josh. I only want what's best for Rose. I hope you believe *that*." He turned and walked out of the room, saying, "I'll say goodbye to her." Once outside, he turned quickly and went to find Rose putting her things together. It wasn't much, and when she turned and saw him, tears came to her eyes. "Oh, Roland, I don't want to go," she whispered.

Roland wanted to put his arms around her but knew that would not be the thing to do. Instead, he took her hands and held them quietly, saying steadily, "I know it hurts, but you've got to pay attention to your family." He bit his lip and shook his head. "I went to the devil and never listened to anything my family said. If I'd listened, maybe I'd have turned out better. I've regretted it ever since."

She looked up, and her green eyes were filled with tears. He could tell her heart was breaking. Holding to his hand tightly, she asked, "Roland, can I ask you something?"

"Of course, anything!"

"Do you—you do care for me, don't you?" Her voice was so low he could barely hear it.

He knew at once that he had to tell this girl the truth. "Yes, I do care for you. You've been like a light in my life, and I've had a dark life. But I'm not fit to take a young wife like you. You deserve better, Rose."

She said quietly, "I love you, Roland."

Middleton flinched as she spoke simply and knew then that he had made a serious mistake. *I shouldn't have let it go this far,* he thought bitterly. Aloud he said, "Sometimes it happens like this. I care for you very much, Rose. But my life is not anything to share."

"You can change," she said. She squeezed his hands hard and said, "You can do anything you want to, Roland. I know you can."

Against his better wishes, Roland said, "I believe I will, but I can't ask you to wait."

Swiftly she reached up, pulled his head down, and kissed him. There was an almost fierce look in her vulnerable face as she said, "I will wait. Come to me, Roland. I'll be waiting." Then she grabbed the small bundle and left him standing there.

"It was difficult for Rose to go back to the farm." Carmen was talking with the Hardcastles. They were having tea in a restaurant near the Spotswood. It was late afternoon, and they had spent some time rehearsing. Without Rose the play was a little different, and they had had to make adjustments for her absence.

"Yes, it was," Elizabeth Hardcastle answered. She touched her white hair, her thin face kind and troubled. "She's such a sweet girl. I don't see why Roland couldn't have married her."

Carmen looked at her. "Why, Roland's not a man to marry."

"He is if he loves the girl." J. Harold Hardcastle slapped his hand on the table, his blue eyes steady. "And I think he did. I think he's making a mistake. They'd have a hard time perhaps moneywise, but if they love each other, they'd make it."

Carmen stared at the two with envy. "You two have made it." She smiled and said, "I don't think there are many in this world that stick together like you have. I wish I could find a man like you, J. Harold." She rose, went over and patted his shoulder, then said, "I think I'll go rest for a while."

When she left, J. Harold said, "That girl makes me sad."

"She's not exactly a *girl*, J. Harold," Elizabeth said. "She's getting old enough to worry about what's happening in her life. She's had a career, but she wants a man—a husband."

"She could've had men lots of times, a good-looking woman like that!"

"Well, I guess she has *had* a few men, but that gets old. She's thinking about a home now." Elizabeth hesitated then said, "I may be foolish, but I thought at times she looked at Frank as a woman looks at a man that she wants to come to her."

"Frank? Why, he's too young for her."

"Perhaps so, but women in love don't always think straight." She looked in the direction of the door through which Carmen had disappeared and said, "I hope she doesn't get hurt in all of this."

If Carmen could have heard their remarks, she would have recognized the truth in them. She was thinking of Frank as she climbed the stairs, wondering how he felt. He had been attentive to her, and once or twice she had seen in him that her presence had affected him. But that was not enough. She was indeed tired of the life she now led. When she got to her room, she began listlessly working with her hair before the mirror. Finally, the desire to talk to Frank came to her, and she rose and left her room. Frank's room was down the hall, and when she arrived there, she saw that the door was half open. Surprised, she stopped, then heard voices. She hesitated for a moment then recognized Lorna's voice. She tensed at once. She glanced around and saw nobody in the hall. Stepping closer to the door, she listened carefully to what they were saying.

Inside the room, Frank was standing in front of Lorna. She had accompanied him to his room after a brief walk, and he had asked her to come in just for a moment.

Now he faced her and said, "I've decided to tell you something, Lorna." He reached out and put his hands on her arms and held her quietly. "This thing that's come to me about God—it's all mixed up. But somehow I know I'm going to have to follow Him—and I know something else."

Lorna was surprised at his intensity. She was conscious of his hands on her arms and said, "What is it, Frank?"

Quite simply Frank said, "I care for you, Lorna. We haven't known each other long, but we do spend a lot of time together. I've never known another woman like you." Hesitating, he said, "I don't know how you feel about me, but I love you as I've never loved another woman."

His simple statement brought consternation to Lorna. She looked up at him with shock in her eyes and said, "Why, Frank!" She was an honest young woman, and now, quickly, the memory of Dennis's betrayal came to her. Somehow, as she looked into his eyes, the past seemed unimportant. And she said quietly, "I care for you, too, Frank."

"You do? That's good to hear." Frank pulled her into his arms and kissed her gently; then he held her. There was a moment's silence; then he released her, saying, "We'll have to talk about this more."

"Yes," Lorna said, "I'll expect a little more courting than this."

A smile flashed across Frank's face, and he said, "You'll get it. We'll be going back to the North soon. As soon as I do this job for Pinkerton."

"What is it, Frank? Can you tell me?"

Frank spoke quickly, revealing the plan, and Lorna said, "Why, I saw that safe when I visited in Taliferro's office."

"That's the one. We'll be going after it tomorrow night, just after midnight. Once that's over, we'll do another week of the play, and then I want to get out of here."

Out in the hall, Carmen had stood stock-still as she listened to the two speak. An anger had begun to rise in her. She had seen the interest Frank had in Lorna, and now she felt rage run along her nerves. A sound behind her caught her attention, and whirling, she saw a couple coming up the stairs. Quickly she walked away. She went back to her own room, and looking into her mirror, she saw that her face was pale but her eyes were glittering. She had not realized how much hope she had placed in making Frank Rocklin love her. And now that that had been suddenly blasted apart, her hope was replaced by a bitterness.

She felt scorned and rejected.

For a long time she tried to get a grip on herself, but she was a woman of emotional instability. She was given to rash impulses, and finally an idea came to her that stopped her dead still. Quickly thoughts ran through her mind, and her lips turned up in a cruel smile. "We'll see if you'll go back to Washington, Mr. Frank Rocklin." Sitting down, she snatched a piece of paper; then, taking a pen and ink, she began to write: "To Major Miles Taliferro: I must inform you of a plot that I have become aware of...."

When she finished the note, she folded it, put it into an envelope, and sealed it with wax. Putting Taliferro's name on the front, she marched downstairs and motioned to one of the young men who helped with the baggage in the hotel. "Timmy, I want you to take this and deliver it for me. It's very important." Then her voice lowered to a whisper. "And very confidential. Can you do this and keep quiet about it?" She handed him the note and a ten-dollar bill.

The young man's eyes opened wide as he took the envelope and the cash. "You bet, Miss Carmen! I'll do it right now."

"Thank you, Timmy." Carmen turned and walked slowly back up the stairs. She went into her room and sat down. Anger still consumed her, and she sat staring blindly at the wall. More than once she had had second thoughts. Once, she had almost risen to go after the messenger, but the memory of the love scene between the two rose in her, and she finally let her lips settle into a straight line. She turned and began to fix her hair again, only this time she looked so hard she scarcely recognized herself.

That night at the performance, Frank noticed that Carmen seemed strangely aloof, unlike herself at all. "Don't you feel

well, Carmen?" he asked.

"I feel very well, Frank," she said. Her voice was very quiet, but her face was pale. She could not resist saying, "How long do you think we'll stay here in Richmond?"

Frank glanced at her quickly, for her voice sounded odd. "We've got an engagement here for the rest of the week. After that, we'll see. Why? Are you getting homesick for the North?"

Carmen did not answer him but turned and walked away. She went into the dressing room she shared with Lorna. With one look at the young woman's face, so glowing with health and beauty—and youth—her heart hardened within her. She said nothing but waited silently for the notice to appear. *They deserve it,* she thought. *He's nothing but a spy!* Somehow that thought did not comfort her, and she grew restless, glad when the call came for her to appear on the stage.

Chapter 22

A Brave Man

Frank started as he heard a sound off to his left. He put his hand in his pocket, seizing the handle of his revolver. It was a dark night with only a sliver of a moon hidden behind a screen of dark clouds. The stars were faint, and he had to peer to see through the darkness. A sentry appeared at the end of the street, stopped, then turned and marched back away alongside the War Department building.

Frank let out his breath and realized that he had clutched the revolver so hard that his fingers ached. *Got to calm down,* he thought. *We ought to make it fine.* He thought quickly of how easy it had been to gain entrance into the building. He had met with Perkins and a smallish man named Simms, the safecracker. Perkins had given orders in a terse voice, and the three of them had moved to the back of the building. There were two guards, but they came along the back of the building once every fifteen minutes. "Plenty of time," Perkins had said. He had jimmied the back door and whispered, "Frank, you stay here. I'll go in with Simms. There shouldn't be any trouble."

Frank had kept his place rather nervously. Twice a guard had made his measured paces along the back of the building. Each time, Frank had jumped inside the door, holding his breath.

Now as he stood outside watching again, he wondered what was keeping them. "How long does it take to open a safe?" he muttered. He was still wondering ten minutes later, when suddenly a sound caught his attention, and he whirled to see Perkins step outside the door. "Did you get the thing opened?" Frank whispered.

"Not yet." Perkins's voice was tense, and he stared up and down the street. "It's taking longer than Simms thought. Anything happening here?"

"Just the guard. He goes by every fifteen minutes. He's due anytime now." He hesitated and then asked, "What if he can't open the safe?"

"Then we'll have to come back tomorrow night and try again—with someone else."

"Once is enough," Frank muttered. "What do you think—" He broke off, for a movement had caught his eye. He whirled quickly to his right and hissed, "We're in trouble, Perkins. Look there!"

Perkins had seen the movement at the same time. He whirled the other way and froze. "They're onto us! We've got to get out of here."

"I'll go get Simms."

"We can't get out this alley. There must be twenty soldiers coming this way. Somebody turned us in. Come on." Perkins stepped inside the door, followed by Frank. He locked it firmly; then the two ran along the hall. Coming to Taliferro's office, Perkins called out, "Come on, Simms. We're caught."

"They'll be waiting at all the doors," Frank said, thinking quickly. "What'll we do?"

"Come on! We'll go up on the roof." The building was

two-storied, and the three men quickly ran down the hall then up the stairs. They found an attic door and quickly clamored up. The attic was pitch-dark, and the three stumbled along until they got to the windows in the gables. Perkins looked down and muttered, "Can't see a thing; it's too dark. But we'll have to go this way. They'll be working their way up."

"That's a long jump," Simms whined. "We'll break our necks."

Perkins hesitated. He knew that Simms was probably right. "Okay, we'll go fight our way out. Come on."

Frank paused then said, "We'd better jump, Perkins. There are too many of them, and you know what it means if we're caught."

Perkins shook his head, the faint moonlight outlining his tense face. "If we break our legs, they'll have us anyway. There are several doors down there, and they can't watch all of them. And in the darkness, we'll have a chance."

Frank hesitated then said, "Not me." He pulled the revolver out of his pocket then handed it to Perkins. "You take this, Dave; I'm going to jump. It's soft ground down there. I think they're in the building, so we've got a chance. Come on, let's try it!"

But Perkins and Simms both protested. Simms, whispering hoarsely, "I ain't jumping out of this building!" turned and walked back down the ladder quickly, and Perkins stopped long enough to say, "I'm sorry I got you into this, Frank. Good luck."

"You, too, Dave." The two men had not been close, but in the darkness of this attic they felt a kinship. Frank waited until the two had gone downstairs. Then he opened the window and put his feet out over the ledge. He could barely see the ground beneath. He could not afford to wait. A strange thought came to him. *I remember once,* he thought, *the preacher preached on Jesus and His temptations. How the devil told Him to throw Himself off some high place. What was that scripture?* "*His angels shall bear you up in their hands.*" He smiled grimly and said, "Lord, if I'm going to get out of this, You'll have to send some angels. I'd appreciate it if You'd help me." He gritted his teeth, hesitated for a moment, then shoved himself free from the window. He remembered hearing once that when you fell from a high place, you should keep yourself relaxed, and he forced himself to do that. The wind whistled by as he plummeted toward the ground. He seemed to fall for a long time. Everything was very clear, and he was concentrating solely on hitting the ground. If he broke his leg, he knew it was all over. His feet struck the ground, and he allowed his legs to fold. He sprawled headlong, but he had fallen on soft earth and not the hard pavement over to his left. There was a flower bed he recognized as he wallowed in the dirt for a moment, pain running through his feet and legs. He gasped, "Nothing broken!" then got to his feet shakily. His fall had made a thumping sound, and he looked around wildly.

Suddenly the silence of the night was broken by the sound of gunfire. *They got Dave and Simms!* Grief ran through him, but he knew he could do nothing. He stumbled out of the flower bed and moved quickly down the street. The gunfire continued, rising in intensity, and then broke off abruptly. As Frank disappeared, heaviness came upon him, for he knew that Simms and Dave Perkins were either dead or captured.

He made his way back to the hotel, and when he got to his room, he examined his clothes. He quickly stripped them off, washed his hands and face, and got into bed. He lay there, thinking mostly of Dave Perkins. "In a way I hope they shot him," he said. "Better to be shot than hanged!"

He had not been in bed for more than an hour when he heard measured footsteps coming down the hall. He had expected it. "They must know I was with them. I didn't think Dave would tell, but I can't blame him."

He waited for a moment; then a hard fist hammered on his door. He let the hammering go on until a voice said, "We know you're in there, Rocklin. Open the door!"

Throwing the cover back, Frank moved to the door. He pushed his hair down over his eyes then made himself look like a man awakened from sleep. Opening the door, he stared at the face of Major Miles Taliferro. Behind him were two armed guards holding their muskets carefully. "You're under arrest, Rocklin," Taliferro snapped with satisfaction.

"Arrest?" Frank feigned the speech of a man awakened out of a sound sleep. He rubbed his eyes and shook his head. "What are you talking about?"

"We know you're a spy, and I arrest you as such. Get your clothes on."

Frank began to protest, but Taliferro stood there coldly, saying nothing. When Frank was dressed, he nodded to the guard. "Bring him along. If he tries to get away, shoot him—and shoot to kill." He gave Rocklin a cold look of hatred. "We know how to handle fellows like you. We've got all three of you now."

"I don't know what you're talking about, Major. What are you arresting me for?"

"You'll have a hearing. It'll be short, and the hanging will be even shorter. One of your friends is dead, but we'll hang you and Perkins. Take him away!"

Frank stood there for a moment while one of the guards put irons on his hands; then he was hustled down the corridor. As they passed through the lobby, he saw the clerk's eyes follow him and knew that his company would soon enough hear of what had happened.

The interrogation had gone on for hours. Frank and Perkins sat at a table across from Major Norris and Miles Taliferro, who shot questions at them endlessly. It was Frank they were mostly aiming at. They tried in every way they could to get Perkins to implicate him. But steadfastly the stubby man refused to speak. Perkins had looked at Frank when he was first brought in, asking, "Who is this man?"

Taliferro had directed most of the interrogation. Again and again he had tried to make a connection between the two. But Perkins had merely said, "I tell you, I don't know the man."

Finally, it was Major Norris, who had said little and allowed Taliferro to do the interrogating, who spoke up and said, "Look, we know you, Perkins. We've been after you a long time. Now we've got you. You know what that means."

Perkins had an iron nerve. He turned to Norris and nodded slightly. "It means the rope. I've always known that."

Norris looked surprised. He said, "You've got courage, Perkins. It's a shame you're on the wrong side."

"I'm on the right side, all right," Perkins said adamantly. "You just do what you've got to do, Major."

Norris lowered his head and thought hard for a moment. Finally, he said, "It doesn't have to be death. If you'll cooperate with us, I'll see that you don't get the death sentence."

"Cooperate? You mean like tell you the names of all my men?"

"Yes," Taliferro snapped. "Including this one," he said, motioning toward Frank Rocklin.

Dave Perkins lifted a gaze that was almost lazy to Rocklin. Their eyes met and for a moment Frank thought, *He's going to do it!* But he was mistaken, as he soon discovered.

"Let's get on with the trial and whatever it is you have to do. I don't know this man."

Frank asked the two men suddenly, "What makes you so sure that I was with these men? You have no evidence at all."

Taliferro said, "We have information that you're a spy."

"Put it before me," Frank challenged.

Taliferro flushed and said, "It's a private communication."

"Anybody can give a 'private communication,'" Frank scoffed sharply. "Either produce it or let me go."

Taliferro flared up. "You're not getting out of this, Rocklin. I'll get the truth out of you."

Major Norris said abruptly, "That's enough for now, Major. We'll continue the questioning tomorrow. In the meantime, you see if you can get more information on Rocklin here."

Frank was taken to a cell, separated from the other man. But as they paused in the hallway to put him inside, his eyes met Dave's. Rocklin admired the man more than he would have thought possible. He could say nothing in front of the guards, but Perkins made it easy. He put his eyes on Frank and said, "Good luck, whoever you are. I wish you well."

"Thanks," Frank said. He had to let his eyes do the rest, for he could not say more. When he was inside the cell, he sat down and thought about Perkins. *They're going to hang him,* he thought bitterly. *And nothing could save him. He could save himself, though, but he won't do it. A brave man!*

※

Morning came, and Frank was given a meager breakfast. Immediately afterward, the interrogation began again. Taliferro this time had him all alone. There was a cold anger in the officer that Frank could not understand. He could sense that Taliferro had no evidence, or little at least, and finally, after what seemed like hours, he looked over and said, "Major, I don't know what's in your head, but you and I both know you've got to have evidence before you can hang a man for being a spy. What evidence do you have?"

Taliferro was coldly furious, and he was disgusted enough to reach into his pocket. "I have this," he said.

Frank took the envelope, opened it, and read it. He recognized the handwriting at once as being Carmen Montaigne's, although it was not signed. He had no idea what was in the woman's heart to accuse him. She had learned somehow of his activities. *She must have been listening outside the door when I was talking to Lorna.* He let nothing show in his face and handed the paper back, saying, "It's not signed. Anyone could've written that note—maybe even you."

"I'll find out who wrote it—don't you worry. And I'll see you swing for this."

Frank was taken back to the cell. Later that afternoon, he had a visitor. He looked up to see Clay Rocklin coming down the hall. He stood up at once, and when Clay was admitted by the jailer, he said carefully, "Hello, Uncle Clay."

"Hello, Frank." Clay stood there silently and then said, "I just heard about the charges. I've been talking to Major Norris." There was a resistance in his voice, and he stood there for a moment saying nothing.

"What did the major say?" Frank asked finally.

"He says some of his people are sure you're involved in a spy ring. Is it true?"

For one moment, Frank was silent. He wanted nothing

more than to deny the charges. But something had come into him that he could not explain. He had betrayed his family and found he could do it no more. "Yes, it's true," he said simply.

Clay stared at him and then said, "Tell me about it."

The two sat down, and Frank told him the whole story, beginning with his service in Vicksburg and his bitterness over the wounding of his brother and the capture of his father. He explained how he was determined to go into the army and fight, but Pinkerton had talked him out of it. Finally, he said, "That's the truth, Uncle Clay. I might add one thing, though," he said defiantly. "You can believe this or not, but before this happened, I'd already determined to go back. I guess it's all right to be an agent—that's part of war, but it's not for me. I agreed to do this one thing, but I've already told—somebody—that it's all over."

Clay Rocklin leaned back in the chair and stared at his nephew. "You didn't have to tell me that, Frank," he said finally.

"Yes, I did have to tell you, Uncle Clay." Frank got up and walked around the cell, squeezing his hands together. "It's been hard. Especially deceiving you and the family. That was wrong, using you like that."

"Has that young woman got anything to do with your decisions—Lorna Grey?"

Surprised and confused, Frank stared at his uncle. Then he nodded slowly. "Yes, she does."

"And what happened at the Thanksgiving service? My mother told me. Does that have anything to do with it?"

Frank sat down and spread his hands. "You know more about me than I thought. Something did happen there. I know this: I'm going on with God, and I'm going to marry Lorna if she'll have me. And I'm not going to be a spy anymore."

Clay's eyes grew warmer. "You made a mistake, Frank—

but not as big a mistake as I made when I was your age." He sat for a while talking to the young man. Once he mentioned Rose. "I think she's in love with the Middleton fellow. I don't know him, but I'd hate to see her make a mistake. Melora's worried about her, and so am I."

"I think that's over, Uncle Clay. Roland told me he'd said good-bye to Rose. He's a better man than you think, though. He could be a good man, if he'd just put his mind to it."

They talked for a few more minutes, and Frank asked about his father. "I tried to see him when we got back from Montgomery, but the guards said he couldn't have any visitors. What happened?"

Clay smiled. "I'm not surprised they haven't told you. It's a pretty embarrassing thing to admit. Your father escaped from Libby while you were away."

"How?" Frank asked, shock evident on his face.

"He had some outside help. Forged orders and fake guards. It was a very convincing charade, the guards say. If you hadn't been in Alabama, Taliferro would try to pin that on you as well."

After a while, Clay rose and called for the guard. He turned to Frank, saying, "I think as long as they don't have any more evidence than they have now, you'll be set free. Taliferro hates you, though. He'll do all he can to get you hanged."

"Dave Perkins won't speak. He'll hang first. I admire that man! Don't know if I could do it. Good-bye, Uncle Clay. Explain the best you can to Melora, would you? And anyone else that needs to hear it, especially your mother."

"I'll tell them." Clay reached out suddenly and gave his nephew a hug. "You'll be all right. You're on the Lord's side now. He's not going to let you fall."

Taliferro had used all his authority and one at a time had drilled every member of Frank's company. He had gotten nothing out of them, however. When he talked with Carmen, he thought he saw something in her and said, "Miss Montaigne, I've received information in the form of a note. I haven't been able to trace it, and it's not signed. But it is from a woman. Did you write that note?"

Carmen shook her head. "I did not, Major. I'm just a member of the company."

Taliferro hesitated; then he kept probing the woman, but she did not bend. Neither did other members of the company. He had saved Lorna for last. Finally, when she sat down before him in the interrogation room, he felt anger run through him. "Did you know about this, Lorna?"

"I don't know what you mean."

"I mean about Frank Rocklin being a spy."

"That hasn't been proven. A charge has not been final. In my country, we hold a man innocent until proven guilty."

Her swift defense of Rocklin infuriated Taliferro. He began to ask her questions, firing them one after another in a slashing manner. But she answered them quietly, and finally she said, "I can tell you no more."

He stared at her and felt the power of her gaze. However, there was nothing more he could do. He released her then went to Major Norris's office.

"Well, do you have anything else?"

"Not yet, but I haven't given up. I'm going to hold Rocklin over until I look further into this case."

"You can't hold him long," Norris said. "We don't have any evidence."

"I know he's guilty!"

Norris's face turned hard. "Your knowing isn't the same thing as proving it. I'll give you until tomorrow."

When Lorna returned to the hotel, the company seemed to be drawn together. All of them except Carmen met in Lorna's room. They crowded in and talked about the problem. They were disturbed, and Hardcastle said, "I suppose this is the end of the play."

"It isn't any such thing!" Elizabeth Hardcastle said. "Mr. Rocklin will be released. There's no evidence on him. Everyone says that."

Middleton said little. He was shocked at the affair and totally unconvinced that Frank was guilty. So was Albert Deckerman, who loudly protested that the government ought to be sued.

Later that evening when Lorna was preparing for bed, she heard a knock on her door. Going quickly, she found Carmen standing there. Her eyes were red from weeping, and she asked, "Can I come in?"

"Why, of course. Come in, Carmen."

When Carmen entered, she stood there wringing her hands for a moment then said, "I have something to tell you. I—I don't know how to do it."

Lorna said, "The best way is just to say it. What is it?"

"I'm the one who gave Frank's name. I heard you two making love."

"We weren't making love. We merely expressed our feelings for each other."

"But you do love him, don't you? I know you do."

"Yes, I do."

Carmen began to weep. She threw herself into a chair and began to sob, saying, "I don't know what got into me! I lost my mind. I do that—I've been that way since I was a little girl. Oh God, how I hate myself!"

Lorna stared at the woman for a moment then sat down beside her. Putting her arm around her, she said, "Let's talk about it, Carmen. God is always willing to forgive, and so is everyone else."

CHAPTER 23

THE COMPANY GETS AN ULTIMATUM

Major Miles Taliferro looked up from his desk with surprise. His face had fatigue lines around the eyes and mouth, and he snapped irritably at the sergeant, who had opened the door wide enough to stick his head inside. "Well, what is it, Sergeant?"

"It's a young lady to see you, sir."

"A young lady? What's her name?"

"Miss Grey."

Instantly Taliferro straightened up in his chair. "Send her in," he said almost harshly. He waited, leaning back in his chair until Lorna entered the room. As soon as she was inside and the door was shut, he said abruptly, "What is it, Miss Grey? I don't have time to waste this morning."

If Lorna felt any rebuke, she did not show it. Coming over to stand before his desk, she said quietly, "I'm sorry to bother you, Major. I know you're busy, but I had to see you."

"Well, you see me," he snapped crossly. "What is it?"

"Might I sit down for a moment?"

"Yes, yes, sit down." Even as Lorna sat across from his desk, Taliferro could not help but admire her appearance. She was wearing a pearl gray dress with white trim around the wrists and neckline. It was smoothly cut and showed off her figure to the best advantage. A small hat with bright feathers was perched on top of her blond hair, and it irritated him that she looked so fresh this early in the morning while he was rather disheveled. Leaning forward, he clasped his hands together on the desk and asked, "What is on your mind? It must be about Rocklin!"

"Yes it is, Major," Lorna said with a nod. "I've come to ask you to think about releasing him."

"He'll be released when I have evidence that he's innocent."

Lorna gave him a direct look. "But there's no evidence that he's guilty, is there? As I understand it, the other man has refused to implicate him."

"He's lying. I know he is!"

"That hardly seems likely. If you offered to remove the death penalty for identifying him, why should he insist on refusing?"

It was a question that Taliferro had asked himself. He had gone over and over the evidence and was well aware that he was not on sound ground. He was as certain that Frank Rocklin was one of the burglars as he was of his own name. Still, proving it in court, even a military court, would be quite a different matter. He started to speak angrily, but at that moment there was a knock on the door, and the sergeant stuck his head inside. "There's another lady to see you, sir."

"I can't see her now."

Sergeant Ames bit his lip and said, "She says she will only take a minute, if you could step outside." The sergeant looked at Lorna and said, "I think it's about. . .the burglary." Instantly Taliferro got to his feet. He was determined to leave nothing untried, and he had sent word to his agents to send anyone who might have seen anything the night of the burglary. "I'll just be a moment, Miss Grey," he said and left the room. As soon as he stepped outside, he saw an elderly woman with white hair and a thin face standing just past the sergeant's desk. He remembered her and asked impatiently, "Mrs. Hardcastle—I'm very busy. Do you have something to say to me about the burglary?"

"I've been trying to think about it all," Mrs. Hardcastle said slowly. "I don't remember as well as I used to. Why, when I was a young woman, I could name you all the presidents of the United States and the dates that they were in office." Her eyes were bright as a bird's, and she added proudly, "And I knew the lyrics to almost any song you wanted to name, and I could—"

"Yes, yes, I'm sure. That's very commendable. But what about the burglary?" He looked around at the sergeant, who was listening, and said, "Step over into this empty room, please, Mrs. Hardcastle."

He turned as she went down the hall and said quietly to Sergeant Ames, "I'll be back. Don't let Miss Grey leave."

"Yes, sir."

As soon as the major was inside the room, he began directing questions at Mrs. Hardcastle. She was a difficult woman to interrogate, for no sooner had he asked a question than she would begin trying to answer it. But her attempts always led her off into some vague memory of years ago. Still, she said enough about the night of the burglary to keep talking for some time. Finally, however, he said with some asperity, "Mrs. Hardcastle, was your employer in the hotel the night the burglary took place?"

"Oh, I'm sure he was. He went to bed early that night, I think."

"But you couldn't know that he stayed in his room, could you, now? Did you see him leave the hotel?" This time the answer was a little vague, but he cut through it by saying, "Yes or no? Did you see him leave the hotel the night of the burglary?"

"Why, no, I didn't, Major, but—"

"Well, what in blazes did you come here for, then?"

Elizabeth Hardcastle looked hurt. "I thought I might help get Mr. Rocklin out of jail. He's such a nice man—"

"Good day, Mrs. Hardcastle." Stomping to the door, Taliferro opened it, and when she left—still protesting that Mr. Rocklin was a nice man—he ignored her. Going back past the sergeant, who gave him a covert look, he entered the office and stood behind his desk. "Can you swear to me that Frank Rocklin was in the hotel all night?" A crafty look came into his eyes, and he said, "Perhaps he was with you all night, Lorna," using her first name almost with a sneer. "That would get him off, if you just tell me he spent the night in your room."

"No, he didn't do that, Major," Lorna said evenly.

"But you are in love with him, I take it, or you wouldn't be here."

Lorna hesitated then said, "Yes, I am. But I just want to see justice done. If you don't have evidence, Miles, you'll have to let him go."

Anger raced through Taliferro, and he shook his head. "You may go now, but I may send for you later."

Lorna rose, and there was a look of regret on her face. "I'm sorry that it's all come to this." She turned and left the room. As soon as the door shut, Taliferro picked up a pen that was on his desk and threw it with all his strength at the wall. The point of it stuck into the pale green wallpaper and quivered there. He stood staring at it with frustration and finally pulled his uniform tunic down and walked out the door. "I'm going down to see Major Norris. If anyone else comes, tell them I won't be back for a while."

He moved through the building, coming at last to Norris's office, and found him busy with a stack of papers.

Looking up, Norris said, "Well, do you have anything on Rocklin?"

"Not yet, but—"

"Then you'll have to release him."

"He's as guilty as Judas!" Taliferro's face grew red with anger. There was a nervous tic in his right eye. "Just give me a few more days and I'll pin it on him. We'll make Perkins talk!"

"I don't think he will." Norris looked critically at Taliferro. "Legally we're on shaky ground. We don't have a thing on Rocklin except your suspicions, and those are not enough."

"You mean we're going to have to turn him loose?"

"Yes, right away." He listened as Taliferro argued; then he snapped, "You heard the order, Major." He hesitated for one moment and said, "I hate this almost as much as you do. You can do this at least—run him out of town. Use any threat you have to."

"Yes, sir."

Taliferro turned and walked slowly away. As he went back to his office, he called the sergeant in. "Have Rocklin brought to my office, Sergeant."

"Yes, sir."

Taliferro sat down, and ten minutes later the door opened and Frank Rocklin stepped in. He had not shaved, but his eyes were clear and his face was filled with curiosity. Taliferro wanted to smash his fist into the face of the actor, but he got a grip on his temper and said, "We're releasing you, Rocklin."

Frank nodded. "Thank you, Major."

"Wait a minute. That's not all." Taliferro tried to take some triumph out of his defeat. "If you're not out of Richmond in twenty-four hours, you and your whole company, I'll arrest you again and every member of your company. Maybe I can't make the charges stick, but I can make it pretty uncomfortable—especially for your lady friend."

Frank stared at him, expressionless, then nodded. "Looks like you hold the best cards, Major. We'll be out of Richmond tomorrow."

"If I hear about you in any other Southern town, I'll follow you. Get out of here. I know you're a spy, and nothing would please me more than to see you hang. I can't do that apparently, but if I find you in Confederate territory, I guarantee you I'll make it unpleasant for you—you and all your troupe. Now get out of here!"

Rocklin stared at him but said nothing. He turned and walked out of the office. Taliferro came to the door. "Write out a release order, Sergeant. See that he's out of here right away."

"Yes, sir, I'll take care of it."

When Taliferro slammed the door, the sergeant looked up with a grin. "Well, I don't see the major losing his temper like that very often." He smiled slyly. "You've been kind of an irritation to him. Come along, and I'll see that you get your stuff."

Ten minutes later Frank Rocklin left the jail and paused to take a deep breath. The air was cool and fresh after the inside of the prison. He made his way back to the hotel, where he was greeted by the entire company. They gathered in his room, and he looked around and said with regret, "We'll be leaving tomorrow."

"We're going back to Washington, I take it," Roland said.

"That's right, by orders of Major Miles Taliferro. It wouldn't be comfortable for any of us in Southern territory." Frank's face showed regret. "I'm sorry for all of you. You'll be paid up until the time we get back. I wish it hadn't turned out like this."

"Why, it's been a rich experience, my boy!" J. Harold Hardcastle exclaimed. "I'm glad you're out of that jail. Maybe we'll do something together back where decent theater is appreciated."

Frank grinned at him and shook his hand warmly. He had noticed that Carmen was not in the room, and when Lorna came to him, he asked about her.

"She's feeling pretty bad, Frank." Lorna hesitated then said, "Why don't you go talk to her?"

Giving her a curious look, he said slowly, "I think maybe I know something about why Carmen's feeling like that."

"Maybe you do," Lorna said. She put her hand on his arm and said, "Be kind to her, Frank. She's a lonely woman."

"Sure, I'll talk to her."

Going to her room, he knocked gently on the door, and Carmen's voice sounded muffled. "Come in."

He entered and she turned to face him. Closing the door, he walked over to her and said, "Everything's turned out all right, Carmen. I'm out of jail, but we've got to get out of the South."

Instantly Carmen's eyes filled with tears. "Frank, I've got to tell you something." She hesitated and then with torment in her face said, "I was the one who wrote the letter to Taliferro. I don't know why I did it. I was jealous of you and Lorna. Frank, I'm so sorry."

"Carmen, it's all over. I'm sorry if you got hurt."

"But you could have been killed."

"Sure could," Frank said cheerfully. He came over, took her hand, and held it for a moment. Finally, he put one arm around her and squeezed her. "We all take wrong turns from time to time, Carmen. I've taken too many to blame anybody else. I don't want you to worry about this. As for me, I forgive you freely."

Carmen looked up then fell against him and held on to him for a moment. Awkwardly, Frank held her. Then she stepped back and dabbed at her eyes with a handkerchief. "We're going back to the North?"

"Yes, so get your stuff packed. If we hang around here, we may see the inside of a jail again. I'm not really sorry to go back, though. I'm really glad." He went to the door, opened it, and then smiled. "Maybe we'll do something in the way of acting together."

"I'd like that, Frank," she said, managing a smile.

When he closed the door, he went to Lorna. "She's all right," he said. "She made a mistake, but don't we all. You'd better start getting ready. I'll go get the train tickets." They looked at each other, and then he put his arms around her. He held her gently and said, "This has been a rough tour, hasn't it?"

"Yes, it has, Frank."

He kissed her cheek then stepped back, holding her hands warmly. "I don't regret it. I found you, Lorna. That's made all the difference to me." He turned and left the room. And as he did, he knew that this was not the end but the beginning.

CHAPTER 24

"A ROLE YOU WERE BORN FOR!"

Buford Yancy looked up from the small anvil where he was pounding on a piece of iron with a ten-pound sledge. He watched as the horseman dismounted somewhat awkwardly, tied the animal to a hitching post, then looked around helplessly.

Tossing the hammer onto the anvil with a clang, Buford moved out of the small shed and said when he approached the man, "Howdy, Mr. Middleton." He had recognized the actor at once. He offered his hand and noted the softness of the actor's flesh. "Surprised to see you way out here, Mr. Middleton."

Middleton gave him an embarrassed grin and shook his head. "I got lost three times, Mr. Yancy. It's not as easy finding your way around here as it is in Washington or New York."

Yancy laughed and shook his head. "I'd get plumb lost in one of them places," he said. "Come on and sit on the porch. I've got some coffee on the stove—or what passes for coffee in these parts lately."

"No, I wouldn't care for any, thank you. I have to talk to you."

"I figured that." Yancy studied the thin face of the actor and said, "I reckon it's got something to do with Rose. What is it?"

"I've come to ask you for your permission to court Rose," he said. He saw the surprise that flashed through Yancy's green eyes and grew intensely sober. "I know you don't have much of an opinion of actors, maybe with some grounds. I don't know what Rose has told you about me, but I want to be honest with you."

For the next five minutes, Roland gave a stark account of his life, leaving out none of the harsh facts. When he finished, he shrugged, saying, "That's what I've been, Mr. Yancy. I didn't hide anything from you. I'll answer any questions that you want to ask. But before you do, I just want to tell you one more thing." Middleton straightened his shoulders, and his gaze was steady as he looked into the eyes of the other man. "I love Rose, and I'm determined to live a different kind of life. I've been a hard drinker. Well, that's all over now. I haven't had a drink in two weeks, and I hope to never take another one. It was something to hide behind, and I wouldn't need that with a wife like Rose. As for my future"—a humorous light came to his eyes—"I'll stay here and work for you on the farm until you see I mean business. I won't be much good at it, but I'll do my best."

Buford Yancy was amazed. He'd expected almost anything out of Middleton—except this. There was an earnestness in the man that he could not deny. He reached up and scratched his head thoughtfully. He thought slowly, turning it over in his mind, and said finally, "Well, Roland, I reckon it'll be up to you and Rose." He looked around the farm and said with a touch of sadness, "This kind of life was all right for the rest of my kids, but it's not for Rose. She wants something more than this. I don't know if she'll be happy with it or not, but I reckon she's going to have to try it." He paused and nodded. "You see that path there? You take that. At the end of it, you'll find some of the finest hogs you've ever seen. Rose is feeding them. You go talk about it with her; then we'll all sit down and see what comes of it."

Roland gave a gusty sigh of relief. He had dreaded facing Buford Yancy, but he saw now that he had a chance. He nodded, and a smile touched his lips. "Thank you."

He took the path, and as Yancy said, it was impossible to miss. It was worn smooth by many feet. Before he had gotten very far, he heard the sounds of hogs grunting and squealing. Slowing his pace, he came out into the opening where Yancy had built pens out of stout saplings. He glanced at the hogs that were gathered around the slender form of Rose, who was putting feed from a wheelbarrow into a trough. The squealing was so loud that she evidently couldn't hear him, and he got within five feet of her before he said, "Hello, Rose."

Instantly Rose whirled, and upon seeing him, her eyes got large and she dropped the bucket of feed at her feet. "Roland!" she cried. She stood stock-still, unable to speak. She had thought of him constantly since coming back to the farm, and there had been a sadness in her that she could not control. When he came to her, she put out her hands and he took them. "What—what are you doing here?"

Roland allowed a smile to touch his lips. "Came to learn how to feed hogs," he said. "Haven't had much experience, but your dad tells me he may need another hand."

"Why, you can't do that," Rose said indignantly.

"I probably won't do very well at it, but I told him I'd stay as long as he wanted." He hesitated; then his face grew serious as he looked down at her. "I told him I was going to stay long enough to prove that I'd make a good son-in-law." He saw her eyes grow large, her lips parted in amazement. "We can talk about it," he said. He pulled her forward, and she came to him, putting her arms around his neck. As he kissed her, she held him tightly. He was very glad that he had not gone back to Washington with the rest of the company. She was firm, strong, and smooth in his grasp—all that a woman should be. Her lips were soft and gentle, yet at the same time demanding. They stood there for a moment, and when she pulled back, she said, "Roland, you can't be a pig farmer!"

"No, I think not. After I've stayed awhile, we'll get married. Then we'll go back. I don't know what's ahead. I haven't been the best actor, but I could be if you'll help me."

"I'll help you, Roland. Oh, it's going to be so much fun!"

He kissed her again then said, "Well, introduce me to your friends here. I'll have to at least try to show your dad that I'm able to take care of pigs."

She laughed and began naming them. "That's Mammie, and that's Paul, and that's Hamlet, and that's Romeo."

"And that's Juliet, I suppose," he said.

She laughed at him and squeezed him. "No, that's Pete. You do have a lot to learn about hogs."

The two of them laughed, and as he held her, he found himself looking for the first time in many years toward the future with hope.

⁕

The makeshift wood-burning engine pulling the dilapidated cars rattled and clanked over the trestle. Frank looked down at the white water below as it rushed around the support, then turned to say, "I'd like to come back to the South someday, when this is all over—the war, I mean."

"So would I," Lorna said. "There's so much good there. The people are so fine, especially your people."

The two had obtained the seat at the back of the car and spoke quietly as the train wound its way along the serpentine pathway through the hills. There was peace in Lorna's face, and she seemed happy.

Frank spoke for a while about his family and how he hoped to make up his wayward years to them, and she said finally, "You're not much of a prodigal, Frank. They'll be glad to kill a fatted calf for you."

He shifted restlessly and put his arm around her shoulders. She protested, but he grinned and held her tighter. Finally, after they had remained silent for a while, he said abruptly, "Only one thing bothers me."

"What's that?"

"Well, I went to all this trouble, took all the risks"—he shrugged with a futile gesture, and his face grew sober—"and all for nothing. I mean, I was no help at all to Pinkerton. Maybe that's something I shouldn't grieve over, but I'd like something to show for what I've invested."

Lorna looked at him with an odd expression in her eyes. "I've got a present for you," she said, her lips turning up into a smile. "I suppose an engagement present."

Curiously, he looked at her. "A present? What sort of present?"

"I'll let you decide." Lorna reached into her reticule and came out with a rather flat box about four inches square. It had a string tied around it, and she handed it to him. She watched as he untied the string, and when he took the lid off and gazed down at it, she was pleased to see him blink with shock and astonishment.

"Lorna! Where did you get this?"

She took his arm and held it, saying, "I wanted to do something. You told me the cipher was in the major's safe. When I was there before, he opened the safe. I have very good eyesight." She smiled at him, and there was a delightful charm about her. "I read the numbers as he opened the safe. Then when you were in jail, Mrs. Hardcastle and I made up a plan."

He stared down at the wax impression of the ring and muttered, "It won't be hard to make a brass impression of this. How did you get it out of the safe?"

"It was very simple. I went in to see the major, and after I'd been there a few minutes, she came asking to see him outside. While he was gone, I just went over and opened the safe, took the cipher ring out, and pressed it into some soft wax that I had brought in my bag. Then I put it back and closed the safe."

"Lorna, you shouldn't have done that! Why, if you had been caught—"

"It only took two minutes. Now, are you proud of your fiancée?"

Frank stared down at the wax impression, and a smile came to him. "Mr. Pinkerton will be impressed."

He turned to her suddenly and said, "I'm going to have to give you a reward for this." He leaned over her, but she pulled back.

"Stop!" she said. "I only take rewards in private, not in a public place like a railroad car," she said demurely.

He laughed at her and leaned back. "Well then, I'll give you a double reward later."

The two rode on, and after a while she said, "Frank, I hate to mention this, but I don't have a cent."

"Neither do I. We're a pair, aren't we?"

"What are we going to do? I've got to get work."

"Don't worry about that for now. You're going to stay with my uncle and aunt and brother Bob. I want you to get to know my family. I'll stay at home and introduce you to my parents." He looked out the window at the rolling hills and said nothing for a while. Finally, he turned to her and said, "God has been good to us."

"I—I don't know much about God," she said. "You'll have to teach me."

"We'll learn together." He took her hand, and they sat there quietly, listening as the rails made a *clickety-clack* steel cadence as the train wound around through the hills.

※

Lorna was sitting alone in the parlor, reading one of Amos Steele's lighter books of theology. It had been Bob Rocklin who had gotten it for her. He had smiled at her, saying, "This isn't quite so heavy. Even I can understand part of it. Why don't you read it to me, and we'll see how it goes?"

Lorna had never felt so comfortable as she did with the Steeles and with Bob Rocklin and, of course, with Frank, who was in the house almost constantly. She had fallen in love with all of them. She had gotten to know Melanie and Gideon only slightly, as Melanie spent most of her time taking care of Gideon, who was still recuperating from illness and malnutrition from his time at Libby Prison. The time she spent with them, however, was very pleasant.

She looked up suddenly as Frank entered and came to sit beside her. "What are you reading?" he asked. "Another one of Uncle Amos's books?"

"It's one I've been reading to Bob," she said. "Written a long time ago by a man called Thomas à Kempis."

He looked at the book and read the title. "*Imitation of Christ*. I don't know this one."

"It's amazing," she said. "Here's a man that lived back in the fifteenth century, but he loved God so much. He said that had to be first before anything else."

Her lips were gentle as she spoke, and there was a calm look in her eyes. "Bob's been telling me that that's what theology is. I asked him once what he really believed about sin and doing wrong, and he grinned at me and said, 'Love Jesus and do as you please.'"

Frank laughed out loud. "That sounds like Bob. He's doing fine, isn't he? He's going to make a good preacher."

"Yes, he is," Lorna agreed. "You're so different, and yet you're somehow alike."

Frank gazed deeply into her eyes, saying nothing, and she looked up at him curiously. "What is it, Frank?"

"It's about a new role for you."

"A new role?" Her eyes grew bright and she asked, "What is it?"

"Well, the story's about a happily married couple. They love each other very much, and you play the role of the wife. I play the role of the husband."

Her lips curled upward and she said, "I see. Do you think I can play that role, Frank?"

He put his arms around her and whispered, "Lorna Grey, it's a role you were born for!" He leaned over, and she turned her face up to him. "It'll be a fine drama—Frank and Lorna love each other and live happily ever after." He leaned closer and kissed her. As he held her, peace ran through him. He did not know what the future held, but when he lifted his lips, he said huskily, "With you beside me, Lorna, I can do anything."

"Frank, I love you as much as any woman ever loved any man!"

The tiny yellow canary in the wire cage by the window had been pecking at a piece of apple that Lorna had thrust between the bars. Now he stopped and put one bright eye, as he cocked his head, on the pair. Then his throat swelled and poured forth a high melodious song that carried with it a joy that filled the room.

Chariots in the Smoke

Part One
Vicksburg

Chapter 1

Barrel Staves and Salt

As the tall, rangy, iron gray gelding plodded wearily down the road, plumes of dust lifted as he planted each foot. The rider, almost as rangy as his mount, glanced up at the sky, which looked hard enough to strike a match on, blinking his eyes against the sun that stared unwinkingly down from above.

"I believe Mississippi's hotter than Virginia!" he murmured through parched lips. Glancing up ahead, he saw a line of trees gathered to the left of the road. Spring had come, filling the trees' bare black branches with green buds, and the rider was drawn to the sight. His face was covered with a film of fine white dust that formed again as soon as he wiped it with the soiled handkerchief he drew from his inner pocket.

Tall, lean, and wide at the shoulders, David Rocklin had a broad forehead and deep-set eyes. His mouth was wider than most, and his square jaw made him look rather determined. When he removed his gray, low-crowned hat to wipe the dust away again, his hair, as startlingly black as his eyebrows, had a crispness to it that didn't seem to go with the fatigue hooding his dark eyes. Replacing the hat, he slapped his shirt, raising a small cloud, and shook his head. "I don't reckon I'll ever get clean again," he said, eyeing again the line of trees that paralleled the road. "Ought to be a creek over there." Turning the gelding's head, he rode slowly toward the line of trees.

When he reached the line of willows, he was pleased to see a stream almost twenty-five feet wide, and at once he moved upstream to find a place to water his weary horse. The trees were thick and the bank so high that it was ten minutes before he finally pulled in at a bank that sloped gradually to the water. Stepping out of the saddle, he loosed the saddle girth to give the horse a breather, then led him down to where the water gurgled over smooth, rounded stones. The horse lowered his head at once, sucking the water in eagerly.

Rocklin leaned against the horse, watching him drink, then finally pulled him away. "Not too much, Ace," he said softly. "Wait awhile and you can have some more." He pulled the reluctant horse around, tied him to a scrub sapling, then walked slightly upstream, where he tossed his hat on the dry grass and lay flat on his stomach. The water was cool and delicious, and Rocklin had to fight off the temptation to gulp it down, realizing that doing so would bring on stomach cramps. He sipped carefully, the water relieving the dry tissues of his mouth, then sighed and sat back to wait.

Rocklin was so tired that fatigue cramped his bones. He'd left his home in Richmond five days earlier, and now both he and his mount were worn thin. He'd left on a search for salt and barrels, a strange combination. But the Confederacy had been stripped clean, at least in the Richmond area, of these two items. David reached down, picked up a handful of pebbles, and began tossing them out, his mind blank for the moment. He was a man who didn't speak a great deal. In this way he was quite unlike his twin, Denton. As he sat soaking up the quiet atmosphere of the glen and enjoying the shade that shielded him from the burning sun, he became aware of the whistling cry of a small flock of birds. "Guess you fellows are Mississippi birds," he said, not recognizing them. They flew downstream, their cries echoing back like tiny trumpets. Glancing down at the water, he saw silvery minnows, rank on rank of them, packed closely together. They all moved together as a body—darting more quickly than a man could ever hope to move, stirring the yellow-brown sands of the stream. When they moved away, he took another drink then watered the horse again. It was almost three o'clock, he judged by the sun, and he had no idea how far he had to go to get to the Cathcart plantation. The small town of Jackson lay twenty miles east, but that was no help for his present problem. He was a stranger to Mississippi, having never been in this part of the world, and had been misled by bad directions.

As he thought again of the long hot ride, he suddenly realized, *By George, a bath wouldn't go down too bad!* He let the horse drink more then pulled him back and tied him again. He went to the edge of the trees and glanced at the road. It was more a trail than a road, rutted with old wagon tracks made in the mud during the winter. There was nobody in either direction and not a farm, not a house, not even smoke in sight. Eagerly he moved back to the stream, lifted his saddlebag cover, pulled his bedroll from behind Ace, and took out a towel and a bar of pale gray soap. He had no clean underwear, but at least he'd be clean. Quickly he moved to the edge of the stream, stripped down, shook his clothes out as best he could, then waded out. The cool water struck him with a force, swirling around his knees, and the soft, sandy bottom yielded under his bare feet. Sinking down to his chin, he lay there floating, letting the water run over his body. For a long time he soaked up the coolness, so welcome after the hot, dry day. After a while, he soaped up and washed his hair. Then, tossing the soap back on the bank, he sat down so that only his head was above water. Downstream a small, furry brown animal emerged, holding itself upright with only its head out of the water. Rocklin watched curiously as the lithe body of the otter moved from spot to spot along the creek.

It seemed warmer now, and he grew drowsier and drowsier as he sat there. *No hurry,* he thought lazily. *I'll get there when I get there. . . .* And he continued to watch the otter's comic antics.

As Leah Cleburne guided her mare through the huge pecan trees, some at least eight feet in diameter, she slapped at the gnats that rose from the ground to swarm around her face, saying sharply, "Get away from me!" She slapped the flank of her horse with a braided crop, and the mare, a small roan, protested by humping her back then breaking into a fast gallop. Her sudden movement didn't disturb Leah, however, for she was an expert rider. She clamped her right leg more forcefully against the horn of the ladies' riding saddle, thinking somewhat irritatedly, *Men can ride astride, but women have to hang on with one leg hooked around a blasted horn!* She pulled the mare up sharply as she cleared the grove, then glanced ahead, seeing the dusty road that wound alongside the river and led to the Cathcart house. Her horse was thirsty, so she turned to cross the road and headed for what Ora Mae Cathcart, her best friend, had identified as the Eleven Point River. When Leah had asked her why it was called that, Ora Mae had shrugged, saying blandly, "That's what it's called. I don't know why."

CHARIOTS IN THE SMOKE

Leah moved across the field toward the river, swaying with the animal's movements. Tall for a woman of that day, Leah somehow managed to appear less than her five-foot-seven-inch height. Her bright red hair was exposed under her black riding hat, and the dark green gown matched her greenish eyes. She had an oval face with a wide mouth and a smooth fullness of neck and figure pleasing to the eye.

Crossing the road, she glanced back to the south, seeing no one, and thought again what an isolated place this part of Mississippi was. She had left Vicksburg to get away from the city's frantic activity, but after a week in this isolated area, where the most exciting event was the Sunday morning service at church, she felt a surge of impatience. She'd spoken sharply to Ora Mae when she'd left for her ride and now was sorry for it. An impulsive young woman, Leah often found herself doing things like this. As she approached the river, she thought, *I'll have to apologize to Ora Mae when I get back. It's not her fault I'm so impatient!*

Noticing a clearing to her left, she led the mare forward. When she reached it, she pulled up short, shocked to see a horse tied to a sapling back away from the stream. Quickly she looked around, but the trees lined the river so thickly except for this one clearing that it would be impossible to see far. She'd been warned about the danger that existed from marauders, from both Confederate and Union troops, so she advanced cautiously. The mare threw up her head, whickering tentatively at the gelding, then stopped at the water's brink.

Looking both downstream and up, Leah wondered at first if someone had fallen in and drowned. But the stream was relatively shallow and not that swift. She then decided that someone had tied the horse and gone hunting along the edges of the river, where squirrels abounded. She tightened her hands on the lines, preparing to turn the mare aside and return to the road, when she remembered she hadn't allowed the animal to drink. Nudging the horse forward with her heel, she sat quietly on the sidesaddle, still alert. When the mare had drunk her fill, Leah realized she, too, was thirsty. Stepping out of the saddle, she held the lines firmly with one hand, stooped down, and cupped her hand into the water. It was awkward trying to drink like this, but she had nothing to drink with.

Suddenly a movement caught her eye, and she gasped involuntarily as fear jolted her. She saw a man in the water—at least a man's head. He was almost hidden behind some willow branches that leaned out over the stream.

"Woman, will you please get out of here!"

The voice was filled with exasperation, but there was no threat in it that Leah could discern. She blinked with surprise then grew stubborn, as she sometimes did.

"I'll go as soon as I've finished getting a drink," she said curtly. Deliberately she turned back and took another scoop of water in one cupped hand and then another.

"Will you kindly get yourself out of here!"

The voice was raspy with irritation, and this pleased Leah since she'd been upset for most of the day without any way to manifest it. She turned deliberately to stare at the man, whose startling hair, longer than usual, glimmered wetly in the bright sunlight. "It's not my fault if you decide to do your bathing at a public place," she said coolly enough. Now that the fear had passed away, she examined the face of the man more carefully. He was extremely good looking, at least the part she could see. His hair was black as a crow's wing, as were the heavy eyebrows that shaded his dark brown eyes. His face, a slight wedge with a broad forehead, sloped down to a prominent chin that now jutted forward aggressively. Because the planes of his face were smooth, Leah judged him to be no more than twenty-one or twenty-two. She could tell from the muscles in the width of his neck that he was a strong man.

As he stared at her with a mixture of anger and embarrassment, she tormented him a little more. "This is a public place," she said again. "If you had any sense, you'd know better than to take a bath here."

"It wasn't public when I got in here. There was nobody in sight. Now get out of here!"

Leah found the situation amusing. "What will you do if I don't? You don't have a gun on, I see."

"I'll—I'll come out of here. That's what I'll do!"

Leah turned to face him, holding on to the lines of her mare tightly. "Why, come right ahead," she said sweetly. "What's keeping you?" And then she was frightened because the man did suddenly move in the water. He came up, the water just over his waist, and she could see the strength in his chest as the muscles in his arms tensed. However, she wouldn't be bluffed and held her ground, hoping to last him out. She was successful; he stopped abruptly, sank back down into the water, and glared at her.

"You won't come out?" she said, arching her eyebrows in mock surprise. "Well then, I'll just have to be moving along." She mounted her horse gracefully and turned the mare's head around. As she left, she said, "Don't forget to wash behind your ears!"

"Hey! Wait a minute!"

Leah turned to see that the man had edged around so he could see her leave. His shoulders glistening with the water, he queried, "Which way is it to the Cathcart place?"

"Oh, you're lost as well as unwise about where to take public baths!" Leah hesitated then pointed with her riding crop. "Go down that road four miles. Then you take a smaller road off to the side. It leads to the Cathcart house."

As she rode off, she heard him calling out, "Wait a minute! What's your name?" But she didn't turn.

When she was out of range of the trees, she laughed aloud. The encounter had pleased her, driving away the bad humor. Then, as she slowed her mare down, thinking about the incident, she said aloud, "What would I have done if he *had* come out of that water?"

She shrugged, knowing she would have been in trouble, but then, after a time, she smiled and said reluctantly, "He *is* a handsome thing! Wonder why he's going to the Cathcarts?"

From the parlor window, Florence Cathcart had watched the man ride up to the front porch and swing out of the saddle. She studied the stranger carefully as he moved up to the house and past her sight. When she heard his knock on the door, she touched her hair then walked out of the front parlor into the wide foyer and to the door. "Yes? What can I do for you?" she asked.

"My name's David Rocklin. I'm looking for Leon Cathcart."

"I'm Mrs. Cathcart. Won't you come in?"

"Thank you." David stepped inside the house, noting with approval the smoothly polished pine floors and rag rugs scattered about the entrance for muddy feet. The walls were papered, and he saw by glancing around at the portraits on the wall—all framed in gilt—that he'd come to a well-to-do family.

"Is Mr. Cathcart at home?" he inquired.

"Why, no, he's not, Mr. Rocklin." Florence hesitated then asked, "Did you have business with him?"

"Yes, ma'am, I wrote him last month. I'm looking to buy a large number of barrels. He wrote back, saying he'd be able to supply me."

"I'm sure he would.... Won't you come into the parlor? I've just made some lemonade."

"That would be good. Mighty hot and thirsty out there," David said, smiling.

Florence Cathcart escorted him to the front parlor, which was well lit by tall windows, and nodded toward a horsehair sofa. "Have a seat, Mr. Rocklin. I'll be right back."

She moved to the kitchen, where she quickly procured a pitcher of lemonade and two glasses. Putting them on a tray, she went back to set them on a low table beside her desk and poured one glassful. "Not too cool, but wet."

David picked up the glass and tasted it, his eyebrows lifting with approval. "That's very good," he said. "I've had a dry, thirsty trip. Is it always this hot in Mississippi in April?"

"No, not at all." Mrs. Cathcart spoke about the weather then said, "I'm sorry you missed my husband."

"Well, when are you expecting him back?"

"He'll be back tomorrow, I'm sure."

David thought of the long road he'd taken then asked, "Is there a village or someplace ahead where I could get a room for the night?"

"Oh no, we're very isolated here." Mrs. Cathcart looked at the young man, noting that his dusty clothes were finely made. There was an aristocratic air about him as well, and Florence Cathcart prided herself on knowing quality when she saw it.

She made an instant decision. "I'm sure Mr. Cathcart would want you to stay here. We have plenty of rooms in this house—six bedrooms as a matter of fact." She let this fact drop to let her guest know he wasn't the only person of quality in the room. "If you'd like to stay, we'd be glad to have you."

"That would be kind, Mrs. Cathcart. I'd hate to be a bother...."

"No bother at all. Come along and I'll show you to your room."

"Let me unsaddle my horse. If you have a place I could put him out to graze, I'd be grateful."

Fifteen minutes later, David was shown into a room on the second floor. He looked around with appreciation, noting the good furniture, mostly walnut. There was a fine rosewood table beside the bed, which had a massive headboard, and pictures of castles, knights, and ladies on the wall. "This is very nice, Mrs. Cathcart," he said, turning to her.

"I decorated it myself. I'm glad you like it. I'll have one of the servants bring you fresh water so you can clean up. We'll be glad to have you take dinner with us."

"I didn't bring any fancy clothes."

"We're informal here. Perhaps you'd like to lie down and rest awhile. Dinner will be at six."

"Thank you, Mrs. Cathcart."

Ten minutes later, a mulatto woman brought water up and David at once pulled off his shirt and moved to the washstand. He lathered his face, took a straight razor, and blinked as it rasped through the whiskers. He had a tough beard, and it was torture for him to shave. His eyes watered, but he worked carefully to avoid slicing his face. Finally, he did a credible job, cleaned the razor, put it back in the leather case, then wrapped the soap up in oilcloth and dried his face carefully. He removed his one change of clothes from the bedroll. Although they were wrinkled, they'd be better than the ones he'd worn for the past three days. "Have to wash them tomorrow," he muttered.

Then he lay down on the bed and dozed off. David had the gift of going to sleep almost instantly under any circumstances, and yet he was a light sleeper. Sometime later a tap on the door sounded and a voice said, "Mr. Rocklin, Miz Cathcart say you come downstairs to eat now."

"Thank you."

David rose quickly and dressed, studying his reflection in the wall mirror as he brushed his hair into place. The shirt was new and bright, with a ruffled collar and a slight ruffle at the sleeves. It was a little fancy for his taste, but these days clothing was at a premium in Richmond. He slipped on close-fitting brown trousers and calf-length boots and, after adding a string tie, left the room.

When he got downstairs, Mrs. Cathcart was waiting for him. "This way to the dining room," she said.

As they entered the dining room, she continued, "My daughter will be down in a moment." Even as she spoke, he heard voices and turned toward the double-wide French doors that opened to the hallway. Two young women suddenly appeared, one in front of the other, and Mrs. Cathcart commented, "This is my daughter, Ora Mae. Ora Mae, this is Mr. David Rocklin."

Ora Mae, a rather plain girl, was wearing a light pink dress that showed off her good figure to the best advantage. Smiling, she said, "How do you do, sir?" Then she stepped aside and added, "I'd like you to meet my friend, Miss Leah Cleburne."

The smile on David Rocklin's face froze, and the greeting

he was about to speak so lightly hung in his throat. The young woman who stepped forward was, without doubt, the woman who had caught him bathing in the stream!

"How do you do, Mr. Rocklin?"

Leah's face was smooth and there was no hint of agitation. However, her green eyes were gleaming with humor.

Why, she's laughing at me! David thought with astonishment. He wanted to be angry, but something about the audacity of the young woman caught his fancy. He smiled more broadly and bowed from the hips. "I'm delighted to know you, Miss Cathcart, and you, Miss Cleburne."

"Haven't we met before?" Leah asked, putting her finger on her chin and tilting her head to one side inquisitively.

"I'm sure I would have remembered *you*," David said, half bowing. He couldn't resist smiling even more broadly.

Mrs. Cathcart said, "Come now. Let's sit down and eat."

Soon the table was covered with platters of fried chicken and fried steak and bowls of butter beans, potato salad, mashed potatoes, and pickles of almost every kind imaginable. There was buttermilk, sweet milk, and lemonade to drink.

During the meal, David stole glances at Leah Cleburne. She was witty, he discovered, several times hinting at the encounter they'd had, daring him to speak of it.

After the meal was over, they retired to the sitting room, where they drank imitation coffee and spoke of the war.

After an hour, Mrs. Cathcart rose and said, "It's time for you girls to go to bed. You have to get up early for church in the morning. You can find your room, Mr. Rocklin?"

David took his dismissal and, after saying good night to the women, went upstairs to bed at once, for he was exhausted from his journey. But he lay awake for a while, thinking what a pleasant combination red hair and green eyes made in a young woman.

The next morning he rose and dressed then went downstairs to find the three women waiting to have breakfast with him. It was a large breakfast, and he complimented Mrs. Cathcart profusely.

On the way to church, he sat in the backseat of the carriage with Leah Cleburne while Mrs. Cathcart and her daughter occupied the front with the driver, a tall man with a face the color of ebony. "You're here on a visit, Miss Cleburne?"

"Yes, my home is in Vicksburg."

"How long will you be staying?"

"I'll be going home at the end of the week. What about you, Mr. Rocklin?"

"My family has a plantation outside of Richmond."

"Oh, you raise cotton, I suppose?"

"No, there's no point in raising cotton," David said, shrugging. "Not when Jefferson Davis has forbidden us to sell it." He referred to Davis's plan to create a market for cotton by refusing to let England have it until they recognized the Confederacy. The plan had backfired, however, because England was in the doldrums economically and had cotton to spare. Besides, they had found another source in Egypt where cotton could be obtained at a reasonable price.

"Is your land lying fallow then?"

"No, not exactly," David said, grinning. "We're raising hogs." When he saw her startled expression, he added, "We plant corn and feed hogs out. That's what I'm doing here. We have a contract to furnish salt pork to the Confederate army, but we're out of salt and barrels to pack the meat in."

They talked on the way to church, and when they got out, he

reached his hand out and took hers. It was warm and firm in his, and she smiled at him. He knew she was still thinking of how she'd caught him in the river, but he dared not say anything in front of the other women.

The service was long and loud. The preacher seemed to have bellows for lungs, and though the building was small, he preached as though there were five thousand people in an amphitheater. His sermon was on hell, and David felt the impact of it, for he was the target of the man's iron gray eyes.

On the way back home, David commented on the service and Leah smiled, answering, "You might not agree with what the reverend said, but he certainly said it loudly and positively enough."

When they arrived at the house, Leon Cathcart had returned. A tall, heavy man with sharp brown eyes, he greeted David with reserve. But later on, when the two men had talked business, he became more open. "I can furnish the barrels," he said, "but it will take a few days. I just sold the last batch I had. We've got the staves already formed, though. They just have to be hooped."

"Well, I'm going to have to find someone to freight them back to Richmond. Perhaps I can get a room at a town close by."

"No need of that!" Cathcart insisted. "Plenty of room here. I'll be around and there's good hunting here. Perhaps you'd like to try a little of that."

David quickly agreed, and for the next few days he got to know Cathcart well. The two men went hunting several times, then sat in the parlor with the family in the evenings. Both girls were musical, Ora being a fine pianist and Leah possessing a rich singing voice. The third night was the first time he was ever alone with Leah. Ora Mae had been feeling ill and had gone to bed early, and the older people had left at nine, admonishing them to turn out the lamps when they went to bed.

David talked with Leah for some time and finally queried, "I've been wondering if you were ever going to say anything about our first meeting."

Leah smiled instantly. "I don't think I'd better, Mr. Rocklin. It wasn't exactly the proper thing a young woman should do."

"I don't think it's the first time you've ever stepped out of that role. You enjoyed it!"

"Why, Mr. Rocklin! Are you insinuating I'm not a proper young lady?"

"Do you claim you are?"

Leah shrugged. "I get tired of the way women are forced to be what men want them to be."

Interested, David leaned back in the Windsor chair and examined her carefully. She was wearing a plum-colored dress with a bodice cut lower than usual. *A daring dress,* he thought, *except at a fancy ball.* He was fascinated by the redness of her hair, which was touched by gold. "I think you enjoy breaking traditions, don't you, Miss Leah?"

"Yes! I wish I'd been born a man."

"I can't join you in that. Much better to sit here with an attractive woman than some dull man."

The more they talked, the more intrigued David was. Leah refused to take the usual mind track most women followed. There was a boldness about her that wasn't arrogance but a willingness to take the less popular side of issues. She could be blunt, as he found out almost immediately.

"Why aren't you in the army, Mr. Rocklin?"

David blinked with surprise at the audacity of her question. It was true that most men of his age were in the army, and he knew people often wondered, especially strangers, why he wasn't. But no one had ever braced him so straight with the question. "I—my family's pretty well represented," he said carefully. "My father and my twin brother are both officers in the Army of Northern Virginia. I have a younger brother who's also served, until he lost a leg. . . ." When he'd finished, he saw she still wasn't satisfied. "As for me. . .well, I can't exactly say. My other brothers were never interested in farming and I was, so I was practically in charge of the plantation when the war came. Then when my father and brothers went off to the army, there was nobody to take care of it. It seemed to me more important to get food to the men who are fighting." This explanation sounded lame, even to him, and his face grew tense as her steady gaze remained fixed on him. Somewhat angered by her obvious refusal to accept what he'd said, he offered no more reasons and instead said, "I suppose I'd better be getting to bed."

They rose to their feet and she said coolly, "Good night, Mr. Rocklin."

"Good night, Miss Leah."

The next morning, however, she seemed to have forgotten the coolness between them. She enjoyed his company, that was obvious, and he enjoyed hers—more than he had any woman's in a long time. He'd never been in love, and he found Leah's beauty and differentness enticing. As the days moved forward, he spent more and more time with her.

On the following Saturday, Ora Mae and her mother spoke of this. "I think he's fallen in love with her, Mama," Ora Mae said firmly as the two were alone in the kitchen making a cake. "For a while he wouldn't do anything but go hunting with Pa. Now all he does is take Leah riding."

"You may be right," Mrs. Cathcart said, nodding. She was

a great matchmaker, and if her own daughter hadn't been engaged to a young officer stationed with the Army of the Tennessee, she might have done more in that direction. However, she was interested in Leah. "I wonder what her mother would think of Mr. Rocklin for a match."

"Oh, you know Claire. She's not going to be satisfied with anybody. I never saw such a picky woman!" Ora Mae said sharply. She looked out the window to where Leah and David were walking slowly along. "He is the handsomest thing! It's too bad he'll be going back to Richmond."

"Well, she'd never have him anyway," Mrs. Cathcart said. "You know what a fiery Confederate she is. Whoever Leah falls in love with and marries will be wearing Confederate gray—you can depend on that."

The next day Leah said good-bye to the family, thanking them for their hospitality. "Now," she said warmly to Ora Mae, "you've got to return my visit. When will you come to Vicksburg?"

"I don't think that would be a wise idea," Leon Cathcart said at once, shaking his head gravely. "Things are looking grim there with Grant trying to take that place."

"He'll never take Vicksburg," Leah said definitely. "Why, they call it the Gibraltar of the South. I wish the Yankees would try it!" Her eyes gleamed with anger for a moment; then she kissed the two women. Mr. Cathcart stepped outside to speak to the driver as David opened the door for Leah. Once outside, Leah turned to David and extended her hand. "I'm glad I got to see so much of you, Mr. Rocklin." Again there was an impish light in her eyes, though her words were demure enough.

David laughed aloud. "Maybe I can return the compliment someday, Leah." The two had gotten very close, on a superficial plane at least, and as he held her hand, he said, "I hope to see you again."

"I doubt if you will. Mr. Cathcart's right. Vicksburg's not a safe place these days."

David couldn't help but wonder if she was referring to his own lack of courage. "If I didn't have to chase all over the country looking for salt, I'd pay you that visit," he said firmly.

Leah stared at him. "Salt! Is that what you're looking for? I thought it was barrels."

"That, too, but we're out of salt in Virginia. You can't have salt pork without salt. It's hard to get in the South, what with the blockade and all."

"Why, I have a neighbor in Vicksburg," Leah said slowly, trying to remember, "who said. . ." She thought for a moment then continued, "He said he had a whole warehouse full of salt that came in on a ship. It was to be shipped, but then the Yankees blockaded the river."

"A lot of salt?" David asked eagerly.

"Oh, he said it was." Her eyes studied him, and then, when Mr. Cathcart called, she said, "Well, good-bye. It's been most entertaining, Mr. Rocklin." She boarded the carriage, and David watched as it drove off.

"Salt—a whole warehouse," he murmured. "And in Vicksburg! Now that's downright interesting. . . ."

Chapter 2

A Soldier of the Confederacy

"William Dabney came by to check on you while you were gone, Leah," Claire Cleburne mentioned, watching her daughter's face sharply. The two of them were sitting on the front porch watching a group of soldiers drilling down on the street. All of them were dressed in ordinary working clothes and seemed clumsy. One of them dropped the musket he was attempting to manipulate, and the sergeant, clad in a Confederate gray uniform, barked his displeasure profanely.

Leah shook her head at the ineptness of the soldiers, then turned to her mother. Well aware that she and her mother didn't hold similar views on the young man mentioned, she asked quietly, "Did he?"

"Yes, he seemed real interested." At forty, Claire Cleburne looked ten years younger. Her auburn hair and clear gray eyes were a complement to her fair skin. She was wearing a well-cut, modish gray dress and sat upright in an oak rocking chair.

Before Leah could comment, a petite woman with light brown hair sprinkled with silver joined them. She had brown eyes and was plain in appearance, but she walked with dignity. She was wearing a simple blue cotton dress, and her hair was done up in an old-fashioned way. This was Amelia Seaton, Claire's aunt. She seated herself in one of the cane-bottomed chairs and began at once to knit a sock out of green yarn.

"I was just telling Leah that William Dabney came by," Claire said. "Such a fine young man—and I think he's very interested in you."

"I suppose so." Leah didn't sound particularly interested, which she wasn't. She continued to watch the soldiers, who attempted to start and stop on time without conspicuous success. "If that's what we've got to stop the Yankees with," Leah remarked petulantly, "I think we have difficulties."

"Where is Grant now?" Amelia kept her eyes on the face of the young woman, listening closely as Leah began to speak of the approach of the Federal general who had been sent by Lincoln with a large army to capture Vicksburg. It was common enough knowledge that Grant, who had been the victor over Fort Donelson, was Lincoln's best chance of subduing Vicksburg.

Claire listened as Leah spoke, then changed the subject. "You haven't said much about your visit with the Cathcarts."

"It's a dull place with nothing at all to do. I was glad to get back home." Leah leaned back in her chair, rocked tentatively, and said, "I did meet one interesting man."

Claire looked up quickly. She was, as most women in her position, keenly interested in her daughter's prospects. After all, she thought, what was there for a young woman to do except marry? And of course, marrying involved a ritual as formal as the mating of cranes. Some things had to be said, other things had to be done, arrangements had to be made. And Leah was so exasperating about it all! So now Claire asked eagerly, "Who was it? One of the Cathcarts' friends?"

"No, his name is David Rocklin. He's the son of a wealthy

planter close to Richmond," she said innocently enough, with a glitter of humor in her eyes. "I saw quite a bit of him."

"What was he doing in an isolated place like that?" Amelia inquired.

"He'd come to buy barrels from Mr. Cathcart." She hesitated, thinking about the young man, then added, "He may be coming here to Vicksburg. He's looking for salt. I told him William Dabney had a whole warehouse full of it."

"Is he acceptable?" Claire asked. By "acceptable"—a code word all three women understood perfectly—she was asking, *Is he single? Does he have money? Is his family respectable?*

Leah smiled sourly. "I suppose so. He's not married and not too old. He's got all of his arms and legs and doesn't chew tobacco that I know of."

"What a thing to say!" Amelia exclaimed, amused by Leah's ribald remarks. "Was he handsome?"

"He looked very well. I don't suppose he'll come here, though. Not with Vicksburg about to be descended upon by the Yankees...."

*

When Amelia answered the door, a tall man removed his hat and asked in a pleasant voice, "I wonder if I might see Miss Cleburne? This is her home, is it not?"

"Yes, it is, sir."

"My name's David Rocklin. I met Miss Cleburne at the Cathcart home."

At once Amelia opened the door, saying, "Come in! She did mention that." As he entered, Amelia's sharp eyes took in the strong figure, the well-cut clothes, and she said at once, "If you'll wait in the parlor, Mr. Rocklin, I'll send her down."

Amelia walked upstairs immediately and knocked on Leah's door.

"Yes? What is it?"

Opening the door, Amelia said, "It's David Rocklin. He's come calling on you."

Leah stared at her blankly then got to her feet, a smile on her face. "What did you think of him, Aunt Amelia?"

"Very handsome!"

"Yes, he is. Has Mother seen him yet?"

"No, not yet."

"Well, try to keep her from proposing, will you? She's so anxious to get me married off, I don't think she'd mind doing that in the least."

Amelia smiled but said nothing as she followed Leah downstairs. She didn't go into the sitting room with the girl, however, but went outside to the backyard where Claire was talking with Deets. Although the black man had put in gardens more years than Claire had been alive, Claire still felt it important to give instructions. When she saw Amelia, she asked, "What is it?"

"That young man Leah talked about—David Rocklin—he's here! They're in the sitting room." A light appeared in Claire's eyes as Amelia continued, "He looks very well. You don't see many men as fine looking as this one."

Inside, Leah had gone at once to the sitting room and, upon seeing David Rocklin, had held out her hand, saying, "You did come! I'm glad to see you, sir."

He took her hand, bent over, and kissed it suddenly. It was an unexpected thing—something he'd rarely done. The sight of Leah affected him strongly. He'd thought of her steadily for several days, and now he said with more fervency than usual,

"You look lovely, Leah."

Leah was taken aback and said lamely, "You've come a long way for salt!"

"I didn't come for salt. I came to see you. The salt's just an excuse."

Leah was pleased with his compliment. "I'm always glad to be esteemed more than a load of salt. Sit down...or do you have to go buy the salt right now?"

"Oh no. There's no hurry at all. Matter of fact," David said as he took a seat on one of the satin-covered chairs that was backed against the wall, "I hope it takes quite awhile to get the dickering done. I'd like to see Vicksburg while I'm here."

The two sat there talking, and finally Leah said, "I'd like for you to meet my family."

"I'd be very happy. I've already met one lady."

"That was my aunt Amelia. I'll go get my mother."

Leah disappeared and soon returned with Claire in tow. "May I present Mr. David Rocklin—and this is my mother, Claire."

David wasn't surprised to see Leah's mother was attractive. He bowed, saying, "I'm happy to meet you. Your daughter has made me feel very welcome in Mississippi."

"Are you in Vicksburg on business?" Claire asked. As David explained his mission, she summed up the tall young man carefully. He was fine looking, as Leah had said, and had a pleasant air about him. As soon as he'd finished, she said, "We'd be happy to have you take dinner with us tonight, if it would be convenient."

"Oh, quite convenient. I don't know a soul here," David responded instantly. "What time shall I return?"

"Come back about six. We'll look forward to seeing you then."

As soon as David left, Leah turned to her mother. "What did you think of him?"

"A well-set-up young man. Tell me more about his family." She sat listening while Leah, amused, told what she knew about David's family. Then she spoke aloud what was troubling her. "He's not in uniform. That's rather unusual."

"His father and brother are in the army," Leah said. "He says his family urged him to stay home and keep the plantation running. They've started raising pigs now, packing salt pork for the troops."

"Very necessary, and I'm sure he does an excellent job. Well, I'd better go talk to Sissy about supper, if we're to have a guest."

※

That evening after supper, they all sat on the porch. It was a beautiful night, with a clear display of the stars. A slight haze settled over the Mississippi, which lay east of them. As they spoke, their voices soft on the night air, lights twinkled from the Vicksburg hillsides. The conversation was pleasant, and David talked more than was customary for him. Claire, who was intense and wore an expression David couldn't quite understand, was nonetheless skillful. David realized she'd learned a great deal about him during the evening.

Finally, at nine o'clock, David was about ready to take his leave when a sudden burst of noise shattered the peace of the evening. "It's the guns!" Leah cried. "The gunboats guarding the Mississippi!"

David stood up, confused. "Who are they shooting at?"

"Grant! It must be Grant and his gunboats. They're trying

to run the Mississippi—come on!" Without even pausing for a coat, Leah ran down the steps.

Her mother called out, but she ignored her. At once David said, "I'll watch out for her, Mrs. Cleburne." He leaped off the porch, ignoring the steps, and caught up with her. She flashed a look at him, her face intent. *She loves this,* David thought. *Any kind of excitement or challenge stirs her up.*

They joined a yelling crowd of people as Vicksburg suddenly swarmed out into the streets. They were all running, and most of them were shouting. Among them were ladies in their most fashionable evening attire, for a grand spring ball had been interrupted. The hoop skirts made it difficult for them, but they ignored this and plunged toward the river. Shrieks rang out when sections of masonry crumbled under the impact of Federal shells.

"They're shooting back!" David said in surprise.

"Of course they are! What did you expect!"

David, feeling foolish, made his way with Leah to the river as shot and shell continued to scream overhead, exploding among the buildings of Vicksburg.

The architect of the advance of the gunboat armada down the Mississippi, Ulysses S. Grant, was standing on the deck of a river transport, his wife, Julia, and children with him. One of the children sat on his knees with her arms around Grant's neck, and as each crash came, she clasped her father closer. Finally, she became so frightened that Grant murmured, "Time for bed!" and a servant took the child away.

Frederick Dent Grant, then twelve years old, later recalled,

"On board our boat, my father and I stood side by side on the hurricane deck. He was quietly smoking, but an intense light shone in his eyes."

Grant had first attempted to take Vicksburg by land, but the bayous of the swampy country had bogged his army down. Now, in cooperation with Admiral Porter, he'd devised a plan to break the long, frustrating deadlock. Grant's army was to pick its way through the swamps on the western side of the Mississippi to a point well below the city. Porter was to take the fleet directly past Vicksburg's batteries in the night. Then, once it met Grant's army, he was to ferry it across to the western banks where an attack could be made on Vicksburg directly. As Grant sat quietly watching the shells explode among the fleet that churned in the muddy waters of the Mississippi, some of the vessels struck by shot that set them on fire, he must have known his reputation rested on this one venture. But he was a bulldog of a man, his chief virtue being the ability to concentrate totally on whatever lay before him. As one man described him, "Grant habitually wears an expression as if he had determined to drive his head through a brick wall and was about to do it!"

A strange sense of depression settled over the entire city of Vicksburg on April 16, 1863, after Porter's fleet successfully ran the batteries of Vicksburg. All understood that the ships would ferry the Union army across the Mississippi—and that that same force would soon be knocking at the gates of the city. It was as if a fatigue drained the energies of the townspeople. During these two days, David got a good sense of the city of Vicksburg itself. On his first day, he went out and made his

CHARIOTS IN THE SMOKE

way through the city. It was a neat town, a river port, laid out in precise geometric patterns. Most of the streets were straight, making right angles, and the buildings and plots were neatly measured into squares. He quickly found, however, that it was different from most cities, being sprawled across an undulating landscape of hills. It was sometimes called "the City of a Hundred Hills." David made his way down roads where houses were found on many different levels, like flotsam scattered over crests and hollows of waves. And on the highest hill, dominating all, stood the new courthouse, its cupola lifted to the sky. It was an impressive structure, standing in eminent solitude. He walked around its freshly stuccoed pillars, ignoring the cannonade that still vibrated through the air from time to time from the wandering gunboats. But the city was silent. Even the bright flag, with its two broad red stripes hedging the single white one, hung limply on the pole, high on the courthouse cupola.

To David, Vicksburg was completely different from Richmond. Along the waterfront, black stevedores worked at the slowest possible rate while white overseers, drained of energy, chewed their cheroots. All along the streets idlers moved silently, if at all, and on the roads, drivers and riders moved in slow motion. All of them, from time to time, stared at the river in dismay.

David found a room, putting off the meeting with William Dabney, for he wasn't anxious to leave Vicksburg. Sunday morning he went to church with the three women. All the denominations were represented, and he supposed each would be praying for deliverance from the villainous Yankees. The various churches were crowded with civilians and off-duty soldiers. St. Paul's, the Catholic cathedral they passed, was no exception. Those who attended mass left as part of the throng that flowed sluggishly down the church steps and onto the streets.

The Methodist church, where the Cleburnes escorted him, was filled to overflowing.

With a salty tang in her voice as she entered the church beside David, Amelia said quietly, "Our church was never this crowded in peacetime. I guess people get more religious when their skins are in danger."

David grinned down at her. She was a cheerful woman, but he'd learned her life hadn't been easy. She'd been married to a man whom she never mentioned except indirectly, calling him "he" without using his name. "He" had been a cotton broker who had died, and after his death, Amelia had discovered he'd wasted his small fortune on women and gambling. Now she lived on a small fund that came from the wreckage of the estate, making her home with her niece and Leah since there was nowhere else for her to go.

During the service, Claire was very much aware of the attention David Rocklin drew. She saw William Dabney straighten up in his chair and frown as they passed, but she only smiled at him courteously.

The service was conducted by a tall, thin minister with a shock of white hair and light blue eyes. He had a soft accent and, unlike most preachers of that denomination, was not a shouter or a ranter. Most of his sermon was given over to exhortation to accept the will of God and to endure hardship with grace and humility.

After the service, David shook hands with the pastor and complimented him on his sermon.

"I don't believe we've met?" Rev. Simms inquired.

"No, sir, I'm a visitor. First time I've been in Vicksburg."

He turned at a touch on his arm, and Mrs. Cleburne said,

"I'd like for you to meet Mr. William Dabney."

At once David recognized the name Leah had given him. "Why, I'm happy to meet you, Mr. Dabney. I believe you're the man I came to Vicksburg to see."

Dabney was a middle-sized man, tending to overweight. He blinked and said, "Sir, I don't believe I understand?"

"This is no time to conduct business," David said, "but if I may, I'll call upon you in the morning."

"Certainly, sir. Certainly." Dabney quickly moved to take Leah's arm and escort her down the steps. "Who is this man, Leah?"

"Oh, I met him last week. He was at the Cathcarts."

"What's this business he has with me?"

Leah smiled and teased him by assuming a pious expression. "It's not right to talk business on the Sabbath, William. Come along; I know Mother's expecting you for dinner."

The dinner was excellent, and Dabney tried every way he could to find out as much as he could about David Rocklin. David was just as determined to keep him from it. Leah understood the duel at once and enjoyed it.

After the meal was over and the two men had left, Amelia observed candidly, "You've got a mean streak in you, Leah Cleburne."

"Mean?" Leah looked innocently at Amelia, raising her eyebrows. "I don't know what you mean, Aunt Amelia."

"Yes, you do. You tormented those two men! You know how jealous Dabney is. I thought he was going to turn absolutely green."

Leah laughed. "It'll do him no good—or harm either."

Claire had come in to hear this last remark. "William Dabney's a good man—I want you to be nicer to him."

"All right, Mother." Leah had long since stopped arguing with her mother. Although she wasn't interested in Dabney as a suitor, he was persistent. For a year now he had come calling regularly as if it were a duty, although he enjoyed her company well enough. He was not at all romantic, which pleased her greatly since she wanted none of that from Dabney.

"We'll have to show Mr. Rocklin our favorite places in town," Leah said, smiling. "All he's seen so far is the Yankees blasting us off the hillside. But we'll do better, I trust."

The next few days were pleasant for David. He'd never met a young woman as charming as Leah Cleburne, and he was in no hurry to get back home. Things were not pressing there, and to be truthful, he was tired of raising hogs. At one time it had been a joy for him to farm, but somehow raising hogs didn't have the romance others apparently saw in it. His quest for supplies was nearly done, but he felt no inclination to return home. He wasn't needed—Josh was an able manager for the time being. *I might as well stay and enjoy myself,* he thought to himself one afternoon as he dressed, preparing to take Leah to a party. *Better than looking at those pigs back home.*

He left his hotel room and made his way to Leah's house. When he entered, she met him at once. "You're right on time!" he said with a smile. "I didn't know women could do that."

"Women can do all sorts of things you don't know about, David," Leah retorted. She was wearing a pale green silk dress, complete with hoop skirt and snowy white lace along the neckline and at the cuffs. She wore small jade earrings, and her red hair hung down her back in heavy waves. As they got into the carriage he had brought, she said, "I think you'll enjoy this party tonight. You'll get to meet most of the officers in charge of the defense of Vicksburg."

This proved to be true, for when they went inside the white three-story house where the party was being held in a massive room, the room was bright with the colors of women's dresses, set off by the ash gray uniforms of Confederate officers. Gold buttons and braid sparkled under the lights of the chandeliers, and the air was filled with laughter and talk.

"You'd never know this place was in such danger," he said quietly to Leah.

"I suppose people would have a party in the evening if the world were coming to an end the next morning. Come along and let me introduce you to my friends."

In the next hour, David met the most illustrious guest, General John C. Pemberton, the Confederate commander. Pemberton was a tall man and rather nervous—as he had every right to be, David thought.

The names, of course, went by David as quickly as they came, but he did remember a young captain of artillery named Raymond Finch. At twenty-five, Finch was husky and had brown eyes and brown hair. His uniform was exquisitely cut, obviously made by a private tailor, and upon finding out that David came from Richmond, he began firing questions about the situation there. A crowd soon gathered about them, and David became the center of attention. He felt out of place without a uniform but was accustomed to that.

"What's Lee going to do?" Finch demanded.

David said, shrugging, "Well, General Lee hasn't let me in on his plans, but I suppose everyone is convinced he's going to invade the North." A murmur of approval went around the room, and Finch nodded emphatically. "It'll be a difficult thing," David continued, "but everyone in Richmond thinks it'll happen."

For some time he fielded questions, and finally Finch asked the one he'd been anticipating. "You are a believer in the cause, Mr. Rocklin?"

"Yes," David said. "Of course, I'm not in uniform, which is unusual for a man of my age—"

He saw agreement in the eyes of Finch, who waited for his explanation. When he gave it, it wasn't satisfactory. Finch studied him carefully and commented, "Well, I suppose someone needs to raise pigs while the fighting men go out and do the work."

David's cheeks reddened at the blatant insult. Quietness fell around the little circle as Finch waited for David to take it up. David Rocklin, however, was a mild young man, and he'd always been so. When the war had come, he'd had none of the fiery zeal to join as had most young men his age. As the war had dragged on, more and more he was aware there would be no happy ending in this struggle for the South. He was convinced that sooner or later the ponderous weight of the Federal war machine would lead to a dire and tragic disaster. Now, however, he knew he had to answer, and he said quietly, "I respect all those who wear the uniform, Captain. Several members of my family serve in the military." It was all the explanation he made and intended to make. As he waited patiently, he was glad to see Finch relax.

Later, on their way home, Leah complimented him on his tact. "It must be very hard for you," she said. "I suppose you get that kind of challenge all the time." They were riding along the deserted streets; the skies were velvet with fiery points of light that burned and vibrated. From time to time they would pass a soldier on guard, but other than that, all was still.

"I don't take offense easily," he responded. "I never did. If you want that, go to my brother Dent. He'd fight a buzz saw or a bear—and give the bear the first bite."

"He sounds like an exciting fellow. Tell me more about him." She listened as David related how his twin had been terribly scarred at the battle of Manassas—and how he'd married a blind girl named Raimey. "They're very happy," he said, nodding as he ended the story.

"He must love her a lot. . .to marry a blind girl," Leah murmured.

"I don't think he even notices that—not anymore." He thought for a time then added, "She lives in fear Dent will get killed, but she never lets him know it."

"Tell me about the rest of your family."

By the time they arrived at the house, Leah knew a great deal about the Rocklins of Virginia. Finally, they reached the house, where he stepped down, went around, and handed her to the ground. When they were back at the steps, she turned to say good night and he surprised her—and himself.

"Leah," he said, "I'm not a ladies' man."

Startled, Leah looked up at him. The silvery moonlight bathed her face in its warm beams. The air was filled with the smell of honeysuckle from the vines that draped a wall to the right side of the house. She was taken off guard and said so. "Most men don't want to admit that!"

"Well, it's true enough."

He was so tall that he seemed to tower over her. Although she herself was more than average height, she looked dainty and fragile in the frilly dress she wore, almost like a mist in the moonlight. "Why are you telling me this, David?"

He made no attempt to touch her. All of his life he'd been compared to his twin, Dent, usually unfavorably. Dent was dashing, romantic, adventurous—and David was the quiet one. . ."the dull one," he usually translated that to mean. Although he had the same good looks as Dent, he'd never been attracted to women, nor had they been attracted to him, strangely enough. Oh, there had been some, but none he really cared for. Now as he stared at Leah, he said haltingly, "I don't know why I wanted to tell you that. It's obvious enough, I guess. Anyway, I did want to say that it's been wonderful, this time with you. You're a fine young woman."

He spoke so simply and without affectation that Leah was speechless for a moment. She was accustomed to more aggressiveness from young men. She had fully expected that by this time, certainly tonight, he would have attempted to kiss her, but he made no attempt to do so. He stood there, the masculine planes of his face outlined by the starlight, with a strength and solid quality about him that she didn't often see. "Why. . .thank you, David. It's been fun for me, too. And it's not over," she said. "You're not going home right away, are you?"

"No, I'm arguing about the price of salt with Bill Dabney. He's so jealous of you, I think he'd *give* it to me to get me out of town. But he's too tight for that!"

"He's close with a dollar, all right. You just keep bargaining. There's lots more I want to do with you." Leah looked up, smiled, and whispered, "Good night, David," then turned and went into the house.

David stepped to the carriage then drove it back to the livery stable. He walked back to the hotel, undressed, and got into bed, where he lay quietly for a while, thinking of how her face had looked in the moonlight. He smiled and said aloud, "No question what Dent would have done. Maybe I should have had him give me lessons on how to be romantic."

***

Another day passed, then two. By this time most of Vicksburg, at least those in the inner circle, knew David Rocklin was not staying to buy salt. He'd already done that, paying a fair price and arranging for the freighting all the way back to Richmond. Dabney had been grudging enough about it and, when he had wished David good-bye, after the deal had been closed, had been disgruntled when David had said cheerfully, "Oh, there's no hurry. I'll stay around for a week or two to see what happens."

During that time, David Rocklin had experienced the most enjoyable time of his life. Away from the pressures of the plantation at Richmond, not having to face the crises that constantly seemed to envelop that city, he felt different about Vicksburg. After all, it was not *his* city!

He and Leah had a grand time together. They went on picnics, and she even took him fishing once on a cutback from the Mississippi where they caught catfish. She shuddered properly over baiting a hook with a worm. They went down to the river to watch the gunboats every day and then had supper at her home. This was usually followed by a time of sitting in the parlor.

David Rocklin was engaged in something new to his experience—falling completely in love with a young woman. He'd always assumed this would come to him sometime, but not so soon. But it was happening now, although he dared not mention it to Leah. The young people in Vicksburg watched all this carefully, because who married whom was the big game in Southern society. Here in Vicksburg, even with the war machine about to grind them to pieces, it was no different.

It was on April twenty-fifth that David stepped out of character. He had gone with Leah to visit one of the two farms Dabney owned outside Vicksburg. Dabney himself had escorted them around. The purpose of the visit was, according to Dabney, for Leah to see to the decorating of the large room for a party, then to be the hostess.

While the two were inside, David wandered around. It was not a well-kept farm, he saw. The slaves looked sullen, and it was with one of these that he was shaken out of his composure.

David was watching when Dabney came out of the house with a white man, evidently the overseer. They went to a barn, where Dabney spoke loudly to a tall slave who stood silently. When David moved closer, he heard Dabney cursing the man. The slave merely shook his head. Dabney yelled, "Tie him up! I'll teach him who owns him!"

David watched as they tied the slave to a fence. The overseer came forward, grinning, a black snake whip in his hand. "Let him feel a taste of that!" Dabney commanded.

"Yes, sah!" the overseer said and at once brought the lash down on the slave's bare back. It left a pale streak that immediately rose up the size of a man's finger, and the lash struck again, crisscrossing the first mark.

David was sickened by the sight. He'd heard of such things and when he was very young had even seen one slave whipped. But this never took place at Gracefield, his own plantation.

The whip rose and fell, and David saw pleasure on Dabney's face as he stood back and watched.

Finally, David moved forward and Dabney caught his eye.

"That's enough," he said, turning to David. "You know what this nigger says? He says he won't work! I suppose you got this kind on your place, too?"

David's face was set, but he said evenly, "We usually don't have to whip our people."

"Then you must have a different kind of niggers. I paid four thousand dollars for this 'un and he's not worth spit! But he will be by the time I get through whipping him."

"He won't be much good to you if you beat him half to death," David said. "Maybe you might try another way."

Dabney stared at him, his face full of contempt. "You come all the way from Richmond to tell us how to treat our slaves? You think you could do better? Then you can buy him—just what I paid for him."

David instantly said, "Why, of course, Mr. Dabney. He looks like a good hand. If you'll make out the papers, I'll write you out a check."

Dabney was aware that Leah was now standing to one side. He took one look at her face and said quickly, "You don't want this nigger!"

When David didn't answer but simply stood there, Dabney knew he had to go through with it. "All right," he said, grumbling. "I'll go make out the papers."

As he left, his back stiff with anger, David looked at the overseer, who was staring at him with wide eyes. "That's all," he said, dismissing him brusquely. Then he stepped over and pulled his knife from his pocket. After slitting the rawhide that held the slave's hands together, he closed the knife and stepped back. The slave turned slowly to look at him. He had not flinched during the terrible beating, and now he stood looking at his new owner, hatred gleaming out of his eyes. He was six feet tall, powerfully built, and a rich brown color. But it was his eyes that attracted David the most. They were intelligent—and bitter.

"What's your name?" David asked quietly.

"Corey...Corey Jones."

"Well, Corey, I think we'd better see about that back of yours."

"I'm all right...sah." The last word was slow in coming, and there was resentment in the slave's attitude.

"Don't be foolish. I'm sure there's something to put on it. My name's David Rocklin. You'll be going back to Virginia with me." He hesitated then said, "I'll see you don't have to go through this anymore."

Unbelief blazed out of the slave's eyes, but he was silent.

On their way home, Corey sat in the back of the carriage, glowering, a sack of meager possessions in his hands. The two in front were intensely aware of him but said nothing. Finally, when they got to the house, Leah said, "Why don't you leave Corey here with us until you're ready to go?"

David said at once, "That would be a help. I don't really have a place." His eyes warm, he turned to the slave. "Corey, I'll be here a few more days. You help Miss Leah all you can, and I'm sure she'll see you're well bestowed."

The slave stared at him, then at Leah. Without a word he got out of the carriage and stood waiting. Leah turned to David, saying, "Well, I doubt if William will want me to grace his party now. He was embarrassed about all this."

"So was I...and humiliated. I never could stand to see anybody mistreated."

"Even a slave?"

He stared at her. "Yes, even a slave!"

She studied him carefully as if seeing something she hadn't

seen. Then her eyes grew gentle. "You're very nice," she said. "There's a goodness in you that I love to see, but don't often find." Then she got out of the carriage, saying, "Come along, Corey. I'll show you where you can stay."

❧

On April 30, Grant and his army were ferried across the Mississippi by the navy of Admiral Porter. As soon as word got to Vicksburg, every person there knew what it meant. David was eating supper with the Cleburnes, and it was Claire who said nervously, "I feel we'll be all right. General Pemberton will certainly be able to keep those Yankees from taking the city."

Amelia, who kept up with military news better than Claire, shook her head. "He's got a big army, and Sherman will be joining him. It's going to be close."

David watched and listened, saying little. Later that night, as they sat on the front porch after supper, all felt the pressure that seemed to be closing around the town like a fist. The women talked of old times.

"I wish you could have known my father, Thaddeus Rayborn," Claire said. "Have you heard of him?"

"I've heard of a Congressman Rayborn."

"That was him; that was my father." Her face glowed as she continued, "He was the best lawyer in the state of Mississippi, maybe in the whole country. He was so wonderful! I used to go watch him in the courtroom. He hardly ever lost a case."

David listened for some time as Claire talked about her father. He found it strange she never mentioned her husband. David had made the mistake once of saying something to Amelia about Claire's "late" husband, and Amelia had answered instantly, "Her husband isn't dead. His name is Matthew Cleburne and he lives in New York. They're separated."

Now as Claire talked eloquently about her father, with great spirit and longing, David realized Leah was listening intently, her eyes fixed on her mother. *I wonder what she feels,* David wondered. *I can't ask her about it, though. Maybe I can ask Amelia later on.*

Later he did ask Amelia about Claire's marriage, and she replied, "It was tragic. The marriage didn't last long. After Leah was born, Claire grew more and more unhappy and finally separated from her husband. He moved to New York and went into business there."

"What was it, Amelia?" David asked, feeling he could ask her honestly.

Amelia looked down at her hands, reluctant to answer. "He drank some...and there was talk about a woman."

There was something in her voice that drew David's attention. "But that wasn't all of it?"

Again a silence—then Amelia looked up at him, misery in her eyes. "She worshipped her father—my brother. She saw everything in him that she admired in a man—and afterwards, when she grew up, she demanded those same things from other men." Silence fell again, cutting across the room like a knife. From somewhere a bird called out in a lonesome fashion, and Amelia waited until the mournful tone had died away. "I don't think," she said in a whisper, "Claire would ever have found what she saw in her father in any other man. I—I liked Matthew very much—but now Claire won't let his name be mentioned."

"Hard on Leah."

"Yes—very hard!"

As the week progressed, David picked up other hints of this situation. When he asked Leah, she said restlessly, "I haven't seen him since I was fifteen years old. Before that, I don't remember when he lived with us. I saw him a few times when I was a child and he came and visited. He took me to a fair once and bought me everything I wanted. But he left after that. Now he writes and sends money."

"I'm sorry," he said. "I know that's hard for you."

She turned to him and David saw tears in her eyes. They'd been walking along the street after supper, and now that they'd reached the porch, she seemed depressed. He said quietly, as if he were saying nothing of particular importance, "Leah, I have something to say to you."

Surprised, she looked up. Thinking about her father always saddened her, although she usually covered it better. But there was something about David Rocklin, something she hadn't felt with any other man, perhaps because she saw no threat in him, that brought out this willingness to share things. Now, as she looked at him, she saw his face was utterly serious.

"I love you, Leah, and I mean to make you love me."

"Why, David—!"

"I know," he interrupted, shaking his head, "I'm not very romantic, am I? I wish I were."

"But you can't...you can't mean it! We've only known each other a few days!"

"I don't think that matters. I've known other women for years, but I've never felt like this. I'm not asking you for anything, but I think it's only fair to tell you how I feel."

Suddenly Leah was confused. *Here's a man Mother would at least accept. He's rich, he has a good family, and he's young, nice looking, and has good manners.*

But that wasn't enough for Leah Cleburne. She looked at him and said gently, "I hate to say this to you, David, but I could never let myself love you."

Her words cut him and he stared at her. "Never?" he asked. "Are you sure?"

"Oh, David," she said compassionately, "It's not *you*. You're one of the most gentle men I've ever known, perhaps the most gentle. You have so many good qualities, but—"

Suddenly he realized what she was saying. "It's because I'm not in the army, isn't it?"

Leah's lips pressed tightly together. "I believe in the Confederacy," she said. "Those of us who do have risked everything we have—and you've risked nothing, David. Two people couldn't live together unless they agreed on the important things, and this is one of the *most* important things."

David stood looking down at her. Her skin was like alabaster in the moonlight, and he could smell the slight jasmine fragrance she wore in her hair sometimes. Finally, he said slowly, "I can see that."

"You can? Then you understand?" she said eagerly.

"Yes, of course I can." He stood there quietly and then said, "Good night, Leah."

He turned and walked away, leaving her alone. As she watched him go, a sense of loss flooded her. "Have I made a mistake?" she whispered aloud. He disappeared into the darkness, and still she stood there, feeling a strangeness she couldn't explain. If he'd been more aggressive, it might have been easier. But now she felt somehow that she'd failed, and she didn't know why. Slowly, she turned and went into the house, not even hearing when Amelia spoke to her.

David stayed away from Leah the next day, May 8, and walked

the streets of Vicksburg in silence. He thought of Corey, the slave he'd purchased, and wondered what would become of him. He thought about taking him back to Richmond. He slept poorly. Finally, on the ninth, he appeared at the Cleburne house late in the afternoon. When Leah opened the door, her hand flew up to her lips.

"Here I am, Leah."

"David," Leah whispered, "I can't believe it."

David Rocklin was wearing the uniform of a private in the Confederate army. It was an ill-fitting uniform made for a smaller man and seemed to pinch. He stood there looking awkward and ill at ease, but he smiled at her, saying, "I've come courting, Miss Leah. May I come in?"

Leah shook her head in disbelief. She put out a trembling hand and he took it. Leaning over, he kissed it and said, "I had to do it, Leah, but I must tell you, I just enlisted for ninety days. At least I'll be able to do something in this battle that's shaping up."

"Why did you do it, David?" Leah asked, although she knew.

Then, for the first time, he reached out and pulled her close so she was leaning against him, with her face turned up. He kissed her slowly, savoring the softness of her lips. Her hands gripped his arms, and she was aware of the strength of the man who held her and the way it made her feel safe and secure. But she was also filled with shock at what he'd done and thought, *A man who would do this for a woman must really love her.*

As if in answer to her thoughts, he lifted his head and said, "I love you, Leah. I won't ask you for an answer now, but you mean more to me than anything in this world."

Leah's eyes grew misty. She said softly, "Come in, David, and let's tell Mother and Amelia."

Chapter 3

A Taste of Fear

On May 11, David Rocklin was introduced to his share of the Confederate army. He'd been connected, in a way, with soldiers and camps before, having spent much time with his father and brothers with the troops in Richmond. This, however, he quickly learned, was far different. Early Monday morning, he found himself in front of Captain Noland Devers, who was in charge of Company C, and the heavy, profane, balding man who looked him over seemed displeased. As a political officer, Devers had never actually seen a battle. He was the sort of officer who was the curse of both the Confederates and the Federals, since neither Lincoln nor Davis learned to avoid such men.

Devers looked across at Captain Raymond Finch, who'd brought David into headquarters, introducing him as a new recruit. Finch smiled superciliously, saying, "Private Rocklin is somewhat late coming to the service of his country, I fear, Captain."

Devers stared at the tall soldier before him dressed in the ill-fitting uniform and grunted, "What brought you to your senses, Rocklin? Finally see the light?"

With Finch's eyes fixed on him, David felt he couldn't

speak the truth—that he'd joined to please his sweetheart. Then he suddenly realized he had no choice. "I'm in love with a young woman," he said evenly, meeting Devers's eyes. "I'm joining the service to prove I can be a loyal soldier."

Devers burst out in uproarious laughter. He cursed colorfully then slapped the table before him with his meaty hand. "At least we got the truth out of you." Then, his eyes crafty and sly, he said, "See to it that he has plenty of opportunity to prove his courage, Captain Finch."

"Yes, sir, I'll certainly do that," Finch replied readily, a grin forming on his lips.

After the two left the tent, he said, "All right, Rocklin, I'm putting you in with a good company."

He took him to a street where some men were drilling, and they met Lieutenant Jacob Turnbridge. "Lieutenant," Finch said, "this is David Rocklin. See to it that you make a soldier out of him."

Turnbridge, a slim man with blond hair, was no more than twenty-three. His blue eyes examined David critically. "After the jailbait we've been having to use, I believe you got a good one. He's big enough. Can you shoot, Rocklin?"

"Yes, sir."

A smile played over Turnbridge's thin lips. "Well, you're not overburdened with modesty. We'll see about that. Sergeant?"

Ballard, a skinny man with blue eyes and red hair, disengaged himself from a group of privates and came to stand before the lieutenant. "Here's your new replacement," Turnbridge said. "Says he can shoot. I guess he'll get some opportunity to prove that, but you'd better check him out."

"Yes, sir."

"This is Sergeant Ike Ballard," Turnbridge said. "Take him,

Sergeant, and make a soldier out of him."

When Sergeant Ballard led David away, Turnbridge turned to Finch and said, "Better quality than we're used to."

"I doubt it," Finch said coolly. "He'll malinger if he can and run away if he gets a chance."

Turnbridge stared at him. "How do you figure that, Captain?"

"He joined up to please a young woman. First smell of powder and he'll be gone. If he'd been any kind of a man, he'd already have been in the army. Keep your eye on him. Let me know if he makes a break. We'll have him shot as an example for the rest."

"Why, yes, sir."

Meanwhile, Sergeant Ballard said to his squad, "You fellows come on. We'll get a little exhibition of shooting from our newest recruit. This here's David Rocklin."

David didn't miss the smirks on the faces of a few of the men, but he followed along to a makeshift rifle range. A target was set up 150 yards away. Ballard picked up a musket and said, "See if you know how to load this thing."

David had loaded guns all his life. All the Rocklin boys were good hunters. Quickly he bit the end off the cartridge, dumped the black powder down the barrel of the musket, then quickly added the lead bullet, tamping it all down and then priming the weapon. "Yes, sir," he said.

It had been expertly done, and Lon Gere, a small man with intense black eyes, said, "Well, he knows how to load up. Let's see if he can shoot."

"Give you two-to-one odds he misses dead center," someone else called.

"No takers," Ballard said. "All right, see what you can do."

CHARIOTS IN THE SMOKE

Without comment, David swept the rifle up, held it steady for a fraction of a second, and pulled the trigger. There was the hiss as the cap exploded, setting off the charge; then the musket cracked, kicking back against his shoulder slightly. He lowered the rifle and stood there calmly.

"Dead center!" Lon Gere said with surprise. "Where'd you learn to shoot like that?"

David shrugged; it had been an easy shot. "My father taught me and my brothers."

"See if you can do it again. This time we'll back away to two hundred yards."

They repeated the process, and David put his next bullet within two inches of the last.

Ballard nodded with satisfaction. "That's enough. We don't have powder to waste. You're a sharpshooter, and we've got use for a lot of them." He looked over at a skinny man in his late twenties and said, "Bones, maybe you need to take some lessons from this fellow."

Bones Detwiler grinned languidly. "I don't figure to be that far away when I shoot," he said.

After David had been tested, he was put to work drilling with the rest, but the drill didn't last over thirty minutes.

Harold Ficker, a seventeen-year-old farm boy with big hands and feet, complained, "Sarge, I don't see what good it does, all this here drilling. Them Yankees ain't gonna come to watch us parade."

Ike Ballard opened his mouth to reprove the young man, then smiled. A tough mountain man from Tennessee, he felt the same way. "You might be right about that, Harold." He looked downriver and said, "Grant has crossed this river. I'm thinking he's headed our way."

The next two days, David was kept under close surveillance, not only by Sergeant Ballard but also by Lieutenant Turnbridge. Turnbridge reported to Finch, "He's a good soldier; he can shoot better than any man in the squad, maybe in the whole company."

Finch, displeased, said, "Keep your eye on him, Lieutenant. Mind what I tell you. He'll run away if he gets a chance, no matter how good he shoots. It's one thing to shoot at a target—another thing to be shot at."

Three days after he'd joined, David got time off. Late that afternoon, he walked down to the Cleburne house and was welcomed gladly not only by Leah but by Claire and Amelia. They went to great extent to put a fine supper on the table, and he ate heartily, for the army food had been bland and there hadn't been much of it.

They were halfway through the meal when Amelia said, "I guess the whole Confederacy's grieving today."

David looked up. "Grieving? About what, Aunt Amelia?" With her encouragement, he'd taken to calling her by this name.

All three stared at him. "You haven't heard?"

"Heard about what?"

Leah's eyes filled with grief. "It's General Jackson. He's dead."

Grief, pain, and shock stabbed David Rocklin. "Stonewall Jackson?" It was as if she'd said, "The sun fell this afternoon." Stonewall Jackson, of all the generals in the Confederate army, had been the best. His men in the Stonewall Brigade and other larger units had won against impossible odds.

"My father and brothers are in the Stonewall Brigade," he said quietly.

"I know," Leah said. "I hated to tell you." She seemed to lose her appetite. "We couldn't afford to lose him. But we did."

The announcement put a damper on the dinner, and only by great effort did Aunt Amelia bring the conversation around to a more cheerful subject.

At last David asked, "What about Corey?"

The three women exchanged careful glances, and it was Leah who answered, "He's very sullen."

"Hasn't offered you any insolence, I trust?"

"No, except he just won't say anything. Does what he's told," Claire said, shrugging, "but you'll never break him. We've seen that kind before. They'll die before they'll give in."

"I'll have a talk with him after we're done eating."

After supper, David found the tall slave sitting outside on a box, watching the sun go down. "Hello, Corey," David said.

The man's head turned slowly, his eyes hooded. "Hello, Mr. Rocklin."

David saw the anger had somewhat faded. "How are you?" he asked. "Getting plenty to eat?"

"Yes, sah." Bare monosyllables were all Corey offered.

"Well, I hope you're able to give the ladies help. It's hard on women having to take care of a house all by themselves."

"I do the best I can."

David sat down, and for a long time there was silence. Finally, David said heavily, "When we get back to Virginia, there won't be anything like what happened to you with Mr. Dabney."

Again, disbelief showed in Corey's eyes.

"Where are you from, Corey? Tell me about yourself."

"What difference does it make, Mr. Rocklin?"

"Why, I just like to know something about a man."

"I ain't no man—I'm a slave."

David clenched his teeth together. It was a matter he'd often thought about, but he had no answer and finally said so. "I tell you this, Corey. I look on you as a man and not a possession. I can't reconcile that with slavery. I don't understand it. I'm in the army now; you know that from the uniform. But I'm not in it because I believe slavery's right."

"What are you in it for then, Mr. Rocklin?"

"Because I'm a fool, I suppose." He found himself talking to the slave as he wouldn't have thought possible. He spoke of how he'd always been fearful of the war, that it was for the wrong cause. "People talk about it being for the states' rights." Then he said, almost in a murmur, "But if a state wants to do something wrong..."

He left the sentence hanging, not seeing the intelligent eyes of the slave fixed on him intently. For a while, Corey didn't speak, filing David's words away in his mind. But after some hesitation, he began speaking of his own life. It wasn't an unusual story. He'd been overworked, mistreated, and had run away and gotten the name of a rebellious slave. When he'd finished the short recitation, he was quiet for a moment then turned to the man across from him. "I thank you for what you done, Mr. Rocklin."

Shocked at the slave's words after seeing such bitterness in his eyes, David nodded. "Well, don't repeat this to anybody else, Corey, but you'll be a free man one day. I'd like to see you free right now, along with all the other slaves. It's what God wants for people.... If you tell anybody this, they'll probably have me shot as a traitor. So there's your chance to get even."

Corey Jones looked at David in a way he'd never looked at a white person. There was something in this tall, dark-haired man he'd often sought in the faces of the white race. He'd found it from time to time, but usually in the faces of women. He couldn't put a name to it, but he knew one thing: Here was one man who wouldn't beat him! Here was one who looked at him as a *man*, not as a piece of property or just another body to be used up to make money. When David rose to leave, he hesitated slightly and then said to Corey, "I want to give you a letter and some papers. If anything happens to me. . .I want you to go to Virginia. Go to my grandmother if my father's not there. Give them to her."

"What do them papers say?"

"One of them will say I've purchased you. It's a bill of sale. That will show whose. . .property you are."

Corey stared at him intently. "And the other one, Mr. Rocklin?"

"I'll write a letter to my grandmother, instructing her to give you your freedom at the end of one year's service."

Corey froze, as if turned to stone. When Rocklin saw that Corey wasn't going to speak, he turned and left. Slowly Corey rose, and for the first time since he'd been a small child, his eyes misted over. He couldn't believe what he'd heard, and yet there was truth in young David Rocklin's face. Corey turned blindly and walked away, his eyes fixed on the horizon as he thought about Virginia—and freedom.

❦

General Ulysses S. Grant's army didn't move all that quickly. Nevertheless, for its time, the Union army experienced many rapid advances and sudden victories in its swift approach to the citadel city of Vicksburg. Grant had sent Colonel Benjamin H.

Grierson sweeping through Mississippi, down into Louisiana, to throw the Confederates off stride. There was no Confederate cavalry on hand to oppose this move, and the raid caused great alarm, diverting attention away from Grant's operations.

Grant's army, including Sherman's corps, still at Vicksburg, numbered about fifty thousand men. The Confederate strength in that area was approximately thirty thousand, most of it concentrated in or near Vicksburg. Only two brigades opposed the crossing, and these were decisively and thoroughly defeated at the battle of Port Gibson on the following day. The Union forces pushed forward, seized the ground, and awaited Sherman's corps, which arrived a week later.

General Pemberton left two divisions idle at Vicksburg instead of concentrating his forces. Furthermore, when some reinforcements reached Jackson, he left them to guard that area. In effect, he strung out his forces on a line all the way from Vicksburg east to Jackson—an impossible area to defend with his smaller numbers.

General Grant proved too swift a thinker for Pemberton. He made for Jackson, where he cut the Confederate supply lines into Vicksburg.

On May 12, Union forces defeated a Confederate brigade at Raymond. On the sixteenth, the Union army won a hard-fought battle at Champion's Hill, the decisive engagement of the campaign.

On the following day, the Union forces lined themselves up at a crossing on Big Black River Bridge, ready to launch the final assault that would lead to the very doors of Vicksburg.

The assault commander was General Michael Lawler, a mountainous man weighing over two hundred and fifty pounds. Lawler was so huge that a sword belt couldn't fit comfortably around his waist. Instead, he wore his sword suspended by a strap from one shoulder. But Grant once said of this man, "When it comes to just plain hard fighting, I would rather trust old Mike Lawler than any one of them."

On the morning of the seventeenth, Lawler moved his brigade through the woods to within four hundred yards of the enemy line. He found a natural gully deep enough to hide his men. "From right here, men," he said, "we'll smack the Rebs so hard they'll never know what got 'em! To get to it, though, we got to cross that open field." He motioned to a field exposed to fire from the Confederate forces. He didn't hesitate, however, and leaving one regiment behind to protect his artillery, he dashed across at the head of the other three regiments, losing only two men. Then he gave a startling order. "Don't bother firing, men. Fix bayonets!" Pouring sweat, he heaved his great bulk up on his horse. Spurring the animal forward, he yelled, "Forward, men!" and the regiments roared out of their shelters toward the Confederate line and took them completely off guard. The shocked Confederates had time to get off one volley before Lawler's column hit them. The charge was one of the shortest in the Civil War, lasting just three minutes. Completely outmanned, and with bayonets and the stocks of muskets raining on their heads, the Confederates turned and fled, throwing down their guns as they ran.

David Rocklin was one of the men who had approached Big Black River. It was his baptism under fire, and as the men were placed in a thin line by Lieutenant Turnbridge, his heart began to beat faster and his hands grew sweaty. Looking around, he didn't see that the other men were going through this sort of struggle. Harold Ficker was arguing with Lon Gere about a horse race they'd planned as soon as the Yankees were whipped. Ficker wore a wild daisy on his tattered hat, and his brown eyes were wide and fearless as he argued.

Bones Detwiler put himself in the line and grinned as he looked at Rocklin. "Gonna see the elephant, I reckon, ain't you, Dave?"

This was a common expression for a man's seeing battle for the first time. David started to speak and found that his throat was dry. He cleared it then managed to smile back. "I guess so, Bones. You reckon they'll be coming soon?"

"I say yes," Detwiler said, nodding almost carelessly.

Sergeant Ike Ballard came by, checking their muskets. "This ain't gonna be no revival meeting," he said crossly. "There's more Yanks out there than weevils in a cotton patch."

Nervously, David checked his musket. He lay there, his muscles tense. He heard a small shrill sound and turned quickly to see a huge cricket not far from his head. Almost invisible, this creature was issuing a tiny chorus, almost like a song. Somehow it stirred David's imagination, and he wondered if the cricket would survive the battle that was surely coming.

Suddenly a loud voice roared across the line and through the air. "All right, boys, forward!" And then Lieutenant Turnbridge came striding along, his eyes gleaming with excitement and his saber drawn. "Get ready, men! They're coming! Don't shoot until—!"

There was a slight thudding sound as the lieutenant's words were cut off. David looked around curiously and saw that a black spot had appeared on the right side of Turnbridge's forehead. The officer stood there one moment, as if thinking deeply, but his eyes had dimmed and he fell face forward, not catching his fall.

"H'yar they come!" Ballard screamed, and then David saw them. He hadn't imagined there would be so many. The Union army swept ahead, a solid blue mass, and broke into small groups, all of them bearing bayonets on the end of their rifles.

Somehow the sight of those bayonets frightened David worse than if they had come shooting. He'd always disliked knives and had never seen how any man could stand up and face cold steel in a knife fight. As Sergeant Ballard moved back and forth yelling, "Shoot! Shoot, men!" he threw his rifle forward, but his hands were trembling so much that he couldn't draw a bead on any of the approaching enemy. He pulled the trigger and knew he had fired wildly over the heads of the charging Yankees.

Then, suddenly, the blue wall was upon them. A tall man with the eyes of a maniac appeared before him, the bayonet held straight at David's stomach. David Rocklin couldn't move. The sight of that bayonet was too much. He could feel it sliding into his stomach, and fear rose like nausea in him. The soldier drew back the bayonet, screaming and lunging at him, but he was driven sideways as a bullet caught him in the jaw. He fell to the ground, clawing at his jaw, scattering great drops of blood on the leaves.

Ballard stepped forward and struck him once in the head with the butt of his musket, and he lay still.

"Load! Load!" Ballard cried, but it was too late. All along the line, the Confederates who had fired the only shot they would get off were facing the steel. Suddenly one man threw down his gun and turned, running as fast as he could. It was a signal for the others, and David, without thought, whirled and ran blindly. He didn't do so consciously, nor perhaps did the others, but they ran. They left the field to the Yankees. It was a blind insanity, and David never remembered running. He heard the screams behind him, and as he fell and scrambled along with the others, he felt no shame, only a determination to get away from what was happening in the battle.

Chapter 4

The Net Closes

The shattered Confederate army tumbled back into the trenches, breastworks, and redans of the city as though an invincible blue tidal wave had washed them back. Emma Balfour, wife of a prominent physician, poured out the spirit of most of the city in a letter to a friend:

> My pen almost refuses to tell of our terrible disaster. From six o'clock in the morning until five in the evening the battle raged. We are defeated! Our army is in confusion and the carnage—awful! Awful! Our poor fellows passed through the streets and every house poured forth all it had to refresh them. We carried buckets of water for them and everything edible was put out. I fed as many as I could. Poor fellows, it made my heart ache to see them. What is to become of all of the living things in this place when the boats begin shelling—God only knows. Shut up as in a trap, thousands of men and women have fled here for shelter.

David and the remains of his company were part of that broken army that stumbled back into Vicksburg. They were as beaten as men could be, and Captain Raymond Finch pulled them up in front of their barracks, his face red with rage, and berated them for being cowards and traitors. "You're not soldiers!" he spat out, venom practically dripping from his lips. "You're cowards and a disgrace to the uniforms you wear! If we didn't need men so badly, I'd have you all shot for cowardice in the face of the enemy."

David stood with the rest of his squad, noting that the loss of Lieutenant Turnbridge, along with several enlisted men, had hit them all hard. Finch's ravings had little effect on David. He was so shaken by his part in the battle that he could hardly separate the officer's words.

I ran away! The shame of what had happened burned in him, and he thought of his father and his brothers who had gone through much worse and hadn't fled at the first threat to their lives. He'd always supposed that if he had been in the army, he could at least have managed to do as well as Dent or Lowell.

But now that illusion had been torn from him. As Finch walked back and forth, stamping his feet so that small clouds of dust rose, David went over the scene again and again, wishing it had been different. But even the thought of those bright flashing bayonets chilled him. *If it had only been bullets,* he thought desperately, *I could have stood it. But I can't stand the sight of that steel!* Later he talked with Lon Gere about it, not revealing his own fears, but asking the small gambler what he felt about their behavior.

"Well, we cut and run," Gere said and shrugged, his features showing nothing. His profession had schooled him to keep emotions hidden, so if he was ashamed of what he'd done, it wasn't apparent in his dark features. "It's happened before to better men than us," he continued. "Just ask some of the fellows that's been in the bad battles—the big ones. The fellow that's a hero today, well, something comes over him and he ups and runs—especially when everybody else is running!"

"That's no excuse," David muttered.

Gere looked at the tall, strong young man whose shoulders now were slumped. He had known Rocklin only a few days but had seen quality in him. Now he added as helpfully as he could, "We'll get 'em the next time, Dave. Don't worry about it. You'll see the Bluebellies turn and run when *we* get the upper hand."

They had the chance to prove their courage, for Ulysses S. Grant, flushed with success, made a tactical error. Convinced he could take the city, he launched an attack on May 19 and was repulsed. Three days later, still hoping he could finish the campaign without a drawn-out siege, he ordered another assault. His troops, as anxious to end the fighting as Grant, rushed forward to the attack. Vicksburg, however, was a naturally strong position, surrounded by steep ravines that were difficult to climb. The defenders had further strengthened the natural defenses, and on May 22, the blue waves of Yankee uniforms were met by a solid sheet of terrible fire that drove them back down again.

Grant, realizing that Vicksburg could not be taken by direct assault, settled down to siege warfare.

*

David made his way down through the streets of Vicksburg, noting the damage that had been done by the heavy guns of the warships in the river. They had sent shell after shell screaming up in the air to fall on the defenseless. Now details were at work everywhere, rebuilding and repairing the work plowed up and torn down by the firing of the enemy's batteries. It was no light task, and he himself had struggled for a week with the other men. After Grant's second assault had been repulsed, David had become a day laborer and, after fighting all day beneath the rays of the summer sun, spent the rest of his strength using pickax, spade, and shovel. He carried heavy sandbags and strengthened the torn-down breastworks with timbers and cotton bales—protection for the next day's combat.

Now as he reached the Cleburne house, he was relieved to see it was undamaged. Just down the street he saw one house—a three-storied mansion—gutted, apparently by explosive shells, and the sight depressed him. He moved up onto the porch and was met before he knocked by Aunt Amelia, who greeted him warmly. "Come in, David." She was wearing a plain brown dress, and her thinning body showed signs of the siege, although it was only the sixth day. "You're late! We waited supper for you, though," she said, a fond light in her eyes. She touched his arm as he stepped into the house. "You look tired. You need more rest."

"Not much of that for any of us," David commented as lightly as he could.

He followed Aunt Amelia into the dining room, where she pushed him into a seat, saying, "Now you just sit there and we'll all be ready to eat in a minute. I'll get Claire and Leah."

She disappeared, and almost instantly Leah came in with a bowl of mashed potatoes and a tray of fresh-baked bread. Noting the fatigue that lined his face, she only said, "I'm going to fatten you up, soldier. We've got plenty tonight."

"Better save it," David warned. "There won't be anything coming in from the outside now that the line to Jackson's been cut."

Leah smiled and shrugged. "We'll worry about that tomorrow. Tonight we feast."

Claire and Aunt Amelia came in and set the table with beef, corn, peas, pickles, and slaw. "Would you ask the blessing, David?" Leah asked.

David hesitated then bowed his head and mumbled a few words. Then he looked up and smiled. "I cleaned up as best I could, but it doesn't do much good."

"What's happening, David?" Claire asked as she took some of the beef then passed the plate along to him. "Are we going to be able to hold out?"

"The officers tell us we will," David said noncommittally. He was determined not to reveal his depression to the three women, so he forced a smile. "We'll last the Yankees out. They can't stay here forever. We've heard that General Lee might send part of the Army of Northern Virginia to take Grant on. That would make a difference."

As the others talked, Amelia watched Leah's and David's faces closely. She took little part in the conversation, although she missed nothing of what was said.

"What will happen if the Yankees do win?" she asked finally. It was a question they had all thought about, although none had voiced it. It was as if they were afraid to mention such a possibility. But now Amelia's brown eyes were filled with a doubt that hadn't been there before the siege began.

"I suppose all the soldiers would end up in a prison camp or else would go on parole," David said, shrugging. He took a bite of a dark green pickle, flinched, and said, "That's strong. Did you make this, Aunt Amelia?"

"Yes. I always say pickles need to be strong or there's no sense fooling with them," she replied firmly. Then she pursued her question. "Well, what would happen to the town? To us?"

"Why, it'd be like New Orleans or Baton Rouge—any other town the Yankees have taken. It'd be under military jurisdiction. Things would be pretty different."

"I couldn't bear to live in a town where a man like Beast Butler ruled over us," Claire said sharply. "Such a man's a disgrace to any uniform, even a Yankee uniform!" She referred to Benjamin Franklin Butler, who had given a special order that any woman in New Orleans who insulted a Federal soldier would be treated as a woman of the streets. It was doubtful you could find a man in the South more hated than Butler. Claire toyed with the slaw with her fork, took a tiny bite, and chewed slowly. She was a woman who liked things to remain the same.

And yet David sensed an unhappiness in her that was rooted more deeply than the siege itself. He had noticed it in her before and assumed her life had been unhappy. Aside from the fact of her separation from her husband, he knew little about what went on behind her smooth, attractive face.

Leah said quickly, "We're not going to talk about losing. Let's talk about when we run the Yankees all the way back to Washington." Her red hair caught the reflection of a lamp behind her, giving off golden glints. Dressed in pale green, with short sleeves and white ribbons at her neck, Leah was vivacious—even under the terrible circumstances. "Tell us what you've been doing," she added. "They won't let us go out to see the fighting."

David didn't want to talk about the war. It was a boring, dangerous, dirty sort of fighting. The Yankees circling the city were throwing up their own breastworks, and now all a man had to do was lift his head—or even part of it—and one of the sharpshooters would end his part in the war immediately. Both sides had sharpshooters posted to inhibit the digging of breastworks. Since David was known as a fine shot, he'd done his part of that duty. But it didn't require courage, and he felt ashamed of shooting the men on the other side as they showed themselves. So far as he knew, he hadn't killed any, but he had winged three and had tried to take satisfaction in putting three Yankees, at least, beyond doing more to root the citizens and soldiers of Vicksburg out of their fortress.

After supper, Leah said, "Come on, David. I want to show you what we're doing now. We're keeping chickens. I bought six of them, and three of them are already laying. Corey built a pen for them. He's as proud of them as I am."

David rose at once and the two left. Claire stared after them and shook her head slightly. "I hope she doesn't get too caught up with him," she said quietly.

Amelia looked up quickly. A spasm of emotion crossed her face, very slight but obvious enough that Claire saw it. "What's wrong?" she asked instantly. "Certainly you don't see him as a suitor for Leah."

"He's a fine young man. I like him a lot."

"Why, I like him, too, Amelia, but we're not talking about a casual acquaintance. We're talking about a possible husband for Leah."

"I think he'd make a fine husband."

"But he's not even an officer...and we don't know anything about him, really. We don't know anything about his family—and you know how important the bloodline is."

Amelia had picked up the platter containing the meat. Very seldom did she say anything that would cross her niece's opinions, but now she said evenly, "Bloodline's not everything."

Claire stared in astonishment at Amelia. So rarely had the woman taken a position opposite to her own that she couldn't remember the last time. "Why, Amelia, what do you mean by that? Of course it's important! Look at my father! We've got his bloodline, and that's important. We know what he was. We don't know anything about the Rocklins, except that they apparently have money." She had risen and picked up the vegetable remains on two separate plates. Sadly she said, "If only Father were alive, we wouldn't be here in all this. I miss him so much!"

Amelia's eyes narrowed; her lips grew tight. She started to say something and then shook her head, almost imperceptibly. She was accustomed to Claire's almost idolatrous feelings toward her father, Amelia's brother. More than once, long ago, Amelia had tried to tell Claire that she needed to put these feelings for her father in the proper perspective but had been so sharply rebuked that she'd ceased mentioning it. Now she saw there was no hope of changing her niece's mind, so she cleared the table and then went to her room to read.

Claire sat on the porch outside, and from time to time, there would be an explosion. The boats on the river had the range and dropped shells on the helpless city in a regular cadence. *I suppose,* she thought, *they've been commanded to do that so we won't be able to sleep.* She leaned her head back, closed her eyes, and thought of earlier days when things had been better. It was a habit she'd fallen into lately. Mostly she thought of her girlhood. She rocked slowly, the chair creaking on the boards of the porch, and smiled as she thought of the times she and her father had made trips together. He had treated her like an equal even when she was a child, and those days had been the best of her life.

Then she thought of her marriage, and her smile vanished abruptly. Her brow wrinkled as she thought of the early days when she'd been so in love with Matthew. But those days hadn't lasted long, and slowly she had drifted apart from her husband. She wondered suddenly what he was doing, what his life was like. He lived in New York now and was apparently successful. He'd been generous with her financially, but the shadow of those days of her marriage when he had proven himself to be unfit as a father—and even more unfit as a husband—disturbed her. Quickly she turned her thoughts to other things.

Later, when David and Leah came back, she said good night to the young man, who then trudged away. "Sit down, Leah," she said. "Tell me, what did David say?"

"Why, nothing, really," Leah answered. She took a seat, and for a while the two women talked, their words punctuated by explosions. "Isn't it strange," Leah continued, "that once an explosion would have had the whole town up, running outdoors to see what it was? Now it's no more than as if a limb fell off a tree. Just part of our way of life." Her voice grew still and a quietness fell over the two. They had been close when Leah was younger, but for the past year or two she had noticed how unhappy her mother was. After a while she said, "I don't suppose we'll be hearing from Father since no mail can get in?"

"No, I suppose not."

The coolness of her mother's tone troubled Leah. She was disturbed by her mother's life and somehow, although she'd never voiced it, had a faint resentment toward the way she'd been brought up. Her mother had never given her a full explanation for the breakup of her marriage, although Leah had asked many times. Now as they sat together on the porch, she tried again. "What does he say, Mother? He's never married again. That's strange for a man his age as fine looking as he is and with money."

"He wants his freedom. He doesn't need to be married anyway. He's...he's not made to be a good husband."

"Why do you say that? What really happened, Mother? You've never told me."

Claire turned to her daughter. The silver light of the half-moon washed across her daughter's face, and Claire was quiet for a moment, as if seeking for words. Finally, she said, "He wasn't the man I thought he was before I married him, Leah."

"Were you in love with him? Before you married him, I mean."

"Of course I was." The answer was quick and almost sharp. Then Claire sighed and leaned back in her chair. She rested her head and closed her eyes for so long that Leah thought she wouldn't speak again. When Claire did speak, pain threaded her voice, something that hadn't happened in Leah's remembrance. Her mother, whatever else, was a strong woman who didn't complain often. But now she seemed to be off guard and spoke softly of her engagement. "He was romantic and fine looking, as you know. He was full of fun—I've never forgotten that." Then her voice grew bitter. "He thought too much of fun—that was his problem. There comes a time when you have to be more serious. But I didn't find that out for a long time." She hesitated then said, "My father tried to warn me against marrying Matthew, but I was a fool and didn't listen to him."

"Grandfather didn't like him?"

"No. He said he had some bad seed in him."

"Bad seed? What does that mean?"

"He was a man who wasn't strong as your grandfather was strong. He was weak."

"Weak in what way, Mother?" Leah leaned forward, her eyes fixed intently on her mother's face. She'd never heard her speak like this, and now a lifetime of questions about her father surfaced. "What kind of weakness was it? You can tell me now. Surely I'm old enough."

Claire opened her eyes and sat up straighter. "Perhaps you are, Leah," she said. "You're a woman now, and before long you will be having to make a decision about a husband.... Marry a strong man." She put her hands together and gripped them firmly as if gathering strength. There was a rigid quality in her back as she continued, "I have to tell you, it was drink and women. Matthew couldn't handle either one."

Leah considered this and asked finally, "Wasn't he in love with you?"

"Yes, he was, in his way. I tried to curb his drinking.... He drank too much. Oh, he wasn't a drunk or anything like that! But that wasn't the worst. He was unfaithful to me, Leah." She turned in the gathering darkness. "I know it's painful for you to hear you have a father like that, but it's true enough."

Leah felt a sharp pain of disappointment, yet she couldn't let it go. "Did he have...many women?"

"No, not that I know of. Only one, but that's enough."

"Was he in love with her?"

"No, he said not and I believed him. He was just weak." She suddenly rose and turned her back, going to the edge of the porch and staring up to the skies. "Look up there, Leah."

Overhead the black velvet sky was spangled with stars that glittered like fiery points of white light. Claire stood studying them for a moment then pointed upward. "See those stars right there? That's the Pleiades. Come and look at them."

Leah moved to stand beside her mother. "Where?" she asked.

Claire lifted her arm and pointed. "You can't see them if you look directly at them. They're almost invisible. But turn your eyes just to one side and you'll see them."

She described the constellation, and finally Leah saw them. "How did you know that, Mother, about the Pleiades?"

"Matthew told me. He knew all about the stars, was fascinated by them. He kept a telescope, and in the summer at night we'd go out and look at them and he'd tell me their names." There was a softness in her tone, and she looked up at the skies again, unaware of her daughter's presence. The warm breeze ruffled her auburn hair, and she said in a voice filled with something Leah couldn't identify, "It's strange about the Pleiades. When you try to look right at them, you can't see them. You have to look to one side. Matthew always said that happiness is like that. If you try to have it, keep your eyes on it, you can't see it or have it. But if you look at something else, it'll come to you."

"I think that's wonderful," Leah whispered. She thought of her father and the few brief days she'd had with him. During their last visit she'd been grown and no longer a little girl. Although both had tried hard, the meeting had been stiff. Now she asked, "Did he often talk about things like that?"

"He was always talking about something. I have to say, he was one of the most interesting men I've ever known, one of the wittiest—and he had great good in him." Claire hesitated, and then, as though a bell had sounded, she stiffened her shoulders. "But he couldn't be what a man ought to be. I wish I didn't have to tell you these things." She turned abruptly and walked into the house, leaving Leah standing on the front porch.

For a while Leah stood there looking at the stars and thinking about her mother's obvious unhappiness. After a few minutes, she entered the house and walked to the parlor, where Amelia was reading. She went in for a moment and sat down. After talking about household details, finally Leah said,

"Tell me about my father, Aunt Amelia."

"Your father?" Amelia looked up, startled, to see a wistful longing in the eyes of her niece. "What shall I tell you?"

"Tell me how he was. Did you like him?"

Amelia hesitated then nodded. "Yes, I liked him. Everyone did."

"Tell me some things about him."

Amelia put down her book and talked for some time. Her features grew soft talking of days long gone, and she lost herself in nostalgia. Finally, she blinked and gave a high laugh. "I don't know when I've gone on like this. Why do you ask about your father, Leah?" But she thought she knew.

"Mother says he was...weak."

Amelia felt a chill as she looked into Leah's troubled eyes. She was a dependent. If it hadn't been for Claire's generosity, she would have had no place to go. For that reason, she had said little to Leah about those days when Claire was married. Now she said simply, "An outsider never knows about what goes on inside a home. Your father and mother did not get on."

"But he took mistresses?"

"I don't...like to say. He was disappointed in his marriage." She hesitated for even longer and then said something she'd never admitted, "Claire loved her father very much. My brother was a great man, but he had weaknesses, too."

Instantly Leah looked up. "What kind of weaknesses?"

But Amelia grew reticent. "We all have weaknesses, Leah. I more than most. Your mother will have to tell you what she wants you to know." She added one more thing: "Don't expect the man you fall in love with and marry to be like anybody else. He'll be who he is. You can change your dress and the way you wear your hair, Leah, but you can't change who people are. The man you marry will have flaws. So do you. The thing to remember is that we love people in spite of their flaws."

She got up as if embarrassed by what she'd said and left hurriedly, leaving Leah wondering what her words meant.

When Amelia Seaton got to her room, she did something she hadn't done for many years. She gave in to the tears. As she sat down on her bed, thoughts running through her head, the tears began to flow. She struggled for some time with them then lay down on the bed, facedown, and her shoulders shook as she thought of the wasted years of the past.

Rumors continued to fly about relief coming to aid the beleaguered city. Pemberton received word that Johnston and Loring were coming with thirty-one thousand men.

That was greatly needed good news, for on the thirteenth day of the siege, the world looked very dark in Vicksburg. It was on that day, June 3, 1863, that David was sitting outside the small chicken house with Corey, talking leisurely. "How are the chickens doing?"

"Fine, Mr. David," Corey said. He had put on weight and looked strong and hearty in the clothes Leah had found for him—a light green shirt, dark brown trousers, and a pair of brown boots. Corey's face was smooth as he asked suddenly, "What's gonna happen, Mr. David?"

"I reckon we're gonna get whipped!"

The simplicity of Rocklin's reply surprised Corey. "Well," he said slowly, "if it happens, I guess it happens."

David, who'd been watching children playing down the street, now turned to Corey and said, "You remember, if anything happens to me, go back to Gracefield."

CHARIOTS IN THE SMOKE

"Yes, sah, I remember. I don't 'spect nothin's gonna happen to you, though."

"It can happen anytime. Yesterday the fellow not twenty feet down the line from me was just sitting there. A shell went off, and one little fragment hit him right in the throat. He bled to death; there was nothing we could do. And it could happen to any of us."

"I guess that's right," Corey said in a deep, resonant voice. He was sitting down on a box and now took a knife out of his pocket and began to whittle slowly on a piece of cedar. He handled the knife easily and carefully, sending long shavings that curled up uniformly. "I always like to smell cedar," he said softly. "Best-smelling wood they is."

"You ever married, Corey?"

"No, sah, never was. And you never was either, Mr. David?"

"No. Not yet." David studied the smooth features of the black man and asked, "What will you do when you're free?"

"I don't think about it, sah."

"Well, it will happen, one way or the other. Either the Yankees will win and all the slaves will be free, or even if that doesn't happen, I've told you, after a year you'll be free."

"I guess I'm just 'fraid to hope," Corey said evenly. When he looked up, his eyes had a curious glint. "Why you doing this for me? I'm worth a lot of money. You don't have to set me free. You didn't have to buy me from that man."

"I guess I need something on my account. I got some things I'm not exactly proud of, so I try to even it up from time to time." Without changing expression or tone, he asked curiously, "Corey, what's it like to be a slave?"

Corey watched the cedar shavings that were curling up beneath the keen blade of his knife. "You remember yesterday, Mr. David, when you touched that hammer that'd been laying out in the sun and it burned your hand?"

"I remember."

"Well, I touched it before that." Corey glanced up and said briefly, "Burned my hand, too."

David instantly smiled. "So we're both alike, you and I?"

"Well, at least we hurt the same when we touch something hot."

"No, there's more to it than that," David said slowly. "The whole system is wrong. You know what I've thought. A slave can't help it if somebody owns him, but when I own a human being, that means I don't see any difference in that human and something else I own. So I'm the one who's made some kind of decision about what men are like."

Corey's interest was held. "I never thought about it like that." He sat there watching the young man who'd come into his life so abruptly and finally said huskily, "Thank you, Mr. David. I ain't much for saying thanks," he said, grinning ruefully. "Ain't had a whole lot to say thanks about, I guess. But now I want you to know that no matter what happens from here on, I ain't never gonna forget what you done for me."

Embarrassed by the slave's words, David stood up. "Let's see if those chickens have done their duty. I could use a good fried egg."

"Wake up! They're coming!"

David had been leaning against the wall of the trench, dozing off. The hours had gone slowly and he'd missed a great deal of sleep. Now, however, as yells ran up and down the trench, he grabbed his musket with both hands and called out, "What is it? What's wrong?"

Sergeant Ike Ballard said, "Look out! They're coming! They're gonna take this trench!"

David looked out, checked his musket, and heard the screams of the enemy as they were running. Ballard was screaming and Finch was calling out from somewhere down the line. *It may be a full-scale attack,* David realized, knowing that the Federals' plan was to slowly squeeze in on the city. His palms grew wet and his hands began to shake. "Stop it!" he said viciously under his breath and slowly raised his head. He received a shock, for it *was* a full-scale attack. Instantly he threw his rifle over, drew a bead, and fired. His man went down and he straightened up and began reloading. He'd heard the Yankees had a breech-loading rifle, that they could just shove a cartridge in and fire, but that wasn't what he had. His hands trembled as he reached into his pocket and pulled a cartridge out. He bit it off and poured the powder down the muzzle, then went through the procedure of ramming home the wads and the musket ball. All the time the screams of the charging Yankees rent the air. Up and down the line, muskets exploded and Ballard screamed out, "They're coming with the bayonets! Fire! Shoot 'em down!"

David straightened up and began to chill as the sun gleamed on the naked steel that flowed toward him in great waves. He straightened his arm out but trembled so violently that he couldn't hold the rifle still. He pulled the trigger and knew he'd fired high—and then there was no time. A Federal soldier suddenly appeared to his left. Harold Ficker was reloading his musket and didn't see him. David seemed to be frozen as the Yankee, a tall, brown-faced man whose teeth gleamed in a wild grin, shoved the steel forward, catching Ficker in the side. The young man screamed, dropped his musket, and reached around.

The Yankee pulled out the bayonet, which was bloodied almost to the muzzle, and drew it back again. Ficker held his hands up as though he could stop the flashing steel. On the other side of Ficker, Lon Gere appeared. His musket wasn't loaded either, but he swung the weapon viciously through the air, striking the Yankee in the face. The force of the blow drove the soldier backward, and Gere reversed the weapon, smashing the man's face over and over with the butt.

All up and down the line individual battles took place. But David could do nothing because his hands wouldn't hold the musket steady enough. Only the fact that on his particular section of the line no Federal came at him with a bayonet saved him. He heard echoing screams of rage and pain, the clash of steel, the explosion of the muskets, and then someone said, "They're giving up! Let 'em have it!"

As David watched the Yankees retreat down the hill, he stood still, unable to move. Soon Bones Detwiler came to stand beside him, his face pale. "They nearly got us that time, didn't they, Dave? I wasn't ready for it." Detwiler looked up and saw that David's face was dripping with sweat. "Are you hit?" he demanded. "Did they get you, Dave?"

David Rocklin shook his head. "No, they didn't get me." His voice was thin and reedy, and he couldn't control the shaking of his hands, so he moved away from Detwiler and fell on his knees beside Ficker. Lon Gere, who was trying to stop the flow from his side, looked up. "We got to get him to the hospital, Dave. Can we get a stretcher?"

"No, I'll take him." David reached down, picked up Ficker, and said, "Come on, Harold."

He bore the weight of the heavy young man easily, and when he got back to where the doctors were already working on the wounded, he laid him down carefully, saying, "You'll be all right, Harold."

"I don't want to go to the hospital," Ficker cried out, his big brown eyes wide with fear and pain. "Don't leave me, Dave!"

"I won't leave you, Harold." David sat there, regaining control over his body. His hands ceased to tremble and his face slowly relaxed. Inside, however, his nerves were still screaming. He knew he'd never forget the sight of those bayonets coming up the hill!

Chapter 5

The Last Straw

Food had become the big question in the besieged city. Cowpeas, small beans, were usually cultivated as feed for animals. However, as regular food supplies dwindled, great ingenuity was expended to use the large supply of cowpeas for table use.

Making peas into bread followed the same process used for corn. The peas were ground into a large amount of meal and sent to the cooks, who mixed it with cold water and baked it. But the nature of cowpeas was such that the longer they were cooked, the harder they became on the outside and the softer on the inside.

When the Federals found out the populace was eating peabread, David had to listen as the Bluebellies hollered for several nights, making fun of them. "Come on over and have a cup of coffee and a biscuit with us," one of them with a shrill tenor voice called loudly.

David hadn't lost his appetite, but he was troubled with nightmares about bayonets. In one of them he was walking on a carpet of green grass with a breeze blowing gently when suddenly, out of the sky, thousands of bayonets appeared, all glistening in the sun—and all headed straight for him! The dream occurred many times and always woke him up as the bayonets were just about to pierce his body. Ike Ballard, tired of David's awakening and thrashing around and mumbling, said in disgust, "If a little thing like being besieged bothers you, Rocklin, you need to become a preacher or something else where there ain't no problems!"

On June 24, David marked the calendar he'd saved from a magazine and noted it was the thirty-fourth day of the siege. He had put in a hard day's work on the reinforcements of the redans and decided to go to the Cleburne house. He was worried about them, for the shells were falling faster and thicker than ever. There seemed to be no limit to the ammunition the gunboats spat out, and the town itself was battered almost beyond repair. As he made his way through the shattered streets, he noticed the magnificence of the courthouse, which caught the sun and glistened pristinely out of the rubble. *I wonder if the Yankees are deliberately leaving it standing so they can use it as a headquarters when they capture the city,* he thought, then realized he'd already given up on Vicksburg enduring the siege successfully. Somehow he knew—and suspected others did—that it was only a matter of time before the city fell.

He made his way first to the hospital, where Harold Ficker was glad to see him. "Hello, David," he said in a faint voice.

Since his wounding, Ficker's face had grown slender and he had none of the health and strength he'd had when David first met him. The brigade hospital was filled, and even now aides carried out the still form of a man who'd died in the night. Turning his eyes away from the sight, David sat down and spoke cheerfully. "You're looking well, Harold," he said. "I brought you a little something special from the mess." He had salvaged a piece of so-called cake and unwrapped the paper from it, holding it up. "Not like your mother used to make," he said, grinning, "but better than cowpea bread."

Ficker tried to smile and reached out a thin hand. As he held the bread, not trying to eat it, he whispered, "They say I've got an infection, David."

"Well, they'll soon take care of that."

Ficker's eyes were fixed on him piteously, almost as if he were begging David for something. "That fellow they just took out. His name was Colin Symington. He's from Alabama. He had an infection, too—and he died last night."

David bit his lip. He knew the dangers of infection were terrible, especially in the hospital. The surgeons moved from man to man, never washing their hands, and it seemed that once infection did set in, it swept through the whole ward. He saw the fear rising in the boy's face and said, "You'll ride it out, Harold."

"I ain't—I ain't really ready to die." Ficker's face was pale, and his mouth moved spasmodically as he spoke. "Most of my friends got saved in a revival we had back home just before I joined up. But I didn't." He held the cake and looked at it, but his eyes weren't really focused on it. He seemed to be looking back in his past, and finally he whispered, "I guess I'll go to hell if I die."

"Why, you can't do that, Harold! I tell you what, I'll have the chaplain come and talk to you."

"Couldn't you do it, Dave?"

David Rocklin swallowed hard. "I don't claim to be much of a Christian. But my people are and I've heard good preaching all my life. I've thought a lot about it myself. The preachers all say you have to repent and turn to Jesus."

"How do you do that?"

Fervently David wished he'd paid more attention. He was a Christian himself but had been timid about speaking to others. Now, however, he breathed a quick prayer and began to explain how to become a Christian. He was surprised to find the sermons he'd heard and the talk around his table at home before the war suddenly bear fruit. The wounded boy looked at him with hungry eyes, and finally David said, "What I think we ought to do is just pray right now that you'll be right with God. I'll pray for you and you call on the Lord to save you."

It was an awkward thing for David Rocklin, but after he'd said a prayer, he looked up and saw tears running down Ficker's face. "Thank you, Dave," he said. "I did it. I called on the Lord. I feel like something happened to me."

David sat for nearly half an hour beside the wounded young man, encouraging him, and finally Ficker dropped off to sleep. He left, making his way out of the hospital.

The scene had disturbed him, and he rebuked himself sternly for not being of more help. He consoled himself by saying, "I'll go back later and sit with him. I'll take the chaplain with me, just to make sure."

When he turned off on Cherry Street, where the Cleburne house was, he was strangely drawn to the place. His feelings for Leah hadn't changed, but the cowardice that had sprung up in him had blotted out all thoughts, except what he might be able to do about it. When he reached the house, he found Corey out back chopping firewood and spoke with him for a few minutes. "Everything all right, Corey?"

"Yes, sah. You all right, Mr. David? You ain't been shot or nothing?"

"Not yet!" He grinned faintly and said, "I'll be glad when this is over."

"So will I, Mr. David. A man don't know when he'll live or die, and I sure hate to see this house get hit like that 'un down the street there. Be bad to see one of them ladies get hurt."

This had bothered David, too, and he nodded. He left, saying, "I'll talk to you before I leave, Corey." When he knocked on the door, Amelia was in the kitchen shelling cowpeas. He sat down beside her and joined in, teasing her about what a bad cook she was.

Amelia replied, "I never noticed you turning down any of my cooking!" She sniffed and gave him a straight look. "I suppose all of you fellows are hungry out there."

"Food's pretty scarce. We're down to mule-meat steaks now."

"I swan! I never thought I'd see the day! Soldiers of the Confederacy, eating mule meat."

"It's better than some I've seen. Some of the fellows had what they called a squirrel stew the other night. I tasted it and found out it was made of rats!"

"Oh my stars!" Amelia said, shocked. "I can't think what would make me eat a rat!"

"Where's Leah and Mrs. Cleburne?"

"They're upstairs, trying to go through all the old clothes. Some of the neighbors lost everything they had. A shell tore up their house completely."

Suddenly David had a strange feeling. Everything happened instantaneously: His ears rang and he wondered if he was getting malaria. The world seemed to rock and the roof to his left caved in. Then he heard a tremendous explosion.

David leaped forward and grabbed Amelia, yelling, "Get out of the house! It's going to fall in!" He quickly shoved her toward the door then turned and ran down the hall, calling, "Leah! Mrs. Cleburne!"

Another shell struck in the house somewhere. This one was even more disastrous than the first. He ran to the stairs and saw Leah and her mother almost falling down. "Come on! We've got to get out of here!" The two women reached the landing, and all three of them ran out the front door. Evidently a barrage from the gunboats had been aimed at this spot, for even as they dashed away from the house, two more shells struck it and blew the walls out. The roof fell in with a tremendous crash.

"Where's Amelia?" Leah cried.

"She went out the back door. I'll go see about her. Go take cover in that ditch!" David ran around the house and found Corey pulling Amelia along in his strong hands.

"Get her out of here! They're dropping a barrage on us!" he yelled.

Corey picked up the woman and ran. David ran alongside, and as the three dropped in the ditch, the barrage increased in intensity. It went on for five minutes, their ears ringing with the force of the explosions.

Then a quiet fell and Leah said, "Look! That house! It's gone, too! We've got to see if they're all right!"

For two hours after the barrage, pandemonium reigned. A little girl had been killed three houses down. Her body was brought out by the weeping mother, and Claire went over at once to comfort her.

David stood looking at the devastation of the house and said to Leah, "You'll have to go to one of the caves, Leah. Let's go through the wreckage and see what we can salvage. I'll go round up a wagon." He looked down and saw she was crying silently. Without thinking, he put his arm around her and squeezed her. "It's all right. Everybody's alive and that's what matters."

"All my things—gone," Leah whispered. Then she looked

up at him and nodded. "You're right, though. *Things* can be replaced. I'll start looking while you get the wagon."

David and Corey stopped working and stood to examine the cave they'd carved out with some help from a few others. It had to be quick, but fortunately Leah and Claire had found enough money in the wreckage to hire other laborers. Now David looked at it with some pride. He winked at Corey and said, "I guess as cave diggers go, we're just about at the top of the list."

Spared from frontline duty, David had thrown himself into the job with all of his strength. They had made the cave in the shape of a T, with a straight entrance being the bottom part and the top part spreading into two compartments. The bottom leg was already being used for cooking and also served to store the furniture they'd been able to salvage. They'd even brought carpet for the two bedrooms and found enough tables and lamps to furnish them. The roof was arched and braced, the supports taking up some of the room.

David now walked in with Leah, and Aunt Amelia came out from one of the side units that served as a bedroom for her and Leah. "Welcome to our new home," Amelia said, trying to smile. A shell went off somewhere down the line and she looked up at the roof. "If they don't score a direct hit," she said, "I think it ought to be all right."

Claire had come out from the other room and added, "One of the caves took a hit." A worried look came into her eyes. "It collapsed and one man died before they could get him out."

Leah walked over and hugged her mother. "We'll be all right, Mother," she said. Then she turned to David. "You and Corey have done miracles. Now then, let's see if we can have our first supper in our new home!"

An hour later they were sitting down to a table just off the opening to the cave. Aside from the cowpeas, Corey had managed to salvage the chickens. One of them had been butchered, and Amelia had fried the chicken over an open fire. There were also some dandelion greens—another of Corey's contributions. When they sat down to eat, Corey waited on them, saying, "I guess I'm a house slave now. Don't know how good I'll be at that."

David took a plate, put three pieces of chicken on it, along with some of the dandelion greens, and offered it to Corey. "Here—you sure earned your keep this time!"

Corey's smile was filled with admiration for David. "You and me could become gold miners," he said. "You sure do know how to dig."

David looked down at the blisters on his hands. "I'd hate to do it for a living."

The meal was pleasant enough. Outside, the air was hot, but inside the cave it was much cooler. This was June 27, the thirty-seventh day of the siege, and David mentally rebelled against going back to the trenches. However, after he finished, he said, "Well, this is all the time the sergeant would give me. I'll have to go back now."

"I'll walk part of the way with you, David," Leah said. She got up and the two left the cave. All along the hills caves had been cut out by homeless citizens, and they had become a community. Leah commented, "You know, we're closer to the people here than we ever were in a house with walls and a roof. We have to trust each other to get along, and we have to help each other."

He looked down at her slightly sunburned face and her red hair tied back in a single braid and smiled. "I guess that's not a bad way to live. Most people never do get to know each other."

They walked along, speaking from time to time. "This is far enough," he said finally, then added abruptly, "I hate to go back. Leah, I hesitate to tell you this, but I'm not much of a soldier."

Leah stared at him. "I expect you're as good as the others," she said quietly.

"No, I'm not." Then he told her what he'd never told anyone. "I think I can stand musket fire and even cannon fire—"

"What is it, David?"

"It's those bayonets. . . ." An involuntary shudder made his body twitch, and his lips thinned. "I can't stand the thought of them!"

Leah watched him closely. "Maybe it'll be over soon," she said. "They can't stay here forever."

"I think you know better than that, Leah." David tried to pull himself together. "It's just a matter of time. We can't hold out here. Surely even Pemberton knows that by now."

Still Leah tried to be positive, as were many others. "It'll be all right," she said. "We'll make it."

David reached out, took her hand, and studied it. "You're getting blisters," he said, looking into her eyes. "I said once that I love you and that I'd make you learn to love me, too. But I haven't had much time for that."

She smiled. "No, you haven't. How do you go about making women love you? I've been waiting for you to turn on the charm."

He answered lightly enough, "I'm afraid to let all my charm out at once. Why, it's been known to stun a young woman at fifty feet."

"Really? I wasn't aware I was with such a man. Why don't you try just a little—not full force, of course," she teased him. Although her dress was faded and needed washing, her body was strong and youthful as she looked up at him. She was intensely attractive and, to some extent, unaware of the impact she had on him.

David held her hand then grew more serious. "I've got to go. Somehow we'll talk about this later. May I kiss you good-bye?"

"Why, you're only going a mile away."

"I know, but it would be nice."

She lifted her head, and taking it for permission, he leaned down and kissed her lightly on the lips. Her lips were warm, full, and firm, yet still soft and yielding, speaking of her femininity. He turned without another word and walked away, afraid to trust his voice.

*

Three days of incessant barrages had frayed the nerves of all the men. Explosive shells went off continually, and now David jumped each time one did. He checked his calendar and saw it was June 30. "Forty days trapped in this place," he muttered, stretched almost full-length against the walls of the trench. It had been quiet for a while now, but he heard the popping of a musket every now and then, reminding him to keep his head down. The Yankees evidently had brought in more sharpshooters, for now all a man had to do was stick his hat up on a stick above the level of the trench and instantly it was shot off. David had tried this himself and pulled off his campaign hat to see a hole right through the brim. He put the hat back on his head and looked up at the sun, which was almost overhead. He lay there for a long time thinking mostly of Leah, who'd come to occupy a large part of his thoughts. He'd managed to block out the thoughts of the bayonets and had had a good night, without nightmares.

But late that afternoon he was jerked out of his ease when another attack was made. Again the sergeant was yelling, the officers were crawling around, keeping down below the parapet, and once again it happened. David was caught in the full fury of a barrage with mortar shells exploding around him. Then he heard the dreaded cry, "They're coming! Get ready!"

As he'd done before so many times, he got off one shot and was loading frantically when Sergeant Ballard hollered, "They're coming with bayonets! Attach bayonets, men!"

David had hated the bayonet he'd been issued. He couldn't imagine himself using it, plunging it into the body of another human being. Now as he fumbled for it, he was aware again that the lines were being broken. It became a melee as men fell and shouted and cursed.

David couldn't attach the bayonet on his rifle because his hands were trembling. Then he heard the screams of men who were dying from bayonets just like his, and something seemed to fall before his eyes.

He had no memory of it later, but somehow he found himself behind the trench, running. He heard a curse and a shout, "Rocklin, come back...."

But he didn't cease running. He ran until his lungs were scorched and burning. He ran until he got away from the sound of those cries. He couldn't face the thought of cold steel. And even as he ran blindly, mindlessly, something deep down inside told him he had turned a corner from which he would never quite recover.

*

July 1 and 2 were days of helplessness for the Confederate officers. Pemberton spent sleepless nights trying to think of a way to achieve some sort of good terms from Grant. He knew that Grant, however, would take the city, no matter what he said. He met his staff, and there was a tremor in his voice as he said, "We're beaten, gentlemen. I'd rather die a thousand deaths, but we must ask General Grant for his terms." Several officers disagreed violently, but Pemberton knew the end had come. "I will write the message to General Grant," he said.

❧

David was in no condition to think about surrender terms. Something terrible had happened to him. When he'd finally stopped running, finding himself on the far side of Vicksburg from the trenches where his flight had begun, he'd stayed out all night staring emptily at the skies.

He'd gone back the next day and had been cursed soundly by Finch, who called him worse names than ever before. Lon Gere had met him with a blank stare, and David saw the contempt in the gambler's eyes. Bones Detwiler had been killed in the attack, so he was not there to know. David had been unable to cope with his world, and now, as General Pemberton wrote his letter to his opponent, all he could do was endure. Inside there was an emptiness, a hollowness, and he knew that no matter what happened to Vicksburg, he, David Rocklin, was a man with nothing inside.

CHAPTER 6

END OF A SIEGE

Captain Raymond Finch stood inside the cave facing the three women. He'd come during a lull in the firing and had made his announcement in a harsh, unforgiving voice. "There's no excuse for a man like Rocklin," he said, his lips drawing tightly together and almost spitting out the words. "He ran away from the enemy in action. I tried to get him shot, but Captain Devers wouldn't listen to it."

Leah's face was pale. "Couldn't there have been some mistake, Raymond?"

"Mistake! I saw him run myself," Finch said. It gave him some gratification to see that his announcement disturbed the three women greatly. "I tried to tell you about that fellow," he said in a more moderate tone, shrugging his trim shoulders.

"Was he the only one who ran away?" Amelia asked quietly.

"Why, I suppose not," Finch said reluctantly, tugging at his mustache. "There'll always be one or two in any action who can't take it."

"Did you ask to have them shot, too?" Again Amelia's voice was gentle, but there was a harsh light in her eyes.

Finch stared at the oldest of the three women and shook his head impatiently. "You just don't understand how these things are, Mrs. Seaton." He turned quickly back to Leah, for it was her face he studied most carefully. He'd once entertained ideas of marrying Leah himself, at least of courting her, but she'd shown little interest in him as a serious suitor. His feelings ruffled, he'd allowed the resulting anger to fall on David Rocklin.

"Well," Claire said abruptly, "I'm sorry to hear of it. I thought he had promise, but evidently I was wrong."

"You were wrong, but you haven't known the fellow long. It's understandable." Finch again examined Leah's face, adding, "Some people look good on the outside, but when you put them under pressure, they crack."

"That's right." Claire nodded, and then she, too, turned to study Leah. "It's well that we found out about him before—" She had intended to say, "Before the courtship got too far along," but changed the subject. "What will happen now to us all?"

"General Pemberton's written Grant asking for terms." The words were bitter on his thin lips, and he shook his head angrily. "I think it's a mistake. We can hold out here."

"I don't see how," Leah said wearily. "Everybody's starving. More lives would be lost."

Her tone was dull as she moved away from the small group walking out of the front of the cave. She stayed away long enough to be sure Finch wouldn't be there when she returned, then made her way back. As she entered the cave, she was greeted at once by her mother, who said, "We'll have to decide something, Leah."

"What do you mean, Mother?"

"Why, I mean we can't stay in this cave for the rest of our lives."

"No, of course not. Will we rebuild the house?"

"I don't have the money," Claire said slowly. "And even if we did, I wouldn't want to live here under the rule of the Yankees. No, we'll have to leave."

"But where will we go?"

Claire Cleburne was a woman who was seldom at a loss for words, who liked to be in control. But some of that slipped from her at this moment. Her cheeks grew tense, and she looked down at her hands blankly. She didn't answer the question for a long time then finally looked up, bitterness scoring her eyes. "I'll have to ask your father to help us."

"I wish you didn't have to do that, Mother."

"*You* wish it! You don't know how much *I* wish it!" Claire's voice was almost a gasp, and her eyes were dull. "I've never asked him for anything—never!"

"But he's sent money all these years, hasn't he?"

"Yes, but I never asked him."

Leah sat down beside her mother. "Let's don't do it. We can think of something."

"Think of what?" Claire stared at her daughter with frustration. "What could we do? There's nothing open. What can a woman do to make a living for herself, especially with this war on?"

"Surely we can find *something*."

But even as Leah spoke, she saw the futility of it all. There was nothing open for a woman, except perhaps teaching school, but in the throes of a losing war, the South didn't put a premium on that. Children would have to be educated the best way they could. She reached over and patted her mother's hand. "We'll think of something," she said and rose to go outside again.

CHARIOTS IN THE SMOKE

David was kept under arrest for only a day, and then Captain Devers told Finch brusquely, "You might as well turn him loose. He'll go into a prison camp with the rest of us."

"I'd like to see him shot!" Captain Finch snapped.

"Well, his chances of getting out of a prison camp aren't too good. You know what they are, Finch," Devers said with impatience. "Now do as I tell you. We don't have time for things such as this."

Finch walked over to the house being used as a temporary stockade. Stepping inside the door, past the corporal who was serving as guard, he looked over and said, "All right, Rocklin. Captain Devers has ordered me to release you. Get back to your unit."

David had been sitting on a cane-bottomed chair, staring out the window. There was no relief in his face as he stared at Finch. He said mildly, "Yes, sir," and turned and left. When he got back to the unit, he found that all spirit had gone out of the group. Even Sergeant Ike Ballard stared at him listlessly and said nothing.

Lon Gere, who was sitting on a box playing solitaire, looked up and said briefly, "You got here in time to surrender, I guess. You don't have to worry about running anymore, Rocklin."

David stared at him, then shrugged and went over to sit down and wait. "Did you hear about Ficker?" Ballard asked.

"No." David knew the truth at once. "Did he die?"

"Yep! Poor fellow. He said to tell you thank you for what you did for him. What was that, Rocklin?"

David said, "Nothing, I guess. I'm sorry—he was a good man."

A lackadaisical air settled over the trenches. The sharpshooters were not firing anymore, for both sides knew this part of the Civil War was over.

Later David rose and made his way to the cave. He called out at the entrance, "It's me, David."

"Come in."

He stepped inside to find the three women looking at him in a most peculiar way. Instantly he knew what had happened. "I suppose," he said quietly, "you heard about me."

"Mr. Rocklin, I think it might be best if you'd not come back here anymore." Claire's voice was firm and her back stiff. "You'll be going anyway with the other soldiers to a prison camp."

"That's true, Mrs. Cleburne." David turned and said, "Leah, I want to have a word with you before I leave. Would you mind coming outside?"

"Very well."

Leah walked out of the cave, and David moved to follow but was stopped by Amelia, who put her hand out. "I'll pray for your safety, David," she said quietly, her hand firm in his. As he looked at her, he didn't see the same hardness he'd seen in Claire Cleburne's eyes.

"Thank you, Aunt Amelia," he said. "That means a lot to me. You take care of yourself now."

"Yes, I will."

Outside, David said to Leah, "Let's walk a little." She fell in wordlessly beside him, and finally he stopped and faced her. "I tried to tell you about myself the last time we talked."

"I remember." Her voice was even and her eyes cool.

"I guess I know how you feel," he said softly. "I feel the same way about myself. I can't explain it, Leah. I'm just what I am."

Leah looked at him calmly. She'd known he would come, and now she said, "I'm sorry it happened and I wish you well. I know it's hard. It'll be hard for you in the camp, you and all the others."

He knew this was a farewell, so he didn't answer for a moment. Finally, he said, "Good-bye. Just remember, I love you. I wish things were different." Then abruptly he walked away.

Leah sadly watched him go. Her conscience seemed to smite her, but her mother had talked to her about the matter. She'd mentioned David's weakness and had said, "If a man is weak in one way, he'll be weak in another. I'm sorry for him, but you don't need him in your life." Leah walked back to the cave. When she entered, she said nothing about their parting. Amelia stared at her for a moment then moved away.

"I've decided we'll have to go to New York," Claire told her. "Your father has a big home there. He's often made it available, mostly to you. We'll go there—at least until we can find something better."

"All right, Mother."

"Are you all right?" Claire queried.

"Of course." Leah tried to blot out the picture of David's face when she had turned from him. She looked up at her mother and said only, "It'll be hard for you, won't it, Mother?"

"Yes, it will be, but we have to do something. Matthew always said he wanted to do something for you. Now we'll see if he's stronger than he used to be."

It was after ten now, and everything was quiet. But as a figure appeared out of the darkness, at once Corey was on guard. He had no weapon, but he doubled up his fists. He'd made himself a shack out of old boards close to the cave where the women stayed, and now he stepped quietly out of the shadows and said, "Who are you? What do you want?"

"Corey?"

"Mr. David!"

"Come on, Corey."

Corey made his way through the darkness. There was no moon at all. "What you doin', Mr. David?"

"We're getting out of here. I'm not going to spend the rest of this war in a prison camp."

"How you gonna get through?"

"Can you swim?"

"Why, yes, sah!"

"We're swimming out of here. We're going down to the river and we're going to steal a boat, paddle out to the middle, and float past the Yankee guards. If they see us," he said quietly, "they'll shoot us. You may not want to go, and you don't have to. They won't keep you here. You're what they call contraband now."

Corey stood there thinking hard. "No, sah," he said. "I be goin' with you."

"You heard about what I did?"

"Yes, sah, I heard."

"You still want to go with a coward like me?"

Corey wanted to reach out and comfort David somehow, but he knew that wouldn't be the right thing to do. "I'm goin' with you, Mr. David. Come on. It's plenty dark. We'll get out in the middle of that river and they won't never see us."

A bit of cheer touched David—the first he'd felt since he'd run away. Although he couldn't see the slave's face clearly, here at least was one who didn't scorn him.

"Thanks, Corey," he said briefly. Then the two men faded into the murky darkness, headed toward the mighty Mississippi.

PART TWO
New York

CHAPTER 7

AN UNCOMFORTABLE SITUATION

Leah was well aware her mother was nervous as the carriage made its way through the crowded streets of New York City. A searing sun overhead poured down harsh rays, and for some reason Leah remembered today was her cousin Tom's birthday, August 10, and wondered what he was doing with himself. Glancing across the carriage, she noted that tension had caused her mother to push nervously at her hairdo, which needed no adjustment.

"You'd never know a war was on, would you?" Amelia murmured, gazing at the crowds filling the streets.

Leah noted there was a richness and a prosperity—a sense of fullness somehow—that formed a stark contrast to the scenes they'd been accustomed to in the South, especially in Vicksburg. As Amelia studied the women's dresses, she smiled. "I don't think they've been forced to do without anything, have they?"

Claire responded shortly, "No, they haven't!" She shifted restlessly in her seat and with an unusual tense note in her voice complained, "How long is it going to take us to get there, I wonder? It'll cost a fortune to pay for this carriage!"

They'd been traveling for a long time. The journey had been

difficult since the Southern railway systems had been decimated by the war. They'd all noticed the differences as soon as they passed into the Northern areas. Even the roadbeds were better and the regular *clickety-clack* of the wheels passing over the seams sounded more solid and substantial.

All three women had been sobered by the journey, Claire most of all. *I hate having to do this—I'd rather go without, myself, but I've got to do something for Leah and Amelia,* she thought. For years she'd deliberately avoided any contact with Matthew except that which was absolutely necessary. Now she was descending upon him, asking for help. Of course, he'd helped financially through their years of separation; she had no complaint about that. But this was different.

Leah cried suddenly, "Look! Look there, Mother! Look, Aunt Amelia!" She pointed to a man and a woman who were making their way along the streets on bicycles. "That looks like such fun," Leah said, delighted. "I want to try it!"

"There are other ways of making a fool of yourself, Leah, than getting on one of those contraptions," Claire snapped.

Leah was surprised, for ordinarily her mother was a good-tempered woman. But she realized it was the situation that had made her mother tense, so Leah said only, "Well, I suppose Father doesn't keep bicycles." Leah noticed that Claire's eyes grew smaller at the mention of her father, and once again she wondered, *It disturbs her so much to come here. . . . Maybe we made a mistake. We should have gone somewhere else. But we don't have to stay long if it's unbearable.*

Finally, the carriage shuddered to a halt then swayed as the driver, a thick-bodied Irishman with a shock of black hair, stepped to the ground. The door opened and he stuck his head in, saying with a gap-toothed grin, "Here it is, 900 West

Twenty-seventh Street. Can I take your baggage in, ladies?"

Claire spoke nervously. "No, let me go up and be certain someone's home." As she stepped down and looked around, she saw the street was filled with solid-looking houses, most of them three-story brownstone. Smoke curled lazily from some of the chimneys, the result of cooking fires and heating water, and nervous as she was, Claire was impressed at the dignity of the wide street. Then she moved forward and marched up the short flight of stone stairs that led to the door, giving the heavy brass knocker three sharp raps. As she stood there waiting, an impulse to turn and flee swept her. But knowing that would be ridiculous, she took a deep breath, got control of herself, and waited.

The door opened almost at once, and a tall man with black kinky hair and a light brown complexion stood before her. "Why, Miss Claire!" he exclaimed, smiling broadly. "It's you! Indeed it is!"

"Hello, Simon." The sight of the tall man brought back sharp memories, but Claire put them aside. "Is Mr. Cleburne here?"

"No, Miss Claire, he ain't, but he'll be back in 'bout two hours. Let me come out and take your bags in." He looked over his shoulder and called, "Lucy—Lucy! Miss Claire's here!"

At his call, a short plump woman with a rich chocolate complexion appeared from down the hall. She came forward quickly, moving agilely in spite of her heaviness, then stopped and nodded briefly. "Hello, Miss Claire." Claire didn't miss the lack of welcome in her tone. "Is Miss Leah with you?"

"Yes, and my aunt Amelia. I'll go tell them to come in."

Claire returned to the carriage and paid the driver. Simon had followed her out and picked up two bags. While he waited for the ladies to go in, he smiled. "Why, this must be Miss Leah!

But you're a grown-up lady now! Last time I saw you, why, you was just a little thing."

Leah smiled back. "I remember you, Simon, and Lucy, too."

"You ain't forgot her good cooking, I bet. Everybody remembers that."

Claire said, "Come along," and, picking up one of the lighter suitcases, made her way back up the steps.

When they were all inside, Simon said, "Lucy, this is Miss Leah. Ain't she growed up to be a fine young lady!"

Lucy's smile was bright. "I remember the time you ate five pancakes and got sick."

Leah laughed. "So do I! They were so good! Will you make me some more, Lucy?"

"Surely I will." Lucy turned to Amelia, saying, "Hello, Miss Amelia. It's good to see you again."

Amelia smiled and said, "Hello, Lucy. You haven't changed a bit. Maybe a few more pounds."

"And looks like you done lost a few," Lucy answered, nodding vigorously. "But I'll put them back on you. You come along now and I'll show you to your rooms. Simon, you hurry up with them bags!"

Simon grinned as he winked at Leah. "You see, she ain't stopped bossing me. Mr. Matthew done give us a piece of paper years ago, said we was free, but Lucy done got another one called a marriage license—and she thinks that's just another way of saying I'm hers to boss around."

"Hush up your mouth!" Lucy said sharply. "Go get them bags." Then she turned and continued, "We'll go upstairs now and you can get all refreshed. Maybe take a nap." She moved down the spacious foyer into a hall only somewhat narrower. At the end, a wide flight of stairs led upward to a landing. When they reached the second floor, she opened the door of the first room on her right. "This here's the dressing room." She stepped aside and the women looked in. At one end, a copper bathtub was set under a large window that let light fall over the brightly colored carpet. The walls were adorned with white wainscoting three feet high, and blue and yellow wallpaper reached to the top of the high ceiling. "Mr. Matthew, he done had one of these baths put in here," Lucy said, shaking her head dourly. "I don't hold with new stuff, but you know how he is—just *had* to have it."

"Oh, it looks heavenly," Leah said. "I'm first!" She'd never had a bath in a tub such as this, and the grimy days of travel suddenly seemed worse.

They moved down the hall to the first door, and Lucy said, "This is your room, Miss Claire." To the left, another door. "This is yours, Miss Leah—and that's yours, Miss Amelia," Lucy said, pointing. There was one more door, but Lucy didn't open that.

Claire felt not only nervous, but ridiculous. She felt sure the door to that fourth bedroom was Matthew's, and it gave her a queer feeling to know he'd be sleeping so close to her. However, she said nothing. When Lucy left, saying she'd fix tea and refreshments for them if they wanted to come down, Claire responded, "We'll be down directly."

After Lucy had descended the stairs, Amelia said with admiration in her voice, "This is a fine house, isn't it? Look at the woodwork, those moldings—such fine work!"

"Yes," Claire agreed reluctantly, "it is nice." Then she added briskly, "Let's get unpacked, and then perhaps we can go down and have something to eat."

"I'm going to take a bath," Leah announced. "I think the dirt's even under my skin." As the other two began unpacking, she grabbed a change of clothes out of her suitcase and proceeded to the bathroom. Closing the door, she removed her travel-stained clothes then turned the faucet on the bathtub. As the water rushed out, she watched it with fascination. "I wonder why someone didn't think of this a thousand years ago?" she wondered out loud. "Instead of having to carry buckets of water, just turn a handle." She waited until the tub was filled, stepped inside, then sat down with a sigh of relief. There was sweet-smelling soap in a dish beside the tub, and washcloths. For a long time she splashed and sputtered and thought about washing her hair but decided that would be too big a project. "Someday they'll figure out a way to dry hair," she said, for her tresses were so thick it took hours in the sun to achieve that.

Finally, with some reluctance, she stepped out of the tub onto a woven cotton carpet, dried off on one of the plush towels, then put on fresh underwear and a green dress with tiny white flowers on the bodice and white ribbons interwoven at the cuffs and around the neck. It was somewhat wrinkled but at least clean. Slipping on her shoes, she looked at the dirty clothes and shrugged. *I'll see about getting them washed later.*

Going downstairs quickly, she found the others in the dining room, drinking tea from fine porcelain cups and eating cookies from a platter.

"Don't eat too much!" Lucy warned as Leah sat down. "We're fixing up a big supper tonight. I don't want you to spoil your appetite."

"I don't think I could do that if I ate this whole plate of cookies," Leah said, biting into one. "They're so good, Lucy! You could always make good cookies."

The black woman sniffed, but there was pleasure in her brown eyes. "I got to tend to the cookin'."

When she left the room, Leah said at once, "You've *got* to

have a bath—both of you. It's just heavenly!"

Amelia took another cookie. "I'm so hungry! That roast beef Lucy's cooking is about to drive me crazy. Maybe she'll let me help her, although she's a better cook than I could ever be."

As the three sat there, Claire was thinking of Matthew. *How will he be after all these years?* Since her childhood, Claire had been strongly determined and had had a clearly defined set of goals. Her strong code of right and wrong, with few gray areas, had ruled her life. But now she thought how empty and fragmented her life had been since she'd left Matthew, and she wondered how it would be when she faced him again.

"I'm sorry I wasn't here when you arrived."

Matthew Cleburne had come into the parlor where the three women were waiting, all of them somewhat nervously. Cleburne stepped into the room, and Leah thought instantly, *He just gets better looking all the time!* She glanced over at her mother, noting that Claire's face was fixed, allowing no emotion to show. Glancing back at her father, she analyzed him quickly—tall, lean, and, at the age of forty-three, looking much younger. He had a thin face with dark blue eyes shaded by heavy eyebrows. His brown hair was gray at the temples, and he had a closely trimmed mustache. His mouth was wide and his lips firm and fully molded. There was an English look about him, especially in the aquiline nose and the high cheekbones.

"I'm sorry to intrude on you like this, Matthew," Claire said at once. She was wearing a light tan dress that showed off her figure to good advantage. Her only jewelry was a pair of small jade earrings and a ring with a small ruby, a gift from her father.

She said hurriedly, as if making an excuse, "I realize that it's inconvenient—"

"Nonsense!" Matthew interrupted. His eyes warm, he stepped forward and took Amelia's hand. "Amelia, it's good to see you again. I've missed you."

"Thank you, Matthew. You're looking so well!"

"And, Leah! I don't know whether to take you up on my lap or bow from the waist." Matthew's lips curved slightly as he saw her confusion. "Perhaps I'd better not do either for a while."

Leah had forgotten how much he liked to tease. She was uncomfortable, for her feelings about her father were complicated. But she managed to say, "You're looking very well! Time has been good to you."

"Thank you, daughter." Then something in his manner changed as he inclined his head, saying, "As always, Claire, you look beautiful. I suppose you're tired after your long trip. Well, come along. Lucy says dinner is ready."

He stepped aside, and the three women made their way out of the parlor, down the hall, and into the dining room, a spacious room with an ornate gaslight chandelier. The table was covered with a snowy white tablecloth and pale blue china with small, darker blue figures gracing each place. The heavy silver tableware gleamed richly under the reflected light, and from a large mahogany sideboard a combination of various silver and porcelain dishes also glowed.

"Well, Lucy, I hope you've prepared a feast," Matthew said, winking at the servant as she came in bearing a large platter containing the roast.

"I 'spect it'll do well enough," she said, sniffing. "I ain't noticed you turning nothin' down lately."

"Ah, but our guests may be fussier than I am." Matthew

smiled, his fondness for the woman obvious. As she went back to the kitchen, he commented, "I would have starved to death if it hadn't been for Lucy." And then, as Simon entered bearing a bowl of beans in one hand and a platter of corn on the cob in the other, he said, "And Simon here makes my life miserable." Simon merely smiled briefly, and Matthew laughed. "I don't know what I'd do without those two. It wouldn't be easy."

"They've been with you a long time, haven't they, Matthew?" Amelia said after the two had left the dining room. "They're very fond of you; I can tell that."

"The feeling's mutual. A good argument against slavery," he said, shrugging. "I can't imagine *owning* Simon and Lucy. There'd be something terribly wrong with it." Then he stopped abruptly and glanced at Claire. "Sorry, I didn't mean to start a political argument. We'll not speak of it again."

Claire dropped her eyes, and as the meal proceeded, she said very little. Strangely enough, it was Amelia who did most of the talking. She'd always been fond of Matthew, although she said little about it. Claire especially was forced to remember how many times Amelia had spoken well of Matthew before her own attitude had put a stop to it. Now, as she was reunited with Matthew, Amelia's eyes were bright with interest in what Matthew was doing.

Cleburne shook his head as he answered, "I'm nothing but a dull, dreary businessman. I steal all the time I can to go hunting and riding. I do that a lot. But with the war on, business is good."

As the meal proceeded, there was a strange mixture of ease and tension in the room. Amelia and Matthew were enjoying themselves, but Leah and Claire both felt strange and out of place. They met each other's eyes once, each understanding the feelings of the other. Finally, when Lucy brought in the dessert, a fine apple pie, they sat nibbling at it until finally Matthew remarked, "I'm glad you got here safely. It's a dangerous time at Vicksburg, at least so I hear."

"Yes," Claire said when the other two didn't speak. "It wasn't a good time at all."

"Well, you'll have to relax and let Simon, Lucy, and me make things easy for you." He hesitated then said quietly, "I'm glad you're here. It's good to have you."

Claire hesitated. There was an honesty in Matthew Cleburne's eyes, but then, he'd always been honest with her. It was his other habits that had separated them. She said softly, "Thank you, Matthew. You were always generous to those in need." Then she rose quickly, as if she'd said too much. "If you don't mind, I think I'll go to bed early."

"Why, of course," Matthew said, rising. "We'll have time to talk later." When Claire had left the room, he said, "What about you two?"

Amelia said, "I'm a little tired myself. When you get to be my age, your bones don't take the bumping around that I got on some of the railroads." She stood there for a moment, and Matthew came over and shook her hand warmly, saying, "I've missed you, Amelia. We'll have lots of time to talk, and I'll show you New York."

"That will be nice. Good night, Matthew."

Leah was not sleepy, and as soon as Amelia left the room, she said so. "I'd like to hear more about what's going on here in the North. We were pretty cooped up in Vicksburg. Will you tell me about it?" She hesitated, not knowing what to call him. She had called him Daddy at one point, but that was in the dim reaches of long ago. Now she couldn't call him Matthew, and

Father sounded stilted. She awkwardly avoided the use of any title at all as the two went back to the parlor.

"Well," he said, "I'll tell you what I know," and began to speak of the news. He was, Leah discovered, a well-informed man who understood the military situation better than most. Leah noticed that he was careful not to speak of the differences over slavery.

Finally, at nine o'clock, she said with some surprise, "It's been a good evening." She'd been prepared not to like her father, since she was firmly convinced he was a wastrel and dishonorable. But he'd been courtly, mannerly, and warm, and she was confused by it all. "I think I'll go to bed."

"I think you should," he said, nodding. "That's a long trip and you've been under a strain for a long time." He stood up as she rose and came over to stand closer to her. "You're a lovely young lady. I'm very proud of you, Leah," he said. "As soon as you're able, I hope you'll allow me to show you off a little bit."

"Show me off?"

"Why, yes, go for rides and let people think, *Who's that old codger with the beautiful young daughter?*"

Leah laughed aloud. "They wouldn't say that!"

"Well, let them say what they want. I know a great many people. I'm not much for society these days, but I get enough invitations. There's a ball coming up that I think you'd enjoy. Maybe you'd let me go with you and do some shopping...but of course, your mother would want to do that. In any case, I don't mean to push you. Now go get some rest."

"Good night," Leah said.

She thought for one moment he meant to lean forward and kiss her cheek, but then he rocked back on his heels as if rebuking himself. "Good night, Leah. Sleep well."

CHARIOTS IN THE SMOKE

She went to her room and lay in bed, restless. In her mind was the image of Matthew Cleburne she'd had for years—a heavy drinker, a woman chaser, a man dishonorable in his marriage vows, an unsteady man.

But that wasn't the man she'd seen this night. *True enough, scoundrels often have fine manners,* she thought, *but there's something different in him. I'll have time now to know him a little bit.* Then she went off to sleep, reveling in the feather bed and the clean linen after the hard, dirty days of travel.

Chapter 8

Flight from Vicksburg

The cottonmouth stretched his length on a decaying cypress log. Except for the long forked tongue that flickered in and out of his mouth, he was virtually invisible. A dark cavity behind his slightly upturned snout gave him the trademark of the pit viper. His eyes seemed dead, yet the mechanisms in his body designed to pick up the scent of blood or slight movements around him were all operating.

A movement stirred the water in slight ripples, and with the sinister smoothness of his kind, the snake slipped off the log, his body twisting sinuously as he swam high in the water, scarcely disturbing the glassy surface. Reaching a point of ground above the tea-colored water of the swamp, he moved onto the land, head lifted.

Two men emerged from the depths of the cypress swamp, wading knee-deep in the fetid waters, their steps stirring up the mold and decay that had settled to the bottom. Their feet made squishing sounds as they pulled them free, and as they moved up on the higher ground, they stopped as if by common consent and looked back at the darkness of the forest behind them.

"This looks like better ground, Mr. David," Corey said,

taking a deep breath. His chest was wet with sweat. He'd removed his shirt and tied it by the arms around his waist. His skin glistened like dark chocolate, the muscles swelling with each movement. "I sho' am glad to be away from that river and through that ol' swamp!"

David didn't answer. His lips were drawn together into a thin line, and his nose was pinched with the effort that had brought him this far. He seemed preoccupied, with a distant light in his eyes, and this troubled his companion. Corey examined David closely then said, "I expect we're gonna get away for sho' now. Them Yankees ain't gonna come through no swamp after us."

David blinked his eyes, as if stirred from some deeper thoughts, and then turned to his companion. "I guess so," he said, his voice no more than a vague mutter. There was an uncertainty in him that wasn't his usual manner. He'd made the swim with Corey down the Mississippi past the gunboats without incident. They'd half floated, letting the current carry them along until they were at least five miles downstream from the gunboats. At night they'd made their way ashore and waited in the darkness until morning. There was no shelter, no hope of a fire, and they'd shivered and suffered the discomfort silently. At dawn they'd left the river, making their way eastward through the cypress swamp without having the vaguest idea of what lay ahead of them.

Now David shrugged unhappily and without a word started across the dry land. But he hadn't taken two steps when suddenly Corey struck him in the back so abruptly and with such force that he fell to the ground, catching himself partially with his hands.

He rolled over quickly in the damp soil, his eyes suddenly

alert, and saw that Corey had turned to one side and was kicking at something. Scrambling to his feet, he saw it was a huge, thick-bodied snake. Catching the white inside of the jaws, he whispered, "Cottonmouth!" and stepped forward, looking for a weapon. But there was none. Just then Corey's foot lashed out, catching the snake and sending him flying backward.

"That'll do you, old cottonmouth!" Corey said, breathing hard. He shook his head. "He were just waitin' for you. Lucky I saw him."

David watched for a moment as the snake swam away, leaving a V-shaped wake as he moved toward the deeper waters of the swamp. Then he turned to Corey and managed a smile. "I never could stand snakes," he said, a slight shudder running through him. "He could have gotten you, Corey. I guess you earned your keep this morning."

Corey examined David's face, pleased to see the action seemed to have picked up his spirits. "Ain't gonna let no old cottonmouth get the best of us, is we now?" He grinned, his white teeth flashing against his dark features. "Come on now, Mr. David. Let's git as far away from this here swamp as we kin. I wants to see some high ground."

The two moved on quickly, and all morning long they trudged along the ground as it rose slowly. They had to fight their way through undergrowth and vines with sharp thorny spines that clawed at their legs, and once they had to detour around a cane thicket that was too thick to plow through.

Just before noon they stopped, and Corey said, "I got to have me a drink of water, Mr. David."

David looked down at the creek that wound languidly along the ground. It moved slowly, almost imperceptibly. He shook his head. "Could be fever in this swamp, Corey. We'd better hold out till we get to someplace with better water. I'm pretty thirsty myself, but that malaria's bad stuff."

"Yes, sah, I reckon you right."

The two of them rested for thirty minutes then continued their journey. Over an hour later they crossed an abandoned road overgrown with vines. Wagon tracks were fresh in the dirt, however, and David remarked, "Not used much, but somebody's there." He looked both ways and said, "Which way shall we go?"

"Well, I guess it leads to sumpin' either way." Corey's brow wrinkled and he studied the tracks. "Reckon that way probably leads back to Vicksburg. Maybe we'd better try this one. You got that pistol handy, Mr. David?"

"Maybe I'd better check it." David sat down on a fallen tree and carefully unwrapped the Navy Colt that he'd brought all the way from Richmond in oilcloth along with the powder and loads. Expertly he loaded the chambers of the Colt and then admitted, "This won't fight off an army, but I'll feel better with it." He stuck it in the waistband of his pants and looked down the road. "Let's see what we can find."

They advanced down the road alertly, not knowing what they would find. The Yankee army had passed to the west of them—David was sure of that—but he was relatively certain that except for a supply line, the bulk of the army was now engaged in besieging Vicksburg. Overhead the skies were clear and a flight of red-winged blackbirds was flying over, making their raucous calls and heading for feeding grounds somewhere to the south.

"That looks like a farm of some kind up there," David said. They halted, and the two men peered around the undergrowth where the road bent.

"Smoke comin' from it," Corey observed. "Guess it ought to

be all right. Ain't likely to be no Yankees this far south."

"Let's check it out." David removed the revolver from his waistband and held it down to his side while they moved down the weed-choked road. As they rounded the bend, they saw a log cabin on a rise of high ground. It was an old place, grown gray with years of rain and the powerful sun of Southern summers. Chickens clucked around the yard, and over to the right, two pigs, caked with red mud, rooted industriously in the soil. They looked up curiously as the men approached. A curly tendril of smoke rose to the sky as David said quietly, "We'd better give them a signal." Lifting his voice, he cried, "Hello, the house!"

A moment's silence reigned; then a tall man appeared in the front door. He had a rifle, David noticed, so he called out quickly, "Just a couple of lost travelers! Maybe you can point us in the right direction."

The man in the cabin door stepped outside, moved off the porch, and advanced, holding the rifle. He was a lanky individual with shaggy brown hair and a pair of steady light blue eyes that he kept fixed on the pair. "What you doing out here?" he called, his voice a high tenor.

Because David was wearing his uniform, he knew there was no point in dissembling. "Don't know if you heard, but the Yankees got Vicksburg sewed up. Me and my servant here had to swim out or get caught." He was still holding the pistol in his hand, and he waited anxiously to see what the man's reaction might be. There were Union sympathizers in Mississippi, and this might well be one of them. But the distance to the man was less than thirty feet, so he hoped it wouldn't come to a shoot-out.

"Waal now, been expecting somethin' like thet." The man slipped his hand down along the barrel and with his right thumb lowered the hammer on the musket. "You fellers was lucky to get away, I guess." He set the butt of the musket on the ground. "Pemberton was a fool to get trapped there. I said so all along."

"In that," David said, slipping the Colt back into his waistband, "I think you're right. Too late now."

"Name's Otis Sudsen. Reckon you fellers could eat some coon and a little corn pone? The pone's fresh."

"That'd go down mighty well."

Ten minutes later David was sitting at the table with the farmer eating the fried morsels of fresh-killed coon. He'd piled a tin plate high with the meat and pone and given it to Corey, who now sat in a chair close to the door, eating and listening to the two men. The talk was of the war, and Sudsen said finally, "I done lost two boys in this war. One at Antietam and one at Fredericksburg. Just got one more boy. He's with Lee."

"My brother and father serve with Lee."

"Do they now? Well, I ain't got a lot of hope with the way this war's turning out. Ain't my war anyhow. Never owned a slave in my life." He looked over at Corey then shook his head. "We been led down the wrong path, I reckon. Don't see no good end to it."

David looked down at his plate. He really wasn't hungry, though he should have been. He managed to eat a little more of the coon then said, "I'm trying to get back to Richmond, where my family is."

"That ain't gonna be no play party," Sudsen said, scratching his growth of wiry whiskers. "Railroad's cut all to pieces, Yankees everywhere you look all through here. I 'spec you'll have to go to Atlanta. Hear tell trains are still running there."

"How can we get to a train to get to Atlanta?" David inquired.

Sudsen stared at the man across the table from him as if weighing something in his mind. Finally, he said, "Reckon I'm about due for a trip to town. I can take you to Kingsburg. There's a spur line there that ought to get you on your way anyhow. You'll have to go around the world, I reckon, to get there."

"Wouldn't want to put you out, Mr. Sudsen."

"Ain't nothing doing here in this place anyhow. If my boy Jimmy don't come home, ain't nothing left. My woman died two years ago. All I do is a little two-bit farming here. One place is good as another." There was a faint despair in the man's blue eyes, typical of the current Southern spirit.

"I'd be glad to pay you for your time," David said.

Sudsen, a proud Southerner, shook his head vehemently. "Don't reckon it's come to me bein' paid for doing a soldier a little favor."

Quickly David said, "That's good of you. We appreciate it."

"Reckon we might as well get on our way. Them mules I got moves like molasses, but I guess they'll get us there."

The roadbed hadn't been repaired and the cars swayed alarmingly as the coal-burning engine wound through the forest of Georgia pines. Once, the cars dipped so deeply that David grabbed for the handle of the seat, thinking they were going to be overturned. "We may have to get out and walk if this gets any worse," he said to Corey.

Corey, who'd never been on a train before, was fascinated by it all. "No, sah," he said with a grin. "This beats walking. Mighty nice of that farmer to take us to the train, wasn't it, Mr. David?"

When David didn't answer, Corey looked at him closely. There was a slackness in his master's jaw, and his eyes seemed fixed on something far beyond the range of the interior of the dilapidated car that clattered and rattled along the narrow-gauge line. He'd noticed during the wagon trip with Otis Sudsen that, from time to time, there was a gap in David Rocklin's attention span. Now he said to himself, *Mr. David ain't right. Somethin's wrong with his mind. Sure be glad to get him home where his family can take care of him.* He tried again. "I got some of that fried coon Mr. Sudsen put up for us. Could you eat a bite, Mr. David?" But there was still no response, as if Corey hadn't even spoken. With a despairing shake of his head, Corey reached into the paper sack, pulled out a piece of the meat, and bit it in two with his strong teeth. He chewed thoughtfully, turning to watch the forest flow by like magic. But always he returned to stare at David and wonder what was going on inside his head.

"All off for Atlanta!"

The conductor, a heavy man who wore a flat-crowned hat with a narrow brim, moved down the aisle. His gold watch chain clinked against his massive stomach as he came to stand over the two men who remained on the train after all the other travelers had filed off. Looking down at David and Corey, he said, "Atlanta! This is as far as the train goes." After staring at David for a moment with his small dark eyes, he turned to the black man. "What's wrong?"

Corey cleared his throat. "Mr. David, he's a little bit troubled, sah, but he'll be all right." He reached over, took David's arm, and shook it. Leaning forward, he said, "Mr. David—Mr. David, we're in Atlanta. Come on, let's get off the train."

The conductor watched and saw that the words didn't seem

to reach the consciousness of the fine-looking young man dressed in the stained Confederate uniform. "He's been in a battle, I guess?"

"Yes, sah, that's it. He's a little bit—wore out. But I'll take care of him. Come on, Mr. David."

The conductor watched as the strong-bodied servant almost pulled the white man to his feet. He gathered a small sack in one hand and, keeping the other on his master, led him off the train.

"Too bad. Looks like he's had more fighting than he can take. Hope the boy'll be all right."

Corey led David down the steps, and when they were on the cinder-covered platform, he said, "Come on now, Mr. David; we'll be all right." He led the man to a bench and looked around almost desperately. "Let's us set here a minute." When David obeyed him docilely, Corey sat down, muttering, "Don't know what to do. What's wrong with Mr. David? We got to get *somewhere*. He got a friend here, so he said." Then he asked his companion, "Mr. David, what's your friend's name? The one here in Atlanta?"

There was no response for some time; then David blinked his eyes and coughed. "What's that, Corey?" he said, looking around. "Why, we're at the station! Is this Atlanta?"

Corey swallowed. "Yes, sah, this here's Atlanta. What's your friend's name?"

"Bernard Dixon."

"I guess we better try to find him. Don't you reckon?"

Weariness tinged the face of Rocklin, and he got up slowly, almost like an old man. He looked around and murmured, "I must have gone to sleep. I don't even remember getting off the train." His voice sounded hollow and he looked, puzzled, at the black face in front of him. "How long have I been asleep?"

"Well, sah, you been mighty tired, I reckon. But you'll be all right. Let's go find Mr. Dixon."

Corey was afraid David would go off into whatever sleep he'd been in and was relieved when they found the carriage and David gave the cabdriver an address. As the two got into the carriage, David said, "I haven't seen Bernard Dixon for a couple of years. We were good friends once. I don't even know if he's still at this address."

As the cab made its way through the city, David noted that Atlanta was somewhat similar to Richmond. But there was a shabbiness about the place that hadn't been here on his last visit, six years earlier. Then it had been a busy, prosperous city, growing and filled with new construction. Now everything seemed to have stopped, and he realized it was due to some of the same genteel poverty that he was accustomed to in Richmond itself.

They reached a section of town composed mainly of white frame houses, most two stories and with fading paint, built along a wide street. The carriage stopped and the driver said, "There she is, sir."

David and Corey got out. David said, "You'd better wait. I'm not sure this is the place."

"Yes, sir, I'll wait."

David walked up to the front door, Corey following slightly behind him. When he knocked, the door opened almost at once and a white-haired woman dressed in black looked him over carefully. "Yes? May I help you?"

"My name's David Rocklin. I'm looking for Bernard Dixon."

"Why, yes, David, I didn't recognize you! Won't you come in?"

"I'd better pay the cabdriver," David said. "I wanted to be

sure this was the right place."

"Bernard will be back in less than an hour, but you can wait."

After David paid the driver, the woman said, "Bernard still speaks of you often, of your days in school together. Why don't you let me take your servant to the kitchen? I'll see that he's fed. You and I can have tea in the parlor."

Corey didn't like to leave his master alone, but he had little choice. He followed the woman into the kitchen, where she said to a large black woman who turned to meet them, "Mr. Bernard has some company, Dinah. See that his man here is fed."

"Yes'm."

Corey stood there uncertainly as the woman left. Dinah examined him almost clinically. "You hongry?"

"I could eat, I reckon."

"Sot down there. I see what we got."

Back in the parlor, David waited for Mrs. Dixon. When she returned, the two had tea together. She was curious about his coming, and he explained his escape from Vicksburg and ended by saying, "I'm trying to get back to Richmond, but I wanted to see Bernard."

"He'll be so glad to see you," Mrs. Dixon said. Then she asked tentatively, "I can see you didn't have time to carry clothes from Vicksburg. You and Bernard are about the same size. Come along; you can get cleaned up and wear some of his clothes."

David went upstairs without argument. When he was alone in the high-ceilinged room, he took a sponge bath, dried off, and put on a pair of Dixon's brown trousers and a clean white shirt that fit him reasonably well. Then he looked at the bed. "Just take a little nap," he said. He lay down and instantly fell into a deep sleep.

"Bernard! Your friend is here—David Rocklin."

Bernard Dixon had entered the house and stopped abruptly at his mother's words. A tall young man of twenty-three with sandy hair and blue eyes, he said with a grin, "Old Dave is here? What in the world is he doing in Atlanta?"

He listened as his mother explained and said, "I think he must have gone to sleep. His servant's out in the kitchen if you want to ask him."

"Yes, I will."

Bernard went to the kitchen, where Corey stood up at once, his eyes alertly fixed on the young white man. When he entered, Corey said, "Mr. Dixon, I'se Corey—"

Dixon, seeing that something was troubling the slave, asked, "What is it? Is something wrong?"

"Yes, sah, there is. I don't know what it is, but Mr. David, ever since we left Vicksburg, he been somehow out of his mind."

"Out of his mind? What do you mean?"

"Oh, I don't mean he acting crazy. I mean he just seem like he passes out. . .like he goes to sleep and I can't wake him up."

"Was he wounded?"

"Naw, sah, he didn't get hit with no bullets, but he been having some powerful bad nightmares—I knows that much."

Dixon frowned. It didn't sound like the David Rocklin he'd known. "Thank you, Corey," he said. "Have you been fed?"

"Yes, sah. I want to help Mr. David get back to his family."

"We'll see what we can do."

Two hours later, David came down the stairs and Bernard Dixon greeted him warmly. "I'm glad to see you! You're lucky you didn't get tied up there in Vicksburg with the rest of Pemberton's army."

"It was kind of a miracle, I think, Bernard. I still don't know how Corey and I managed to get away."

"Well, come on; I want to hear all about the battle. I'm going in the army myself next month. Maybe you can give me some pointers."

David looked at Bernard Dixon, a strange expression twisting his face. "I don't think," he said woodenly, "I'd be able to do that, Bernard."

Bernard Dixon sensed his friend was greatly troubled. But, being a sensitive young man, he knew better than to plunge right in. *I'll have to find out what's going on in Dave's head*, he thought, then said, "While you're here, we'll get caught up. You don't have to leave right away, do you?" He waited, but no answer came, and he was shocked to see David appeared not to have heard him. He said quickly, "We'll talk about it later. Come along. Let's see if Mama's got any of that chocolate cake left. You always were partial to chocolate cake."

˙

Later David put the tip of the pen into the inkwell and then slowly began to write:

> *Dear Grandmother,*
> *I know you've been worried about me, but I've been somewhat ill since I escaped from Vicksburg. Perhaps it's some form of malaria, I'm not sure. I hate to tell you this, for you have enough to worry you on the farm. God willing, I'll be well soon. Try not to worry.*

CHARIOTS IN THE SMOKE

I've been here in Atlanta, staying with Bernard's family for two weeks now, and most of that time I've been merely trying to gain my strength back. I've lost considerable weight and have no appetite, which seems to be part of this sickness. Bernard and his parents have been most gracious. They wouldn't hear of my finding a room in Atlanta while I recovered. They've had their family doctor to see me, and while he hasn't yet identified what sort of fever it is, I feel sure he'll find the cure.

I have a servant with me now, a slave I bought in Vicksburg, named Corey. He is a treasure and I intend to free him at the end of a year. He takes good care of me, fusses over me like a mother hen, and is a combination manservant and nurse.

Please write me with any news of Pa and Dent. We hear about the awful loss of life at Gettysburg and I'm very concerned one of them might have been wounded. I'd feel better if you could write at once. And please tell me how things are there on the farm, and how Josh is getting along with everything, especially the salt pork.

I'll stay here with Bernard until I'm recovered and can make the trip home safely. Please pray for me and write as soon as you can.

Your loving grandson,
David

David put the pen down, exhausted by the weight of it. He closed his eyes abruptly, put his arms across the writing desk that sat beside his bed, and rested his head on it. He hadn't told his grandmother of the blackouts that had come to him, nor of the terrible nightmares. Both were coming more often now, and he knew that the Dixons were concerned. Corey was also worried.

For a long time he sat there, feeling himself slipping away again. Almost wildly he jerked himself upright and shook his head, gritting his teeth. "I can't go into that again!" Panic and fear tingled through his body and almost exploded in his brain.

"I can't go mad! I can't—!"

Chapter 9

Very Nice—for a Yankee

"Git yo' worthless self out and bring some firewood in!"

Simon had been sitting in a cane-bottomed chair reading the newspaper, but at Lucy's irritated tone, he lowered the *Tribune* and looked up, a quizzical expression in his eyes. "Why you jumpin' on me so much?" he inquired mildly without moving. "I ain't done nothin' to you, woman."

Standing in the middle of the kitchen, her forearms covered with flour, Lucy gave the tall, lanky man a disgusted look. "Don't argue with me," she said firmly. "You ain't done nothin' but set around this house all mornin'. Now git busy!"

"I know what's aggrafrettin' you. You ain't been fit to live with since Miss Claire came here two weeks ago. That's a long time for a man to put up with a rebellious wife."

"Never mind about no rebellious wife!"

"The Bible say, 'Wives, don't persecute an older man.'"

"Where it say dat? You tell me where!"

Simon grinned. "The book of Titus, I think. You ought to read up more on the scripture about how to treat a husband." He creased the paper gently, his face growing more sober. Shaking his head, he added, "I know how you feel, Lucy. I ain't shore it's good for Miss Claire to come here. Just about the time Mr. Matthew gets over her, she pops up again—and down he goes."

"That's a truth," Lucy said. She picked up a wooden spoon in her right hand, cradled a huge bowl in the crook of her left arm, and stared thoughtfully out the window as she stirred vigorously. It was a beautiful August afternoon with birds singing outside, but there was no contentment in her face. "I don't know what she have to come here for."

"Didn't have no place else to go."

"That ain't no excuse. Mr. Matthew always sent her and Miss Leah money." The spoon moved strongly and rhythmically in the bowl, slapping the dough. "She ain't changed a bit—never will."

Slowly Simon climbed to his feet, stretched carefully, then turned toward the door. "I'll get the wood," he said. As he moved across the floor, he spread his hands out in a gesture of helplessness. "You right about it, though. Mr. Matthew, he ain't happy. She always do that to him. You reckon he still love her after all these years?"

"I don't know, but she is done made one big mess out of raising that girl. Don't even love her own pappy. That ain't *right*, Simon."

"Maybe Miss Leah can get to know Mr. Matthew better if they stay a long time. He sure is trying hard, taking her places and all."

"That ain't gonna do no good. Not with that mama of hers whispering in her ear about what a bad man Mr. Matthew is." The spoon reached a pinnacle of speed as Lucy allowed the anger in her to exit through her strong right wrist. "Now she's taken up with this Yankee soldier, Miss Leah has. That might be a good thing, though," she added thoughtfully. Looking down at the dough and testing it, she moved over to the table and set the bowl down. "She still got that Confederate mess in her mind. I surprised she even running around with that lieutenant."

"Her mama don't mind. Miss Claire maybe sees he'd be a good husband for Miss Leah. Comes from a rich-type family. I guess Miss Claire's smart enough to know there ain't gonna be nothin' left in the South when this here war's over. Anyway, I kinda like that soldier."

"You like him 'cause he gives you money," Lucy said, snorting. "Now get out of here and bring that firewood in!"

Later in the afternoon, Simon encountered Leah as she was walking around the small flower garden in the backyard.

"Howdy, Miss Leah," he said. "Them flowers about gone. Gonna be nothing but old dead weeds in a month or two." He stopped and looked down at the chrysanthemums. "They was real pretty when they first came on. Wish you'd been here to see 'em."

Leah was wearing a pale blue dress with yellow lace at the neck and small figures of white in the skirt, and her hair was carefully done. As Simon looked at her, he asked, "You must be steppin' out tonight, Miss Leah—all dressed up like that?"

"Yes, I am. Lieutenant Decatur's taking me to the theater."

"Sure 'nuff? Well, ain't that nice." Simon was insatiably curious and at once began fishing for information. "He shore is a nice gentleman. I 'spect you been out most every night since you met him at that ball?"

"That's right. He's been very insistent." Leah smiled and touched her hair in a feminine gesture. "I never thought I'd let a Yankee officer take me anywhere."

"How come you do it, Miss Leah?" Simon asked.

"Oh, I don't know. When I met him at the ball, I snubbed him. I thought it would be enough to get rid of him, but. . ." A thoughtful light came into her eyes, and she shook her head slightly. "He just wouldn't take no for an answer. I believe he's the stubbornest young man I've ever seen! And he is nice—for a Yankee."

"Ain't that the truth! Well, what's your mama think about you going around with a Yankee?"

"I'm sure you've asked her already, Simon," Leah said innocently.

"Who, me? Why, I don't poke around in folks's business!"

"No, so I've noticed. Well, Mama, for your information, thinks he's a very suitable young man. She approves thoroughly, at least of my going to the theater with him."

"What's yo' pappy think about him?"

The question startled Leah. "Why. . .he hasn't said." This particular remark troubled her, and she said quickly, "I suppose he doesn't care one way or the other."

"Now that ain't so, Miss Leah," Simon spoke up quickly. He scratched his head vigorously and kicked at the clod of dirt in the flower bed at his feet. "Mr. Matthew, he's interested in everything you do—always has been. You don't know how much he 'preciate them letters you write to him once in a while. He still got every one of 'em."

"Has he really? I wouldn't have thought that."

"'Deed he do. He read them to me over and over again. And that picture you sent two years ago, you know where it is? Right in his bedroom. He think a heap of you, Miss Leah. Never saw a pappy more attached to a young lady."

Just then a bumblebee lumbered down over a dead blossom as if perplexed. He flew haphazardly among the dying flowers, hovering in the air hopefully, then moving on hesitantly. Finally, finding nothing to satisfy him, he rose slowly, made a circle of the garden, then headed out over the fence. Leah watched him until he disappeared, then lifted her eyes to the tall, dark-skinned man. "He always wrote to me. Every time I wrote to him, a letter would come back."

"When you was just a little girl," Simon said thoughtfully, his voice almost dreamy, "he'd take you for a walk every day, when you couldn't even walk. You'd fall down and he'd pick you up." The memory was pleasant to him, and he seemed to savor it. "And he got you that dog. Miss Claire had a fit. You remember Jigger?"

"Yes, he was so sweet. I think about him all the time. Daddy gave him to me when I was just four years old." The name Daddy had jumped to her lips without thought, and Leah glanced quickly at Simon to see if he'd noticed. However, he merely stood there, the late-afternoon sun falling on his craggy features. Then she continued, "When he died, we had a funeral."

"Why, I remember that! It was me who got the box. It was a soap box, and Mr. Matthew—nothing would do but he'd find some satin from one of Miss Claire's old dresses and line it. Then he made a regular casket out of that."

"Yes, and we had a funeral, you remember?" Leah's eyes were misty. "We even read out of the Bible, out in the backyard by the little grave. And Daddy preached a little sermon. I still remember that," she said quietly. "I think I remember it more clearly than anything that happened in my childhood. He was so busy then, but he took time to have a funeral for Jigger."

"He give you anything you want back in them days," Simon murmured, "and I guess today he'd do the same thing."

He looked up, his wise old eyes fixed on Leah and his voice summer-soft as he said, "You miss Mr. Matthew, Miss Leah?"

Leah couldn't meet his eyes, nor could she answer his question. She realized suddenly that she *had* missed her father, more than she'd known. Speaking of the funeral for the dog had brought back other memories that rushed through her. To shut them off she said, "Oh, I suppose so," then hurriedly left, saying, "I've got to get ready to go."

Simon stared after her then turned slowly and made his way into the kitchen, where Lucy was taking a pie out of the oven. "Maybe I'd better sample that," he said.

"Keep yo' hands off it!" Lucy snapped.

"That chile still loves her pappy in spite of everything," Simon said. "It's a shame that them two ain't had no time for each other." He didn't mention Claire's name, for he knew Lucy carried a deep-seated resentment against the woman. Indeed, she blamed Claire Cleburne for bringing sorrow and distress to the Cleburne family. Simon resumed his seat in the chair, tipped it back, and, as he leaned his head against the wall, inhaled the fragrant incense of the pie that hung over the kitchen. Then he sighed, thinking of what might have been.

Lieutenant Brian Decatur was a handsome young man, fit and trim. At five-foot-ten, his one hundred and sixty pounds was firm and solid. He moved athletically into the parlor, where Claire Cleburne was sitting in a chair beside the window. "Well, hello, Mrs. Cleburne," Decatur said, smiling easily. He had curly brown hair and a mustache. He was sharp featured, and there was something unsettling about his gaze, for he had one brown eye and one blue. He moved across to bend over and kiss Claire's hand when she extended it, then said, "You really ought to be going to the ball with us, you and Mr. Cleburne."

"Oh no, I think not, Lieutenant."

Her tone was so abrupt that Decatur paid attention instantly. He'd met Leah less than two weeks ago at a ball where she'd been escorted by her father. He'd been taken by the girl's attractive manner and rather saucy ways. Escorting a Southern girl around had been a challenge to him, but Decatur liked challenges. Now he realized, however, he'd stepped into a family matter that was somewhat precarious. Being a tactful young man, he smoothed over his remark by saying, "Why, of course, maybe some other time."

As he was saying this, Leah entered and said at once, "What was it you said last time, Lieutenant—that a woman's never on time?"

"I apologize and ask your hearty forgiveness, Miss Cleburne." He advanced to where she stood, taking in the trim figure and smooth, clear complexion. "You look beautiful," he said. "No one will be able to watch the actors or actresses, not with you in the hall."

Leah laughed. "You Yankees are the romantic ones, not Southerners, as rumor has it." She turned to her mother, saying, "We're going to see *Hamlet*. I've never seen it—have you?"

"Yes, I saw it with—with your father once, many years ago. Who's in the starring role?"

"I'm not sure," Brian Decatur said. "I've heard he's not the best actor in the world, but he's very popular."

"Well, try to get home before it's too late."

"Certainly. Are you ready, Miss Leah?"

Decatur and Leah left the house, and he escorted her into

the carriage he'd hired for the occasion. "Capitol Theater, driver," he said then got in beside her. As the horses clip-clopped along the streets, Decatur spoke cheerfully of the evening. "There won't be many more of these, I'm afraid. I'll be leaving soon."

"Where are you going, or is that a military secret?"

"Oh, not really. I suppose everybody knows that the next big battle will be somewhere around Chattanooga."

After the crisis of July 1863, both armies had reassessed their positions. The North was more optimistic and confident now that the Mississippi valley was clear and Lee was back in Virginia. Lee, however, was far from beaten, and practically every expert agreed that General Rosecrans, with his Union Army of the Cumberland, would be attacking General Braxton Bragg somewhere around Chattanooga.

Leah sat quietly as the lieutenant spoke of the war almost lightly. She'd noted before his confidence, and now she remarked, "You seem very sure the war will go your way."

"Why, yes, I believe it will. I don't want to injure your feelings, of course, but I think it won't be long before all of this is over."

"Not everyone agrees with you in the North. Just last month, here in New York, there were draft riots."

Brian dropped his eyes, unable to answer for a moment. "I'm embarrassed about that, to think people here have so little vision!" He spoke of the crowds that had looted and actually killed during the draft riots, protesting against conscription and the war itself. "But there's always people like that," he said, shrugging his trim shoulders. "Now let's put all this behind us and enjoy ourselves...."

Leah did enjoy herself that evening. She'd never been to a first-class theatrical production, and the actors, she had to agree, put on a good show.

She looked out the window and by the gaslights saw that people were walking the street even at this late hour. "It seems so strange to see people going on with life as if there were no war," she remarked.

Decatur glanced at her quickly. It was dark in the carriage and he could only see the outline of her face. He'd found himself almost bewitched by this young woman. For some reason, the fact she was Southern and Confederate in sympathy seemed to make the attraction stronger. "It'll be over soon," he said. "Then we can put it all behind us, North and South." The horses' hooves drummed on the pavement, iron against stone, and the two sat there quietly until they finally arrived back at the Cleburne house. Then he got out and escorted her inside.

"I'd ask you in," she said, "but it's rather late."

"Of course...now about tomorrow night—"

Leah laughed. "You *are* persistent, Lieutenant! No wonder you Yankees are doing so well. Don't you ever give up?"

Brian shook his head. "I've only got a few days. Now what I propose tomorrow night—"

"I can't go out with you every night," Leah protested. "The neighbors will be talking."

"They're all in bed. Look! Almost every house is dark."

"Well, that one isn't." Leah pointed to her own house. "My mother will be waiting up for me."

"Then I'd better go in and make our excuses," Brian said quickly.

"No, I think not, Lieutenant." She put out her hand and smiled graciously at him. "I must admit, you are a charming young man—for a Yankee."

Brian laughed at her audacity. "And you are a beautiful

young woman—for a Rebel."

The two stood there, speaking lightly for a moment, and then his face turned serious. "I'll be leaving soon. The army's already on the move. I'm just staying later to take my company toward Tennessee—maybe a week, no more."

"I'm sorry you have to leave. I've enjoyed our times together," she said, her voice light.

No one ever accused Brian Decatur of being a timid or bashful young man. As the smell of her perfume wafted faintly in the air, he reached forward and saw her eyes change as his arms went around her. He expected her to pull away, but she didn't—and then he kissed her.

Leah had known, of course, that he was going to kiss her. She was experienced enough in the ways of amorous young men to know such things. She held herself slightly apart, not giving in to his embrace, but not pushing away either. This Yankee was attractive; that she couldn't deny. It couldn't be serious, of course, she told herself, but he'd been nice to her. When he had held her for a moment, she put her hand against his chest and moved back. "There," she said, "that's enough."

"For you!" Decatur said, grinning. "I'll be here tomorrow at two o'clock. Wear some clothes that aren't so fancy."

"What in the world for?"

"You'll see," Decatur said, bowing slightly. "It's been a great evening. I'll see you tomorrow, Leah."

Leah watched as he got into the carriage and rode away; then she went into the house. Claire was sitting in the parlor, although it was after eleven. "You shouldn't have stayed up, Mother."

"I couldn't sleep." Claire put down the book she'd been reading and stood up. "Was it enjoyable?"

"Yes, it was different. I'd never seen anything quite like it." She sat down, and for a while the two women talked, Claire listening, a smile on her lips as Leah recounted her evening. "He's really very nice," she said finally, "but he's leaving next week, I think."

Claire nodded as if she found this reassuring. "It's just as well. He is nice—but he is a Yankee."

The two women rose, and as they did, Leah asked, "Has Father gone to bed?"

"Yes...."

There was a hesitancy in Claire's tone. Matthew had come in earlier, and for a time the two had spoken. She'd fixed him a cup of tea, and they'd sat at the dining room table. The conversation had been mundane as he'd asked about her day and the things she'd done. Finally, he had given her an odd look and said, "I'm glad you're here, Claire, no matter what the reason."

His words had echoed in Claire's mind, disturbing her somehow. She'd gone to bed then tossed and turned for so long that finally she'd risen, put on her robe, and come downstairs to read and wait for Leah to come in. Now, as she stood there, she looked unusually vulnerable.

"What's the matter, Mother?"

"Oh, I don't know. I feel so...so out of place here. I wish we could go somewhere else."

Leah sensed a rare uncertainty in her mother. "Have you and Father been quarreling?"

"Oh no, not that. He's been...very nice. It's just that—" She broke off then and said abruptly, "Good night, Leah." Moving hastily out of the room, she ascended the steps and turned into her own bedroom. She put the candle down on the nightstand then looked at the bed. She was restless, not sleepy, and she rocked in the chair a long time before finally sighing deeply and getting into bed.

The courtship went on for a week, and on Sunday, young Decatur presented himself at the door with a carriage to escort the family to church. The entire family attended the Methodist church, where the sermon was on forgiveness.

"That was a good sermon, wasn't it, sir?" Decatur asked Matthew.

"Very good," Matthew responded. "Rev. Haws is a fine preacher."

After dinner, the two men sat out on the porch talking. The ladies joined them for a while, and the conversation drifted back to the sermon.

But Claire took no part in it, for somehow the sermon had pierced her. Finally, she excused herself and left the porch. As she moved away, she thought, *I've got to get away from here. I can't bear it any longer.*

Chapter 10

A Grim Picture

"I don't understand it, Mother. It's like—it's like David is a different man!"

Bernard Dixon had come to sit beside his mother, who was crocheting a doily out of light blue thread. She looked up at him, worry in her fine gray eyes, and shook her head. "Your father says he saw men like him during the Mexican War. He said they just seem to retreat back into their own minds after their hardships."

"Yes, I know," Dixon murmured. He picked up a book lying on the table, riffled the pages impatiently, then tossed it down. "Dave just goes back into—some kind of a *cave* almost and piles rocks up until nobody can get at him. I've never seen anything like it."

"Dr. Summers says it's not physical."

"I know that. He didn't get wounded or anything. I've talked to Corey about him. He says he's changed so completely he hardly knows him."

"Has he written to his family?"

"Yes, but I don't think he's told them anything. As far as I understand, he just tells them he's got a physical sickness—a fever of one sort or another. It's not like Dave to lie like that."

"I'm not sure he's lying, at least not completely," Mrs. Dixon remarked. She put the crochet material down in her lap and clasped her hands together, easing the cramped muscles. She had the beginnings of arthritis and dreaded to see it come on, for she loved to do fine work. "I don't know him well, but it seems to me he's afraid to face up to what's happening to him."

"I've noticed that, too. Every time I've tried to talk to him about it, he just shuts me off. But he's got to do *something*."

"Dr. Summers says there's really not much he, or any doctor he knows of, can do. If it's in Dave's mind, then medicine won't help much, will it?"

"I suppose not, but I hate to see this happen to Dave! He's such a good man—and such a fine family! I think they ought to be told. I've thought of writing them myself."

"I wouldn't do that!" Mrs. Dixon said quickly. "Let David handle it. All we can do is just be available."

"I suppose so." Bernard got up and walked around the room aimlessly. "He's gone off on another of those long walks of his. What if he blacks out while he's outside? That'd be terrible."

"Usually Corey goes along with him, but he didn't go this time. He was chopping wood and David walked out of the house without saying a word to anyone." She glanced up at the clock on the mantel. "He's been gone over three hours. I didn't want to say anything, but I'm worried about him."

"I've got to do something!" Dixon exclaimed, turning to leave the room. "I'll go see if I can find him."

At that very moment David was wandering through the streets

of Atlanta. He'd found his way to the center of the city and passed along the thronged streets, only vaguely aware of the conversation and activities of the large city around him. He'd left the house almost desperately, for he'd felt himself dropping off into what he'd come to recognize as a "spell." It was like falling asleep in a way, but he'd learned these periods could last as much as three or four hours. Corey had stayed close beside him during such times, and David had become very dependent upon the black man. Now as he meandered along the streets of Atlanta, desperation swept over him. A heavyset man came out of a butcher shop, his white apron red with blood, reminding David of the fighting he'd seen in Vicksburg. Quickly he averted his eyes and walked rapidly along the street. Wagons and carriages and carts rumbled along the broad street, but he ignored them, thinking, *I've got to do something. I can't stay at the Dixons' forever—but I can't go home again either.*

He paused and waited while a six-horse team, pulling an enormous wagon loaded with barrels, went by. Then he crossed the street, returning to his train of thought. *I've got to tell my family something. They must be worried sick about me.* For another twenty minutes he walked, then made his way back to the Dixon house. *I've got to tell them,* he thought, *and I'd rather die.*

A vision of Leah's face came to him, clear as a photograph. He let the memories of their times together flow through his mind, savoring them to the fullest. There had been no woman in his life who had stirred him as this one had, and now she was as lost to him as if she were dead. *I'll never see her again,* he thought, and the sweet memories became bitter. He forced his thoughts away from her and moved down the street, his head bent and shoulders slumped.

Thoughts fluttered through his head like bats in an old barn, and he finally said aloud, "I'd rather die than lose my mind!"

This thought was both the root and the effect of his problem. He was so horribly afraid of losing his mind that the very thought of it seemed to bring on the blackouts that plagued him. But as he wrenched his thoughts away from the notion of insanity, they kept swarming back. He had awful visions of what it would be like for his family, as well as for himself, if he went mad.

I don't know what to do. If it were a physical wound, it would be different. But I can't stand this awful thing that's hanging over me!

As the light filtered in from the tall window in his room, David opened his eyes then closed them quickly. He stirred carefully, turning his head away from the light. When he opened his eyes again, Corey was leaning over him, his face tense, his lips drawn tightly together.

"What—what is it, Corey?"

The eyes of the black man half narrowed, and he said, "You feel all right now, Mr. David?"

From the tone of the slave's voice, David instantly knew he'd had another episode. Looking down, David saw he was virtually undressed, wearing only his underwear with a sheet pulled up to his waist. Alarm jangled his nerves and he sat up abruptly, staring wildly around. He licked his lips, found them dry, and asked, "Can I have some water?"

"Yes, sah!"

David sat there while Corey jumped up and poured water from a pitcher into a glass and handed it to him. He gulped it down thirstily then handed the glass back. He watched as

Corey put the glass down and sat down slowly in the chair. As the slave leaned forward, concern on his face, David asked, "Have I been—sick?"

"Yes, sah!"

"How long have I been here?"

Corey swallowed hard and looked down at the woven carpet on the floor as if reluctant to answer. He moved his feet and twitched his shoulders but finally decided there was no evading the question. "You done been here three days, Mr. David."

"Three days!"

"Yes, sah. You didn't come down for breakfast, and I come up to see 'bout you. You was just standing there at that window looking out. You hadn't even dressed and you didn't know me. You didn't know *nothing*, Mr. David."

A sick feeling rose in his throat, for this was the worst he'd imagined. "Tell me," he said, his voice harsh. He swung his feet out and sat on the side of the bed listening as Corey described what had happened. He'd been like a child, obedient to commands but unable to respond. Corey stumbled over the words but then said urgently, "We done had the doctor here every day."

"He's no good for what I've got."

"Maybe he is. The preacher, he wuz here, too. He pray over you every day, Mr. David. He's a good man."

But David Rocklin wasn't listening. He knew now that something terrible was wrong with him—something so awful he didn't want to say it aloud. And then he realized he had to.

"I'm losing my mind, Corey," he said quietly. He faced the slave, seeing compassion in the large eyes, then stood up and walked to the window and looked down. Outside, a red-brown, bushy-tailed squirrel was busily digging a hole in the ground with sharp erratic movements. When he'd finished, he stuffed something into the hole and covered it up. Then he scurried along the ground, scampered up a tree, and paused to look alertly around. David saw the shining glow of his quick eyes; then the squirrel twitched his tail and disappeared around the tree trunk.

David turned around slowly. Corey had risen and was watching him silently. David wanted to say something to reassure the slave, but he felt more alone, helpless, and alien from his world than he'd ever been in his life. In his hopelessness, he saw nothing ahead of him but a life of complete misery.

Chapter 11

The Verdict

"Lucy, can you help me a minute?"

Leah had donned her corset and now turned to Lucy, who'd just brought her dress from downstairs.

"What is it?" Lucy demanded.

"Help me lace this corset, please." Leah held on to the massive oak headboard on the bed and waited. There was a moment's pause; then the strings in the back of her corset jerked tight. Lucy's touch was so rough that Leah gasped several times until the operation was finished and the final knot was firmly tied. Then she said with a smile, "Thank you, Lucy." Taking a deep breath, she shook her head, a wry expression on her lips. "I don't know why women put up with this, cutting the life out of themselves just so they can have a small waist."

Lucy didn't answer. She moved back to the dress she'd brought up and placed across the bed. Picking it up, she examined it critically.

For a moment Leah stared at the woman, thinking back to the past. When Leah had been little more than a child, Lucy had been a smiling woman, always willing to nurse Leah's bruises and to show her affection. But that warmth was entirely missing now. Ever since Leah had come back to her father's house, she'd noticed this hardness in the servant.

"Well, Lucy," she said finally, "it would appear you don't like me anymore."

"Got nothing to say about likes or dislikes."

"You don't have to say anything. It's written all over you." Leah's temper flared for a moment. "What's the matter? Why are you upset with me?"

"Nothin' was said 'bout bein' upset."

Stepping in front of the woman, Leah stood there until Lucy lifted her eyes. "What have I done? Why don't you like me?"

"No, I don't like you." Lucy's words were flat, and she lifted her head defiantly to look up at the taller woman. "You don't treat Mr. Matthew right."

"That's not for you to say!" Leah replied angrily.

"I didn't say it till you asked me about it. If you don't want to know, don't ask." Lucy's lips twisted downward in a scowl. "He done everything for you that a man can do for a daughter, and all you do is put him down! If you don't like him, why'd you come here?"

"We didn't have anywhere else to go."

"That's right—and all these years he been sendin' you money, ain't he, now?"

Reluctantly Leah agreed. "Yes, he's always taken care of us in that way. That's not why—" She broke off then shook her head so violently that her hair swung up and down her back. Then she straightened with indignation; she didn't have to talk about her father with a servant. "Just help me put this dress on."

Silently Lucy assisted the young woman, and when the dress was in place, she asked, "You want me for anything else?"

"No—and thank you, Lucy." She waited till Lucy left the

room and then, when the door slammed louder than necessary, said loudly, "You're welcome!" She turned to the mirror, troubled by the encounter. She'd always had a special affection for Simon and Lucy. But although Simon was the same, Lucy had changed.

Forcing the issue from her mind, she looked at the peach dress trimmed with emerald lace. Her father had given her the money, saying, "If you're going to a ball, you need a new dress." She'd enjoyed going with Amelia to look for it and now saw it fit extremely well. There was not a wrinkle from bosom to waist, and the skirt flared out perfectly over the hoops. Sitting down, she dressed her hair then added a touch of rice powder and a little carmine on her lips. Taking a deep breath, she stood, picked up the small reticule and the cape that really wasn't needed in such warm weather, and went downstairs.

She heard voices as she descended the staircase. Turning on the landing, she saw Brian Decatur, dressed in his blue uniform with shining brass buttons and polished black boots. His eyes lit up as he saw Leah. "So this is the new dress I've heard so much about," he said. "You look wonderful."

Leah stepped off the last stair and took in the uniform. "Not as wonderful as you look! If you drop dead," she remarked blandly, "we won't have to do anything to you—except stick a lily in your hand."

"Leah!" Claire exclaimed as she stood beside Brian. "You say the awfullest things!"

Decatur laughed, however, saying, "I hope she's not that impudent at the ball. There's going to be some important people there, maybe even the governor."

Just as Claire started to speak, the outer door opened and Matthew stepped in. He was wearing a light gray suit, a white shirt, and a string tie. He stopped abruptly and looked at the three. "Well, are you coming or going?"

"We're going to the ball, sir," Brian answered. He hesitated for a moment then said, "If you and Mrs. Cleburne would like to go, I'm sure you'd be welcome."

Embarrassed silence fell over the three, and Claire said quickly, "No, thank you, Brian. I'm not feeling well tonight. You two go on. Have a good time."

Matthew waited until the door was closed and said to Claire, "It might be good for you to get out. Won't you change your mind?"

Surprised, Claire looked at him strangely. "That would be rather odd, wouldn't it?"

"A husband and a wife going to a ball? What's odd about that?"

Aware of the irony of his tone, she responded, "I don't think of us as husband and wife anymore. I haven't in a long time."

Matthew clasped his hands behind his back and rocked on the balls of his feet. "Have I missed something?" he asked quietly. "Did you get a divorce and forget to mention it to me?"

Claire flushed. "You know I haven't. I never will." Then she said almost angrily, "You can have your other women, but you'll never get a divorce from me."

Matthew Cleburne's face showed no anger—and that troubled Claire. He continued softly, "I've never asked for a divorce." As she made a move to leave the room, he said, "Claire, wait a minute." When she turned to him, he asked quietly, his voice somewhat strained, "What about young Decatur?"

"Why, what about him?"

"You know what I mean. Is Leah serious about him?"

"I don't think so."

"Well, what does she say? Does she talk to you?"

"Of course she talks to me."

"Well then—?"

"I'm not sure he'd be a suitable husband."

Matthew's eyes half closed and his lips grew tight. "Doesn't meet your standards, is that it? I'm sure they're still very high."

They were on the verge of a quarrel, and Claire forced herself to say calmly, "Let's not argue about it, Matthew. I'm not sure about Brian, and neither is Leah. As for my *standards*, I just want her to have a good husband."

"What you want is for her to marry your father."

Claire's face grew pale. "What do you mean by that?" she whispered, anger rising in her. "How dare you mention my father!"

Matthew smiled bitterly and stepped closer to her, saying sharply, "That's who *you* wanted to marry—your father—or someone just like him."

"That's not fair!"

"Fair? You're an odd one to talk about fair." He reached out and grabbed her arms so quickly that she had no time to avoid him. Her eyes grew wide and she opened her mouth to protest, but his words beat at her almost like blows. "You were so filled up with your father and what a glorious saint he was that no man could have pleased you. I'm not saying I was perfect. I told you then, years ago, that I was wrong. But you drove me to some of it."

"That isn't true."

"It isn't true?" His eyebrows lifted in mock surprise and his powerful hands closed more tightly on her arms. "You weren't the one who locked me out of your bedroom?"

"Only after you were seeing that woman!"

"And until then you'd been a warm, loving wife? Is that it?"

His words struck her heart, for she knew he spoke the truth. "Let me go, Matthew," she said.

But still he held her, looking down. What he saw still was the beauty that had captivated him as a young man: the lovely face and large gray eyes that had always been her best feature. Even now, at forty, she had no gray in her auburn hair, and her figure was that of a much younger woman. After a minute of silence, he loosed his grip and stepped back. "You never forget. . .and you never forgive, do you, Claire? How nice it is that you've never made a mistake or done anything wrong!" He wheeled and walked stiffly down the hall without saying another word.

Claire listened as the door to his room at the end of the hall closed. Then she realized her hands were trembling. She hadn't had a scene like this for years, and now she wanted to cry out, to protest that it wasn't all her fault, that *he* was the one who had been wrong. She thought back to the time when she'd left him—how, although she'd never admitted it, she was filled with loneliness and despair. "I did love you, Matthew!" she whispered, staring down the hall. A longing she thought was dead and buried years ago rose in her. Now, however, as she moved blindly to the stairs, groping at the mahogany banister, she thought suddenly of the first years of their marriage, how ecstatic and happy she'd been in his arms and how much she'd loved him. As she entered her room, she stood there almost frantically possessed by a desire to run away, to leave the house because she still remembered his arms around her, his lips on hers, and the sweet way he'd treated her. Slowly she sat down on the bed, staring numbly at the rose wallpaper. Then she said so softly that her voice barely stirred the air, "I did love you once. . . !"

"I've never seen such a glutton before!"

"Glutton? I'm not a glutton." Brian Decatur sat beside Leah in the carriage and, with a purpose in mind, put his arm around her shoulders. "I don't know why you'd call me that."

The two had left the ball after midnight; then Brian had insisted on taking her to a restaurant that apparently stayed open to all hours. They'd eaten fried johnnycakes and drunk strong coffee for over an hour. He'd kept her entertained with his stories of army life. Leah had never laughed so much and had enjoyed herself thoroughly. He was a clever, witty man, and now as they rode along, she said, "I've had a fine time, Brian."

"Have you?" His arm closed around her shoulder, and he suddenly drew her close.

"Brian! You mustn't!" she protested. But in the seclusion and darkness of the carriage, she turned to him and met his kiss halfway. His arms were strong and his hands on her back pulled her against him. His lips were firm and demanding, and almost to her shock, she found herself responding. She'd been curious about her feelings about Brian and thought, *This is one way to find out!*

Finally, she pulled away, putting her hand on his chest. "There now!" she said. "You're as greedy for kisses as you are for johnnycakes."

But her light teasing tone didn't seem to touch Decatur. He did remove her arm but reached out and took her hand. He held it firmly, and the only sound that broke the night silence was the steady, clopping beat of the horses' hooves on the paved streets. Outside, a full moon shed its warm beams over the buildings that loomed on each side, and there was an almost holy peace about the setting.

Brian said abruptly, "I'll be leaving soon, Leah."

"I wish you didn't have to go."

His hand tightened and he turned to face her, the moonlight illuminating his sharp features. His large eyes were fixed on her carefully. "I wanted to go. I was ready to go down and whip Johnny Reb—but then you came along."

"You can't blame it on me," Leah teased, then, at the look on his face, said quickly, "I'm sorry, I didn't mean to be light. I wish you didn't have to go—really I do, Brian."

Brian seemed to struggle then said, "Your parents, they never go anywhere together."

"No, they're separated. I thought you knew that."

"I've heard rumors, but I didn't know for sure." He hesitated then said, "I'm asking for a reason. It's not just out of curiosity."

"A reason? What do you mean?"

"I'm going to ask one of them for permission to marry you."

At first Leah was almost amused, thinking it was another one of his light remarks. But at once she saw he was serious. "Why, you can't mean that! We haven't known each other but a few days."

"I can't help that. I wish we had a year to get to know each other, but we don't. Things happen fast in wartime."

Leah was troubled. "You shouldn't even think of such a thing, Brian. You can't love me. You can't fall in love with someone in a few short weeks."

"Why do you say that? You ever hear of Garibaldi, the Italian patriot? He was riding along a street, looked up, and saw a young girl in a window. He stopped his horse," Brian said and grinned slightly, "took off his hat, and said, 'I love you; I want to spend my life with you.'"

Leah waited a minute then said, "Well, what happened?"

"Oh, he married her and they lived together for fifty years. Just one look was all it took."

"I'm not very romantic, Brian."

"That's all right," he said. He lifted her hand, kissed it, then lowered it. "I'm romantic enough for both of us." He hesitated slightly then continued, "I love you and I want the truth. Do you feel anything for me?"

"Oh, Brian, I can't—"

"You'll love me before I'm through," he said. "I'm a very stubborn fellow." He put his arms around her again and pulled her close, whispering, "You'll get used to me. One day you'll look up and be surprised and you'll think, *Why, I've been married to this fellow for forty years, and what a good husband he's been.*" Then he kissed her again, and Leah felt his urgency. She was stirred—if not by his ardor, then by some desire for order in her life.

But even as Leah was moved by his caress, a sense of shame touched her. The thought of David Rocklin coursed through her like fire: *I let him kiss me like this and I thought it meant something....* She drew back, murmured a quick farewell to Brian, then hurried into the house. Once inside, she shut the door then leaned against it, her eyes closed as troubled thoughts came almost against her will. *I thought I was in love with David, but only a few weeks later, I'm letting another man kiss me.* Disgusted with herself, she thought angrily, *I've got to forget David—it's all over.* But as she ascended the stairs, the memory of David Rocklin came even more strongly and so powerfully that she was vexed with herself. *He's out of my life—that's all there is to it....*

The Atlanta *Constitution* had placed a massive headline across its cover: Fort Sumter Bombarded. David Rocklin read the story as he rode along in the carriage. It recounted how eleven Federal guns on Morris Island, aided by naval armament, had fired 938 shots in the first bombardment on August 17. This was now the nineteenth, and the heavy bombardment continued.

Back to Fort Sumter, where it all started, David thought, shaking his head silently. He opened the paper and read that Rosecrans's advancing Army of the Cumberland was approaching Chattanooga in a major offensive. The editor had written almost in a frantic tone: "The Yankees must be stopped! They must not take Chattanooga or we will lose all our territory in that area!"

David folded the paper, put it down on the seat, and leaned back and closed his eyes. The war somehow seemed far away. For several days now he'd battled his own war. Four times he'd slipped off into the nightmare land where his mind ran to hide—four times that he and Corey or others had known he was out of this world. But there had been other times—times only he himself was aware of. Short times, sometimes only an hour, usually when he was preparing for bed, dreading closing his eyes in sleep. The nightmares of bayonets had returned so that every night he seemed to see a forest of bright glittering blades marching across fields, all aimed for his heart. He'd either wake up fighting the bedcovers and moaning or sink into the black oblivion, which was even worse.

The carriage stopped and the driver said, "Here we are, sir."

David got out and looked at the ancient gray building, half covered with ivy. The mortar between the dark red bricks was crumbling in places. He asked doubtfully, "This is the place?"

"Yes, sir. This is the asylum." The cabdriver, a small man with sharp black eyes like a mouse and a thin line of mustache, asked offhandedly, "You got people in here?"

David didn't answer the question but said, "Wait for me. I don't know how long I'll be, but I'll pay for your time." The cabdriver gave David an odd look then shrugged and pulled his hat firmly down on his head as David walked away.

David approached the building, which was surrounded by a high wall made of wrought iron. The uprights had spearlike tips on them that looked as if they could pierce any man who fell on them. A few men were out in the yard down the way, cutting the grass without enthusiasm. The building itself loomed four stories high, a massive affair sitting by itself beside a country road.

It was simply called "The Asylum." David had come here to see Dr. Carl Steiner. After a long conference, Dr. Summers, the Dixons' family physician, had admitted frankly that David's trouble was not physical and said, "There's not much we doctors can do about cases like yours." He'd hesitated then continued, "There is a man, Dr. Carl Steiner, out at the asylum. I don't know much about him, but I've heard he's been able to help some people with your...trouble."

At first David had revolted against the idea of going to a mental institution but in desperation had finally left the house and made his way to this place. As he approached, he climbed the three steps and knocked on the massive door, then waited. After a time the door opened and a man wearing a loose-fitting shirt, brown trousers, and flat-heeled shoes said, "Yes, sir?"

"I wonder if I could see Dr. Steiner?"

"Come in and I'll see if the doctor can see you now."

David followed the man down a broad hall and looked

around carefully. There were no ornaments on the wall, no pictures whatsoever. It had been papered once with some sort of blue paper with small designs, but they had faded now and the paper hung in place limply, ready to give up its grasp on the wall. Beneath the peeling paper he saw nothing but ancient gray plaster.

There was a rank smell about the place, an odor partly of age and partly of decay and hopelessness.

"You wait right in here, sir."

"Thank you."

David entered the room that the man indicated and saw a rolltop desk fronted by a chair, several bookcases with large thick books, and a framed diploma. Moving to read it, he saw that it was a certificate that Dr. Carl Steiner had been awarded—his medical degree from a German university in Berlin.

Sitting down in one of the hard straight-backed chairs, David waited, his fists clenched so tightly together that they ached. Deliberately he forced himself to relax and prepared for a long wait. He was surprised when the door opened almost at once and a tall, portly man, wearing a white jacket that came to his knees, entered the room. David stood and the man said, "I'm Dr. Steiner," in a heavily accented voice.

"My name is David Rocklin."

"Ah—Mr. Rocklin. Will you have a seat?" Steiner waited until David sat back down, then took his seat in the leather padded chair before the desk. He turned and put his full attention on David. His eyes were very light blue, almost as pale as the tiny wildflowers David had seen growing beside the road back in Virginia. The doctor's Germanic face had tightly drawn lips and a high-domed forehead capped by a heavy mop of coarse salt-and-pepper hair. A scar traced its way down his right cheek, starting at the corner of his eye and angling back toward his earlobe. It must have been a terrible cut, for although it was old, it drew his eye permanently half closed.

"And how may I help you, Mr. Rocklin?"

David took a deep breath and began speaking. "I've been having some problems—mental problems. I go off into some sort of blackness and can't seem to come out of it. . . ."

Steiner listened without saying a word until David had finished. Then he leaned back and studied the tall young man. "How long has this been going on?" He listened as David answered, then shot questions at him for ten minutes. Finally, he sat without a word, staring at the man before him.

"What is it?" David asked almost frantically. "I've never had any trouble like this."

"Tell me again about the dream, about the bayonets."

David was startled. "You think that has something to do with it?"

"The blackouts didn't come until after that. Is that not so?" Steiner inquired.

"Why, yes, that's true."

"Tell me again about the dreams—everything you can remember."

The conference went on for over an hour. At the end of that time, David felt as if he'd been put through an ordeal, which he had. His face shone with perspiration, and finally he said in an unsteady voice, "I don't want to talk about those dreams anymore."

"No, I can see that—and that is why you go off into this place you speak of. . .why you leave this world and go to another."

David started at the doctor's choice of words. "What's the

matter with me?" he asked hoarsely.

"There's something in your life that you cannot face up to," Steiner said slowly. "Most of us have things like that. Sometimes we hide them in some place and nobody ever knows about it." He shrugged his burly shoulders and tapped his fingertips together in an almost effeminate gesture, strangely incongruous to the massive strength of the hands. "What is it that you are hiding?"

"I'm not hiding anything," David said stiffly. "I've told you everything."

A silence fell across the room. The walls were well insulated and there was no outside sound at all. *It's like,* David thought, *being entombed.* He insisted, over and over again, that he was hiding nothing, but Steiner kept prying. Finally, David grew angry. "This is not helping! Don't you have medicine or something that will stop me from whatever this thing is?"

"No."

David blinked at the harshness of the word. He stared at the physician, who stared back at him with a steadiness that was disconcerting. "I cannot help you until you're ready to help yourself."

"I'll do anything," David insisted, his hands trembling. "I can't go on living like this."

Steiner dropped his eyes and turned to his desk. Reaching up, he pulled down a book—a rather new book, David noticed. He leafed through it, found what he was looking for, then read aloud, "'If the patient refuses to discuss his problems freely, he is hiding something. As long as he hides these things, he will not get better. He can only get worse. If he persists, the chances are great that he will fall into a condition of total insanity.'"

The words chilled David Rocklin. He swallowed hard and

couldn't answer. He heard Steiner say, "Come along; I'll show you something."

David rose, glad to get out of the room, and followed Steiner through the door. They went down a long hall and up the stairs, their footsteps echoing hollowly. When they left the landing, there was another long hall with three doors on each side. Steiner took out a key from a chain that was attached to his belt and inserted it, and it clicked solidly. "Do not be afraid," he said quietly, "but you must see this."

Pulling the huge door back, Steiner stepped inside and motioned for David to enter. At least twenty men occupied a room that must have been at least twenty feet wide and thirty feet long. They were all wearing light gray uniforms, bulky and shapeless. Two or three of them were walking rapidly back and forth from one end of the room to the other as if their lives depended on it. One of them was talking to himself or arguing with someone who wasn't there. "I tell you," he said frantically, "it wasn't my fault. You've got to forgive me, Carol...."

His voice droned on, and a horror came over David as he saw that the man was speaking to someone not there. "Come this way, over here," Steiner said. He led David through the men, whose faces all seemed pasty and dead. One of them was sitting in the middle of the floor staring down at his hands, not moving, almost like a small statue of Buddha that David had once seen. He was very fat and didn't move or speak as they passed him. It was as if he were carved out of white stone.

"Here is the man I wanted you to see."

David looked at a man who was sitting on a chair. He was of medium height, and his face was pale and heavy. His eyes were brown, and as David stared into them, he felt a shock: there was nothing behind the eyes—no mind, no thought, nothing!

"This is Henry Patton. He came to me three years ago," Steiner said quietly. "He had a successful business and a good family, was well thought of in society."

David stared at the man, who obviously heard none of what Steiner said. There was something eerie and frightening about a body with no mind. David's voice was unsteady as he asked, "What happened to him?"

"He started having mental problems," Steiner said softly. "I was called in before he fell into this condition." He looked over at the man and put a hand on his shoulder. "I tried my best, Henry," he said sadly, "but you wouldn't share your problem." He removed his hand and said, "This is what happens to those who hide from the truth. Come along now; it isn't good for you to see too much of this."

He led the way out of the room then back down the stairs. "Can you come and see me on a regular basis?"

David stared at him. "I've told you all I know."

"That's what Henry Patton said, over and over again." Steiner shook his head. "It's so tragic that there was one thing in that man's heart and mind—if he'd said it, he would have been free, but he couldn't bear to have anyone know what it was. Now you see what he's become." Steiner's face grew sterner. "I don't want to frighten you, but perhaps I should. These blackouts you've been having, they're very bad. One day you may go out and never come back."

The words echoed in David's mind. He muttered, "I'll come back," and put out his hand. Steiner shook it, and David left.

Steiner watched the door as it closed then turned back and stared up at his medical degree. "What good does it do for me to see people if they won't let me help them? Nothing in that young man is so bad that it cannot be fixed—but he won't say."

He'd seen many like this, and a hopeless despair came to his light blue eyes. He shook his head then began reading the book before him.

David left the asylum and got into the carriage. "Take me back to town."

"Yes, sir." As the cabdriver looked at David's face, he thought to himself, *That's a bad 'un. If he's got folks in there, he didn't get no good news from them.* Aloud he said, "Git up, Babe! Come on, Nancy!" and the matched bays leaped forward. As the carriage wheeled back to the city, a plume of dust rose high in the air then settled back onto the road.

CHAPTER 12

IT'S NEVER TOO LATE

Claire had been more disturbed than she liked to admit since the scene with Matthew. For two days she'd thought about little else and had slept fitfully, rising at dawn, her eyes puffy from lack of sleep.

"Don't you feel well, Claire?" Amelia asked as Claire came into the kitchen where Amelia was forming biscuits out of dough that she'd mixed.

"Oh, I'm all right—just didn't sleep well." She moved over to take down a pan, saying, "Suppose we make pancakes this morning?"

"All right. You always did make the best pancakes I ever saw."

Claire looked at her aunt with a faint smile. "It's the only thing I can make better than you can, and Lucy makes them better than any of us. But since she's off today, we'll have to be the cooks."

The two women worked on the meal. When they were almost finished, Matthew stepped into the kitchen. He glanced quickly at Claire and said, "Good morning," then moved over and looked down at the pancakes. "Special treat for me?" he asked pleasantly.

Amelia looked up and smiled. "You think everything's for you. I remember you used to promise me anything to get me to make you a blackberry cobbler. Do you still like them?"

"I haven't had any in a long time, not good ones like yours," Matthew said, seeming preoccupied. "I'm going to town after breakfast. Can I bring you anything back?"

"Yes," Amelia said. "I've heard about a book called *Leaves of Grass*. I got a letter from my friend Doris Heilman, and she says there's nothing like it."

"What kind of a book is it?" Matthew inquired.

"Oh, it's a book of poetry." She smiled and said, "I'll let you read it, if it's good. It's written by a man called Walter Whitman, a New York man. Have you heard of him?"

"No, but then, I don't read much poetry, not anymore."

Unexpectedly Claire said, "You used to read a lot of Longfellow and Whittier."

Unsmiling, Matthew answered, "Yes, I did," then left the room. Claire watched him go with a strange expression. Amelia noticed, but she said nothing.

Later they ate breakfast together, and afterward Amelia said, "I'll do the dishes since you made the pancakes." She began to gather the plates, and Matthew said, "It was a fine breakfast. Almost as good as Lucy's, but don't tell her I said so." He nodded as he rose and went to his study.

Claire ignored Amelia's protest and helped clear the table, and as they were doing the dishes, Amelia said, "It's amazing how Matthew keeps his good looks. He doesn't look any older than he did ten years ago. Some people are like that, I suppose."

"Yes," Claire murmured, "he's still fine looking. He always was."

Amelia glanced at her sharply and saw that Claire's face was tense. She wanted to inquire into Claire's problems but, knowing her niece well after staying with her for years, didn't feel it would be wise. "I think I'll go out and tend to the flowers. They need water," she said instead.

"All right, Amelia. Maybe I'll join you later."

It was an overcast August day with rain threatening from time to time but not quite coming. A strong wind unexpectedly kicked up, and finally raindrops, fat and thick, began to fall. Amelia hurried into the house, grumbling, "Here as soon as I start watering those blasted flowers, the rain comes. I think it brings it on sometimes."

Claire smiled at her but didn't answer. She was sitting on the screened-in porch reading a book, or at least holding it open. When Amelia left, she put it down on the table beside her and closed her eyes. For a long time she sat there and then got up and began to move through the house. There was little to be done, for Lucy kept the house spotless, but she was restless and created work for herself.

At noon someone knocked at the door and Claire answered it. The young deliveryman who was standing there asked, "Are you Mrs. Cleburne?"

"Yes, I am."

"A letter for you. Mr. Cleburne sent it. Said it come to his office."

"Here...." Claire searched her pocket for a coin and passed it to the young man. "Thank you." She closed the door and stepped inside, then recognized the handwriting.

Amelia, who'd also come to answer the door, stopped as she saw Claire opening the letter. When Claire's brow furrowed, she asked, "What is it?"

"It's Mother!" She looked up, trouble in her eyes. "She's very sick."

"What's wrong with her?"

"It's her heart, I think. Her old trouble." Claire stared back at the letter, which was no more than five lines long. "I think I'll have to go take care of her. There's nobody else."

"I'll go with you," Amelia said at once.

"I'm sure Matthew would be glad to keep you here."

"No, it would be awkward without you. What about Leah? Do you think she'll want to go?"

Claire's mouth tightened. "Yes, she must go. She can't stay here."

Leah received the news when Claire came to her room. She'd slept late and her hair hung about her shoulders as she listened. "Do you think it's very serious, Mother?"

"I'm sure it is. She's not one to complain. She says she needs help, and I'm afraid it's rather critical."

"I'll go with you, of course," Leah said at once. She'd never liked it around Chattanooga at her grandmother's house, but she had a strong sense of loyalty and knew she couldn't desert her mother. "When do you think we'll be leaving?"

"I'll ask Matthew to make the arrangements," Claire said.

***

That night after supper Matthew waited until Amelia and Leah had gone up to their rooms to pack. Then he said, "Claire, I'd like to speak with you."

"Why—of course."

"Come into the parlor. It's quieter in there."

Puzzled, Claire moved to the parlor, and he followed her.

She turned to him, expecting he'd have something to say about the arrangements for the trip. Instead, he said, "Claire, I want you to consider coming back here when you're sure your mother is all right."

Claire's eyes opened with surprise. "That's very kind of you, Matthew, but then, you always were thoughtful of our needs."

Matthew shook his head. "I don't mean what you think." He was a tall man and she only of moderate height, so she was forced to look up at him. His blue eyes were utterly serious as he said evenly, "I still love you, Claire."

His words so shocked Claire that she couldn't think what to say for a moment. She opened her lips slightly, but the words that came weren't suitable. For a flickering instant, she thought again how handsome he was. Still, she said only, "That's all passed, Matthew."

"Not for me. Tell me," he said, stepping closer to her, his voice low and intense, "did you ever love me, Claire?"

"You know I did." Her voice was low and she couldn't meet his eyes.

"I thought so. I thought that very few people ever had a love like we had. I think of those times every day." He fell silent for a moment then admitted, "I don't think there's been a day I haven't thought of our early years together. They were the best years of my life. Nothing's been right since you left."

"Oh, Matthew, we've been through all this...!"

"Have we? I don't think so." He thought of the bitterness and the separation, and his cheeks twitched at the sharpness of the memory. "Are you happy? If you loved me once, is there anything left of it?" He waited, looked down into her face, and saw that his words had disturbed her greatly. She had a natural control that had increased over the years so that she'd become difficult to read. Yet now her lips trembled slightly and her gray eyes masked something she didn't want revealed. "If there's anything at all left in you, any kind of love or affection for me, please tell me, Claire," he pleaded.

Knowing it took great courage for this strong man to beg her, Claire felt something akin to pity. She also thought of those early days and the sleepless nights she'd had since their last encounter. Then the old bitterness came over her. "That's all over, Matthew," she said firmly. "You can't go back to what things once were."

Standing before her, Matthew squared his shoulders and waited. He was silent so long that she wondered if he'd ever speak. Finally, he sighed. "I've always hoped that somehow we would get over our difficulties. I thought that no matter how bad they were, somehow we'd find a way through them and come together again. That's been my dream," he said softly, pain and regret in his eyes. "I guess you'll never change."

"Matthew, I wish it didn't have to be like this, but we can't go back again."

He studied her carefully and then said, "I'll make arrangements for your trip."

❧

Brian Decatur took the news with a mixture of disappointment and frustration. "Chattanooga? That's no place for you to be going!" he exclaimed when Leah told him of their plans. "Why, the war is moving there! Braxton Bragg's got the Army of the Tennessee lined up, and I'm headed there right now along with Rosecrans's army. It may be the biggest battle of the war. You *can't* go there!"

"We've got to go. My grandmother's very ill."

Decatur had been shocked but then finally said, "Well, at least we'll be in the same part of the world."

"But I'll be on the Confederate side. You won't be able to come courting there," Leah said with a smile.

Brian Decatur, a self-confident young man, took her hand and kissed it. "I told you once, Leah, I'm a very stubborn fellow. Don't be surprised if you don't look up someday and see a young Union lieutenant coming up to the front door of your house."

Leah had laughed and allowed him to kiss her. Later she reported to her mother as they were packing, "The lieutenant is threatening to come calling in Tennessee—along with about forty thousand others of the Army of the Cumberland."

Claire turned, holding a dress she was packing in a trunk. "How do you feel about him? You've never really said."

"Oh, I don't know, Mother. It's not the time to think of such things. He's Union and we're Confederate. I don't see any good ending to that."

Claire stared at her daughter, suddenly swept with doubt. "These are hard times, aren't they, Leah?" The doubt and despair in her voice drew Leah's attention. She looked at her mother for a moment, studying her carefully. She was well aware that living in Matthew Cleburne's house had been a strain to all of them but especially to her mother.

Tentatively she picked up a blouse and folded it mechanically, then handed it to her mother. "Have you ever thought you and Father might. . . ?"

Claire looked up quickly. When she saw the hope in her daughter's eyes, she said at once briskly, "No, I don't think that could ever happen." As the expression in Leah's eyes faded, Claire returned to the packing, thinking, *I can't let her think like that. It would bring nothing but disappointment.*

⁂

Many days later the three women stepped out of a carriage as Claire paid the fare. "Just bring the bags in if you will," she said to the driver, then turned to look at the house. "It hasn't changed," she said as the three moved down the walk. "I grew up in this place. It has lots of memories."

Amelia said nothing, for she was depressed at the sight of the place. She had stayed here for short visits with Claire and hadn't been happy. It was not the kind of country she liked, although the mountains were beautiful. She wished they were back in New York.

As they entered the house, they were greeted by a black woman who threw her arms around Claire. "I so glad you're back, Miss Claire. Yore mama needs you bad."

"How is she, Bessie?"

"She ain't no good," Bessie, a tall, angular woman with white hair and chocolate-colored skin, responded. "She ain't no good at all, Miss Claire. She gonna be with the Lord purty soon."

Leah felt compressed, as if she'd been put into a box and was being squeezed. She'd spent summers at this house and they'd been bearable. Now, however, with the shadow of war hanging over Chattanooga, she knew nothing pleasant or good was going to happen. She accompanied her mother and Amelia to the sickroom, where all three were shocked by the frailness of the woman who lay in bed. Death was written on her features, and her voice was feeble. Claire said, "You're going to be all right, Mother," trying to keep her voice cheerful.

GILBERT MORRIS

Later Leah thought, with a sharp regret, of her father's house in New York: the busyness, the activity of that city. She thought, too, of Brian Decatur and wondered if he was as stubborn as he claimed to be.

PART THREE
Chickamauga

CHAPTER 13

A RASH DECISION

Hearing footsteps on the back porch, Bernard Dixon set down his coffee cup, rose from his chair, and left the library. He passed through the kitchen, where Dinah, the Dixon cook, was cutting a chicken into pieces, then saw Corey enter with a cotton sack in his hand. "Hello, Corey," he said. "Where have you been?"

"I been out looking for some herbs, sah."

"Oh! You're an herb master, are you?"

"Well, sah, I done study it a little bit. Some folks say I was right good at it."

"I had an aunt who lived in Tennessee. I swear she knew every bush and herb in the world. Some of them did good, too. Let's see what you've got."

Dinah came over to watch as Corey unloaded his bag, laying various leaves and bunches of grass and vines on the kitchen table, explaining them carefully. "This here is saffron—good for measles, and it ain't bad for fever either. This is saxifrage—it cures infected eyes; and this one is neat stone for stomach problems...."

Dixon examined the herbs skeptically then said, "Come out

to the backyard, Corey."

"Yes, sah."

Corey followed the trim young man outside, stopping when Dixon turned to face him. "I really am worried about your master, Corey. He's getting worse, isn't he?"

Corey met Dixon's eyes squarely then shrugged his muscular shoulders. "Yes, sah, he is. He has bad dreams every night." Dinah had fixed Corey a pallet on the floor beside David's bed, and now as he thought of the nights that had passed, he shook his head dolefully. "I 'spect these herbs ain't gonna help Mr. David. What's wrong with him ain't in the body."

"No, it's all mental. I wish it *were* a physical wound. It would have been better if he'd been shot in the leg or shoulder. Those wounds heal up." Dixon shifted his feet to watch a young mockingbird as it teetered on a clothesline. Just then a black cat with white breast and four stocking feet began slinking across the yard. Suddenly the mother mockingbird swooped down out of a pear tree and rapidly pecked the huge tom on the head. The cat blinked, shut his eyes, then fled the barrage in disgrace.

"That stupid cat will never learn," Dixon observed mildly then turned his attention back to the slave. "Has he said anything to you about the doctor he went to see at the asylum?"

Corey shifted his weight uneasily then shook his head. "Well, sah, he did say the doctor didn't give him much hope."

"I think he ought to go home."

"That's what I told him, Mr. Dixon," Corey said energetically. He was wearing a pair of cast-off brown trousers somewhat too large for him and a blue cotton shirt open at the neck. He pushed the sleeves up nervously before continuing. "I done told him that, sah. Man in his condition needs to be with his people. From what he done told me, they a mighty fine family."

"They are. The Rocklins are the finest people I know," Dixon responded. "Look, I'll try to talk to him, Corey. I know he's mighty low, but we mustn't give up hope."

"No, sah!"

Dixon left the yard and reentered the house. He ascended the stairs, stopped before the door to David's bedroom, and knocked. "Dave? Are you up?"

"Come in."

Bernard entered to find David sitting in a straight chair, a book on his lap unopened. He was staring out the window, and only slowly did he turn his head, as if it were an effort. "Hello, Bernard. Sit down."

Bernard pulled a chair away from the wall and sat down across from Rocklin. As he did so, he noticed the wan, drawn expression on his friend's face. David had always been physically strong, Bernard remembered, but now he was losing weight rapidly because he had no appetite. Instead of talking about the problem, Bernard began by discussing the military situation of the two countries. "I've been reading the papers, Dave," he said. "It looks like everything's changed since Vicksburg fell and Lee was beaten at Gettysburg."

He waited a moment for a reply, but David merely sat there loosely, his muscles lax, his lips drawn together tightly. Bernard hurried on, saying, "It looks like the action is going to be somewhere in Tennessee now that Grant's won at Vicksburg. Port Hudson's fallen, too. The Mississippi River belongs to the Union." He frowned, and despair touched his clean-cut features. "They've got the Mississippi now—cut the Confederacy right in two. Now we can expect them to hit some other targets closer to home."

David appeared not to have heard. He was staring intently

out the window, and Bernard moved slightly to follow Rocklin's gaze. Across the street a young woman in a yellow dress with a white broad-brimmed hat was moving around a flower garden. Although the flowers were faded, she was trying to coax some last bit of color from the small plot of ground. Her yellow dress made a bright splash against the light brown grass, which had died early from lack of rain, and as she looked up, Bernard said, "That's Helen Raines. She was engaged to marry Tony Hardin, but Tony got killed at Antietam." He waited for a reply but, receiving none, went on. "Well, I look for the Federals to hit in Tennessee—at least that's what Father says. He says that Chattanooga's on the main east-west railroad line and that if the Yankees can cut that, it'll leave our men there without supplies. Then, too, Lincoln's always wanted to do something about Knoxville. Lots of Union folks there."

A fly moved about the room humming briskly, then lighted on Bernard's forehead. He slapped at it. "Blasted flies! I don't know why we can't keep them out of the house." He looked then at David and saw that he was getting nowhere. Leaning forward, he put his hand on David's shoulder and shook him, drawing the young man's attention. "Dave!" he said in a different tone, now totally serious. "Let's talk about this. . .problem you have."

David shook his head, and there was a dead quality in his voice as he said, "Nothing to talk about, Bernard. . . . It's not the kind of thing the doctors can do anything about."

"It may pass away like it came," Bernard insisted, his great affection for David Rocklin evident. "Look, I'm not trying to get rid of you, Dave. You know that. We'd be glad to have you stay here as long as you like." He hesitated, running a hand through his sandy hair. "But I think you ought to go home.

When a fellow has trouble, he needs to be with his people, and I know your family would help you."

"I can't let them see me like this." David's statement was tinged with an underlying current of despair.

"Why, they won't think less of you, Dave."

"No. I just can't do it, Bernard." David got up and moved about the room nervously, looking down at the circles containing pale pink flowers in the carpet under his feet. He lifted his eyes then and stared blankly at the pictures of dogs and cats on the wall. Then he said flatly, "If I'm in your way, I'll leave. But I can't go home, not till I get this thing whipped."

Instantly Bernard rose and clapped his arm around David's shoulders. "There's no question of that," he protested. "Stay as long as you like. I'm believing this thing will go away. You're not going back to see that doctor anymore?"

"No, there's nothing he can do."

"I tell you what. We'll go out on the town tonight. There's a new play that might be amusing."

"All right, if you like."

Bernard hesitated then said, "We'll leave about five, go out and have a good supper. It'll take your mind off. . .your troubles."

As Dixon left David's room and descended the stairs, Corey came out of the kitchen, asking at once, "Did you talk to him, Mr. Dixon?"

"He won't go home, at least not now." Dixon's brow wrinkled. "I wish he would. It would be the best thing for him. But he's a stubborn fellow."

༄

It was already mid-August. The trees had lost their spring greenness and were beginning to be tinged with the heat that late summer brings. The grass died slowly each day as fall loomed somewhere beyond the horizon. Fall was a time David Rocklin usually loved—the crispness of it, the smell of the earth, the sharp bite of the wind—but now the reminder of its coming depressed him. On Sunday morning he went to church dutifully with the Dixon family. He sat in the pew and listened as the minister announced the subject: "'As it is appointed unto men once to die, but after this the judgment.'"

It was a fine sermon, well organized, filled with scriptures that underlined the main points, and preached with vivid illustrations. But as David sat on the hard pew, bolt upright, he heard echoes of his own mortality. Perhaps it was connected somehow to the approach of winter. Always he was conscious of the terrible dreams and blackouts that came to torment him.

Even as he sat there, he felt himself receding and prayed, *Oh God, don't let me pass out, not here!* He threw his will against the coming of the blackness. It was almost as if he were being sucked down into an ebony pool, and he struggled against it, not moving a muscle but with a terrible spiritual clash of his will against whatever it was that drew him into nothingness.

When the benediction was finally announced, he rose and kept his hands half concealed so Dixon wouldn't see they were trembling. He wiped his face quickly with a clean white handkerchief and shook hands with the minister, murmuring, "Thank you very much," mindlessly. He sat in the carriage on the way home, listening to the family discuss the sermon. Although there were several attempts to draw him into the conversation, he said almost nothing. His presence, he knew, was a burden on the others, and he thought, *I've got to get away! I can't impose any longer on these people....*

The following Tuesday he was still wrestling with the

problem of what to do and had begun a difficult letter home. Masking his true condition, he kept up the pretense that he was suffering with a physical affliction and would come home as soon as he could. But filled with disgust at his own prevarication, he left the letter unfinished and went down to the main streets of Atlanta, unable to bear his own solitude. After some time he entered a small café, where the proprietor, a short, muscular man with a drooping gray mustache, took his order. He wasn't hungry but ordered coffee and pie for the privilege of sitting at the table. It was a small restaurant, and he sipped the coffee slowly, ignoring the other customers. His mind beat inside his brain like a bird trapped in a box, moving from one impossibility to another. Still, there was no peace nor even a glimmer of a solution for him.

Slowly he became aware of a loud voice coming from his right. Turning his head slightly, he saw a tall, rawboned sergeant with a shock of black hair and a ferocious beard that bristled wildly. He was not old, not over thirty, but there was a rough-hewn quality about him that suggested a hard life. The coffee cup in his hand was dwarfed by the size of his huge paws—hands of a man who had done hard labor. David listened as one of the men beside him asked, "What was it like there at Gettysburg, Rafe?"

"Why, it was purely out of the pit."

David had heard from his grandmother that his uncle Gideon had been captured at Gettysburg and was in a Confederate prison in Richmond. David had been tremendously relieved to discover that Clay and Dent had not been killed or even wounded, despite the terrible battle.

Rafe's loud, raspy voice continued. Here was a man who clearly enjoyed an audience. He sipped the coffee with a noisy slurping sound then sighed in appreciation. "Aaaah! Now I ain't had no good coffee like that for nigh onto two years 'cept that which I liberated." He winked, and a laugh ran around the civilians who listened to the soldier. "What was it like? Why, it was pure perdition. That's what it was like."

"What outfit was you with, Rafe?"

"I was in with Pickett."

One of his listeners, a smallish man wearing a neat black suit with a string tie to match, picked up on that. "I heard about that charge. I don't see how men stood up to it. Was it as bad as I heard?"

"I dunno what you heard, but it was the wust I seed—and I been in since Bull Run." Rafe slurped his coffee again, picked up a pork chop with his hand, and tore off a bite with strong white teeth. He seemed not to chew at all but swallowed it almost in its native condition. He held the bone, stared at it contemplatively, then clawed at his whiskers with his free hand. "I dunno as I'd ever want to do a thing like that again."

"Tell us about it, Sergeant," one of the onlookers, a young man not over seventeen, said. His eyes were bright, and he leaned forward toward the rawboned sergeant. "That must have been something. All that advance by Pickett."

Rafe stared at the young man thoughtfully. "I reckon people got funny ideas about what war's like," he said almost roughly. "I did myself. I always thought it'd be like in a picture—some big plain somewhere and two armies marching toward each other out in the clear where you can see everything." He shook his head almost in disgust. " 'Taint like that, though. Most of the times you're in the woods. . .can't see no further than ten feet away. Then after the first volley, the smoke's so thick you can't see *five* feet away. Sometimes you shoot your own fellers or they shoot you. You don't never see no battles. All you see's the ten feet away."

"But it wasn't like that at Gettysburg, was it?" the small, neatly dressed man persisted.

"No, it warn't. That was different." Rafe leaned back in his chair fingering the coffee cup, and a peculiar expression stiffened his face. His voice grew somewhat harsher as he growled, "We all lined up. There was this big field and a hill right in front of us. Right up on top of that hill was the Yankees. They must have had a thousand artillery pieces up there, probably ten thousand men, all with a loaded musket. They was behind a fence, lots of 'em were, and there we was, ready to march right into that."

"Why'd you do it? It sounds like suicide to me." A burly man with pale gray eyes and thick reddish-brown hair spoke. "Don't sound like good tactics to me."

"Looking back, I don't see that it was, mister, but General Lee, he said, 'Go.' I heered that Longstreet didn't want to go at all and was late gettin' up—but there we was, and General Pickett, he rode up and down on that fine hoss of his tellin' us that we was all Virginians. 'Course, I wasn't no Virginian, but I took it all in anyhow." He hesitated, sipped his coffee once again noisily, then shook his head. "We all stepped out, started out across that field all in order, line after line. The flags was whippin', and you could hear the officers barkin' like hounds, gettin' their men to form their lines right. The grass was green that day; I remember that. Pretty farming country, it was. There was a bunch of the prettiest cows I ever saw when we started across that field. They all run off scared when they saw us coming."

"How far was it from where you had to go up to the top of that hill?"

"I guess most half a mile mebbe, and there was a big ditch

right across in front of us. We had to break our lines, crawl across that ditch, and reform."

"Was the Yankees shootin' at ya?"

"Not hardly; they was just waitin'," Rafe said grimly, "and we knew it, too. They was just waitin' for one volley. I was right in the front of our line, and I knowed whut was comin'. I heard the fellow next to me, a corporal named Patterson, say, 'Lord, for what we're about to receive, may we be duly grateful. . . !'" Rafe's eyes grew small, and he continued, "He went down the first volley—throat shot plumb away. Good man. . .was from Alabama."

Rafe continued telling how the lines had advanced, and David found himself caught up in the story. He turned his chair around without pretense, listening as the soldier continued. He'd heard some stories of battles from his father and brothers, but somehow this particular incident caught his attention.

"And that's the way it was when we was no farther than fifty feet away. They opened up with the guns—they just tore huge holes in our lines—and the muskets, they all went off. As soon as they fired once, them men stepped back to reload and another line stepped in place. It wasn't no way to escape. I dunno yet how they missed me," Rafe said almost hoarsely. "On both sides of me my buddies went down—good friends. I got to where I didn't even care if I got kilt. I was so mad at the Yankees! I was screaming and hollering." He laughed almost gutturally. "I remember I was hollering, 'Come on and kill me! See if you can!' I expected it, too."

A silence fell across his listeners, and the neatly dressed man said solemnly, "I don't see how men can go in to face certain death like that. They had no chance at all."

"Me nuther," the sergeant remarked, shrugging. "I don't

CHARIOTS IN THE SMOKE

know whut makes a man do a thing like that. I couldn't do it right now by myself. But when you're in a line like that, there's fellers on both sides of you and fellers behind you. You just can't stop even though you know you're gonna get kilt. Somehow you got to go on." He looked down at his empty cup then ran his gaze around the small circle of men and said with a note of finality, "After all, when you're dead, all your troubles are over with. I reckon that's part of why men are able to go right up into the lion's mouth like we done at Gettysburg."

For David, the sergeant's words seemed to be framed in large black letters: *"When you're dead, all your troubles are over...."* Over and over the words repeated themselves, like an echo coming back from a long distance that faded finally into a whisper and insistently tapped at his brain.

David never knew how long he sat there. Finally, he got up, paid his bill, and walked out of the restaurant. Evening was coming on, the light in the east fading and turning to a murkiness as the sun began to sink. He walked slowly along the streets, unaware of his surroundings. Wagons bumped down the cobblestone pavement, the horses chuffing and hooves clattering against the stones. There was a murmur of talk from a group he passed, but this was all outside him. Inside he felt a strange, fatalistic peace. He reached the residential areas then slowed his steps under the large oak trees that met overhead, forming a canopy. There was almost a cathedral atmosphere at this time of twilight, and he walked on until the light faded completely. Finally, he found himself far from the Dixon house, almost at the outskirts of the city. He had no desire to return, but as the darkness closed around him, he turned and made his way back.

The sable darkness brought out night birds, swifts tumbling in the sky, and then finally the shudder of black wings as bats feasted on mosquitoes and bugs.

Silence enveloped David Rocklin as he shut out the scenes that broke through his senses. He heard again the sergeant's words, this time in a gentle whisper: *"When you're dead, all your troubles are over. . . ."* For hours he walked. Finally, when he knew the Dixons would be in bed, he returned and went up to his room. Being as quiet as possible, he undressed and lay down on the bed. He put his head on the pillow and stared up in the stygian darkness of the room, darkness broken only by faint moonlight that filtered through his window.

With startling clarity a thought came to him with such force that he sat up on the bed and clenched his fists together as his mind reacted strongly.

"Of course!" he said softly, breaking the quietness of the room. The thought grew in his mind until it became almost palpable. A grim smile touched his lips. "I don't know why I didn't think of it before."

He felt strangely relieved after the pressures that had literally crushed him. He rose, moved to the window, and stared down on the earth across the yards and at the streets vaguely outlined by the pale moonlight. It was so simple! *All I have to do is join the army, get in a fighting outfit, and when they charge, put myself at the front of it. Maybe I'll be a color-bearer. They always go for those fellows first. If they shoot me in the leg, I'll hobble on, standing up until they finish the job.*

For a long time David Rocklin stood there, his eyes fixed on nothing, as he thought about the solution to his problem. *I've been a coward,* he thought, *afraid of bayonets. I've run away in battle, but nothing's worse than what's happening to me. I'd rather be dead anytime!*

Finally, he went back and lay down on the bed, knowing

CHARIOTS IN THE SMOKE

what he must do. It didn't seem cowardly to him, because he would fight as best he could. Many of his friends and neighbors from home had died on the field of battle.

I can die as well as they can, he thought, *and when they kill me—why, my troubles will be over!*

Chapter 14

The Army of the Tennessee

Perhaps if David's dire symptoms had left after he'd made his decision to seek death at the cannon's mouth, he might have changed his mind. However, the next day after he'd firmly decided to end his life honorably by throwing himself into the fury of battle, he suffered one of his blackouts. Fortunately, Corey was there to watch over him, and it lasted less than half a day so that the Dixons weren't even aware of it.

The result of this, however, was that David's resolve was hardened. He spent the next day writing letters to his grandmother, to his father and brothers, and to other family members and friends. His letter to his grandmother was the one that gave him the most difficulty. He made several drafts and finally in desperation wrote:

Dear Grandmother,
 I know you'll be surprised to learn I'm in the army again. As you know, I have not been eager to rush into this war, but now for many reasons I feel I must do so. You might expect that I would come home and join the Army of Northern Virginia, but somehow I feel I cannot do this.

CHARIOTS IN THE SMOKE

I wish I could come home and see you before I enlist, for as you know, leave is sometimes difficult to obtain. However, I feel so strongly about this that I am leaving for Tennessee tomorrow. I am sending this letter back by Corey, the slave I've told you about. He has proven himself faithful and loyal beyond all my expectations. If anything should happen to me, please see he is set free at once. In any case, I have promised him that after one year he will be freed.

David went ahead to express his gratitude for the many good years that his family had provided for him, thanking his parents from the bottom of his heart for being the best any boy or young man ever had. He said things he'd been reluctant to express aloud and finally closed by saying:

It may not be that we shall meet again on this earth. I do not want to grieve you by speaking of this, but you both know this is a possibility for all in our army. If I do not return, do not grieve for me. I go knowing Jesus Christ as my Savior. This you taught me as a boy, and although I have not served God as faithfully as I should have liked, still I am confident I stand under God's merciful hand.
Your dutiful and loving son,
David Rocklin

The best part of two days went by before he had all the letters finished and ready to mail. It was his plan to have Corey take them back to Virginia, but he encountered a stubbornness that took him unawares. It began when he took Corey aside and explained what he intended to do. Corey listened, his eyes fixed on David as he explained that he'd be leaving to join the Army of the Tennessee and that Corey was to go at once to Virginia.

"I've got everything ready, Corey." David pulled an envelope from his pocket. "Here are the papers showing you belong to me. They'll be honored by any who stop you. I have included evidence that my father and brothers are officers in the Army of Northern Virginia. I've also included plenty of money for your transportation and for food along the way. I want you to give this letter to my parents when you get there."

"No, sah, I won't do it."

David blinked with surprise. "What did you say?"

"I said, Mr. David, I ain't goin' to Virginia."

"But—"

"No, sah, I'm going with you to the army. You bought me and I'm gonna be with you."

A warm shock ran along David's nerves, for this kind of loyalty certainly couldn't be bought. "Why, Corey, that's fine of you," he said with a smile. He put his hand on the tall slave's shoulder then said, "Really, it's the best thing for you to go back." He wanted to tell Corey more, but his secret couldn't be shared with anyone. However, Corey was staring at him with suspicion in his brown eyes as David said hurriedly, "I'll be all right. You go on home now and in a year you'll be free. Maybe we can help you buy a farm there. Anyhow, you'll be free."

When Corey started to argue, David snapped, "I'm telling you, you're going back to Virginia and don't argue with me!" He hardened his expression harshly. "I appreciate your offer, but it's got to be this way. Now take this and don't argue anymore." He thrust the envelope containing the money and the letter to his parents in Corey's hand and turned and walked away.

That evening at supper he told the Dixons he'd be leaving.

"You going back to Virginia?" Bernard asked. "I think that's wise."

CHARIOTS IN THE SMOKE

David avoided the question. He expressed his gratitude to all the family. "You've been so kind to me. I don't know how to thank you."

"Why, it's nothing at all," Bernard said warmly. "You tell your family when you get home that we're expecting them to take good care of you."

"Why, of course," Mrs. Dixon said. "You'll be all right when you get home among your people."

Later that night, just before bedtime, David had a farewell word for Bernard. He shook his hand, saying warmly, "You're one in a million, Bernard. Can't tell you how much you've done for me or what it means to me. I'll be leaving early, so we'll say our good-byes now."

Bernard was immensely relieved by the decision he assumed David had made. Shaking his hand, he reached around and clapped him on the shoulder. "I've been worried sick about you, David, but God's going to be with you. He's the Healer, you know, and He can heal a mind as well as a body. You'll write?"

"I'll write!" David said.

The train that left Atlanta heading north was scheduled to leave at four fifteen in the morning. David had made arrangements to borrow a horse and leave it with the station agent, who was a special friend of the Dixons. He slept poorly but had no nightmares that night. At three o'clock, he rose, dressed, and packed his few belongings. He left the house quietly, moved to the barn, and saddled the gelding, patting him on the neck and leading him out of the small barn behind the Dixons' house. He swung into the saddle and walked the horse out into the road, then headed toward the south part of Atlanta where the train waited.

Stars were still twinkling overhead as he moved along. A quietness hung over the city, and all seemed asleep. He felt a strangeness in the air as he swayed with the movement of the gelding. He thought of many things, flashes of his time at Vicksburg...and of his times with Leah. She'd been driven from his mind by his mental lapses, but now as he saw his life as a book with only a few pages left to turn, his mind went back to her. He saw her face suddenly in his memory, oval, with alert greenish eyes and the red hair that always shone gold in the sun. He thought of the faint odor of lilacs that always hung about her and the firmness of her body as he'd held her and kissed her.

Then he shook his head, murmuring, "I've got to put all that behind me now."

He'd gone approximately halfway through town when he was aware of soft noises behind him. It was still dark, and only a faint light from the sky touched the earth, for the moon was hidden behind skeins of clouds that scudded across the velvet blackness. Here and there a star or two put its feeble light over the city streets, and only rarely did a gaslight offer a pale gleam.

David's hearing was better than most, and he was sure he heard something or someone behind him. He thought of a thief and slipped his hand into the saddlebag where he kept the Navy Colt. Pulling it out, he tried to remember if it was fully loaded but could not. He rolled the cylinder, feeling it with his hand, and the heft of it told him there were loads. Suddenly he wheeled the horse around and drove his heels into its sides. The gelding snorted wildly then half reared. David kicked him again and leaned over his neck as the horse thundered back at a dead run. He hadn't gone more than fifty yards when he saw a form ducking to one side.

"Hold it!" he said, throwing the Colt down and pulling the horse to a shuddering halt. "Don't move or I'll shoot!"

The shadowy figure made no answer. David gathered the reins more firmly then moved the horse closer to the man who stood waiting for him. He was a tall man, but that was all David could see as he held the pistol on half-cock. "Why are you following me?" he said.

"It's me, sah...Corey!"

David's teeth clicked together. "What are you doing here?" he demanded.

"I told you, I'm goin' with you, Mr. David."

David slipped off the horse, took the pistol off half-cock, and shoved it back into the saddlebag. Then he turned to Corey, coming close enough to see the slave's face in the dim starlight. "You fool!" he said angrily. "I told you what to do. You're not free yet. You go on back to the house."

"No, sah, I ain't goin'." Corey's voice was so calm and even that David knew any argument was useless. "I'm goin' with you, Mr. David. You done bought me and you done promised me my freedom. Until that time comes, I'm your man."

"But I'm going to join the army. You can't go with me."

"I don't know much 'bout no army, but I know some of the men take their body servants with 'em, and that's what I'm gonna be. I'm gonna do your cookin' and take care of your uniform and your gun, and if you get hurt, I'm gonna take care of you. And if you get kilt, I'm gonna take your body back to Virginia to your family."

David stood there transfixed. Finally, he pulled off his hat, ran his fingers through his hair, wildly trying to think of a better argument. Then the last remark Corey had made, "If you get kilt, I'm gonna take your body back to Virginia to your family," caught him.

He thought swiftly, *Pa and Grandmother would like that. It won't mean anything to me, but it'd mean a lot to them.* He jammed his hat back on his head, settled it firmly, then muttered with a smile, "You're the stubbornest man I ever saw."

Corey saw the smile and knew he'd won. "I guess we'd better get goin', Mr. David. It's a long way to Tennessee, ain't it?"

"Pretty far. Well, if you've got to do it, let's go." He moved to the horse, swung on, and kicked his foot free. "Put your foot in there and get on behind me."

Instantly Corey was behind him. He was carrying a sack containing his possessions in his left hand, and with his right he held on to David's waist.

"You're a stubborn fool, Corey," David said again. "Don't you know that people besides soldiers get killed in battles?"

"Ain't nothin' gonna happen to me," Corey said. "Now let's get goin', Mr. David."

David, for the first time since his illness, laughed. It was a soft sound on the air, and he was amazed to find he had any laughter left in him. But Corey's gesture had disarmed him. He'd been so concerned with his own problems that he hadn't thought of anything else. Now as the horse moved along at a fast walk, he thought, *This man is what we've been trying to own in the South. It'll be a good thing when it all stops. I won't see it, but men like Corey will be free someday.*

The two men swayed with the movement of the gelding and soon saw the lights of the station far down the road. An aureole circled the gaslights outside, and David commented, "There it is, Corey. It won't be long till we'll be in Tennessee."

"Yes, sah, I guess that's right."

Chapter 15

Shock of Battle

After the trying times at Vicksburg and the bustle of activity in New York City, life on a farm outside of Chattanooga was placid and almost dull to Leah. She spent a great deal of time strolling through the woods as September came, and all the battles seemed far away. She heard with regularity from Brian Decatur, who informed her that the Army of the Cumberland was on the move at last and headed for Tennessee. "I told you I was a stubborn fellow," he said in his letter, and she smiled as he insisted, "I'm going to be hard for you to get rid of, Leah. You might as well get used to having me around, for I intend to be with you for a lifetime!"

Leah read his letters, for the most part, to Claire, who listened with mild interest. Once she asked, "Do you feel anything for him, Leah?"

"He's entertaining and a fine young man," Leah said. "I don't know if it will ever go past that."

She said as much to Amelia, who shook her head, saying, "I doubt if you'll ever think of marrying a Yankee. They're different from us, Leah."

Claire spent a great deal of time nursing her mother.

Martha Rayborn had been ill before, but this time Claire had seen almost at once that her mother was in worse condition than she'd imagined. Martha's face was drawn and sunken, and the dullness in her eyes frightened Claire. She spent long hours sitting beside her mother's bed and was surprised when her mother, whose habit was not to dwell on the past, wanted to speak of those days long ago. Somewhat to Claire's surprise, her mother didn't speak a great deal of her husband, Thaddeus.

Finally, late one afternoon, Claire asked her, "Tell me some more about Father." As the sun streamed down in golden bars through the window, it fell upon her mother's face, emphasizing the gauntness of the stricken features and making the sunken eyes even more cavernous. At Claire's question, the pale lips drew more tightly together. "What do you want to know about him, Claire?" Martha Rayborn asked, her voice flat and unemotional.

"Why, I think about him so much. . .how he used to take me places and how he was always so good to me. I remember how people would come to the house," Claire said dreamily, "famous people, anxious to meet him. I thought there was nobody like him. I still think that."

A fly buzzed in the room with an insistent drone, landing on the sick woman's forehead, but Martha Rayborn didn't have the strength to brush it away. As Claire fanned it away with a folded newspaper, she seemed deep in thought but finally murmured, "He was admired by everyone. I've kept all the letters from the president and the senators. He even received a letter from Henry Ward Beecher, the famous preacher, commending him for his work." Claire leaned forward, her face intent and still. "Tell me about your courtship. You've never said much about it, Mother. Was he romantic?"

"No, not really. There was a—a magnetism to your father. When he came into a room, nobody could look at anyone else, and I was the same. I was so young, and I was shocked when he began to court me. I couldn't believe that of all the women in the world, he'd be interested in me. There were others more beautiful, more charming, and certainly more rich. Some of the most prominent young women in the land practically threw themselves at him."

"When did you fall in love with him?"

Martha's eyes half shut, and she didn't speak for a moment. Finally, she said slowly, "I don't know as I would call it that. It wasn't like in the romances. I admired him and thought he was a great man...and he *was* great in his way."

Something in her mother's voice caught Claire's attention. "What do you mean, Mother? Didn't you have a good marriage? I thought it was wonderful."

"You only saw it from a child's eyes. Your father was gone a lot of the time. He was very busy, very popular, with everyone seeking his attention...." Martha talked for a while, and then her eyes opened and she examined her daughter with a strange curiosity. "You've always been enamored of your father, Claire—too much so, I think sometimes."

"Why, Mother! How can you say that?"

"He wasn't a saint. He had his faults."

"Why, we all have our faults. But he was good to us."

Martha Rayborn hesitated then said slowly, "I may have done you an injustice, daughter." Seeing a look of incomprehension on Claire's face, she breathed heavily as if drawing on some inner resources. A spasm of pain took her and she closed her eyes for a moment, clasping at the coverlet with her skeletal fingers. She waited until it passed then breathed carefully.

These spasms always left her with the feeling her heart was made of fragile crystal and the slightest shock could destroy it in a moment. When she'd regained her strength, she said, "My time is short—oh, don't bother, Claire; we both know I can't live long in this condition. I've had a lot of time to think, and there's something I want to tell you."

Claire loved her mother and hated to see her suffer so. "What is it?" she asked quietly, picking up her mother's hand.

"It's about your father. I have to tell you something. . . something you won't like and may not even believe."

A cold wind blew through Claire. She'd never been able to listen to criticism of her father from anyone, and now, with it coming from her mother, she had a sudden urge to turn and leave the room. But she knew that she mustn't. "Go ahead, tell me," she said, holding her mother's cold hand tightly as if to ward off a blow.

"Your father was one man in the public eye and quite another in his private life. He was unkind to me. He never loved me as I wanted to be loved—"

"What do you mean 'unkind'? What did he do?" Claire asked, bewildered. She'd never seen this in her parents. Their relationship had been formal, but she'd assumed that was merely their public appearance.

"He was cruel in many ways. Some of them were of the mind. He verbally abused me, taunted me with not being what a woman should be. He said I was cold, and that was why he. . .why he went—" Martha's voice broke and tears appeared in her eyes. Her voice grew husky. "That was why he had other women."

Claire Cleburne couldn't have been more shocked if the roof had suddenly collapsed. *No!* something inside her screamed. *It can't be true—it can't be! Not Father!* As she sat there trying to assimilate what she'd heard, she couldn't speak to save her life. She released her mother's hands and clasped her own hands tightly together, for they were trembling. Her eyes were fixed on her mother's face as if searching to refute the words.

"I know—this is terrible for you, Claire. I never wanted to come between you two, so I never told you any of this. And I always hoped he would change," Martha whispered. "He never abused me physically. That would have been easier." She lay there exhausted, her eyes closed, her lips barely moving. "I'm sorry to destroy the dream you've had, but you needed to know." She opened her eyes briefly and said, "I saw how you compared Matthew to your father, and I knew I should have said something. You tried to make your husband live up to a man who never existed. It was unfair, but I was a coward and afraid to speak." And then, in the way of the very ill, without warning she abruptly closed her eyes, her breathing deepened in a ragged fashion, and she was asleep.

Claire Cleburne rose and walked blindly from the room. Her world had been shattered in a few minutes, and she couldn't think clearly. Visions of the past appeared before her, her father's face smiling and laughing. But then she thought, *I never saw him kiss my mother, not once!* She went to her room, shut the door, and fell across the bed, her body wracked with sobs.

❦

"What's the matter with Mother?" Leah asked Amelia, a puzzled tone in her voice. She was putting the finishing touches on her hair, preparing to go to a rally held in Chattanooga to encourage the soldiers. She looked over and saw that Amelia's face was noncommittal. "She hasn't said ten words in the past two days. Is it Grandmother's illness, do you think?"

Amelia, as a matter of fact, didn't think that was the case. She knew Claire too well, and besides, she'd had her own talks with Martha and knew of the scene that had taken place. "That may be so," she said guardedly. Then, preferring not to talk about it, she continued, "We'd better get all these eatables in the wagon if the soldiers are going to get any of them."

Bessie and Amelia had been baking pies, cakes, and cookies all the previous day, and now Pax, Martha's manservant, came to load them into the wagon. When everything was safely loaded, Amelia and Leah got onto the seat beside Pax. As they pulled out, Pax said, "Them soldier boys sho' is gonna enjoy them goodies you been makin', ladies. I wouldn't mind a bite myself."

Leah laughed, reached back, pulled a large box from the pile, and opened it. "Here! Try some of these cookies. I made them myself, so they're probably not as good as Bessie's or Aunt Amelia's. But you're welcome to them."

Pax opened his hand happily and bit into one of the cookies she'd put on his pink palm. "Gingersnap!" he said. "That sho' is fine, Miss Leah, and they ever' bit as good as Bessie could make. But don't you tell her I said so. . . . Giddup now, hosses, we got to go to the doin's."

When they reached Chattanooga just before noon, the city was humming with activity. Military bands played martial airs, and people from the outlying areas packed the streets.

When Leah asked a short, fat private the way to where the food would be served, he looked up and answered with a roguish grin, "I'd better 'scort you there. All these soldiers ain't the gentlemens they appear." He scrambled into the wagon, stood behind them, and pointed the way. When they arrived, he jumped down and helped Leah and Amelia, holding to Leah's hand a little longer than was absolutely necessary.

"You deserve an award, Private," Leah said and reached into a box and removed a thick slice of chocolate cake. "Sorry, no lemonade to go with it."

The soldier plopped half the cake into his mouth and mumbled, "I'll help you unload this stuff, Miss. There's the tables right over there."

Leah and Amelia joined the women who were laying out the refreshments on long tables made of planks placed across sawhorses. Leah enjoyed the frivolity of the day, and for over an hour she was besieged with soldiers hungry for female company as well as for cookies.

Later there was a speech by General Braxton Bragg. The crowd gathered down at the far end of the street to hear him, but Leah stayed at the table so she could get a clear view. "He doesn't look like much," she observed aloud, "and his speech-making isn't very inspiring. I wish we had Robert E. Lee here or Stonewall were still alive. We'd show those Yankees!"

"Hello, Leah."

Startled, Leah whirled to see David Rocklin standing before her, dressed in the butternut uniform of a private. For one moment she thought she was mistaken. *He can't be here!* she thought wildly. *And not in uniform!* She was so confused she couldn't speak, and David smiled at her, his face thinner than she remembered.

"It's me all right. I didn't mean to startle you."

"David...what are you doing here?"

He looked down at his uniform and in a wry tone said, "I'm defending the Confederacy, can't you tell?" The scene flashed before her eyes of the time when she'd said good-bye to him so coldly and rebuked him for his cowardice. But somehow the face of the man who stood before her now was changed. He looked as if he'd been ill, but he was somehow calmer than she remembered him.

"I am surprised to see you—and in uniform."

"You've got a right to be surprised. After I ran away, no one would expect me to put myself back into a uniform again."

Leah was baffled and intrigued. She had, in her mind, blotted David Rocklin out, never wanting to see him again. Indeed, she never thought she would. But now, as he stood before her with his hat removed, his black hair moving slightly in the fall breeze, she suddenly said, "Come along. While they're listening to the speech, we can visit a little." Turning, she went back, put a piece of cake on a plate, and handed it to him. Then she poured a glass of lemonade, saying, "Come on, there's a space back here where we can have a little privacy." She made her way behind the tables and around a corner to a large open space. It was vacant now, and after they sat down, she asked at once, "What have you been doing, David?"

David entertained the idea of telling her the truth but had purposed never to let anyone know of his illness. As he looked at her, admiring the clearness of her eyes, the smoothness of her skin, the youthful beauty of her face, the love he'd felt for her at Vicksburg surged through him. "You haven't changed," he said slowly. "I've thought about you a great deal." Then, when she didn't speak, he realized he'd embarrassed her. "Oh, don't worry. I'm not here to pursue you. We won't be here that long. The Yankees will be here probably within a week." He bit into the cake, nodded his approval, then asked, "Where are you staying? I didn't expect to see you here at all. I thought you went to New York."

"My grandmother's very ill. She has a place just outside of the city here. Mother, Aunt Amelia, and I are staying with her. I don't expect she can live long, so we had to come."

"I'm sorry to hear that."

"But you—what are you doing in Chattanooga? And in the army?"

David shook his head. "It's not a very interesting story, Leah. I never thought I'd see you again, so let's not talk about the past."

Leah couldn't put it all together. She had put David Rocklin out of her mind, but here he was now, sitting relaxed before her. True, there was a shadow in his eyes that hadn't been there before. She wondered if he hadn't been able to live with his cowardly behavior and if the shame accounted for the change in him. He'd also lost weight. "How long have you been in the army?" she asked.

"Not long," he said briefly then changed the subject abruptly. "I would like to see Aunt Amelia. I don't suppose your mother would like to see me, though."

"Why, Amelia's gone to hear Braxton Bragg, the general, speak. You'll see her when she comes back."

As Leah talked to David, she grew more amazed at how much he'd changed. Sometime later Amelia came back. Her eyes brightened and she cried out, "David," coming at once to put her arms around him.

David, who had stood up, was somewhat surprised at her display of emotion, but he embraced her and looked down at the petite woman, saying, "Bad penny turned up again, Aunt Amelia."

"Never that, my boy!" She reached up to touch his cheek fondly then sat him down and insisted on feeding him cookies and cakes as Leah watched.

Later on, the crowds came back and Leah said, "Come and see us, David, if you can get away." She read his thoughts and responded, "Mother will be glad to see you, and so would we."

"All right. I'll come if I can, but I doubt there'll be time. The Yankees are coming with three hundred thousand men, so they say." He stood and left abruptly, his back straight as he made his way through the crowd.

After he left, the two women talked of his strange appearance and of his decision to join the army. "I don't understand it," Leah murmured, her brow furrowed. "He's different, isn't he?"

"Yes, he is. I can't explain it, but he's changed somehow. He's more serious than he was, but it's more than that. He looks troubled—and yet he's somehow more of a man than he was. He's been through a hard time. We've got to help him all we can."

"Yes," Leah agreed, thinking it even stranger that David Rocklin, who she thought was forever out of her life, could walk back into it on one sunny afternoon and be an even stronger presence in her life than ever.

※

The Union Army of the Cumberland, led by General Rosecrans, had begun moving toward Chattanooga in August. By August 21, General Bragg, the Confederate commander, received reports that the bulk of the Federal army was moving toward him. His own army now totaled only thirty thousand men. Bragg was justly nervous, for he knew he didn't have a large enough force to combat the Federals. On August 31, the Army of the Cumberland started to cross the river at Stevenson

CHARIOTS IN THE SMOKE

and poured into the mountains that were south of Chattanooga. Three times during that week, General Bragg started to pull his men away from Chattanooga, each time reversing his decision. At last, however, he made his decision: On September 7, Bragg and his Confederate army gave up Chattanooga and moved south over dusty roads. They hadn't fired a single shot.

Bragg's retreat from Chattanooga led General Rosecrans into a serious mistake. Assuming the Confederates were in a full-scale retreat, Bragg thought he had a once-in-a-lifetime opportunity to destroy the Army of the Tennessee. But Bragg wasn't fleeing for his life; his withdrawal from Chattanooga had been orderly. On September 9, he stopped close to La Fayette and reorganized his infantry units, preparing for battle. He was also being reinforced with new troops. General Thomas and his twenty thousand Federals were marching into a trap.

On the evening of September 9, Bragg gave orders for the trap to be sprung the next morning, and all along the Confederate line excitement was generated. At last they were to have their chance at the Yankees, and this time on their own terms! But due to disorganization in Confederate ranks, nothing came of the promised battle with the Federals.

It wasn't until the morning of the thirteenth that David found himself moving forward with Company H, with Sam Watkins on his right. "Looks like it's gonna be a good 'un," Sam declared almost blithely. "Don't reckon they gonna be countin' how many cartridges we shoot off this morning long as we get a Yankee with 'em."

They were advancing over rough terrain studded with second-growth timber, making progress difficult. It was a weird scene in a way, but picturesque. As David stumbled through the dark wilderness of woods, vines, and overhanging limbs, somehow everything looked very solemn: the trees, the men, and even the horses. He thought about the nights he'd passed since leaving Atlanta. To his shock (and relief), he'd not had dreams of bayonets, nor had there been any reoccurrence of the black pit into which he'd fallen so often before. That morning Corey had wakened him early with breakfast already cooked. The slave had bent over and looked into David's eyes, and what he saw in his owner reassured him. "You all right, Mr. David," he had said, grinning. "Your eyes is just as clear as a mountain stream! Here, come and get some of this breakfus'."

Now as David marched along, conscious of being in the first line of battle and of men on his right and his left, he felt he wasn't a single individual, but part of some complicated machinery. *I couldn't run if I wanted to!* he thought grimly, glancing down the lines of infantrymen. But he didn't have time to think further, for Lieutenant Archie Biers suddenly shouted, "There's the Bluebellies! Get ready! They're coming our way!"

"We'll give 'em the best we've got in the house, Lieutenant!" Sam Watkins called out. He turned and flashed a wild grin at David. "Let's get more of them than they get of us, David. What do you say?"

"All right," David promptly replied.

He felt a calmness he couldn't explain, even when he suddenly saw a line of blue ahead of him. He also saw bayonets glinting in the morning sunlight, but amazingly he felt no fear. *I'll be shot before they get to me with those bayonets,* he thought. Then the colonel came galloping down the line on a fine bay stallion, waving his sword and screaming, "Charge! Charge! For the Southern cause and the Confederacy! Men, protect your homes and your wives!"

The whole Confederate line surged forward, and David

began to run at full speed. He was conscious of the humming of bullets about his ears and felt a tug as one of them touched his slouch hat, but he didn't slow his pace. As the din of battle increased in pitch, men around him began to fall and gaps opened in the blue line ahead. Black smoke obscured the scene, and finally the blue line retreated. Wild screams came up from the Confederates, and Lieutenant Biers, his face blackened by powder and yelling like a demon, cried out, "Come on, we've got 'em on the go!"

Again the line charged. There were fewer of them this time, and the fire became more intense. Artillery pieces and shells fell in the midst of the Confederate lines, lifting men into the air and then down, still, on the leaves beneath their feet. The Confederates wavered; then just ahead David saw the color-bearer go down. Without conscious thought he ran forward, grabbed the colors, and lifted them high, yelling, "Come on!" and ran straight into the terrible fire.

Colonel Bleeker, seeing this, called out to his aide, "Who is that man?"

"I don't know him, but look at him go! Right into those guns! He'll never make it, though," the lieutenant said, shaking his head regretfully. "That fire's too hot."

Somehow, however, David did make it, and as he ran directly into the fire, his courage inspired others. Sam Watkins yelled, "Come on, don't let that rookie show us up!" and threw himself forward. The Confederate line charged once again, and David was the first man to reach the blue line. The Federals were, however, not waiting; they'd turned and fled, throwing their rifles down and running wildly as if in a race.

A cheer rang out as the Confederates overran the Union lines, and men pounded David on the back. Lieutenant Archie

Biers came to him soon, grabbing him by the arm. "I never saw anything like that!"

Colonel Bleeker had ridden up also, his face wreathed in smiles. He looked down from his horse and said, "What's your name, Private?"

"David Rocklin, Colonel."

"Have you got room for another sergeant in your company, Lieutenant Biers?"

"Yes, sir!"

"Well then, Sergeant Rocklin, you're now promoted."

That night David was amused at the warm admiration that came his way. Corey insisted on hearing the story over again from as many men as would tell it and was as proud of his master as a man could be. His black face glowed, and he said finally to David, "I guess you showed 'em, sah, what a real soldier's like!"

David Rocklin was seized by a grim amusement as Company H extolled him that night. He listened to it all, smiled, and took the teasing that came with his sudden promotion well. Later, when the camp had gone to sleep, he lay on his blanket, thinking of the strangeness of it all. Here he'd sought death—and hadn't found it. Instead, he'd found something far different, something he thought he'd never have: the approval of brave men!

If they only knew what a coward I am, he mused, *it would be different.* Then he thought of the next day. *There'll be another line of battle and I'll rush right into it just like I did today. A man only has so many chances, so much luck. So many good fellows went down today, better men than I am.*

He was exhausted, but the sleep he fell into was a healthful sleep. Corey came once to stand over him, his black face filled

CHARIOTS IN THE SMOKE

with admiration. As he pulled David's blanket up, he whispered, "You is some soldier, Mr. David! Your family gonna be downright proud of you!"

Chapter 16

Leah Has a Visitor

The abrupt knock on the door startled Leah. Glancing up at Bessie, who was standing across the kitchen from her cutting up a chicken, she asked, "Who can that be? I'll go get it." She made her way through the house's central hallway and opened the door, expecting to find one of the neighbors. Instead, however, David Rocklin was standing there, smiling at her surprise.

"I took you at your word, Leah."

"Why, David! Come in!" Leah was conscious of how pleased she was to see him. She'd thought of him almost constantly since their encounter a week ago and had finally decided he wouldn't come to visit. Now she took him by the arm, drawing him inside. "I didn't expect you. What are you doing away from the army?"

David followed her into the front parlor, where he took a seat in a rocking chair and explained, "Neither army's doing much. There's a big battle coming up, but it looks like both generals are afraid to make the first move." He was wearing his uniform and had gained a little weight, but he still wore the same look of relaxation and ease that Leah had noted before. He continued, "I still feel odd about coming here. I know your mother doesn't have much use for me."

"I think you'll find her different now. I told her all about you joining the Army of the Tennessee, and we had a visitor from your regiment who passed through. He's a neighbor boy who lives down the way. He told us how you'd showed such courage that you were promoted to sergeant." She looked at the chevrons on his sleeve and saw his flush of embarrassment. "I'm so proud of you, David—and Mother is, too. She wants to see you. Now tell me all about it."

"Why, it wasn't all that much...," David protested, feeling like a fraud, but at her insistence he gave a quick sketch of the battle.

Leah listened to him relate the tale then said, smiling, "Jed Thompson tells it a lot different. He said none of the officers had ever seen a man run head-on into fire like you did. It was almost," she said, a fleeting frown crossing her face, "as if you didn't care if you were killed or not."

David looked down at the carpet, unable to speak for a moment. *If she knew how close to the truth she is!* Then he shook his head, saying, "I didn't come here to talk about the war. What about you and your mother and your grandmother? Is she well?"

"No, she lives from day to day, I think sometimes. She's in a shadowland, David, but she's ready to go—anxious actually." She saw that her words had struck some sort of response in David, for he nodded slightly as if he read a meaning into her words that she herself had missed. "Why do you look like that?"

"Oh, I don't know. It seems a good thing to be ready to go, I suppose. I've thought about it a lot lately."

The two of them sat there talking, and when Claire came in, she fulfilled Leah's words by smiling warmly and coming over to offer her hand to David. "I'm so glad you're here," she said. "We've heard all about your promotion and how well you performed. You're staying for supper?"

"Just dinner, if it's not too much trouble."

"Of course not! You stay here and talk with David, Leah. Bessie and I'll see what we can do about dinner for this young soldier."

It was a pleasant day for David. He and Leah took a long walk through the fields, once stopping to watch a white-tailed deer go bounding across in effortless flight. Later, before they got back to the house, she stopped him, saying, "David, I'm glad you came." Once again David was aware of the richness of her complexion and her inner excitement that seemed ready to bubble over. As the cool winds flushed her cheeks, blowing her red-gold hair in tendrils down her back and over her simple light blue dress, her vibrant figure spoke to David of life, youth, and hope.

"Leah, I—" He hesitated then said, "I've got to go back." He wanted to say more, but he was walking now in the shadow of what he knew must come. True enough, he'd had no more blackouts, but it was a menace that was always with him. He was frightened, not of death, but of losing his mind—and now this honorable way of avoiding madness had become a way of life to him.

"David, be careful!" Leah whispered, disturbed again to find that his return into her life stirred her so strongly. As she reached up suddenly to touch his cheek in a half caress, she saw a clearness and purpose in his eyes that she hadn't seen before. "I don't want anything to happen to you," she murmured.

David felt helpless, for in his own mind he was already a dead man. *This is the last time I'll ever see her,* he thought, and reaching forward he took her in his arms. "I shouldn't do this," he whispered, "but I want to tell you something. Of all the women I've ever known, you're the loveliest and sweetest and dearest." He leaned down, hesitating, and gave her time to pull away. But she didn't draw back. Instead, she lifted her arms, pulled his head down, and he felt the sweetness of her lips under his. For that one moment he forgot the war, forgot his madness, forgot everything except Leah and the richness of her as she held him tightly. There was a rushing in his veins, and his ears tingled as he inhaled her fragrance—partly lilac, partly rich young womanhood. He'd never experienced anything like this, and he held her for a long time. But finally, drawing back, he said huskily, "Good-bye, Leah." Then he pulled himself away abruptly and walked away, not turning around.

Leah stood and watched him until he disappeared down the dusty road, then walked slowly into the house. Her mother was in the kitchen cleaning up. Bessie had gone and the house was silent. "Is he gone?" Claire asked.

"Yes, he's gone."

Claire looked up suddenly then put down the glass she'd been drying and came over to stand beside her daughter. "He's different, isn't he, Leah? I could see something in him that wasn't there before."

"Yes, and I don't know what it is. It's strange, but I wish he didn't have to go." She turned suddenly to her mother, misery in her eyes. "This war is awful," she said bitterly. "It tears people apart, ruins families; it's nothing but death! I think sometimes I can't bear it."

Claire put her hand on Leah's shoulder. "You're a grown woman now," she said, "but there's something about you that reminds me of when you were just a little girl." Her voice grew soft and her face tender. "You used to come to me when you'd stubbed your toe or put a splinter in your finger or cut yourself. I'd take you in my lap and hold you. . .and I think at times," she said with a half smile, "you'd hurt yourself on purpose."

"I did," Leah confessed. "I didn't think you knew it, though. I needed that." Her eyes brimmed with tears. "I guess I still do."

"Leah—" Claire pulled her daughter close and held her as she hadn't in a long time.

As the two women stood there, Leah said, "I'm so afraid for him, Mother!"

"I know." Claire wanted to offer words of comfort, thinking of herself when she'd been Leah's age. It was about then that she'd married Matthew, and the thoughts that came of that time were sweet, strong, and poignant, as always. They'd become even more so lately, especially since she'd discovered the truth about her father. She felt sharp remorse, for now she'd accepted her mother's words as truth.

Finally, Claire stepped back and said, "A woman needs a strong man, Leah. That's the way we are. No woman is complete by herself, and I suppose no man is, either, without a woman to love."

Leah stared at her mother in surprise. She'd never heard her talk like this. She said slowly, "Do you still feel that way? That you need a man after all these years?"

"I didn't think I'd ever need anybody or want anybody. But I'm not as strong as I thought I was, Leah."

Claire turned and walked away, saying no more. For a while Leah simply stared at the door through which her mother had disappeared, the meaning of what she'd heard sinking into her.

Startled, Leah realized, *She still loves him! After all these years, she still loves him. I never knew that!*

CHARIOTS IN THE SMOKE

The Battle of Chickamauga was almost a reenactment of a famous line of poetry in which the poet spoke of "ignorant armies that clash by night."

On September 19, Union forces moved forward through the densely wooded areas. They had marched over unfamiliar territory where landmarks were practically nonexistent and every tree looked just like the last one. The front line stretched about six miles through the woods. As the battle began on the morning of the nineteenth, brigade after brigade, both Union and Confederate, entered the fray all along the line. First one side, then the other would attack. Before the day ended, almost every unit of both armies had been engaged, yet neither side had made any substantial progress. That night Lieutenant General James Longstreet arrived to reinforce Bragg with two Virginia brigades. Other units also filtered in. For the attack the next day, Bragg organized the Confederate forces into two parts: The right half of his army he put under Lieutenant General Polk; the left under Longstreet.

When the Confederates advanced the next day, however, they found out that the Union forces were not where they had been. David marched along with Company H in this part of the battle, and General Polk ran up against such terrific fire that the Confederates went reeling backward.

Longstreet did his best and found a large gap in the Union line. Through this hole he poured his army. In this attack, General Hood, who'd been severely wounded at Gettysburg, lost a leg.

It was the great opportunity for the Confederates, but

Bragg failed to understand the situation. Instead of following through the line with Longstreet, he insisted on sticking with the original plan, which simply threw brigade after brigade against Union commander Major General George H. Thomas. Thomas had been a former lieutenant in Bragg's battery in the Mexican War. He was a man slow to act, methodical, careful. It was here on this field that he gained his nickname, "Rock of Chickamauga." And it was against Thomas's men that David and the remains of the already-thinning brigade were thrown. "I ain't never seen such fire!" Sam Watkins complained. He was lying down behind a small fallen tree with other members of his squad to his right and left. He glanced over at David and grunted. "We done lost some mighty good fellers, Dave."

David's heart was pounding. He knew there was no way they could live through the fire if they were commanded to charge. Somehow he'd forgotten or put in the back of his mind his purpose in coming here. He'd thrown himself into the battle, determined to do his part. He owed that to his commanders and to his squad. He was watching down the line where Lieutenant Biers was speaking to the colonel. The pair was sheltered by a large oak tree, but chunks of iron from artillery still flew through the air. Explosions from the Union guns punctuated the afternoon with mighty bursts of sound, and muskets popped all along the line like firecrackers going off.

After studying the colonel and the lieutenant, David turned to say, "Sam, I think we're gonna have to charge. It looks like that's what the colonel's telling Lieutenant Biers."

Sam lifted his head over the tree, and immediately a bullet took his hat off. He ducked back, scrambled after his hat, and pulled it down almost to his ears. "Why, Dave, we can't make no headway against that! We'd all get killed!"

CHARIOTS IN THE SMOKE

David heard Watkins's remark but had turned again to watch the lieutenant. Biers suddenly dropped down and came wriggling on his stomach behind a slight hummock. Dave watched as he came closer and turned to meet him. "What is it, Lieutenant?"

Biers replied, "There's a nest of sharpshooters right over there. If we can wipe them out, we can get out of this artillery fire. But they're dead shots, and I believe they've got some of them seven-shooting Spenser rifles. Get your squad together, and we'll go see if we can knock 'em out."

"Yes, sir!" David looked up and down the line and called out, "All right, Company H. Let's go get 'em!"

Sam Watkins complained, "Why do we always have to be the heroes and pull the chestnuts of them generals out of the fire?" But he followed nevertheless, as did the rest of the squad.

As they moved out of the line of artillery fire, David could see what the lieutenant meant. There, on the crest of a hill, was the rifle fire that was decimating the Confederate lines. "We've got to get those Yankees out of there!" Biers exclaimed.

"We can't get across that open field, Lieutenant," Sam said. "At least I don't see how."

Biers's face was pale. "We've got to try. Are you with me?"

Seeing the fear on the men's faces, David responded, "We can do it. You stay here, Lieutenant."

But Biers rose, pulled his pistol, and said, "They're not looking this way. Let's work around a little bit more; then we'll charge across that open field."

David followed the lieutenant and, glancing back, saw that at least thirty of the company were creeping along, keeping down to avoid the fire. When they reached the end of the timberline, Biers gasped, "All right. We've got 'em flanked."

"They'll spot us before we get across that open field," Watkins warned.

Biers shook his head. "We've got to stop 'em. Come on!" He jumped out of the timber and started across the open field. David followed, finding himself yelling. Somehow all fear had left him. All that mattered was taking that small hummock where the enemy was killing his fellow soldiers.

They were halfway across the field when a cry rang out and suddenly musket balls began to whistle and men began to drop. They hadn't gone more than another ten steps when Lieutenant Biers suddenly fell, his face bloodied by a musket ball. He lay still, and there was no question he was dead. David reached down, picked up Biers's pistol, and yelled, "Come on, we've got 'em!"

From across the field, Colonel Bleeker saw what had happened. "They're going to make it!" he exclaimed. "Look, they are! Rocklin's leading them in!" There was more musket fire, and then David stood up and waved.

"They've flanked them! Come on! We can get around through that gap!" Bleeker led the remnants of the company around the edge of the timber and, when he got to David, said, "Somebody's got to take the men on in. It'll have to be you. Right now I'm appointing you a lieutenant—brevet, of course."

"Brevet!" David said. "That means I get to be a lieutenant until I get killed!" Amazed at his own ability to joke under such circumstances, he continued more soberly, "Yes, sir, I'll do it."

He turned back to the company and grinned at Sam. "You can now address me as Lieutenant Rocklin, Sam. At least for the next ten minutes." He looked around at the men who had gathered and said, "The colonel says for us to keep going and flank these Yankees—get behind that artillery. I hear the Bluebellies brought some candy with them. I'm going to get some of it. Any of you boys got a sweet tooth?"

CHARIOTS IN THE SMOKE

Surrounded by laughter from the men, Sam Watkins said, winking at the squad, "I can always stand a little of that. Any of you fellows feel like following Lieutenant 'Candy' Rocklin?"

That was how David got his nickname: Lieutenant "Candy" Rocklin. Some later would think it was his real name on first meeting him. That day Rocklin led the men in a flanking maneuver, and by the time night fell, the battle was over. The Union general, Thomas, held his position for a time then marched back to Chattanooga.

Chickamauga was merely a tactical victory for the Confederates, who captured thousands of small arms and fifty-one guns. Coming less than three months after bitter defeats at Vicksburg and Gettysburg, this small gain gave new hope to the people of the South.

The Union army retreated to Chattanooga, and General Bragg followed, laying siege to the city. That night David and Corey sat before a campfire and celebrated the victory. The colonel came by and said, "Well, Rocklin, you can be a lieutenant—brevet, of course—for another few weeks at least."

David was still shocked at being alive since he'd fully expected to be killed, and now he said sadly, "That should have been me instead of Lieutenant Biers. He's worth a lot more to you than I am."

The colonel looked at David, his eyes filled with compassion, and laid his hand on David's shoulder. "He *was* a good man, but so are you. I hear they're calling you Lieutenant 'Candy' now. Well, they can call you what they want. We've got a lot of hard fighting ahead, my boy, and I'll be depending on you."

David talked to Corey later on when all the rest of the men were asleep. "Corey," he said quietly, "do you know why I joined the army?"

"No, sah."

David said abruptly, "I joined to get killed. I couldn't stand the thought of going crazy."

Corey's ebony face glistened in the firelight as he nodded slowly. "Yes, sah. I can see how that might be better—but you ain't gone crazy, Mr. David. And you ain't been killed either. You reckon the good Lord's got something else on His mind for you?"

"Well, if I don't go crazy and I don't get killed," David said simply, "maybe He has."

Chapter 17

"I Was All Wrong...!"

After retreating from Chickamauga, the Federals attempted to reform their broken lines on Missionary Ridge. David was in the force that moved on them at once, but there was little action, and the shattered Union army fell back to Chattanooga.

"We ain't never gonna blast them out of Chattanooga," Sam Watkins said mournfully to David. It was almost noon, and they'd had nothing but a little salt meat for breakfast. Sam gnawed on the last bit that he'd saved, shaking his head. "We built them breastworks and forts, and I know whereof I speak."

David looked down on the city from Missionary Ridge, where his company was stationed, and saw a beautiful panoramic view. The whole city of Chattanooga, with the Tennessee River curling around it, lay at his feet. The position the company had taken seemed to be on a precipice, and as David looked down he commented, "We may not be able to take Chattanooga, but the Yankees sure can't take *us*. Why, it would take a mountain goat to climb up to this place!"

Sam swallowed the bite of salt meat, took a swig of water out of his wooden canteen, then shrugged his thin shoulders. "Well, time for preaching. We might as well go get it over with."

Amused, David asked, "Don't you like preaching, Sam?"

"Yeah, I like preaching, *good* preaching, but what we're gonna hear this morning ain't gonna be much."

"Who's the preacher?"

"Rev. P. D. Holmes." Sam made a face. "One of our fellers used to hear him when he was a young man and said he knew how to turn his wolf loose. But he went off to school somewhere and learned to read Greek...and that just about ruint him! And then he's bought a dictionary somewhere along the way and studies how he can get the biggest, longest, most highfalutin words he can into every sermon."

"Doesn't sound like much of a treat," David offered, getting up and brushing off his clothes. "But we might as well go."

As they made their way toward the opening where the company had gathered for the Sunday service, Sam Watkins said grumpily, "I think Rev. Holmes is scared to death that somebody's going to understand what he's talking about, but he don't have to worry about that."

The two men settled themselves along with the other members of the company. Soldiers of the other brigades began filtering in, and soon a large crowd had gathered. P. D. Holmes got up on a small knoll formed by an outcropping of gray rock spotted by lichen and began by saying a prayer the likes of which David had never heard in all his life!

"O Thou immaculate, invisible, eternal, and holy Being, the exudations of whose effulgence illuminates this terrestrial sphere, we approach Thy presence, being covered all over with wounds and bruises and putrefying sores, from the crowns of our heads to the soles of our feet. And Thou, O Lord, art our dernier resort. The whole world is one great machine, managed by Thy puissance. The beatific splendors of Thy face irradiate the celestial region and felicitate the saints. There are the most exuberant profusions of Thy grace, and the sempiternal efflux of Thy glory. God is an abyss of light, a circle whose center is everywhere and His circumference nowhere. Hell is the dark world made up of spiritual sulfur and other ignited ingredients, disunited and unharmonized, and without that pure balsamic oil that flows from the heart of God...."

David was highly amused by Holmes's prayer and the sermon that followed in the same vein. It contained little spiritual food, for indeed Holmes seemed to be enamored with the sound of his own voice—which was smooth and of sufficient volume to reach almost to the city of Chattanooga.

But at the end of the sermon, Holmes seemed to change. It was as if now that the prayer and the sermon were out of the way, he could be himself again. He looked over the men who were watching him and said earnestly, "Men, you have fought bravely for our cause. There's much hard fighting ahead. Some of you may not be at the next service. We are that close to eternity. I want to simply say that if you do not have Jesus Christ as your Lord and Savior, this is the hour for you to make that decision."

He went on in a simple manner, and something about the earnestness of the plea brought tears to David's eyes. When Holmes asked those who wanted prayer to come forward, at least a dozen men made their way to the front. David turned away, and as they left, Sam asked, "Are you a Christian, David?"

"Yes, I am. Not much of one, though. How about you, Sam?"

Sam hesitated. "No, I ain't."

David gave him an astonished look. "Why, I thought you were! You never miss a service."

Sam Watkins was an engaging young man, full of fun. He was courageous, David knew, to an extreme degree. He'd seen many of his friends shot to death, others maimed beyond belief, and yet he was always in the forefront whenever the call was made for dangerous work. "What's wrong, Sam? Why aren't you a Christian?"

Watkins shook his head. "Don't rightly know, Dave. Who knows about things like that? I do know one thing. That last little bit of talking the preacher done, that was preaching! That other stuff, he was just tickling his fancy."

David marched along silently, and finally, when the two were clear of the crowds and settled down alone looking down at the city, he said, "Sam, you ought not to put it off. I'm no preacher, but I know all of us are in poor condition here. No longer than I've been in the army, I've seen that we live on a tightrope. Why, that young man Jed Hotchkiss..." David spoke a minute about one of the young men in his company whom he'd met the day he entered service, then continued, "I'd grown close to that fellow. He was going home to be married. His girl was named Sylvia. Now he's dead and in the presence of God. He was a Christian, he told me. I'm glad of that."

Watkins picked up his musket and began running his hand along the barrel. "I reckon he was, Dave. A real one, too—not like some of the imitations I've seen. I thought a heap of that young feller." He let the silence run on for a while then said, "I know the Bible is true. Just can't understand why I've let it go."

"Be a good time right now to call on the Lord," David prodded gently.

Watkins looked at him carefully. "I been watching you, Dave. You shore ain't afraid to die! Matter of fact, sometimes you skeered me half to death the way you charge into them guns! I think maybe there's such a thing as being a little bit *too* brash. I know you're ready to meet God, but, shoot, I wouldn't be in no hurry about it if I was you."

David continued to talk with Watkins for some time. He had a real affection for the young man and was sincere in his desire to see him come to know God. But Sam's last words stayed with him after he left the young man: "Don't be in too big a hurry to meet God."

As he walked along the ridge, noting the usual activities of the soldiers who were playing cards, digging latrines, patching their clothes, and reading books, he thought, *You haven't had a single blackout since you decided. . .* For a moment he couldn't frame the rest of the words. Then they came to him: *to die.* Somehow he hadn't put this together in his mind. Now he wondered, *What's happened? Maybe just giving up on the idea of life has made a difference in my head.* He'd had several fleeting bad dreams of bayonets, but they had been mild compared to the awful nightmares that had blackened his life before. Now as he walked along, he tried to puzzle out the confusion in his mind.

"Lieutenant Rocklin!"

Turning, David saw Colonel Bleeker walking rapidly out of the grove of trees where the officers had pitched their tents. David hurried forward. "Yes, sir? What is it, Colonel?"

"Come along with me. Got some special duty for you." Bleeker gave him an odd look then grinned. "You're always ready for hard, difficult tasks, aren't you?"

"Why, I'm always ready to do what you order, Colonel."

"That's fine. Come along." Bleeker moved away down the winding path that led to the officers' tent. The Confederates had commandeered some Sibley tents captured from the Yankees, and Bleeker had made one of them his own command post here.

"Here we are," he said abruptly, his bulky form blocking Dave's view. Then he suddenly turned aside, and a shock ran through David. Leah was standing there, wearing a plum-colored dress, and a broad-brimmed hat with flowers on top was tied under her chin with a green ribbon. David thought she looked somewhat subdued.

Bleeker grinned at David's surprise. "This young lady tells me she's a friend of yours. I don't usually let my officers receive ladies, but for 'Candy' Rocklin, I suppose all things will go. You two have a good visit."

As Bleeker moved into his tent, Leah stepped forward, her face somewhat pale. "I know you're surprised to see me, David."

David had seldom been more surprised, but he said quickly, "It's always good to see you, Leah." Looking around, he noticed that several of his fellow officers and the corporal who served as the colonel's personal servant were grinning at him. He mumbled, "Come along. I'll show you the view of Chattanooga." He swung around, and she moved forward and took his arm lightly.

They moved back down the path and were shortly standing on the brink looking down once again at the city. Leah said, "I've never been this high before. It's beautiful, isn't it?"

"Yes, it is." David couldn't think clearly. He'd been thrown off guard by her coming. Then he asked, "How is your grandmother?"

"Not well at all," Leah answered slowly. "Could we go somewhere and sit down, David? I feel rather foolish coming this way."

"Of course. Look, there's a big old tree that's down. No chairs, but it's a little more private than most places."

He led her to a small glade set back from the brow of the hill. The rocks had been scoured out by geologic action, making a flat surface across which an uprooted oak tree three feet in diameter lay. The spot was sheltered by undergrowth, but there was still a partial view of the city below. Leah sat down, and when David joined her, she said seriously, "I have to congratulate you on your promotion." Then, thinking of the colonel's words, she asked, "Lieutenant 'Candy' Rocklin. . .how do you like that name?"

David made a face and shrugged. "Oh, it's a bit of foolishness."

"Why did he call you that?"

David repeated the incident where he'd incited the soldiers to take some candy away from the Yankees.

"Was it a hard battle, David?"

"I suppose they're all hard. I lost some good friends. Hadn't known them long, but it's hard to see men go down, shot to pieces."

"What's happened to you, David?" Leah asked suddenly, her clear greenish eyes fixed on him appealingly. The sun, past the meridian, touched her reddish hair, bringing out the gold glints and making her look very feminine—and somehow vulnerable—as she sat there. What David didn't know was that Leah had been going over her relationship with him almost constantly. All the affection she'd felt for him at first—that which had been driven away by his cowardice—had come back. Now she said quietly, "Something is different about you. I can't explain it, but I want to know. . .that is, if you'd like to tell me."

David sat on the log, suddenly desiring to share what had gone on in his life. He'd kept it bottled up so that, except for Corey, no one really knew what had happened. Still in his mind was the knowledge that he had been a coward, that he had run away. He still felt shame over that and thought he'd never get over it. Even his way of fleeing from it—to deliberately throw himself into battle, to seek death as a release from what he'd become—seemed cowardly now in the light of day.

And then as he sat there, a determination swept over him. His jaw set tensely, he began to speak. "You saw what I was at Vicksburg—nothing but a coward." He spoke for some time of how he'd never been afraid of being killed by a musket or by artillery fire but how the sight of bare naked steel somehow drained his manhood from him. It was difficult to speak, and he clasped his hands tightly together and looked down at his boots, avoiding her eyes. Several times he thought he couldn't go on as he spoke of what it was like to endure those nightmares. And then, when he spoke of running away, he said, "All my people have been courageous, Leah—all of them. The Rocklins may have been many things, but if they were cowards, nobody ever found out about it. I'm the only one. Do you know what that means?" He looked at her, his eyes almost wild. "I couldn't stand to have my father and brothers know they had a coward in their family."

A great wave of compassion rose in Leah. She'd never seen David like this before, and somehow as he spoke she knew she loved him no matter what he'd done. She didn't tell him this, however, for he continued to narrate what had happened. He told her then of the blackouts that had occurred, and his hands trembled as he buried his face in them. "I couldn't stand the idea of going mad. Anything would be better than that...anything." He straightened his shoulders. A wry expression on his lips, he said, "The doctor told me that that was where I was headed, more or less. I couldn't face a lifetime of madness. I wouldn't put my family through that. So I decided—"

CHARIOTS IN THE SMOKE

He broke off, and Leah waited quietly. Around her echoed the sounds of a soldier singing and a woodpecker rattling a tattoo on a dead tree. The sweet smell of evergreens and the smoke of a wood fire surrounded her. But she was unaware of all this, focused on the torment in David Rocklin's face. Then suddenly she knew!

"You joined the army to get yourself killed, didn't you, David?"

Astonished, David turned to her, his eyes widening. "Yes," he whispered. "You see that?"

"I don't think it's as unusual as you think."

David shook his head. "It's a coward's way out, but I'd rather be dead than insane. I couldn't stand the thought of that, Leah! I decided to join the army, and when the call to action came, I'd just throw myself in and...get killed, as you say."

Leah reached over and put her small, well-shaped hand on his. When he took it in his strong hands, he squeezed it so tightly that it pained her. But she said only, "I'm so sorry, David. If I'd shown more understanding, it might not have come to this."

"I don't think it would have mattered," he answered slowly, aware of the warmth of her hand and of the strength it held despite its size. He reached over with his left hand, stroked it, then looked up. "Something has happened. I didn't think I could ever speak of this to anyone." A look of surprise came into his eyes, and he said quietly, "The doctor tried to get me to tell him what was in me. I couldn't even tell him how I felt about being a coward."

"You are *not* a coward, David!"

He stared at her. "Why, of course I am!"

"You are not a coward! Everyone in your company knows it,

and the colonel is as proud of you as if you were his own son. He said he'd never seen such courage."

"He didn't see me at Vicksburg."

"You've got to put that behind you," Leah said firmly. "It was a fault, but you were caught off guard. Have you seen bayonets since?"

David realized, *Why, I have seen them, but I guess I was so intent on getting myself killed that I didn't pay any attention.* Some of the Union soldiers he'd charged had had bayonets, but the fear that had paralyzed him before hadn't taken him.

"You see," she said, reading his thoughts, "that's the way it is, I think, with fear. If we face it honestly and earnestly, with God's help we can overcome it."

David sat there, her hand still in his. Suddenly he raised it to his lips and kissed it. "Thank you, Leah," he whispered. Then in the quietness of the glade, with her face turned toward him, he leaned over and kissed her lips. They were sweet and innocent, but there was also a warmth and a passion in them as he put his arms around her and drew her close.

Leah surrendered herself to his embrace, and when he lifted his head, she said, "Be careful, David. I know you have to fight, but don't throw yourself away."

David looked at her tenderly. She was soft and yielding in his arms, and yet she had the same strength in her face that first attracted him. She was a daring girl and yet she had a sweet femininity. David had never found this mixture in any other young woman. "I love you, Leah. No matter what happens, I want you to always remember that."

Leah reached up and laid her hand on his cheek. She was about to speak when voices approached and David stood up.

A squad of soldiers marched by the opening of the small

glade where they were sequestered, and David said, "We'll talk later."

"All right, David."

The two left the glade and spent an hour walking along the ramparts, David speaking of the men in the company and introducing her to Sam Watkins.

"This is a particular friend of mine, Miss Cleburne," he said, "Sam Watkins."

"Proud to know you, ma'am. Won't you come and have dinner with us?"

Leah, liking the look of the cheerful young fellow, said, "Why, I'd be glad to."

"Right this way," Sam said. He led the two to where the rest of the squad were gathered and introduced Leah as "Lieutenant Rocklin's lady friend."

Leah was treated with respect, as well as astonishment. When the meal was set out, it turned out to be parched corn. "Is this all you've got to eat?" Leah exclaimed.

"Rations are a might shy right now," Sam admitted, "but I'll go out and liberate some if the Yankees give us a little breathing room."

"We've got a pig at home that's about half grown," Leah said abruptly. She turned to David and said, "Lieutenant, if you'll prevail upon Colonel Bleeker to allow you to escort me home, I think you could bring back that porker."

"Do it, Lieutenant!" Sam said. "And let me go along. I'll dress that there hog out, and we'll have cracklin' bread and pigs' feet."

David grinned. "You can have the feet," he said, "but some pork chops would go mighty good. I'll go ask the colonel for a pass."

Colonel Bleeker was pleased to grant his request but added, "I'll expect some ribs. I'm mighty partial to barbecued ribs, Lieutenant."

"Yes, sir. I'll see that you get them."

David and Leah made their way through the lines. The Rayborn place lay east of Chattanooga, sufficiently far from the Yankee lines so that there was little danger. When they arrived, Amelia and Claire greeted David with smiles. "I'm glad to see you, Lieutenant," Claire said, and David noticed there was something different about her.

Later, as Sam Watkins took over the butchering of the hog, David walked with Leah among the trees.

"There's so little time," Leah said as they paused under the shade of pecan trees that towered overhead. "It seems that's the way it's always been."

David looked out over the farm. "This reminds me a little of our place in Virginia." He ran his hand down the hair that hung freely down her back. "Maybe you'll see it after the war."

Leah wanted to say, "David, be careful," but she knew there was no way for an officer in the Confederate army to be careful. So she said aloud instead, "Have you had any more of those black spells, David?"

"Not a one."

"Maybe they've gone away," she said hopefully.

The thought had been in David's mind. "Maybe they have. Maybe when a man meets fear in its worst form, there's nothing else that can happen worse than that. I think I gave up when I decided to join and let the Yankees kill me."

Leah took his arm and said what she'd planned to say. "David, I—I think I love you. I don't know much about love, but I was all wrong to turn away from you as I did. Love shouldn't be like that."

CHARIOTS IN THE SMOKE

David stared down at her, touched by her admission. "We're all wrong, I guess, from time to time, and maybe you're right. Love is forgiving as much as it is anything else." He touched her hair gently; then the two moved toward the house.

Chapter 18

Love Never Changes

After the battle of Chickamauga, the Federal general, Rosecrans, attempted to shift the blame of the loss to his subordinates. Nonetheless, Lincoln was well aware of Rosecrans's shortcoming. Lincoln did what he could to support Rosecrans; however, it was becoming clear to everyone that Rosecrans was unable to handle the situation. He was, Lincoln said, "stunned and confused, like a duck hit on the head." The solution came with the decision to send Major General Ulysses S. Grant to assume command. After a frustrating summer in Vicksburg, Grant had suffered a fall from a horse and his leg was swollen from the knee to the thigh.

Some suggested that Grant was drinking, but he was firmly supported by General Sherman. Sherman had had mental problems at one time, and Grant had stood by him firmly. Now he said with a flash of wit, "Grant stood by me when I was crazy—so now I'll stand by him when he's drunk."

Chickamauga was not a clear-cut victory for either side, the Confederate capture of Union equipment being the only real gain. And so the Confederate command was also in turmoil. Braxton Bragg blamed General Polk for the loss and relieved the general. He also sacked General Thomas Hindman and in general tried to avoid all blame.

However, on October 4, a group of corps commanders, including Longstreet, D. H. Hill, Polk, and Simon Buckner, sent a formal petition to President Davis. They accused Bragg of being incapable of command and unfit physically to lead the army.

Since Bragg was a personal friend of Jefferson Davis, the president interceded as best he could. When his efforts failed, he took a train to Bragg's headquarters outside Chattanooga and gave a speech, rebuking the soldiers for their poor opinion of Bragg. However, that night he presided over a council of war consisting of Bragg's staff. Davis begged the commanders to support Bragg, but in response Longstreet declared, "Our commander could be of greater service elsewhere."

Unfortunately, Jefferson Davis was perhaps the only man in the Confederate government who liked Bragg. In addition, he couldn't find anyone capable to replace Bragg. Therefore, when Davis departed a few days later, he left the unpopular General Bragg in command. This pleased no one—possibly not even Bragg himself—and the entire army fell into a depression over the president's choice.

***

A knock at the door startled Leah, who was sitting in the parlor reading *Ivanhoe*. She'd buried herself in the romantic novel, wishing life itself were as romantic and idealistic as the world the writer had created. Rising to her feet, she called out, "I'll get it, Aunt Amelia," and made her way to the front door. When she opened it, she exclaimed, "Why, Father—!"

Matthew swept his hat from his head and smiled at Leah. "I should have let you know I was coming," he said briefly, "but the mail to this part of the world seems to have broken down."

"Why, come in," Leah said, stepping back. "How did you get here?"

"By train. Some of the lines are still intact, even in this area—the Union lines, that is." Matthew was wearing light brown trousers, a frock coat of darker brown, and a shirt of fine quality that was somewhat wilted. His brown hair had been pressed down by the soft felt hat he wore, and as he handed it to Leah, he asked, "Is your mother here?"

"No, she's gone over to a neighbor's. But I'll send Pax over to fetch her. Come into the kitchen. We've got some lemonade."

"That sounds good."

The two of them went to the kitchen, and after seating her father and giving him a glass of lemonade, she went out the back door to where Pax was chopping wood in slow motion. "Pax, go down to Mrs. Jamison's. Tell Mother that Mr. Cleburne is here."

"Yes'm, I'll do that."

Moving back inside, Leah sat down and questioned her father about his journey. She didn't want to ask outright about his purpose, but she was intensely curious.

As Matthew talked quietly, Leah noticed he looked tired. There were lines about his eyes that she hadn't seen before. Finally, he said, "I've come to try to get your mother to come back to New York. We can take your grandmother with us. This place is a powder keg, Leah. The battle could go right over this farm. It's just not safe."

"I don't think Grandmother can be moved," Leah said.

"Is she that bad?"

"I'm afraid so. Would you like to see her?"

"Yes, I would." Draining the rest of the lemonade from his glass, Matthew stood up then followed Leah through the house to the bedroom. When he stepped inside, he found Martha Rayborn much changed, but he'd been prepared for this. The last time he'd seen her, she'd been in good health. Now, however, her face was pasty and drawn and there wasn't an excess ounce of flesh on her body. However, her eyes still had a brightness and she whispered, "Matthew—," as he came across the room.

Taking her hand, he kissed it and held it as he sat down. "I'm sorry to find you so ill, Martha." Matthew had always liked his mother-in-law and she him.

The separation had hurt her, he knew, and she'd told him once, "Claire is making a terrible mistake; she'll never find a man like you."

Matthew thought of this as he sat beside her, speaking quietly for fifteen minutes. She was interested in his life, and Matthew noticed that Leah had seated herself in a chair across the room and was listening. Finally, Martha looked at him directly and asked, "How is it that you never sought a divorce? A man like you wants a wife and a family."

Leah studied her father's youthful-looking face. Now that her grandmother had asked the question she herself had wondered about, she leaned forward unconsciously and waited.

"I can't really answer that," Matthew said slowly. Then, realizing Martha Rayborn wanted an honest answer, he continued quietly, "I think love never changes."

His simple reply surprised Leah. She drew a sharp breath and her eyes flew to her grandmother, whose eyes met hers. *Why, that's not what I thought he'd say!* Again she remembered those few precious times she'd had with him as a child. Finally, she heard her grandmother say, "You always had strong feelings, Matthew. I've always respected you for that. Still, a man needs people, and you've had no one."

Matthew Cleburne shifted his weight uncomfortably. He hadn't spoken of these things to anyone. During the long separation, he'd struggled with loneliness. There had been many women anxious to share his time, for he was handsome, strong, virile, and had enough money to satisfy most. More than once he'd been tempted to throw himself into clandestine affairs, but he never had. Now in the silent room, he said quietly, "A man's word is about all he has in this world, and when he breaks that, he doesn't have much left. When a man gives his word, it's like he took water in his hands and held it there. If he opens his fingers and lets the water go to the ground, he needn't expect to gather it back again. I've done some things I'm not proud of in my life, but I like to think I'm a man who knows how to keep his word."

"You mean your marriage vows?" Martha whispered.

"Of course."

"Most men wouldn't have felt that way."

"Well, they must do as they see fit." Matthew once again moved his shoulders uncomfortably. "Now then, what can I get you to make you more comfortable, Martha?"

A slight smile tugged the corners of Martha Rayborn's thin lips. "I'll be very comfortable shortly, Matthew," she said, humor touching her fine eyes. "There have been times I've wondered about Christianity, about death, about judgment, but now that it's upon me, I find it most comforting to look back and remember that always, even with my doubts, I've been convinced of the truth of the Lord Jesus."

He held her hand gently and glanced over at Leah. "Your

grandmother was responsible for leading me to the Lord, Leah—did you know that?"

"No, I didn't."

"I was fairly wild, I suppose, and some had given up on me, but you never did, did you, Martha?"

"I saw something in you the first time you came to our house that I admired and liked. I wish it—" Martha broke off her words, giving a slight gesture of despair. "Why did you come, Matthew? Just to see an old woman make her exit from this earth?"

"I came to take you back to New York, Martha. You'll be safe there and we can take better care of you. There are fine doctors, and it would be a comfort to have you."

"That's like you, son-in-law," Martha said. It was what she'd always called him, and Matthew was touched by hearing the old phrase. Then she shook her head. "But I'd never live to see New York. I wish you would take Leah and Claire. I'd feel better if they were safe."

"I won't leave," Leah insisted. She rose, came over and took her grandmother's free hand, and smiled down. "You're not getting rid of me that easy." Then she looked at her father. "I'll go down and start fixing something to eat. You and Grandmother visit." She left the room and found Bessie, saying, "Bessie, I want us to fix a good meal for my father tonight."

"Yes'm. What you want?"

"His favorite food was always steak. Do we have any of that?"

"Yes'm. Paxton killed that yearling and we can have 'bout anything you want."

"Let's have T-bones, then, and potatoes and carrots if there's any left." She was still planning the meal when her mother walked in. "Mother," Leah said, "Father is with Grandmother."

"Did he say why he came?"

"Yes—he said he came to take us all back to New York."

Claire bit her lip. "She'd never stand the trip, I'm afraid."

"That's what she said. She said she wants you and me to go back to New York with Father."

"We can't do that."

"Of course not, but it was nice of him to come, wasn't it?"

"Yes." Claire hesitated. "Your father is always a thoughtful man in things like this. How long will he stay?"

"He hasn't said, but I'm fixing a good dinner tonight. Why don't you go and sit with him?"

"I'll let them have their visit. Your grandmother always thought the world of Matthew. From the very first time he came to the house, she liked him. But my father didn't care for him."

"Why not?" Leah was intensely curious. "Why didn't Grandfather like him?"

It was a question Claire had often asked herself, and now that she was faced with it, she spoke impulsively. "He was too strong a man, I think, and—he'd come to take me away."

"Well, it should have pleased him to give his daughter to a strong man," Leah said, astonished. "I don't understand."

Claire shook her head. "I didn't either for a long time. Perhaps I still don't." She walked out of the room, and Leah followed her to the parlor. "I thought about it so often," she said quietly, her eyes troubled. "I fell so in love with Matthew. He was everything I wanted, everything I'd dreamed of as a young girl. I thought Father'd receive him with open arms. He always liked strong men, and Matthew was that. But he didn't."

"Did he ever say why he didn't like him?"

"No, but he tried to persuade me not to marry him."

"I didn't know that."

"Oh yes, and Grandmother, for once in her life, stood up to him. They had an awful argument about it, and I guess for once she won." Claire smoothed her dress over her knees and sat looking at the figures in the carpet. "I think now about those times and I see that Father was very possessive, most of all of me. I was his little girl, and he didn't want to turn me loose."

Leah watched her mother's face quietly. "Do you think he was wrong?"

Startled, Claire looked up. She'd never once admitted that anything was wrong with her father, but now she said finally, "I think in this case he may have been." She would have said more, but at that moment Matthew walked in the door. Claire got to her feet at once and said nervously, "Hello, Matthew."

"Hello, Claire." There was a hiatus of silence, and feeling somehow out of place, Leah said, "I'll go help Bessie with the dinner."

When Leah left, Claire felt awkward and couldn't put into words what she was feeling. "I'm glad you've come, but you shouldn't have."

Matthew moved closer to her. "Claire," he said quietly, "I need to talk to you."

Surprised, Claire looked at him. "Why—certainly. Shall we sit here?"

"No, let's go outside for a walk. The air's cool out there."

"I'll get my cape." Claire put on a lightweight cotton cape and a bonnet, and the two left the house. As they walked along, the leaves that were falling from the trees rustled dryly at their feet. "I always liked the fall," Matthew said. "My favorite time of the year."

"I remember you couldn't wait until the hot summers were

over and the coolness would come." She smiled as she looked up at him. "I always like spring best, but you like fall." They moved to the deserted road that led to the north. Far-off fires from the fireplaces of houses scored the sky, the breeze driving the smoke out of tight spirals into long skeins as it left the chimneys. Overhead a flight of red-winged blackbirds argued noisily in the crisp, invigorating air.

Finally, they came to a bridge over a small creek and stopped to look down at the clear water. "Look at that!" Matthew said abruptly. "See him? That's a bass. I wouldn't mind catching one that size."

"Do you still fish sometimes? You always loved it so."

"I did for a while. It's not so easy in New York City. You have to go out of town. I miss the country. Remember how you used to go with me? You'd never fish, though."

"I didn't like to bait the hook," Claire said, smiling. Then she asked quietly, "Do you still think of those days, Matthew?"

He turned to her at once. "I've never stopped thinking of them, Claire. That was the happiest time of my life. I think of it all the time, those days we had together."

There was a silence in which they occasionally met one another's eyes. Finally, Matthew said, "Claire, let me take you back to New York."

"Mother would never stand the journey," Claire said simply.

He looked at her quickly. "If it weren't for that, would you come back?"

"I—oh, I can't say, Matthew. It's impossible anyway." She turned from him, the wind blowing her auburn hair about her face. She pushed it back under her bonnet, her heart too full to speak.

He put his hands on her shoulders and leaned down, his

cheek against her hair. He felt her stiffen, but he whispered, "Claire, I still love you. I always have—I guess I always will."

Startled by his touch, Claire felt a sudden rush of emotion. As Matthew pulled her back to lean against him, she felt the strength of his body, felt his lips kissing her hair. A sudden thickness in her throat prevented her from speaking, and tears rose in her eyes. She was a woman who needed love, who needed a man's warmth and presence, and she knew she'd stripped this from herself. The years had been long and cold and lonely—and now as he held her, his strong hands on her shoulders, she knew she had missed so much. For a moment she wanted to turn to him, to throw her arms around him. She couldn't trace the exact moment it had happened, but somehow she had gradually come to understand that she'd made a terrible mistake in her life. But she was a proud woman, and now as she struggled with her feelings, she realized she couldn't give him what he was asking for. So with large, wide eyes, she moved away and turned to face him. "I—I can't come back to you, but I want you to have all of the time you can with Leah." She dropped her head and bit her lip. "I've been unfair about Leah. I've robbed her of her time with a father, and I ask you to forgive me, Matthew."

Matthew Cleburne knew her pride. It was keen and sharp—and sometimes too hard. But now he saw she was vulnerable in a way he'd never seen before. He said instantly, "Of course. I'd like that very much."

They stood there for a moment, Matthew wanting to say more. But he saw that Claire had drawn inward, and though there was a sadness he couldn't quite identify about her mood, he knew this wasn't the time to speak of it. "Come along," he said. "We can talk about some of the good things. Do you remember the time that...?"

Late in October, the Army of the Tennessee prepared for the onslaughts that were coming. For weeks they'd watched Grant's army build itself down below. Chattanooga, they knew from the spies who came almost freely back and forth, was bristling with soldiers from the Army of the Cumberland. Grant, Sherman, and General Thomas were there, ready to launch the well-fed, well-clothed, and well-armed Union soldiers against the thin, ragged line of Confederates that lay rank along Lookout Mountain and Missionary Ridge.

David was standing at twilight one Monday, looking down at the city. It was almost invisible now except for the lights that twinkled through the falling darkness. He almost fancied he could hear the Union army as it hustled, pulling itself together for a massive strike against the mountains where their Confederate adversaries lay.

A sound caught David's attention, and he turned to find Corey bearing a cup in his hand. "Coffee for you, Mr. David. 'Bout the last there is. You better enjoy it."

David took it gladly. "Did you get some for yourself, Corey?"

"Yes, sah! The cook, he always eat good." Corey's white teeth flashed in the darkness as he stood there looking down on the city with David. "Lots of them soldiers down there in them blue uniforms, ain't they, sah?"

"Yes, there are. Quite a few." David sipped the coffee, which was bitter but hot and welcome. "Corey, I've talked about this before, but I'd like it if you'd go on to Virginia."

"Ain't no use, Mr. David," Corey said quietly. "I belongs to you and I'll do anything you says—'cept leave you."

David again felt a warm surge of affection for this tall young man. He'd understood for some time that slavery was the basic flaw in Southern culture—a cancer eating away at civilization. He knew his father and the rest of his family felt the same way. But although he'd been around slaves all his life, he'd never understood what it meant to accept a black man as an equal until he'd met Corey. He knew it had something to do with the fact that Corey had seen his weakness and had accepted him in spite of it. Now he looked at Corey and asked, "Why do you insist on staying with me, Corey?"

"Because," Corey said, his voice slow and strong and rich, "you the first one ever treat me like a man, Mr. David. To ever'body else I was no more than a mule or dog—but not you. I ain't never gonna forget that, and I ain't never gonna leave you!"

"You'll be free sooner or later, Corey."

"Well, then you and me'll be partners—on a farm, maybe." Corey smiled at Rocklin. "Wouldn't that be sumpin'? I 'spect you and me'd be about the best farmers there was."

"I like farming."

"I knows you do. You talk about that farm, Gracefield, all the time. I'm anxious to see it, sah, but I ain't going back without you."

"One day, Corey, all your people will be free. It'll be a better world then," David finally said.

"It'll still be hard, Mr. David. No piece of paper's gonna make black folks and white folks love and trust each other."

"No, that's true, but you and I love and trust each other. So we know it can happen, don't we?"

Corey Jones looked at the man who owned him—at least on paper—and smiled. "Yes, sah, I guess it do prove that."

PART FOUR
Chattanooga

CHAPTER 19

TWO WOMEN

The decision to send General Ulysses S. Grant to assume command in Tennessee was quickly made but not so easily implemented. Grant's rough fall from his horse caused him severe physical problems. His score of critics insisted his fall was the result of his being drunk. In any case, Grant spent fourteen days in bed but on October 16 received orders to report to Louisville, Kentucky. He was also ordered to take his staff with him for immediate duties.

Grant was met in Indianapolis by none other than Edwin Stanton, the irascible secretary of war for the United States. Stanton had never met Grant, and when he moved into the railroad car, he ignored the small, unimpressive man in the shabby uniform. He at once shook hands with Dr. Edward Kittoe, Grant's staff surgeon, saying, "How are you, General Grant? I knew you at sight from your pictures."

A smile crossed Grant's face; he was accustomed to such things. When he identified himself, Stanton, in some confusion, gave Grant command of the armies and called upon him to make a decision. "Do you want to retain General Rosecrans as commander of the Army of the Cumberland—or would you prefer General George H. Thomas?"

Instantly Grant chose Thomas. He regarded the man as too slow, but a vast improvement over Rosecrans. The two men talked strategy for the rest of the day, but they were both shaken when the secretary received alarming news that Rosecrans intended to abandon Chattanooga! Stanton at once commanded Grant that under no circumstances could the Union afford to lose that city.

Grant at once left for the Tennessee, stopping in Alabama, where he met Rosecrans, then proceeding to Chattanooga over a long Federal supply route. This trip showed Grant how difficult the problems he faced were, for the narrow and steep stone road was, in Grant's words, "strewn with the debris of broken wagons and the carcasses of thousands of starved mules and horses."

"If we don't find some way to supply our troops," General Grant told his staff, "we may very well lose Chattanooga to the Confederates."

Brian Decatur had come earlier to Tennessee and now was informed that the first priority on the commanding general's list was to see that the supply line was open. The Confederates were solidly entrenched on Missionary Ridge and Lookout Mountain to the south of the city, and there seemed no hope of rooting them out. It was not the kind of war Decatur had envisioned, and he grew restive. Finally, in late October, he obtained permission from his colonel to be gone for a short leave.

"I don't know where you'll be going," Colonel Smith said, grumbling. "There's nothing ahead of us but Rebels, and nothing behind us but mountains. But go on! Young men will find adventure in anything, I suppose."

Taking Colonel Smith at his word, Decatur managed to liberate a thin horse well past his prime from the quartermaster. Following rather vague instructions in a letter he'd received from Leah, he left the city, moving to the west. Actually, he had little trouble finding the Rayborn house. He stopped at two farmhouses, but the inhabitants slammed the door in his face. However, at the third house he found an elderly woman who had, he discovered, been born in Michigan and was staunchly Union despite the disapproval of her neighbors. "Who you looking for?" she demanded, cupping her hand over her ear. Then, without waiting for an answer, she said, "When's the Union army going to run those Rebels off those ridges?"

Brian grinned at the old woman's fiery spirit. "I was talking with General Grant about that this morning, Auntie," he said. "I figure it won't be long now." Then, leaning forward, he continued, "Do you know of a family named Rayborn?"

"Rayborn—Rayborn?" The old woman stared at him with eyes bright as a crow's. "Why, I know four Rayborns in this valley. Been here most of my life," she said, nodding firmly. "Which Rayborns would you be wanting?"

"Mrs. Martha Rayborn—her husband's name was Thaddeus Rayborn."

"Why, everybody knows Thad Rayborn's place. I'm surprised you had to stop and ask."

"I'm a stranger here, Auntie. Which way is it?"

The old woman gave him complete instructions and would have welcomed more talk about the Union invasion. Decatur stood talking with her for a time then finally made his apologies and galloped away. She cried out in a surprisingly strong voice,

"Get them Rebels out of Tennessee! Tell Mr. Lincoln we're ready to see the end of this thing!"

The incident had amused Decatur, and he was happy at his luck. He followed the old woman's instructions and two hours later pulled his weary horse up in front of a large two-story frame house set in the midst of a grove of pecan trees. He was somewhat apprehensive, for, naturally, Rebel sympathies were strong in this part of the world. Sharpshooters and even plain citizens had picked off more than one lonely Union officer who wandered from the city. However, he tied the horse to the fence, walked up to the front porch, and was delighted when Leah herself stepped out of the house. "Why, Brian!" she said with a smile. "I never expected to see you here."

Swooping off his hat, Decatur ran up the steps. He reached out and took the hand she offered and kissed it. "Why, I told you I was a stubborn fellow, Leah!" All the weariness from the tedious days of siege faded from him, and he pulled her toward him, intending to kiss her.

Leah, however, put her hand on his chest. "Now," she said, "come inside. Mother and Amelia will be glad to see you."

Decatur wanted to say, "I didn't come to see your relatives. . . ," but had more judgment than that. He entered the house and was quickly surrounded by the three women. Amelia and Claire seemed glad enough to see him, and as they sat down for a while in the parlor, he accepted tea and a slice of cake that Leah had made.

"Nothing this good to eat in Chattanooga." He grinned, shoving a huge chunk of the cake in his mouth. Washing it down with a cup of tea, he added, "We're mighty hungry back there."

"What's going to happen, Brian?" Leah asked. Then she

instantly added, "But I suppose you can't tell us that since we're the enemy."

"Well, I don't think I'd be shot for mentioning that things are picking up. Everybody in this area knows that General Grant's come and new forces are moving into Chattanooga. Sooner or later there'll be a battle."

Claire leaned forward, her eyes curious. "Have you ever met General Grant?"

"Of course. I've been in on several staff meetings," Decatur said. "I'm just a lowly lieutenant, but I'm Colonel Smith's aide. I was there waiting on him mostly. Naturally I wouldn't dare to open my mouth in that sort of company."

"What's the general like, Brian?" Amelia asked. "We've heard so many things about him."

"He's not much to look at," Decatur admitted. "Small and almost insignificant. When he first got here, he wore a private's uniform with only his stars on his shoulders to show that he was a general. Take those stars off and you'd walk right by him—never even notice him. But evidently Lincoln and Stanton think a lot of him. Made him overall commander of the Union armies."

The talk went on for some time about the war, but there was a stiffness to it all. Finally, Leah said, "Come along and I'll show you around the farm. We've got a litter of pigs. I'm sure you're interested in that," she said, smiling slyly.

Brian rose at once. "Nothing I like better than looking at a litter of new pigs! If you ladies will excuse us. . ."

The two left the house, and Brian followed Leah around to the back to a pigpen that held nine squealing pigs that sounded the alarm as they came close.

Brian leaned on the fence, looking at them with interest,

then turned his eyes on her. Leah was watching him curiously. She found his gaze disconcerting, partly because of his one brown eye and one blue eye, but even more because of his expression that she couldn't quite identify. "I didn't really come down to look at pigs. Are you a farm girl, Leah?"

"Not really. We spent some time here at my grandmother's when I was younger and I loved it. But I'm always glad to get back to the city."

This answer pleased Decatur, and he nodded. "I'm glad about that. I love you, but I don't think I'd make much of a farmhand."

"You don't love me, Brian."

Leah was practical in many ways, and she'd thought a great deal about Brian's proposal. Now, looking at him as he leaned negligently against the fence, she remarked quietly, "I don't think a marriage between a Yankee and a Rebel will ever work."

Decatur examined her thoughtfully. He looked up in the sky, where a red-tailed hawk was circling silently, then gazed back at her. "You may be right about that. But when this war is over, we can't be Rebel and Yankee anymore. We'll have to be one people again."

"After all that's happened?" Leah shook her head. "Almost every family I know in the South has lost sons or brothers or sweethearts, and so many women are without husbands. We've been stripped of the finest of our men. How could the women of the South forget that—or the men, either, for that matter?"

"There are lots of empty places at tables in the North, too, Leah. I believe in this country." Decatur was totally serious now. "We've been torn in two by this terrible war. I feel it had to come because slavery isn't right. That may not have been the only quarrel between the North and the South, but it's the issue at the heart of this war. But when that's gone, after a time we'll have to learn to forgive each other."

"I don't know if that's possible, Brian." Leah thought of her own mother, who had harbored unforgiveness toward her father as long as she could remember. Her mother was a good woman, Leah knew, and if she couldn't forgive one she'd loved, how could the South and the North become one people again?

The pigs crowded against the fence, squealing and grunting. Leah picked up an ear of corn and held it down, watching as they fought to get at it. "I sometimes bring the leftovers down here," she said, more to take her mind off the way the conversation was going than anything else. Looking down at the pigs, she said, "I doubt they'd love me so much if they knew what we had planned for them. They'll all end up as pork chops one day not too far off."

They talked for a time; then she took him on a quick tour of the farm. When they returned to the house, Claire asked, "Can you stay for the night, Brian?"

"As a matter of fact, my pass *is* overnight—but I don't want to intrude."

"Nonsense!" Claire said briskly. "We'll be happy to have you. Come along; I'll show you to your room."

That night Decatur had a fine time. He learned that Amelia had a fine wit and enjoyed teasing him. However, Claire Cleburne's behavior puzzled him. When he and Leah were alone, he asked, "Is your mother depressed about your grandmother?"

"Well—yes, she is. She's very fond of Grandmother." Then Leah hesitated. "My father was here for a visit. He wanted us to go back to New York with him."

"I think you should have gone, but I suppose you couldn't leave your grandmother."

"No, that would be impossible."

"Your parents...they've been separated for a long time, you said. Is there any chance they'll ever be reconciled?"

"I don't think so."

Her answer was so bleak that Decatur didn't pursue it. "It's a bad situation," he said. "Your mother's such a lovely woman. When I met your father, he seemed like a respectable gentleman. What's he like?"

The question troubled Leah. "I haven't been around him very much because Mother took me away when they separated. But I do remember things about him that I like very much." She went on for some time speaking of her father, and Decatur saw the longing in her eyes. *She's been robbed of part of her life. Everyone should have a good home to grow up in, and Leah's missed out on all that,* he thought sadly.

Even as the two were speaking downstairs, Claire, who had gone to sit beside her mother, was thinking of her past life with Matthew. She'd given her mother some painkiller, but it hadn't taken effect yet. Suddenly her mother asked, "Claire, did you talk to Matthew while he was here?"

Claire looked at her mother with surprise, wondering if she was falling under the drug's power. "Of course I talked to him, Mother."

"No, I don't mean that. I mean, did you talk to him about...about you and him?"

Instantly Claire realized her mother was not wandering in her mind. The eyes sunken back in the sick woman's head were clear enough, and she seemed to be resting easier. Very uncomfortable beneath her mother's steady gaze, Claire finally said, "There's nothing to talk about, really."

The room was almost silent, except for the rhythmic ticking

of the Dutch clock that had been placed on the mantel over the fireplace so Martha could know the time without asking. The clock made a rhythmic ticking sound, sharp and clear, as it broke the silence.

"Mother," Claire said suddenly, "I've been thinking about what you said about Father."

Martha Rayborn's lips tightened, as if she'd been expecting this. "I should have talked to you long before. I made a mistake, Claire, about your father and about you."

"A mistake? What kind of a mistake?"

"I thought it would be unsuitable to tell you about your father when you were a child. And then after you grew up to be a young woman, somehow it was too late," she replied, her face shaded with a pain that came from deep within.

Claire clasped the frail hand and said quietly, "I'm *glad* you told me, Mother. I made a mistake about Father, too, but it's too late to go back and fix things."

"It's not too late for you to fix your marriage."

"I could never do that!"

"Most of your trouble with Matthew stemmed from your love for your father. I saw it. I tried to talk to you more than once, but I couldn't do it without destroying your father's reputation in your sight, and I didn't want to do that." Bitterly she added in a whisper, "I wish I had now. You're a woman made for love, Claire."

Soon afterward Martha dropped off to sleep. Claire sat there, her face highlighted by the amber light of the table lamp, and studied her mother's face. She thought back over the years since she'd left Matthew and realized there had always been something missing from her life. Now she felt she knew what it was, but the past couldn't be reclaimed.

CHARIOTS IN THE SMOKE

Finally, with a heavy heart, she rose and left Martha. As she went to her own room, she was aware that Leah and Brian Decatur were talking in the parlor. Her daughter's voice brought a fresh pain to her, and she breathed an urgent prayer: *Oh God, don't let her marry the wrong man. Give her a good home. Don't let her make the mistake I've made!*

Chapter 20

A Startling Discovery

For the most part, life went on with great difficulty for the Confederates perched on Missionary Ridge and Lookout Mountain. The supply lines were thin and usually broken. In a book of recollections, Sam Watkins wrote about that time:

> *In all the history of the war I cannot remember of more privations and hardships than we went through at Missionary Ridge. When in the very acme of our privations and hunger, when the army was most dissatisfied and unhappy, we were ordered into line of battle to be reviewed by the Honorable Jefferson Davis. When he passed by us with his great retinue of staff officers at full gallop the cries went up from the troops, "Send us something to eat, Massah Jeff. Give us something to eat, Massah Jeff. I'm hungry! I'm hungry!"*

David Rocklin spent most of his time learning how to be an officer. Much to his surprise, he learned more from Private Sam Watkins than the higher-ranking officers. The wiry young man was full of native wisdom. He was "country smart," as they called such men back in Virginia.

David quickly discovered there was considerable communication between the two armies. He was out once checking on a detail, talking quietly with Sergeant John Tucker and Sam Watkins, when the three heard the pickets calling from across the river. Sam began hollering at the top of his voice across the river, which was about three hundred yards wide at this point. Sam said, "Look, Lieutenant, there's an island out there!"

About that time a Yankee voice cried out, "Oh, Johnny! Johnny! Meet me halfway in the river on the island."

Sergeant Tucker said at once, "Is it all right if I go, Lieutenant?"

"Go ahead, Sergeant. Maybe you can find out something about our friends over there."

Tucker immediately undressed, wearing only his underwear and a hat in which he carried tobacco, the Chattanooga *Rebel*, and some other Southern newspapers. He swam across to the island and stayed for quite a while. When he got back, David asked, "What did you find out?"

"Well, we swapped a few lies and some tobacco for some coffee. You know what, Lieutenant? That wasn't no private out there—that was General Wilder his own self!"

David stared at him in disbelief. "That can't be right!" General Wilder commanded the Federal cavalry and was known as the best at his job in the whole Union army. "A general wouldn't be out on an island talking to a Rebel."

"Oh, it was him all right," Tucker insisted, his head bobbing up and down. "I seen his picture in the Chattanooga paper. And besides that, he had an aide with him. The general wasn't wearing no uniform, but his aide whispered something and he called him General Wilder. That was him all right!"

David laughed aloud. "We should have captured him—but I guess that wouldn't have been fair, seeing as how he'd just come to swap for tobacco."

Although David wasn't aware of it, General Grant himself had become involved in a similar action. He'd ridden down to water his horse one day when a Federal picket had called out, "Turn out the guard for the commanding general." Grant said, "Never mind the guard," and the men went back to their tents. At the same time he heard from across the river, "Turn out the guard for the commanding general!" and Grant thought they mentioned his name. Later he wrote, "Their line at a moment fronted to the north facing me and gave me a salute which I relished."

David had one brush with the high and the mighty. He was very low down on the chain of command—as officers were counted, he was the lowest of the low, being a mere second lieutenant and a brevet at that—but he was witness to a scene that he was never to forget. It concerned General Nathan Bedford Forrest, probably the best cavalry commander on either side of the Civil War.

Lieutenant Rupert Allen had become interested in Rocklin, and the two had become friends. He called him one day, saying, "Come along if you want to see an explosion."

"What's going on, Rupert?" David asked curiously.

"Bragg's decided to send Joe Wheeler to attack the Yanks, and he's commanded General Nathan Bedford Forrest to turn over his entire command to Wheeler, except for a single regiment and one battery."

David whistled and lifted his eyebrows. "From what I've heard about General Forrest, he's not likely to take that sitting down."

"Not him! He's coming over, we've heard. Come on, let's just mosey over to General Bragg's headquarters. Maybe we'll get to see some of the fireworks."

The two men made their way to Bragg's headquarters, where they made themselves as unobtrusive as possible. They hadn't been there long when General Forrest, accompanied by Dr. J. B. Cowan, his chief surgeon, rode into camp. Forrest was a tall, strong man with handsome features and a well-cared-for beard. There was a power that emanated from him, and it was known that he'd killed more men personally than any staff officer on either side of the forces of the Civil War. David tried to make himself invisible, as Bragg, looking sickly as he always did, stepped out of his tent. There was fear in his eyes as well as he met Forrest.

Bragg put out his hand, but Forrest ignored it. "I'm not here to pass civilities or compliments with you, but on other business," he said brusquely. He drew himself up to his full height and stared down at the commanding general. There was a harsh ring in his voice as he said, "You commenced your cowardly and contemptible persecution of me soon after the Battle of Shiloh, and you've kept it up ever since. You did it because I reported to Richmond the facts, which you reported to be lies." Forrest spoke loudly, not caring who heard. His voice carried over the clearing so that Bragg's entire staff of officers, as well as many of the enlisted men, heard his voice clearly. He used such epithets as *scoundrel* and *coward* and finally shouted, "You may as well not issue any more orders to me, for I will not obey them." Then he hunched his shoulders, looking absolutely deadly. His piercing eyes fastened on General Braxton Bragg. "If you ever try again to interfere with me or cross my path, it will be at the peril of your life."

There was a silence in the glade as Forrest waited for the general to speak. Every officer there, David included, expected Bragg to take up the challenge, but he didn't. He sputtered, growing pale, and finally said, "Now, now, General Forrest, let's not lose our heads."

Forrest stared at the man with disgust, turned away without a word, and mounted his horse. He and his companions rode away at a dead run, and Braxton Bragg ducked into his tent.

As Allen and David made their way back to their own campsite, David said, "And *that's* the man who's supposed to lead us while we whip the Yankees? He's not much, is he?"

"Nobody can explain Braxton Bragg," Rupert said, shrugging. "I don't think there's a man in the army who likes him—except Jefferson Davis." A dark shadow crossed his face and he shook his head in disgust. "Nobody can explain that either. Of all the men Davis might admire, such as General Forrest, he has to form a friendship with a weakling like Bragg."

David later learned the outcome of Forrest's challenge. General Forrest took his complaints straight to the president. Jefferson Davis, instead of punishing him, gave him an independent command in western Tennessee far from Bragg.

꩜

Despite David's feverish activities to learn the rudiments of military procedure, his own problem was never far out of his mind. He spoke of it to no one except once to Corey. Late one evening Corey was preparing a meager meal out of what could be scraped together. David was slumped on a nearby log reading a book on tactics.

"What you readin', Mr. David?"

"How to be an officer and fight a war." David looked up and gave the book a disgusted slap with his free hand. "It's all about how to march men across fields, make them all turn together—forward march, about face, oblique right." He glanced down at the steep drop-off of the mountain and smiled at the foolishness of his words. "I'd like to see someone march men right up that mountain, or down it, either, for that matter!" He went back to the book as Corey came over and sat down on a cracker box across from him. He studied the young man's face carefully. David had become the single most important thing in Corey's life. He'd given David a devotion that had been withheld from other men, and he knew it was returned. He waited quietly then finally said what had been on his mind for some time.

"You ain't had no spells lately, Mr. David."

Looking up quickly, David saw Corey's eyes fixed on him steadily. "No, I haven't," David said briefly.

"I think that's a good thing. Maybe your troubles be over."

"The doctor said it wasn't. He said it'd come back."

"Well, doctors don't know ever'thing."

David didn't answer. He got up and walked away, leaving Corey to look after him with a strange expression in his eyes. "You sho' is in a mess, Mr. David," he commented sadly then went back to the meal he was cooking.

None of David's unit knew his background. Only Leah, her mother, and Amelia knew of his cowardice back in Vicksburg—and only Leah and Corey knew he had joined the army in desperation, hoping for death.

He walked for a long time then finally went back to his tent and pulled out an encouraging letter he'd received from Bernard Dixon a few days earlier:

Dave, there's a medical officer, Major Tom Dillard, who's a friend of mine. He did a lot of work with people before the war who had mental problems. He resigned to serve in the army. He's got a lot of sense—knows a lot about such problems. Why don't you see if you can find him? Maybe he'd help.

David put the letter back in the box where he kept his personal effects and tried to analyze what was happening to him. The likelihood that Major Dillard was anywhere close by was small indeed. Still. . . . At last he sighed deeply and murmured, "It won't hurt to try."

Surprisingly, finding the physician wasn't difficult. David went to Rupert, who said, "I never heard of the doctor, but our own medical officer knows them all. I'll find out for you." He disappeared and came back shortly, saying, "Major Dillard is serving with Joe Wheeler's cavalry. They're camped out beyond Missionary Ridge right now, but Wheeler's leaving to go on a raid. He'll probably take the doctor with him, so you'd better get over if you want to see him." He gave David a sharp look, asking, "Feeling poorly?"

"No, I wanted to make an inquiry, something about a friend," David said quickly.

Fortunately, there was little to occupy him that day. He made his way behind the lines and found out where Wheeler's cavalry was stationed. He saw great activity going on and discovered without much difficulty that the cavalry was going to be sent to attack the Federal supply line.

"Can you tell me where I can find Major Dillard?"

The tall private he had stopped nodded. "Yes, sir, he's right down over that way behind the horse pen. I seen him not thirty minutes ago."

CHARIOTS IN THE SMOKE

"Thank you, Private." David made his way past the milling horses, noting that they all looked lean and hungry. The cavalrymen themselves, for the most part, were undersized. Most of them had only parts of regular uniforms, but there was pride and a cocky spirit about them. Joe Wheeler was one of the Confederacy's best cavalry commanders, known for his aggressiveness and innovation in combat. Finding a line of tents, David asked a lieutenant, "Is Major Dillard about, Lieutenant?"

"There he is, right over there."

David looked up to see a powerful man with a full black beard smoking a long cigar. He advanced and saluted, saying, "Major Dillard?"

"Yes, what is it, Lieutenant?"

Now that he was here, David felt insecure. "Sir—" He hesitated, wondering how to put it and knowing he was making a poor show of it. "You're probably busy. I'll come back later."

"Wait a minute, Lieutenant." Dillard took the cigar from his lips and stood there studying the tall man before him. "Is it a private matter?"

"Yes, sir, it is."

"Come along. I've got some time on my hands just now." Major Dillard turned and led the way to one of the tents, stepped inside, and waved to one of the two camp chairs. "Have a seat. What's your name?"

"David Rocklin, First Tennessee up on the Ridge. I know you're busy. This is a very personal matter." He took a deep breath and said, "Sir, I've been losing my mind. I don't know any other way to put it."

Dillard leaned back and puffed on the cigar, sending purplish smoke rising to the top of the tent. He had large hands, more like the hands of a blacksmith than a physician, but there was a keenness in his dark blue eyes that revealed a great intelligence and discernment. "Tell me about it if you can."

David halted at the words "if you can." "Why, I think I can, sir."

"Not many can who are going mad. Most of the time they want to cover it up. What makes you think you're losing your mind?"

David replied, "It goes back to Vicksburg. I was in the army there, and I ran away. . . ."

The physician listened carefully as David spoke, his eyes never leaving the young man's face. Finally, when he'd heard it all, he asked, "Have you had any nightmares lately?"

"No, sir."

"What about blacking out? Have you done that?"

"Why, no, sir. It's been a few weeks, but—"

"Have you ever told anybody about this? About your running away, about your fear of disgracing your family—the things you've just told me?"

"Yes, sir, after I ran away and I felt pretty much alone. But I have a servant who's with me. He's very faithful, stayed with me when most would have left. Matter of fact, he saw me through those black spells. I told him what I intended to do, join the army and get killed and be done with all of it."

"Tell anybody else, Lieutenant?"

David dropped his head and couldn't answer for a moment. "Yes, sir," he said finally, lifting his eyes. "A young lady I'm very fond of."

"I see. Tell me about her."

"About her, Major?"

"Yes, about her. Why'd you tell her?"

David couldn't speak for a moment; then he looked the

physician firmly in the eyes. "Because I love her. I'd failed her, and I wanted her to know that she was right to have nothing to do with a coward like me."

Major Dillard sat so still he might have been carved out of stone. The quietness filled the tent and mounted, although outside men were dashing about, noisily getting ready to leave. Finally, Major Dillard said, "You know why many people lose their minds, as you put it, Lieutenant?"

"No, sir. I don't know much about things like this. We never had any of it in our family."

"They lose their minds because they bottle everything up. Finally, it doesn't have any outlet and the mind just blanks out. You were very ashamed of running away, weren't you?"

"Of course I was, sir! Who wouldn't be?"

"You'd be surprised how many men wouldn't be," Dillard said dryly. "But you're of a different sort. From what you tell me, your family has an honorable tradition, men of courage and honor."

"Yes, sir, that's right."

"That would make it all the worse for you. You couldn't face being the one coward in your family, so that's why you started blacking out. You didn't like this world, in other words, so you just went into one of your own where there wasn't any shame, because there was nothing there. . . ." Dillard went on explaining the reasons for David's blackouts. His voice was low, but his eyes were steady and they pierced David constantly. "I've studied this for years, Lieutenant Rocklin, and as best as I can tell you, it's a very simple matter. All of us do things we're ashamed of. When we do, there are only two things to do with them: We either bury them, or else we confess them. If we bury them, they begin to stink just like a dead body. Later they'll fill the whole house, the whole world, the whole mind. And that's when we can't stand it, Lieutenant—that's when we lose our minds."

"And what's the other way?" David asked, although he felt he knew.

"Why, I think you've already done it. If we confess what we've done, just *say* the thing, why, we're rid of it. It may be hard to take the consequences from those around us, and it's hard to confess that we've been wrong." The major paused for a moment. "There's a lot of this in the Bible. Are you a Christian, Mr. Rocklin?"

"Yes, sir, I am."

"Then you know what the scripture teaches. 'If we confess our sins, He is faithful and just to forgive us our sins.' The Bible also says that 'he who covereth his sins shall not prosper.'" He leaned back and puffed again on the cigar. "I've thought about that a lot—covering up our sins. God knew what He was talking about when He said that." Major Dillard smiled suddenly. "But He always does, doesn't He?"

"Yes, sir, I believe so." David was stunned by what he was hearing. Hope had begun to rise in him. "Are you telling me, Major Dillard, that I'm cured?"

"I think you have the answer to that. You were afraid of bayonets, but who wouldn't be? The bayonets weren't your problem. Oh, they caused you to run away, but the bravest men run away when situations are just right. As for your being cured, I think you began the process when you confessed what was going on inside you to your manservant, then to the young woman, and now to me. There's only one more step, and I believe you'll be completely recovered."

"Yes? And that step is...?"

"I think you need to tell your family all of this."

David seemed to shrivel. "I'd hate to do that." When the major didn't answer, he grinned suddenly. "But I've known all the time that I'd have to."

"Now there's just one more thing," the major said. "I just recognized you. You're 'Candy' Rocklin, aren't you?"

"That's just a foolish name that got attached to me."

"Yes, and the word is you're fond of leading charges straight into the center of the hornet's nest. Everyone says you're like a man trying to get killed—and they're right. But that's got to stop, Lieutenant Rocklin!"

David suddenly blinked. A thought occurred to him, a rather appalling thought, which he spoke at once: "I was anxious to die before, because I was losing my mind, but now that I'm not, will I run away again—dodge the fight?"

"That's what I want you to face up to." The heavy officer leaned forward, the cigar between his teeth. He puffed on it for a moment then removed it. "You're back where you were at Richmond. You're facing battle, you're afraid to die, and it may be you'll face some more bayonets. Whatever it is, your courage will be tested. You had an automatic out before—just get killed and you wouldn't have to worry about anything. But you can't lean on that anymore, can you?"

David shook his head slowly. "No, sir, I can't." He thought again about the bayonets that had come at him and had driven him to flight and wondered, *Can I stand up to that again?* Aloud he said, "Thank you, Major, for helping me. But I guess no one can help me when the battle starts."

"I'm glad you see that, Lieutenant," Dillard replied. "It's one thing to talk about courage and theorize about it. I think a wonderful thing's happened to you; you've been given another chance. But when the firing starts, it'll be whatever's within you that'll keep you in place with the rest of your men."

David rose, saying, "I've got to get back to my unit, Major Dillard."

Dillard rose with him and shook his hand. "Write to your parents, my boy, and your brothers. Tell them how you feel, what's in your heart." There was an urgency in his grip and in his eyes. "Don't put it off. Word has it that we're going to be attacked. Grant won't wait long."

"Yes, sir. That's what everyone says. Thank you again, sir." He turned and left the tent then made his way back through the lines until he got to his own unit. Corey was feeding the men, so David sat down, taking his plate of parched corn and a small piece of meat. When he didn't join in the conversation around the campfire, Corey noticed instantly. Moving over to David, he whispered, "You all right, Mr. David?"

David saw Corey's concerned expression. "Yes, Corey, I think I am—and I think you ought to hear what the doctor said." He explained the essence of the doctor's words and ended by saying, "So you see, I'm not going to lose my mind, and there's no need of getting killed on purpose."

"You see! I done told you that, Mr. David!" Corey exclaimed with delight. "We're gonna make it all right, jus' fine!"

David smiled. "All we have to do is stand up to about a million Yankees."

"You can do whatever you has to do. You got yo' mind, and we're gonna see great things, you and me." Corey's face was wreathed in smiles. He half laughed and said, "You know what, Mr. David? I almos' put my arm around you and gave you a hug just like you was black just like me. Too bad you white or I'd a-done it."

Instantly David moved over and put his arm around Corey's

CHARIOTS IN THE SMOKE

shoulders. He felt the muscles tighten, for no white man had ever touched Corey—except to hurt him. "Someday, Corey, you'll be able to do that without any fear. In the meantime, I guess I'll have to tell you, you're a mighty good friend."

Corey dropped his eyes. The warmth of his owner's hand and arm burned into his shoulder. When he looked up, there were tears in his eyes. "You take good care of yourself, Mr. David. I can't afford to lose you!"

Chapter 21

Fall of an Idol

As October passed and November brought colder weather, the siege wore on in Chattanooga. It became almost impossible to feed the mules. Half starved, the poor beasts chewed on anything that was vaguely edible—trees, bushes, fences—anything they could reach. During that period over ten thousand draft animals died.

Those trapped in Chattanooga were scarcely better off. Men stole corn from the horses or hunted for it on the ground. W. F. G. Shanks of the New York *Herald* reported, "I have often seen hundreds of soldiers following behind the wagon trains which had just arrived picking out of the mud the crumbs of bread, coffee, and rice which were wasted from the boxes and sacks by the rattling of the wagons over the stones."

But if the army suffered greatly, the population suffered even more. They had no one to help them, and they lived in squalor in what had once been a prosperous town. The thirty-five thousand army men were jammed together in an area of about one square mile. The civilians, their houses having been demolished for the sake of firewood, were crowded together with the army. "Their shacks," Shanks reported, "surpassed in filth, number of occupants and general destitution, the worst tenements in New York City."

The Confederate army suffered just as badly, as did their counterparts living in Chattanooga. Captain Fitzgerald Ross, an Austrian army officer and visitor to Bragg's camp, wrote, "The army is in a bad way. Insufficiently sheltered and continually drenched with rain, the men are seldom able to dry their clothes and a great deal of sickness is the natural consequence."

One of Longstreet's officers observed sourly, "There is a tradition among these flats that there has been a time in the past when it wasn't raining."

As winter approached, both sides were aware that a conflict was building. There was no turning back for either side. The Confederates couldn't afford to lose the area around Chattanooga, and the Union army couldn't afford to let them keep it. Thus, as the skies overhead darkened with the oncoming winter, darkness also fell upon the spirits of the men of both armies.

ଔ

The civilians on the farms outside of Chattanooga didn't suffer as greatly as those in the city itself. The harvest had been good. Since both armies were guilty of allowing their men to steal from civilians, most farmers grew wary and learned to hide their livestock and keep their smoked food and preserves under careful guard.

Pax and Bessie had taken over that particular task, and together they formed a formidable pair. Pax slept lightly and more than once had let off his shotgun when stirrings in the brush around the house told of pilferers. It was a game that delighted Pax, and he told Leah, "Miss Leah, I'm just as good as an army around here, ain't I now?"

"Would you really shoot someone stealing our pigs, Pax?" Leah asked with a smile.

"Why, sholey I would! The Bible say so, don't it?"

"That you ought to kill anyone stealing pigs? I don't remember that particular verse."

"Well, I don't remember it either, but if it ain't in there, it *ought* to be!" Pax, carrying the shotgun proudly, said adamantly, "I don't care whether they is Union or Confederate—they gonna leave our pigs and our chickens alone, or I'll fill their legs so full of buckshot they won't be able to walk!"

Amused, Leah went into the house and said, "Amelia, I think Pax has found his true calling. I'm afraid he's going to hurt someone, though."

"I think he's just loaded with bird shot," Amelia said placidly, knitting as usual. She looked up to study her niece's face. "Claire tells me that Martha had a bad night."

"I know. I think Mother was up with her all night, Aunt Amelia. I'll go up and give her a rest." She left the parlor and mounted the stairs to the second floor, where her mother was sitting beside the sick woman. Going over to stand beside Claire, she put her hand on her shoulder and said, "Mother, you go rest awhile. I'll sit with Grandmother."

"I'm not really tired."

"You need the rest. Go on, don't argue."

Claire got up, stretched, and looked down at her mother, who was breathing shallowly, obviously in a fitful sleep. "She gets weaker every day, doesn't she?"

"I'm afraid so, Mother."

"There's only one end to that." Pain touched Claire's eyes, and she left the room without speaking again. Leah sat down, picked up the Bible that lay on the table, and began reading it. She had spent many hours reading this book to her grandmother, who could no longer hold the book nor see clearly enough to read it. Her grandmother's favorite had been the Gospels, and Leah had been surprised at how much she herself had learned simply by reading for hour after hour. She opened it now and began reading in the book of John. After a few minutes, she heard her name called. Looking up quickly, she saw that her grandmother was awake and struggling to move. Quickly putting the Bible down, Leah stood and said, "What is it, Grandmother?"

"Can't. . .breathe." Martha's face was ashen, and Leah was alarmed. "Let me help you sit up," Leah said, knowing this posture often helped. She leaned over and pulled her grandmother into a sitting position, putting the pillows behind her. She was relieved to see some color come back into the thin face. "Thank the Lord! That frightens me so when you do that."

Martha was breathing rapidly. She turned now and said, "I'm such a bother, Leah."

"You're no such thing!"

"I always hated to be a burden on anyone, and now that's all I am."

Leah leaned over, fluffed her pillows up a little more, then kissed her on the cheek. Sitting down, she said, "You're not a burden. I'll read to you some more."

She opened the book to the Gospels, but her grandmother said, "Read in Revelation, the last chapters."

"In Revelation? All right, Grandmother." Leah found the last book in the Bible and at her grandmother's instruction began reading. She herself had never found this part of the scripture a favorite, but when she finished, her grandmother said, "That's a marvelous chapter, isn't it? I've always loved it."

"I never read much in Revelation," Leah said quietly.

"It's always been one of my favorites. Life down here's been so tiresome sometimes. It changes so much and usually not for the best." Her eyes half closed. "I've had a good life, but some of it has been hard. When I read about that scene in heaven, it makes me yearn to be there."

Leah was somewhat disturbed. "You're going to be with us a long time yet, Grandmother."

Martha turned her head and smiled. "I should have taught you better than that, Leah, to face up to the truth. I won't live long and I wouldn't want to. I'm ready to go—anxious, really." She looked at her granddaughter with a mildness in her fine eyes. "You can't understand that now because you're young and strong, but the day will come when you'll feel like someone on a long, hard journey. The closer you get to the end of it, the closer you'll be to what's most precious. To me, the most precious thing has been the Lord Jesus. Soon I'll be seeing Him. How could earth itself or anything in it compare with that?"

"That's beautiful, Grandmother," Leah whispered. She reached out and took the thin hand and said, "You love the Lord, don't you? You always talk so much about Jesus. My father always saw that in you. You helped him become a Christian."

"Your father was ready to become a Christian. He was hungry for the things of God. I never saw anyone hungrier."

Leah hesitated. "I haven't treated him fairly, Grandmother. I should have been kinder to him."

"Yes, you should, and so should we all. We've all failed Matthew, but it's not too late. He's a young man and has a long time to live if the Lord is willing. Do you want him back as your father?"

"Why—it's too late for that!"

"Don't say that." Martha's lips grew stern. "It's never too late for God." Martha plucked at the yellow, red, and blue checkered quilt with her fingers, then looked up at Leah. "I made this quilt the first month after you were born. Every day Amelia and I, along with all the women from around here, would work on it together. Those were good times. We sat together and talked while we quilted and then embroidered the lambs and birds in each square. When you came to this house as a baby, I thought you were the sweetest child I'd ever seen."

Leah looked out the window at the sun falling in golden bars on the yard. "This house...I remember it so well. We moved often, but always when we'd come here, it felt like home."

"I never knew you felt that way."

"You were always so kind. You spent so much time with me, especially when I was a little girl. I was very lonely."

"I know you missed your father."

Leah dropped her head. "Yes, I did." It was the first time she'd admitted this aloud to anyone, and now she looked up, her eyes sad and poignant. She was a sensitive woman—strong, yet at the same time full of hunger for the things of life. "I always felt incomplete somehow because I had no father...or at least he wasn't there. And I blamed him for it. I've seen lately how wrong I was to do that."

"Then you should tell him so, Leah."

Leah bit her lip uncertainly then said with fierce determination, "I will, Grandmother! I'll go back to New York, and I'll ask him to forgive me for the way I've felt and acted."

Happiness lighted Martha Rayborn's pale face. "That will mean a great deal to him. And I'm praying your mother will come to see she needs to do the same thing."

"Do you think that's possible?"

"With God," Martha Rayborn said softly, "all things are possible."

David had grown quite adept at persuading Colonel Bleeker to grant him leaves. Bleeker was amused by his fledgling lieutenant. It was quite an honor to have "Candy" Rocklin in his troop, for the word of Rocklin's daring exploits had spread through the Army of the Tennessee. When David had asked for a day off, Colonel Bleeker had said indulgently, "I believe you've earned it. Lieutenant Allen tells me you've learned quite a bit about how to be a soldier, and Sergeant Hickman, whose recommendation I find invaluable, tells me the same." He smiled then and asked, "You're going to see that young woman of yours?"

David flushed. "Sir, she's not exactly *my* young woman—but yes, I'd like to go calling on her."

"Go on, then. Have Captain Davidson write you out a pass. Bring me back some of that cake your young woman baked for you last time."

"Yes, sir, I'll see what I can do."

As David made his way across the country, he was highly alert. There had been reports of Yankee cavalry in this area, and the *last* thing he wanted was to be captured and spend the rest of the war in a prison camp. So he traveled under cover of darkness and waited until dawn before approaching the house. He had just passed the front steps when somebody called out, "Hold it right there!" David looked around, startled, as Pax appeared around the corner of the house peering at him suspiciously.

"Hello, Pax. You're not going to shoot me, are you?"

Pax blinked with surprise. "Mr. David! I didn't know it was you. We been having trouble with some chicken thieves."

"I'm glad you ask questions and shoot later." The door opened and Leah stepped out. David said quickly, "Pax is about to gun me down, Leah. Put in a good word for me, will you?"

Leah laughed and said, "Get away from here, Pax. Nobody's gonna steal chickens in broad daylight." Then she took David's arm. "Come inside. You're just in time to help me cook breakfast."

The two went into the kitchen, where he sat and drank imitation coffee made of roasted acorns. It tasted terrible, and they both laughed at the faces they made trying to drink it. She cooked bacon and fried ham and a large portion of grits. When Amelia came in, the three of them ate together. Afterward Claire entered, and when David rose, she said, "My mother said last week that she'd like to see you if you came back. Would you go up and visit with her?"

"Of course, Mrs. Cleburne."

"I'll take him up, Mother," Leah offered. "You sit down and eat." David followed Leah out of the kitchen and up to the sick woman's room. As they entered, Leah said, "Look, Grandmother, David's here."

David sat on the chair on one side of the bed, and Leah took the other. "How are you feeling, Mrs. Rayborn?" he queried.

"Very close to heaven," was her simple answer. Martha, noting his look of confusion, put out her hand, saying, "That startles people, but I'm more in the other world than I am in this one. It's very real to me."

"I think that's a wonderful thing," David said quietly. "You know, you remind me of the women in my family, especially my grandmother."

"Tell me about her."

David talked about his family for some time, Leah listening with interest. Finally, he said ruefully, "I've become a regular chatterbox!"

Martha shook her head. "No, it's good to hear such things."

Sensing that Martha Rayborn wouldn't live long, David said gently, when it was time for him to go, "I'll be going into battle soon, Mrs. Rayborn. I may not see you again."

Martha Rayborn looked at him steadily. "We live from day to day, David. You're a young man and I'm an old woman, but you may be in heaven before I am."

"That's very true. I've thought about that a great deal lately."

"Do you know the Lord Jesus?"

"Yes, ma'am, I do."

A smile wreathed Martha's face. "I'm so glad." She turned her head toward Leah. "You have good taste in young men, granddaughter."

Leah flushed then smiled almost roguishly at David. "Yes, I do. I demand the best."

Looking at the pair, Martha said, "I have no time for subtleties. Do you love my granddaughter, David?"

"Yes, I do," David responded. "I've told her so."

Then Martha turned to Leah. "Do you love David, Leah?" As confusion washed over her granddaughter's face, Martha continued, "I have no tact or manners, but when a man loves you, you should at least have *some* idea how you feel. But I won't embarrass you anymore. Go along now."

"I'll visit you again before I leave, Mrs. Rayborn."

When Leah and David were outside, David said thoughtfully, "She's a very beautiful woman. Her spirit, like I said, is much like my grandmother's."

"Yes. I'm just now realizing how wonderful she is. Why can't we learn to value people while they're still with us?"

They were alone in the hall, so he paused uncertainly then turned her toward him. "I'm sorry she embarrassed you. I know I love you, but that's never enough." She started to speak, but he shook his head. "Perhaps it's just as well you don't love me, Leah. The battle that's coming is going to be pretty bad. But I've got some things to tell you about myself."

"What things?"

"Not here. Later. Now let's go."

The two enjoyed their day together. Amelia and Claire watched them leave the house, Leah heavily bundled in a red and green coat with a bright red hat over her red hair. As they disappeared across the road and entered into a woods, Amelia sighed. "They make a beautiful couple."

"Yes, they do," Claire said quietly. "He's a fine young man."

Amelia asked, "Would you approve of him if he came asking for Leah's hand?"

"I can't imagine he'd ask, not with this war going on. But then, people do fall in love and get married even in a war."

"*Especially* during a war." Amelia looked down at the garment in her hands and then asked herself aloud, "Why am I constantly knitting these things?"

"Why, you always give them to people who need them. I think it's a noble deed," Claire said with a smile. "What do you think of him? David, I mean."

"I think he's the finest young man I've seen since Matthew Cleburne came to our house."

Startled, Claire stared at her aunt. Amelia's face flushed then turned pale. Amelia had said almost nothing about Matthew during recent years, but Claire knew he had been a favorite of hers. "You haven't talked about Matthew in a long time," she said quietly.

"No, because I knew how you felt. Every time I mentioned his name, you added a brick to that wall you'd built around yourself. I hated to see you bury yourself alive, Claire, but that's what you've done."

Claire looked down at her hands, unable to speak. Finally, she lifted her eyes and whispered, "Mother's been talking to me. Was my father really like that? He was your brother. You'd known him all of his life."

Amelia thought for a few moments then shook her head. "He was a strange boy and he became a strange man. There was greatness in him—you saw that. So did everyone. But there was another side to him, a dark side that he kept concealed. I found out about it, of course, when he was very young, but he could charm almost anyone. I don't suppose you remember, Claire, but I tried to tell you about it before you married Matthew. It was at our house when you'd just announced your engagement."

"I *do* remember," Claire said softly. "I got upset, even angry. For a long time I didn't like you because of what you'd said."

"I should have said more," Amelia responded, "but you wouldn't have believed me."

"No, I wouldn't have. I wouldn't have believed anyone."

Amelia said abruptly, "I hope they *do* get married. It might be short. He might not outlive the war, but then, people die every day. Leah needs a man like that, I think. I think she loves him, although for some reason she's afraid to say so. She's been very choosy about men."

"So have I," Claire admitted bitterly. "As I look back over my life, I've made almost every mistake a woman could make!"

Her admission surprised Amelia, and she said quickly, "It's not too late for you. Matthew loves you, and he always has."

"No." Claire's voice was almost harsh. "I can't go back. Not after all this time!"

"That's your pride speaking, Claire, but pride is a cold and lonely thing. A woman like you needs the warmth of a man's love and the touch of his hands. Go back, Claire!"

Claire got up and left the room at once, her face stiff. But Amelia wasn't discouraged. "I think she still loves him," she whispered to herself. "When love is there, no matter how small, it can work miracles."

Outside, Leah and David walked along a pathway that led through the woods. "This is an old logging trail," Leah said. "It goes way deep into the woods."

"I'd like to go to the end of it," David said, "so far back that there wouldn't be any war, any killing. . .but that can't be." He turned to her suddenly. "I've found out something about myself."

"What is it, David?" Looking up in his face, Leah saw an utter seriousness there. "Is something wrong?"

"No, although I'm not quite sure that's an honest answer." He caressed her cheek, which was smoother than anything he'd felt in his life. He let his hand rest there for a moment then touched her hair. "You're so beautiful, Leah!" he said, his voice quiet and gentle. "But I would love you even if you weren't."

"What's the matter, David? What did you want to tell me?"

"It's about myself," he said, seeing she was troubled. He related his conversation with Major Dillard as she listened intently. Finally, he concluded, "So I really believe I'm cured." He laughed lightly. "I cured myself, according to the doctor, by confessing what a rotten scoundrel I was. Somehow that makes it all right. But I don't think it can be that simple. It can't be!"

"You haven't had any bad dreams, nightmares about bayonets?" Leah queried softly.

"No, not a one."

"And you haven't blacked out anymore?"

"No, I haven't, and that's what gives me hope. Those things frightened me to death, but as I think back, it's only after I confessed it to Corey and to you and then finally to the doctor that I've been freed. The doctor's a Christian man, and he said confession of our wrongs frees us from bondage."

"I think he's right." Thinking of her father, Leah hesitated, not wanting to speak. "Something's been wrong in my life for a long time. I've never told anyone about it, but I'd like to tell you."

"What is it, Leah?" he asked, not being able to imagine what was making a shadow in her greenish eyes.

"I've been terribly unfair to my father. I've just found it out by talking to Grandmother. And Mother—she's changed, too." She went on speaking almost feverishly and finally said, "I wish you could meet my father, David. You'd like him."

"I'm sure I would." David took her arm, and they began walking slowly through the woods. "Tell me about it. Maybe it will help. It surely helped me."

As they moved along under the trees that were shedding their orange and red leaves, making a multicolored carpet on the forest floor, Leah spoke of her father. She related that somehow she had hated him for leaving them, even though now she realized it wasn't his fault. She also told of how she'd held herself back from him when he tried to do things for her, to be with her.

"I was so *unfair*, David, so cruel! I've got to go to New York and ask him to forgive me. . .and that's going to be so hard." Her lips trembled. "I don't know if I can do it."

"I think you can." As he pulled her close, she rested her head on his chest and began to weep. David said nothing for a long time, knowing this release of tears was something she needed. After a while she lifted her head. Her lips were soft and vulnerable as he kissed her. "I think that doctor was right," David said, still holding her tightly. "We have to *say* things to make them right. You need to tell your father, and I've got to go to my people, too. Or write them. I've already started, and it's very hard."

They walked through the woods for a long time until she finally said, "We'd better go home." As they retraced their footsteps, a rabbit started up right at their feet, startling them both for a moment. They laughed, relieving the tension of their talk, as he ran away, ears wildly flopping. But before they got home, David said seriously, "I may not have a chance to say good-bye properly, but I want you to know I'm a one-woman man, Leah." He kissed her again. "If I live through this battle, I'll find out whether I'm going to be able to be a man. I may run away at the first shot—just like that cottontail."

"You won't," Leah said firmly. "I know you won't. Your doctor friend *was* right. We have to face the thing we fear most. If we turn and run from it, it will pursue us and destroy us."

Now back at the house, they stepped up on the front porch. Instantly a hard voice startled them both. "Hold it right there."

David whirled to see a Union officer, a lieutenant, holding a gun on him.

"Brian!" Leah cried. "What are you doing?"

Brian Decatur had come, obviously, to call on Leah. He'd seen the two of them go into the woods and had waited. Now he held the gun steady, saying, "Don't move, Lieutenant. I'm taking you prisoner."

David, not carrying a gun, felt a moment's helplessness. Then he said, his voice steady, "I think this is neutral ground, isn't it, Lieutenant?"

"What are you doing here?" Brian asked, as if barking an order.

"He came to see me. He's an old friend." David's eyes turned toward Leah, but she ignored them. "Brian, this isn't right."

Decatur looked at her with surprise. "This is war, Leah. If he'd caught me, he would have taken me prisoner. Wouldn't you?"

David shook his head, not answering. The despairing thought foremost in his mind was, *Now I'll never know whether I'm a coward or not. I'll be rotting in some prison. That'll be worse than some battle.* But he wouldn't beg. Leah put her hand on his arm as she said, "I won't let you take him, Brian. Please let him go for my sake."

Decatur stared at her, an unreadable expression on his face. "You're asking this of me? You know I'm a soldier bound to be true to my oath!"

"This isn't a battle," Leah insisted, "and I'm asking it of you—as a friend."

This wasn't something Brian Decatur wanted to hear. Nevertheless, he lowered the revolver. Staring across at David, he said almost bitterly, "You're a lucky fellow, Lieutenant." Then he holstered the pistol. "I feel in the way here," he said briefly.

Knowing Brian was dreadfully hurt, Leah stepped toward him. "Please, my grandmother's ill. This is our home. We've tried to keep the war out of it. That's all I mean by this, Brian. I'd ask the same of David if he'd captured you."

"You would? Really?"

"Of course I would."

Decatur took a deep breath then eyeballed the taller man. "I think I'll have to honor Miss Leah's request, Lieutenant."

"Thank you, Lieutenant," David said, studying the sharp features of the other. "I'd like to think I'd do the same thing."

He turned to Leah and said, "Good day. I can't speak before my opponent here, but it seems unlikely I'll be back anytime soon. So good-bye for a while. Tell your grandmother I'll be praying for her." He nodded at Decatur, saying, "Your servant, sir," then walked away.

Decatur watched him go. "Quite a fellow there," he said softly to Leah.

Disturbed, Leah offered immediately, "Come inside, Brian. I'm a little upset, but I'll be better." She led the way into the house.

When David got back to the camp, Corey asked, "How was the ladies, sah?"

"They were fine."

"Sho' would like to see them again. They mighty fine, all of 'em."

"Yes, they are," David said briefly. He glanced in the direction of Chattanooga, where the enemy lay, then toward Leah's home. After the encounter with his enemy, he wondered what Decatur's relationship with Leah was.

"Well, old boy. We'll be tasting battle smoke soon," said a voice beside him, interrupting his thoughts. Startled, David turned to find Lieutenant Rupert Allen standing beside him.

"Did you hear something, Rupert?" David queried.

"I think the Yankees are moving into position. They'll hit us pretty soon. I'm glad we've got you, Lieutenant 'Candy' Rocklin, the famous fighting Virginian, on our side!"

David summoned a smile, accustomed to being teased by the use of this nickname. But as he turned to go with Rupert to headquarters, his thoughts were with Leah.

Chapter 22

The Battle above the Clouds

At the Battle of Gettysburg, the Union army had occupied the top of a series of ridges. Perched there above their enemy, they could plainly see the Confederates as they approached across open ground and made their way up the hill.

Now, just outside of Chattanooga, Tennessee, the situation was almost completely reversed. Up above Chattanooga and the bend where it's nestled in the Tennessee River, the Army of the Tennessee stretched itself along a long ridge called Missionary Ridge. The left flank of this army was planted on top of Lookout Mountain, the right flank at the end of Missionary Ridge. The officers in charge of defending Missionary Ridge were Breckenridge, Hardy, and Cleburne on the right flank. Rarely has it been so easy to diagram a battle. The Confederates were stretched in a thin line across Missionary Ridge. Approaching them was Grant's army, with Hooker on the right, General Thomas in the center, and Sherman on the left flank.

The chronology of the battle is equally simple. It took place on three separate days. The first day, November 23, 1863, was little more than a skirmish, known later as the Battle of Orchard Knob. This involved General Hooker striking the Confederate force on the left and driving them back to Lookout Mountain. This proved to be the outpost from which on the following day, the twenty-fourth, the battle for Lookout Mountain was launched. This battle has become known by the poetic name "the Battle above the Clouds," but in fact, the battle wasn't fought on top of the mountain but in a heavy mist on a rocky slope about five hundred feet below the crest. Hooker's force outnumbered the Confederates about six to one, and the outcome was never in doubt. The next day a detachment planted the Stars and Stripes on top of Lookout Mountain.

Brian Decatur found himself temporarily detached to Sherman's army. That unit, instead of attacking directly, moved around north of Chattanooga itself, shielding its movements, and came to attack the right flank of the Confederate army. The army had to cross the river, and did so on pontoon bridges. Decatur was on one of these bridges, which were over 1,350 feet long.

"I don't think we'll ever get across. This bridge won't hold," Decatur complained.

The bridge rose and fell with the current of the river, seeming to be more of a toy than a real bridge. His fellow lieutenant Gerald Colvin agreed with him. "I'd rather fight the Rebs than cross a thing like this! I can't swim."

Decatur grinned at him. "Well, if you drown, you won't have to put up with these bad rations anymore."

Colvin gave him a sour look. "That's not much of a comfort," he said, grunting. Then he looked ahead, saying, "Come on, let's get off this bridge." They stepped off the bridge and joined the troops who were hurrying about. Colvin said suddenly, "Look, there's General Sherman over there." They moved forward, expecting some sort of orders. Instead, they found Sherman, livid with rage.

"What's the matter with the old man?" Decatur asked.

"Don't know. Let's find out." As they moved closer, Colvin asked the colonel of their brigade, "What's General Sherman so mad about?"

Colonel Jones stared at him. "We're on the wrong hill. That's what's the matter."

"The wrong hill, sir?"

"Yes. We did all this sneaking around Chattanooga to get on the foot of Missionary Ridge. Now look at that." He pointed forward and they saw a valley. At the top of the hill across from them, Confederate troops were plainly evident, digging in with artillery and lining up along the top looking down on the Union.

"*That's* where we're supposed to be, but the general had the wrong map, I guess."

Sherman called a brief council of war. "We'll fortify this mound, but tomorrow morning we'll take that hill over there, gentlemen." He looked up at the right flank of the Confederate army. "I understand General Cleburne's up there. If he is," Sherman said, his mouth stubborn and intense, "if Pat Cleburne's up there, we'll pay for every foot of ground we take!" Then he kicked at a rock, running his hand through his wild red hair. "But we'll take it. Yes, we'll do it if we have to crawl our way up with our fingernails!"

The next morning both Union and Confederate troops stared at the heights of Lookout Mountain, but Grant downplayed the mythology that surrounded the battle. He later said that reports of an incredible victory at Lookout Mountain were "one of the romances of the war...it is all poetry."

At first light they looked up at the heights of the ridge where two Confederate divisions under Patrick Cleburne had arrived during the night, shifted from Lookout Mountain. The fact that the defending Confederates knew the rugged terrain helped to compensate for their deficit in numbers.

Standing on top of that line, David stood shoulder to shoulder with Sam Watkins and Sergeant Baker Hickman.

"There sure is a heap of 'em, ain't there, now?" Sergeant Hickman murmured.

"There's a passel," Sam agreed. "But they got to climb that hill."

David looked down, seeing that Sherman's troops would have to climb down the hill they occupied, cross a valley and an open field under fire, then ascend a steep slope—all against troops who were protected by log-and-earth breastworks. "If we just keep our heads," he said, "they'll never make it. I just wish we had more ammunition."

Even as he spoke, down below, Sherman, the Union general, signaled the advance by saying to his brother-in-law, Brigadier General Hugh Ewing, "I guess, Ewing, if you're ready, you might as well go ahead."

As the movement toward the top of Missionary Ridge began, Colonel Bleeker moved up and down the line of the First Tennessee Infantry, encouraging the men. "Don't fire till you've got a good target, men, and remember, you're shooting downhill, so fire low."

The Federal advance began, and at once three Confederate batteries opened fire on the blue line.

"Hold your fire! Hold your fire!" the officers were crying, David among them. Already he could see the sun glinting on the bayonets that the attackers had attached. Then they disappeared from his view as they climbed up the six-hundred-foot incline.

As David Rocklin stood there, he thought of his past and of Vicksburg and how the bayonets had driven him from the field. Stiffening his back, he pledged to himself, *I won't run this time. If they run me through a hundred times, I'll stand right here on this spot.*

Soon the battle began to rage all along the line. As the Federals attacked in the center, directly in front of David, hissing lead flew between the two armies.

All morning long the fighting raged with intensity. About three o'clock that afternoon, David, his face blackened like everyone else's in the line, was still clinging to his ground desperately. Line after line of the Union troops had been thrown forward, and Sam Watkins said, "Them Yankees got nerve, I'll say that. They just keep on a-comin'!"

Even as he spoke, David said, "Look! There's the general." His companions watched with him as Patrick Cleburne leaped on top of the Confederate breastworks. Then, flourishing his sword, he led a Texas brigade in a charge on the Yankees.

Instantly Colonel Bleeker stood up. "Come on, men. Let's give the Texans a hand."

David ran his eyes down the Confederate line. "Come on!" he cried at the top of his lungs and plunged forward.

At first the Union troops were shadows, dodging behind rocks and scrub trees; then they were separated into individuals. He felt the *hiss* of musket balls close to his ear, humming like angry bees. Beside him a man stumbled and fell, but David never turned. He was still determined to stop the oncoming blue line. "You won't get this hill!" he cried. "Come on, men!"

Beside him Watkins yelled, "Lieutenant Candy'll show us the way!"

They hadn't moved forward more than twenty yards when a

Union private, a large man with wild eyes and a ruddy face, suddenly appeared in front of David. He'd evidently fired his musket, but his bayonet gleamed in the sunlight. He came straight for David, the bright bayonet aimed at David's stomach. He was so close that David saw him with absolute clarity, noting that he had a large mole on his right cheek.

David lifted his pistol, pulling the trigger—and it clacked on an empty chamber. The keen blade on the end of the soldier's musket seemed to grow larger, but David threw himself forward, directly at the bayonet that the soldier thrust at him. As David twisted his body to one side, the blade sliced across his chest, tearing his uniform. David then swung the pistol, knocking the soldier to the ground. When he attempted to get up, David reversed it and struck him in the head with the butt of the heavy Colt. The man collapsed at once, and David picked up the rifle he'd dropped. There was blood on the tip of it, and he saw he'd been grazed by the blade, which had a razor edge. Staring at it for one brief second, he noted with relief that his nerves were steady. *You can't get closer to being stuck by a bayonet than that!*

"Are you hurt, Lieutenant?" Sam Watkins called as he ran to stand beside him.

"No, I'm all right. Let's get these Yankees out of here," David replied.

Since they were reinforced almost at once by the Thirty-sixth and the Fifty-sixth Georgia infantries, the fighting was shortly over.

Sherman at last halted the fighting. After suffering two thousand casualties, his troops still weren't any closer to taking Tunnel Hill than they'd been at the beginning of the day.

David helped gather the prisoners, who were soon herded

off, and then assisted in carrying both Confederate and Union wounded to where the doctors could care for them.

Rupert Allen, who hadn't been scratched, said to David, "Let's see that wound."

"It's not much," David replied. Although his uniform was torn, when he unbuttoned his shirt there was only a thin red line on his chest. "Just a scratch."

Allen eyeballed the wound. "Better try to bandage it up, I guess." He studied it for a moment then shivered. "I never could stand cold steel. I saw you go after that Yankee with nothing but an empty gun. I don't think I could have done that."

Amused, David answered wryly, "I don't think I could either."

Rupert stared at him, "But you did. You ran right at him. I thought you were a goner for sure."

As David Rocklin stood there among the frantic activity of the army getting ready for the battle they all knew would come the next day, he was suddenly sure of one thing: that he could stand as a man and face death without fleeing.

On the morning of November 25, General Grant stood looking up at the heights of Missionary Ridge. At last his army was ready. He turned to General Thomas and, with his teeth clamped on the everlasting cigar, said, "I think we'll see if we can take those rifle pits at the foot of the mountain, General Thomas."

Thomas, an expert drillmaster, nodded and left. He formed his ranks precisely, the lines perfectly straight. As all twenty-five thousand men appeared on the plain, with bands playing and banners waving, the Confederates, watching from the mountaintops a mile away, were struck with fear.

At Thomas's signal this great mass of infantry began marching toward the Confederate line. They seemed remorseless and unstoppable. Later, Confederate General Arthur Manigault wrote in a letter that the Union army struck with the order and regularity of a juggernaut.

Bragg had given orders that the Confederates should fire one volley then move up the ridge. This order proved to be disastrous, for as the men fired their guns and then moved upward, it encouraged the Federals, who thought they were watching a retreat. It also disheartened the rest of the Confederate army high up on the hill who didn't know their comrades were retreating by Bragg's orders.

Grant watched as his army rolled over the rifle pits, capturing many of the Confederates who'd stayed. Then, through his binoculars, Grant saw an astonishing sight. Long lines of blue-clad Union soldiers were laboriously pushing their way up the hill.

Dismayed, Grant turned to Thomas, demanding, "Thomas, who ordered those men up the ridge?"

"I don't know," said Thomas. "I didn't."

Grant questioned the rest of his officers, including General Granger, who responded, "They started without orders." Then Granger added with grim satisfaction, "When those fellows get started, nothing can stop them!"

Grant turned back, his jaw tense. This was a battle out of control—a general's nightmare. Never once had he considered taking Missionary Ridge, since it seemed impossible any troop could take it because of its location.

"If it turns out all right, fine," Grant said, muttering. "If not, someone will suffer!"

Someone *was* suffering, and it was the Confederates. David and the First Tennessee fired as the men in blue advanced up the side of the hill, then began rolling rocks down the hillside. But nothing could stop the force of the charge. As the Confederate men at the bottom of the slope raced for the safety of the summit, they made it hard for the defenders, who were afraid to fire for fear of hitting their own men.

There was something uncanny about the soldiers of the Army of the Cumberland. They came on, determined to reach the crest of the ridge, and as they did, the men of the Army of the Tennessee threw down their arms and fled.

As General Bragg came upon the fleeing soldiers, he shouted, "Here's your commander!" But the soldiers only mocked him and ran past.

General Breckinridge was cool enough. "Boys," he yelled, "get away the best you can!"

David held his little company together along with the other officers but soon saw it was a hopeless task. Flags from sixty Yankee regiments began to float along Missionary Ridge from one end to the other. As great cries of victory went up from the Federals, Colonel Bleeker told David, "Get the men out! Make an orderly retreat, Lieutenant."

"Yes, sir." David turned to his men and ordered, "Move back! We'll be all right! They'll win this time, but there'll be another day!"

The Army of the Tennessee moved backward and to their rear. No one has ever explained how panic can strike an entire army, but on that day, the First Tennessee was not itself.

As they retreated, David found himself, along with his company, trapped between two forces of Federal troops. Skillfully he

CHARIOTS IN THE SMOKE

maneuvered them back, but just as they were free of the trap, something struck him in the side of the leg. There was no pain and he thought he'd run into the branch of a tree. But when he looked down, he saw that his uniform was crimson with blood and thought with shock, *Why, I've been shot!* Then the pain came, but he gritted his teeth and continued to direct the retreat.

It was Sam Watkins who saw it first. "Look, Lieutenant!" he said to Lieutenant Allen. "Lieutenant Candy—he's been shot!"

Allen rushed at once to David's side. "Are you hurt, Dave? Let's see."

"I'll be all right," David muttered. "Just don't leave me here."

"Here, you fellows! Help the lieutenant! Get him out of here!" Allen yelped.

Sam threw down his musket and, along with Sergeant Hickman, took David's arms and looped them over their shoulders. As they started moving, David protested, "It's all right—I can walk."

But he couldn't walk, and suddenly the rattling of guns and the booming of cannons was muted. He tried to say something to Sam, but his lips wouldn't work. His legs were also losing their power. After what seemed like a long time, he heard Corey say, "That's all right. I take care of you, sah."

As the darkness began to close over him, the last thing David saw was Corey's face in front of him. As Corey lifted him, holding David in his arms like a child, the blackness swept over him like a mighty wave and he knew nothing.

*

David's world had grown strange. For some time he had felt hands working on him, and sometimes there was pain. At other times he'd wake with a start. But through it all, he knew he was part of the wounded, of those who were moaning in a makeshift hospital about him. Only one factor remained constant: Whenever he awoke, Corey was by his side instantly.

"Am I going to die?" David whispered once.

"Die? Why, no, sah! The doctor, he got that bullet out and you gonna be fine."

David smiled briefly but passed out almost at once.

He awoke again sometime later, but in a different place. Once again Corey was there, this time with food. "You got to eat, sah."

As Corey pulled him upright, David noted they were in a room of some kind, but there were no wounded soldiers there.

"Where are we, Corey?" he asked softly. Then, clearing his throat, he said in a stronger voice, "Where's the rest of the army? Is this the hospital?"

"No, sah, the army done moved. Now here, you eat this, and if you eat it all, I tell you what you need to know."

David ate two servings of the soup then looked down at the bandage that swathed his leg. "All right. Where are we, Corey?"

"The army done gone. The doctor got the bullet out and you didn't get no fever, which they said was unusual."

"Where's the army gone to?"

"Done retreated, sah. But you wasn't fit to go with 'em nor to ride in one of them wagons they took 'em in. So I kept you here. I used some of your money to pay for you a room with these folks. Them sympathizers to the South. Soon as you get able, we gonna get out of here. I done 'ranged with the gentleman that owns this place to take us to the railroad."

"Where are we going, Corey?"

"Going back home to Virginia, sah."

"But I'm in the army!"

"Colonel Bleeker, he done told me to take you home and get you all healed up. You ain't gonna be soldiering for a while, I don't reckon."

David looked down at the wound and said nothing. When he did look up, he smiled at Corey. "It'll be mighty good to get back to Virginia. You're gonna like it there, Corey."

The black face split in a wide grin. "Yes, sah. And you and me, we gonna be the finest farmers in all the whole state of Virginia!"

CHAPTER 23

"YOU HAVE TO TRUST LOVE!"

The grave had been dug in ground that was frozen at least a foot deep. Now the small company of neighbors and friends who had known Martha Rayborn most of her life stood silently as the tall, white-haired minister read passages from a worn black Bible.

Claire, Amelia, and Leah wore black, of course. Martha's death had come quietly. She'd spoken with them all on Thursday evening and seemed to be doing better. All three of the women had sat around her bed, and the sick woman had been livelier than she had been for some time. She'd asked Leah to read to her again the last chapters of Revelation, and when Leah finished, Martha Rayborn had smiled, exclaiming, "What a time that will be when we all fall down and worship the Lord Jesus Christ and the Father!"

The next morning, as Leah was eating breakfast with Amelia, Claire had entered the room, her face pale. The other two women knew before she spoke. "Mother's gone. She died with a smile on her face. I don't think she knew a moment's pain."

Now as the cold breeze whipped Claire's skirt, she listened to the final prayer and then turned away from the graveside.

She endured the duty of receiving the condolences from friends well, but she was glad when she was back inside the house. Taking off her bonnet, she hung it up carefully then removed the heavy coat and did the same.

The three women went about their duties at once, cleaning house in that unnatural atmosphere that follows hard upon the death of a loved one. They spoke little that day, but the next morning at breakfast, Claire surprised them all. She waited until they were finished with the pancakes that Bessie had made then said, "I've got to go back to New York. We can't stay here."

Leah nodded. The fond memories of this place had been replaced by new ones of war and hardship and now the death of her grandmother. "Are we going back to Father's house?"

Claire hesitated then said, "Yes," and nothing more.

After Claire had left the table, Amelia said quietly to Leah, "I'm surprised we'll be going back so soon."

"Mother's been very quiet. I suppose Grandmother's death has hit her hard."

"It's more than that," Amelia remarked. "I think there's been some kind of change in her. I've never seen her like this before. She was always a little too—well—too *hard* in her ways."

Leah looked up quickly. "You mean toward Father?"

"Yes. I think she's been thinking a great deal about her life and the way things have gone."

After that, the two said no more about it. It took a little over two weeks to get ready to go. Martha had left the property to Claire, and although it was devalued by the war, still it had potential to be a good farm for someone. The farmer who lived on the adjoining place had expressed an interest in buying it, and Claire had asked the assistance of the local banker in concluding the sale. The buyer didn't have all the cash, but he had a good down payment and agreed to pay the rest in yearly payments.

The three women went through the house packing the things they wanted to keep—mostly pictures and letters and photographs. Finally, they made their way to the station, relieved to discover it wouldn't be hard to get passage out. Supplies were pouring into the city now for Grant's army, and the trains were filled with troops, but they returned to the North mostly empty.

As they moved out of the Chattanooga station, the steam engine huffed coarsely, sending large clouds of smoke and steam against the iron gray sky. But instead of looking around, Claire was thinking about what she would say to Matthew when they returned to his house.

New York was gripped in the fist of a hard winter. By mid-December, ice and snow were piled high on the sidewalks, having been cleared from the roads by plows and crews with shovels. The three women dismounted from the train, and Leah saw to the luggage while Claire found a carriage. When they were all inside, Claire gave Matthew's address, and the horses responded to the driver's cheerful "Giddup, you lazy hosses!"

Leah noticed her mother was pale. Claire had spoken very little on the journey, which had been, as usual, difficult. Although a woodstove was kept blazing near one end of the car, the cars were drafty and cold and offered little comfort. Now as they moved along the streets of New York toward the residential area, Leah thought, *Father's going to be surprised to see us coming.* She herself had practiced her speech to him over and over, but now that the time approached, she felt uncomfortable and wished it were over. She had a rootless feeling that she hadn't been able to shake off. Glancing over at Amelia, she noted that the older woman was more cheerful than she'd been in a long time. As they drove along the frozen streets, Amelia spoke of the future with some hope...but Claire did not respond.

※

Matthew was in his study going over his accounts when he heard a knock at the door.

"I'll get the door, Lucy," he called out. Stiff and tired of the book work, he stretched as he moved out of the room. Down the hall, Lucy stuck her head out of the kitchen but withdrew it as she saw him headed for the door.

Opening the door, Matthew stood stock still, unable to speak for a moment. Disturbed by his silence, Claire was unable to speak. Finally, it was Amelia who said cheerfully, "Well, Matthew, you have a houseful of company, it seems."

Matthew at once exclaimed, "I'm so surprised to see you! Come in—come in, all of you."

When they were inside, Claire found her voice. "I apologize for barging in like this, Matthew—"

"Don't be foolish, Claire! Here, let me take your coats and hang them up." He took all of their coats but didn't inquire more than to say, "You must have had a hard trip from Tennessee. Come on into the parlor. I'll stir up the fire and we can talk."

Fifteen minutes later they were all seated in front of the fire, and Leah, standing beside it, held her hands out to the yellow flames. "That's good! I've been freezing to death on that drafty old railroad car!"

Matthew smiled at her. "Winter's not a good time to travel." He turned to Claire and said, "I was grieved to hear of Martha's death." He stroked his chin thoughtfully. "She was a fine woman. I loved her a great deal."

"She was very fond of you," Claire said quietly. "She spoke of you almost every day. I think it was one of the regrets of her life that she didn't get to see more of you during these last years." Embarrassed, Claire turned her face away, studying one of the pictures on the wall.

Matthew looked up quickly. From the time she'd stepped into the house, Matthew had sensed a new quality in Claire. But for the moment he said only, "She's always meant a great deal to me. I'll miss her."

Lucy came in to ask, "I'm fixin' dinner. You all staying?"

"Of course they're staying," Matthew replied quickly, seeing a strange look cross Claire's face. "You are, aren't you?"

"If—if we won't be in the way," Claire stammered.

"Of course not," Matthew said with a smile. "I'll get Simon, and he can carry your bags upstairs. I think he's out in the back."

When he left the room and the three women were alone, Claire said miserably, "I don't know why I'm so awkward."

Amelia examined her niece, seeing a brokenness in Claire that hadn't been there before. *She's changed,* Amelia said to herself. *She's changed a great deal.*

The noon meal went well, though Claire hardly spoke. Matthew talked with animation. "It's good to have you here. I just rattle around in this big old house by myself." He looked over at Leah and said, "You and I may get to take in a play or two." Then he winked at Amelia. "A little bit racy for you, Aunt Amelia, but these young folks, you know how they are."

Leah, suddenly feeling warm, said, "I'll look forward to it." She was thinking ahead to the time she would have to speak to her father—and that time came the next morning. She'd gotten up early, dreading the thought of the meeting, and gone downstairs to find Matthew sitting in the kitchen. He'd built up the fire and made a pot of coffee. "I expected you to sleep late," he commented, teasing her. Then he studied her face. "You didn't sleep well?"

"No, not very." She took a quick breath and said, "Father, I have to talk to you."

"What is it, daughter?"

"I've been very unhappy lately. I want to ask you to forgive me."

Matthew Cleburne was silent for a moment. "Forgive you for what?" he asked finally.

"I haven't been the kind of daughter I should have been. As I was growing up, I resented you a great deal. I blamed you for not being with us, and I was lonesome. But it wasn't your fault; I know that now. I wish I could go back," she said quietly, hesitating. "But I can't do that. None of us can. Will you forgive me?"

Matthew stepped forward and put his arms out. Leah moved into them at once. "Of course I will," he said. "We'll start from right now."

Leah stepped back, quickly wiping the tears from her eyes. "Well now, tell me all you've been doing." The moment was over. Later Leah would speak more about her childhood, but presently she wanted to get away from the tension.

As the two talked, he finally asked, "What about that young man, David Rocklin?"

"I don't know. He was with the army when they retreated. A great many men were killed and more of them wounded. I did let him know where I was, but I haven't heard anything."

Matthew examined her critically. "You were very fond of him, weren't you?"

"Yes. I treated him badly, too." Leah shook her head in despair. "Seems like I need a lesson in how to treat men. I haven't had much success."

"What about young Decatur?"

"He's still with the army in Chattanooga. I saw him before I left."

"He was pretty serious about you."

"Yes, but he could never be more than a friend. I told him that when I left." She smiled and continued, "He'll find somebody. I think he was really infatuated with the idea of having a Rebel sweetheart. He's a fine young man, but not for me."

The two talked for a long time, and finally Matthew looked up at her from across the table, saying warmly, "It's good to have you here, Leah. We'll have to make up for lost time."

*

Claire Cleburne was more miserable than she'd been in years. She'd thought coming back to New York might solve her problems, but somehow she couldn't seem to fit in. She was happy to see Matthew and Leah growing close and had brought it up to Amelia, who said, "They always loved each other very much, but now it'll be different."

These words made Claire feel even guiltier. She'd struggled with her feelings for some time, and now that she was back in New York in Matthew's house, despair gripped her. Finally, she determined that she must leave for a while. At least knowing Leah and Amelia had a place made it easier. She waited, not wanting to tell them. But one Thursday evening, after Leah and Amelia had gone to hear a local minister, she stayed at home, knowing she had to speak to Matthew.

For over an hour she sat in her room, wondering how to speak of their past, then finally shrugged. "I've *got* to tell him! I can't stay here."

She walked down the stairs and went to his study. Once there, she stood in the open door and asked quietly, "Matthew, may I speak to you?"

Looking up from his book, Matthew got to his feet at once. "Of course, Claire. Come in and sit down over here by the fire."

"No, I can't stay long. There's something I have to say to you."

Matthew looked at his wife—for so he still thought of her—and saw that she was disturbed. Her smooth features were marked with signs of tension, and unhappiness shone in her gray eyes. "Is there anything I can do?" he queried.

Claire, her hair fixed in an old-fashioned way that framed her face, couldn't face him. She walked to the window, staring at the streetlight for a moment, trying to put her words together. Finally, she turned and said with effort, "I talked with Mother a great deal before she died—and before that with Aunt Amelia." When she saw he didn't understand her, she continued with difficulty, "They talked to me about—my father."

When Matthew saw that the words almost had to be wrung from Claire, he waited. Finally, when she seemed to find no words, he asked, "What about your father, Claire?"

"He wasn't the man I thought he was. I always put him on a pedestal. I see that now." The words began to flow faster, and Claire put her hands together, holding them tightly to control the trembling. "Ever since I was a little girl, I thought he was the greatest man alive. I measured all other men by him."

Matthew Cleburne had long known this, but he'd never expected to hear Claire say it. As he stood there quietly, Claire shook her head and cried in despair, "I was wrong about him, and I treated you shamefully!" Her throat seemed to close up and her voice trembled. "I've got to say this to you. *I* was the one that ruined our marriage, not you. It wasn't your fault. It was me that drove us apart. I've ruined our lives, Matthew. Can you ever forgive me?"

For one moment Claire thought Matthew would leave her without a word. Then he came to stand before her. Putting his hands on her arms, he said simply, "I've always loved you, and I always will."

"Oh, Matthew!" Claire began to weep. She buried her face against his chest as his arms went around her. She hadn't been held like this by a man for years, and it all but broke her heart. She wept until there were no tears left, and still he stood holding her as if protecting her from a storm. She felt his lips on her tear-stained cheek as he kissed her, bringing back memories. She clung to him fiercely then, and he lifted his head and said, "Of course I forgive you. We'll start all over again."

"Can love be put back together like that?" Claire whispered.

"You have to trust love," Matthew said gently. "Do you love me, Claire?"

Echoes of years gone by sounded deep within Claire Cleburne. She remembered the first time she'd given herself to this man. There had been a freshness in their love and a stirring in her that she'd never forgotten. And now she knew that she'd longed desperately for his love for years. As he held her tightly, she said, "Yes, I always have, but I was such a fool!"

He kissed her again then smiled. "I think it's time for another honeymoon. What would you say about a voyage to the South Seas? There would be warm breezes and blue skies, and we can get to know each other all over again. Would you come along with an old man?"

Claire looked up at him, returning his smile through her tears. "You're not old!" she protested. "And yes, I'll go with you. Oh, Matthew, I can't believe it. Can we really start over again?"

"If you trust love," Matthew responded, "you can always start over again."

Chapter 24

Freedom

Corey looked up from the forge where he was tapping a red-hot horseshoe with a ten-pound sledge. "Why, Mr. David," he said in surprise, "I didn't 'spect to see you down here the day before Chrissmas. Why ain't you with the family?"

David carried a cane. He still favored his left leg, but the weeks of recuperation at Gracefield had brought almost a complete recovery. He'd been released from the army, and for the past four weeks he and Corey had been together every day.

"Leg's getting better all the time, Corey. What are you doing?"

"I'm makin' a new shoe for that little strawberry mare you like so good."

"Nice to have another blacksmith on the place. Box is getting a little old for much hard work. He's been telling me that you're the second best blacksmith in the South."

"I lets him talk like that. He's a good man," Corey said. "You set down over there and let me finish this horseshoe. Then we'll see can we scare up some of them groceries they been makin' in the big kitchen." David sat down on a box turned on end with his leg stretched out in front of him. The minié ball had missed the big bone but had torn a deep furrow in his flesh. Now he watched as Corey tapped the horseshoe from time to time, reaching over to the bellows and sending sparks flying upward.

As he sat there, David thought of his return home. He'd been received with open arms by his grandmother especially, and with hands that had trembled—something that didn't happen often, for she was a steady person. His father, Clay Rocklin, had managed to come home once on leave and had listened carefully as David had told him the whole story of what had happened to him.

As Clay listened, he was thinking, *He's so different from Dent, far more sensitive than he is—or me, either, for that matter.* He had a special love for this young man, so quiet in his ways, so unobtrusive. Now he saw something different in him, a firmness that hadn't been there before. Just then David said, "I couldn't stand being a coward. What I did may have been wrong, but I would rather have died than live with that."

"I'm glad you didn't," Clay said quietly, hesitating. "I could tell you some stories about myself—about the time I ran away once in the war in Mexico. But you're all right now. God brought you through it all." Then he'd embraced David.

As David watched Corey form the horseshoe, feelings of gladness and peace, which he hadn't known for many months, came over him.

When Corey finished the horseshoe and sat down beside David, he commented, "Lots of Chrissmas doin's up at the Big House."

"Not as many as we'd like. My brothers are still gone—couldn't come home. But still, it's good to be here."

"You got a fine family," Corey said simply.

"Yes, I do. . . . Liable to be pretty active tomorrow,

Christmas and all, but I've got your present right here."

"A present for me?"

"Yes." David reached into his inner pocket and pulled out an envelope. He handed it over and watched as Corey opened it. Inside was a single sheet of paper. Corey had learned to read, despite obstacles, and now as he formed the words with his lips, he seemed suddenly turned to stone. Finally, he looked up and whispered, "This says you done give me my freedom, Mr. David."

"I told you I'd wait a year, but I thought it would be a good Christmas present. Merry Christmas, Corey. You're a free man now," David said, smiling. "Go anywhere you want to; you're not tied to anything."

"That ain't right," Corey said, having trouble breathing. He stared down at the words on the paper and then repeated them as if they were an incantation. Finally, he looked up. "I ain't belonging to nobody. That's right and I thank you forever for that, Mr. David. But I guess in one way when a man's got a friend, why, he ain't completely free. He owe that friend something, and nothing will ever change what I feel for you."

David's throat thickened with emotion, and he slapped the big man's knee. "Well, that's over," he said briskly. "Now all we have to do is make this into the best plantation in the South."

"I reckon we kin do that. Come spring you gonna see some plowin' like you never seen before!"

The two sat there for a long time until, finally, David rose to his feet. Corey stood also and put out his hand. When David took it, he gripped it hard. "Jubilee Day for Corey Jones! Free at last. Never thought I'd see the day. Thank you, Mr. David!" Corey said gratefully and reverently.

David left the blacksmith shop and hobbled back to the

house. He could hear voices as he entered the kitchen, and for a while he joined his family. However, there was a sadness to the planning of the upcoming festivities, for the whole family wasn't there. David knew some might never be there again, but he kept these feelings to himself.

Christmas came the next day, and little gifts were passed around. There was good food, and they savored it to the fullest, perhaps even more so because they all knew it couldn't last long and they must go back to the grim specter of war. When Clay asked David, "Will you be going back to the Army of the Tennessee?" David shook his head. "I don't know, sir. Depends on how well this leg does. It doesn't look good for us, does it?"

"No," Clay Rocklin said firmly. He'd never been in favor of the war; he'd fought against the South's entering it with all he had. "There's only one end—they're just too strong for us." He hesitated then said, "And we had the wrong cause."

"Slavery's got to go," David said. "I think it would have gone anyway if the war hadn't come." He'd thought a great deal about this and had talked with his father about it often. It was a bad system morally and even worse economically. "I'll be glad when it's all gone."

Clay examined this young son of his carefully. "It's men like you, David, who are going to have to rebuild the South. It'll be hard, but with God's help we can do it."

"Yes, sir. We can."

※

Two days after Christmas, David was sitting in the study going over the records and planning for the spring planting. He was surprised when his stepmother, Melora, came to say, "Corey wants to see you, David."

"All right." David put his papers aside, picked up his cane, and hobbled to the door.

"Put your coat on if you're going out," Melora scolded. "You're just like a little boy! That's all you'd need, to catch cold again."

He laughed and said, "You're too young to be my mother, and I'm never going to call you anything but Melora."

Melora sniffed teasingly. "You always were a disrespectful young man. Now put on that coat."

David shrugged into the coat Melora held for him and saw she was smiling. "What are you laughing about?" he asked suspiciously.

"Oh, nothing. Go on along with you now; then come back and we'll have tea or coffee or something."

"It'll have to be 'or something' I guess. The tea and coffee are all gone."

"I'll make some sassafras tea. You always liked that."

"All right."

David left the house and saw Corey standing beside the area that held the scuppernong vines. Although they were stripped of leaves now, they were so thick they practically formed a wall. As he approached, he noticed that Corey was struggling to suppress a smile. "You're grinning like a mule eating briars, Corey. What are you laughing about? What's so funny?"

"Chrissmas gif', Mr. David!" Corey announced. "Two days late, but I got it for you!"

David frowned. "Christmas gift? Oh, you didn't have to do that."

"Well, no, sah, but I thought you deserved it. You want it now?"

"Why, yes."

Corey waved his hand and said, "Go right in that grape arbor and you'll find it all waitin' for you."

Giving Corey a quizzical look, David moved past him, his cane tapping hollowly on the stone walkway. He turned the corner, not knowing what he would find, then stopped dead still.

"Hello, David."

"Leah!"

David heard Corey laughing behind him, and then he heard departing footsteps. The sun overhead was a pale disc and the air was cold as David stepped toward Leah, putting out his left hand. As she took it, he said, "I can't believe you're here!"

"You said in your letters you were lonesome for me," Leah said. "I hope you meant it, because here I am."

Leah had received three letters from David in New York. Each time he'd told her he loved her and promised to come to New York as soon as his wound healed completely. She'd finally talked with her mother and Amelia about it, and it had been Claire who insisted, "If he can't come to you, you'll have to go to him. I don't know if you love this young man or not, but now's the time to go find out." Claire radiated joy these days. As she and Matthew prepared to leave on their trip in a week, she had told Leah, "I'll get the money from your father. You can go in style this time and dazzle that young man. If he's the one you want, then go after him and never let him go!"

Her mother's words—and the happiness on her face—had propelled Leah to come. But now that she was here, she was somewhat embarrassed at her own boldness and very conscious that he hadn't released her hand. "How—how is your wound?" She faltered, afraid that she'd presumed too much.

David stared at her. She was wearing a beautifully tailored

hunter green wool dress with a coat to match. A small black hat perched on her head, and her face flushed as she stood before him.

"Leah," he said huskily then pulled her forward. His cane fell, but neither of them seemed to notice. He very naturally leaned on her, and she very naturally supported him. "You'll have to hold me up a little," he said, smiling at her. "My leg's not very strong."

Leah put her arms around him and looked up at him. "I was afraid to come," she said simply, "but I found out that I couldn't forget you."

"I hope you never do." He held her for a moment, searching her eyes, then drew her close. "You fit right here in my arms," he said. "Have you come to stay?"

Leah smiled impishly. "I've come to be courted. You needn't think you're going to get out of that! I'll be staying in town. You can bring your guitar and sing love songs to me in the middle of the streets of Richmond."

"I can't do that! I can't even sing!"

Suddenly he pulled her closer. As she felt the strength of his body, Leah Cleburne knew that she'd come home. She clung to David as he kissed her firmly. Then when he pulled his head back, she said, "I love you, David. I don't know what's going to happen, but I wanted you to know that much."

He touched her cheek. "You're here," he murmured quietly. "That's all that counts."

For some time they stood there; then, suddenly aware of where she was, she struggled in his grasp. "We can't stand here kissing in this arbor! It would cause a scandal if anyone saw us."

David smiled. "All the Rocklin men bring their sweethearts to this arbor to be kissed. That's what it was built for."

She took his hand, bent down, and picked up his cane. "Come along," she said. "I'm anxious for your family to meet me. They'll say I'm some brazen woman come chasing after you! You'll have to protect me."

David laughed and hugged her tightly; then the two of them made their way out of the arbor.

Standing off to one side where he was concealed, Corey shook his head and grinned broadly as the two moved slowly toward the house. When they went inside, his grin grew even broader.

"Well now! I guess I done brought Mr. David a Chrissmas gif' he ain't *never* gonna forget!"

Witness in Heaven

Part One
Dream of a Man

Chapter 1

Memories

As the stars rested in the velvet canopy over the mountains, faint pulses of light from the east began to dilute the cold blackness of the earth, revealing a still figure wrapped in a single blanket. On every side the narrow valley, surrounded by tall, craggy peaks, turned amber and crimson, the light streaming over the tops of the sentinel-like peaks that glittered like icy diamonds. The shadows from the cliff disappeared as the sun stained the earth gray.

As the staccato drumming of a woodpecker broke the silence, Charlie Peace rose from her blanket, throwing it back with a quick gesture, and when she was upright, stamped her feet. Worn buckskin pants were stuffed into knee-high elkskin boots. As she moved to fold up her blanket, the fringe of her soft deerskin hunting shirt swayed gently. Picking up a coonskin cap, she clapped it on her head then stared around her at the dense stand of fir that covered the mountainside. For a moment she considered cooking a hot breakfast, then murmured, "Ain't no time for that if I intend to get me an elk."

She moved to the horse that was staked away from her blanket, patted him on the nose, and asked, "You hungry,

Sonny?" She laughed when the horse nickered, and she pulled out a pouch of feed, pouring it on the ground. "You wait here, and I'll be a-comin' back to get you to haul me and my elk back home." She patted the animal on the shoulder then picked up her knife, a pouch, and her rifle that leaned against a tree. Quickly she checked the priming, found it dry, then left her camp.

As Charlie moved through the trees, her feet making no sound on the thick carpet of needles, her eyes were constantly in motion. They were the darkest possible blue, and the short-cropped, curly hair that fell out of her cap was a deep black. She had high cheekbones and olive skin, part of her Crow ancestry, and a wide mouth set in an oval face. At age eighteen, she was a strong-bodied young woman.

At dusk the night before, she had located a watering hole with an abundance of tracks—elk, deer, and mountain lion—so she was confident of making her kill. She took long strides to cover the ground rapidly, her feet avoiding rocks and dry sticks that might snap and alert the game she sought. Now as she approached the stream, she stopped, tested the air, then stepped past a grove of towering blue spruce so as to come in downwind. She moved cautiously, stopping once for more than five minutes, remaining so motionless she might have been one of the trees, or even one of the stones that glittered in an outcropping behind her. Patience was part of her makeup, for her father had taught her that only patience can bring down the game. "You got to learn to set still, Charlie," he had told her when she was but a girl. "Try to turn yourself into one of them stones. Don't move no more, nor even breathe no more'n you can help."

Slowly she worked her way in behind a clump of stunted firs, so crowded they could not attain their full growth. Her eyes narrowed as she settled down, the rifle cradled in her arms, ready to be aimed at once.

At first nothing happened, except a black squirrel ran out along an extended branch over her head. Looking down, he chattered at her angrily to leave his domain. The brisk wind that rustled the pine needles overhead was the only sound then for a time—until a faint rustling reached her. She pulled the hammer back on the rifle and half turned to face the creek. For a time she saw nothing, but she knew how shy these animals were. Finally, a flash of movement caught her eye, and a six-point mule deer stepped out of the shadows of the timber and halted, head high. He seemed frozen for a time as his nostrils flared, testing for scent. Satisfied all was well, he moved forward to the water and lowered his head to drink.

Disappointed it was a deer instead of an elk, Charlie decided to still take the shot. Moving almost imperceptibly with the rifle lowered, she waited until the bead was on the side of the buck by his heart. Then she pulled the trigger. The kick of the rifle jolted her arm and lifted the barrel several inches, but she saw the buck fall sideways to the ground. He kicked wildly, staggered to his feet, then ran toward the woods. He had not gone more than a dozen steps, however, when he fell to the earth, his antlers crashing against the stones that lined the stream.

Charlie smiled with satisfaction. "You ain't no elk, but you'll be prime good eatin'," she said. Speaking aloud to herself was a habit she had formed from being alone so much of the time. Aside from her parents, there was no one for her to talk to—no brothers or sisters. So she talked to her horse, her dog, and herself.

Reaching into the pouch at her side, she reloaded the rifle. Pouring the powder into the barrel, ramming the ball on top of it, and then adding the powder to the pan to explode the charge took less than thirty seconds; then she rose and walked to the stream. The deer was on the far side. Since she didn't want to get her feet wet, she moved down until she found a narrow spot studded with rocks that could serve as a walkway. Lightly holding the rifle, she skipped across then walked to where the deer lay, his eyes already glazed. Leaning the rifle carefully against the trunk of a dead fir, she pulled a large knife from its sheath and expertly skinned the deer. Rising, she washed her hands in the stream, replaced the knife, then grabbed her rifle and headed back to camp. Throwing the saddle on Sonny, she said, "Got us a good 'un, Sonny. Too bad you cain't bite up on deer meat. It's plumb good, but not for hosses, I guess."

She threw her gear onto the horse behind the saddle, stepped aboard in an easy motion, then drove the big bay at a gallop through the forest. When she reached the deer, she tied Sonny up and again leaned the rifle against the tree. Then she began to put portions of meat into the aged, rank-smelling canvas bags she had brought for this purpose. Her mind was so engrossed with the task that it took Sonny's shrill neighing to catch her attention.

Fear shot through her nerves as she turned, for there, emerging from the thicket, was one of the largest grizzly bears she had ever seen! Lean from hibernation, he still looked monstrous. *It's too early for bears to be out,* she thought wildly, but there was no time. The bear was no more than forty feet away and coming at her with incredible speed.

Charlie Peace had spent her life in the woods and had had her share of close calls. Acting on pure reflex, she leaped for the rifle, glad she always kept her rifle primed. Sonny had broken loose and was running away, but she paid no heed. She threw the rifle to her shoulder, putting the sight right on the bear's mouth. Bears could be hit by half a dozen bullets and not be killed, so she knew it had to be a head shot. If she missed, she would be mauled and probably killed. In the few seconds she had left, she steadied her arms and hands and, as her father had taught her, gently squeezed the trigger. The powder exploded, kicking the barrel up, and Charlie at once turned to run in case she had missed.

But she had not missed. The bullet took the bear right in the open mouth, driving upward through his brain. He took four or five more paces; then his front legs collapsed and he rolled over, awkwardly coming to rest not ten feet from where Charlie stood. Blood stained the back of his head, and his paws made paddling motions for a few moments then grew still.

Staring down at the dead grizzly, Charlie slowly lowered the rifle until the butt of it rested on the ground. Her breath began to come faster then, and she swallowed hard. "Wal now. That was a mite close!" Her voice was somewhat hoarse and sounded overly loud in the stillness of the glade. She smelled the burning powder and heard far off the sound of Sonny as he continued to run through the thickets. But as she looked down, pride swept through her. "Reckon Pa would have been proud of that shot," she whispered. Reaction came then, and her hands began to tremble. *I didn't think nothin' could do that to me,* she thought. *But a full-grown grizzly about to tear your heart out—I calculate even most men would be a little shook up by that.*

She whipped her hat off and wiped her damp forehead. Then she loaded the rifle again before marching off in the direction Sonny had gone. He had not gone far and came back to her call, somewhat skittish. Charlie waited until he was calm. "Reckon you'll have to tote double, because I intend to bring some of that bear meat back to Ma. She always was partial to bear liver. Come on now. I'll skin the critter, and you haul 'em both back."

The cabin that Noah Peace had built for his wife was far better than most found in the rugged mountains. He had built it himself without any help, out of the blue spruce that abounded on the Rockies, and now as he sat in a chair built out of oak that he had hauled from the lowlands, he still felt as he had nineteen years ago when he had first notched the logs and raised them. Noah, a tall, rangy man of fifty with dark blue eyes, a short beard, and a thick growth of auburn hair sprinkled with gray, was not a man who thought deeply. His life in the Colorado mountains had tempered him, and he had lived with the seasons, enduring the frigid blast of winter, often snowed in for weeks at a time. As he glanced over toward the woman who sat across the room, reading by the light that streamed in through the window, his mind went back to the time he had brought her from the western plains to the high mountains. Naomi had been the most beautiful woman he had ever seen, one-half Crow, the other half white—her father a mountain man named Dollar, who had been killed by a hostile tribe. But now whatever disease was attacking her had weakened her and dulled her coppery skin. *She's worse,* he thought, studying her countenance, and sadness flooded through him. *She's gettin' weaker every day. I've got to get her to a doctor or somethin'—though I never had no use for 'em.*

Naomi Peace looked up from the Bible she was reading and caught her husband's glance. She was an astute woman and knew that the sickness she had was more serious than any of them had thought at first. Seeing the concern in Noah's eyes, she smiled faintly. "I'll feel better now that spring is almost here."

"Why, shore you will." Getting up from his chair, he came over, knelt down beside her, and took up her hand, thinking how thin it was and remembering how strong and plump it had been before the sickness had come. Awkwardly he raised it to his lips and kissed it, bringing a look of astonishment into Naomi's eyes. "Well," he said, "I'm gettin' to be quite a Romeo, ain't I now?"

Squeezing the big hand that held hers, Naomi said nothing for a moment. Silence was customary with her, though she often sang as she worked in the cabin and outside in the garden—sometimes the old songs of her people, other times the hymns she had learned at the missionary school where she had been when Noah had come by and seen her. The memory of that day flooded back to her, bringing warmth.

The sun was bright, and the mission school was surrounded by young women working in the garden, some of them washing clothes in a big black pot. Naomi had been hoeing beans, and she had looked up when a shadow had fallen across her. A big man with the bluest eyes she had ever seen and a rash grin looked down at her from a tall buckskin horse. He wore faded blue trousers, a deep blue shirt, and a gaudy yellow neckerchief. For a long time he said nothing; then he slipped off his horse and stood before her, so tall she had to look up. She had waited for him to speak, and when he had, his voice had a softness unusual in the men she knew. He had said, "Howdy, miss. My name's Noah Peace."

The memory remained rich and full in her heart, making her happy. She put her hand out and brushed back a lock of his auburn hair. "You're getting gray," she said.

"Yep, you're married to an old man."

Naomi smiled and let her hand remain on his cheek. They stayed there for a moment, and then a pain took her. To conceal it from him, she took her hand back and said, "I wish Charlene would come back." Naomi always called her daughter by her given name instead of her nickname, Charlie.

"I 'spect she'll be gettin' on home. I told her not to stay out more'n one night."

Noah straightened and walked toward the window. It was midafternoon, and the blue sky seemed hard enough to strike a match on. The snow was melted, except for the high peaks, and spring would soon be here, although the winds were still numbing. He stood quietly for a while then leaned back against the wall of the cabin. Looking down, he said, "I'm gonna take you down to town to have the doctor take a look at you, Naomi."

"If you say so, but I doubt it will help."

Concern flared in Noah's eyes. He opened his mouth, but one look at her face caused him to cut off the words. Naomi was a firm woman; he had long known that, and he could not break through the Indian part of her. So he walked the floor nervously then stepped outside the cabin and did the afternoon chores. He had just finished them when he heard a shout and looked up to see Charlie riding in from the trail at full gallop. She brought her big bay to a stop and slid off in one fluid motion, her eyes bright with pleasure.

"'Bout time you was gettin' home, Charlie."

"Pa, I got a six-point buck—and guess what else?"

"Couldn't venture a guess."

"A bear."

"You shot a bear? Didn't know they was out of their winterin' yet."

"This'n was. He's plumb skinny, but I brought some of it home with me."

"How'd you nail him, Charlie?" He stood there proudly as she related the story of her hunt, her face mirroring her excitement, the small dimple appearing at the left side of her mouth. As she spoke, he saw the hint of her will that revealed itself in her eyes and lips—features that showed the swift changes of her mind.

"I brung the head in, Pa," she said, pulling a smaller canvas sack off the horse. "Look, he had his mouth open, and I put the bullet right inside it. Came out the back here, see?"

Taking the head, he studied it then drawled, "I reckon you done good. I couldna done better myself, daughter."

"I'll go show it to Ma."

"Well, she ain't feelin' the best right now, Charlie. Maybe later." Her dark blue eyes, so much like his own, reflected unhappiness whenever Naomi's illness was mentioned. She did not argue but nodded, and he said, "I'll unpack the meat. You go set by her a spell. I reckon she'd like that."

"All right, Pa."

As she turned to go, Noah called her back. "Charlie, I been thinkin' a lot about you and your ma—the way we live out here."

Puzzled, Charlie looked up into her father's eyes. He was, she knew, a man who reasoned things out slowly and could not be rushed into quick talk. It was a way he had of going logically from one fact to another, and now as she waited, she felt a rush of affection for him. She could not remember a time when he was not by her side. When she was barely able to walk, he had taken her into the woods and taught her the language of the forest, the names of the trees, the tracks of the animals, and every bird in the mountains. Now she saw something was troubling him.

"I think I made a mistake buryin' us out here in these mountains," Noah said finally.

"Why, Pa, it's a good life."

"Maybe for a mountain man or Indians, but you ain't neither one of 'em."

"I'm part Indian," Charlie said quickly, proud of her Indian heritage. She lifted her head and studied her father carefully, then touched his arm in an unaccustomed gesture. "What's the matter, Pa?"

"Well, this ain't no life for a young woman," Noah said. "You don't never get to go to dances or wear pretty clothes. You don't learn how to sew or do things that young women do. Back when I was a younker growin' up in Virginia, I didn't live in no big mansion, but I worked for Mr. David Radke. Had him a big plantation and a passel of daughters. I'd go by there, Charlie, and there'd be all them girls dressed in pretty white, yellow, and blue dresses. They'd be out on the lawn sometimes havin' a party, their hair all done up, and there'd be young fellers comin' by in carriages and on fine-blooded horses. They'd be dressed real fine, and you shoulda heard 'em laugh and sing and dance, too. I went to one of them dances. Not personal, you understand, but I seen it. The floor was shiny, and Mr. Radke's house had chandeliers overhead with lots of candles, and music with fiddles playin'. It was real nice, Charlie."

"I guess it was, but it's nice out here, too." An impudent light flickered in her eyes. "I bet one of them girls couldna shot that bear like I did with him a-chargin'."

"Likely they couldn't," Noah said, smiling. Then he continued, "I been worried about it. This ain't no life for a young woman."

"I wouldn't want to be nowheres else, Pa." Charlie studied her father's face, not knowing what else to say. He had never talked like this before, although he often talked of his boyhood and young manhood in Virginia. She had asked him once, "Do you wish you'd stayed in Virginia, Pa?" And he had replied slowly, "I don't reckon so, daughter. I always loved the mountains." Now, however, she saw a longing and an unhappiness on his lean face but did not know how to speak to it. Although they were close, this was something she had not learned how to handle. "I'll go in and set with Ma a spell, then fix us a bite of supper." And she walked inside and sat beside her mother, telling her about the hunt, all the while wondering what her father was thinking and why he was so disturbed.

Charlie was sitting cross-legged on her narrow bed with a turkey quill in one hand and a large tablet on her knees. She studied the date then nodded in self-approval at the writing. Although Naomi had learned how to write at the mission school, Charlie had not taken well to instruction up to this point, preferring to hunt and trap with her father rather than study with her mother. Now she attacked the job of writing as she did everything else where skill was lacking—with determination. Dipping the turkey quill in the inkwell, which was set on a shelf nailed into the wall beside her bed, she began to write, the quill scratching as it moved across the paper. Her tongue, from time to time, would creep out from between her lips as a particularly hard word had to be written, and her brow would wrinkle.

GILBERT MORRIS

February 17, 1863

Ma aint doin well atall. I worry bout her somethin awful. She is losin wait, and you can see it in her face and in her neck. She caint eat much and I can tell she hurts real bad—which makes me hurt, too. Pa says he is goin to take her to town to see the doctor, though he dont have much confidense.

Irritation swept through her as she tried to spell through *confidence* in her head several times and then finally shrugged. "It don't make no never mind. I can tell what it is, and ain't nobody else gonna read this here diary anyhow." She steadfastly plowed on through bad spelling and grammar.

Pa has got me worriet. Ever since I kilt the bear last week, he aint said hardly two words together. Its the way he is when he is thinkin bout somethin, and there aint no way to hurry him up. I wisht he would tell me what it is cause its more worry to me not nowin than it would be nowin whatever it is. Maybe he is just worriet about Ma, but then, I am, too.

Pete Ledbetter come by yesterday. He brought a quarter of a deer he had kilt, but I reckon as how that was just an excuse. I been suspectin him for some time of wantin to get his hands on me, and yesterday he done it. We was out at the corn crib, and I was showin him the new shoat. He said he wanted to see it. Well, theys mighty fine shoats if I do say so my own self, and I raised em all by hand. When we went out there I was just fixin to show him the shoats when he reached out, grabbed me, and hugged me, and would have

WITNESS IN HEAVEN

kissed me right on the mouth, but I just had time to turn my head. I got mad at Pete. I swung on him and hit him smack in the eye as hard as I could. He went a staggerin back and then got mad, askin me what kind of a girl I was that didnt want to be kissed. I told him I would be the one to say when there was a kissin to be did, and if he tried it again I would black his other eye. He went roarin off, and when Pa came out and asked what happened, I told him. He laughed at me, which I didnt like, and said, "You might as well get used to men wantin to sweeten up to you," and I told him it wouldnt be Pete Ledbetter anyway.

Before Charlie could start another sentence her father called from downstairs. "Charlie, come down here, will you?"

She took a little box of fine sand she had gotten from the bed of the river, sprinkled it over the red ink, and then swished it around the paper before blowing it off on the floor. Then she carefully closed the tablet, put it back on the shelf, wiped the turkey quill off, and capped the bottle of ink. Springing off the bed in bare feet, she started down the ladder, jumping the last six steps and hitting the puncheon floor with a slap.

"You're gonna break your ankles jumpin' out of that attic. I done warned you about it," her father said mildly.

"What you want, Pa?"

"Guess I want to talk to you. Come on over here and sit down. Me and your ma got somethin' to say."

Alarmed, Charlie sat down on a stool before the fireplace. The fire had burned down to glowing coals that radiated heat throughout the cabin. She glanced over at her mother, huddled in a blanket, and saw that her face was stiff and unnatural.

"Charlie, I been doin' a lot of thinkin' all week long, and I done made up my mind about somethin'." Noah glanced over at Naomi and paused, but she said nothing. "Your ma don't quite agree with me on this, but it's somethin' I guess I gotta do." He stood up, back stiff, and went over to the window and looked out. It was an involuntary action, for he was an outdoorsman, and the cabin was confining to him. "It's like this, Charlie. I been considerin' that this kind of life ain't no good for a young girl. I done told you that."

"Pa, I like it here. I don't wanna go nowheres else."

"That's what you say because you never been nowhere else. But you cain't live out here the rest of your life, or you'll have to marry up with somebody like Pete Ledbetter."

"That no-account! I wouldn't have him on a bet!"

"That's all there is around here, trappers and hunters. Some of 'em is mighty fine men, but rough." Noah struggled to put his thoughts into words and finally threw his hands apart in an impulsive gesture that showed his unhappiness. "I been thinkin' 'bout what it was like when I grew up, about them planters back in Virginia around Richmond, and I done decided the best thing to do is to go there."

"You mean—live there? What will we do in Richmond? That's a town, ain't it? It ain't woods like this, and mountains."

"That's right, and that's where you need to be. But the trouble is, I ain't got the money to buy a plantation."

"Then we cain't go," Charlie said swiftly. "I don't keer, Pa. I'm all right here. Me and Ma like it, don't we, Ma?"

"Your pa has always dreamed of goin' back there." Naomi's voice was low, for this was not one of her good days. She had listened as Noah had explained what he intended to do, and now her Indian blood came to the forefront. She would no more have thought of arguing with him than she would have reached out to strike the sun. "Perhaps he's right. This is a wild place, and you have no hopes here."

"That's what I say," Noah replied. "What I got to do is to make some money."

"You mean trappin'?"

"No, there ain't no money in that. The fur trade is dead." Noah leaned forward, his eyes alight as memories came back. "Before your ma and I married, my friend Lavelle Cole and I went out to Denver huntin' for gold."

"Did you find it?"

"Well, there was lots of gold found all over the West, but it got so bad that the people come floodin' in from everywhere, and I couldn't stand it no more, so I came to the mountains."

"But ain't all the gold took?" Charlie demanded.

"Most of it is, but me and Lavelle went out chasin' some of them creeks back a ways. And, Charlie, we found good color. But Lavelle, he took sick, and I had to bring him back. The poor feller died two months after we got back here to the mountains. I always intended to go back and get that gold."

"You mean we're gonna go gold huntin'?"

"Not *we*, Charlie," Noah said. "Just me. I'm gonna go back and pan enough gold to buy us a plantation in Virginia."

Charlie could not have been more surprised. She shifted her glance to her mother, but Naomi's head was down. Charlie wanted to argue, but she knew her father well. He was indulgent toward her, but from time to time he would speak in a certain tone, and fire would flash from his eyes. When that happened—as it had now—Charlie knew protesting would be foolish.

"All right, Pa. I'll stay here and take care of Ma while you're gone."

Relief flooded Noah Peace, and he expelled his breath with a rush. "That's my girl." He came over and caressed her raven hair with a rough but affectionate hand. "You'll like it back in Virginia when we git on that plantation—wearin' pretty dresses and dancin', and young fellers tyin' their hosses up out at the rail and comin' in to see you. And I'm gonna get me a white suit and a bunch of black cheroots and walk around and be a big plantation owner just like Mr. David Radke."

"How long will you be gone, Pa?" Charlie asked.

"Just long enough to git the gold. I'll send word to you by way of Silas Warmerdam, the fur buyer in town. There's always trappers comin' out this way. He kin ask one of 'em to drop a letter off."

"Kin we write to you, Pa?"

"Well, once I'm at where I'm goin', I'll send word where you kin write. Most likely the post office in Denver."

Charlie *was* worried, although she had better manners than to show it. "All right, Pa," she said. She went to sit down on the floor beside her mother and took her hand. "We'll make out fine until Pa gets back with all that gold, won't we, Ma?"

Naomi Peace knew more than she said. Deep within she knew that unless Noah hurried back, she would not be there to greet him. Her pain was growing much worse, but she stoically refused to reveal it. Now she could do no more than to encourage her daughter as best she could. Although Naomi knew somehow she would probably never live to see Virginia, she managed to smile. "Yes. We'll take keer of each other."

Chapter 2

Two Are Better Than One

Despondent, Noah Peace rode his horse down Black Mountain, leading another packhorse. Up until the time he had said good-bye to Naomi and Charlie, he had been excited about his journey. He had left just after daybreak, embracing Naomi and whispering, "I'll be back, and we'll see all the doctors you need and get you well again."

But as he guided the horses down the old Indian trail, a grayness came over his spirit. He knew Naomi well, and despite her attempts to cover her pain, he knew she felt worse than she would admit.

By noon he had reached the foot of the mountain and crossed the north fork of the Powder River. Turning west, he pushed the horses on until nightfall, where he hit the main body of the river and made camp.

Since the spring grass still had not appeared, he fed his horses the grain he was carrying. Collecting firewood, he made a roaring fire. *I couldna made a fire like this seventeen years ago,* he thought. *I'd have lost my scalp.* As he cooked his bacon and made coffee, then sat back to eat it, he thought of the old days. He wondered if, as men grew older, they lived in the past more than in the present, and certainly not in the future. Overhead the wind whistled through the firs, and the river gurgled beside him, its icy water flowing down from the mountain toward the lowlands. He took a bite of the bacon and chewed it thoughtfully, recalling his youth and strength. He remembered the days he had competed with Crow warriors and when he had first begun to think of Naomi as a woman he might love. She was the most beautiful woman he had ever seen and had turned down many men. A smile creased his tough lips as he gazed into the fire, watching as a log shifted, sending myriad sparks upward like tiny stars to tangle with the larger stars overhead. It reminded him of many campfires of his youth. Finally, he rolled into his blanket and fell asleep.

Arising at dawn, he cooked breakfast, ate it, then saddled his horse and put the load on the packhorse. He continued to follow the path of the river. By late that afternoon he reached Fort Collins and stayed for the night. He had not been in the settlement for years, but now he saw it had changed little. Tying his horses up outside the single hotel that decorated the town's main street, a place he had stayed once before when he passed through, he entered the mirrored lobby. A raw pine desk and a stairway were attached to one of the walls, and through an archway he could see the dining room. He gave his name, made his mark at the register, then went up the creaking stairs and opened the door on the left.

Sealed with rough lumber with cracks between the beams, the room allowed anyone to observe his neighbor. A single window covered by green roller shades discolored by sun and rain opened onto the main street. A lamp was set on a table, and the bed was a mahogany four-poster covered with some lumpy quilts and a pillow without a slip. The floor had once been covered with a lead-colored paint, but now that was mostly faded to a leprous gray and brown.

Back a few years ago, I could have made this trip and still been ready for a night of howling like a wolf. A man gets old. Comes up on him all of a sudden. He still thinks young inside, but when he looks in the mirror, he sees that he's nearer the end of the trails than he is to the beginning, Noah thought, realizing he was tired.

He stripped off his shirt, washed his face, and shaved, grunting as the razor pulled through his whiskers. He had not shaved for some time, and it was a painful chore. Finally, he dried his face, put on a clean shirt, then descended the rickety stairs, turning left into the dining room, directly across from the saloon. Once entering the dining room, he saw a blackboard sign: T-BONES, MASHED POTATOES, AND APPLE PIE—FIFTY CENTS. The notice beneath it made him grin: IF YOU DON'T LIKE OUR GRUB, DON'T EAT HERE.

Sitting down, he waited until a slovenly Indian girl with obviously unwashed hands brought his meal. She gave him a sultry look but, when he did not respond, shrugged wearily. As he ate, he studied his fellow diners, who consisted mostly of roughly dressed miners and a few townspeople, including some farmers and their wives.

After the meal, he filled his pipe and sat smoking it. When it was consumed, he tapped it on his heel, letting the ash fall to the floor. Rising, he threw four bits on the table and made his exit. When he reached the foyer, he hesitated. It was early, and the food had quickened him somewhat. When he heard a tinny piano, he entered the saloon—more out of a desire to escape the leprous floor upstairs than for any other motive. It was a long room with a few battered tables where several games of blackjack and poker were going on, while across the far wall a mirror reflected a long bar. The walls were decorated with elk and deer antlers, and a badly stuffed mountain lion scowled from a table beside the east wall. The smoke was thick, covering the clink of glasses and the murmur of poker players' voices.

Noah became aware of an argument going on over to his left and turned to see the source of it. Three roughly dressed men wearing guns had engaged the few men who stood at the bar. One of the toughs, a large, muscular man wearing a garish yellow shirt and red neckerchief, was belligerently arguing with a tall, elderly man who regarded him steadily. "I ain't lettin' no Yankees tell us what to do! If I want to have slaves, I'll have 'em!"

"That's right, Dud," the slender man on his right said. He was more finely dressed, with charcoal slacks and a pale blue shirt, and wore a .44 pistol on his left hip. "These nigger lovers here need to get back to New York or to Chicago."

The man named Dud was showing off, Noah realized, for his audience. With a squat neck, curly red hair, and a scarred face, Dud had the look of a professional fighter. Something about his attitude warned Noah that he wanted trouble. *He's the kind that likes it,* he thought, *and he'll have it out of somebody.*

The argument spoiled the saloon for Noah, and he started for the door. But before he could reach it, the man in the pale blue shirt stood up to bar his way. "Which side are you on? Are you a Yankee?"

Noah was not carrying a gun. He had one in his gear upstairs, but it hadn't occurred to him he'd need one. So he just said mildly, "Don't know anything about politics." As he moved to go around the man, Dud joined them. "Well, what is he, Slick?"

"Says he don't know nothin' 'bout politics."

Dud grinned, his teeth large and stained with tobacco. "Don't know 'bout politics. That sounds like some kind of a yellow dog to me. A man that don't know which side to take in this here war ain't worth a lot, is he?"

The third man, tall and gangly, had come to join them. His hazel eyes were rimmed with drink. "If I had my way, we'd rat out all these Yankee nigger lovers and run 'em out of town on a rail!"

Noah suddenly realized these three had located innocent strangers and humiliated them before. Although he was more Southern in view than Federal, he determined he was not going to let hooligans like these force him to give his views. "If you three will just stand aside," he said quickly, "I'll go to my room. I don't want no trouble."

"He don't want no trouble, Devoe. Did you hear that?" Dud said, winking at the hazel-eyed man. "He's one of them Yankees all right. They don't never want no trouble, but they're gonna come down south and tell us how to live and whether we kin own slaves or not." He stepped forward, his eyes hard. "I think I'm gonna make an example out of you, Yankee."

"I wouldna do that."

Dud laughed aloud then, driving his elbow into Devoe's side, and said, "I'm gonna bust you up, Yankee. I'm gonna break your teeth out into stubs and bust your nose so you'll whistle when you breathe. Then I'm gonna kick you until you walk straddle-legged."

Noah knew he had a beating coming. He did not have to look around the room to understand no one would come to his aid. This was a country where a man took care of his own quarrels. Fervently he wished he had brought a gun, for he would have used it if he had. Instead, he tightened his lips in preparation.

The three stood before him, anticipating the fun. Cruelty in his eyes, Dud lashed out, his huge right fist grazing Noah's cheek. Managing to step aside, Noah threw a strong punch that caught Dud in the nose and set him back. As blood immediately spurted over Dud's shirt, he looked down at it with disbelief. Then, seemingly immune to pain, he wiped his nose with his sleeve and grinned even more broadly. "Well, looky here. We got us a live one. Come on, boys. Let's bust him up."

Noah watched as the three separated, Dud in front of him, the other two moving to his left and right. Noah had just doubled his fists and held them up when a voice behind him said, "You boys like good odds, don't you?"

Dud had been poised to attack. The voice set him back on his heels. He lowered his huge fists and stared at the man who had come to stand beside Noah. "You buyin' into this?" he demanded.

"Always like to see even odds."

Noah turned his head to look at the man who had come to his aid. Over six-feet-two, he was about twenty-eight and lean, lithe, and muscular looking. He reminded Noah, somehow, of a mountain lion at rest but ready to spring into action with blinding speed. Deep-set hazel eyes and light brown hair showed beneath the tan hat he was wearing, and he had a scar on his right cheek. Noah noticed that he was smiling. Although most men before violence get tense, there was an ease in his expression. *He's seen the elephants,* Noah thought, relieved. When Noah saw the man had a worn Colt on his left hip, he felt obliged to say, "Don't need to buy into trouble on my account, though I appreciate it."

Dud stared at the tall man. "You'd better butt out of this— or are you a Yankee, too?"

"I'm not givin' my past history today. Why don't you and your two friends go to the bar and have a drink?"

"Easy won't do it," Dud said. He had won many fights, mostly because of the heavy bone that surrounded his brain and his bulky muscles. He needed a fight as most men need food, and now, being deprived of one, he glanced at his two friends and found the odds comforting. "Well, I think you Yankees are gonna get a whippin'. Just like you got at Bull Run." He pulled his fists back and lumbered forward, his eyes glittering with anticipation. His two friends moved around to the side, and Noah stepped back. He had decided to take on the smaller one and try to put him away so that the odds would be two against two. Somehow he felt the tall man would be able, at least, to handle the muscular Dud.

But even as Noah glanced to one side, he was shocked to see that somehow the revolver at the tall man's side had been lifted and then brought down with a crushing blow on Dud's head. It almost drove him down, but the thick cushion of bone kept him from total unconsciousness. He stirred and put his fists up again as blood stained his cheeks, this time from the cut made from the gun barrel. But he had no chance, for once again the gun was lifted and fell on the other side of his head. A hard blow drove him down, where he sprawled loosely on the floor. The muzzle of the gun instantly swiveled to cover the man called Slick. Slick's eyes were blank with shock as he looked into the eyes of the man who had just destroyed his friend. He swallowed hard and said hoarsely, "I ain't joined."

"Better take your friend out. He may need a few stitches."

Noah watched as the eyes of both toughs changed. They were unused to being beaten, but something in the tall man's attitude gave them pause.

"Come on, Devoe. We'd better get 'im to a doctor."

The two men grabbed the unconscious Dud's arms. He was so large they could not carry him, so they dragged him out with his heels bumping across the rough floor of the saloon. They turned to go outside, and the barkeeper yelled, "Look at that blood! Who's gonna get it off the floor?"

Noah turned to the tall man. "I'm obliged." As Noah put out his hand, the tall man's gun seemed to disappear, almost as if by magic; then his hand was met by a firm grip. "Never could stand fellows like that."

"Me neither. My name's Noah Peace."

"Boone Manwaring."

"Got time to sit down?"

"Got nothing but time."

As the two men moved over to a table in the corner of the room, Noah said, "You saved me a beatin', mister."

Boone shrugged. "Glad I was around. This war fever's making men act crazy."

Noah grinned. "Actually, I guess I'm more Southern than I am anythin' else, but I wasn't going to let that hooligan tell me what to believe."

"I feel the same way. Lots of self-constituted committees roaming around Colorado these days. Most of them never heard a shot fired, but they think they know exactly how to run the country and the railroads."

The two talked of the war for a time. It was going badly for the South, although they had won victories like Bull Run.

"I grew up in California," Boone said mildly. He sat loosely in his chair, relaxed. "I guess if I'd grown up in the South, or even in New York or Chicago, it would be a lot more real to me."

"Your people, they ain't aligned?" Noah inquired.

"Don't have any people, really. My father was a captain on a schooner. My mother died when I was fourteen. I've been at sea most of my life." He hesitated, and an odd expression crossed his face. "We had a shipwreck last year. Only seven of us got off. My father was the captain, but he didn't make it."

"Sorry to hear 'bout that. It must have been hard."

"Most things are hard in this life, I guess."

The remark caught Noah's attention, and he examined Manwaring's face more carefully. Something about this man set him apart. The corners of his lips had a tough, sharp set, as if he had both a sense of humor and a temper that could come out hot as fire behind his quietness.

"That's all the family you had?" he inquired gently.

"Yes. That's all."

The brevity of the reply stirred Noah. "Not good for a man to be alone. That's what the Bible says."

"That's right. In Genesis, talking about Adam."

"You know the Bible?" Noah asked with surprise.

"Know it—don't do it."

Noah smiled at the laconic statement. "That about describes my condition. I got a good wife. She's a fine Christian. So's my girl."

"You got a family? Where are they?"

"Back up in the Rockies."

"Don't know it. Don't know anything about this country."

It was against Noah's inclination and habit to pry into other men's business, but somehow he felt easy enough to ask, "Where are you headed?"

"Guess I lost my compass," Boone said. "I had enough of the sea—for a while at least. Thought I'd see what this country looks like. It came in my mind to go prospecting." He smiled, his teeth white against his tanned skin. "I don't know any more about prospecting than I know about being a lawyer. But it sounds like something a man ought to do once in a lifetime."

Caught by surprise, Noah said, "I kinda got that idea myself."

"Is that right? Have you done any prospecting?"

"Some years ago I did some. Never hit it really big. Me and a partner of mine was in California. But he got sick, and I had to bring him back home."

Boone leveled a gaze on Noah. "What would a fellow need to go prospecting? I'm nothing but a greenhorn. Sometimes I feel like a fool even talking about such a thing." He reached up to scratch his eyebrow with his right forefinger. He looked at the finger and said, "Look." He doubled his fingers under with the forefinger extended. "I can't bend that finger."

"What's wrong with it?"

"Got crushed when I tried to catch a shark when I was at sea. My old man put it back together. I didn't lose it, but it won't bend."

"That's your trigger finger. How do you manage that?"

"I shoot with my left hand. I do most things with my left hand. Didn't use to come natural to me, but it does now. Sometimes I think it would have been easier if it had been lopped off." He gave Noah another look and said, "Where would you figure to go looking for gold?"

Noah Peace was a fair man. "If it wasn't for you, Boone," he said quietly, "I wouldna be doin' any prospectin' at all. Them fellas woulda left me with busted ribs, if I was lucky. I figger I owe you somethin'."

"No need to feel that way."

Although Noah sometimes worried an idea for days or even

weeks, he made up his mind instantly. He liked the look of this man. "You saved me a beatin', Boone. That means somethin'. Look, back when me and my partner was prospectin', we found color in a stream that I bet nobody's found to this day. That's been some years ago, but it's the most unlikely lookin' spot I ever seen. It comes out of the mountains and then runs for no more than a few miles before it disappears in a hole in the ground. I always intended to go back and check it out."

"That's where you're headed now?"

"Yep. Be glad to have you go along with me. Fifty-fifty. We'll split what we find."

"You don't know me, Noah."

"I doubt if any man knows another complete, but a man needs a partner in this country. If he's out there, falls down, and breaks a leg, what does he do? Probably dies. The Bible says two are better than one."

Boone leaned forward. "I wouldn't want to be butting in on your find."

Noah laughed. "May not *be* a find, Boone. You've got to understand that. I found some color there, but the creek may have been found and panned out, or it may have been just a flash in the pan—no gold to speak of. But I'd like to have you. There's still a few Indians around there. I'd feel pretty good havin' you by my side."

Boone Manwaring was somewhat taken aback. His life had been hard, and he had found men often to be less than honorable. Now as he looked into Noah's dark blue eyes, he made his own decision. "I'll go along, but I don't know about the fifty-fifty. I don't know the first thing about mining."

Noah flattened his hands on the table. "Not much to learn about it. Once you find it, you dig it out of the ground or get it out of the river. It's a lot of hard work either way. But fifty-fifty is the way it will be. There'll be no more talk, all right?" He stuck out his hand and felt the impact of Boone's gaze. Somehow he knew he had done the right thing.

※

The two arose before dawn, left the hotel, and began moving south. They did not stop to make camp until dusk. The road was well traveled, so there was little chance of Indians, and for two nights they found a place beside a stream where they could camp and rest the horses. On that second night Boone heard the details of Noah's decision to go prospecting.

Sitting beside the fire, Noah had been thinking about Naomi. "My wife ain't been well," he explained to Boone. "I'm worried about her. That's one reason I'm goin' prospectin'—to git money for good doctors."

Two days on the trail had given the men confidence in one another, so Boone listened as Noah spoke freely about his wife and daughter, Charlie.

"Her real name's Charlene, which is what her ma calls her, but somehow I got used to callin' her Charlie."

"How old is she, Noah?"

"Eighteen years old. She's one-quarter Crow. Naomi is half Crow. Good-lookin' people, the Crows. Best lookin' of all the Indians."

"I don't know much about Indians."

"They're fine people, but they're gettin' pushed aside. That's one reason I went to the mountains, I guess. I lived with the Crows for a while, but I saw their ways was disappearin', so I married Naomi, and we went up to the high country. Charlie was born the next year. We've stayed up there."

"I like that," Boone said. "On a ship you're never alone. Most crowded life on earth, I do believe."

The fire burned cheerfully in the darkness as Noah finally began to speak of his dream. "When I was a boy in Virginia," he said, "I was poor, but I always watched the rich plantation owners...."

As Noah continued to speak of his desire to go back and buy a plantation and make his daughter into a fine lady, Boone felt a gust of compassion. Brought up in a hard school, Boone had decided somewhere along the line that most of life was drudgery and trouble—and that the most fun came only when you worked very hard for it. However, fun came and went too quickly. The emptiness in Boone's soul didn't easily receive good things. Although he was moved by his new friend's dilemma, at the same time he felt there might be trouble ahead.

"It's just a dream I got, but a man's got to fight for his dreams, I guess," Noah concluded.

Boone picked up a stick, stuck the end in the fire till it blazed, and then tossed the whole thing into the flames. "Dreams don't work out—that's been my observation."

Seeing the hardness and doubt in the younger man, Noah said grimly, "This one will, Boone."

Boone didn't move or speak for a time. Then he summoned a grin. "I hope so, Noah. I'd like to see you sitting on a porch in front of a big white house down in Virginia drinking a mint julep and smoking a thin cheroot, and your girl all dressed up. I'd like to see that."

Noah Peace allowed himself to smile. "That costs money, and we're goin' to get that, Boone. Better get some sleep. Once we get to the gold country, there won't be much of that."

GILBERT MORRIS

Later, as Boone stared up into the sky, spangled with a million points of light, he wondered about what had happened. His father always taught him that a man's life was out of his control—*"What's going to happen is going to happen."* Now he had met this man who had a dream he desperately wanted to see come true—if only to refute his own grim philosophy. Finally, the night closed around him with all of its darkness, and he fell asleep.

Chapter 3

The Long Good-Bye

Pale bars of sunlight filtered through the single window in the loft. Charlie blinked and came awake, instantly turning her head to one side to avoid the glare. The corn-shuck mattress rustled as she sat up and stretched her arms high, while from outside, as regular as the sun itself, the rooster lifted his clarion call—shrill, clear, and urgent as it announced the beginning of a new day.

"Reckon you think the day couldna start without you servin' notice." Charlie stood and went to the window, loving the mountains and the hills that lay beyond the valley. In some ways, Charlie was a creature of firmly fixed habit—she liked the way things were and was suspicious of change. Now she performed her morning rituals.

Slipping out of her cotton gown, she donned her underwear then poured water from a pitcher into a basin. She took some soft soap on her fingers, spread it on her palms, and lathered her face until it glowed with a rosy tint. She had made this soap herself and added a bit of scent that her father, at some distant time, had brought to her mother. As she rinsed off and dried her face, she thought with some sadness, *But Ma never uses perfume.*

As she slipped into her jeans and one of her father's old cotton shirts, she stopped long enough to sit down on her bunk.

Picking up her worn Bible, she opened it at the place marked by a dried wildflower. She sat there, letting the light play over the words of the Psalms for ten minutes, then bowed her head and prayed softly, "Oh Lord, You know Ma's sick, and You know they ain't nothin' we kin do for her. It's plumb out of our hands. I'd be obliged, Lord, if You would see fit to give her a good day. Take away all the hurtin'. And be with Pa. Keep him safe on his travels and bring him back again, for, Lord, You know how bad we need him. And I pray this in Jesus' name."

Placing the Bible back, she picked up her tablet and removed the top from the jar of ink. The ink she had also made herself out of pokeberries and soot from the fireplace. It was not as good as store-bought ink, and she reminded herself to get a supply the next time anyone went into the village. Dipping the turkey quill into the ink, she began to write, as always, haltingly.

July the fifth, 1863

>*Well, yesterday was Independence Day, but it didnt make no difference to us. Ma had one of her bad spells, and I set by her most of the day tryin to ease her, but it wasnt no good. She never makes no complaint, but I know she is hurtin fierce. I would give anythin to just take it off her, but there aint no way one person can hurt for another, I reckon. I dont like to think about it, but I wonder what it would be like if Ma went to be with Jesus. It would be bedder for her though, I know that, but it shore would be hard for me and Pa. We would miss her so much.*

Leaning back, she perused what she'd written, crossed out a word and wrote in a different spelling, then began again.

We had another letter from Pa last Thursday. He claims he was doin good. We got three letters from him, and the writin is the finest you have ever seen. Its writ by a feller called Boone Manwaring, which is a funny sort of name for any man. Reckon he was named for Daniel Boone, but I aint never heered of no Manwaring in all my born days. Anyhow, he writes as nice as anything you ever seed. I wisht I could write like that, but I caint.

Pa said that him and Mr. Manwaring was workin hard lookin for gold, but they aint found much yit. He was plum worriet about Ma and me. When I writ him back I told him there wasnt no sense worryin about me. Ma was doin poorly. I didnt ask him to come back, but I sure wisht he would. I dont care nothin about no gold, and I aint goin to no Virginia and becomin a lady. These mountains was good enough for Ma, and they is good enough for me.

Anyhow, I got to thinkin last night. Ma is mighty partial to turkey, so I reckon I will go out this mornin and see if I caint get one for her. I wisht Pa was here, for he shore is good on shootin them things, and I aint as good as him. But if it would help Ma, I wouldnt keer if I had to stay out all day.

After finishing the words and sprinkling sand over the writing, she got out of bed. She slipped her feet into the elk-skin boots then descended the ladder to the main living area. Moving quietly, she went to the door of the single bedroom and looked inside to see if her mother was awake. "Are you awake, Ma?"

"Yes. Good mornin', Charlene."

Moving inside, Charlie put her hand on her mother's head and smoothed the hair back. "You ain't never called me Charlie in my whole life. Why is that, Ma?"

"I think Charlene's so pretty. I wish your pa would call you that."

"He won't never do that." Charlie noticed with some shock that some of her mother's hair was white. "I'll fix you up some nice grits and maybe a soft-boiled egg, Ma. Maybe two."

"One will be enough."

"All right, Ma. You lay easy there."

Charlie built up a fire, got the water boiling, then boiled an egg and made grits. She added a cup of fresh milk and took it in to her mother, then went to fix her own breakfast. She fried up a piece of ham and two eggs easy-over, for she liked the yolks runny, and ate them, along with a biscuit left from the day before.

When she went back into her mother's room, she found the egg only half eaten and the grits hardly touched. "Cain't you eat no more, Ma?"

"I'm not hungry. Maybe later," Naomi said. She reached over and took her daughter's hand. Her face was very pale with strain, and her lips were drawn tight as she whispered, "You have a time takin' care of me. I wish you didn't have to."

"It's okay, Ma." Words came hard for Charlie, for neither of her parents were great talkers. So they sat there saying nothing, both of them aware that the illness that had come the last six months was not going to pass away. Then Naomi looked at her daughter, whom she loved so deeply and strongly, and said, "Charlene, after I'm gone, you must not grieve for me."

"Don't say that, Ma!"

"You're a Christian, Charlene, and so am I. We've talked so much about how hard this life is and how it will be when we are with the Lord." Naomi's eyes were filled with pain, and not all of it was physical. In the smooth face of her daughter she saw the blue eyes, a part of Noah, and the black hair and olive skin that were her own contribution. "I'm glad you're a good girl and know Jesus. It would be hard to go if you wasn't."

Charlie was not a young woman to show emotions, but her eyes began to sting. Despite herself, tears formed. She dashed them away and threw herself on her mother, holding her close. The thinness of her mother's body was a never-ending shock to her, for, like Charlie, Naomi had always been a strong woman. As Charlie's body shook, her mother stroked her back. The two stayed that way for a long moment, and then Naomi said, "Now you go 'bout your business. Sometime this afternoon we'll read the Word a little more. All right?"

"All right, Ma." Charlie straightened up and tried to smile, wiping her tears away with the backs of her hands. "I'm goin' to get you a turkey, Ma. You always liked fresh tom turkey."

"Thank you, Charlene."

Leaving her mother's room, Charlie cleaned the dishes and then picked up the rifle and ammunition pouch. She went to the small, sturdy box where the ammunition was kept and got the shot out, adding it to the pouch she wore slung on a belt around her waist. Moving over to the mantel, she picked up the turkey call her father had made for her. She held the wooden box with paper-thin sides gently in her hand, then picked up a whetstone and drew it across the top edge of one side. The action produced a low, rasping crooning that sounded like a hen turkey; she made it yelp by jerking the stone across. Satisfied, she stowed it in her upper pocket and left the cabin.

Since she had heard turkeys calling not a mile from the cabin, she walked across the yard and through the fields and finally climbed a rise. When she reached the top, she looked down into the valley that glowed in the summer sun like a jewel. It was studded with trees, none very tall. However, long grasses grew there, and the grasshoppers were thick, which drew the turkeys.

It was late to be on the field, and she knew she would have to be patient. She reached a blind made out of deadwood stacked in a rough fence and covered with brush. She and her father had come here often, and now she lay down and checked the priming in her rifle. Carefully she slipped it out through a gap and could almost hear what her father had said the first time he had brought her here. *"Now you cain't move that gun. Don't you even bat an eye, because them turkeys can see better than folks. Just call to him, and if he gobbles as much as twice, that's all you need. You might have to wait an hour, maybe longer, but if you call another time, he'll suspicion somethin'. After he quits gobblin', he'll make out like he's goin' the other way, but don't you fear—he'll slip back."*

For the next thirty minutes the young woman lay still. She had given the turkey call twice, and the last time, after a few seconds, she had heard what seemed to be an echo but was really a turkey responding. Finally, she was rewarded by a flicker to the right. Moving only her eyes, she saw a magnificent tom turkey step out. He nervously stepped forward, making a rapid pecking motion with his head, then uttered a clucking sound again. Charlie did no more, and after nervously making a half circle, the turkey advanced with regular steps. From behind him two female turkeys followed, and Charlie thought, *They'd be more tender than that male. I'll take the second one there.* As it happened, however, as the turkeys marched across the line where her rifle was held, the two hen turkeys were side by side for one instant. Charlie squeezed the trigger, and when the gun went off, the tom charged away into the brush with a thunderous beating of wings. Both of the hen turkeys were knocked to the ground, and as Charlie rose up with an exultant cry, they kicked their last. "Two with one shot! Even if it was bird shot, Pa won't never believe this!" she cried. Running over, she picked up the two turkeys by the feet.

She returned to the house at once, stepped inside, and called, "Ma, I got *two* turkeys. I'm gonna fix you the best turkey you ever had."

"Sounds good, daughter."

After she had dressed the turkey, she rubbed the outside with lard, sprinkled it with salt and pepper, and put it inside the oven, where she baked it for about three hours. When that was done, she combined flour, the cooked chopped liver and gizzards, and water in the saucepan to make gravy.

By two o'clock the meal was ready, and her mother was up watching her as she cooked. She set the table, adding two glasses of sassafras tea, and said, "Ma, yesterday was the fourth, so I guess this is *our* Fourth of July."

"It smells wonderful," Naomi said. She started to get up, but then her face went taut, and she fell back in the chair, gasping for breath.

"Ma, what is it?"

Naomi could not answer. Her eyes were opened wide, and her lips moved as she tried to speak. Charlie reached out and held her hand, crying, "What is it, Ma? Is it bad?"

Naomi Peace struggled with the pain of the white-hot brand in her breast, knowing it was time for her to depart this earth. Struggling to speak, she managed to say in a weak voice,

"Tell your...pa I always loved him...." She reached out and held Charlie's face between her palms. With loving eyes, she gasped, "You are my faithful daughter, Charlene. I will..." She was suddenly taken by another tremendous pain and closed her eyes for a moment. Aware Charlene was holding her hands, she prayed for strength for a moment. Then she said, "I will wait for you in...our Father's house."

Then the pain lessened, and she opened her eyes. But she seemed to be drifting away. The outline of the cabin walls, the home that had been hers for so long, faded while her daughter's face grew sharp and clear. Naomi whispered, "I have always treasured you, my daughter," then closed her eyes as strength went out of her. She slumped back, her head turned to one side.

"Ma! Ma!" Charlie cried. She touched her mother's face, but she knew her mother was gone. She began to weep violently, holding her mother's head close as tears rolled down her cheeks and her body shook.

Charlie went to Lyle Gunderson's cabin after she had gotten her mother back into bed and said, "Lyle, Ma has gone to be with the Lord."

Gunderson, at forty-five, was a widower. Having lost his wife two years previously, he stared for a moment with shock at the young woman who stood before him, her back so straight, her lips a white line. "I'm mighty sorry to hear that, Charlie," he said finally. "I wish your daddy was here. There ain't no way to get him, I don't reckon."

"No. Will you help me, Lyle?"

"Why, shore. I'll go right now to get the preacher, and then

I'll get the word out to everyone that your ma's passed." He hesitated and said, "Can you watch the kids while I go?" He had three children, all under the age of ten.

"I'll take keer of them, Lyle. I'd like to have the funeral as soon as we kin."

"I won't waste no time, Charlie."

The funeral was over, and the neighbors had left. Several of them had urged Charlie to come and stay with them, but she had shaken her head, saying, "I'll wait here for Pa."

There had been more than twenty-five people at the funeral, and the preacher had come from the village. It had been a good funeral, for Rev. Smith had known Naomi Peace well. She had attended his meetings, and he had preached a fine sermon. Later he had expressed his condolences, saying, "Child, she's with the Lord, but I know it's still hard." When Charlie had not answered, he said, "What will you do until your pa gets back?"

"I'll be all right, Reverend."

The preacher had looked at her then said quietly, "I believe you will, Charlene. Let me know as soon as your pa gets back. I'll be wantin' to talk to him."

Now only Lyle Gunderson remained after the grave had been filled, and he came to stand quietly beside Charlie. He was a red-faced man who was habitually silent, and the task of raising three lively children had put lines in his face. He hesitated until she finally said, "Come in, and we'll eat some of this here food, Lyle. I'm beholden to you."

"'Twern't nothin', Charlie. I wish I could have did more."

The two moved inside the cabin, and Charlie, glad to have

something to do, heated some of the turkey, thinking it had been years, rather than little more than a day, since she had brought the turkeys home.

"Fresh kilt, ain't it, this turkey?" Gunderson asked. He was wearing his only suit, which was small for him. Before eating, he took off his coat and hung it on a peg on the wall. He listened as Charlie told how she had killed two with one shot.

"Don't reckon I ever heered of a shot like that." Admiration shaded Gunderson's eyes as he ate quickly and hungrily. Outside, his children were playing, their voices keen in the air.

Charlie thought, *Death means so little unless it's one of your own.* Inside, however, there was a dull, empty ache. "Would you keer for some more turkey, Lyle?"

"Reckon I've had aplenty." As he sat up, Charlie noticed he was nervous. Not fathoming why, she began to clean the table off.

"Charlie, I thought I might say somethin' to you. I hope you take it right."

Surprised by his tone, the young woman asked, "Why, what is it, Lyle?"

Gunderson shifted uneasily and ran his big hand over his taupe-colored hair. "This ain't no time to speak of it, but I figured I ought to say it now. What it is, Charlie—well, I got three kids and don't know how to raise 'em. Now you're a growed woman, and I been thinkin' on it for some time. You got no man, and if you ain't spoken for, it appears to me like we need each other."

Charlie's olive skin flushed, and she dropped her eyes for a moment. Gunderson's announcement did not come as any great surprise to her, for she and her parents had often talked of how he needed a wife to share his life. She also had been aware of his eyes on her from time to time, but to her he was an old man.

WITNESS IN HEAVEN

It was not, however, uncommon for young girls to marry older men in the mountains. They needed husbands, and the older men, after they lost their wives, needed a companion.

She liked Lyle Gunderson. He was always polite, a slow, soft-spoken man she had always admired for his kindness to his neighbors, his willingness to help. He also was a good father. But there was nothing that moved inside her toward him, so she said gently, "I thank you for your offer, Lyle, but I reckon I'll just go on like I am for a time."

"It's your say, Charlie," Gunderson said, disappointed. "But if you ever change your mind, I reckon I'll be ready."

Gunderson left soon after that, and Charlie, unable to bear the cabin with the many reminders of her mother, picked up her rifle out of pure habit and walked the woods until dark fell. It was hot and sultry, but she did not heed the weather. Her mind was full of her mother, and she knew that for days, or weeks, she would not be able to stop the rush of fond memories.

Finally, going back to the cabin, she stood irresolutely for a moment then put the gun over the mantelpiece and climbed the stairs. Lighting the candle beside her bed, she got out her writing material. With an unsteady hand, she began to write, *Dear Pa, I got reel bad news for you. Ma went to be with the Lord just yesterday....*

Chapter 4

Yellow Dust

March 1863

By the time Noah and Boone reached Denver, the mountain peaks to the west of the fledgling city still glittered with snow, but a lush smell of fresh earth and vegetation pervaded the air.

"Not much of a town, is it, Noah?" Boone observed as the two entered by the north of the city. He took in the treeless, dusty streets lined with false-fronted buildings and dotted by an occasional brick edifice. Boone had seen many cities in his travels, and here the brick buildings were strangely incongruous in the incivility of their surroundings. The two rode on through the population of miners, merchants, Indians, town boomers, drifters and drovers, lawyers and gamblers, and it was Noah who said, "The town's a lot bigger than it was the last time I was here. Weren't no brick buildings here then."

"Are we going to stay in Denver?"

"Just for tonight. I reckon we'll get a room if we can and see if we can't get some wind of what's goin' on."

The two pulled up in front of a three-story yellow building with white-framed windows that bore the sign

Hamilton House. "This ought to be good enough for us," Noah said, grinning.

They dismounted, tied up their horses, then stepped inside. The lobby was busy with men talking loudly of the war. "I guess there's no way to get away from this war," Boone said.

"I reckon not." Noah waited his turn in line then asked the pimple-faced young clerk, "Got a room?"

"If you got ten dollars, we do."

"Ten dollars for one room?"

"That's the price, mister." The clerk's hair was slicked back with grease, and there was a nervous tic in his right eye. "Do you want the room or not?"

"Reckon so." After Noah made his mark on the register, Boone wrote "Noah Peace" after it then signed his own name.

"Number 208," the fledgling clerk said. "Next!"

Carrying their gear upstairs, the two men entered the room and saw one sad-looking bed with a sagging mattress.

"Reckon I'll take the floor," Boone observed.

"We'll cut the cards for it. Come on, let's wash up and go downstairs. I need to find out what's happenin'."

The two men washed, changed shirts, and went downstairs, walking leisurely down the dusty street. As they moved along, they heard many accents—sharp-clipped voices of New England, Irish brogue, and the soft tones of Virginia and the South.

"It looks like there are people here from all over the country," Boone observed. "Gold draws people like honey draws flies—and most of it ends up in places like that." He pointed at the Golden Horseshoe, a saloon with a man out in front begging customers, "Come on! Give us a bet! Step inside, sports! Pretty ladies and win your fortune at the wheel of fortune!"

"That's where most of it winds up," Noah agreed.

"Does a meal occur to you?"

"Reckon so. I'm hungry enough to eat a buffalo, hide and all."

Ten minutes later the two were seated in a large restaurant filled with men determined to speak as loudly as possible. The din was tremendous. "I wonder why they all talk so loud," Boone said.

"They don't get to talk much when they're out workin'. I guess they try to make up for it here."

"Are most of these miners?"

"Shore. That's what Denver's here for. If it wasn't for the mines, this wouldn't be nothin' but a dusty spot at the foot of the mountains."

After the meal, they made their way to the Golden Horseshoe and sat at the bar, each nursing a beer. The talk was either of the war or of mines and claims and strikes. Boone Manwaring knew the talk of the sea, but all of this was like a foreign language to him, so he kept quiet until finally they were outside, stepping along the boardwalk. "Did you find out anything about where to prospect, Noah?"

"Why, I wasn't figgerin' to find that out." Noah gave Boone a surprised look. "I thought I explained that. We could stay here for ten years and never hit a strike. Our only hope is that one spot I found last time I was here with my partner. Reckon we'll pull out in the mornin'. We'll stock up on supplies today. Load our packhorses down."

"Will it take a lot of equipment?"

"Not as much as you might imagine," Noah said. "Come on. Let's go buy our supplies; then we'll rest up today. Get a good night's rest and start out in the mornin'."

WITNESS IN HEAVEN

❧

Boone looked at the creek that meandered between large outcroppings of rock down the slope of a ridge. Somehow he'd been expecting something different, and he lifted his eyebrows as he turned to his partner.

"That's it, Noah?"

"What did you expect, the Mississippi?" Noah grinned at Boone. "Greenhorns come out here expectin' gold to come poppin' out of the ground, maybe like popcorn. It ain't like that!" He reached over to his packhorse, opened a canvas bag, and pulled out a tin pan twelve inches in diameter and several inches deep.

"Guess you're due fer a little education, Boone. Come on. Let's set up the tent and cook us up some supper. This trip's done wore me out."

The two had left Denver at dawn that morning, covering thirty miles that day. Weary and dusty, they set up the tent and installed the cots with mattresses, for Noah had said, "I've done slept on the ground enough. We're liable to be out here for weeks."

When the tent was up, they had a quick meal of flapjacks, which Noah made expertly. "Reckon you'll get sick o' these before long."

"I don't know. They're mighty good. We didn't have these on board ship."

Noah speared a fragment of flapjack, mopped it in the molasses he'd poured in beside it, and then stuck it in his mouth. When he had chewed it thoroughly, he washed it down with a cup of scalding coffee and then waved his cup toward Boone.

"It's time fer a little education," he said.

Boone finished his meal and took a swallow of coffee, making a face. "That's strong enough to raise the dead!"

"You'll get used to it. Now if we was comin' out here to *mine* gold, that'd be a different story," Noah explained. "We'd have to have shovels, and picks, and dynamite, and saws to make timber—all kinds of stuff. Why, in the winter when the ground freezes, you have to build a fire over the ground to soften it up. Then you dig down a couple of feet to where you hit frozen ground again, then build another fire. A foot or two a day is mighty good goin'."

"Sounds like a lot of work."

"Work? That's the name of gold huntin', Boone. Tenderfeet come out here, and bank clerks, and ribbon clerks, and lawyers. Ain't never done a hard day's manual work in their life. They don't last long as a rule. Farmers make good miners. They're used to hard work. And cowboys, they don't last long. All they want to do is ride a horse, although they're tough enough."

"So we're not really miners, then?"

"No. That takes a long time and a lot of capital. And time's the one thing I ain't got—or capital either." He picked up the pan. "We'll be lookin' for 'placer gold'—means gold in a creek or a river."

"How did it get there? What's it look like?"

"Well, I'll show you what it looks like tomorrow. Maybe, maybe not. But it gets there from being washed down from the high country. See those hills over there, where this creek comes from? It winds all around almost from the top, and if there's gold there, over a lot of years, it picks up a flake here and there, washes it along the bottom of the stream, and finally sometimes it bangs up against a rock. I've found pockets of gold as yellow as a hound's belly, but usually that ain't the way. I'm tired, Boone. I'll give you your first lesson tomorrow."

The two slept soundly, and after breakfast—pancakes again—Noah picked up a pan and handed it to Boone. "You're gonna get them fancy boots wet. You'd better put on the ones you bought in the store."

He waited until Boone had put on the rough brogans, then went down to the edge of the creek. "Here's all there is to it," he said, squatting down. Dipping the pan into the water, he dug at it until it was half full of pebbles and sand. "The trick," he said, staring down inside the pan, "is to get everythin' out of this pan except the gold—if there be any."

Boone watched as Noah rocked the pan back and forth, letting a little of the sediment at the bottom clear the edge. It looked simple enough, just a twist of the wrist, and finally when the pan was almost empty, he asked, "Any gold?"

"Not a particle."

Somehow, despite the warnings from Noah, Boone was disappointed. "Does that mean there's no gold here?"

"It means there wasn't no gold in that pan I just did. I'll move here and try again. Sometimes you get nothin' and move six inches and find that yellow dust. Have a try at it."

Boone imitated Noah's actions. "How do I know what I'm looking for?"

"Anythin' that glitters is suspect. May not be gold, but it might. Here, I'll just watch you fer a spell."

Boone eagerly tried several experiments, feeling awkward, but Noah encouraged him. "Ain't no great art in it," he said. "You're doin' fine." Then he stopped abruptly and said, "Look! Right there!"

Peering down into the pan, Boone saw a flicker of light as

the sun shone into the pan. With excitement, he asked, "Is that gold?"

"Let me see." Noah peered at it. "That's gold all right."

"How much is it worth?"

"Probably about ten cents."

"You mean only a dime?"

"That's right." Noah was enjoying the look on his partner's face. "Now if you did that about a thousand times today, you'd make a day's wages." He laughed at Boone's astonished face. "But the next pan might be worth fifty dollars. Who knows?"

That was the beginning. The two men worked the creek slowly, but Boone's legs soon ached from the unnatural squatting position. Noah spotted this and said, "You'll git toughened up soon. I guess I'd have some kind of problem if you had me on your boat haulin' sails up."

Boone soon discovered there was nothing really difficult about panning for gold. It was just tiring and enormously hard work. Hour after hour, he worked doggedly on. They paused at noon long enough to cook a quick meal, then went back to work. All afternoon under the glittering sun they kept at it until finally, at three o'clock, Boone said, "Well, I reckon that's enough for us today."

As Boone arose, his legs protested, pain shooting through the backs of them. "My legs are killing me!" he groaned. He looked over at the older man, who was peering at the bag where they carefully kept the gold they had panned. "How much did we make, Noah?"

"Maybe ten dollars. Maybe a little less." When he saw the expression on Boone's face, he continued, "But wait till tomorrow. We'll probably strike it rich."

"I think I'll have to lie down tomorrow. That squatting is killing me!"

"You'll get used to it. A man can get used to anythin'. Come on. I'll fix you some more pancakes."

"None of that. Let's have some steak tonight before it spoils."

⚜

As the weeks wore on into April and then became May, Boone's legs grew stronger. He was able to match Noah hour for hour as they moved slowly upward toward the mountains. It was dull, boring work, but no more so than some of the duty he had put in on board ship. He did not complain and thus won Noah's approval.

"I reckon you're doin' good, Boone," Noah said as they roasted the jackrabbits he'd caught. The odor of the cooking meat made both men ravenous. "You ain't afraid of work, and you got a strong back. That's about all you have to have to be a prospector."

Pulling the stick back, Boone tested the flesh with his knife and found it to be done. He began tearing strips off and, careful not to burn himself, chewed on the tough meat. From time to time he took a spoon and dipped into the can of beans he'd opened.

The two men ate quietly and then, as usual, opened up a can of peaches to share for dessert. They drank the bitter coffee and listened to the sounds of a night bird. Looking up into the sky, over toward the timber, Boone said, "Mighty quiet life."

"Like bein' at sea?"

"No, not like that. A ship's a noisy place. Usually crammed with more men than there's room for, and not beds enough for the hands."

"Where'd they sleep?"

"They have watches at different times when they're on duty. They get to sleep in a bed when somebody's gone on watch."

"Don't think I'd keer for it. Too crowded."

Boone nodded but said nothing. The two sat there in warm companionship. Boone had learned over the past weeks that Noah was a single-minded man. He worked like a machine and never seemed to grow discouraged, where Boone himself was not so motivated. But Boone knew that sooner or later, as he did every night, Noah would begin to speak of Virginia and then of his family.

"Back when I was a younker, I remember the planters used to go huntin' foxes. Somethin' to see."

"Never saw anything like that," Boone remarked.

"Well, I don't know what they do it fer. Don't reckon a feller could eat a fox. Probably taste about like a hawk."

"You've tasted hawk?"

"Oh, shore. Once I got lost for a day or two and had to eat somethin'. Hawk was all I could git."

"What did it taste like, Noah?"

Noah laughed aloud. "About like fox, I guess. Tough as saddle leather and wild. I guess Naomi could have made it better, but she weren't there." His rough face softened as he began to speak of his days back in Virginia. They were very real to him, Boone discovered, though many years had passed. Noah had a fixation about the gentry in Virginia. Finally, Noah said, "I'm gonna git me one of them plantations. Maybe not a big one, but Charlie, she'll like it, I bet."

"Might be different with the war on. It's bad enough out here," Boone commented.

"Oh, I reckon there's fightin' all right, but that'll be over soon. Them Yankees, they'll give up and go home soon enough."

Boone had doubts about this, for he had studied the political situation more than his companion. He knew Abraham Lincoln was not a man to quit, and the North had the edge in manpower and munitions. However, he did not attempt to persuade Noah, for he had discovered there was a blind spot in the man's thinking. He had his dream, and he was going to achieve it—war or not.

"I thought we'd hit good color before this," Noah said after a long silence. "I found another little spur of this here creek. Ain't more'n three or four feet acrost, but sometimes you find color there. Maybe we'll move over and try it tomorrow."

⚜

They did try the creek, which was barren, and finally in early June had to go back into town for supplies. When they got there, they were astonished, for they found that most of the town had burned down. They stared at the blackened skeletons of buildings and on an inquiry found out that flames had burst out in the night on the roof of the Cherokee House on Blake Street in the middle of town. The wind had pushed the flame around, and the fire had leaped from false front to false front. Men had tumbled out of their beds to form ragged bucket brigades from the South Platte River, but their efforts were useless.

"Looks like Denver's about gone," Boone murmured, looking at the wreckage.

"Guess it is, but they'll build it back. Where there's gold, men'll build. Let's go see if there's any supplies to be had. I'll bet they're pretty short."

The two managed to get what supplies were available, paying a high price for them, and then returned to their camp. They worked hard for three days. It was on the third day that Boone said, as they pulled their blankets up, "I don't think we'll ever find it, Noah."

Noah lay silently for a while. Then he asked, "Do you want to give up?"

"Just about."

"You go on, then. Me, I ain't leavin'."

"What about your family?" Boone had written several letters to Noah's family and had read the two letters that had come from Charlie. He had picked them up in Denver on his trips in for supplies. The spelling was abominable and the writing only passable. He had a picture in his mind of the young woman from Noah's description, and now he thought of the last letter that had spoken of Naomi Peace and her illness. He did not feel qualified, however, to remind Noah of this. He knew Noah was worried, but the fixation in his mind of finding gold and getting his family out of the high country and back in Virginia was too strong.

"I'll try awhile longer, Noah," he said finally.

It was two days after this conversation that Noah came crashing across the creek where Boone was panning. "We got it, Boone—we got it!"

Boone stood up, his face alive with excitement. "What is it, Noah?"

"Over there!" Noah grabbed Boone's arm and shook him, then began to dance around like a wild man. "I found it for shore! Look!" He opened his bag with trembling hands and poured out a stream of yellow nuggets and dust. "That's one pan, Boone! Just one pan, and it's all collected right there in a little bend smashed up against a rock ledge. All we gotta do is git it out!" Then he stopped dancing, and tears ran down his face as he stared at the yellow dust. "I reckon the good Lord led us to this place."

"I'm glad, Noah. Now you can take care of your family."

"Come on. We gotta move camp."

The two moved hurriedly, Noah frantic with urgency. The creek that Noah led Boone to was inconsequential. "Probably dries up in the summer," Noah said, "but right now it's here. Come on—I'll show you."

He led Boone to a bend in the creek that dead-ended into a solid sheet of rock. Noah waded out into the middle then drove his pan up against the rock. "Try it, Boone!" he yelled.

Boone followed him out and scooped up half a pan of rock. As he lifted it, his breath grew short, for he saw at least half a dozen nuggets, some no bigger than a pinhead, but two at least as large as a pea. His hands began to tremble, and he looked up wildly at Noah. "I never saw anything like it," he whispered.

"I did when I was here before, but I was afeered somebody would git to it. Come on, Boone, we got work to do."

⁂

Boone Manwaring had known hard labor at sea, but never had he worked as hard as he did for the next several months. Every day he rose before first light, ate a hurried breakfast, then went at once to the creek, which they named "Mogo." He worked steadily throughout the day until nearly dark; then the two staggered to camp for a meal. Supplies ran low over time, so one of the two would go hunting. For if they went to town, Noah warned, there was always a chance that somebody would follow them back to their strike.

"It's happened plenty a times, Boone," Noah told him. "Man finds gold, he goes into town, shows a nugget—then everybody in the whole creation is out diggin' elbow to elbow with him."

"But we got to get grub, and we're out of salt, Noah," Boone finally protested. His bones were aching with the unaccustomed work, toughened as he had become. He had watched the yellow dust grow in the bag Noah had brought as an act of faith, and every day he waited for Noah to say they had enough. Now it was almost September.

At last Noah relented. "You go on to town, Boone, and git some supplies. Take both pack animals. Bring enough back to last another month. I'll stay here and pan out some more dust."

Boone left the next morning for Denver. He got the supplies then moved to the brand-new post office, built out of raw timber and smelling of rosin. As he stepped inside, he nodded to the postmaster, who remembered him. "Hello, got a letter for your friend. His name's Peace, ain't it?"

"That's right. Noah Peace."

"Right here."

"Thanks. Get this one off, will you?" Boone asked.

Boone took the letter with the familiar writing he knew to be Charlie Peace's. He stuck it in his inside pocket then went out, mounted, and led the packhorses out of town. He made the trip back quickly and arrived at dusk.

"You made good time, Boone."

"I was afraid I might go into a saloon and get drunk and tell about the Mogo out here, but I didn't. Letter from Charlie."

"Let's unload them supplies and cook up some of this grub. Then you can read it to me."

They unloaded the supplies and turned the animals loose to graze before Boone said, "I'm the cook tonight. I brought a bunch of canned stuff."

"I could eat shoe leather," Noah said eagerly. "You do the cookin', and I'll do the cleanin' up."

The meal was different, for it included canned oysters, canned corn, beef, and for dessert a pineapple that had somehow found its way to Denver. After the meal was over, Noah leaned back and patted his stomach. "Reckon that'll keep me fer a spell. Now read me Charlie's letter."

"All right." Reaching into his pocket, Boone used his knife to slit the envelope. He pulled out a single sheet of paper and started to read. "'Dear Pa, I got reel bad news for you. Ma—'"

Boone broke off abruptly, and Noah Peace grew very still. "What's it say, Boone?"

Boone bit his lip and couldn't answer for a moment. "It's bad news, Noah."

"Is it—Naomi?"

"Yes," Boone said.

"Read it."

I got reel bad news for you. Ma went to be with the Lord yesterday. She went easy, and the last thing she said, almost, was to tell you how much she keered fer you. I am rite sorry that I have to tell you this. I know how it will hurt. I will wait here til you get back, or if you will write to me maybe I can come and be with you. I am sorry, Pa. I miss her a lot.

Your loving daughter,
Charlene Peace

Noah held out his hand, and Boone put the letter in it. As the older man ran his fingers over the writing, the fire crackled, and from somewhere far off a wolf sang his lonely song to the night sky.

"She was a good woman, Boone."

"I'm sure she was, from what you tell me."

Noah said quietly, "I got to git back, Boone. We've got enough gold here to buy that place in Virginia. I'm gonna take Charlie and go there."

Although Boone still had his doubts about Noah's plan, he saw the sorrow in the big man's dark blue eyes. "I'm right sorry, Noah." He tried to say something comforting, but there was nothing except, "You need to get back with your daughter."

"I'll start first thing in the morning."

"That'll be best."

"What you figure to do, Boone, with all this gold we dug out?"

"No plans, Noah. I'm like a ship without a rudder." Boone sat there looking into the fire.

Abruptly Noah said, "Wisht you'd trail along with us, Boone."

"You mean back to the mountains?"

"No, I mean go with us back to Virginia. You ain't ever seed that part of the world, have you?"

"No. Never been to the South."

"You'd like it there, Boone. It's mighty good country. They ain't got big mountains like these, but they's got the Shenandoah Valley. Ain't nothin' prettier than the Smoky Mountains. Not even the Rockies, to my judgment."

Boone's curiosity was stirred. He had heard much of the fighting, and he knew that Noah Peace was doomed for some disappointment. "I guess I'll go along just for a while," he said.

"I'd like to see those Smoky Mountains, and I'd like to meet that girl of yours, too."

"She's like her ma in a lot of ways."

They were silent for a while; then Noah finally said, "I feel like I been shot right in the middle, somehow. A man stays with a woman long enough, she gits to be part of him, and when she's gone it's like losin' an arm or a leg. But with me it's more like I done lost a heart."

There was nothing Boone could say, so he made no attempt. *I'll go with him,* he thought as the two went to bed. *He doesn't need to be alone. Maybe I'll like it in Virginia.*

The next morning they got up, packed their gear, and left. As they took one look back at the creek, Noah said, "We didn't get it all. Someday you might git a notion to come back and take the rest."

"Don't think I'll do that," Boone said softly. He let his eyes run over the creek and felt the solid weight of the gold in the canvas sacks slung over his pommel. "I don't think a man should go back too much. If you look too much at what's behind you, you can't know what's going on now, or what may come tomorrow."

Noah nodded. "That's true, but it's hard fer a man not to look back. Come on. Let's get to where Charlie is...."

Chapter 5

Promise to a Friend

The late-afternoon sun had dropped behind the barricade formed by the Rocky Mountains by the time Noah and Boone reached Denver. Casting a critical glance at the long shadows that were beginning to fall, Noah murmured, "Let's treat ourselves to a little celebration, Boone. We can put up in a hotel, have a good meal, and start out by first light."

Stretching high in the saddle, Boone arched his back and nodded. "That might be all right, as long as we don't get into a poker game and show some of this color we're packing."

"You're right 'bout that. We'll put our dust in the stage office for safekeeping." Noah laid his hand on the bulky canvas bag tied on behind his saddle. Looking thoughtful, he said softly, "More money here than I've ever seed in my life. It'll be plenty to buy that plantation for Charlie." He turned his attention toward the saloons that were already belting out their tunes. "I'm not gonna throw any away on things like that. I might have, though, when I was a young feller like you."

Sensing the unspoken question, Boone returned Noah's gaze. "Don't worry about me, Noah. A good meal and a bed is celebration enough. There's the stage office down there."

The two men wound their way through the traffic that lined the streets, for though it was only approaching dusk, Denver was winding up for its nightly spree. When they reached the false front of the stage office, they slid off their horses and removed the canvas bags from behind the pommels of their saddles.

When they entered the stage office, an elderly man with blue eyes asked pleasantly, "May I help you with something?"

"Like to keep this in your safe overnight," Noah said, dropping the bag on the counter. Boone followed suit. The agent studied the bags for a moment then picked one up, his eyes widening at the weight of it. "Where'd you dig this out?" he asked, not expecting an answer.

"Over that away," Boone said, waving irresolutely toward the east.

"Don't blame you for keepin' a tight lip," the agent replied. He was an old hand and knew that prospectors went to any lengths to avoid telling their secrets. He started to speak again, but two men came in and stood waiting. Glancing at the two who had fastened their eyes on the canvas bags, he murmured, "I'll just put these in the safe for you gentlemen." He turned and opened the safe at the back of the building to his left. Then, grasping one bag in each hand, he put them in, shut the door, and twirled the combination wheel.

"It'll be here for you," he said when he returned.

"Appreciate it. We'll be back in the mornin'. What time do you open?" Noah asked.

"Eight o'clock."

As the two turned to leave, one of the men who had entered smiled. Wearing an ornate, colorful vest and a long, fashionable black coat, he was certainly no miner. "Struck it rich, I take it," he commented.

"Just fair," Noah said then left the building.

"Sometimes I think folks can *smell* gold," he remarked to Boone as they mounted their horses.

"It's only yellow gravel," Boone replied as he turned his horse's head and the two started down the dusty street. "Butter's yellow, too, and you can spread it on bread. You ever try that with gold?"

Grinning slightly, Noah asked, "That may be right, but did you ever try to buy a mansion with butter?" The two laughed, for there was a lightness, a release of tension as they rode to the hotel and entered the lobby. After signing in, they carried their gear to their second-floor room then washed up.

Leaving the hotel, they ambled in a leisurely fashion down Denver's main street. Some of the saloons were already in full roar. As they moved down the street, the spielers were crying, "Come on over and give us a bet!" Lights beamed through the yellow windows, glittering against the dusk, and bedlam hammered out of the joints. A man stood on one corner as the two passed, lifted his gun and shot into the air, then gave a high-pitched yelp and walked away. Overhead a woman stuck her head through a window and screamed but drew no attention from the passersby, except for Noah and Boone.

"A rough place," Boone observed.

"All towns are bad," Noah said sarcastically.

"Well, you're going to Richmond. That's a town."

"It's different in the South. And anyway, we won't be inside Richmond. I want a place at least ten miles away with cotton fields, corn, and a garden."

Later the two stopped at Franklin House, where they ate a leisurely meal of the usual beefsteak. But there were also fresh vegetables. Curious, Boone asked the waitress, "Where do you get the fresh vegetables?"

"A Chink grows them just outside town." Although the short, heavyset waitress had a harried look on her face, she stopped long enough to give Boone a speculative look. When his eyes rose to meet her gaze, she waited, expecting him to say something. When he did not, she was surprised. "Ain't you gonna ask me what time I get off?"

"What time do you get off?" Boone asked, returning her smile.

"Nine o'clock."

"Too late for me, I guess. I'll be pounding the air by that time. I never have any luck," he said to soften his remark, then shook his head regretfully.

The waitress snorted. "A grown man like you goin' to bed at nine! What's wrong with you?"

"A lot of things, but nothing you could fix, I guess."

Noah had taken in this encounter with interest. "Right pretty. You ain't interested?"

"I'm just interested in getting to bed and getting to your place, Noah. I'm anxious to meet Charlie."

"You'll like her," Noah said, his thoughts on home and the mountain cabin. "She won't like leavin' the mountains," he admitted. "A time or two Naomi and me tried to get her to put on dresses and go to dances and things in town. She tried it out a few times, but she always came back and said she liked huntin', fishin', and bein' away from people."

As Noah spoke, Boone thought, *If she hates towns, people, dances, and dresses, how in the world does Noah think she's going to fit into Richmond society? From what I hear, they're a pretty snooty bunch. Almost like royalty, those planters are, with everybody else a serf.* But since Boone himself felt much the way Charlie did, he simply said, "It'll be interesting seeing the South. I've heard a lot about it, but what you hear isn't always the way things are."

"I been gone a long time, but I remember enough to know I liked it. Good country, Boone, and good people, too. A might high-tempered, but generous and hospitable."

The two men lingered at the table, and when they rose, Boone put the price of their meal on the table then added a silver dollar for the waitress. "If I'm going to be rich, I might as well start tipping like a rich man," he said. Then he moved out of the restaurant, aware of the gaze the waitress fixed on him, but he did not return it.

The two men went back to their room and went to bed at once. They were more exhausted than they knew from the long months of panning gold, for there had been almost no time when they had gotten good rest. Now they dropped off to sleep at once and were not awakened by the noise on the street below or by their sometimes noisy neighbors.

*

The next morning, as Noah and Boone visited the agent to reclaim their gold, a thought struck Noah. "Boone, it just occurred to me it might not be so easy to get gold dust broke up into spendin' money."

"I can do that for you," the agent said, his eyes alert.

"Be a good idea," Boone said.

The agent weighed up their gold, figured the worth, and then asked, "How will you have it? Gold coins or greenbacks?"

"Gold coins," Noah said instantly.

But Boone shook his head. "They'd be too hard to carry, Noah. Greenbacks will spend anywhere."

"Even in the South?"

The agent answered at once. "They'll spend better there. Confederate money's gone down to nothin'. If you're headed that way, you can live like a king on U.S. greenbacks."

Noah hesitated. "All right, mostly greenbacks, but I want some gold coins, too." He stood there while the agent counted out the fresh greenbacks, all brand-new notes, and then made up the rest in gold coins, which he put in small canvas bags.

"You leavin' town now?" he asked after the two had counted their money.

"Reckon so."

"Wouldn't travel after dark—that's a lot of cash you're carryin'."

"Thanks for your interest," Noah said as they left the office. The two had already had breakfast and loaded their pack animals, so they swung into the saddle. "Let's be on the way," Noah exclaimed. "I'm hungry for home."

They left Denver, and when the sounds of the city faded, Noah took a deep breath and expelled it excitedly. "I'm always glad to be out of towns," he said, picking up their earlier conversation. He looked over and asked curiously, "Do you like towns, Boone?"

"They're interesting. I went to China once. Now *there* were some towns for you."

"You went all the way to Chiney?"

"Sure. Once."

Noah pondered this amazing fact and finally asked cautiously, "That's on the other side o' the earth, ain't it?"

"Just about, Noah."

"Hard to figure why they don't fall off." He laughed at his own foolishness. He felt lighter, as if the darkness that had dwelled in him since the news of Naomi's death had lifted. "Let's make time," he said and kicked his horse into a fast trot.

The September air was cool and fresh. The mountains glittered over to their left, and to the right were the beginnings of the flatlands, the plain country of Colorado. They followed the road that curved between two groves of evergreens as it lifted in a steep incline. The horses, laboring, slowed to a steady walk. Noah and Boone had almost reached the top of the grade when, without warning, three men dashed out of the thick woods to their right. They had been hidden behind a massive outgrowth of rock, and their intent was obvious, for all were masked.

"Stand where you are! Don't move!" one of the men shouted.

Although both Noah and Boone were wearing guns, they had been taken unaware and were helpless. Two men, with guns out and loaded, flanked a fancily dressed man—a man wearing a colorful vest. With a flash, they realized it was the man they'd seen in the stage office when they had deposited their dust.

"Stand easy and you won't get hurt! We know you got money. If you want to live, toss it down, along with your guns."

With a bitter taste in his mouth, Boone realized they had no chance. He reached into his inner pocket slowly to pull out the thick wallet containing the bills that constituted his share of the money. But while his hand was still inside, he was startled, for Noah had let out a sharp cry and pulled his gun. Boone wanted to shout, "Don't do it! It's suicide!" but it was too late. Noah got off one shot, and it knocked one of the men out of the saddle. He threw his hands up, uttered a short cry, hit the ground, and did not move.

But the other two men opened fire at once, and Boone, who reached to pull his .44, heard one of the slugs hit Noah, who grunted in the saddle but continued to fire.

As Boone lifted his Colt at the chest of the man with the fancy vest, a slug raked along his ribs, throwing his aim off. Other bullets hissed beside his ear. Noah slumped to the ground, still firing blindly.

Pulling down on the hammer again, Boone could not get a steady bead, for the horses were plunging wildly. Another shot took his hat from his head. When he said, "Steady boy," and his horse steadied, he stretched his arm out, drew a bead, and got off one shot. It struck the vested man so that he slumped, but it didn't kill him. Boone then turned his fire on the other man, who apparently had exhausted his ammunition. Boone's next shot grazed the man's neck, and he dropped his gun and reached up to grab the wound. Then Boone heard him yell, "Let's get out of here!" Boone shot twice more, but the men's horses were plunging, so he missed both times. He pulled the trigger again, but the hammer fell on an empty chamber.

As soon as the men were gone, Boone swung off his horse and ran to where Noah was writhing in the dust on his face. Rolling him over, he demanded, "Are you hurt bad, Noah?" Then he saw that he was. Blood seeping out of his chest had stained his shirt, and his right thigh was also crimson.

Boone whipped out his and Noah's neckerchiefs and made a tourniquet to stop the bleeding of the leg. Pulling the shirt back, he saw that the bullet had entered high and to the right. *If it got a lung, he won't make it*, Boone thought.

"Take it easy, Noah. Don't move."

"Did you—git 'em, Boone?" Noah gasped.

"They're gone. You lie still. I've got to work on this leg."

As he cut away the pant leg and studied the wound, Boone's mind raced. *This is bad. I've got to get him back to a doctor, but I don't know how he'll stand the ride.* His face and mouth grim, Boone considered the options. He was a man of quick decision and action and now said, "Noah, you lie here. I'll make you a travois. You can't sit in the saddle."

"They didn't git—the cash, did they?"

"No, they didn't get the cash." Boone was thinking, *I wish he had let them have it. We could have gone back and dug more gold.*

✥

Edward Fitzgerald was a man of culture, immaculately dressed, hardly fitting into Denver's schemes. But he was the best doctor in Denver. He stood looking down at the still form of Noah Peace, his eyes speculative. He was accustomed to dealing with bullet wounds—indeed, they were his chief stock-in-trade. And now as he looked at the wounded man, he was clinically weighing his chances. Finally, he seemed to have made a decision. "We got the bullets out, but you lost a lot of blood, Mr. Peace."

"Am I gonna make it, Doc?" Noah asked. His voice was thready and weak, and his face pale as paper. But his dark-blue eyes were alive, and he studied Fitzgerald's face as a man might study a book.

"I can't say. I've done the best I can. If you don't get infection, I think you might make it." Fitzgerald turned to Boone and said, "You'll have to keep him here until he recovers."

"I thought that," Boone said.

"No, I got to git home."

"Don't be a fool, man," Fitzgerald said with irritation. "You're not going anywhere! Come along, Mr. Manwaring!"

WITNESS IN HEAVEN

Leading Boone out of the room, which was adjacent to his main office, Fitzgerald said, "It's pretty bad."

"What are his chances?"

"I'm not a gambler. I don't deal in chances."

"You've got a pretty good idea, Doctor. You've seen a lot of men shot."

"Too many." Fitzgerald's reply was glum and his eyes bleak. "The leg will be all right, but he's lost so much blood. It's a wonder he didn't die on the way in. You did a good job getting him here," he admitted grudgingly. "But infection's the problem. When a bullet goes into a man, it carries some of the clothing in. I can't get it out. If it gets an infection..." He hesitated then said, "If you're a praying man, I'd suggest you start praying. Are his family close?"

"Up north. Almost at the border."

"I wish they were here."

"Is it that bad?" Boone asked soberly. He searched the doctor's face but found no hope there. "Do all you can for him, Doctor. Money's no problem."

"I'll do the best I can."

Boone walked back into the room where Noah lay, pulled up a chair, and sat down beside him. "Well," he said cheerfully, "it looks like we've got a little change in plans."

"Boone, you reckon you might go git Charlie? I got a feelin' I might not see her if you don't."

Boone had considered this, but he knew it was a hard trip, and he hated to leave Noah alone. "Let's wait a day or two and see how you make out," he said finally. But as he leaned forward and looked at Noah, he knew there was no way he could fool this man. "You've got a good chance, Noah. The doctor said so."

Noah kept his eyes locked on Boone's and smiled faintly. "I

don't kid myself 'bout things like this. Somehow it don't seem I'll make it."

Boone tried to think of a cheerful rejoinder but could not. Finally, he said, "I've seen men hurt worse than you make it. I'll be right here, Noah."

✦

"I still think it's a fool thing to do."

Noah looked up from the wagon bed where he was lying. Boone had gotten some help and brought him there, but the pain had been worse than he had thought. "If I'm gonna die, Boone, I want to die on my own place, and I want to be buried beside Naomi."

"You don't know you're going to die," Boone said with some irritation. He had been shocked when Noah had told him the previous day that he wanted to go home. He had argued and pleaded and brought in Dr. Fitzgerald, who had told him it was next to suicide, but Noah had been adamant. "If I'm gonna die, I'd like to see my girl one more time," he had said and finally demanded Boone take him there.

As Boone squatted beside him, arranging the pillows and blankets, he remembered Fitzgerald's comment. *"You may as well take him, Mr. Manwaring. He's got an infection. I don't think he'll make it here, and there's a chance he might get to see his family."*

"Are you comfortable?"

"Yes. Just go."

Boone stepped over the wagon seat, sat down, and took up the lines. He had traded in the two packhorses on a wagon and team, and now he slapped the reins on the backs of the bays. "Get up!"

WITNESS IN HEAVEN

As they left Denver, depression settled over Boone. He was totally aware that Noah was likely not going to make it. Barring a miracle, he could not live, but it was Boone's avowed purpose to get him home before he died.

He drove slowly all morning, avoiding the potholes as best he could. He passed by freighters and solitary riders and once a stagecoach, but paid them no heed. At noon he pulled up, made a fire, and heated the broth that he had brought in sealed glass jars put up by the hotel cook. He did not attempt to take Noah out of the wagon and could get him to take only a few swallows. Finally, he gave up, and when Noah asked for water, he poured him a cupful out of the canteen and held his head up while he drank thirstily.

"I guess we'll go on if you feel up to it, Noah."

"Yes," was the single monosyllable Noah was able to manage.

Stepping back into the seat, Boone started the team again and drove steadily all afternoon. He paused at dusk to camp beside a swift mountain stream. He took care of Noah's needs, built a fire, and cooked up supper, but once again Noah refused to eat. He seemed to have lost his appetite completely, and nothing Boone could say could cause him to put down more than a few swallows.

After Boone had eaten, he moved back to the wagon and sat beside Noah. He seemed to have drifted off into a coma, and his fever was up, which Dr. Fitzgerald had warned about. Never had Boone Manwaring felt so helpless as when Noah tossed and threw his arms around.

The next morning he rose at sunup, ate a quick breakfast, then changed the bandages on Noah's chest and leg. Noah was more alert, was able to eat some breakfast, and drank a great deal of water. His fever, however, had not gone down. He said softly, "Go as fast as you kin make it, Boone."

"All right, Noah. I'll do my best."

※

Noah died two days away from his home. Both men recognized it was coming. The fever grew worse, so that Noah passed into unconsciousness, tossing and turning, his skin dry and burning. Boone was helpless. He tried to bring the fever down by bathing the parched body with cold water from the mountain streams, but it did no good.

The end came at dusk where Boone had just made camp. He heard his name called and at once sprang into the wagon. "What is it, Noah? Can I get you something?"

"Ain't gonna. . .make it, Boone." The voice was such a dry whisper that Boone had to lean forward to hear it.

For two days Noah's eyes had been cloudy with the fever, but now when he opened them, they were clear. His mind, too, was clear for the first time, and he reached up a tentative hand to touch Boone's chest. Boone took the hand and held it tightly. It was hot and dry, and fear swept through him. "What can I do, Noah—anything?"

"I hate to lay a chore on you, Boone, but I got no one else to ask."

"Ask it, Noah."

Noah studied the bronzed face that loomed over him. "I got to ask you to. . .take keer of Charlie. She's a woman growed in body, but she's just a child inside."

"I'll help her all I can, Noah. I promise."

"It's more'n that." Noah closed his eyes. He tried to swallow, and it seemed hard. Boone thought he had passed out again, but then he opened his eyes and whispered, "Take her. . .to Virginia."

"You want me to do that, Noah?"

"I'm askin' you to do so."

Boone desperately wanted to refuse. He could already guess the problems that would ensue, but the dying man's eyes were on him, so he cast aside his reservations. "All right. I will, Noah. I'll take her to Virginia."

"See she's treated right. Find her a place. Stay with her, Boone."

"I promise, Noah."

"And. . ." The chest heaved as he fought for breath. There was a rattle in his throat as he said, "Find her. . .a good man. I'm askin' it."

"I'll—I'll do my best, Noah. I promise."

The eyes looked at him then with something like startled surprise, and the voice was suddenly clear. "I. . .thank you, Boone." Noah was quiet for a while, and he only spoke once more—this time in a faint whisper that came out twenty minutes later. As Boone held his hand in despair, he saw the lips move. Leaning over, he asked, "What is it? What did you say, Noah?"

"Reckon. . .I'll see Naomi. . .!"

The end was easy, for Noah simply ceased breathing. The chest grew still, and the hand that was in Boone's relaxed.

Boone sat there in the darkness, holding the limp hand with great sadness. He had learned to love and respect this man in a manner that was unusual for him. He was basically a loner, and Noah's friendship had become a vibrant and living thing in his life. He had looked forward to going to Virginia with Noah, and now the man was gone, blotted out in a moment of senseless violence.

Boone looked up into the dark sky and saw only clouds and a few scattered stars. Doubt and almost anger washed over him. He had wondered for a long time about God, for he had seen the savage side of life, and nothing seemed fair. Now as he held his friend's hand, he wondered, *Why did You have to take him, God? He had a dream that was good, and he's got a daughter. I don't feel equal to doing it, but I gave my word.* He looked up, shooting his mind's questions to the velvet canopy overhead, but received no answers. The clouds rolled on, and the earth's silence enveloped him, yet still he sat there, wondering why a man like Noah had to die when others less worthy lived.

Lowering his eyes, Boone realized that he had no alternative plan. He had nothing better to do with his life than to fulfill this promise to Noah. Boone may not have been a cultured, rich man, but he considered a man's word to be his bond. And he felt responsible, at least partly, for Noah's death. Boone looked to the sky again and knew what he must do.

Chapter 6

"I Don't Need No Man!"

The wind in the trees around the cabin had a soothing effect on Charlie, bringing restful, easy sleep. Since her mother's death she had slept poorly, and her appetite had dropped off. With every day that passed, she realized more and more how great her loss was. But tonight she had gone to bed early and fallen asleep at once.

Then, through the curtain of her subconscious mind, she heard a sound, and at once her eyelids opened. She lay in the bed listening, not frightened but alert, like an animal that has scented danger.

Again the sound came, and she slipped out of bed, pulled on the buckskin trousers she had started wearing when fall had come and a wool jacket, then thrust her feet into the deerskin moccasins beside her bed. Moving quietly, she descended the ladder and crossed the room, lit only by moonlight. She reached up over the fireplace mantel for her rifle and checked the priming. Since the sound had come from the front, she slipped out the side door, standing still in the murky darkness.

Charlie was aware of the source of most sounds at night. The cry of a night bird or the howl of the wolf were familiar enough, but this sound was different. She had not been able to identify the source of the sound, but then she picked up on movement coming down the trail. Slipping out from the shadows of the cabin, she crept to the stand of pines that her father had left growing to create shade for the cabin. The sounds were clearly coming to her now, the sounds of footsteps. Living alone had made her more conscious, for there were rough men in these mountains. Lifting the rifle, she waited, and a shadowy figure emerged. He seemed bulky, and she saw he was tall. He also was carrying a gun, but she could not see the face, for his hat shaded his features.

The figure walked slowly forward, almost as if he were uncertain. He came so close to Charlie she almost could have reached out and touched him. At first she thought it might be her father, but he was bulkier than that, and the moonlight had revealed just a glimpse of his features—a face she had never seen. Moving out behind him, she stepped on a dry stick that snapped, and the man whirled, throwing the rifle up. Instantly Charlie brought her rifle down over his head. The hat cushioned some of the blow, but she heard the solid clunk as the metal hit his skull, and he collapsed bonelessly at her feet.

Breathing hard, Charlie bit her lip. *I'm glad I didn't have to shoot him*, she thought. *But I may have to yet*. Carefully she rolled him over, and the hat fell off. She saw a lean face, rather handsome, and as she studied it she wondered what had brought him to the recesses of the mountains. If he'd come in daytime, she might have welcomed him. But he had come like a thief, and now she reached down and pulled the revolver from the holster at his side. It was a heavy gun, and she stood up and checked the load as best she could by the silvery moonlight. She waited patiently, studying his face, her lips drawn in a tight line.

WITNESS IN HEAVEN

Consciousness came back to Boone with a rush—and a splitting pain that made him shut his eyes and groan. He felt the dry grass under him and knew he was lying full length, but for a moment he couldn't even remember where he was or what he was doing there. Startled, he opened his eyes and sat up, which made the pain worse. Something moist ran down his forehead, and, reaching up, he touched a raw wound on his scalp. Then a voice said, "Set right still!"

Looking up, Boone saw a young woman whose face was illuminated by the faint starlight. The moon came out from behind a cloud, throwing its silver beams across her, and he took in the high cheekbones, the oval face, and the wide mouth.

Boone sat still but explored the bump that was already beginning to rise. The gash was bleeding freely.

"Do you always greet people by knocking their brains out?" he said angrily. As he slowly got to his feet, he saw she was standing clear but was holding his revolver leveled steadily at his stomach.

"I'm keerful when strange men come bustin' onto our place in the middle of the night totin' a gun." The voice was cool and steady, rich with mountain dialect, but he couldn't see her eyes.

"Are you Charlie Peace?"

"That's my name. How come you know it?"

It was an awkward moment for Boone Manwaring. He stood there for a moment, unable to think of a reply. She watched him carefully, and then he said, "I—" He could not finish the sentence, for to tell her that her father was dead was a hard thing. Finally, he said, "My name is Boone Manwaring. I came—to tell you about your father."

The gun wavered slightly, and the light from the moon made a silver line along the barrel. "My pa?" she asked quietly. "You know my pa?"

"You been getting letters from him. I'm the one who wrote them."

And then suddenly Charlie remembered. This was the man who had written with such beautiful handwriting. "You're Boone Manwaring?" she said. She looked past him. "Where's Pa?"

The howl of a wolf from the neighboring ridge floated over the still air as Boone tried to think of some way to break his terrible news. At last he cleared his throat. "I've got bad news for you, Charlie."

Instantly the young woman grew still, and she lowered the revolver. "Is it about Pa? Is he hurt bad?"

There was no way out, and Boone would rather have been any place on earth than facing her dark eyes. "He's dead, Charlie. I'm sorry."

The words hit the young woman like a blow. She dropped the revolver and walked blindly away toward the cabin. Not knowing what else to do, Boone reached over, picked up the revolver, and stuck it back in his holster. He picked up the rifle that she had leaned against the base of a tree and stepped forward until he was only a few feet away. As he stood there silently, he noticed that her shoulders were shaking. He wanted to go forward to put his arm around her, but he was a stranger.

Finally, the young woman seemed to recover. Without turning, she said, "Come on in. I'll fix your head."

"You don't have to do that."

She did not answer but went inside and lit a lamp. Boone followed her and stood helplessly, but she did not speak. She moved stiffly toward a shelf nailed to the cabin wall, and he saw that her face was pale. "Set here," she said, and when he obeyed, she filled a basin with water and tore a strip from a piece of cloth. "It will hurt a mite," she said then began to cleanse the wound. After she had washed the blood away, she said, "This here will sting," then applied some sort of salve that smelled like balsam. Boone gasped at the fiery bite of the ointment then asked, "Does it need sewing up?"

"Reckon not. Have to be washed out fer a few days."

Turning abruptly, she emptied the basin, replaced it on the shelf, then said, "I'll fix you up a bit to eat." Going to the fireplace, she raked up the coals and threw some sticks on. Almost at once a fire began to crackle, sending tendrils of smoke up the chimney. Boone took a chair over by the rough-hewn table, feeling more uncomfortable than ever before in his life. He thought of leaving but knew that wouldn't do. He watched as she made coffee, fried ham, then threw some eggs into the skillet. She took a plate off the shelf and laid it in front of him, along with a knife and fork.

"Reckon this'll have to do you, Mr. Manwaring."

"Boone will do." Boone began to eat. He was not really hungry, or if he was, he was so disturbed he could not think of it. She poured a cup of coffee and sat down across from him. When he had eaten, he murmured, "That's mighty good, Charlie."

"Tell me 'bout it. What happened to Pa?"

Boone began, "I met your pa in Denver. We got on very well...."

Charlie listened with hungry eyes, as if the words had sustenance for her. When Boone finally talked about Noah's last words, he did not face her but looked down at his hands that were folded on the table. "He asked me to make him a promise,

Charlie. He had it in his mind to take you to Virginia. You and your mother at first, but when the word came that she died, the dream was even stronger in him."

"I know. He always figured he'd missed somethin' there. I don't know if he did or not." She held her coffee cup with nervous hands, turning the cup. When she looked up at him, her pale face made her dark blue eyes look almost black. "I told him the mountains was good enough fer me, but he wanted me to go there. He wanted me to put on purty dresses and learn how to dance."

"That was his dream," Boone said. "And I promised him I'd take you there, Charlie, and I will if you want me to."

Neither of them spoke for a time. Finally, Charlie said, "I'll think on it."

"It's your say, but I'll do my best because I promised your father." He hesitated and said, "He was a fine man. Maybe the finest I ever knew."

She looked up at him then, and he knew her heart was empty and at the same time filled with grief. She rose suddenly and motioned toward the bedroom. "You kin sleep in there—Boone."

"All right."

She banked the fire then picked up the rifle and headed for the door. "I'm goin' out fer a spell." As she began to disappear into the darkness, he remembered the wagon. He ran outside and caught up with her. "I stopped the wagon about a quarter of a mile down. I couldn't get it up the trail in the darkness. I've—I've got your father there."

"You brought Pa with you?"

"He wanted to be buried beside your mother. . . . Charlie, he wanted more than anything else to see you before he died. I did my best to get him here, but he just couldn't make it. He said he loved you then asked to be buried beside your mother."

"I'm thankin' you, Boone," Charlie whispered. "Reckon we'll go git him now."

❧

Charlie carefully penned *October 5, 1863* at the top of the sheet then wrote:

We buried Pa today right beside Ma like he always said he wanted. I am proud they are together now. In a way its funny. It makes me feel better bout Ma that she aint lyin out there alone. It seems like I been walkin around without much sense ever since Boone brought Pa back, but now that they are side-by-side I feel considerable better.

Reaching over, she dipped the turkey quill into the ink. It was late afternoon, when the sun was going down over the peaks, spreading its rosy rays over the valley. She admired it then began to write again.

Boone aint said much, but from what I kin make out Pa wanted me to go to Virginia and become a lady. I aint got no hankerin fer that, but if its what Pa wanted, I reckon I will have to do it. It will plum tear my heart out to leave this place. I reckon I will sell it to Jed Tompkins. He made an offer to buy it just after the funeral, in case I wanted to sell. I guess I will be glad to go. Every place I look now I would be thinkin about Pa on the outside of the cabin, just like I been thinkin about Ma on the inside. Maybe the best thing is to git away, and thats what Pa wanted. So I have made up my mind that I am goin.

She finished writing then went downstairs. Boone was not there, but she heard the sound of an ax splitting wood. Stepping outside, she saw him wield the ax and called out, "Boone!"

Boone turned toward her. The paleness had gone somewhat, and he admired the smoothness of her olive skin. She was, he thought, the most beautiful woman he had ever seen. "What is it, Charlie?"

"I reckon I'll go to Virginia."

"You sure that's what you want?"

"It's what Pa wanted, the last thing he asked, so I got to do it."

"I think it might be the best," Boone said thoughtfully. "When would you want to go?"

"As soon as we kin. It makes me sad to be around here."

"It's not easy to lose someone."

"What 'bout your folks?"

"Don't have any."

"They're both dead?"

"Both of them. I guess I'm all alone in the world."

Charlie regarded him carefully. She had done so since he came, for he was different than the other men in the mountains. There was a fineness about Boone Manwaring that interested her. But the fact that he had widely traveled and was educated made her feel somewhat awkward around him. Once, she had put in her diary, "I wonder if he thinks I'm nothin' but a country bumpkin', which I guess I am." Now she said quietly, "I got to do it, Boone."

"Whenever you're ready, we'll go."

"Pa wanted to buy a big mansion and make a lady out of me."

Alarmed, Boone felt constrained to say, "I tried to talk to your father about this, Charlie. It was his dream, but dreams sometimes don't turn out well when we get them."

"What do you mean by that?"

"I don't know how to say it, but sometimes a man or a woman will think, *If I just had this, I'd be happy*. Then they get it and find out that it wasn't what was lacking in them." Seeing she was puzzled by his words, he continued, "But I think it's right to go to Virginia. From what I hear, the people there are hospitable. They're brave, too, taking on the whole United States army and navy."

"I reckon they are. You don't have to go with me," she said abruptly.

"I promised your father."

"But I'm releasin' you if you want it that way."

"No. I did promise your father, but I always wanted to see the South. We'll go when you're ready."

❦

"We're ready for sunup tomorrow," Charlie said. The two were standing on the path outside the cabin. They had stepped outside after supper into the night, and now long shadows reached out over the hills. Quietness had fallen in the cool fall air.

"Are you glad to be going, Charlie?"

"I reckon I am. I won't be comin' back here, not fer a long time anyhow." She looked around and whispered, "I'll miss this place."

"Always hard to move on, I guess." He was standing close

enough so that his shoulder almost brushed hers. "Care to walk and take one more look around?"

"All right."

The cows lowed as they passed, and she spoke fondly, saying, "I'll miss you, Betsy." Then she added, "I'm glad Jed Tompkins wanted all the critters. I'd hate to just turn them loose."

The two walked under the whispering trees until finally they stopped at the edge of the forest. "I—I ain't thanked you proper fer what you did fer Pa. Ain't many men woulda did it."

She seemed very vulnerable at that moment, and Boone felt a rush of pity. "It's been hard on you, Charlie—losing your mother and then your father. I'm sorry."

She looked up at him, tears in her eyes. She had not wept, at least in his sight, since her father's funeral. But now he saw that the thought of leaving was oppressive to her, and her lips trembled.

"Charlie, it'll be all right," he said softly. Impulsively reaching forward, he drew her close and held her against his chest. For a moment she pressed against him, then suddenly struck him in the chest and stepped back. She dashed the tears from her eyes and flared out, "Don't you ever tetch me!"

"I meant nothing by it, Charlie."

"You heered me, Boone! I don't ever want to be tetched! I know right well what men say—and what they do! They've been around here often enough! But I don't need nothin' like that!"

"Your father asked me to get you settled, to help you find a good man for a husband."

Charlie Peace straightened her back, a fierce glint in her eye. She said almost vehemently, "I don't need none of your help to get a man, Boone!"

Boone stepped back, not willing to argue. "I'm sorry," he

said again. "I won't interfere."

"Best that way!" Charlie said. As she walked back toward the cabin, she threw these words over her shoulder: "We'll leave first light in the morning."

Ever since Boone Manwaring had made his vow to Noah Peace, he'd been apprehensive. Now, watching Charlie's disappearing form, he felt almost angry at himself. *Why'd you have to get into this?* he thought. *Why didn't you just leave things alone?* But he knew why: When a man has a friend, he stands by him. Now he stood in the falling daylight and wondered, *How am I going to keep my promise to Noah? She needs a father, and she doesn't have one.* Finally, he went back to the porch and sat there for a long time, watching as the sun finished going down. Then he went to bed, dreading what was to come.

PART TWO
The Misfits

CHAPTER 7

YOUNG LOVE—AND NOT SO YOUNG

In November 1863, winter came to Virginia almost with a single bound. One day the air was mild with fall's gentle breezes and the land bathed in sunshine. Then the beast of winter arrived, shriveling the grass to a deadly gray.

Clay Rocklin sat in the parlor with his wife, Melora, who was sewing the new symbol of his authority onto the sleeves of his gray Confederate army uniform. Outside, low-lying clouds formed. "I think there's snow coming."

Looking up from her needlework, Melora said, "It will be a bad winter, I think. Paul said the pecans had extra-thick shells."

"And the caterpillars were more woolly than usual. He said that, too, didn't he?"

Melora Yancy Rocklin's green eyes crinkled as she smiled. "Paul always knows what the weather's going to do."

"I expect he does," Clay answered, shrugging. "Are you about through with that uniform?"

"Almost." Melora took a few more stitches. As she did, Clay watched her. She was only twenty-nine to his forty-three, and sometimes he wondered if he had done the right thing in marrying such a young woman. She had waited for him, however, since she was a young girl. Quickly he thought of his first wife, Ellen, who had made life such a misery to him and everyone around her—and to herself most of all. He recalled her death with sorrow, for she had not had a happy life, and Clay had never reconciled himself completely to the fact that he had not made her any happier. He had married her on the rebound after being rejected by Melanie Benton, who had married his cousin Gideon.

As Clay studied Melora, taking in her black hair and smooth cheeks, he was grateful. Although it had been difficult, for he had loved Melora for years, he had been faithful to Ellen even though their marriage had been a travesty. And now it seemed that the Lord was rewarding them. Melora was nearly two months pregnant and due in June. "How are you doing today?" he asked, smiling at her.

"We're fine. Both of us."

"Take good care of that new son of mine."

Melora stood up, holding the coat out for him. "I'll take good care of our *daughter*," she said. It was a long-standing, teasing argument between the two of them. Although neither actually had strong preferences for either a boy or a girl, it was one of those little games they had played since their marriage. When she had discovered she was pregnant, Melora had been ecstatic. But Clay had looked solemn, worried about Melora and the baby because of his dangerous line of work. When he voiced his concerns that he might die in battle, she had touched his cheek, saying, "God didn't let me wait for you all these years to lose you, Clay. We're going to grow old together. You can shout into my hearing trumpet, and I'll keep up with your false teeth."

Slipping into the coat, Clay looked down at the sleeves of his uniform where the curling insignia of a lieutenant colonel wound in a serpentine fashion. "I think they made a mistake making me a colonel."

"They don't make mistakes like that."

"Well, it's only a brevet rank, you understand. You know what that means?"

"Not quite," Melora said.

"It means I'm not really a colonel and that when they get a real one, I'll go back to being a major. You'll have to pick out all those stitches." He grinned, tenderly putting his arms around her and drawing her close. "I love you, Melora."

Melora pulled his head down and kissed him. One of the things she loved about him was the fact that he wasn't embarrassed to tell her of his love. She kept her arms around his neck, pleased just to hold him. Knowing that time was short, that soon he would ride out with the regiment, she put aside her apprehension and instead looked up into his eyes. He was the handsomest man she knew. His raven hair had only a few gray hairs, mostly along the long sideburns, and his olive skin was smooth and clear. Known as one of the "Black Rocklins," he was still muscular and trim.

"Your coat's a little too large," Melora chided. "You've lost weight."

"Well, you've gained it," he teased her.

"There's that much more of me for you to love!"

"Right! Now let's sit down, and you can tell me what a beautiful *son* I'm going to have."

He led her over to the horsehide couch in front of the window. It was a favorite place for both of them, for they could look out on Gracefield's sprawling lawn and circular drive. Over to the east, the hills formed a cup that held the valley; to the west the land leveled out to the cotton fields, filled only with stalks, and after that the second-growth timber that lay between them and Richmond.

Clay listened as she talked about the child who was about to come. But Clay could tell, even in their brief time of marriage, that she was worried, because the right side of her lips tightened. It was unconscious with her, he knew, so he finally said, "Are you concerned about something?"

She murmured, "You know me too well, Clay."

"Is it about the baby?"

"No, it's about the war." She ran her fingers down the back of his hand then asked, "What's going to happen?"

"We're going to lose."

Startled, Melora looked up. She had known Clay was filled with doubts about the war. He had not wanted the South to secede in the first place, and he had joined only out of a desire to help Lowell, his youngest son, who was going through a difficult time. He had enlisted and risen rapidly through the ranks, becoming an officer very quickly, but all the time, through the hard-fought battles of Bull Run, Antietam, and Gettysburg, she had seen that his hope for victory had been quietly put away. He served now out of duty, she understood, to his state and because he could not lift his hand against his family or his people. She suspected there were many in the South who were in the same position, for most men in the Confederate army owned no slaves.

"Do you think there's no hope at all?"

"Look at it this way, Melora. Every time we have to keep a line of battle, every time one of our men gets wounded or killed, that leaves a hole in that line. There's no one else to put in that hole, Melora. We've taken every young boy of fifteen to man of fifty, and they're all gone now. If the North loses twenty thousand men, all they have to do is reach back into their reserves and bring up another twenty thousand. Their factories are turning out munitions at an unbelievable rate. We have hardly a factory left in the South we can count on. If Atlanta falls, or Richmond, it's all over."

"Why doesn't President Davis simply surrender?"

"He'll never do that," Clay said sorrowfully. "He's too proud. We'll go on as long as we have an army. That's all that keeps them out—the Army of Northern Virginia here in Richmond, and Joe Johnston's Army of the Tennessee."

"Things didn't go well in Tennessee, did they?"

"No, we took a terrible beating at Lookout Mountain. We won Chickamauga, perhaps, but it didn't help. Now Sherman is gathering a huge army, and he'll begin to push Johnston back toward Atlanta."

"Can General Johnston hold him off?"

"No. All he can do is retreat. There's only one end to that."

Melora listened as Clay spoke, and she saw the air of fatality that gripped him. He would never quit, she knew; he loved his men too much for that. Fiercely she wished the war were over, but she knew women in the South—and North—were wishing for the same thing.

Finally, sensing she was depressing Clay, Melora said, "Well, it's as God wills. Whether we win or lose, we'll have our family."

"That's my girl. You always had more faith than any woman I ever saw."

"Not more than your mother."

"I think you're a close tie," Clay said. Then he frowned. "I'm

WITNESS IN HEAVEN

worried about Marianne and Claude."

He spoke of his aunt Marianne, his father's sister, who had married a stranger named Claude Bristol. It had been a very romantic courtship, but Clay knew they did not have a happy marriage. Claude did not fit into the Rocklin family as well as Marianne had hoped. From a French background, he had a volatile temperament and a store of good looks, but bad luck. The family was kind enough to call it "bad luck," although Marianne's brothers knew it was more than that. Claude Bristol was a sportsman, a gambler, and he drank too much. Although his charm and wit had carried him along in the society, and one could not help liking him, Clay wished he had more sense and less charm.

"What's wrong with them?"

"I'm afraid they're in financial difficulties."

"Why, aren't we all?"

"I know, but I think it's worse for them. If something doesn't happen, I think they're going to lose Hartsworth."

"Why, that can't be true, Clay! It isn't that bad, surely!"

"I think it's worse than anybody knows. Marianne doesn't talk to me much about things like that, but I picked up the idea from Paul and Austin."

Paul Bristol, the older son, had married a woman named Frankie Ames. He had become a fine photographer and had moved to Birmingham, Alabama, where he continued his profession.

"Paul told me the finances were in an absolute mess, and Austin said the same thing."

"I talked to Marie last week," Melora said thoughtfully. "She didn't say anything about trouble." Marie was Marianne and Claude's only daughter, a beautiful young woman. "She usually says whatever's on her mind."

Clay shook his head. "I don't think she would—not in a case like this. I'm going by there and see. Maybe I can talk to Claude. Not that we have any money to help anybody with." He reached over and hugged her. "We're pretty well broke ourselves." Then, anxious to get away from the talk of finance, he said, "I'm more concerned about Rena than I am about our finances."

"She's all right," Melora said quickly. She had always been fond of Clay's daughter, now seventeen. The two were close friends, and Melora was proud she had become a mother, indeed, to someone who had had great difficulties earlier in life. Rena had been ashamed of her mother, Ellen, and ashamed of being ashamed. Melora looked up at Clay and asked, "Are you worried about Josh?"

"I guess I am a little bit," he admitted, "although he's a fine young man."

Josh was Melora's seventeen-year-old brother. They came from a large family, and Josh was, perhaps, her favorite among the boys. "Why are you worried, Clay?" she queried.

"Rena keeps talking about wanting to get married, and I think it's a bad idea right now."

"That's what people said about us."

"I know, but it's different with us. We're older."

"Young love—and not so young," Melora said. "What's the difference?"

"I guess young love may be more impulsive. I'm afraid they'll get married, and sooner or later Josh is going to be in the army. He's already begged me to take him into the brigade."

"I know. He's talked to me about it. He wants me to influence you. I hate to see him go. We've already lost Lonnie."

"He'll go; there's no question about that. I just wish they'd wait until the war is over."

"That's easy to say, Clay," Melora mused. "But when you're seventeen and in love, it's hard to think logically."

The two talked for a while, and finally Clay arose. "I've got to get back to camp," he said.

"When will you be able to get back again?"

"I'm not sure. It depends on Ulysses S. Grant. When spring comes he'll move his army down from Washington. And from what I hear of that fella, he won't stop until he gets to Richmond or dies trying."

"Come back as soon as you can, Clay. I want every second with you."

"You can believe I'll do that." He put his arms around her and kissed her cheek, then her neck. "You're so beautiful, Melora," he whispered. "When I leave here it's like tearing part of myself away. Sometimes I want to just let everything slide and stay with you."

"I feel that way, too, Clay, but we can't," she said, her eyes tender. "Come back, Clay. Come back soon!"

"Do you know what this arbor's for?" Rena asked, her eyes twinkling with mischief as she regarded Josh Yancy, who sat beside her on the cold bench. They had come to the arbor covered with scuppernong vines shortly after Josh had arrived at Richmond. Josh was tall, lean, and muscular like his father, and Rena was convinced she'd been in love with Josh forever. Now she waited for his answer. It was slow in coming, for he was not a quick-speaking young man. In moments of distress he often exhibited the slight stutter that had plagued him most of his life.

"I reckon it's to raise grapes," he said, admiring Rena shyly.

"No, that's just an excuse. This arbor's where all the Rocklin men bring their girls to court them. Look, no one in the house can see a thing because of the vines." She pulled the vines back and pointed toward the house. "See, no one can see what we're doing. Does that give you any ideas?"

Josh's lean face flushed, for he knew she was teasing him. "I reckon I do," he said. He leaned forward and kissed her on the cheek, then hesitated and said huskily, "You're mighty sweet, Rena, and the prettiest girl I know."

Rena waited for him to kiss her again and to pull her into his arms as he had done on a few occasions. Josh had a reserve that sometimes pleased her—and other times, such as now, got on her nerves.

"I declare, Josh Yancy, you have no more romance in you than a—than a doorknob!"

"A doorknob!" Josh blinked with surprise. "Why, I don't know what you're talking about!"

"Why, I mean here we are all alone, and all you can do is give me a peck on the cheek! I bet if Henry Watson were here, he'd do better than that!"

"Well, I'm not Henry Watson!" Josh's eyes kindled slightly as he mentioned the name, for this wealthy planter's son was not a pleasant thought to him. It seemed that every time Josh went to Gracefield, Henry Watson was parked there in the parlor with Rena. "If you want Henry Watson to paw you out in this arbor...!"

"Oh, I didn't mean that!" the vivacious Rena said quickly. She touched Josh's cheek. "I was just teasing you. Don't take things so seriously."

Josh knew he was not as lively as some of the young men

who came to court Rena, but he was held back by the knowledge that they were the sons of wealthy planters or merchants in Richmond, while he was the son of a small farmer who had nothing but a few acres back in the deep woods. It troubled him, and he wished he could express himself better to Rena. He remembered when he had first met Rena—how he had stuttered so horribly that he would not say a word in her presence. But over a period of time, as they grew up, she had won his confidence and encouraged him so that, during the war, he had learned to love her as he had never thought he could love anyone else.

Rena leaned back on the bench. "You don't seem very happy today."

Josh shot her a glance. "I guess you know me pretty well.... I came over to talk to your father."

Rena's eyes flew open, and words involuntarily leaped to her lips. "You're going to ask him if we can get married?"

"Why—no! Not that, Rena!" Josh stuttered somewhat, for he knew that they had talked about this before. As the excitement in her eyes died down, he took her hand. "I came to ask him to let me join the Stonewall Brigade."

All the joy went out of the morning for Rena Rocklin. "I knew you were going to do it."

"I've got to do it, Rena. You can see that, can't you?"

"I suppose so."

Her bleak reply did not encourage Josh, so he went on to defend his actions. "I'm seventeen," he said. "All the other fellows my age are already in the army."

Rena listened with a sense of gloom as he spoke. She had known it was coming. Her father and Melora had warned her, and Josh himself had insisted that sooner or later he would have to go. Now that the moment had come, however, she said despairingly, "Let's get married before you go to the army. We can take a few weeks."

"Why, it wouldn't be fair, Rena. What if something happened to me?"

Rena had thought of that also. The country was filled with eighteen- and nineteen-year-old widows. The toll of the war had been harsh, but Rena put all that out of her mind. "I love you, Josh," she said simply.

"Why, I love you, too." Josh Yancy threw his arms around Rena, and she nestled close to him. He lost himself in the pleasure of the moment as her soft lips found his, and her hands clasped his neck.

Rena drew back and whispered, "Please, Josh, let's get married!"

"I can't do it, Rena. It wouldn't be fair."

That was the beginning of the quarrel. Rena argued gently at first, and then when Josh was stubborn she grew more demanding. Finally, she said stiffly, "You don't love me at all!" Rising to her feet, she started for the house.

Josh hurried after her, saying, "Oh, Rena, don't say that! I do love you, but it wouldn't be fair!"

"Well, go on and join the old army, then!" Tears now blinded Rena's face, and she did not want him to see her crying. He caught her, however, turned her around, and when he saw the tears, exclaimed, "Don't cry—please don't cry!"

So the quarrel was made up as it is by young lovers—with a sweet kiss. Later Rena watched Josh as he swung aboard his strawberry mare with the natural grace of a born horseman. He waved at her and smiled as he galloped out of the yard, shouting, "I'll stop back and see you after I get signed up!"

Rena called back, "I'll wait for you!" and then went at once to the kitchen, where Melora was making a pie. Taking a tall stool, she set it by her stepmother and asked, "Are men always so stubborn, Melora?"

Startled, Melora's eyes flew open, and then she laughed quietly. "What do you mean?"

"Josh always has to have his own way. He's going to join the army."

"You knew it was coming, didn't you? He's talked to you about it."

"Oh yes, but I thought we'd get married before that happened."

"You won't?"

"I asked him to marry me. He said it wouldn't be fair."

"Josh is very levelheaded. He's always been that way," Melora remarked, beginning to speak of how Josh, even as a young boy, had been steady and reliable. Melora noticed that although the talk pleased Rena, she still seemed dissatisfied and unhappy. Finally, Melora said, "You'll have to wait a little, I guess."

"Melora, what's it like being married?"

"Why, what in the world do you mean, Rena?"

"Well, I don't know anything about—well, about marriage." Rena's cheeks were tinged with pink. "Most girls had a mother, I guess, to teach them what a woman's supposed to do, but Mother never talked about those things with me. So if I get married, I won't know anything."

"There are worse things than that," Melora said quietly. "Some girls know everything. They bring their husbands nothing fresh. Be thankful you can come to your husband with a sweetness that hasn't been touched."

"But shouldn't I know something?"

For the next half hour the two women talked quietly of the physical intimacies of marriage and then of what a marriage really meant even beyond that. Rena listened intently as Melora concluded, "God gave us two sides of marriage, Rena. The physical side and the spiritual side. Both are important, and no one can tread the way for you. But if you love Josh, and he loves you, you will discover the joy of marriage."

"I can tell you and Pa are so happy," Rena said. "I hope Josh and I will be like that."

Melora opened her arms, held Rena for a long moment, then whispered, "You will, daughter—you will!"

A general air of dilapidation hung over the city of Richmond. There was nothing shining or polished about the streets as Clay threaded his way between the wagons, horses, mules, and throngs of people.

"Colonel—Colonel Rocklin!"

Clay, at first, was shocked, for he was not accustomed to his new office title yet. Turning, he saw Sam Birdwell, the tall, thin owner of the Crescent Saloon, coming across the street. Stopping his horse, Clay called, "Hello, Sam." Then, seeing the agitation in Birdwell's blue eyes, he asked, "What's wrong?"

"Well, I hate to bother you with it, Colonel," Birdwell said, "but I got to." Birdwell ran his hand through his salt-and-pepper hair. "It's your uncle, Mr. Bristol."

Alarmed, Clay asked, "What is it, Sam? Is he drunk again?"

"Dead drunk this time, Colonel. I tried to make him leave, but you know how he gets sometimes. He threatened to shoot me if I didn't leave him alone and serve him whiskey."

"Where is he now?"

"He passed out, and I took him into my office. Got him on the couch. I won't mind if you want to leave him there."

"No, Sam. That's good of you, but I'll have to get him home. I'll have someone come by as soon as I can."

"Sorry to bother you about this, Colonel."

Clay offered his hand. "I appreciate your concern, Sam. It was good of you."

"Nothing a'tall. Nothing a'tall, Colonel."

Clay nodded then moved on down the street. Spurring his horse into a fast gallop, he headed for the camp, which lay just north of Richmond. His mind worked quickly, trying to think of a way to handle the situation, but he could not. "I can't go back now. I've got to get to my duties. Austin will have to handle it."

Five minutes later he pulled up in front of the large white building that housed several of the government agencies, one of them being the War Department. He stepped out of his saddle, tied the horse, then saluted the young sergeant who stood guard at the door. Once inside, he mounted the stairs two at a time until he came to the second floor. He entered the third door on his right and saw Austin Bristol sitting at his desk.

"Hello, Austin."

"Why, Clay—" Austin jumped up, his blue-green eyes shining with pleasure. "I mean, Colonel! Sorry about that, sir!"

At the age of thirty-one, black-haired Austin Bristol was one of the neatest young men Clay had ever seen. He always looked freshly barbered and shaved, and his clothes were meticulously right, as if whatever Austin Bristol put on achieved a sort of grace. He came forward limping slightly, for he had been wounded in an earlier skirmish and had complications. Now he served as one of General Lee's liaison officers in the War Department. "How does it feel to be a colonel?"

Clay shook his head. "Somebody made a mistake somewhere. If they have to have me for a colonel, we're in real trouble."

"I don't think so, sir."

Clay shifted his feet nervously. Usually he was a straightforward man, able to handle most things by "setting them on the front porch." Now, however, as he looked at Austin, he hated to bring him more trouble. He already knew that Austin and his sister, Marie, were very concerned about what was happening on their plantation. But it had to be done.

"I hate to bother you with this, Austin, but Sam Birdwell down at the Crescent stopped me."

Instantly Austin's eyes hardened. "Is it Father?"

"I'm afraid so. He drank a little too much and passed out."

"Where is he?"

"Sam put him to bed in his office. I'd like to take care of him, but I'm just getting back."

Austin settled back on his heels, his jaw hard. "I'll take care of him, sir. Would you give me permission to be absent from my desk?"

"I'll see to that. Take him home. Come back in the morning, Austin."

"Yes, sir."

"I'm sorry about this."

"We're all sorry about it." It was unusual to hear bitterness in Austin's voice, since he was normally a cheerful, easygoing man. But Austin was ashamed of his father, so now he simply said, "I'll be going."

"Austin, don't be too hard on him," Clay said quickly. "He's not a happy man."

Austin gave Clay Rocklin a look that was almost harsh. "He's made his life, Clay," he said, forgetting to use the title.

There was nothing Clay could say, so he watched as Austin left the room hurriedly, then moved out to find the officer of the day to get belated permission for Austin to be gone. As he walked down the busy hallway, he thought with a twinge of anger toward his uncle, *He doesn't have to be like this! He could do better if he wanted to!*

Chapter 8

The Wrong Man

"How old are you, Ketura?"

The black woman who walked alongside Marie Bristol did not answer until the pair of them reached the end of the section set off for the slave quarters. The cabins the Bristol slaves inhabited were neat, though small, and carefully whitewashed. They reflected the sun that spread itself over the earth and warmed the November breeze that came in from the north.

"How old I be? Why, laws, Miss Marie, I ain't got no ideer!" The idea intrigued the black woman, for she stopped in front of a three-foot-high wooden structure and rested her hand on it as she considered. A fine network of wrinkles crisscrossed her face; even her lips appeared shriveled. Finally, she said, her old dark eyes glowing with humor, "As far as I can calculate, I must be somewhere between eighty-five and ninety."

Marie, who had been partially raised by Ketura and loved her, smiled and took the woman's hand. It was bony now, not strong and hard like Marie remembered it as a child. But even then Ketura had seemed old to her. "Do you remember much about when you were a girl?" she asked gently.

"First I remember I belonged to Mr. Tom Hadley in

Louisiana. My ma, she worked in the rice fields there, and my pa, he cut timber for Mr. Hadley. He was a fine man, my pa," she said, struggling to bring the memories into focus. "Once, the men tried their strength to see who could throw an anvil the farthest, and my pa threw it a full ten feet past what them other men did. He was a powerful strong man, my pappy!"

Twenty-six-year-old Marie Bristol hesitated for a moment, thinking. The breeze caught her rich brown hair, ruffling it slightly, and the sun added a slight reddish tinge. Her deep eyes were full of intelligence—and also known for the hint of deviltry that would leap into them at times. Her plain woolen work dress, which had been dark red, was now faded after innumerable washings. "I don't remember him," Marie finally said.

"Oh no, child! He was sold downriver. We heard he went to a man in Georgia, and my ma, she was sold to Mr. James Clifford when I was fifteen."

Such sadness filled Marie that she asked what she probably would not have asked another slave woman. "Did it hurt you a lot to be separated from your ma and pa?"

"Of course it hurts, child. Why you reckon it wouldn't hurt? Think how you would feel if you was separated from your ma and pa."

"I know. It was a stupid question."

Ketura patted Marie's arm, a fondness in her eyes. She shifted the sweet-gum stick that protruded from her mouth as she answered, "I guess people hurt whether they're black or white." Then, seeing Marie's depressed mood, Ketura said more cheerfully, "But 'bout that time I married up with my first husband. His name was Roscoe, and whooee—he was a scutter!"

Loving to hear the tales of Ketura's youth, Marie grinned broadly. "Was he good looking, Ketura?"

"Good lookin'? I speculate he was! He was tall and strong, and every gal that ever got close to him couldn't keep her eyes off him!"

"Did you have trouble keeping him honest?" Marie teased.

"No, ain't had no trouble with nothin' like that!" Ketura said. "Woman's got to know how to keep a man happy if she wants to keep him close to home. 'Specially if he's good lookin'."

"Maybe you'd better tell me how you did it in case I ever stop being an old maid and get a husband of my own someday."

"You get you a man; then I'll tell you how to keep him!" Ketura said. "Now let's get started on this here soap. We done run nearly plumb out, and Mr. Austin say they ain't none to be had much in Richmond. I don't like that soap he buys nohow! I can make better than that!"

It was not unusual for Marie Bristol to spend time with Ketura. She had learned a great deal about the myriad details involved with plantation life, and early in the morning she had asked Ketura to let her help with the soap making. Now the two stood there before the V-shaped affair that was wide at the top and came to a point at the bottom. It was nailed together with boards and lifted up on poles. Out of the bottom ran a spout, and under the spout was a large tin bucket.

"We make the lye first of all," Ketura announced. "This here is ashes from the hickory you done burned already. Hickory ashes make the best lye for soap. Sometimes you have to use oak or somethin' else, but hickory's the best. You just start pourin' water in over these ashes."

Marie watched as Ketura's grandson Isley brought bucket after bucket of water from the nearby well. As he poured the liquid in, it soaked into the ashes at once.

"I don't see how this makes lye, Ketura," Marie said when

the black woman finally cautioned Isley to stop.

"I don't know neither, but it do! And soon as that bucket under that spout fills up, we're ready to get to our soap makin'."

The two women went back to the house, where Marie sat back, listening to more of Ketura's tales of her youth and drinking sassafras tea. Sometime later Ketura said, "Appears to me like that lye ought to be about done. Let's go get that bacon fat we been savin'.... If you want this soap to smell sweet, go get some rosewater or some of that perfume you got."

"All right, Ketura." Marie ran at once to her room to look through the bottles of perfume that she had collected from time to time. Finding one bottle her father had given her three years earlier, she snatched it up and went back downstairs and then outside. She found Ketura speaking strictly to her grandson, Isley. "You better get that fire built! You're as slow as molasses! And get some more buckets of water, too!"

"Yes, Granny. I'm doin' it fast as I can."

Soon a hot fire was going under the black pot, and Ketura shooed Isley away. "You get on 'bout your other business now!"

As soon as Isley disappeared, she said, "You put about two pints and a half of water; then put your lye in there."

Following Ketura's instructions, Marie filled the pot then went over to get the bucket full of lye. "How much do I put in?" she asked.

"I don't never measure nothin'. Just pour it in till I says stop." She watched critically; then finally as the brownish fluid poured out of the bucket, she said, "That's 'bout enough! Now you stir it until it dissolves good."

As Marie began to stir the mixture with a paddle whittled out for that purpose, she suddenly thought, *We might lose this place.* That idea disturbed her more than she liked to admit.

Hartsworth had been home all of her life. She knew every inch of the house and practically every foot of the fields. She had ridden over it from the time she was a girl and could sit a horse. But she knew that being forced to leave was a real possibility, for she did part of the bookkeeping work and knew exactly how heavily mortgaged Hartsworth was.

Unaware of Marie's disturbance, Ketura continued her instructions. "Now it looks 'bout like chicken gravy, don't it, beginnin' to thicken up. Pour that perfume in there, child." She watched carefully as Marie uncapped the bottle and poured the cologne into the thick mixture. "Now pour that bacon grease in." Marie again followed her instructions. "Now there ain't much else to it. We just keep on a-stirrin' and a-cookin' until finally it's all right."

Thirty minutes later Marie's arm was tired, for she had agitated the liquid steadily. "Now we're gonna dip some of that out in these pans."

Marie carefully spooned the thick white mixture into flat pans, then asked, "Is that all there is to it?"

"That's all. We let it cool then cut it up into blocks. You done good, honey."

Sometime later, after the mixture had cooled, Ketura cut the soap up into blocks about three inches square. Marie took one of the blocks and said, "I'm going to try it out right now." Turning, she made her way back toward the house. As soon as she cleared the large hedge that blocked the house from the slave quarters, she stopped with surprise. There, coming down the road, was her brother Austin driving a wagon. *Austin never drives a wagon,* she thought. *I wonder where his horse is.*

Glad to see him in any case, she waited until he pulled up. "Hello, brother! It's good to see you!" She stopped then, for she saw that Austin's face was set with an emotion she could not identify. "What's wrong?" she asked, still holding the soap with both hands.

"This is what's wrong!" he said, motioning toward the bed of the wagon. He stepped down, looking down at the ground.

Puzzled, Marie peeked into the wagon and saw her father lying on a blanket. His face was pale, he was snoring heavily, and his clothes were filthy, for he had evidently thrown up on himself. Her heart turned sick within her, and she moved away from the sight. "Where was he?" she asked.

"In the Crescent Saloon. Birdwell put him back in his office. I suppose everybody in town had a look at him, though. Why can't he do his drinking in private, and why does he have to do so much of it?" Not waiting for an answer, Austin said, "I'll get some of the slaves to help me carry him to his bed."

As he strode toward the slave quarters, Marie heard him calling out, "Solomon—Solomon!"

She looked down at her father again, although she hated the sight of him. It was not the first time this had happened. For Claude Bristol, getting drunk was common enough, but to get "helpless drunk" in Richmond with all the world to see was something else again. She stood aside when Austin came back, followed by Solomon and Alexander, two husky slaves who said nothing as they carried him inside the house. With a flash, Marie thought, *This is going to hurt Mother.* The only thing Marie could do was comfort her.

In midafternoon Marie stood at the kitchen table polishing the silver. It was something one of the slaves normally did, but she was restless. She had come in to find her mother alone and had tried to find some way to open the conversation but found none. Finally, she looked across the table and said, "I had hoped this would never happen again, Mother."

Marianne Rocklin Bristol, at the age of fifty-three, was still an attractive woman. Although her black hair showed traces of silver, her blue eyes were clear and she was still shapely and attractive. She looked up now and shook her head. "It's happened before," she said briefly.

Marie could not meet her mother's eyes. "Why does he do it?" she murmured.

Marie expected no answer, for her mother never spoke of her marriage to Claude Bristol. But something had broken within the older woman this time, and she looked out the window, her hands idle. "I wish you could have seen him when he was a young man, Marie. I met him at a ball in Charlotte. He was the most handsome man I ever saw—and the most charming. You can't believe how witty he was. All the young women were after him, although he was not wealthy." She continued to speak of that time, her voice soft but tinged with bitterness. Finally, she looked up with pain in her fine eyes and said, "I knew he was a gambler, but I wouldn't listen to my parents. I thought I could reform him. But I couldn't. . . . I knew that before we'd been married a year. It's like a disease with him, gambling, and then he drinks to forget."

Marie felt helpless, for her mother had never spoken like this before. She moved to put an arm around her. "I'm sorry. Maybe this will be the last."

"I doubt it." Marianne's eyes were sober. "Never marry a man on your emotions, Marie."

"Why, you have to love a man, don't you?"

"Yes, but love is more than a palpitation of the heart. I had that, for Claude could make a girl feel like the most beautiful, wonderful woman in the world. He still can, or could the last time he tried. . . . But he hasn't tried in a long time, since he's ashamed." She continued, "Be wise, daughter. It's easy for a woman to be swayed by a handsome face and a trim figure—by a man who knows how to use words. But marriage is more than that. I want you to find a man who's solid, who doesn't have the—the faults your father has." Marianne broke off her words then finally said, "I shouldn't be speaking like this. We have to love him no matter what he does."

"I do love him, and I know you do, too, Mother."

Marianne Bristol gave her daughter one more searching look then said in a terse voice, "Make sure your man has something besides romance. It's a thin diet for a marriage." She turned and left the kitchen, leaving Marie to stare after her.

A little later, when Marianne called Marie and Austin in for supper, Austin said briefly, "I'll stay over tonight. I've got to talk to Father about this business."

"No, let me do it," Marianne answered.

"Are you sure, Mother?"

"Yes, I'm sure."

"You'll have to be firm. I don't even know where he got the money that he lost. It was considerable. I think he gave an IOU. I don't know how in the world we'll pay it."

None of them enjoyed the meal—all were glad when it was over. Austin went to the study and closed the door. Marie helped her mother and Ketura with the dishes then went to speak with Austin. Going to the door, she knocked and called out softly, "Austin, can I come in?"

When he answered in the affirmative, she entered and found him sitting behind the rosewood desk. "Sit down,

Marie. We've got to talk." He waited until she was seated, then said, "What can he be thinking of?"

"He's not happy. That's when he gambles."

"Well, if he has to gamble every time he gets dissatisfied, he's going to spend the rest of his life at a poker table!"

Although Marie and Austin had always been close, even with the five years in age separating them, Marie found herself unable to meet her brother's eyes. Marie knew he had joined the army full of high expectations. But after being wounded and spending weary months in the hospital, then at home, he seemed to have become discouraged. She also knew he was bored with his duties at the War Department. But in spite of herself she blurted out, "What's going to happen to us, Austin?"

"We're going to be thrown off this place! That's what's going to happen!"

"Oh, Austin, we can't let that happen!"

"It's not going to be our choice! Father's run up so many bills, and he's gambled away what little profits we made. Now with cotton not worth a dime a bale, what else can we do? I'd be in favor of selling out, but nobody's buying land these days."

"There's got to be another way!"

Seeing the distress in her eyes, Austin rose and walked over to put his hand on her shoulder. She covered his hand with one of her own.

"I guess," he said with a flash of his usual humor, "one of us will have to marry well."

"You mean you'll have to get a rich wife?"

"Or you'll have to get a rich husband."

Marie disagreed almost violently. "Don't be foolish!"

"Not as foolish as it sounds. People do it all the time. Look at Frank Burrows. That place of theirs was down to nothing until he married Mary Delchamp. It seems to have worked all right."

"He didn't love her! Everybody knew it! Even Mary knew it!"

"Well, she thought he was her best bet. At least she's got a husband now and a baby on the way. And Frank's got what he wants—a fine plantation. They'll survive whoever wins the war."

"You can't be serious, Austin!" Marie said. She couldn't believe he really meant what he was saying. Then she relaxed. Austin often was guilty of teasing her like this. "You'd never think of doing such a thing!"

"Not in normal times, but these aren't normal times, Marie. The name of the game is going to be survival." His shoulders slumped as he said, "The North's going to win this war. We might as well make up our mind to that, and when they do, they're going to be hard on the South. Anybody whose land isn't paid for will lose it! You watch what I tell you!"

Marie did not like to hear her brother talk like this, but she saw that he was serious. "Well," she said quietly, "I guess we'd better do some shopping."

"Might be a good time for you to think about Malcolm Leighton." He saw her face darken. "I know he's a little flashy, but he's got those two ships, and he seems to have success running the blockade. He's making money hand over fist."

"He's bringing in perfume and patent leather when he ought to be bringing in bandages, gunpowder, and muskets."

"Not much money in those. There is in perfume, though, for those who have the cash. Malcolm's not a bad fellow." He saw her shake her head firmly. "You're too romantic. That's what your trouble is. Now, me, I'm practical." He stood up straight, put his hand over his heart, and announced, "Here I am, ladies! For sale, one slightly cynical, prospective husband! Bathes often, no bad habits to speak of, would make an excellent flatterer! Come make your bids!"

Marie stood up and laughed. "You fool! You could never do it!"

Austin's foolishness left him then. "I'll tell you the truth, Marie. I'd do anything to keep this place. I love it just like you do! Don't be too sure that I wouldn't marry any woman, providing she's got enough cash."

The two went to bed shortly after that, and the next morning at breakfast they were already eating with their mother when their father came in.

"Good morning, Claude," Marianne said quietly, ignoring the wan, harried look in Claude Bristol's eyes.

"Good morning," he said, including them all in his greeting. He was, at fifty-eight, still a fine-looking man, despite his heavy drinking. He was an inveterate rider, and the exercise kept him trim and strong. He removed a biscuit from the plate and looked down at the eggs that Marianne spooned onto it for him along with two pieces of bacon. Taking a bite of the eggs, he chewed them slowly then swallowed and reached out for the coffee. He tasted it and made a face. "What is this?"

"It's not coffee," Marianne said. "It's impossible to get that, Claude. It's a recipe Sally Tompkins gave me, making coffee out of burned acorns."

"I'll just take water," Claude mumbled. He could not meet any of their eyes, and none of them said anything about the condition he had come home in. Finally, Austin stood and dabbed at his lips with a napkin. "I've got to get back to the War

Department," he said. He gave his a father a hard look, as if he appeared ready to say more. But with a glance at his mother, who shook her head slightly, he said only, "I'll be going, then." He went over and kissed his mother on the cheek then said quietly, "Good-bye, Father."

Marie got up soon afterward and left the room, leaving Claude and Marianne alone. When their eyes met for a moment, Claude dropped his to the table. Picking up a fork, he traced an intricate design on the white tablecloth until the silence grew unbearable. Then, without looking up, he said, "Doesn't do any good to say I'm sorry. I've said it too many times." When she didn't answer, he looked up and saw a strange expression on her face. "Why are you looking at me like that?" he demanded, his head beating painfully from a raging headache.

"How long is this going to go on, Claude?"

"Time for a sermon, Marianne?"

Usually this would be enough to stop Marianne, but now she was desperate. "I think you *need* a sermon, Claude. You set out to destroy yourself some years ago, despite all I could do." Her voice was cool, and there was a steady light of anger in her eyes. "Now you're going to destroy Hartsworth, your children, and your wife! Is that what you want?"

"No, it's not what I want!"

"Then why do you act as you do? What's *wrong* with you, Claude?"

Claude Bristol wanted desperately to answer her. He wanted to say, *What's wrong with me? I'm no good! That's what's wrong with me! I never have been, and I never will be! You're used to the Rocklin clan—strong, noble men. And instead you got me—a gambler and a drunk!*

Not being able to read Claude's thoughts, Marianne finally

said firmly, "Claude, there's no more money. Do you understand that? I don't see how we can save Hartsworth, but I've talked to the banker, and you won't be able to draw any more funds." She saw his eyes fill with shame. "I hate to do this to you. It's not the way a marriage should be, but I must try to save something for the children." She hesitated then said, "You're not the man I thought I was marrying, Claude."

Claude Bristol sat quietly for a moment then tossed his napkin down. He got up and headed for the door. But he had to grope for the doorknob before he could find it and leave.

Chapter 9

A Shopping Trip

Stepping off to the platform, Boone automatically turned to help Charlie Peace down from the train, but she ignored his hand and leaped to stand beside him. "So this here is Richmond, is it?"

"Guess so. That's what the conductor said." Manwaring was very much aware of the curious glances the two were drawing from the crowd that had apparently come to meet the train. To their right was a line of soldiers, corralled by a short, muscular sergeant with a full beard. They were not watching him, Boone realized, but Charlie. *I should have made her buy a dress. Those buckskins stick out like a sore thumb on a young woman around here—or anywhere for that matter.* "Come on, Charlie," he said quickly. "Let's get out of here."

"Shore is a busy place," Charlie said. She was carrying a plaid carpetbag in her right hand and had pushed the coonskin cap back on her head so that her black hair hung down in curly masses around her forehead. "What are them fellers starin' at?" she demanded, glaring over at the grinning soldiers. Before Boone could speak, she stepped over closer to the sergeant and asked, "What's the matter with you fellers? You act like you ain't never seen nobody from Colorado before."

The sergeant and soldiers laughed loudly.

"Well, guess I ain't seen nobody like you, missy. You're from Colorado, you say?"

"Shore! Where you from?"

"Arkansas."

"Well, you ought to teach them fellers of yours to keep some manners! They shore ain't got any!"

"That'd be a pretty big job," the sergeant said. "They're a rough bunch, but I don't reckon they see a sight like you every day of the week."

Charlie was about to answer when Boone grabbed her arm and pulled her away, shouldering his way through the crowd. He was exhausted after the long trip from Colorado, which had involved more than he had thought. The train service had not been bad traveling through the North, for their lines were intact. But the Southern railroad system had been so ravaged by the war that the trip had involved many detours, including once taking a coach ride around a section of line that the Northern troops had captured. Now Boone just wanted a bath, a shave, and a bed.

When they reached the outer perimeters of the station, Boone saw a carriage with a For Hire sign on it. He hailed the driver, who was leaning against the wheel eating an apple. "Can you take us to a hotel?"

"Shore. Which one you want?" The speaker was a hollow-cheeked individual with a patch over his left eye.

"What's the best hotel in Richmond?"

"That'd be the Spotswood."

"All right. Take us there." He moved to help Charlie with her baggage, but she simply tossed it in the back and leaped agilely up and seated herself beside the driver. She looked around and repeated the same words she'd said at every city of more than five hundred they'd passed through: "Shore is a big place." As the driver climbed up beside her and picked up the lines, he lifted the eyebrow over his remaining eye but said nothing except to the horses. "Get up there, Babe! Come on, Dixie!" The horses started up, and as the hooves clattered over the cobblestones, he finally asked, "Just got in, I see?"

"Yes," Boone responded. "Came in from Colorado."

Charlie sat upright between the two men, her eyes alert as she studied the milling crowds that filled the streets of Richmond. "Where are all these people goin'?" she asked the driver.

"Well, I reckon they're goin' to work, some of 'em. Lots of soldiers here. They're gettin' ready for the next battle. Some just come out to see what's goin' on. You never been in Richmond afore, I take it?"

"Nope. Never been in Virginia," Boone answered.

"Well, you come at a bad time. Was a nice town before the war. It's gone to perdition in a bucket now!"

They wound their way through the heavy traffic, passing by several factories that belted out black smoke. Finally, they pulled up in front of a four-story building with a sign saying SPOTSWOOD HOTEL over the front. "How much?" Boone asked.

"Confederate or U.S.?"

"U.S." Boone said.

"Well, that'll just be a dollar. It'd been fifteen Confederate." He took the coin Boone handed him and shook his head ruefully. "Don't see much of this kind of money around these days."

Boone grabbed his two valises and watched as Charlie

jumped to the ground and retrieved hers. She looked up and said, "It looks pretty fancy, Boone."

"Well, that's good. I'm ready for a fancy hotel." Boone strolled inside, Charlie keeping step with him. The lobby was expansive and humming with the sound of people coming and going. Moving over to the desk, Boone waited until the clerk, a man with alert gray eyes and red hair, asked, "What can I do for you?"

"Two rooms, please."

"Yes, sir. Just happen to have two. You're lucky. Got a cancellation. They won't be together."

"That doesn't matter."

Boone signed the register for himself, hesitated, then signed "Charlene Peace" beneath his own.

"You need help with the luggage?"

"No, we can take it, but we're pretty tired. Do you suppose we could get some hot water hauled up for a bath?"

"Yes, sir! Mackey!" The clerk waved his hand to a young man who stood nearby. "We need two baths, Mackey. One for this gentlemen and one for this—lady." Charlie didn't notice he hesitated over her status.

"Take 'em to rooms 204 and 221, Mackey."

"Yes, sir! This way, please!"

Mackey reached over to get Charlie's suitcase, which surprised her. She jerked it away from him, saying, "What do you want? What are you doin' tryin' to get my things?"

Boone laughed aloud. "He's not going to steal it, Charlie. He just wants to carry it for you."

"I guess I carried it from Colorado; reckon I can make it upstairs."

Boone sighed. "Here, you can take mine, Mackey."

"Yes, sir. This way." Mackey smiled at Boone then led the way up to the second floor. He stopped at the first room and said, "Will you take this one, sir?"

"Are they just alike?"

"Yes, sir. Both pretty much alike."

"Doesn't matter, then. Charlie, you take this one. This young fellow will bring you a tub and some hot water. Guess you could use a bath."

"A bath? You mean all over?"

Mackey stifled a laugh and then looked away, trying to keep his face straight.

Boone gave Charlie a disgusted look. "You do what you want to! Usually a bath is all over, but that's up to you. I'll come back in about an hour, and we'll talk."

Mackey then led the way to Boone's room. Opening the door, he stepped inside and deposited the suitcases on the floor beside the bed. "Anythin' else besides the bath?"

"Where's a good place to eat, Mackey?"

"Well, our restaurant's about the best, I guess." As he saw the coin Boone handed him, his eyes opened wide. "We don't see much of this hard U.S. money, sir."

"Things are pretty bad, are they, with the cash situation?"

"Just terrible! Have to practically take a wheelbarrow to the store to get a little load of groceries. They keep printin' the stuff, but it don't mean nothin'." He flipped the coin up in the air, caught it adeptly, then nodded. "I'll be right back with those tubs and have plenty of hot water for you. I didn't catch your name, sir."

"Manwaring."

"Right, Mr. Manwaring. Glad to have you stayin' at the hotel."

When the door shut, Boone sat down on the bed and pulled his boots off. He examined his socks, stiff with sweat, and ripped them off, too. He tossed his coat on the bed then sat down in the chair to rest and let the weariness flow out of his body. Watching the crowd outside his window, he noticed that clothes were worn and patched and that even the men's uniforms were in a sorry condition. Then, thinking of Charlie, he muttered aloud, "We may have made a big mistake, Noah. I don't think that girl of yours is ever going to fit into this place!"

Meanwhile, Charlie was looking over her room, saying aloud to herself, "This is the best room I ever saw! Better than any of them places we stayed on the way." They had stayed in several hotels on their journey, most of them very rough—especially when they had reached the South. More often they had slept on the train, which had been difficult for Charlie. She was used to privacy and quiet, and there had been little of that on this trip. Now she walked around and touched the wallpaper, which was a design of strange beasts she had never seen. She looked at them in wonder, especially an exotic-looking animal with a tremendously long neck and long legs. "Don't know what you are, but I wonder if you'd be good to eat."

Taking off her coat, then her moccasins and socks, Charlie walked around in her bare feet, enjoying the somewhat chilly sensation of the carpeted floor. Then she moved over to the window to watch the activity in the streets below. She was fascinated by the traffic, for it included cannons drawn by horses that were driven by soldiers. Wagons passed in a steady stream. The women's dresses particularly interested her, for she knew Boone would insist on her becoming more feminine. Some of them wore skirts that stuck out in the shape of a bell. "They can't be that big under them dresses!" she said, puzzled. "I wonder why they do a thing like that? It looks plumb silly!"

More exhausted than she knew, she went to sleep in the chair. Awhile later a knock at the door startled her. She leaped out of the chair and opened the door. The young man, Mackey, was there with some black servants. "Got your tub and some hot water, miss," he said.

"Well, I guess you kin come in." They brought the tub in and set it in the middle of the floor, filling it from huge kettles. The steam rose in the air. "Brought some fresh towels for you, ma'am," Mackey said. "Anythin' else?"

"I reckon I can handle it from here," Charlie said, giving him a level glance. She had thought he was making fun of her, but he only smiled and said, "Let me know if you need anythin', miss," then left.

As soon as the door closed, Charlie looked warily at the copper tub. She had never had a bath, except in the creek during suitable weather, so she approached it cautiously. Reaching down, she touched the water and found it was very hot.

"Why, I kinnot get in that! It'd cook me like a boiled squirrel!" she exclaimed. But as she set about to simply wash her face and hands as she ordinarily did, curiosity got the better of her. She picked up the bar of soap and said, surprised, "Why, it smells like roses!" The two towels were large and thick, and there was a smaller one for a washcloth.

Finally, she made up her mind. "You don't know till you try!" she said aloud then stripped out of her buckskins and underwear. Throwing them onto the floor, she felt strange, so she put a chair underneath the door handle then hastily looked out the window to make sure no one could see in. She waited until the water was bearable, stepped in, and then sat down, gasping as the hot water splashed over her. Gingerly she took the soap, dipped it in the water, and worked up a lather for her face. She soaped her upper body then held one foot up. "I reckon you need washin'!" She began to scrub. "Didn't know takin' a bath was this much fun! It's a little bit different from them cold creeks up in the mountains." She scrubbed every inch of her body then decided to wash her hair. After rinsing it, she lay back in the now-tepid water and relaxed. Her eyes drooped, and without volition she went to sleep.

When someone outside the window fired off a gun, Charlie started and splashed wildly for a moment, unable to recognize where she was. "What in the cat hair—! Reckon I musta gone to sleep!" She got up and shivered, for the room was cold. She took the towels and rubbed herself down fiercely. Stepping to the carpetbag, she pulled out her clothes—long underwear, a pair of men's wool trousers, and a plaid wool shirt—and quickly slipped into them, then pulled on a pair of thick socks. Refreshed by the brief sleep, she plunged again into the carpetbag and pulled out her tablet, ink, and quill. Putting them on the table beside the bed, she sat down and began to write.

November 12, 1863

> *Well, here we are in Richmond. Caint say as I would like to make that trip again. It shore was a humdinger! We rode trains till I got plum sick of em. Sorry way to get from one place to another, but Boone said it was the only way.*
>
> *We took a long time to make this last leg of the trip. Boone said it was because of the war. Trains was all messed up. I kept lookin out the windows to see if there was any fightin, but we didnt see none. We did see lots of soldiers,*

and Richmond has got more soldiers than dogs got fleas. I got to say though I dont see why Pa liked it so much. It dont look no better than no other town to me, but then I dont like no town no ways. I git lonesome sometimes for the cabin, but they aint no way I kin go back there, I dont reckon.

She paused, dipped her quill into the ink bottle, and sat musing for a few minutes before she continued:

I can tell Boone is ashamed of the way I look and dress. Well, I caint help that, but he has been tellin me the whole trip that when I got to Richmond I would have to put on dresses and learn how to fix my hair and be a lady. Peers to me like thats too much of a job, but he says it kin be did. He has been real nice to me on this trip. I kept expectin him to take liberties, but he never done such. As a matter of fact, there was a feller that came up and tried to make up to me on the train when Boone was gone to the bathroom. The feller just set down in Boones seat and started talkin to me, and when I ignored him, he put his hand on me. I was gettin ready to bust him one when suddenly there was Boone. He had his pistol stuck in his belt, and when the feller saw it he kinda swallowed hard, got up, and said, "Guess I must have got the wrong seat." When Boone set down, I said, "He didnt get no wrong seat! He was tryin to put his hands on me! If you hadnt come, I was fixin to hit him in the mouth!" Boone laughed and said, "I guess thats another thing you will have to learn, Charlie. How to get rid of unwelcome attention." I asked him what unwelcome attention meant, and he said it was men comin around me that I didnt want around me, and I told him I didnt want none of em. He laughed at that too.

I guess I will have to say that Boone is a nice feller. I dont spect he would be as good a man in the woods as Pa, but he shore knows how to get from one place to another, how to find hotels, and how to eat right. Got more good manners than any ten men I ever see.

Just then a knock sounded at her door. Charlie went to answer it. "Hello, Boone," she said.

"Hello, Charlie." He glanced at the bathtub. "Did you enjoy your bath?"

Charlie flushed, for there seemed something wrong with the question, but she could not figure out what. "It was all right."

"I guess it's about time to go down and eat, unless you want to sleep first."

"No, I slept on the train, and I'm hungry as a bear!"

Manwaring looked at her clothes. They looked terrible, but there was nothing he could do about it. He had cleaned up his own clothing as best he could, but it, too, was wrinkled.

"They say the restaurant's got good food. Why don't we eat and then try to find something to wear?"

"All right with me."

The two made their way down the stairs. As they entered the lobby and then the door that led to the restaurant, Boone was uncomfortably aware of how much attention Charlie was drawing. *No help for it, I suppose, but I'll be glad to get her some decent clothes. Feels like we're a traveling circus!*

A waiter came over and, deliberately not looking at Charlie, asked respectfully, "Yes, sir?"

"Table for two."

"Yes, of course. Right this way, sir."

As they walked toward their table, whispers and eyes followed them. Most of the patronage was composed of army officers and the upper strata of Richmond society, Boone realized. *Well, let them look!* he thought. When the waiter reached the table, he pulled out a chair for Charlie, who just stared at it. "What's wrong with the cheer?" she asked.

Boone grinned. "Just sit down on it, Charlie." He winked at the waiter, whose face broke into a slight smile. He pushed the chair under Charlie, put two menus down, and said, "I'll be back for your order, sir."

"Does he think I'm crippled?" Charlie demanded. "Cain't sit down by myself?"

"He was just being polite. Waiters do that."

"Oh!" Charlie realized she had made another mistake, and her face reddened. In the woods she was steady and never had a moment's doubt about what to do, but this new world was alien to her—frightening. Now she looked covertly around the room and noticed that many were watching her. A woman in a bright green dress a few tables down was staring at her with hard eyes. She leaned over and said something to the man with her; then both of them laughed.

Charlie turned to the menu with an absurd temptation to weep. *I'm just tard,* she thought. *What do I care what them people think 'bout me!*

"See anything you like, Charlie?"

"Whatever you get will be good enough for me."

"Well, the selection's kind of limited. But it'll be better than what we've had."

Boone ordered fried chicken and mashed potatoes and asked if there were any vegetables. Upon finding that there were none, he said, "I sure would like some fresh milk and bread."

As the waiter left with their order, Charlie was strangely silent, so Boone asked her what was wrong.

"I'm right tard," Charlie admitted. "Travelin' on them trains is worse than walkin' through the mountains."

"I think you're right there," Boone agreed, studying her and her clothing.

Charlie had steadfastly refused to buy any clothes on the journey, saying, "What I've got is good enough for these old trains. If I have to have a dress, I'll buy it when I get to Richmond."

"What are we gonna do, Boone?" she asked abruptly, lifting her dark blue eyes to his.

Under the light that streamed in from the window, he was almost startled to see how beautiful her eyes were. And she had washed her lustrous black hair so that it was shiny and soft, lying in curls around her head. "I guess we'll go buy some clothes if you're up to it after we eat."

"I mean after that. We gonna buy us a place somewhere?" As she spoke the words, Charlie suddenly realized she spoke of them as if they were somehow married. The thought gave her a jolt, and she wondered if Boone had noticed it. However, he leaned back and shook his head.

"Well, that's a big item. You don't just run out and buy a plantation like you buy a new dress or a pair of shoes. We'll have to ask around, find out how much places cost, and where would be a good location. Unfortunately, I'm the wrong man for this. We'll have to find somebody here who knows property."

"You think we kin do it? I don't know anythin' 'bout farmin' really. 'Cept how to raise a garden. I don't guess you do either?"

"No. All I know is how to run a ship, Charlie." As he smiled at her, she was aware of how fine looking he was. She had not missed how other women had let their eyes linger on his tall figure. *Reckon he could have any woman he wanted,* she realized.

After the waiter came with the food and left, Charlie said, "Do you want to ask the blessin', or do you want me to do it?"

Boone had run into this before. He himself was not a person of faith, but Charlie was. "I told you, Charlie, the Lord wouldn't hear anything I had to say. You'd better do it."

Charlie lowered her head, but she did not lower her voice. She spoke the prayer so loudly that several people in their vicinity listened carefully, looking surprised.

Charlie said, "Amen," then picked up a chicken leg and bit into it. "Hey, Boone, this is good chicken!"

"I always heard people in the South knew how to cook. I had a first mate from Mississippi who was always talking about the fried chicken, how he missed it." He bit into a piece of the breast. "I reckon Motley was telling the truth!"

The two ate hungrily, for it was the best meal they had had since leaving Colorado. They cleared their plates then had apple pie and coffee. Afterward Boone lit up a cigar he had bought.

"I didn't know you smoked," Charlie said.

"I don't. Just saw one of these and thought I'd try it. Charlie, you have to give up chewing that tobacco."

"Why would I do that?"

"Well, it's not ladylike." Boone had been appalled the first time Charlie had pulled out a plug of tobacco. She did not chew it often, but from time to time she would, and he was both amused and repelled by the sight. "Young women don't do that in Richmond society."

"How do you know? You ain't never been here!"

"I just know, that's all. Now I'll tell you what—I'll quit smoking cigars, and you quit chewing tobacco."

Charlie stared at him. "You talk like you're my daddy! I'll

chew what tobacco I please!"

"I guess I am your daddy," Boone said with a grin, imagining what it would be like if Charlie pulled out a plug of tobacco and chewed it at a fancy ball in Richmond. "That's what your pa wanted me to be."

"Well, you ain't my pa! You're too young for one thing, and you just ain't for another!"

"All right. I'm your manager, then. If you're through, let's go shopping."

⁂

Finding shops in Richmond was not difficult, and soon after their meal Boone led Charlie down along the street that was lined with dressmakers and general stores.

"I guess this one's a good place to start." Boone waved his hand toward a sign that said ANDERSON'S DRESS SHOP. "Let's see what they've got to get you dressed up like a queen."

"Don't reckon I hanker to be no queen."

"Just a manner of speaking. Come on."

The spacious shop smelled like cloth as they walked inside. Several dressmakers' dummies were spotted around, and Charlie, who had never seen one of these before, was fascinated. "Ain't that somethin'! Just like a real person!"

"May I help you?"

Boone removed his hat and nodded to the matronly woman who approached with a genteel air. "My name's Manwaring, and this is my—uh, ward," he said, finally settling on a word, "Miss Peace. We've just come in from the mountains and couldn't bring any luggage with us."

"Oh, so you need complete outfits, Miss Peace?"

Charlie stared at the woman and nodded curtly. "I reckon that's the way it is."

"Well, we don't have as good a selection as we have had in days gone by—the war, you know—but we'll do the best we can."

What followed next was rather a nightmare for Boone. He had not grasped how uncertain Charlie was, nor how she covered this uncertainty with a brash, loud manner. As Charlie began to speak loudly, he noticed that a young woman to his right was trying not to show curiosity. However, he met her gaze, and she flushed delicately then turned away from him. *She probably thinks we're both crazy,* he thought. *Sure is a fine-looking woman, though.* Then his attention turned to the argument Charlie was having with the clerk, Mrs. Jones, over a dress.

"All I want's one dress! A woman can't wear but one dress at a time no matter how fancy she is!"

Mrs. Jones gave Boone a startled look. "I understood you wanted a complete wardrobe!"

"That's right. We do. Charlie, will you listen to Mrs. Jones?"

"I guess I kin have a say in what kind of clothes I'm gonna wear! You're not gonna wear 'em, and neither is she!"

Embarrassed, Charlie did not know how to act. She wished heartily she were back in Colorado. She was also angry at Boone, somehow, for putting her in this situation, although she knew he was trying to help her. Stubbornly she thought, *I'll do what I please, even if this is a fancy shop in Richmond!* She reached into her pants pocket and pulled out a plug of tobacco. She glared at Boone, daring him to say something, then bit off a piece. Stuffing the plug back in her pocket, she tucked the bite of tobacco inside her cheek and said, "Now let's get on with our rat killin' here."

This time Boone heard a distinct giggle from the young woman and turned toward her, admiring her trim figure, but was embarrassed to meet her gaze.

For some thirty minutes Mrs. Jones struggled violently to help Charlie, and finally after considerable argument in which Boone could say nothing that pleased Charlie, several items were selected.

"I guess that'll be all for today," Boone said, anxious to get out of the place. He had felt like a fool, for the young woman across the aisle from him had remained to see the show—or so he thought.

Charlie stared at the collection of clothes, which included two dresses, two skirts, and two blouses, then said loudly, "Well, what 'bout underwear? I cain't go neked under these things, kin I?"

Mrs. Jones gasped, and Boone, if he had not been so irritated with Charlie, would have laughed. Instead, he turned to the young woman who was concealing her smile well. "Hello, I'm Boone Manwaring. This is my friend, Miss Charlene Peace."

"How are you, Mr. Manwaring? I'm Marie Bristol. You're just in from the West, I take it?"

"Yes, just in from Colorado."

Charlie took in Boone and Marie's conversation with interest. She was more impressed by the woman's bearing and good looks than she wanted to admit. *That's the way he wants me to look*, she thought. For some reason she was irritated—and she grew more so as Boone and Marie Bristol continued to talk. Finally, Marie put out her hand and said, "I'm glad to know you, Miss Peace. Welcome to Richmond."

The woman's smile was so winsome and her air so generous that Charlie could not help but be impressed. She took Marie's hand and found it to be soft but not weak. "Thank you," she said. She looked around the store and said, "I ain't never been in a big store like this, and I don't know how to buy clothes, neither."

"Perhaps you would let me help you, if you wouldn't mind. I love to shop, but I can never afford to buy what I want."

"That's most kind of you, Miss Bristol. Why don't I give you ladies a chance to finish up? I'll wait outside." Boone found the cold outside a welcome relief. "Blast that girl! Why can't she act like a woman instead of some kind of wild mountain man!" he growled. He thought then of Marie Bristol with pleasure. "Now *that's* what a woman should look like. Maybe she could give Charlie some pointers."

Pleased that Marie Bristol had offered to help, Charlie had to admit that the woman was kind. She did not insist on anything but just recommended certain items of clothes. But after Marie had helped her select some underthings and another outfit, Charlie began to grow restless. "I reckon this is enough to wear for a year."

Marie Bristol laughed and nodded toward the purchases. "You have some nice things here. I hope we haven't spent too much."

"No, I got enough money to burn a wet mule," Charlie responded.

"Really?" Marie said, startled by that evaluation.

"Yep, my pa and Boone found gold out in Colorado."

"I see! Well, in that case this won't be too expensive."

Marie Bristol went to the door and waved Boone inside. "I think we're all finished."

"I appreciate your help, Miss Bristol."

"Since you're strangers in town, perhaps you'd like to come

to the Charity Ball tomorrow night."

"Why, that's very nice of you to ask us. What do you say, Charlie?"

"I don't keer."

"We'd be glad to come," Boone said, sensing Charlie's uncertainty but not understanding why. "Where is it to be held?"

"Down at the Fenway Hall. Anyone can tell you where that is."

"We'll see you there tomorrow. Perhaps you'd save a dance for me?"

"Certainly. Maybe I can introduce you to some of Richmond's finest."

"That would be most kind."

After Marie left, Mrs. Jones packaged the purchases and then said breathlessly, "That will be four hundred and fifty dollars, sir."

"Is that Confederate?"

"Why, yes, of course!"

"How much in U.S. notes?"

"Oh my! Let me see!" Mrs. Jones figured rapidly with a pen. "Forty-eight dollars and fifty cents."

Boone reached into his pocket for some gold coins and counted them out. "Mrs. Jones, you've been very nice to us. Keep the change. We'll probably be back for more later."

Leaving the shop, they made their way back to the hotel. Entering Charlie's room, Boone put the packages down. That's when Charlie said, "I don't like it here, Boone."

Shocked, Boone looked up to see her face set stubbornly in displeasure. "What do you mean you don't like it? We just got here! And already we're meeting people. That Miss Bristol, she can help you."

"I don't like her!"

"Don't like her? What do you mean you don't like her?" Boone demanded.

"She's stuck up!"

"That's foolish talk, Charlie. She was very helpful."

"I don't keer! Let's go back to Colorado, Boone."

For the first time Boone saw beneath Charlie's brash exterior. She was a strong young woman, mannish in her ways, but how could she be anything else? As she lifted her eyes, he saw her fear. *How would I feel if I were thrown into a new life as she's been?* he thought, leading him to speak gently to her. "I know it'll be hard, Charlie, but we'll make it. You and I, we've come here to do something that your pa wanted. I promised him, and in a way, you did, too."

Thinking of how Boone had used "we" made Charlie feel better. "All right, Boone," she said finally, "if you say so. But I don't think we kin ever make a lady out of me!"

"I think the good Lord already did that, Charlie," Boone said, smiling. He reached out and grasped her hand, holding it warmly in both of his. "We just need to polish up your manners a bit. After all, a diamond is only a rough piece of rock until a jeweler polishes it until it sparkles. That's what we'll do with you."

Charlie could not speak for a moment, but then she whispered, "All right, Boone, if you say so."

CHAPTER 10

A MATTER OF FAMILY

Josh Yancy took a deep breath and approached the corporal who had his left arm in a sling. "I'm Josh Yancy," he murmured. "I'd like to see the colonel."

The corporal looked up at the young man with a critical light in his eye. "The colonel's busy," he said.

"I'll be glad to wait."

The corporal shrugged. "Okay. Sit over there. What's your name again?"

"Josh Yancy."

"I'll tell the colonel you're out here when I get time."

"Thank you, Corporal."

Josh moved away from the tent. The Stonewall Brigade was only a small part of the Army of Northern Virginia, but it was not an unimportant part. It had become famous under the leadership of the famous Stonewall Jackson, and after Jackson was killed in the Battle of Chancellorsville, the unit had remained intact. All around soldiers were being drilled by sergeants, and over to his left an artillery crew was going through gun drills without actually firing.

With the hint of bitter weather in the air, Josh pulled his

wool coat up close to his ears, thinking mostly of Rena, whom he loved. Josh Yancy was an imaginative young man who dreamed vividly, so he had no difficulties summoning up her face, scenes, or events. He remembered how, the previous summer, her eyes had sparkled as they were fishing on the creek—how, when he had pretended to throw her in the creek, she had screamed and thrown her arms around him, begging him not to. That was a good memory, and Josh's face softened. So he was startled when the corporal said, "All right. You can go in now, Yancy."

Josh stepped into the interior of the Sibley tent, a canvas structure that rose to a high peak, and stopped before Clay Rocklin's portable desk, waiting until Clay lifted his eyes.

"Why, Josh!" Clay set down his goose quill and put out his hand. "I can guess why you're here."

"Yes, sir. I think I've got to join the army, and I'd rather be in your outfit than any other, if you'll have me."

Clay sighed heavily. "Of course I'll have you. You'll be as good a soldier as Lonnie was." He spoke sadly of Josh's brother who had died in action. He had looked much like Josh, with the same lean look and slightly freckled face. Brushing the memory aside, Clay continued, "We'll get you signed up. You've told Rena about this?"

"Yes, sir, I have. She wanted us to get married, but I told her it wouldn't be fitting with me leaving right away."

A warm feeling came to Clay Rocklin then. This young man had character like an iron bar, and although he had no wealth and did not come from aristocracy, still Clay was not displeased with Rena's choice. He could remember several marriages among his kinfolk that had turned out badly when young women married simply for those reasons.

"I appreciate that, Josh. I'm not much of an example,

because Melora and I married knowing I'd have to leave and go into action. But you're younger than I was. Come along. We'll get you signed up."

Clay made the arrangements with the corporal then said, "I've got to make a trip to see my aunt, Corporal. I'll be back before dark. Tell Major Evans he's in charge until I get back."

"Yes, sir."

Moving to where the horses were kept, Clay said to the private who saluted him, "Bring my horse out and saddle him for me, Private."

"Yes, sir!"

Ten minutes later Clay was on the road out of Richmond. It was a relief to him to be away from the camp for a while. Since his return he had worked almost night and day, and his mind was exhausted with the myriad details. Finding enough food and proper uniforms for his men was difficult enough. Since the Confederacy had been encircled by the blockade by sea and the armies of Grant and Sherman by land, the South could only count on what they could manufacture themselves. Many of the men were armed with muskets and bayonets taken from the Yankees after battles, and as for new arms, so few were smuggled through the blockade that they were almost nonexistent.

The sun was a pale disk overhead as Clay made his way toward Hartsworth. He arrived there shortly before noon and handed the lines of his horse to Solomon, who greeted him with, "Hello, General."

"Not a general yet. Probably never will be, Solomon. How are you doing?"

"Oh, fine, suh! You go right on to the house. I'll take care of this fine hoss of yours."

Clay approached the steps of the large, two-story brick

home that was painted white with dark green shutters. But he had no chance to knock on the door, for he was met by Marianne, who opened it. "Come in, Clay."

"Hello, Marianne." He gave her a hug and kissed her cheek. "You're still the second-best-looking woman in Virginia."

"Melora will be glad to know she's still number one. Come into the parlor. I've got a fire there."

Clay followed Marianne into the parlor, and the two sat down in front of the fireplace. Clay relaxed and stretched out his legs, holding the soles of his boots toward the fire. "It's cold outside," he said. "I wouldn't be surprised if we have snow for Christmas."

"A white Christmas. We haven't had one of those for a long time."

"No, about three years, I think."

As Clay sat loosely in the chair, Marianne called for tea then asked, "Can you stay for supper, Clay?"

"No, I've got to get back. Mainly I just wanted to get out of camp. But I can stay for lunch."

"Are you going by Gracefield?"

"I sure am. I wouldn't pass this close without going to see Melora. I'm still a new bridegroom, you know."

"And about to be a father again! Are you happy about that, Clay?"

"Yes, I am! For my own sake, but also because Melora's so happy," he said simply. "It's good for her, I think." He sat up straighter as Ketura brought tea, and they went through the business of putting in sugar and cream. He sipped the hot liquid gratefully. "I'm concerned, though, that something might happen to me."

"Melora would manage. She's the strongest woman I know.

I've always admired her."

"So have I," Clay said, grinning. Then he frowned slightly. "Josh came in and enlisted this morning. I knew it was coming, but I hate to see it."

"Are he and Rena talking about getting married?"

"Rena wants to, but Josh said it wouldn't be fair. That was fine of him, wasn't it?"

"Yes, it was. I worry about him, though, Clay, and all the young men. So many of them are gone now."

"The best rushed out and joined up when the war started. Too many of them are buried in shallow graves out by Antietam and Gettysburg."

Fond of each other, Clay and Marianne found solace in one another's company. When Marianne mentioned the Charity Ball, Clay said, "I guess I'll take Melora. Are you and Claude going?"

"I'm not sure, Clay," Marianne said. You know what it's like. There's no money, and we've got mortgages on this place."

"Who hasn't?"

"I suppose that's true." But Marianne didn't want to talk about Claude, so she said quickly, "Malcolm Leighton is taking Marie."

Clay lifted an eyebrow. "Is she serious about him?"

"I don't think so, but who knows these days? I hardly ever see Austin. You probably see him more than I do."

"No, I don't go near the War Department any more than necessary. They're liable to make me a general. Then where will I be?" he said comically.

"In any case, I asked Marie about Leighton, and she just laughed and said, 'He's working his way through all the young women in Richmond alphabetically. He's on the *B*s now.' She wasn't serious, of course, but I don't know. It's a bad time for young women. So many young men are gone now."

After a while the two went in to the lunch that Ketura had prepared. They were eating chicken salad and pork ribs when Claude came in. He took one look at Clay and nodded. "I'm glad to see you, Clay."

"Hello, Claude. I'm eating your food up. Sit down before I devour it all."

Claude Bristol sat down. He wore a tan double-breasted jacket with a narrow collar, a red tie, a white shirt, and baggy white trousers. As usual he looked neat, but his face was rather drawn, and he could not meet Marianne's eyes. After the meal Marianne said, "Why don't you two go into the study? I'll join you later."

Claude rose with alacrity and led the way into the large study, carpeted with multicolored pastels. Its walls were covered with light tan and floral paper and pictures in thick gilt frames. One wall held many books on dark wooden shelves. Between two long windows was a comfortably padded sofa and two brown and ivory armchairs. "Claude, this is a beautiful room, but then, Hartsworth's the most beautiful place I know."

Claude stared at Clay nervously, trying to find some meaning in his words.

Knowing Claude Bristol well, Clay was aware something was on the man's mind. He waited for Claude to bring it up.

After some light conversation, Claude suddenly stood up and said, "Clay, I want to join the army."

For a moment Clay Rocklin thought he had misunderstood Claude. His mind raced as he tried to find an answer. "I don't think that's the best idea you've ever had, Claude."

"You think I'm useless! Well, you're probably right." Claude pulled out a cigar and lit it, watching the smoke rise in the air. "I haven't been any help to Marianne or to the children. In fact, I've dragged them down." He made a hopeless gesture with his hands. "It would have been better if Marianne had never met me, Clay."

Clay shifted uneasily in his chair, since he'd often thought that himself. But he had never said one word about Claude to Marianne or anyone else. "If you want to help Marianne and the children, the best thing you can do is straighten up. Be some help around the plantation here."

"I'm no good at that. Marianne does a better job running this place. And she's the real heart of Hartsworth. Always has been. All I've done is throw money away with both hands, but that's over, Clay."

"Why the army?"

"It's the only thing I can think of where I might be of some use. I thought of just leaving Marianne, going off and getting out of the way, but—I love her, Clay, and miracle of miracles, somehow she still cares for me. Even after all I've been."

"Yes, she does, Claude."

"I saw Austin the morning after he hauled me back drunk. There was disgust in his face, and I don't blame him. Marie covers it up better, but she has no respect for me either. Why should she?" Claude paced the floor nervously. He came to stand over Clay, looked down at him, and said, "I know I'm not a soldier, but there must be *something* I can do rather than be deadweight around here. At least I'd like a chance."

For a few minutes Clay argued with Claude then saw the man was adamant. "I still don't understand why you want to do this, Claude," he said finally.

"It's a matter of family, Clay. You're a Rocklin, and I know your pride in being a Rocklin. Marianne's the same way. But I take no pride in being a Bristol! If I could do one thing right, I think I might be a part of the Rocklin family, even if it's secondhand." His eyes caught Clay's, his lips tense. "I don't know how to beg, Clay, but I wish you'd give me a chance to do something."

"The Stonewall Brigade is a fighting outfit. We'll be leaving Richmond soon because Grant's coming down. If you go with us, you could get killed."

"That's all right with me," Claude said bitterly. "Better to die than to go on like I've been going. Will you do it, Clay?"

As Bristol waited, the pleading in his eyes was more than Clay could stand.

"If you're serious, Claude, I'll do what I can. No combat, of course, at your age, but you can be my clerk until you're ready to be made adjutant. You'll come in as a second lieutenant, but you'll be in for some trouble. This is a fighting outfit, and they'll scream that I'm showing you special treatment."

"I can stand it if you can, Clay. Will you do it, then?"

Clay nodded. "Come when you get ready. I'll enlist you, and we'll find you a uniform. You'd better hurry if you're going, because when Grant strikes, we'll be pulling out overnight."

"I'll come the first thing in the morning."

"Have you told Marianne any of this?"

"No."

"You'd better have a talk with her. It's a big thing. I don't know what she'll think about it. She may blame me."

"She won't do that." Claude put out his hand. "I know this is charity on your part, and I'm thanking you. If I die, that's all right.... I'm hoping that I can do this one thing, and that my wife and children won't think so badly of me."

As Clay shook the man's hand, he thought, *Claude Bristol has never done anything unselfish in his life, so I'm probably making a big mistake. But he's right about one thing—it is better to die than to live as he has been.*

&

"I'll be leaving in the morning, Marianne."

Marianne was preparing for bed. She had on her nightgown and had paused long enough to take the combs out of her hair. As it fell down, she turned to her husband with surprise. "Leaving for where, Claude?"

"I'm joining the army," Claude said nervously and seriously. "Clay has agreed to take me as his clerk. I'll be a second lieutenant."

Marianne stared at her husband, her mind swirling. "Why are you doing this, Claude? You've never shown any interest in the Confederacy."

"I still don't have much, but I'm interested in—"

Bristol broke off, embarrassed. He stood before Marianne and put his hands on her shoulders. "I'm interested," he said slowly, "in doing one thing that you admire before I die."

"Why, Claude!" Marianne said, still in shock. "Why do you think this would please me? You might get killed!"

"So I might. That's what Clay said. But I've not been a man you could admire, Marianne. When we first met, and when we married, I thought I might be, but it hasn't happened. Maybe it never will, but if there's any chance at all you could see something in me that's good, I've got to take it."

Marianne was aware Claude was asking her for something. It had been so long since he had asked her for anything, she could not believe it nor understand it. She knew he was an unhappy man, that under the gaiety he often showed outwardly, there was a sadness, for he recognized the failure of his life. Slowly she reached up and touched his cheek, then said softly, "Be very careful, my dear."

"I still love you, Marianne, and one day I hope you'll think better of me." His face working with emotion, he walked out of the room. When he did not return, Marianne lay in bed wondering what had happened. A faint hope began to grow in her, and she prayed then for this husband of hers who had been such a trial. Finally, she whispered to herself, "Nothing's too hard for God...."

CHAPTER 11

A DISASTER AT THE BALL

Charlie stepped out of the copper tub and stretched luxuriously. The water dripped down her arms as she reached to pick up a towel. *A body could get used to this here bathin'. It ain't as bad as I figured it'd be.* She had learned, almost at once, to love the feel of cleanliness, both in body and in clothes, and now as she dried off and slipped into the undergarments that seemed very soft after the rough underwear she was accustomed to, it made her feel odd. Actually, it made her feel feminine, but she would not have thought of it like that. After she had donned her underthings, she stared at the apparatus Mrs. Jones, the store clerk, had called a bustle. Marie Bristol had mentioned that many women were wearing them, so Charlie put it on, tying the strings in front. She looked back and found herself grinning. "I guess they figure women didn't have enough behinds, but you sure do with one of these things." Then she turned to the fashionable blue silk dress, both fearful and admiring of it. The bodice was edged with a delicate white frill, and the overskirt was looped up at the sides and accented with black lace. A black ribbon tied around her neck would complete the outfit.

Carefully she pulled the dress over her head. It was tight

enough that she had to work at it. Finally, it slipped over, and she turned to the mirror fastened over the washstand and gasped.

"Why, I can't wear a thing like this!" Even though she was alone, her cheeks flushed as she saw how much of her neck the dress revealed.

But it was too late now, for she had no choice. She tried first pulling it up, but it slipped right down again. Finally, she stripped the dress off. Going through the underwear she had bought, she found what the woman had called a vest. At least *it* buttoned all the way and covered up her front. She slipped it on, nodded with satisfaction, then pulled the dress on again. Staring at herself in the mirror, she said, "Now that's more like it! Can't imagine a female runnin' around not wearin' no more clothes than this! That woman must've forgot part of it!"

Moving over, she picked up the pair of shoes and slipped them on her feet. Taking several experimental steps, she found that they pinched her more than she remembered at the shop, and she teetered back and forth in them. "Don't know why women have to try to be tall. It's like standin' on your toes—and they hurt."

For a while she moved around irresolutely, stopping to look at her hair. She had seen some ornate hairdos, but there was nothing she could do. In the first place, she didn't know how, and in the second place, she was rebellious enough to say, "If my hair don't suit 'em, let 'em look at somebody else." Defiantly she ran a comb through her black curls. Picking up a small box marked RICE POWDER, she opened it carefully and stuck her finger down in it. "It looks like flour you can make flapjacks with," she murmured. Gingerly she spread some on her face, leaving streaks. "That looks plumb silly! I just ain't gonna wear it!"

When she got up and walked around, she liked the crinkling noise the dress made, but the shoes still hurt. Finally, she reached down, removed them, and slipped her feet into her moccasins. "Don't see what difference it makes. Ain't nobody gonna see my feet as long as this here dress is." A knock sounded at the door, and she marched over and pulled it open. Boone stood there, as she expected, and she saw his eyes widen. "Well, that's a pretty dress!" he said.

"Come on in, Boone." The two examined each other. What Boone saw was a very attractive young woman who had something strange on underneath her dress. "What is this thing, Charlie?" he said, pointing to the garment that covered her from neck to below the front of her dress.

"I think they forgot part of this here dress, Boone. Why, I was plumb scandalized when I put it on! It hardly covered me up a'tall!"

Boone restrained a smile, since it was no time for a lesson. But he thought, *She'll have to talk to Marie Bristol about some of these things.* "You look fine," he said.

"So do you, Boone. Well, you look as good as a lawyer or an undertaker."

Boone laughed aloud. "I suppose I should say thank you, but I don't care for either breed." He was wearing a dark gray jacket, a white shirt, a black waistcoat, and black-and-gray-checked trousers. A red tie was knotted around his neck.

"You look powerful good," Charlie said; then a worried look passed across her features. "I still think I'd rather not go to this here dance. Do you suppose they'll do any hoedowns?"

"I don't know," Boone said. "Never been to a dance in Richmond."

"That's the only kind of dancin' I know, and I don't know

much 'bout that." Her eyes narrowed. "I bet you're a good dancer, ain't you, now?"

"Well, just fair."

But Charlie knew better, for she had learned that Boone was a quality man. During the brief time they had been together, her attitude had changed. Back in the cabin when he had tried to touch her, she had grown angry. All during the trip she kept waiting for him to make some kind of move again, but he never had. Somehow this had irritated her. Now as he picked up her coat, a pearl gray wool coat with a fox collar she loved, and slipped it over her shoulders, she thought, *He knows women*.

"All right," Boone said. "I hope Richmond's ready for us."

"Boone, don't let me get into no trouble."

"Trouble? How could you get into trouble?"

"I don't know. I feel funny goin' out dressed like this. You know how to do things like this. I ain't never been out of the woods, Boone." Her eyes were so large and vulnerable that he wanted to run his hand across her hair. But he knew better than that, so he smiled instead, saying, "Why, you'll do fine, Charlie. A month from now you'll have Richmond at your feet."

"You really think so?"

"I know it! Come on. Let's go to the ball."

Malcolm Leighton leaned back in the carriage and allowed his shoulder to touch Marie Bristol's. She instantly removed her own a fraction of an inch, amusing him. "You don't exactly make a fellow feel good, Marie. Every time I try to touch you, you run like I was a copperhead or something."

"Sorry you feel like that, Malcolm," she replied, "but a girl has to be careful with young men. Especially young men with your reputation."

"Who's been giving me a bad word?" Leighton asked, affecting surprise. "I'm only a poor country boy trying to get along."

"I know all about that," Marie said. Malcolm Leighton *was* a country boy. He had grown up poor, as he had told her once, and determined to be one thing—rich. He had gone to sea as a cabin boy, had risen rapidly in his profession, and now at the age of twenty-eight owned two ships, both excellent blockade runners. He was also sought after by half the eligible unmarried ladies in Richmond and in the surrounding countryside. "You know what I told my mother about you, Malcolm?"

"I'm not sure I want to hear."

"You've heard worse, I'm sure." Turning to stare at his handsome features, which consisted of a straight nose, high cheekbones, and glossy brown hair, Marie said, "I told her you were looking for a wife but that you had started at the *A*s and were working through alphabetically."

"Oh, that's foolish!"

"Is it? What about Betty Ashland? You chased her for two months, and after that was Charlotte Allison. You worked your way through the *A*s and now you're down to the *B*s."

"I don't know what to make of you, Marie," Leighton said lightly. He had known women perhaps more beautiful, but none with a wit sometimes so sharp it hurt a little bit. To tell the truth, he was tired of being successful with women. With his good looks and money, he could take his choice, and it seemed all he had to do was smile and the victory was won. With Marie Bristol, however, it was different. He had known that from the beginning. And now as he smiled at her through the growing darkness, he thought, *Why is it I always want something I can't have? Marie doesn't have a dime. Her folks won't have a pin after the war's over. . . . But I guess as long as one of us has money, that's enough, and she is a handsome girl!*

The carriage clattered over the brick streets and stopped in front of the large building where the Charity Ball was to be held. The door opened almost at once, and a tall black man offered her a hand down. She looked up in surprise to see that it was Solomon, one of the slaves from her own plantation. "Why, Solomon, what are you doing here?"

"I'm the doorman, Miss Marie." Solomon's white teeth flashed in the reflection of the lanterns that lit up the street and the front of the building. "They payin' me ten dollar just to help folks out. I do it for nothin' all the time. Ain't that somethin'?" Then he nodded toward Malcolm. "Good evenin', Mr. Leighton."

"Hello, Solomon." Reaching into his pocket, Malcolm pulled out a coin and passed it over. "Buy yourself a new necktie."

"I shore will! A red 'un! Thank you, suh!"

Marie took Leighton's arm, and the two entered. As they stepped inside, Leighton whispered, "It looks like everybody in Richmond is here. I never saw such a crowd."

"It's for a good cause."

The cause she spoke of was to help pay for medicines and supplies for Chimborazo, the large Confederate hospital outside Richmond. Marie was a fervent supporter of that and spent much of her time there. Now as they made their way through the packed room and across the white marble floor, she said, "There aren't many places this large, and they fixed it up for the ball so nicely." Chandeliers glittered from the high domed ceiling, and a fire blazed in the two large fireplaces on each side of the room. Long tables clothed in white linen were heaped high with silver plates, bowls, and platters of delicious-smelling food.

At the far end of the room, double French doors led to a large porch, then a beautiful garden.

Over at one end of the ballroom, ten musicians were playing. The brilliant reds, greens, and yellows of women's dresses swirled around the room, counterpointed by the brass buttons and epaulets of the many officers.

Marie heard her name called and turned to see Austin exiting the floor with Ida Campbell. Austin was wearing his uniform, and Ida was wearing a new red silk dress with layers of flounces pinned up at the back with a fabric bow. She could well afford it, Marie knew, for she was the daughter of Clara Campbell, a wealthy widow. Her father had owned an immense plantation, but now Mrs. Campbell stayed most of the time inside Richmond mingling with the affluent. Ida came at once to Marie, and the two women hugged each other. Ida, at twenty-seven, was a year older than Marie. She was not exceptionally pretty, but Marie liked her honesty and openness. They exchanged compliments on their dresses while the two men talked.

Suddenly Ida said, "Who in the world is that, Austin?"

Austin squinted through the yellow light from the candles, lanterns, and chandeliers. "I never saw them before."

"I have," Marie said. "The man's name is Boone Manwaring."

"How do you know that?" Malcolm asked with surprise. "Is he a friend of yours?"

"No, not really, although I invited them to the ball." She felt their questioning eyes upon her. "I was in Mrs. Anderson's dress shop when they came in. They're from Colorado."

"His wife's a pretty woman," Ida said.

"Oh, she's not his wife," Marie replied.

"Not his wife? You mean she's his mistress?"

"I don't think so. I don't know the whole story, but he introduced her as his ward."

"Well," Leighton said with a grin, "that's one way of saying it. She's a pretty thing, isn't she?"

"There's something strange about her. Look how she walks," Austin said, watching the two cross the floor. He could not put his finger on it for a minute; then he said, "Look how long her steps are. She keeps up with that tall fellow with her. Manwaring is his name?"

"Yes, and her name is Charlene Peace, but she prefers to be called Charlie."

"She sure walks like a clodhopping farmer," Leighton said, studying the pair. "And what's that she's got on? I can't make it out."

Ida said, "Introduce us, Marie. It looks like they might be interesting. He's a fine-looking fellow!"

"Remember, I'm the fellow who brought you to this ball, Ida," Austin said quickly. "He may be taller than I am, but surely he's not better looking."

Ida laughed. "I like to make you jealous, Austin. . . . Look, they're coming this way!"

Boone Manwaring had seen Marie Bristol and her party. He had leaned down to whisper, "Come on, Charlie. Here's a way to get introduced."

As they moved across the floor, Charlie's heart was thumping. She was stunned with all the activity, the colorful dresses, the loud music, the couples whirling around the floor, and now she wanted desperately to leave. But there was no hope for it. Boone's hand was on her arm, and he guided her through the crowd until they stood before Marie Bristol and her friends.

"How do you do, Miss Bristol? I took you up on your

invitation," Manwaring said, smiling.

"I'm glad you did, Mr. Manwaring. This is Boone Manwaring. May I introduce my brother Austin. This is Mr. Malcolm Leighton, and this is Miss Ida Campbell."

"I'm happy to know you all, and may I introduce Miss Charlene Peace."

Charlie could do no more than swallow and nod as the others returned her greeting. Aware they were all looking at her peculiarly, Charlie clung desperately to Boone's arm, far more frightened than she had been when attacked by a grizzly bear. Finally, Boone said, "I think this is our dance, Miss Charlene, but if I may put in my bid, Miss Bristol and Miss Campbell, I would like the honor of a dance with you later on in the evening." He received assurances from both women and then pulled Charlie away.

"Boone," she said in a horrified whisper, "I cain't dance!"

"Sure you can. You said you could do a hoedown."

"Well, this ain't no hoedown!"

Noticing that people were staring, Boone said almost roughly, "Look, Charlie, there's nothing to it! Here, give me your hand! Now put your other hand up on my arm! Try not to fall over my feet!"

Charlie swallowed hard. "I don't know how to do this, Boone, but I'll try."

He was careful not to do anything complicated and was pleased to discover she had a natural rhythm. "That's fine, Charlie—you're doing real good!"

"Am I really?"

"Sure you are! Why, you'll be bragging someday that you had the best teacher in Richmond. Here we go now; we're going to try a little turn."

The four they had left were watching them. "What was that thing she had on under her dress? It looked like undergarments," Ida said.

"I think it was," Marie said. She hesitated, then feeling it might be kinder to give a little detail of her meeting, explained how the two had just come from Colorado. She ended by saying, "The girl just lost her parents, and somehow Mr. Manwaring is taking care of her. I don't know the details, but in the dress shop it became obvious she had never had a dress on before. She was wearing buckskins with fringes and a coonskin cap."

"You're joking!" Leighton said. "You made that up!"

"No, I didn't. Can't you see how frightened she is? I feel sorry for her."

Ida turned toward the couple and smiled. "Well, she seems to be learning quickly. Come on, Austin; let's dance."

Austin agreed at once, and when they were out on the floor halfway through the dance, he said, "I'll tell you what, Ida. I'm going to give you a chance to dance with that fellow, Manwaring, that you think is so handsome."

Suspicious, Ida asked, "You're going to dance with that girl, aren't you?"

"I'm curious about her. Maybe I'd like to find some sweet, unspoiled young girl, totally innocent. Sort of a noble savage."

Ida liked Austin tremendously and considered marrying him often. She had turned down more than one offer, for she was a quick-witted girl and could read men rather easily. They had been after her money and little else. In all honesty she did not think this of Austin, but now as she glanced at Manwaring, she said with humor, "All right. Let's trade partners."

Austin maneuvered Ida out until they were even with Boone and Charlie, then tapped Manwaring on the shoulder. "I don't know about out west, but here we always cut in on strangers. Would you exchange partners with me?"

Boone saw the terror in Charlie's eyes but smiled encouragingly. "Why, of course! You'll dance with Mr. Bristol, won't you, Charlie?"

He gave her no chance to say no. Instantly he bowed to Ida; then the two moved off. As Charlie stood there almost paralyzed, Austin astutely realized she was frightened. "There's no need to be afraid," he said quietly.

"I ain't scared!" Charlie fired back. But then she bit her lip. "I ain't a good dancer, Mr. Bristol."

"Well, I'm an excellent dancer, so we'll average out. You step on my feet, and I'll step on yours in revenge." When he smiled at her, Charlie felt much better. This was an honest young man, she saw, and when he put his arm around her and took her hand, she did her best to follow. As they moved around the floor, he questioned her cautiously. "You've just come to Richmond, then, Miss Peace?"

"Yes. Me and Boone, we come in three days ago from Colorado."

"And how do you like Richmond?"

"Don't like it! Wisht I was back in the mountains!"

Amused by this blatant honesty, Austin smiled broadly. "I don't blame you a bit! I don't like it myself, but I live here, so I can't leave. Are you here for long?"

"My pa wanted me to come here. He grew up in Virginia. He wanted to buy a place and bring me and Ma here, but she died. So did he."

"Sorry to hear that." The dance moved on and he asked, "So you still intend to buy a place, a house?"

"Not a house. Pa wanted to get a plantation." By this time

Charlie did not have to give all her attention to her feet. She had found that all she had to do was follow Austin on the floor, which to her surprise she did rather easily. She explained her father's dream, and Austin listened carefully then said quietly, "I'm sorry he didn't live to see his dream come true. It's a shame."

Charlie looked up to see the genuine concern in the young man's eyes. "That's neighborly of you to say so, Mr. Bristol."

"Look, why don't you just call me Austin, and perhaps you'd let me call you by your first name."

Shyly Charlie said, "Everybody calls me Charlie. My real name's Charlene, but only my ma ever called me that."

"I think I like Charlene, if you don't mind."

"I reckon it'd be all right." Charlie was pleased, for she did like the name Charlene, but her nickname had stuck so firmly that she did not know how to reverse it. As they continued to dance, she found herself enjoying his conversation and little knew how his tact made things easier for her.

Across the room Boone Manwaring kept an eye on the two. "Your escort is a very good dancer," he said. "I was worried about Charlie."

"Everyone's curious about her, of course, and about you."

"I understand why they would be," Boone said. "She lost her parents recently, and she's not over the shock of it yet."

"Do you intend to stay in Richmond?"

He started to tell Ida the story, then decided it was too complicated. "I hope to find a place somewhere and get Charlie set up. She needs a home, a place of her own," he said simply.

"There's some fine old homes in Richmond. I could find out which ones are for sale."

"That's very gracious of you. I'll take you up on that, but we'd rather have something outside town. Something with some land."

"How much land?"

"I'm not sure." Again he almost told the story but said instead, "I'm a sailor, Miss Campbell. I don't know farming or plantations, but I guess I'll have to learn since I have to look out for Charlie."

Ida Campbell burned with curiosity to find out the relationship between the two, but she knew this was the wrong place and time to ask.

As the two danced, Ida found herself intrigued by Boone Manwaring. Boone himself, as he looked down into her face, was entranced by her smooth complexion, sparkling brown eyes, and gracious manners. *If all Southern women were like this, it'd be a heaven for bachelors,* he thought.

When the dance ended, Boone escorted her over to the refreshment table, where Charlie and Austin stood beside Malcolm Leighton. "I think I'll have to claim this dance, Miss Peace," Leighton said at once.

Charlie glanced at Boone for reassurance. He nodded, and she moved out to the dance floor. Boone asked Marie Bristol to dance and was amused at how she tried to find out more about him and his ward. "Are you and Miss Peace related, Mr. Manwaring?"

"Not at all. I was a good friend of her father."

"I see," Marie said, but she did not at all. "And her parents are both deceased?"

"Yes. She doesn't have any family."

"And what about you? Excuse my curiosity," she responded, "but my mother says I have the curiosity of ten cats."

Boone liked the woman instinctively, so he sketched his background, his experiences on the sea, and finally said, "Not a very exciting biography. It was really more exciting looking for gold with Charlie's father."

"And you found the gold?"

"We found some of it," Boone said cautiously, not wanting to reveal the extent of his wealth. After the dance, they went back to the table, where he found Charlie fielding questions from Malcolm Leighton.

"Ah, I was just asking Miss Peace about you, Mr. Manwaring. I understand you're a seafaring man?"

"All my life," Boone said.

"So am I. If you're interested in a place, I can find room for you on one of my ships."

"That's very obliging of you, Mr. Leighton. I don't anticipate going back to sea anytime soon."

"Sooner or later someone will ask you about your politics, Mr. Manwaring," Leighton said. "We can't ask what time it is without asking that in this part of the world."

"I noticed that," Boone said, grinning. "My politics are to get rich, I guess."

His answer pleased Malcolm Leighton, and he laughed aloud. "I think we belong to the same party, sir. We'll have a drink on that." He proposed a toast. "To making money!" But it was Marie who said immediately, "And to the Confederacy!"

"To the Confederacy!" Malcolm said. "I stand rebuked!"

Staring at Boone, Marie said, "I'm afraid you'll have to be a little more specific. Making money is nice, but how do you stand on the war?"

She was, Boone saw, very serious, and the others were also listening carefully. *I've got to say this right, or I'll get off on the wrong foot,* he thought almost grimly. Speaking deliberately, he said, "Out in the West, you wouldn't believe how little the war matters. I know that sounds odd to you, for it's your whole life here. But when you're in the middle of the mountains, or when you're out at sea, it's another thing. As for my politics, I really don't have any. I've spent much of my life at sea, and all I know about the war is what I read."

"Are you saying you don't care one way or another about the war?" Leighton asked sharply.

"If I had cared about it," Boone said, shrugging, "I would have joined either the Union or the Confederacy. I suppose right now you'll just have to put me down as undecided."

"End of questioning!" Austin said quickly. "A very fair answer, Mr. Manwaring. I hope that when you do decide, it will be for the Confederacy."

At that moment they were interrupted by a civilian, a bulky man almost as tall as Boone, who wore a fine suit of clothes. Without preamble he said, "Excuse me, Austin. I see we have some visitors. Could I ask that you introduce me?"

"Certainly," Austin said with reserve. "This is Miss Charlene Peace and Mr. Boone Manwaring, and this is Mr. Jack Cowling."

"We're glad to welcome you to Richmond, sir," he said, bowing slightly to Manwaring. Then he turned to Charlie. "Miss Peace, may I have this dance?"

Once again Charlie was frightened, but she had gained enough confidence to murmur, "I reckon so."

As she moved out on the dance floor with Cowling, Austin said, "He's one of the most influential men in Richmond, but nobody knows exactly where his money comes from."

"Part of it comes from making rotten uniforms that fall apart the first time they're worn!" Ida Campbell said, looking with distaste at Cowling.

Coming on the heels of Leighton's questions about Boone's

politics, it was an uncomfortable moment—as if someone had exposed a secret that had been better off unmentioned. Boone understood at once that there were people in the Confederacy who weren't particularly admirable. He asked, "May I have this dance, Miss Bristol?"

"Of course."

The two moved out on the floor, and Boone said little. When the dance was half over, he stopped abruptly, causing Marie to miss a step. They both had heard a voice that could only be Charlie Peace's because it was loud enough to be heard over half the ballroom: "Keep your slimy hands to yourself!"

Instantly sensing trouble, Boone said, "Pardon me," and pushed his way through the crowd. He came upon Charlie, who was glaring at Cowling. Cowling's face had a red mark on it.

"What's the trouble, Charlie?"

"Why, he put his hand on—" Charlie stopped short then said, "He put his hands on me in a place he shouldn't, and I punched him fer it!"

"I'll have to ask you to excuse Miss Peace, Mr. Cowling," Boone said.

Cowling was unaccustomed to being slighted. Certainly no one had ever struck him in public in a ballroom, and his rage was evident. He had been drinking, for his eyes were slightly bloodshot. "If you want to make more of this, you can have your man call on me! I'll be glad to oblige you!"

For a moment Boone was tempted to take up the challenge. Instead, he said, "I try to delegate all the fighting to my dog."

Cowling's face turned pale and he opened his mouth, but a friend came quickly to his side and said, "Come on, Jack. You're drunk."

"I want to go home, Boone! Let's get out of here!"

GILBERT MORRIS

"All right, Charlie."

Boone threw one look at Marie Bristol and shrugged helplessly; then he and Charlie left the room. When they were outside, Charlie said emphatically, "If that's your fine society, I don't keer much fer it!"

"I don't think Jack Cowling was a good sample."

"I don't like any of this, Boone!" Charlie whispered almost plaintively. "Cain't we go away from here?"

Feeling sorry for the girl, Boone stood there silently as the music floated out of the building toward them. "I'll tell you what, Charlie," he said, "let's try it for a while. If it doesn't work out, I'll take you back to Colorado. Is that fair enough?"

Charlie knew she had behaved badly, and she was humiliated. After all, she had only done what she would have at a dance back in the mountains. She had expected Boone to take up the challenge and was surprised when he did not. Looking up now, she saw the concern in his hazel eyes and suddenly realized how much she had come to depend upon this man since her father had died. He was, in one respect, the only friend she had.

"I reckon that's fair enough, Boone."

Chapter 12

A Favor for Boone

Marianne was sitting in the parlor working on a new quilt. She would have the women in for a quilting later that afternoon, so she was gathering the material together. Ketura came to the door and said, "They's a gentleman here to see Miss Marie."

"Who is it, Ketura?"

"I can't say his name. It's funny."

Wondering who it could be, Marianne rose and went to the foyer, where she saw a tall man dressed in a new suit. "I'm Mrs. Bristol, sir."

"Mrs. Bristol, my name is Boone Manwaring. I don't know if your daughter has spoken of me or not."

"Why, as a matter of fact, she has! She mentioned she met you at a dress shop."

"Yes, and then again at the Charity Ball three days ago. I would like to see her if she's home, Mrs. Bristol."

"I believe she's up in her room. If you'd care to wait, I'll go get her."

"Thank you, Mrs. Bristol."

Marianne showed Boone to the study and then went upstairs. She found Marie reading a book before the fireplace. She was wearing a simple gray dress with white buttons.

"You have a visitor, Marie."

"A visitor?" Marie put the book down. "Who's out in this kind of weather?"

"It's Mr. Manwaring. The one you told me about. You didn't say he was so good looking, though."

"Boone Manwaring?" Marie cocked her head in puzzled surprise.

"Didn't you invite him here?"

"Well, in a general way, but it looks like he took it specifically."

Marianne smiled, saying, "He didn't bring his young woman with him. I was hoping to see her after what you told me about the incident at the ball."

"I'd better go down," Marie responded. "I'll tell you about it later, Mother."

"Very well. I'll be anxious to hear."

When Marie reached the parlor, Boone was standing in front of the fire. He came forward at once. "I'm sorry to impose on you, but I hope you'll forgive me."

"Certainly! I'm glad you came in. Let me have some tea brought in."

Happy to be warmly received, Boone said, "That would be nice."

Marie went to the door and called to Ketura. They spoke of unimportant things until the tea came. Then when it was served, she sat back and waited for the reason he had come to see her.

Boone went over again in his mind what he intended to say. Since the ball, he had spent some time investigating land prices but had been too concerned about Charlie to do much more.

He had taken her out to meals, and they had walked around to see the sights, but she was obviously unhappy with life in Richmond.

"A man hates to ask favors," Boone said abruptly, "but that's what I've come here to do."

"What is it, Mr. Manwaring?"

"Do you suppose you could call me Boone?"

"Oh, I suppose so, and if I'm going to do you a favor, perhaps Marie would be better than Miss Bristol."

"Thank you. That's very charitable of you." Now that the moment had come, Boone was at a loss for words. He stared down at his boots for a moment then looked up, a serious expression on his face. "It's complicated. Do you mind if I tell you how I met Charlie?"

"I'd be interested to hear it." A dimple appeared in Marie's right cheek. "You have no idea how curious I am."

"Not just you. Everybody's curious. I'd call it nosy, at sea, but I suppose it's natural enough. An unmarried man and woman ride in, and with Charlie dressing like she does and acting like she does, I suppose it's inevitable."

"How *did* you meet her?" Marie asked quietly. She sat very still while Boone went back over the story of how he and Noah Peace had met then worked together to find the gold. She knew he was taking special pains to prepare the way for the favor he wanted to ask, but she still couldn't imagine what it was. Finally, when Boone got to the part where Noah had died and had made his last request, Marie began to understand. She leaned forward. "I suppose that's why you're here, then, to fulfill her father's last request."

"That's it, Marie," Boone said, "but it hasn't been easy." Marie refilled his tea, which had grown cold, and he held the cup in his hands. "You see what she is. She's a good girl, but a disaster at a ball. She doesn't know what to wear. She doesn't know how to act. I don't know how in the world I'm going to handle it. That's why I came here."

"I'm afraid I'm a little dense. Why exactly did you come here?"

Boone took a deep breath, for the dreaded moment had come. He appeared ill at ease, but he was a determined man. "I've got to have help, Marie, with Charlie. I've got to buy a place and see that she's not cheated, and I don't know anything about land prices. I can learn a thing like that, but I can't help her with the other things—like what to wear, how to talk, and what not to say. Did you know she chews tobacco?"

"I remember she had a plug at the dress shop!"

"I think she does it to irritate me." He paused then and shook his head despairingly. "I've got to have some help! So that's the favor. Will you help me make a lady out of Charlie?"

"Why, I'd be happy to do anything I could."

"Would you really? That would be so much help. Why, I could tell in the store you knew what to do with her."

"I didn't think she liked me much."

"She's afraid of you, Marie. When she sees somebody like you, so beautiful and poised, why, it scares her. I guess it would scare anybody."

Inwardly pleased at his evaluation, Marie asked, "What does she say about all this? Would she be willing to learn from me?"

"Oh, I haven't said a word to Charlie," Boone responded. "I wanted to ask you first. It wouldn't do to disappoint her."

"Exactly what did you have in mind?" Marie queried.

"Well, this is the hard part to say. I wish there was a school of some kind where I could send her. I guess there are schools like that, aren't there?"

"Yes, there are. Several, but Charlie's a special case. For instance, the school I went to wouldn't know what to make of her."

"That's exactly right, but you do. I could see that right away." Boone floundered for a minute then hurried on. "Could I hire you to teach Charlie? I know you don't need the money, but it would make me feel better to put it on that basis."

Marie almost said, *Need money? Why, bless your heart, we need all the money we can get.* But somehow she could not bring herself to say these things. Times were not that hard yet!

"I'll be glad to do what I can, Boone, but there's no question of money." She leaned back in her chair. "As a matter of fact, I've always wanted to create a new person. Maybe I could practice on Charlie."

Boone was immeasurably relieved. "That's what I came to ask, and I have to say I expected to get thrown out. I'll have to make this up to you some way, Marie."

Marie's quick mind came to a decision. "It would be hard to train her for just an hour or two a week. What would you think about having Charlie come and stay here at Hartsworth? Say, for a week? Then we could see how we get on."

"Why, that's more than I would ever dare to ask. Are you sure it would be all right?"

"Oh, of course. There's just me and my mother here, besides the servants. My father is leaving with the army soon. He's in camp already. We just rattle around this big old house. It would be a pleasure to have her."

Boone expelled his breath. "Sometimes I think we spend so much time worrying about things that never happen that we never have time to worry about the things that do happen."

"I've thought the same thing. Do you think she'll come?"

"I think she might. She's sick of that hotel room. She might be a little afraid of you, but you've got a way that puts people at ease."

He rose and squeezed her hand, saying fervently, "You don't know how much I appreciate this, Marie."

"Well, let's wait and see if I'm able to help. But somehow I think it can be done."

"Charlie learns fast. She's stubborn as a mule, but then, so am I."

Marie smiled, pulling her hand back. Apparently he'd forgotten to turn it loose. "Bring her anytime."

"Would today be too soon?"

"Not at all. I'll have her room ready."

"I thank you very much, Marie. And Charlie will, too, when she's had a chance to think about it."

After he left, Marie went at once to find her mother, who was in the kitchen. Marianne listened to the story until Marie concluded, "He wants me to make a fine lady out of her—and I think I might be able to do it."

Marianne was more doubtful. "It's not safe to play with people's lives, Marie."

"You don't mean that. You're always 'playing with people's lives.' Only you call it trying to help them."

Marianne laughed then. "I suppose you're right. The poor girl needs help. Do you really think it can be done?"

"I think it's a dangerous thing—you're right about that. Not because it's about learning better manners and how to dress, but because it's a dream her father had. I'm not sure that same dream will work for Charlie."

Marianne was silent for a while. "No," she said sorrowfully, "dreams usually don't come true."

WITNESS IN HEAVEN

Marie knew her mother was thinking of her father and their life together. She rose, saying, "Well, I'll go get her room ready." As she moved upstairs, calling Ketura to come with her, she thought, *Boone Manwaring is some man. Most men I know wouldn't have taken a promise this seriously, especially a promise to a dead man.* "Well, I'll see what I can do, but I can't promise Charlie will like what we make of her."

PART THREE
Confederate Christmas

CHAPTER 13

LOVE IS MORE THAN A KISS!

"Rex, you'll have to get down—how can I write with you perched in my lap like this?" The big yellow tabby cat who had plopped himself on top of Charlie's journal did not find her statement particularly impressive. He closed his eyes and began to purr deep in his throat, the tip of his tail switching wildly. The big tom had taken up with Charlie as soon as she had arrived at Hartsworth and now felt it was his prerogative to interrupt any of her activities. Desiring Charlie's full attention, he put his claws out and began flexing them, digging them vigorously into her thighs.

"Stop that, Rex—it hurts!" Charlie exclaimed, then put down the quill and began to stroke Rex under the throat. He raised his head, eyes closed in ecstasy, and rumbled noisily.

Rubbing the thick fur, Charlie smiled faintly. "I wish I didn't have any more problems than you do, Rex. All you have to do is eat and catch a mouse once in a while, then come and get tickled. That's some life you've got there."

Outside, the sky was gray, but there was a hint of snow in the lowering clouds. Charlie missed the snow from the mountains and wished sometimes she were back there, forging her way on snowshoes through the deep drifts with a rifle, looking for an elk. No matter how easy things were at Hartsworth, she felt out of place—and lonely.

Charlie picked Rex up and dropped him gently over the edge of the bed. "Go catch a varmint, you worthless critter!" She smiled as Rex yawned hugely then lay down with his head on his paws to sleep. Then she opened the tablet again and intently began to write.

Boone come over here twice this week. He said he was lookin round for a place, but he did not seem too eager bout it. I did not complain, although I shore wanted to. Its been a hard thing tryin to learn all that stuff Marie wants me to know. Theys a million things to learn just bout dresses. Seem like these women in the South dont do nothin but put on clothes and take off clothes. Got to have a different dress every time you spit! I told Marie there wasnt no sense in so much clothes changin and she just smiled and said that is the way ladies done in the South. And I told her it wasnt the way you done in Colorado. A pair of buckskins was all you needed cept for goin to meetin. She laughed at that and said sometimes she wished she could just wear pants and a shirt like a man.

Outside, the wind began to moan like a wounded creature, causing Charlie to look up. The limbs of the walnut tree outside her window began to scrape the side of the house. Charlie remembered how, back in Colorado, the aspens had whispered overhead and brushed against the side of the loft where her bed was. She sat still for a time then began to write again.

> *Seems like I been here forever, and they aint no end to it. I told Boone again it would suit me to go back home again, but he said this was gonna be home. I know he gets put out with me, and I caint help it. Seems like he is the only one I got left now. I been thinkin bout him a lot lately. I was thinkin about the time before we left home—well, the old place, anyhow—and he put his hands on me and I yelled at him. As I think on it, there werent no sense in that. He was just tryin to be nice, and I acted like he was a bear tryin to claw me or somethin. I told him never to touch me again. Well, I hate to admit it, but theys been times when I wish he would touch me!*

Charlie looked back at the sentence she had just written, mesmerized by her thoughts. *What in the cat hair am I thinkin' 'bout? I was the one to tell him to keep his hands to his self, and now I'm wantin' him to put 'em on me again? Reckon I've gone crazy since I come to this place, but it would be nice if he would put his arm 'round me a little bit and tell me he liked me. I don't know how to tell him to do that. He'd think I was makin' up to him, for sure, and he ain't thinkin' 'bout me like a woman. To him I'm a wild colt he's got to break to halter.*

The tree again brushed the house, interrupting Charlie's thoughts. She flushed slightly at what was in her mind, then began writing again.

> *I cant help but see why Boone wouldnt want to be foolin with me. I dont know much about courtin and all that, but it sure is plain Boone likes Marie. Caint blame him fer that. She is bout the prettiest woman I ever seen, and when he looks at her I kin tell there is somethin in his eyes. He somehow acts different round her. I dont know how to*

word it, but he is stuck on her, that is fer sure. Well, who cares? Let him like her! Dont make no never mind to me! I will git me a big house like Pa wanted, and I will git me a man bigger, finer lookin, and smarter than any old Boone Manwaring!

Dissatisfaction and longing swelled in Charlie Peace as she sat on the bed. She had been happy back in the mountains, hunting and fishing and taking care of her mother. Now, however, that world had passed away, and she was lost and confused in a new one. What it was she wanted she could not say. It had something to do with Boone Manwaring, she knew that much, and now as she balanced the tablet with her pen held loosely in her hand, she wondered if this was only a part of growing up—of becoming a woman. "I've got to have me a man someday," she muttered. "Every woman's got to have a man, but I ain't never worried about it. Not till now, anyways."

Closing the tablet abruptly, she put it away then cleaned the quill and laid it down on the shelf. Swinging her feet over the side of the bed, she stared down at the red carpet that covered the pine floor. *Maybe it would be better to git away from Hartsworth,* she thought sadly. But she had grown very fond of the people here, especially of Marianne Bristol, and knew she would miss them—that she would be even lonelier. Then Charlie said aloud, "Me and Boone can get us a place somewhere and git away from all this. I ain't never gonna learn to be the kind of lady he likes anyway!"

It had not taken Boone Manwaring very long after the Charity

Ball to learn that when one lived in Richmond, it was necessary to think about the war. When he had been at sea, he had lived in a microcosm with the captain as the monarch, the officers as the aristocracy, and the sailors as the serfs. The captain's word was law, right or wrong, and it could be death to disobey him. The land world had been far away, and things such as politics were alien to his thoughts.

But Richmond was no ship. It was a beehive of activity, and the thoughts of every man and woman were intertwined inextricably with the struggle for survival in which they found themselves. Everyone avidly watched for news from the fronts. The battles that had taken place in the west around Lookout Mountain had been something everyone talked about. Boone was amazed to discover that even the very young knew the names of the commanders. Sherman and Grant and Thomas, for the Union, and the Confederate generals—Cleburne, Hardee, and Breckinridge—were as familiar to them, almost, as their own names. The story of the fierce battles of Lookout Mountain and Missionary Ridge had been brought back by some of the wounded, and the whole city listened as they told of the fighting above the clouds.

As Boone finished shaving and put on a clean shirt, then tied his cravat carefully, he was baffled over the whole matter. "I don't see why they keep on fighting," he murmured as he slipped into his frock coat and put on his wide-brimmed black hat, settling it firmly on his head. "They must all be fools to think they could win. Almost every day they get news about losing a battle—and everybody, even the kids, knows that Grant's got an army of a hundred thousand men. He'll be knocking at Richmond's door before spring, but they keep on acting like they're going to win. I don't understand."

Transferring his wallet from the table to his inner pocket, he eyed the .44 and considered carrying it, but then left the room without it. Going downstairs, he entered the restaurant and was surprised to see Malcolm Leighton sitting alone at a table. When Leighton saw him, he waved him over. "Come and keep me company. Always did hate to eat alone."

"Thanks, don't mind if I do." Boone took the chair and ordered bacon and eggs, then picked up the cup of coffee that the waiter poured. He tasted it then made a face. "I thought this was coffee! It's tea!"

"Coffee's mostly gone. I meant to tell that waiter." He hailed the waiter when he went by and said, "Bring Mr. Manwaring a cup of that coffee you keep back for me."

"Yes, sir!"

"Well, how's the experiment going?"

"Experiment?" Boone asked, slightly puzzled. "You mean coming to settle in the South?"

"Yes, we don't have many folks coming this way. Most of them are leaving Richmond if they've got enough money to get away." Leighton, who wore black wool trousers, a green jacket, a crisp white shirt, and a green and black tie, toyed with the eggs on his plate while his sharp eyes probed Boone carefully. "How is it going with your ward, Miss Peace?"

"Very well. She's been a guest of the Bristols for the last few weeks."

"So Marie tells me. Sort of a finishing school, I take it?"

It angered Boone to hear Leighton put it this way. Boone had a quick temper that he had learned, after hard examples, to keep under control, so now he let nothing show in his face. Instead, he said smoothly, "Charlie hasn't had many advantages. It was very generous of Miss Bristol to offer to help."

"Yes, it was." The coffee came then, and the waiter poured it from a silver pot into Boone's cup. As he left, Leighton asked, "What about yourself? Are you going to settle here around Richmond? You'll have to forgive me, but strangers are fair game for speculation. As a matter of fact, quite a few people are wondering about you two."

"I suppose the gossip system is effective wherever you go," Boone said, smiling slightly. "No great mystery about it." He sipped the coffee then continued, "Charlie's father was a good friend of mine. When he passed on, he asked me to look after her until she married. He was from Virginia himself, although he hadn't been here for many years, and he wanted to come back and let her have a life here. So after he died, I decided to try to do what he wanted."

Leighton pursed his lips. "A pretty big order, Boone."

"Well, Noah Peace was a good man. He would have done the same for me."

"Fine thing, loyalty." But the statement fell flatly from Leighton's lips. "Have you had a committee yet, investigating your politics?"

"Not formally, but I get a lot of odd looks. I guess any man my age who isn't wearing a uniform is suspect."

"You're right about that. The South is scraping the bottom of the barrel now. You may get a few insults, since some of our firebrands here get pretty blunt when it comes to the Cause. It'll probably get worse. That is, if you decide to stay."

"I'll stay until I do what I came to do. You can depend on that."

"I figured that might be the way of it. Well, I don't know much about plantations. I guess you and I know about ships and not much else."

The truth of the remark struck at Boone. "That's about the story." He would have said more, but the waiter came back with his breakfast. He plunged into it hungrily as the two men spoke of the war and the prospects of the South. Boone found it difficult to read Leighton, who was certainly not a firebrand. In fact, he seemed almost indifferent to the war news. *I guess he's mostly interested in making money,* Boone thought, *which I suppose is not uncommon, even in the Confederacy.*

As they finished breakfast, Leighton said, "I'm going out to the Bristol place this afternoon. Can I take any word to Miss Peace?"

"Tell her I'll be out later, if you would."

"Be glad to." As Leighton rose, he said idly, "You might go see Colonel Clay Rocklin. He's Marie Bristol's relation. Knows pretty much everything about land and plantations. He might have some ideas on a place that would suit you."

"Thanks, Malcolm. I'll do that."

When the two men separated, Boone decided he did need advice. Moving down to the livery stable, he rented a horse, a rather undersized bay, but all that was available. "Do you think he'll make it to the camp?" he asked the hostler with humor.

"If he dies, you get your money back."

"Good enough." Boone swung into the saddle and rode through the town. He had been anxious to see the camp, in any case. Even in Colorado he had heard of the legendary Army of Northern Virginia and its equally famous commander, Robert E. Lee. He was not sure Lee was in Richmond now, but he suspected so. When he reached the camp, he asked for directions, and twenty minutes later he was stepping down before what was apparently a commander's tent. A flag with a military insignia he did not recognize flew over it, and as he tied his horse to a sapling, he turned to see an officer approaching. The man wore the uniform of a second lieutenant and looked oddly familiar.

"May I help you, Mr. . . . ?" the lieutenant asked. He was not a young man, Boone observed.

"Manwaring."

"Manwaring? Boone Manwaring?"

Boone was astonished. How far had his and Charlie's "fame" spread?

The lieutenant laughed, and again Boone wondered if they'd met before. "My daughter has told me of you and your friend. I am Claude Bristol of Hartsworth!"

The truth dawned. *Marie's* father. Austin's father. No wonder the resemblance. "Well, hello, Mr. Bristol. I didn't expect to see you here."

Claude Bristol smiled wryly. "You're echoing the sentiments of most people. Ever since I joined the army, people have been in a state of shock."

"Why should they be surprised?"

"Because I've never done anything before that was unselfish or right. I think they're all waiting to see if I'm not a spy for Lincoln."

Boone was surprised at the frankness of the older man. He had picked up a little bit of the Bristol family's problems from Charlie, and other information he had gleaned from things other members of the family had said. Now as he looked Bristol over carefully, he noted marks of dissipation from years of self-indulgence, but found no viciousness. Bristol had a lean, aristocratic face, and his uniform fit perfectly. Although there was a cynical air about the man, he was cheerful enough as he asked, "I don't suppose you came to join up?"

Boone grinned. "Not quite, sir."

"I thought not. Well, what can I do for you?"

"I came to talk to Colonel Rocklin. You probably know I'm trying to find a plantation that would be suitable for Charlie. Malcolm Leighton said the colonel knows land and values as well as anybody around. And also that he's honest."

"That's a good evaluation, I think. I wish I could help you, but I was never a businessman. I think the colonel's free if you'll wait here."

Boone waited as Bristol disappeared into the tent then reappeared almost at once. "Go right in, Mr. Manwaring."

"Thank you, Lieutenant." Stepping inside, Boone saw that Colonel Rocklin was wearing a heavy coat and there was no fire inside the tent. But he stood up from his desk at once and put out his hand.

"How do you do, sir? Mr. Manwaring, isn't it?"

"Boone Manwaring. I'm glad to meet you, Colonel. I've heard a great deal about you from Mrs. Bristol. She thinks a lot of you, of course."

"Well, I think a lot of her. Won't you sit down? Wish I had some coffee, but I'm afraid we're all out, unless you can drink acorn coffee."

"No, thanks. I only need a few minutes of your time." As Boone explained his mission, he grew more and more impressed with Clay Rocklin. No wonder men and women alike spoke so well of him—there was a strength and kind power in the man. Boone finished his story by saying, "I wouldn't want to make a bad buy, Colonel."

Clay had listened carefully. "I can't tell you whether it's a good time or a bad time to be buying land. If you have greenbacks from the United States government, you can get a good price. There are some good places for sale, but what will happen in the future nobody knows."

"I understand that. It was Miss Peace's father who wanted to come here. I tried to tell him things would be different than when he was growing up as a boy, but he wouldn't listen."

"Those days are gone," Clay said at once. "We'll have to start over again after this war is over, and it'll be hard. In all honesty, Mr. Manwaring, it would be better to invest your money in land elsewhere. If you want to stay in the South, even a border state like Kentucky would be safer."

"If it were my choice, I would do that at once, Colonel. But I'm bound by my promise to Charlie's father."

"Let me think on it. Plenty of places for sale, but you'll want to do the best you can for the young woman."

Boone said, "Thank you very much for your time. I'm staying at the Spotswood if you get word of anything good."

"I'll put out some feelers right away. In the meantime, I hope to see you again." Colonel Rocklin cocked his head. "Don't suppose you'd be interested in joining a good outfit?"

"No, I think not. Thanks for your offer."

"Never hurts to ask. Good day, sir."

"Good day, Colonel."

Boone stepped outside and waited until Lieutenant Bristol finished speaking to a sergeant. Then he said, "I'm on my way to your home. Can I take any message?"

"Why, I don't believe so, except to tell them I'm healthy."

"I'll do that, sir."

Boone left the camp and made his way toward Richmond, taking the side road that led to Hartsworth. It was a cold day, and by the time he reached there, his face stung from the bitter weather. When he stepped off his horse, he could not feel his feet. Solomon came running up to take his horse, and he murmured his thanks then climbed the steps to the front door carefully lest he turn an ankle. When the door opened, Charlie stood there, her eyes bright. "Boone, I'm glad to see you. Come in out of the cold."

"How are you, Charlie?" Boone asked as he took off his coat and hat. He watched as she put them on a coat tree and then turned to him. She was wearing a dress he hadn't seen before. "That's a pretty dress."

"Miss Marie helped me pick it out. Do you really like it, Boone?"

Boone looked at the dress more closely. Simply made of brown wool with tan stripes, the dress was modestly cut with white lace around the edge of the neckline and around the bottom of the full skirt. "I sure do. It goes well with your hair." Then he remarked, "Your hair is getting longer. Are you going to let it grow?"

"I don't know. What do you think?"

Boone laughed. "I'm no expert in ladies' fashions. Is there a fire around here?"

"Yes. Come on in. Are you hungry?"

"I'm starved."

"Let's go to the kitchen. I'll fix you somethin' to eat."

The two went to the kitchen, where Charlie bustled around, fixing a meal. "Dinner ain't ready yet, but we got some biscuits left over from breakfast, and I'll fry you up some bacon. That ought to do you till dinnertime."

"That's fine, Charlie. Tell me what you've been doing."

Charlie chattered on, and Boone was amazed at how lively she seemed. When she brought the meal and sat down across from him, she folded her hands and asked, "Did you find us a place yet?"

"Not yet, Charlie. It's a pretty big job, and I don't have a head for things like this. Now if it was buying a ship, I could do something."

He continued to tell Charlie about his goings, for she was always interested, and as he spoke, Austin Bristol came in, accompanied by Marie. Boone stood up at once. "Hello, Austin—Marie. How are you?"

"When did you get in?" Austin asked, shaking his hand. He seemed genuinely pleased to see Boone.

"I went out to the camp and met Colonel Rocklin this morning. Your father was there, too. He said to tell you he was well. Marie, please pass that along to your mother."

"Thank you, Boone. Now don't eat any more! We'll fix a proper meal." Marie was glad to see Boone, for she'd been thinking about him a great deal. Now she began instructing the cook about the meal, then said, "I want to hear all about what you've been doing, Boone. Come along."

Austin happened to be watching Charlie's face as his sister spoke. He saw the change in it and knew Charlie was disappointed. *Why, she's jealous of Marie!* he realized with astonishment and said, "Charlene, I want to show you my new horse."

For a moment he thought Charlie would decline, but then she said quietly, "All right, Mr. Austin."

"Not *Mr.*—just Austin."

They put on coats and walked to the barn, where Austin exhibited his new horse, a rangy bay, with pride. "Maybe you'd like to ride him? He's a bit of a handful, though."

"Let me git my britches on, and I'll show you I kin ride him! I cain't ride nothin' in this here dress!"

Austin laughed. "You ever ride sidesaddle like Marie?"

"No, that's a foolish way to git on an animal, with your leg all crooked 'round the horn."

"I guess it is. I don't think I could stay on. Tell you what, you go put on some 'britches,' as you call them, and I'll saddle another horse." As he saddled the horse, he puzzled about the relationship between the two who had come to Richmond. The girl was beautiful, though rough around the edges, but that wouldn't stop a man. Marie had told him Charlie was learning quickly, and though it would take time, one day she'd be able to take her place in the ballrooms and tea parties of Richmond society.

Charlie came back wearing a pair of jeans, a wool shirt, and a black coat. She mounted the horse expertly, asking, "What's his name?"

"Thunder."

"Well, I'll race you, then!"

Caught off guard, Austin grinned. "All right. We'll race to the tree down by the creek. You ready?"

"When I count three, we'll go. One—two—three!"

They had their race, and Charlie was delighted when she won. "This is a good hoss!" she said. "If an Indian had him, he could git him a good squaw fer just this one hoss."

"Is that right? I never thought of a horse in terms of how many brides it would buy."

"Indians do it all the time. Hosses are money fer 'em."

After a cold ride, they started back, and Charlie grew quiet.

"You're very fond of Boone, aren't you?"

Charlie's cheeks reddened. "He's been good to me," she said simply.

"You ever think of marrying him?"

The tinge of red grew deeper. "I don't think 'bout things like that, Austin."

"Oh, I guess I was mistaken, then. I thought—"

"I don't want to talk 'bout it."

"All right, Charlene."

He thought the conversation was over, but when they were inside the house, she asked, "Why ain't your sister, Marie, ever got married?"

"Never found a man she loved, I guess."

"Was she ever spoken fer?"

"Two or three wanted to marry her, but she didn't feel anything for them."

"You reckon she'll marry someday?"

"Oh yes, I'm sure she will." Glancing at Charlie, Austin saw she was deep in thought. "You'll have a man of your own one day, Charlene."

"I don't think 'bout it much."

"Well, you're probably the only girl in Virginia who doesn't."

"What 'bout you, Austin? Why ain't you ever got a woman?"

"Just looking around."

"You're pretty old not to be married."

Austin laughed with delight at her bluntness. "You come right out with the thing, don't you, Charlene? You don't know how refreshing that is after listening to women hint and scheme."

"Why should I do a thing like that? And what did I say? 'Bout you being old?"

"Most women wouldn't put it that way."

"How old are you?"

"Thirty-one."

"That ain't old," Charlie said, smiling. Her hair, black as night, curled out, rich and lustrous, from beneath the soft gray hat she wore, making her eyes look even darker.

Austin leaned forward. "Why, you have blue eyes, dark blue! I thought they were black."

Charlie stared at Austin and said, "I guess so. You think you ever will git a woman?"

Austin hesitated. His weeks-old conversation with Marie about marrying for money brought a jolt of shame to him. "Maybe someday."

"Be sure you git a good one. You deserve a good woman."

※

Boone had been asked to stay over, which he did. Charlie was extremely quiet, but when he had tried to find out why, she simply said she didn't feel like talking.

Before supper, Marie and Boone took a walk on the grounds of Hartsworth. It was almost dark when they again approached the house, and she stopped, looking around. "I'd hate to think of living anywhere but here."

Boone said quietly, "It must be nice to be in one place all your life. I never had anything like that."

"You never had a home?"

"We had a house, but I was mostly at sea. Some say they liked to call the ship a home, but it's not like this."

"That must be lonely, not having a place," Marie said. This was the first time they had been alone, and he was suddenly aware of the curve of her mouth, her lovely throat, and the way her face mirrored her change of feelings. As she spoke of Hartsworth, he sensed her love for the land and felt a stirring inside. He couldn't decide whether it was Marie's beauty or the loneliness that had been with him for a long time.

As the darkening light played over her form, her soft fragrance slid through the armor of his self-sufficiency.

Marie stopped speaking and looked up with surprise, seeing in his eyes that Boone was thinking of her as a woman.

As for Boone, he could not have told what he was feeling. But as the last glow of the sun touched her face, he strained against the leash of his reserve and put his arms around her. As he kissed her, he felt her relax and thought, *This is what I've been looking for.*

As for Marie, she was in shock that she had allowed Boone to take her in his arms and kiss her. She was not a woman who gave caresses easily. Although she had been kissed, it had not always been her choice, and now she knew as she lay in his arms, with the pressure of his lips against hers, that this was something she had chosen. But she was also troubled by the emotion she felt when his arms pulled her closer. Perhaps it was then she realized how she needed a man's strength, so she surrendered, allowing the kiss to go on longer than she had intended. Then she drew away.

"When a man's alone," Boone said quietly, "he's what he is. But when he sees a woman and gives something to her, he never gets it back. If he wants to be whole again, he's got to go to that woman."

Marie stared at him, taken by his words. "Do you think things like this often, Boone?"

"When I think of you, I do."

"Have you thought of me often?"

"Yes." He would have pulled her forward again, but she put her hand on his chest. He stepped back, put his hands behind his back, and clamped them together. "I never met a woman like you before."

"You've known women, Boone."

"Every man, maybe, knows something about women, but it doesn't amount to much. And then one day, maybe at dusk like this, he kisses a woman and sees what he really is—what's been driving him all his life."

Impulsively Marie wanted to step forward, throw her arms around his neck, and feel the touch of his lips on hers again. But she fought against it and said instead, "I think we'd better go inside."

"All right."

"What do you think about Boone?"

Marie had been sitting beside Austin at the desk, going over the figures of the plantation. The question surprised her, and she blushed. "What do you mean by that?"

"I mean about him and Charlene."

"I don't understand you, Austin."

"Why, the girl's foolish about him. Surely she's told you that."

"No, she hasn't. What makes you think so?"

"Why, she practically told me—and she's jealous of you, Marie. You didn't notice?"

Marie remembered how reticent Charlie was whenever Marie spoke of Boone and how strangely silent Charlie had been during Boone's most recent visit. "I suppose you're right. It would be only natural. She doesn't have anybody else."

"I don't know how he feels, but she's in poor condition, ripe for the wrong man to come along. I hope it doesn't happen."

The two turned back to their figuring. Austin finally said,

"We've got to do something, Marie. I don't see how we can last another month. The bank's screaming for money and talking foreclosure."

"They've done that before."

"They mean it this time. I know this sounds odd, but have you thought of Boone as a man you might marry?"

Marie rose abruptly, eyes flashing anger. "Because he has money? What about you? All you have to do is ask Ida. She has more money than Boone, I'd say."

Austin dropped his head. "I'm a fool," he said, "but it's driving me crazy, Marie. I don't know what to do. I can't stand the thought of losing this place."

Marie loved Austin deeply. She got up and stood behind him, putting one hand on his shoulder and brushing his hair back from his forehead with the other. "I know," she whispered. "I've thought of it, too. But wouldn't it be wrong?"

"I don't know anymore what's right and what's wrong."

"Neither do I." She thought of the kiss, knowing she would not forget it for weeks. But then her mind spoke rebelliously, *Love is more than a kiss!*

Chapter 14

A Matter of Courage

Major Olan Ferguson was too old to be an officer, but Robert E. Lee was scraping the bottom of the barrel. Ferguson had graduated from West Point and, like Lee and many others, had resigned from the United States Army at the beginning of hostilities. He was a martinet, and the sight of a missing button on an enlisted man's uniform was, to him, the sign of complete degradation, militarily speaking.

Clay Rocklin had inherited the major and was not certain that the brigade was better for having him. He remarked once to Melora, "He's about ready for a rocking chair somewhere, and I wish he'd go there. He's driving me crazy, and I don't know what to do about him."

Claude Bristol was the current catalyst that stirred Major Ferguson's ire. He had, upon hearing of Bristol's recent acceptance as Clay's adjutant and clerk, sputtered angrily, saying loudly in an open meeting of the officers, "What good will he do? Has he ever been to the Point?"

"The Point doesn't converse saintship on men, Major," one of the officers suggested, which did no good to the major's state of mind.

"He'll not be worth a pin to us! Watch my words!" Ferguson had snapped. He had almost welcomed Bristol's coming then, eagerly awaiting with a vulturelike attitude the first mistake that Claude Bristol would make.

And the mistake was not long in coming. It was on his second day that Major Ferguson publicly rebuked him over failing to return a salute.

"I will not put up with this sort of behavior among our officers! Things have gotten too slack, and I intend to see that it stops!" he had ended by saying.

Clay, later that afternoon, heard a private report and took time out from his busy schedule to say, "Lieutenant Bristol, let's take a walk around and see what the brigade looks like."

The two strolled along the line of tents where men sat outside, gathered around fires. Snow was in the air, but there was a general air of contentment among the men that Clay noticed and approved of. When he spoke to a sergeant, commending him for his work on getting his men into good condition, the sergeant's eyes lit up.

"I don't think I'll ever be able to please the major," Bristol said sadly.

"You mustn't pay too much attention to Major Ferguson," Clay said encouragingly. "He's a relic from the old army. He should have been retired and probably will be very soon. You're my adjutant and my clerk, and you're going to be very helpful to me." Clay grinned ruefully. "I'm not the best record keeper in the world."

"Neither am I, Colonel, but I'm going to do the best I can."

For the next week Claude Bristol threw himself into his quest to become a soldier with more energy than he had ever used on anything—even gambling and horse racing. He stayed up late at night by the light of a candle going over the manual of arms and the various regulations that are necessary for any army. At dawn he was up early studying again. Soon it became familiar around camp to see him walking with his nose in a book. Len Baylor, a grizzled sergeant, took him under his wing. He also had been doubtful of Bristol, knowing he was related to the colonel. But Bristol had admitted cheerfully, "Sergeant, I don't know the first thing about the army. I'd appreciate it if you would be patient with me and give me some of the basics."

The sergeant had nodded approvingly then reported this to Clay. *Maybe it'll be all right,* Clay thought to himself, satisfied by the sergeant's report. Perhaps it would have been, but Claude could not avoid the blistering criticism of Ferguson. It grew so bad that he dreaded to see the old man coming, and finally Clay noted that Bristol was growing tense and nervous.

"Lieutenant, I think you've put in some good time, and you've learned a great deal. Sometimes, if you're like me, you soak up all you can and then you have to wait for it to settle down." Clay had looked up over his desk, speaking to Claude, who was reading *Cooke's Cavalry Tactics*, his brow furrowed. "I think it might be good for you to take a few days off."

"You don't have to make exceptions for me!" Bristol protested. "That might look like favoritism!"

"No, it won't, because I'm sending you on detached duty. We're desperate for horses to pull our artillery. I want you to make a swing through the countryside and see if you can come up with some." Grimacing, he added, "We don't have much money, and only Confederate, so I don't think you'll have much success. All I ask is that you don't steal any. But maybe if you can come up with even two or three, that will be a help. And go by and touch base at Hartsworth. Stay there for a couple of days.

It'll be good for you, and you'll be fresher when you get back."

"Yes, sir. If that's what you want," Bristol responded. He half suspected Clay was getting him out of Ferguson's way and was grateful for it. Leaving Clay's tent, he went to his own quarters, which he shared with First Lieutenant Maylin Meyers, a short, muscular twenty-five-year-old who had been amused at Bristol's eagerness to learn, but pleased by it.

"So you're on detached duty. Bring me back some fresh ham or maybe even a chicken if you can find it."

"I'll do that, Lieutenant," Bristol said. "You can depend on it."

Claude drew an ancient horse from the quartermaster. "I have to respect my elders," Bristol said, smiling. "What's his name, Sergeant?"

"Methuselah, I reckon, sir," the sergeant replied, grinning back at him.

"An apt name indeed. Come along, Methuselah. I'll try to get him back to you alive, Sergeant."

Claude took his orders seriously and before going to Hartsworth did make a sweep of the country. He was actually successful in buying three horses, none of them prizes, but at least they were able to walk around and could pull the weight of a cannon. Claude well knew the terrific toll the war had taken on horseflesh, and it had saddened him, for he loved horses best of all animals on the earth. He took turns riding them, sparing Methuselah, and finally, on the morning of December 20, rode up to Hartsworth, where he was met by Solomon, who greeted him ecstatically.

"Why, Marse Claude, look at you now! Ain't you fine in that pretty uniform!"

"A uniform doesn't make a soldier, Solomon." Bristol slipped off Methuselah and handed the lines of all four horses to Solomon. "Take these fellows out to the pasture and see if you can't find them something to eat."

"Yes, suh! You gonna stay for a while, Lieutenant?"

"No, I'll be leaving tomorrow or the next day."

Claude was surprised at the eagerness with which he approached the house. Although he had been gone only a short while, he had felt the separation keenly. Almost every day it had entered his mind that he might never see it again. Although he wasn't on the front line of battle, he well knew that the location of the "front line" was sometimes flexible. Now he paused for a moment, looking at the familiar structure. Shocked at his happiness, he murmured, "I didn't know I was such a homebody. But this place means more to me than I ever understood." Bristol was not a sentimental man, and yet, under the cynical exterior he had covered himself with over the years, he suddenly realized that life was a precious thing—and that this house was more than wood and glass and carpet. He had spent many years here, and now he felt a thread of disgust at how he had wasted his life. *If a man could go back again and do it all over, I wonder if he would do it any better. When I came here, I had all sorts of dreams, and yet I haven't fulfilled one of them. I've wasted my money betting on horses and cards, and it's hurt Marianne and the children. Why did I do it? Why does a man allow himself to fail like that?*

"Claude, come into the house!"

Claude glanced up to see Marianne holding the door open. He moved forward quickly, putting his morbid thoughts behind him. When he got to the door, he saw that Marianne had a smile and an embrace for him. *She's still as beautiful as ever,* he thought. He kissed her and then, when he lifted his head, whispered huskily, "If I had known I'd get such a welcome, I would have joined the army a long time ago."

"Claude, what are you doing here? We didn't expect you."

Thirty minutes later the two were sitting in the kitchen, and Claude was ravenously attacking the fried ham, hominy, and fresh bread Marianne heated for him. He washed it down with two glasses of sweet, fresh milk and then, when he had finished, said, "It's the best meal I've had since I've been in the army."

"You look thinner," Marianne said. "Isn't the food good?"

"Not like this," Claude said. He looked around the kitchen, taking it all in. "It seems like I've been gone for a long time. I've discovered how much I miss Hartsworth."

"Do you, Claude?"

"Yes. It surprised me. When I rode up and saw the house—well, it got to me, Marianne. I realized how much I love this place."

Marianne Bristol felt a surge of hope. She'd been praying that Claude would develop the same kind of love for the land, house, and tradition that went with it that she herself held.

Claude reached over the table and captured her hand. "I was standing out in front of the house, looking at it and thinking how glad I was to be back," he said thoughtfully. "And I thought how different it should have been. I haven't been the kind of husband I should have, Marianne. And just in case, I want to tell you now. You've been the best wife a man could ever have, and I've been a failure."

For years Marianne had longed to hear this simple statement from Claude, and now it had come! She squeezed his hand tightly. Somewhere along the way, she had lost the first love she had had for this trim, handsome man. He'd had such great gifts, and he'd squandered them like a prodigal. But now as he sat there, his hair still brown without a touch of gray, and pain in his fine eyes, she found herself thinking of their first meeting, their courtship and marriage. It had been a time of wonder and pure joy. Only afterward had it grown bad. Finally, she whispered, "It's never too late for love, Claude."

Claude Bristol blinked with surprise. "I think it may be for us, but I want you to know that whatever happens, you have never failed me, Marianne. You're the pride of my life."

That evening Marianne listened for two hours in the parlor as he told her of life in the camp. He was excited, she saw, and pleased with being able to do something. Finally, they rose and went to bed. When he lay beside her in the darkness, her arms went around him. She kissed him softly at first, then with a hunger she had thought was buried deep within her.

The next day Charlie was sitting alone in the study, laboring over her handwriting exercises. Marie had given her several lessons, but she still found herself grasping the delicate pen as if it were a plow handle or a musket. Her tongue appeared at the edge of her lips as she moved the quill across the paper, trying to make the same smooth, graceful strokes that Marie made so easily. Finally, she gave it up in disgust. "Rats! I won't never learn how to write pretty!"

"Oh, I wouldn't give up!" Claude Bristol had been passing by the library door as Charlie uttered her cry of despair. Now he stepped inside and went to stand beside her. "You're doing very well, Charlene."

"Do you really think so, Mr. Bristol?"

"Why, you can write better than I can write now, but of course that's not saying a lot," he said, smiling. As he sat down in the chair beside her, admiring her freshness and innocence, he noticed how the blue dress she was wearing matched her dark blue eyes. Claude Bristol was a perceptive man, and Charlene Peace's story had attracted him. He felt a great interest and even compassion for this young girl so alone in the world, and being a witty man, he was soon able to make her smile.

Charlie liked Claude Bristol. During the time he had been at Hartsworth, he had gone out of his way to speak to her, and the previous afternoon he had asked her to join him for a ride around the place. She accepted at once, always eager to get on a horse, and when he saw how well she rode, he praised her highly.

Now, however, she was in one of those moods that had occupied her lately. Boone had not been back for several days, and she was beginning to feel that she could not stay at Hartsworth much longer. She grew so quiet that Claude asked quickly, "Is something wrong, Charlene?"

"I reckon I just got the mullygrubs."

"Mullygrubs?" Claude said, grinning. "I don't think I've ever heard of that particular ailment."

"Just down in the mouth, Mr. Bristol. Don't you ever git that way?"

"Frequently, but then, I'm an old man and you're a beautiful young lady."

"No, I ain't! I may be young, but I ain't no lady, and I ain't beautiful! I cain't talk right neither!"

"Why, Marie tells me you're making wonderful progress. My wife has seen it, too. And surely Boone has noticed it."

"No, he ain't noticed it," she said. And then before she could think, the words slipped out. "He's too busy spendin' time with Marie to pay any attention to the way I talk!" Looking shocked, she clamped her hand over her mouth. "I didn't mean to say that. Ain't none of my business if he wants to come courtin' Marie."

Claude Bristol instantly realized, *Why, she's in love with the man—or thinks she is.* He said quietly, "It's not easy being young, Charlene. You ever see a magnifying glass?"

"Yes, I seen one of them things."

"Well, when you're young, you see everything through a magnifying glass. When something goes wrong, you hold that glass up and the trouble looks about five times as big as it really is. So right now you're having a hard time, but the troubles aren't as bad as you think."

Charlie listened gratefully as Claude Bristol spoke. Somehow just being able to talk with this easygoing, friendly man relieved her. When he began to tell her stories of his foolish mistakes as a soldier in camp, she found herself laughing. Finally, she said, "I feel a lot better, Mr. Bristol. Maybe I *kin* learn to be a lady."

"I'm sure you can, Charlene," Claude said fondly. "I'll be going tomorrow, but I'll be expecting to hear good things. Maybe you'd write me from time to time and tell me how things are going. Soldiers like to get letters—at least I do, although I don't call myself much of a soldier."

"Oh, you wouldn't want to read stuff I might write."

"That's where you're wrong. We're friends, aren't we, Charlene?"

"Yes, if you say so, Mr. Bristol."

"Austin will be coming out to the place from time to time. Any letters you might write, you could give to him."

On his way back to camp the next day, Bristol thought of Charlene Peace and Boone Manwaring. *I wonder if he knows the girl's in love with him. If he's not a fool, he must.* He had met Boone only once, but he determined the next time he saw him to find out how the man felt about this young girl. "She's very vulnerable," he mused quietly. "I hope she doesn't get hurt."

The closest thing to a gentlemen's club in Richmond was the billiard room of the Spotswood Hotel. There was a ladies' parlor adjacent, which could have been half a world away, so different were the activities of the two rooms. The ladies' parlor was designed much like a parlor in a fine home, but the billiard room was far different.

Austin Bristol leaned back in his chair, taking in the two billiard tables, neither of them occupied at the moment. The billiard room itself was spacious, being twenty feet wide and thirty-five feet long. Sofas, chairs, lamps, and tables were arranged so that a man could come and read or meet friends. The two bigger tables, imported from New Orleans, were the pride of the owner even though the green felt was worn. At one end of the room, four tables were set up for card games; however, only two of them were occupied, for the day's crowd was rather thin.

Austin was tired, for the paperwork at the War Department bored him out of his mind. He had applied for active duty on numerous occasions, but each time his superior officer, Brigadier General Thad Cornwallis, had briskly denied him with the words, "Can't do without you here, Austin. Too much work for me. You'll just have to fight your war from your desk as I do. All of us would like to go, but we're doing important work here."

Now Austin moved over to the poker table and sat in an

empty chair. He received a greeting from the players, which included Malcolm Leighton and Boone Manwaring. "Deal you a hand, Austin?" Leighton asked. As always he was dressed immaculately and expensively, this time in a black suit, white frilled shirt, and string tie. "I'd like to get some of that army money," he said, grinning.

Austin returned the smile but shook his head. "Too rich for my blood," he said then turned to Boone. "How's it going, Manwaring?"

"Very well," Boone said, nodding. He motioned toward a large stack of chips in front of him. "I've had a lucky streak."

Across the table Earl Dillon, a sleek man with cold eyes, spoke his challenge. "A bit too lucky, I think."

Earl Dillon, Austin knew, was one of the shady characters who floated around wartime Richmond. He always appeared to have money, although to Austin's knowledge he never worked. Most had decided that he made his living with the cards since he was a good gambler. Now, however, the stack in front of him was small, and Austin sensed he was angry. He also knew Dillon was quick tempered and that he had already fought three duels, killing two of his opponents and badly wounding the other.

Silence fell around the table, with every eye on Boone, waiting for him to respond to Dillon's remark. It had not exactly been an insult, but there was a bold sneer on Dillon's lips.

But Boone well understood men like Earl Dillon from his career on the sea; he knew that Dillon was a bad loser and that it wasn't worth taking up the challenge. So he simply shrugged and said, "Sometimes I'm lucky; sometimes I'm not, Dillon."

Seeing that Boone was not going to respond to Dillon's challenge, Leighton picked up the cards. "Another hand, then. Maybe you'll be luckier this time, Earl. I never saw such a run of bad luck."

Austin sat back. He was not much of a cardplayer himself, but as the game went on, he sensed that Dillon had lost heavily and was now trying to restore his fortunes with a single big win. As the time droned on, everyone in the room came to stand around the tables, for Richmond loved drama.

As Dillon's complexion turned ruddier and ruddier and the tension in the room grew, Boone was very much aware of the situation. He would like to have pulled out, but it was against the code of cardplayers to quit while a big winner, and he knew he would have to tough it out. He also had heard stories of Dillon's prowess with a dueling pistol, and even with his own skill he had no desire to fight the man.

The stack in front of Boone continued to grow as Dillon's diminished. The climax was coming. Boone had just dealt himself three eights, which he thought would be enough to win the hand. "I'll stand on these," he said, making his voice as pleasant as possible. Dillon stared at him, dislike evident on his face. "I'll meet that and raise you," he said, counting his chips and shoving them into the center of the table, "two hundred dollars."

For a moment Boone was tempted to fold, but he assumed Dillon had a good hand to bet that much. "I'll see that," he said and shoved out chips. He turned his hand over. "Three eights is all I've got."

Dillon's face paled, and his lips tightened. Then he threw down his hand. "You're a cheat, Manwaring!"

Boone narrowed his attention on the gambler. "I'd be careful about names like that," he said softly. He was not sure whether Dillon was wearing a gun. He himself was not, so he put his hands carefully on the table, waiting to see what would happen.

Dillon stood up, his voice tense. "I'm saying you're a cheat, and a coward, too!"

In that moment Boone Manwaring knew that his future in Richmond was hanging in the balance. He had just been called a name no one would take, and as he glanced around, he saw every man was expecting him to take up the challenge. He was not afraid, for he was of more than average skill with a gun, although he had never fought a formal duel. Now he knew that if he walked out of this room without challenging Dillon, he would be a marked man. Yet why should he kill a man over a few dollars? Boone wished he could just shove the money back and walk away, but he knew the situation had gone far beyond that easy solution. "I won't fight you, Dillon," he said, getting up. He gathered the chips into his hands and left the room.

Austin felt sick. His eyes met Leighton's, who shook his head. Both men were thinking the same thing: Boone Manwaring was a coward.

Dillon began to curse. "He's a no-good Yankee! A coward and a cheat! Wouldn't take my challenge!"

Austin rose slowly and left without another word. Somehow the scene of a man breaking under pressure was nauseating to him. He had grown up in a culture where physical courage was necessary. No man could exist in his world without it. Austin himself would have answered Dillon's challenge, even though he would die the next moment for it.

Leaving the hotel, he went about his duties for the rest of the day. Later that afternoon he saw Marie coming into his office. "Why, Marie," he said. "Didn't expect to see you."

"Have you got time for a woman with nothing but time on her hands?"

"Of course. Let's go down the street. We'll maybe find some ice cream."

"Ice cream in Richmond?"

"Well, that's optimistic." Soon the two were seated inside a restaurant where there was no ice cream, but they both had slices of fresh raisin pie.

Marie spoke of the plantation then said, "I brought a list into town of things that we need, but I don't have the money to pay for it. Our credit's stretched pretty thin. What do you think, Austin?"

"We'll get it somehow, if those are things we have to have," Austin responded, somewhat preoccupied. Then he continued, "Pretty bad thing happened in the billiard room at the Spotswood this afternoon." He went on to relate the incident and watched Marie's face as he ended. "It was a sorry sight. I thought better of Boone. He just turned and walked out."

Marie had listened to her brother carefully, and now she sat silently, saying nothing for a time. She had no doubt about Austin's reaction, for she knew, like all the men in her acquaintance, to prove oneself to be a coward was the worst possible thing that could happen. Finally, she said, "Maybe he just doesn't like to kill a man over cards."

"It wasn't over cards, Marie. It was a matter of honor. No man can let himself be called a name like that."

"I suppose not." But Marie was not altogether sure what she thought. She knew men who fought over things that to her were utterly ridiculous—and to her it was a tragedy. Although she wasn't sure of her feelings for Boone Manwaring, she knew they weren't mild. He had stirred her with a single kiss.

"I may be wrong," Austin said, "but I thought I saw something in you for this man." When she did not speak, he continued, "Don't mean to pry, but I'd hate to see you involved with a man who had no spine."

WITNESS IN HEAVEN

Marie saw the concern in Austin's eyes. "I don't think you have to worry about that, Austin."

Austin sighed with relief. "I guess I was mistaken, then."

Marie kept up the thread of their conversation then left Austin to go on her errands. As she moved along the cold streets, however, she drew her coat closer around her. She could not reconcile what had happened at the Spotswood with what she had seen in Boone. *But I know so little about him,* she thought. *And there are men who are not courageous.* Turning into the hardware store, she tried to put him out of her mind. However, she knew she wouldn't be able to, for Boone Manwaring had gained a larger place in her thoughts than she had imagined.

Chapter 15

At the Chesnuts

By December 1863, it was not, perhaps, apparent to either the North or the South, but a turning point had come. It was like a small leak in a large dike, unnoticed for a time and allowed to become more and more damaging until finally the entire structure was threatened. So it was with the Confederacy. The year of 1863 had produced some great victories for the South, and some may have argued that the South still held the advantage. They were defending their home grounds, and Robert E. Lee had proven himself to be a fine general.

But by this point in the war, the North had transformed itself into an industrial giant, pouring out arms, ammunitions, uniforms, wagons, buttons, canteens, and the myriad pieces needed to put an army in motion. The South, on the other hand, was producing barely enough to keep the thin lines of the Confederacy together. The men were often hungry, and heaven help Union prisoners who were in Confederate prison camps, for, unable to feed themselves, the Confederacy could do little for its prisoners.

What Jefferson Davis needed was a miracle, for it would take that to save the South. The government was bankrupt.

Paper money was not worth the paper it was printed on, and a larger burden would have to be borne by fewer people if the Confederacy were to stand. Yet Jefferson Davis refused to listen to proposals for peace.

Several weeks earlier, across the brief distance that separated Richmond from Washington, D.C., another president, Abraham Lincoln, had been invited to the little town of Gettysburg to dedicate the new National Soldiers' Cemetery.

When November 19, 1863, arrived, parade marshals wore mourning rosettes. Abraham Lincoln stood up to make a few appropriate remarks. His words were brief, and he spoke of peace—words that have been repeated more than any other words from any other speech by any other president in history. Americans have never forgotten them and never will. When he sat down, there was long applause. Then the crowd broke up, and people began their long journeys home. Soon Gettysburg grew quiet again.

"I don't want to go to no old party, Marie!"

Marie Bristol was patient but adamant as she helped Charlie pull the dress down over her head. "You've got to go. We've already accepted the invitations, and I promise you'll like it. There'll be a lot of young people there." Stepping back, she admired Charlie's rose-colored dress trimmed in black lace. "You look so nice!"

"I feel like a big dressed-up doll!" Charlie complained,

shaking her curls in front of the mirror. "All we ever do at them parties is talk."

"Not *them* parties. *Those* parties."

"*Those* parties, then! But all we do is talk!"

"What else would you want to do?" Marie demanded. "It's what people do at this sort of thing. And besides, I want you to meet the Chesnuts."

"I can't remember the names of half the people I done already met!" Charlie exclaimed. "I mean that I already met!" she corrected herself, seeing Marie's lips framing a rebuke.

"You're doing much better with your grammar, Charlie." Marie smiled then said, "I mean, Charlene. I'm so used to calling you Charlie, I don't know if I'll ever change."

Charlie ran her hands over her hoop skirt. Secretly she liked to dress up but would die before admitting it. Indeed, Charlie had made almost every step of her education more difficult. She could not have explained to herself why she did this, for she knew Marie Bristol and her mother worked hard to smooth out her rough edges. But Charlie was basically an independent, stubborn young woman and hated to be pushed in a direction that was foreign to her. For weeks now she had practiced for hours every day on her writing and her grammar, and she had even been taught how to dance by Austin, who had come often to the house. Still, she had the feeling she was living in a world not her own, and she longed for her simple life back in the mountains.

"I guess we'll have to go," she said resignedly, then commented to Marie, "You sure look pretty." Marie's baby blue taffeta dress had a full skirt with layers of flounces at the bottom, all edged with white lace. "I bet Malcolm Leighton will think so."

Marie shrugged. "He's seen this dress before."

"Does he aim to marry up with you?"

"He hasn't asked me."

"I expect he will, though. He looks at you funny all the time."

"What do you mean *funny*, Charlie?" Marie demanded.

"I mean he cuts his eyes 'round when he thinks you're not lookin'. It's like he was sizin' up a horse he was aimin' to buy."

Marie Bristol burst into laughter. "I expect that's pretty close to the truth," she admitted, her eyes sparkling with amusement from Charlie's directness. "After he's looked over all the other young ladies and evaluated our worth, I expect he'll make an offer on the one who will bring him the most value for his money."

Struck by Marie's offhanded reply, Charlie asked, "You don't mean that, do you? It's not really like he's going to buy you."

Marie, suddenly serious, bit her lip and wondered what Charlie would think if she spoke the exact truth. *Yes, he's going to buy me, and I'm going to have him because he has money.* She could not bring herself to say such a thing and struggled as she attempted to explain. "It's rather complicated—this matter of marriage."

"Wasn't where I come from. Feller just came by and courted a girl, and if she liked him, she'd marry him."

"I wish it were that simple here," Marie said fervently.

"Well, why ain't it?"

"You mean, why *isn't* it? Why, I don't know, Charlie. It's more complicated than it should be, I think." Disturbed by the conversation, Marie said, "I think you're all ready now. Let's go to the Chesnuts'."

The two left the house wearing heavy coats and wrapped

up in blankets, for the weather was turning steadily colder. The horses moved along rapidly toward the Chesnuts' house until they arrived. Solomon helped Marie out, but before he could turn, Charlie had already leaped to the ground. "I don't reckon I'm old enough to be helped out of a carriage, Solomon."

"I reckon that's right, Miss Charlene," Solomon said, grinning. He was quite taken with the young woman, as were all the slaves. She had free and easy manners with them and thought nothing of going into their quarters and eating corn pone and ham with them for supper. "You be careful now, Miss Charlene," Solomon said. He winked at Miss Marie. "There's some of them mens that ain't the gentlemens they should be. Young ladies has to be careful about 'em."

"Austin will protect you," Marie said.

Austin had ridden up and was just getting off his horse. He tied him up and came over, saying, "Well, just in time for the festivities."

"Don't you ever do any soldierin', Austin?" Charlie asked.

"Not very often." This was a sore spot with Austin, for he was sensitive about his lack of frontline duty, so he turned quickly and said, "Let's get inside. It's getting cold. I think it's going to snow."

"I wish it would," Charlie said, taking his arm. It felt strange to do this, but it was something Marie had taught her to do. "I wish it would snow two feet deep, or three, or four! I always liked it when we got snowed in on the mountains. Once, we got snowed in for a month! Good thing we had plenty to eat, or we'd have starved to death."

"What did you do all that time?" Austin asked. "I think I'd go crazy if I was shut in a cabin for a month."

"Oh, Ma read a lot from the Bible, and me and Pa listened.

WITNESS IN HEAVEN

We made moccasins and a pair of buckskins fer Pa. It wasn't so bad." Almost wistfully, she continued, "I wisht I could do it again. I shore miss Ma and Pa."

Marie and Austin exchanged glances; then Marie changed the subject. "It looks like everyone in Richmond has come tonight." As they stepped inside, a man took their coats. They moved down the hall and, turning to the left, entered the large parlor used by the Chesnuts for entertainment. At once Mary Chesnut spotted them and came over. "There you are, Marie and Austin. I'm glad you could come in this bad weather."

As she took their greeting, Mary Chesnut smiled at Charlie. "And who is this delightful young woman? I don't believe we've met."

"This is Miss Charlene Peace," Austin said. "She's a visitor to Richmond, hoping to settle here."

"Oh yes! I believe I have heard your name. You're here with Mr. Manwaring."

"You know everyone in Richmond and what they do, Mrs. Chesnut!" Austin exclaimed with surprise.

Mary Chesnut, indeed, knew most people in the upper regions of society. Her home was often visited by President Davis, for he was an intimate friend of the Chesnuts. She was not a beautiful woman, but nobody ever noticed this. Her eyes were lively and expressive, her complexion lovely, and she had a wit and charm that attracted others to her.

"Yes, ma'am. Me and Boone come down from Colorado—came down from Colorado. Do you know Boone?"

"I met him yesterday in town. He spoke with my husband about a piece of property that we once owned. I'm glad to think you're considering settling here."

Charlie nodded, feeling awkward yet charmed by the

woman. Mary Chesnut loved young people and was especially fond of beautiful young ladies. She took great pride in pairing couples together. Now she took Charlie's arm, saying, "Come along. I want you to meet some of our guests."

Charlie did not remember the names of all of the guests, but she did remember one. She was introduced to General Robert E. Lee, a fine-looking older man. He bowed when they were introduced and welcomed her to Richmond.

Nearly half an hour later, Charlie looked up in the crowded parlor and saw Boone entering. He spotted her at once and came over, smiling. "That's a pretty dress. I haven't seen that one."

"Marie helped me pick it out. I feel silly wearing this here bird cage." She patted the hoop that held the skirt out. "Thing's big enough to keep a flock of chickens under."

A laugh arose from those close enough to hear. Charlie flushed then noticed there was good humor in all the faces.

"Have you found any property that looks good, Boone?" Marie asked, not really thinking of the property, but of Boone's encounter with Earl Dillon.

Boone was not easily fooled. He was aware of the tenseness of the situation. He knew that word of his encounter with Earl Dillon was all over Richmond. Although he himself had said nothing to either Austin or Marie and they hadn't mentioned it to him, there was a stiffness and restraint in their manner that hadn't been there before. So he began to speak of the property and finally ended by saying, "I don't know if it's a good buy or not."

Mary Chesnut had listened to this with some interest. "I know that property. It's close to our old home place. The Dillons had it for a while."

At the name Dillon, a hush fell over the group. Mary

Chesnut added, "The Dillons both passed away a few years ago. Their son, Earl, had it for a while, but I believe he has sold the property to the Thompsons."

Boone had never felt more vulnerable in his life. Looking directly at Marie, he saw an odd expression on her face. *She thinks I'm a coward,* he thought, and then his eyes shifted to meet Austin's, seeing regret and dislike there. Quietly he said, "I expect that's the same property."

Mary Chesnut, an astute woman, knew she had said something to create the silence. Later she found her way to Austin and asked, "What did I say?"

"You haven't heard about the quarrel between Boone and Earl Dillon?"

"No, I haven't." She listened as Austin briefly explained, then said, "What a shame! Such a fine-looking man!"

Austin looked at the floor for a moment. "I guess fine looks don't mean much. It's what's inside a man that counts."

Chapter 16

Christmas at Hartsworth

Snow began to fall on December 24. As Boone stood in his room at the Spotswood, looking out at the tiny flakes drifting down, laying a white glaze on the dirty streets of Richmond, his mind went back to the mountains of Colorado. He thought of how he had first met Charlie and felt a loss he couldn't explain. Somehow Noah's plan had not worked out as he had expected—but then again, he wondered what it was that he had expected. Despite his reservations concerning Noah's plan to bring a new life to Charlie, Boone had summoned up a hope that it would all work out. As they had traveled south, he had let this hope grow in him until finally, despite his normally cynical way of looking at the world, he had come to expect better things. But those things had not happened, and now he wondered what would come next.

Turning from the window, he picked up a week-old newspaper that almost fell apart in his hands. Even worse than the quality of the paper were the editorials that threw all the blame for Confederate hardships onto President Jefferson Davis's shoulders. The editor of the *Mercury* wrote in such a shrill tone that finally Boone threw down the paper in disgust. "He sounds like a whining kid!" he muttered. "Why doesn't he toughen up and do what he can to encourage people!" It surprised him that he thought like this, for he had settled the matter in his mind that this cause for the South was lost. He knew in his heart that the Confederacy could not stand, although he was careful not to speak of this when others were around.

A knock interrupted his thoughts, and he opened the door to find Charlie and Marie Bristol there. Surprise washed over him, but he recovered quickly, saying, "What a nice surprise! Won't you come in?"

"Oh, Boone, we cain't stay!" Charlie said hurriedly. She was smiling vivaciously as she added, "You've got to come to Hartsworth for Christmas Eve and Christmas!"

Shooting a glance at Marie, Boone said, "I wouldn't want to impose. That's a family time."

Marie had come to town with Charlie to buy a few last-minute gifts, and in her forthright fashion, Charlie had asked if Boone could come to spend Christmas Day at Hartsworth. With some reluctance Marie had agreed, but now she covered this, saying, "Don't be silly! We'll be glad to have you, Boone. As a matter of fact, we have plenty of room. You could go back and stay the night there."

"Come on, Boone!" Charlie urged, her eyes shining. "There's no point staying in this old room by yourself!"

For an instant Boone hesitated, not sure a "coward" would be welcome at the Bristols', but not wanting to spend the evening alone with his thoughts. "All right," he said. "Let me throw a few things together, and I'll meet you in the lobby in ten minutes."

As Marie and Charlie moved down the stairway, Charlie said with satisfaction, "Now he won't have to be by himself."

"He seems like a man who can bear solitude," Marie answered. They reached the landing and stepped toward the brocade sofa on one side of the lobby. "I wonder if he has any family."

"No, he doesn't. I guess that's why I feel close to Boone.... I didn't really like Boone at first, but I just didn't understand him then."

"You like him very much now, don't you, Charlie?"

"I guess so," she replied cautiously, then asked, "Do you like him, Marie?"

Marie Bristol was a woman who usually spoke straight out, but at this moment she was uncertain. She *had* liked Boone Manwaring very much, but the thought that he might be less a man than she had at first thought troubled her deeply. Yet determined not to hurt Charlie's feelings, she answered diplomatically, "Why, I expect I do. We haven't known each other long, of course." As they waited, Charlie spoke volubly about the celebration to come. But when Boone came downstairs looking handsome in a brown suit, white shirt, and shiny black boots, Marie thought, *It's a shame he's not what he ought to be on the inside.*

That evening, talk ran cheerfully around the large white-clothed table. Set with china, crystal goblets, fine silverware, silver candlesticks, and sprigs of holly, it was a sight to behold. A large turkey, cooked slowly in the cast-iron cookstove, was placed at the head of the table, and silver bowls were filled with cabbage-and-apple salad, corn pudding, green beans, corn bread stuffing, sliced potatoes with onions in a cream sauce, and fresh bread and butter.

WITNESS IN HEAVEN

As Boone sat at the table, he felt strangely out of place, despite their hospitality. Claude Bristol, who'd been allowed to come home for the holiday, sat happily at the head of the table, wearing his spotless gray uniform. To his left was Marianne Bristol, her mulberry-colored dress setting off her patrician beauty. Across from her sat Austin, wearing a light blue coat and dark blue trousers. Occasionally his eyes rested on Boone with a silent displeasure. Next to Austin sat Marie, wearing an emerald dress and jade earrings that caught the light from the candelabras.

As Boone sipped the elderberry wine, he half wished he had not come. Turning, he studied Charlie, who was wearing a pale orchid dress. She looked at him often, as if she wanted to say something, but there was little privacy at the table.

Austin watched carefully, for he was concerned about Marie's feelings for Boone. He had liked Manwaring very well at first, but being a son of the South, he could countenance nothing like cowardice in a man. It troubled him to think Marie might be seriously interested in the tall man who sat down the table from him. As he swirled the dark red liquid in his glass, he thought, *Surely Marie knows better than to be interested in the fellow. But he does have money, and I think either of us would do anything to save Hartsworth. Still, it would be a bad match.* Involuntarily his eyes went to his father, who seemed to have lost the depression that had settled on him before he had joined the army. *He looks well,* Austin thought, *but he still has been a failure, and I think he knows it.* Then Austin looked fondly over toward his mother. He admired her more than any other woman, and now he saw, despite her youthful appearance for her age, that the years had laid their hand on her. Most of it, he thought resentfully, was due to his father's behavior.

Claude Bristol tasted the blackberry cobbler that had been brought to each member of the table. "Why, this is fine, Blossom! You always made better blackberry cobbler than anyone!"

"You always say that, Mr. Claude," Blossom said, smiling ear to ear. She was a short, heavyset woman with enormous brown eyes and had been the cook at Hartsworth for many years. "You just hopin' to git a second helpin', ain't you, now?"

"And maybe a third," Claude said.

"You'll be too fat for your uniform, Father," Marie said, smiling. She was pleased that her father looked better and also that he seemed to be more at peace with himself. He was not a man, she knew, to worry greatly about the future, while she, Austin, and their mother thought about it a great deal. Now, however, it was Christmas, and she wanted to take this moment and shut out the rest of the world. Wistfully she said, "It's nice being here, not having to think about Grant or Lincoln or what to plant instead of cotton."

Austin shifted uncomfortably. "Yes, it is," he admitted, "but that world's still out there."

"But we don't have to think of it tonight," Marianne said quickly. She looked down the table and smiled at Charlie. "What did you do for Christmas back in the mountains, Charlene?"

"Oh, Pa would always go out and chop down a tree. Ma and I would string red berries for decorations and pop popcorn and make strings of it. I'd go out and shoot a turkey, and we'd have roasted turkey and sweet potato pie." Her eyes grew nostalgic as she spoke. "It was fun! Pa always made a big thing out of Christmas. He'd go into town and git Ma and me some nice presents and bring them back, callin' himself Santa Claus. Last Christmas it snowed us in pretty bad, but Pa put on some snowshoes and hiked all the way to town. He came back near frostbit, but he loved Christmas."

All were silent around the table, for they were aware of Charlie Peace's aloneness in the world. As Austin saw once again her vulnerability, he noticed again what an attractive woman she was, with her beautifully textured olive skin, black hair, and dark blue eyes. "I'm glad you could be here with us, Charlene," he said quietly, smiling at her when she looked up with some surprise.

Marie saw this interchange. She was very fond of her brother and worried sometimes about what the world would bring to him. He was a young man of superior qualities—she felt sure of that; and his position in the War Department had kept him out of the fierce battles that had laid so many young men in unmarked graves throughout the South. But hard times were coming, and her heart caught suddenly as she thought what would happen if this vibrant brother of hers were to die.

Down the table, Boone Manwaring caught Marie's look. *She loves her brother a lot,* he thought, *and he cares for her. Nice to see a family close like this one.* Once again, feeling like an outsider, he kept quiet until Marie, sensing his awkwardness, finally said, "Tell us about some of your voyages, Boone. I've never been on an ocean trip. What's it like?"

Boone leaned back in his chair, masking what he was feeling. He ran his hand through his thick brown hair, touching the scar on his right cheek with the index finger of his right hand. He held it up for a moment and said, "Every time I think of the sea, I think of that finger."

"How did it happen, Boone?" Marianne asked.

"I threw a line overboard to catch a shark. Got one all right, but the line got snarled, and my finger got caught in it. The shark weighed probably eight hundred or a thousand pounds. I thought I'd lose the finger. It was crushed, but my old man put a splint on it and I kept it. Never could bend it, though." He pointed at Charlie and smiled. "It's good for pointing but not for much else."

"Do you like the sea? Will you go back there?" Marie asked.

"I doubt it. I went to sea a lot with my father as a young boy. It was a hard life. Exciting for a boy, but it's not a good life for a man—especially a married man."

"Do wives often go with their husbands on board ship?" Marie asked.

"Only the captain's wife from time to time."

"Did your mother go?" Marianne asked curiously. Drawn to Boone because she sensed his longing for something better, she sensed that Boone didn't give his trust easily.

"No, my mother never liked the sea. She stayed home, and sometimes my father and I were gone for a year or even more. I think she grew very lonely at times and wished my father had followed some other trade."

"Tell us about some of your adventures, Boone," Charlie said. "Tell about the time you nearly got shipwrecked down in the South Seas. The one you told me about."

Boone related the story of the terrible typhoon and how the ship had been tossed about like a poker chip. When he finished the story, they pressured him to tell more about life at sea until he finally said, "Strange things come to the minds of sailors. They are very superstitious."

"Do they have a girl in every port?" Charlie asked impudently.

"I don't know about that," Boone said, smiling at her. "I didn't." His thoughts went back to his days at sea. "I think sailors develop some kind of sixth sense about life."

"What do you mean by that?" Claude asked, puzzled.

"Sometimes you feel almost prophetic. You know something's going to happen, but there's no evidence for it. Do you know what lee shore is?"

"No, what's that?" Marie asked.

"It's a shore you don't want to get too close to because the wind will carry you into it, not away from it. And when you get caught off a lee shore, you're almost lost. The funny thing is," he mused, his voice dropping, "sometimes even when I couldn't see a lee shore, like in the middle of the night when there were no stars out and it was absolutely black, I would know somehow that lee shore was there."

"How could you know that?" Austin demanded. "If you couldn't see anything, I mean."

"That's what I mean about superstition. It came sometimes when there was not a sight of the sun or an observed shoreline for days. You don't have any idea where you are within a hundred or two hundred miles, but at night you feel the loom of that shore under your keel. You can see nothing, but you can almost hear the rocks grinding out the bottom of your ship." He paused then continued, "And it's not just at sea. Sometimes I've felt bad things were about to happen and had no reason for supposing it to be."

"Do you feel that way now, Boone?" Marie asked, intently listening, aware he had revealed part of himself. Now he was tense, she saw, and his hazel eyes looked disturbed as he lifted them to her, considering her question.

"Yes, I do feel like that." When he saw the effect of his words on the group, he gave a short laugh. "Why am I talking like that? Don't pay any attention to a superstitious sailor!"

"I know how you feel," Claude said soberly. "I've never been at sea, but I've had feelings like that."

After the meal was over, they moved into the parlor. Marie entertained them by playing the pianoforte and singing with her fine contralto voice the hymns of Christmas, insisting they join in with her. Charlie sat beside Boone, her shoulder touching his, and once she whispered, "This is nice, isn't it, Boone?"

"Yes, it is. I haven't been in a home like this for many years." What he really meant was never, but he did not say so.

Finally, it grew late, and Claude and Marianne excused themselves, going to bed. "We'll get up early and have a good breakfast, then open a few presents."

Austin, sitting beside Charlie, turned to ask, "Are you sleepy, Charlene?"

"No. I hate to go to bed at night."

"What are you afraid of?"

"Nothing. I'm just afraid I'll miss something." She smiled at him.

"I'm the same way," he admitted. "Maybe we'll sit up all night and watch the dawn."

"Not me," Marie said. "I'm sleepy."

Boone rose and nodded to her, saying, "Good night, Marie."

"Good night. Good night, Charlie and Austin."

After she left, depression settled over Boone. Finally, Austin, sensing the silence, said, "I guess I'll go to bed. I'll see you all in the morning. Good night."

When he had left the room, Charlie came over and sat down beside Boone. "That was fun, wasn't it?" she said, slipping her shoes off and holding her feet out to the fire. "You know, I miss my moccasins more than anythin' else. I don't see why women around here love shoes that hurt their feet." She wiggled her toes. "Did you have a good time, Boone?"

"Yes," Boone said, not quite truthfully. He turned to her and saw the reflection of the fire blossom in her eyes. "You know," he said, "you've got the most beautiful eyes I've ever seen in a woman."

Charlie was stunned. It was the first remark Boone had ever made like that, and she could not think how to answer him. She dropped her eyes, unable to meet his, very much aware of the pressure of his shoulder on hers. "Thank you," she said. "That's the nicest thing you ever said to me."

"I guess it is, isn't it? Now you say something nice to me. Tell me how pretty my eyes are."

Knowing he was teasing her, Charlie met his eyes again. "You have funny eyes. They're hazel. I never seen a man with hazel eyes like that." She reached up and touched the scar that traced its way down his right cheek. "How did you get that? In a fight?"

"Yes. Back when I was young and foolish."

"Young? You're still young, Boone!" she protested.

"I'm twenty-eight. Not a boy any longer." He was very conscious of the touch of her finger on his cheek and also of the sheen of her hair. He had always admired black hair, and he barely refrained from running his hand over the curls as they cascaded around her face and down the back of her neck. "You like Marie very much, don't you?"

"Yes. She's been very nice to me. You do, too, don't you?"

"Yes, I do."

Troubled by his brief answer, Charlie was quiet for a while then said, "I like Austin, too."

"Fine man."

They sat there speaking from time to time, and there was a comfort about it. Finally, Boone turned to her. "You know what

I like about you, Charlie? A man doesn't feel he has to keep up a line of chatter. I can be quiet with you and not feel like I'm letting you down."

"Why, I feel the same way, Boone," Charlie said. "People do talk a lot in the South, don't they?"

"No more than elsewhere, I wouldn't think."

"Yes, they do, too!" Charlie argued, waving her hand for emphasis. "Pa and Ma would go, seem like, four or five hours without saying a word."

Boone laughed at this and reached out to catch her hand.

The next day Austin was sitting in the study when Charlie burst in. "Austin, where's Boone? I can't find him."

"Why, Marie invited him for a ride around the place. I think they left about half an hour ago."

"Oh, I see!"

Seeing the happiness in Charlie's eyes fade, Austin said, "I don't see why they should be the only ones to go outside. Let's you and I join them."

"No. I wouldn't want to do that," Charlie said flatly.

"Well, we don't have to, but I would like a ride. We need some exercise."

Charlie hesitated, but she loved to ride, so she finally nodded. "All right."

Twenty minutes later the two were riding knee-to-knee across the hills west of Hartsworth. As the horses' hooves moved silently, cushioned by the freshly fallen blanket of snow on the low-lying ridges, Austin said, "We don't get much snow down here. I suppose you've missed it."

"Yes, I have."

Austin tried to keep the conversation going, but Charlie was silent. Then she blurted out, "Do you aim to marry up with Ida Campbell?"

Caught off guard, Austin stammered, "Why—what makes you ask that, Charlene?"

"That's what everybody says."

"Who's everybody?" Austin demanded.

"Oh, I don't know." Actually, she had heard Blossom say to another of the house servants, "Ain't no doubt in my mind but that Mr. Austin is gonna marry up with that Ida Campbell." Now Charlie turned in the saddle to ask, "You ain't gonna marry her, then?"

Although Austin liked Ida's wit and warmth, he knew, however, that these were not the qualities that had made him consider marrying her. At a loss for words, he finally said, "It would be a good marriage for both of us."

Charlie looked puzzled. "A good marriage? I thought all marriages were supposed to be good."

"I mean—well, it would have advantages."

"What does that mean?"

Again set back by Charlie's directness, Austin fiddled with the lines of his horse. "It means that you have to think about what comes after marriage."

"I reckon you have kids. Is that what you mean?"

"Of course there's that. What I mean is—Ida needs a husband, and she's a fine woman." Then honesty compelled him to say, "And if you must know, Charlie, it's likely that our family will lose this place."

"Lose Hartsworth?" Charlie was shocked. She had thought the Bristols were immensely wealthy. With the large house, the servants, the spacious fields and timber, she could not imagine money being any kind of a problem. "How could that be?" she demanded.

"Well, things are pretty bad right now in the South. And some unwise decisions were made. As a matter of fact, Hartsworth is mortgaged to the hilt. If we don't come up with some money, we'll lose it."

Charlie leaned over and patted the sleek side of the chestnut mare, letting this information sink in. Then she straightened up to look at Austin. "Is that the 'advantage' you're talkin' 'bout? That she's got money, and you'd marry her to keep from losin' your place?"

Her directness made Austin feel foolish. Then he realized she was merely showing the same response he himself had felt. He had despised himself at times for even thinking about marrying for money, and now he could not answer except to say, "I guess that's about it, Charlene."

A heavy silence lay over the land as the two made their way along. Heavy drifts came up to the horses' fetlocks, and overhead the sky was unmarked by even a single cloud. Finally, Charlie asked quietly, "Ain't there more to a marriage than that, Austin?"

Austin lost his temper. "If you had more experience, Charlene, you'd know it's not that simple." He clamped his lips together, sorry he had been provoked into such a reply, and moved his horse closer. He grabbed her arm and pulled her toward him so he could read her eyes. "I guess you think that's terrible—a man marrying a woman because she has money."

Very much aware of Austin's hard grip on her arm, Charlie answered quickly, "I heard of women marryin' men for money, but I never knowed it to be the other way 'round."

"Happens all the time," Austin said briefly and released her arm. Then he wheeled his horse around. "Let's head back to the house." He waited until she had turned her mare around, and then the two trotted through the drifts of snow. When they dismounted and handed the lines to one of the slaves, Austin said, "Pretty cold. We'd better get inside." He glanced down at her face as they waded through the snow, and before they reached the house, he stopped to face her. "It may sound pretty bad to you, Charlie, but I really like Ida and I think we'd get along. She needs a husband, and I'd try to make her a good one. Can't you see that?"

Far away a dog barked frantically. Although Charlie noticed it, she paid no heed. She was trying to find a way to put Austin at ease since she had embarrassed him. "It ain't any of my business, Austin. If you like Miss Ida and she likes you, there ain't no reason you shouldn't git married up."

Feeling he'd explained the matter badly, Austin said, "Marie hates to lose this place as bad as I do. It's not impossible that she would marry. A rich husband could come up with enough to save Hartsworth."

"You mean she might marry that Malcolm Leighton?"

"Him or somebody else." Then he said almost involuntarily, "She might even marry Boone."

Eyes wide with shock, Charlie could not speak for a moment. Finally, she said, "You don't reckon she'd do that, do you?"

"I hope not."

"So do I," Charlie said. "You reckon he cares for her?"

Hearing an uncertainty in Charlie's tone, Austin said, "I'm not sure, but I am sure of one thing. After the way he's run away from Earl Dillon, she wouldn't be happy with him."

"He ain't no coward!"

"He's given a mighty good imitation of one, Charlie. I know he's your friend, but he can't stay in this country. A man can't live down a reputation like that. Men will be laughing at him behind his back." When he saw the hurt in Charlie's face, he said gently, "I'm sorry to speak so plainly, but I know it's something you've probably already heard."

As a matter of fact, Charlie had been aware of this, but now she replied fiercely, "I don't care what they say! Boone ain't no coward!"

Almost at the exact moment Austin and Charlie were standing outside the house, Boone and Marie had stopped their horses by a grove of towering pine trees. Marie had pulled up first, and when Boone had stopped his mount beside her, she said, "Boone, I've got to talk to you, and it's not going to be easy."

Boone was aware of Marie's intensity. From the first time he had seen her, he had guessed at her depth. She showed a great deal of pride, and he was aware of the powerful emotions that lay beneath the surface. Now he noticed that she was attempting to control her eyes and lips, as though she feared to reveal herself.

"Before you tell me what you've got on your mind, Marie," he said, "I want to say one thing." The saddle creaked as he shifted his weight, and the metal of the bridle made a musical jingle as his gelding tossed his head. "Every man, I guess, goes through this world looking for some kind of beauty." Seeing the guard in her eyes, he almost didn't go on. But then he said softly, "Tough on me, but you're the kind of beauty I see nowhere else. No other woman possesses it for me."

Marie Bristol dropped her eyes, breathing rapidly, for his words had come as a shock to her. Finally, she lifted her eyes and met his. "That makes what I have to say a little harder, Boone."

"I can guess what it is."

"Can you?"

"Not too hard to know what people are saying. You want to know why I'm running away from Earl Dillon."

"Yes." Other women might have dodged, but Marie Bristol was not that sort. And she knew she could not let the matter rest. "You know what's being said about you, I suppose."

"That I'm a coward? That I'm afraid of Earl Dillon? That I'm no part of a man. Is that it?"

"Some people don't say that out loud, but if you'd been in the South long enough, you would have known what people think of a man who won't defend his honor."

Boone wanted to answer rashly, but he managed to control himself. "Would you have me kill a man over a card game, Marie?"

Marie shot back, "It's more than that, and you know it!"

"Marie," Boone said slowly, "a man comes out of nothing and heads toward something. He can't turn and go back through nothing. I know what's behind me, but I don't know what's ahead. All a man's got at the end of his life is a set of memories—things done well, things done poorly. I can't kill a man because of words he spoke over a card table. A man's life has got to mean more than that."

Marie knew there was wisdom in what he was saying. In fact, for a brief second she thought, *Perhaps the whole war is like this. Men can't put up with an insult, so hundreds of thousands of men are dying because of it.* But Marie was still a daughter of the South, where the code of honor was strong, so she said aloud,

"But there are certain things a man must do."

"That's right, Marie. A man is full of things meant to be used or given away—or maybe destroyed. The more he spends, the more he gets back." He suddenly wanted Marie Bristol to understand him. "I can't speak for others, but I know there's something more to life than what I've seen in the past. . . . And whatever it is I'm searching for, I've seen part of it in you, Marie."

"Don't—don't say that to me!"

"You would turn down a man because other men called him a coward?"

"I wouldn't marry a man I couldn't respect. I've seen too much of that in—" She almost said "in my father" but bit the words off. She saw, however, by the expression in Boone's eyes that he understood her. "You can't live like that, Boone. When you live among people, you have to live up to their expectations."

At that moment Boone knew that Marie Bristol cared for him because of the pain in her eyes. But he responded, "I can't kill a man because of some rules somebody made up. If it were on board a ship, I could fight him with my fists. We'd get our heads bloodied, but then we'd heal up and get on with life. But that's not the way the code is around here, is it? Somebody's got to die for a rude remark. I don't see it, Marie."

Marie held her hands over the saddle horn firmly so that Boone would not see their trembling. Her emotions ragged, she examined his face and saw the tough set of his lips. She knew he had a temper and that sometimes he was moody, hot as a flame. As he considered her steadfastly, she felt he was weighing in the balances what kind of woman she was. Finally, she could bear his gaze no longer. "I need to get back to the house."

As they moved rapidly through the snow, Marie wondered

WITNESS IN HEAVEN

why the scene had been so disturbing. *Do I care about this man? What has shaken me so much? If a woman loved a man, she would love him even if he wasn't perfect, right? And he may be right. Is killing a man for an insult, or maybe dying yourself, worth it?* However, she could not answer these questions, and when they dismounted she went into the house without saying another word. He followed, knowing that they'd both lost something precious during their encounter under the pines.

Chapter 17

Austin and Ida

The large blue-and-gold-wallpapered room in which Ida Campbell and her mother, Clara, sat was most pleasant. Light blue draperies edged with gold fringe delicately framed the windows and the looking glass over the fireplace. Brightly colored oil paintings adorned the walls, accenting the burgundy, light blue, and dark green design in the carpet. A corner bookcase contained hundreds of books. "I've always liked this room," Ida murmured. "It's my favorite. It seems so livable."

Clara Campbell sat on the blue sofa in the center of the room, sewing on a delicate piece of material. "It should be," she told Ida, glancing around. "I spent more time decorating this room than on the rest of the house put together." Clara paid careful attention to her stitching for a moment then put the cloth down, carefully plunging the needle into a crimson pincushion. Rubbing her eyes for a moment, she murmured, "My eyes aren't as good as they used to be." Leaning back in the walnut rocking chair covered with emerald plush, she asked, "Austin hasn't been here in a few days. Did you two have a spat?"

"No," Ida said quietly, smiling at her mother. "You think a lot about Austin, don't you?"

"I think about you."

"About my getting married." Ida's smile left her face. "Maybe I'm destined to be single."

"That's foolishness!" Clara Campbell snapped. "You could have had half a dozen men. Why, there's that nice Bobby MacIntyre. He was very serious about you a few months ago. What happened? I thought you might make it a match."

"I can't say. I suppose he would be a good husband. I could get him back, I think." It was unusual for Ida to speak like this, and she got up and walked to the fireplace. Standing over it, she looked into the flames, soaking up the heat from the bed of coals. "I like Bobby a great deal, but he's not very exciting."

"Exciting!" Clara exclaimed. "You're not talking about going to a play! Some of the most *exciting* men I know turned out to be terrible husbands."

"I know," Ida said. "I'm being foolish. I really do like Bobby. Maybe I've always wanted more romance than I found."

Just then a tiny bird emerged from the door of the room's clock, uttered three shrill cuckoos, and then went back into hiding. Staring at the clock for a moment, Ida mused, "I never did like that clock."

"It came all the way from Germany. It cost a great deal of money."

"I know, but it seems silly."

"You're not in a good mood today. I take it you and Austin must have had some sort of problem."

"No, Mother, really we didn't. He said he'd be by this afternoon. I expected him before now, but he's never sure when he can get off."

"He's a fine man, and good looking, too." Hope was scarcely hidden in Clara Campbell's voice. She herself had been married at the age of nineteen, and now here was her only daughter at the age of twenty-seven, still unmarried. Since her husband had died, Clara had been even more anxious to see Ida marry and perhaps have a family. Now for the first time she said with a trace of regret, "I'd thought by this time I'd have grandchildren, Ida."

The words hurt Ida, and she dropped her head for a moment. She had no answer for her mother, realizing the only thing she could do to help her was to do as she requested—marry and have children. It was true enough that she could have married. She had been asked three times, but one suitor was nearly sixty; the other two were young, but both were obviously after the Campbell treasury.

"Now that I think on it," she said finally, "I cared more for Bobby than for any man I've ever known."

"Not Austin? I thought you were very attracted to him."

"He's not really attracted to me, Mother. For a while I thought he was, but he's not really." She went over and patted her mother on the shoulder. "I think we'll have Bobby over for dinner Sunday."

Clara Campbell had always favored Robert MacIntyre, the son of a local banker who was rising in his profession. He had served in the army, then was wounded, and now walked with a slight limp. He was a cheerful young man, full of energy, and not at all bad looking, though a trifle thin. "That will be fine," she said. "I'll fix his favorite dishes."

Austin stared down at his books. As often before, he had come to the conclusion that the work he did had almost no effect on the war itself. Now as he critiqued the fine handwriting he had used to fill up sheet after sheet, he grew disgusted, rose, and pulled on his coat, then settled his hat firmly. Leaving the office, he murmured to Corporal Jenkins, "I'll be out for the rest of the day."

"Yes, sir. See you in the morning, sir."

Leaving the War Department, Austin spoke briefly to the men he knew, but his mind was elsewhere. He had not slept well over the past several nights, and now he was at loose ends. Remembering he had promised to visit Ida Campbell, he mounted a horse at the quartermaster stables and rode out of Richmond. The Campbell plantation was only four miles outside Richmond. He enjoyed the bite of winter air and the azure sky with patches of clouds sailing along in a stately fashion. Austin took a deep breath. "This is what a man ought to do. What good is it being stuck in a stuffy office?" As he thought this, again the impulse came to transfer out of the War Department and get in some branch of the service that offered some action. He had seen action before and knew there was no glamour in it, as many had thought at the beginning of the hostilities. He remembered how young men had flocked into Richmond, fresh-faced, eager-eyed to be in battle. But after the massacres at Shiloh and Antietam, everyone realized the war was going to be a grim business with little romance about it. Yet in spite of knowing this, Austin still felt useless, as if life were passing him by. More and more he thought about after the war. He had settled it in his mind that the South had no chance and the only hope he had was to make Hartsworth a good plantation. Now even that hope was slipping from his grasp.

When he pulled up in front of the Campbell mansion and stepped down out of the saddle, a short, muscular black man took his horse. "Good afternoon, Lieutenant."

"Hello, Bill. Are the folks at home?"

"Yes, suh. You go right on in."

Austin moved up the steps, his eyes taking in the elaborate three-story redbrick home with black-shingled roof. Six enormous Corinthian columns set off the front of the house, and two colonnades connected the main house to its two wings, one housing the kitchen, the other now a spare room that had once been used as a schoolroom by Ida. Surrounding the mansion was a carriage house, cotton gin, sugar mill, guest houses, dovecotes, and slave quarters. *This certainly isn't a poor man's home,* Austin thought as he stepped into the rich polished-pine foyer furnished with antiques brought from Holland. Ida came at once to him. "I saw you ride up, Austin. I'm glad you could come."

The two moved to the cozy parlor, the fire sparking a note of cheer that reflected in Ida's eyes. But Austin was in a complaining mood, so she listened as he sipped tea and talked about his useless existence. Finally, he said, "I guess I'm not very good company today."

"I know it must be discouraging. Actually, you weren't made for that kind of job. Seems someone made a mistake putting you there."

"Well, after I got wounded, I couldn't move around too much, so it was the best I could do. But I've been thinking about transferring out."

"To what branch?"

"The artillery. I've always been interested in that branch of the service."

"It's pretty dangerous, isn't it? Doesn't the other side always try to put the artillery out of action?"

"Oh, I don't know. I suppose they do, but it's what I'd like to do."

WITNESS IN HEAVEN

As they talked, Austin grew more restless. When he began shifting uneasily in his chair, Ida knew he was struggling with something he wanted to say.

Finally, Austin, who had pondered this moment for many weeks, gave up on subtlety. Without warning, he looked straight at Ida. "Ida," he said in a restrained tone, "have you ever thought about me as a man you might marry?"

Ida Campbell had a great inclination to say yes. She was not a girl any longer, and she needed a husband. She also longed for children. Austin Bristol was one of the most attractive men who had ever come calling on her. But she had never expected him to ask, for deep down she knew he did not love her. She was well aware of his family's financial problems, yet out of kindness did not resent the fact that this was a factor in the question he had just asked her.

"Yes, I have thought of it, Austin," Ida said, her voice low. "But I don't anymore. You don't really love me, Austin, any more than I love you. We've always been such good friends, but that's not what a marriage is based on."

Austin was taken by surprise. He had expected Ida to accept his offer at once, or at least to give him encouragement. But she was firm, and he knew that a further move would be useless. "I thought husbands and wives should be good friends," he said. "Some of the couples I know can't stand each other."

"I can't argue that. I know some couples like that. I've been waiting a long time to marry, and you're one of the finest men I know, Austin—but we simply don't have the love that should exist between two people. I haven't hurt you, have I?"

"You have in a way," Austin answered, "but I suppose I'll get over it. I'm not romantic enough to go out and shoot myself because you turned me down."

"Austin," Ida said, reaching to hold his hand, "I don't have many good friends. I can't afford to lose you. Let's not destroy that."

Austin had always liked Ida Campbell, but now he felt a tremendous admiration for her. He knew her honesty had cost her, so he said, "Good friends always." He leaned forward and kissed her on the cheek. "I suppose I should go out and get drunk, as a rejected suitor."

"Don't do that," Ida said, laughing. "There's a young woman somewhere waiting for you. Go and find her."

"You may be right about that. In any case, I'll be going now." When she escorted him to the door, he said, "The best of luck to you, Ida. Some man will find a good woman when he finds you."

"Good-bye, Austin. Come often."

When Ida closed the door, she realized with a sudden pang what she had done. But she was a straightforward young woman, and she murmured, "All right, Bobby. You're going to get your chance, but you're going to have to be more romantic than you have been in the past." Then she turned away from the door, putting the idea of Austin Bristol out of her mind forever, except as a friend.

※

When Austin returned to his room, he found a note from his father:

Let's have dinner together if you've nothing else to do. I'll be at the Spotswood at seven if you can come.

Austin did not want to be alone. The break with Ida Campbell had put a closure on something that had been a great deal in his thoughts. In truth, he was ashamed of himself, for looking back he realized he had come very close to bringing tragedy into both of their lives. *I'm glad she spoke up,* he thought as he made his way toward the Spotswood. *We would have been one of those couples who get along very well but are bored with each other. Ida deserves better than that.*

Entering the dining room, he saw his father over at a table at the far side and went at once to greet him. "Hello, Father."

"Glad you could come, Austin. Have a seat."

The two put in their order, and after the waiter disappeared, Austin said, "How's everything going? Are they still giving you a hard time?"

"Oh, a little bit, but that's to be expected. The old-line army officers resent being saddled with a greenhorn like me. I get along with the men," he said with a slight smile, "better than I do with the staff, except for Clay, of course."

The meal, which consisted of roast beef, potatoes, and carrots, came after a time. "I wonder where they got these carrots? They must be tinned," Claude said. "They taste like it anyway. We grow better than this at Hartsworth, don't we, son?"

"A lot better." The mention of Hartsworth stirred Austin's thinking. He hesitated for a moment then decided it would do no harm to talk about the situation. "I've been wondering how we're going to make it. It looks pretty grim financially."

A shadow came into Claude Bristol's eyes, and he put down his fork. "My fault," he said briefly.

"Not entirely," Austin countered. "A lot of plantations are in trouble over this embargo."

"The great regret of my life is that I didn't look to a time like this. If I hadn't been such a wastrel, we could have been out of debt. A man thinks about things like that when he finally comes to himself." Bitterly he continued, "All the years I was out racing horses and gambling, I could have put that time and money into our home. Your mother deserved it, and so did you, Paul, and Marie. I've let you all down, Austin, and in case I haven't said it, I'm sorry for being that kind of father."

Austin was taken aback. One glance at his father's face told him Claude was more serious than he'd ever seen him before. Austin finally said, "We all make mistakes."

"Well, I made a bad one. God gave me a wonderful woman and fine children, better than anything I ever expected when I was a young man. I haven't told you much about my life before I married, but my father was a gambler. I don't remember much about my mother." The din of the tables made a pleasant hum as Bristol spoke in a low tone, regret etched on his features. "I grew up thinking I'd get rich, then I'd quit gambling. Well, that's a fool's paradise. All gamblers have it, I suppose, but now that I've grown old, it's hard to realize what a fool I was."

Suddenly Austin felt again the affection for his father that he thought he'd lost long ago. "We're not lost," Austin said. "It'll be tough, but we can survive."

Claude Bristol straightened and blinked rapidly. Then in an unsteady voice he said, "It's generous of you to say that, Austin. I don't deserve it, and I know that better than anyone."

"I wish we could take a day or two off and go home. Maybe we could make some plans and get to know each other better. Maybe go hunting."

"Would you really do that, Austin?"

"Why, sure. It would be good for both of us. Can you get a couple of days' leave?"

WITNESS IN HEAVEN

"I think the regiment will somehow survive my absence," Claude said, a light of amusement in his eyes. "What about you?"

"I don't think they'll even know I'm gone. Tell you what. Let's go in February, for a couple of days anyway."

"Good. I'd like nothing better."

Grasping the quill firmly, Charlie drove it across the page of the tablet, paying careful attention to the instructions Marie had given her. Now her writing was even and rather beautiful, and she took pleasure in the act. It was one of the things she could point to and claim as an improvement in her life. Steadily she wrote:

January the fourth, 1864

> *I aint seen Boone—I mean I havent seen Boone—since Christmas, and that is over a week ago. He sent word out by Austin that he would come, but he hasnt.*
>
> *What I think is that he has got his mind on Marie, and since nobody will ever see this I guess I can put it down. It makes me feel bad because I like Marie so much. She has done a lot for me and so has Boone. To tell the truth, I guess I am in love with Boone, but I am afraid he will never think of me as a woman. All he can think of, I guess, is me runnin round in buckskins and shootin a bear. No matter how many silk dresses I put on, he can only think of that.*
>
> *I been thinkin bout what Austin said bout him marryin Ida, or Boone maybe marryin Marie. It bothers me a whole lot. Of course, Marie Bristol is probably the prettiest*

woman I ever saw and any man would be lucky to get her, but somehow I hope it wont be Boone. I am gonna write Boone a note and have Solomon take it in. I am gonna ask him to come out here so we can talk about what we are goin to do.

Charlie ceased writing. Somehow the writing had not pleased her. She was more unhappy than she had been at Christmas, and she knew somehow that it had to do with the artificial life she seemed to be living. More than once she had said, "I can't stay here forever. I've got to get on with things." Now as she stood in the center of the room, a determination came to her, and she said, "I'm goin' to see Boone! I cain't stay here no longer!"

She changed clothes, went at once to the stable, and had Solomon hitch up the buggy. When she got in it, she said, "I'll take good care of this horse, Solomon."

"Yes, ma'am. He's a good hoss. He'll get you there and back."

All the way into Richmond, Charlie's mind was tumultuous. "If I love Boone," she said, "I reckon he likes me some. He just don't know it yet. But if we git away from here, just him and me, on a farm of our own, why then maybe he'll see that I'll make him a good wife."

This thought, in one form or another, stayed with her until she drew up in front of the Spotswood. She stepped down and handed the lines to a servant.

She went directly to Boone's room, knocked on the door, and was relieved when he opened it. "Hello, Boone."

"Why, hello, Charlie," Boone said with some surprise. "Is something wrong?"

"No—well, maybe a little bit. I got to talk to you, Boone."

"Let's go down to the restaurant."

Charlie knew his words were to avoid compromising her, so she waited until he slipped into his coat and stepped outside. On the way down he questioned her about what was going on at Hartsworth. Finally when they entered the restaurant, were seated, and had been served, she said, "Boone, I cain't live the rest of my life out at Hartsworth."

"Don't you like it there? The idea was that you would—well, learn things from Marie."

"I know, but it would take me forever, and I never would be as fine a lady as she is."

"You don't know that, Charlie," Boone said. "You're very quick. You need to give it a chance."

"No, Boone, I don't want to do that! We come to Virginia to buy a place. That's what Pa wanted. Well, fur as I kin see, we ain't gettin' nowhere!" She looked at him so fiery with independence that he knew an easy answer would not do.

"I've been looking around and mostly trying to learn what places are worth. It's hard, Charlie, because all I've ever really done is operate a ship. Here I'm lost."

"You got to try, Boone. Will you?" she asked, her dark eyes intense.

He stared at her for a moment. "All right," he said. "I'll see what I can do."

Relief washed over Charlie, and she somehow felt that a load had been lifted from her. Impulsively she clasped his hand and said rather shyly, "I know I'm a pest, Boone, but I gotta git a place of my own."

Conscious of her hand on his, Boone smiled. "I guess I know the feeling. I've felt the same. We'll get at it right away. Now maybe you and I can ride around and look at the countryside today. It's pretty cold, but—"

"That's all right, Boone," Charlie said quickly. "Let's do it."

⚜

A month later, Austin found out that his father could not get leave as he had hoped. "It's that Major Ferguson," Claude had said. "His chief occupation in life is to stop people from having fun. Some other time."

Austin had been disappointed but had still gone to Hartsworth. He had stayed for two days, spending most of that time with Charlie. During the days, they loved to ride. In the evenings, he, Marie, his mother, and Charlie would sit around the fire. On the last night of his stay, Charlie and Austin found themselves up late, almost midnight, in the kitchen. It had been a good evening: They had played cards and Marie had sung. Finally, Marie and his mother had gone to bed, and now Austin had said something about being hungry. Charlie at once had said, "Come on. I'll fix up a bite."

They had gone to the kitchen, where she had made a huge omelet, something Blossom had taught her. When she had divided it onto plates, Austin bit into it. "Why, this is better than anything I've had in weeks! I didn't know you could cook like this, Charlene."

"Oh, Blossom's teachin' me to cook."

"Well, she's done a good job." He ate heartily, and they also enjoyed coffee, for he had brought a half pound with him. "Drinking coffee these days is like drinking gold. When this is gone, I doubt if we'll have any more."

As they talked, they began to laugh so loudly that once Austin had to say, "We'd better keep it down. They'll be getting up to send us both to bed." They stood before the large fireplace sipping the last of the coffee, and when it was gone, they put their cups on the mantel. "The last of the coffee," he said. "There's always the last of everything, isn't there, Charlene?"

She looked at him, puzzled. "What do you mean?"

Austin looked at her, thinking how much she had changed. Rather than her buckskins, she was wearing a gray dress with a pink sash. "Let's draw up some chairs and toast our feet. I'm still not sleepy."

"All right, Austin."

They drew up a deacon's bench, and he said, "Here, there's room enough for both of us." She sat beside him, conscious of his nearness when he continued. "I was thinking about church last Sunday, when the preacher preached on the brevity of life. It was a good sermon. It made me feel kind of little."

"Me, too."

"Well, I guess I couldn't get away from that text. What was it? Man's life is like a flower—here today, and then it's gone. So I got to thinking. Sometime I'll see my mother for the last time, I'll have the last sip of coffee, the last kiss from a woman." He grew serious. "Do you ever think of things like that, Charlene?"

"Not much. I guess I'm not much of a thinker."

Laughing, he grabbed her hand. "Don't say that. You're quick. I've always said that. Look how much you've learned."

"Do you think I've changed, Austin?"

"Why, of course you have! When you first rode to town in man's clothes and packing a musket, I thought you were a mighty attractive young woman. But now, why, you can stand up in any drawing room in Virginia."

Charlie swallowed hard. "I'm mighty proud you think that."

As the fire cast its warmth on them both, Austin did something he had always wanted to do. Her black, curly hair had always intrigued him, so he whispered, "Charlene, your hair is the most beautiful thing I've ever seen." He stroked her curls with his hand. "It's lovely. No other woman has hair as pretty as yours."

Charlie Peace, although she did not know it, was hungry for this kind of attention. She wanted to be told she was pretty, and the touch of Austin's hand on her hair released something in her. She sat there not protesting, lips parted slightly, her eyes large.

As for Austin, the feel of her soft hair released something in him, too. He suddenly saw her not as a rough, boyish figure but as a beautiful and enticing young woman. As he looked at her sweet, wondering face and generous mouth, he put his arm around her and drew her close. As he bent his head, her lips came up, quick and eager, and for Austin it was like falling into softness. Prolonging the moment, he did not release her.

The strength of his arms and the pressure of his lips on hers were like nothing Charlie Peace had ever felt. She drew back finally, the light in her eyes glowing warmly.

For Austin, Charlene had become a fragrance, a melody. Despite what she had been, Charlene Peace had grown into a beautiful and desirable woman.

Afterward, neither of them could speak, and finally Austin said, "I suppose I ought to apologize for that, Charlene—but I won't."

If he had apologized, Charlie would have been hurt deeply. Now she saw something in his face that pleased her. She rose

WITNESS IN HEAVEN

and whispered, "Good night, Austin." She made her way out of the kitchen, went upstairs, and went to bed. But she could not sleep. Austin's kiss had confused her even more. She could not help thinking, *If Boone had kissed me like that...*

Chapter 18

Death at Sunrise

Charlie was standing in the kitchen looking out the window as she peeled potatoes when Boone drove a buggy up the driveway. At once she dropped a half-peeled potato along with the knife and ran out of the kitchen. "Boone!" she called out. "Boone! Here I am!"

Pulling up the pair of matched bays, Boone grinned then laughed as Charlie took a leap and cleared the front wheel of the buggy, landing beside him. "Don't be bashful," he said. "Just climb right in."

It was now March, a month since Austin had kissed her, and she had been unable to put the incident out of her mind. She had finally recorded in her journal, "I guess I'm just a country girl, but he is a good-lookin' man, and I don't reckon he meant anythin' by it." Now as she looked at Boone, she said eagerly, "I'm glad you're here. Come on in, and I'll fix you somethin' to eat."

"No. Go get changed. We're going to look at a plantation; then we'll go into Richmond and have supper together. I reckon it'll be too late to bring you home."

"Boone, you found a place?"

"Well, I found a place for us to look at."

"Let's go now."

"All right, but you'll have to stay in the hotel tonight. Go pack a suitcase with whatever you need overnight. Hurry along with you now!"

Jumping back out of the wagon, Charlie stormed back into the house. She nearly ran into Marianne in the hall. "Oh, excuse me! I'm goin' with Boone to look at a farm. I won't be back tonight. He says it'd be too late."

Racing upstairs, she rapidly changed into a pale blue dress, pulled on calf-high shoes, then yanked a dark blue wool coat from the chifforobe. Running down the stairs, she yelled, "Good-bye, Miss Marianne! I'll see you tomorrow, probably, unless we buy the place—then I might just stay."

Marianne watched the pair leave. "That young woman is certainly impulsive," she murmured.

The day had been exciting for Charlie. Boone had taken her to a small plantation that was not more than five miles outside Richmond and less than six from Hartsworth. He had warned her, "It's not fancy like Hartsworth or Clay's place. Don't be expecting too much."

Charlie had not expected too much and had been delighted with the property. She knew little enough about farming, and Boone knew not much more, but the owner, a tall man with gray hair and mild blue eyes, informed them, "It's an easy place to farm. Don't take many hands to do it." His name was Stafford, and he told them within five minutes that his wife had passed away a year ago and he wanted to move to his daughter's home in North Carolina. "Nothing around here for me now," he said, "except memories. I'll make you a good price on the place."

Charlie was fascinated by the house, which was, indeed, not so large as Hartsworth. It had four bedrooms, however, plus a sitting room and a huge kitchen with a magnificent fireplace. She moved from room to room, followed by Boone. "Look, Boone! These ceilings are high as our old cabin back in Colorado." She marveled at this and at the wallpaper that evidently Mrs. Stafford had taken a special interest in. "Shore is pretty, ain't it? I mean, *isn't* it, Boone?"

"It's a nice house," Boone agreed. They investigated every nook and corner inside and then went outside so Stafford could drive them around the perimeter of the place.

Finally, Stafford said, "You and your wife will want to talk about this. Come back and see me when you make up your mind. Reckon we can handle the financing between us."

At the words "you and your wife," Charlie had flushed and shot a look at Boone. He had winked at her and shaken his head, as if to say, *He'll find out soon enough.*

They left for Richmond, arriving about dark to obtain a room for Charlie. But she turned to Boone, saying, "It's too early to go to bed."

"Sure is," Boone said. "Let's get something to eat, but not here. I've eaten here until I know every biscuit that's coming."

The two went to a restaurant called the Pioneer, a place Boone had found on one of his nightly excursions. It was frequented mostly by officers of the army stationed outside of town, bachelors who were looking for a meal to break the monotony of the army diet. The room also held several civilian families.

When the meal came, Charlie said, "This is good cookin'! I could do this good, though."

WITNESS IN HEAVEN

Boone sipped his coffee, or what passed for coffee. "Maybe you can get a job here," he suggested. Then he frowned, "I wonder what they put in this cup."

A waiter overheard him and asked, "Something wrong, sir?"

Boone winked at Charlie. "If this is coffee, bring me tea. If it's tea, bring me some coffee." Charlie giggled.

The waiter, rather disgruntled, said, "If you don't like it, sir, I can get you some sassafras tea."

"No, I'll muddle along with this." Boone waited until the waiter left, then said, "I guess it doesn't do to complain about the food here. That fellow is downright sensitive!" He sipped from the cup again and shook his head. "Too much for me. What did you think about the place, Charlie?" He sat there listening as she, with a glowing face, spoke about how much she liked it. Finally, he said, "Not fancy like Hartsworth."

"Well, I'm not very fancy myself," Charlie said happily.

"We'd be a pair trying to farm, wouldn't we? Probably plant crops under the trees so we wouldn't have to work in the sun."

"Oh, I know better than that!" Charlie said indignantly. "Did you ever farm at all?"

"Not even a garden. It's hard to farm when you're out on the sea in a schooner. Might be fun to learn, though."

The two talked until a crowd came in and the waiter looked at them with impatience. "I guess we'd better leave. The waiter's liable to throw us out if we try to hang on to this table any longer," Boone remarked.

He picked up Charlie's coat, which was draped over the back of her chair, and held it for her. When she slipped her arms into it, he smelled the freshness of her hair. "You've been sneaking around washing your hair again, Charlie. It smells good."

Charlie turned and said, "That's not very polite, Boone, to

talk about a girl's washin'."

Boone only grinned at her and stepped aside to let her walk toward the door. They had almost reached the entrance that led from the main dining room into the large foyer when Earl Dillon appeared with three men. He stopped to stare at Boone. "Well, look what we got here! Fighting Boone Manwaring!"

An alarm as clear as a bell rang inside Boone. He saw Dillon had been drinking and, indeed, was weaving slightly. His eyes were red-rimmed, and his speech was loose, slack with drunkenness. Stepping forward, Boone took Charlie by the arm and pulled her slightly to one side without speaking, hoping Dillon would pass on, but keeping his eyes steadily on the man.

"This here's the famous mankiller. You may not have heard of him." Dillon raised his voice so everyone in the restaurant turned to watch the scene. Only the clattering of dishes in the kitchen could be heard.

Boone felt something begin to burn inside and recognized it. When he had become angry, a few times in his life, it had built up like a volcano and then burst with such violence that when the fight was over, it had sobered him. He knew he was capable of killing when he fell into such a mood, and now, in order to still the rising violence that troubled him, he said quietly, "Come on, Charlie."

"Wait a minute!" Dillon stepped forward and grabbed Charlie's other arm. He leered down at her. "What's a pretty thing like you doing with a yellow-belly like this? You deserve a real man!"

The fiery anger boiling inside Boone turned into a coldness, for he knew it was hopeless to try to pacify Dillon—indeed, he did not want to. Now he stepped forward and with one blow struck Dillon in the chest, driving him backward. Dillon cartwheeled into his friends and would have fallen if two of them had not caught him.

"Step over there, Charlie," Boone said then turned to face what he knew was coming. Dillon had caught his balance now, and his face had turned white. He pulled his coat together then said, "I don't take a push from any man! If you're too much of a coward to face me like a man, then I'll whip you like a dog!" His hand flashed out and would have struck Boone on the cheek, but Boone easily blocked it by grasping Dillon's wrist in a vise and squeezing it.

As he heard a slight gasp come from Dillon's lips, Boone said, "I'm tired of you, Dillon! You've been pushing this. You're the kind of man who has to be seen. I have some things to do first, but I'll see you the day after tomorrow at dawn. My man will call on you. If you need an excuse, here it is." Boone swung his free arm in an arch, short and powerful, and threw his body into it. His open hand caught Dillon squarely on the left cheek and drove him backward so that he fell into a table. Two women sitting there screamed as the table fell over beneath the careening body. Dillon got to his feet slowly, the mark of Boone's hand on his face.

"Enjoy your meal, Dillon," he said. "Come along, Miss Peace." He took Charlie's arm and guided her outside.

The violence had shaken Charlie, since it had seemed to explode from nowhere. As they walked down the street toward the Spotswood, she finally took a deep breath. "Does this mean you're goin' to fight him, Boone?"

"No choice. I'll have to."

Looking up, Charlie saw that his lips were set in a tight line and thought, *What will I do if Boone dies?* The idea struck her like a physical blow. She found it difficult to imagine where she would turn. Since Boone had come into her life, she had unconsciously learned to look to him, and now she felt it was more than that. When he stopped at the door of her room, she awkwardly laid her hand on his chest. "Boone, don't do it! I've heard 'bout him. He's already killed two men and shot another."

"There's no way out, Charlie. Go to bed now. I have things to do."

Charlie watched, unable to move, as Boone walked down the hall then disappeared down the stairway. She entered her room and sat down on the bed, feeling empty and almost paralyzed by the fear that Boone might die and leave her.

"You haven't heard about Boone, Marie?" Austin Bristol had looked up the next morning when his sister entered his office. As he saw her smile fade, he knew instantly she had not heard the news. "He came to me last night. Seems that Earl Dillon insulted Charlene down at the Pioneer."

"What happened, Austin?"

"Well, I guess I've been wrong about Boone," Austin admitted. He stroked his cheek thoughtfully. "I wasn't there, but I heard about it later. From what Boone told me, Dillon put his hands on Charlene, and Boone knocked him across the room."

Marie could not think for a moment. Duels were not uncommon in Richmond and in the countryside, although they were illegal. She had always taken them for granted as a part of the Southern way of life, but now she looked at Austin in consternation. "I don't know what to say."

"I don't think anyone else does either. We've all put Boone down, but I guess he had other reasons than cowardice for not wanting to fight. I'll have to help him with this."

"Isn't there some way to avoid it?" Marie asked, her lips dry.

"You know what Dillon is. It's what he's been screaming for." Austin shifted nervously, running his hand over his hair. "I don't like it, though. He's a dead shot and quick as a snake. I talked to a man who saw him when he killed Jerry Fowler. He said Fowler never even had a chance. It was like a murder."

"We've got to stop him, Austin."

"I've talked to him, but it's too late for talk. I think we're responsible for this, and that's what worries me. Boone's a pretty sensitive man, and he knows the talk that's been going around about his being afraid of Dillon. His eyes used to be sort of laughing, but now they're cold as ice."

"I'm going to talk to him! Do you know where he is?"

"It'll do you no good."

"I have to try anyway!"

"You can probably find him in his room."

Marie went at once to the Spotswood and knocked at Boone's door. When he opened it, she saw exactly what Austin had meant. Boone's eyes were not the same. "I just talked to Austin. He told me about Dillon."

"Pretty common knowledge. We ought to fight in public and charge admission. We could make a fortune." Bitterness, something Marie hadn't heard from Boone before, tinged his speech.

"Boone, you don't have to do this. Everyone knows what kind of a man Dillon is."

"That wasn't the way you felt before."

Boone's words hit Marie hard. She dropped her eyes, feeling ashamed, and worked to regain her composure. When she looked up at him, there was a vulnerability in her mouth and eyes. "I deserve that," she said quietly. "It's the way we've lived around here, but I've never been this close to the thing before. It was always a story about two men I didn't know, but it's real enough now." When he did not answer, she said, "I'm sorry I misjudged you, Boone, and Austin is, too."

"I suppose it had to come. Dillon would never have given it a rest. I'm just sorry Charlie had to get involved in it."

"Where is she? That's why I came to town. She didn't come home."

"She's got a room down the hall—202. It might be good if you'd go be with her. She's pretty upset."

"I should imagine. So am I."

Boone cocked his head to one side. "I don't want to be impolite, Marie, but I'd appreciate it if you would leave me alone. Go down and see Charlie."

Desperately Marie wished she had never let Boone suspect her feelings about his courage, or lack of it. Now she saw it was hopeless, but still she had to try. "I remember once you said that a game of cards wasn't worth killing a man for. It sounds odd coming from me, but let me ask you this. The man didn't hurt Charlie. Is it worth killing him because he insulted her?"

"I don't know the rules. I didn't make them up. I only know that sometimes a man has to fight, and this is one of them." A serious light touched his hazel eyes, and he paused to gather his thoughts together. "I expect there's many a man in the army who doesn't feel anything about slavery in particular, or states' rights either. He's there because of pressure, what his people would think of him, and what his friends would think. So finally, regardless of what he thinks about the political situation, he goes into the army, and sooner or later he has to kill—or be killed. It seems like it's something that's built into men. I don't like it, and I wish it didn't exist, but it does."

"But, Boone, what if you're killed?"

"Then I'll be dead."

"Don't be foolish. I know this is no time to preach, but I've sensed that you don't know God personally. That's what frightens me the most, although I—" She started to say, "I've come to care for you," but cut her words off. It would sound false and hollow now. In truth, anything she said sounded foolish to her own ears. If she really cared for him, why hadn't she spoken to him about things like God and eternity before? "Boone, please put it off for a while. Give it time."

"I can't do that, Marie. Go to Charlie." He hesitated then said, "If all goes well, I'll see you tomorrow."

Marie had no choice. She wanted to hold him, beg him not to go, but her pride would not let her do that. And now that this moment had come, she realized how much her feelings for Boone had grown since he had kissed her.

"Good day, Marie," he said then closed his door. It sounded like a death knell to her as she stood outside numbly, unable to think, devastated by fear. Then she moved down the hall to the room Boone had mentioned and knocked on the door. When it opened, she saw Charlie's pale face and eyes red with weeping. "Oh, Marie!" she said. "He's gonna git killed!" She threw herself into Marie's arms. Marie held the trembling young woman close and heard her desperate words. "He's goin' to die, and I love him, Marie! I love him!"

Marie could only stand there, her hand patting the back of the sobbing girl ineffectually. Although she had suspected Charlie loved Boone, now it had come from Charlie herself. Without a doubt, Marie now knew that this young woman's life was tied up with the tall man who, down the hall, was preparing himself for death.

That night Boone went to bed. After lying there for a long time, he finally went to sleep. He awakened, however, after an interminable period, not knowing how much time had passed. Looking out the window, he sensed dawn was not far off. He rose and shaved, using cold water, and then dressed as carefully as if he were going to a formal wedding. He had finished brushing his hair when a tiny knock sounded, and his eyes narrowed. He moved to the door and asked, "Who is it?"

"It's me—Charlie."

Opening the door, Boone said, "You shouldn't be here, Charlie. Go back to your room."

"Boone, I couldn't help it." Charlie looked exhausted. "You don't have to fight that feller. Let's get away from here. We've got enough money to go anywhere. Please, Boone, let's go!"

Astonished by her emotion and the tremor in her lower lip, Boone grasped her cold hand. "Charlie, I've got to do this thing. Then if you don't want to stay in Richmond, we'll go someplace else."

When she started to speak, he said, "There's no point talking, Charlie. I wrote a letter and delivered it to the bank yesterday. If I don't make it through this, it's all yours. So you won't have to worry about anything."

"I don't keer 'bout the money! I just keer 'bout you!"

Charlie threw herself against Boone, holding him tightly. He felt her trembling. "I've got to go, Charlie. It's time. I'll be all right. I'm a tough old bird."

Charlie lifted her head and locked her hands behind his neck, pulling his head down for a kiss. Boone tasted the saltiness of her tears and her soft lips. As she clung to him desperately, Boone was astonished at his own feelings for her.

"You cain't go," Charlie said, releasing him at last. "It don't mean nothin'. He didn't hurt me."

"A man has to live with other men, Charlie. I couldn't stay in this place unless I faced up to Dillon. Most duels," he said, grasping at straws for the most part, "don't get anybody killed. Shot in the arm or the leg, maybe, but if I don't make it, I'll say this: I've become very fond of you."

"I love you, Boone," Charlie said simply.

"Why—you're just a child, Charlie. You see me as a father." He saw her shake her head and knew then he had to get away. He carefully pushed her away then picked up his coat. "Stay here at the hotel. I'll be back."

And then he was gone. Charlie stared after him then took a ragged breath and went back to her room. She sat down on the edge of the bed to begin her long vigil, her thoughts on the encounter that would take place outside Richmond at sunrise.

*

"Are you all right, Boone?" Austin asked nervously. He shifted his feet and looked over the slight rise where three men were waiting. "Maybe he'll apologize; then we can all go home and forget it."

"You can forget about that, Austin. You know Dillon better than that."

"I guess that's right." Austin saw the grim determination in Boone's face. "You've got to be fast and get in the first shot. From everything I hear, that's what Dillon does."

"I doubt if I can beat him; he's had more practice than I

have. But he'd better hit me in the brain, or he's a dead man."

They were approaching rapidly now, and Boone saw that Dillon had already taken off his heavy coat. He was wearing a white shirt, and it occurred to Boone, *You'll get that shirt bloody if things don't go your way.*

Austin said at once, "Gentlemen. I think, Masters, we would be ready to consider an apology."

Masters, a bulky man with cold eyes, said, "My principal will make no apologies. Is your man ready?"

Austin said in a thin voice, "Yes."

The third individual now produced a case and opened it. "You may have first choice of the weapon, Mr. Manwaring."

Carelessly Boone picked up one of the pistols and glanced at it. It was a fine dueling pistol, but he would have preferred a Colt .44. However, he made no complaint. Dillon sneered but said nothing as he took the other pistol.

Boone watched as Austin and Masters carefully charged the pistols. When Austin handed him the weapon, he held it loosely at his side and listened as the third man gave the instructions. "I will count to ten as you march away from each other. On the count of ten you will turn and fire. Is that understood?"

"Yes," Dillon said and turned his back. Boone merely nodded and took his place. He heard the count begin almost at once. "One—two—three—" His mind seemed to be working more rapidly than usual. He was not thinking of his own death, although that might be only seconds away. His thoughts were of Charlie and what would happen to her. If he had fear, it was that she would not be able to make her way in the world, and then he thought, *Marie will help her.*

"Eight—nine—ten!"

Boone turned quickly, holding his body at a right angle,

presenting the least possible target. As his own weapon swung up, he saw he was not going to be fast enough, for Dillon had already whirled and leveled his weapon.

He's going to get me, Boone thought, but his arm continued its upward sweep. It was as if he moved underwater, so slow did he seem, and then as his finger tightened on the trigger of the pistol, he was aware a great blow had struck him. As his own pistol discharged, the earth began to grow quiet; the rising sun darkened. Then, as if he were struck with a powerful fist, he fell over backward, not feeling his body as it hit the ground.

PART FOUR
Shadow of the End

CHAPTER 19

A TIME TO LIVE

Charlie Peace had never spent such a bad day in her life. Dawn came, rosy and bright, but she had no eyes to see the beauty of the sunrise. Slowly the crimson disk turned to a harvest yellow and rose over the city as Charlie sat mutely at the window. From time to time she would get up and pace the floor, her face tense, agitation spreading throughout her as she thought about the outcome of the duel.

"I shouldn't have let him go!" she murmured. "I could've found *some* way. We could've left this place and gone someplace else. What do I keer 'bout this place if Boone dies?"

She moved over to the washstand, filled the basin with fresh water, and, soaking a washcloth, pressed it against her face. Then she assumed her lonely vigil, sitting in the chair and staring down at the street. Her reverie was broken by a sharp rap on the door. Leaping to her feet, she sprang across the room and, seizing the doorknob, jerked it open. "Austin!" she cried, and then could say no more. The words "Is he dead?" had almost passed her lips, but somehow it seemed unlucky to even let the words be spoken, although they were in her heart.

Austin exhaled what was almost a gasp. "He's alive, Charlie!"

"Thank God!" Charlie said. As her face paled, the room swayed around her, and Austin leaped forward to put his arm around her.

"Here," he murmured, "sit down awhile." He guided her to the bed and sat down beside her, keeping his arm around her. "It takes you like that sometimes. I don't know why. Good news can hit you as hard as bad news."

"Is he bad hurt, Austin?"

"Well, he's not going to die." His mind went back to the scene of the duel. A vivid image of Boone's face and hair covered with blood filled his mind. He had thought at that moment that Boone was killed instantly. "He took a slug along the side of the head. He's down at Dr. Malone's office now."

"I got to go to him, Austin."

"That's why I came." Rising, Austin watched carefully to make sure she wasn't still dizzy. But she had regathered herself. Taking her arm, he said, "Better put on a coat."

Charlie grabbed her coat from the armoire then said hurriedly, "Come on! Let's go, Austin!" Her unbrushed hair framed her face with curls.

"He was unconscious," Austin said, "but I wouldn't want him to wake up alone."

The two hurried out of the hotel, and Austin led her to Dr. Malone's office, which was upstairs over the general store. They ascended a rickety stairway and went in to find Malone. He was a burly man of fifty, thick-fingered, broad-shouldered, and with the beginnings of gray in his brown hair and beard. His eyes sharpened as he took in the young woman, but he said nothing.

"How is he, Doctor?" Austin asked quickly.

"Same as when you left. Unconscious." Malone had a New

England way of speaking, for he had been born in Massachusetts and studied medicine there. He had married a Southern girl and had come to take up his home in Virginia. Even though his heart was not in the Confederate cause, he stayed, like many others, because of family ties. Now his blue-gray eyes caught the agitation in the young woman. "You can sit beside him if you wish," Malone said.

Charlie followed Dr. Malone through the door that led off to the right and at once saw Boone lying stretched out on a cot. The sunlight threw golden bars across his face, and the white bandage he wore around his head made him look odd and out of proportion. Quickly moving across the room, she knelt down beside him and took his hand. Oblivious to the stares of the two men, she searched Boone's pale face for signs of hope. Finally, she turned and met the doctor's eyes. "How is he, Doctor?"

"I think he's going to be all right. If that bullet had been a half inch to the left, he'd be dead. As it is, it's given him a pretty bad concussion. The wound itself isn't so bad. I cleaned that out, and it shouldn't get any infection, but the concussion is what I'm worried about."

"Anything else we can do?" Austin asked.

"Just wait."

"Kin I stay with him?" Charlie asked.

"Don't see why not. May be a little noisy when patients start coming in, but they won't bother him." Questioning in his mind, *Sweetheart? Wife? Sister?* Dr. Malone finally said, "I don't know your name."

"Charlie Peace."

"Well, Miss Peace, this may go on for several days. I hope not, but I hate to give false hopes."

"I won't be in your way, Dr. Malone."

Malone nodded brusquely then walked out. Austin followed him. "I've got to get back to my office, Doctor. Send for me if anything develops, will you?"

"Nothing likely to happen," Malone answered. "That girl, is she his intended?"

Austin always had difficulty explaining the relationship between Boone and Charlie. Now it came again, and finally he gave it up as a bad job. "They're just good friends," he stated flatly. "Let me know if he wakes up."

Malone's eyes narrowed as Austin left. "Just good friends," he muttered. "What the devil does that mean?" He went over to a table and began rolling pills and stuffing them into glass bottles. In spite of the many illnesses and injuries he'd treated over the years and especially during the war, Dr. Malone had somehow retained the gentleness and goodwill he'd had as a young man just leaving medical school. "Just good friends," he said, rubbing the side of his nose with a thick forefinger. "Now they'll get married and live happily ever after." He continued with his task for ten minutes when the door opened. "Why, hello, Marie," Malone said. "You just missed your brother."

"I know. I was at his office waiting for him." Marie's face was drawn and her clothes wrinkled. In truth, she had not slept at all but, like Charlie, had waited for news. When Austin had not returned to his office, she had heard from one of his officers that there had been a duel and that one of the survivors, a Mr. Manwaring, was in Dr. Malone's office. She asked quickly, "How is he?"

"Not bad, considering he nearly took a bullet in the brain." Malone hesitated then nodded. "Miss Peace is in with him." He had delivered Marie into the world as a young doctor, and now his eyes took in his handiwork. She was, and always had been, an attractive young woman, but now he noted that her hands were unsteady. "You can go in and join Miss Peace."

"Thank you, Doctor." When Marie entered the room, Charlie looked up. "Has he awakened yet?"

"No," Charlie whispered. She was still holding Boone's hand. She had drawn up a straight chair and was sitting beside him. "He looks so weak and helpless. I'm scared, Marie."

Marie touched Charlie's shoulder then looked down at Boone's still face. "Dr. Malone says he'll be all right. It'll just take a little time." She said this more to comfort herself than Charlie, for she, too, was accustomed to a healthy, bronzed Boone Manwaring. Now he was weak, and his helplessness stirred her instincts, maternal and otherwise. She put her hand on his brow. "No fever," she said.

"Dr. Malone said it wasn't a bad wound as far as a cut's concerned, but he said something else. A con-something."

"Concussion, I expect," Marie said, finding another chair and sitting quietly beside Charlie. Finally, Marie asked, "What about Dillon?"

"I didn't hear."

"Austin didn't tell you?"

"I guess he was too set on takin' care of Boone, and I was too troubled to ask." She patted Boone's limp hand then stroked it gently. "He don't look good to me, Marie."

If Marie had been alone, she would have done exactly what Charlie Peace was doing, taken Boone's hand and held it. But somehow that office was taken—and by a person hopelessly in love with Boone Manwaring. As Marie mutely watched the two, she wondered what was going on in the young girl's heart. She knew Charlie was innocent as far as men were concerned, that she had not known a man. And there was something almost pathetic about the way she held on to Boone. *He's all the family she has. I can't begrudge her that,* Marie thought.

Finally, Marie arose and said briefly, "I'll be back in a moment, Charlie."

Stepping inside the office, she found Dr. Malone dismissing a patient with, "Take this home and give it to your wife. I'll be by early tomorrow."

"Thank you, Doc."

Marie waited until the man had left and then said, "Dr. Malone, just how bad is Boone?"

"I think he'll be all right." Then, studying Marie, he asked, "You got an interest in this young fella?"

Flustered by the doctor's question and the curious look in his eyes, she blushed. "I... He's a good friend."

"That's what Austin said he is to that young woman in there. He's got a lot of good-looking lady friends," Malone observed. Then, enjoying teasing Marie, he said, "A Yankee of some sort, ain't he?"

"No, he's from the West."

"Some talk around town about him, even before the duel." Malone clasped his hands behind his back. "I don't guess there'll be any more talk about his courage. From what Austin told me, he was as cool as a cucumber."

"What about Earl Dillon?"

"The devil looks after his own," Malone said wryly. "He didn't get a scratch."

"That's good."

Malone's eyebrows lifted. "How do you figure that?"

"Boone didn't want to kill a man—not over something like a card game or an insult. He wouldn't have fought this duel if Dillon hadn't insulted Miss Peace."

"Well, be that as it may, I think it's going to be all right."

"Dr. Malone, would it be all right if we took him to Hartsworth?" She saw a greater interest spark in the doctor's eyes. "We can take better care of him there. There will be three of us. My mother, Charlie, and me."

"I don't see why not. He ought to wake up soon, but I've got my rounds to make and nobody to stay with him." He pondered for a moment then nodded. "Get a wagon and fix a bed in it; then we'll get someone to carry him down. Drive slow and easy, and put him in bed the same way. I don't want that head shaken any more than it's already been."

"Thank you, Doctor." When Marie was back at Charlie's side, she said, "We're going to take him to Hartsworth, Charlie."

"Oh, that'll be good, Marie!" Charlie's eyes brightened. "We kin take real good keer of him there, cain't we?"

"Yes, Charlie. We can take care of him real good."

※

"Do you think he's looking better, Marianne?"

Charlie and Marianne had been changing the dressing on Boone's head while he lay still as a statue. They had made the trip very slowly, having to hold the horses back to their slowest possible walk. Finally when they had reached Hartsworth, the two women had dismounted, and soon Marie had gathered up enough strong men to put Boone in a blanket. They had each taken a corner and, as Charlie held the door open, had gone into the house.

Marianne had been caught off guard but at once said, "We'll put him in the green room at the end of the hall."

"That'll be good, Mother," Marie said. "It's bright and sunny there. When he wakes up, it won't be so gloomy."

They had installed Boone in the room, putting him into bed, and it had been Marianne who had removed his clothing with some help from Ketura—and had gotten him into a clean cotton nightshirt. She had been ready to bathe Boone's face when Charlie had come in and said, "Let me do that."

So Marianne watched as Charlie bathed Boone's face. "His breathing is steady," Marianne said reassuringly. "We had a man who fell out of the loft three years ago and got a bump on the head. He was out of it for two days. When he came back, he was good as ever. Still here as a matter of fact. That's Solomon, who works with the horses."

"He's just got to be all right," Charlie whispered.

Marianne Bristol studied Charlie for a moment then left the room. Once in the kitchen, she found Marie staring out the window. "Marie, are you all right?"

"Oh, Mother, I didn't hear you." As Marie turned around, Marianne could tell she was tense. "It could have been much worse," Marianne said.

"I know it could, and it would have been my fault if he had been killed!"

Surprised by her daughter's vehemence, Marianne asked, "Why would you think that?"

"Oh, not my fault alone!" Marie struggled to find the words to express the tumult within her breast. "I egged him into this! We all did it!" Angry, she said, "I get so sick of this *honor* business! How many young men do we know who are in their graves because of it—and older men, too! Remember Roy Jacobson? He had a wife and four children. He went out and fought a duel with shotguns, no less, with Henry Rodgers. Now does that give his wife any satisfaction? She's trying to raise those children alone. Her husband should have thought of that!"

Marianne had had the same sort of thoughts that Marie had just expressed, so she said, "Unfortunately, if men have courage, we think they're fools. But if they're cowards, we despise them."

"I know—and I was the biggest fool of all!" she said, her eyes narrowed. "I'll never make that mistake again, God willing."

Wanting to turn the conversation, Marianne asked, "What about Dillon?"

"Alive and well. Dr. Malone said the devil takes care of his own. But I'll tell you one thing, Mother. If he pursues this, I'll shoot him myself!"

"That's strong talk, Marie," Marianne said, staring into her daughter's determined eyes. "Do you feel that strongly about Boone?"

"I don't know. It bothered me, this dueling business, and it bothered Charlie worse." She paced the floor energetically then faced her mother. "Charlie's in love with him."

"I don't know about that. She's very attached to him, but that's only natural. With her family dead, he's the only friend she had who could come to her rescue."

"I expect they'll marry."

Marianne knew this fiery daughter of hers well. She noticed that, besides her typical determined spirit, something new had been added to her daughter's character—a tenderness and softness due to the near death of Boone Manwaring. It showed in the relaxed set of her shoulders and the gentleness that came when she spoke his name. Marianne wanted to pursue the matter but knew that it was not yet time. "Well," she said firmly, "we've got to get him well first."

"That's right. We'll do that, won't we, Mother?"

"Of course. Now I think *you* need to get a little rest. You don't look like you've slept in a week."

"All right. I'll lie down for a while." Once in her bedroom, Marie removed her dress, washed her face, and stretched out on her bed. She closed her eyes, but her mind was like wild birds in a cage. Thoughts fluttered and came like ghosts, whispering to her until she drifted off into a troubled sleep.

Darkness was all there was, except for tiny spots of light that would flicker on like candles far off in the distance. He could not see them clearly, and somehow his arms and legs would not move, and this frightened him. Sounds then came, but he could not understand them. They were voices—he knew that much—different voices. From time to time, as he struggled to free himself of the darkness, hands touched him and his brow and face would grow cool.

Although a week had passed, time had lost all meaning. The same troubled dream came to him again and again, and he tried to drive it away. Someone was standing close, but he could not see a face, for it was too dark.

Then one day light crept under his closed eyes. Cautiously he opened them, but the light was so strong he quickly shut them again. He stirred and found he could move. He reached his hand up and touched something around his head. He could not understand where he was or what was on his head. His thoughts swirled, confused and formless, until he heard a voice calling his name.

"Boone—Boone, are you awake?"

Carefully he lifted his eyelids and turned slightly away from the light. He was lying flat on his back; he knew that much. Someone bent over him as he opened his eyes. He saw Marie's face then grew dizzy. As he shook his head to clear it, agony shot through him.

"Don't move, Boone! Keep your head still!"

Marie's voice was gentle but insistent. "Do you know me, Boone?"

"Sure, but—" He opened his eyes again and once again grew dizzy. "I can see—two of you!" he exclaimed.

His words frightened Marie. She had never heard of such a thing, and she said quickly, "Just keep your eyes shut, then. You're just dizzy, I suppose."

Boone lay there, and memory flooded back. The scene flashed through him of Dillon turning, the muzzle of his pistol looming like a giant tunnel. "I got shot in the head, didn't I?"

"A crease along your temple, but you're going to be all right."

"What about Dillon?"

"He's all right."

Boone relaxed. "That's good," he said, aware of the faint scent of violets that Marie used. Weakly he asked, "Where am I?"

"At Hartsworth."

"How long have I been here?"

"About a week. Charlie and I didn't want to leave you in the doctor's office, so we brought you here where we could care for you better."

"Is Charlie here, too?"

"Yes, do you want me to get her?"

"I guess she'll come when she takes a notion."

Despite himself, Boone could not keep from trying to open his eyes. It seemed the natural thing to do, but every time he did, the double vision created havoc with his mind. He found, suddenly, that he was not as strong as he had thought. Desperately peering at Marie, he said, "Don't want to be trouble."

"How could you be that?" Marie put a hand over his lips. "Don't try to talk."

As Marie watched, she saw him begin to pass back into unconsciousness. She was frightened by the phenomenon of the double vision but did not know what to do. When he lay completely still, she leaned forward, kissed him lightly, and whispered, "Get well, Boone."

Suddenly the eyes opened, and Boone said clearly, "What's the kiss for?"

"I—I thought you were asleep."

"I was, but every time a beautiful woman kisses me, I wake up." Tired and dizzy, Boone wondered if he'd dreamed it. As he drifted back into the shadows, he said, "Glad you brought me here, Marie."

"He's going to be all right." Dr. Malone had arrived before noon to examine Boone carefully and discovered that the double vision was fading, now coming back only intermittently. "Not unusual," he said to the three women who gathered outside Boone's room to get the report. "It's something the brain does when it gets a pretty bad jolt. The eyes don't work right for a time, or the brain can't pick up what they're seeing. I don't know, but he tells me it's better." He smiled, saying, "He's got lots of good-looking nurses. I'd get sick myself if I could have you three wait on me."

Marianne and Marie were accustomed to Dr. Malone's teasing, but Charlie was not. She looked startled until she saw the twinkle in his eyes. Then she said, "We'll take good keer of him, Doctor."

"Don't let him get up. He'll be trying to, but he needs to lie down for several more days. A week would be better, but you'll never keep him in bed that long. But I want him to stay still. I've seen cases where people got better, then rushed it."

"I'll make him stay in that bed if I have to hog-tie him to it!" Charlie vowed. She lifted her head, determination in her dark blue eyes.

Malone grinned. "I expect you'd do it, Charlie. Well, I'll come back day after tomorrow. Nothing I can do that you three can't."

As Marianne left to see the doctor off, Marie said, "That's good news, isn't it, Charlie?"

"Yes, I was real worried."

"I was, too."

"Guess I'll go set beside him fer a spell," Charlie said.

"That's good. I'll see if I can cook something he can eat. Maybe just soup or something like that."

Marie left for the kitchen and spent the morning without seeing Boone. Charlie came in twice, once to get water and once to get some soup. "He says he's hungry," she said, her eyes bright.

"That's good, but just give him this soup. If he does all right with that, he can have something more solid tonight."

Late that afternoon, Charlie, who had left the house, looked up from her walk to see Austin riding up. She ran to meet him, and when he dismounted, her eyes were sparkling. She said at once, "Austin, he's much better."

"That's good." He reached out his hand, and she took it unthinkingly. "You look tired. I'll bet you've worn yourself out."

"No, I haven't done much. Just sat beside him. He's asleep now, though."

"Tell me about it while I unsaddle."

The two of them walked slowly to the barn, and Charlie spoke of Boone's condition as Austin put the saddle over a beam and turned the horse out into the pasture.

"Let's go down for a walk," Austin said. "I'll show you where I caught my first five-pound bass."

The two walked down around a copse of trees on the east side of the property where a large creek, still patched with bits of snow, gurgled among mossy stones. Reaching a pool twenty feet across, Austin said, "Right there. I still remember how my heart beat when I caught that big fish."

"How old were you?"

"Must have been about ten, I guess. Do you like to fish, Charlene?"

"Sure do. We caught a lot of trout up in the mountains."

"No trout around here that I know of. Here, sit down. We'll watch the sunset." Crisscrossing his legs, Austin began to speak of his boyhood. "I must've come to this pond a thousand times. I still miss it."

As the faint rays of sun bathed Charlie's face, she shook her head, sending her black ringlets into motion. When she smiled at him, there was a restfulness in her face that caused him to remark, "You were pretty worried about Boone."

"I sure was. I don't know what I would have done if he had died, Austin."

Seeing the warm innocence in Charlie's expression, Austin

asked suddenly, "What do you feel for Boone, Charlene?"

"Feel fer him?" Charlie looked down for a moment. "Why, I reckon I feel a lot fer him. If it wasn't fer him, I'd be all alone."

"No, you wouldn't, Charlene. You've got me, and Marie, and Mother," he said, longing to follow up the question, but not knowing how.

His words touched Charlie Peace. "I never knew there were folks as good as you, Austin, and your ma and your sister. We kind of lived alone, and all I knew was Ma and Pa. But you've taken me in, and I appreciate it." She wanted to say more but did not know what words to use. So instead she grasped his hand, then laughed. "I guess I'm pretty forward, holding hands with you."

"Don't mind a bit," Austin said, admiring her freshness and gently releasing her hand. Then, changing the subject, he said, "I've got to get out of that office, Charlene."

"You mean git out of the army?"

"No, I mean out of the office. It's driving me crazy."

"It sure would drive me crazy," Charlie said, "to be cooped up in a little place like that. What do you want to do, Austin?"

"I want to join the real army."

"You was wounded, wasn't you? When you were in the real army before?"

"That's all gone now. I'm fit enough."

Troubled, Charlie said, "I'd hate it if you had to leave."

"Would you, Charlene?"

"Why, sure I would! Don't you know that?"

Austin was amused. "I forgot how honest you are."

"Honest? What do you mean by that?"

"I mean many people aren't. They're always pretending to be something they're not."

"Why would they want to do that?"

"Why, I guess to catch a spouse."

"I'd want no man I'd have to catch!"

"Why, sure! You catch him, and he catches you!"

"Maybe it's so," Charlie said.

"So what about you and Boone?" Austin blurted out, unable to help himself.

"Oh, I don't know, Austin."

Austin thought she did know, but he said nothing. Finally, he rose and said, "It's getting dark. Let's go home."

When the two arrived back at Hartsworth, Austin was greeted by Marianne and Marie. While supper was being prepared, Austin visited with Boone. "You got it made, Boone. Just lie around and get waited on day and night. Some men have all the luck."

Boone smiled. "You're right about that. I'm a natural-born sponge. Take all the attention I can get. What's happening with you, Austin?"

Austin expressed his desire to be out of the office and into an active, fighting outfit. He ended by saying, "I'm going to get into this fight if I have to desert and enlist as a private."

"I wish I felt that strongly."

"It's different for you," Austin said. "I've been thinking about what you said about people in the far-off parts of this country, way out in Colorado and Oregon. This must seem like another world, but for us it's everything."

Cautiously Boone asked, "Do you really think you can win this war, Austin?"

"I don't think there's a chance. But one of these days I'll have to explain to my sons what I did, and I don't want to have to tell them I shuffled paper in an office."

Austin stayed until suppertime then sat in the parlor afterward with Marie while Charlie was in with Boone.

Marie was unusually quiet, so Austin asked, "What's troubling you, Marie?"

"I've been going over the books, Austin, and I visited with Mr. Keith down at the bank. I don't see how we're going to make it."

"What did Keith say?" Keith had been their banker for years and had been kind, but times were hard, Austin knew. "Is he going to give us time to pay the bills?"

"He'd like to, but I could see he's getting pressure from others. We've got to get some money to pay at least the interest, Austin. Maybe sell some land."

"No! Not that!" Austin said quickly. Then gloom descended on him. "I've tried to put this all out of my mind, but we've got to face up to it, Marie."

"Maybe we could go to another bank in another place. Maybe in Charlotte."

"If our own bank won't lend us money, why should they lend us money in Charlotte?"

"I know. It was just a thought."

"It's going to take some faith," Austin said. "God will have to help us through this, sister."

"He never fails. He may not come always right when we want Him," she said, forcing a smile, "but He never forsakes those who trust Him."

"What do you think about Charlene and Boone?" Austin asked abruptly.

"I think she's in love with him."

"What about him?"

"I don't know. . . . Good night, Austin."

WITNESS IN HEAVEN

"Good night, Marie." Austin watched her go then went to his own room, thinking of the enormous debt that had gathered around Hartsworth. He wanted to get angry at his father, who was responsible for a goodly portion of it, but then he thought, *At least he's trying what he's never done before. I can't let myself get bitter. Something will turn up. God won't let us down!*

Chapter 20

"Stretch Forth Thine Hand"

In early April Boone sat in the rocker at Hartsworth, his feet planted firmly on the floor, listening as Marie, dressed in cobalt blue and ivory, read aloud. From outside the window came the sound of laughing voices, black and rich. Solomon and Alexander, who had helped carry Boone from the wagon in to his bed, were working in the flower garden, and with half his mind Boone was listening to Solomon tell about catching an enormous catfish on a trotline. He smiled at the exaggerated report: "...and I tell you that fish was as big as any *man* you ever seed, Alexander! Why, if I had 'nother 'un like that, we could feed this whole plantation for a month!"

"You find Solomon's fishing feats more interesting than this book, don't you, Boone?"

Looking up swiftly, Boone saw that Marie had closed the novel and was smiling at him quietly. "Well, I guess I'm not much for novels."

Marie laid the book down on the table beside her and examined Boone. "Your color's better. I think I'll change your bandage."

"It's all right. I don't need it."

"That's what *you* say. You just hate to be fussed with." Marie rose and carefully untied the bandage. It adhered a little to the raw wound, and he winced. "Sorry," she said, "I'm not a very good doctor." She looked down at the red scar and murmured, "I think it's finally healing up. I believe you're going to have a permanent scar, though." Boone reached up to touch it, and she slapped at his hand. "Don't meddle with that! I think we'll leave it open to the air for a while, and then I'll put some ointment on it and bandage it before you lie down again."

"It itches! I'd like to claw at it!" Boone protested.

"Well, that's all you need to open it again! Now leave it alone!"

Boone grinned at her, his eyes suddenly alive. "You're a hard taskmaster, Marie. When are you going to let me out of this room?"

"Dr. Malone said tomorrow, but you're not going far. Just for short walks."

Marie sat back down beside him, and they both listened to the voices of the men working in the garden. "They sound happy, don't they?" Boone said. "Do you ever talk to them about what it feels like to be a slave?"

Startled, Marie shook her head. Even dressed as simply as she was, Boone noticed she had the gift, as did Austin, of making the poorest of clothing look somehow graceful and right. Her hair was bound by only a single thong, for she had washed it and it was not quite dry. The rich chestnut color gave off glints of a reddish color as the sun struck it, and unconsciously she patted it as she thought about his question. "It's something we've always taken for granted here, up until the war—but we won't anymore. I don't think slavery will last even if the South wins. It's such a bad system."

Boone gave her a curious glance. "What does that mean?" he asked. "You'll just set them free?"

"That's what I'd like to do, and I know many others who feel the same way," she replied, continuing to talk about slavery. Boone, not being from the South, had not seen slavery firsthand. But he had read Harriet Beecher Stowe's *Uncle Tom's Cabin* and wondered if the mistreatment of slaves was as bad as the woman had presented it. When he brought the matter up, Marie said, "It's very bad, to be honest, Boone. In some places, I mean. It all depends on the owner. None of our slaves have ever been mistreated that I know of. If we sold a slave now, we would be paid in Confederate money, which is worthless. And without selling a slave, we'd have no money to hire labor—which is what we'll have to do once this war is over anyway."

Boone said thoughtfully, "It looks like the South is in a no-win situation. Even if you win the war, slavery's not going to be in existence forever."

"I think that's right."

"Do you worry about the future, Marie?"

For one terrible moment, Marie thought Boone had become aware of the fact that she and Austin had talked about marrying for money. But when his hazel eyes were guileless, she realized he was simply asking out of interest. "Things are very bad, Boone. You can see the place going down. I wish you could have seen it before the war. We can't afford to fix anything now. Cotton's not worth raising, and there's no cash money if you raise other crops."

Although Boone had seen many dilapidated farms and plantations on his search and encountered the hopelessness that existed among many of the planters, he was still disturbed by Marie's attitude of failure. However, he hadn't known how bad it really was until now. Finally, he said slowly, "It's too bad. This is a fine plantation."

"It's been our life, I suppose you might say, Boone. My brothers—Paul and Austin—and I know every foot of it. Paul's now in Alabama, and Austin is in the army. So it's rather ghostly. A lot of memories bring back those days when we were all here and there was no war."

Wanting to change her mood, Boone asked, "Why don't you read some from the Bible?"

Immediately Marie pushed her thoughts away. "You like that better than novels?"

"I never read the Bible much. My people weren't religious."

"That's a shame. Some of my earliest memories," Marie said, "were listening to Mother read the Bible." She opened her Bible and riffled through the pages. "I always liked the story of Zacchaeus. Do you know it?"

"No," he said.

Marie began to read from the book of Luke, chapter 19, her love for the scriptures evident. That puzzled Boone, but at the same time he was drawn to it.

" 'And Jesus entered and passed through Jericho. And, behold, there was a man named Zacchaeus, which was the chief among the publicans, and he was rich. And he sought to see Jesus who he was; and could not for the press, because he was little of stature. And he ran before, and climbed up into a sycomore tree to see him: for he was to pass that way. And when Jesus came to the place, he looked up, and saw him, and said unto him, Zacchaeus, make haste, and come down; for to day I must abide at thy house. And he made haste, and came down, and received him joyfully. And when they saw it, they all murmured, saying, That he was gone to be guest with a man that is a sinner. And Zacchaeus stood, and said unto the Lord; Behold, Lord, the half of my goods I give to the poor; and if I have taken any thing from any man by false accusation, I restore him fourfold. And Jesus said unto him, This day is salvation come to this house forsomuch as he also is a son of Abraham. For the Son of man is come to seek and to save that which was lost.'"

When Marie stopped reading, Boone said thoughtfully, "That's a strange story. He was a short little fellow, wasn't he? Couldn't see over the heads of the people."

"Yes. I've always loved this story," Marie murmured thoughtfully. "Perhaps because Zacchaeus stands for all the people who somehow get hungry for the Lord."

"I guess I've never had anything like that happen to me."

"I think," Marie said quietly, "that God calls every man and every woman at some point. I was only fourteen years old when I felt the Lord speaking to my heart."

"Were you in a church?"

"I'd been in church all my life, but it happened when I was out in the fields. I was gathering wildflowers and not thinking of God at all, and then suddenly I was thinking about God."

Boone, intently interested, leaned forward slightly. "What was it like, Marie?"

"Oh, it wasn't anything very dramatic. At first I thought it was just something in my mind. I thought of the sermon the pastor had preached a few weeks earlier about a woman who touched the robe of Jesus. She had been sick a long time, and when Jesus came by, she thought, *If I can just touch his robe, I'll be healed.*" Marie smiled and continued, "It came into my head, or my heart, or whatever part of us hears God, that I needed to touch Jesus, too."

"What did you do?"

"I sat down under a big chestnut tree, and somehow I knew God was there—not just under the tree, but inside my heart. And as I began to think about Jesus dying for the sins of the world, I began to cry." Marie was silent, remembering. Then she said, "I began to pray and asked God to come into my heart somehow—and He did." Her eyes filled with tears, and she dashed them away. Looking rather shamefaced, she took a handkerchief out of her pocket. "Sorry, I didn't mean to subject you to all this."

"That's all right. I can see it was very real to you."

"It still is," Marie said. "From that day on I've been a Christian. That's why I like the story of Zacchaeus, I suppose. He got so hungry for something in his life that he made a fool out of himself by climbing up in a tree. Don't you suppose his friends must've laughed at him? After all, the Bible says he was a prominent man."

"A lawyer or something like that?"

"Probably a tax collector!" Marie laughed. "Can you see one of the government officials here climbing up a tree to see a preacher come to town? Not very likely! In any case, Zacchaeus must have had something happen to him up in that tree."

"I suppose so. You say he offered to pay back everybody he had cheated four times as much as he had gotten?"

"Yes, and that's not like a tax collector, is it? I think the Lord Jesus calls to everyone, but we don't all hear it the same way. Sometimes people are in church. I've been at camp meetings, Boone, when the Spirit of God moved, and I've seen people fall to the ground, struck with the power of God."

"I've heard about that. Dave, a friend of mine, said his great-grandfather was at one of George Whitefield's meetings, back about the time of the Revolution, I think. He told the story so many times, about how whole acres of people fell over. Dave never forgot it. I've wondered about that."

"I think it's far more common for people to just know that God is calling them, and then somehow or other they ask Him into their lives.... The last verse is one of my favorites. I think it was the first verse I ever memorized: 'For the Son of man is come to seek and to save that which was lost.'" She put her finger on the Bible and held it where he could see it. "Look, I've underlined what I think is the most important word."

Boone looked and then said with surprise, "You think the word 'that' is more important than the other words?"

"Yes, because I think God wants to save every part of us. Not just our soul, but our body and all that we are. *That* which was lost. Whatever we've lost, God's going to save it for us."

"That's pretty deep for me."

"Maybe I'm oversimplifying, but back in the book of Matthew, in the twelfth chapter," she said, riffling through her Bible to find the place, "there was a man in the synagogue who had a withered hand. The enemies of Jesus wanted to catch Him healing somebody on the Sabbath because that was against the Jewish law. Can you guess what He did?"

"From what I've heard about Jesus, I guess He healed him."

"That's right. In verse 13 He said to the young man, 'Stretch forth thine hand. And he stretched it forth; and it was restored whole, like as the other.'" Marie looked up. "I think God is saying that most of us have problems, and Jesus saw this man's problem as his crippled hand. So He told him to stretch forth the thing that needed fixing, and He healed it. Sometimes there are things in life that are a lot more troublesome than a bad hand."

"How do you figure that? It's pretty bad to have a crippled hand."

"Is it worse to have a crippled mind or a crippled heart, Boone?"

"I—I've never thought of it."

Seeing the astonishment on Boone's face, Marie said, "I've seen so much death since the war started. Our neighbors down the road lost their only two sons in the war, one at Shiloh and one at Fredericksburg. The father wasn't a Christian, and he grew very bitter. I wondered if he'd actually die of grief. But then he was able, with the help of a pastor and some good Christian friends, to hold that grief out to the Lord. Don't you see, Boone? It was as if God were saying, 'Stretch forth thy loss, and I will heal it.'"

"That's asking a lot even of God!"

"I think God's the only One who can heal us from things like that, Boone, and there are other things. Some men are lost in lust and others in drink; some get caught up in making money. Every one of us clings to something."

"You couldn't have had much sin in your life when you were fourteen years old."

"I had enough that I knew I needed a heart change. I was very envious, for one thing, of what other girls had, and I had to ask God to heal that in my own life. . . . Boone, I don't want to preach at you, but Jesus did come to seek and to save that which was lost. You almost lost your life, and I can't tell you how distraught I was thinking about your going out to meet God unprepared."

Boone looked down, unable to meet her eyes. "I had a bad time myself. All I could think of was, if Earl Dillon kills me, I'm lost forever."

"But you don't have to be lost forever, Boone."

"My life's a little more complicated than a fourteen-year-old girl's."

"You know better than that, Boone. Some people don't find God until they're in their sixties or seventies. We all need peace in our heart, and Jesus is the only peace there is."

As Boone listened, he felt a strange mixture of fear and hope. He saw the honesty and the love in Marie Bristol's eyes, heard the certainty in her voice, and knew that he lacked what she had.

"No one can force anyone to become a Christian, though," Marie said. "No one twisted Zacchaeus's arm. He was so hungry for God that he climbed a tree to find someone to help him. I don't know what kind of pain, or grief, or loss was in his life, but when he took Jesus home, a miracle happened inside his heart. And that same miracle—of Jesus coming into your heart—is what every man, woman, and young person needs."

"Jesus Christ is very real to you, isn't He, Marie?"

"He's more real to me, Boone," Marie said, "than this chair I'm sitting in. And that's why I want you to know the same peace."

Shocked at the feelings inside him, Boone knew he could not leave this behind him. The decision would only grow more and more demanding. "Thank you for talking to me, Marie, and for explaining this. I'll—I'll think on it."

"Would you do one thing for me, Boone?"

"Why, certainly, if I can."

"Would you let me pray for you?"

Boone was embarrassed, but he nodded. She began to pray very quietly, "Oh Lord, this is your wandering child, Boone Manwaring. You've known him even before he was born, when he was in his mother's womb, and now I'm asking You, Lord, to increase the hunger in his heart until he has to climb a tree, or stand up before the world, or whatever, in order to find his peace with You through the Lord Jesus Christ. Make this for him more important than anything in life, and I will thank You for it in the name of Jesus. Amen."

Boone opened his eyes and whispered huskily, "You're some woman, Marie Bristol."

Marie shook her head impatiently. "I'm not much, but I have a great Savior. And one day you'll have that same Savior, Boone."

*

Austin looked up with surprise to see Charlie Peace, who had entered and stood over his desk. "Well," he said, "this is a welcome relief. What are you up to, Charlene?"

"I've come to go shoppin', and you're takin' me," she said, smiling, dressed prettily in a green dress with matching shawl. "Come along now."

Austin rose with alacrity. "Yes, sir! I mean, ma'am! Anything to get out of this office." He turned to the sergeant who was standing over to one side and said, "As you can see, I have urgent duty. If any of my superiors call, tell them I'm on urgent military business."

The sergeant grinned broadly. "Yes, sir! I can certainly do that!"

Charlie took Austin's arm as they left the War Department. The sun was shining, and she seemed happy. "I've finally decided," she said, "that I've got to do somethin' to pay my own way. I've been like a leech livin' off of you and your people."

"Don't be foolish, Charlene! You've been a guest."

"A nonpayin' guest, but I've got a purse full of gold coins, and we're goin' to load the wagon up with everythin' we kin find that will help back at Hartsworth. I talked to Solomon, and he gave me a list of things they need in the forge and some of the equipment that's got to be replaced. Then I want to git some groceries, whatever's to be had here in the way of staples."

Surprised but pleased with her generosity, Austin spent the next three hours escorting her up and down the streets of Richmond. She had driven the wagon in herself, and Austin moved it several times, loading it until the axles creaked.

"I don't think the wagon will hold any more, and you've spent a fortune!"

"Not enough. I want to buy somethin' nice for your mother and Marie." She tugged at his arm, and he laughed, accompanying her into Anderson's Dress Shop. "The first time I came in here," she said as they entered, "I was wearin' buckskins, and I chewed tobacco."

"You didn't!"

"Yes, I did! Just to make Boone and the store clerk, Mrs. Jones, mad. Hello, Mrs. Anderson," she said, smiling at the owner. "Got to have somethin' very nice fer Mrs. Bristol and Miss Bristol."

Austin enjoyed the buying spree. He watched as Charlie picked out some things for the two women. As she paid for them, she said, "Now I guess we can go." Turning, she smiled graciously. "Thank you, Mrs. Anderson. You've been a great help." Austin could not help but think how much she had changed since the first time he had met her. Her grammar was still sometimes prone to go off course, and when she forgot, she would walk with the open stride of a mountain man. But no one looking at her now would have thought it was the same young woman he had met such a short time before. When they got outside, he said, "Why don't you stay over tonight? We'll go out and get something to eat."

"You know, I believe I will. Maybe," she said with a mischievous light in her eyes, "I kin git my old room at the Spotswood. I had my first all-over bath there, except fer the creek."

Austin laughed aloud, attracting the attention of several passersby. "You do say the most audacious things!"

"I guess a young woman ought not to talk 'bout bathin' to her escort."

"Well, it's not the most common conversation." He looked at her warmly. "You've changed a lot, Charlene."

"If I have, it's because of Marie and you and your mother. I know I still ain't a lady like those two—"

Austin took her hand and kissed it. "I think you're a lady," he said quietly.

Charlie stood there, shocked, for no one had ever kissed her hand before, and she did not know what to say or do. Seeing her confusion, Austin said, "Let's get your room."

It was a fine night for both of them. There was a minstrel show passing through, and Charlie had never seen one. She laughed until her sides hurt, and when they got back to the hotel, she said, "They shore kin play them banjos, cain't they? And how do they think of all them things to say?"

Austin was pleased Charlie had enjoyed her evening. They were now alone in the hallway outside her room. "I guess they say it over and over again," he quipped. "It was fun, wasn't it?"

"You reckon Boone ever went to a minstrel show?"

"I'm sure he has."

"I don't know," she reflected.

Austin plunged in. "I've been wondering about you and Boone, and so has Marie. How do you feel about him? I don't mean to pry, but it's only natural we'd wonder."

"Well, I think a lot of him, Austin. I guess you see that."

"Do you love him?"

"I—I'm not rightly sure I know what love is. I didn't go in fer courtin' and such up in the mountains."

Her statement bothered Austin. "Does he love you?" he asked quietly.

"I—I don't know." Charlie turned her head away then said swiftly, "Good night, Austin. It was fun going to the show." She slipped inside the door, shut it, and then leaned back against it, thinking about what Austin had just said. *Does Boone really love me? Do I care for him?* She sat down at the desk, turned up the lamp, and, taking her quill, began to write rapidly:

> *Austin just asked me if Boone loved me, and I sed I didnt know. And then he asked me if I loved him, and I didnt know that either. Austin looked kind of funny when he asked the question, and I dont know what he thinks bout me. It sure is hard tryin to grow up and be a lady!*

Malcolm Leighton had come to Hartsworth with a set purpose, and now he faced Marie out in the scuppernong arbor. The two had come out, at his insistence, to where the spring breeze shook the tender vines, shutting off the view from the house. "I guess I'll get right to it, Marie," he said. "I want you to marry me."

Leighton's bluntness threw Marie off balance. Startled, she knew she could no longer put the matter off. "You've put up with a lot from me, haven't you, Malcolm?"

"It isn't that, but a man needs to know where he stands. I

know you think I've been a woman chaser, and maybe I have, but that's all over. I want to get married and start a family." He looked around and said, "I know, Marie, that you've been worried about Hartsworth."

"It's common knowledge," Marie said in an acid tone. "Everybody knows everybody's business in Richmond."

"Your situation's not much different from others'," Leighton said, shrugging. "There's no money, and with this war on, there's not likely to be any. I know how much you love Hartsworth, and I could keep it. The ships have done well, and even if the South loses, I've got enough money to pay off the loans."

"How do you know how much they are?"

"I talked to Keith down at the bank. He didn't give me the exact amount, of course, but roughly. He let slip what it would take to clear all the paper off this place."

Despondent, Marie knew that Malcolm Leighton had an affection, of sorts, for her, but this was not her idea of romance. So she said at once, "Malcolm, I don't love you as a woman should love a man whose bed she'll share the rest of her life."

Leighton blinked with surprise at her bluntness. "That's coming right out with it," he said. "I know you're an honest girl, Marie, but you've got to be practical. I've already told you I care for you. Maybe you don't love me now, but," he said, smiling and pulling her to him, "I can make you love me. After we're married you'll find out what it's like to be a wife. You'll love me then."

Marie wanted to protest, but he kissed her then. Something in her protested, but at the same time she was thinking, *Maybe he's right. Maybe I could learn to love him.* He was strong, and practically every unmarried young woman in Richmond would have loved to be in her position. But when he lifted his lips and said, "Marry me, Marie," she said, "I think there's more to marriage than a plantation." She thought this might discourage him, but he merely shook his head and insisted. Then finally she said, almost in desperation, "Give me a month."

"All right. One month it is. Are we engaged?"

"No, not even that. We have an *understanding*. In one month I'll give you my answer. I know this seems hard to you, but a woman can't make a mistake about things like this."

Leighton stared at her. "A man can't make a mistake either. I care for you, Marie, and you'll care for me, too. I promise you."

***

The next morning Boone came downstairs for breakfast, surprising Marie and Marianne, who were already seated. "I think I've been an invalid long enough," he said, taking a seat. "I'll be moving back into town today."

"Don't go yet, Boone," Marianne said. "It's too soon."

"I'm fine, Mrs. Bristol. You're a good nurse. You, Marie, and Charlie have been more than I deserve."

At that moment Charlie entered. "What are you doin' downstairs? I didn't tell you you could come down to breakfast! I was takin' it up to you!"

"I'm afraid I'm going to get spoiled," Boone said. He looked fit in spite of the bandage still around his head. He touched it lightly, saying, "This is all healed up pretty much. It's just so ugly I want to cover it, but I feel I've got to go to town."

All three women protested, but in the end Boone left. Charlie wanted to drive him, and he permitted that. When she dropped him off at the Spotswood, she said, "Why cain't I git me a room here, too, Boone?"

"You're much more comfortable at Hartsworth. I'll be looking around for a place."

"Don't you do too much," she warned.

"I won't."

He watched as she drove back out of town. Then he entered the Spotswood and again signed up for a room. It was a strange feeling, and soon he grew unhappy with the smallness of the room and left to walk the streets. He hadn't thought much of religion before his talk with Marie, but now he was aware of God's presence. He knew for a certainty he'd have to make a decision about what to do with Jesus. *A man has to face up to this matter of salvation sooner or later—and I think with me it's going to be sooner.*

He encountered Clay Rocklin as he walked. Pleased, the colonel said, "Well, you're up and around, Boone."

"Yes, Colonel, I am. I hope I don't meet Earl Dillon."

"You haven't heard about Dillon?"

"I guess not."

"Well, you won't have to be worried about him. He joined the army. Some kind of a political appointment. He'll be serving in the western theater around Atlanta. He'll have his hands full there, and all the fighting he wants."

"I'm glad it turned out as it did. I'd hate to have his blood on my hands."

Clay studied Boone then said, "Things are happening. We're taking the army up to meet Grant."

"Didn't Marie say that your wife will be having her baby soon?"

Clay's eyes grew cloudy. "That's right," he said. "Although I don't have any choice, of course, this battle couldn't have come at a worse time for us."

After the men talked and Clay moved away, walking rapidly down the street, Boone thought of Austin Bristol. *I'd better go tell him I'm here. Maybe we can see each other.* When he reached the War Department, the sergeant informed him, "Why, he's not here anymore. Just transferred today."

"Transferred to where? To what?" Boone demanded.

"This mornin' he pitched a regular fit, the lieutenant did. Said he wasn't going to shuffle one more piece of paper. Got himself transferred immediately into the Stonewall Brigade. Guess he'll be serving under Colonel Rocklin. Got to be kind of a family affair. Colonel Rocklin, his boy, his uncle, and now his cousin."

"What about you, Sergeant?"

"Well, I'm goin', too. As a matter of fact, I think about every able-bodied man who can carry a gun's gonna go. It's gonna take that to stop Grant, from what I hear. Word is, he's got a hundred thousand men, and we don't have half of that. We'll stop 'em, though. The Lord will be with us."

Boone told the burly sergeant, "Wish I was a praying man. I'd pray for you all."

"Never too late to start," the sergeant replied.

Leaving the office, Boone noticed the excitement in the air. When he reached his hotel, he sat outside and watched the activity—wagons rumbled up and down the street carrying supplies, and men moved quickly. Somehow he felt left out, like a man without a purpose. Finally that night he went to bed, and early the next morning he saw the Army of Northern Virginia leave. He heard the trumpet and saw flags flying high as the troops began their march northward. The men, some of them in ragged uniforms but looking determined, formed a serpentine line that headed out from the camp. He saw Clay

WITNESS IN HEAVEN

at the head of the brigade and looked for Austin, then finally caught sight of him walking alongside the troops.

"I wish I were going!" he whispered. "But it's none of my fight." He left town, riding restlessly as he struggled with his own heart. He'd heard Marie quote one of the fathers of the church once, saying, "'Man has a hollow spot in his heart—and will never be content until it is filled with God Himself.'" Now as his horse's hooves pounded along the road, he said, head down and weary with life, "Guess I'll have to get that spot filled if I ever want any kind of peace."

When he went to bed that night, sleep would not come. Finally, he arose, feeling depressed, as if he had no hope or aspirations for the future.

Then just as dawn began to color the skies, he knelt beside the bed and cried out, "God—I'm not even fit to pray to You, but I've got to find some kind of peace!"

Chapter 21

Sacrifice in the Wilderness

Ten miles west of Fredericksburg, Virginia, lies a region known as "the Wilderness." It had been called this long before the Civil War, and in the early eighteenth century German colonists had tried to tame this wild section of country and failed. They'd cut timber to shore up mine tunnels, planked roads, and chopped wood to fuel iron-smelting operations, then abandoned their endeavors. The forest grew back quickly, so by the time Ulysses S. Grant brought the Army of the Potomac out of Washington to face the Army of Northern Virginia, led by Robert E. Lee, the country was nothing but an impenetrable second-growth woodland.

Battles had been fought here before, for in May 1863 Lee and Stonewall Jackson had fought the battle of Chancellorsville, defeating General Joe Hooker in a savage and confused battle. At this spot Stonewall Jackson had been shot in the faint light of dusk by his own men and had died on May 10 from his wounds. Now, almost a year later, Robert E. Lee's army was drawn up near Orange Court House just west of the Wilderness. It straddled a broad turnpike that led to Fredericksburg, and it was on May 5 that these two rival armies marched into the heart of the Wilderness and began a fight that actually lasted to the end of the war, since it proceeded southward until Grant's army was knocking at the gates of Richmond.

The Army of Northern Virginia had 65,000 men, led by Generals Richard Elwell and James Longstreet. Grant's Army of the Potomac was 120,000 men, led by staunch commanders such as Hancock, Warren, and Sedgewick. Meade was ostensibly in command of this particular army, but Grant, knowing that Robert E. Lee and his Army of Northern Virginia were the real adversary, came personally. So in all truth the battle of the Wilderness, and those following in rapid succession, was fought by Grant against Lee.

Grant's advantage in numbers would count for much less in this theater, due to the impenetrable thickets. His artillery would be nullified, for few guns could be used over this terrain. Neither could masses of men be marched rapidly from one place to another through the undergrowth. As the two commanders eyed the spot that fate had chosen for the battle, both of them must have been apprehensive, for it would not be a classic battle. Here there would be no long lines of men neatly arranged in regiments and brigades, but small, struggling groups, broken up and fragmented, hidden from even their own lines by the thickets, vines, and saplings that clawed at their faces.

The collision point came promptly on May 5. Advancing Confederates were met by skirmishers of Grant's army on the turnpike, and from that point both Lee and Grant began to feed men into the furnace of war, much as men would feed wood into a stove to make the fire burn hotter. The battle was almost impossible to control. No man could see more than a few yards in any direction, and movements ahead of him might be his own fellow soldiers. In truth, many men were killed by those wearing the same uniform. Soon the rattle of musketry filled the Wilderness, and the roar of cannons added a solemn refrain as the men fought, almost blindfolded by the terrain. General Hancock said later, after the battle, that men who tried to make a charge could not tell where their enemies were until they ran full tilt into them. The generals knew where the battle lines were only by listening to the sounds of musketry, which was not very helpful, for musket fire made a staccato series of explosions throughout all the battlefield. Often whole divisions broke up into fragments, running into flanking fire. Gaps in the opposing line suddenly appeared but went unexploited because nobody could see them.

As the sun rose and fell, the battle was fierce. In many cases, men fought hand to hand, clubbing each other with muskets, stabbing with bayonets or even with pocketknives. The Battle of the Wilderness was, for all practical purposes, not one battle but hundreds or even thousands of battles where men stalked blindly and bled their lives out into the red clay. The wounded lay where they fell, for no medical assistance could be brought into the furnace of battle. As the night came on, many died alone, crying out for their mothers or to their God, and some simply and silently stepped across the threshold into death. Perhaps the most terrible part of the battle occurred when the dry leaves caught fire, sparked by musket fire, and a wall of flame began sweeping across the Wilderness. Men fled in panic, more frightened of being burned to death than of being shot down by their enemies.

But the wounded could not flee. Those who were too badly wounded to walk had to lie there, watching the flames licking the dry timber and knowing that their doom was sealed. After the war was over, many hardened soldiers would say, "I saw many hard things during the war, but nothing was harder than to hear the screams of wounded men as they were burned to death in the Battle of the Wilderness."

※

Clay Rocklin ducked behind a tree as the roar of musket fire shook the earth around him and yelled, "What's your report? I can't hear!"

The lean lieutenant, who had a bloody rag wrapped around his forehead, said, "It's General Longstreet, Colonel. He's been shot."

"Was he killed?" Clay asked rapidly.

"No—no, sir. Badly wounded, and by our own men."

"What else is happening?"

"General Ewell wants you to move your brigade over to the left. He thinks he sees an opening in the line there."

Clay's eyes swept the battlefield that was like no other he had ever seen, looking for an opening in the dense woods. "Report back and tell him we'll move forward, but it will be slow work."

"Yes, Colonel."

As soon as the courier turned to make his way through the thickets, Clay turned to Major Tom Merrick, saying, "Orders from General Ewell, Major. He says go forward. Over to our left." Then he added, "General Longstreet's down. Not dead, but badly wounded."

Merrick's blue eyes fastened on the colonel. "We can't spare him, can we?"

"I suppose somebody will have to step in his place, but I don't know who it will be. How many men have we lost?"

"Hard to say, Colonel. We haven't got reports back from down the line, but it hasn't been cheap. When do you want to move forward?"

"You go down that side of the line, Major. I'll go down this one. We've got to move together as much as possible. You have a watch?"

"Yes, sir!" Merrick pulled out a large silver watch. "Belonged to my grandfather."

The two men compared times, and Clay said, "We move out in exactly thirty minutes. Tell the men to try to stay together."

"Yes, sir!"

Clay moved down the line as musket balls whined through the air, some of them ricocheting off trees and crying like a banshee, the most unnerving sound of all. Clay came upon the third company, where his son Denton crouched behind a log, looking over into the smoke-filled woods. "Dent, we move forward in thirty minutes!"

"Yes, sir!" Denton turned to look at his father. His face was already scarred from an earlier wound, but his eyes were bright with battle. "You're not going forward with the line, are you, sir?"

"You can't lead from behind," Clay said, grinning. "Keep your head down, son." He wanted to say more but knew that Dent understood. Moving on down the line, he spoke to the men, encouraging them. When he reached the edge of the regiment's line, he looked at his watch. "Still fifteen minutes to go." He traversed the line of battle again and moved the other way, running into Major Merrick. "Just checking, Tom. I'll say a word to the boys."

As he made his way along, speaking to as many of the men as he could, he ran into Claude Bristol.

"What are you doing here, Claude? I left you back at headquarters!"

His face blackened with powder, Bristol said, "I thought I'd come and help the boys out a little bit."

"You don't need to be here, Claude."

"Don't send me back, Clay," Claude said quickly, looking down the line. "Austin's down there. I wanted to show him I'm good for something."

"You put me in a bad position, Claude. Marianne would hate me if you got yourself killed."

"No, she wouldn't." Claude Bristol's mouth tensed. "As long as we've been married, Marianne's been waiting for me to do one thing that was unselfish. I've gotten this far. Let me go the rest of the way."

Clay hesitated. He knew Claude was not in fighting condition, that he was soft from easy living, but then, so were many of the other men. But after studying Claude's face, he said, "You stay with me, Claude. We'll go along with the line together."

"Yes, sir!"

Clay moved down the line and found Austin, who was peering into the thick smoke. Turning around, Austin grinned. "A little different from my usual job, Colonel."

"You watch yourself."

"You, too, sir." He glanced down the line at his father, an odd expression in his eyes. "You're not letting him go, are you?"

"He'll be with me," Clay responded.

From down the line, Claude winked at his son. "A little warm work for an old man."

"You shouldn't be here, Father," Austin yelled down the line, then moved toward his father so he could hear his response.

Claude did not answer. "I wish you weren't going in, Austin.

I haven't said this before, not as I should, but I've been very proud of you and Paul." He put his hand on his son's shoulder and squeezed it warmly. "I'm praying God will spare you in this battle and that you'll become a better man than I ever was."

Austin started to reply, but there was a lump in his throat. Then his father was gone, striding after Clay Rocklin. Austin turned back, tears in his eyes. He dashed them away, trying to focus his mind on the battle that was to come.

Clay studied the hands on his watch, and when the time came, he called out, "Charge! Stick together as close as you can!" This was the last command he was able to give to more than a handful of men. Then the brigade moved forward through the tangles into the very teeth of the enemy.

Clay had intended to stay back, but within ten minutes after the brigade moved forward, it was hard to tell where "back" was. All around him the fury of battle surged. He saw men drop silently to the earth; others kicked and screamed. Clay fought blindly, but finally, as the sun began to go down, he was miraculously reached by a messenger with word to fall back. He lifted his voice, saying, "All to the rear! Everyone to the rear! Withdraw slowly!"

The withdrawal took some time, but only when they were back out of the immediate range of the guns of the enemy did Clay have time to check their losses. His heart bounded with relief when he saw Denton stride over, his face grim as he said, "We lost a lot of good men."

"Have you seen Austin?"

"No, he was on the other side of the line, wasn't he?"

"Yes. I'm going to pull the men together. You help Major Merrick."

For the next hour Clay searched vainly for Austin and

Claude. Already he could hear the screams of the wounded as the fires, which had been reignited, swept over the battlefield. The sound grated on his nerves, and he was relieved when he came face-to-face with Claude.

"Have you seen Austin?" Claude asked. "Is he safe?"

"I can't find him. Come on. Get back to the rear."

Claude hesitated. "You go on, Colonel. I think my boy's out there. I'm going to get him."

Clay snapped, "You can't do that, Claude—Claude, come back here!" He shouted this last, for Claude had plunged back into the Wilderness. Clay took two steps forward then realized he had the entire brigade as his responsibility. He called one more time to Claude then shook his head and turned back.

As the musket fire diminished, the blaze from the trees and dead leaves grew louder, and Clay could not keep from looking with agonizing anxiety toward the furnace into which Claude had disappeared.

"God help them! Bring them out!" he whispered then turned to his duty.

Austin had crawled as far as he could after being shot in the upper part of the leg. He did not know if the bone was broken or not, but he feared so. Standing was impossible. He had already fainted twice when he tried it, and crawling was no better. Casting his eyes back over toward the wall of fire that approached him, he gritted his teeth and, using his arm and his good leg, tried to drag himself along.

Five minutes later he passed out again. The world around him seemed to be nothing but heat, and the roar of the flames dimmed his senses. He knew he had no hope, and he began to pray that death would come quickly. A great sadness came to him as he realized there were so many things he would never do now. Then with startling abruptness, he saw Charlie's face. He was delirious and weak from loss of blood, but her face was as clear and sharp as a portrait in a gallery.

"Son—son, are you all right?"

Austin awoke to find himself staring up into his father's face.

"I've got to get you out of here. Can you sit up and get on my back?"

"Pa, what are you doing here?" Austin had not called his father "Pa" since he was a small boy, but now it came to him easily. "You can't do it! Leave me here!"

"Not likely! Come on. It isn't far, but we've got to get away from the fire."

Claude hauled Austin to a sitting position and then stooped before him. As best he could, Austin threw his arms around his father's neck.

"Hang on, son!" Claude Bristol said, plunging forward as the vines grabbed at his feet and slashed at his eyes. He shut them and reeled on blindly, thanking God that He had led him to his boy. He gasped, "Hang on! Almost there!"

Austin was aware of very little. He felt the jolting as his father staggered across the tangled ground and held on as best he could. The sound of the fire muted, and then he heard the sound of musketry, for the battle was still going on in various parts of the Wilderness.

Finally, Claude, gasping for breath, looked up and said, "There's some of our men! We've made it, son!"

Austin heard his father's labored breathing, and then there

was a sudden sound off to his left that sounded like a giant had exhaled his breath. He felt his father's body jerk and then fall to the ground. Agony shot through Austin as his leg struck the ground.

"Pa, are you hit?" Passing out from the pain in his leg, it was some time before Austin was aware of gray-uniformed men standing over him. Then he saw Clay Rocklin.

"Pa! He got shot—artillery shell!"

"I know." Clay helped Austin sit up. "It's pretty bad. He's still alive, but I don't think he can make it, Austin."

Austin turned his head and saw his father lying on his back. "Let me speak to him."

Clay nodded to Dent, who was there, too. "Hold him up, will you, Dent?"

The two wounded men, father and son, were facing each other then, their legs out in opposite directions. Austin was supported by Clay while Dent Rocklin held Claude up. Reaching out, Austin touched his father. Seeing the blood that stained the left side of his uniform, he knew there was nothing to be done. "Pa!" he cried out, seeing Claude's eyes flutter then open.

"Son—you're all right." Claude Bristol's face was pale. "I'm glad—that you'll be the man God wants you to be."

"Pa, you saved me! I'd be burned alive if it hadn't been for you!"

Claude Bristol smiled then. It was a gentle smile, almost as if he were in a drawing room back home. He reached out his hands, and when Austin awkwardly embraced him, his arms went around his son. He whispered, "Tell your mother, at last I did something she can be proud of."

Austin held his father tightly. Tears of anguish ran down his cheeks, and he said huskily, "I love you, Pa!"

"That gives me great pleasure," Claude said, his eyelids starting to close. "Good-bye. Tell your mother I loved her—to the end." And Claude's arms fell lifelessly to his sides.

Clay watched as life passed away from Claude Bristol. His eyes met Dent's, and then Clay put his hand on Austin's shoulder. "He was a brave man, Austin. You must always be very proud of him."

Austin shut his eyes as Dent lowered his father to the ground. Then he said softly, "I will, Clay—and Mother will be, too!"

Chapter 22

A Soldier Comes Home

"I wonder who that can be." Marianne Bristol looked from her position at the dining table, and her eyes narrowed. "I don't believe I know that man."

Last light had come, that hour between daytime and darkness when the world begins to grow murky. The Bristols had postponed the evening meal until almost eight o'clock. "I don't know him either," Marie said. She got up and walked to the window, peering out into the gathering darkness. "He's an officer, but I don't remember him from the regiment."

Charlie and Boone sat beside each other to Marianne's left. As they waited for the visitor to be announced, Boone thought, *Charlie's changed so much.* Then, shifting his gaze, he looked over at Marie. The night before, as he and Marie had walked along the garden pathways, he'd asked her finally if she intended to marry Malcolm Leighton. She had simply said, "Malcolm and I have an understanding." The words didn't satisfy him then or now, for he knew he loved Marie.

"A Lieutenant Bates be here," Ketura announced, waiting at the door for her instructions.

"Have him come in, Ketura."

"Yes, ma'am."

"I don't believe I remember any lieutenant. Maybe I did meet him. There were so many of them."

Marianne watched as the young lieutenant came in, his uniform dusty. "Lieutenant Bates, ma'am, of Colonel Rocklin's brigade," he said nervously.

"Good evening, Lieutenant," Marianne said. "You have a message from my husband or son?"

Lieutenant Bates shifted his feet then said, "Perhaps I could speak with you alone, Mrs. Bristol."

"Is it bad news, Lieutenant?" Marianne asked, rising to her feet. "Is it about my husband?"

"I'm afraid it is, ma'am."

Marianne straightened, and Marie came to stand beside her. "Has he been wounded—or is it worse, Lieutenant?"

Bates dropped his eyes. "I'm afraid," he said, then lifted his gaze, compassion in his eyes, "your husband has been killed. I'm—I'm most sorry, ma'am."

Marie uttered a choking cry, and her mother took her in her arms. Marie's body shook, but Marianne Bristol was dry-eyed. She would keep her tears for later. She waited until Marie's sobbing had slowed, then said, "Thank you for coming, Lieutenant. It was kind of you."

"Well, ma'am, I have another message." Again Bates seemed embarrassed. "It's your son, Lieutenant Austin. He's been wounded."

"How bad is it?" Marie asked, turning to face Lieutenant Bates.

"I didn't get that word. The messenger just came in. We lost a lot of men, and the Yankees did, too. But General Lee is moving the army southward toward Richmond. It won't be good for the wounded."

Marie exclaimed, "We've got to know! Is that all the word you have, Lieutenant Bates?"

"I'm afraid it is, ma'am." Bates looked sorrowful. "It's going to be pretty bad. Grant came down with the biggest army, I guess, that's ever been in this country. When the Army of the Potomac got whipped before, they turned and ran back to Washington, but not this general! They're already calling him 'Butcher' Grant. He doesn't mind losing ten men to our one because his men can be replaced, and ours can't." Bitterness tinged his reply. "I've got to get back, ma'am. I'm very sorry."

"Where will my son be?" Marianne demanded.

"Hard to say. They'll be bringing some back in wagons, those too bad off to walk."

Marianne hesitated then asked, "Will you take some refreshments, Lieutenant Bates?"

"No, ma'am." Bates stopped at the door. "I'm sorry about your men," he said then wheeled and left. His boots echoed on the hardwood floor of the foyer; then the door slammed, and horse hooves began to clatter.

"We've got to do something, Mother!" Marie said, her voice weak and hands clasped together.

"There's nothing we can do, I'm afraid, except pray."

Then Charlie spoke, her dark eyes glowing and determination in her lips. "We'll go git him and bring him home."

"Why, you can't do that!" Marianne exclaimed.

"Yes, I kin! If I kin find my way 'round in the mountains with bears and panthers, I reckon I kin find one man."

"I think I might do it, Marianne," Boone said. Then, turning to Charlie, he added, "But you're not going."

"That's what you think!" Charlie snapped back. "I'm going with you or without you, Boone Manwaring! Now make up your mind!"

For a moment Boone considered running away and leaving her, but he knew Charlie Peace well. He understood that if he did leave without her, she would go alone. There was no use arguing against her deep streak of stubbornness. "All right," he said, "we'll leave tonight."

"Why, you can't travel in the dark!" Marie said, astonished that Boone had suggested such a thing. But her grieving heart warmed toward the young woman and Boone.

"I reckon we kin. Full moon tonight," Charlie said. "Come on, Boone, let's go!"

Marianne hugged Charlie, her heart filled with anxiety for her son and grief for her husband. "Charlene," she said, "I couldn't ask you to do this. But if you must go, God go with you," she said.

Charlie looked at the older woman with love. "Don't you worry. We'll bring 'em both back." Then she said abruptly, "I'm gonna shuck this here fancy dress."

"Wear anything you want," Boone said as Charlie ran out of the room and headed upstairs. "We'll do the best we can, Marianne. I'm sorry. I'd grown very fond of your husband. . . . I'll go out and see to the horses."

"You'd better take the wagon to bring Claude home, and you can make a bed for Austin, too."

"All right, I'll see to it."

Boone left the house. He rounded up Solomon and soon had the wagon hitched with two fine horses. Solomon, upon hearing the news, said sorrowfully, "Po' Mr. Claude! He done just found his way, and now he's gone to be with the Lord." He patted the horses on the rump. "These are the best hosses in the state of Virginia. You be careful now, Mr. Boone. Don't you be gettin' yourself shot—and take keer of Miss Charlie."

"I'll do that, Solomon. You watch out for things here."

Turning toward the house, he was surprised to see that Marie had stepped outside. When he went to meet her, he said, "Words don't mean much at a time like this, but I know a little about what you're feeling—since I've lost both my parents."

"Thank you, Boone." Marie had gained some control, but she knew sorrow was beginning to form within her. "He was doing so well, and now we've lost him."

Boone said nothing. Aware of her trembling, on an impulse he put his arms around her. She surrendered to his embrace, tears streaming down her cheeks. "It's mighty tough," he murmured to her softly. "We'll find Austin and bring him back."

"I'll be praying for you, Boone."

Boone held her a moment longer then drew back. "I've got something to tell you, Marie. Two nights ago I got down on my knees and asked God to do whatever needed doing in my life." He related his experience then said, "I guess it was my time to find God, Marie. After you read the verse about Jesus telling the man with the withered hand to stretch out his hand," he continued, wonder touching his eyes, "something changed for me—like it did for you when you were fourteen."

Joy coursed through Marie as she touched his cheek. "I'm so happy for you, Boone—" And then Charlie's voice was heard, and he released Marie quickly.

Wearing a dark green traveling dress and carrying a suitcase, Charlie's eyes narrowed as she took in the fact that Boone and Marie were standing together. But she merely said, "Are we ready?"

"I guess so, Charlie." He went around, climbed into the wagon, and picked up the lines as Charlie jumped up to sit beside him. Turning back to Marie, he said, "I guess you can pray for all of us."

"I will," Marie murmured. She watched as the team stepped smartly out at Boone's command and then stood in the darkness. The sun had gone down completely now, and finally, as the wagon disappeared, she felt her mother's presence. She put her arm around her, and they made their way back to the house to begin their vigil of grief.

Boone drove the team without speaking for some time. Then he said, "About that place we looked at, Charlie—I haven't forgotten it."

"It don't matter now, Boone. I reckon if God wants us to have a place, why, He'll let us know."

"We'll look at it again after we get all this done."

"All right, Boone—if you say so."

※

Boone pulled the weary team to a halt in front of the white frame house. Both Boone and Charlie were exhausted, for the trip had been hard. They had changed horses at one point the day before to give the team a rest, promising to exchange again when they made their way homeward. Charlie's shoulders were slumped, and he knew she had slept practically not at all during the rapid trip from Richmond. Now he said, "I'll go in and see if this is the Payton place." He stepped down from the wagon and stretched, then walked on stiff legs to the front door. It was two o'clock in the afternoon, and the sun was still high in the sky. As he approached the porch, an elderly woman dressed in black came out. "Mrs. Payton?" he asked.

"Indeed. I'm Mrs. Payton." The white-haired woman examined Boone. "Have you come to see about the lieutenant?"

"Yes. I'm Boone Manwaring, Mrs. Payton." He turned and said, "Charlie, this is it."

Mrs. Payton watched as Charlie slid off the wagon with one swift move and walked toward her, eyes expectant. "Is he here?" she asked.

"This is Charlie Peace. We've come to see about Lieutenant Bristol. We ran into a cavalry unit that said you had kept him here."

"Yes. I didn't think he could stand the jolting of those wagons they took the wounded off in." Her eyes clouded. "Poor boys!"

"Is he all right?" Charlie asked. She had done little but think of Austin on the journey, and the strength of her compassion had surprised her. She had thought over and over again of the times he had been with her, his kindness and wit, and especially of the time he had kissed her.

"He's doing very well. You didn't hear any details?"

"No. Only that he was wounded," Charlie said. "Is he hurt bad?"

"Not as bad as some," Mrs. Payton said. "I had three of 'em here, keepin' 'em, but two of 'em died already. I had my man bury 'em out there in the family cemetery."

"Can we see him?"

"Of course." Charlie and Boone followed Mrs. Payton inside the house then walked down a short hallway to an open door. Charlie stepped in, her eyes sweeping the room. It had a bed, nightstand, chifforobe, and several pictures of family members on the wall. Austin lay on the bed, eyes closed, a brightly colored quilt covering his lower body. Charlie moved toward his side and took his hand. "Austin, can you hear me?"

Austin Bristol's eyes fluttered then opened. He seemed

confused for a moment and licked his lips before saying, "Charlene—?"

"Yes, it's Charlene, and Boone's here with me."

Austin turned his head with some effort to see Boone, who had come to the other side of the bed. "Hello, Boone," he said, his voice raspy. "Didn't expect to see you two here."

"Manwaring and Peace Ambulance Service." Boone squeezed Austin's shoulder gently. "We've come to take you home."

Austin's eyes sought out Charlie. "Father's dead," he said, sadness in his feverish eyes.

"I know," Charlie said. "I'm right sorry. He was real nice to me."

"He died getting me out of a fire. The woods were on fire, and I was going to be burned up. He came in and carried me out of there. Just as he got me free, a shot caught him. He—almost made it." Austin shook his head feebly. "We'd just gotten to know each other, and now I've lost him."

"He ain't lost. He's with the Lord Jesus," Charlie said, smoothing his hair back from his forehead. "You're gonna be all right. We'll take you back to Hartsworth."

"We've got to take Father back, too. Mrs. Payton has been wonderful. She had her husband make a fine coffin. I've been trying to think of a way to get him home. He wanted to be buried at Hartsworth."

"We'll start in the morning at first light," Charlie said.

Boone asked Mrs. Payton, "How's the leg?"

"It's better now. There won't be any infection, I don't think, if you keep it clean. Can't tell if the bone was hurt. I don't think it was broken, though. At least that's what the doctor said. You going to move him tomorrow?"

"If we can," Boone said. "He'd feel better at home, and so

would his mother and sister."

"I think if you go real slow, it will be all right, but don't bump him around." Mrs. Payton hesitated then added, "I lost a boy at Chickamauga. My only son. I thought if I could help with this one, it might save some mother the grief I've had."

"We're right grateful to you, Mrs. Payton," Charlie whispered. "I'm sorry 'bout your boy."

"I'll fix you a place to stay tonight and have my man take care of your team," Mrs. Payton said.

Aware that Austin was still clinging to her hand, Charlie squeezed it. "You'll feel better when you get back home." She saw, however, the grief on his face and knew he was thinking of his father. There was little one could say at a time like this, but she was conscious of a tremendous lift in her own spirit. *He's alive,* she thought, *and he's gonna be all right.* Puzzled, she realized, *I didn't know I cared so much fer him. It woulda killed me if he had died!*

⁂

The next day Boone made a comfortable bed for Austin in the wagon, then thought, *He can't ride with the body of his father beside him.* When he mentioned this to Charlie, she said, "Oh no, Boone, that wouldn't be right! We'll have to get another wagon!"

Buying a wagon and another team presented no difficulty, for a neighboring farmer had one he was willing to sell, especially for gold coins. Boone placed Claude Bristol's coffin in it and covered it with a tarpaulin, and by ten o'clock they were ready. They gave their deepest thanks to Mrs. Payton, with Boone saying, "Mrs. Bristol will be writing to you. I can only give you my thanks, but you have done a great service for a fine family." Then Boone, driving the wagon bearing Claude Bristol's body, led out, followed by Charlie with Austin.

Boone took the easy route, traveling carefully so that Austin would not be jostled. When they stopped at noon for a quick meal, Boone said, "We can stop if it gets too bad, Austin."

"No," Austin said, "I'm fine." He was indeed looking better, with more color in his cheeks. He ate a little of the food Mrs. Payton had fixed for them, drank a great deal of water, and then went to sleep.

They drove steadily through the afternoon, pausing that night beside a stream. Boone fixed a fire, and Charlie cooked a hot meal. She made a dish called Hoppin' John out of rice, beans, and bacon, seasoned with salt and pepper, and also corn bread. Now she sat beside Austin in the wagon bed. As she helped him prop himself up, perspiration came to his forehead as the pain in his leg grew sharp. He made no protest, however, but ate hungrily.

"That's good for you. You got to keep your strength up," Charlie said, smiling. She was sitting across from him, her back braced against the wagon side as she ate her own food. "You look better."

Although he was light-headed, Austin was feeling better. "I'm lucky," he said briefly, glancing toward the wagon where his father's body rested. "So many of our fellows never made it out of the Wilderness." As darkness fell over the land, an owl drifted toward them in the still air, drawn perhaps by their activity. Austin took another drink of the water. "I can't tell you what it means, Charlene, your coming to get me like this. I thought I'd have to bury Father here in a strange land. Didn't look like there was any hope of getting him back home. How did you hear about us?"

Charlie related how Lieutenant Bates had come, and when she had finished, Austin asked curiously, "You were the one who decided to come after us, weren't you?"

Charlie flushed. "I reckon I was. Somebody had to do somethin'."

Austin smiled. "It's just the sort of thing you'd do. You're the only woman in the world, Charlene, who would come into the middle of a battle to get a friend who'd been hurt. I don't see how I can ever thank you enough for it."

"Why, you don't have to do that, Austin."

"I guess I do. When someone does something for us, we have to thank them, don't we? And I know Mother was worried about me."

"Yes, she was, but I don't think I could've got you if Boone hadn't been with me."

"Good man."

"He sure is. Never even hesitated 'bout comin' to git you. When he looked like he was gonna leave without me, we almost had a fight. I told him I was comin' whether he went with me or not." She laughed. "I guess I'm a stubborn woman."

"Good thing for me you are," Austin said, knowing he felt something for her that he could not identify. "I guess I'd better lie down. I'm getting a bit feeble."

"Let me help you." Charlie maneuvered him back onto the mattress they had brought, and when he drew his breath in sharply once, she put her hand on his cheek. "I'm sorry. I didn't mean to hurt you, Austin."

"It's all right." Austin lay back, his head on a pillow. Charlie bent over him, trying to adjust him to a more comfortable position. Seeing the brightness of her eyes, even in the darkness,

Austin suddenly reached up and without thinking gently touched her face. "I guess I'll have to tell you how much I admire you, Charlene." He pulled her head forward and waited, and then she lowered her face and kissed him softly on the lips.

"I guess any woman would have done it," she said, straightening up and pulling the coverlet over him. But the touch of his lips had stirred her. "I'll be up if you need anything."

"All right, Charlene. Good night—and thanks for the kiss. Nobody's done that for me since I was a child. Mother used to come in every night to kiss me and say a prayer over me."

"I guess it was right forward of me." Kneeling beside him, she touched his cheek. "You're going to be all right, Austin. We'll get you home."

He said sleepily, "Sit by me awhile, Charlene."

Charlie hesitated for a moment then sat down, bracing her back against the wagon side. By the starlight she could see that his face was no longer tense but relaxed and young looking. Her lips broad and maternal, she stroked his hair. In the background she could hear the fire crackling and once glanced over to see Boone sitting in front of it, staring into the blaze. As she sat in the wagon with Austin, she silently compared the two men. Boone had come out of nowhere and had been her strength, and she felt a gratitude, an affection, an admiration for him for that. If it had not been for Boone, she would not have had a place to turn. She had thought herself in love with him, but now she realized she felt more at home with Austin. He knew how to make her laugh, and he had sensed her apprehensions and had gone out of his way to make her feel wanted and accepted. There was a goodness and a gentleness in him that she had not often seen in a man in her limited experience. As the silver light of the stars outlined his face, she knew she could no longer deny her love for this man.

⁂

Ketura came running in, crying out, "Miss Marianne, they's here!"

Marianne leaped up from the stool in the kitchen. She had been sitting there waiting for the bread to finish baking, but now she ran outside. When she saw the two wagons, her heart swelled with both joy and grief. She waited while the drivers stopped and Charlie met her, saying, "Austin's fine! He's gonna be all right, Marianne!"

"Thank God! Bring him into the house. I've got the bed all ready." She ran quickly over to the wagon and, discarding dignity, climbed up into the bed. She kneeled down beside Austin, who was watching her. "My boy," she whispered, "you're home."

"I'm sorry about Father. I'll have to tell you all about him. He saved my life, Mother."

Marianne glanced involuntarily at the other wagon. "I'm glad you're both home, son. I want to hear everything."

Solomon and two other servants carried Austin in gently, as if he were a child. As they did, Marie came outside to stand beside Boone. "Did you have much trouble?" she asked. It was not what she wanted to say, for now that Austin and the remains of her father were actually home, she felt a great debt to this tall man and young woman who walked beside Austin as he was carried into the house. She wanted to speak what was in her heart, but somehow could not do it.

"Not too much. Austin was lucky. A lady took him in and cared for him."

"I—don't know how to thank you, Boone."

"No need for that." His hazel eyes searched hers. "It's been hard for you waiting and not knowing. We came as fast as Austin could take it."

"It has been hard," Marie said, feeling as if a great weight was lifted off her. When she saw how tired Boone was, she said, "I know you're exhausted. You need to go to bed."

Boone, however, was thinking of their trip. "That Charlie is some young woman. I don't think she slept five hours since we left here, especially on the way back. She's cared for Austin better than any nurse."

"She's a wonderful woman. I know you're proud of her."

Her comment surprised Boone. "Why, I suppose I am. Not many young women could have done that."

The two stood there feeling ill at ease, both somehow thinking of Marie's "arrangement" with Malcolm Leighton. In the last few days, Marie had grown even more confused. In between the mixed feelings of elation that Austin was home safely and the grief that her father was dead, she had begun thinking of Boone Manwaring as a woman thinks of a man. She wanted to be comforted, and she thought, *If he just touched me, I think I'd collapse and fall into his arms—but he won't do that. He'll expect me to go to Malcolm with my grief, and I can't do that.*

Straightening, Marie said, "I'll go see what I can do for Austin."

As Boone watched her go, Solomon came to stand beside him. "You done fine, Mr. Boone. You and Miss Charlie done real good."

"Thanks, Solomon," Boone said, watching Marie as she left. "Find me a horse. I'm going back to town."

"You ain't gonna stay?"

"No," Boone said. "You take good care of Mr. Austin." Then

he moved toward the stable, wondering if the next day would bring some wisdom that he seemed to lack. Ten minutes later he rode out of Hartsworth, exhausted, weary, but strangely satisfied over the task he and Charlie had accomplished.

Claude Bristol's funeral was memorable, in spite of the many funerals that had already occurred during the war. The church was packed as Rev. Eli Samuelson delivered the sermon. An old friend of Claude Bristol's, Rev. Samuelson was honest in his evaluation. He spoke of the hope of the Resurrection and then finally on a personal note said in a ringing voice, "Claude Bristol, like all men, made his mistakes, but he died in a fashion that many of us would envy. He died saving the life of his son. The scripture says, 'Greater love hath no man than this, that a man lay down his life for his friends.' If we change the word 'friends' for 'son,' we have the crowning triumph of our brother's life." His eyes took in the family in the front pew. Insistent on attending, Austin was in the aisle with his wounded leg stretched out on a chair. Now his eyes glowed at the reverend's words. "As long as there are Bristols in the world, they will remember this man's sacrifice," the reverend finally concluded.

Afterward, when the family got back home, Austin was put to bed. The trip had not done him any good, and Charlie said to Marie, "He's got fever. I hope that leg don't git infected. We're gonna have to nurse him real good, Marie. I can't bear to think of anythin' happenin' to him."

Marie put her arm around the young woman. "You're good, Charlie," she said.

"No, I'm not good!" Charlie said with surprise. "It's just

that—well, I'm right fond of Austin."

"And I think he's fond of you. He watches you all the time."

The remark confused Charlie, and she turned away, unable to answer. She went at once to Austin's room, picked up a basin, filled it with cool water, and began to bathe his face. "You done too much," she said quietly. "But you had to go; I know that."

"I'll never forget him, Charlene," Austin said softly. "He wasn't always the kind of father I admired, but he made up for it at the last."

Charlie nodded. "I reckon your pa and my pa are both with Jesus now. That's a good thought, ain't it, Austin?"

"Yes. Real fine." Austin moved restlessly. "I'm going to miss him. Just like you miss your father."

Charlie continued to mop his brow. "You lie quiet now. You're gonna take some real nursin' to git over this. I think you've got some fever, and we don't want infection in that leg."

But as his temperature shot up over the next few hours, Charlie grew fearful. She began to pray, *God, don't let nothin' happen to him now—not after all of this!*

CHAPTER 23

A TIME TO EMBRACE

The campaign that had begun on May 5, 1864, in the Wilderness transformed itself into a dance in which the two armies moved in almost minuet precision. General Lee had hoped that the Army of the Potomac might retreat at the end of such a hard-fought battle—which had been the pattern in the years gone by. But for the first time during the war, Grant's hard-bitten army that had suffered so many losses *advanced* instead of retreating to Washington. Their object was Richmond.

When Lee pulled his forces out of the Wilderness, one of his aides asked him where they were going. "To Spotsylvania," he replied. When asked by the officer, "Why there?" Lee responded, "Because General Grant will be there. It is the right thing to do militarily." Lee had a respect for Grant that he never had for the other generals he had faced, and now he moved his Army of Northern Virginia toward Spotsylvania. On the night of May 7, General Grant also headed toward Spotsylvania, which was in the direction of Richmond, but when he arrived there he found General Lee's Army of Northern Virginia squarely across his path. Stubbornly, Grant threw his men against the emplaced Confederates and, during the next twelve days, mounted many assaults. The Union losses were horrendous. The Confederate losses were much less, but they had no replacements and so the lines grew thinner and thinner. There were too few men left in the South to refill the ranks.

Grant stopped at Spotsylvania as predicted, pulled out, and again launched a movement toward Richmond. Once again, at the North Anna River, he found Lee in front of him. Grant swung by his left flank, only to find Lee waiting for him again. At Totopotomoy Creek a frustrated Grant kept doggedly at the task. Richmond lay to the south only a few miles, and only the thin ranks of the Army of Northern Virginia lay between him and the trophy that could mean the end of the Civil War.

Charlie carried the tray into the room where Austin lay propped up in bed. He shook his head and said grumpily, "How long have I got to stay in this bed?"

"Until I tell you you kin git out!" Charlie said emphatically, putting the tray down. "Do you want to feed yourself, or shall I do it?"

"I'm no baby!" Austin growled. He flexed his leg upward, bending it, and made a slight grimace. The pain was not as severe, indeed had been growing less severe every day. But the two weeks that he had been cared for by Charlie had been hard ones. The wound had gotten infected, and his fever had risen. Day after day had passed, and always it seemed that when he awoke Charlie was there beside him. Sometimes, of course, it was his mother or Marie, but nearly always Charlie was there. As he cut up the meat on his plate, he asked, "Don't you ever get tired of waiting on me?"

WITNESS IN HEAVEN

"I never had a baby to take care of," Charlie responded, "and that's about what you've been."

Austin looked up quickly, a sharp retort on his lips, but then laughed. "I've been a lot of trouble to you, haven't I, Charlene?"

"I don't mind." Charlie sat down and watched him eat. "You know, I like it when you call me Charlene."

"Do you now?"

"Yes, it always makes me feel—I don't know—more like a woman."

"Beautiful name."

Charlie thought of the days just passed when she'd been frightened that he might die. She had found out what it meant to live with praying people. Her mother had been a woman of prayer, but she, Marie, and Marianne had prayed not only individually but together, joining hands. Now as he sipped milk from a tall glass, she said impishly, "You got milk in your whiskers."

Austin grinned and picked up his napkin. "I never had whiskers before. I think I'll grow a beard all the way to my chest."

"No, don't do it. It wouldn't look right on you."

"How about a mustache? Would that be all right?"

Charlie smiled. "I suppose that would be all right. You already got a start on one. Maybe I ought to git my scissors and trim it."

"How big a mustache? One that droops down, or just a little one?"

"Not a droopy one. I'll take keer of it. I used to trim Pa's whiskers all the time. When he got sick once, I even shaved him a time or two."

When he finished eating, she removed the tray. "I think maybe you could git up out of that bed and sit in a chair for a while."

"Good. I'm sick of this bed!"

Pulling the rocker up close to the bed, Charlie helped him lift his leg over. She had changed the bandage earlier. "The wound's 'bout all healed up."

"You're a good nurse, Charlene." He put his weight on her, his arm falling over her shoulders. She was firm and strong beneath his grasp, and he groped with his free hand for the chair, then sat down in it with a sigh of relief. "That feels so good—just to sit on a hard chair!"

"You'll be walkin' soon, and before long we kin go ridin' again."

"Good. I won't feel like a man until I'm able to sit on a horse." He enjoyed the sensation of sitting up and finally commented, "You know, it's strange how little things can mean so much. When I was lying in that fire and it was coming toward me, I was pretty sure I wasn't going to make it."

"What did you think 'bout when you thought you was goin' to die?"

"I thought about you."

Charlie's eyes flew open. "No, you didn't!" she exclaimed.

"Well, I thought about Mother, and Marie, and about how I wished I'd made it up better with Father. But when it got closer, all of a sudden—" He stopped and looked at her. "Your face—your eyes and hair, all black and curly—came to my mind. Even when the fire was creeping up." He dropped his head and said, "You know, Charlene, I think one of my biggest regrets was that I wouldn't see you again."

"That's sweet of you, Austin," she said huskily. What he had said pleased her, made her feel warm.

"Nothing like that ever happened to me before. . . . You know, Charlene, you're the easiest young woman to be with."

"Me? Why would you say that?"

"Well, with some people there's always a reserve, especially between women and men. But with you, I'm always at ease." He looked up. "Why should that be, I wonder? I guess it's because," he said, answering his own question, "you're the most natural person I've ever known."

Charlie ducked her head. "I'm glad you feel that way, Austin. I've—I've grown right fond of you."

"Have you? That's good to hear." Feeling suddenly better than he had since his injury, he said, "Get the scissors. Let's trim this mustache; then you can let me beat you at another game of checkers."

※

In late May Marie realized Malcolm Leighton was restless. He came to see her and fidgeted all through the visit. They went outside to where daisies, hyacinths, and roses dotted the garden with yellows, blue-purples, and reds and sat down on a bench.

"Something's wrong, Marie," he said bluntly. "You haven't been yourself lately."

"I suppose not. Since losing my father, I suppose, I haven't been in very good spirits. I'm not very good company for you, Malcolm."

"Have you been thinking about our engagement?"

"I hate to say so, but I really haven't. When Austin got so sick, it took most of my time, that and the loss of Father. I haven't thought of anything very much."

"Well, that's understandable. I'm sorry to intrude, and I don't want to pressure you." He rose abruptly. "I'll give you a little more time; then maybe you can give me your answer."

"Perhaps. Come back tomorrow, Malcolm."

After he left, she went back into the house and about her work. But she said so little that finally Marianne asked, "Marie, don't you feel well?"

"Oh yes. I feel very well."

"You're exhausted. I think all of us are." She sat down and folded her hands, then gave her daughter a more careful look. "Malcolm didn't stay long," she commented.

"He wants to announce our engagement."

"Oh! What did you tell him?"

"Nothing really. Just that I've been too upset over Father's death and Austin's sickness. . . . I feel so confused," she said finally.

"About Malcolm?"

"Yes. It seems so—so *businesslike*. It's not his fault. He's—well, he's not very romantic."

Then Marianne spoke what had been in her heart for a long time. "Be very careful. It's a dangerous time for you. You've had a great loss, and the burden of the plantation and financial pressures are terrible. I know you and Austin both have thought about losing this place. . . . Are you marrying Malcolm simply because he has money?"

"I'd hate to think I'm doing that, but it's a factor."

"Then I'd say don't commit yourself. There should be nothing at all like that between a man and a woman."

Relief broke free in Marie Bristol. "That's what I've been thinking," she said. "Malcolm's a charming man, fine looking, and so many young women have tried to catch his attention. I suppose I should be flattered that he wants me."

"He's all those things, but marriage is more than that. You know that, Marie. At least I hope you do."

WITNESS IN HEAVEN

Knowing she had a big decision to make, Marie got up. "I think I'll go for a ride." She left the house and rode the hills and paths of the surrounding countryside all afternoon. But even the beauties of the May season could not drive away the heaviness in her heart. Finally, she drew up on top of a ridge that overlooked Hartsworth. She caught her breath as her eyes took in the emerald lawn, the fine old house with its stately beauty, and the outbuildings. For a long time she stood there, on the precipice of her decision, as her horse chomped at the fresh grass. Finally, she shook her head in a gesture that was almost defiant. Looking down at her home, she spoke aloud. "I'll hate to have to leave this place, but a marriage is more than a plantation." Then, impetuously, she swung up on the horse and rode rapidly down the road that led toward her home. When she arrived, she dismounted and handed the reins to Solomon. Then she walked into the house and stood in the middle of the foyer, seeing it through different eyes. When she finally walked into the parlor where her mother was sitting, she said, "Mother, I have something to tell you...."

"What's the news on the fighting, Marie?" Austin asked three days later. He was standing with the aid of a cane as his sister entered the house. She'd been talking to the man who delivered mail—at least whatever mail came through in these troubled times.

"He says there's been a terrible battle at Cold Harbor," she said. "Can you stand up like that? Does your leg hurt?"

"Cold Harbor? Why, that's just outside of Richmond!"

"I know. We're surrounded now. Grant lost five thousand

men in one hour."

Austin took this in then said quietly, "It'll be over soon. It can't last long."

"I hope so. Oh, I hope so!" Marie said.

She turned to leave, but he detained her. "Marie?" When she looked at him with a questioning air, he asked, "What about Leighton?"

Marie hesitated. "I ended our agreement. It wasn't really an engagement," she said, smiling wryly. "It was all wrong from the beginning. I hate to think I've been so uncertain."

"You've told him?"

"Yes, day before yesterday. He took it pretty well, I must say. Not at all like a man dying of love."

"Are you sure about this, Marie?"

"Yes. I feel like a load's been taken off my back. We might lose this place, but I couldn't marry just for money."

"I'm glad you did it, sis. I could tell you didn't care for him." Then he said shyly, "I've got news for you."

"What is it, Austin?"

"Would you think I was crazy if I said I'd fallen in love with Charlene?"

Marie kissed him, exclaiming joyfully, "I think it's wonderful, but what about Boone?"

"What about him?" Austin asked.

"I've always thought Charlie was in love with him. She's practically said so a couple of times. Have you said anything to her?"

"No, but I'm going to right now. I like Boone, but if he wants Charlene, he'll have to fight for her."

"He might do that," Marie said, a strange expression crossing her face. "I don't know what he feels."

She left the room with Austin staring after her, wondering what his sister was thinking. Then he hobbled into the kitchen, where he asked Blossom, "Where's Miss Charlene?"

"She's out there in the garden, Mr. Austin."

Austin limped out of the house to where Charlie was trimming the arbor. "Charlene," he said, "do you have to work all the time?"

"Not all the time." Charlie stepped down from the stool she was on, put down the shears, and gave him a critical look. "You're walkin' too much on that leg."

"Well, let me give it a rest. Come on and join me."

They sat down on a bench that had been painted white but now was peeling. "Needs paint," he said. "Maybe I'll do that tomorrow."

Charlene was wearing an older dress, and her hair was bound up with a green bandanna. She pulled it off now, tossing her hair and letting her curls fly free. Looking at him curiously, she said, "Did Marie tell you 'bout her and Malcolm Leighton?"

"I just asked her. I'm glad that's over."

"I am, too. She didn't care fer him. Do you know what I think? I think she's in love with Boone."

Startled, Austin was silent. Then he said, "I don't know how Boone feels."

"If you ask me, I think he keers fer her," Charlie responded. "Watch him sometime. He never takes his eyes off her."

Not knowing what to say, Austin let his hand drop to Charlie's shoulder. "I'm sorry, Charlene."

Astonished, Charlie turned to face him. "Sorry? Don't you like him? You wouldn't want him to be married to your sister?"

"Why, I wouldn't mind that, but—Marie and I both thought you cared for him—as a man, I mean."

Charlie could not meet his eyes for a moment. When she looked up, her voice was quiet. "I reckon I did keer for him like that at one time, or I thought I did. He was so good to me, bringin' me here and takin' keer of me after Pa died. I couldn't help but admire him for that."

"Do you love him, Charlene?"

"No—not like you mean." Charlie dropped her head again, for her heart was full. She had decided that Austin was the man she loved, but she didn't know how to tell him.

Suddenly Austin reached out his arm and pulled her toward him. He said abruptly, "Charlene, I've got to tell you something, and it's not going to be pleasant."

"What is it, Austin?" she asked, not taking her eyes off his face.

"A man does a lot of things he's ashamed of, and one of the things I'm most ashamed of is—well, at one time I thought about marrying for money."

"I know that, but you didn't. You never married Ida."

"Because she had sense enough and wisdom enough to see that it would never have worked. I can't say what I would have done otherwise, and that's not a thing a man likes to admit."

Aware of his arms holding her, Charlie said, "Austin?" But she found she could not ask the question.

"What is it, Charlene?"

"I don't know how to talk to men," she said haltingly. "I never learned how to court or nothin' like that, but I want to know somethin'. Will you tell me the truth?"

"Yes. What is it? Ask me anything."

Her lips soft and vulnerable, her eyes dark and intense, Charlie asked, "Do you love me, Austin?"

Stunned by the simple question and the courage it had

taken for her to ask it, Austin said urgently, "Yes, I do. That's what I wanted to tell you, Charlene. You've got money and I don't, and that's galling to a man. But I have to tell you that I do love you. I'd love you if you didn't have a penny." Then he pulled her closer and kissed her.

As Charlie put her arms around Austin's neck, she felt peace, joy, and exhilaration. Drawing back after the lengthy kiss, she said, "Let's don't ever think 'bout money. It won't be mine or yours. Everythin' will be ours. Just love me, Austin. That's all I ask."

"I'll always do that, Charlene," he said, embracing her again. As they kissed again, he knew the exultation of finding what he'd been searching for all his life.

CHAPTER 24

"WHITHER THOU GOEST"

For Clay Rocklin the struggle to keep the Union army out of Richmond never ended. Each day he arose, mustered his men as best he could, buried the dead, tended the wounded, and then advanced to the line across which the Confederate army faced the Army of the Potomac.

The struggle that had begun at the Wilderness had not stopped for a single day. Skirmishes took place constantly, and Sheridan's Union cavalry was constantly in movement, countered by the Confederate cavalry. Always before, the Confederate cavalry had been superior, but now missing its great leader, Jeb Stuart, and worn down to a mere shadow of what it had been during its days of glory, the cavalry was almost paralyzed.

The worst day of fighting had come at the battle of Cold Harbor on June 3. Hoping to eliminate his adversary in one crushing blow, Grant sent his men forward against the Confederates, who were firmly entrenched. In one hour, six thousand men in blue were wiped out, and afterward Grant was to say, "The attack of Cold Harbor was the worst mistake of my military career." In the North men were shouting, "Relieve Butcher Grant!" But in the White House Abraham Lincoln hung on grimly. He knew the Confederacy was tottering, and though he walked the White House at night alone, a tragic figure mourning the death of so many young men, he refused to relieve Grant.

Over the South gloom was thick, and in the North men and women began to hope that the end of the terrible war would come. But all knew by now that there would be no real victory. Too many men were dead and wounded for there to be rejoicing.

Boone had come to Hartsworth often, mostly sitting with Austin. The two were both chess players and carried on some lively battles. So when Charlie met him the day after Austin had told her of his love for her, her eyes were shining.

"What are you so happy about?" he asked, handing his lines to Solomon. "You look like it's Christmas."

"I guess it is, for me anyway. Cain't you guess?"

Boone stood there baffled. "I don't guess I can. What is it?"

"It's Austin, Boone! He loves me!" She watched almost anxiously until his face broke into a broad smile; then she threw herself into his arms. "We're goin' to git married, Boone! It's goin' to be like Pa always wanted. We'll stay here at Hartsworth and use the money from the gold to pay the bank off."

Boone hugged Charlie then stepped back. "That's the best news I've had in a long time, Charlie. You're getting a mighty fine man, and he's getting a fine girl, too."

"Come on! He wants to talk to you!" She took his hand and tugged him into the house. Soon Boone was seated in the study, where Austin held hands with Charlie, both faces beaming with delight.

"I guess this catches you by surprise, Boone," Austin said, looking fondly at Charlie. "I can't believe it's really happening."

"I can," Charlie said, her face wreathed with smiles. She patted Austin's arm. "We're goin' to take the money Pa found and pay off all the bills, ain't we, Austin?"

Frowning slightly, Austin shrugged. "I hate to be a beggar, but it's what Charlene wants."

"Of course it's what I want!" Charlie said indignantly. "This is goin' to be my home!"

"I think that's wonderful," Boone said. He listened as the two talked happily about the future, then asked, "Will you go back to the army when you get healed up?"

"I don't think there'll be any army left. It looks like the end, Boone," Austin said.

"The news is pretty bad. Have you heard from Clay?"

"No, but Dent came by on leave. He said all the Rocklins are fine. None of them got killed, but he was worn down. They're about fought out."

Boone shook his head. "What will happen, Austin?"

"Nobody knows. Lincoln is pretty well hated in the South, but he'll be the best friend the South ever had after the war ends. He's said many times 'with malice toward none.' He wants to put the country back together again."

"You know, I believe he might be able to do it," Boone said. "Everything I hear about that man is good."

Marie came in at that moment, and Boone rose to greet her. "Hello," he said. "How are you today, Marie?"

"I'm fine, Boone." Conscious of a certain stiffness between herself and Boone, Marie wondered if Boone was displeased with her for her semi-engagement to Malcolm Leighton. Both of them were quiet while Charlie and Austin did the talking.

But from time to time Marie would glance at Boone, who was watching the happy pair. Finally, she rose and said, "You'll be staying for supper, Boone?"

"I guess I will, but this may be the last time."

"The last time?" Marie said. "What do you mean?"

"I guess my job's about done," Boone said, addressing Charlie. "You've got what your pa wanted, Charlie, and I can see he would have been very happy, he and your mother. I never was sure it would work. It's kind of like a fairy tale." He smiled then but seemed sad. "I'm glad for you, Charlie."

"But where are you goin', Boone?" Charlie asked plaintively. "Why cain't you stay here?"

"Guess I'll go back to the sea. Thought I might make a cruise to the South Seas. Never been to some of those islands. I hear they're pretty nice."

Marie suddenly left the room.

Watching her go, Charlie said quickly, "Don't leave now, Boone."

"I think I'll have to, Charlie," Boone responded.

Austin asked, "When will you be pulling out?"

"Tomorrow, I think."

"I hate to see it. I'd hoped you would settle around here."

"Things come to an end, Austin," Boone said thoughtfully. "Never know what the next day will bring."

The rest of the day went badly for Boone. He felt out of place, and Marie scarcely looked at him during supper. *I've got to get away from here and try to forget her,* he thought. But he promised he would not leave before seeing them all again.

Later that night, after Boone left, Charlie went to Marie's room and knocked on the door. "Marie, are you awake?"

The door opened, and Marie said wearily, "Yes, I'm awake.

What is it, Charlie?"

"I thought I'd come and talk to you 'bout Boone."

Marie bit her lip. "You'll be sorry to see him go. We all will."

"I don't think you ought to let him go," Charlie announced. She had stepped inside the room and shut the door and now turned to Marie with a determined look on her face. "I guess you've taught me a few manners, but back in the mountains I got pretty much in the habit of sayin' whatever came to my mind, and now it comes to my mind that you're in love with Boone."

Marie shook her head quickly. "There's nothing to that."

But Marie's answer was too fast, so Charlie continued, "I don't think that's right. You're goin' to let him git away, and you'll be sorry the rest of your life."

"He doesn't care for me."

"I think he does. He watches you all the time. When you're not lookin', he keeps his eyes fixed on you. And when he talks 'bout you to me, I kin tell he feels somethin' for you."

"It's just friendship, Charlie. I know you mean well, but there's nothing to say. Boone's a fine man, and I admire him. I'll always be grateful for what you and he did for my father and for Austin, but that's all there is to it."

Charlie argued for a while then left, wondering if the situation was hopeless. As she moved down the stairs, she heard a knocking at the door and arrived there at the same time as Marianne.

Marianne took one look at the man outside and said, "Is there trouble, Eli?"

"Yes, ma'am, I guess, in a way." The tall slave shifted his feet nervously. "It's Miss Melora. Her time's done come, and she ain't doin' good. Mr. Clay ain't home, and Miss Melora sent me over to see if you would come and be with her while she has her baby."

"Of course! Tell her I'll be there as soon as I can get there, Eli."

"Yes, ma'am. I'll sure tell her."

"I'll go with you," Charlie said.

"No, you'd better stay here with Austin." She looked at Marie, who, hearing the commotion, had come down the stairs. "It's Melora," she said. "She's having her baby and it's not going well. We'd both better go."

"All right, Mother. I'll be ready in five minutes."

The two made record time to the Rocklin plantation, which was only a few miles away. When they arrived, they found that their doctor had come from Richmond. When he answered the Rocklins' door, he looked surprised. "Well, I didn't expect to see you ladies this time of the night!"

"How is Melora?"

"Why, she's fine," the doctor said, his eyes twinkling. "She fooled us, though. Sent Eli over to get you because it looked like a difficult delivery, but it wasn't."

"You mean the baby's already born?"

"That's right. Both of them."

"Twins!" Marie gasped.

"Yes, a boy and a girl. I don't know what she's named them. You can go see them if you want to."

The two women hurried into the bedroom, where they found Melora, her black hair framing her pale face. She was holding both babies, one in each arm, with an expression of love that Marie and Marianne would never be able to forget. Melora had loved children all her life, and now she had her own. "The Lord gave me a double blessing," she said, her voice clear but the lines of strain still on her face. "This is Jonathan, and this is Ruth."

Marianne and Marie went to either side of the bed, each taking one of the babies. Marie moved the blanket back and said, "She's beautiful!"

"Yes," Melora said, pride in her eyes. "I wish her father could be here."

Marianne traced the silky cheek of the other new arrival, Jonathan.

Melora watched as the two women held the babies, thinking of Clay. She knew he might be fighting for his life at this very moment, but she was a woman of tremendous faith. She felt that God had promised her Clay would be spared.

Melora soon drifted off and slept soundly the rest of the night. When she woke up just before dawn, Marie was sitting beside her holding Ruth in the crook of her arm. Jonathan, over in the cradle, was awakening, and soon the cries of both babies filled the room.

"I guess it's feeding time," Marie said, smiling. She brought both babies to Melora, thinking she'd never seen a more beautiful sight. "You're a happy woman, Melora. You've got two beautiful children and a fine husband."

"Yes. God has been good to me."

"It wasn't easy, was it? Did you love Clay all those years you waited for him?"

"I think I loved him," Melora murmured, "from the time I first saw him. I was just a child. He had been hurt in a hunting accident, and Jeremiah Irons had brought him to our house. I took care of him. I was just a little thing, but I bossed him terribly."

"It must've been hard all those years, knowing you might never have him."

"It was hard, but I believed God was going to do something. I didn't know what, of course." Melora looked up from the two infants. "I've been meaning to talk to you, Marie. I've been thinking so much about you these last few days, and I wanted to ask you how you feel about Boone."

Instantly Marie became evasive. "I—I thought I cared for him once, but he doesn't care for me."

"He hasn't told you that."

"Well, no. Of course not."

"Has he ever kissed you?"

"Yes." She had not forgotten the strength of Boone's arms nor the tumult in her heart, and now she couldn't face Melora's eyes. "I do care for him, but he doesn't care for me," she confessed. "Besides, he's going away."

"He came by here yesterday to say good-bye. We talked a long time. I think you're making a mistake, and so is he. He told me about how you led him to Jesus. When he speaks of you, there's something in his voice. And I can take one look at you, Marie, and tell you'll never forgive yourself if you let him get away."

"He's the one who decided to leave!"

"He thinks you don't care for him. I could tell from what he said." Melora lifted her voice. "Don't be a fool, Marie! Go to him! Tell him you love him!"

"Why, I can't do that!" Marie said, aghast.

"Why can't you do it? You do love him, don't you?"

"Yes," she said softly, humbly. "I love him."

"Then don't miss out on what God has for you. Go tell him."

Marie was as confused as she had ever been in her life. In truth she had thought more than once of telling Boone of her feelings, but she'd been raised to think a man should speak first about such things. She bit her lip. "You mean—right *now?*"

"I mean this morning!"

Realizing that if she missed this chance she'd never forgive herself, Marie said courageously, "All right. He'll probably laugh at me, but I'll do it."

"He won't laugh. Come back as soon as you talk to him."

"I will." She left Melora, but as soon as she was outside, she began to doubt the wisdom of what she had made up her mind to do. Then, shaking off her fear, she said, "Eli, hitch up my buggy. I'm going into Richmond!"

Boone had packed his few belongings and now stood looking out the window. He was unhappy, feeling somehow that he was making the biggest mistake of his life. He stared blankly outside, not really seeing the crowd below, but wondering where he would go. The sea was always open, and he had tried to put a good front on it, but he had no desire to go to the South Seas nor to become a sailor again. The spell of the land was on him, and he had failed utterly to convince himself that going back to his old life would bring him peace.

A tap at the door interrupted him, and he sighed. As he opened the door, he said, "Marie!"

"Can I come in, Boone?"

"Why, of course." Stepping aside, he asked, "Is something wrong? Has Austin taken a turn for the worse?"

"No. Melora had her babies last night. Twins—a boy and a girl."

"Why, that's wonderful! Clay will be thrilled, I expect."

"Melora named them Jonathan and Ruth. They are

beautiful babies, Boone."

"Sit down, Marie."

"No, I can't." Now that she was here, Marie wondered if she had the courage to go on. But his eyes were fixed on her, so she thought, *Well, I'll be a fool, then.* Aloud she said, "I can't let you go, Boone, without telling you something. You probably won't want to hear it, but I've got to say it anyhow."

"Why, I think I'd like to hear anything you have to say, Marie."

Taking a deep breath, Marie said, "Austin and I talked about marrying for money. Both of us thought it might work out. You knew that, didn't you?"

"I guess so. You couldn't do it, though. Neither could Austin. You have better judgment."

"Do you hold it against me, Boone?"

"Why, of course not!" Boone was astonished. "What would make you think that?"

"I thought so many things," Marie said, unable to meet his eyes. She walked to the window and felt him come up behind her. "I wanted so badly to hold Hartsworth for the family, and then I saw I was wrong about that. And I thought you cared for Charlie—that you were in love with her."

Boone turned her around, his hands clasping her shoulders. "There was never anything like that. She's a fine girl, and she and Austin are very much in love."

"I know that now. Oh, I've been such a fool! In the school I went to, young ladies were carefully prompted on how to speak to men, but I'll say what's in my heart. I—I love you, Boone."

Boone Manwaring had expected anything but this. He blinked with surprise as she looked up at him, eyes pleading. When he didn't answer, she said, "Never mind, Boone. I didn't

GILBERT MORRIS

expect you to love me, but I think when a woman loves a man, he ought to know it." She tried to move away, but his hands tightened, and he began to smile. "Boone?" she whispered. "Is it with you as it is with me?"

Instead of answering, he gathered her in his arms, bent over, and kissed her. And Marie Bristol knew then, from the hunger in his lips and the pressure of his arms, that she had done the right thing.

When he lifted his head, Boone said, "I've loved you for a long time, Marie, but I was mixed up, too. I still am, I guess. I don't have a place, but I know one thing. Wherever I am, I want you to be there."

"Do you want to go back to sea?"

"No, I never really wanted that! What I'd like to do is stay here." He smiled then. "Maybe you can teach me how to raise pigs."

Amused, Marie caressed his cheek. "I think you and I can do more than raise pigs," she said, then grew serious. "It's going to be hard. The war will be over, but it won't really be. It'll take years for the South to recover."

Boone loved the smell of her perfume and the soothing touch of her hand on his cheek. As he pulled her even closer, he said, "Whatever I do, as long as you're with me, it'll be fine." He leaned forward, and just before his lips kissed hers again, he said, "We're going to have a fine marriage and seven or eight children."

When Boone released her from his kiss, her eyes danced. "We'll have to talk about *that*, Boone Manwaring! Now how does it sound?"

"How does *what* sound?"

"Why, didn't you know women always experiment by putting their first name with the last name of the man they intend to marry?" She looked thoughtful and tapped her cheek in mock seriousness. "Marie Manwaring."

"It sounds wonderful to me," Boone said. Then he laughed aloud and, seizing her, swung her around. "Come along, woman; we're going to make our announcement to the world! The future Mr. and Mrs. Boone Manwaring are ready to be recognized!"

If you enjoyed

Appomattox Saga

(Part 3)

then don't miss

Appomattox Saga

(Parts 1 and 2)

ISBN 978-1-60260-178-9   ISBN 978-1-60260-179-6